P9-DTQ-106

DAW BOOKS PROUDLY PRESENTS THE SCIENCE FICTION NOVELS OF W. MICHAEL GEAR:

The Donovan Series

Outpost

Abandoned

Pariah

Unreconciled

The Team Psi Series

*The Alpha Enigma**

The Spider Trilogy

The Warriors of Spider

The Way of Spider

The Web of Spider

The Forbidden Borders Trilogy

Requiem for the Conqueror

Relic of Empire

Countermeasures

***

Starstrike

The Artifact

*Coming soon from DAW

UNRECONCILED

UNRECONCILED

DONOVAN: BOOK FOUR

W. MICHAEL GEAR

DAW BOOKS, INC.
DONALD A. WOLLHEIM, FOUNDER
1745 Broadway, New York, NY 10019
ELIZABETH R. WOLLHEIM
SHEILA E. GILBERT
PUBLISHERS
www.dawbooks.com

Jacket illustration by Steve Stone.

Jacket design by Adam Auerbach.

Book design by Fine Design.

Edited by Sheila E. Gilbert.

DAW Book Collectors No. 1853.

Published by DAW Books, Inc.
1745 Broadway, New York, NY 10019.

First Printing, May 2020
1 2 3 4 5 6 7 8 9

TO MY BEAUTIFUL

KATHLEEN O'NEAL GEAR

WHO HAS FILLED MY LIFE

WITH THE KIND OF MAGICAL LOVE THAT ONLY

EXISTS IN FAIRY TALES.

IRREDENTA

I sit—as I often do—in the observation dome. A transparent bubble, it protrudes from Ashanti*'s hull on Deck Three. I look out upon an infinity of stars, see the swirls of nebulae, marvel at patches of dark matter that appear as blemishes upon the composition of light. Gazing at the heavens, I experience the full meaning of awe. To sit here is to dimly, feebly perceive the majesty of Creation. The magnificence of the universe beyond the dome defies comprehension. Reconfirms how small, how absolutely insignificant my existence is.*

A mere mote. Not even a speck upon the face of the deep.

I need but look out at the universe and the words of the Prophets resonate within me. Understanding pervades my soul: I have been chosen.

We *have been chosen.*

Here, in this most unlikely place. Among these most unlikely circumstances.

Only after years of doubt, of faltering faith, do I begin to understand: The universe does not make mistakes. It had to be Ashanti. *It had to be on this spacing. And it had to be us, the Irredenta, who were chosen to initiate such an immense task.*

What we believed to be tragedy, injustice, and horror was nothing more than the universe preparing us for the ultimate revelation. As seemingly insignificant as we might appear, we are the beginning, the spark that shall ignite the flame. Great things come from tiny beginnings. Consider a microRNA. It, too, seems insignificant at first glance. A mere twenty-two base pairs. It can turn a gene on or off, initiating a chain of events that will change an organism, a species, and an entire biome. From the microscopic to the multiverse.

So it is for us.

The Harrowing and Cleansing was necessary to ensure that when we were given the Revelation we would understand. The universe had to lock us in Ashanti*'s belly. Onto this one miserably cramped deck. It had to confine* *us to these few rooms, these short corridors and dim halls. An entire universe condensed into this compact existence. The perfect place to break us, to shatter our illusions. Only through the Harrowing and the Cleansing could we be prepared, made malleable like white-hot iron in a furnace, purified through heat, and ready to accept Revelation.*

The Revelation ran counter to all we once believed, which is the way of illumination. It was the only way we could learn, could see, and finally accept ultimate Truth: The universe is conflict. It is polluted and unclean. The only way it can be purified is by consuming itself and being reborn. Think of the ancient image of the snake devouring its own tail.

It has fallen to us—to me—to initiate the pulse of rebirth that will cleanse and renew the universe. And I am desperately afraid that I am unworthy of so great a task.

If Deck Three didn't have this observation dome, I would never have found the strength to endure the burden. But looking out at the infinite dots of light, the frosting of stars and galaxies that mottle the endless black, I manage to carry on.

The universe doesn't make mistakes.

If it has chosen me to be its messiah, it is because somehow, I will prevail.

I finger the scars on my arms, remembering the words of the Prophet Guan Shi. How we were horrified as she took a knife to her own skin and began to cut herself, saying, "Pain is purification. It is the path."

1

Watch began at 06:00 ship's time as *Ashanti* continued its long deceleration into the Capella star system. For Captain Miguel Angel Galluzzi it was anything but another day in the countdown from hell. He strode down the long corridor from his cabin. Every other light panel had been removed years ago to save energy. Didn't matter, he could have walked it blindfolded.

Around him, *Ashanti* hummed, and he could feel the familiar vibrations of a living ship. Could feel the movement of air on his face as he passed one of the ventilators. It surprised him that he could still detect the stale odor of confinement and clogged filters.

It had been seven years, ship's time, since *Ashanti*'s generators had ceased to maintain the fields that inverted symmetry. When they did, the ship had popped back "inside" the universe and found itself in black empty space. Low on fuel, and 0.6 light-years from the Capella system.

Since then he'd lived an eternity—one from which he wasn't certain he'd ever recover. A waking horror without end.

As if perdition began in *Ashanti* and would end there.

Sometimes he wondered if it wouldn't have been better to have overloaded the reactors. Blown the ship into a brilliant miniature sun. Ended it all.

He'd committed crimes against humanity, and in the process, he'd heroically saved his ship. But when one sells his soul to the Devil, the dark one will always have his due.

Galluzzi contemplated that as he passed the Captain's Lounge and hesitated at the hatch for the Astrogation Center, or AC for short. In another day and age, it would have been called the bridge. After the advent of quantum qubit computer operational systems, navigational functions had been completely removed from human control.

That didn't mean that people didn't have to monitor systems, that decisions didn't have to be made.

A feeling of excitement—mixed with nervous anxiety—began to burn in his breast. And something he hadn't known for years stirred: hope.

Staring at the featureless hatch, he swallowed in an effort to still the crawling sensation in his stomach. If the conference came off as scheduled, he would be talking to a Corporate Supervisor. For the first time he would have to confess and defend his actions. Didn't matter if they hauled him out and shot him as long as his crew didn't have to pay the price for his decisions.

The sick anxiety in his stomach worsened; that damnable nervous spasm began: his right hand was twitching like a poisoned mouse. He used to function with stone-cold competence under stress. The twitch had manifested in the hard months after they'd popped back "inside" so far from Capella.

Doesn't matter what they do to me. It will all be over soon.

For the last month, his first officer, Edward Turner, had been in contact with the Corporate survey ship, *Vixen.* The messages had been simple photonics, which due to the difference in relativity had been a rather drawn-out affair. This morning, as *Ashanti* came out of its occulted position from behind the system's primary they were finally close enough for a visual conference. Entangled photonic communications would allow them an almost simultaneous transmission.

Galluzzi girded himself. Wouldn't let the others see how fragile and anxious he was. Couldn't let them know how close to tears he felt.

The trembling in his right hand was getting worse. He knotted it into a fist.

Back stiff, composed, he cycled the hatch and stepped into the Astrogation Center to find his officers already in their seats. In the rear, Benj Begay, the forty-five-year-old Corporate Advisor/Observer was seated in one of the two observation chairs. Director of Scientific Research Michaela Hailwood, from the Maritime Unit, sat in the other.

"Good morning," Galluzzi greeted, snapping out a two-fingered salute from his brow. For today he'd worn his dress uniform. It felt good, professional, to be dressed for the part. Not that there were any illusions left when it came to his crew or the scientists. Not after a decade of living in such close quarters. But today, for the first time since inverting symmetry outside of Neptune's orbit, he'd be face-to-face with total strangers. Powerful strangers. And they would judge him.

"You ready?" Begay asked wryly. "I'm so wound up I could almost scream. Half of me wants to get up and dance, another part of me wants to throw up."

"Hard to believe. I know," Galluzzi replied. "But we're still not out of the shit. We've got a couple of months left before we're in Cap III orbit. And there's no telling what's going to happen when we finally inform the Unreconciled that we're closing on the planet."

"Do we have to tell them, Cap?" Second Officer Paul Smart sat at the com console and worked the photonic data.

"Might be better," Turner said, "if we just established orbit first. Shut most of the ship down. Then, when there was nothing left to go wrong, we could let them know."

Begay shifted uneasily. "Just leave them in the dark? Then spring it on them? Surprise! We're here."

Galluzzi, who'd been wrestling with the problem for days, raised a worried brow. "We're in uncharted depths. And remember, it's not our sole decision. There's Supervisor Aguila to consider. She's the Corporate authority here."

"Captain?" Second Officer Turner called, voice tense. "Might have been our synch that's off, but the signal's coming in." He bent to his projected holo data, using his hands and implants to manipulate the photonic gear and refine the signal.

Shit on a shoe. I'm not ready for this.

Galluzzi gritted his teeth, slipped into the command chair. Fought to control his trembling hand. He stared at the communications holo, dark now for a decade. The realization that he was about to face a strange superior sent an eerie chill down his spine.

The image formed up, faces magically appearing as if out of

empty air. Then, under Paul Smart's and the *Vixen* com officer's competent control, the photonics linked and the projection seemed to solidify.

Galluzzi was looking at a raven-haired woman, perhaps in her thirties—though with the benefits of Corporate med, who knew? What would have been a very attractive face was lined with fine white scars. Scars? On a Corporate Supervisor? The piercing blue of her eyes had a laser-like intensity. In her form-fitting black suit, the woman exuded a sense of command, had to be Supervisor Kalico Aguila.

A small brown man sat at her side. Looked Indian, with a round face and flat-mashed nose. His unruly shock of thick black hair—graying at the sides—rose a couple of inches above his head. Curious brown eyes and an amused smile suggested an amicable nature. The biggest incongruity was the man's dress. Like he was some peasant in a homespun brown shirt embroidered with yellow flowers, and a sort of shimmering rainbow-colored cloak hung around his shoulders.

"Do we have sound?" the blue-eyed woman asked.

"We can hear you on our side, Supervisor." Galluzzi fought a tightness in his throat. "I'm Captain Miguel Angel Galluzzi, of The Corporation's *Ashanti.* IS-C-18. Behind me is Corporate Advisor/Observer Benj Begay. Seated to his left is Scientific Director Michaela Hailwood."

"I'm Corporate Supervisor Kalico Aguila, in charge of all Corporate property and activity on Donovan. What you probably know as Capella III. With me is Shig Mosadek, one of the administrators of the independent town of Port Authority."

An independent town? What the hell was that?

An eyebrow lifted, rearranging the woman's scars. "Welcome to Donovan, Captain. From what I gather, you've had a much longer and vexatious journey than you anticipated. I've reviewed your communications with *Vixen.* Somehow, I suspect there's a lot more to your story."

His hand began to jerk spastically. He stuffed it into his belt. Hoped Aguila hadn't noticed. Forced himself to begin damage control. "We've had to make some difficult choices. *Ashanti* wouldn't be here were it not for my crew, ma'am. No matter what, I want it on the record that they have acted with the utmost professionalism under difficult and soul-trying circumstances. We're anxious for the day we can set foot on Donovan."

"I suspect that you will find conditions on Donovan somewhat, shall we say, unique."

Galluzzi felt like he was choking. Okay, get it over with. "Supervisor, we've got our own 'unique' problem. One of the reasons we've been looking forward to this conversation."

Was that a lie, or what?

From behind, Begay said, "Ma'am, as the Corporation's Advisor/Observer, I want you to know that I backed every one of Captain Galluzzi's decisions when it came to the Unreconciled." He paused at her blank look. "Um, the transportees, Supervisor. They also call themselves the Irredenta to signify their difference and isolation from normal human beings."

Galluzzi quickly added, "Given circumstances, we've had to take some rather distasteful and unorthodox actions. While I appreciate the Advisor/Observer's support, ultimately the responsibility is mine, and mine alone. Under no circumstances did my crew do anything but follow orders. They exhibited the most professional—"

The Supervisor cut him short with a raised a hand. "Start at the beginning, Captain."

Like a man condemned, Galluzzi took a deep breath. "After a two-and-a-half-year transit, *Ashanti* popped back into our universe. For the first couple of days, we hadn't a clue as to where we were. Just lost in the black. The reaction among the crew and transportees was dismayed to say the least.

"We didn't have enough fuel to invert symmetry, restart the qubit computers, and run the math backwards in a bid to return to Solar System. Not only that, we were so far out in the empty black, the figures were pretty grim when it came to hydrogen/oxygen scavenging."

"I can well imagine, Captain. Go on."

"After Astrogation Officer Tuulikki finally established our

position, it turned out that we were zero-point-six of a light-year from the Capella star system. We made the decision to run for it. Used what was left of the fuel for a burn, fully aware of how long it would take to reach Capella. But we were moving, which increased hydroxy scavenging. Had a couple of months where we weren't sure we were going to make it. At least until we hit the break-even point."

Call that a mild understatement.

Aguila's expression remained inscrutable, and in association with the scars, it suggested that he was dealing with one hard and tough woman.

"Of course, as we got closer to the Capella system, scavenging increased, which increased our thrust. Bootstrapping, you see. Then, two and a half years ago, we reversed thrust. Began the process of deceleration."

"Doesn't sound like anything but prudent and competent spacing, Captain."

"Yes, ma'am. The problem was the transportees. The hydroponics system had an operational life of four years. We were looking at ten. The only way to extend the hydroponics to last ten years was to reduce the demand put upon the system."

Aguila's face might have been carved from cold stone. No trace of emotion showed in her glacial-blue stare.

Galluzzi's heart began to pound. His mouth had gone dry. "I gave first priority to my crew. If they died, the ship died. We survived the cut in rations because we had a command structure. Discipline. A purpose. A bond that went deeper than mere shared humanity. But the transportees . . ."

Aguila's eyes narrowed the least bit, her lips pursed. "Did you euthanize them all?"

Euthanize?

"No, ma'am!" Galluzzi choked down a swallow. "They were panicked. Desperate. They could do the math as well as we could. Enough of them worked in hydroponics that it was common knowledge: Over time, feeding that many people, the vats were going to break down. Didn't matter that we didn't have enough fuel to invert symmetry in an attempt to return to Solar System, some of them decided they were going to seize the ship, space for Solar System. They made a violent try for the AC."

Galluzzi winced, remembering the bodies in the corridors. Blood pooling on the sialon.

"We held the ship, ma'am. Beat them back. They withdrew to Deck Three. Before they could reorganize and try for the command deck again, I had the hatches sealed. Welded. But for that, we'd never have saved *Ashanti*. Or the crew. Or any of the transportees."

"But you saved some?" she asked thoughtfully.

He couldn't stop the shiver that ran through him. Tried to still the memories. His hand was jerking despite being stuffed under his belt. The images that lurked behind his every thought drifted up like vaporous apparitions. To tell it to another person, someone who hadn't lived the horror, left him on the verge of tears.

How did he explain?

"What they did to each other down there? We saw, ma'am. At least in the beginning before they blacked out the cameras. It was . . . It . . ."

He couldn't stop the shakes.

Stop it! You're the captain!

He sucked in a breath, flexed every muscle in his body.

"I take it they turned on each other?" Aguila asked softly.

"With the critical ship's systems isolated from the transportees' deck, *Ashanti* continued to function as best she could. A food ration, insufficient as it was, was delivered to them by conveyor from the hydroponics, air and water circulated. Yes, we isolated the transportees, sealed them into Deck Three, but we gave them every support we could. Those were human beings in there. Families. Men, and women, and children."

"How many are still alive, Captain?"

"Not sure, ma'am. We inverted symmetry off Neptune with four hundred and fifty-two aboard. Eighty-seven were crew. Three hundred and sixty-five transportees, including the Maritime Unit. As of today, I have sixty-three crew. Counting the children born since transit began, there are thirty-two in the Maritime Unit. We estimate the population of the Irredenta at around ninety to a hundred."

"So, they're still sealed in your Deck Three?" Aguila's expression betrayed nothing. She seemed to be taking the news with an almost stoic acceptance. Why?

"Yes, well . . ."

After the "rats" had devoured themselves, they had "evolved" to be such . . . what? How did he describe the Irredenta without sounding like he'd lost his mind?

"Supervisor, we have a voice com still linked to Deck Three, and on occasion messages are passed. The Irredenta—the word refers to a culturally autonomous region existing under foreign control. Well, they don't exactly carry on sophisticated conversations. Mostly it's just propaganda about their Prophets. Their leader is a man named Batuhan. Thinks he's some sort of messiah. They say he interprets for the Prophets, whoever they are. What they send us sounds like raving. Supposed prophecies about what they call the coming 'Annihilation.' Some sort of violent spiritual cleansing of the universe."

"Messiah? Prophets?" Shig Mosadek, who'd sat silently, now asked.

"The Irredenta's leader, this Batuhan, is a fifty-year-old electrical engineer. Trained at the university at Ulaanbaatar, he was contracted on Transluna to install a new solar panel array for one of the outlying research bases on Capella III. Instead, after all the bloodshed, he's ended up as a sort of messianic leader among the Irredenta."

"Messiahs come in all forms," Mosadek replied.

"Sir." Galluzzi fought the urge to pull at his too-tight collar. "If I told you some of the things Batuhan's Irredenta have done down there, you'd call me mad. That human beings could descend to the kind of demonic . . ."

He winced, trying to keep the panic out of his voice. He didn't dare lose it. Not in front of the Supervisor.

Thankfully Benj said, "We're forwarding all the records to *Vixen.*

We want you to have plenty of time to review them before we arrive at Capella III."

Aguila had pursed her lips. "What happens if you unseal their deck?"

Benj spoke. "They'd murder us wholesale. Turn us into sacrifices. Cut up and eat our bodies. All in the name of their—"

"Did you say *eat*?" Aguila arched a scarred brow.

Shig had straightened, a gleam of curiosity in his eyes.

Benj's voice strained. "Some sort of belief that the universe must consume itself to be reborn in purity. That's according to Batuhan and his doctrine of holy annihilation. They think they're divine soldiers, chosen to carry their truth into the universe. They see existence as warfare. That the universe was designed to hone the fittest through perpetual self-consuming conflict. According to Batuhan's propaganda, their first trial will be the elimination of all the heretics aboard *Ashanti*. They see the ship as an interstellar womb, and as soon as they burst out of Deck Three, it will be like a birth of rage and fire."

"Fascinating," Shig murmured, his gaze intensifying.

Aguila asked, "Have they said anything about what happens after their arrival at Donovan?"

"Sure," Benj said. "Capella III is supposed to be the home that nurtures their development. Their 'childhood' as they call it. As they mature, the planet is supposed to be the springboard from which they shall spread out into the universe and either convert or destroy anyone who stands in their way."

"How did this happen?" Aguila asked.

Galluzzi winced. "I don't think you can understand until you realize the horror that engulfed Deck Three, ma'am. Like I said, they did the math. Knew that hydroponics could only produce enough to support around two hundred people in the long term. They started with a lottery. Some of the families that were chosen to starve to death didn't think much of the idea. Embarked on a more sanguine means of decreasing the population."

Benj said, "Things got ugly in a hurry down there. Think

atrocity and horror and no way out. The ones who survived committed the kind of abominations that defy description. They've been locked away on that deck for close to seven years now . . . lived in the midst of their self-reinforced insanity. They've prepared themselves for the moment of their emergence from Deck Three, and when they do, they expect to initiate a wave of horror that is so terrible it will both consume and regenerate the universe."

Aguila's brow had knit. "What kind of lunacy . . . ?"

Shig placed a mild hand upon the Supervisor's arm. "Unfortunately, depending upon the reality in which one has existed, atrocity might seem the only possible explanation for existence."

Aguila asked, "You think people can make a religion of violence?"

In an oddly calm voice, Shig said, "Human beings can create a religion out of anything. It's hardwired into our genetics. And, when you think about it, it's a lot easier to make a religion out of mayhem than salvation. Let's hold judgment until we see what's on these records *Ashanti* is sending."

Aguila turned her attention to Galluzzi. "And what about you and your crew, Captain?"

Here it came. He ran a hand over the back of his neck. Hated the feel of nervous perspiration. "Supervisor, it's been rough. Most of us who are left, we're hanging on by our fingernails. Not so many suicides these days. We've gotten good at patching ourselves together when we're on the edge of insanity. Would have given up long ago except that we could see the finish line. We knew there was an eventual end to the nightmare and could count down the days. As soon as we have *Ashanti* in orbit around Capella III, it's going to be all I can do to keep my people from storming the shuttles to abandon this ship."

"Yeah, well, Captain, I don't want to rain on your hopes, but you might not find Donovan to be the nirvana you've been led to believe."

"After *Ashanti*? We'll take our chances."

"Unfortunately," she told him dryly, "you will." A pause. "One last question. Is Derek Taglioni on your passenger manifest? Is he, perhaps, still alive?"

"He is, Supervisor. And I daresay, he'll be as delighted as the rest of us to set foot on Cap III."

The Supervisor's smile had taken on a grim set. "Captain, please understand, this is a fragile colony. A dangerous world fraught with perils to life and limb. As the Corporate Supervisor, I will be enforcing all stipulations as set forth in Corporate contracts. We'll give your people time to recover, but we're barely hanging on here ourselves."

"After *Ashanti*, anything would be an improvement."

"Really?" Aguila chuckled. "We have a joke here, we share it with all newcomers: Welcome to Donovan."

2

"What do you think, Shig?" Kalico Aguila asked as her A-7 shuttle dropped into Donovan's gravity well. Through the cabin windows on the command deck she could see the reddish glow as atmospheric friction built.

In the pilot's seat ahead of her, Ensign Juri Makarov monitored the descent.

Shig had been oddly quiet—and more unusual, he'd had a perturbed expression on his usually placid face as he reviewed the hand-held holo that displayed *Ashanti*'s logs. He sat in the seat beside hers on the command deck. Normally, in the shuttle, he reminded her of a schoolboy, fascinated and delighted by everything. As if the shuttle were a new and magical marvel.

He didn't look up as he casually asked, "Who is Derek Taglioni? Why did you ask specifically about him?"

"Derek's a first cousin to Boardmember Miko Taglioni."

"Ah, I see. The Boardmember is your superior and benefactor, as I recall."

"That's a mild way of putting it." To change the subject, she said, "The way you reacted to news about these Irredenta, that's not like you. Seriously, what set you off?"

Shig looked up from the holo display. "You must understand. The human brain is more of an analog rather than a digital organ. It's plastic, and by that, I mean it can be molded, shaped by events. When traumatized, it will struggle to make sense of the violation. Attempt to reconcile and explain the insult. If the trauma is too terrible, the brain will grasp for disparate facts, string together unrelated—even impossible—data to create understanding in the new conditions. Give meaning to everything it has endured."

"Sure. I understand how brain chemistry works. The bizarre things human beings will allow themselves to believe in an effort to cope."

"These were Corporate people," Shig reminded. "Families for the most part. People who were, and I quote, 'well integrated' in the Corporate system. They were educated, affluent, and prosperous families who lived their lives in secure and very comfortable upper-status surroundings. Had nice dwellings. Played by the rules and never suffered deprivation—let alone confronted a serious threat to their wellbeing. Living as they did in the center of the Corporate cocoon, they were coddled and protected. Call them the middle of the bell-shaped curve when it came to living the Corporate dream."

"I'm well aware of the demographic," she replied. "The Board wanted well-balanced families, the kind whose profiles didn't indicate potential trouble when they reached the colony. Families who'd immediately and seamlessly integrate into colonial society."

"Right," Shig agreed. "Kindly folk who'd just do their jobs and expect to be taken care of in return. If they had any overriding passion, it was for their family and raising their kids. Perfect young trade professionals."

Kalico stared out at the curve of Donovan's horizon as the shuttle's pitch changed; g-force pushed her down into her seat. "And then they come out of inverted symmetry. They've just spent two and a half years of ship's time living inside cramped quarters. Their nerves are already frayed when they're told that if they survive the next few months, it might be another seven years before they reach their destination. The hydroponics, designed for a four-year life span, can't support four hundred and fifty people for another seven."

"Things begin to degenerate. They panic. Some try to seize the ship, and Galluzzi seals them into a single deck." Shig rubbed his brow with a nervous hand. "Galluzzi's people recorded the condition of the stripped human bones that came down the chutes for hydroponics reprocessing. My suggestion is that you don't mistake these reports for cozy bedtime reading. At least not if you want a good night's sleep."

"That horrible?"

"The transportees were dying of starvation. Each corpse represented protein, fat, and life. But what does it mean? How do you justify surviving by eating your companions?" Shig smiled wistfully.

"In religious studies, we have a term: sacred abomination. It's when something is so abhorrent and appalling, its very profanity makes its practice sacred. The ultimate reconciliation of opposites."

"What do you mean by abomination?"

"The people locked on that deck were receiving insufficient rations. They were murdering men, women, and children. Their best friends. People they had lived with, laughed with, and knew intimately. Dismembering their bodies, stripping muscle from bones, removing and eating organs. Sometimes even the bones were smashed for marrow. Brains removed from skulls. How did they justify such atrocities? They made it a religious event. A form of communion."

"Dear God."

"And, of course, they understood that sex was the reconciliation of death. Its polar opposite. If you are going to celebrate one, you must pay tribute to the other."

"Maybe I'll skip the reading."

"Suffice it to say that all those cheery, happy, normal, coddled-and-protected families suddenly found themselves trapped in the kind of violent and profane terror that shattered their psyches. The only way to survive atrocity was to commit even greater atrocity. And they did it year after year. Locked in that seeming eternal hell of Deck Three."

She didn't have to know the intimate details to understand, having spent too many hours on *Freelander.* Just the thought of the ghost ship made her stomach turn queasy.

Shig raised a finger. "And into the mix, you must throw agency: Batuhan. The charismatic leader who tells you that it isn't your fault. It's just the way the universe is. You aren't an abomination but a divinely selected agent about to remake reality. Suddenly you are serving a higher calling. Sure, you murdered and ate babies, cut fellow human beings apart and drank their blood, but through that communion they are reborn into purity."

"That's creep-freaked."

"That's the religious mind at work in an attempt to rationalize and condone abject horror," Shig replied. "Or have the lessons taught by *Freelander* eluded you?"

"Believe me, I was half expecting Galluzzi to tell me that, like Captain Orten on *Freelander*, he'd ordered the murder of all the transportees."

"Fascinating, isn't it?" Shig tapped fingers on his chin. "Aboard *Freelander* the crew developed their curious death cult, worshipping the ghosts of the people they murdered and threw into the hydroponics. On *Ashanti*, it's the transportees who are murdering each other, who have developed their own cult. Leaves us wondering if this is random coincidence. Or, with a sample of only two, if there is something about being locked in a starship—faced with starvation, atrocity, and time—that triggers the religious centers of the brain."

"So, what do you think they've become?"

"Smashana Kali."

"Excuse me?"

"I think they have turned themselves into the most terrible manifestations of the Hindu demon-goddess, Kali. The black goddess who is descended from endless time, who decapitates her victims, drinks their blood, and wears the heads of the dead around her neck. By devouring her victims, she purifies them, and the world is reborn."

"And what happens to Kali in Hindu texts?"

"She only ceases her rampage when she steps onto Shiva's chest."

"This is the twenty-second century! And we're talking cannibals? Like some primitive forest tribe?"

"Just because it's the twenty-second century, what makes you think human beings have become a different animal? Because we have The Corporation and space travel? People are still fundamentally nothing more than technologically sophisticated chimpanzees."

"Back in Solar System we could reprogram them at a psychiatric facility." Kalico mused. "Treat the madness."

"We're not in Solar System."

"Shig, you're the professor of religious studies, the proponent of ethical behavior, what do we do with them?"

"I haven't a clue."

3

The captain's lounge aboard *Ashanti* seated six. Located just down the central corridor from Astrogation Control, the lounge was a cramped room jammed against the curve of the Command Deck hull. One of the few perks of "officer's territory," it even had a small galley on the back wall. Not that ten years of ship's time had left many choices except two: tea and ration.

Miguel Galluzzi—cup of said tea in hand—nodded to the rest as he entered, stepped around to the rear, and settled into the worn duraplast of his captain's chair. On the one working holo, an image of Donovan spun against a background of stars.

In their long-accustomed seats, First Officer Turner sat at Galluzzi's right, Benj Begay on his left. Second Officer Smart had the watch, so his chair remained empty. Michaela Hailwood hunched in the seat beside Begay's. Finally, at the far end near the door, Derek Taglioni slumped in his usual place.

Galluzzi took their measure. Begay was descended from Native American stock. He was forty-five now, kept his hair in a bun tied tightly at the back of his head. His dark eyes were thoughtful as he fingered the line of his blocky chin.

Turner, who stood six-foot-five, was now in his fifties. A faint English accent still lurked in the man's speech. Galluzzi couldn't be sure, but Turner's washed-out blue eyes seemed to grow paler by the year. Like all good spacers, he kept his head shaved.

Galluzzi's gaze lingered on Michaela Hailwood, forty-seven. The lanky black-skinned woman had been born in Apogee Station. A curious origin for someone who would become chairperson of the Department of Oceanography at Tubingen University on Transluna. She headed the group of scientists dispatched aboard *Ashanti* to establish the first research station for the study of Capella III's oceans.

Still slumped in his chair, Derek Taglioni had laced his fingers together. The man's genetically engineered yellow-green eyes fixed on Galluzzi. Turns out that designers of fine haute couture on Transluna didn't tailor their snazzy garments for longevity; Taglioni's exotic clothing no longer looked natty and sharp. Derek, Dek for short, might have been in his mid-thirties, but given the medical benefits of being a Taglioni, who knew? Today his sandy-blond hair was combed over. The guy looked classic; his chiseled jaw even featured a dimple in the chin.

In the beginning—being a Taglioni—Dek had been a real self-inflated prig. Imperious. Demanding. But something about survival, about realizing that no amount of power or wealth made him any more valuable than a lowly hydroponics tech, Class III, had wrought remarkable changes in his personality and approach to life. The condescending arrogance had begun to break down during the transit. For years he'd even shaved his head like crew. But during those long months when it looked like they were all going to die? That's when something fundamental had changed in Taglioni.

Amazing what kind of man can evolve when he's knocked off his high horse and face-first into the shit.

Galluzzi stared down into his cup of tea. Not like the real thing, mind you, but a green liquid made from boiled spinach, algae, and leaves. Stuff that still grew in hydroponics, though the nutritional content was down considerably from the early days.

They all showed signs of malnutrition.

"What do you think?" Galluzzi asked. He was long past formalities with these people.

Benj, still fingering his chin, said, "Aguila's not like any Corporate Supervisor I ever knew. When I saw the scars, it scared hell out of me. Like she was one of the Unreconciled. Sent a shiver right up my spine."

Michaela placed her long-fingered hands flat on the table. "She didn't bat an eye when we told her we sealed the transportees on Deck Three. Not a single protest. Nothing about what the contractual implications might be, or what it was going to cost The Corporation in litigation."

"Tough lady," Turner said thoughtfully. "Sounds like Cap III has fallen on hard times while we've been in transit. I don't know about the rest of you, but I'm not sure how the crew is going to take this. We've sold them on the belief that when we reach Cap III, it's going to be like a paradise."

Benj chuckled. "Hey, just being out in fresh air, under an open sky, is paradise."

"After what we've been through, you'd think the universe would cut us a break." Galluzzi sipped his tea. Tried to remember what it was supposed to taste like. Nothing had much taste anymore.

Turner shot him a sidelong glance. "I think you just got your break, Miguel. Aguila didn't immediately order you arrested for what we did. I thought she'd take that a whole lot harder."

"Something's not right," Benj added. "We lost two thirds of the transportees, and what's left are man-eating monsters. Drop that kind of bombshell on a Corporate Supervisor? You expect to let loose a shitstorm."

"She almost took it as a foregone conclusion." Galluzzi rubbed his face, thankful that his hand was no longer shaking. Damn, he'd been on the edge. Like the others, he'd expected to be relieved of command, pilloried, maybe even charged with mass murder.

He glanced at Taglioni. Had hoped that if Corporate was going to flush him down the shitter, that Dek would be his only chance. Betting on a Taglioni? It showed how desperate a man could be.

"Think it's some kind of political gambit?" Begay wondered. "You know. The kind of intrigue the Board is into: layers within layers. Maybe we're suddenly pawns in some complex game she's playing. Like she's going to use our failure to keep the transportees alive as a means to destroy some adversary."

Was that it? Galluzzi's stomach began to roil. He felt the first tremors in his hand. "I just wish it was all over."

"Hey, Miguel," Michaela told him, "you're getting ahead of yourself. We all are. Think, people. There's going to be an inquest. There has to be. You can't just seal three hundred and sixty people into a confined space, let them mutilate and eat each other, and expect to walk away without some sort of questions."

She glanced around the table. "We've known since the beginning that a day of reckoning is coming. In the meantime, we stick together. Let's not forget that by doing what we did, we got the ship to Cap III. And we did it with most of the crew alive. The entire Maritime Unit is not only alive, but with the kids there's a lot more of us than spaced from Solar System."

"Steps had to be taken," Benj agreed. "Remember what it was like? We all agreed that if we made it, we'd stand together. That what they did to one, they'd have to do to all of us."

"Here, here," Turner muttered, watery eyes fixed on infinity.

Benj turned to Taglioni. "Dek? Your word is going to carry the most weight."

Taglioni's lips bent into a thin smile. "You're assuming my family's still in power."

"Aguila asked specifically if you were aboard," Benj reminded.

"That has as many ominous interpretations as it does positive ones, Board politics being what it is."

"Let's wait and see," Galluzzi told them. "If it comes down to it, and there has to be a sacrifice, it is my responsibility."

"You're not doing that holy martyr thing again, are you?" Michaela asked. "We didn't like it the first time you pulled that shit."

He smiled, sipped his tea, looked around at the familiar faces. He'd alternately shunned these people, loved or hated them, sought their company, and periodically despised them. Between them, they had no secrets. Well, maybe but for Taglioni. Not that he hadn't done more than his share, pulled more than his weight, but he'd always kept himself apart. Maintained a distance.

"No martyrdom. It's just that the end, at last, is in sight. Mostly, however, it's because after what we've been through, if they need a sacrifice, I don't give a damn. I'm just . . . tired."

Taglioni was watching him with those piercing yellow-green eyes. Even after all these years, they still sent a shiver up Galluzzi's spine.

There would be a price. There had to be.

4

The tavern in Port Authority was called The Bloody Drink; the moniker dated back to a more sanguine period in the colony's early existence. Most folks just called it Inga's after the proprietor. Inga Lock was a large-boned blonde woman in her forties with thick arms, a no-nonsense disposition, and a talent for brewing, distilling, and producing extraordinary wines from local grains and fruits.

Inga's tavern had originally been housed in one of the midsized utility domes, but as it was the planet's only public house, the crowds had necessitated expansion. Since the dome couldn't be enlarged—and with Donovan being a mining planet—Inga had dug down to create the cavernous stone-floored room that now sported locally made chabacho-wood tables, benches, chairs, a restaurant, and on the west end, the curving bar from which Inga dispensed her liquid refreshments.

A ramp in the storeroom behind the bar led up to street level and the two-story stone building that housed her distillery, brewery, and winery. The upper floor she rented out to itinerant miners and hunters—called Wild Ones—who might be in town.

On the righthand side of the bar, Security Officer Talina Perez perched atop her usual stool. She wore mud-spattered and smudged quetzal hide: a rainbow-color-shifting leather made from one of the native predators. Next to her knee, her rifle was propped against the bar. Hung from a strap around her neck, a floppy leather hat flattened Tal's raven-black hair against her back.

"Hard day?" Inga asked as she approached with her rolling gait, a bar towel over her shoulder. Talina's glass mug—filled with a thick stout topped by an inch of creamy head—was in Inga's right hand. This she deposited on the scarred wood with a thunk.

"Step Allenovich and I spent the last three days out in the bush, working the breaks leading into the Blood Mountains. Tracked Whitey that far. Storm hit. Winds were too strong for the drones. Had to wait it out. Once we could fly again, we'd lost the sign."

"You look all in."

"I'm eating whatever you got, sucking down a couple of glasses of stout, and then I'm off to sleep for a week."

"You sure it was Whitey? One quetzal pretty much looks like another."

"We managed to get a drone right on top of him. Crippled left front leg? Couple of bullet scars on his hide? Slight limp in his right leg? Gotta be him."

Down in Talina's gut, Demon—piece of shit that he was—hissed in approbation at the mention of Whitey's escape. But then Whitey's molecules where part of what made Demon such an insufferable beast.

Talina could feel Rocket shift on her shoulder—the little quetzal's presence as illusory as Demon's. In the words of Talina's ancient Maya ancestors, she was *Way*. Pronounced "Wh-eye." A spirit-possessed dreamer, transformed, one-out-of-many. Her quetzals were *Wayob*. Dream essences. Spirits who lived within.

"When it comes to Whitey, you'd know. You were the one who shot him up." Inga wiped the bar down with her towel before slapping it over her shoulder. "Food'll be up in a minute."

Tal tossed out a five SDR coin.

"You're still up two fifty on your account, Tal."

"Put it toward my tab. Day might come, Inga, when I'm caught short."

The big woman snatched up the coin. "Yeah, as if that would ever happen."

"You forget, I have a habit of pissing people off in this town." And, hero to them she might be, but Talina Perez was still a freak, infected as she was with quetzal TriNA.

"This far down the line, Tal, it would take some real doing for you to make it permanent." Inga shot her a wink and retreated down the bar to note the amount on her big board where she kept her accounts.

Talina chuckled under her breath. Inside, she was what the Maya called *pixom*—of two conflicting souls. In her case, that of killer in opposition to that of protector.

Funny thing, to travel thirty light-years across space in order to discover that her ancient heritage was the only way to make psychological sense of who she had become after quetzal molecules began playing with her brain.

Down the bar, Stepan Allenovich, mud-spattered himself, was calling for whiskey. Three days in the bush hunting quetzal, and the lunatic was going to spend the rest of the night drinking and singing. Then he'd no doubt wander over to Betty Able's brothel where he'd drink some more, pay to screw Solange Flossey, and finally make his way to The Jewel casino. The man was an animal.

Talina sipped her stout, let the rich beer run over her tongue. Damn, she'd missed beer. Three days of hardscrabble hunting on foot and by air, and that pus-sucking Whitey had put the slip on them again.

"*Yes,*" Demon hissed from behind her stomach.

It only felt like the quetzal lived in her gut. The Port Authority physician, Raya Turnienko, had repeatedly proven to Talina that there was no quetzal hiding out behind her liver. Rather—like the presence of Rocket on her shoulder—that was how the thing manifested. Used transferRNA to communicate with the nerve cells in her brain. Not that Demon was a single quetzal, but existed as a composite made up of the TriNA molecules from a quetzal lineage. Whitey's lineage.

Nor was that the only quetzal TriNA that infested her. The one she called "Rocket," the *Wayob* that perched on her shoulder, was made up of several different quetzals from the Mundo, Briggs, and Rork lineages. Her blood and tissues were thick with the stuff.

One and many at the same time.

Only a Maya shaman would understand.

Talina just wanted the shit out of her body.

"But I'll get you in the end," she promised both Whitey and Demon.

"*Or we'll get you.*"

"Been trying that for the last four years, you piece of shit." She sipped her stout.

Rocket's spectral presence chittered quetzal laughter in her ear. She gave the little twerp a wry smile in reply.

Talina turned to take in the tavern. Inga's was half full: miners, the local trades people, and the weekly rotation from down at Corporate Mine now came trickling in. The few local troublemakers, like Hofer, seemed to be in a convivial mood.

Good. She'd hate to have to go bust heads.

Talina saw Kalico Aguila descending the steps. Beside her, Shig Mosadek was saying something, his hands gesturing in emphasis. Kalico was dressed in her last fancy Supervisor's uniform—the one she was saving for special occasions. That the woman would dress up like . . . Ah, yes. This must be the day she'd taken the shuttle up to *Vixen* to contact *Ashanti.*

Captain Torgussen had delayed *Vixen*'s departure to rendezvous with a particularly intriguing comet in order to allow Aguila to use *Vixen*'s photonic com. By now the survey ship was accelerating hard to catch the comet as it rounded Capella.

Shig, who had also attended, was wearing his locally milled fabric shirt with the squash-blossom flowers Yvette had embroidered on the front. To Talina's knowledge, the comparative religions scholar didn't have anything resembling formal attire in his wardrobe. Shig's only concession to fashion was the quetzal-hide cape he reserved for rainy days.

Talina arched an eyebrow as Aguila turned her way, strode across the fitted stones in the floor, and hitched herself into the elevated chair beside Talina's. Shig clambered onto the stool on Aguila's right.

"What's with the fancy dress? Trying to impress the new folks?" Talina asked.

"Just back from *Vixen.*" Aguila had a thoughtful look on her scarred face. "*Ashanti*'s finally close enough that we could have a conference on the photonic com. Talked to the captain, the Corporate Advisor/Observer, and the science director. Not that it's a huge surprise, but the situation on *Ashanti* is a bit grimmer than we'd been led to believe on the text-only long-range com."

"How grim?"

Aguila grinned humorlessly; it rearranged her scars. "Grim enough that I told Shig he's buying the whiskey."

"Couldn't be worse than *Freelander*." Memories of Talina's last time aboard the ghost ship still sent fingers of ice slipping down her backbone. And to think she'd condemned Tamarland Benteen to that eerie and endless hell.

"Maybe not," Shig agreed. "But trouble still. We finally got an explanation for some of the hesitation they've expressed through their messages. They've been ten years in that bucket. Out there in the black for almost seven now. Popped back in more than a half a light-year from Capella."

"Shit. And let me guess. Didn't have the fuel to pop back out?"

Aguila's gaze thinned as she gestured down the bar to Inga. "Miracle and tragedy all in one. The miracle's that they're alive. The tragedy is what they had to do to stay that way for seven years in a ship that couldn't feed them all."

"They murder the transportees like the crew of *Freelander* did?"

"Might just as well have," Kalico told her. "Captain Galluzzi sent his official log to *Vixen,* along with the Observer/Advisor's reports. Shig and I gave them a quick scan. The transportees tried to take the ship. It got bloody. Failed. So Galluzzi had them sealed onto the transportee deck. And left them there."

"Bet they're ready to get the hell out."

Shig glanced at her. "It's just Galluzzi's word, of course, but it may be a bit more complicated than that. If the good captain and the records are to be believed, things turned remarkably brutal among the transportees. Over the last six years they have apparently developed some sort of messianic cult based on the notion of controlled violence and eating one's fellows as a reflection of the universe. At this stage we can only guess at the depth of the belief and its intricacies. If there's good news, it is that there's only about a hundred of them left."

Aguila added, "Just talking about it, Galluzzi broke into a cold sweat. The guy's almost a basket case, and he's scared. Really scared." She shot Shig an evaluative look. "So much so that he sent me a private com just before we stepped off *Vixen.* Asked me to consider blowing up *Ashanti* as soon as he could get his crew off."

Shig's round face puckered. "That's a bit extreme, even for cannibals, don't you think?"

"Excuse me? Cannibals?" Talina asked.

Kalico gave her a dead stare. "Think locked on Deck Three with insufficient food. It's eat your neighbor or be eaten by him. One or the other."

"Oh, shit."

"Blowing up the ship would solve some of Galluzzi's problems," Shig mused.

"Hey?" Talina asked. "What about the cargo? *Ashanti*'s holds must be full of things we need. Equipment. Parts. Seeds, maybe cacao, or cotton, or who knows what? And unlike *Freelander* it wasn't lost in space for a hundred and twenty-nine years."

Aguila laid a 10-SDR coin out for Inga, saying, "My party tonight. Put whatever's left on my tab."

"Thought I was buying," Shig said. "That was the deal."

"How's the vegetable market these days?" Aguila asked.

"I sold a couple of squash last week," Shig told her proudly.

Shig made most of his income from his garden. One of the most influential men on Donovan, Shig Mosadek was also one of the poorest. He was a third of the triumvirate—the three-person government of Port Authority. Shig was the conscience, the public face, and liaison to the community. Yvette Dushane—a pragmatic woman in her fifties—did the nuts and bolts daily administration and record keeping. Talina Perez served as security chief, enforcer, and protector.

Inga set a whiskey down before Aguila and placed a half-full glass of wine before Shig, saying, "My latest red from those sirah grapes they transplanted from Mundo Base." Then she scooped up the coin, heading back down the bar before reaching up to credit Kalico's account on her big board.

Talina asked, "We're not seriously blowing up a starship, are we?"

"Of course not." Aguila raised her whiskey and swished it around, inhaled, and took a sip. "Oh, that's her new barrel. Much better than last month's."

"So, remind me. That leaves us with how many traumatized maniac religious cannibal nuts?" Talina asked. "A hundred, you say? What are you thinking? Put 'em in the domes in the residential section? Let them rub elbows with us locals until they come back to their senses?"

Shig studied his half glass of wine. "I think that would be a bad idea. At least given what we currently know about them."

"I can't put them up at Corporate Mine," Aguila said. "First, I don't have the dormitory space. Second, we're a pretty tight organization down there these days. If I drop a hundred soft meat into the mix, I'm going to have chaos. And who knows what kind of skills these people have?"

"Not to mention that they eat people. That will go over big in the cafeteria," Shig noted.

"So that brings us back to some of the empty domes in the residential district." Talina shrugged. "If they start to get out of line, it may take a couple of head whacks, but my guess is that between us, we can civilize them."

Shig held up his hand for attention. "I don't think that's wise, let alone an operative plan of action."

"Okay," Talina told him. "Since when is having someone like me, Talbot, or Step coming down on a bit of misbehaving—"

"I took the opportunity to read some of the ravings the Irredenta sent to Captain Galluzzi."

"The irrawho?"

"The Irredenta," Shig told her. "That's what they're calling themselves. That, and they often refer to themselves as the Unreconciled. The words attributed to their Prophets reek of demented religious fanaticism. These people believe that they have passed through a brutal selection, that they have been given absolute truth. That they've been chosen to possess the one true understanding of God and the ultimate reality of the universe. Worse, they've been locked away, isolated, and survived a most terrible winnowing. Events stripped them of their humanity. They committed atrocities, acts that abnegated the kind of people they were before the trauma."

"So what? Donovan is no one's idea of a picnic," Talina retorted.

Shig softly said, "In my view, turning them loose in PA or Corporate Mine would be to unleash a calamity."

"Bit melodramatic, don't you think?" Talina asked.

Shig arched a bushy eyebrow. "After the rise of The Corporation, religious fundamentalism was suppressed, monitored. But think back to your security training. You must have run across historical references to fringe beliefs, fanatical interpretations of scripture. Millenarians. Radical cults. Most were led by charismatic individuals thought of as messiahs by their followers."

"Yeah," Talina said, "but this is Donovan. That kind of silliness doesn't last long here. You know how I'm always joking about the Buddha never existing on Donovan? 'Cause if he'd seated himself under a mundo tree, a nightmare would have eaten him. Same for a self-proclaimed prophet. They all digest the same in a quetzal's gut."

Aguila had been listening; from her expression she'd been accessing her implants, scanning data. Now she said, "I side with Shig. If these people are as indoctrinated to violence and their holy cause as Galluzzi says and their writings indicate, turning them loose in either PA or Corporate Mine would be a major mistake at worst, horrendously destabilizing at best."

Shig dryly asked, "Do you really think that practicing cannibals preaching apocalypse can just move into the dome next door without repercussions?"

"So? Leave them up on the ship?"

Aguila's wary smile rearranged her scars. "We want that ship. We need that ship. I've got a fortune in rare metals, clay, and gemstones in containers up in orbit. You've got shipping containers full of clay and plunder stacked seven-deep around the shuttle field. Maybe *Turalon* arrived on schedule back at Solar System last year. Maybe it didn't. But *Ashanti* is coming in. If we can load her to the gills with wealth, ship her back to Solar System—even if we have to do it on AI—it's another shot at long-term survival."

"We could lock the cannibals up with crazy old Tam Benteen on *Freelander*," Talina mused.

Aguila shook her head. "What? Compromise our only platform for freefall and vacuum manufacturing?"

"You'll have *Ashanti*," Shig pointed out.

"Not if we can convince someone to space her back to Solar System and make us all rich," Aguila added. "Galluzzi really wants me to blow them up."

"Morally unacceptable." Shig declared as he fingered his wine glass. Talina grunted in agreement.

"Which leaves the planet. Maybe they're crazy as the quanta. Maybe in the end, they can't be reconciled with the rest of us. We won't know until we can see for ourselves." Aguila lifted her whiskey, studying the amber fluid in her glass. "Put them down at Mundo Base? Buy it from Mark Talbot's family?"

"Not that they'd sell," Talina said. "And the quetzal lineage down there's really hostile."

"Tyson Station," Shig said. "Way out west. On that mesa top. Five domes. Just right for about a hundred people. Good garden space. Enough cisterns and capacity to handle a population that size."

"Never been there," Aguila said.

Talina sipped her stout. "Might work. Somebody needs to go out there. Check it out."

Aguila shot Shig a sidelong look. "You all right with that? I mean, given your moral imperatives, all that talk about freedom? About government staying out of people's lives? Isn't this a form of playing god? Making these decisions for those people?"

Shig gave a half-hearted shrug. "One of the few tenants of government in a libertarian system is that the state should provide for the common defense. If these people arrived in our skies infected with some contagious disease, we would be within our moral rights to place them in quarantine for the protection of the general population."

"But this is a cult."

Shig's eyebrows lifted. "And what makes you think that zealous adherence to a messianic religious cult isn't just as dangerous as smallpox, rubella, or ebola?"

THE PROPHETS

I sit among the Prophets. The room we placed them in has come to be called The Temple. It used to be a recreation room, the walls surrounded by monitors and VR holo projectors long gone black and now decorated with drawings based upon the holy utterances. In places quotes that have passed the Prophets' lips are written on the walls.

This room, these three holy people, are the repository of Truth.

Their beds are laid out in a triangle, and I sit in the exact center between them.

At the top—in the position of honor—lies Irdan, once a specialist in the use and maintenance of scientific equipment like microscopes and centrifuges. He was the first who was called. As the sacred presence of the universe slowly possessed his body, took his coordination, and began giving him visions, the initial Prophecies passed his lips.

Within days, Callista, young, dark, and insecure, was the second to be called. Her specialty was medical equipment: scanners, imaging machines, and diagnostic equipment. She'd started to stumble, her hands to twitch, as the universe took possession of her.

Not another week had passed before Guan Shi, a plumber by trade, began to drop things. Started to stumble in her walk. Her speech grew slurred, her train of thought inconsistent. By then, we knew the signs of the calling.

As the years have passed, the Prophets have fallen deeper and deeper into the universe. As they have, their voices have become more profound and ever more cryptic. I suppose this makes sense. Like newborn infants, we need to learn the language. A neonate does not immediately comprehend Shakespeare, Mak Shi, or Sophocles.

What worries me as I sit here is that as the Prophets fall deeper into the universe, their health is deteriorating. They have no control over their bodies and can barely swallow when food is placed on their tongues. But even more ominous, these days I can rarely understand their Prophecy. Statements like,

"Waa wass glick faa faa," which Callista has uttered as I sit here, have no meaning to me.

It begs the question: When the universe chooses a Prophet, does it inevitably suck them down and devour them, much in the same way as we consume the impure? Is their fate the most enviable of all? Or, is it that we—myself in particular—despite being the repository of so many lives and souls, are only capable of limited understanding? Perhaps I cannot learn the language past a certain level of comprehension, similar to a learning-impaired child whose linguistic abilities are forever capped at the age of five?

In the former case, we are reassured, for we have others now—Shimal Kastakourias in particular—who have begun to show the initial signs of incipient Prophesy.

If the latter—which is the nightmare that keeps me awake in the night—then I am unmanned by the possibility that I might not be capable of performing the daunting task for which I've been chosen.

Irdan's legs twitch; his sunken eyes flicker sightlessly as he says something that sounds like, "Thaaweenaah."

In that moment, I fear I am not only unworthy, but too stupid to comprehend the remarkable Truth that Irdan has just shared.

If that is the case, I am a failure.

I hang my head and weep.

5

The Taglionis were one of the few true dynasties in The Corporation. Back in the mid-twenty-first century, when it became apparent that national governments couldn't be trusted with the responsibility of running the planet, the family had been instrumental in the establishment of Corporate control over the world economy.

The algorithms had taken care of the rest. Remarkable what a settling effect comprehensive monitoring and perfect resource distribution had when it came to keeping the populace mollified and compliant. But then the Romans had figured out the rudiments clear back when it was just bread and circuses.

Since the establishment of The Corporation, through adroit skills, a lack of preoccupation with ethics, and no little daring and guile, the Taglioni family had maintained its position on the Board of Directors. And that—in the face of competition from the likes of the Radceks, the Grunnels, the Suhartos, and Xian Chan families—took some doing.

Derek had grown up as a well-connected and influential scion in the midst of the family's treacherous web. Though they'd vied to dominate the power elite, his parents had been outmaneuvered from the start by Miko Taglioni's mother and father: They'd had a lock on the Board.

Nevertheless, Board politics being what it was, Derek and his other cousins had been kept in the wings, waiting, each constantly being groomed in case he or she should be called upon by the family elders to step into the role of Corporate Boardmember should anything happen to Miko and his immediate siblings.

Yet here I am.

Derek stood in the Crew Deck observation dome on *Ashanti*'s port side and stared at the now-familiar swirls and splashes of stars.

He kept thinking back. How he'd thrown a petulant tantrum, told Miko that he was tired of being a sidelined ornament. That if he wasn't given his due, he'd make it on his own.

And Miko had laughed in his face.

Hands clasped behind his back, Derek contemplated the interstellar majesty beyond the transparency. This day he wore a secondhand set of coveralls, the elbows and knees patched. Secondhand? And stained from the hydroponics lab? How far the mighty had fallen. At the thought, a dry chuckle broke his lips.

"Something funny?" Miguel Galluzzi asked from behind.

"Didn't hear you come in."

"Just wanted to take a look outside before I call it a day."

Derek shot the captain a sidelong glance as the man took a position beside him. The captain's gaze was fixed on the dot of light just to the right of Capella. He pointed. "That's Cap III. Right there. In plain sight." A pause. "So many times over these last endless years . . . well, I never thought I'd see this day."

"That's what I was chuckling about." Derek rocked on his heels. "I'll remind you that I came on this trip in a fit of pique. If they wouldn't give me what I wanted, I'd show them. I'd ship off for Cap III and make my own way, build my own empire."

Galluzzi gave him a wary glance. "So you've said. From the reports we've seen, Donovan isn't exactly Transluna. They've got less than a thousand people down there. And government is split between Corporate and this Port Authority. It's starting to sound like growing a garden is the most successful thing a man can do dirtside."

"Aguila is the Corporate authority. If there's anything for me, it will be through her."

"I see."

"No, you don't. Miguel, you come from a normal family. The Taglionis? We have a lot more in common with the Irredenta than we do with normal people. It's just that we devour each other in more figurative terms. Looking back at who I was the day I stepped aboard *Ashanti* compared to who I am now? Well . . . I wonder why you didn't step up when I wasn't looking, shoot me in the head, and drop me down the chute to feed the hydroponics."

"Thought about it a time or two," Galluzzi said. "You might think that being a Taglioni is an imposition, but family reputation isn't without its rewards. It kept you alive back when you'd have been of more value to us as nutrients in the hydroponics vats."

Derek stared thoughtfully at the pinpoint of light that was Capella III. "I'm sorry I was such a miserable shit, Miguel. I just . . . well, I'm sorry." He barked an amused laugh. "Pus in a bucket, imagine that. Derek Taglioni just apologized to another human being for being an asshole. Don't let *that* get back to the family."

"You make it sound like a first."

"You may be most assured that it is." Derek, lifted his chin. "We're taught to never, ever, under any circumstance, apologize to anyone. To do so would imply that we were at fault. A Taglioni, you see, never makes a mistake."

"That seems a bit unrealistic."

"What does reality have to do with it? I have discovered—to my undying horror over these last seven years—that people can be such self-deluded idiots. Given what we've survived? The choices I've watched you make. It's like having my skin ripped off to leave my naked quivering muscles and nerves exposed to a most painful truth."

"Neither of us will ever be the people we once were. I'm still not sure that something terrible isn't waiting for me when we reach Cap III. There has to be a price paid for what I did."

"You made a choice and saved the ship."

"I condemned three hundred and forty-two innocent men, women, and children to starvation and the survivors to a living hell. I locked them in and left them no alternative than to become monsters in a free-for-all of murder, inhumanity, and suffering."

"I saw the holo. Supervisor Aguila didn't bat an eye when you told her that you'd sealed the transportees in."

"I expected her to order my immediate arrest." A pause. "I think I know why she didn't."

"Oh?"

"There's another ship in orbit around Donovan. She's called *Freelander.* Something went really wrong when she inverted symmetry.

Went someplace 'outside' where time is different. Some effect of relativity. She aged one hundred and twenty-nine years during a two-and-a-half-year transit. *Freelander* was carrying five hundred transportees. When her captain, Jem Orten—a man I knew and admired—figured out that they were marooned in time, he and his crew killed them. Asphyxiated them. Then froze the corpses and added them to the hydroponics over the years as the molecules began to break down."

"Did you ever consider going to that extreme?"

Galluzzi pursed his lips, nodded. "Funny, isn't it? I could seal them up in Deck Three, let them murder each other and become psychotic cannibals, but simple euthanasia was morally reprehensible. I guess, after what happened with *Freelander,* my actions with the Irredenta didn't have quite the same impact they once would have."

"Then maybe Supervisor Aguila has a pragmatic streak to her personality. And who knows? She may actually live up to her reputation."

"Which is?"

"She was one of Miko's protégées," Derek noted. "As of when we spaced, she was the Supervisor of the Transluna district. Met her a couple of times back in Transluna. The circumstances of which I hope she's forgotten. She has a capability ranking of 9.8."

"What does that mean?"

"Means Miko thinks she could go all the way to Boardmember. Me? Best rank I ever got was a 7.6. My flaw was always emotional volatility. The kind that would make me lose control. Do something dumb. You know, like throw a temper tantrum and stomp off to join a ship headed for Cap III. Teach the bastards a lesson. Show them all what a real Taglioni could do." A pause. "And you can see how well that worked out."

Galluzzi chuckled. Pointed at the planet, and asked, "So, what are you going to do now?"

"Haven't a clue, Miguel. That old original plan of making planet, throwing my weight around, taking charge of some money-making and high-prestige venture doesn't have the same appeal. Not only that, but the files *Vixen* has sent on Donovan indicate it's not the thriving colony we were told to expect. It never was. Even way back then. Supervisor Clemenceau, who I figured I could manipulate, has been dead for as long as we've been in space."

He stared at the dot of light that was Cap III. As if he could feel it across the distance. Calling to him in a way that bordered on the mystical. As if the planet was in harmony with his blood.

Sheer silliness. But still . . .

"I'm sure Supervisor Aguila, if she's in the Taglioni fold, will find something for you."

"Maybe."

"Why do you say that?"

"I know that you told her I was on board. Since then I haven't heard a word from her."

"So? She's busy. She's a Supervisor in charge of an entire planet."

"You don't understand. I'm a first cousin to Miko, and she's in his stable. Kalico Aguila should have immediately placed a call to my com. Should have offered up her compliments, inquired about my welfare, asked what she could do to be of service. Doesn't matter that we didn't part on the best of terms, such a call is required protocol for a high-ranking member of the Taglioni family."

"I see." The look on Galluzzi's face indicated that he was happy to only have a ship to worry about.

"That she did not immediately initiate contact is about as disturbing as my own reaction."

"And what's that?"

Derek lifted an eyebrow. "Supervisor Aguila is no longer playing the Corporate game. Either that or she's switched allegiances to another Boardmember. But if she had, why would she tip her hand? That doesn't make sense. You don't just telegraph hostile intent to a potential opponent."

"What are you going to do if she's changed sides?"

"That's the second remarkable thing. The miracle of my reaction to Aguila's slight. Hey, I've scrubbed corridors and toilets, worked in hydroponics, bumped elbows and starved with you and your crew, worried from day to day that I was going to die. I've watched the rise of the monsters down in Deck Three. Spent nights in terror, unable to sleep for fear they would break free and cut my intestines out while I screamed. That *Ashanti* was my tomb. Do you think that after that, I could give a damn over a skipped courtesy call?"

But that still left the question: Now that the impossible appeared to be happening—that they were going to actually live long enough to get off *Ashanti*—what was he going to do once he set foot on Capella III?

And worse, what did it mean when Kalico Aguila wasn't acting the way she should? Derek might not have wanted to play the game, but that didn't mean that Aguila wouldn't still use him as a pawn in a game of her own.

6

The thing about living on Donovan was that it always seemed to take a series of unexpected twists. Just when a person figured he or she had a handle on life, it was only to find oneself zipping off at a ninety-degree angle from the expected path. Traveling in a direction never anticipated—and initially so stunned from the trajectory-altering impact as to be incapable of reacting to the change.

Security Second Mark Talbot's life had taken exactly those kinds of hits. He'd arrived on Donovan as part of Kalico Aguila's Marine detail. He'd backed Lieutenant Spiro's faction of "loyal" marines when Cap Taggart resigned from the Corps. When *Turalon* was about to space, he'd joined fellow marines Shintzu and Garcia for a quick trip into the forest. Just a chance to say they'd been face to face with Donovan's wilderness.

The forest had immediately crushed their aircar. A nightmare had finished off Garcia. Slugs had eaten their way through Shintzu's guts. Talbot had found himself alone; only his armor had saved him on his march across the forest to Mundo Base.

Again his life had been smacked sideways: Within months he was a polygamist married to three women, had a family and responsibilities as a father. Only to lose it all when Mundo Base fell apart, the local quetzals turned against humans, and he and his wives and children had to flee to Port Authority.

In the curious calculus that was survival on Donovan, he'd been there to save Talina Perez's life when a rogue marine would have shot her from ambush.

Since then he'd been a jack of all trades, with his time spent between Corporate Mine and PA. Father, husband, teacher, advisor, and finally, somehow catapulted into the position of Security Second.

He considered that as he studied Talina from the passenger seat. She was piloting the aircar due west over the vastness of endless forest.

They'd passed the Briggs River and given him a longing glimpse of the homestead at the head of Black Canyon. His eldest surviving daughter, Kylee, now lived there. A half-human, half-quetzal child who teetered precariously between two different worlds.

And then there was Talina Perez, the woman who had murdered two of his wives' first husbands. A once-despised enemy who had miraculously appeared at his family's moment of greatest need. A quetzal-haunted woman who was now his superior.

They couldn't ask for a better day for flying, with the temperature in the low thirties, sunny, and no chance for rain. The forever forest stretched off to the horizon, a lumpy mat of greens, blues, and every shade in between. Here and there rivers cut winding paths through the verdure, and ridges, bluffs, and hills receded in distant hazy lines toward infinity.

Talina seemed to be in better control of herself today. Working around her was always interesting, but at times the woman was locked in combat with her inner quetzals. Generally, if a comment contained the words "you piece of shit," it was a dead giveaway that quetzal molecules were whispering in her mind.

Talbot had lived with his daughter Kylee and her pet quetzal, Rocket, for long enough to have at least a hazy understanding of the symbiosis. And his wife, Dya, had explained the best hypotheses that she, Turnienko, and the chemist, Cheng, could come up with: That essentially quetzal TriNA was a "smart" molecule that interacted with human brain cells through common transferRNA.

But all it took was a glance at Talina Perez to know it did more than that. The woman's eyes were striking, larger, darker, peculiarly shaped. Then came the planes of her face, the cheekbones sharper, the jawline pointed at the chin. Her muscles were faster, stronger than any human Talbot had ever known, and she moved with fluid grace that reminded him of a prowling lioness.

She scared hell out of half of Port Authority. The other half treated her with a wary respect—even if they were unsure of who and what she'd become.

"What's up, Mark? You're looking at me like I'm some sort of lab specimen."

How did she do that? He thought he'd been circumspect. "You're quiet today. Not even a single growl under your breath. Demon hasn't been making a pest of himself?"

"This whole *Ashanti* thing. That's got me thinking of ships. Which reminds me of *Vixen*. Which makes me think of Weisbacher. Kalico was up there. I noticed that she artfully didn't mention if she'd seen the good doctor."

"Which made you think of Trish," he finished. Mark turned, squinted out at the forest. Here and there he could pick out more turquoise patches in the various shades of green. Some sort of unknown aquajade species? They passed the first of the curious ping pong paddle trees in their circular clearings. "It's been over two years, Tal."

Talina frowned. "Seems like yesterday. Still don't know what I'd do if I walked around a corner in PA and came face to face with him." A pause. "Think I'm responsible enough to keep from blowing a hole through his sorry hide?"

"Kylee still calls him Dortmund Short Mind. Says he's the biggest waste of skin she's ever known." Talbot gestured amusement. "Of course, her total exposure to humanity can be numbered in the low tens." He paused. "I'm sorry Trish isn't here. I know what she meant to you."

"Six of one, half dozen of the other, Mark. The kid had that innate sense of place that comes from growing up here. She was rock-solid when it came to a tight situation in the bush. A dead shot with a rifle. If she had a fault, it was that she was young. Made the kind of dumb mistakes young people make. Still needed to completely find her feet. Hated herself for letting Benteen scare her."

"Benteen would have killed her."

"Yeah. Maybe. The thing is, she always figured she'd die in the bush. Quetzal, bem, some skewer, or maybe mobbers."

"Odd that you'd say that. I was just thinking about the way life on Donovan changes in an instant."

She shot him an evaluative glance from the corner of her eye. "You're as good as Trish, you know."

"I'll take that as a compliment."

"Better in a lot of ways. You know more about the bush. More mature. Tougher down in your core. Like Trish, I know you've got my back. You proved that when you shot Chavez. You don't have that gut-level handle on Port Authority yet, but you're learning."

"Trish grew up with those people. To most I'm still a stranger, and as the town's only polygamist, something of a curiosity."

"You were Wild Ones, you get more leeway."

Talbot grinned. He hadn't been in Port Authority for more than a couple of months before he became fully cognizant of the fact that he was comfortable in his own skin. Funny thing, that. Knowing exactly who and what you were meant that other people's opinions didn't have nearly the weight they once had.

"What's the story behind this Tyson Station we're going to?"

Talina rested her hand on the wheel, her alien-dark eyes scanning the forest ahead of them. "Tyson's colony was fifth ship. The research base was established on a mesa top way out west. The idea was that, like Mundo down south, it would be a stepping stone for the exploration of the continent. The site was chosen since it had a different ecology, was considered somewhat defensible from wildlife, and could be easily expanded as the population grew. The big dome, with full basement, contained the cafeteria and kitchen, communications, admin offices, storage, and meeting rooms. Separate domes for the barracks, science labs, shops, and support staff. Last we knew, they had about five acres in farmland. Like everywhere, the bems, brown caps, chokeya, and slugs began to take a toll. There were rumors of other creatures, different from what we know back east.

"Clemenceau demanded that the base be held no matter what. After learning of his much-too-delayed departure, most of the people loaded up and flew back to PA. Five stayed behind, trying to finish up a few last projects."

"What happened to them?"

"When we finally got around to sending a car out a couple of months later, we found three skeletons. No trace of the other two. Not even a pile of quetzal crap."

"And this is a place for *Ashanti*'s kooks?"

"You've got me, Mark. Hey, Shig's the comparative religions teacher. He's been reviewing all the stuff these Irredenta dropped on *Ashanti*'s crew. Shig's worried." A beat. "Worried? Shig? Those are two words I never thought would collide in a sentence. You know Shig. End of the world coming? Fine. Make a cup of tea, read the *I Ching* and a couple of the Vedas, then smile as sattva fills your last days."

Talbot stared off to the right, caught sight of a flock of flying creatures. Pulling up his binoculars, he made sure they were scarlet fliers and not a deadly swarm of mobbers.

"There it is." Talina pointed ahead.

Mark used his binoculars to inspect the mesa that rose above the forest. The thing reminded him of a fortress jutting out like an extended shoulder below what was obviously a volcanic peak. Amazing what he'd learned about geology since coming to Donovan. Even from here he could tell the sheer sides were either lava or basalt. A few trees clung precariously to the precipitous and rocky slopes. As they approached, he estimated the vertical relief at over two hundred meters. A substantial slow-moving river curled around beneath the southern end of the mesa, the waters a translucent green.

Talina climbed, crested the flat, and leveled out. She made a wide swing around the five domes that stood in a clearing on what looked like bedrock. Many of the early research bases had been established on bedrock. Not as many slugs. People could see the quetzals, bems, and sidewinders coming.

Sheds had been laid out in a row on the western side, the doors closed. A solar array consisting of five panels stood on the south. Three of the panels were still tracking Capella's course across the sky. Between them and the landing field just this side of the domes, he could see the garden.

Talina dropped lower, slowing to a hover. As she used her quetzal vision to survey the place, Talbot relied on his binoculars. The base gave every appearance of being abandoned. Right down to the thin soil that was devoid of tracks. Pieces of equipment looked rusty and dusty; an old pair of coveralls lay wadded beside one of the doors, tattered and faded. Tarps were frayed by wind, torn loose from their bindings. They'd once protected corroding pieces of equipment that Talbot couldn't identify.

"What do you think?" Talina asked.

"Well, at least a swarm of quetzals didn't come charging out of one of the domes with their collar membranes glowing crimson and their claws out. Can't tell about bems, skewers, the occasional sidewinder, spikes, or whatever the hell else there might be."

She arched an eyebrow, then descended to the landing field on the south side of the domes. Talbot retrieved his rifle as she let the fans spin down.

"How's the charge?" he asked.

"Twenty percent. Smart people would plug into the spare powerpack before stepping out of the aircar."

"I like smart," he suggested, watching her plug the auxiliary cable into the spare powerpack and then check as the indicator flashed back to eighty-nine percent. Nothing went to one hundred, given the age on the batteries.

He stepped out carefully, having had four years of Donovan's hard lessons to keep him from acting irresponsibly. The plants here were terrestrial. Some sort of scrubby low weeds that didn't writhe under his foot the way the native flora did.

Talbot kept his rifle up, safety off, finger on the rest just above the trigger. He cocked his head at the chime, different here. Deeper, with a bass rhythm unlike anything he'd heard before. The air, too, had a different odor, more of a saffron and sage than the more familiar cardamom and cinnamon scent around either Mundo or PA. The breeze had a muggy feel. The air heavier and hot.

Talina on his right, he started for the first dome, scenting the air for any hint of vinegar that would indicate a bem or skewer. Got nothing but the background of vegetation. A small herd of roos burst from behind one of the domes, fleeing like a shot across the flats.

At the first dome, Talina tried the latch, found it unlocked. She let the door swing in, swept the room with her rifle. Talbot followed, covering. Standard security room-clearing procedure. Nothing looked out of place, the chairs were upright, desks slightly dusty, but nothing suspicious. Room by room, they cleared the first dome, then moved on to the next. An hour later, with nothing but a single sidewinder and an infestation of invertebrates in the sheds, Tyson Station appeared to harbor no immediate terrors.

The cisterns were full and overflowing into pipes that drained down to the garden patch. To Talbot's eyes the water looked skuzzy, but that could be addressed without much effort.

"Skeletons were all out in the open," Talina told him as she led the way from the last of the domes. "We didn't know it then, but they were probably killed by mobbers. That, or something we haven't seen yet."

"It's a big planet," Talbot agreed, thinking of the various creatures that had attacked him while he trekked through the forest down south. He could count at least five creatures that weren't on the list of known predators. And that included an oversized cucumber-looking thing.

Talbot followed Talina down to the garden. Located on the southern end of the base, it grew on soils that had washed down from the higher exposed basalt. The place reminded him of a smaller Mundo: lettuce, cabbages, pepper plants, lots of garlic, mint for tea, some tomatoes, broccoli and squash all growing in a riotous mixture.

"What do you think?" Talina asked. "Enough to feed a hundred people?"

"Maybe. They'll need corn and potatoes from PA, some grapes, an apple and cherry tree or two, some blueberry bushes. Now that I get a better look, I make this to be about seven acres. From the height of the surrounding trees, the soil's deep enough the garden could be expanded. Maybe all the way down to the end of the mesa."

Talina nodded, her careful gaze scanning the edge of the forest. "Let's check the solar panels and battery packs. Looks like two aren't working. And if the batteries are shot, that's really going to compound our problems."

Turned out that if there was a weakness to Tyson Station, it was the power. The motors were burned out on two of the solar towers, and whoever last had been responsible for the batteries had left them untended, only two took a charge, and even then, they only tested at fifty percent.

"We really going to strand nearly a hundred people out here?" Talbot asked.

"We could drop them at Mundo. Maybe hope they'll kill Diamond and Leaper. On the other hand, as much as I've got a grudge against those two quetzals, I'm not sure that dropping the Unreconciled on top of them wouldn't be a crime against quetzaldom."

"It's just hard to get my head around. All right, so they ate other human beings. What kind of sins do people have to commit to leave them totally beyond redemption?"

"I'm not the person to ask, given some of the things I've done. And to members of your family, no less. But here's the thing: I know the sins I've committed. If we can believe Shig's analysis of the Unreconciled, they think everything they've done is in preparation for the coming struggle."

"And you think that putting them out here will keep us all safe?"

"Guess we'll see, huh?" She pursed her lips as she looked around the base. "And maybe they're not the psychotically insane and twisted monsters that everyone thinks they are. I mean, I don't know what really happened on Deck Three, but dropping the Irredenta out here gives us the chance to see just what kind of trouble they might be."

"Tal, I was trained, wearing combat armor, and I almost didn't make it. You and I both know that no matter what these people did, it's going to be a death sentence for a lot of them."

She turned her alien-dark eyes on him. "Doesn't matter where we put them, people are going to die. How many of your marines, let alone the *Turalon* transportees are still alive? It's just how things are here."

"Yeah. Welcome to Donovan."

Talina had walked to the western side of the escarpment, was staring out at the endless tops of the trees. A tension lined her forehead, pinched her full-lipped mouth.

"What is it?"

Talina hesitated, started to speak, then shook her head. "You feel something out there?"

Talbot let his gaze roam the treetops. "Feel . . . like what?"

Talina turned, grunted. "Probably nothing."

But Talbot noticed that she kept looking back over her shoulder at the thick forest, as if something unseen were nagging at her.

THE CLEANSING

Now, with our internment coming to an end, I can take a moment and look back. Remember the Harrowing and Cleansing, and what it meant for all of us.

I understand now: Had we just been given the Revelation, it would have been rejected out of hand as an insane abomination. We had to be broken down, our illusions about life and morality destroyed. It's an old cliché, but like a field, we had to be prepared before a seed could be planted that would eventually bear fruit.

First was the fear. When Ashanti *reinverted to normal space and we understood the full scope of the disaster that had befallen us, we realized that, no matter what, some or all of us were going to starve to death. Trapped. Here, in this ship, in the black immensity of space.*

Then came the fight: the attempted mutiny led by Irdan and Brady Shaw. Its failure at the hands of the crew. How could they just have shot human beings down like that? We'd lived with these people for close to three years during the transition. Only to have them murder our leaders in the hallways.

We knew disbelief and rage when we discovered that the hatch had been sealed. That we were not only doomed but trapped in the limited warren that was Deck Three.

What followed was a mind-numbing despair—the kind that left even me weeping, defeated, and broken.

Then the rations were cut.

How clever the universe is. It let us observe the worst in humanity while teaching us the ultimate lesson: Survival is conflict.

Raised within the warm and secure womb of The Corporation, we could not have been more shocked by this rude and disturbing awakening. The depth of the deception we had been living back in Solar System was as traumatic for us as the ensuing starvation. As we wasted away in an agony of hunger, it became clear that altruism was a myth. Everything The Corporation had taught us to believe was a sham and a lie.

We witnessed the base brutality of the human soul.

In the beginning, when the interpersonal violence broke out, we dropped the bodies down the chute. Sent them to the hydroponics.

It was Irdan—who would become the first of the Prophets—who realized that it was a waste. All those calories, the protein, and fats. He was the first to begin the Harrowing.

See the cunning of the universe? Indeed!

Upon the revelation of Irdan's actions—that he had cooked and eaten another human being—most had a feeling of revulsion. Thought the consumption of human flesh was abhorrent. A few sought retribution; Irdan killed them when they came for him. Nor did he leave them to waste, but promptly processed their meat and organs.

The Harrowing was over and the Cleansing began.

With it, so did the beginnings of the Revelation.

I remember the guilt I experienced the first time I ate human flesh. The self-revulsion. At the same time, I relished the sustenance. The relief from the hollow pangs of starvation.

This was meat.

This was life.

I knew it was Sally McKendricks, mother of two, whose meat I was cutting up and chewing.

But that night I slept with a full stomach.

For a time, following that, I was lost. Guilt. Guilt. Guilt. Disgust. A loathing of who I'd become. How low I would sink just to live another day. To keep breathing. To be rid of the hunger pangs.

Irdan—always in the forefront of the universe's will—was the one who told me: "Batuhan, they're not dead. They're inside us. Living through us."

And that night I had the dream, a vision.

Nothing like those bestowed upon the Prophets.

This was just a simple understanding: The universe had put us in such dire circumstances to serve a purpose: This was its will.

If killing and eating another human being was the universe's will, it could not be a crime, an abomination, or a sin.

Consuming another human being was immortality.

7

The increase in gravity was the first indication of the beginning of the end. Security Tech II Vartan Omanian felt it as he rose from Svetlana Pushkin's bed. Cocking his head, he could hear it, feel it through his bare feet. *Ashanti* had changed. The sound and vibration of the ship, the air, even the surrounding sialon hinted of hard acceleration.

Vartan made his way to the toilet, relieved his full bladder, and re-crossed the small room to Svetlana's bed. Nominally, as a member of the Messiah's Will—as the enforcers were called—he slept in the men's dormitory. His rank, as Second Will—or the second in command of Batuhan's enforcers—granted him certain privileges. That included access to available women as long as they weren't ovulating.

Among the Irredenta, the tracking of a woman's cycle was of paramount concern. During those critical days during ovulation, she became the sole property of the Messiah—and if more than one female was fertile at the time, the responsibility of the First Chosen to inseminate.

Those who had objected to the True Vision of the Prophets when it came to women and reproduction had long since become immortal. Vartan had been responsible for most of the disciplinary actions. The one thing the Irredenta couldn't afford was any hint of division or strife. Those who might have doubted, who suffered from a lack of faith, would finally discover Truth in their next existence. After they'd been consumed, purified, and reborn.

Vartan himself had once doubted. Back then. In the beginning. But he had learned, adapted, and as the universe taught, survived.

Privately he wondered if his ex-wife, Shyanne Veda, didn't still doubt. As Second Will, he had her and her few friends watched.

With the death of her year-old son a little over a year ago, she'd had a period of recalcitrance and grief, but had acted in no overt manner to demonstrate any apostasy or disbelief in the revelations of the Prophets. Now she doted on six-year-old Fatima, her remaining daughter.

But then, they all had secrets. Private thoughts that each of them desperately hoped the universe wasn't privy to.

We live in fear.

Vartan stopped at the side of the bed, staring down. Svetlana slept on her right side; her long body lay mostly exposed, a twist of sheet around her midriff and left thigh. The swirl of her long brown hair curled behind her head. Her arms were bent, hands tucked next to her lips.

He settled himself on the side of the bed and dialed up the room light to dim. As he did he felt the ever-so-faint change in acceleration. The ship had just kicked it up a bit.

"Hey, wake up."

She shifted onto her back, blinked her brown eyes. "It's been three times already. You're an animal. Let me sleep."

"Ship's boosting. Gravity's changed. I think we're starting the long burn toward Capella III. Listen. Feel."

She did, coming fully awake. Sitting up, she wiggled past him, stood. "I feel heavier."

"*Ashanti* is killing delta vee. It's actually going to happen. Just the way the Prophets said it would."

She studied him, brown eyes pensive, the light casting shadows across the complex patterns of Initiation scars that marked her as the second of the Messiah's four wives. After the Cleansing, she had been one of the first to offer herself to the newly acclaimed Messiah, had borne his first two children, and was waiting to see if she'd conceived the third.

Vartan reached up where she stood before him, ran his fingers along the long scars that marked her body. At his lingering touch, she shivered, closed her eyes, and leaned her head back to let her hair cascade down her back.

"The path of souls," he whispered, tracing down the line of scar that led to the thick mat of her pubic hair. He gave the curly mat a light tug, causing her to stare down at him with irritated eyes.

He softly asked, "Do you really believe that the souls of the dead have followed the same route my fingers just did? That they were reborn inside you?"

She chuckled just as softly. Said, "I could feel it. Both times I conceived with the Messiah. Wasn't anything like a regular orgasm. What began as more of warm honeyed feeling burst through my hips like a brilliant light that filled my uterus. An explosion of life that wracked my entire body."

From her expression, the tone in her voice, he wasn't sure if she was having fun at his expense. Or might have been just parroting the Messiah's lines.

That was the thing about Svetlana. He could never quite know if she believed the revelations of the Prophets, or if she was the penultimate survivor who accurately assessed the situation and sided with the man most likely to prevail.

All of which made his relationship with her so fascinating.

"I see that look," she told him with a grim smile. "You still wonder, don't you? But let me ask you, do *you* really believe? Because I think, like me, you're a survivor."

Another lurch, increasing the sensation of weight.

She looked up, as if she could see through the decks to *Ashanti*'s AC. "It's really going to happen. So, how do you think this will play out, Mr. Policeman?"

Vartan rubbed a hand on the back of his neck. "No matter what the Messiah says or believes, they're not going to welcome us with open arms. To them, we are going to be monsters."

She reached down to lift his chin and stared into his eyes. "We're alive, Vartan. As long as we are, there is hope and opportunity. And many of us are still under Contract. You were trained in law enforcement and security. You know of any law that says eating another human being is illegal?"

"No. But killing them for apostasy or heresy most certainly is." He raised a hand to take hers. "We plead that Galluzzi, by starving us, forced us into the practice. That we could either die or bow to necessity."

"Batuhan and the Prophets insist we're the tools of the universe. The chosen," Svetlana told him. "They believe. And so do most of the rest. After the Harrowing and Cleansing, the Revelations were like a straw floating on a sea of fear and guilt. The desperate not only grabbed onto it with two hands, it's become the only salvation left to keep them afloat."

He nodded.

Still staring into his eyes, she said, "You and I both know who among us might just be playing the game, keeping their heads down until the hatch opens. And when it does, they're going to run right to the Corporation and condemn us all."

"Why are you telling me this now?"

Another lurch of acceleration pulled at his body.

"Figure it out for yourself. Maybe we are the mystical chosen, and the universe will see to our ultimate triumph. Works for me. But when that hatch is finally open, I want to be positive that I, and my children, have a way out."

8

Dan Wirth surveyed his domain. He was lord and master of The Jewel. As night fell on Port Authority, Dan leaned on the bar and chewed a chabacho-wood toothpick. The stuff wasn't really wood, but close enough. The cells, so he'd been told, were a sort of polymer rather than cellulose—whatever the hell that was. Anyway, the wood was different than wood back on Earth.

Science wasn't really Dan's kind of preoccupation. Money was. And he was good at it. He'd made himself the second-richest person on Donovan—second only to Kalico Aguila.

Second.

Once upon a time, that fact had bothered him. He'd plotted various ways of murdering Aguila, seizing her assets, and turning himself into the richest man on the planet.

But then, just because Dan might have been a psychopath didn't mean he was stupid.

Killing Aguila would have meant the collapse of Corporate Mine, because he sure as hell wasn't going to go down and try to run the damn thing. Far better that the cunning slit of a Supervisor spent her time ensuring that fabulous wealth kept pouring out of those holes in the ground.

As long as her miners continued to patronize The Jewel, betting at Dan's tables, drinking his booze, buying his pharma, and paying for sex with his whores, he kept making money.

He had enough trouble maintaining good will with the kind and gentle people in Port Authority. When it came to the Wild Ones who lived out in the bush, prospected and hunted, at least a fella could whack them up alongside the head to get their attention. It was the "upstanding" and "decent" folk that drove Dan to the brink of distracted madness. They had to be treated with kid gloves. It was a full-time job.

The result was that nothing that happened in Port Authority took place without his knowledge, and as it turned out, his blessing.

Thankfully, he had Allison Chomko to carry some of the load. Originally, he'd targeted her because she'd been vulnerable, beautiful, and he'd needed her knowledge of Port Authority. Back in the old days, he'd drugged her. Prostituted her for all the benefit he could get. What he hadn't calculated into the equation was that she might be cutting-edge smart down under all that voluptuous beauty. He should have had a clue, given that both of her parents had been PhDs.

As she had taken over more of the management, become integral to the workings of Dan's little empire, their relationship had become a great deal more complicated. He now wondered when, and under what circumstances, he might be forced to remove her from the equation.

That would be a tricky piece of work. Allison had her backers, including Step Allenovich, Talina Perez, Shig, and even Yvette. Not to mention a lot of the "respectable" women who had once been Ali's friends. These days the righteous bitches might spurn Allison as a whore, but if there were so much as a hint that Dan had murdered her, the hypocritical slits would come after him with a rope.

Even as he thought about her, Ali emerged from the back with Desch Ituri hanging on her arm. The contrast was almost laughable. Ituri stood maybe five-foot four, stocky and black-skinned, with short curly hair and eyes like balls of obsidian. Allison towered over him, stately, elegant, a perfectly shaped Norse goddess of a woman with pale skin and silky silver-blonde hair that hung down her back. Sparkling blue eyes were set in a classic face. Laughter bubbled off of her lips as she reacted to something Ituri said.

Dan watched as they parted; Ituri headed for the door. Every eye in the place was glancing back and forth between Ituri and Allison, and most of them were covetous. No doubt imagining with salacious detail what Ituri had just enjoyed in Allison's bed.

For her part, Allison stopped to deposit something in the cage at the back of the room. First and foremost, Allison was a businesswoman. Dan could count the men she'd sell her sex to on two hands. Whatever Ituri had offered to bed Ali, it must have been worth a small fortune. But then, the man could pay. He was Kalico Aguila's head engineer down at Corporate Mine.

Dan inclined his head graciously as Allison turned his way. She paused only long enough at the tables to share a greeting and smile with the patrons. Called, "Vik! Another whiskey for Lee Halston."

With an almost predatory smile, she sidled up next to where Dan was keeping an eye on the roulette table as Shin Wong called for bets.

Dan asked, "Have a nice time?"

She gave him a conspiratorial wink. "I wouldn't screw him if I didn't. No matter how much plunder he offered."

"So what did he offer?"

"Turquoise. Ever hear of it before?"

"Yeah, I might have. Blue-colored stone, right? What's the big deal?"

"The deal is that Lea Shimodi, that Corporate geologist that works for Aguila, was down on the south continent. Found a big copper deposit. I guess it's a kind of desert down there. Something about it's got to be dry, and there's aluminum involved, and anyhow, the conditions are right for this deep-blue turquoise. The first ever found on Donovan."

"What's it worth?"

"Haven't a clue. It's a chunk the size of my fist. The important thing is that it's the first piece ever found on Donovan. Shimodi wrote it up in her notes. Described it."

"How'd Ituri get it?"

"He made a bet with Shimodi. Some technical thing about the Number One mine down at Corporate. She lost."

Dan flipped his toothpick to the other side of his mouth, delighted to watch as C'ian Gatlin lost an entire stack of chips betting odd on the roulette table.

"Anything else interesting down at the mine?" Dan asked.

Allison twitched her lips in disappointment. "Ituri made some kind of deal with Aguila to get to come back here. He takes it seriously. He doesn't let slip about anything critical or salacious. Any kind of talk about the mines or the Supervisor is strictly off limits."

"Yeah, too bad. It's like the good Supervisor has stopped all of her leaks over the last year. Did you ask about Kalen Tompzen?"

"No. I didn't want to even hint that we had an interest in him." Allison stopped long enough to greet the bootmaker, Rude Marsdome, and Bernie Monson from the clay pit as the two strode in the door.

As they retreated to the pinochle table, Dan said, "Listen, it's been over a year since we've seen or heard from Kalen. We've had feelers out to the other marines that serve with him. We know he's still alive down there. So my best guess is that she finally figured out that he was our agent. That we had our claws into him."

Dan made a face, gestured with his toothpick. "I gotta hand it to Aguila, if she finally narrowed it down to Kalen, she's put the screws to him. Not that Kalen is the toughest of birds to start with, but she'll have sweated him for everything we had on him."

Allison waved to Fenn Bogarten as the chemist entered, headed back to join the others at the pinochle table. To Dan she said, "Just be glad she didn't order this place off limits after she found out."

"If she wanted to make something of it, she'd have sent Tompzen's corpse, or at least a couple of his body parts our way. That she hasn't speaks volumes."

"At this stage, given time for tempers to cool, perhaps we could make her a deal for Tompzen. Buy him back. Ever since Benteen killed Art Maniken, we've needed a good enforcer." She gave him an amused sidelong glance. "You don't have the same brute touch that Art had. By nature, you're much too subtle."

"I'll mention it the next time I see the wily cunt." Fact was, he did need a good enforcer. Not that he was above slitting a throat now and then, but too many such doings affected his standing in the community. Who the fuck would have ever thought that maintaining a reputation could be such hard-sucking work?

Allison arched a slim eyebrow. "Why don't you let me? Aguila and I don't have the same history that the two of you do. But enough of that. While I was relieving Desch of his built-up stress, what did you learn at the meeting with the triumvirate? That ship really coming in?"

What's your game, Ali? Building an alliance with Aguila? Strengthening your position at my expense?

Dan gestured his dissatisfaction. "Oh, *Ashanti*'s coming in, all right. But she's a mess. Turns out they've been locked in that bucket of air for ten years. Word is that the transportees got out of hand, so the captain, a guy named Galluzzi, welded them in. Bottled them up in their quarters."

"God, that sounds . . ."

"Yeah, gets worse. Shig said that according to the ship's records, they gleefully murdered each other to start with, and ended up eating their dead. Having been sealed in without crayons or color markers, they practiced art on each other with knives. And in the process, they've elevated some guy called Batuhan into a sort of guru messiah who interprets for three babbling prophets. Batuhan's calling for some sort of galactic jihad that's supposed to end in the universe having itself for supper and being reborn in purity like him and all his fawning acolytes."

Allison's lips tightened in distaste. "That for sure?"

"I guess so. Shig's clap-trapping weird over it. Remember Shig? The bipedal Buddha? Never-got-his-balls-in-a-knot Shig? That guy? Well, he's fart-sucking freaked about the transportees." Dan glanced at the palm of his hand where he'd written it down so he wouldn't forget. "They call themselves Irredenta. Means something about being culturally unique in someone else's territory."

"They still scheduled to make planet in a couple of months?"

"Give or take."

"So, what's the plan? Just let a bunch of cut-up cannibals land at the shuttle field?"

"We're thinking of Tyson Station. Supposed to be an abandoned base somewhere out west."

Allison grunted under her breath. "I lived out there for a while. My parents died there while I was in school here in Port Authority. After Clemenceau was no longer in the picture, they were going to close the station down. Mom and Dad stayed behind to finish up some research. They found Mom's skeleton. Never did find what happened to Dad. Not a trace."

"Apparently some of *Ashanti*'s scientists and some of the crew are still sane. Since the ship's Corporate, the cargo manifest has gone to Aguila. She'll share it with the rest of us as soon as she has a chance to go through it. As to what happens to *Ashanti*, that's up in the air. Word is that the crew just want to be dirtside for a while. That for most, ten years in that bucket is enough."

"Aguila going to claim them like she did the *Turalon* deserters?"

"Maybe. I don't know. My take was that Aguila's still figuring this thing out."

"We'd better be figuring, too," Allison mused. "Ship's crew? They're going to be hitting dirt, looking for any kind of diversion, and they're going to be coming here."

"Yeah, all looking for a good time, and the randy marks aren't going to have a cent to their names." He paused. "There's opportunity in that."

She tapped a slender finger on his chest. "But carefully this time, Dan. We don't want a replay of the Tosi Damitiri mess."

Figures you'd bring that up.

Was she trying to piss him off? Remind him of how that had almost turned into a disaster?

Dan nodded, thinking. "You might want to talk to Aguila sooner rather than later regarding Tompzen. Something makes me think we're gonna need a good enforcer. And the thing about Tompzen is that he's proven that he's not squeamish if it comes to a little blood and pain."

9

Ashanti looped around Capella, using the star's gravity to decelerate. As it did the ship's energy fields scooped up the dense solar wind, harvesting hydrogen for the reactors. With fuel to burn, and the generation of one-and-a-half gravities of thrust to slow their velocity in relation to Donovan, *Ashanti* entered the final course corrections on her seemingly eternal voyage.

The ship might have been structurally rated for a two-g acceleration, but after having been lived in for ten years, many of the constructions, such as ad-hoc shelving, plant stands down in hydroponics, and make-do repairs were not.

For Miguel Galluzzi and his crew, it was a constant scramble to deal with one minor calamity after another. Pumps failed, pipes began to leak, and so far as Galluzzi was concerned, the activity was a godsend. His people were constantly occupied, and they had to be extra careful. Every move had to be planned. He went to the extent of having them employ safety harnesses to go up and down stairways. Even a simple slip or fall at 1.5g could have dire consequences. No one had time to think about Donovan and what disembarking was going to necessitate.

Of course, Galluzzi's crew weren't the only ones to notice. Every time the captain stepped into the AC, the board was flashing messages from Deck Three.

He checked a few. In among the usual propaganda about the coming end of the universe as he knew it, were demands for information. Unsurprisingly, each came with a threat, that if it were to be unanswered, dire consequences would ensue.

Galluzzi considered that as he stared at the holo of *Freelander* where it was projected over his worktable. He had taken to wondering about the derelict, had spent hours staring at the dead vessel. Had read all of the reports and logs Supervisor Aguila had sent him.

He'd barely survived ten years. How did he get his head around Jem Orten facing what he thought was an eternity lost in nothingness? On *Freelander* they had murdered the transportees. Jem and his first officer had welded themselves into the AC and ultimately used a pistol to blow their brains out.

Just because my actions weren't as extreme, it doesn't absolve me of my failures.

Galluzzi—seated in his captain's chair—was reading through the latest list when Derek Taglioni minced his way into the captain's lounge on carefully placed steps.

"Can't believe my back hurts so much," Taglioni noted. "Makes me wish I'd built up to this. That, or we'd practiced for a couple of hours every day."

Galluzzi glanced up at the bulbous shape of *Freelander* where it was projected from the holos. "Won't be long. Another couple of days. Just about the time you start to adapt, we'll shut down. *Ashanti*'s got the final course plot. It's just a matter of watching the hours count down."

He flicked the image of *Freelander* off and replaced it with a holo of Cap III, Donovan, as he reminded himself to say.

Moving like an old man, Taglioni seated himself in Turner's seat at the nav panel. "Hope the Unreconciled are enjoying it. Wonder what they make of all this?"

Galluzzi tapped the side of his head. "Playing some of their latest demands and threats on my implants now. 'As the fire is to the wood, so are the Irredenta to you and the rest of humanity. You are about to burn, for only as ashes will you finally reap the true reward of being.'

"And here's another: 'You cannot hide the truth. We know we are nearing Capella III. As we emerge from the womb of transformation, it will be to expand upon a wave of blood. Upon it we shall ride, consuming the ignorant, devouring their being, until reborn in blood they shall be made whole and will know illumination.'"

Galluzzi winced. "This one is my favorite: 'The moment of our release is at hand. The universe shall see to this. Upon the instant of our release, you shall know the fulfilling rapture of terror. In it, you shall be reborn and find immortality.'"

"I've heard it all before." Taglioni stared absently at Donovan where it spun before them. "You don't think that just maybe we've got it all wrong, and he's talking in metaphors?"

Galluzzi shot him a chiding look. "Want me to access the photos of the butchered remains they've sent down the chute to hydroponics?" He paused. "And don't forget that we sampled their sewage before it was sent to the tanks. More than enough human myosin II was found in their feces to pretty much discount the notion they were only biting their nails."

"So what does Supervisor Aguila say about all this?"

"She sent a message to the Irredenta that she asked me to forward on for her. It stated that a research station was being made ready for them on Donovan. That upon disembarkation, subject to contract, each individual would be evaluated and suitable employment would be provided."

"She's got to be kidding."

"Whatever else she may turn out to be, she is a Corporate Supervisor, and by making the offer, she's covered all of her contractual obligations. The Irredenta replied in a most colorful way. They informed the Supervisor that they would consume her corpse in a community feast. That the pollution of her existence could only be purified through the concerted action of each and every true believer."

"You forwarded that to the Supervisor?" Taglioni asked. "I'd have loved to have seen the expression on her face."

"My take on Kalico Aguila is that the woman isn't your rank-and-file Corporate Supervisor. A fact you might keep in mind when dealing with her. Her reply, which was radioed in almost immediate return, was 'Please inform them that they're going to have to age me for a couple of weeks since I'm a lot tougher than they realize. And they'd better have an ample helping of salt and pepper on hand.'"

Taglioni smiled at that. "Tell me you didn't send that on to Batuhan and his merry band of man-munching fiends."

"I do have some good sense."

"I've been reading the reports the Donovanians have sent up. What do you make of them?"

Galluzzi fixed him with a measuring glance. "I had to look up the word 'libertarian.' If there's a total and complete opposite of Corporate, that's it. Dek, that planet down there is a free for all. Corporate Mine, for what it's worth, is structured, ordered, and Corporate in nature. A person can know where he or she stands. Where he or she fits.

"Port Authority on the other hand? It's chaos. How do they live? Who takes care of them? What's this market economy they're so taken with? No one's in charge. Just stumble along on your own. Who keeps people from making a mistake? And if they do, they have to take full responsibility for it. No equitable redistribution. No management whatsoever. How do they even make it through a day?"

Taglioni said with smile, "Funny thing. I *dreamed* of that planet last night. Like it was singing to my bones. Call me crazy, but it's like I'm coming home to a place I've never been before. I can't wait to set foot down there and see what chaos feels like. Sounds remarkably liberating and terrifying all at once."

"You're kidding, right? Port Authority exists in defiance of everything your family has believed going all the way back to the founding of The Corporation. And they live behind a fence for shit's sake. Because the wildlife can creep in and eat people. You read that, didn't you? That the gates are locked at sundown. And if we're not inside, that they won't come out looking for us."

Taglioni grinned wider. "I went to one of the rewilding reserves on Earth when I was a kid. Stepped outside at night. Knew that there were lions and tigers out there. That I could be eaten. Liked to have scared myself to death."

"You've seen the holo taken during the *Tempest* expedition? Of Donovan? The first guy to die down on that rock? That thing, the quetzal, eating him alive? And you find that exciting?"

Taglioni nodded, expression turning thoughtful. "Looking back, Miguel, I have trouble remembering who I was the day I stepped on board *Ashanti*. I'm not that Derek Taglioni." He looked down at his hands, spread the fingers, inspected the palms. "I've scrubbed caked shit out of the insides of toilets. Fought to keep from puking while I hung over the ferment tanks to repair the agitators down in hydroponics. Hell, I could qualify for a Ship's Technician Level I rating. I've crawled into raceways, come within a whisker of electrocuting myself. Carried the dead bodies of men and women I considered friends down to hydroponics after they committed suicide. I eat at the common table in the crew's mess. So, compared to that arrogant scum-sucking Corporate prick who strolled aboard back in orbit off Neptune, who the hell have I become?"

Galluzzi gave him a slight nod. "Once I would have died before I said this, but perhaps you have become a human being?"

"Makes you wonder, doesn't it? Looking back, I was a sort of monster once. Now I have become human, and down on Deck Three all those perfectly humdrum humans have become monsters. How—on the scales of universal justice—does that balance out?"

Galluzzi stared thoughtfully at the projection of Donovan. "Maybe you'll find an answer on Cap III."

"What about you?"

Galluzzi shook his head. "I don't have a clue. Once the last of those people are down-planet, I wonder if I won't just disintegrate into atoms and fade into nothingness."

10

The one-and-a-half gravities had been like an endless torture. Locked as they were in the confines of Deck Three, it wasn't like the Irredenta had any avenue open to them but monotonous endurance. It didn't matter that over the years, more and more ration came tumbling out of the conveyor in the mess. These days—eat as much as a person might—he or she just didn't gain flesh.

"Ration" consisted of a cake-like composite of protein, fat, carbohydrate, and glucose injected with synthesized vitamins and recaptured minerals. The stuff was made from algae, plant tissue, and bacteria that grew in reprocessed nutrient-rich water.

From the loose teeth and thinning hair, the frail bones, the slightly sunken eyes, and occasional motor coordination troubles, malnutrition was simply a fact of life. Things might have been better if the ship's physician and medical techs hadn't been killed in the initial rioting.

Vartan stood in the back of what served as the infirmary. His ex-wife, Shyanne Veda—she'd gone back to her maiden name—was treating the scars on one of the little boys who'd undergone Initiation. It didn't matter that the infirmary had some of the best lighting left in the whole of Deck Three; she still had to bend down to inspect the scabs that ran down the little boy's arms and legs.

With a sigh, Shyanne straightened. Shot Vartan a look through weary umber-colored eyes. Like Svetlana, she was another tall, thin woman who crowded six feet. The similarities were enough to make him wonder if he cleaved to a certain type. Thinking back, most of the women in his life had been taller than him.

"'M I okay?" little Pho asked, staring up at Shyanne as if she were an oracle.

Fat chance that, the job already had been taken by the Prophets.

Shyanne gave him a nod. "You're healing. Be careful not to tear the scabs off like you did on your leg. I want you under the UV light for a couple of hours a day. It's the only thing we've got to get that infection under control."

She helped the little boy up off the table, watched him limp stiffly out of the room. Then she glanced at Vartan. "So, Security Officer, what can I do for you?"

"They'll be coming soon."

She crossed her thin arms under the scarified spirals that covered her small breasts, lifted her brows. "Given the shutdown of the ship, the sudden return to normal gravity, that doesn't take a Prophet to figure out."

He turned, glanced to make sure the hallway remained empty. Turning back, he said, "A Supervisor has been in touch."

"I've heard. But not the details. What's it mean, Vart? Incarceration? Psychiatric confinement? Some kind of prison camp? Given the things we did . . ." She lifted a hand, turned away.

"A research base," he told her. "Somewhere out away from the main settlements. That's not common knowledge."

"Then why are you sharing it with me?"

He shrugged. "You're not like the rest. I know that. You don't buy the Prophets and the Universe. But most of them do. It's the only way they can cope."

"Vart," she told him, a distant look in her eyes, "I'm not a fool. I bought in the first time I looked down on a plate and told myself: 'It's eat it, or die.' Understood that if I died, it would be cooked pieces of me on the plate. After that, the rest was easy. Well, all but the shit-sucking Initiation with the all the cutting, the screaming in pain, bleeding, and weeks of agony as the scars healed."

She stared into the distance of memory. "The first time the Messiah came to my bed, I was creep-freaked. But I figured I could lay there while he did his thing. I let my mind go somewhere else. It wasn't like there was anything left of me to lose."

She cocked her head. "And now, after all this time, why the hell do you even care?"

"I've heard that there are a few who are planning to demand their rights under Contract as soon as the hatch is open. I don't want you to be one of them."

The way she looked at him, the light of her soul might have gone dark. "I told you, I'm in. So far as I'm concerned, we're the chosen. The universe speaks to the Prophets, and the Messiah is their voice. We are the living dead. Through us, they are reborn. Pure."

"Why don't I believe you?"

"Because, Vart, there's little else left to believe."

11

The feeling was surreal. After all that Derek had been through, it had to be the way a convict felt: Like his sentence was finally over. That he'd served his time.

He looked around the small sialon room that had been his cell. The once-stately quarters—with a bed, desk, the separate toilet and shower—had been a most remarkable luxury. Almost sixteen square meters of living space. At times this had been a refuge, and at others a confinement. A place of soul-numbing fear, endless hunger, and desperate hope.

He laid a hand on the wall, feeling the ship's vibrations through the hard material. "*Ashanti*, access please."

"Hello, Dek," the ship's com said. *"What can I do for you?"*

"Nothing. Just wanted to say thanks for keeping us alive and getting us here."

"You are welcome. Safe travels."

It was said with feeling, but then the AI was programmed that way. When all was said and done, the ship's intelligence was incapable of emotion, but still smart enough to evaluate a human's behavior and tone, then respond accordingly.

Dek took a final look at the room, thinking, *Maybe I'm not so different from the Unreconciled. Maybe I was gestated within these walls just to be born as someone different.*

He cracked a parting smile, lifted his two bags and gun case, and stepped out into the familiar corridor. It struck him that he, a Taglioni, was carrying his own luggage—all that remained of the two large trunks of fine clothing, special foods, entertainments, expensive jewelry, and the ornate plates, pitchers, and engraved silverware. Even his family tea service had been traded away to different members of the crew during the long years.

Beyond that he hadn't frittered away the two shipping containers in cargo. One contained his airplane—the one he had intended to use traveling between his holdings. The other had various recreational gadgets, exercise equipment, a home VR theater, interactive furniture, sports equipment for his leisure time, and other indulgences suitable to a Taglioni.

Given what he now knew about Donovan, he was wondering what exactly the use of a squash ball might be, or the value of his self-aware drink caddy.

In his two bags were his com equipment, a couple pair of worn coveralls, a set of utilitarian tools, and a few keepsakes he couldn't abide to part with. The gun case contained his hunting rifle, pistol, bullets, and powerpacks. He was wearing his last, best, formal wear. Shabby as it was.

Walking down the corridor for the last time, filled him with a curious remorse. *Ashanti* had brought them through. Carried them across thirty light-years of interstellar space from Solar System. The error that had almost killed them hadn't been the ship's fault. It had been in the math hidden down in the quantum qubit computers in the ship's core. Something that someone back in Solar System had programmed into the complicated statistics that governed inverted symmetry.

When *Ashanti* had popped back inside the universe a half light-year away from her target, she'd still managed to get them to Capella III.

A man couldn't help but have a fondness for a ship like that.

He took the lift down to Deck Four, made his way to the shuttle deck, and stepped into the Number Six hatch area. Passing through the decompression doors, he found Captain Galluzzi at the airlock in conversation with Michaela Hailwood.

"We the first ones here?" Derek asked. "It's not even 15:00 hours."

"Hardly," Michaela told him. "The entire Marine Unit's already aboard, buckled in. Kids included. Have been for the last fifteen minutes. And that's after they'd been waiting nearly an hour at the airlock. You'd think they were in a hurry to get off."

"Just waiting on you, Dek," Galluzzi told him with a smile.

"Thought there'd be a riot to get on the first shuttle." Derek glanced around at the empty hallway.

"Funny thing," Galluzzi told him. "Yeah, we got some real anxious sorts who can't wait to shuttle down. Set foot on dirt again. But the closer we got, the more people began to waver. It's like they're suddenly unsure. It's a bit intimidating to leave what's comfortable, you know what I mean?"

"Guess I do."

Galluzzi waved toward the lock. "Welcome aboard. Soon as you're strapped in, Ensign Naftali can dog the hatch, uncouple, and see if the shuttle still works."

"What if it doesn't?" Michaela asked, her dark eyes thoughtful.

"Another reason a lot of us aren't in a hurry to leave." Galluzzi gave her a wide grin. "If you explode and burn up on reentry, we'll know to stay aboard."

"Cute," Derek told him. Dropped his bags. Took Galluzzi's hand in a hard shake. Pus and blood, the look in the man's eyes was like that of a suffering martyr. "See you dirtside, Captain."

"Yeah. You, too."

Derek followed Michaela through the lock and into the main shuttle cabin.

"You and I get to ride on the command deck," Michaela told him as he handed over his luggage. "Benefits of status."

He let Tech Third Class Raptu stow his bags and followed Michaela through the hatch into the command deck. He got the right-hand seat in the row of three behind Naftali and copilot Windman's command chairs. Begay, the old, familiar, pensive "don't disturb me" look on his face, was in the left seat. The Advisor might have been meditating given the lines of concentration.

Derek buckled in. Aware of Michaela's curious appraisal as she snapped her harness tight.

"What?"

"Just thinking. About all we've been through. You and me. All of us."

He arched an eyebrow. "Ten years in that bucket of air is a long time, Micky." He called her his old affectionate name from one of the two periods when they'd been lovers. "I haven't a clue about what awaits us down-planet. Whatever it is, if you need me, let me know."

She glanced away. "It's not like there're many secrets left after all this." A beat. "I'm sorry for the way I . . . Well, I could have been more diplomatic that last time."

"I just wish that things would have worked out better between you and Turner."

"All right, people," Naftali's voice carried from the command chair. "Let's go see a new world."

Thumps could be felt through the deck. Servos whined and hydraulics moaned.

"Hatch is sealed and secure." Raptu's voice announced through the com.

"Begin undocking sequence." Windman's voice couldn't mask the excitement.

A bigger thump shivered the shuttle. "Locking latches free."

Looking through the right-side window, Derek watched the shuttle rise, clear *Ashanti*'s hull, and Capella's bright light spilled through the transparency. As they rose, Derek got a good look at the ship. Could see the occasional pits in the sialon hull, and then they were above it.

Ashanti seemed to glow in Capella's light, radiant. Part of the ship's hull lay in shadow. And behind it the wash of the Milky Way—in a billion stars—gave it a special sort of beauty.

Then the shuttle changed attitude, banked, and the stars—masked by a pattern of black nebulae—took the ship's place.

"I can't believe this is happening," Michaela whispered. "It's really over. We've made it. There were times when I almost gave up."

Derek chewed his lips, the surreal sensation increasing as acceleration pushed him into the seat. As it did, they passed *Freelander* where it hung in orbit. Unlike *Ashanti*, the big ship's hull was dark behind the terminator line. Dek had read the reports, seen the images of the temple of human bones in the cafeteria.

There, but for the grace of God, go I.

The ghost ship seemed to hold his gaze as it cried out to his sense of tragedy and horror. People had committed mass murder, died of old age, gone mad. Now, studying the dark vessel, something wasn't right. The light, it didn't reflect. The sensation was like looking at one of those 50% mirrors that passed half the photons. Which was clap-trapping crazy, of course.

But something about the derelict sent a shiver up his bones.

As if *Freelander* took the trials and tribulations that *Ashanti* endured and magnified the horror tenfold.

With a sense of relief, he felt the first turbulence of atmosphere, watched the reddish haze trace its way across the wings and past his window. A faint roaring filled the cabin, the shuttle bouncing down out of the sky.

They shot over the terminator, looking down on an eerily dark planet. He could barely make out the continents, the seas, and islands.

Dark.

How odd after Earth, Moon, and Mars, all of which were stitched with patterns of light while in their nighttime phases.

As they shot into the sunlight, dropping down, Derek picked out the signature outline of the giant meteor impact crater. The sight of it reminded him of a bite taken out of the continent. Knew it marked the location of the human settlements on Capella III.

G-force threw him into his seat as the shuttle banked out over the ocean, leaving him a view of a sky that seemed to have a deeper blue than Earth's.

The shuttle's nose lifted. The roar grew louder. The ground seemed to rise, as if to smack them. Only to have the shuttle flatten out, almost skimming over the blue waters. Patches of white cloud flashed past the window.

They were over land now, a reddish soil dotted with what looked like trees. And nowhere, to Derek's amazement, could even a speck of civilization be seen.

I belong here.

The planet might have been a magnet, drawing him. A thrill, like a vibration in his bones, had him staring down at the terrain flashing below. The feeling was . . . mystical!

And then they were down, the shuttle dropping on its landing struts. Dust blew out to curl before a wall of stacked shipping containers.

Dust?

"Welcome to Donovan," Naftali called. "If you'd keep your seats until we spool down, we'll have you off as soon as possible."

Derek could hear whistles and cheers coming from the main cabin.

It's real. I'm actually here.

He could feel the gravity. Stronger than on the ship.

As he stepped back into the main cabin, it was to see people in tears. They were hugging each other, crying, smiling. These were mostly the Maritime Unit people and their families. But a few of the crew had managed to snag some of the open seats.

Raptu got the all clear. The crafty tech opened the hatch, lowered the stairs, and raced to the bottom, ostensibly to offer people assistance, thereby getting to claim that he'd been the first from *Ashanti* to set foot on Cap III.

A decade ago, Derek might have had the guy's head. Now he just chuckled as he grabbed up his bags and took the stairs to the ground. At the first contact, the electric thrill in his bones intensified. Could have been his body turning into a tuning fork.

I am home. This is my place.

With the seared clay under his feet, he took a moment to get his bearings. Stacked cargo containers blocked the view in every direction except toward the town. But the scent! Perfumed, a sort of cardamom and sage with a trace of cinnamon. For a moment, he closed his eyes, filled his lungs. Pure bliss.

Benj and Michaela clumped down the stairs, and both sighed in unison as they stepped onto the ground.

As Derek turned his attention in the direction of town, the first thing that struck him was the fence. Fully fifty feet tall, composed of cobbled-together sections of woven, welded, and chain-link wire, it looked like something from a maximum-security prison.

Behind it he could see weathered duraplast domes, peaked roofs that looked somehow medieval, and a collection of people who crowded against the fence. They were calling, waving, obviously happy at the shuttle's arrival.

From a gate came four people who . . .

Derek stared, wondered what he was seeing. Escapees from the circus? A sort of freak show? The notion of old-time pirates came to mind. They were dressed in gaudy, wide-brimmed hats and shimmering, rainbow-hued leather boots, vests, and cloaks. Each wore a shirt of some light fabric embroidered in colorful patterns. Okay, maybe Gypsy clown pirates.

It took him a moment, but Derek picked out the Supervisor, tall, raven-haired, with her scars. Hard to believe this was the same stately beauty he'd coveted in Transluna. The one who had once perched on Miko's arm like an exotic ornament. She walked forward with a swinging stride and stood out only because she wore a black business suit beneath the dancing colors of her prism-colored cloak. Disconcerting was the holstered pistol upon which she rested her right hand.

She picked him out immediately, recognition flashing. And then distaste and barely masked loathing turned to puzzlement as she noticed he was carrying his bags and gun case. Good. Let her stew on that.

Shig Mosadek was the short one with the unruly hair, brown face, and amiable grin. Beside him strode a tall silver-blonde woman with piercing green eyes. She might have been in her fifties, or with the right med, even older. She had a curious, almost mocking smile on her lips.

And finally, the fourth woman was mesmerizing. Thirtyish, maybe five foot six, with long blue-black hair and angular cheekbones unlike anything Derek had ever seen. Then he fixed on her inhuman, almost alien-black eyes. She walked with the same innate grace and flow as a hunting panther. The military-grade rifle slung on her shoulder, the big knife and the use-worn pistol on her pouch-filled belt, added to her look of deadly competence.

Supervisor Aguila stepped ahead, offering her hand as she said, "Advisor/Observer Begay, I'm Supervisor Kalico Aguila of Corporate Mine. To my left is Shig Mosadek, Yvette Dushane, and Security First Talina Perez of Port Authority. Welcome to Donovan."

That she'd deferred to the Advisor/Observer irritated something deep in Derek's chest. Yes, Begay was the senior Corporate official. But to spurn a Taglioni? What was the woman trying to prove? What was her game? What percentage did she play by antagonizing him and throwing down the gauntlet . . .

Stop it. You're not that guy anymore.

Derek fixed on Begay's face, realized that the man looked stricken. On the verge of tears, Begay said, "Thank you, Supervisor. A lot of us, well, we thought we'd never see this day."

Michaela, too, was looking shaken. Her mouth was working, a glitter of incipient tears behind her eyes. At the moment she seemed too overcome for words.

When Aguila finally looked his way, Dek stepped forward, dropped his bags, and offered his hand. "Derek Taglioni, Supervisor. Good to see you again. Allow me to introduce Michaela Hailwood, in charge of the Maritime Unit and our lead scientist."

She ignored his hand, a mere quiver of distaste at the corner of her mouth. A thousand questions lay behind the look she gave him.

He tried not to be distracted by the tracery of scars across her face. Oh, yes. She remembered that last meeting. Her blue gaze seemed to shoot through him like lasers. "Welcome, sir. I hope the vicissitudes of your journey weren't unbearable."

Derek felt an old part of himself bristle at the reserve she tried to keep from her voice. She still loathed him. That brought him no little amusement. And yes, had he stepped down from the shuttle ten years ago . . .

Have I changed so much?

Aguila had shifted her attention to Michaela, saying, "Welcome to Donovan." She had no trouble offering the woman her hand in a firm shake.

Mosadek—a beneficent smile on his lips—said, "I look forward to getting to know you all. Port Authority is delighted to welcome you."

Dek could hear the buildup of people behind him as the Maritime Unit came flooding down the stairs. Children were crying, people wondering at the smell of the air, the feel of sunlight on their skin and ground underfoot. He could hear complaints about the gravity.

Grabbing up his luggage, he stepped off to the side, happy to be out of the limelight.

In a loud voice, the alien-eyed Perez called, "Welcome to Donovan. I'm Security Officer Talina Perez. If you'll all follow me, my associate, Corporal Abu Sassi, has a registration and orientation set up in the cafeteria."

Aguila turned to the crowd. "Please stay close. We don't want anyone to stray off on this side of the fence. Once you are in the cafeteria and have completed orientation, your Corporate status will be determined. Temporary housing will be assigned, and we'll get you fed." A beat. "With *real* food!"

That brought a round of happy cries and applause.

As Perez lined them out, Dek matched Aguila's step, asking, "Is the fence to keep people in, or something out?"

"Out." Aguila shot him a measuring glance. "Sir, forgive me for being blunt, but Donovan is not Solar System, and Port Authority is not Transluna. In the next few moments you are going to hear yourself referred to as 'soft meat,' a 'Skull,' and who knows what else? The terms are not disrespectful, but a reference to your having been aboard a ship. It's a difficult request, but if you would be so kind as to grant the locals a bit of leeway, I would sincerely appreciate it."

Derek tried to decipher the message she was sending him. Obviously, a warning, but not even Miko's woman would dare hint to another Taglioni that he not behave like an ass.

They were nearing the gate, and behind the fence he could see the crowd, all dressed in insane costumes of leather, boots, worn coveralls, and looking like ruffians from a VR fantasy. The number of weapons alone should have sent prickles down his back. Would have, once upon a time. What kind of lunatic gave weapons to the common people? They couldn't be trusted.

Is that what living two decks up from the Unreconciled for all these years has done? It's left me numb to physical threat?

The gate was a big thing, ten meters wide, fifteen tall, but the smaller "man gate" was set into the side. His Donovanian escort led the way through, and Derek followed them into Port Authority proper.

He returned greetings called from the cheerful Donovanians and delighted in the fact that though they carried them, none were waving guns around. Gravel crunched under his feet. Gravel? Not paved?

The domes to either side appeared old, weathered, streaked with what looked like fungus. Here and there he could see pieces of cannibalized equipment, much of it sitting up on blocks. The sunlight seemed harsher, the sky a deep shade of turquoise that hinted of lapis.

Stopping before the double doors at the cafeteria dome, Aguila said, "Sir, rather than attend the orientation, how about you and I get some things straight on our own?"

"Listen, Supervisor, given our last meeting, I don't blame you for the chilly reception. Just for the record, I'm not here to cause you any grief. Not after what I've been through."

Skepticism filled her laser-blue eyes. "Actually, nothing would delight me more than to leave you on the other side of the fence. But I'll tell you what you need to know to stay alive. Call it the Aguila crash course."

"And where are we going to do that? Your office?"

"Hardly." She barked a laugh. "Follow me. And don't worry about the rest of your luggage. They'll send it to a dome. Two Spot will tell me where."

"This is it." He raised his bags and gun case. "Well, there are a couple of containers in cargo. An airplane. Some other toys. But this is all I've got."

"You're kidding."

"It's all that's left."

For a long moment she tried to dissect him with her cutting gaze. "Whatever game you're—"

"No game. I don't have any left to play."

He watched the others as they passed through the doors into the cafeteria dome. All those expectant faces, men and women, their children. People he'd known so intimately for all those horrifying years. And here and there a crewman. Including Koikosan, with whom he'd worked hydroponics. How had she managed to snag a seat downplanet?

"Long story, Supervisor. Call it a beautiful terror, a wondrous nightmare. A numbing epiphany."

She was giving him that you're-more-disgusting-than-shit-on-my-shoe look again. "Let's just get this over with as painlessly as possible so I can be shut of you."

She led the way down what looked like the main avenue. Domes were interspersed with stone-and-wood buildings of local manufacture. He saw signs proclaiming ASSAY OFFICE, GUNSMITH, GLASSWORKS, and FOUNDRY. The street was empty of traffic. The town's entire population, it appeared, was back at the cafeteria and shuttle field.

"Not even a stray dog," he mused.

"According to the records, dogs rarely lasted more than a couple of months before Donovan got them. The invertebrates took out the cats even faster."

Derek had started to pant. His feet heavy, the two bags like sodden weights. He could feel the strain in his shoulders, wondered if they'd be pulled out of joint. When had he gotten so soft?

Fortunately she led him to a dome a block down. The place looked old; oddly matched benches sat in front of a double door. A faded sign proclaimed: THE BLOODY DRINK.

Derek glanced at it, then at the I'll-take-no-shit-off-you Supervisor as she opened the door.

What the hell have I gotten myself into?

12

Kalico took the chair to the left of Talina's. Indicated that Taglioni seat himself on the stool generally occupied by Shig when he chose to join her. Or sometimes by Step Allenovich, the part-time biologist and security third.

Puffing to catch his breath, a sheen of sweat on his too-pale skin, Taglioni dropped his bags and the expensive gun case on the fitted stone slabs. The guy was way out of shape, and Donovan's gravity was a couple of points higher than that provided by the ship's rotation.

He looked sallow, half-starved, and he probably didn't have a clue that he smelled bad. But then, after ten years in the same ship, they all did. Hard to believe this was the same man as that foul-mouthed maggot back in Transluna.

"What is this place?" Taglioni asked, glancing around at the tables, the benches, the stairway that led up to ground level, and the high dome overhead.

"It's called Inga's. The local tavern. And this is Inga herself." Kalico gestured to the big blonde woman who made her way down the bar. "Do treat her respectfully. Or not, if you want a quick one-way trip up to a grave in the cemetery."

"What'll it be?" Inga demanded in a tone that obviously shocked Taglioni's patrician sensibilities.

Kalico indicated Taglioni. "Meet Derek Taglioni. Fresh in from Solar System. Sir, this is Inga Lock, master brewer, distiller, and winemaker. She's also owner of Donovan's finest and only tavern."

"My pleasure." Inga shook Taglioni's hand. From the guy's expression, it looked like she was crushing his bones. "What'll you have?"

"Um . . ." Taglioni looked suddenly unsure. "It's been so long."

"You name it, we got it."

Kalico asked, "Sir, do you prefer wine or beer or spirits?"

She watched the corners of his mouth quiver. "Something mild, I suppose."

"I recommend the blond ale," Kalico said. "Me? I'll have the new-cask whiskey."

Inga inclined her head. "He on your tab?"

"Yeah. You eaten, sir?"

"Ration this morning." Taglioni replied, a curious insecurity growing behind his eyes.

"Two plates of the lunch special." Kalico added.

"You got it, Supervisor." Slapping her bar towel over her shoulder, Inga went bundling off down her bar, bellowing, "Two lunch specials!" at the top her lungs. As if she'd need to, given that Kalico and Taglioni were the only people in the place.

Kalico considered the man next to her, watched the interplay of emotion behind his too-perfect face. He was still handsome, striking actually, with his yellow-green designer eyes and sandy hair. "I doubt you would recall, but you and I have actually met before, sir. Several times. The last was at a Board reception in the Heiman Hotel. You were rather intoxicated. Knew I was accompanying Miko. Offered your own—"

"Loud, lewd, and vulgar offer of . . . um, companionship." He finished, followed by a crestfallen look and a humorless laugh.

In a weary voice he said, "I am deeply and sincerely apologetic. Not that I remember the totality of the occasion. I'd like to blame my behavior on the liquor or whatever mood-altering substance was dulling my brain. Unfortunately, I can't, knowing that it was the man himself who proved himself a rude boor."

Kalico blinked. Of all the . . . Was this really Derek Taglioni? "You're not exactly what I expected, sir."

In a soft voice, he said, "Can we dispense with this 'sir' thing? At least for the moment."

"Would you prefer that I call you Mr. Taglioni?"

"Most call me Dek."

Dek? Kalico arched an eyebrow. "Okay . . . Dek. An apology from a Taglioni? Whatever game you're playing—"

"I meant what I said. No game. After what I've been through . . . well, I'm just sorry for the way I behaved back then. I mean that."

"Just like that?"

He seemed to fidget, and for an instant, gave her a crafty sidelong glance. "You're not exactly what I was expecting, either. Back on Transluna, you were in the game for keeps. You're . . . let's say, a little different."

"Welcome to Donovan. If you survive here for long, you'll get the humor in that. Start with why you were aboard that bucket of air in the first place."

"You are still in my cousin's service?"

"Miko helped wrangle me this appointment. One of my tasks upon arrival here four years ago was to ascertain your whereabouts and status. Obviously, if *Ashanti* never arrived, neither had you, so I forgot about it."

"Back on Transluna . . . Can we just say I was angry and feeling slighted? In a fit of irrational and puerile rage, I ran away from home. Thought I'd come to Donovan and make a name for myself."

"You say that with a good deal of regret." *Real or faked?*

"*Ashanti* reinverted symmetry and popped back into the universe way off course." Taglioni's lips twitched. "Thought we were lost. Not enough fuel. Surely you've read Miguel's report. He told you the God's awful truth. Damn noble fool thinks he's going to get the ax for what he did to the transportees. Supervisor, I was there. At that time, at that moment, the smartest thing Miguel could have done was seal the transportees into Deck Three."

"No other choice?"

"Looking back with twenty-twenty hindsight, he could have taken the *Freelander* option. But no. No choice." Taglioni shook his head, eyes fixed on some internal hell. "Oh, if he'd let the transportees take the ship, under some freak of fate *Ashanti* might have arrived here under the ship's AI. But it would have been filled with corpses."

"Like *Freelander.*"

"Right. All dead. Even with Miguel's actions, it was a close-cut thing. For nearly six months it was nip and tuck as to whether we lived or succumbed to starvation. When it finally became clear that we were going to make it, I weighed eighty-nine pounds." He smiled into infinity. "That sort of thing changes a man."

"What about these others? This Maritime Unit?"

"They got the same ration as the crew and I did. Their director, Michaela Hailwood, she got them out of Deck Three before the shit came down. Kept them together. They're supposed to start the first oceanographic survey of Cap III." Taglioni's brow lined. "It's like three worlds up there in *Ashanti*. There's the Maritime Unit and there's crew. But no one knows the Unreconciled. They're locked away in their own private hell."

"Okay, Dek"—awkward calling him that—"let's step off the record."

"Seriously? Does anyone really go OTR?"

She chuckled at his skepticism. "You haven't lost all of the Taglioni wits. But, yes. We do. On Donovan. What's your call on what to do with the Irredenta?"

"Heard you had someplace where you could isolate them."

"We do."

"Hope it's far away. 'Cause if you're putting them here, inside this fence, I'm shuttling back up to *Ashanti* the moment they're off board."

"See, this is the thing I don't get: If they've been sealed on that deck for seven years, how do you have any idea what kind of people they really are?"

His haunted look was more eloquent than his words. "Because I worked hydroponics. I *saw* the remains that slid down that chute from Deck Three. You putting them here, in Port Authority? I want to be outside that fence when you do. And I'm still beating feet into the hinterlands as fast as I can."

Derek Taglioni worked hydroponics? Was she seriously supposed to believe that? But then, he carried his own bags. Claimed they were all he owned. "As soft meat you wouldn't last a day out there."

"Wouldn't last a day in here with the Unreconciled, either. I'd rather be eaten by your local monsters, thank you."

Inga thumped one of the handblown beer mugs onto the battered chabacho-wood bar in front of Taglioni. It was filled to the rim with golden ale. She set Kalico's whiskey in front of her. "Food's coming up. Good news is that you didn't have any orders in front of you."

And then she was gone.

Kalico lifted her whiskey. "To Donovan."

Watched Derek raise the ale. "To Donovan."

He took a sniff and closed his eyes. Then the man touched the glass to his lips, sucked a small taste. A look of other-worldly transcendence filled his face. Then he took another drink, deeper. Made a moaning sound of ecstasy down in his throat.

Kalico signaled Inga for another ale as he drained his mug and sighed in contentment.

"I remember exactly what you're experiencing," Kalico told him. "And that was after only two years stuck in *Turalon*."

Then came the plates. Hot, steaming, and smelling of crest meat, beans, peppers, and recado with a side of fresh cherries and blueberries. She watched the man eat like it was the fulfillment of dreams.

This was Derek Taglioni. She'd never forget the eyes, the dimple in the chin. But where he'd been arrogant and vile, the guy was now like a pastiche of hard and soft, clever and mellow. It was the damaged-but-strong part of him that intrigued her. Still, she remembered that old Derek Taglioni. The one who'd wanted to "fuck Miko's squeeze inside and out." Was that man truly gone? Or was this just his quetzal side, working under a most convincing camouflage?

Never trust a Taglioni.

When he'd finished, she asked, "What the hell are you doing here? Seriously. With everything you had back in Solar System, you left because of a temper tantrum?"

He ran thin fingers through his sandy-blonde hair, a bitter smile on his sculpted lips. Then he turned those yellow-green eyes her way and said, "I was going to prove that they'd misjudged me. That when it came to guts and daring, I could tame an entire world."

"And?"

"Something funny happened during the months when we didn't

know if any of us were going to live out the week . . . if *Ashanti* was going to be our tomb. That man who'd been Derek Taglioni was slowly leeched away. For a while, I thought I could see him go. Sort of like a faint dye, swirling around and disappearing down the drain every time I washed. When I started working hydroponics, I looked carefully in the vats. Tried to see if anything of him was left. All I ever saw was brown goo."

In her ear bud, Kalico heard Two Spot announce: *"The alert is about to sound. This is a drill. Repeat: This is a drill."*

At the wailing siren, Taglioni straightened, looked around. The piercing note rose and fell, an involuntary shiver running through Kalico's flesh and bones.

She said, "That's a quetzal or mobber alert. Now, pay attention. It means that either a quetzal is in the compound, or a flock of mobbers has been spotted flying this way. If it's mobbers, the siren will continue to sound. Your first priority is run like a striped-assed ape to your dome and lock your door."

"I saw images of a quetzal on the holo. What's a mobber?"

She pointed to the scars. "Five of them did this to me in less than twenty seconds. When you hear that siren, don't hesitate. Don't stand around like a gaping idiot. Drop whatever you're doing and run. Flat out. Get undercover, out of sight, where you're supposed to be, and don't come out. And for God's sake, don't try and 'help' the search teams. You'll just get somebody killed. Somebody who's a lot more valuable and important when it comes to keeping people alive than you are." She glared into his eyes. "We clear on that?"

To her surprise, he took her warning without getting his back up. She figured he'd bristle, make some remark about being a Taglioni. Instead, all he said was, "Clear."

"Some things might turn out to be worse than your Irredenta."

"So, you're telling me I might have just left one kind of hell for another?"

"Welcome to Donovan."

At the sound of the two short blasts of the siren, and then the repeat, she said, "That's the all clear. After you hear that, you can come out."

She signaled Inga for a refill of Taglioni's mug. After he'd taken a swallow and had that mellow look on his lean face, she casually asked, "So tell me. Now that you're here, what specifically do you want?"

For couple of seconds Taglioni stared thoughtfully at his beer. A puzzled look grew behind his yellow-green designer eyes. "You know, Supervisor Aguila? I don't have a clue."

She searched his face for any hint of guile. But to her surprise, the guy really seemed to mean it.

She cocked an eyebrow. Was he playing her? After all, she had a real live Taglioni on her hands. Close cousin to Miko. Not the sort she could allow to wander out into the bush and be eaten by a quetzal.

So, what the hell was she supposed to do with him?

Especially when she couldn't get that last image of his leering face out of her head. Leopards, the saying went, didn't change their spots.

13

The pounding was like someone was pumping hydraulic fluid inside Dek's head in a bid to explode his skull. Worse, his mouth was dry, his tongue like a senseless lump. He tried to swallow, gagged when his tongue stuck in the back, managed to conjure enough saliva, and finally got some moisture down his throat.

He blinked, squinted against the light pouring through a square window in the side of a dome. Pus and blood, but that was bright!

Straightening, he pushed back an old-fashioned blanket and sat up. Didn't recognize his surroundings. Where the hell . . . ?

And it came back.

Donovan. Port Authority.

The last thing he remembered was Inga's tavern. Eating another meal of beans, peppers so hot they left him crying and wiping his nose. But the *taste*. The *marvelous* taste. It made it all worth it after years of ration.

And beer.

He remembered beer. Lots of it. Wonderful beer. And then whiskey. Tasty and . . .

His stomach twisted. Tried to squeeze itself inside out.

Easy. Just breathe.

Somehow, he staggered to the small bathroom, figured out how to operate the sink, and stuck his head under the flow. Then he scooped water into his mouth with cupped hands.

He used the toilet, stepped into the shower, and turned the water on hot. To his surprise, it didn't stop after thirty seconds like the ones on *Ashanti*.

When he stepped out, no vibradry slicked the water from his skin for recycling. Took a moment to realize the old-fashioned towel wasn't a quaint decoration but the real thing. Fascinating. He'd never used a real towel before.

He was wondering if he was supposed to rehang it on the rack when a woman said, "Thought you might like a cup of tea. Mint is the local favorite."

He spun around, startled. The woman stood in the doorway, a cup in her hand. He fixed again on her eyes. So large and dark. The almost inhuman angles of her face gave her an exotic look.

"Talina Perez," he reminded himself. "I remember you from last night. But . . . Damn. It's all a bit fuzzy. Think I'm sick. Maybe some local fever. Head hurts like it's about to split."

She grinned, handed him the cup. "It's called a hangover. Sorry, but no pills. We get over it the old-timey way here." She gestured. "Not that I mind naked men traipsing around my house, but I've laid out a couple of your suits. Me? I'd go for the coveralls."

He stumbled out of the bathroom, caught a hint of the mint tea, and found the temperature just right. He sighed as he let the taste spill over his tongue. "Of all the things I've missed. Taste is the one. Damn! I feel terrible. This is a hangover? That's, like, for the drunken and ignorant masses."

She was watching him through those incredible alien eyes. "I forget that you're a Taglioni, and then you can't help but remind me."

He figured she was probably right about the clothing, so he chose the secondhand overalls. Once dressed, he followed her out to the main room, separated as it was from the utility kitchen by a breakfast bar with four stools.

By the door two rifles were racked. He did a double take. Rifles? In her house? But then, a gun belt with pistol and knife, hung on the couch back.

The smell reoriented all of his thoughts as he climbed onto one of the stools and stared at the plate she set in front of him. He took a moment to inhale the fragrances of real food. "What is this?"

"Breakfast tamales. Reuben Miranda has a farm on the southeast side. He grows the corn and chilis. The meat is from something we call chamois. We have an annatto tree in the greenhouse. Some of the other spices, like turmeric there, come from local herb gardens in the green houses. I make my own recado."

Dek picked up the fork and—despite the queasy feeling in his stomach—ate as if it were the last meal in the universe.

She was watching him, seemed to be seeing right through him.

"So, how did I get here? The last thing I remember, the Supervisor passed me off to some big guy for safekeeping. Is that right? And how did I get drunk in the first place?"

A crooked grin bent her lips. "Kalico wanted to know what you were really here for. There's an ancient saying that in wine, there is truth. In beer, with whiskey-shot chasers, there is a window to the soul."

"She got me drunk to discover if I was a threat?"

"In your previous encounters with Kalico, you didn't exactly endear yourself to her."

He toyed with his fork. "She's right to despise me."

"Loathe is probably a more accurate term. She told me that when it came to a choice between suppurative pus and you, she'd take the pus any day."

Dek winced, studied the woman through a pain-slitted eye. "Okay, I probably deserve no better. But why all the suspicion about my motives?"

"The last high-ranking official to arrive by ship was Tamarland Benteen. Yeah, the one from the history books. He tried to take over Port Authority and got a lot of people killed. We're a little gun-shy when it comes to mucky mucks."

"Mucky mucks? Is that a . . . what?"

"Means the high and mighty. And the way Kalico tells it, the last time you and she were face to face, you acted like a toilet-sucking prick."

"That was my usual operating parameter back in those days."

"So, what happened?"

"I had to become someone else." He smiled, wished his head would stop hurting. "This hot and spicy food. Is that the best thing for my stomach?"

"Trust me. It is."

He took a long moment to really study her, trying to put his finger on what made her so . . .

"It's quetzal," she said. "I'm part quetzal. Infected with their genetic material. That's what you were wondering, isn't it?"

"I, uh, sorry. I guess I was just—"

"I'm used to it."

"Double sorry then." He forced his thoughts away from the thousand questions that popped into his head. Tried to access com through his implants, but couldn't. "Something's wrong. I can't access the net."

"No net to access. You're on Donovan. It'll take a while, but some people claim they like the silence in their heads once they get used to it."

"That big guy I was drinking whiskey with last night?"

"Step Allenovich. Kalico tasked him with keeping you out of trouble."

"He kept calling me 'Skull.' Referred to me as soft meat."

"You just came off a ship."

Dek took a deep breath, trying to remember. "How did I get here?"

"Step and I alternately walked, dragged, and carried you. Be glad you tossed your guts in the avenue last night. If you hadn't, that hangover would be making you consider a single gunshot to the head as a viable remedy."

"This is your place?"

"Yep."

"You slept on the couch?"

"Yep." She arched a thin brow. "Not the first time."

"So . . . where do I live?"

"You remember Shig from last night?"

"Short guy. One of the Corporate Administrators?"

"Nothing Corporate about him. He's like a third of the government, such as it is. He said that if you'd like, you're welcome to his study. It's a small dome out back of his place. Sits in his garden. Has a charming view of the perimeter fence."

"I can bunk down with the contractees. I don't need anything fancy."

"We're a market economy. Yes, I know you have Corporate

credit. Which is meaningless here. We transact business with real currency, plunder, and trade. You'll get a period of grace, but you're going to have to figure out a way to support yourself."

"Like . . . what?"

"What can you do? Hunt? Mine? Farm? Medicine? Security?"

"I can fix things. I like to joke that I could qualify for a Ship's Tech I rating. And there's hydroponics. But you have farms here."

"Well, you've got a couple of days to figure it out." She frowned slightly. "What?"

He realized that he was staring again. "Sorry. I've just never met a woman that was so . . ."

"Go on."

"You seem so competent. Exotic. In control and somehow invincible."

She threw her head back and laughed. "Wow! You should be locked in here with me and the quetzals. It's chaos. Their thoughts popping into my head, one bunch trying to get me killed, another trying to find a bridge with humanity. Their memories get all mixed up with mine. And the physical changes? My face and eyes? I miss the old me."

"I'm new here, so I can tell you that the way you look? Well, you're doing just fine. Remarkable in fact. And before I make a fool of myself, let me say thank you for taking care of me last night."

"You're welcome." She frowned. "Not exactly what I was expecting given the stories I've heard about the vaunted Taglionis."

To change the subject he asked, "So, what happened to Benteen? I remember something about him. He killed one of my great uncles. Assassination."

"He's locked up on board *Freelander.* We needed a jail so we sealed him into the ship's astrogation center. You guys on *Ashanti* aren't the only ones to employ that option. We left him with hydroponics and water recycling. As long as he doesn't screw it up, he could live his life out in there. You've heard about Schrödinger's cat? He's our Schrödinger's assassin. You don't know if he's alive or dead until you unseal the AC and look inside."

"Screw vacuum. Isn't *Freelander* supposed to be, like a ghost ship, or something?"

"No supposing. You set foot on that bucket of air, and weirdity happens. You see things. Parts of that ship are still tied to wherever it went; it's leaking part of itself back to that place. Every hair on your body will stand on end."

"Thanks, but I had enough of that living with the knowledge that the Unreconciled were eating people, and only a sialon hatch was between me and their next meal."

Again she turned those unusual eyes on his. "We have a saying here. People come to Donovan specifically to leave, to find themselves, or to die. Why have you come?"

He sopped up the last of the bean juice with a tortilla. "Maybe I came to eat your breakfasts. I swear, after ten years of ration and weak spinach tea, I'm in heaven.

"As to the rest, Officer Perez, if those are my only choices, all I can tell you is that I'm not leaving. So that means I'm either going to find myself, or I'm here to die."

CONFRONTATION

I am like a man balancing upon a precipice. Within hours I am to be face to face with this Supervisor. My stomach flutters, and I want to be sick. Since the Harrowing and Cleansing, this is the first real trial.

The universe expects me to look into a demon's eyes, and not quail. I am the warrior who must face down evil, ignore its lies and deceit. She cannot see so much as a flicker of weakness, or know the churning anxiety gripping my heart.

I must *be invincible. A pillar of belief. Any doubt has to be discarded as a distraction given the great responsibility now looming before me.*

"Faith fills the hollows of the soul," Callista whispers. She lies on her bed, curled in a fetal position. Her spasming fingers flutter where they're positioned before her mouth. She's a frail thing, little more than a living skeleton, but today the universe has left her coherent. I assume for my benefit.

"Faith fills the hollows of the soul," I repeat, taking strength from her words.

The anxiety and uncertainty fade.

The other two Prophets, Irdan and Guan Shi, blink vacant eyes, their lips moving soundlessly.

At that moment First Will Petre enters the Temple. He glances uneasily at me. In his hands he carries two containers. One filled with white paste, the other, smaller, with a charcoal-black concoction made from burned cloth.

"They're ready," Petre says.

He places the containers beside the box of jewelry and the blue makeup I keep for my third eye.

"The com device?"

"Inserted through the hole they drilled in the main hatch. As you ordered, I've had your throne carried into the corridor."

I swallow hard, clench my teeth. Petre cannot be allowed to see so much as a crack in my armor. "Send me Svetlana."

He inclines his head and steps out.

"The true life whispers in the flesh," Callista murmurs. *"Like leaves in a wind. Whispers . . . around in a bowl they go."*

I take a deep breath.

Svetlana, my second wife, steps in; her light brown hair is pulled back, her dark eyes wary.

I untie my waist wrapping and let it fall so that I am naked. "Prepare me."

She steps forward. "How, Messiah?"

"This Supervisor, she's the embodiment of evil. She's everything the universe calls on us to defeat. Irdan told me, 'Go forth in white.'"

"In white?"

I point at the container. "White is the color of good, symbolic of purity." I raise my arms. "It will be my armor. Paint it all over me."

"You're facing her naked?"

"She will be dressed in finery. Is there any more powerful way to emphasize our differences? I go naked before her, a mark of ultimate humility. Representative of the fact that I am clad only in truth."

Svetlana uses her fingers, rubbing the white paste onto the patterns of scars and over my skin.

When she is finished, I indicate the small jar filled with black grease. "For my eyes and lips. I want this woman to see a living skull. To know that we are the living dead. That I am not facing her alone, but as the repository of all the souls and bodies inside mine."

Svetlana's expression remains grim as she attends to my eyes and lips. I even let her blacken my teeth to enhance the effect.

As she paints, I feel the righteous strength of Revelation swelling within me. I begin to pulse with the universe. One with its purpose.

She finishes by painting the eye in my forehead in bright blue.

When I face her, I see a startled look. A hesitation, and she bows before me, obviously upset.

"Wife?" I ask.

"You are someone else," she whispers. "What next, Messiah?"

"The jewelry," I tell her. "I want to wear as much as I can. The emblems of the dead. Actual mementos of the lives for which we are responsible. The rings, necklaces, and bracelets are the physical presence of those for whom I speak."

I inhale as I feel the dead pulse within me.

As I begin to don the jewelry, it is as if each piece burns against my flesh.

"Yes!" Guan Shi cries from her bed. Her eyes—sharp for once and seeing this world—focus on the polished gold and silver. "Today . . . rises . . . the glory . . . all the sunshine . . ."

Finally I am done.

The universe fills me.

"Let us go and engage the enemy," I say jauntily.

But down deep, I pray I am good enough, strong enough, to carry this off.

Believe, Messiah. You must believe!

14

The shuttle thumped, rocked, and was slammed sideways as the grapples clamped onto it. Not the best docking Talina had ever experienced, but then Ensign Naftali was ten years out of practice.

The ship's voice said, "*You have hard dock. Establishing hard seal.*" A pause. *"Hard seal. Welcome aboard."*

Tal glanced over at Shig, who sat in the seat beside her. The man looked absolutely nonplussed. But in the seat beyond, the Corporate chemist and design engineer, Fenn Bogarten, had a slightly amused expression on his tanned face. Kalico Aguila was riding in the copilot's seat.

"Welcome to *Ashanti*," Naftali called over his shoulder. "We have hard dock. Grapples engaged. Hatch has a hard seal. You are welcome to deboard."

Talina unbuckled, almost launched herself as she misjudged the angular acceleration. Shuttle deck didn't have the same circumference as the crew and cargo decks did; the effect was as if she were in seven tenths of a gravity. As a result, she had to mince her way out of the seat, walk carefully from the command deck to the hatch where a crewman gave her a smile and welcomed her aboard.

Tal followed Kalico through the main cabin and into the small airlock. As she exited it was to see a crisply uniformed Captain Miguel Galluzzi. He was in the process of greeting Kalico. And doing so with obvious relief.

In person, the man was smaller than Talina had expected. Looked emaciated. Nevertheless, he greeted her with a smile and an extended hand, saying, "Welcome aboard, Security Officer. *Ashanti* and her crew are delighted to have you."

With her quetzal-enhanced senses, Talina tried not to notice the odor: *Ashanti* stank. Not the musty-and-clinging scent of rot and death like aboard *Freelander*. This was more of a packed-humanity smell of long-unwashed socks, stale sweat, and fetid breath.

"My pleasure, Captain."

She stepped past as Shig shook the captain's hand, followed by Bogarten.

Dogging Kalico's heels, Tal was introduced to First Officer Edward Turner, Second Officer Paul Smart, and finally the A.O. Bekka Tuulikki, all in their dress uniforms. Tuulikki was a pale Nordic woman with steely blue eyes.

The *Ashanti* officers kept looking at Talina as if she were some sort of freak. Or it had been too long since they'd seen a different human face.

As Shig made the round of introductions, he said, "We have a present for you. If you'll have your people attend to it, we've packed the hold with fresh vegetables and fruits from the farms around Port Authority. It should come as a welcome relief in the crew's mess."

At which point Shig offered the captain one of his acorn squashes, proudly announcing, "I picked this from my own garden just this morning. I hope you like it."

"What is it?" Galluzzi asked warily, taking the squash.

Shig, his expression still mild, seemed confused.

Aguila gave the short Indian a crooked smile. "Shig, the captain's a spacer. Hydroponics are for growing yeasts, leafy vegetables, and tubers. My guess is that he's never seen a squash before. Am I right, Captain?"

"So this is a squash!" Galluzzi cried in delight. "What a wonderful gift."

Shig, still his amiable self, said, "I'd be delighted to tell your kitchen staff how to cook it."

"While you show the Supervisor to the conference room and discuss recipes, how about Bogarten and I take a look at the Deck Three situation?" Talina suggested.

"This way," Turner told her, taking the lead.

Something about the ship, the way it smelled. The dingy corridors and sense of despair. It all sent quivers up her spine. Like the thing was a trap—a prison that might close down around her in an instant and crush the soul out of her body.

Her demon quetzal squirmed in her gut.

"Yeah, you piece of shit. Welcome to space."

She figured Demon wasn't going to settle down until she was back dirtside. At least, it had been that way every time she'd been aboard *Freelander.*

"Not right."

Talina grinned to herself. The only thing quetzals hated more than space was deep water.

Turner led her and Bogarten past the hatch and into a curving corridor. The ship's angular acceleration was even weaker here. To her surprise every other light in the corridor had been removed.

"You saving lighting panels?" she asked.

Turner, a thoughtful look on his face, said, "In the beginning we took them out to cut the draw on the electrical system. Every amp we could save was one we didn't have to generate. Could put that much more energy from scavenged hydrogen into the reaction engines. We even tried ditching the cargo ring to reduce mass."

"Why didn't you?" Bogarten asked.

"Couldn't figure out how to detach it without structurally damaging the ship. And without being able to balance the counter-rotation, it would have played hell with stability."

Talina told him, "Well, you may not know it, but that cargo is going to make all of our lives a whole lot better. We're hoping you've got a lot of spare parts and equipment we need. The biggie, however, are the cacao seeds. We're hoping, desperately, that they're still viable, and we can grow the trees."

The lift carried them up a deck, and the radial corridor took them to the transportee ring. Talina was relieved that the ship's rotation left her feeling more firmly planted. Took a while to get used to the difference between gravity and angular acceleration.

Bogarten asked, "Is this the only route to the shuttle deck? Using the lift? Or is there a companionway? Ladders? Something where we can have better control?"

"Companionway's around that bend." Turner pointed. "We can close off the lift. Block the corridor just past the stairs if we have to."

"That or use armed guards." Talina hooked thumbs in her utility belt as she studied the hall.

Bogarten gave them both a wary look. "And you don't think they'd just walk down to the shuttle deck on their own?"

Turner shrugged. "After all this time? Who knows? Maybe. But as for the crew, we've got a say in this, too. We'll feel better if we give them one possible route: a straight shot from Deck Three to the cargo bays and the shuttle. Once they're locked in the shuttle's hold, off the ship, and unloaded dirtside, we're all going to be sleeping a lot better."

"You make them sound like a disease," Talina noted.

"Whatever." Turner didn't argue. "You didn't have to live with them. See the things they did to people before they dropped the fragmented bones into the hydroponics chute."

Turner stopped before what would have originally been the pressure hatch that led into the transportees' section. Sialon was a ceramic composed of silicon, aluminum, oxygen, and carbon that was molded and superheated in vacuum. To say that the hatch was welded was something of a misnomer. Rather it was glued with a thick bead of bonding material.

The machine that stood before the door was a hypersonic drill. Sialon—being harder than any metal—didn't cut. But the atomic bonds would separate under intense heat and the right hyperfrequency vibrations. A four-inch hole had been bored into the door, a remote holo com device having been installed.

"So this is it." Turner told them. "Maybe five temporary bulkheads to install, and we can make an alley that runs all the way to the shuttle. Then it's just a matter of securing the cockpit and command deck so they can't commit mayhem once they're aboard."

"You'd think you were transporting wild animals," Bogarten noted as he used his laser scribe to measure the corridor. Then he went to the companionway, checking out the stairs.

Turner softly whispered, "I guess you'd have to define what's human, and what's animal."

In Talina's ear com, Shig's voice said, *"We're about ready, Tal. If you could meet us in the captain's lounge?"*

"Be right there," Talina and Turner said in unison, apparently getting the same message from ship's com in their implants.

"This way." Turner, again, took the lead, leaving Bogarten to inspect the route back to the shuttle.

The lift deposited them on the Crew Deck. Turner showed her to the small lounge just down from the AC. Inside, Shig and Kalico were already seated. Galluzzi was in the captain's chair in the rear. Turner took what was obviously his seat, and Talina settled for the chair near the door.

"Are we ready?" Galluzzi asked hesitantly. Talina noticed that his right hand was trembling as he rubbed it nervously on his pantleg.

"We're all curious," Kalico told him, a shadow of smile on her lips.

"Supervisor, please. Just be aware that I have no idea what kind of reception we're going to get."

"It's all right, Captain." Kalico lifted a scarred hand. "Proceed."

The image formed up on the holo. A projection of the corridor just behind the sealed pressure hatch on Deck Three. The walls were decorated, painted with skeletons in various poses. It hit Talina that had they been fleshed bodies, the postures would have been erotic.

What really grabbed attention, however, was the naked male seated in an ornately carved chair that blocked most of the hallway. Behind the chair back—two to either side—stood four women.

Talina fixed on the seated man. He slouched, almost insolently. His entire body was painted in blotchy white, as if it had been daubed with clay. It took Talina a moment to realize that what looked like designs covering his skin were intricately patterned scars. Combinations of chevrons, interlocking squares, a Grecian key style, overlapping circles and loops ran down his arms and legs. A series of lines ran down his belly to converge in the man's pubic hair at the root of the penis, and fantastic spirals—centered on his nipples—covered each breast.

Then there was the jewelry. His fingers were thick with rings. A myriad of necklaces hung at his neck, and a row of bracelets ran from wrist to forearm above each hand.

But it was his paste-white face that mesmerized. The cartilaginous part of his nose was missing, leaving a gaping hole split by the septum. The scars on the man's cheeks each created a maze that opened at the corners of his mouth. His eyes were blackened with what looked like kohl to make them dark in contrast to his white-pasted face. And in the middle of his forehead someone had carved the image of a single eye, painted blue and surrounded by a white sclera. The black pupil was like a window to darkness.

Whatever Talina had been expecting, it wasn't this. The guy looked like a character in a VR holo from hell. Even his hair was greased up into a macabre fan that ended in a series of black spikes.

A faint smile bent his black-painted lips. He more whispered than said, "Blood and pain and terror."

"Excuse me?" Kalico asked, leaning forward.

"The holy trinity of birth, but then you wouldn't remember." A pause. "Who are you?"

"I am Corporate Supervisor Kalico Aguila, in charge of all Corporate property and holdings on Donovan. What you'd know as Capella III. To whom am I speaking?"

"The ending and the beginning, the purification, the living repository of the dead and the initiator of life. I am the holy vessel."

"That doesn't answer my question," Kalico barked back.

Talina couldn't take her eyes off the man, kept trying to understand what kind of pain he must have endured to have his body mutilated like that.

"It tells you everything," the man replied.

"So, cut the crap," Kalico snapped. "Whoever you are, you're under contract. That means you answer to me. Now, do you want to . . ."

Shig held up a hand, gently urging Kalico to desist. "If I could rephrase the Supervisor's question, who were you prior to your illumination?"

"The past is a meaningless term. There is only being and becoming."

"Perhaps," Shig said. "It would help us to understand who and what you are if we could know what person you came from. I assume you were once Batuhan."

"That was another existence." He lifted the hand that had been lying on the exotic chair's arm, and part of the arm detached like a scepter. The thing was a couple of feet long, slightly curved, and remarkably carved in relief, the spiraling designs incredibly intricate. It reminded Talina of the ancient ivory carvings done on tusks in East Asia; the delicate relief was too tiny to make out in the holo.

"All right," Kalico continued, clearly annoyed, "So you're Batuhan. I understand that you and your people have had a most difficult passage from Solar System. But you're here. Given that you are under contract, I have the right to—"

"Neither you, nor The Corporation have rights. The Corporation is pollution, and you are its agent. Not that you could know, drowning in ignorance as you are, but you are suffocating, wallowing in self-delusion. Until you are freed from the black and engulfing prison of your lies and unquestioned deceit, you cannot grasp the simplest or faintest sliver of illumination. Let alone understanding."

Talina shot Kalico a sidelong glance. Saw the roiling anger mixing with confusion.

Again, Shig raised his hand to still Kalico's incipient outburst. "Illumination and enlightenment aside, we need to deal with some more pragmatic and immediate concerns. I have read many of your tracts and revelations. You think your current confinement is the universal womb. That you will be born the moment you set foot on Donovan."

"Nothing you can do will stop that," Batuhan said softly.

"Stopping you is not our wish. We are finalizing plans to shuttle you down to the planet. To a place called Tyson Station. There you will find housing, a garden, water, and everything your people will need to survive."

"We know." Batuhan made a shaking gesture with his scepter, baton, or whatever it was.

"You know?" Shig asked amiably.

"Of course. We serve the universe. In order to consume darkness and corruption, the universe will first free us from the confinement of the womb. As it eventually will free us from this planet when we mature from childhood. Only then can we begin the task of purifying the universe itself." He smiled, exposing dark and vicious-looking teeth. "We are the chosen. Through us will come redemption."

"Heard that before," Kalico snorted.

"Of course you have. We are the culmination of the Kali Yuga, the turning of the katuns, the End of Days, Ragnarok, the monsters who devour the universe. We are the terror. And we are the rapture. Chosen, harrowed, tested, and purified within the womb to redeem the universe."

Kalico asked, "Just how do you plan to redeem us all?"

Batuhan shifted his dark gaze, fixed his intense eyes on hers. "You must be consumed. The three holy Prophets have said so."

"Who are the three holy Prophets?" Shig asked.

"They are here, with us. Irdan, Callista, and Guan Shi. They hear the voice of the universe and shall go with us, lead us through childhood, and their teachings shall be universal."

Shig's face lined with curiosity. "So you are not the Prophet?"

"I am only the beginning and the end. I am the receptacle of souls. The interpreter of Prophecy. The first and last of the eternal graves of the martyrs."

Kalico said, "I don't understand this first and last, this whole graves thing."

Batuhan gave her a pitying look. "It's simple semantics. By consuming the dead, my people and I become the end. The last receptacle for the dead person's physical body and a pathway for his or her soul. Each piece of jewelry is the physical manifestation of a human being who lives within us. The proof of their existence."

He pointed to the mazes on his cheeks. "Thus, we become their living graves, their breathing tombs. They live through us since we are but repositories for their essences. And when my semen impregnates one of my wives, I am the vehicle through which a renewed and pure life is once again born. I plant that purified life to grow in a field fertilized by the essences of the dead who reside within that woman."

Kalico looked stunned.

Talina's stomach turned.

Where he sat, looking enchanted, Shig whispered, "Absolutely fascinating!"

"You see," Batuhan insisted softly, "we are blessed by the universe as the vehicles of immortality."

15

Vartan stood back in the shadows next to Petre Jordan, the Messiah's First Will. Just behind Vartan's shoulder, the Third Will, Tikal Don Simon, had his arms crossed, a sour look on his round Yucatec face.

The four Chosen—the men who originally accepted Batuhan as the Messiah—along with the First Wives who had offered themselves to the Messiah, stood in ranks behind the Throne of Bones.

As the holo that displayed the Corporate officers flickered out, the Messiah chuckled. For a moment he sat there, facing the hatch. His back to them, he waved his intricately carved thigh bone back and forth as though it were a cat's tail. Then, standing, he turned.

Vartan studied the man, saw the cunning in his kohl-darkened eyes, the confusion of polished jewelry. Had to admire his audacity. Not only had he gone to the meeting nude, but they'd made a white paint from finely ground white duraplast. With the black accents on the eyes and lips, along with his hole of a nose, it had given his face a skull-like appearance.

If Vartan remembered anything about the Corporate mindset, it was that they liked things neat. According to plan. Without deviance. They wouldn't have had the first clue about the meaning of the scars as offerings and self-sacrifice, or the pain the Messiah had endured as penance for past sins. Rather, his appearance would have shaken them to the core.

Walking around the throne, the Messiah paced his way down the hall, beckoning for the others to follow him to the cafeteria. There, he waited while the Chosen placed his throne in its traditional spot. Only after he'd seated himself did the rest slip into their chairs.

"Now you know the measure of the opposition." The Messiah closed his eyes and looked at them, one by one, through the great blue "spirit" eye carved in his forehead.

A shiver always ran down Vartan's spine when that gibbous blue orb was focused on him. As if the "spirit" eye really could see into his soul as the Messiah's physical eyes could not.

"I see worry, hesitation. Some among you are unsure." The Messiah's voice came as a husky whisper.

"Messiah?" Petre asked, bowing his head so deeply that his long white ponytail rode up his back.

"You are my First Will," the Messiah replied. "Speak."

"You know they're going to take precautions. Limit or even deny us access to the crew. After all this time, the moment has come to unleash our wrath, the long-held anger of the dead we host. We've promised—"

"They will indeed plan, devise, and do all in their power to keep us from the *Ashanti* and her crew." The Messiah fingered his long-bone scepter. "The Prophets heard the universe last night and they sang. I heard them, and they allowed me to see." He pointed a finger at the eye in his forehead.

"What did you see?" Petre asked.

"The time is not right to purify the crew. But it will be. When the universe determines we are ready. Look around you, at each other. We're weak. Starved by *their* ration and tea. In the song of the Prophets I heard what their visions had seen. I have been given a glimpse."

"Messiah?" Svetlana asked. "A vision of what?"

"Ah, Second Wife. An infant doesn't run into battle before he can so much as crawl. In this ship, we are nothing more than a fetus. On the planet, at this Tyson Station, we shall become infants. Who then grow into children. Who finally become adults. When adults fight, they win. But only after they've grown, learned the arts of combat."

"Messiah?" Vartan asked with respect.

"Second Will?"

"How, then, do we deal with the evacuation? What do the Prophets wish of us?"

"We will act submissively. Follow the Supervisor's orders. Do as they ask. The Prophets tell me that our goal, and our only goal, is to get to the planet. To a place where The Corporation and its agents no longer control us."

"And then?" Svetlana asked.

"Then we finally come into our own."

Vartan chewed his lips, thinking back to the unending rage they'd lived with after the hatch was sealed. For so many of them, it had been the anger, the promise of retribution against Captain Galluzzi that had kept them alive. Given them purpose in the endless hell of their gopher-warren of a deck.

"Messiah," Petre said. "We have detained five who would betray us. Just as you foresaw. They are bound, awaiting purification and immortality."

"Five?" The Messiah shook his head, exhaled through the ruin of his nose. "The universe provides. This is my Will. Listen. Hear it. Make it so. We have but two days. At the end of them, we shall need our strength. To have fortified our bodies. To do that, we must feast. Each and every one of us must eat, fill our stomachs in anticipation. We are leaving the womb. Being born, and birth requires strength and energy."

Petre reached down and removed the cleaver from its scabbard on his belt. Finely polished steel caught the light, gleamed along the razor edge.

Vartan ground his teeth. Glanced at the Messiah. Beneath the ruined nose, a grin split the man's face. Raising his thigh-bone scepter, he said, "We shall need all of the buckets this time. I don't want a single drop of the blood to be wasted."

ENGAGED

I sit in the observation dome. An odor that one of the Prophets once called mutton-pork—that sweetly cloying and unmistakable scent of cooked human flesh—hangs in the air. The others are still feasting. Preparing for our "birth" as the figurative release from Deck Three will be. I absently run my fingernail down the lines of scars. Think of all the souls that have followed that path to rebirth and immortality. It is for them, for the universe, that I fight.

And the battle is now engaged.

My people do not understand the depth or intricacies of that combat.

After all these years, I have a face for my True Enemy. Since we were confined on Deck Three, I filled the role with Captain Galluzzi. Not that he really was the enemy, being nothing more than the universe's tool, the one it used to create us.

If there was a parallel in human history it might have been Rome and the early Christians. But for Rome, there would have been no Jesus. But for The Corporation and Miguel Galluzzi, there would have been no Irredenta. Pontius Pilate had to play his part in the creation of the Christian messiah, Galluzzi served the same purpose in creating us.

But now I have Kalico Aguila.

The physical embodiment of The Corporation.

The Corporation had to play its role. The Irredenta had to be raised in the midst of its lies, deceit, and inhumanity. Trust me, we'd bought it all, been faithful followers and believers. Never questioned that The Corporation—and all it stood for—served the ultimate good. That it was kind, just, and caring.

Which made the Harrowing and Cleansing epically traumatic. When faced with brutal Truth, it was to discover that The Corporation had deceived us on every level. To discover that we'd been played for complete fools had been soul numbing.

So much so, that some never could justify themselves with the Truth.

But they've since been purified and will be reborn with a full and better appreciation for the universe and its fundamental Truths.

When first looking upon Kalico Aguila, I must confess, her scars gave me the slightest bit of hesitation. The woman has undergone an Initiation of her own, made her own sacrifices of pain and blood. I hadn't expected that from a Corporate figurehead. But then, the universe makes no mistakes. The scars are there to warn me: Here is an opponent you must not underestimate. She will try and pervert the Truth. Seek to mislead the Irredenta from the Revelation, the True path, and the teachings of the Prophets.

She will be ruthless.

Praise be to the universe. I am warned.

To do battle with Kalico Aguila, I need my people united. The feast serves not just as a means of eliminating dissension among the ranks, but as a reminder of our unique identity. We are the chosen. We are the living dead. The vehicle through which they shall become immortal.

Staring out at the billions of stars, I am made humble. Aware once again of my failings, my weaknesses, and overwhelmed by the responsibility that has been laid upon my shoulders.

I am Blessed by the knowledge that I am no longer alone. It's not just me, but all the human beings I have incorporated into my flesh and bone. They pulse with my blood, live in each cell of my body. I am they, they are me.

As long as the Irredenta are united, without divisions and rancor, we shall win. The universe, in its wisdom, has prepared us. Marked us as separate.

At the time, I didn't see the genius of the Initiation. I was lost in the moment and trying to comprehend when Guan Shi began to scarify her flesh. I thought it a penance. That the pain and mutilation was a way to atone for guilt and previous sin.

And yes, the terrible agony of scarification is an offering to the universe—each of us sacrificing and suffering at the most personal level. What more intimate and honest sacrifice is there than to proffer from our own bodies?

Accepting that belief, I have given more of myself than any of my people. I can think of no other way to prove my devotion.

And the scars serve the dead. Not only are they a path leading to immortality, they demonstrate the willingness of the pure to suffer on their behalf.

How simple of me to think that's all that the Initiation was.

Only today—face to face with Kalico Aguila—did I realize the universe's true genius: the scars set us apart. The Irredenta will never *fit into Corporate society. They separate us from the rest of humanity in a way that can never be bridged. They unite us as a people in a way that no feasts, no shared experiences ever could.*

So, now, as we emerge into our inheritance, I am reassured that no failing or inadequacy of my own, no heresy, or doubts on the part of the Irredenta, will cause us to fail.

I pity Kalico Aguila.

She has only The Corporation to serve.

I have been chosen to fight for the universe.

16

When she peered down into the glass of whiskey, Kalico could see no facial features, just an outline of her head and hair against the gleam of the dome overhead.

Inga's was full—the suppertime crowd having trooped in for whatever the kitchen offered. The place felt reassuring; the clank of mugs on chabacho wood, the tinking of silverware on plates, and the jovial calls from the miners and locals somehow came across as jarringly normal after her day on *Ashanti*.

She barely acknowledged Shig as he climbed onto the stool beside hers and flicked a finger Inga's way for his traditional half glass of wine.

Kalico shot him a sidelong glance. "If there was ever a day when I'd expect you to drink a full glass, this is it."

He shifted on the stool, expression thoughtful. "I've canvassed the literature. The Unreconciled are delightfully unique."

"Excuse me?"

"They've taken an entirely novel approach to anthropophagy and mixed it with teleological eschatology."

"Repeat that in a human language, please."

"Religious philosophy has always preoccupied itself with what happens at the end of time. For Christians it's the rapture, the four horsemen, and judgment day. End of Days for the Muslims, or perhaps the return of the Twelfth Imam for the Shia. In Hindu mythology Kali and Shiva destroy the fourth cycle and restart time at the end of the Kali Yuga. Among the Central Americans, it was the turning of the Katun, the great wheel of time. For the Zoroastrians, a monster comes to destroy the world. The Norse thought it would be Ragnarok, the battle of the gods."

"Got it."

Shig gave Inga a smile as she placed his half glass of wine on the bar before lumbering off to mark it on her board.

"Usually," Shig said, "the end is preceded by an apocalypse. You know, the usual chaos of famines, plagues, warfare, boiling oceans, maybe a meteor, or flood, or wildfires. Cannibalism? Consuming the universe, purifying it through digestion and sexual reproduction? Becoming a living grave for the dead you have consumed? That's remarkably novel and innovative."

"How can you be so jazzed over something that creep-freaked me half out of my skin?"

He gave her a wink, his other eye twinkling with amusement. "When I was young, I was constantly amazed by the workings of the religious mind. It doesn't matter what the tradition, each one depends on some mystical acceptance that defies common sense: an immaculate conception; a great tree that holds up the sky; gods who can change sexes and colors; bringing the dead back to life; emerging from a hole in the earth; or maybe they fell from the sky. No matter how outlandish, people choose to believe this stuff. Can't help it really."

"That's why The Corporation regulated religion as thoroughly as it did. No one has ever figured out whether—when you chalk up the total body count—religions or governments killed more billions or caused greater suffering. When you get into those kinds of numbers, it's a wash. Both are equally dangerous to human life, liberty, prosperity, and happiness."

"The Unreconciled are proof of that." Shig fingered his glass. "I've studied cults like the Aghori Hindus who seek to immerse themselves in corpses as a means of achieving purification. By embracing death and corruption, they seek to attain a state of nonduality. The hope is that it will help them break the eight great bonds that keep the soul from achieving *moksha*. Um, *moksha* is the transition into illumination, emancipation, and spiritual fulfillment."

"But not cannibalism?"

"Only by a matter of degree. The Aghori may ingest something derived from a corpse, but in doing so, they're hoping to find their own illumination. Not acting for the benefit of another by eating a whole person in an attempt to purify him or her."

Kalico suppressed a sense of panic. "These were normal, everyday people, Shig. What we saw . . ."

Shig stared thoughtfully at the back bar. "Understand that as bizarre as their beliefs are, those people reflect the horror and despair they lived every day for seven years. The transportees didn't have enough to eat, so they ate each other. To assuage the guilt, they chose to believe they were keeping the dead alive within themselves.

"And the entire time each of them was asking, 'Why did this have to happen to me?' The only thing that made sense was that the universe chose them specifically for the purpose of bringing about its renewal. The reason their ordeal had to be so terrible was because of the grand scope of their coming endeavor: universal purification and renewal. Not only did that assuage survivor's guilt, but it made their actions inevitable and heroic."

"What was with the white makeup? The too-much jewelry? Being buck-assed naked? Is Batuhan out of his fricking mind?"

Shig arched a knowing brow. "Everything he did in that display was calculated. The white color? Symbolic of purity? Accented by the black eyes and mouth? Perhaps to represent a living corpse? And he wanted you to see the scarification, the lines leading to his penis. Death and sex, the ancient dance and balance of life."

"Then what was with the jewelry? He said it was taken from the dead."

"That they might be witness. In place of a name, he wore a possession from the dead."

"You ask me, they were nothing more than a collection of trophies. The kind a serial killer keeps as mementos of his victims."

"Anything but. That man *believes*."

"So, how do we fix them? Reprogram them?"

"You don't. At least, not on Donovan. A psychiatric hospital in Solar System might. For now, this cult of theirs is how they cope. Maybe, in a couple of years, you might start trying to talk sense to them."

She sighed. "Let me guess. You're telling me that offering counsel to them now would be a waste of time because they're too close to it. Bonded by a rite of passage. They'd just see it as an attack and hunker down on the core belief."

"Correct."

"A true believer? Is that why Batuhan had to be such an arrogant prick? It's like he was purposefully picking a fight. Daring me to do my worst. What would possess him to act like such a hard ass?"

"You really don't know?"

"Do I look like I do?"

"It's the only defense he has. Sheer blind faith in himself and his cause. Unwavering, unquestioned. As his makeup symbolized, it's all black and white."

"Come on, even mystics question. Can carry on give-and-take conversations."

"Not when they're scared."

She gave him a disbelieving glare. "Batuhan? Scared?"

"Oh, yes, Supervisor. If you ask me, that's the most frightened man I've ever seen. Shaken, terrified right down to his bones. His nightmare—the terrible fear that haunts his soul—is that he's unworthy, incapable of attaining the task before him."

"Came across as pretty sure of himself and his cause."

Shig's expression turned thoughtful. "Most great mystics are terrified. What they often call 'The Dark Night of the Soul.' Or sometimes, 'The Cloud of Unknowing.' It's the sense of being unworthy of the task God has chosen for them. Think St. John of the Cross, or St. Teresa of Calcutta. The only defense Batuhan has against his gnawing and deep-seated self-doubt is to project a complete, absolute, and unwavering certainty in his cause. The greater his self-insecurity, the more absolute and unbending his public face will be. His greatest fear will be that his mask will slip, that someone will glimpse his terror."

"Shig, seriously, do you think that putting them down out at Tyson Station is the best thing we can do? Even telling them what to watch out for, half of them will be dead within six months."

Shig lifted his glass of wine, touched it to his lips, but she wasn't sure that he actually tasted it.

After he placed it back on the bar, he said, "Supervisor, Donovan is all about making the best decision out of nothing but bad choices. Do you choose what is just, what is moral, or what is correct?"

"God, I hate you sometimes."

"That's why being me is so much fun."

17

Allison Chomko descended the stairs into Inga's and found the tavern doing a good business. The first rotation of *Ashanti*'s crew had come down with the latest shuttle. People had volunteered to personally escort the malnourished and frail crewmen, to ensure that they didn't get into trouble. And, most of all, to be sure that no one got devoured by the local fauna. Donovanians considered it bad luck to be eaten on a person's first night planetside.

She and Dan had been of two minds about allowing the *Ashanti*'s crew into either The Jewel or Betty Able's until it was learned that the Supervisor had provided each spacer a hundred Port Authority SDRs in advance of their Corporate pay back in Solar System.

Granted, it was only thirty crew people, and with only a hundred SDRs to their names it wouldn't be good business to pick them completely clean the first time they set foot in either establishment. The best that could be hoped for was that they'd think kindly of The Jewel or Betty Abel's. That they'd come back sometime when they were flush.

Allison picked out Kalico Aguila seated at the bar next to Talina Perez's chair. Even as she spotted her, a bowl of the house chili was placed in front of the Supervisor. Would have been—in the old days—that Aguila would have had a marine guard to watch her back. That she didn't showed how far the woman had come since that long-ago day she set foot on Donovan surrounded by twenty marines in battle tech who were toting hot weapons.

Allison nodded to and returned calls from patrons, gave a wave to others.

It no longer bothered her that old friends, people like Mellie Nagargina, Friga Dushku, or Amal Oshanti never so much as met her eyes. Losing their respect had been a price she'd had to pay. Odd notion that. Once she'd been one of them. An aspiring wife and mother, a homemaker for Rick. Only to lose him to an accident and then her infant daughter, Jessie, a year later to a quetzal.

So, where would she be if Dan Wirth hadn't sniffed her out with the same acuity as a slug in the mud homed in on a bare foot? Remarried? With another two children? Teaching at the local school? A housewife bustling about her garden, preparing suppers, and ensuring the kids were properly dressed and supervised?

It brought a tired smile to her lips as she walked up to the chair beside Aguila's and slipped onto the cushion.

"Good evening, Supervisor." To Inga, she gave the hand sign for a glass of whiskey.

"Allison Chomko," Aguila said in a flat voice. "To what do I owe the pleasure?"

"At first I thought maybe we'd try girl talk. You know, chat about the weather and gossip about who's doing what. Then I figured fuck it, we'd talk business."

"And just what business did you have in mind?"

"How much do you want for Kalen Tompzen?"

Aguila laid her spoon down, fixed those laser-blue eyes on Allison's as she asked, "You really want to go there?"

"Supervisor, history is what it is. You and Dan had to learn a few things before you could understand what Donovan is all about. There's enough here for everyone, but it takes all of us together." She grinned. "You beat Dan at his own game. Got to admire a woman with that kind of acumen."

"What makes you think I don't hold a grudge?"

"Fine. That's your concern. Mine is business. How much do you want for Tompzen?"

"You assume he's still alive."

"I figure we'd have heard if he wasn't. As for myself, I suspect you've had him doing whatever unpleasant thing you could possibly find or invent. At this stage, he's probably so miserable that an up-close-and-personal encounter with a quetzal might come as a welcome relief compared to the crap he's got to look forward to."

"What do you want with him?"

"He has skills."

"On Dan's orders, he killed three people who worked for me. Threatened my life. I don't forget."

"I'm not asking you to. Twenty thousand?"

Aguila chuckled, returned to her chili.

Allison read the wariness in Inga's eyes as she set the whiskey on the chabacho bar. Allison slid a five-SDR coin across the wood, saying, "Keep the change."

"Hope this batch is better than that last," Allison noted, swirling the amber liquid in the glass and inhaling the aroma.

"It is," Aguila told her.

Allison sipped, swished it around her tongue. "Never had a taste for the stuff until I had to start drinking it as part of the job." She paused. "You were up at the new ship today. You really putting the transportees out at Tyson Station?"

"Believe me, you wouldn't want them here."

"I lived out there for a while when I was a kid. My folks died out there. It's about as far as you can get from anywhere. And these people are soft meat."

Aguila finished off the chili, washed it down with a slug of whiskey, and turned to face Allison. The scars on the woman's face rearranged as she smiled humorlessly. "I got to meet the leader. The guy's sitting naked in a chair carved out of duraplast with human-bone insets. His skin's all cut into fancy scars and he's painted white. He cut his nose off to leave a hole. Says he's a walking grave because he's become a repository for all the people he's eaten. The guy thinks he's a messiah who will lead the universe as it consumes itself. Now, even if he doesn't speak for them all, don't you think we'd better get a handle on who these people are before we let them loose?"

"That bad, huh?"

"Before I came to Donovan, nothing scared me. Then there was *Freelander,* followed by *Vixen,* and now *Ashanti.* Not to mention Donovan itself. Makes you wonder what kind of moron would agree to be locked into a starship, confined in a small space for a minimum of two or three years, popped out of the universe by an energy field, to hopefully pop back in somewhere light-years away.

And only then discover they were going to die of starvation or old age in that tiny little tomb?"

"Not all ships end that way."

"No. But too many of them do." Aguila shook her head. "There's something going wrong with the theoretical physics that we don't understand. What's really frustrating is that with the time lag, unless *Turalon* made it back to Solar System, they don't have a clue back there that there's a problem."

"You were high in the ranks. What do you think they'll do when they find out? Stop sending ships?"

"It's a possibility. The Corporation was founded on the principle of limiting risk, controlling business cycles, providing social value through efficient distribution of resources. The biggest aspiration was getting rid of uncertainty and the destabilizing effects of nationalistic governments. Extraction, refinement, manufacturing, production, logistics, distribution, and consumption. All perfectly monitored by AI and ever-evolving algorithms."

"And you think The Corporation will balk over the number of dead aboard *Freelander* and *Ashanti*?"

"You think The Corporation gives a shit about people? Human beings are a renewable resource." Aguila's expression tightened. "It's the cost of the ships verses the potential returns. We'd just damn well better hope that *Turalon* made it back on schedule, and with all of its cargo intact."

Allison took another taste of her whiskey. "Welcome to Donovan. Which means we're on our own. And that brings me back to my purpose: Will you take twenty-five thousand for Tompzen?"

"Wirth getting tired of cutting his own throats these days? By the way, in case you haven't noticed, that's a real nice playmate that you're in bed with."

"Dan is more than capable of keeping the chuckleheads in line and assuring that the marks cover their bets. But that's not always good business. It behooves us to have another person in the position of enforcer. A layer of insulation between the occasional strong-arm tactic and the loftier position to which Dan has aspired in the community."

"Doesn't want to have to build any additional schools to rehabilitate his image, huh?"

"As he says, 'Once was enough.'"

Aguila chuckled. "Fifty thousand."

"Supervisor, you're not thinking this through. A great many of your people from Corporate Mine patronize our establishments. Knowing that we've taken one of your ex-marines as an enforcer reminds them that certain standards of behavior are expected. And that Corporate Mine's interests are aligned with ours when it comes to their welfare."

Aguila's gaze had sharpened. "You're not exactly the woman I thought you'd be."

"Let's just say I had a rough patch a couple of years back. Life didn't deal me the cards I thought it would. When I came out of it, I realized that where I found myself wasn't where I wanted to be. Or who I wanted to be."

"And who are you now?"

"The second-richest woman on the planet. One who can sit here as an equal, dealing with the most powerful and richest. For the moment, we're dickering over the value of a man's life. And no, I don't have aspirations when it comes to your mine or authority. I'll do everything in my power to keep you where you are and successful."

"Why?"

"Because you and your people are making millions down there. As long as you do, Dan and I get to take our cut, and we get to do it without the headaches of administration."

Again, Aguila gave her the probing look. "So you're sitting on all that wealth. What are you going to do with it?"

"Me? I'm young. The day is going to come when The Corporation figures out the problem of the missing ships and the navigational errors inherent in inverting symmetry. When they do, I might send them a couple of shipping containers of the finest gemstones on the planet, buy myself a townhouse in Transluna." A beat. "Or maybe I'll buy Montana, or that island they call Fiji."

"Assuming that in the process, you don't run afoul of the good Mr. Wirth."

Allison took another sip of her whiskey. "You're right. He is a dangerous playmate. There isn't so much as a whisper of empathy, remorse, or regret in his body. The man's as forgiving as a side-winder. So far I've been smart enough to avoid any conflicts that would incline him to slitting my throat in the middle of the night."

"Who said that only the wildlife was deadly around here?"

"Welcome to Donovan," Allison agreed, clinking her glass against Aguila's.

"All right, twenty-five thousand. And one other thing: Derek Taglioni? He's hands off. Get my meaning? I don't care if he plays the tables, buys a whore every now and then, but that's it. Just simple business. You and Dan don't try and play him because of who he is."

Allison shrugged, wondering just who Derek Taglioni was and why Aguila would be worried. "Done and done."

18

The mine gate on the north end of town was a huge square opening in the fifty-foot-high monstrosity of fence. The size was large enough to pass the haulers coming down from the clay pit. The gate itself rolled on large wheels and cammed into place when closed. Truly a remarkable piece of engineering.

Unlike so many of Dek's kin, he'd spent time during his youth in many of the re-wilded areas on Earth. He had enjoyed the open air, hunted—as only a Taglioni could—and come to relish the out of doors.

Maybe that's why Donovan called to him. He'd been ten years stuck in the confines of *Ashanti*'s few decks. When a person is removed from nature for any length of time, coming back into contact with it is an almost mystical experience.

He extended a hand—a futile attempt to touch the ethereal. Closing his eyes, he let the breeze caress his outstretched fingers.

Better than nothing.

Dek laughed at his folly and raised his face to the partly cloudy sky. He let his gaze rest longingly on the dusty haul road where it vanished into the scrubby trees. The curious scent that he equated with cardamom and a hint of cinnamon tinged with the lightest touch of saffron teased his nostrils.

The sound of the place was just as enchanting with its melodic rising and falling of harmony. Something similar to a symphony that was on the verge of finding the perfect musical score. But each time it was almost there, it would drift off into an atonal direction and have to start all over again. He'd been told that those were the invertebrates—a series of species of winged, shelled, and legged creatures that made up one of the lower trophic levels of Donovan's biome.

"Kind of a treat, huh?" the guard asked. He was a red-haired, brown-skinned man with a large triangular nose and knowing black eyes that stared out from under a shelf of brow ridge.

"I could listen to it for days on end. There's a magic here. Something that echoes in my soul," Dek told the man. Then offered his hand. "Derek Taglioni."

"Wejee Tolland. I'm part of the security detail. I like being posted at the mine gate the best. You see, that's the bush out there. Right close and personal. The other gates, they all let out on farms, the aircar field, the shuttle field. But that's pure Donovan running right up to the fence."

Dek took a long step, planting it firmly beyond the high wire enclosure.

"Uh, sir? I gotta ask you to step back inside."

Dek retreated, asking, "Is there a problem?"

Wejee gave an offhand shrug. "Orders are that we're not supposed to let you—and especially you—get eaten. Of all the gates, the quetzals try this one the most often. Whitey brought two others of his lineage right through here last time we had a major incursion. And that's not counting the bems, spikes, sidewinders, and skewers. Cheng's slug poison is working pretty well, and dry as it is, slugs aren't a major threat. At least not today. But I wouldn't trust it to be out with those soft town shoes of yours, sir. You'd be a heap better off in boots."

A man had to appreciate orders that said he wasn't to be eaten. "Can't set foot outside the gate, huh? Those are Kalico's orders?"

"No, sir. She don't give orders here. That comes from Tal. And if Talina Perez asks me to wrestle a quetzal bare-naked, shoot a hole in the moon, and toss *Freelander* out of orbit with one hand, I'm going to do it."

"I guess you and I see Talina Perez in the same light. Where you from, Wejee?"

"North of Alice Springs in the red center of Australia. Mother made the trip out from the city so I'd be born on the ancestral lands. Family's lived in Sydney for a couple of generations. I'm the first to qualify for deep space. I came here on the seventh ship. Never wanted to go back."

"Worked for Talina the entire time?"

"Yes, sir."

"I'd rather you called me Dek. I wasted too much of my life being called 'sir.'" He turned his gaze out to the bush. What the hell was it? This incredible longing, as though some unseen thing was beckoning him from just beyond that line of trees. After ten years in *Ashanti*, he really wanted to go wander, smell the land. "Who do I talk to about going out there?"

"Talina Perez."

"What *is it* about her? I'm not sure yet, but she may be the most amazing woman I've ever known."

Wejee's grin wrinkled the brown skin around his mouth. "Don't go getting a thing for her, Dek. Half the men in this town cast covetous eyes at Tal. Problem is, she's got quetzals inside her. That, and she'd break any man in two if he riled her the wrong way."

"So, she doesn't have a man in her life?"

"Here's the thing about Tal: I'd die for that woman, and she's saved my skinny Aboriginal ass more than a couple of times. But she's had her share of heartache. Buried her first man, Mitch, when he died from an infection. Cap, the second, got broken up by a quetzal, crippled, and somebody overdosed him. Then there was Trish. As close as Tal was going to come to a daughter. Trish's in a grave up at the cemetery after some soft-meat piece of shit shot her by accident. That was a couple of years back. Since then Tal's been different. Aloof."

"Tell me about these quetzals inside her. I overheard her talking to herself this morning. Not that I don't talk to myself, but this sounded like she was answering questions."

"She say, 'You piece of shit,' on occasion?" At Dek's nod, Wejee said, "Yeah, those are the Whitey quetzals. The ones she calls 'Demon.' Local lineage around here. They've got a blood vendetta against humans."

"Hold on a second. How does she have these creatures inside her?"

"It's the molecules, Dek. We humans got DNA: two strands of nucleic acid. Quetzals got what they call TriNA. Three strands. With three they can encode three times the information for a given length of molecule. I get a little hazy on this, but Cheng, Dya, and Dr. Turnienko, they figure the molecules are intelligent. That they think, or at least process information."

"So Talina has smart molecules running around inside her? And they talk to her?"

"Talk is the wrong word. They communicate through transfer-RNA, just like in terrestrial cells. Hey, I'm a security guy. You want details? Take the microbiology up with Cheng and Dya Simonov."

"The quetzal molecules don't just interface with her brain, do they? Is that the difference in her eyes and face?"

"She can see into both the UV and IR spectra. Hears way better than any human should. And she may not look it, but she's twice as strong as any man I ever knew."

"How does she deal with it? Must be, well, unsettling at best."

"She had a tough go of it a couple of years back during the Benteen excitement. Then, to lose Trish? That girl was like a daughter to her. Damn near broke her, but somehow, she put it all together, keeps the quetzal part of her separate."

"Hell of a lady."

"Yep."

"Hey! There you are!" a voice called.

Dek turned to see Michaela Hailwood's tall and slender form striding down the avenue; her long legs were clad in some dark fabric; an embroidered shirt was tucked in at the waist. She had one of the quetzal-hide capes over her shoulders.

"New wardrobe? Looks good on you."

"Hell, yes," she told him with a wide grin as she came to a stop; Capella's harsh light glinted in her fuzz of short black hair. Sticking out a hand toward Wejee, she said, "Doctor Michaela Hamilton. Maritime unit. Glad to meet you."

"Wejee Tolland," he replied with a grin. "What's a maritime unit?"

She gestured east, past the fence. "We're supposed to establish the first research base for the study of Donovan's oceans. We've got a submersible research module aboard *Ashanti*. I've spent all morning with the Supervisor and Dr. Shimodi about where to set up. Looks like it will be on a series of reefs five hundred kilometers out from the coast."

Dek gave her a grin. "That's the best news I've heard all day."

She gave him a wan smile in return. "Hard to believe after all we've been through. But, yeah, we're finally in business. They'll start downloading cargo as soon as the Unreconciled are safely planetside."

Dek made a face. "Glad I don't have to be part of the team that has to clean up Deck Three. Something tells me it's going to be a nightmare."

"You and me both." She looked out the gate. "So that's the storied bush, huh?"

"It is," Wejee told her. "The sound you hear is what we call the chime. It's the invertebrates singing to each other. Not sure if it's something they do to distract predators, or attract mates, or locate food. And since we've figured out about the intelligent molecules, it could even be language for all we know."

"Bugs with language?" Dek wondered.

Wejee shot him a cautioning glance. "Now, Dek, don't go making judgments based on Terrestrial life. On Donovan that can get you killed. Things don't work the same here."

To Michaela, he said, "And we haven't even begun to look at the oceans and rivers. But if an old hand can give you any advice, Doctor Hailwood, you'll live a lot longer out there if you'll take for granted that everything on this planet is trying to kill you."

"We'll be taking care to make sure we don't expose ourselves to any unnecessary risks."

"Good. Take that care, and then take it twice more, if you get my meaning. Nobody has ever died of old age on Donovan."

"I hear you, Wejee. We'll be extra careful."

"Good. But prepare yourself, Doctor. If I'm any kind of a guesser, you're going to lose a couple of people in the first month."

"Isn't that a bit extreme?" Dek wondered.

Wejee's knowing eyes had no give. "Just the opposite, Dek. That's unbridled optimism on my part."

PARTURITION

I sit in the observation dome, knowing it is the last time that I shall do so. This has been my haven. My retreat. I have come to this place when I was drowning in self-doubt. When my faith wavered, and I was frail and terrified that I wasn't worthy of being chosen for such an immense responsibility.

Here, looking out at the universe, I drew sustenance. In this place I was able, somehow, to summon enough courage to meet the challenge. Even if only for one more day. But it carried me through.

As the Prophets had said it would. Back in the beginning, before their language became that of the universe.

I so desperately wish I could appreciate the profundity of their words and utterances. But I fear they've fallen so deeply into the universe, that our frail and stumbling brains can no longer comprehend. This saddens me, for I am desperately envious of the Truths they now understand.

Sometimes they sing.

Used to be they'd sing in a sort of unison, now it's only occasional, and one at a time.

We've tried to record their songs. Learned the words to the early ones. Today we will sing their "ecstasy" song as we leave Deck Three. Depart the womb where we have gestated for these last ten years.

Everything goes back to procreation, be it peoples or individuals. Figurative birth. Literal birth. Life and death.

Sex is the inverse of death. Like Siamese twins, one cannot exist without the other. Opposites crossed. The divine reconciliation of opposites.

The universe laughs.

In the background I can hear the Irredenta. Excitement fills their voices. There is banging, the sound of crates being slid across the sialon deck. The preparations have been going on for hours. Kalico Aguila sent a list of things for them to do. Orders. Bring this, don't bring that. Wear shoes or boots. Hats are necessary. A long list of reasons for the above had been included.

We have no way of knowing what might be true or what might be a lie.

Being Corporate, whatever she tells us is probably a lie. What we do know is that the universe has brought us this far. It has taught us that we can only depend upon ourselves and the Prophets.

The universe will provide. We will continue to live with that faith and take with us only what we can carry.

I gave the order based upon something the Prophet Callista said a couple of nights ago. Sounded like, "Taaa whaaa ya c . . . c . . . carree."

Take what you can carry?

So often, I can only guess. But for the most part, the universe has backed my guesses. None, so far, have been proven horribly wrong.

Given that three hundred and forty-two people once lived here, that's a lot of possessions. Why the universe wants us to leave so much behind is beyond me, but it is not my place to question.

Somewhere in the background I hear a crash. Perhaps a shelf has collapsed or been torn down?

Cackling laughter breaks out from one of the children. They're half manic with excitement. Born here, they've never known anything else. Deck Three is their world.

As Ashanti *rotates, I see Capella III come into view: a green, blue, and brown globe with white polar caps, its oceans and continents brilliant in the star's light. Within moments the terminator is visible like a black line through the middle of the planet.*

Before I sleep again, we will be down there.

I catch a gleam of silver off to the right. Crane my head.

With a smile on my lips, I recognize the shuttle. Watch it close until it slips beyond the observation dome's field of view.

I rise, tilt my head back, and whisper, "Thank you for the strength and vision to do what I must."

I turn. Walk unsteadily out of the dome and into the chaos that is Deck Three. I see old belongings strewn about. Once-precious possessions too large or heavy to be carried. Not our concern. Let the Ashanti *crew clean it up. A reminder of their original sin.*

Many of these things will be missed in our new home. But then perhaps that is the lesson we're supposed to take away with us. We will leave here humbly. Wearing nothing that so much as hints of hubris or vanity. As the living graves of the dead and vessels of their immortality, we go as near to naked as we can. No one has ever been born wearing clothes. This is our womb. The hallway to the shuttle shall be our vagina. The shuttle shall deliver us into the sunlight.

When we walk out into a new world, we shall be as infants.

And then the hard work really begins.

19

The amiable ship's voice said, *"Shuttle Corporate One. You are on approach to* Ashanti. *Request permission to take control of your navigational functions prior to docking."*

"Thank you, *Ashanti.* Corporate One prefers to maintain manual control. Please notify us if there is any deviation during our approach." Ensign Juri Makarov replied.

"Roger that, Corporate One."

Where she sat in the right-hand seat behind the pilot, Kalico Aguila smiled to herself. Word was that any able shuttle pilot would decline surrendering control. Docking was about a pilot's only way to show off given the automation that was space travel.

Through the transparency, Kalico watched the A-7 shuttle drop down into *Ashanti*'s docking bay. Ensign Makarov eased them onto the grapples without so much as a quiver.

But then, Makarov had been flying almost constantly since *Turalon*'s arrival more than four years ago.

"We have docking," *Ashanti* said through the com. *"We have hard seal. Welcome aboard. Captain Galluzzi will meet you at the hatch."*

"Hard dock, hard seal," Makarov confirmed from the pilot's chair.

"Deal with it, you piece of shit," Talina Perez muttered where she sat beside Kalico. The expression on the woman's face was the one she adopted when she and the quetzal presence she called Demon were sparring over control of Talina's limbic system.

"Quetzal's don't like flying?" Kalico asked.

"Hate it," Talina told her, unbuckling. "Good news for us. Means that Whitey and his bunch aren't going to have any desire to commandeer a shuttle, steal a starship, and invert symmetry in a desperate attempt to space back to Earth and invade it."

Kalico stepped free of her seat, head cocked. "Too bad. I'd

consider giving them *Freelander* if they ever wanted to give it a try. Might be worth it just to see them attend their first Board meeting. Ultimate predators finding themselves face to face with ultimate predators. Wonder who'd win?"

Tal grinned, glanced at Mark Talbot where he rose from the left seat. The man was dressed in full and battered combat armor, his helmet clipped to his belt. From the seat rack he retrieved his service rifle.

"You ready?" Tal asked, slinging her own rifle.

"Good to go, Tal." Talbot stepped forward, the slight whine of his servos distinct in the shuttle's silence as the turbines spun down.

Sheyela Smith had managed to cobble together a small power-pack that had allowed Talbot to salvage his worn-out armor. The system wasn't military grade, but Talbot and the rest of the marines had their tech back online, at least for the time being. For the most part the remaining marines only wore armor during quetzal and mobber alerts. Today they would wear it to keep the so-called Irredenta in line. After all, there was no telling what kind of surprise the Unreconciled might have cooked up to "celebrate" their release, birth, or whatever.

Tal, dressed in coveralls, her knife and pistol on her utility belt, led the way.

Stepping into the cargo bay, it was to see it set up as a passenger cabin with rows of seats. Kalico gave it a preliminary inspection.

Corporal Abu Sassi and privates Dina Michegan and Katsuro Miso rose from their seats, all dressed in shining combat armor, their helmets clipped to their belts. The rows of seats looked oddly out of place given that the shuttle had been used for shipping cargo into orbit for the past few years instead of as a people hauler.

Kalico took a stance, calling, "All right, people. You've been briefed on the Irredenta. Your mission is to ensure that they are deposited at Tyson Station with the least amount of disruption. Your opinions about them, your reaction to them, is not part of this operation. You will ensure that they board this shuttle, that they are seated, and transported to Tyson without incident. Any last questions?"

Of course there weren't. She, Galluzzi, Bogarten, and Abu Sassi had planned this down to the final resort, which was to gas the entire cabin if things started to get out of control. Separated from the command deck by the hatch—and with the marines in full combat armor with their breathing systems—the Irredenta could be rendered unconscious and harmless.

"Let's do this," Talbot muttered, leading the way to the hatch.

On the other side, Galluzzi waited; the man looked like he had an electrical short in his underwear given how he was bouncing on his feet. The way his right hand twitched reminded her of a spastic mouse.

"Good to see you, Supervisor," he greeted. "Welcome aboard."

"Got the corridors sealed?" Kalico asked, taking the captain's salute.

"They've got one route to take. From their main hatch, right down here and into the shuttle."

"All right." She turned. "Mark, you and Abu Sassi have the enviable job of bringing up the rear to ensure that no one is left behind."

"On it," Abu Sassi said, giving her a salute. Then he and Talbot disappeared into the corridor.

"My people will sweep the entirety of Deck Three as soon as you've spaced, Supervisor." Galluzzi was still fidgeting. "Don't think they'd leave us a lethal going-away gift, but Batuhan comes across as the kind who might carry a grudge. Or at least might want to make a parting statement."

"See to it." She looked around. "I'd hate to have them compromise the ship. It's the only reliable one we've got."

Which was true. *Freelander* was a ghost ship, and *Vixen,* besides only being a survey ship, had a programming flaw that would take her fifty years into the future if she spaced for Solar System. At least *Ashanti* had made the transit to Donovan in the expected two-and-a-half-year time frame. It was the next seven and half years that hadn't been anticipated. They'd just have to take on faith that she'd return home a lot closer than the navigational error that had left her so far from Capella.

That was the thing about life on Donovan. One always had to pick from bad choices.

"*F.O. Turner reports all is ready,*" *Ashanti*'s voice sounded from the speakers.

"Supervisor?" Galluzzi asked in a voice filled with tension.

"Proceed," Kalico told him.

In his com, Galluzzi said, "You have the okay. Open the hatch."

The captain gave her a salute. "Supervisor, I wish you good spacing. I'll see you on the planet after we've secured the ship."

He turned on his heel, stepping through a hatch, and sealing it behind him.

"I guess that's our cue to lock ourselves in the command deck." Talina turned. "So how about that, Demon? You're about to ride down to the planet with a bunch of human cannibals. Given the way your kind treats their elders, that ought to have you feeling right at home."

Kalico wondered what sort of retort the beast in Talina's gut made to that.

At the command deck hatch, she followed Talina in and watched as Juri Makarov flipped the switch that sent the dogs clicking home to lock the door.

Retreating to her seat, Kalico accessed the holos that interfaced with *Ashanti*. In the image, First Officer Turner dissolved the last of the bonding agent on the Deck Three hatch and beat feet for the secure hatch that led up to Deck Two.

Abu Sassi moved into view; dressed in full armor, he tapped the panel control beside the sialon hatch. Through his helmet, Kalico could hear the whine as the latches retracted.

With a tug, Abu Sassi pulled the hatch open.

Talbot's armored form stepped to the far side, rifle at the ready.

"Attention please," Abu Sassi used his helmet speaker to project it into Deck Three's dim recesses. "Your transportation is ready. Please proceed forward, down the companionway, and to the shuttle."

The familiar drawings on the side of the hallway could be seen, the skeletons erotically posed. But beyond lay a dark haze.

Kalico waited; each beat of her heart measured her rising tension.

Where the hell were the Unreconciled? They'd had ample notice that this was their relocation day.

Unless they were planning something else.

"Supervisor?" Galluzzi's stressed voice asked through com. *"Think we should send someone in?"*

Talina muttered, "You don't think they did us some big favor like committing mass suicide, do you?"

"We're not that lucky." Into com, Kalico said, "Sergeant, send a drone in."

"Yes, ma'am."

She watched as a recon drone detached from Abu Sassi's shoulder; the little flying sensor whirred off down the hall. A separate monitor snapped on, showing the halls bathed in the green-and-shadow glow of IR and UV. The walls were all decorated with images, the effect spookily reminiscent of the scrawlings in *Freelander.*

And there were the people, reflected in visual spectrum and IR heat signatures. All lining up. Just as the drone fixed on them, the parade started forward. Kalico stared in disbelief. Where the hell were their clothes? Men, women, and children—they had only fabric wraps around their waists.

Batuhan was in the lead, followed by four young men who carried his ornately carved chair. Behind them were the four women with babes in arms, and following were three people borne on litters carried by men.

Kalico tried to get a better image of the people being carried. Looked like two women and a man, all three of them emaciated, looking half dead, but their hands were working spastically, their legs kicking and trembling.

Immediately to their rear were the rest of the people, dressed in the skimpy patchwork of clothing. Their hair long and unkempt, they shuffled forward in ranks.

"They're going down dressed like that?" Talina wondered. "To Tyson Station? What do they think it is, a beach?"

As the people passed the hatch, a weird and eerie song burst from their lips. They locked step, walking in time to the rising and falling half-chant. Kalico tried to make out the slurred-sounding words, something about an ecstasy of everlasting life, eternal salvation, and being the living graves of the purified.

At the hatch, Abu Sassi had stepped back. As per orders, he and Talbot had taken positions to either side, standing at attention, rifles at port arms. The pose was to make them look more like an honor guard than a threat. But if the situation went sideways, they could both tap the gas grenades on their hips, use the stun guns on their belts. And if worse came to worst, fall back on the non-lethal rounds in their rifles.

Emerging into the full light of the corridor, Batuhan walked barefoot ahead of his chair. For the exodus he had at least draped his loins in a sheet. Like a king, he strode with back straight, head up, his weird spiky hairdo in a great fan sticking up from his head. The man's skin was still covered with the splotchy white makeup, and the intricate scar patterns on his face and the eye carved on his forehead contrasted with the missing flesh of his nose.

The four young men bearing his chair—though less intricately scarred than Batuhan—had large sections of their bodies scarified; their half-glazed eyes flashed in every direction, taking in the marines. She could see them swallowing hard. One was almost shaking, looked to be on the verge of panic.

Why?

"Sergeant, keep that drone searching." Kalico rubbed her chin. "Check for anything unusual in there. Any odd heat sources. I want the chem sensors to reconfigure for anything explosive."

"Roger that."

She wasn't sure what to watch—the drone or the continuing procession of the Irredenta. The amount and patterning of the scarring, she realized, was different depending upon the person. Batuhan, in the lead, had the most and greatest intricacy. Then the four throne-bearers, then the four women. After that, the amount of scarring dropped, with fewer and fewer designs.

It's a sign of rank.

To her surprise, most of the women were either carrying an infant, or showed some degree of pregnancy where they walked under shouldered burdens. Like the men, they, too, only had a wrap around their hips and went barefoot. And of the children—all of them clad only in breechcloths—none looked to be over the age of six.

The children walked with a bouncing excitement, eyes aglow with the adventure. All of them were skinny little specimens, with hollow guts and too-well-defined ribs. To Kalico's disgust they'd all been scarified, but nothing like their parents. Their hair, with varying measures of effectiveness, had been done up in the fan. Looking closely, Kalico couldn't tell the little boys from the girls.

On the lower screen the drone continued its search, whizzing in and out of rooms, rising and falling as it inspected discarded personal items, old bits of clothing, looked under beds and into gaping closets. The rooms were rife with trash and abandoned belongings. Why were they leaving so much behind? Most of the light panels were dark. Looked like what was left behind in the poorer parts of Earth when a slum was cleared.

Following along at the back of the exodus came young men in their twenties and teens, each bent under the weight of a crate, bundle, or duraplast container. Apparently, they were the porters for the few assembled belongings of the Irredenta.

The drone buzzed, getting her attention. It was in the women's locker room, hovering over a pile of five skeletons. Most of the soft tissue had been half-heartedly stripped off, leaving the still-articulated bones looking red and ill-used. The skulls had been chopped open, the brains extracted.

"What do you make of that?" Talina asked.

"Reminds me of what mobbers do to a person, but they're a lot more efficient when it comes to cleaning the bones."

"You want to do anything about it?" Talina asked.

Kalico shook her head. "Not now. Maybe later, after they're planetside and safely contained at Tyson. There'll be plenty of time to ask questions then."

At the companionway to the shuttle deck, people were filing down. The children, of course, had never encountered stairs. They were having a wonderful time, jumping down, step by step, giggles of laughter rising, smiles bending their scarified cheeks. Their bare feet slapped onto the treads.

"You know the eye carved in Batuhan's forehead?" Talina asked.

"Yeah. That's creep-freaked, isn't it?"

"Just caught the light right. Got a good look," Talina told her. "Those three on the litters, they've got the eyes carved in their foreheads, too. But it's just them. Batuhan and the three on the litters."

Kalico thought back to the interview she'd done with Batuhan. "You think they're the Prophets?"

"Could be. Something's not right about them. And look, there, that young woman." Talina pointed. "See the way she's walking? Like she's got issues with coordination. And she's not the only one."

Tal was right. Something about the woman's coordination was off. Intoxicated? No, this was different. Like impaired motor control. Might have been the result of a brain injury. Kalico kept seeing odd movements, loose steps, curious wobbles of the head. Or a rocking tremor of the hands.

The continued sing-song chanting—the words being distinctly and purposefully slurred—sent a shiver down Kalico's spine. With a gesture, she muted the sound.

"*We have a total count of seventy-seven,*" the com informed.

In the transportee quarters, the drone was continuing its search, only to stop at a collection of shoes in one of the rooms. They'd been piled, maybe a meter high. A carefully built pyramid with the toes pointed outward.

"What's that all about?" Talina wondered. "We told these people they needed shoes. And what are they doing? On top of being damn near buck-ass naked, every mother's son and daughter of them is barefoot."

"Sent them an entire checklist for how to dress, what to expect."

"We dusted Tyson with slug poison, but that's not one hundred percent effective. And stepping on the wrong invertebrate is going to get a lot of them bitten." Talina made a face. "Thing is, it usually only takes once before the lesson is irrevocably learned."

The last of the Irredenta were descending the companionway.

In the shuttle's monitors, Batuhan strode imperiously past Dina Michegan where she stood before the hatch. His chair bearers had to fit the thing through the door and into the limited clearance between the first row of seats. At the hatch to the command deck, Miso snapped to attention, his helmeted head faced forward, but you could bet he was watching everything on the heads-up display inside his helmet.

Batuhan took the chair in the middle of the first row, his bare toes not more than a foot from Private Miso's armored feet.

The chair bearers clambered around, bracing the "throne" awkwardly on the seats immediately behind Batuhan's. People continued to file in; those bearing the litters carefully laid them on the deck where space could be found, thereby blocking the aisles.

As the rest tried to crowd in, bedlam ensued, with people trying to step around the three litters, scrambling over seat backs, and chattering.

But no one, Kalico noticed, crossed in front of Batuhan. The Mongolian tech sat motionless, back straight, head up, eyes forward as if he were a carved statue.

To Kalico's relief, none of the Unreconciled tried the locked hatch. No one brandished anything that looked like a weapon. The sensors picked up nothing that indicated an explosive was hidden on any person or in the various containers, bundles, and baskets.

"Sergeant?" Kalico contacted Abu Sassi. "Looks like we're about loaded. But before we seal the hatch, I need you to take a cargo net back and collect that pyramid of shoes."

"*Roger that.*"

Talina gave off a weary sigh. "So far, so good."

"Yeah," Kalico was rubbing nervous fingers over the backs of her hands. "Why do I have a really bad feeling about this?"

20

The sound of the shuttle lifting off had brought Dek wide awake. His dreams had been filled with forest and the smells of Donovan. In them, he'd been out there beyond the fence. Some intangible temptress—like a siren of old—had danced and beckoned him. Just a fleeting shape among the bushes and scrub. But the harder he pursued, the more elusive the phantom had become.

He blinked, taking in the small and neatly furnished dome. The walls were stacked with books—the old-fashioned bound-paper kind.

Shig had explained to him about the books: "These are old, valued because various preeminent scholars of religion have underlined passages and left notes in the margins. Oh, I have them in the implants." He'd tapped the side of his head. "But when I open to a page in the *Vedas*, I have the thoughts of Ramanadas, Irrawiri, and Raja Sing right there, written in the margins in their own handwriting."

Dek sat up in the small bed—something called a futon; it folded out from a bench. Not the most comfortable thing he'd ever slept on. Shig had called it "surprisingly restful," and after having spent two nights on the contraption, Dek suspected you never took an ascetic at his word when it came to basic creature comforts.

Within a matter of moments, Dek had attended to his toilet, made the bed, and dressed. He chose the coveralls, figuring he might want to save the last of his "good" clothing.

Stepping out into the day, he was surprised to find Shig bent over the plants in his garden. The short scholar had an old plastic gallon container labelled "mayonnaise" into which he was dropping green beans. Another quart container, by his foot, was already filled with blueberries from the bushes that were growing into the perimeter fence.

"Good morning!" Dek called, blinking in the light.

"Shuttle awaken you?" Shig asked.

"How did I sleep so long?"

"It's the gravity." Shig collected his containers and straightened. "And wholesome food. Not to mention being able to sleep in a proper bed after all those years in a starship."

Best not to tell him about the futon's shortcomings.

"Kind of early for the shuttle to be going up, isn't it?"

Shig shrugged. "They're going to transport the cannibals down to Tyson Station today. Strange, isn't it? As of the moment they step off of the shuttle, they won't be the Irredenta. They'll be their own people in their own place and responsible for governing themselves. Have to come up with a new name, I suppose."

"The Unreconciled." Dek glanced covetously down at the green beans and blueberries. "That's what they told us aboard ship. The Universe had picked them specially, and they would never find reconciliation with the rest of humanity until they had purified it."

Shig's knowing brown gaze had picked up on Dek's preoccupation with the beans and berries. "I suppose that given their history, reconciliation might be beyond hope. But what about you?"

Dek laughed at the thought, heard his stomach gurgle with hunger. Screw him in vacuum, but ever since he'd set foot on the planet, he was always feeling as hungry as he had during those starvation months aboard *Ashanti.*

"Shig, I can reconcile with anyone over anything." His stomach sounded its discontent with greater volume. "Well, but for my nether regions."

The brown man raised his buckets. "I was just on the way to trade these to Inga. I think it's enough that she'd give us both breakfasts. Care to join me?"

As he matched pace, Dek said, "Funny, isn't it? The way a man's life changes. Were you to transport me back to Transluna, to the man I was, you wouldn't recognize me. And seeing me, as I am now, they wouldn't recognize me either. Me then. Me now. Same man? Or two different men? Begs the question: Do we ever really know ourselves? Can we ever define a constant whereby a person can say, 'This is who I am regardless of the environment I'm in or the events I'm experiencing'?"

"The mystics in the Eastern religions would tell you that you cannot know yourself until you break the bonds of samsara and experience moksha. Only then do the scales of illusion fall away, and even the notion of 'self' is discarded because it perpetuates duality."

"How does that work on Donovan?"

They had stepped out into the main avenue, and Shig closed his garden gate. "Talina tells me that had the Buddha ever come to Donovan, he would have seated himself under a mundo tree. That the moment he did, a nightmare would have reached down with its tentacles, impaled him, and yanked him up into the tree to spend the next couple of months devouring him."

"Leaves me thinking Talina will never be a mystic."

Shig gave him a wide grin. "She has a young soul, one balancing between tamas and rajas. That's darkness and passion in case you were wondering."

"She's a most remarkable woman." He remembered the way her eyes looked, how she moved. "Something about her . . ."

Shig was giving him the eye, a slight lift to his left eyebrow. "She is our warrior. Being a society's warrior sets a person apart. The warrior is the one who is called upon to do the distasteful, to act for the protection of others. But in Talina's case, she has also been chosen by Donovan to be an intermediary. She is a bridge between humanity and the planet. A role that leaves her in even greater isolation. Because of that, she lives in constant fear."

Dek pursed his lips. "I know what that's like."

"Why would you say that?"

"Being a Taglioni means you're always apart. Perpetually worried whether you're worthy of the name. I think I see something Taglioni-like in Talina. Makes me wonder who she would be back in Transluna."

Shig's curious look had intensified as Dek held the door to Inga's; Shig led the way down the long flight of wooden stairs to the tables below. At the bottom, people called greetings, to which Shig replied with waves and cheery responses.

He didn't lead the way to a table, but to the bar stools, taking the one where Supervisor Aguila had sat, and indicating the empty stool to the left.

Dek climbed up, noting, "I sense a definite hierarchy in the seating. You pick this for a reason?"

Shig set his containers on the bar and indicated the empty stool beside him. "That's Talina's. Turn around. Look out at room. That's what she does, resting her elbows on the bar behind her in the process. It's how she looks out at her people."

"Why are you telling me this?"

"Because she can't go back to Transluna. You asked who she'd be back there? She'd be a freak. A human contaminated with Donovanian genetic material. A warrior in a land of neutered and autonomous worker bees. The Corporation would destroy her. You must understand: The kind of people necessary to survive the vicissitudes and dangers of frontiers are not tolerated by the civilized and tamed."

"I see."

"I hear that you want to go out beyond the fence. That you want to learn how to live out there. That you've been asking about the Wild Ones."

At that moment, Inga appeared, hurrying down the bar and looking flustered. "You drinking or eating?"

Shig gave the woman that remarkable beaming smile. "Good to see that business is booming. How are you today?"

"Up to my ass in quetzals. What's in the containers?"

"Green beans. All that were ripe. Oh, and blueberries. Dek and I were wondering if you'd trade us for two breakfast specials?"

Inga shot Dek a who-the-hell-are-you look, lifted both eyebrows, and chuckled. "Yeah, but don't push your luck, Shig. If it were anyone but you . . ."

With that she scooped up the containers and bulled her way back down the bar toward the kitchen.

Dek spread his hands wide. "Yesterday I stood at the fence for what seemed like hours. Wejee puts up with me. Answers my questions. Says I should contact some of the farmers, that they'd trade labor for information. But, yes, I want to get to know the Wild Ones. I've heard of the Briggses, the Philos, the Shu Wans. And then there's the prospectors. I figure I can work while I learn. Pay my way in this clap-trapping crazy free-market economy of yours."

"What would you do to get out there?"

"Anything, Shig. You name it."

"Why?"

"I feel it. Here." Dek touched his breast. "Donovan, I mean. Like it's a sort of presence."

"Odds are that a skewer, a slug, or a sidewinder will get you. Even with a knowledgeable guide. If you had someone like Tip Briggs and Kylee Simonov as mentors, I'd say you still had a seventy percent chance of being killed in the first week."

Dek took a deep breath. "But maybe I wouldn't. What the hell, let me go, Shig. You can order it, can't you?"

Shig's gaze softened, seemed to see right down into Dek's soul. "I might. But say you do go, that you manage to make the deal with Donovan. You understand, don't you? You'll be just like Talina. Donovan will claim you. You'll never be able to go back. No reconciliation with that old Derek Taglioni, let alone your family."

"That man's already gone. I want to know who this new one will be."

"Even if it comes at a price?"

Dek looked at Talina's chair, a symbol of isolation. Smart man, this Shig Mosadek. "Nothing comes without a little pain, Shig."

"I'll remember you said that."

21

With his hands clasped behind him, Miguel Galluzzi stood in the observation dome and watched the Supervisor's A-7 shuttle as it lifted from the bay. Capella's harsh light gleamed on the sialon hull, the craft's aerodynamic delta shining against the dark interstellar background. The sleek vessel turned gracefully, like a thing alive, and began to accelerate.

Within moments it had passed out of sight, leaving only the empty majesty of the galaxy as it glowed in righteous splendor against the black.

Righteous?

Galluzzi snorted to himself, curious about the sudden emptiness that hollowed his core. Surprised at the intensity, he staggered to the side, tears welling in his eyes. His heart began to pound against his breast.

He blinked, jaw quivering.

They are gone.

The notion left him dazed, reeling.

What the hell was this? He'd never experienced the like. This sucking emptiness of body and soul. A vertigo of self—all whirling and disoriented. He swallowed against the sudden nausea, put a hand to his mouth.

For long moments he sat half crouched against the side of the dome. Seemed he could barely get enough to breathe. That everything that he had been was looted away.

They are gone.

From the moment he'd learned of *Ashanti*'s arrival so far off course from Capella, in the wake of his decision to seal Deck Three, he'd lived in guilt, terror, and desperation. Every breath. Every beat of his heart. Each pulse of blood in his veins had been with the knowledge of the horror he'd unleashed upon his transportees.

Now that living shame was gone.

Deck Three was quiet, dark, empty. Halls, decking, and rooms that had shivered in time to the screams of murdered and butchered human beings now lay thick with ominous silence.

Years of desperate yearning to deliver the Unreconciled to their destination—once an almost impossible dream—was now a fact. That terrible weight was lifted. It no longer lurked like a beast on his shoulder, exhaling its fetid stench into his waking thoughts, his nightmares, or deepest fears.

They are gone.

The reality should have left him ebullient. Filled with life and hope. It should have been freedom.

Instead, Galluzzi just huddled against the transparency, his arms tucked tightly against his aching gut.

I just wish I was dead.

Out in the black, the endless patterns of stars mocked him in silence.

22

As the shuttle lifted from *Ashanti*'s bay, Talina kept her attention on the monitors that showed the main cabin. There, just behind that locked hatch, seventy-seven of the Irredenta sat, waiting. Some trembled with anxiety, others chatted in an almost manic fashion with their neighbors. Still others kept singing that oddly atonal, slurred-sounding song. Over and over, as if it were a mantra.

"What do you think?" Kalico asked, her gaze uncertain.

"Reminds me of an anthropology video from the twentieth century, like some sort of long-lost tribe discovered on an isolated island or deep in the jungle."

"Does, doesn't it?"

Talina crossed her arms, feeling herself growing weightless as Makarov changed attitude. At the I'm-falling tickle down in her stomach, Demon, like usual, panicked. The quetzal sent filaments of anxiety through her limbic system. Tried to paralyze her with fear.

Failed.

On her shoulder, Rocket chittered softly.

Back in the main cabin, people who hadn't followed the instructions to buckle in, especially the children, screamed and yipped. Some floated up from their seats. As Makarov applied thrust, acceleration returned to a reassuring 1 g and a concurrent resettling of half-panicked bodies in the back.

"They are not us," Kalico mused. "They have become something other. Different. Alien."

"I wouldn't have believed it. Not after just seven and a half years."

"That can be an eternity, Tal," Kalico noted. "We're off the map. First *Freelander* and then *Ashanti.* The patterns are similar. The crew does their best to save the ship, but in the case of *Freelander* it's the crew who develop the weird death cult. In *Ashanti,* the crew and the maritime unit stay sane, and it's the transportees who become . . . well, this."

Talina's frown incised her forehead. "I think The Corporation needs to rethink deep-space travel. That, or don't pack as many people into the ships. It always comes down to food. Essentially being stuck in a can and making the choice as to who lives and who dies as the hydroponics break down and begin to fail."

Makarov, taking extra care—given the mess of unsecured humans and their luggage—eased them into the atmosphere and juggled the stick as the shuttle hit turbulence.

"Be happy to get this load off," he growled just loud enough for Talina to hear.

"That's a unanimous decision."

Down in her belly, Demon shifted, still teetering on the verge of panic.

To make his point, Makarov took the fast way down, pulling as much as 1.5 gs as he used atmosphere to brake their descent. Then, roaring in a tight circle, he dropped down toward the endless mat of green, blue, and turquoise forest that covered the land west of the Wind Mountains.

With a howling whine, he settled the shuttle over the pad at Tyson Station and eased the big A-7 down onto its landing struts.

"Welcome to Tyson Station," he said into the com, adding with irony: "Please remain seated while we spool down."

"All right, let's get this circus unloaded," Kalico stood, palming the hatch.

Talina followed her out to see a cowed and almost silent crowd. Some of the children were crying, clinging to their ashen-faced mothers. Others looked like they were on the verge of throwing up. But puking what? Raw red meat from the scavenged skeletons back in the women's locker room on Deck Three?

In his seat immediately in front of her, Batuhan was doing his best to appear aloof, but the tension in his face was bunching his scars into an unpleasant grimace. Face to face with the guy, his missing nose, the scars, the weird fake blue eye in the middle of his forehead, it sent creepy crawlies through her bones.

"I'm Security Officer Talina Perez," she told them. "I'm responsible for your introduction and orientation to Tyson Station. You will disembark, one by one, through the hatch and down the stairs. At the bottom you will proceed to the admin dome. There you will be processed by medical personnel before assembling in the cafeteria. We've got a hot meal prepared the likes of which you haven't had in years. After that, I will tell you what you need to know to survive. Now, Batuhan, if you will follow me."

She turned, not caring if he did or didn't. At the hatch, the ramp lowered and she stepped out into Capella's bright light. Privates Sean Finnegan and Paco Anderssoni, dressed in combat armor, had stretched lines of plastic ribbon to create a lane that led to the doorway of the admin dome.

Talina started down the route, hoping that Batuhan would follow. Not that it mattered in the end. Once the Irredenta were off the shuttle and the hatch was buttoned up, they could run wild all over the place. The marines would evacuate Raya Turnienko, Dya Simonov, and the kitchen staff. Kalico's A-7 would take them back to Port Authority.

If the Irredenta played by the rules, they'd get what help PA and Corporate Mine could give them.

She glanced back, seeing Batuhan plodding along behind her, almost hobbling on his bare feet. Donovan's gravity was having its effect, and the guy didn't look healthy at all. His white-powdered makeup looked even more bizarre given the scars and his kohl-black eyes and lips. She could see into his severed nose to where the turbinate bones were visible.

"Whatever you're planning," he told her through heavy breaths, "it won't work."

"We're not planning anything except to give you a fighting chance."

"We are the universe's chosen."

"Good for you. So, here's the deal: You and your people are malnourished, unaccustomed to the gravity. It'll take you about a month to adapt. We'll help you through that, but if you threaten any of our people, hurt anyone, or try to eat them, we're out of here. You're on your own. No second chances. Get my message?"

"You are only a vehicle," he said. "The universe's way of opening our path to the stars."

"Yeah, right. Well, Donovan's going to have some say about that. In the meantime, those are the ground rules."

He chuckled under his breath. "Of course. We only need to bide our time. In the end the universe will ensure our triumph. Until then, we will only become stronger, more numerous."

"Whatever."

"You don't understand, Security Officer Perez. As time passes, there are going to be more and more of us, all preserved in these bodies, passing through time, existing, being consumed, and continuing along."

"Uh-huh."

"When you look at me, you see a body that once belonged to Batuhan, but on the inside there are a couple hundred of us. Interred in this flesh. Waiting. All those souls, all those bodies. And the day will come when we break free in purity and light."

She kept her expression under control.

He followed her into the dome, and she was able to look back and see his poor acolytes staggering under the weight of the carved duraplast chair. In the light of day, she got a good look at it. The seat had been made out of a desk. Someone had spent a huge amount of time shortening the legs, carving remarkable bas-reliefs that depicted human corpses, skeletons, various bones, phalluses in full erection on the verge of penetrating gaping vulvas, all mixed with spirals, mazes, and geometric designs. The intricately rendered chair back had been carved into artistically intertwined skeletons and might have once been a part of a wall that had been carefully mortised into the chair's frame.

The four manhandled it through the doorway and down the hall in pursuit of Talina and Batuhan.

Not my parade. And thankfully so.

At the end of the hall, Raya Turnienko had set up her station. The lanky Siberian waited on the other side of a table. The woman was tall, slender, with almond eyes in a severe round face.

She greeted Batuhan, saying, "I'm Dr. Turnienko. If you'd extend your hand, this will only take a second."

Batuhan stared at her. Raya stared back, clearly fascinated by his mutilations.

"Just do it," Talina growled. "That, or we're out of here. It's nothing more than a medical sample to see if there's anything we can do to help you and your people."

Batuhan warily extended his ridge-scarred hand. Raya efficiently ran a U-shaped device around the web of his thumb. It snapped and Batuhan jerked his hand back.

Talina said, "After what you've done to yourself, that had to be like a soft scratch. Come on. Let's go feed you."

She led the man into the cafeteria, the place smelling of broccoli, chili, chamois steaks, and freshly baked bread all backed with the scent of mint tea.

Batuhan might have considered himself a walking living graveyard, and the soft part of his nose might be missing, but his ruined face betrayed a deep anticipation as he inhaled. Nor did he waste any time stepping to the table and eagerly accepting the plate that Millicent Graves handed him.

Batuhan missed the horrified look on the woman's face as she gaped at his mutilated face and the rest of his scars. He was too busy staring in disbelief at the food. Seemed to stagger to a table, sinking down to begin shoveling morsels into his mouth.

The bunch with the throne had made it through Raya's blockade, the duraplast chair intact.

Talina gestured to the side of the room. "Set it there. No one here's going to steal the thing."

The three on the litters were brought through next. Their bearers, placed them reverently in a row on one of the tables before taking their turn in the chow line.

As the Irredenta filed through, taking plates, attacking the food, often with fingers given their hurry, Millie asked, "Are they really cannibals?"

"They are." Talina told her. "And as soon as you're finished dishing out plates here, one of the marines is going to hustle you right back onto the shuttle."

"Won't be quick enough for me."

Seeing the last of the young men pass the door, followed by Raya's high sign, Talina stepped to the center of the room.

"Welcome to Donovan. This is Tyson Station. It will be your home from here on out. The term *Irredenta* means a culturally distinct people living under a foreign or culturally incompatible rule. You are no longer Irredenta. This is now yours. For you to rule as you see fit. Welcome home."

Scarred faces turned in her direction.

"Everything you need to survive is here. A farm, water collection and cisterns, shelter. I know you consider yourselves newly born after leaving *Ashanti*. Hold onto that thought. In terms of Donovan, you are infants cast loose in a world you don't understand and where everything will kill you."

She looked around the room, at the scarred faces, heard the crying of the infants. "First rule, no one sets foot outside barefoot. We tried to poison the slugs, but we can't be sure that we got them all. They'll burrow into your foot, divide, and eat you from the inside out.

"Second rule: No one sets foot outside the compound. If you venture into the forest, you'll be dead or dying within a half hour at most. We've left you fencing supplies out back behind the sheds. Until you put the fence up, quetzals, bems, skewers, sidewinders, and fifty other predators can wander in at will and eat you."

"How do we recognize these things?" one of the men who'd followed Batuhan asked.

"We're leaving you a holo." Talina told him. "Study it. I mean that. Your lives will depend on it. In the meantime, we've provided you with a siren for an alarm when predators are inside the compound. You have to train yourselves to immediately find shelter when there's a threat.

"Third rule: And this is the hardest one. You are in mobber territory. These are flying predators who will strip a person down to a skeleton in less than a minute. Your only defense for the time being is to get under cover. Failing that, you must fall flat and *don't* move.

Mobbers may have killed the last people here more than a decade ago. Our hope is that they've forgotten that humans are prey since then."

"Just hold still?" someone called. "That's the best we can do?"

From the back of the room, Kalico called, "We can make you a couple of cannons at Corporate Mine. Provide you with shot shells. But that will take a while."

Talina was actually relieved. The questions were the sort she'd expect from a human audience. "I mean it. Stay close to the domes for the first week or so. Organize expeditions to the farm plot. Keep your eyes open. And wear your shoes. We've brought them from *Ashanti*."

"That was an offering to the ancestors!" one of the throne bearers cried, standing and raising a fist. "Symbolic of the fact that while the immortal could no longer walk on their own, we now walk for them!"

Angry cries of assent filled the room.

"Fine." Talina threw her hands up. "Make your own damn shoes. Personally, I suggest boots." She lifted her right foot up to show them the quetzal-leather that rose to the top of her calf.

"Don't! I repeat: don't try to eat the local vegetation. It will just go through at best, but nine times out of ten, it will poison you dead. The plants here move. Stay away from them. Same with the roots, they will grab hold of you, and if they get a good grip, you're going to regret it."

"The plants move?" someone asked.

"We're leaving you a radio with the frequencies marked for Corporate Mine and Port Authority. You can contact us any time if you have questions. Both Supervisor Aguila, and I and my people, will be happy to send you what advice we have."

"We have the Prophets," a voice chimed up from the back. "They've brought us this far."

Grunts and mild applause came in response, and people turned to look at the three gaunt figures who rested on the litters. They were twitching, being spoonfed—without much success—by a couple of the younger women.

Batuhan was looking pleased, his slight smile bending the maze-patterned scars on his cheeks.

"Disregard my advice if you will, but here's the last and final rule: On Donovan, stupidity is a death sentence."

Around the room, she could see the skeptical expressions. Everyone was looking toward Batuhan or off to the side where the Prophets reposed on their litters.

As if he could sense their reliance on his reaction, Batuhan stood, spread his arms as he faced the room.

In a hollow voice he said, "The universe has brought us this far. It will not let us down now. We are the chosen, the possessors of the Revelation. We are the living dead. We are the ending and the beginning. We shall have no fear."

Whatever that meant.

Talina took a deep breath. Turned to see that Millicent had indeed departed.

Kalico stepped up beside her, saying, "I am Corporate Supervisor Kalico Aguila. I control all of Donovanian Corporate assets and—"

"You are in control of nothing," Batuhan thundered. "You are deceit, darkness, and corruption."

Applause sounded across the room.

Talina couldn't help but drop a hand to her pistol.

"Do you need anything else from me?" Kalico asked the room. "Any concerns under contract that—"

"No," Batuhan told her. "You have served the universe's purpose. For that we thank you."

Kalico's soft laugh was filled with wry irony. "Then, I take it there are no contractual issues. But I need to hear it from the room. Any of the rest of you have a claim under contract?"

"The Messiah speaks for us," one of the women declared hotly.

Kalico turned to Talina. "Then, I guess we're done here."

Talina gave the room one last thoughtful appraisal. "Welcome to Donovan."

Then she turned, following on Kalico's heels as the woman led the way from the room.

23

As Second Will, Vartan had command of the small detachment that watched the Supervisor's shuttle vanish off to the east; a final gleam of silver flashed as its sound faded away.

He turned, along with the rest, to stare warily around at the remarkable new world in which they found themselves. The hot sun felt like a miracle on his pale skin. How long had it been? Twenty years since he was last on Earth and had seen the sun? And then it had only been for a couple of hours total as he shuttled back and forth between classrooms. Most of his security training had been on Transluna given that his specialty was institutional security for factories, mines, processing plants, and the like.

"Smell that," Tamil Kattan said reverently. The man closed his eyes, head back, sniffing the warm air. "Never smelled nothing like that in my life."

"And listen to the sound. What is that? Like singing." Wonder filled Shimal Kastakourias's voice as the woman turned, staring out past the edge of the escarpment at the tops of the surrounding trees. Hands twitching with the early signs of prophecy, she shifted her feet, used her toes to scrape the loose dirt. "This is . . . a dream. The kind I never had before."

"What do you think, Vart?" Tamil asked. "This is, like, too good to be true. All these buildings. That farm down there. It's our own town."

Vartan squinted around in the bright light, raised a hand to shield his eyes and take in the features of Tyson Station. The domes, the weathered sheds, the solar collectors down on the point.

"It's a prison," he decided. Laughed self-derisively. "No fences, no guards, but it's still a prison."

"The universe will provide," Shimal told him. "The Prophets will guide us."

Tamil was giving him that sidelong look. "You were Corporate security. What did you make of that orientation? That sample the doctor took. All the things that Perez woman said? More Corporate lies?"

Vartan shrugged. "They want tissue samples. Tells them who's really here when they check it against the *Ashanti* records. As to Perez, she was telling the truth. There are dangers here. Why wouldn't there be? It's wilderness, yes? And we all know that guy, Donovan, was killed on this rock way back when."

"The universe will see us through." Shimal repeated the familiar mantra. And, maybe it would. It had gotten them this far.

Even as Vartan tried to absorb his surroundings, the doors from the admin dome opened to spew children, all of them whooping and running on their skinny little legs.

They were staring around as they jumped, pointing up at the sun, shielding their eyes. Some were so recently Initiated that their preliminary scars were still pink lines. Pho was in the back, having just lost the last of his scabs.

Didn't take long, the gravity being what it was, for the exuberant dancing to taper off. It was replaced by wide-eyed exploration as the children fanned out about the complex, looking at this and that. Given that they'd never seen dirt, a sky, or even a plant, they were rapt.

Somebody ought to be keeping an eye on them, Vartan thought as he turned his steps for the admin dome.

Not his job. Petre had assigned him to ensure that Aguila had really left them alone. His next responsibility was a reconnaissance of the domes in order to develop a plan for their security.

Stepping inside, he made his way to the cafeteria, the smell of the food still lingering in the air. Damn! But that had been the most marvelous meal he'd ever eaten. Turned out he'd missed taste, had missed color, and open air, and . . . Well, so much.

His muscles, atrophied from all those years, pulled, and his lower back could feel the strain, but he made his way to the cafeteria, joining the group around the Messiah.

"Second Will, report?"

He nodded respectfully to the Messiah. "She's gone. Disappeared into the east."

"You were trained in security," the Messiah noted, his eyes straying back toward the kitchen with a certain longing. Hell, they were all hungry. "What do you suggest we do next, Second Will?"

"Messiah, first thing, my task is to conduct a complete inspection of this place. Determine the lay of the land. Start an inventory of the station's resources. We've got most of a day. We need to be organized by nightfall. The rest of the Will should assign lodging and duties. And someone has to be detailed to begin the next meal. I see that there are crates of provisions back there."

"First Will?" The Messiah turned to Petre, "Can you do that?"

"Of course," Petre bowed his white-haired head, the ponytail bobbing.

"See to your reconnaissance." The Messiah turned back to Vartan. "Take a small group. I think there's a map back in that pile on the rear table."

"Messiah," Vartan added. "The children . . ."

"Yes?"

"They're running around outside. Unsupervised."

"I have the women and young men attending to the placement of our belongings. If you think that's a problem, detail Shyanne and Marta to keep track of them and make sure they're safe."

Vartan nodded and turned to leave.

"Second Will?" the Messiah called.

Vartan turned back, squirmed as that blue eye in the Messiah's forehead seemed to bore into his soul.

"What do you make of this warning the Supervisor and that Perez woman gave us?"

"I think we should heed each and every one until we can separate the lies from reality here."

The Messiah puckered his black-painted lips, sucked at them for a moment, and nodded. "I agree. While the universe has indeed brought us this far, it doesn't expect us to be fools. Develop whatever security protocols you think necessary."

Vartan fixed on Petre. "You and I should put our heads together and—"

"Deal with Tikal on that. I'm afraid the First Will and his picked team have other priorities," the Messiah said, an absent look in his dark eyes. "He's going to be arranging for our next meeting with the Supervisor. You saw the scars on the woman? That's a sign, a warning from the universe itself. Worry about the wildlife and plants, yes, but ultimately, she might very well turn out to be the death of us."

Vartan kept his expression neutral. Bowed his head again. "Of course, Messiah."

"To defeat her, we must first reassure her. She must believe that we are not a threat. I need Shimal, who understands these things, to cause a malfunction in the solar panels. Something easy to fix that will require the Supervisor to send a party out. One that we can convince that we are humble, grateful, and thankful for our new home."

"Of course, Messiah," Vartan told the man. "I'll see to it immediately."

But as he walked off, he glanced back at the piles of boxes Aguila had left for them. Aguila might be the long-term threat, but he worried about the I'm-not-giving-you-shit tone in Talina Perez's voice as she talked about the dangers surrounding them.

Seemed to Vartan that they'd be better off figuring out how to deal with Tyson's dangers before going to war with Kalico Aguila and the rest of the planet.

Where the Prophets lay on their litters in the back, being tended to by the Chosen, Callista cried out, "Whaaa . . . whaaa . . . shoot."

Watch out?

At the door he shot a look back at the Messiah. *Hope you're right about all of this.*

24

"Never figured I'd see the like of those people." Marc Talbot perched on his chair with a knee up as the Corporate shuttle arced above the clouds where they packed against the eastern side of the Wind Mountains. He glanced over to where Talina and Kalico sat in the row of seats behind the pilot.

Aguila said, "The human brain has given us the keys to the universe, allowed us to travel across thirty light-years, banish all but a tiny number of diseases, colonize distant worlds, and control the laws of physics. Can those human beings really be related to us?"

"The religious mind," Talina mused, gaze unfocused. "It operates on faith. They choose to *believe* the universe has chosen them. They have *faith* it will protect them for its own purposes."

Talbot rapped his fingers on his knee. "This is Donovan. Sometimes I think even the most basic laws of the universe don't apply here. So what's going to happen the first time they figure out that nothing's working the way the Prophets want? And what's with them, anyway? Looked to me like they're spastic."

At that moment, Raya Turnienko leaned in the hatch. Her round face was thoughtful. "Supervisor? Are you in a hurry to get back to Corporate Mine this afternoon?"

"Yeah, one of the first things unloaded from *Ashanti* were a pair of Semex 81-B roto mills. Brand new. We can replace our old, broken-down jury-rigged mucking machines. And besides, Talovich has half of my people building shoring in the Number Three."

The Number Three had seemed like a good idea. Tunnel in from the bottom of the mountain, then the ore could be rolled downhill on tracks all the way to the smelter. What no one had counted on was the shattered rock zone they'd hit about two hundred meters into the adit. The impact-shocked rock was rich with exotic metals, but so unstable as to come tumbling down if it was disturbed by so much as a loud sneeze.

"What have you got, Raya?" Talina asked.

"Preliminary data on the Irredenta. I won't know for certain until I can run some of these data through the lab. Especially their so-called Prophets."

"Anything you can share with us now?"

"Outside of anemia, vitamin deficiency, malnutrition, and atrophy? No. But once we're back in PA, I've got some serious research ahead of me."

"You look pretty grim," Talina noted.

Raya arched her thin eyebrows. "Yeah, they've got the dead inside them. No doubt about it. The problem is, if I'm right, the dead aren't happily going along for the ride."

"Zombies?" Talbot asked, making a face.

Raya didn't rise to the bait. "Actually, pending results of the tests, this could be a whole lot worse. I'll know in a couple of days." She glanced at Kalico. "Want to be there when I figure this out? They are your people, after all."

"Sure."

And then Raya ducked back through the hatch, her concentration locked on her handheld monitor.

25

On the monitor, Miguel Galluzzi watched as the last of the containers dropped into Donovan's atmosphere. In the telemetry, the rectangular box began to tumble, the corners glowing from dull red to orange to fiery as the duraplast heated.

Like the others that had preceded it, they'd accelerated the container, shot it out so that Donovan's gravity would increase its speed for maximum effect when it hit atmosphere. The tumbling container glowed now, streaking through the planet's upper skies, leaving a trail behind.

Didn't take long. Given the velocity, friction disintegrated the container's sides, spilling the contents into the fire. The combustibles, things like clothing, bedding, woods, and plastics, immediately flared into ash. The metals, sialon, and glass all lasted a little longer, tiny streaks of light as they incinerated. The bigger items, furniture and the like, splintered off from the main mass, trailing fire into oblivion.

And then it was gone. Only vapors and tiny particles marking the path of the Unreconciled's last belongings.

Far beneath, dotted with patterns of white cloud, Donovan's ocean gleamed in serene blue, Capella's light adding a golden sheen along the planet's curve.

Galluzzi sighed, turned, and strode down the hallway to the Deck Three hatch. He'd had the crew working in hazard suits as they packed everything loose into sacks. The room fixtures, beds, furniture, the kitchen wares, the tables and chairs, anything that wasn't structurally attached to *Ashanti,* had been packed into the containers. Then, one by one they'd been jettisoned to burn up in Donovan's atmosphere. A symbolic final resting place for anything having to do with the Unreconciled.

At the hatch, Galluzzi pulled on his hazard suit, flipped down the hood, and sealed it. Then he palmed the hatch. As it slid open, billowing gusts of steam and cleanser rolled out.

Stepping inside, Galluzzi sealed the hatch behind him, staring through the clouds of cleanser. The air here was toxic, filled with chemicals, soot, particles, and hot enough to sear a man's lungs, should he inhale.

But along with the Unreconciled's trash and belongings, the filth was gone. The macabre art had been blasted off the walls, partitions had been removed, every surface scoured of as much as five millimeters of material. A combination of fire, chemical, and abrasive had stripped *Ashanti* of every last vestige of the horror that had thrived here.

It is gone from everywhere but my memory.

That, Galluzzi couldn't scour.

As he looked around at the snaking hoses, the pressure machines, and blow torches, he wondered what The Corporation was going to say about his modifications to Deck Three. Assuming he ever made it home.

Not that it mattered. That was then. This was now. He and the crew wanted every last trace removed. Even the notion of trying to space *Ashanti* with the reminder of Deck Three had been too horrifying to countenance.

Turner, in his trademark hazard suit with a yellow duck emblem on the chest, appeared out of the infernal fog. "Last one burn up?"

"It did. Just like the others. Whatever's left can float down on Donovan now. Food for their fishes."

"Wonder if they even have fishes. Guess Michaela's team will find out."

"Do I hear regret in your voice?"

"Cap, do you believe in temporary insanity?"

Galluzzi waved a gloved hand at the surroundings. "You ask me that? Here? Given what we're doing to the ship?"

Turner's expression through the transparency communicated a wry humor. "I'm thinking that when it came to Michaela, I'm going to be spending a lot of the rest of my life thinking I was an idiot to let that one get away."

"Might not be too late."

Turner's shrug was masked by his bulky suit. He turned away, saying, "Come on. Let me show you what we've done."

The finer details were masked by the noxious atmosphere, but for Galluzzi, he might have been on another ship. Dark, dingy, Deck Three was transformed. With all the light panels in, most of the walls removed, the kitchen-cafeteria and rec room as one large open space. The cabins and barracks were scoured; the entire deck was foreign, new, pristine.

Galluzzi even like the rounded effect. The cleansing hadn't left a single sharp corner to be found. The place had a melted look, creamy and open.

"What do you think?" Galluzzi asked.

"It's a miracle," Turner told him. "Got a question: You sleeping better, Cap?"

Galluzzi paused, surprised when he said, "I am. What makes you ask?"

"Crew was talking about it. How the nightmares have been going away. It's like with each day's work, the more we clean down here, the better we're doing. Like a weight lifted off. A terror that's now becoming a really bad memory. Like we're never going to be the same again, but we're all going to make it."

"Yeah, I hear you." Sure. Easy for Turner to say.

Galluzzi stared around through the swirling mist. *Ashanti* was cleared of the physical reminders of the Unreconciled. They were all feeling better, but it wouldn't last. The things that had happened here, the things Miguel Galluzzi was responsible for, those haunting memories would cling to him like the albatross of legend.

Ultimately, *Ashanti* might be cleansed of the corruption, but looking around at the scoured surfaces, it was to see the scar. A scar might be healed tissue, but it also served as an enduring reminder.

Like my ship, I will never outrun my shame.

26

Mark Talbot couldn't believe it. It hadn't been twenty-four hours and he was on his way back to Tyson Station. All he'd had in between was a pleasant evening with his family—a rare night when his two wives, Dya and Su, along with the kids, had been home at the same time. After dealing with the Unreconciled, the evening had been a reminder of the blessings that had befallen him. To be part of a family, to have women who loved him, children to be proud of.

Sure, they had suffered tragedy enough on Donovan, but with the exception of Kylee, they'd come through it. Adjusted. Dya's skills had earned her a valued position as one of the preeminent researchers on Donovan. Her insight into the biology was going to revolutionize humanity's chances for success on the planet. Su was reworking the PA computer systems, her coding abilities allowing for increased data manipulation in the town's single quantum cubit computer.

The kids had finally integrated into the local academy, a transition made somehow easier because Dan Wirth had built a new school. As though everyone moving into the new building had leveled the playing field, hadn't left the Mundo kids feeling as much like outsiders.

Talbot had sprawled on the couch, watching as Damien, Sullee, Tuska, and Taung had led the rest of the children in a game of snap. He'd had one arm around Dya, the other tucking Su close.

This, he had thought, *is the meaning of existence.*

That lingering knowledge had made his lovemaking with Su even more tender and fulfilling than usual—though he had slept that night with nightmares of the Unreconciled, recoiling from tortured dreams in which they stalked his children from the shadows, their eyes burning red in intricately scarred faces.

And what do I wake up to this morning?

Two Spot had called on the com. *"Mark? We've got a plea from Tyson. Something's wrong with the solar generators out there. They're losing their electricity. Kalico wondered if you could take Sheyela Smith out with a squad of armored marines and see what's wrong?"*

So here he was, at the wheel of one of the new airtrucks, scooting along some thousand feet above the rumpled and mounded carpet of forest. Tyson Station was just ahead, a flat mesa jutting out from the broken and tumbled hills that marked the old volcano. He could see the white dots of the domes, the paler green of the agricultural fields to their south. And there, on the point, were the culprit solar collectors.

"All right, people, gear up."

Behind him, privates, Paco Anderssoni, Dina Michegan, Wan Xi, Russ Tanner, and Briah Muldare strapped into their combat armor. The sound of the armor clicking into place was like music to Talbot's ears. He could hear the hum of the servos as his former team checked their systems. The *slick-slick* of weapons check meant that rounds were being chambered.

In the rear, Sheyela Smith, a woman in her thirties, called, "Whatever you do, don't let the freaks eat me."

"You're our electrical guru," Dina Michegan told her. "Didn't even need to hear it from the Supervisor. We'll level that shit-sucking station before we let them harm a hair on your head."

"Indispensable," Wan Xi agreed, a smile on his mobber-scarred face.

"Yeah," Muldare agreed. "Second only to Inga, but that's only 'cause while you can keep electrical shit running, you can't brew a keg of IPA that wouldn't gag a slug."

"Hey, guys," Talbot warned, "Kalico wants us to go in, fix the solar, and get the hell out without an incident. Job one is to keep Sheyela safe. Job two is to fix the electricity. Job three is to get out without an incident. In armor, with non-lethal tech, that shouldn't be an impossible mission."

"Yeah, Mark," Anderssoni replied. "Who do you think you're talking to? After all the shit we been through, you're not going to find a tighter squad in the Corps."

Mark turned, grinned, and slapped hands with Anderssoni. Donovan had honed them, shaped them, and compressed them. Cap Taggart, Deb Spiro, and Kalen Tompzen had torn them apart and Donovan glued them back together. What was left of the original twenty marines were closer than family.

God help the Unreconciled if this were a trap.

Mark wheeled the airtruck around, wishing he had the A-7 with Makarov at the helm, but the big bird was in orbit, tied to *Ashanti* for a refit.

He cocked his head, seeing people as he circled the compound. They were all outside, clustered before the domes, waving.

"Looks friendly enough," Muldare noted as she peered down.

"Don't see any weapons," Wan Xi agreed. "Hell, they're half dressed."

"Let's go down and see," Mark told them. "Helmets on, kiddies. Sheyela, the marines will jump down first, form a box. You and I will climb down after them. They'll proceed in a diamond formation to the solar collectors. You and I stay in the middle while the marines use their tech to keep eyes on the man-eaters. Russ?"

"Yo!"

"You're in charge of the airtruck. Keep it secure. We might have to beat feet out of here, so do what you have to. And, Russ, as soon as we hit the dirt, get some drones in the air to keep an eye on things."

"Roger that, Mark."

Talbot set them down on the landing pad, powered down the fans, and asked, "Ready?"

"Yut yut!" came the call from the marines as they opened the door and began dropping to the ground outside.

Talbot climbed down, took Sheyela's toolbox, and helped her to the ground. The Unreconciled were crowding around just beyond the marines, waving, calling excitedly.

"It's just women and kids," Anderssoni muttered.

"Fuck me," Michegan growled uneasily. "I'll never get over those scars. Who'd do that to themselves?"

The crowd parted, a man and woman walking through the press.

The man was white-haired, a long ponytail hanging down his back. The scars gave his thin face a pinched look. The woman was tall, maybe late thirties, intricately scarred. Both were naked to the waist, and to Mark's curious relief, they were both wearing shoes.

"I am First Will Petre Jordan," the man introduced. Indicating the woman, he added, "This is Second Wife Svetlana Pushkin."

"Call me Svetlana," the woman added with a smile. "The formal titles really are a bit over the top. On behalf of the Messiah, we want to thank you for coming at such short notice." She glanced askance at the marines in their gleaming armor, rifles at port arms. "The guns and soldiers won't be needed. It's just an electrical problem. Probably something simple. But we don't have anyone left who can fix it."

"The marines are just a formality," Mark told her with a smile. "If you could tell us what the problem is?"

Again, it was Svetlana who extended an arm. "Something down at the collectors. If you'd come this way?"

To the people she added, "I know you all want to talk to the newcomers, and you have a thousand questions, but please, stay back. Maybe, when some of the suspicion has been allayed, we can truly welcome these people to our homes."

Mark felt that warning bell go off. After Batuhan and the first impressions, this was just a little too good to be true.

Nevertheless, Svetlana and Petre started south, leading the way.

"Screw me with a skewer," Sheyela whispered. "So that's a cannibal?"

"Shhh." Mark waved her down.

Svetlana had dropped back, seemed nonchalant as she matched Mark's pace, apparently unconcerned about Muldare artfully staying between them. "So, you're Mark Talbot, right?"

"Yeah. I'm security second for Port Authority."

"I saw you when the Supervisor brought us down. We would have liked to have talked then, gotten to know you all, but you've got to understand, we were scared. After what had been done to us on that ship, we didn't know what to expect."

"Welcome to Donovan."

"Yeah," she shot him a grin. "This is like a paradise."

"One that will kill you before you know you're dead."

"Oh, we're taking precautions."

"Half those women and kids following us are barefoot."

"Mark, you've got to understand, we're still trying to cope. Those kids have never had shoes. Didn't need them in Deck Three. What we endured? Well, it's going to take a while to come to terms with it. We've barely survived a holocaust. Probably be a while before we're normal again."

Amen to that. Aloud Mark said, "We'll do whatever we can to help. Get you a start, at least. I lived on a station like this one down to the south. Everything you need is here. Use the radio. Call if you have questions."

She indicated the marines who tromped along in their armor. "Listen, combat-ready soldiers don't exactly send a reassuring message to our people. I know where the Supervisor is coming from, and I can only guess what that shit-sucker Galluzzi has told you. But if you'd give us a chance . . . well, maybe today can be a first step. You follow what I'm saying?"

"Sure. Just let us get your electricity fixed, and we'll call it a win all the way around."

She shot him a warm smile. "Then we'll consider this the first step. What do you need from us? How can we help?"

"Just let us do our job."

Svetlana crossed her arms under her small breasts and frowned as they passed the agricultural fields. "It won't be easy for us. We're not in the habit of trusting strangers. Any consideration you could show would be helpful."

"One step at a time." He knew the marines were monitoring their tech. Into his com, he asked, "Russ? What do your eyes in the skies see?"

"Not a thing, Mark. You're definitely the center of attention, but it's just a bunch of women and kids, most of the men are working in the fields, harvesting crops. Nothing that looks like a weapon anywhere. Looks to me like they're good."

It took Sheyela five minutes to bypass a fried circuit board. As she closed and latched the access door, she said, "Looks like, old as it is, it just couldn't take the load. They'll be good to go."

As they started back, Mark's com announced, *"Mark? The men from the fields are headed in my direction bearing baskets."*

To Svetlana, he said, "My marine tells me that a bunch of the men are headed for the airtruck."

"Good," she answered. "It's the only thing we could think of."

"Think of what?"

"Fresh food. It may not be that noteworthy or valuable to you, but after years of ration, it's the most valuable thing we have to offer as a way to express our appreciation for your kind help."

Five minutes later, as he piloted the airtruck up from the landing pad, Talbot wondered what had just happened. Behind him, the marines crowded around baskets of green beans.

And yes, he understood the symbolic offering it represented.

So much for salivating cannibals.

Maybe they'd been overreacting to the threat from the beginning?

Vartan stepped up beside Svetlana and Petre as the airtruck sped its way eastward. The sound of its passing had long since faded. Now it was but a dot in the distance, barely visible against the clouds. Then it vanished.

"Well, what do you think?" Vartan asked.

Svetlana shrugged, rubbing nervous hands up and down the scars on her arms. "We could have been more convincing if the marines hadn't been wearing that armor. Talbot was skeptical right up until we gave them those baskets of food."

"That almost broke my heart," Petre said with a sigh. "My mouth watered at the sight. I kept thinking what that lot would have tasted like broiled over a grill."

"You did well," Vartan told Svetlana. "Me, I've never been good at lying. Too much honesty in me, I guess."

"It's not like a lie, Vart," Petre told him. "That's the enemy. Deceivers. We owe them nothing but destruction."

27

The small conference room midway down the hall in the Port Authority hospital was packed. Kalico Aguila sat in the chair just back from the door. Across from her, Talina Perez was listening to something in her head. Given her expression, it must have been Demon. The woman's eyes had that penetrating, almost alien look that reeked of quetzal.

Dya Simonov was using her implants to scroll through a complicated holographic display Kalico couldn't quite make out given her angle at the table.

And in the chair beside her, Lee Cheng was fiddling with some sort of protein that was projected in the air before him. He kept using his fingers to flip the projection this way and that as if studying the protein's geometry.

Mgumbe, Cheng's assistant, sat back in his chair, his fingers crossed. A pensive expression gave his face a sagacious quality. Beside him, Iji Hiro, the Port Authority botanist, was doodling on his tablet.

Raya Turnienko came bursting into the room in a long-legged stride, her lab coat flapping behind. She abruptly pulled out a chair and dropped into it. For all the haste of her entry, she sat for a moment, staring as if at some distance beyond her mental horizon.

"What have you got, Raya?" Dya asked, breaking the woman's almost trancelike stare.

Kalico shifted, curious as to what Raya's big mystery might be. It wasn't like it was a secret that the Unreconciled were cannibals—as tough as that was to comprehend in the twenty-second century.

"Cheng," Raya said, "could you turn the display so that everyone can see it, please?"

He did, and Kalico got a good look at something that resembled a warped oval that had been bent out of shape. At the same time, Cheng said, "Is this it?"

"It is."

Cheng blinked. "No pus-sucking way!"

"Way." Raya replied flatly.

Talina, beating Kalico to the punch, said, "Fascinating conversation. Mind cluing the rest of us in?"

"Kuru," Raya said without emotion. "A disease that vanished in the early twenty-first century. What you are looking at is called a prion. Specifically PrP^{sc}, a misfolded protein that causes a form of transmissible spongiform encephalitis. It's similar to Creutzfeldt-Jakob disease, though kuru has a slightly different etiology. In this case, transmission of the disease is via the consumption of infected tissues found in the human central nervous system. Particularly the brain. Though it can also be found in other bodily fluids."

"Where did they get it?" Talina asked. "I mean, who passed it through screening back in Transluna?"

"Maybe no one," Cheng said with a shrug. "Could just be a chance folding of the protein."

Mgumbe grunted, said, "If they even screen for prions. It's not like a whole host of cannibals are applying to The Corporation for space travel. It should have been extinct."

Raya added, "Even if the prion was present in one of the transportees when he or she boarded *Ashanti,* most people have a genetic resistance against kuru. Paleoanthropologists have proven that our evolution is rife with anthropophagy. That's the fancy word for people eating other people. Like for the last two million years. No matter how hallowed you think your ancestors were, go back far enough, and someone was chowing down on his or her fellow man."

"You're joking," Kalico said.

"Not at all. According to the anthropological literature, cannibalism served four different functions: survival, ritual, political, and pathological.

"Survival speaks for itself: A dead body represents a lot of calories to a starving person. Ritual? As with the Fore people where kuru was first identified, they ate their dead ancestors as a sign of respect. Political cannibalism is what we see in places like the prehistoric American Southwest. There, if you rebelled against the rulers, they'd eat your family in front of you. And, finally, there's pathological, like the psychiatrically disordered who kill, dismember, and eat their friends or lovers. The Unreconciled seem to have incorporated all four functions at once."

Dya said, "Let's get back to the initial infection and why it wasn't detected back at Solar System. Where did this come from?"

Raya cleared her throat. "So whoever the original patient was, he or she might have lived a normal life. Never known the prion was in their system. When he or she died, the disease would have dead-ended.

"But there are two mutations on the 129th location on the PrP gene; if they turn up homozygous recessive, and the individual is exposed to the prion, they will develop the disease."

"How contagious is this?" Talina looked grim, thinking no doubt of her time in contact with the Irredenta.

"You don't want to handle any brain or body tissue from the infected. You don't want to expose yourself to sores on their bodies. Nor do you want to stick yourself with anything contaminated by their blood or body parts. Oh, and if I were you, I'd be very careful if I got a lunch invite from the Irredenta." Raya was back to staring at infinity.

"What about the *Ashanti* crew?" Kalico asked. "Are they in danger?"

Raya said, "Only if they ate infected Irredenta. The standard precautions taken in hydroponics would have been sufficient to protect them."

Dya ran fingers through her blond locks. "I'll send Galluzzi's people an update. Ensure they take the appropriate measures as they sterilize Deck Three. As to hydroponics, the systems are designed to denature proteins down to their constituent amino acids. The design ensures that microviruses are rendered incapable of transmission, which should similarly denature prions. But be aware, prions are durable, long-lasting, and resistant to most simple sterilizations."

"How do we cure this?" Talina asked. "Some vaccine?"

"You don't," Raya told her. "You saw their prophets. Those must have been the first cases. Their dementia is so advanced they've lost motor control. Remember how they were being fed? The trouble they were having eating? That's because they can't swallow. Their brains are full of lesions, holes, that will kill them within a month, I'd say."

"And their prophecies?" Talina asked.

"The ravings of dementia," Raya told her. "The slurred speech and disjointed words. Mumblings, jumbled utterances. Sometimes they'll break out in laughter, other times, tears. Not the first time in human history that the demented were believed to be oracles, or to have a direct line to God, or whatever."

Raya then added, "And there are others who are in the initial stages. Go back to the holo of the Irredenta leaving *Ashanti*. The ones lacking coordination? The trembling? The ones with odd facial expressions? Those are the early stages. Along with slurred speech. The patient has trouble with basic motor function."

"Slurred speech?" Kalico mused. "Remember that eerie song they were singing?" She paused, putting it together. "I thought it was so odd that they'd pick a chant that mimicked being drunk or drugged. That they'd sing something like that with such enthusiasm. Bet it was one of the prophets who sang it first."

Cheng, always the hard scientist, muttered, "Wait a minute. I mean, sure, things were pretty grim on Deck Three. But we're supposed to believe that when these prophets started going crazy, saying demented things, that all the rest of the survivors just bought into it? I mean, there had to be somebody sane who said, 'Wait a minute, this isn't divine revelation, these guys are going clap-trapping insane.'"

"I wouldn't doubt but you're right." Talina was squinting, as if picturing it in her head. "But it's a traumatized population looking for answers. Wouldn't surprise me if good old Batuhan himself wasn't the one to sidle up behind the naysayers and whack them in the head. Probably noted the event by saying, 'And such are the wages of disbelief.'"

"Believe or die?" Mgumbe rubbed his jaw.

"Religion has always flourished as a means of maintaining group identification, solidarity, and harmony." Raya was staring at the prion holo where the oval-shaped protein was displayed, the fold running through its middle.

Kalico asked, "What happens when we tell them it's a prion disease and not divine revelation? These are educated people, professionals, the kind who understand cause and effect in the physical world. It's not like being Unreconciled is the only reality they've ever known. Surely we can appeal to the sane and intelligent among them to give up this crazy belief that they're going to devour and thereby cleanse the universe."

Dya had been thoughtful, tapping her fingers on the tabletop. Now she said, "I suspect you're right. Most of them probably had that underlying skepticism all along. Probably went along with the belief. As long as they were locked away on Deck Three, they were surrounded by reinforcement. What other reality was there?"

Dya lifted a finger. "But say that we show up, having done genetic scans from the samples we took as they got off the shuttle. We tell them: 'These people will develop kuru and die of dementia. The rest of you are immune to the prion. There is no divine revelation. It's just a simple illness.'" She paused. "What happens next?"

"They realize that they've been duped." Cheng shrugged. "Go back to being normal people again. Problem solved."

"Hardly," Dya shot back. She glanced around the table. "They murdered, dismembered, and ate their fellow transportees. These were people they'd known intimately over the years that they were in transit. They committed acts of repulsive abomination. Scarified their bodies. And did you notice? Every woman is either pregnant or breastfeeding a newborn. And, reviewing the preliminary genetics, about half of the children are sired by Batuhan and—with a few exceptions—his four lieutenants."

"So you're saying Batuhan and his Chosen have preferred sexual access to the females?" Cheng leaned forward and frowned.

Dya fixed him with hard blue eyes. "I'm saying that there's no 'normal' for any of these people. Sure, the sane among them are going to understand that what comes out of the prophets' mouths is demented babble. What does that do to their feelings of guilt when they realize it wasn't divine revelation, wasn't the universe telling them it was all right to murder and eat people? Wasn't God telling them to scarify their skin, or to surrender their bodies to Batuhan to sire his children? It was just a disease. Sorry."

"So what do we do about it?" Talina asked.

Kalico rubbed her eyes, a growing sense of distaste down in her gut. "We tell them the truth."

"That might split those people right down the middle," Raya warned. "It's not like they're novices when it comes to murdering each other."

"Can we offer them anything?" Mgumbe asked. "Maybe a chance to relocate the nonbelievers?"

"Put them where?" Talina asked. "Three Falls? Wide Ridge? Rork Springs?"

Dya had turned introspective. "Interesting moral question, isn't it? What do we, as the surviving humans on the planet, owe these people?"

Raya leaned back in her chair. "Someone's going to have to go give the Irredenta the bad news."

"Want to draw straws?" Mgumbe asked.

28

Working outside on the farm, out past the fence, felt like a tonic. The heat from Capella's rays was in the process of baking Dek Taglioni's hide. He'd peeled off his thin jacket and was down to an undershirt. Not only that, but he'd drunk four liters of water from the jar Reuben Miranda had provided.

Nor was the heat his only problem. Every muscle in his body was aching and his joints were creaking. The gravity was sapping every bit of reserve, but he was feeling better. Toughening up by the day.

Nevertheless, he kept shooting glances at the bush, that aqua-and-green-colored band of scrubby trees and low vegetation beyond the edge of the fields. The sensation was eerie, the kind a person got when hidden eyes were watching him. Judging his every action and thought.

Get over it. It's just trees and wilderness. There's no sentience behind it. Donovan's only a planet. Not a consciousness.

"Yeah, right," he whispered under his breath and forced himself back to the task of picking peppers.

The quetzal-hide boots Reuben had loaned him shot rainbows of color along their length with each step he took. He looked like a vagabond, wearing the light claw-shrub-textile pants of local manufacture. A wide-brimmed fiber hat topped his head. And on his hip now rode his Smith & Wesson 3-41 electro-rail pistol. An expensive, engraved, and elegant weapon made with sculpted grips carved from finely figured black walnut. Gold inlay gleamed along the three rails and in the scroll work on the receiver.

So now, not only did he look like a pirate, he felt like one, too.

Pirate he might be. Nevertheless, he'd picked five whole baskets of peppers and was almost finished with a sixth. Something about that filled him with an incredible sense of purpose.

This wasn't just work, it was food. Until *Ashanti* had found itself in trouble, he'd never given a second thought to what he ate. Food was just there, ready, whatever he wanted to order, prepared in any way he desired, and provided for his gustatory pleasure. No limits. Not on variety. Not on quantity. Nor had he ever so much as wondered where it came from. How it was produced.

That had all changed when Galluzzi ordered rations cut. When Derek Taglioni had gone to bed hungry. When he'd laid, night after night, tortured by the craving in his belly. Knowing it wouldn't be filled. Not tomorrow. Not the next day, or the day after. He had lived with the knowledge that hydroponics couldn't continue to feed the number of people they had on board. That when the tanks finally broke down far enough, he and everyone around him would starve to death. Didn't matter that he was Derek Taglioni. He was just as condemned as the lowliest ship's tech.

His relationship with food had been forever altered.

Panting in the heat, he blinked sweat from his eyes and reached down to pluck another couple of jalapeño peppers from the bush. These he dropped into the basket Reuben had provided. Feeling crafty, he slipped over to the poblano plant and used his little knife to cut the stems on two large green peppers. They brought his basket up to the brim.

All it would take was another . . .

"Dek?" An irritated call carried over the chime.

He straightened from the row of green plants, seeing Talina Perez as she came striding across the field at a no-nonsense pace. The woman was dressed in a black chamois-hide one-piece that was most likely supposed to be utilitarian but conformed her curves in a most enticing way. Still, there was nothing feminine about the utility belt with its pistol and knife, or the service rifle hung from her shoulder.

He pulled the wide-brimmed straw hat from his head and wiped sweat from his face with a sleeve. Reuben looked up from where he was plucking beans. "Hey, Tal!" He threw the woman a lazy wave. "You didn't need to come out. I'd 'ave had one of the kids drop off the latest at your dome."

"I'm not here for beans, Reuben." She stopped before Dek, gave him a distasteful appraisal, and then shot Reuben a sidelong squint. "Dek here isn't supposed to leave the compound. You know better than to bring soft meat out past the fence."

Reuben's expression bent into an amused quirk. "Since when are you getting between me and my hired labor? The man asked me for a job."

"And what are you paying him?"

"A tenth part of whatever he picks."

"He's soft meat. And not the kind we can let get eaten by a slug. The guy doesn't know a bem from a toilet plunger."

Dek crossed his arms, feeling that old irritation raising its ugly head. "Hey, I'm right here. That's right. Look me in the eyes. Now, what's the trouble?"

"Do you know the repercussions if something happened to you?"

"I'm not an ornament."

"You're a Taglioni."

"Congratulations. You've read the passenger manifest on *Ashanti*." He raised a hand, cutting off the response that was bubbling up on her lips. "Stop it! That's an order." Turned out he could still summon that old brook-no-nonsense tone of voice.

To Reuben he said, "Thanks for the chance to get outside. If you don't mind, the security officer and I have to clear some things up."

"Yeah, Dek. Take that last basket. We're square." To Talina, Reuben said, "Cut the man a little slack, Tal. He's got grit."

Dek picked up his basket, adding, "I'll get the boots back to you."

"No, you keep them. You're gonna need 'em, and they're too small for my feet as it is."

Tucking his basket of peppers under his arm, Dek started through the rows of crops, Talina matching stride.

"Look at this," he told her, patting the basket. "Aboard *Ashanti* I could trade this to someone for a whole month's work scrubbing hydroponics."

She ignored him, snapping, "Do you have a death wish?"

"Not on me right at this moment, but if you're in desperate need of one, you might try the Unreconciled."

"Hey, don't fuck with me!"

"That makes two of us." He shot her a look of warning. "Yes. I got the message the first time Supervisor Aguila gave it to me: Donovan is dangerous. It'll kill me, and I don't have the first clue about what to look out for. So I asked around. With the exception of the Wild Ones and some of the security folks, the farmers know best how to stay alive. They live on *this* side of the fence. And among the farmers, the best are Miranda and Sczui. Some folks said Terry and Sasha Miska, too. I ran into Reuben first. Good man. Said he'd trade a part of the harvest for the labor."

"Yeah, they're good and solid. All of the farmers are." He could hear a little give in her voice. "Well, at least you're armed. You know how to use that thing?"

"I have an implant. Spent a lot of time at the range. Same with the rifle."

"An implant and range time. I am *so* reassured." The sarcasm in her voice was heavy enough to sink a ship.

"Talina, here are the facts: Transluna and Solar System are thirty light-years away. As incomprehensible as it might be for anyone back home to even conceive, on Donovan being a Taglioni—along with a one siddar coin—will get me a beer at Inga's." He lifted his basket of peppers. "This might get me supper and breakfast along with a beer. For the time being, it's all I've got."

She was watching him sidelong through her alien-dark eyes. Walked quietly for a time. Then asked, "What do you want, Dek?"

He stopped, turned, and pointed to the bush where it lay beyond the verdant fields. The aquajade and thornbush were shimmering in the mirage. "I want to learn the things I need to know in order to go out there."

"Why?"

"Because I have to. You see, when I ordered my name added to *Ashanti*'s manifest, I was coming here to show Miko and the rest of the family that I was a man to be reckoned with. When things got bad on *Ashanti*, when I realized I was going to die, I wanted to die with the knowledge that I'd done everything I could to keep the ship and crew alive. Now that we're here, I want to know and savor Donovan."

"I'm not sure that anyone can 'savor' Donovan. It has its own agenda." A pause. "You know why Aguila has all those scars?"

"Said it was mobbers."

"But for a handy crate, they'd have stripped her down to a skeleton before anyone could have saved her. And that was inside her compound, surrounded by her people, behind her fence. The point I'm trying to make is that Donovan kills nine out of ten people who come here. You ready to accept those kinds of odds?"

Dek shifted his basket. "I am."

"You might talk to Mark Talbot, ask him about the way people die on Donovan. What it's like to be eaten alive from the inside or digested over a couple of months as a nightmare's tentacles wiggle their way through your guts. Nothing about death on Donovan is glorious or noble."

"Who's Briggs?"

That got a start out of her. "Well, that might be Chaco or Madison, or their boy, Flip. He's eighteen, just finishing his studies in minerology and chemistry here in town. Wants to go to work for Kalico down at Corporate Mine. Where did you hear of them?"

"Over a beer. Heard about a lot of people, Wild Ones, who live in the bush. Makes me think they know something the rest of us don't. Like maybe I could go and learn what they know."

"And what would you do with this stuff you'd learn?"

"I'm not sure yet." He glanced back at the distant bush. "But here's the thing: Do you think I'm bonked out if I tell you that I can feel it? Like some sort of summons." He gestured off toward the west. "It's out there, like a siren's call. I really need to go find it."

She took a deep breath, slowly shook her head. "What is it about me and men who hear Donovan calling?"

"So, there have been others?"

"Yeah."

"Can I talk to them?"

"They're all dead."

THE TERROR

Terror is nothing new. I have known it before, during the Harrowing and Cleansing. In those days I feared my fellows. Lived with the constant knowledge that with even a small shift in alliances, I'd be the next meal. We all spent our days that way. A shared anxiety that made it impossible to sleep. Hard to explain the psychological impact it has to anyone who's never suffered that kind of fear. What it does to a person. How it can wear away at hope and endurance until a part of you screams: "Get it over with! Just kill me!"

There's a worse kind of terror compared to that anything-is-better-than-this fear of one's fellows.

It is the terror of knowing that the whole of the universe is depending upon you. Looking up to you. Expecting you to be perfect, omniscient, and omnipotent.

The realization that you are not any of those things is like acid poured upon the soul. It eats into your every thought, and the fumes bring tears to the eyes—sear through the nose and into the very brain.

I live this terror: I am not good enough. Smart enough.

That knowledge is indeed my personal acid. Not only has it eaten holes in my resolve, in my faith in myself, but I can see it the eyes of those around me.

It is the middle of the night.

I sit alone on my throne of bones, the symbol of our strength as a people.

"You are no longer the Irredenta." *The words uttered by that damned Perez woman rattle around inside my head like loose parts. The implications are too disturbing to even consider.*

I finger the long-bone scepter, stare at the intricate carvings of people who are struggling up a spiraling ramp. The little figures are no more than a centimeter tall, and perfectly rendered in the slightest detail. Fodor Renz spent a year in the carving of it. Rendered it from the thigh bone of the first woman I ever ate.

Now, I fear it is a mockery.

What is the fate of a false Messiah? One who cannot intercede with the universe on behalf of his people? One who can no longer understand the sacred voices of the Prophets? One whose people are dying all around him?

29

Sunlight amazed Fatima Veda, as did soil, plants, color, and the magical terror of an endless sky. She had just turned six. That wonderful age where awe, fear, and curiosity seesawed back and forth, each constantly giving way to the other. At first, she and the other children had been terrified of the open. The unsettling notion that there were no walls had slowly given way to curiosity.

On Deck Three, the only off-limits had been the temple and the observation dome. Children were not allowed to disturb the Holy Prophets. Otherwise they could go where they wished, play where they wished. Every nook and cranny had been known.

Once the great dome had been explored, the next fascination was the outdoors. A huge, awe-inspiring universe of space, places, sights, and light.

Fatima, at age six, was one of the oldest children. And, because she was, the little ones looked up to her. Shimal, Bess, her mother Shyanne, and the rest of the women had told her she was to help keep the little ones out of trouble.

And she would do that. Just as soon as she decided where they could and could not go. The women were all in the kitchen. Cooking something called vegetables.

Fatima wasn't sure she liked vegetables; ration was what food was supposed to be. Mother had assured her that there was no more ration. How could that be? Ration just was. Instead, in this new place, there were vegetables. That they pulled out of the dirt. Seemed a lot of work when ration just fell off the conveyor.

Fatima stepped outside, raised a hand to block the hot light pouring down from Capella. Hard to think that wasn't a ceiling. Just open space forever overhead.

She blinked around. Amazed at the smells, the moving air, the feel of loose dirt under her feet. She giggled as she scrunched her toes in the stuff. So different from hard and smooth deck. The air sounded magical, the rising of the chime, the breeze in the forest. She giggled in delight.

Everything here was new. She wandered over to the pieces of machinery. Wondered at the purpose of each, and ran her fingers over the steel, duraplast, and sialon, amazed at the shapes of hoses, fittings, and levers. At six, she was old enough to know the machine was supposed to do something. It even had a weathered seat that she climbed up to perch on.

Tired of that, she hopped down, stomped her way across the green plants. She bent down for a closer look. Mother had said they were alive. Like people. Fatima fingered the leaves and stems, pulled one of the stems loose and sniffed and nibbled it.

She made a face at the bitter taste. Tossed the stem away.

A change in the musical chime drew her to the edge of the cliff to stare out at the forest. She tried to imagine the ends of it, couldn't. And looking down brought her heart into her throat. She instinctively stepped back, vertigo causing her to gasp. Long way down! She'd never felt anything like that.

Something red flashed down by the vegetables, and she turned, trotting to see. The thing was pretty, the brightest red she'd ever seen. Something else alive. And it flew, fluttering through the air as it dropped down to snap something up from among the plants.

"A bird!" Fatima cried with glee. Mother had told her about birds. Animals that flew. She'd seen her first animal!

Giddy, she chortled to herself, clapping her hands. Rubbed her shoulders, surprised at how hot the light was making her skin.

One of the pipes running down from the dome dribbled water onto the ground next to the plants. When she stepped in it, her foot sank. Stepping back, she stared in amazement at the impression her foot had made. Stepping forward, she pressed her foot down into the mud again. Felt it squish up between her toes. A sensation like she'd never known. Again and again, she stomped her foot down. Each time she made another track.

Delighted, she stomped her way to the end of the muddy spot.

And with the last jump, a stinging pain made her scream.

She dropped to her butt, pulled her muddy foot around, and stared at the bloody puncture in the sole of her foot. She screamed again as the pain burned its way through her foot.

She'd known pain. She had wailed and screamed during the Initiation. This was as bad. And worse, it was moving.

Moving *inside* her foot!

She tried to stand. Couldn't. Hurt too much!

"*Mother!*" she screamed.

But the women were inside. Cooking in the kitchen.

The only sound was the rising and falling of the chime, and it seemed to mock her.

30

Talina was sitting on her stool in Inga's; the tavern was full of locals and a few *Ashanti* crew. The rise and fall of conversation echoed from the high dome. The occasional scrape of a bench across the flagstone floor was augmented by Inga bellowing an order to her kitchen.

Talina's gut kept tying itself in a slipknot, and then releasing. Half of it, she was sure, was Demon making a nuisance of himself. The rest was the result of her conversation with Dek Taglioni. Shit on a shoe, what was it about the guy?

So what if he had rich-man's designer eyes and a dimple in his chin?

"*The chemicals say you would mate with him.*"

"Oh, go fuck yourself."

"Quetzals do not fuck."

"Okay, go share spit with yourself."

"Takes three."

"Asshole."

Demon chittered its amusement.

She kept half an ear open to the chatter that rose and fell behind her as the supper crowd came in. The clunking of mugs on chabacho-wood tables was reassuring, as was the sound of people calling to each other. The big news was that the first cargo shuttles bound for PA had landed from *Ashanti.*

Picked out from among the multitude of containers slated for the marine unit, Pamlico Jones and his crew were unloading the first lots of medical supplies, spare parts, farming equipment, and a new set of yard lights ostensibly for the Wide Ridge Research Base up north, but that had been abandoned for ten years. The good news was that Port Authority would have streetlights again. Assuming they could broker a deal with Kalico; this was, after all, Corporate property.

The distant rumble of thunder boomed above the rising din of conversation. Figured. Hot day like today, of course there'd be rain rolling in from the east.

She gave Inga a nod as the woman brought Talina her stout with one hand, whipping the five SDR coin into her pocket with the other.

"I'm still thinking about what I want for supper."

"If you want the chili, don't wait too long. Don't have that much left."

Which left either chamois steaks or the squash bake.

"Chamois steak with broccoli and cherry pie," she decided.

"You got it!" Inga pivoted on her heel, bellowing the order in the direction of the kitchen.

Talina lifted her stout, took a sip as Shig climbed up onto the stool beside her and slipped his water-spotted cloak from his shoulders.

"Looks like it's going to be a hard rain," he noted. "I checked with Talbot on the way over. He's got everyone on the gates. The *Ashanti* people from the shuttle field are safely inside the compound."

"Good. We can use the moisture. It's been a couple of weeks. I was out in the fields. Things are looking a little dry."

"Indeed, but the Sczuis got their wheat, barley, and rye harvested. Worked out perfectly for them." Shig paused. "Trouble out at the farms today? Heard you had to make a trip out to Reuben's."

"No. Well, maybe. Dek Taglioni was out there, picking peppers for Reuben. I gave specific orders that he wasn't supposed to go outside the gates." She gave him a sidelong glance. "Ko Lang tells me that someone named Shig told him that good old Dek could go work for Reuben for the day."

Shig was giving her his mildly reproving look. "It might seem churlish of me to remind you Dek's a free man, an adult, of sound mind, and seemingly healthy if malnourished body. You have no right to tell him what he can or can't do."

"The guy's a pain in the ass!" she snapped.

Demon hissed down in her gut.

She thought she heard Rocket laughing somewhere in the back of her head.

Shig's knowing gaze fixed on hers. "I see."

"Don't go dropping any of that Buddhist crap on me. I'm not in the mood."

"There is something in his personality that reminds me of Mitch. Some quality of having been tested, of not knowing the answers, but willing to tackle whatever it takes to find them."

"Don't even think of going there."

Shig smiled his thanks as Inga rushed down the bar just long enough to place his half-glass of wine before hurrying back to fill more mugs with beer.

"He's different from Cap. Didn't land with that cocksure, I'm-gonna-kick-asses attitude. But at the same time, he's similar in that he's fascinated just by being here."

"Do you want me to break your jaw?"

"Unlike both of them, Derek Taglioni has a different depth of personality. Mitch never faced the kind of desperate trial Taglioni did. And Cap, of course, had a head start from his training. He didn't have to begin his reevaluation of self until he was faced with disaster."

Talina gave Shig her most evil I'm-going-to-make-you-hurt-like-you-never-thought-you'd-hurt glare. "If you say one more word, I'm knocking you off that chair."

Shig lifted his glass, sipped. He studied the wine, a nice translucent red. Worked it in his mouth. "Very pleasant," he told her as he set the glass down. "I think it has possibilities."

"Glad you can talk about something besides Taglioni."

"What makes you think I was talking about the wine?"

Tal slapped a hand to the battered chabacho bar. "That does it! I'm shooting you through the knee."

Shig stared thoughtfully at the backbar with its glasses and containers of liquor. "History can be a burden. It accumulates. Becomes a weight and a hinderance. In its own way it can become blinding, so that the only thing people see is who you once were. They see you gunning down Pak or Paolo. Eliminating Clemenceau. Burying Mitch. Saving the town from disaster. Facing down Kalico Aguila, and walking out of the forest with Cap. Or they remember you taking down Spiro or standing up for quetzals. Maybe they remember you shooting a shipping crate when you thought it was Sian Hmong. Or single-handedly hunting three quetzals in the rain. They might—"

"Does this have a point?"

"The point is, they might not see Talina Perez."

"Well, duh! Right here. Filling this chair."

Shig's amiable smile bent his lips. "But do they see you, Tal? Or do they only see your history? The legend?"

"Let's just say that I'm too dense for the holy mystical shit. The learning-by-analogy crap. So stop with the hocus pocus, already. What's your point?"

Shig gave her one of his bemused looks. "If you were truly as dense as you attempt to portray yourself, you'd have been turned into quetzal shit years ago."

"Yeah, well, I've come close to ending up that way more times than I like to remember."

Demon made that broken gurgling that quetzals thought sounded like laughter, then hissed, *"Yes."*

"Very well, I shall be as blunt as a boulder." Shig twirled his wine glass on the counter. "When it comes to raw material, Taglioni is as good as I've seen over the years. I think he would be a real asset to Donovan for a lot of reasons. For one, his name, assuming we ever hear from Solar System again. For another, he's got that spark of soul. What should have snuffed it dead aboard *Ashanti* has given it additional illumination. He has the makings of greatness in him. My fear is that he will never be allowed the chance to discover it within himself."

"Why not?"

"He is going to pursue his calling. Follow his Tao where it will take him. And do so in the company of whomever will serve as a guide. Perhaps Rand Cope? Or maybe Bernie Monson?"

"They'll get him killed within a week." A beat. "He was asking about the Briggses today."

"They'd be adequate for the time being, though insufficient for what I think Taglioni's ultimate needs will be."

She gave him a distasteful look. "So, you're playing matchmaker?"

He studied her with an intensity she wasn't used to. "Tal, over the years, I've developed a certain fond regard for you. In truth, I never figured you'd live this long because of the *tamas* in your soul. Not to mention that you're the tip of our sword. There's not a man, woman, or child in Port Authority who doesn't owe you their lives. Taglioni needs a teacher. I think you need a student, even if you don't recognize that fact."

"I need a student?"

"Since Trish died, you've existed alone. You distance yourself from your people in Security. You only socialize with Kalico when she's up from Corporate Mine, with me, and on rare occasions Yvette when she comes in. Otherwise, your beloved bar stool might as well be on up on Donovan's moon."

"And what would I talk to people about?"

After the silence dragged for a bit, Shig said, "Precisely my point."

31

Fatima's arrival interrupted Vartan's concentration; he'd been going over the inventory of supplies, equipment, and stored items. Jon Burht, the first of the First Chosen, had heard the girl screaming down by the garden.

Burht brought little Fatima in just before dusk. She was bawling, said that something had hurt her foot. And there, inching up her pencil-thin calf, was a lump as big around and as long as Vartan's thumb. Moving. The thing was crawling along under the skin.

"Call Shyanne!" Vartan cried as he tried to soothe the child. "Hey, it's all right. Your mother's coming."

"It hurts!" Fatima declared as tears streaked her cheeks. "I'm scared. I want my mother!"

"Coming. She's coming."

The Messiah, disrupted from his reading, walked over, stared down. "What is it?"

"I don't know," Vartan told him. Lifting the girl's foot, he could see the wound, a bloody puncture where the child's foot was caked with mud. "What was it that they said? Something about slugs?"

"And shoes," Burht reminded. "That we needed to wear shoes."

The Messiah tipped his head back, eyes closed. The blue eye in his forehead continued to stare aimlessly at the light panel overhead. "Perhaps we should."

"It's moving faster," Burht noted.

The Messiah reached down, pressed on the lump moving slowly up Fatima's lower shin.

The girl screamed, and the lump slipped down behind her tibia and fibula, as if hiding. As it did, Fatima shrieked and kicked, as if trying to dislodge the pain.

"Fatima!" Shyanne cried, her expression panicked as she raced into the room. "What's happened?"

"Something bit her," the Messiah replied thoughtfully, a curious stirring behind his dark eyes.

"Bit her?" Shyanne bent down, taking her daughter's hand. "Baby? What happened? What bit you?"

"It hurt my foot! It's in my leg! Make it stop, Mother! Please. Just make it stop!"

Vartan ground his teeth. He'd always had a soft spot for Fatima. But for the universe, she might have been his child. Even after the Harrowing and Cleansing, he still had feelings for Shyanne. Couldn't help but remember how it had been before.

His soul ached at the expression on Shyanne's face as her quick hands began to press on the girl's swollen lower leg. As she did, Fatima screamed her pain.

"Sorry, baby. So, sorry." Shyanne glanced at the Messiah. "What do I do?"

"You're the vet tech," the Messiah told her. "The closest thing we have to a doctor."

"I'd better call Port Authority," she said through a nervous exhale. "They'll know what to do."

"No." The Messiah's tone left no room for doubt. "That is forbidden. We want nothing from those people. All they intend for us is harm."

Shyanne's brown eyes had taken on that gleam Vartan knew so well. He laid a hand on her shoulder. Felt her flinch as he told her: "Deal with it. You can figure it out on your own. It's just like an infection, right?"

Shyanne blinked, winced as Fatima screamed again.

"Please. Let me call."

"No. I will not tell you again," the Messiah told her. "You are our medical expert. You've seen the materials they left us. What do you think this is?"

"Probably something they call a slug." Shyanne was wavering on her feet, her hand clutching Fatima's. Tears were rimming her eyes.

"A slug," the Messiah said softly. "I thought they poisoned them all."

"Lies!" Burht snapped. "Corporate deceit."

Fatima began to whimper.

Vartan looked down in time to see the lump shift behind the little girl's skinny knee. "It's in the lower thigh now."

Shyanne clamped her eyes closed, both hands holding her daughter's. "They said it could be cut out."

"This is the universe's will," the Messiah said with finality. "This is a lesson to us."

"Get me a knife." Shyanne's voice had that high waver on the verge of hysteria. "I'll need something to sew with. I've got to get that *thing* out of my daughter."

"And risk yourself?" the Messiah asked. "Shyanne, think. Yes, she's your daughter. But you are our only medical person. What if, in trying to save your daughter, it infects you? We can't let that happen. You are too important to us."

Vartan watched the interplay of anger, fear, and worry behind his ex-wife's expression.

Before she could do herself irreparable harm, Vartan spun her around to face him. "I need you to run back to your room. Read everything you can find on these slugs. That Perez woman left the notes. Once you do, we'll know how to proceed. So go now. There's not a moment to lose. Find the answer for sure."

Shyanne shot him a look of disbelief.

"Yes," the Messiah agreed. "Go read the notes. See if there's anything mentioned besides surgery. Hurry!"

Vartan, praying, watched Shyanne hesitate, saw the skepticism, but the woman nodded. Bent down. "Baby, I'll be right back with the cure."

Shyanne left at a run. Almost bowled First Will Petre off his feet as he met her at the door.

Vartan wiped sweat from his forehead. "Maybe it won't be as bad—"

"Take her to one of the back rooms," the Messiah ordered. "I read the section on slugs. They are probably dividing inside the girl's leg as we speak. I want Fatima quarantined."

To Petre, he said, "Your job, First Will, is to keep Shyanne away from her daughter. Whatever it takes. But remember, as our only medical person, she's not to be too badly harmed."

Vartan fought down his urge to protest. Glanced at the agony reflected in the little girl's face. This was going to break Shyanne's heart. It was already breaking his. "Yes, Messiah."

As he reached down and gathered up the writhing little girl, he heard the Messiah say, "And no one goes outside barefoot from here on."

As Vartan carried the whimpering little girl down one of the dim hallways, he couldn't help but wonder.

If they lost the children, they lost everything.

32

A roiling muddle of thoughts filled Miguel Galluzzi's head as the shuttle's pitch changed, g-force pressing him down in the copilot's seat as Ensign Naftali placed them on approach to Port Authority.

Ahead the blue expanse of Donovan's ocean was broken by the continental mass; the old impact crater made it look like a bite had been taken out of the coast. They were shooting through clouds now. Flashes of cumulus that momentarily blotted the view.

Galluzzi might have been an old space dog—and he had to maintain his decorum—but inside he bubbled with excitement. This, after all, was the culmination of everything. The entire purpose of space flight. He was living the dream that had filled human imagination all the way back to the moment the first hominin looked up at the stars and wondered.

For that one moment, it didn't matter that *Ashanti*'s voyage here had been disastrous. If anything, knowing how close they'd all come to dying made this arrival even more fulfilling.

To get to this point, Galluzzi had crossed thirty light-years of space, lived for nearly three years "outside" of the universe. Brought his ship, the survivors, and cargo to this distant world.

G-force increased as the shuttle cupped air, the roar of it loud through the hull. Then the nose dropped, Naftali caressing the thrusters as he crossed the coast, put them into a glide over a vegetation-dotted landscape, the colors oddly vivid compared with Earth.

The shuttle slowed into a hover, and Naftali eased it down. Galluzzi caught sight of another A-7 parked off to the side of a stack of shipping containers. Then a billow of dust spewed out, and the shuttle settled onto its landing skids.

"Welcome to Donovan, Captain," Naftali told him as he spooled the thrusters down.

Galluzzi could feel the change through his seat. Planetary gravity. So different from the angular acceleration that served as a surrogate aboard ship.

I am on a distant world.

For a moment he wanted to giggle, to shake his fists with delight. Didn't, of course. He was the captain. Captains didn't do those sorts of things.

Even if they had survived the kind of spacing he had.

Rising, he emerged from the command deck hatch and crossed aft through the cargo-packed main cabin to where Windman opened the aft ramp and let it drop.

The acrid smell left by the thrusters gave way to fresh air as Galluzzi minced his steps down the ramp. Gravity, after all these years, was a tricky thing. He could feel the strain in his muscles.

And then he was out in the light, blinking, aware of the air on his skin and its incredible perfumed scent. The direct heat from Capella was a marvel, the light so bright it hurt his eyes. In wonder, he extended his hand to the breeze, feeling it trickle over his fingers. Eyes closed, he leaned his head back to the sunlight; for a moment, with breath going in and out of his lungs, he savored the miracle of fresh air.

The whine of machinery began to seep through his consciousness. Opening his eyes, he forced himself back to reality.

"Miguel!" Benj Begay called. The Advisor/Observer came striding across the landing field. The man wore a freshly pressed suit. Something obviously retrieved from one of the crates of personal possessions that had been locked away in cargo. Begay might have just stepped out of an office on Transluna. The professional cut of the clothing, shining a metallic blue in the light, looked oddly out of place against the background of dirt, shipping crates, and the high fence surrounding the domes.

"Benj. Good to see you."

"What's the word on the ship?" Begay stepped close, shaking

Galluzzi's hand as if it had been years instead of days since they'd seen each other.

"Got Deck Three cleaned out. I wouldn't leave until that had been taken care of."

Benj's expression soured. "I can't imagine the kind of . . . Well, was it bad?"

"Call it macabre, grisly, insane . . . Hey, words don't convey the kind of things . . ." He shook his head. "Forget it. The whole deck's sterilized. Stripped down to the hull." He looked around at where forklifts were whining and moaning as they lifted shipping containers. "What's happening here?"

"Getting the first loads out of *Ashanti* now that Corporate Mine has been taken care of and the Maritime Unit has been happily dropped out on their reef. Figure that if you're done with Deck Three, with the additional crew to help, we can have the Cargo Deck emptied within another couple of weeks. Most of what you see here is ready to be shipped up. Loaded and sent back to Solar System."

"Given what the Supervisor's got floating up in orbit, and the number of containers I see here, we're not even going to come close to taking it all."

If I can even stomach the thought of spacing again.

"I've got a manifest of what goes first. Miguel, you're not going to believe it."

"Believe what?"

"The wealth." Begay took his arm. "Come on. I've got the manifest on my tablet. Let me take you on a stroll through town. Buy you a drink and the finest meal you've ever eaten. Then I'll brief you on what's at stake."

Galluzzi let Benj take the lead, followed him through a huge gate just before a giant hauler wallowed its way past, cloaking him with a light coating of dust. To his amazement, a man dressed in quetzal hide and coarse cloth stood guard with a rifle. And, yeah, he'd heard. Seeing it, however, was shocking.

"What's that?" Galluzzi hooked a thumb at the departing hauler.

"Clay," Benj told him. "Makes the finest sialon in the galaxy. As if that means shit. Most of those containers out there are full of it. Enough cubic kilometers to fabricate a dozen *Freelander*-sized ships. But forget the clay. It's inconsequential."

"What? That's why they founded Port Authority here in the first place."

"Those containers up in orbit? They're full of beryllium, rhodium, cerium, terbiums, ruthenium. All being kept pristine in vacuum. And then there's the gems, like nothing Earth has ever produced. After that, the gold, silver, platinum and the like are almost boring."

Looking around at the central avenue just past the admin dome, Galluzzi asked, "When do we get to the good part of town?"

"You're here." Benj spread his arms to take in the entirety of the graveled north-south thoroughfare. "I give you the Transluna of Capella III."

Galluzzi's brain stumbled at that. He saw weathered domes interspersed with buildings made of stone, timbers, and some sort of plaster. Barrels, pieces of equipment, drying racks, little gardens, hand-painted signs, everything was a jumble, right down to the mismatched light poles that lined the street.

The people ambling past were just as bizarre. The colors, the outlandish cut and style of the clothes, the rainbow-effect quetzal hide, the wild and unkempt hair styles. Most men were bearded. Not to mention the big floppy hats and guns. So many guns. Hard to think that they hadn't all murdered each other upon the outbreak of the first discord. Even the women looked like cutthroats.

"This is the richest planet in the galaxy?" Galluzzi asked.

"Sum and total," Benj told him. "Me, I can't wait to get out of here. Even if it means shipping back aboard *Ashanti*, but I'll get to that in a bit. Want to see the worse parts of town?"

"I think I'm fine with first impressions."

A loud bang made him jump. Turning, he realized it came from the building with GUNSMITH burned into the curious wood sign over the door.

"They build and fix firearms. Sell them to anyone, can you imagine? I mean, you could just walk in there and buy a rifle. No questions asked, no one watching."

"Insane!"

"The whole place is, Miguel." Benj shook his head. "It's one thing to hear that they're a bunch of libertarians. But once you set foot down here? Realize that, no shit, there really isn't any government to speak of? I mean seriously. No one takes care of these people. They're completely on their own. What kind of insanity is that?"

"Sounds scary."

"Yeah." Benj motioned. "Come on. After years of rations, I promised you a meal the likes of which you've never eaten. They might be a bunch of lunatics, but, by damn, can they cook!"

"What's the Supervisor say about all this?" Galluzzi tried to take in a whole new order of shabby as he walked beside Benj. "Why hasn't she restored order here?"

"According to the story, she tried. Quickly figured out it would be open warfare, and she'd have to kill them all to reestablish Corporate control. Now, that said, Aguila herself is off the rails if you ask me. She and her Corporate Mine are little better than the local savages."

"You been down there?"

"I have. They might call themselves Corporate, but it's in name only. You ask me, it's a sort of co-op. But one that's corrupted by Port Authority's cash economy. Miguel, there's no redistribution here. Even Aguila's people, they're rich in their own wealth. What they call plunder. And they're a clannish bunch. You say anything critical of Aguila, they're ready to reach down your throat and pull your lungs out through your mouth."

"What's Dek say about all this?"

"Dek?" Benj laughed almost hysterically. "I never knew that insanity was infectious, but he's gone as crazy as the rest of them. Figured that as a Taglioni, he should have come uncorked at first sight of this place. Instead, he's out in the bush, like he's fallen headlong into the absurdity that is Donovan."

Benj led him to a dome with benches out front. "This is Inga's. The local drinking and eating establishment. Well, there's the cafeteria, but the name pretty much says it. Down the street, The Jewel is a casino and whorehouse. One of two brothels if you can believe it, but that's a story for another time."

Galluzzi stepped inside to find the floor in need of sweeping and followed Benj down into a subterranean room with a stone floor and long tables crowded by benches.

Benj found a spot in the back, off to the side, and told the young man who walked over, "Two of the lunch specials and two glasses of the amber ale."

The waiter said, "Uh, you're Skulls. You got cash or plunder?"

With careful fingers, Benj placed a coin on the table. "That's a ten. That enough?"

"You got it," the lanky twentysomething told him, turning to bellow, "Two specials, two amber ales." Then he was off to a table full of hatted, cloak-wearing, pistol-packing locals up front.

Galluzzi just stared at the coin, having never seen the like. Finally asked, "Why didn't we just stand up and shout?"

"Some of us try to cling to the illusion of gentlemanly conduct."

Galluzzi threw his head back, laughing with gusto for the first time in how long? "Hard to believe this place is for real."

"Oh, it is."

"What do you hear about the Unreconciled?"

"Guess they're out in some distant research station. The latest news is that the Prophets got turned into raving morons because they ate other people's brains. Some sort of protein malfunction that eats holes in gray matter. Spongiform encephalitis." Benj barely suppressed a shiver. "Damn, but I'm glad to be rid of them."

Galluzzi grunted.

Benj fixed him with a hard stare. "Miguel, I need to know. Once the cargo is loaded, how soon do you expect to space?"

Galluzzi leaned back, experienced a quivering in his heart. "I don't know, Benj. It's going to depend."

"On what?"

"The condition of the ship and crew. What the Supervisor orders. I don't know. Just how we all feel."

"How we *feel*? You heard anything I've said? This place is a lunatic's asylum. The closest thing to Corporate order is Aguila's mine. And *there's nothing there*. Just a mine, barracks, and a cafeteria. *This*"—he waved around—"is the best this shithole has to offer."

"Benj, take a breath. Listen to me. You were there. You know what kind of condition my people are in. It's been ten years. We almost died. Most of them are out of contract. If I post an order that we're spacing as soon as we're loaded, half of them will refuse. The half that I order aboard will hate me for cutting their shore leave. . . . And it's not like murder hasn't been committed on *Ashanti* before."

Benj rubbed his face with the flats of his hands. The old gesture of frustration having grown so aching familiar over the years. "Miguel, do you understand? We're talking about the kind of wealth that will make us all famous. Look back in history. The Spanish treasure fleets of galleons? The Venetian merchants of the Renaissance? They are *nothing* compared to the splash *Ashanti* will make when she's unloaded. Your photo will be holoed from one side of Solar System to the other."

Right. They'll have a face to put to the name. "So that's what a monster looks like. He's the one who left the cannibals to die."

Galluzzi asked, "And you, my friend?"

Benj's lips twitched before he said, "Who knows? Supervisor of Transluna? It wouldn't be out of the question."

"What if Aguila wants to go back? Take her own wealth. Put herself at the forefront of the discovery."

Benj's expression went tight. "I guess we'll just have to wait." A beat. "As the locals say, 'Welcome to Donovan.'"

"Meaning?"

"Meaning anything can happen."

Not that it mattered to Miguel Galluzzi. What did was the question that bounced around inside his head: *Can I space again? Do I even want to?*

33

The last time Shaka Mantu had walked under the stars, he'd been nine. Memory of that night, of the warm and moist air, and the South African sky, had clung to him during the long and terrible eternity of Deck Three. When the horror and hopelessness had grown too much to bear, he'd tuck himself away in his bunk and remember. Go back to his life as a boy before he'd traveled off to Academy.

Those hours he would spend with his mother and brothers, reliving life when there was a sky, home, and a future without death, pain, and misery.

On this night, he finally walked free under the stars. Different, it was true. Here no Southern Cross, no Magellanic Clouds, no Coal Sack were visible. And the Milky Way was brighter, wider, and stunningly different.

"But I am finally free," he said, raising his hands as he strode out beyond the northernmost dome.

His way wound through the scrubby trees; he let the curious sound of the night chime bathe him in its subtle music. If he thought about it, he could almost call the intonations tribal.

Warm air caressed his skin.

"God, I have longed for this." Inhaling, he filled his lungs and savored the perfumed scents. Tried to catalog them. Sort of a saffron? Maybe mixed with cilantro? A hint of tang similar to steeping honeybush tea?

Movement under his foot surprised him. He skipped sideways, startled. Then laughed. Yes, it was the roots. He'd heard that they moved. To experience it was a marvel. He tried to tread lightly, wearing his soft leather boots as the Messiah had ordered.

Odd that. It flew in the face of tradition.

"We are no longer like a fetus in the womb!" the Messiah had de-

clared. *"As newly born infants, we must now learn to dress for our new world. Shoes will be worn at all times while outside. Just as children must learn to wear clothing."*

Seven years barefoot. Now he had shoes again. It felt oddly restraining.

Call it a happy tradeoff for the ability to stroll under an open night sky. He tried to mince his steps, to mitigate the disturbance to the roots. Even in the darkness, with a sliver of moon to light the sky, he could see the trees shifting their branches, as if the leaves were watching him.

"Mama? I made it. I'm standing on a distant world. Tough times to get here. I did things. Things I hope you never have to know. But I lived."

Funny thought that she might be looking up at the night sky outside of Johannesburg, perhaps looking right at him, as he might be looking at her. And it would take thirty years for the light to travel between them.

How did the human brain synthesize that?

His path had taken him to the edge of the cliff. He sniffed, catching the faint odor of vinegar mixing with perfumed scents on the wind. The vista overwhelmed, and he marveled, looking out at the humped confusion of treetops that vanished into an indistinct horizon marked with stars.

What a miracle. This was an alien forest.

And he, Shaka Mantu, was seeing it firsthand.

Not bad for a Zulu boy. That day he'd received his first scholarship, who would have guessed that he'd . . .

The boulder he was walking around jumped. Something lanced through his left shoulder, the impact of it shearing through his scapula, upper ribs, and clavicle. Knocked him back. He would have fallen, but the spear took his weight. Dangled him.

Pain—like nothing he'd known—stunned him. Before he could draw breath, his body was grabbed. In the darkness, he barely saw the two tentacles that drew him close against the boulder . . . that was no longer a boulder.

He tried to draw breath.

To scream.

But his chest, fiery with pain, was frozen.

As his mouth worked soundlessly, the *thing* that held him pressed close. Warm tissue spread along his bare thighs, over his wrap, and onto his stomach. Like a jelly bath, it began to surround him.

And then the burning began.

He finally managed to draw breath.

Was about to scream, when the spear through his upper chest jerked sideways. Stunned with pain, he didn't realize one of the tentacles had shifted. He barely felt it seize the back of his head. Then he was pulled down, bent double, and his face was shoved into the warmth as the *thing* engulfed his head . . .

34

Not for the first time did Dan Wirth wonder if he was a moron, deluded, or just plain crazy. Right. *So, stop with the psychopath jokes, already.*

He'd swung the safe door open and was staring at the packed shelves. This was the second safe. The first—hulking in its place in the corner—he didn't bother to open anymore. It was packed with stacked ingots of gold, platinum, something called rhodium, and bars of ruthenium. Hell, he'd never heard of such stuff as that last. Now he had safes so full of it the legs had buckled.

He scowled, taking in the contents of safe two. The thing was a five-foot tall by four-foot steel box that Tyrell Lawson had welded together. This time Dan hadn't bothered to bolt it to the floor. By the time it was full, it would take a heavy-lift shuttle to pack the thing off. And where was he going to find a thief on Donovan dumb enough to chance stealing from him?

"Oh, Father, if you could see me now, you worthless piece of walking garbage."

But the old pedophile couldn't. And Dan hoped the cocksucker never would. The old man was the only living being in the galaxy who knew who Dan Wirth really was. And if there were any justice—real or imaginary—dear old Dad was either dead before his time or brain-wiped for the sick shit that he was.

"So, what the hell do I do when this one's full?" Dan wondered. Wasn't going to take much. Maybe another couple of months. He stuffed the bag of rubies in the right-hand side. How many damn rubies could a single planet produce?

Allison had suggested using some of the gems to inlay the bar, and then covering the whole thing with glass. Sure as hell, that would be a crowd pleaser. The richest bar in the universe. After all, he already had a dozen fifty-to-sixty-karat "pigeon-blood-red" rubies, not to mention all those thirty-to-forty-karat rocks that constantly trickled in. And then there were the emeralds, the diamonds, sapphires, and all the rest.

"Fucking pain in the ass." He slammed the door shut and wrenched the locking lugs closed.

As he stood, Kalen Tompzen—dressed in a black shirt and wearing tight chamois pants—knocked and leaned in the office door.

"Uh, boss? Got something you might want to keep an eye on."

Dan walked over to his big desk, ensured the ledger book was up to date. Bless Ali for a good girl—it was. He raised his eyes. "What sort of something?"

"Guy's winning a lot of hands, boss. Dalia gave me the high sign. I've had Vik watching. Shin, too. Can't see how he's cheating."

"What's his take?"

"He came in with nine SDR. He's up to about three fifty now."

"Nine to three fifty? Now there, by God's ugly ass, is a man after my own heart." Dan stepped over to the mirror, adjusted the fine white silk scarf tied at his throat. Real silk. The only one on Donovan. He'd obtained it from Amal Oshanti, one of the local housewives. The slit had traded a bedroom addition on her house for the scarf. She'd brought it all the way from Solar System back on sixth ship.

Traded, for fart-sucking sake!

Here he was, a man with two safes full of plunder, and he couldn't *buy* a scarf. No, he had to *trade.* But so be it. He now owned and wore the *one-and-only* silk scarf on the whole toilet-sucking planet.

He slipped his form-fitting quetzal-hide vest over his shoulders, looped the gold and rhodium chains into place, and strode for the door.

In the hallway he could hear the rhythmic thumping of the bed as Angelina provided some john with horizontal glee. Ali's door was closed, but then, she was supposed to be down at admin, dealing with Muley Mitchman's deed. Nice that she'd been seeing to the nitty shitty little details needed to manage property. And it kept him from getting frustrated, cutting throats, and making more trouble for himself.

Stepping into the casino, it was to see a new guy seated at the back table playing poker with Step Allenovich and Lee Halston. Obviously soft meat from *Ashanti,* the guy was nevertheless dressed like a farmer. Quetzal boots, local-fabric shirt, canvas pants.

He might have been in his thirties, sandy hair, and those eyes . . . ah, custom. Genetically designed. The pistol on the guy's belt was like nothing Dan had ever seen. Looked like a presentation piece, all wood, gold, and inlaid. Electronic no less. Fancy.

Had to be Taglioni, the one that slit Aguila had warned Ali not to exploit. All of which brought Dan's curiosity to full boil.

"Why, I do declare. A new face. What a welcome relief after the butt-ugly mugs I've been staring at for all of these last long months." Dan thrust out a hand. "Dan Wirth, owner, proprietor, and lord and master of The Jewel. Most pleased to be at your service."

"Derek Taglioni," the Skull replied, his handshake firm, and to Dan's surprise, a confidence lay behind the man's designer eyes. Something that reeked of power and influence. Be just Dan's pus-sucking luck if this guy turned out to be another fucking Tamarland Benteen.

"Mind if I sit in?" Dan asked, swinging a chair around from the next table. "Been a while since I've played a few hands."

Step Allenovich carefully swept his remaining SDRs into his pocket, saying, "Me, I've bled enough. I'll leave it up to you to get my siddars back from Dek here."

"Makes two of us," Halston muttered as he picked up his plunder. "I want enough left to cover my meals until the Supervisor pays me for that last load of timber I cut for her."

Dan took the deck, cutting and shuffling. The entire time Taglioni was watching him through those unsettling eyes. No change of expression, just taking his measure.

"What's your pleasure?" Dan asked.

"Anything you like. We were playing five-card draw."

"Works for me."

Taglioni tossed out an SDR.

As Dan shuffled again and dealt, he asked, "So what tempted a man of your obvious good sense to entrust his life and sanity to a long space voyage? Not that anyone would expect a ten-year transit, but I was half-crazed after a mere two years in *Turalon*."

"A small family disagreement," Taglioni told him without inflection. "I found myself in need of new opportunities, new challenges."

"You may have come to the right place. Anything I can help with? Property? Perhaps offer my services when it comes to making the right introductions? Not that a man of your means would be short on capital, but Corporate credit isn't negotiable in Port Authority. Our libertarian brethren insist on hard cash or plunder. Wouldn't be the first time I funded a promising venture when the right person was at the helm."

A faint smile played at Taglioni's lips. "What if I wanted to open a casino in that nice stone building across the street?"

Dan experienced that cold slowing in his chest, the keening of incipient combat. "I would wish you good luck. In the first place, Sheyela Smith is our local electrical wizard. Considered a non-replaceable asset, and she likes her building just fine, thank you. In the second, being the bustling metropolis that Port Authority is with its four hundred thriving souls, the traffic really wouldn't support two such specialized institutions." A beat. "Not even if they were clear across town."

Taglioni answered with a knowing nod. "Yeah, not really my sort of thing. How about I leave any such dealings to you and Allison?" He checked.

That little spear of relief made Dan chuckle. The guy was good. He'd dangled the bait and studied the reaction.

"So, what are you after?" Dan asked, folding to give the mark a false sense of security.

Taglioni took the cards. His shuffle was good. Almost professional. Dan was dealt two fours, took three cards. Was stuck with his pair.

God, he wished Art Manikin was still alive. Tompzen was too new, didn't know the game. Wasn't trained to give the signals. No telling what Taglioni had in hand.

Dan bid it up to ten, lost to three sixes.

"Word is that people come to Donovan to leave, to find themselves, or to die." Taglioni gave him a grim smile. "Me? I'm not leaving, so it's one of those last two."

"Let's hope it turns out to be the former and not the latter," Wirth told him with a placid smile. At that moment, Allison entered, shot him a victorious smile, and tapped a slim index finger to the corner of her jaw. Her signal that the Mitchman deed was taken care of.

Dan laid his hand on the table, two queens. He was surprised to see Taglioni lay down three twos. What the hell?

For a moment Dan stared at the cards, then shot a glance at Taglioni's yellow-green eyes, noted the challenging curl at the corner of the man's lips.

Oh, so that's the game, is it?

Outside thunder crashed and boomed. Rain began to hammer on the roof. For the next two hours Dan played poker like he hadn't in years. Every bit of his concentration, skill, the benefits of his implants and fancy tricks. He barely broke even.

Playing Derek Taglioni, he might have been playing a chunk of granite. The guy had no tells. Not so much as the flicker of an eye, not a tick, nor even a slight shift of posture. A robot couldn't have played it better.

And through it all, Taglioni kept up a constant stream of small talk. Told of the cannibals, his hopes to get out in the bush, even asking about Dan and his background. Might have been the kind of meaningless chatter to be shared over a cup of tea.

By then The Jewel was starting to fill with locals, some calling for drinks, others catching on that a new guy was playing Dan at poker. As a crowd started to build, Dan thumped the table. "As enjoyable as this is, I've got to go to work."

He stood, saying, "Come back with me, and I'll exchange those chips."

Taglioni rose, following Dan into the back hall and to his office. Shutting the door behind them, Dan asked, "Whiskey?"

"Sure."

Dan poured, studying Taglioni as the guy took in Dan's big and ornately carved chabacho-wood desk, the two safes and the mismatched furnishings. "Where did you learn to play poker like that?"

"Implants backed by a program that monitors data." Taglioni didn't even deny it. "That and I've been raised since I was a kid to study strategy, negotiation, statistical analysis of risk. Everything a budding Corporate cutthroat might need to succeed in the deadly world of high-stakes politics." A faint smile. "Works for poker, too. Though I admire your ability when it comes to sleight of hand. That had to take years to perfect."

Dan handed him the glass of whiskey. Shit, the fucker had seen the bottom deals, the hustle. "Let's keep that last as our own little personal secret."

Seating himself behind his desk, Dan asked, "So, as one card shark to another, what can I help you to accomplish? That is, aside from setting up a running game in my establishment? I don't want the chuckleheads to figure out just how easily they can be skinned at the tables."

"They haven't figured out that the house always wins?"

"Oh, to be sure, they've heard the words before." Dan tapped the side of his head. "It's just the comprehension where they're a little slow on the uptake."

Taglioni pulled the big stuffed chair around in front of the desk, settled himself comfortably across from Dan, and stared thoughtfully at his whiskey. "So fill me in. I've heard the chitchat. You run the games and sex trade, have fingers in most of the local pies, loan money, investment. People who cross you end up dead of mysterious, and, yes, not-so-mysterious causes. Shig, Yvette, and Talina run what government there is, but you're always there. Sort of in the background. Something needs doing for the community, you see that it gets funded. In the old days, the word was gangster, mafia don, or maybe *capitan.* Some say the Supervisor is the most powerful person on the planet. Others say it's you. Which is correct?"

Dan rubbed the links of his vest chain between two fingers. "Aguila and I came to an unspoken agreement a couple of years back that we would never try and answer that question. But the fact that you asked it, well that makes you even more interesting. The last major player who showed up here was Benteen. Got a lot of people killed. Precipitated a disaster. He ended up as a science experiment up on *Freelander.* I would hope you're not entertaining similar delusions."

"Not even close." He studied Dan with those peculiar and evaluative eyes. "All I can figure is that you had leverage on someone in personnel to get a posting on *Turalon.* Some last-minute substitution for the real Dan Wirth. Which means he's dead, and you can never go back to Transluna."

Dan felt the cool calm seeping through his guts. His heart slowing. That clarity of purpose was taking possession of his brain and body. His pistol hung in its rack just below the top of the desk. He need only . . .

Taglioni waved it away. "Relax. I could give a rat's ass."

"Really?" Dan asked, trying to keep the emotionless tone from his voice.

"Mr. Wirth, how about we come to an agreement?"

"You have my undivided attention."

"Good. But first, answer me a question. Answer it honestly. What do you intend on doing with all that wealth? Word is that both of those safes are full to bursting. Are you eventually thinking about shipping it back to Solar System? Maybe going back as a rich and powerful man one of these days?"

"Maybe."

"Okay, so here's the agreement: You leave me alone. Stay out of my hair, don't cause me any problems. For my part, I'll do my absolute level best to stay out of yours. In return, if and when *Ashanti* spaces back, you can be on her. With all of your plunder. I'll use my connections to ensure you get to spend that wealth. No questions asked."

"Just like that? Out of the goodness of your heart?"

Taglioni grinned. "Well, all right. There might be a fifteen percent service fee tacked on."

"Ten."

"Ten . . . with the provision that you pay all additional expenses for bribes, fees, gifts, entertainments, and the associated graft that will be an unavoidable necessity when it comes to the Corporate Board."

Dan arched an eyebrow, the subtle feeling of satisfaction rising within. There might actually be a way out of this.

"So, Mr. Taglioni—"

"Call me Dek."

"So, Dek, outside of ten percent and expenses, what do you get out of this? Seems to me, you could get the plunder back to Solar System, turn me in for a reward, and claim a lot more than your ten percent."

Taglioni took a full sip of the whiskey, ran it over his tongue as real whiskey drinkers did, and held it. After he'd finally swallowed and savored the finish, he said, "The Derek Taglioni who boarded *Ashanti* off Neptune would have done exactly that. The one who scrubbed toilets and mucked the hydroponics tanks for the last seven years in a bid to stay alive discovered different priorities."

"Such as?"

"I'm not sure that a man with your form of narcissistic and anti-social psychopathy can understand. It's more attuned to Shig Mosadek's kind of world view, but for me, there's now a need to measure myself against my soul."

"You're right. Only Shig could understand shit like that."

Taglioni laughed. "So, there it is. Laid out. I've no designs on your operation here. If, in the future, for whatever reason, we come into conflict, I'd prefer that we figure it out over a glass of whiskey before we go to cutting each other's throats."

Outside, lightning flashed and thunder boomed. Rain came down in earnest.

"Yeah, I can live with that." But why the hell is it that I don't really trust you?

35

The sense of despair was hardly an unknown companion as Miguel Galluzzi ambled his way down the main avenue. After parting with Benj, he'd taken the opportunity to stroll the length and breadth of Port Authority. Not that there was a whole lot of either before running headlong into that impossible soaring conglomeration of fence.

This is the height of human achievement on Donovan? This miserable collection of disabled vehicles, ramshackle housing, junk, clotheslines, toys in the dirt, and makeshift warehouses?

His feet hurt. His back ached, and his limbs were tuckered from the gravity. The yawning sense of despair just wouldn't turn loose from him.

Didn't matter that people had been friendly, had greeted him with a smile, and almost to the last, had introduced themselves. Hadn't even recoiled when he told them who he was. All had been most cordial—a fact that surprised him given that even the women had been armed.

Galluzzi had never been too taken with airs, but the fact remained: He was a captain. Here, even the children treated him with a most unsettling familiarity. What irked was that he was *not* one of them. Never would be.

Nevertheless, he'd been polite, done his best not to offend. After all, it was their town. Their world and ways. Not to mention that good manners seemed particularly prudent when talking to an armed man or woman—even if they were of menial status.

Glancing up at the clouding sky, Galluzzi sighed. How damn forlorn could a man be? He hadn't expected much of Port Authority. What he'd discovered, however, made him want to drop his head into his hands and weep.

He passed The Jewel. Considered entering, having not been in a casino since Macao some twenty years ago. But after laying eyes on the brown-haired man in a quetzal vest who was watching him from the doorway, he'd had second thoughts. Benj had already given him fair warning, and besides, after the glory, color, dash, and excitement of Macao, what depths of disappointment could a Port Authority casino plumb?

So he had forced his tired feet to carry him past, headed back . . . Where?

He stopped short in front of the admin dome, could see the hospital marking the south end of the avenue. Was about to turn and follow the side street to the shuttle field, when Shig Mosadek stepped out of the admin dome's double doors.

The short Indian was clad in a quetzal-hide cloak, his embroidered fabrics looking rumpled. The man squinted at Galluzzi, then smiled and waved. He shot a look at the sky, and called, "Just a moment. I shall be right back."

Then he vanished back inside for all of twenty seconds before emerging with a second hat and another of the quetzal-hide cloaks. These he presented to Galluzzi, saying, "I heard that you were in town, Captain. Forgive me for not finding you sooner. We had to work out a title dispute on a couple of claims out west. The previous owner was killed by a rogue quetzal we call Whitey. Old Mao had left his claim to Muley Mitchman but owed a gambling debt to The Jewel."

Even as Shig spoke, a most remarkable blonde woman, tall, dressed in a suggestive form-fitting sheath crafted from some local fabric, emerged from the admin dome.

Galluzzi instinctively straightened, squared his shoulders, as he reminded himself not to stare. What the hell was wrong with him? Damn, he hadn't been locked up in a ship for so long that he'd gape like a drooling idiot.

If the woman noticed, she didn't let it show, but stepped up next to Shig, dwarfing the Indian as she fixed enchanting blue eyes on Miguel.

"Don't let me interrupt," she told him in a melodious voice.

"No interruption," Shig told her. "In fact, I'd like to introduce

Captain Miguel Galluzzi, master of the *Ashanti*. Captain, this is Allison Chomko, one of the partners in The Jewel."

"My pleasure," he told her, taking her offered hand. The touch sent an electric pulse through him. In that instant, he could have lost himself in her smile and those wondrous eyes. His heart began to hammer in his breast.

To Shig, the woman said, "Thanks for your help in there. I'll give Dan the rundown. I think Muley is happy with the settlement. If not, we'll work something out."

"He's young. If he can stay alive out there long enough, it could be the turning point for him. Mao had high hopes for that new diggings of his."

Again she fixed that miracle-blue gaze on Miguel, adding, "My honor to meet you, Captain. Do come by. I'd find it a pleasure to buy you a drink, and you'll find me a rapt audience if you'd be kind enough to share your experiences."

"I . . . well, of course. I'd be delighted." What in hell was it about her? She'd turned him into a stammering idiot.

He remained mesmerized as she gave him a radiant smile, turned, and strode away in a walk that hinted of almost feline grace. She seemed to float, the sway of her hips, the straight back, the way the light was shining in her . . .

Galluzzi blinked, tried to shake it off.

Shig, an amused smile on his lips, glanced up at the sky. "Might want to get indoors. This one's going to come down hard. I don't have Ali's allure, but I'd stand you a drink. Perhaps we could talk about your plans. Have you a place to stay?"

"I, uh, assumed there would be Corporate housing somewhere around the shuttle port."

"Ah, well, even when we were Corporate they never quite got around to such basic facilities as spacers' quarters, let alone an officers' lounge. As Dek has recently relocated to a dome of his own, you'd be more than welcome to use my study. My futon has a reputation for remarkable comfort. I've passed many a pleasant night on it myself."

"I couldn't—"

"Oh, no inconvenience. I assure you. It's a separate building. I won't even know you're there." Shig smiled. "Come. This hat and cloak are for you. By the time the night's over, you'll be thankful to have them."

"Where to?"

"Inga's of course. There really is no other place except the cafeteria, and though Millicent's cooking is filling, it's rather uninviting for extended conversation."

Back to the tavern?

The first drops of rain began to fall as they made it to the tavern door. Galluzzi fingered the thick quetzal leather, amazed at the patterns of rainbow light that ran under his thumb. Had to be the crystalline scales on the hide.

Inside, and down the stairs, Shig led the way to the right side of the bar, propped himself up on one of the stools, and indicated the second from the end for Miguel, saying, "We keep that last one for Tal. Not that we're much for status and ceremony around here, but she's earned it the hard way."

"That woman, Allison. She's a partner in The Jewel? I mean, I've heard rather unsavory things about it." He couldn't shake the image of her. Figured she'd be haunting his dreams for a while.

"Owns forty-nine percent of The Jewel; and she's branched out into various real estate, mining, and development ventures. Let's just say that her start was a little rocky. Various tragedies left her ill-used and wounded. A fact that she realized and corrected. Once she took the bit in her teeth, she's made a rather impressive turnaround."

"I see." Wasn't the place also a brothel?

Shig lifted his hand in Inga's direction, asking, "What will you have?"

"I would kill for a cup of coffee or hot chocolate."

"Wouldn't we all? The coffee trees are supposed to produce beans this year. Meanwhile, we have a variety of teas, all of which, to our horror, are herbal and without caffeine."

"The amber ale was good."

After Inga had taken the order, Shig asked, "So, what are your plans? How can we be of service here?"

Galluzzi turned, looked over his shoulder at the people trickling down the stairs and into the tavern, water shining on their cloaks. "I haven't a clue." He laughed. "It's odd to admit, but I figured after what I'd done to the transportees—and if I ever lived long enough to make it here—I'd be arrested, tried, and executed." A beat. "Looked forward to it, actually."

"Might have happened that way, once upon a time," Shig agreed. "*Freelander,* up there in orbit, however, has taught us all an interesting moral lesson: Sometimes the universe leaves us with nothing but bad decisions."

"Sounds remarkably like situational ethics."

"Welcome to Donovan."

IMPOTENCE

Two people are missing. Mauree Baktihar and Shaka Mantu. Third Will Tikal has been out searching with his team. Shaka told one of the women that he was going for a walk last night. Tikal said he tried to track him. That there wasn't even a scuff in the dirt.

Mauree Baktihar, mother of two, was last seen on the south end of the garden. The young men working in the field with her said that one minute she was there, the next she was gone. They wondered if maybe she'd stepped into the bushes to relieve herself.

Again, not a sign can be found.

As if my people would know what to look for.

I don't know what to do. Call everyone into the admin dome? Bar the doors? Tell my people that we're going to have to live like we did on Deck Three? Locked away? And that if we travel outside, we must do so in large parties for mutual protection?

Around me, the cafeteria is silent but for a humming from the air system and the rattling of the refrigeration back in the kitchen. On their tables, the Prophets are still for the most part. Occasionally one of them will twitch, jerk a leg, or utter a rasping snore. I envy them their peace as they fall ever deeper into the universe.

As for me, I cannot sleep, cannot rest.

I think I have been played by Kalico Aguila. Led here to a sort of trap. Vartan, however, has found something in his search of the sheds. Something that, if we play it right, will give me Kalico Aguila. Assuming I can allay her suspicion and lure her back here, I look forward to adding her to my collection. I want to feel her soul as it winds its way toward immortality.

That might turn out to be my lone victory.

Vartan—who knows these things—also tells me that Tyson Station might not have walls, fences, or cell blocks, but that we're as incarcerated here as we were on Deck Three. He told me that privately, just before retiring for bed. I suspect he's with Svetlana tonight. They seem to favor each other.

I find myself somewhat jealous.

Instead of wrapping myself in a woman's arms and celebrating the act of procreation, I sit here, alone, and in fear.

What can the universe's purpose be? What are we supposed to learn here? Am I too stupid to figure it out? Am I so blind with my three eyes that I cannot see?

The universe might not make mistakes.

But humans do.

36

As the supper crowd chattered on with raucous volume, the sound echoed off Inga's high dome. To Miguel Galluzzi's mind, it almost gave the place that hollow echo he'd heard in great cathedrals back on Earth. Above it all, the occasional bang of thunder and the soft pattering of rain made a most remarkable backdrop.

Now he placed a hand to his overstuffed stomach and shot Shig Mosadek a sidelong appraisal where the small man perched on his bar stool, the untouched half-glass of wine before him. "Is it always this loud?"

"New people in town. This is the first time some of your crew members have been here. We're a curious bunch. And visitors, especially after three years, are a novelty. Not to mention the, shall we say, unique events you've survived getting here. Makes you and your people the center of attention."

Galluzzi stared into his glass of beer. Fought the urge to belch. How long since he'd had a full belly? Let alone the enjoyment of tastes so long forgotten? He had forced himself to eat slowly, drink with moderation, and savor each bite. After what ration had become on *Ashanti*, he'd have sold his soul to the devil if it meant gustatory satisfaction the likes of which poured with such little fanfare from Inga's kitchen.

Except that Satan already owns my soul.

"That was a rather rapid transition from a look of bliss to one of misery," the observant Shig noted.

"You are a scholar of comparative religion?"

"I am."

"Do you believe in damnation? In a form of higher justice? That we are condemned to be judged for our actions?"

Shig's dark eyes fixed on his. "I do. But not in the way that concerns you at the moment. Parsing religious philosophies down to the grossest of blunt fundamentals, the Eastern traditions assume that existence is a struggle to rise out of the chaos of creation to attain the sublime state of nirvana. The essence of the Western traditions is that divine good and evil are in conflict, and the goal is to act in the service of good in such a manner whereby the soul is granted salvation.

"Your, torment, Captain, is whether your decision to save your ship and crew came at the expense of your humanity and soul."

Galluzzi rolled his glass of beer on its base. "I thought by scouring out Deck Three, it would make it easier. I wish there was a way to scour the soul."

"The Western faiths provide the penitent with paths to forgiveness, some as easy as simply declaring yourself to be a believer. In a single stroke—or a dunking—your sins are washed away. All is forgiven. In other traditions, it's a little more difficult."

"That sounds remarkably like a cheat."

Shig chuckled to himself. Smiled. "Indulge me in a little experiment. A mind game. Looking back with the God-like clarity of hindsight, let's put the 'you' of today—knowing what you do now—back in that place. In that terrible moment of decision, what would you change? What would you decide differently?"

"I don't know, Shig. I chose my ship and crew, and in the process, condemned three hundred and forty-two people to starvation, murder, and madness. That was a crime against humanity. Those people were under my care, my responsibility. Given what they suffered? Well, someone has to pay."

"Thought you'd be arrested upon arrival, didn't you say?"

Galluzzi's right hand began to twitch. "And here I sit, with a full stomach and a tasty beer. Where's the justice in that? I feel . . . disgusted with myself."

"You haven't answered my question: With the benefit of hindsight, what would you do differently?"

"That question tortures me every night. Lurks down under my every waking moment. Those were innocent, good, and amiable men, women, and children. They were decent human beings guilty of nothing. They were deserving of the best."

"Having thought it all through, you still can't find a better solution than the one you made?"

He shook his head, a leaden emptiness in his gut. "If there is justice, why am I still alive and so many of those good people dead? I turned the ones who survived into monsters. And in the process, became one myself. God, karma, the universe, even the quanta should see me blasted and burned for eternity."

He tried to keep his voice from breaking. Damn it. He jammed his spastic right hand behind his belt.

Before Shig could reply, he said, "But if I'm not to be held responsible? If the Supervisor isn't going to arrest me, try me, punish me? There's part of me that urges me to walk down to the shuttle deck, key in the override, and cycle the lock. Let it blow my body out into vacuum." Galluzzi smiled wistfully. "I find a certain solace in the notion that for the rest of eternity, my body will tumble through the frozen and empty black. Staring sightlessly, limbs fixed, the moment of horror caught forever on my face. That out there, like that, I can finally atone."

Shig sat for a moment, head cocked, frown lines deepening on his forehead. "Tomorrow morning, will you take a ride with me? There's something I want to show you."

Galluzzi snorted his displeasure with himself. "What have I got to lose?"

37

Out on the aircar field, Talina Perez walked up and slapped a hand against the hull of Kalico's heavy airtruck. The vehicle had been unloaded from *Ashanti*'s hold the day before. Had spent all night with its powerpack on charge from Port Authority's grid.

Kalico had been living the high life back in Transluna when the last airtruck on Donovan had failed, stranding its cargo and passengers atop a ridge out in the Blood Mountains. The hull, stripped of anything useful, still sat there as a lonely beacon of dying dreams.

"You really think this is a good idea?" Talina asked, squinting in Capella's reflected light where it beamed off the polished duraplast bodywork.

Kalico turned as a wagon was trundled up to the tailgate and Terry Miska began handing crates of produce up to his wife Sasha. They'd had a bumper crop of okra and broccoli. Not to mention that they'd managed a good harvest from the wheat and rye crop. All staples that didn't grow at Tyson Station.

"They're still technically Corporate," Kalico told her. "Legally, they remain my responsibility." She indicated the containers of wheat being loaded into the back of the airtruck. "After the food offering they gave us last time, maybe this will soften the blow. No telling how they're going to react when I tell them that their prophets are victims of dementia."

"Why don't you wait? Give it a couple of days. At least until I get back. Then I'll go along."

"I'll be fine. They didn't even raise a finger last time Talbot was out there. If we have to eat another meal of Tyson green beans, I'm going to puke. Privates Carson and Muldare will be backup. They'll handle security."

"They going along in combat armor? With tech?"

"Thought about it. But after Talbot's last trip, I think the

Unreconciled have figured out how much they need us. Besides, I can handle it." She tapped the butt of the pistol on her hip. "Compared to mobbers, *Freelander*, and Tam Benteen, what are some whacked-out cannibals?"

"It's a cult."

"They're unarmed. Mostly malnourished women and children. It's just a hop out to drop off a load of food and to let them know what we discovered about the prophets. Give them a heads up that the people susceptible to kuru, the ones who are infected? Well, there's nothing we can do for them."

"So, why can't you do that with Carson and Muldare wearing armor?"

"Like that woman, Svetlana, told Talbot: Someone has to start treating them like human beings. By now it's sinking in that they're really going to make it, and they have to be asking questions: What's the future? How are we going to be treated? Are we abandoned out here? Cut off like pariahs? Are we condemned to be monsters?"

"Uh, yeah."

"Oh, come on, Tal. You, of all people, should know what it's like when everyone is looking at you like you're some sort of freak. Or have you forgotten why you ran off to Rork Springs?"

"My point is that they're not going to break down and sob over the future if your marines are in armor."

"Maybe, but it's a symbol that they're not trusted."

"Damn straight."

"If they were going to cause trouble, they'd have tried something with Talbot."

"So why you taking this?" Talina thumbed the side of the airtruck. "I'd be a hell of a lot happier if you rode out there in the shuttle."

"The A-7's up in orbit for repairs. Makarov's got the *Ashanti* shuttle techs doing a refit. Hell, we were only about four hundred hours overdue for maintenance on that bird. It'll be about a week, and she'll be back to as close to pristine as we can get without a space dock. This has the battery capacity to fly me out and back without a recharge."

"So you're placing your faith in an untested airtruck to meet with a bunch of cannibals, tell them their holy men are demented, and your marines aren't wearing armor when you do it."

"You make it sound insane."

"No shit."

At that junction Mark Talbot—pack and rifle slung over his shoulder—rounded the airtruck; his wife, Dya Simonov walked at his side. "We ready?"

Talina called, "Dya, tell me you're not part of this insanity."

"Hey, Tal. I'm the biologist and geneticist tagging along to answer any technical questions about the prion. Besides, they radioed in that they've got a couple of sick kids. I'm going to take a look at them. Decide if we need to bring them back to Raya for treatment."

"And where are you headed to?" Kalico asked, obviously happy to change the direction of the conversation.

"Taking Taglioni out to the Briggs' place. He wants to meet Wild Ones."

"And you call me crazy? You know what'll happen to you if that guy gets so much as a scratch? Let alone parasitized by a slug? Or worse, eaten?"

Talina arched a suggestive eyebrow. "The terrible Taglionis don't worry me."

"Well, they should." Kalico gave her a humorless grin. "I was in bed with Miko. Literally. When I got here, discovered *Ashanti* was missing and Derek with it, I breathed a huge sigh of relief."

"He may not be such a bad guy," Talina said.

"The scum-sucker I met a couple of times back on Transluna? A real piece of work. Maybe he's changed. Maybe, down under all that Taglioni cunning, he hasn't. He's a quetzal, Tal. And you think I'm crazy?" Kalico turned. "Come on, folks. Let's saddle up, as they say. Carson? Muldare? You aboard?"

"Here, Supervisor!" Carson's dark face appeared in the doorway.

A slam from the rear tailgate was accompanied by Terry Miska's call, "You're loaded, Supervisor. Thanks for the business."

Kalico put a foot in the step and swung up to the cab. "See you when I get back."

"Hey," Talina slapped the airtruck again. "This thing starts giving you trouble, remember, the Briggs homestead is your closest refuge. If you're down on charge, don't even think of flying it all the way back here."

"Got it." Kalico took a place in the front where she could see.

As she waved at Tal, she reassured herself. It would just be out and back.

38

Beyond the shuttle view ports, Donovan's sky darkened above the curved haze of atmosphere. Capella hung low over the eastern horizon as the shuttle arched its way into the indigo reaches that gave way to star-frosted space.

Miguel Galluzzi glanced to the side where Shig sat at the window seat, his eyes wide, rapt at the sight as the planet seemed to drop away below them.

"I'd think you'd never spaced before," Galluzzi noted.

"It remains a miracle, you know." Shig's voice was filled with awe. "This experience should never be commonplace. Should never be taken for granted."

"It's just a shuttle ride."

"Is it?" Shig turned thoughtful eyes his way. "Think, Captain. For at least a couple of million years as human imagination evolved on Earth, endless generations of proto-humans and then humans dreamed of the ability to defy the bonds of gravity, first to fly, and then to tread among the stars. What we do today is magical, and I revel in it. Not just for myself, but for all those millions upon millions of dreamers who lived out their lives craving."

"Never thought of it that way."

"No. But then my hope for today is to open your mind. To expose you to a broader understanding. I want you to learn to see from outside yourself."

"My eyes only see from one direction."

"And that, my friend, is the root of the problem."

Galluzzi laughed. But then, that was the thing about Shig. The little brown man said the most confusing things with such absolute surety.

And now, here he was. Headed, who knew where? *Ashanti,*

Vixen, perhaps some view of Donovan from orbit? It seemed a bit extravagant. But Shig had been insistent.

The light patter of rain on the dome had brought Miguel Galluzzi awake at dawn. He had been lying on his side, in his underwear, on a much-too-hard mattress. A moment of terror had seized him. Gray light was pouring in a small square window to illuminate a desk, bookshelves filled with old-fashioned books, a small but neat room.

Where the hell am I?

He had sat up in panic, having no clue as to why he wasn't in his cabin, surrounded by his . . .

Another patter of rain sounded on the dome roof.

The dome roof . . .

Donovan. You're on Donovan.

It all had come rushing back to him. An evening of drinking and eating with Shig Mosadek. Well, he'd drank. Shig, somehow, had managed to make a half-glass of red wine last him the entire night.

Shig had tapped on the door as Galluzzi was dressing. With two pails containing breakfast, the short scholar had led Galluzzi out through the misty rain, through the fence to the PA shuttle where the pilot was already spooling up the thrusters.

Throughout the liftoff, Shig had resolutely refused to declare their destination.

If anything, the mystery deepened as the shuttle climbed higher into orbit.

"Coming up," the pilot, a man dressed in quetzal hide and named Bateman, declared.

"From the off side, if you don't mind," Shig added. "I'd like the captain here to get the full effect of our arrival without bias."

"Shig," Bateman announced, "sometimes you don't make any sense."

"If sense could be made," Shig riposted amiably, "they'd sell it by the gallon bucket, and at a premium."

Galluzzi, from long experience, felt the shift in attitude, estimated that Bateman was making a 1.2 g burn to change delta-*v*.

Then came careful maneuvering, the starfield wheeling beyond the shuttle's windows.

It came as a surprise as the sialon walls of a shuttle bay appeared outside, and Bateman neatly dropped them onto grapples. The resulting thunks could be felt through the deck.

"Hard dock," Bateman announced. "Powering the hatch, and . . . yes, we have hard seal."

"*Vixen,*" Galluzzi declared. If it had been *Ashanti,* the ship would have announced itself, asked to bring the shuttle in. Odd, however, that Captain Torgussen didn't have the same protocol for his ship.

Shig unbuckled, stood, and extended a hand. "After you, Captain."

Galluzzi noticed that the short scholar had picked up a pack, was slinging it over his shoulder. "So, Shig, you think a little heart-to-heart with Torgussen's going to make me see myself from the outside? As I understand it, it was his crew who voted to stay here. *Vixen*'s circumstances are entirely different from *Ashanti*'s."

"They are indeed." Shig paused long enough to cycle the hatch. As the sialon door slid to the side, he said, "Be my guest."

Galluzzi strode forward, relieved at the feel of angular acceleration as compared to gravity. He walked right into . . .

What the hell?

The room was poorly lit by a couple of flickering overhead panels. To one side, rows of chairs stood in the gloom. Trash, not to mention marks on the floor, gave the place an abandoned look.

And then there was the air! What was it? A musty and thick odor. Something that smacked of an ancient tomb.

And then he felt the first . . . What the hell did he call it? A smearing of reality, as if time and normalcy wavered? Whatever it was, for an instant the effect was as if he'd viewed the room from underwater. Felt himself shifted sideways through time and space.

The hair on his head lifted, gooseflesh rising on his arms, and a shiver twisted its way down his back.

"Where the hell . . . ?"

"Welcome to *Freelander,*" Shig said softly. "Come. I have something to show you."

Galluzzi—a quiver of fear like a sprite in his guts—stood rooted as Shig walked past, paused at the dark corridor beyond, and looked back. "Come, Captain. I know you're frightened. To date, however, none of the ghosts have proved malicious to the living. Though they are hard to ignore."

"Ghosts? You talk about them like . . ." Galluzzi winced, owl-eyed enough to believe in ghosts for once.

"Yes. I do," Shig told him amiably. "Do come."

It took all of Galluzzi's will not to turn and dash full out for the shuttle's lock.

Instead, throat stuck, nerves electric, he forced himself to follow the short scholar into the corridor, the way illuminated only by Shig's handheld light.

And then something reached out from the blackness and touched the back of Galluzzi's neck.

39

The comparison was hard to avoid. The last time Talina had flown this route with soft meat it had been with Cap Taggart sitting in the passenger's seat. That time, as this, she'd been headed to Briggs' place. Then it had been to ensure that Madison was transported to town. This time it was to allow Dek Taglioni the opportunity to visit one-on-one with Wild Ones.

And why the hell was she risking her butt flying a privileged member of the aristocracy anywhere?

Because Shig had asked her to.

Sure. And quetzals could fly.

At the thought, Demon shifted in her stomach. Other quetzal images played in the back of her mind. Scenes from Kylee's childhood with Rocket, the little quetzal and Kylee playing fetch with a knotted rag. For an instant she was Rocket, feeling the joy as he charged out, his third eye keeping track of the tumbling knot of rag, air rushing through his . . .

She blinked it away.

Pay attention, or you're going to get yourself killed.

She was entering Mainway Canyon. This was the easiest route through the towering Wind Mountains. A gigantic crack in the high range, Mainway Canyon's massive vertical walls of faulted stone rose to either side. Metals gleamed where veins crisscrossed the black, green, and red-brown rock. Overhead, the canyon rim made a silhouette a couple hundred meters up. And beyond it, snow-capped and soaring peaks shot up into the sky.

"Now that's stunning," Dek said, rising from his seat to stare in awe at the bent and folded geology. Not only were the colors vivid where the strata were exposed, but the sheer walls, the deep and ink-black depths of the canyon, were some of the most awe-inspiring on the planet.

She kept a careful hand on the wheel as the always-vicious winds batted them back and forth. If there was any good news, it was that no sign of airtruck wreckage was visible splattered on the walls, so Kalico's vehicle hopefully made the passage without incident.

When they crested the summit of Best Pass, they hit the winds head on. Bucked up and down. Talina fought the controls. Dek went pale, grabbing the support bar for all he was worth. Then they were through. Tal gave her geological lecture as they crossed the exposed deep-crustal rock, then skimmed over the two-billion-year-old ocean bottom.

As they picked up the head of the Grand River, it hit her that unlike Cap, Dek Taglioni sat listening intently, his questions short and to the point. His eyes might be alight, but they gave off the intensity of a student trying to absorb all he could. As if his life depended upon it.

On Donovan that was never just an academic concern.

"See that distant knob? Closest to the right on the southern horizon? That was our refuge when Cap and I went down in the forest . . . just about . . . there." She pointed to the approximate spot in the dense tangle of trees.

"Once you were down, how did you orient yourself?"

She pointed to her wrist unit. "Compass. The trick, as I'm sure you've heard, is to keep moving. In deep forest like this, if you stop, the roots will get you. My task was to get us to that knob. On Donovan, roots can't penetrate rock. Not enough to grab onto if another tree wants to topple them."

"The trees topple each other? Why?"

"We're not sure yet. Might be that they're some form of sentient life we haven't figured out. Maybe it's just instinct. Iji wonders if perhaps a tree gets sick, and the surrounding trees uproot it, cast it down as a means of keeping the illness from spreading. On the other hand, maybe it's like children on a playground: One just pisses the others off."

She expected some snide reply. Instead, he nodded as if storing that tidbit. Then asked, "And if there's no bedrock around?"

"Climb. Lower branches are the best. You can sleep in the axial joint where the flat on the triangular branch juts out from the trunk. Nine times out of ten nothing will show up to eat you."

"And that tenth time?"

"Welcome to Donovan."

"So, tell me about this nightmare I've been hearing about? Are they around here?"

"We've never found one this far north. Or in any kind of tree except a mundo. Nightmares live up in the branches. Dangle wispy looking tentacles down to ensnare their prey. You'll know a mundo tree by the big leaves. And I mean big, like a blanket."

"So nightmares don't prowl?"

"Seem to be solitary and sedentary. What this country is, however, is mobber territory. We see a flight of them headed our way, we run for it. They top out at a little over a hundred kph, and can't hold that for long."

"And who was the lucky bastard who found that out?"

She gave him a wink. "You're looking at her. Kylee and me. Outran a flock of the nasty shits back down at Mundo Base."

"Then I guess I couldn't have a better guide."

"Yeah, you could. Kylee for one. Mark Talbot. Tip Briggs. Listen, I'm going to introduce you to Kylee and Tip. Doesn't matter that they're little more than children. If you've got a lick of sense, you'll listen to every word they say. Those kids have been living in the wild since they were born. And they're still alive. You follow what I'm saying?"

"I do. And just in case I haven't said it enough, thank you."

"Just hope I'm not making a mistake." She shot him a look. "You know, I'm crazy for taking a Taglioni out into the bush. Something goes wrong? Eventually I'm going to end up in a pile of shit."

He chuckled, eyes fixed on the vastness of forest as they followed the Grand River west. "If I could have any wish, it would be that I could ditch the name. Just be Dek Smith. Or Dek Garcia. Being a Taglioni's a pain in the ass."

"You're kind of a puzzle."

"So are you, which makes us even."

She ignored his riposte, saying, "Okay, so you're a rich guy.

Corporate royalty who wants to be like the common everyday kind of Joe. Wants to turn himself into just another nameless cog in the giant wheels of life. Happens every day. Why should I be surprised?"

"Let's just say I'm here to find myself, and you're free to attribute the reasons behind the quest to a peculiar idiosyncrasy on my part."

"That's nebulous enough. How am I a puzzle?"

"You're the most capable and competent woman on Donovan. A third of the Port Authority triumvirate. Head of Security and the living legend who wants to be rid of her quetzals. Given the advantage that gives you on this planet, why would you want to be rid of such an asset?"

She uttered a bitter laugh. "It's like having strangers inside my head. I get images from the past. Unrelated memories of quetzals long dead. Visions of times and creatures I can't comprehend. Understanding of things I don't have a conceptual framework for. Screws with my sleep. And there's times they butt in at just the wrong moment."

"My point, exactly. There, see? Now we understand each other."

She wheeled the aircar, turning north to follow the Briggs River where it cut down through the basalt, remembering the overland trip she and Cap had made. Ahead, broken hills beckoned where an upthrust fault had exposed metamorphic rock rich in metals. And atop the cliff next to the waterfall where the Briggs River thundered down into its chasm, Chaco and Madison Briggs had established their claim and farmstead.

Talina took a turn around the place and settled the aircar on the farmstead flat just back from the canyon's edge. The landing pad was on open ground next to the utility shed with its plug in. The garden looked lush where it stretched to the south, tall corn, beans, peppers, heads of cabbage and tangles of squash vines all mixed together. A trellis supported flowering hops vines. The wheat and barley were turning amber, almost ready for harvest.

"Welcome to the bush," Talina told Dek as the fans spooled down. She picked up the handset for the radio, keying the mic. "Two Spot? This is Talina. Made it to Briggs' safe and sound."

"Roger that, Tal. Be careful out there."

"Any word from Kalico?"

"Roger that. She set down at Tyson an hour ago."

"Let me know if you hear from her."

"Roger that. Give Chaco my regards. Tell him I haven't forgotten I owe him that twenty."

"You got it."

Talina pulled her rifle from the rack on the dash and grabbed the pack she'd laid in the rear. Taglioni lifted his war bag and gun case, then followed her over the rail. She paused only long enough to plug the aircar into the Briggs' grid to recharge.

The Briggs farmstead consisted of a collection of drying and storing sheds, the workshop, and the solar collection array. A radio mast rose above the workshop roof to provide their link to the outside world.

Chaco, an oily rag in hand, emerged from the shop, a wide grin on his face. He was third ship, had grown up on Donovan. Now edging forty, his broad face was tanned to a perpetual brown. Sandy hair hung down to his collar and contrasted with the gleaming black beard. The man wore chamois and quetzal, with a fabric shirt from town hanging on his muscular torso.

"Hey, Tal! Always glad when you make it here on the first try."

"How you doing, Chaco?"

He lifted the oil-blackened rag. "Rebuilding the bearings in the main pump. We'd be fart-sucking up the creek if ol' Tyrell Lawson hadn't found some salvage bearings the right size. Just got the thing back together."

He walked over, offering an oil-stained hand. "Chaco Briggs. Glad to meet you."

"Dek Taglioni."

They shook like equals, and to Talina's surprise, Taglioni didn't immediately wipe his hand. Didn't even so much as glance at the smudges left on his skin.

"Madison's got crest and cabbage cooking." Chaco glanced her way. "You eaten yet?"

"Not since chili this morning. Brought your shopping list. Got everything except the pipe-elbow-thing. It's all in the crate on the back seat."

Chaco was giving her his infectious grin. "Think I fixed the pipe-elbow-thing. Made a mold and cast it out of gold. It's not like we don't have gold running out of our ears around here, and it's a soft metal. Squishes under pressure, so it makes its own seal. Don't need a gasket. And being soft, it takes vibration well. It's only a day since I put it in, but we've got water back to the house."

Taglioni had been listening intently. "Gold melts at over a thousand degrees centigrade. How do you get it that hot?"

"Used to be tougher to do. Chabacho doesn't burn as hot as hardwood on Earth. Lot easier now that Ollie Throlson's got those wells producing hydrocarbons. As it is, I had to trade the guy ten chamois hides for the cylinder of gas."

"I love it," Taglioni said with genuine amusement.

Tal added, "Two Spot says he owes you twenty."

"Yeah, I made him a knife. Used quetzal bone for the scales in the handle. Did you know that when it's buffed right, quetzal bone almost looks like mother-of-pearl?"

"And how do you know what mother-of-pearl looks like?" Tal asked.

"Madison has a brooch. Belonged to her mother back on Earth. Come on. Let's eat."

Tal followed Chaco to the stairs, descending the fifty feet to where the main house was built into a cavern in the side of the canyon.

"Wow," Taglioni drawled as he stopped at the railing, looking up the canyon to where the Briggs River plunged some two hundred meters in a magnificent waterfall. Layers of mist shimmered in rainbow streamers. Here the canyon was narrow, not more than one hundred meters across. Sunlight sparkled in the mica, quartz, and veins of metal exposed in the bent and faulted strata below the layer of basalt.

And in a dazzling display below them, the Briggs River tumbled over boulders and gravel banks as it roared its way south toward the Grand.

"Not bad, huh?" Talina asked, stopping to share the view.

"Back on Earth this would all be a Corporate-owned tourist attraction."

"Hey, Tal!" Madison Briggs called, stepping out on the deck to give her a hug. She stood tall and straight, just over six feet; her smooth dark skin had a satin tone. The high cheekbones and the unusual slant of her almond eyes made her one of the most beautiful women Tal had ever seen.

"And you must be Derek Taglioni," she greeted, taking Dek's hand. "Welcome. Come. We'll eat."

Madison had set a table just inside by the large window overlooking the falls.

Taglioni was seated—as the guest—with the best view. For a time the man sat motionless, staring out the window. Chaco noticed, grinned. That window was his pride and joy. Just getting it here had been a feat. Then it had to be carefully lowered by ropes from above before it could be framed and set.

"I understand," Taglioni said, as if from a distance.

"How's that?" Madison asked as she set a plate of steaming meat and cabbage on the colorful aquajade table.

"I see why you're here. Why you'll always be here. You have found what humanity has forgotten. You have made a dream."

Tal caught the look of shared communication between Chaco and Madison. Some sort of approval.

"There's worse places to be." Chaco dug into the food with a big serving spoon. Splashed some on Tal's plate. Then Taglioni's before he saw to Madison and himself.

"Where are the kids?" Talina asked.

"Tip, Kylee, and Flute are out checking on a rogue quetzal. Youngster, maybe ten or so. Probably just passing through, but if it's trouble for the local lineage, we want to know. They were going to try and make it back before you got here." Madison gave her that irritated-mother look. "As to Maria and Skip, girls who don't get their chores done don't get to enjoy company until all the laundry is folded."

"Tip is your son," Taglioni noted. "Kylee is Dya Simonov's, but who is Flute?"

"That's their quetzal," Chaco noted, an unaccustomed reserve in his eyes.

Taglioni took a bite. Closed his eyes. Chewed as if in bliss and finally swallowed. "What *is* this taste? I've never known such a . . . an interesting, mellow, what? How do I describe this?"

Tal tried hers. This wasn't just meat and cabbage. It had a sort of anise saffron mixed with . . . No, there was simply no Earthly comparison to the delicate taste.

Chaco looked triumphant. "Cool, huh? Made barrels from aquajade, then charred them on the inside, right? For Inga's whiskey. But that raised the question: What if we fermented cabbage in one of the barrels. Shazam! That's the taste."

"Inga will buy all you can produce."

"If I could sell this in Transluna," Taglioni declared, "we could all retire."

"I like this guy," Chaco said with a smile.

Taglioni gave him a companionly wink.

"So, what's the trouble with Flute?" Talina asked. "Something going on there?"

Chaco leaned forward on his elbows and used a napkin to clean the grease from under his fingernails. If Taglioni noticed, he didn't so much as blink. Another point for Taglioni.

"Tal, it's like they're a threesome. The good news is that we don't worry nearly so much about the wildlife. Haven't seen a skewer, a bem, or a sidewinder around the shops for more than three years now. Makes it a lot safer for Maria and Skip. On the other hand, it's like the three of them are more of a family than we are."

Madison added, "Getting harder to get Kylee and Tip to make it through their lessons. And it's weird, they seem to share thoughts. Like telepathy."

"Molecules," Tal said, knowing intuitively. "TriNA reads our memories through transferRNA. Encodes them. Then, when the molecule is handed off to another person, it uses tRNA to code the memory to another brain. I have flashes from Kylee's youth all the time. Memories of her and Rocket and Mundo Base. All from when we shared molecules."

"Worries me about what else they might be sharing out there," Chaco muttered. "You know what starts to happen between boys and girls when they turn thirteen?"

"Sometimes it's funny to call them children," Madison said. "They're a lot more mature than I was when I was thirteen. Kylee in particular. Sometimes I think I'm talking to a grown woman."

Talina gestured with her fork. "Kid's had the crap kicked out of her by life. Don't know what would have happened if you hadn't taken her in."

"Got her language mostly straightened out. Took two years to keep her from cussing like a marine. Where'd she learn that foul mouth, anyway?"

Talina winced, made a face, and raised a guilty hand. "Uh, I was under duress at the same time she had the misfortune to think of me as a role model."

Taglioni, though wolfing food, and having gone back for more, was watching with rapt attention. Seemed to be hanging on every word. What was it about the guy? He might have been studying for his comps.

"She still hate people?" Talina asked.

"Not as badly. I think it helps that Dya and Talbot fly out every couple of weeks. I don't know what to think of her. She's different. But so is Tip." Madison took another helping.

"So, Dek," Chaco turned his attention. "Heard you had a pretty rough transit from Solar System."

"Some damn fool once said that wisdom comes through adversity. Looking back on it, now that I'm so wise, I'd have been a whole lot happier to have remained arrogant, dumb, and unenlightened."

"Taglionis," Madison noted. "As I remember they were pretty high up in The Corporation."

"Yeah," Dek agreed. "Most of the time when I went to family gatherings, we had to be on oxygen."

"So what brings you to us?" Chaco asked.

"I guess I'm like a pilgrim from the old stories: a man in search of some illumination or understanding. The part of me that I lost on the way here? I need to replace it with something else."

"You any good with tools?" Chaco asked. "Want to help me put that pump I just fixed back in the water system?"

Slugs in the mud! Chaco had just asked a fricking Taglioni to . . .

Instead of the rude response or explosion Talina expected, the man said, "Sure. Be my pleasure."

Well, what the hell other surprises lurked inside that unassuming shell?

40

It hit him like an explosion. The scintillating pleasure shot through Dan Wirth's pelvis, up his backbone, and tingled the bottoms of his feet. He gasped, crying out as Allison's practiced muscles tightened and she rocked her hips. Rode his orgasm for every delicious instant of it.

Panting, Wirth rolled off of her, leaving his arm to drape over Allison's chest. "Wow," he rasped as the tingle faded. He blinked up at the ceiling. He'd had Hofer's best man hand-plaster the bedroom. Like Allison, there was nothing to match it on the entire planet.

"No complaints?" Allison asked, reaching for a cloth to mop up.

"You do that for all of the marks?"

"Of course. But you're the only one that gets it on demand and for free."

"Lucky me, eh?"

She was watching him with those calculating eyes. He missed the old Allison. The innocent one with the wounded-bird expression and hesitant, almost desperate approach toward life.

"You've been preoccupied." She tossed the cloth to the side.

"What's your take on Taglioni?"

"Not sure. He's different. I've given him the eye, he just nods. Has that strange smile like he knows and understands, is actually appreciative, but not interested."

"Think he's into men?"

"No. Definitely heterosexual, just not into a casual fuck." She shifted. "You remember, don't you, that we promised Aguila we wouldn't take him down."

"He says he can fix it. Make it so that I can go back. Live like a fucking Boardmember and lord it among all those high and mighty cocksucking assholes in Transluna. The slate wiped clean. A whole new life for Dan Wirth."

He waggled a cautionary finger. "All for ten percent and expenses. You know, the unsavory bribes for the Board and the rest of the ass-fucking bureaucrats. Now, why do I smell a quetzal in the bushes? What's wrong with this picture?"

"He say why he'd do it?"

"As a fuck-you to his cousin who's on the Board. And I'm supposed to believe that?"

Allison raised a pale shoulder in a shrug. "What else did he say?"

"That he's staying here. That he's not going back. And I'm supposed to believe that a child of that kind of wealth and privilege just lets it all go?"

"Depends on what happened on *Ashanti.* From the crew I heard that he scrubbed toilets. Lived with them, worked with them, no job too tough. Their story is that he changed when they all thought they were going to die. Maybe he doesn't want to chance that again. Aguila didn't. Not after *Freelander* showed up."

"So I trust the fancy prick?"

Allison reached out, turned his head to face hers. "You've been getting moody. You've got an anger building inside. Then, after you talked to Taglioni, you've been more like the old Dan. Like you're plotting and planning again. So tell me. The truth. What do you want?"

"I'm the richest man on the fucking planet."

"You are."

"I had to trade a bedroom addition for a toilet-sucking scarf. Those two safes. They're bursting. That's real wealth. Not on paper, or a line of credit. The triumvirate or Aguila need something, they come to me. I own half of this miserable planet. So, what's the point?"

She considered, the ghost of a smile molding her lips. "Wondered if that wasn't the trouble."

"Hmm?"

"He dangled the carrot, and you can't help but bite at it, hoping it's for real." A beat. "Might be. If it is, you'd go back?"

"To play in the big game? Baby cakes, I'd go in a second."

"So, he's offered you the chance to go back on *Ashanti*? Is that the fool's play? Or is it the lucky draw? How do you tell if it's real, or a sucker's bet on red twenty-two?"

"Oh, I don't trust the fucker for an instant. I think he's playing me. Wants to use my wealth to bitch-slap that cousin of his. Now, knowing that, am I smart enough to sidestep the landmines before they blow my fucking foot off?"

"Are you?"

He made a face. "See, that's the gamble. Those Corporate cocksuckers play a rigged game. But tell me, who knows more about rigged games than me, huh?"

"You got any insurance that good old Dek won't have you arrested the moment you step off *Ashanti*? Then he gets all the plunder, and you're fucked."

"Oh, angel, you have no idea how that very thought rolls around inside my head. But, no. Sometimes you've got to go with instincts. Rather than making a fast fortune, I think he's playing a long game. Wants to use me as a pawn on the Corporate chessboard."

"Pawns get sacrificed."

"Uh-huh. And if they make it all the way across the board, they get turned into queens who can really kick ass."

She shifted, stared at him with an uncommon intensity. "You're seriously thinking about going, aren't you? Even knowing the risks."

He smiled, slapped a hand to her toned stomach. "What about you? Want to go with me?"

"Not for the time being."

"Oh?"

"Like you, I'm willing to play the long game." A pause. "What happens with The Jewel? This house? Your interests here?"

He gave her his coldest, threatening look. "You asked for forty-nine percent once. I'll give you half of everything. Anything you establish from here on out, that's yours. But don't fuck with my half."

"What about the house here?"

"Yours. But in return, you fucking damn well better be sending plunder back in my name. You see, Dek's right about one thing: If

Ashanti makes it back to Solar System, they *will* be sending more ships. If my share of the plunder isn't on board, I'll still be rich enough to hire some nasty shit-sucker to pay you a visit."

"I'm smarter than that."

"Yeah. I think you are. You got the balls to do what has to be done?"

She gave him a taunting smile. "Only one possible problem."

"What's that?"

"Your good Mister Taglioni? He's out in the bush at the Briggs place. Odds are better than forty to one the silly son of a bitch is going to get himself killed before he can do either one of us any good."

TRAP

I live in a state of confusion that I cannot confide to anyone. To do so would be a sign of weakness. If there is anything the Irredenta do not need at this point, it's even the suggestion that I am not in complete control. That I doubt—in any way—the Will of the universe.

That's on the surface. The façade I present. The persona that I adopt.

Inside, I wish I could drop to my knees, raise my hands and implore the universe: Did I not sacrifice everything for you? I murdered my fellows, ate their flesh and organs in an act of holy sacrament. I committed myself, without reservation, to your Truths. I followed, without question, the wisdom of the Prophets. Endured the hideous agony of scarification as I sliced my skin and repeated the process time after time. Used a cleaver to amputate the soft flesh of my nose. Made my body a repository for the dead and destroyed relationships to ensure the dead I harbored would be reborn in the next available female.

How is my faith and sacrifice repaid?

Fatima continues to suffer. Three more people are missing, two of them children.

And still another child, young Pho, is dead. This time, we know what happened. Manram saw the plant reach down, wind itself around the screaming child. The little boy was lifted off the ground and the plant began eating him. Manram ran forward, tried to pull little Pho away, and was grabbed up herself. She barely managed to tear free; large chunks of her arms, the flesh of her hands, a large patch of her shoulder are missing.

Another, Renzo Demopolis, age six, was found at the edge of the escarpment. He was in convulsions. Something blue staining his mouth. He's now laid out in the cafeteria in hopes the Prophets will, through some utterance, tell us how to cure the boy.

The impact is devastating. The children are the reborn souls of the dead. Purified. The universe promised they'd be immortal. That the Irredenta were the way—the vehicle through which all of humanity, the universe itself, would be purified.

I am achingly, painfully, aware that each of these children who dies at the hands of Donovan will be lost. For them, death is once again eternal and absolute. Renzo and the slug-infested Fatima, we can save. We can consume their remains again and insure their eventual reincarnation.

At least, I hope so.

I need the Prophets! I need their counsel. But to my absolute frustration, Irdan is mute this morning. Won't eat. His breathing is shallow, his limbs barely twitch. Callista and Guan Shi are mumbling so softly I can't hear, seem to be fading just as fast. I really look at them now, realize how wasted their bodies are. Living skeletons draped with sallow and loose skin. Their eyes have sunken so deeply into the sockets, they remind me of those Mexican Day of the Dead masks.

And what happens when they die?

With people bustling around the cafeteria, I dare not show despair. I cannot drop my head in my hands.

Cannot weep.

I am the Messiah.

I am contemplating the uncomfortable realization that I am the loneliest man alive when Shyanne Veda hurries in from the hallway, stops before me, and bows.

"Messiah," she says, avoiding my eyes. "There's a call on the radio. Supervisor Aguila is flying in. Says they're bringing provisions and want to give us some information. Should I answer?"

I give this consideration.

Is this the universe coming to my aid? And so much faster than Petre, the Chosen, and Vartan had anticipated?

That old and innate sense of opportunity fills me. "Tell the Supervisor we are delighted to accommodate her." Raising my voice, I call, "Someone! Find Petre! Call the Chosen. The Corporation is coming! You know the plan. It's time to spring our trap."

And in that instant, relief pours through me like a cool and refreshing wave.

I chuckle like a gleeful child.

I finally understand.

Of course we're suffering. Once again, the universe is teaching us a lesson: Just because we're in a new place doesn't mean we forget the holy Truths.

In this case, the Truth is that there is no progress without sacrifice, pain, and purification.

We need a new sacrament, and Kalico Aguila shall be our first. But we must play it perfectly. Petre and Svetlana have worked this out, planned every aspect of how to lure Aguila and her people to the right place. As The Corporation is the epitome of deceit, we must be even more cunning. As long as they are not wearing armor, if we play this correctly, it will make no difference.

41

Donovan's immense and endless forest gave way to the escarpment upon which Tyson Station perched. The day had gone from uncomfortably warm to downright hot. Kalico shifted her quetzal-leather hat where it hung down her back, the strap tight at her throat. Anything to get a little air. She wished she'd worn something lighter.

She stood beside Mark Talbot as the ex-marine kept the airtruck skimming a good two hundred meters above the highest treetops. Thickly packed forest stretched off to the irregular horizons—a lumpy mass composed of aquajade, various species of chabacho, stonewood, broadvine, and the curiously turquoise trees she'd never heard a name for.

And then, here and there, they would overfly an open spot, something she'd never seen except around Tyson. Usually it was a round hole in the forest, maybe a couple hundred meters in diameter and surrounded by towering trees. In the center, all alone, stood a most unique tree. Another uncatalogued species. This one a bright lime green with branches that ended in oversized round-shaped flat spatulate structures—could you really call them leaves? They reminded her of supersized ping pong paddles on flexible stems. The tall tree occupied the exact center of the opening; apparently the rest of the forest wouldn't dare to intrude. Given the way Donovanian forest jostled, shoved, fought and crowded, that made the plant, tree, or whatever it was, more than a little ominous.

Talbot pulled back on the wheel, and the airtruck climbed as it approached the dark basalt cliff upon which Tyson Station had been built. He crested the caprock and hovered while Kalico, Dya, and the two marines studied the research base. A couple of people were out, watching, hands to their brows to shade them as they squinted against Capella's bright rays.

"Try them again," Kalico said to Dya.

The woman lifted the mic, saying, "Tyson Base, this is the Supervisor. We're inbound with a load of provisions. We have issues we need to discuss. Please respond."

"We see you. You are free to park. Look forward to serving you."

"Serving us? Hope that isn't a cannibal joke." Private Muldare observed where she stared thoughtfully out at the five domes. They looked out of place—white and round as they were against the green, blue, and gray background. The sheds, made of chabacho wood, had more or less faded into the scenery as they weathered.

"Park? What is it with these people?" Kalico muttered under her breath. "All right, set us down in the landing field, Mark. But be ready to fly if they make a run for the airtruck. Carson, Muldare, be ready. Weapons on safety, but chambered."

She heard "yes ma'ams" all the way around.

Kalico braced a hand on the grabrail as Talbot swung the airtruck in a wide circle, settling onto the landing pad with the lightest of touches.

Kalico waited, counting the seconds. The people standing out before the domes just watched. A couple were talking back and forth, obviously about the airtruck's arrival. Nothing, however, indicated the slightest apprehension, not the least bit of concern. People didn't look off toward any of the sheds or other domes like they would if an armed party were hidden there and were expected to issue forth at any moment.

"Nothing," Talbot said through an exhale. "That's a relief."

"Very well," Kalico said. "Let's get those crates of food offloaded. Carson, Muldare, you're on guard so keep your eyes open."

Talbot lowered the tailgate, jumped down, and started offloading the crates that Dya and Kalico handed him.

Can you believe this? Kalico asked herself as she manhandled another crate to the tailgate. *I'm a pus-rotted Supervisor, working like a dockhand.*

Kalico muscled another of the heavy crates around. Imagine what Miko Taglioni would have said. Perhaps something like: "My, how the mighty have fallen."

It took them all of fifteen minutes to stack the crates off to one side. In that time, another three people appeared to watch the proceedings.

Finishing, Kalico wiped the sweat from her forehead and ordered, "Carson, you stay here. No one gets access to the airtruck."

"Yes, ma'am." Carson snapped a saluting hand to his brow.

"Why is my gut doing flip flops?" Dya asked as Kalico led the way toward the large dome that housed admin, the cafeteria, and the offices.

Kalico nodded to the watching people as she approached, asking, "Where's Batuhan? Um . . . the first and last? Your leader."

"In there," one of the young men told her, averting his eyes in the process of pointing toward the admin dome. Then he scuttled away, as if afraid he'd be tainted just by her presence.

"Something's happened," Talbot half growled. "Last time, it was all a happy parade."

"Wish we were in armor." Muldare tightened her grip on her rifle.

"On your toes, people," Kalico muttered, her hand on her pistol. She led the way, pushed open the double doors, and strode down the hallway. Glancing in doors as she passed, it was to see the rooms vacant. Arriving in the cafeteria, she recognized a couple of the throne-bearers huddled around a little boy who'd been laid on one of the tables in the rear.

One looked up and started before saying, "Oh, it's you. What are you doing here?"

"Don't you listen to your radio? We've brought a load of groceries, things that don't grow here. It's all stacked out on the landing pad. Where's your boss?"

"Our boss—as you say—is the universe."

"Batuhan. Where is he? We need to talk."

"Then, let us talk, Supervisor," Batuhan announced, stepping out from one of the side doors. The big weird blue eye painted on his forehead and the amputated nose were always disconcerting. He carried his human-thigh-bone scepter in his right hand. The man was dressed in a breechcloth; his skin—apparently unwashed—still showed evidence of the white stuff he'd been plastered with aboard *Ashanti*. He walked over to the throne, seated himself, and crossed his legs as he studied first Kalico, and then Dya, before shifting his gaze to Briah Muldare, who stood at attention. Talbot, he ignored.

"Nice," he murmured. "Three beautiful, strong, and healthy females of breeding age. Such a change. But then, as the fetus, upon exiting the womb, transitions from the umbilical to its first solid sustenance, so to do we metaphorically make the change during our own birth."

"Right," Kalico told him. "And you'd damn well better stick to your metaphors. We're not your acolytes. But tell me. What's with the scars? Why the mazes on your cheeks? What's that all about?"

He raised a finger to the corner of his mouth, flat black gaze on hers. The blue eye on his forehead sent a quiver through her. Seemed to look right through her. She noticed that his fingernail was long, stained black with something that looked like dirty axle grease.

"I am the way," he said. "The beginning and the end. Only through me will you find salvation. But the body and soul are different, a duality of existences. Upon a person's death, through the sacrament of consumption, the body begins its transition to purification."

"Yeah, I got that part," Kalico told him.

Dya was looking at the guy like he was her worst nightmare. Talbot was fingering his pistol. Muldare's expression hinted that Batuhan was the most disgusting human she'd ever seen.

Call it unanimous in Kalico's eyes. "You left five butchered skeletons on *Ashanti*. They do something to piss you off, or just have an unlucky day?"

"At the last moment, their faith wavered. Salvation depends upon unity of spirit."

"And they didn't live up to your expectations, huh? So, what's with the patterns of scars? How does cutting designs into living skin purify the soul?"

Batuhan adopted the same tone he would use when talking to a child. "When we consume the body, it follows the path past the lips, over the tongue, and down the throat. In the stomach it begins its assimilation, passing through the guts until finally only the profane—the summation of darkness, foul, and refused of salvation—is voided from the anus."

"No need to elaborate on that," Dya muttered.

Batuhan didn't even bat an eye. "The rest of the body, the pure portion, has begun its journey toward salvation. It is assimilated into our living flesh, made part of the whole. In the receptacle of my body, it lives on.

"But not being physical the soul releases itself from the flesh. It enters here"—he tapped the side of his mouth at the opening to the maze—"separating from the body at the time of consumption. Keep in mind that the soul is light, airy. Adrift without the flesh that once anchored it. Seeking any path, it enters the maze. A receptacle. A place into which the soul must lose itself. It must try this direction and that, slowly working out its way. Learning. Experiencing the twists and turns, feeling out the dead ends."

"Screw me in vacuum," Talbot whispered just loud enough for Kalico to hear.

Batuhan closed his eyes, leaned his head back. The big blue eye in the middle of his forehead stared mockingly as he played his long black fingernail through the various paths in the maze scarring his right cheek. The expression on the man's face was rapturous.

Dya looked sick. Muldare's face had gone pale.

Through a long exhale, Batuhan said, "Only when the soul has matured in the maze and found its way does it locate the exit." His black nail had wound through the twists and turns to the opening just in front of his ear. "From here it follows the path."

Batuhan's black nail traced the long line of scar tissue down the side of his neck, then forward to the suprasternal notch. From there the scar tissue split into three lines: the left into one pectoral spiral, the center ran straight down the man's belly, and the right into the right pectoral spiral.

Batuhan tapped fingers against his chest, saying, "The paths, one on the right, one on the left, lead to the spirals." The black fingernail traced the routes. "There, the souls that have not yet reached illumination are led in an ever-decreasing radius to the nipples. There they reside until a woman suckles them into her own body."

"Excuse me?" Dya snapped. "Did you say suckles?"

Batuhan fixed on her with dark and intense eyes. "Of course. In the same way a woman provides an infant with milk, I provide a supplicant woman with one of the souls that has lodged in my right or left nipple. She produces physical sustenance when an infant sucks from her breast. I produce a spiritual essence when she sucks from mine."

Kalico couldn't stop the shiver from running down her spine.

Fixed on Dya, Batuhan smiled. "I have the feeling that you are empty, a void that longs to be filled. Would you like to partake?" He shifted and offered his right breast in Dya's direction.

Kalico shot out a restraining hand as Talbot started forward.

"Not on your life," Dya managed through gritted teeth.

"And the center line?" Kalico asked, desperate to get off the subject of Batuhan's breasts.

"Ah, that is the route chosen by those souls that have achieved true purity." Batuhan shifted his dark-eyed gaze to hers. The black fingernail traced down the line of scar tissue to the separation around his navel, and then down under his breechcloth.

Kalico remembered the scars ending at the root of his penis. "Where, along with your semen, they can be deposited into a fertile female," she finished.

"Quite so." Again he leaned his head back, eyes closed, and took a deep breath. "I am the beginning and the end. I am the purification of the body and the soul's route to immortality."

"Then," Dya asked, "what's with the eye cut into your forehead?"

"It was a gift from the Prophets, who know the universe's will."

Kalico ground her teeth, feeling ill. Pus and ions, but she wanted to be shut of this place. Maybe nuke it from space. "Yeah, about your Prophets. We've got some information about them. Have you ever heard of prions? Or something called kuru? Spongiform encephalitis?"

"No."

"It's a protein disease, one communicable to people with a

homozygous recessive genetic predisposition. It's called kuru, though it hasn't been seen since the early twenty-first century. It comes from eating another human being's brain, spinal fluid, or infected—"

"Stop it! Of course you'd manufacture such foolishness. Not only do we have no desire to hear, but we anticipated your heresy. The universe told us in no uncertain terms that you would do anything in your power—corrupt and tainted as you are—to mislead us."

Dya said, "It's not misleading, don't you understand? Your prophets are going to die. Their brains are already riddled with lesions. And you have other people—"

"Enough!" he barked, straining upright. "You are the mouths of deceit. Lies incarnate sent to tempt the pure back into perdition. By your very declarations, you betray yourselves. And in the end, we will finally rid you of your pollution. You will come to understand." He paused. Smiled to himself. "Soon."

Yeah, right. But Kalico gestured for silence on Dya's part as the woman drew breath to object. Saw the almost pleading look the woman gave her.

Batuhan studied his scepter as if something fascinating were to be found in the intricate carvings. "I need you to tell me what's wrong with two children. And then I need you to leave. And when you do, I want you to never come back. Our people don't need your kind of duplicity."

Kalico fought to keep her expression under control.

"Is that one of the children?" Dya asked, indicating the boy on the back table.

"It is. The other is a little girl. We think something is inside her body, so we put her in a back room where, if the creatures get loose, we can contain them."

"What's with the boy?" Kalico asked, stepping close to the kid. She looked down to see a half-wasted little urchin, his skin puckered in patterns of scars. That they were already white indicated he couldn't have been more than three or four when the boy had been scarified.

"Don't know," the first man said. "Found him like this at the edge of the cliff."

Dya leaned over, squinted at the faint blue stain on his swollen lips. "He ate berries off one of the bluelinda vines. They're pretty, almost a crystal blue, and deadly." She sighed, stepped back. "If you could see inside his mouth, you'd discover it's already blistered. Blood vessels are breaking in his tongue, the back of his throat, clear into his brain. The same in his stomach, and as soon as the enzymes eat through, his liver and kidneys will be riddled."

"What's bluelinda?" the third man asked. "How do we know which of the native plants to keep the children away from?"

"Keep them away from *all of them*!" Dya almost shrilled. "What part of 'all the native plants are dangerous' don't you get?"

"Hey," Kalico said, "easy. Now, what's with this little girl?"

"She's in the back," the first man told her, his eyes a flat brown, as if no emotion remained there. "Something's wiggling in her leg. Like a moving knot."

"Want to bet it's a slug?" Talbot managed to say through gritted teeth.

"Take us," Dya snapped. "If it's a slug maybe we can still save her."

"Might cost her the leg," Mark noted as they followed the man toward the door in the rear. "Was she barefoot?"

"To be barefoot is a sign of humility." Their guide had a prim, superior tone in his voice.

Dya turned to where Batuhan still sat in his throne. She snapped out, "This is Donovan, do you get it? There is nothing, *nothing* on this planet that won't kill you. Now, round your people up, get them dressed, and keep the kids out of trouble."

Before following the man down the hall, Kalico turned one last time to Batuhan. "Did you hear what she said? Otherwise, you're not going to have any children, let alone people."

Dya was almost vibrating with rage as she stomped along behind their guide. "They just let children wander? Are they mad?"

"Just ignorant," Talbot said in a calming voice.

Private Muldare had kept quiet, her hazel eyes shifting this way and that, clearly uncomfortable. Her hand remained on the action of her slung rifle as they followed a hallway to the rear.

"Why'd you put her clear back here?" Talbot asked, a wary tone in his voice.

"Thought that if something was alive in her, and it got loose, we could catch it here in the back room." Their guide shot them a sidelong look. "You still don't get it, do you?"

"Get what?" Kalico asked.

"These children really aren't dying. The universe might be killing their bodies for the moment, but they're going to be purified and reborn. There is no such thing as permanent death among the universe's chosen."

Kalico made a desist gesture in Dya's direction to keep the woman from leaping for the guy's throat.

They had laid the little girl on a table in one of the storage rooms at the back of the dome. She lay naked on the duraplast surface, and Kalico winced. She could see three lumps moving slowly under the little girl's scarred skin. One on her upper thigh, two more slipping along under the delicate skin of her stomach.

"Shit!" Dya hissed, coming to a stop.

The little girl was writhing, her arms flexing, hands knotting, while whimpers broke from her throat. Behind the delicate lids, her eyeballs were flicking back and forth. The kid looked to be in agony as the slugs slithered through her guts.

"That's two we can't help," Talbot said. "Not with the slugs in her belly already."

"Supervisor!" came the cry in her earbud. *"Carson here. They're making a try for the airtruck. I'm . . ."*

Kalico was turning for the door when the distant bang of a rifle sounded. The throne-bearer whirled, leaped from the room, and slammed the heavy door shut behind him.

"Carson! Carson! Stat report! Carson!"

Even before Talbot could get a hand on the knob, the sound of the lock clicking home could be heard.

"The only way Carson wouldn't be responding is if he's dead,"

Talbot said laconically, a finger to his earbud as he glared at the locked door.

"Lot of good that's going to do them," Muldare noted dryly as she unslung her service rifle. "Mark, step back. I've got an explosive round chambered. I'll blow the damned door straight off its hinges."

As Talbot leaped back, Batuhan's voice sounded through the room speaker overhead. *"If you attempt to shoot your way out, we will detonate the magtex charge in the ceiling. Most likely, so my people tell me, it won't kill you outright. They assure me, however, that you will be sufficiently stunned that we can disarm you and secure you without issue."*

Magtex? Where did they find the magtex?

But then, it was a mining colony. Could have been in any of the boxes out in the sheds.

"What about this little girl?" Kalico demanded, stepping forward. "You going to blow her up, too?"

"Fatima is already dying. Her body will become one with us, purified, and she shall be reborn into a better existence."

"Sick son of a bitch," Dya hissed, hands clenched.

"So?" Batuhan's voice asked reasonably. *"What will it be? Will you lay down your weapons? Or shall my people simply remove them from your stunned and disoriented bodies? For our purposes, it matters not if you are a little bruised and tenderized. Purification is a painful business either way."*

Talbot leaned close to whisper, "I don't see a camera. He can't see us, just hear us."

"Got something in mind?" Kalico mouthed the words.

"Plan B." And so saying, Talbot shoved a crate against the door knob to block it. Then he pulled his knife, stepped over to the BoPET polyethylene terephthalate wall, and with all his might, drove the blade into the plastic.

42

For this to work, everything must happen exactly as planned. That thought kept rolling around in Vartan's head as he paused behind a rusty piece of mothballed equipment at the edge of the landing field. The rear of the airtruck lay no more than thirty meters from his hiding place.

Capella's hard light burned down on his bare head, scorched his already sunburned shoulders. The heat waves rising off the hard basalt and low vegetation amazed him. Sort of like looking across the top of a hot stove. He'd never seen such a thing, even when he'd been on Earth those few days.

Being out in the open was still too new, the light, the moving air, the endless sky, all that musical sound from the wildlife. It scared him. Way down deep. Not to mention that he might be dead in a matter of moments.

The plan had made so much sense when he pitched it to Petre. But it was one thing to propose such an absurd idea while sitting in the cafeteria over a cup of delicious mint tea. Quite another to be creeping up to the airtruck, knowing that if the marine guarding it peered over the side, he'd be shot within an instant.

His heart hammered in his breast. A sheen of nerve-sweat had broken out on his face, neck, and chest. He felt sick to his stomach, muscles quivering.

Step by step, he made his way closer, and yes, right on cue, here came Svetlana, five of the children in tow as they emerged from the garden. The children—having been coached—caught sight of the airtruck, and at a whispered command, charged forward, shouting, laughing.

Perfect!

For the first time, Vartan entertained the faint hope that he might survive this after all.

Sure, the Messiah always promised that anyone who died would be reborn. That through the Irredenta, they were all immortal. It came across as such a reassuring thought: His flesh would be consumed, purified, and his immortal soul would travel the maze, find its way into a woman's womb during intercourse. That he would be born again.

He licked dry lips and wondered if he really and truly believed.

The children were almost to the airtruck. The guard would have his attention focused solely on them.

Vartan sprinted for the airtruck. Reached the side. He flattened himself. Panting, he tightened his grip on the tape-wrapped stave of flexible steel.

It had come to him: If the Supervisor had left them defenseless, they'd have to craft their own weapons. Rail guns and rifles were too complicated. But humans had been building weapons for all of their existence. Bows were still used in sporting competitions back in Solar System.

He'd found the length of steel, tested its flex, and fashioned the bowstring from thin cable. The arrow, he had crafted from a dowel. To create fletching, he cut plastic to shape.

Not only that, but in practice, he could hit a man-shaped target dead center from ten paces.

"Hey, back away!" the guard bellowed from the cab door.

"They're just children!" Svetlana's voice protested.

"I said, get away!"

Vartan's heart had turned manic. Sweat was trickling down the side of his face. Fright bunched in his throat.

He crept around the front of the vehicle, saw Svetlana's subtle gesture to wait. She shooed the children away, stepping close to the airtruck. "What would you do? Shoot me? An unarmed woman?"

"Listen, we don't want trouble."

Vartan crouched, Svetlana at the edge of his vision as she walked up to the airtruck. "Step down here. Let me see you. Been a lot of years since I've seen another man."

"Can't ma'am."

Svetlana looked around. "Hey, uh, there's only you and me. The kids are gone. I mean it. I want to look at you. Surely an undernourished and naked woman isn't a threat to a big man with a rifle."

The guard laughed, clearly uncomfortable.

"It's the scars, isn't it?" she said after a pause. "That's what fascinates you. They all mean something. It's for the souls of the dead. Oh, come on. You're not going to be able to see from up there."

Vartan heard the man step down from the cab. Svetlana backed away, giving him room. Asked, "Is it the spirals on my breasts? That's for the souls to follow when an infant suckles."

"Clap trap in buckets, but that had to hurt."

Svetlana had maneuvered him so that the guard's back was fully exposed. Vartan stepped out from the airtruck, nocked his arrow, and pulled it to full draw. It was all his muscles could take. The arrow wobbled as he centered the tip in the middle of the man's back.

The seemingly broad expanse of the guard's dark shirt became Vartan's universe. Time seemed to slow. In that instant he felt Capella's heat, the sweat beading on his skin. Heard the rising and falling of the chime. Was aware of Svetlana's dark gaze holding the guard's, willing the man's attention into her own.

Vartan's fingers slipped off the bowstring. The stave shivered in his hand as the aluminum arrow leapt forward, caught the man just to the right of the spine, punched through the chest.

For a moment, the guard staggered, glanced down, as if in shock.

Svetlana wheeled on her heel, sprinting for all that her thin legs could carry her.

The guard managed to shout: "Supervisor. Carson here. They're making a try for the airtruck."

Then he lurched sideways, crashed into the side of the cab. Tried to prop himself. The rifle discharged with a booming concussion. Dirt exploded as the bullet tore a divot from the ground.

Vartan watched the rifle drop from the guard's hands to thud into the dirt. Then the man sagged, seemed to wilt. When he coughed, it was to blow a spray of blood across the side of the airtruck. A moment later he was down, gasping as frothy lung blood gushed from his lips.

"I'll be . . ."

Any revelry was cut short by the bang, muffled as it was from the inside of the admin dome. Scratch one Supervisor. Though it would break Shyanne's heart that Fatima's life had been the price.

Vartan, wiped his hot face. Stepped warily forward. He reached down, snagged the rifle away, awed by how heavy it was. Then he jerked the pistol from the man's belt.

He caught a momentary glimpse of the man's wide and straining eyes. Gaped at the blood, so much blood, gurgling up from his throat.

Then Svetlana was there, grinning. "Worked! Good shot!"

"Feast tonight, huh?" he mumbled, still too amazed at what he'd done to think straight.

The sound of gunshots could be heard from inside the dome. What the hell?

She clapped him on the shoulder. "Sounds like trouble in the admin dome. Now, you do know how to work that rifle, right?"

"Oh, yeah." He performed a chamber check, finding a round loaded. "Guess I better go make sure the Messiah and Prophets are all right."

He was panting by the time he arrived at the dome. People were crowded into the cafeteria, pressing around bleeding bodies who'd been laid onto the long tables.

The Chosen. Three of them. Looked like Burht, Shyute, and Wamonga.

Hurrying down the hall, he found Petre and the members of the Will huddled at the junction of two hallways.

"Got the airtruck," he told them. "What's happening here?"

"They slipped out of the trap. Shot three of the Chosen." Petre spared him a worried glance. "They're holed up in a stairwell at the far end of the hall. There's no way to rush them without being shot."

"Don't be a fool. They're in the basement, headed for another stairwell, figuring to get out behind us. Make a try for the airtruck. Quick. The rest of you! There're three more stairways. Block them. Seal them any way you can. Pile whatever, but be sure they can't get out."

He turned, seeing Tikal. Tossed him the marine's pistol. "Get to the airtruck. Keep it safe. Shoot any of the Supervisor's party who try to take it."

People seemed to explode into action, flying off in all directions.

"Should have thought of the other stairwells," Petre said sheepishly.

"If they break out, I can still stop them with this." Vartan slapped the side of the automatic rifle. "Military grade. I can disable that airtruck if they try and lift off. Assuming they get that far. And if they don't shoot me before I can finish the job."

"Just see that they don't, huh?"

43

Cutting a hole in the plastic wall took all of Talbot's strength. Good thing it wasn't a load-bearing wall like the one on the other side of the room.

Talbot muscled the flap back. Dya, Kalico, and Muldare scrambled past a couple of crates. They slipped through the slit and into the darkness of the adjoining room. As a sensor picked up their movement the light panel flickered to life. The way the ceiling curved meant they were in the rear of the dome. One of the axial hallways would be just beyond the closed door.

"This way," Talbot whispered, hearing Batuhan's demands for a response issuing through the hole behind them.

"Shoot our way out?" Muldare asked, flipping her safety off.

"It'll mean killing a lot of people," Kalico ground her teeth.

"What part of 'them or us' don't you get?" Muldare hissed back.

"Is there another way out of here?" Dya whispered. "One that doesn't leave dead bodies all over?"

"Yeah," Talbot said. "But you're not going to like how we're going to have to do it."

Kalico said, "Get us to the airtruck without turning this into a bloodbath. There's women and kids out there."

Talbot nodded. "Fenn Bogarten and I were all through this installation. We've got a way out, but it's down, through the basement, into an old lava tube in the basalt. While Fenn and I didn't check it out, it should take us into the forest. From there we can circle. Get to the airtruck from behind."

Kalico gave him a slap on the shoulder. "Lead forth."

Talbot unslung his service rifle, opened the door a crack, and leaned out. Seeing no one, he led the way into the hall. Lights flashed on as the sensor detected their motion.

The air seemed to pulse, suck, and blow; the dome shook as

concussion literally blew Muldare through the doorway and into the hall.

"Briah?" Kalico asked the disheveled marine, "you all right?"

Muldare shook her head, worked her jaw back and forth to clear her ears. "Good to go, Supervisor."

"Hey!" someone shouted from down the hall.

Talbot didn't hesitate, but wheeled on his heel, lifted the rifle, and sent a shot in the direction of the young man who'd stepped into the hallway.

"There went our period of grace," Talbot growled. "Beat feet, people. Follow me."

He shoved past, heading for where the hall dead-ended against the dome. At the last door, he wrenched it open, tapped the light pad, and told the women, "Stairway. When you hit the bottom, we can't get through the walls down there. They're all load-bearing, so we've got to go back to the center. When you get there follow the first radial hallway to the left. Take it all the way back to the circumference. I'll be right behind you."

As the others started down the stairs, Talbot watched the hallway, took the time to thumb a replacement round into the rifle's magazine.

Shouts sounded, and yes, here they came—a knot of men led by the throne bearers and carrying what looked like clubs and spears.

Talbot took his time, braced his rifle, and shot the leader through the chest. As the leader fell, Talbot's second shot took the next man in the left shoulder. His last shot hit the third man center of mass. As they tumbled, howled, and screamed, those behind turned and ran.

Talbot bellowed, "That's just the start! Next man to come down this hall, I'm popping out this door and shooting the dumb pussucker."

He dropped back, eased the door closed, and pulled a screwdriver from his belt. This he hammered into the jamb with the rifle butt. Wouldn't hold them for long, but it might slow them down.

In the hallway, shrieks and mayhem told him that the Unreconciled were too busy retrieving their dead and dying to follow for the moment.

Scrambling down the stairs, Talbot hit the hallway, running full-out for the center. At the hub, he took the left in time to see Muldare at the far end, bringing up the rear. The light panels, being old, flickered, but illuminated the way.

Talbot pounded down the hallway after them.

"Now what?" Kalico asked as he arrived, panting, his rifle at the ready.

"Forget the doors to either side. It's just unfinished storerooms. They excavated this, figuring the base was going to grow. The assumption was that it would eventually house more than a thousand colonists."

He stepped past to the big cabinet that blocked the end of the hall. Handed his rifle to Dya. "Briah, give me hand here."

Together they grabbed the cabinet, muscled it to the side to expose a sialon door set in the basalt. Talbot clapped the dust from his hands, saying, "Bogarten and I didn't figure the Unreconciled needed to know this was here. It would have just gotten them into trouble."

"What the hell did they need that big a lock for?" Kalico asked as she gaped at the oversized bolt on the door.

"Maybe we don't want to know what they were trying to keep locked on the other side."

Talbot slid the heavy bolt back and opened the door, looking into the black maw beyond. "Briah, tell me you've got a light in that utility belt of yours."

"Sure."

"Inside. Now," Talbot ordered. After the women hurried in, he slid the cabinet back as far as he could to block the door, then closed it behind him.

"You were right." Dya eyed the darkness, running nervous hands up and down the backs of her arms. "I'm not liking this at all."

Muldare was shining her light around the irregular sides of the old lava tube. "What is this place?"

"Volcanic eruption," Talbot told her. "As a result of the meteor impact. There are places where the lava runs hotter than the surrounding rock, and when it drains out it leaves these tunnels behind."

"What now?" Kalico asked. "Where does this go?"

"Supposedly all the way to the base of the escarpment," Talbot told her. "But no one's been down this since the base was built."

"I can't do this," Dya whispered.

"Sure, you can," Talbot told her, hugging her close.

"There's something in here with us. You can feel it, can't you?"

Kalico turned to the woman. "Hey, it's either this, or you can go back. Batuhan will kill you, chop you up, and eat you. Then as your flesh is purified by digestion, your soul can figure out the maze, avoid getting sucked out his nipples, or finally ejaculated into a fertile female."

Dya made the most horrible face Talbot had ever seen his wife make. "You're right. There're worse things than dying in terror. In the dark."

He kissed her fondly on the lips, saying, "I'll be right here with you, wife."

DISBELIEF

I stand over the bodies of the Chosen. Petre and his members of the Will have carried the bodies of my dead friends to the cafeteria, have laid them out one by one on the tables. Blood drains from the holes blown in their chests. Their eyes are half-lidded, lips parted, the bodies limp in death.

Three friends, three believers. The repositories of so many of our dead. They were my priests. They helped me bear the burden.

Jon Burht was the first to declare his faith. I stare down at his face, remembering those terrible days during the Harrowing and Cleansing when he stood at my side.

Then came Felix Shyte. I step over, take his hand. It is cold and limp as I run my thumb over the scars running back in thin ridges from the tops of his fingers.

Will Wamonga was the third to join me. Now he lies shot clear through and bleeding, taken far too soon.

For the moment all I can do is stare down at them. At the terrible wounds that heartless bullets have torn through their flesh, bones, and organs.

Only Ctein Zhoa is left of the Chosen. He stands to the side, expression traumatized, as if he cannot come to grips with the horror. He is wringing his hands. Tears streak down, losing themselves in the maze of scars carved on his cheeks.

The Chosen must be processed, of that there is no doubt. We must attend to them first thing, before the dead they host can dissipate.

Or so I hope.

We are in uncharted waters here. What are the spiritual ramifications of so many living hosts all dying at once? How do we save the dead they contain, as well as themselves?

I glance over at the Prophets where they have been reinstalled in the cafeteria. Irdan isn't moving. For the moment I wonder if he, too, is dead, and then I see his chest spasm. Callista and Guan Shi are staring out with empty eyes, but only Guan Shi still flexes her fingers as if she's playing an imaginary piano.

Petre, a pistol in his hand, rushes in from the back, saying, "They're in a stairwell, Messiah. I've got Vartan covering the doorway with that rifle we took from the marine guard. I've had the other stairwells sealed off. They can't get out."

He is looking at my dead Chosen, a barely suppressed horror in his eyes. Like me, he has to be wondering how this could have gone so terribly wrong. We are supposed to have the Supervisor and her people on the tables, to be preparing their bodies for sacrament.

Instead, my Chosen are murdered, and we have a single dead marine to show for it. He's still outside and unclaimed, given as busy as we have been here.

"How did they escape the explosion?" I ask.

"Cut a hole in the wall, Messiah," Petre says, swallowing hard.

"So we have armed and deadly intruders in our basement. How do we determine their whereabouts? How do we deal with them?"

"Vartan says we need a drone. I remember seeing some in the science dome. They'll need charging—that is, if the batteries are still any good."

"See to it. And have Vartan arm one with explosives. I want a flying bomb I can use to kill those people without additional casualties." I close my eyes and let the rage build. As if the universe is staring over my shoulder, watching, waiting to see if I am capable of solving the crisis.

"No matter what the cost," I mumble through gritted teeth, "I will see them dead."

Nothing else is acceptable.

44

Night had fallen. The roar of the waterfall generated its own music—a kind of background that made sitting out on the Briggses' deck in the warm damp air, drink in hand, a most special event. Overhead, in the narrow band of sky visible from the canyon, the Milky Way painted the Donovanian heavens in glowing swirls of light.

Talina sat in the back, having surrendered the seats closest to the crackling fire to Dek and Chaco. Chaco had built the blaze in his homemade steel fireplace. It perched atop its tripod out on the corner of the deck. The smell of burning aquajade and chabacho lent the air a familiar and reassuring perfume. One Talina had never quite been able to get enough of.

Kylee, who'd appeared just at sunset, sat off to the side, partially obscured by the night. She'd shared that special hug with Talina, given her a knowing look from those almost sagacious and oversized blue eyes. Definitely not the eyes a thirteen-year-old girl should have.

"Kip and Flute are keeping an eye on the rogue," she said. "I think he's got the message. No new opportunities here. Looked like he was moving on."

Which meant the Briggs quetzals wouldn't be hunting it down and killing it for invading their territory. Maybe. One never really knew with quetzals.

Kylee had been circumspect during her introduction to Dek Taglioni; she had been the minimum of polite and very much wild-thing suspicious. Now Kylee sat back in the shadows beside the railing, listening to the conversation as Chaco and Dek drank their beer.

The irony of it fascinated Talina: Derek Taglioni—one of the most privileged scions in The Corporation—side-by-side with

Chaco Briggs, the ultimate do-it-yourself stand-on-your-own-two-feet self-made man.

Briggs was one of the original Wild Ones. He'd fled here after killing a man who'd had the ill grace to pester Madison with his attentions when, clearly, she wasn't interested. Briggs had come from nothing in Argentina. But to listen to him and Derek swapping thoughts about the pump they'd fixed, about the work it had taken to get the water system back to perfect, Talina was witness to the ultimate in male bonding.

Talina tossed off the last of her beer, rose silently, and stepped into the house. At the crude tap, she refilled her glass with home-brew amber ale. Madison had Maria and Skip industriously employed at the sink, finishing the last of the supper dishes.

"How they doing out there?" Madison asked, glancing up.

"You'd think they'd been replacing pumps and getting sprayed by broken water pipes their entire lives. Prince and pauper, a match made in heaven. Who'd have thought?"

"Chaco had one of the best days he's had in years." Madison dried her hands with a towel as she walked over. "Pour me one. I'm ready." To the kids she said, "You two get them dishes put away, and it's off to bed."

"But there's a fire," Maria complained with a little girl's pique at cosmic injustice.

"Bed." Madison accented her will with a pointed finger.

As the kids shuffled off, Talina grinned and poured Madison's beer.

The tall woman lifted it to her lips, sipped, and sighed. "I needed that." Then she gave Talina a thoughtful look. "So, what's with Taglioni? Really?"

"Shig's taken with him. Hell, half the town is."

"And you?"

"Me?"

"He watches you with the eyes of a man who knows what he wants in a woman. For the time being, he's learning, figuring out what it will take to get it."

"And you think I'm 'it?'" Talina leaned her butt back against the counter beside the sink. "He's soft meat, Madison. And me, I'm not sure I want his kind of trouble."

"It's almost four years since Cap died. Three now that you've been learning to live with the quetzals inside. What are you saving yourself for? To be a holy relic in the name of chastity?"

"I don't know. Guess I'm a little scared. I'm not sure that I'm not part crazy. I don't have clue if I could carry on an intimate relationship with anyone. I sure as hell don't know if Dek Taglioni, of all people, would be that man."

"You watch him with a woman's eyes."

"Most people think my eyes are too filled with quetzal."

"I mean a *woman's* eyes. The ones she uses when she's interested in a man. He keeps doing the right things, doesn't he? And he's not half bad to look at. He's been tested, this one. And better, he knows he is ignorant, that there are things he has to learn, but he is not afraid to take chances learning them."

"He's also got another side. The guy crossed swords with Kalico back in Solar System. When I asked her about it, she said, that when they met that last time in Transluna, Dek was scuzzier than toilet water."

"Maybe he was." Madison took a swig of her beer, bracing her butt next to Talina's. "That was how many years ago? We all have heard how close *Ashanti* came to being another *Freelander.* People change when they are living with the knowledge that each breath might be their last." A beat. "You still the same woman who spaced from Transluna all them years ago?"

"Well, I guess he's got your vote."

Madison gave an offhanded shrug. "If he were still a spoiled Corporate candy ass, he'd have quit the first time a seal failed, and he and Chaco got drenched. He stuck it out. Stood there with a wrench on that fitting. Not only that, the guy not only enjoyed it, but he knew his shit. Pointed out a couple of things Chaco had never thought of. And more to the point, Chaco doesn't take to many men. Finds that most of them don't measure up. Don't have what it takes. And there he is, drinking beer like he's with a kindred soul."

"Okay, so the guy walks on water." Seeking to change the subject, Talina said, "If I were you, I'd be more worried about Tip not coming home. He's out there in the dark hunting a rogue quetzal. That would have my undershorts in a lot tighter knot than Dek Taglioni could ever tie them in."

Madison's expression strained the least bit. "Yeah, I worry. We've lost too many kids to Donovan over the years. Every time Tip and Kylee don't make it back for supper, the trepidation's there. Is this the time they don't come home? Is my child out there hurt and in agony? Maybe dying, and I can't do a thing about it? That's the worst. The not knowing."

"So?"

"So, it's who Tip and Kylee are going to be, Tal. That's the price I pay as a mother out here. Living is a dangerous—and often too-short—business. So you get on with it."

"Yeah, I guess."

She heard the laughter as Dek and Chaco shared some story out by the fire.

Madison gave her a pat on the shoulder. "You and Dek are in the back rooms. Neither you nor he are ready yet, but there's a connecting door should the day ever come."

Talina was giving Madison a "no way" look when Dek stepped in, a grin accenting the dimple in his chin. He had an empty glass in his hand.

"Chaco's out of beer. The good news: Kylee's taking me hunting in the morning. Chaco talked her into it."

Talina pointed with a no-nonsense finger. "I can't stop you, but if that girl gives you an order, even if it sounds crazy, you do what she tells you!"

"Yes, ma'am," Dek told her as he gave her a two-finger salute. "Way ahead of you."

He paused only long enough to refill the glass, give Madison a winning smile, and vanish back onto the deck, where the talk promptly turned to where chamois might be found in the morning.

Talina took a deep breath to still the sudden tension in her chest. Anything could happen out there. "I hope this isn't a mistake," she murmured.

Madison had a sliver of smile on her lips. "Yep. It's back."

"What is?"

"The way you look at him with a woman's eyes."

45

Every muscle and joint in Vartan's body ached; his brain had that fevered feeling of fatigue. His thoughts had gone muzzy in a head that felt stuffed with wool. When he blinked, the lids seemed to scrape over his eyeballs. The ability to carry a thought to its conclusion had congealed. He'd forgotten how much he hated exhaustion and fatigue. All he wanted to do was sleep.

The cave had been terrifying. Draining. First the descent filled with mind-numbing fear of being shot from the blackness, then the sapping ascent back to the door. Climbing the stairs from the basement took every bit of his concentration. His muscles screamed, his lower back ached under the weight of the rifle. Just those fifteen stairs—not to mention Donovan's gravity—had him winded by the time he reached the ground-level hallway.

The way his feet kept tripping over themselves it was as if they had become disconnected from his brain. His legs had a loose and rubbery feel.

Vartan plodded his weary way into the cafeteria where the Messiah slouched in his throne. The man sprawled more than sat, chin propped on his chest, dark eyes dully fixed on the wasted body lying prominently on the table just before the throne. The eye in the middle of The Messiah's forehead seemed to stare at infinity.

Vartan thankfully slipped the heavy rifle from his shoulders, let it clunk onto the nearest table. He pulled a chair out, slid it around, and dropped into it with a sigh.

Irdan. That's who lay upon the table.

Off to the side, Callista and Guan Shi were each being sponged by a couple of the children. Not that either of them looked more than half past the shade of death.

"What news, Second Will?" the Messiah asked softly.

"We followed the tunnel as far as a drop off, Messiah. By then the hand lights were failing, getting too feeble to see into the depths. We turned back. Blocked the door with enough heavy items they can't shoot their way back inside.

"Meanwhile, Tamil has discovered a blueprint of the admin dome. The tunnel apparently has an outlet down in the forest. That's where they'll come out. The cliff is pretty sheer immediately above the lava tube. The trails they'll need to climb back up are to the north and south. We have enough people to defend them if they try and return that way in an attempt to get the airtruck."

The Messiah kept his gaze fixed on Irdan's corpse, as if momentarily expecting the dead Prophet to utter some startling revelation.

"What of the armed drone?" The Messiah's words were barely a whisper.

"Petre has it on the charger again. It should have a full charge, or as much as it will take anyway, in another hour or two."

"Tell the First Will that my orders are as follows: He, you, and Tikal will each take a squad of fifteen people. He will descend the north trail. You and Tikal on the south. Once down the escarpment, you will have your teams fan out in three groups of five to comb the forest floor. You will sweep your way forward, closing on the vicinity of the cave exit. Where—"

"Messiah, I don't think—"

"What you think doesn't matter." The Messiah shifted his gaze, eyes like cold black stones in his head. The hollow created by his missing nose whistled as he inhaled.

The mad power of the Messiah's gaze and the intensity of his anger sent a shiver through Vartan. The painted blue eye in the middle of the man's forehead seemed to bore right through Vartan's soul.

Implacably, the Messiah said, "Each team of five will search. When they locate the Supervisor and her party, they will not engage. They will only alert you or Petre as to the Supervisor's location. You will then use the drone. Fly it right into the middle of the Supervisor's party. There, you will detonate the explosive. At that time, everyone will converge upon the location, recover the bodies, and bring them to me."

"Messiah, I—"

"My orders are not up for negotiation, Second Will."

Vartan chewed his lips. Blinked in the glare cast from the cafeteria lights and jerked a short nod. It took all of his effort to push himself up from the chair. Took three steps before he remembered the rifle and plodded back to retrieve it.

Ten years in Deck Three, doing nothing. Now he was planetside, malnourished, dealing with a heavier gravity. His physical endurance was spent.

Outside, he glanced up at the starry sky, wondering when night had fallen.

"You all right?" Shyanne asked as she appeared out of the dark.

"I just want to sleep for a week. Lay in the sun and eat steak before sleeping again. He's ordered us to put together teams, to go into the forest in search of the Supervisor." He hesitated. "You heard about Fatima?"

"She's dead. And they never even let me see her. For that . . . Well, never mind. It's all going to shit anyway."

"Be careful, Shyanne. I know how you're—"

"Vart, you don't have the first fucking notion about how I'm feeling." The anger and grief in her voice made him wince. To change the subject, she said, "You heard about the prions?"

"Something."

"Vart, everything that happened? The Prophets? It's a disease." She hooked her fingers in quotation as she said, "Divine revelation? Hardly. It's dementia from a physical source. From eating contaminated brain matter. We weren't *saving* the dead. They were poisoning us."

"Best not say anything about that where any of the Will could hear. You'll be sliced up, boiled, and put on the table next."

She chuckled humorlessly. "Look around. Okay, we're off the ship. But we're still on our own. And so what? Think back. Remember who we were when we first set foot on *Ashanti*? Remember those people? The things we believed in. The kind of human beings we were? We've given up so much of ourselves to madness. Justified . . . well, everything as the price of survival."

"Yeah." He hung his head, rubbed the back of his sore neck. "Used to be human."

"You were a security officer. I was a vet tech." She shook her head, curled her hands into desperate fists. "I look back to the woman I was, to the man I was in love with and married to, to all the dreams."

"Those were good days. Maybe . . ."

"Maybe would be a lie. We're monsters, Vart. That's what Batuhan and his supposed Prophets have made us. Look at the scars." She traced fingers along the lines that led to her breasts. "This is the mark of Cain. The visible proof that I participated in the sick murder of my friends, that I willingly seared their flesh and ate it. That I sold my humanity and self-respect to keep breathing, whored myself to that twisted Mongolian monster and his minions in order to bear their children. So I lived? To become . . . what kind of *thing*?"

"Hey, Shyanne, don't—"

"Vart, wake up. We'd have been better off dead. You, me, all the rest of us. Now we're, well . . . Let's just say we're a sort of human pollution."

The words stung. He'd loved her once. With all of his heart. Could remember how they'd delighted in each other. They'd been so young, so possessed of each other that they'd soared. Like two souls who'd fit like meshed gears . . . and lost it all.

"I've got work to do."

"Vart. There's a way, you know. An out. You know Batuhan's batshit crazy. This whole living graves and immortality sham is a lie to justify the most heinous crimes human beings can commit. But just 'cause we played along to save our worthless lives doesn't mean we still have to."

"Shyanne, don't. If the wrong people hear you—"

"You can fly the airtruck, can't you? It's a way out of the insanity. We can find a place. Somewhere—"

"I'm going to pretend I didn't hear that. Now, Shy, take my advice: Don't. Say. Another. Word. Not to anyone."

She stared at him in the dark. Nodded. Finally said, "You take these search parties down into that forest, most of those people are not coming back."

"Oh? Think they'll just wander off looking for Eden?"

"I've read the reports. The ones Batuhan says are all lies. I've tried to treat the ones Donovan's already claimed. You were a smart man once, be one again."

He yawned, wished the fatigue would let him clear his head. "Sorry, Shy, I've got to get ahead of this thing with the Supervisor."

"You really believe that Batuhan's a divine messiah?"

"You keep your head down, Shy. I know you're hurting. And I'm so sorry about Fatima. But promise me you won't do anything stupid, all right?"

Her laughter sounded heartless. "Oh, you know me, Vart. I don't have any stupid left in me."

He laid a gentle hand on her shoulder, took a deep breath, and forced his trembling and weary legs to leave her standing there as he plodded toward the dormitory to form his search parties.

What he would have given for a short, quick nap.

46

Time vanished in the cold black of the lava tube. Was it only hours, or a day? Kalico Aguila wasn't sure. And she had started to regret her once-flippant remarks that being in the tube was better than being eaten by Batuhan's cannibals. She'd been in some dark places before, especially her mine. But nothing as dark, cramped, and terrifying as this.

When Muldare had occasion to flip her light off, the blackness was complete. Total. Literally the stygian depths of the tomb.

And worse, there were things. Invertebrates that scuttled around in the black recesses, always running from the light.

"How you doing?" Talbot asked his wife.

"There's something in here. Watching us. Waiting," Dya told him, shivering. "Mark, promise me. If something happens, if it looks like we're trapped here, you'll shoot me. You will, won't you? You won't leave me to die in the dark."

Kalico swallowed hard. From the tone in the woman's voice, she was clap-trapping serious.

"We're going to make it, wife." Talbot told her in a voice dripping love.

What was that like? To be loved so completely? Kalico took the moment to wonder—not that she'd ever allowed herself such a fantasy. Still, here, in the evil blackness, she envied Dya Simonov that warm reassurance.

Up in the lead, Muldare took a deep breath, as if nerving herself as she crawled up and over a hump where the floor rose. "Got another drop ahead," she said before shining the light back so Kalico could slither across the clammy wet rock in the marine's wake. Only to find herself perched on a shallow ledge before the tube dropped off into inky depths.

Kalico reached back, took Dya's hands, and helped the botanist negotiate the hump. The woman was trembling, her jaw quivering with fear as she swung her feet around to find purchase on the ledge. Then came Talbot, his rifle clattering on the unforgiving stone.

When Muldare shone her light into the depths, the invertebrates scattered like perverted lice. Skittering this way and that, they hid in cracks, huddled in shadow, and seemed to flow down into the depths.

"I hate this place." Briah Muldare's voice was a hoarse whisper.

Talbot was staring down into the hole. "Shit on a shoe, but that's a straight drop."

"So, what now?" Kalico asked—felt something drop onto her head. She panicked, clawed with frantic fingers to rip the skittering invertebrate out of her hair. The little beast, legs thrashing, sailed out into Muldare's light and vanished into the blackness below. Kalico willed every ounce of her courage to get her heartbeat back to normal.

Pus and ions, I'd give a kilo of rhodium for a drink of water. Give up the whole damn Number One mine to be out of here and back in Port Authority chowing down on Inga's chili and drinking whiskey.

Talbot took Muldare's light, flashed it around the walls of the shaft, and then leaned out, saying, "Bless you, yes!"

"What?" Kalico craned her neck, trying to see.

"Got a rope here." Talbot handed the light back to Muldare, dropped to his knees, and backed over the ledge, feeling his way with his feet.

"Mark, damn you, you be careful," Dya cried, leaning forward. "So help me, if you . . ." She couldn't finish.

"What makes you so brave?" Muldare asked, trying to hold the light for him.

Talbot grinned weakly. "I survived four months in the forest. Alone. Every time I figured I was dead, I wasn't. When I eventually do wind up dead, I'll know I've either just made a really dumb mistake, or that the odds finally caught up with me." A pause. "Ah, there. Little bit of a foothold here. Don't mind the invertebrates, they crunch under your boot."

"Did you *have* to say that?" Dya cried, on the verge of tears.

Talbot lowered himself, feeling for footholds. "Got another one. Ouch. *Shit!*"

"What?" Kalico's heart starting to hammer again.

"Don't put your fingers in the crushed invertebrate." Talbot wiped his hand on his coveralls. "Their guts really burn."

We're all going to die in here.

Talbot eased himself over the edge. "Okay, got the rope. So, the good news is that someone passed this way before. And better yet, left us the rope. Best of all, the invertebrates haven't eaten it. The bad news is that while it's knotted, it's still just a rope. Means we each have to climb down, one by one."

Kalico—seeing Dya shaking and on the verge of tears, and Muldare looking pretty rocky herself—said, "You go first, Mark. Then Dya, Muldare, and I'll be last."

"You'll have to do it in almost total darkness," Muldare told her, a worried look in her hazel eyes.

"So?" Kalico shrugged. "I'll manage."

God, can I lie to myself, or what?

Screw this being strong for everyone shit. She wanted to drop to her knees and throw up.

Talbot was already descending the rope. She could hear his clothing rubbing against the stone, the occasional clunk as his rifle butt hit rock. The man's breath kept coming loud in the cavern. How long? Ten seconds? Twenty?

"I'm down," Mark called. "Come on, Dya. Feel with your feet as you lower yourself over the lip. If it feels like a step, it is. Once you grab hold of the rope, use both of your feet to grip the knots."

In the flashlight's glow, Dya's face was a mask of terror. She tried to swallow. Couldn't. Tears glistened at the corners of her eyes. Who would have thought that rock-solid Dya, woman of steel, would have been afraid of the dark?

"I can't." It came as faint whisper.

Kalico bent down, placed a hand on the woman's shoulder. Forced a kindly confidence she didn't feel into her voice. "You going to let a Corporate bitch like me show you up? Besides, down that rope is the only way back to Su and Damien, Tweet, Tuska, and the rest of the family. Nothing you couldn't do in the light of day. The only difference is that now you do it in a tunnel."

"It's okay," Talbot called from the bottom. "Not more than five meters."

"I don't want to die in the dark," Dya whispered. Her entire body shook, but somehow, looking numb, she swung her feet over the edge. "Something's here. Feel it? Watching us."

Kalico couldn't help herself, a shiver playing down her arms as she stared at the surrounding black, and damned if she didn't feel some presence. Cold. Heartless. And malevolent.

Muldare took Kalico's hand for stability, leaned out to shine the light as far down as she could to help Dya see.

Foothold by foothold, the trembling Dya lowered herself, tears streaking down her face. She was below the lip, said, "Got the rope." Then added, "Fuck me. Here goes."

For a moment there was silence, then a yip of fear echoed in the shaft.

"Dya!" Kalico and Talbot cried in unison.

"It's . . . It's . . . I'm okay. Just . . . Just . . ."

"Take your time," Talbot called. "Feel your way."

"*Shut up!*" Dya shrieked. "I've been on a rope before."

At the terror in the woman's voice, Kalico closed her eyes.

She's going to lose it. She'll freeze. Won't be able to move. When her fingers cramp, she's going to fall.

And what? Land full on Mark? Leave them both crippled here in the terrible black?

She glanced sidelong at Muldare, wanted to shout down to Talbot to stay out of the way.

Oh, sure, and that would really seal Dya's fate, wouldn't it?

"How you doing, wife?" Talbot called up.

"Okay," Dya squeaked. "I found the rope. Got my feet on the knot."

Kalico sucked her lips, her heart hammering. *Come on. You can do it.*

Then came the sound of clothing sliding on rock. The softer sounds were Dya sobbing, struggling. But the sliding on rock continued, getting ever more faint.

Then, "I . . . I'm slipping! I can't hold on any . . ." It ended with a shriek. Then a muffled thump.

"Mark? Dya?" Kalico called, hanging out as far as she could over the edge. All she could hear was whimpering, the sound of someone broken.

47

Kalen Tompzen's words, "Boss, I could handle this," kept repeating in Dan Wirth's head as he stalked through the main gate that opened out onto the shuttle field. Fact was, he never liked going out beyond the fence. Somehow, leaving the protective barrier behind with nothing between him and Donovan was like walking down the central avenue buck-assed naked with his prick and balls wagging in the wind.

Not that being inside Port Authority was all that safe. Since landing on Donovan, he'd spent how many nights huddled in The Jewel while search teams scoured every square inch of town for a man-eating monster? Good old Dube Dushku had been torn in two and swallowed by a quetzal just on the other side of the wall where Dan hid in his office.

Yet, here he was, Tompzen's assurances echoing in his head. Sure, the ex-marine could have hunted Windman down. Made the appropriate example of him. Beat the guy to a pulp, broke an arm, or dislocated a shoulder. Got the message across that a mark didn't waltz out, leaving The Jewel holding the bag. Not when said mark lost more than five hundred at roulette. The guy wouldn't have had the chance to skip if Vik Schemenski hadn't been so busy at the table.

But Windman had, and now the situation must be dealt with.

Dan squinted, staring across the shuttle pad. The place where the PA shuttle usually sat lay vacant; the clay was baking under Capella's hot glare. To the right, just before the seven-tall wall of shipping containers sat an A-7 shuttle from *Ashanti*. That had to be where Windman, a copilot, would be found.

In fact, wasn't that him? The guy lounging on the open loading ramp where it was lowered in the rear?

Dan took a deep breath and started across the hard red soil. In places hot exhaust had melted it to a glassy texture. In the distance the chime kept rising, almost finding harmony, and falling into that awful discordant and atonal fugue before rising again.

I could be gone from here.

Dek Taglioni's offer hung in his imagination like a desert mirage: alluring, and just out of reach. If only Dan could trust the guy. The opportunity was just too good to be true, but what if it was real? On Donovan, at least he was safe, secure, and alive. But that was where it ended.

The conundrum just added to Dan's foul mood: knowing that he wasn't trapped. That this wasn't the end of the road. That if he'd just keep his wits, he could be off this rock, back in the game. The *real* game, where it wasn't just pissing around with a bunch of broke-dick colonists on a backwater world, but Transluna! Where absolute power awaited anyone with the cunning and moxie to seize it.

All of which had caused him to give Kalen Tompzen a wink and say, "I'll take care of the guy."

Dan *needed* to get the hell out of The Jewel, away from the wary gazes his people kept giving him. Damn it, he was desperate for action, any kind of action. And thumping the shit out of copilot Windman was going to be a relief, a way to vent the growing frustration.

"Don't kill him," Allison had warned as Dan had settled his hat on his head and checked his knife.

Of course I won't kill him. He's Ashanti *crew.*

But that was part of it, the whole frustrating thing. It was the pissant little rules. Like having to trade a fucking bedroom addition for a scarf. By God's ugly ass, he was tired of placating a bunch of candy-dicked and self-righteous bastards.

He grinned, a swell of anticipation rising within as he walked up to the shuttle ramp and called, "Ensign Windman in the flesh! Why, of all the people to encounter. Luck is with me for sure."

Windman, who'd been doodling on his tablet looked up. The guy was spacer pale to start with. Now he went two shades whiter. Swallowed hard.

"Oh, no need to fret," Dan reassured the rabbit-eyed Windman. "You and I just need to talk."

Dan glanced around. "But not here. I mean, anyone could walk by, and you do have a reputation to maintain. So, how about we both saunter over past that shipping container and enjoy a bit of privacy while we figure out our little dilemma."

"Uh, I'm not an ensign. Just a copilot." Windman wobbled unsurely to his feet.

"Either's good enough for me." Dan placed a reassuring hand on the spacer's bony shoulder. He could feel the guy flinch down to his toes.

Windman nerved himself. "Listen, I know how it looks. Me slipping out like that. But, uh, hey, you've got this reputation. Like, I know I screwed it, shouldn't have made that last bet. But you need to know that I'll make it—"

"Sure you will. That's what we're going to discuss. How to make it right. 'Cause I suspect you really don't have any five hundred siddars hidden away up in that ship, am I right?"

"Well, no. But when I get back to Solar System, after *Ashanti*'s been this long in space? I mean, with bonus and time, and being over contract, I'll have more than enough—"

"But that's then. Not to mention in way far off Solar System. We have to talk about now."

Dan propelled copilot Windman past the last of the stacked shipping containers. Caught a glance of Pamlico Jones where he ran one of the forklifts toward the *Ashanti* shuttle. Jones was smart enough to leave matters be that didn't concern him.

Behind the towering crates, a couple of big transparent plexiglass boxes—some sort of shipping crates—stood in a haphazard line. No telling what they had been used for. Given the rows of air holes in the tops, whatever had been in them must have been organic.

Beyond them, it was no more than fifty meters across the ferngrass to the bush. There a low line of aquajade, sucking shrub, claw shrub, and scrubby chabacho trees shimmered in opalescent greens and turquoise. A flock of scarlet fliers fluttered in aerial dance among the branches. The chime grew, louder, wavering in the heat.

Dan stopped Windman before the transparent crates, the guy's escape blocked from behind by a low hillock covered by ferngrass.

"Listen, Mr. Wirth, I really am sorry." Windman was craning his head, eyes searching for any possible route of escape. It had to be dawning on him that for whatever was about to happen, there would be no witnesses.

"Sorry is a good word, but it doesn't have any value. Get my point? I could say, 'I forgive you' but it wouldn't mean anything either. Now, let's say you have five hundred SDRs in that pouch on your belt. You hand that over, and we're all square. Even. The accounts balance. But you don't have five hundred, and sorry's just a word. No more than an exhalation of air."

Windman's mouth must have gone dry because it took him three tries to swallow. A growing terror turned his quivering eyes glassy. "Wha . . . What's going to happen to me?"

"Well, that's a problem isn't it? How do I get any value out of a broke spacer who can't cover his debts? I guess the only thing I can figure that would make you of any worth to me is as an example."

"Huh? What kind of example?"

Dan put the whole weight of his body behind the swing, drove his fist deep into Windman's gut. The spacer, malnourished and skin-and-bones as he was, didn't have a chance. Air whooshed from his mouth as he bent double. Stumbled back three paces and dropped hard on his butt.

"So, this is going to hurt," Dan promised, taking a step forward. "Sorry, but it's the only way you can . . ."

The hump of ferngrass behind Windman shifted, seemed to liquify and flow. Rising, the ground was swelling and expanding, beginning to take shape. The three eyes that blinked open on the great triangular head were fixed on Windman's back.

The spacer sat hunched on his ass, legs out straight, had both hands on his gut. His eyes were bugged, mouth open, expression that of a man in pain.

Dan froze. Stared in disbelief as the huge creature formed behind the clueless Windman. Large. Easily two meters at the shoulders as it seemed to materialize out of thin air. But what the . . .

Quetzal.

Dan had seen enough of them. Dead, of course. Never in the flesh. Never this close.

Tears were streaking down Windman's now-red face. He gasped for air. Started to throw up. Never got the chance to finish.

The quetzal struck, remarkably fast for so big a beast. The movement was a blur, the head twisting sideways. Mighty serrated jaws snapped shut on Windman's torso, crushing his shoulders, chest, and gut. The beast twisted Windman sideways and lifted as it straightened its head. With a claw, it ripped most of the shirt off the man's body. The spacer's head, forearms, and hips protruded from the jaws like doll parts.

Like some grotesquely oversized terrier, the quetzal shook Windman, his limbs flopping loosely. Where the serrated jaws clamped tight, they severed Windman's neck, an action that pitched the man's head like a volleyball to bounce and roll just short of Dan's feet.

The quetzal's hide now flickered in crimson and black patterns. Dan heard the crackling and snapping of Windman's bones, watched the thing gulp the man's upper body down. Straightening its neck, the great quetzal reached out with its claw-sharp foreleg and ripped Windman's pants from his legs. The cloth sailed out to flutter to the ground.

With another shake and gulp, the hips and arms vanished.

Dan stumbled back, gaping in horror as the quetzal stripped off Windman's boots and choked the rest of him down.

The big plexiglass box stopped any further retreat when Dan's back slammed against it.

The last of spacer Windman was an oversized lump traveling down the quetzal's throat. The three eyes fixed on Dan. Opening its mouth, the creature sucked air, venting a low harmony from the vents back by its tail.

Dan shot a quick look, as desperate for an escape as Windman had been such a short time earlier. Backed against the transparent container as he was, his fingers slipped off the latch.

Faster than a heartbeat, Dan flung the door open, darted inside, and closed it. A millisecond later, the quetzal hit the thick plastic with enough force to rock it back precariously.

Desperately, Dan studied the latch, figured it out, and shot the bolt home that would lock it. As he did, the giant quetzal charged again, hit the plastic hard, and toppled it backward. The impact jarred Dan down to his bones. Then the quetzal leaped full onto the box, its weight flexing the plexiglass as it twisted its head this way and that, biting at the box.

Fuck me, but if that latch breaks . . .

Through the transparency, Dan had a close-up and mind-numbing view of the creature's blade-like and bloody teeth, the red gullet, and swelling throat tissues.

For what seemed an eternity, he and the quetzal stared at each other. The thing's bloody jaws now pressed against the clear plastic, leaving crimson smears.

That's when Dan noticed the crippled left front leg, the bullet scars along the beast's muscular hide.

"Whitey," he whispered.

48

The shape in the sucking shrub thirty meters away might have been a small boulder. The bulk of Dek's body was hidden behind the bole of an aquajade tree. In the early morning light he squinted, shifted his focus slightly to one side. As if . . . yes.

"See it?" Kylee Simonov asked from where she hunched beside him. She was peering out from the other side of the tree. She'd been the one to spot the thing, having picked it out through a mere gap in the dense growth. That she'd seen it at all amazed him.

"Kind of that rounded shape," Dek told her.

"That's it. Now, on the left, you see that pointed part? Sort of blends into the branches? Notice how it's not moving like the rest of the plant?"

"I do."

"You want to put your bullet back where that pointed part merges into the rest of the body. That's actually the back of the head and neck."

Dek carefully eased his Holland & Holland hunting rifle up to his shoulder. Braced it against the trunk of the aquajade to steady his aim and sighted through the optic. Sure enough, the IR gave him a complete rendering of the fastbreak. Dek placed his point-of-impact dot on the thing's . . . well, neck. As the dot settled, he caressed the trigger.

The pop of the bullet leaving the rails at fifteen hundred feet per second was surprisingly mild. But then he'd dialed down the velocity for such a close shot. The Holland & Holland could accelerate a bullet as fast as eighteen thousand feet per second. Assuming one really wanted to blow a hole in something. The down side was horrendous shoulder-pounding recoil, and the powerpack would have to be ejected and replaced after three such hyper shots.

At the impact, he watched the fastbreak explode from the bush, make a fantastic leap, and collapse on the ground. As it did, the shrub thrashed its branches, irritated by the disturbance.

"Good shot," Kylee told him. "But you've got to hurry. See how it's over by that claw shrub? The roots will have your fastbreak in another thirty seconds. And once they do, you don't want to try and wrestle it back. You'll end up being sliced clear to the bone."

Dek cycled another bullet into battery, rose, and trotted out to the fastbreak. Yep, the roots were squirming in the thing's direction. He picked it up, awed by the weight, by the warm limpness of the body.

My God. I just killed something.

The sense of elation faded into a feeling of unease. He stared thoughtfully at the beautiful creature. The soft hide was covered with a sort of feathery pelage that now took on a sheen of color—like oil made rainbow patterns on water. How did it do that? What passed for blood was leaking from the bullet wound, splattering red-brown on the soil. The three eyes in the triangular head were already sightless, growing dim.

This creature, this living thing, had been happily going about its business. Had thought itself hidden, without a care. And from out of nowhere its life was suddenly blown out of its body by a carnivorous monster from a planet thirty light-years away. Where was the justice in that?

Kylee propped callused hands on her young hips. She was giving him a thoughtful appraisal. The kid was supposedly thirteen, just entering that period of transition from a girl to a young woman. The changes in her body were evident. If she continued the way she was, she'd be stunning. Except for her alien-blue eyes, the almost triangular cheekbones. And her legs—maybe because of a growth spurt—appeared a bit too long for the rest of her body.

Not exactly an everyday blonde blue-eyed northern European kind of girl, she exuded a sense of danger, of otherness. From the moment he'd made her acquaintance the night before, he'd wondered if she wasn't as likely to stick a knife in his guts as give him a smile.

"It's called hunter's remorse," she told him. "Instead of torturing yourself for taking a life, blame it on the universe. It's how being alive works. Something has to die for something else to eat. Same on Donovan as it is on Earth. Maybe more so here."

"Why's that?"

"Because on Donovan, it's how information as well as sustenance is transmitted. TriNA is ingested, passes through the gut wall, and is incorporated into another organism. Pretty tidy actually. But that means if you want access to information, as well as nutrients, you have to eat it. Take quetzals. Among them cannibalism is an expected part of the life cycle. You want to know how to hunt chamois? Eat one of your elders who excels at hunting chamois."

"That's . . . um, unsettling." And hewed too closely to the crap trap the Unreconciled claimed to believe. He studied the fastbreak, noticed how the stripes and shadows on its hide were fading to brown. So amazing that everything on Donovan changed colors.

"Come on," she told him. "We need to get your kill back and cut it up. It will be lunch." With that she turned her steps down the trail toward the farmstead.

Dek followed, careful—as he'd been instructed—to put his feet where she did, to pay attention.

"I really appreciate you taking me out hunting this morning. I've never done this before."

She gave him the slightest twitch of the shoulders. "I wanted to see how stupid you were."

"I . . . see." Which, of course, he didn't.

"Talina's my friend."

The way she said it, Talina was a lot more than that.

"I really appreciate her bringing me out here."

"Yeah, I know you do."

"Oh?"

She shot him a knowing look over her shoulder. "You're way more interested in her than just as a friend."

"I am?"

"You give her more eye contact, heartbeat changes, pupils dilate. Your smell goes more musky. Sexual interest. Male attraction. The hormones are working."

"Oh, come on."

"Yeah, you're probably only partially aware. That over-civilized part of you has spent most of your life trying to keep the limbic system under control."

"Listen, I don't know where you get all this, but I—"

"Watch out for that blue nasty. Step wide."

He did, realizing his attention had wandered. Amazed at the same time that she'd known he'd strayed from her path even though he was behind.

"What about me being stupid?" he asked. "I didn't understand that."

"The last time I got stuck with soft meat, it was Dortmund Short Mind. He was a professor and about the most stupid man alive. Letting him live was a mistake. He ended up killing Trish through gross incompetence, and that broke Talina's heart. If I had let the quetzals eat him, the world would have been a lot better place." A beat. "Though it might have been an act of malicious injustice to the Rork quetzals."

The way she said it, so matter of fact, sent a shiver down Dek's back. "Remind me not to be stupid."

"You pay attention. That's more than I expected. I can see what Talina likes about you."

That caught his interest. "She likes me? She seems kind of stand-offish."

"She's waiting to be disappointed."

"She tell you that?"

"Didn't need to." Kylee pointed to her head. "Part of her is in here. I've got a lot of her memories. Her thoughts."

"You've shared molecules," Dek guessed, shifting the fastbreak to his other shoulder. The damn thing was heavy. His muscles were still adapting. He didn't want to start panting. Not in front of Kylee. The need to make a good impression had become a great deal more important.

"Yeah." She fixed her attention on one of the aquajades, slowed. "Changes the way you think."

She held up a hand, head cocking as she stopped in the trail.

Around them, the chime was rising and falling, the music slightly different than what he'd grown used to outside Port Authority.

"Something's wrong," she told him. "We need to make time. Hand me the fastbreak."

He did, unsure of what might be wrong. All he could hear was the background of chime, the faint whisper of the morning breeze in the aquajade and chabacho leaves.

"Got to hurry now." She flipped the fastbreak's body over her shoulder like it was a sack of cloth. "Concentrate, Dek. Do as I do. Follow me. Footprint for footprint. If I veer wide, so do you."

"Got it."

"That will be an uncommon change from the usual soft meat."

And then she was off, seeming to float as she trotted effortlessly along the winding path.

Concentrate. Don't be stupid.

Within a hundred meters, he was panting and staggering. His Holland & Holland, not weighing more than four kilos, had started to feel more like a bar of lead.

Under his breath, he whispered, "Oh, Dek, what have you gotten yourself into?"

That's when the sound of the approaching airtruck finally penetrated his thoughts.

49

The dark corridor reeked of something more than just a dead ship. A presence filled it. Something Galluzzi couldn't quite manage to comprehend—a quality that seemed to slip off at a ninety-degree axis from reality. That it did so at the very instant Galluzzi began to grasp its essence made it even crazier.

"Where are the lights?" Galluzzi tried to keep the panic from his voice.

"The *Turalon* crewmen supposedly fixed them. Not up to their usual standards."

When Shig shone his light down the corridor, Galluzzi would have sworn that something devoured the photons. As bright as the beam was, it should have penetrated more than just a mere ten or fifteen meters. Light didn't disappear that way; that it did here was plain unnatural.

Shig added, "I don't think their hearts were in any of the repairs. Hard to concentrate when you're constantly looking over your shoulder. I suspect only fear of Supervisor Aguila's wrath enabled them to patch up the few systems they did. Get the ship stabilized . . . and get the hell off. Workmanship wasn't a priority when things were sneaking in at the edges of their vision."

"I'm creep-freaked enough to understand where they were coming from," Galluzzi said through an exhale. "Next time something touches me, I'm out of here."

He kept wanting to ask the ship for light, for air, for an explanation as he would aboard *Ashanti*.

They chopped the ship's AI out with cutting torches, he reminded himself.

Shig continued to plod forward, his light a truncated cone of reality in the dark insanity that was *Freelander.*

"I saw her," Galluzzi whispered. "*Freelander.* In the yards outside

Transluna. They were fitting her structural members. Just the rude skeleton that would become this ship. I remember how amazed we all were. Knowing that we were on the leading edge of ever bigger and better ships."

And now she has come to this.

Shig stopped at a hatch. Then he turned, shining his light past Galluzzi and back the way they'd come. "Consider this: We're looking at the transportees' deck. All this black and empty space. They voided this deck. Five hundred people suffocated here, most of them in their bunks. Then they turned off the heat. Let them all freeze. Think of that. Five hundred corpses, frozen solid. An entire deck as a deep freeze."

Given the difficulty with which Galluzzi managed to swallow, someone might have jammed a knotted cloth into the bottom of his throat. He stared back into the depths, tried to imagine the frozen corpses, eyes frosted white, lips pulled back from teeth that glinted with icy crystals.

The voice beside Galluzzi's ear whispered, "*. . . wasn't but two days ago when Melanie . . .*"

Galluzzi whirled, threw up his arm, crying out. "Get away!"

Shig flashed his light back. "Hear something?"

"A woman. Whispered something about two days ago. Melanie something."

"If you want, you can look her up on the transportee manifest. That, or search long enough, you'll find her name on the wall."

"What wall?" Galluzzi put a hand to his heart, trying to still it as the shadows closed in around him. He could *feel* them. Kept turning his head, trying to see behind him, fearful of another touch like the one he'd felt outside the shuttle bay.

"You'll see. This way." Shig cycled the hatch manually, opened it to a corridor where the lights flickered on. The panels glowed in what Galluzzi would have called malaria yellow and cast a urine-colored tone on the corridor that led to the Crew Deck.

But the walls . . . Galluzzi tried to understand. Dark, as if poorly covered with...what? Scribbling? Scrawling?

"That's writing." He bent to peer at the looping script. Layers and layers of it. Sentences written over sentences. Thousands upon thousands, until the original meaning was hidden in a mass of looping black ink.

"We've never bothered to scry them all out, given the overwriting, but one of the most frequent is 'The exhalation of death is the breath of life. Draw it fully into your lungs.' My personal favorite is: 'The fingers of the dead wind through our bodies, stroke our hearts, and caress our bowels.' I've always wondered if it was metaphor or factually derived."

Galluzzi stepped warily along the corridor, awed by meter after square meter, the countless layers of overwriting covering walls, ceiling, and floor. He finally saw a legible line that read: "I am vacuum. A cloud of emptiness. I am vacuum. A cloud of emptiness. I am vacuum . . ." and then it was submerged in a tangled chaos of overwritten lines.

"How many days . . . No, how many *years* did they dedicate to this?"

I am reading the ravings of the long dead.

His hair was on end again, a tremble in his muscles. Every fiber of his body wanted to turn, chase pell-mell back through the dark corridor and to the shuttle. To be rid of this . . .

He jerked to the side, sure that something had just passed him. A faint image of a human. It vanished as quickly as it had appeared.

"Did you see that?"

"No." Shig told him. "But I don't believe you've glimpsed the bits of movement I have, either. One seemed to appear out of your right side, only to evaporate. Your only response at that instant was a slight flinch."

"They *lived* in here for one hundred and twenty-nine years?"

"Correct." Shig ran his fingers over the black mass of scrawl, as though it were braille. "They are writing to the dead. This hallway was the only one they left unsealed. Through this door, they brought the bodies, one by one, over the years. Carried them right through here before dropping them into the hydroponics."

Galluzzi endured a flashback. Saw again the stripped and broken human bones sent down the chute from Deck Three to find their ignominious end in *Ashanti*'s hydroponics.

"We are all monsters," he whispered.

"Perhaps. Among other things. All of which makes the study of humanity so engrossing, if not particularly illuminating."

Shig fought off a shiver, turning his steps forward. Took a companionway up, having to turn his flash on again.

Then they stepped out on the Command Deck where again the lights came on with that off-putting urine-yellow glow.

"It's the light in this place," Galluzzi growled. "Like it's sick."

"Captain Torgussen has a theory. When *Vixen* puts her sensors on *Freelander*, it's as if the ship is still tied to wherever it went on the 'other side.' They think it's leaking particles, photons, energy and what have you, back into that universe."

"That's . . ." But no, apparently it wasn't impossible. "My God, Shig, what happened to these people?"

"Mass murder. What they believed was an eternity trapped aboard *Freelander.* And, well, I want you to see this."

"Crew's mess, isn't it?" He stepped through the hatch as Shig shone his light into the room's center.

For a long moment, Galluzzi squinted, trying to make sense of the dome-like structure in the exact center. Some sort of yurt, or cupola. Rounded on the top, perhaps two meters across, two-and-a-half tall at the peak. But what was the lattice-like dome made of? He couldn't place the rickety looking materials.

Shig slapped a palm to the wall, and dim lights flooded the two-story room with a faint glow that cast eerie shadows across the scraped and dirty floor.

"Holy shit." Galluzzi fought for breath.

Bones. The whole damn thing is made of bones.

It put Batuhan's carved throne to shame as a mere pipsqueak's mockery.

Galluzzi felt himself pulled, almost staggered his way to the front of the thing. Stared in disbelief at the incredible artistry. Vertical femora held up the walls. Then came the lines of columnar shin and arm bones, the rows of staring skulls. Thousands and thousands of bones.

"Where did they get so many? My God, there must be hundreds of people here."

"All of them." Shig stopped beside him, rubbing the backs of his arms. "Even the last one."

Galluzzi followed the nod of Shig's head to where the wasted skeleton lay in the doorway. "How come they left that one lying there?"

"Because she was the last. There was no one to wire her bones into the temple."

50

Talbot clutched Dya's body close to his chest as she wrapped her arms around him. Whimpering and sobbing, she buried her head in his neck. The surrounding cavern was blotted with shadow where the weak light of the flash high above didn't penetrate.

"Hey, it's all right," he crooned, petting her hair.

"Damn it! What's happening down there?" Aguila's voice thundered from above.

"We're all right," Talbot called back. "I caught her. Dya's fine. But, hey, you guys might get down here. It's pitch fucking black."

He lowered his wife to her feet, saying, "Keep a hand on my belt. The footing's a little treacherous." Then he fingered around for the rope, felt an invertebrate scuttle its way across the back of his hand.

I really hate this place.

"I thought I was going to die," Dya whispered behind him. "God, Mark. I've never been so scared."

"You were almost to the bottom. It was only about a meter. I could see your silhouette as you fell. Told you I'd be here for you."

"Do you know how much I love you?" she whispered. "If I don't make it . . ."

"We're going home to Su, Kylee, and the kids. You'll see."

He felt it when Muldare's feet found the rope. "That's it, Briah. Just like basic training."

"Fuck you, Talbot," she called down. "I was always your beat on a fast rope."

He held it for her, watching the flashlight beam darting this way and that as she descended, the light obviously held in her teeth. As she reached the bottom, he could see the gallery they were in. Sickly pale invertebrates kept fleeing like a receding wave before the light. The floor continued to slant down, a second tube coming in from the side to join theirs.

"Supervisor?" Muldare asked, shining her light up.

"Damn, it's dark up here," Aguila's voice called down. "Okay, there's a little light refracted. Hold the flash steady. Right there. That's good." And then, "I'm coming down."

Mark got hold of the rope, thankful that Muldare's light was shining up. At least he'd have warning if the Supervisor's body came plummeting down.

"I should have been last," Muldare noted. "I'm trained for this."

"Yeah? Fleeing through lava tubes on a planet thirty light-years from Solar System? Pursued by twenty-second-century space cannibals who are going to save the universe by dismembering and eating people? All the while knowing that if nothing in here kills us, we still have to survive virgin forest full of things that want to make a meal of us? What part of training did I miss?"

Muldare gave him a wry twist of the lips as she said, "Asshole."

Aguila found the rope. He felt it whip as the woman clamped her feet on the first knot.

Talbot grinned to himself as the rope snapped back and forth in his grip. Not that he needed to worry about Kalico. After the three of them had descended, no way the Supervisor wasn't going to make it to the bottom. Didn't matter that her heart was going to be in her throat, Kalico Aguila was going to hit bottom looking like she'd never even broken a sweat.

And she did, almost stumbling for footing, as she stared around at the sloping tunnel.

"How far do you think?" she asked.

"No telling," Talbot told her, taking the lead and feeling his way down the slope.

"Any of the rest of you as thirsty as I am?" Muldare asked.

"Dryer than the desert," Dya agreed, seeming to pull courage from somewhere deep inside.

"Turn the light this way. PA should be scrambling. We're way overdue." Aguila held up her wrist monitor in the flash's glow. "Shit. It's been ten hours since we started down this tunnel. How far does this go?"

That's when Muldare said, "Maybe you haven't been noticing,

but as the bearer of the light, I have. Eyes adjust to illumination so it's hard to keep track. When we started, my beam was good for close to a hundred meters of tunnel. Now we're down to maybe thirty. My advice, people, is that we make time while we've still got light."

Talbot glanced at the beam. Realized it didn't hurt his eyes as badly.

"Yep. Move it. Muldare, you're right behind me lighting my way. Supervisor, Dya, you stay hard on her heels. Let's go."

And he hurried down the sloping surface.

Problem was, he had to have Muldare's light tucked close behind him. He dared not step into a shadow—since on more than one occasion it was a hole that dropped away into unknown depths. Nor did he trust the occasional huge invertebrate that skittered from their path. The things were supposed to be bug-sized, right? So what was with the big ones—the size of lobsters—that fled this way and that? The things looked lethal with barbs, claws, and spikes sticking out of their bodies.

Anyone who'd lived on Donovan knew that when it came to critters, anything that looked like a weapon was. They also knew that while Donovanian wildlife was deadly to humans, in many cases, a person's only safety lay in the fact that said wildlife had never seen a human before, and usually didn't know they were edible.

But if so much as one of the big bugs figured that out?

As the light began to dwindle, Talbot had to ask himself: *Shit on a shoe, where's the end of this thing?*

With the others crowded close, he edged around a vertical stone column, scattering a chittering horde of clicking and scurrying creatures. Here the tube divided. So, which way?

"There!" Muldare pointed with the dying light.

A faint arrow was scratched in the basalt pointing to the left-hand tunnel.

"At least it's not an A.S.," Muldare noted.

"A what?" Dya asked.

"Arne Saknussemm." Muldare glanced back and forth. "Didn't any of you read Jules Verne?"

"Who?" Aguila asked.

Talbot hurried into the tube, stumbled, and almost fell headlong into a dark hole that dropped away on the left side of the cavern.

"Dya?" Talbot called as his heart tried to hammer its way out of his chest. "How you doing?"

"Okay, Mark." But her voice was shaky, on the edge of panic.

"Supervisor?"

"You forget, Marine. I run a mine." Aguila's voice had a forced joviality. "I'm used to holes. And these don't have explosives drilled into the rock at the end."

Yeah, but you also have elevators that you can ride out into the sunlight.

Talbot shinnied past on the lip of the hole as Muldare's fading light illuminated the way. Ahead, he could see nothing in the depths but an eternal blackness.

Under his breath, Talbot whispered, "Get me out of here, God, and I'll live the rest of my life in the out of doors under an open sky."

But the slanting tunnel just kept winding ever deeper into Donovan's depth. They made their way, step by step, clambering over humps of rock, squeezing through tight spots, avoiding bottomless drops, for another three hours.

As the light flickered out, they found the end of the line: a door set into the basalt. Wouldn't have been a problem, but the damn thing was locked.

From the outside.

And then Muldare's beam went dead, leaving them in the pitch black.

51

When did a nightmare end and mind-numbing terror begin? Where was the line? Nothing had prepared Vartan for the things he'd just survived. Nothing. Not even the Harrowing and Cleansing.

During those terrible days people had been ritually murdered, their bodies carefully cut into pieces, cooked, and reverently consumed. If it was truly the universe's will, it made sense.

What he had just witnessed? Just survived?

Incomprehensible.

Vartan staggered back, away from the last of the trees and onto bedrock, making sure he kept his feet moving. That the thin roots here couldn't take hold. Twisting, he turned the rifle to cover every approach; the fear-shakes finally took possession of his muscles.

Tried to swallow.

Couldn't.

That slimy feeling down in his guts urged him to stop. To void his now-liquid bowels of their fear. Breath chattered in his panic-spasming lungs.

Nothing made sense.

Stop. Think. What happened?

Fifteen people had accompanied him down into the forest. Per orders, he'd broken them into three teams. Given each a direction to search. His team had consisted of Mars Hangdong, Hap Chi, Sima Moskva, Will Bet, and Tuac Sao. With Tikal's teams, they had made the long climb down the south trail, the slow and awkward descent from the heights evidence of the poor physical condition they were in. They'd reached the bottom, exhausted. Were resting on a stone outcrop, away from the roots, when the airtruck had roared off overhead.

Vartan had seen a body fall from the side. Thought it was a female. Tried to make sense as to who would be thrown out of the vehicle so wantonly, let alone why the thing was in the air. Svetlana and Hakil were supposed to be guarding the vehicle.

Leaving that for later—once his party had caught their second wind—he had waved farewell as Tikal's parties had spread out from the base of the trail.

For him and his team it had been magical; the journey north along the basalt had been a revelation: the sights, the realization of life in every direction, and most of all, the colors, smells, and sounds. After so many years locked in the prison of Deck Three, here, spinning all around them in a tapestry of blues, greens, cerulean, and yellows and reds, the forest was like a dream come true. Just inhale and pull the perfume into the lungs. Listen to the rising and falling chime.

Magic.

They'd laughed, leaped from stone to stone, marveled at the roots that squirmed under their feet. Stared up at the brilliant blue of the sky and the beams of light cast through the branches by Capella.

They'd located the door that marked the tunnel exit. Chained and locked, it meant either the Supervisor's party had found it open, chained it to keep pursuit from following, or they were still locked inside. He'd studied the ground. Could see no tracks, but that didn't mean anything. Vartan was a city person who wouldn't know a track unless it was glaring.

If his quarry was locked inside, well and good. He had them. If not, he needed to know. Leaving Mars Hangdong to guard the door, he'd taken Sima, Will, Tuac, and Hap Chi to run a quick sweep into the forest as insurance that Aguila wasn't ahead of them.

Nothing big, just check a couple of hundred yards into the deep forest. Besides, he wanted to see. To walk under the towering giants and marvel at the sights and miracle of the place.

At the edge of the basalt flow, some weird plant had grabbed Will Bet as he stepped beneath it. What looked like giant yellow-black-and-red-striped flowers had fastened onto Will's neck and arm. Jerked him up high and out of reach. The flowers had proceeded to bite down on the screaming Will. Damn thing wasn't fazed when

Vartan shot a couple of rounds through the thick stalk. The only reaction came from the plant's roots as they slithered out of the ground in his direction, cutting off retreat back the way they'd come.

In horror, they'd fled down the tumbled basalt and into the darkness of the forest. Scrambled across a tangle of giant roots. Realized the damn things were twisting! Slowly, but surely.

Sima Moskva, mother of two, was next. Something resembling knee-high stalks, pale on the bottom and dark brown on the tips, exploded in some kind of spores that puffed into Sima's face. Sent her into convulsions on the spot. She had fallen, bucking, gagging, her eyes protruding from her head.

. . . And died within moments as the roots she lay on began to writhe and wind around her body. Trying to resuscitate her, Tuac Sao was seized by the same convulsions, having caught a whiff of the spores.

With the roots slipping around their feet, Vartan and Hap had fought a battle to pull away. Barely managed to jerk their way free. Each got a grip on Tuac, tried to hoist the choking, gagging man from the encircling roots. Couldn't.

They'd stumbled back, watched in awed horror as the roots wound around the dead Sima and dying Tuac. Didn't take more than ten minutes total before the thick bunching of squirming root mass had totally engulfed both bodies.

"Vart?" Hap had said. "We've got to get out of here."

"Yeah," he'd panted, consumed by fear.

But trying to get back?

Which way? He was all turned around.

The faintest of screams carried through the chime. Had to be Mars. Vartan hurried off across the roots, realized that the ones that were squirming marked his back trail.

Hadn't gone more than ten meters before he heard the hollow impact. A sodden thud. Like someone dropping a melon from a height onto a duraplast floor. Vart had scrambled the rest of the way down the root mat. Turned, figuring that Hap had fallen, and he would help him back to his feet.

Nothing.

Hap was gone.

Vanished.

Looking up, Vart thought he saw movement up in the trees. Couldn't be sure.

Again, a scream from the direction of the basalt flow.

Somehow Vartan had staggered up onto the basalt flow, panting, falling, tripping over his own feet. He'd kept the rifle, hadn't lost it in his panic. He'd veered wide around where the flower-thing was chewing on Will's head and arm.

The door remained chained.

"Mars!"

Nothing but a slight variation in the chime answered him.

Vartan paced before the door, looking for any sign. Blood. Scuffed dirt. Something dropped.

But he found nothing. The only thing moving was the thin layer of roots that quivered and extended in sinuous patterns across the shallow soil.

"Mars? Where are you?"

Only the endless chime filled his hearing.

Vartan came raggedly to his senses. Realized he was sobbing. Had been for some time.

Terrified down to the marrow in his bones, he wiped tears from his eyes and turned his steps back for the trail. They'd been what, no more than fifteen or twenty minutes here? And he was the only one left?

Veering wide around the gaudily colored plants—shivers wracking his muscles—Vartan tried to cover everything with the rifle. Not that shooting the monster-flower plant had saved Will.

At the trail up, he flopped onto the exposed stone, panted for breath. Tried to find some sort of sanity down in his reeling and tumbling thoughts.

I'm supposed to be the strong one. Trained in security.

And all he had left was consuming terror.

A scream. Barely audible, carried from out in the forest.

Vartan turned to stare out at the vast expanse of green, blue, and turquoise. Was it human? It had been so faint, almost drowned by the chime.

Tikal's parties were supposed to be out there. They'd been sweeping the forest behind Vart's group. Had fanned out from the bottom of the trail.

Scarlet birds burst from the forest canopy, started flying his way.

Vartan cried out, remembering the stories of some flying creature that sliced a man's flesh from his bones.

He pulled up the rifle, fired a burst. Missed. Nevertheless, the flying things veered off and dove into the trees.

Got to get out of here.

Some deep well of terror gave life to his exhausted muscles. Whimpering, sometimes sobbing, he scrambled up the steep trail. He climbed until exhausted. Flopped onto the unyielding basalt, unable to go farther. Panting, spent, he gave up. Closed his eyes, waiting for . . . what? Surrender?

Death?

Nothingness?

He came to. A sound, a shadow, a hint of movement at the edge of his vision sent him scrambling in panic. Breath tearing at his lungs, he swung the rifle around. Couldn't place the threat. Climbed. His feet kept slipping and sliding for purchase given his slick-soled city shoes.

And he made it. Fell weeping on the basalt caprock atop the mesa. The sight of the domes and fields just past the solar collectors was like a miracle of salvation.

After gathering his wits, he struggled to his feet; the heavy rifle hung from his trembling hands. Thirsty. So thirsty. Exhausted like he'd never been.

He managed to stumble his way to the admin dome. Stared at the mangled remains of a woman laid beside the door.

Her face was a bloody wreck; the limbs were broken, rudely askew. The oddly short and contorted torso didn't make sense—at least until he realized her back and hips had to be broken and compressed. Like a human who'd been crushed five inches shorter by a macabre hammer blow. Which explained why her left leg was dislocated so high up on her hip, as if growing out of her waistband. And then there was the bruising and blood.

The scars. So familiar.

Svetlana?

He wavered on his feet, blinked. Kept trying to understand the impossibility of what he was seeing.

This broken bone and meat wasn't Svetlana. She was his lover. His friend.

"She fell from the airtruck," Marta's soft voice said from behind him. "Shyanne and Tamil stole it. Flew it away. Svetlana and Hakil tried to stop them . . . were clinging to the outside. Svetlana landed in the garden. Hakil fell into the forest off to the east."

Svetlana?

Could this cold and brutalized pile of maimed flesh be the woman he'd come to . . .

The world turned glassy in Vartan's vision: He saw it waver, fade, and slide slowly to the side. Thought he heard the distant chatter of automatic weapons fire from somewhere below the rim. Then a singing and ringing sound drowned it out.

The last thing he remembered was his body hitting the ground. Even that faded into a gray haze.

52

As Kalico watched—hands clamped hard to her ears—muzzle flash worked to illuminate the door. Even so, the sound deafened in the confines of the lava tube. Talbot adjusted his aim. Fired another burst. Without hearing protection, the guy had to be in physical pain, given the way Kalico's ears rang.

Holes, shining light could be seen in the door.

Talbot threw his weight against the door, slamming the thing open. Daylight spilled in and Kalico, holding Dya's hand, stumbled out into Capella's blinding glare. Here, near the base of the cliff, scrubby aquajade and stonewood—stunted by the thin topsoil—poked up through some curious species of ferngrass. It had a paler blue tint than what she was used to at Port Authority.

"They're going to have heard that," Briah Muldare said as she turned, staring up the steep slope that rose behind them. They had to be at the bottom of the Tyson escarpment, though nothing could be made out at the top a couple hundred meters above them.

So had PA sent in the cavalry?

Muldare indicated the bullet-severed chain that had secured the duraplast door. "Makes you wonder what used to live in that tunnel that they'd have brought a door down here and chained it shut."

Talbot slammed the portal, fiddled with the broken chain, and gave it up as a bad idea. He rolled an angular chunk of basalt over and used it to prop the door closed.

They all looked disheveled, hair in tangles, clothes filthy, smudged, stained, and scuffed. Kalico assumed that her face, too, was smeared with, well, who knew what that greasy-looking stuff might be? Invertebrate shit?

Her mocking internal voice chided: *You look like you've been locked in a cave for a day.*

Kalico took in the surroundings. The lava tube had opened onto a flat that stuck out on the west side of the Tyson escarpment. Sheer basalt, tumbled boulders, and the aforementioned trees that could find enough soil to cling to rose to the rim where it loomed above them.

From the angle of the sun, partially hidden by trees, and according to her wrist unit, they'd emerged in late afternoon. Crap. Night would be falling in a couple of hours; they were all suffering from thirst and hunger. And they were heading out into the forest without a lick of shelter in any direction.

Talbot pulled his radio from its belt pouch. "I'm resetting the broadcast frequency so the Unreconciled won't monitor us." He hit the mic, and said, "Port Authority, this is Mark Talbot. Do you copy?"

The only answer was static.

"They have to know we're overdue," Muldare groused as she fingered her rifle.

Talbot asked, "Does anyone read? Hello. Can anyone hear me?"

Kalico tried her personal com, knowing it would only link as far as the airtruck, assuming it was still up top. "This is Supervisor Aguila. Does anyone copy?"

Nothing.

Muldare was trying her own radio.

"Sure wish *Vixen* was still in orbit," Kalico groused. "With their survey array, they'd have a chance of picking up our signal."

"Too far out for the handhelds," Talbot agreed, reholstering the unit on his belt. "Where the hell are our people? Two Spot should have half the town here to look for us."

"What now?" Muldare asked.

Around them lay nothing but forest. A flock of scarlet fliers had appeared, perhaps drawn by the unusual sound of gunfire. The chime was rising and falling, adapting in the invertebrates' eternal quest for a symphony.

"Whatever we do, we've got to move," Talbot warned, his eyes on the roots and ferngrass they'd walked out onto. Several of the sucking shrub plants were swiveling branches in their direction.

Kalico turned her attention to the escarpment. The cracked

basalt, much of it columnar, would be an impossible climb. "Where are the trails up?"

"Back to the north," Talbot told her. "And another one down on the point at the southern end. We going back up? They'll be waiting if we do. It's easy to monitor those trails. Lay an ambush."

Kalico squinted. "The airtruck is up there. We've got two service rifles, three pistols. Assuming they got Carson, they've got his rifle with forty rounds and his pistol with twelve."

Dya arched an eyebrow. "You want to go to war with the Unreconciled? You're going to have to shoot down a lot of people to get that airtruck. Thought that avoiding that scenario was why we took to the tunnel in the first place."

"We're overdue by a whole day," Talbot reminded. "What the hell is wrong? Where's Step, Talina, and the posse?"

"And what kind of reception will they be flying into?" Muldare wondered as she fingered her rifle.

"Batuhan had fifty-seven adults to start with," Kalico mused. "Mark shot three. Carson might have taken one down with that gunshot. Given the number of children it's killed, Donovan might have taken out a couple of adults by now, maybe more."

Dya stuffed her fingers in her back pockets as she eased her weight off the shifting roots. "The radio and the airtruck are up top. That's where rescue is going to head first. That's where we've got to be."

"And that's where Batuhan and his cannibals are going to expect us." Muldare, too, was staring up at the high rim, as if expecting to see people staring down from above.

Talbot re-slung his rifle. "Doesn't matter. We've got to move. I've got point. Dya, second. Supervisor, you're third, and Muldare, you've got the six. Walk carefully, people. Try not to disturb the roots."

"Which way?" Kalico asked.

"West off this point, then north through the forest, skirting the base of the basalt to where the slope isn't as steep and rocky," Talbot said. "Even if we can't take the trails, there should be an easier climb leading up into the high ground. We can circle and come around from the north. But be careful, this kind of terrain is just made for bems and skewers. And God alone knows what else might live in the cracks and crevices. Things we've never seen."

When it came to wilderness, Kalico did as she was told. No one—except maybe Talina and Kylee Simonov—knew the backcountry better than Talbot. If there was a chance they could make it, it would be because of his and Dya's forest skills.

Assuming this section of forest had the same threats and followed the same rules they were familiar with.

Dya's skills had been honed in the south, outside Mundo Base. As had Talbot's. That was nearly a thousand kilometers away, in a different ecosystem. Who knew what sorts of deadly creatures lurked in these forests? Especially given that of the last five occupants of Tyson Station, only three had been found, and they'd been skeletonized.

Kalico fell into step behind Dya. The change in the woman was like night to day. A literal analogy. Dya Simonov was once again herself: calm, in control, capable. As if stepping out from that black hole, she'd shed her mind-numbing fear like an old coat.

Well, everyone had his or her weakness.

"There's your bluelinda," Talbot noted, pointing with his rifle as he entered the trees. The thing was indeed beautiful; the little berries, like a string of royal-blue glass pearls, hung from the undersides of the branches where the plant climbed up the side of an aquajade.

The aquajade here were smaller, more widely spaced. Biteya bush, thorncactus, and sucking shrub hung on as understory, and the numerous gotcha vines reminded her of spiderwebs strung between the trees.

Talbot led the way carefully, rifle up, eyes scanning.

Overhead, tree clingers—the first Kalico had ever seen in the flesh—leaped from branch to branch, staring down with their three curious eyes.

The chime seemed to change as they walked farther out onto the point.

"Hold up," Dya called. "Got a bem. Smell it?"

Talbot sniffed, trying to sample the morning breeze. "Your nose is always better than mine. But, yeah. It's there."

Kalico realized the roots were reaching for her feet.

Step by step, she followed Dya forward until Talbot called, "Got it. On the right. About ten meters ahead. By the base of that aquajade."

Kalico followed where he pointed, seeing what looked like a tumbled basalt boulder. Scenting the breeze herself, she thought she picked up the slightest scent of vinegar. Took a long gander at the bem. "Damn, they're good. Even knowing what to look for, I'd have thought it was a rock."

Talbot cut wide, leaving plenty of distance between them. Bems weren't fast, depended on their perfect camouflage for success in hunting.

They had reached the edge of the flat, the ground dropping away on either side into deeper forest. Kalico was wishing she had eyes in the back of her head, trying to see everything in this deadly world of greens and blue. The leaves were all either moving on their own accord or stirred by the slight breeze.

The chime covered any forest sound. Movement on the branches was caused by the vines, invertebrates, or the shifting of the trees.

She almost ran into Dya's back, so quickly did the woman stop.

"Damn," Talbot, up in the lead, cursed.

Kalico craned her neck, looking around Dya to see a body. Well, okay, most of a body. Naked, obviously male, the thing was suspended a good two meters off the ground, having been wrapped up in dark green vines that wound around the legs, the torso, and single remaining arm. Other vines were woven into the chabacho and neighboring aquajade to support both plant and victim.

The main stem of the plant looked as thick as a man's thigh, the upper part engorged. Two stalks ending in . . . well, hard to call them flowers, were expanding and contracting, taking slow bites out of what remained of one shoulder and the bloody neck. Didn't matter that an arm and the head had already been devoured; the scar patterns identified the remains as one of the Unreconciled.

Below where the body hung, a flock of invertebrates scuttled around and through the man's scanty clothing as they snapped up any bits and drops that fell from above.

"What the hell?" Muldare asked through a horrified exhale.

"Tooth flower," Dya said woodenly. "One of the biggest I've ever seen."

"It's eating . . ." Kalico couldn't finish. Could only stare.

"Come on," Talbot almost barked the command. "Poor bastard was probably searching for us. Keep an eye out, and let's get the hell off this point."

"To where?" Dya wondered. "It's going to be dark long before we can work out any trail back to the top."

"Don't know," Talbot said, cutting wide around the tooth flower and its feast. "Rock outcrop? Maybe a low crotch of a tree if we can find a chabacho big enough and without any of the carnivorous vines."

Kalico swallowed hard, wishing again that she had something to drink. Wishing she were away, back in Corporate Mine. Wishing she were anywhere but out here in the forest.

As she passed, she could hear one of the tooth flowers contracting; the sound was accompanied by the snapping of human bones as the teeth sheared through the man's clavicle, upper ribs, and vertebrae.

Dya whispered, "Judging from that poor bastard back there, I guess the Unreconciled aren't as pure in the eyes of the universe as Batuhan thought."

"Yeah," Muldare said in a tight voice. "Maybe the universe found Batuhan's methods wanting and decided to improve upon the process."

53

Talina watched the airtruck drop toward the Briggs pad to land beside her aircar. Dust swirled up, blowing out in curling clouds to dissipate as the vehicle settled onto its skids.

Capella's harsh light gleamed on the sialon and metal sides, glinted from the windshield up front. Airtrucks weren't masterpieces of elegance, being built strictly for utilitarian function.

As the fans spun down, a thin woman opened the door, climbed wearily down. She was naked but for a wrap around her waist; her ratty brown hair was confined with a tie at the back of her neck. Talina could see the lines of scars crisscrossing her pale flesh. Some sort of spirals—centered on the nipples—covered each of her small breasts.

"Pus-sucking hell," Chaco whispered where he stood beside Talina. "So that's a cannibal?"

A rail-thin man appeared in the door behind the woman and stepped carefully to the ground. He, too, only wore a breechcloth; his bare feet, like the woman's, looked so incongruous on the raw dirt. No one went barefoot on Donovan. At least not if they wanted to avoid a most hideous death as slugs slithered around their insides, eating their guts and muscles. The man was dark-skinned and the scars stood out—lines of them running down his torso, arms and legs, and around his face. They'd been patterned like triangles to accent his broad nose.

"Hello," the woman called, starting forward, a hand shielding her eyes from Capella's strong light. "I'm Shyanne Veda, and this is Tamil Kattan. Thank you for the beacon. We didn't know what to do."

Talina stepped forward, hand on her pistol, wary eyes on the airtruck. The thing could carry up to fifteen, maybe twenty people if they didn't mind being packed in like sardines. "How many of you are there?"

"We're all that's left. We started with six. Batuhan's First Will got the other four. Tamil, here, he was the important one, he could fly the airtruck."

"Where's Supervisor Aguila, Dr. Simonov, Talbot and the marines?"

Shyanne had a panicked look on her face. Her lips parted, and she was panting. From the heat? From exertion? Or fear? "One of the marines, the one they left to guard the airtruck, he's dead. The others got away. At least I think they did. The Messiah had people searching everywhere. Even sent teams down into the forest. Batuhan sent so many after them, it gave me and Tamil our chance to break away. But damn him, he knew. Tried to stop us. We shook Hakil and Svetlana off as we were climbing from Tyson."

"Who are Hakil and Svetlana?" Talina asked.

"They're some of the Messiahs' 'Will.' That's what he calls them. Police. Enforcers. The ritual executioners. They ensure that what he wills is done."

Chaco made a wait-a-moment gesture with his hands. "Hey, I'm Chaco Briggs. This is my place. So relax, huh? Start at the beginning. You're not making a lick of sense."

Tamil had stopped a couple of steps behind Shyanne, dark eyes glancing uneasily from Talina to Chaco and back. The guy kept licking his lips. Couldn't quite figure out what to do with his hands, so he started wringing them.

Shyanne fought down what looked like a surge of panic. Swallowed hard. "Listen. I'm a veterinary tech Level I. There were six of us. With scientific backgrounds . . . or maybe just the kind of people who didn't buy the bullshit, you know? But it was survival. Who the hell wanted to have their throats cut and be eaten? The things we did to . . . to . . ."

When she couldn't finish, looked on the verge of breaking down, Talina snapped, "We know. What happened at Tyson?"

Tamil told her, "Shyanne was listening from the kitchen. Hoping to get back to see her daughter. Understood the moment the Supervisor said it was a prion that was giving the Prophets their visions. Shyanne explained it to us. Not that we'd bought the clap-trapping holy prophet shit. We'd already figured that once we got dirtside, we'd get away. Figured that out clear back on *Ashanti*. Then, seeing where we were? Surrounded by wilderness? It was like being crushed."

"Then Aguila shows up with the science." Shyanne had found her voice again. "There were six of us who thought we'd finally gotten our chance. Here was proof that would debunk the whole 'we're chosen by God and the universe' thing."

Tamil added, "But Batuhan had members of the Will in place, waiting. Tricked the marine guarding the airtruck. Killed him. Closed the doors to the dome, figured he had the Supervisor trapped, right? But they pulled guns. Shot some of the First Chosen. Those are the ones who carry the throne and attend the Messiah. The Supervisor and her people managed to get down into the basement."

Shyanne said, "Stalemate. Batuhan can't attack them head on. They've got enough firepower to kill everyone in that stairwell. Meanwhile, the rest of us, the disbelievers, we're waiting for rescue. Someone's going to come for the Supervisor. But it gets dark.

"So we plan. Come morning, with Tamil at the wheel, we'll fly out. Find help."

"But somehow Batuhan knows; he has the Will grab four of us." Tamil chuckled in what was clearly gallows humor. "Cuts Jilliam's and Cumber's throats right there. Starts butchering them for feast. Don't know what happened to Kleo and Troy."

"We play the game." Shyanne's eyes had gone dull. "But we're being watched. Then, at daybreak, there's a cry. Turns out that the Supervisor and her people have found a way into some tunnel. It takes a while to figure out, but this tunnel goes down somewhere on the west side. So maybe they've escaped into the forest."

Kylee—a fastbreak over her shoulder—with the panting and sweating Dek Taglioni stumbling behind her, rounded the workshop and pulled up. The way Kylee fixed on Shyanne and Tamil was like a mongoose on a cobra. Talina gave her a hand signal to wait and listen.

Shyanne might have been oblivious. "First thing this morning Batuhan sent search parties to hunt them down, and we made a break for the airtruck. Thought we had a chance. Barely got if off the ground. And that was with Hakil and Svetlana clinging to the side, swearing they'll kill us."

Tamil spread his hands like a supplicant. "If you hadn't heard us on the radio, sent us that beacon, we'd have never found this place."

"Get back to the Supervisor." Talina stepped close. "She, Dya, Talbot, and one marine escaped into the forest, right? So, they're still out there?"

"As of when we left." Shyanne nodded.

"There's about thirty of the chosen hunting them," Tamil added. "More than enough to chase four people down."

"Shit on a shoe," Chaco muttered.

Kylee stepped close, shooting the scarred woman and man a scathing glare. "So my mother and father, Kalico, and some marine are out in the forest? Being hunted?"

"Yeah, kid," Talina said softly, the quetzals in her blood having quickened. In her mind she was seeing forest trails, smelling the scent of prey, vision going keen in the infrared and ultraviolet.

"How much chance can they have?" Tamil asked, almost pleading. "There's only four of them. With the airtruck gone, Batuhan has nothing to keep him from sending everyone in pursuit."

"It's not the Unreconciled I'm worried about," Talina said.

"We've got to go get them." Kylee's gaze had gone vacant. Her eyes seeming to enlarge.

Yeah, she was sharing the same images Talina was.

"What about the rest of Batuhan's people?" Tamil asked, a look of desperation in his dark eyes.

Kylee—in a voice thinner than wire—said, "Sorry. They had their chance. Nothing we can do for them now."

"What does that mean?" Shyanne's gaze flicked from face to face.

"On Donovan, stupidity is a death sentence," Talina told her. "Let's tell Madison what's coming down and get packed."

"Not me," Shyanne cried, on the verge of tears. "I'll die before I go back there."

"Me, too," Tamil said in a hoarse whisper.

From the look in Kylee's eyes, she was more than ready to help them along.

"We'll take care of you until this is over," Chaco said.

"Let's beat feet." Talina turned, images of deep forest playing in her head. Four people, without armor, in unfamiliar territory. And just because they were among the best on the planet, this was still Donovan.

They didn't have much time.

54

When Dek appeared on the landing pad with his rifle and packed war bag Talina demanded, "What the hell do you think you're doing?"

"Packing my shit to go along. What do you think I'm doing?"

"Hey, soft meat, the last thing I need is a newbie Skull stumbling around in the forest and turning himself into supper for the nearest sidewinder."

"The last thing you need is to set down somewhere in the forest, only to have good old Batuhan stumble over the airtruck. Who guards it while you search? Or did I miss something?"

A sliver of smile bent Talina's lips. "Bound and determined to get your ass in a sling, huh? Okay, get your gear on board."

As Dek turned away, he heard Chaco say, "You sure that's a good idea? He's a solid guy, got potential, but you're going to get him killed."

Dek turned back. "You just keep an eye on Shyanne and Tamil. Maybe they're really refugees. Maybe not. But you figure that after what they've been through, what they've done, they're still Unreconciled. Probably not as soft and cuddly as they are trying to appear. Think: Broken goods."

"Gotcha." Chaco stuck out a hand. "Hey, Dek. You make it through this? You gotta place out here with us. You understand?"

"Thanks, Chaco."

He placed a foot in the step up to the airtruck and noticed Talina's evaluative stare. "What?"

She arched a slim eyebrow. "Must have been some day down in the canyon fixing that pump."

"Turned out to be a little more complicated than Chaco thought. We got it working, why?"

She rolled her lips between her teeth, her gaze going alien on him. "Nothing. Get aboard."

He slung his pack onto the deck, climbed in, and racked the Holland & Holland next to Talina's service rifle. He made sure he had his bullets and a spare powerpack for the gun in his web gear.

Kylee was fastening the straps on a backpack, glanced sidelong at him. "Told you she liked you."

"You see different things than I do."

"Yep." She didn't look up. "You might want to move out of the doorway."

"Huh? Why, I—"

Kylee reached out, grabbed him by the web gear, and jerked him sideways. Damn near yanked him off his feet.

As Dek struggled for balance, something huge, flashing yellow and black, scrambled through the space he'd occupied. The thing blocked the light, filled the doorway. The sound of claws could be heard as they sought purchase on the sialon deck.

Dek planted a foot, whirled to stare at the creature that now took up way too much of the compartment. Big, fully two meters at the shoulders, the beast swung its muzzle to within inches of Dek's nose.

A great triangular head filled Dek's vision, and he had to look from eye to eye to eye, so widely were they spaced across the top of the monster's head. Black, gleaming, they seemed to see right through to Dek's bones. Patterns of violet, mauve, and orange replaced the yellow and black designs running over the beast's hide.

"Wha . . . ? What?" Dek staggered backward, slammed into the duraplast wall. Knees gone weak, his heart now hammered so hard it might burst his chest. He fought to get a breath.

A yip of terror escaped his throat as a membrane, like an unfolding sail, ringed the creature's neck and began flashing colors so brilliant they almost hurt the eyes.

Dek opened his mouth in the attempt to cry out. A blur shot from the beast's mouth. Like a hard leather rod, it jetted past Dek's lips, flicked over his tongue and bumped off his molars. The force of his reaction banged the back of his head off the wall. As the leathery thing glanced off Dek's soft palate, his gag reflex tried to bend him double.

An overpowering taste—like concentrated peppermint extract—flooded his mouth. Saliva began to pump. Paralyzed, he stared across the great triangular head into the top eye. It seemed to have expanded, filling Derek Taglioni's entire universe.

"*Flute!*" Kylee's barked command barely penetrated Dek's fugue. "*Back off!* Leave him alone."

Just as quickly, the tongue was gone. Somehow Dek kept from collapsing, managed to lock his knees, back braced against the airtruck's cargo bay.

For long seconds he fought to fill his lungs, to keep from throwing up.

"They don't know how rude humans find that," Talina muttered from the wheel where she was checking the battery indicator and fans.

"What the hell?" Dek squeaked in terror as he gaped at the . . . the . . . what? Dinosaur? Dragon? Or . . .

"This is Flute," Kylee told him. "He's a quetzal. Don't mind the French kiss thing. It's how they say hello."

A quetzal? Here?

Dek gaped at the creature in rapt horror. Quetzals ate people. He could well imagine, looking as he was at that big mouth filled with wicked serrations that served as teeth. They ran from one side of the wide triangular jaw to the other.

He wanted to spit the terrible taste out. His mouth kept watering.

"You sure you want Flute along?" Talina asked. "This is last call for him to get off."

Kylee stepped over, placed a hand on the beast's . . . um, shoulder? With her other hand, she pointed toward the rear of the compartment. "You better go lie down. And don't look out the windows. When Rocket flew, he almost went catatonic."

Flute flashed a riot of orange and sky-blue; the intricate designs ran down his hide as if flowing. That sail-like collar had deflated flush with the beast's neck. Then, with remarkable agility for a creature that large, it curled itself along the floor, conforming to the back bench.

"Shit on a shoe," Dek wheezed. "It's going with us?"

Kylee fixed her alien-blue gaze on him. "That's my mom and dad out there in the forest being chased by cannibals. Get it? And Flute likes Mom."

Dek jumped as the fans spun up, Talina at the wheel. Still shaking—and as scared as he'd ever been—he stepped to the door, gave Chaco and the cannibals a farewell wave, and slammed it before anything else could leap in with him.

Talina was on the radio. "Two Spot? Got trouble at Tyson. If we can believe the source, Carson is dead, and Kalico, Dya, Talbot, and Muldare are hiding out in the forest. I'm heading that way from Briggs. I'll let you know what's up as we get closer."

"Roger that. But, Tal, we're on lockdown. Got a quetzal. At least one is in the compound. Got another five outside the fence trying to get in."

"Shit. Figures. I'll send an update as soon as I know anything."

"Roger that. We get this resolved, we'll come on the run."

It hit Dek that everything had happened so fast. Now, as they soared out over the forest, it was with the realization that he was flying out to confront the Irredenta, to attempt the rescue of Supervisor Aguila and her party, accompanied by a quetzal-infected teenager and Talina Perez. And he was locked in a small compartment with a man-eating monster. One that—of all things—had stuck its tongue into Dek's mouth. What part of this wasn't insane?

Oh, Derek. You were the one who wanted to get a feeling for the real Donovan.

Which left him shuddering. If this turned out wrong, if the quetzal didn't eat him, it would be the Irredenta who'd be picking his bones clean.

Hard to believe that he'd considered that nightmare safely left behind the day he'd shuttled out of *Ashanti*.

55

A quetzal in the compound? Five more trying to get in? The desire to wheel around, fly full-throttle for PA, tore at Talina's soul. She should be there. No one knew how to hunt quetzals like she did.

Down in her gut, Demon hissed, *"Got you, didn't we?"*

"Yeah? Bet there's going to be nothing but steaks and leather by nightfall, you creepy little shit."

Talina took her heading for Tyson. As much as she yearned to head for PA, Kalico, Dya, and Talbot needed her. First hand, she knew the sense of desperation that came from being lost in the forest.

"So, from Two Spot's report, it was six of them. Three on the Mine Gate, three from the shuttle field." Talina shot a glance at Kylee. "That's a whole new tactic. And in the middle of the day."

"Whitey really hates you, huh?" Kylee gave Talina an evaluative blue-eyed stare.

"Yeah, lucky me."

Demon tried to claw at her stomach, hissing in rage.

Piece of shit.

Talina checked her compass and airspeed. Below her the wild Donovanian terrain unfolded and flowed. The airtruck responded instantly to the touch. The fans and gimbals were all tight, within tolerance. Ungainly as the airtruck looked, it handled like a dream, a reassuring feeling after all of these years. Hard to believe that the power indicator really meant what it said. Reliable. So good that she could partially ignore that constant and nagging worry about what to do if they went down. How damn long had it been since she could fly without fear?

Dek was scrunched in the corner of the cab, back to the door. He kept staring in disbelief at Flute. The look on his face was priceless: Like the guy just knew the terrified quetzal was going leap across the cargo box and eat him.

Not a chance given that Flute was flashing the bright yellow-and-black patterns of terror mixed with teal anxiety spots in addition to glowing way down in the infrared.

Quetzals really hated to fly. That he'd dared it at all was mark of the beast's affection for Kylee and perhaps Dya. Or—who knew?—it was some other quetzal experiment cooked up by his lineage.

Kylee stepped up to the dash beside Talina, her gaze fixed on the landscape. In a voice barely above a whisper, she said, "He's not ready, you know."

"Flute? Then why'd you insist he come along?"

"I mean Dek."

"He wanted a taste of Donovan. As long as he just stays in the airtruck, keeps it out of the cannibals' hands, he'll be all right."

"You're not setting us down at Tyson, so that means we're setting down in the forest. You've got a place in mind?"

"Ridgetop, a couple of kilometers north and above. Mostly basalt bedrock. If Dek locks the doors, shoots anything that tries to force its way in, he'll be all right. And I'll set the radio on the PA frequency before we go. If something happens, Shig can have Manny Bateman run the shuttle out to pick him up after they mop up this quetzal trouble."

Kylee shrugged.

Talina shot Kylee a questioning look. "Did he shoot that fast-break this morning, or did you?"

"He did. He listens well, but he's still weak from being on that ship. I get what you see in him. With the right luck, he might make it. Really different than Cap, though. This one's more centered. If Donovan doesn't kill him, he could be a full partner."

"Got it all figured out, huh?"

"He's a world of improvement over Bucky Berkholtz."

"There's times I wish you didn't have so much of me in you."

"No, you don't."

"And why's that, kid?"

Kylee flipped her hair back, grinned. "Because every time I want to lose it, want to fucking scream, and cry, and beat the crap out of Tip, or unload all my frustrations on Madison, you're there. Down deep. It's like having a big sister inside my head. At first, I hated it. Really, really, hated it. Now I'm the most thankful girl on the planet."

"Glad to be of service. Having you inside me . . . well, it's a balance. Keeps me on track with all these asshole quetzals running around inside my skull."

Kylee nodded, her worried gaze fixing on the horizon. "Think Mom's okay?"

"Don't know, kid. Nobody in their right mind wants to take a chance on the forest, not without a full set of armor and tech. If it was anybody but your mom and dad, I'd say write it off. And as good as your mom is, Talbot's even better. Maybe as good as anyone on the planet when it comes to staying alive."

"He's not us," Kylee countered, referring to the quetzal in their blood. "And we've got Flute."

"Which is why we'll find them."

"You think this lockdown could be Whitey?"

"Bet on it. That snot-sucker's still ahead of me. Killed a prospector last month. Old Chin Hua Mao. As good a veteran Wild One as you'll find in the bush. Somehow Whitey, or of one of his lineage, got old Chin by surprise while he was working his claim in the Blood Mountains."

"There," Kylee pointed. Having spotted Tyson in the distance.

Talina keyed the radio. "Kalico? Mark? Dya? Do you read? Come in. Kalico? Mark? Dya? If you can—"

"Got ya, Tal," Kalico's voice came faintly through the receiver. *"We're about a half klick west of Tyson, moving slowly. Where are you?"*

"Coming in from the east in the airtruck. Anyplace I can set down?"

"Negative on that. We're on the floodplain below the basalt. Trees are four hundred meters tall if they're an inch. We'll have to find someplace open enough you can drop down."

"What's your situation? Who's with you?"

Beside her, Kylee went as tight as a coiled spring.

"Me, Talbot, Dya, and Muldare are still out here. We think Carson's dead and the Unreconciled have his weapon. Consider Tyson hostile. Repeat, Tyson is hostile. You copy that?"

"Roger that." Talina keyed the mic again, calling, "Two Spot, you get that relay?"

"Affirmative."

Talina circled wide of Tyson Station, peering down through the windscreen as she did. It was to see a handful of people watching from the domes, some waving her in. As the angle changed, she spotted a few more. Not more than seven visible in the whole compound.

"What do you think?" Kylee asked as they curled around to the west. A person need only look down on the vegetation to know where the deep forest lay and where shallow bedrock restricted the size of the trees.

Talina keyed the mic. "Supervisor? If my calculations are correct, we should be right above you. Trees are definitely too thick to attempt a descent here. Canopy looks like it's woven as tight as a blanket."

Talbot's voice came through. *"You find a safe place to put down. We'll beat feet to wherever you are."*

Talina drifted them north, searching. There had to be a hole, something with a rocky outcrop where the roots hadn't taken hold. The last thing they needed was to set down and have roots wind themselves around the fan blades.

And there, she saw it. An opening in the canopy. One of the weird lime-green trees with those monstrous paddle-shaped branches. It stood like an isolate out in the center, but if Talina could slide down along the margin of the branches, she could drop them at the edge of the root zone.

"Kalico?" Tal keyed the mic. "We're maybe a kilometer to the north and west. Got a hole. We're going to ground."

"Roger that. Got a reading on my signal?"

"Affirmative." Talina plotted the fix, glanced at her compass. "We're north, twenty-five degrees west. Figure that we'll meet you halfway. After we're all loaded, it'll be three hours to supper and beer at Briggs' place."

"Best news we've heard all day. Got any water? Repeat: We need water."

"We'll bring some." Talina smiled at that, gave Kylee a reassuring wink, and began her descent. She dropped the airtruck down just out of reach of the waving branches. As she did, the chabacho and aquajade leaves kept turning her way, pulling back from the downdraft created by the fans.

Even the vines retreated, and here and there, some forest creature vanished into the darkness, fleeing in panic as the airtruck roared past.

"Kylee, grab a couple of water bottles. Dek, you lock the door after the last of us is out. I'm putting us on the edge of the root mat. If you see them creeping toward the airtruck, you call me ASAP on the radio. I'll beat feet back and lift us off before they can latch hold of the frame or tangle in the fans."

"You sure you don't want me to just take the controls and hover?"

"You can fly this thing?"

Taglioni shrugged. "It's been a while. Looks like standard controls. Nothing different from my old Beta Falcon."

Talina grinned as she set them softly on the dark-gray soil just beyond the edge of the roots. "My, you're just one surprise after another, aren't you? Why didn't you say something?"

"You never asked." He was watching out the side window, staring at the weird lime-green tree where it stood maybe fifty meters away in the center of the clearing. "What is that thing? You got a name for it?"

Tal glanced, noticed the gigantic leaves—somehow reminding her of the woven handheld palm fans of her youth—had turned their way. Reacted to their descent.

"Nothing official," she replied. "Iji calls them lollipop trees. I heard Talbot call it a ping-pong-paddle tree. We've never had the time or people to fully study them, let alone a lot of Donovanian life. That's what Tyson Station was originally all about. If there were any notes about those trees, they never survived the evacuation."

Kylee unlatched the door to stare out thoughtfully, her nose working, as if she'd pick up anything beyond the stench of exhaust and hot motors.

"Let's go, people," Talina called, pulling her rifle from the rack. "We've only got a couple of hours before dark. Flute? We're here.

You can open your eyes and turn blue and pink now. You survived your first flight."

An eye popped open on the top of the terrified quetzal's head. It focused on the open door. The beast damn near bowled Kylee off her feet as it rushed to make its escape.

"Hey! Don't be an asshole!" Kylee shouted at the departed quetzal, then slung her backpack with the extra water over one shoulder, grinned, and leaped out after Flute.

Talina handed Dek his rifle, saying, "Keep the door closed. Anything tries to get in that's not us? Shoot it."

"Yes, ma'am." Dek took his rifle.

"*Talina!*" Kylee's scream brought Talina to the door, her heart skipping a beat.

Kylee was standing at the edge of the root mat, staring up over the top of the airtruck. Flute, too, was fixed on whatever was up there, his panicked colors instantly gone, replaced by perfect camouflage as he hunched down and blended with the background. Only his three gleaming black eyes were visible.

Talina leaped to the ground, whirled, bringing her rifle up.

For a moment, she could only blink at the impossibility of it.

The ping pong paddle tree was moving, bending. The fifty or so giant paddle fans—each maybe ten to fifteen meters across—were glowing in eerie viridian as it leaned toward them, the bulk of it hidden by the airtruck.

"Dek!" she screamed. "Get out of there!"

As she did, the first of the big paddles slapped down on the top of the airtruck with a solid thump. Another pasted itself against the tailgate, shivering the truck. Dek, in the open door, was knocked free. Rifle in hand, he tumbled to the ground—barely kept himself from landing face-first.

"What the hell?" Talina barely whispered as the airtruck was shaken as if it were a toy. The huge paddles had conformed and latched onto the top and sides. And then the tree began to straighten, lifting the vehicle as if it were a feather.

Behind her right ear, Rocket's sibilant voice told her: *"Run!"*

56

When Talina Perez shouted "*Run!*" Dek was still stumbling forward. Using his rifle for balance, he staggered to a stop, tried to understand what had happened. One instant he'd been in the door, looking down at Talina, Kylee, and most astonishing of all, the way Flute had seemed to vanish before his eyes.

The next it was like the hand of God had pitched him out onto the ground.

As he caught himself, he turned to look. Couldn't believe what he was seeing: the airtruck was being lifted, something big and flat, glowing lime green, stuck to its top. More of the great pads had attached to the sides and front. And behind them, the rest of the giant fan-shaped green spatulas waved and fluttered, as if trying to get to the airtruck.

"What the hell?" He stood rooted.

A hard hand pulled him around. Talina glared hotly into his eyes. "I said *run*! Follow me. Now!"

She dragged him violently backward.

Kylee was already sprinting across the roots to disappear into the shadows under the trees.

"Flute!" the girl called as she vanished into the forest. "Come!"

The quetzal materialized out of apparent nothingness, seeming to just pop into existence. The beast moved like nothing Dek had ever seen. Literally a streak of yellow and black as it shot into the shadow of the trees.

Following on Talina's heels, Dek spared one last look over his shoulder. The lollipop tree had lifted the airtruck a good sixty or seventy meters into the air. He could hear the buckling of metal; the loud popping as sialon and duraplast ruptured and broke.

As pieces fell from the crushed vehicle, the lower leaves caught them, fielding the wreckage like baseball mitts caught fly balls. The whole huge tree seemed preoccupied with the bits and pieces.

And then he was in twilight, heart hammering, a cold sweat like he'd never known turning his skin clammy.

Kylee had slowed, staring around. Flute, his colors still a riot, was making a weird tremolo from his tail vents.

"What the hell?" Talina asked, rubbing a hand on the back of her neck. "You ever seen that?"

"Nope." Kylee muttered. "I got nothing from quetzal memory, either. But my quetzals aren't from around here."

"Keep moving," Talina told Dek. "Don't let the roots grab hold of your feet. And you follow us. Do as we do."

All he wanted was drop to his knees and shake, but somehow, he nodded. Said, "Yes, ma'am. So . . . what do we do now?"

"Link up with Kalico," Talina muttered. She checked her wrist compass, said into her com, "Kalico? You there?"

Dek couldn't hear the response through Talina's earbud.

"Yeah, well, I've got bad news. One of those ping pong trees just destroyed the airtruck. Crunched it up like it was made of paper."

A pause.

"No shit! And I'll add a fuck, cunt, damn, and hell, to boot!"

Talina's expression communicated distaste as she listened.

Then: "Yeah." A pause. "It's that or nothing." Another pause. "We're headed your way."

Talina took the lead, walking softly across the thickening mat of roots. "Wow. Turns out the Supervisor can really cuss when big trees eat her airtruck. Too bad you weren't listening in, kid. You could have learned some great new swear words."

"Never knew anyone could out-cuss you, Tal. So, what's next?" Kylee had one hand on Flute's side as they stepped over a thick root. To Dek's amazement the root was squirming, as if uncomfortable with the very soil in which it was embedded.

Talina told her, "We've got to link up with your folks and Kalico. Find shelter for the night. Then, in the morning, we've got to get to high ground. That, or a radio where we can get back in touch with PA."

"That sucks toilet water," Kylee murmured, then pointed. "Dek, see that? That's called you're screwed vine. Don't get close to it."

"And don't touch *anything*," Talina warned.

"No shit." He took a real good look at the you're screwed vine, committing it to memory. Clutched his rifle close. As he followed, he kept staring down at his booted feet. Weird feeling how the roots squirmed underfoot.

Around him, in the dim shadows, the world seemed to close in. In places the roots crowded into great bundles that merged into the monstrous trunks of trees that in turn rose to impossible heights. Vines, their stems the diameter of oil drums, wound up into the overstory. Here and there he could see clumps of inter-knotted roots as if neighboring trees were wrestling and trying to strangle each other.

The sound! The chime here was louder than he'd ever heard. Rising, falling, shifting. And when he looked closely, he could see the invertebrates scrambling through the root mass. Keeping a wary distance from their passage.

Flute uttered a gurgling chitter, his hide flashing teal and sky blue. Kylee turned her attention to the quetzal, asking, "How so?"

Flute, his colors going muted green, displayed in a riotous pattern followed by royal blue and a deep purple.

"Flute says there's something bad here. It's an old memory. Almost mythical. He thinks we should veer a little more to the east. He's just catching hints."

"Flute?" Talina called. "Take the lead. Your call. We just have to get to Dya. You understand?"

A harmonic sounded from the quetzal's vents, the color patterns turning sunset-orange as the beast hurried on ahead.

Talina must have had an incoming communication. Dek heard her answer, saying, "All I can see from here is roots and tree boles. Something's spooked Flute. We're headed a little more east before we veer south. Should have eyes on you sometime soon."

A pause as Talina listened.

"No," Talina told her com as she hurried along. "Can't hear a thing over this chime, but we'll be listening for your call."

"I wouldn't have believed it," Dek whispered, watching in awe. "Quetzals are intelligent? They can understand something as complicated as that?"

"Well, duh," Kylee muttered under her breath, gaze turned up as something shifted in the branches above.

The pace picked up with Flute in the lead. Dek found himself pushed to the edge of endurance, panting, trying desperately to keep up. When had his rifle grown so heavy? And the damn thing was always in the way.

"Flute?" Talina called. "Got to slow down some."

Dek grinned under his layer of sweat. "Sorry. Ship muscles."

"Yeah, and don't think forest travel is always this fast," Kylee added. "It's remarkable how many predators run for their holes when a quetzal's out front."

"But don't get cocky," Talina growled, gaze roving. "Tooth flower, biteya bush, brown caps, claw shrub, and the like couldn't care less. They'll still kill you."

Dek funneled all of his concentration into just keeping up. Putting one foot after another where Talina put hers. In the trees overhead, something screamed, the sound agonized and unearthly.

At a bundle of giant roots—all laced together like a nest of monster worms—Flute bounced gracefully to the top. Froze there.

Laboriously, Kyle, Talina, and finally Dek climbed up, scrambling from one massive root to the next, like ascending giants' stairs.

At the top, Flute remained motionless, his collar fully expanded, muzzle lifted, mouth open as he sucked in air and vented it behind his tail. For Dek the process was fascinating to watch.

"What's up?" Kylee asked, her own nose lifted and sniffing.

Talina, too, was scenting the air.

Something about the way they did reminded Dek of hunting dogs.

For the moment he was happy to crouch in the half light, pant, and wipe the sweat from his face. Damn hot in here. Moist. Felt like a low-level steam bath.

Talina cupped her hands and bellowed *"Talbot? Kalico?"* at the top her lungs, then cocked her head to listen.

Up in the high branches, some creature tweeted, cackled, and cooed in an unearthly juxtaposition of sound. Might have been something from a bad dream, but none of the others seemed bothered by it.

He glanced around, wishing he had better light. Wondered at the smells of the place: all musty, damp, and curiously mindful of mold-slimy cilantro. When he concentrated on just one spot, he had the eerie realization that things were moving. Slowly, to be sure, but moving nevertheless. The roots, the vines, the shadows, all alive.

A distant scream was followed an instant later by the sound of gunshots.

And then silence.

Viscerally, Dek understood: That scream had been human.

57

What the hell was it? Talbot stared at the oddity. Some sort of seed? No, had to be a creature. Reminded him of a picture he'd seen of a sea urchin back on Earth—a big ink-black ball-like thing bristling with countless slender needles pointing out in all directions. But this wasn't under water, it rested on the forest floor. The beast was at least a meter in diameter, and clearly had three eyes. So, animal then. What sent a shiver down his back was the hundreds of gleaming needle spines, and each of them was quivering.

Kalico was still spouting the occasional colorful curse word. She'd started cussing upon receiving word of the airtruck's fate. Kept muttering the occasional acid-laced profanity.

Behind him, Dya said, "Never seen anything like that before. Looks like a . . . a . . ."

"Giant sea urchin?"

"Yeah. But this thing's bigger than an oversized beachball."

Talbot glanced around; the masses of roots piled and interlocked like a giant knot. Tough to go around.

The forest began to chime with a greater intensity, as if building to a crescendo. A few faint beams of light shown through the high canopy a couple hundred meters overhead. The vines swung as if in a breeze—though the muggy air pressed down, still, heavy, and damp.

Reaching into his pouch, Talbot dug around for an obsidian pebble he'd picked up during a geologic survey with Lea Shimodi. Squinting, he pulled his arm back and threw.

The pebble arched, hit the pincushion dead center.

Talbot figured the thing would threaten, wave the long needle-thin spines around. Instead, to his horror, a haze of them shot out from the round body. Deadly little arrows traveled five or six meters, sticking into the surrounding roots like wicked spears. The roots immediately began to writhe as if in great pain.

"Guess we don't want to go that way," Dya said dryly.

"Guess not," Talbot agreed, rising from his crouch. "All right, it's backtrack or nothing."

"Great," Kalico whispered. "What I'd give for a bottle of water."

"Wish it would rain," Talbot agreed. "That aquajade we tapped didn't have enough to more than wet our whistles." Not to mention the heavy metals that had to be in the sappy and thick liquid.

He turned back the way they had come, seeking to avoid stepping on the same roots they'd disturbed earlier. The chime seemed to mock them as the invertebrates played their rhythmless symphony.

Talbot retraced his way around the old chabacho with its five-meter-thick trunk, took his heading as best he could. North. They had to keep going north and a little west. Once they hooked up with Talina and Kylee, they could keep better track of Kalico and Muldare. When it came to forest, nothing beat Talina and Kylee's quetzal sense.

Face it, Mark, he told himself, *you've just been lucky so far.*

He'd avoided disaster by the merest hint of luck since leaving the cave. Just that innate sense of his, developed during all those months in the forest down south. But it was only a matter of time before the odds caught up to him.

Here, outside Tyson Station, the pincushion-sea-urchin thing was just the latest of the threats he'd barely recognized in time. So, too, had been the purple-burst flower, as they'd called it. The plant had just been too gorgeous: a riot of crimson, canary-yellow, and deep purple. He'd poked at with the extended barrel of his rifle and barely managed to keep his gun when it shot out and tried to eat the muzzle.

But so far, the only casualty was Muldare, who'd somehow gotten too close to the local variety of gotcha vine, which, it turned out, was significantly more mobile than the varieties Talbot and Dya were used to. Unexpectedly, it had leaped out far enough to brush the marine.

They'd had to pull sixteen of the wicked spines out of Muldare's arm and shoulder. Briah, trying to be stoic, wasn't succeeding. Her face remained a mask of pain.

"Kylee?" Dya shouted as they started back around the big chabacho.

The chime mocked her in response. Overhead a flock of scarlet fliers swooped low from the branches, apparently drawn by the change in the chime. A few of them managed to snatch a couple of inattentive invertebrates, and then they were gone. Vanished back into the heights.

Again, Talbot took the lead, climbing over roots, lending a hand to Dya, who lent a hand to Kalico, and then to the grimacing Muldare as she brought up the rear.

"Do you know the difference between roots and a marine boot-camp obstacle course?" Muldare asked as she clambered over the latest pile of slowly writhing roots.

"Obstacle courses don't eat you?" Dya wiped at her sweaty brow.

"And they don't move," Kalico groused as she jerked her foot away from a closing gap where two roots pulled themselves tight.

"We can't be more than a couple hundred meters from them," Talbot insisted as he helped Dya down to what he assumed was ground level.

Kalico tried her com, asked, "Talina? Where are you?"

A pause.

Kalico nodded, said, "Yeah, we're still headed north. But in this shit? We could miss you by fifty yards and never know it."

To the rest she said, "Talina says that all she can see is trees and roots."

"When we get home," Dya insisted, "Su's making us spaghetti with that red sauce and chamois meatballs."

"Damn, that sounds good," Kalico said between panting breaths. "Me, I'm pouring a bathtub full of water and drinking it dry."

"Watch it," Talbot told her. "Slug there."

The thing was stretched out on a rare bare patch of damp soil. Odd to see one just out in the open like that. They usually liked having a layer of dirt between them and their predators.

"Shit," Kalico skipped sideways. Her boots were probably thick enough to stop the creepy little beast, but why take chances?

"Yeah, I see it," Muldare declared as she leaped down. With a quick draw, she used her combat knife to slice the thing in two. It contracted, spilling goo onto the nearest root. Even as they watched, spindles of root began to suck up the fluids and entwine themselves in the twitching halves.

"Spaghetti, huh?" Kalico said longingly as Talbot started toward the next bundle of straining and bunched roots. They blocked the way between two of the towering broadvine trees, their trunks almost obscured by thick coils of vines.

"You're welcome to come," Dya told her. "We can always set an extra place."

"Do you know how long it's been since I've had spaghetti? Don't imagine it will be the same as Luigi's in Transluna, but I'm already salivating."

"What's Luigi's?" Talbot asked. "Never heard of it."

"You wouldn't of," Kalico told him. "It's a favorite hangout for white-assed soft-belly Corporate types. I'll bet Su's sauce is better. What about the noodles? Homemade or does she buy them from Millicent Graves?"

"Homemade," Dya told her. "The only thing this Luigi's might have on us is eggs for the noodles. As if any of us can remember what an egg noodle tastes like."

"Count me in," Kalico said through what was obviously a dry mouth. "I'll bring the wine."

"Deal," Dya told her.

From his position in the lead, Talbot grinned. Funny how their relationships had changed over the years since Kalico had tried to seize Mundo Base out from under Dya, Su, and Rebecca. But then that was Donovan for you.

Talbot clambered up, hoisting himself from one thick root to the next. It was maybe a three-meter climb to the top. There he stopped, staring ahead in the gloom, half expecting to spot Talina and Kylee struggling over the next root mass. Only to see nothing in the dim half-light but more roots. A vast expanse of them fading into the shadowed recesses.

"Crushed the airtruck?" Kalico wondered under her breath as she grasped Dya's hand and let the woman pull her up the last of the climb. "What would have possessed Talina to set down next one of those damn lollipop trees?"

"It was close to where we were?" Talbot guessed. "Let me guess: No one's ever reported that lollipop trees can crush airtrucks? Sort of like no one's seen purple-burst flowers or sea urchin pincushions before, either."

"At least no one who lived through it," Muldare said wearily and winced as she climbed to the top of the roots. "How long was Tyson occupied?"

"Maybe four years," Kalico answered, dropping to sit on the top root and rest her feet on the one below. "Most of that time was spent building the base, establishing the garden, flying regional cadastral surveys."

Again Dya cupped hands and shouted, "*Kylee?*"

The forest seemed to scream back as the chime shifted up a notch and something screeched a mocking mimicry from above. No answer from the girl could be heard.

"Fire a shot?" Muldare suggested.

"Maybe. In a bit," Talbot said. "If we don't run into them soon. Sure as hell, we don't need to worry about the Unreconciled. Dressed the way they are, if they tried to make it this deep into the forest, they'd be a meal."

"They'd know where we are though," Kalico noted as she leaned her head forward and massaged the back of her neck.

"Think they wouldn't have seen the airtruck go down?" Muldare shifted her rifle and rolled her sore and swelling shoulder. "Surely they would have had someone watching from the cliffs."

"Get me out of this," Dya whispered to the empty air around her, "and I'll never leave PA again." She chuckled. "Funny, isn't it? I just want to hug the kids again. Sit on the couch and listen to Su complain. Hear the kids playing."

"I want a jug of water," Kalico whispered. "A big one. Like a couple of gallons."

Talbot nodded, shifted his rifle, and rubbed his shoulder. Damn, his empty belly was like a hole in his gut. He worked his mouth to stimulate enough saliva to swallow. Of everything, he hated being thirsty the most. Miserable as he was, he knew Dya and Kalico had to feel even worse. Unlike him and Muldare, they'd never undergone this kind of deprivation.

He glanced up at the trees on his right, in the direction of Tyson Station. That was the closest food and water. Up there. Right under the noses of the Unreconciled. With the airtruck gone, that was the only choice left.

So, what are we going to do? Shoot our way through the middle of them?

With Talina, that would give them three rifles, five pistols. Firepower enough to murder every last cannibal up there.

Murder?

What else could he call it? Batuhan hadn't seemed like the type who could be bluffed. The guy *believed* he was a messiah who had a direct link to the divine universe. How did anyone rational deal with that?

Fact was: They had to get back up to Tyson. Soon. Dehydration was taking its course. Not to mention lack of sleep. It—along with hunger—was making them stupid. Slowing their thoughts and reactions.

It had been pure dumb luck that no one had been killed so far. It wouldn't hold.

He glanced down at Dya. Wished she wasn't here. Wished, with all his heart, that she was still back home.

Dear God, I love her.

Yes, he loved Su, too, but Dya had always been special. Not only had she been the first of the Mundo women to become his lover, wife, mother of his first child, but more, she fit the best. Together they'd shared the most. Been the strength in the marriage after Rebecca's death.

If anything happens to her . . .

It would kill him.

And then there was Kalico Aguila, once the unassailable

Supervisor who looked down on him from on high. Still one of the most formidable women on the planet, here she was—a dependent partner in the desperate bid for survival that was Donovan.

He cupped hands around his mouth, filled his lungs to shout . . .

It came from the side. A blur. He'd barely started to turn, to try and identify the movement, when a blast of something ripped through his chest like a fountain of fire. Lifted him bodily from the roots.

Stunned agony.

Pain like he'd never known.

He was being lifted. Could feel his legs jerking. Felt and heard his ribs breaking. His chest torn in two.

The forest spun, his body flopping like a rag doll's.

He had the horrible realization of something big stuck through his center. Bloody. Impossible to conceive.

A scream could be heard from somewhere far away.

As his consciousness began to fade, the distant sound of shots could be heard.

And then he was rudely . . .

58

The weight of the room, the dark shadows, and most of all, that insidious dome of moldering human bones, pressed down. The air like a miasma. What kind of sick minds built a monument to the people they'd murdered? The light played weirdly over the skulls, the polished leg and arm bones seemed to dance in the shadows cast by the intricate rosettes made of vertebrae and phalanges.

The dead stared out from the dark recesses, peered between the cracks, and filtered through the myriad of wired femora, humeri, and jaws. Each empty eye socket glared with malicious intent.

In all of his life, Miguel Galluzzi had never known a sensation as disturbing as this. His soul felt besmirched and fouled.

He turned, fought the tickling wetness that preceded the urge to throw up. As if the mere act of puking his guts out would rid him of the pollution, filth, and contamination that now clung to his skin like a film.

In the corner of his eye, he caught a flash of a long-haired man in yellow overalls as he hurried past. Hardly enough to recognize. Just that fleeting impression.

The temple of bones might have been a malignancy. It loomed, seemed to expand. Began to suck at Galluzzi's soul. The sensation akin to the structure pulling a hazy thread of his spirit into its low-arched doorway, past the sprawled skeleton that lay like a broken doll.

"I have to get out of here," Galluzzi whispered hoarsely.

"I understand," Shig said reasonably and turned on his heel. As he passed the double doors, he slapped the wall panel. Darkness fell over the monstrosity of bones with a solidity that sent a quake down Galluzzi's back.

Though left behind in darkness, he could *feel* the dome of bones—its looming presence. That the thing was alive, sentient, watching him with the gaze of an inquisitor. In judgment of his life, soul, and sanity.

Galluzzi stumbled under the impact, braced himself against the hallway wall as he fought for breath. Tried to still the pounding.

The light smeared, slipped sideways, momentarily blurring Shig's concerned features.

"Death is here," Galluzzi whispered. "It's all around us. Feeding on our souls."

Shig's features solidified again as the man said, "Curious that you'd use those words. It's one of the phrases in the hallway we passed through. You read that there?"

"No. Just . . . just came to me."

"You've gone pale."

Galluzzi blinked, finally able to get a full breath into his starved lungs. "I knew Jem Orten. Have I told you that?"

"No."

"Like so many of us, he was hopeful of getting *Freelander.* Would have sold his soul to sit in the captain's chair." He fought back tears. "Maybe that's what he did, huh? He just didn't know it when he spaced out of Solar System."

"Can you walk?"

Galluzzi managed a weak nod, pushed himself off the wall. It was like the surface didn't feel right. Sort of rubbery, not quite . . . well, real.

When Galluzzi looked down, his right hand was jumping around like a wounded songbird. The staccato clicking sound came from his chattering teeth.

Unseen *things* kept touching him. But when he looked, there was nothing there.

"I want out of here," he told Shig without the least bit of shame. "This place is hell, and I want no part of it."

"Just this way, and we'll be gone."

Following Shig through the half-light down the hall took all of Galluzzi's will. They passed the Captain's Lounge, the door ajar to expose a dark room. Unseen eyes peered out at their passing. Whispers and hisses, barely below the threshold of hearing, issued from within.

Before the door to the AC, Galluzzi started, sure that he'd seen someone peering at him from the wall. Familiar dark eyes were watching him. The lips were in the process of forming words. When he fixed on the sialon, the woman's face wasn't there. Just. Blank. Fucking. Wall.

I saw her. Black hair. Asian features. Like I knew . . .

"Oh, shit. That was Tyne."

"Excuse me?" Shig had stopped before the duraplast and steel door that led to Astrogation Control.

"Tyne Sakihara," Galluzzi said, voice rasping. "Someone I knew back in Solar System. Spaced with me on a couple of my early runs. We were . . . well, intimate. I loved her." He choked on the memory. "Once upon a time." Galluzzi balled his fists, used them to scrub at his eyes. "What the hell is wrong with me? Why would I see her face? Like it was coming out of the fucking wall?"

Shig watched him with eyes that almost glowed. "You *saw* her?"

Galluzzi forced himself to breathe. Glanced back at the blank and featureless wall with its faint coating of grime. "Has to be my imagination. She's somewhere back in Solar System. Bet she's got her own ship by now."

"She's here." Shig's voice carried no emotion. "Behind that wall. In Astrogation Control. Or at least her skeleton is. She was locked in with Captain Orten. When it became apparent that there would be no exit, he shot her in the head before he turned the gun on himself. Her bones were still on the floor when Talina sealed Tamarland Benteen behind this door."

Shig reached out, reverently running the tips of his fingers over the battered surface of the AC's door.

As the words sank in, the hallway slipped sideways, seemed to spin around Galluzzi. Voices whispered in the air around him. He slumped against the far side, tried to steady himself.

"She's behind that door? Dead? With Jem?" He ground his teeth. Tried to understand. "Why the *hell* did you bring me here?"

"So that you would understand."

"And Tamarland Benteen is in there, too?" He could hear the panic in his voice, the incipient insanity. "Should we knock and announce ourselves?"

"No, we should not. If Benteen's alive in there, pounding on the door would be a cruel form of baiting. If he's dead, like Jem and Tyne, the action would be futile and without meaning."

"What the *fuck* are you saying?"

"I'm saying, Captain, that reality can be many things. That behind that door, Benteen may be alive, or he may be dead. You cannot know until you open the door."

Shig leaned close. "You, Captain, had a choice to make: You could save your ship and crew, or you could suffer the same fate as *Freelander.* Like knocking on the AC door, you could not know the outcome until you'd made the decision and observed the results. Your reality is illusion."

Something cold, like an icy finger, slipped along Galluzzi's ribs. Tyne had stroked him like that when they were lovers. The sensation was real enough that he yipped and leaped sideways. With a nervous hand he batted at his side.

Looked down to see . . . nothing.

"I want out of here. *Now.*"

"After seeing all this," Shig gestured grandly at the ship, "do you still think that blowing yourself out an airlock would be in the interest of cosmic justice?"

Galluzzi stared woodenly at the battered and welded AC door. The last refuge of Jem Orten and Galluzzi's once-beloved Tyne Sakihara. The final internment for Tamarland Benteen.

"I don't know what to think anymore."

"Ah," Shig said through an exhale. "With that realization, you have just taken the first step on your new Tao."

"My what?"

"Your path. Only after you stop questioning will the answers come to you."

Galluzzi flinched as maniacal laughter echoed down the hallway, vanished.

As loud as it had been to Galluzzi's ears, Shig apparently hadn't heard it. Not even a hint.

59

Kalico Aguila was sitting wearily atop the highest root, staring out over the dim forest floor with its tangles of roots, vines, and immense tree trunks. Her only concern was how miserably thirsty, hungry, and exhausted she was.

Talbot stood beside her, Dya squatted at his side. Muldare, to Kalico's right, was scanning the surrounding forest through her rifle's optic in search of any sign of Talina's party.

Something tore through the air. Mark Talbot's body jerked under a mighty impact. Was flung forward and up off its perch. The man's rifle clattered down across the roots, torn from his hands by a force that catapulted him into the heights.

Kalico froze, gaped, unable to comprehend what she was seeing: Talbot's body—skewered through the chest—was being hauled skyward by some long tentacle. The man's arms, legs, and head jerked and swayed, limp like rubber. Then he was gone. Pulled into the high branches. Vanished.

It seemed impossible.

Couldn't be happening.

Dya's piercing scream shattered Kalico's dazed disbelief.

Briah Muldare—her instincts true to her training—pulled up her rifle. She didn't hesitate. The blasting racket of a burst hammered at Kalico's ears as bullets shredded the branches high above. Bits of detritus came floating down, but no body. No terrifying alien.

"*Mark!*" Dya screamed, her throat straining until the veins stood out. She leaped to her feet, almost tottering on the root. Her fists like rocks, muscles flexed as she stared up in absolute horror at where her husband had disappeared.

"What the hell?" Muldare whispered hoarsely, her rifle at the ready, muzzle pointing toward the dark branches overhead.

Kalico scrambled down, recovered Talbot's rifle. She raised it, worked her mouth to try and swallow. Felt her heart hammering against her chest as if fit to burst.

Overhead, only the slow shifting of the branches—the apparently endless dance that was Donovan's forest—could be seen. The chime rose and fell as if nothing had happened.

"Mark!" Dya screamed again. She struggled to keep her balance on the high root as it slithered to one side.

"We've got to get off of here," Kalico said, shifting the heavy rifle as she scanned the heights.

"Come on, Dya," Muldare said as she started down, leaping from root to root. "There's nothing—"

"That's *my husband*!" Dya continued to stare up, tears leaking down her cheeks.

"Damn it, Dya," Kalico cried. "He's gone! You saw that same as I did. Whatever that thing was, it punched a spike, a tentacle—whatever the hell that was—right through his chest!"

"We can't lose him," Dya almost whimpered. "Not again."

"Dya, come on!" Muldare shouted, starting back up the roots to physically drag the woman down.

Dya began, "This will break Su's heart! Leave us . . ."

This time the spike came from behind. Unseen. Caught Dya Simonov between her shoulder blades. The point of it, black and sharp like polished horn, shot out between her breasts. It jerked her upward so hard and fast the weight of the woman's head could be heard snapping her neck.

Kalico, taken aback, stood paralyzed as Dya Simonov disappeared up into the high branches.

"Supervisor?" Briah Muldare scrambled down, grabbing her arm. "I need you to leave this place now!"

Talina's voice was yammering in Kalico's earbud, demanding to know what was wrong. What the shooting was.

Kalico nodded, struggled to think. Let Muldare pull her sideways, ahead. Somehow Kalico managed to run, to put one foot ahead of the other.

Lost track of the mad scramble as she climbed up over masses of roots, half-leaped, half-fell down the far side, only to stagger onward. She couldn't think, couldn't answer Talina's frantic call for information through the com.

Panic. It was all panic.

Until something deep inside her screamed *Get a grip!*

"Wait!" she cried, pulling up, slowing, aware of what their mad flight was doing to the roots. Looking back, she saw a writhing trail. *"Think!"*

"Think what?" Muldare cried, the glaze of panic in her hazel eyes as she scanned the trees, shifting her rifle this way and that. "There's something up there!"

Kalico spun the woman around, glaring. "And there's things down here! You want worse than thorncactus to worry about? Now, think! We've got to go slow, go smart, or we're as dead as Dya and Mark. You hear me?"

"Yes." Muldare swallowed hard. Jerked a nod.

"Good." Kalico fought for breath. Thirst, hunger, exhaustion, and now horror. Could this get any worse?

Have to find Talina!

Signal shot.

Or would that draw the beast?

She pressed her com. "Talina? Where are you?"

"What the hell is going on?"

"Something in the trees. Something big, Tal. Like nothing we've ever seen. It took Mark and Dya. No warning. Just speared them through the chest and jerked them up into the trees!"

For a moment there was silence as Kalico tried to catch her breath, shifted the rifle, eyes on the darkening branches above.

"Mark and Dya?" Talina's voice came softly.

"It's in the trees! Something big!" The panic was building again.

"*Roger that. In the trees. We'll keep an eye out."*

"Talina, you don't understand. If it's hunting you, you won't have a chance. No warning. It's that fast. That deadly."

Again there was silence.

Say something, damn it!

Then, *"Kylee's coming. She's riding a quetzal, so don't shoot it."*

"Roger," Kalico repeated. "Kylee's riding a quetzal. Don't shoot it." She repeated for Muldare's benefit.

"Yeah," Kalico whispered to herself, desperately searching the high branches. "As if a quetzal would stand a chance against this thing."

And worse, it was getting dark.

60

Talina watched Kylee climb up on Flute's back. The sight never ceased to amaze her. As if the camouflage-mottled quetzal was a pet horse instead of an alpha predator.

"You be damned careful," Talina warned again. "Aguila sounds like she's on the edge of a breakdown. No telling about the marine she's with. They could shoot at anything that moves."

"What about Mom and Dad?"

"Nothing new there, kid. Kalico says whatever this thing is, it speared them and hauled them up into the trees. That's all I've got so far. *Pay attention!* First priority: Find Kalico. She'll tell you more."

"Someone's going to pay for this," Kylee vowed, tapping Flute and saying, "Let's go."

With Dek beside her, Talina watched Flute stretch out; the blonde kid on the beast's back bent low as the quetzal leaped to the next batch of roots and disappeared on the other side.

"Dek, you stay close now. We can't afford a mistake." Talina shifted her rifle, staring up at the darkening branches overhead.

"I don't get it," Dek said as he followed behind her. "Hauled them up into the trees? What can do that?"

"Nightmare hunts that way." Talina experienced that familiar crawling in her gut, and for once it wasn't Demon. "Maybe that's what this is."

But as she glanced up, it was to wonder what kind of nightmare could reach that far, lift that much weight that fast. Mostly they suspended their prey like dangling fruit as the tentacles wound down and into their victim's guts. It took days.

Spearing the victim's body? Jerking it up? It just didn't sound right.

Or it's something we haven't seen.

And worse, it had taken two of the most important people on

Donovan. Dya Simonov had revolutionized their understanding of Donovanian genetics, was in the process of developing local plants that humans could actually digest in case anything happened to the terrestrial species upon which survival depended.

And if Talbot was dead, too? Another talented second in command at Port Authority security? A friend? Just gone like that? Poof? Hauled up into the high branches to be eaten?

"You look grim," Taglioni noted as he panted along behind her.

"Just thinking what it means to lose Mark and Dya. On the com Kalico said this thing speared them through the chest. Yanked them up into the branches. Said it took just a couple of seconds."

Taglioni shot a furtive look up at the darkening branches overhead. "That's what? Forty, fifty meters up? That's a lot of muscle to haul a body up that high."

"Now you're getting the idea." Talina shook her head as she climbed over a bundle of interlocked roots, reached back, and helped the struggling Taglioni as he clambered awkwardly over the mess.

"You know, it's starting to get dark." Stress thinned Taglioni's voice. "We going to be able to track down Kylee and the Supervisor in the dark?"

She tapped the side of her head. "Part of the curse of being infected is that I can see in the dark. We're fine. At least I am. You? If you can't see where you're putting your feet? If you blunder into a chokeya vine? Guess you'll be the main course for some lucky critter out here."

"And to think, I used to worry about being eaten on *Ashanti*. That was my night terror. That the Unreconciled would get loose in the night. Come slipping up from Deck Three. Sneak into my room, and I'd be helpless as they started carving on me." He chuckled hollowly, eyes on his feet as he tried to match her steps. "Why does it always come down to being eaten?"

"Stop. Take my hand. We're climbing this knot of roots. There's a tooth flower off to the side. I need you to follow my lead. Don't do anything dumb."

"You got it."

"Give me your rifle." She took it, slung it next to hers. "Okay, let's go."

She eased Dek over the tangle, ensuring he didn't accidently close the distance with the tooth flower. Damn, the thing was bigger than the ones she'd seen previously. And it was aware, watching them where it hung down from a thick vine that spanned the space between two aquajades.

On the other side, she took a quick look around. Noted a sidewinder that was easing out from a dark hole. The thing had probably hidden as Flute passed this way. The roots were still squirming but starting to relax after the quetzal's passage.

"How much farther do you think?" Dek asked.

She gave him a sidelong glance. Dark as it was getting, the guy probably figured she couldn't see the outright fear in his face.

In the branches high overhead, something uttered a whistling, almost hypersonic scream. Taglioni jumped half out of his skin.

"Don't know, Dek. Guess you'll just have to trust me."

She saw the flicker of amusement behind his fear as he said, "Oh . . . sure." A beat. "Gave myself up for dead back when the ping pong tree crushed the airtruck."

61

To say that night fell like the flick of a switch wasn't quite right. But the analogy wasn't too far off the mark. At least, not as far as Kalico Aguila could tell.

For the moment, she had effectively been brought to a dead stop. Couldn't tell where to put her feet. Wasn't able to see more than a couple of feet in any direction. Go bumbling around? Stick her head into a cutthroat flower, or maybe a biteya bush? Offer a tempting leg to a sidewinder?

"We're fucked, aren't we?" Briah Muldare asked, stepping uneasily to the side as roots squirmed under her feet. The woman kept sweeping with her rifle, using the optic's IR to search for approaching danger.

"Kylee will be here." Kalico tried to say it with assured bravado. Fact was, she'd never been as sure that she was about to die. Terrified that some spearing thing was going to lance through her chest. And she'd never know it was coming.

The voice, from the darkness off to the right called, "It's us! Don't shoot!"

Kalico laid a hand on Muldare's rifle, just to be sure the woman understood.

Given all that had happened, the sight of a slim blonde girl riding up on a quetzal like it was a quarter horse didn't seem as incredulous as it should. Kalico figured her sense of reality had taken so many blows, nothing was beyond belief.

"Damn, we're glad to see you."

Kylee unhitched her backpack, slung it down. "There's water. Talina's right behind us. Which way to my parents? Back there? Follow the roots?"

"Kylee, listen. Whatever this thing is, you really don't want to—"

"We'll be back."

"—take any . . ."

The quetzal—Kylee on its back—wheeled, leaped to the top of the root mass Kalico and Muldare had just climbed over, and vanished into the encompassing darkness.

"Did I just see that?" Muldare asked hoarsely. "A kid riding a quetzal?"

The water was the finest Kalico ever drank. She and Muldare emptied the bottles, heedless of saving even a drop. The water hit her stomach like a gift from God. She was already feeling better.

Now she peered around in the almost charcoal black. Kept shifting her feet, wishing she could see what the roots were doing.

"Supervisor?" The rising stress in Muldare's voice couldn't be missed.

"Yeah, I know."

Got to do something.

They couldn't just stand there. The roots were going to be grabbing hold. Kalico could feel them underfoot, becoming more agitated, starting to cling.

"Here, take my hand." She reached out, got Muldare's hand.

Step by step. That was it. She thought she was headed north. The darkness pressed down around her, thick, almost solid.

"What do you see with your rifle sight?" Kalico asked, lifting Mark's rifle, trying to hold the heavy weapon one-handed, to see through the optic. The thing was too heavy, or she was too weak. It would take two hands, and she couldn't convince herself to turn loose of Muldare's hand.

"Root mass ahead," Muldare told her. "Maybe four meters."

It was foolish. A sure recipe for disaster. But so was standing still, letting the roots entangle their feet. Get stuck in them? Unable to pull free? They'd entomb a person. Surround her, crush her, and absorb the decomposing body.

At least this way I'm doing something.

Kalico wanted to throw her head back, to howl with insane laughter. She was going to die here. In the darkness. From something horrible. Like that tooth flower that had been eating that man's naked corpse. Why? Because she was running from a bunch of cannibals. In the twenty-second century? Shit, who'd believe it?

"This isn't going to end well, is it?" Muldare asked softly.

"Probably not." Kalico squeezed the woman's hand in a gesture of solidarity.

"For the record, ma'am. I want you to know that while I sided with Cap back during the *Turalon* days, it has been an honor and the finest privilege of my career to serve you these last four years."

"I appreciate that, Briah. But we're not gone yet. Kylee and that insane quetzal should be back at any moment."

"Maybe. Ma'am, whatever that *thing* was that got Mark and Dya, no child, and I daresay no quetzal, can stand up to that." A return squeeze and a tug stopped Kalico. "And that's why I'm taking the lead. If there's anything out here, I'm stumbling into it first."

"Can't do that. You're as blind as I am. If it were daylight, with your training, yes. You'd have a better chance of spotting the danger than I do. But here, in the black? I can't ask you to take a risk I'm not willing to take myself."

"You think I don't know that? That any of us don't know that? Besides, I can scan with my optic." Muldare shifted to the lead, took a step. Kalico thought she saw the woman sweep the night with her rifle sight. "Wonder if any of those assholes back in Transluna would have had a clue?"

Kalico pulled Muldare to a stop. "You hear that?"

"What?"

Kalico turned, let loose of Muldare's hand and raised her rifle. "To the right, Briah. I'd swear I heard something."

"Got to go," the marine said. "Roots are pulling on my foot."

Kalico cocked her head, allowed herself to be pulled another step forward, worried she was just antagonizing the roots Muldare had trod upon.

She was on the verge of taking another step when a voice off to the side said, "I wouldn't do that. You've got a couple of brown caps about three meters ahead of you. Step off to the right."

"Kylee? That you?" Kalico asked.

"Yep. We're going to hop down from these roots, Supervisor. Don't shoot us."

Kalico heard the thump as a heavy body landed on the root mat.

"Okay, walk toward my voice. We've got to get you out of this little bowl and into someplace where the roots aren't as pissed off."

"How the hell can you see?" Muldare asked.

"She has quetzal TriNA," Kalico answered when Kylee didn't bother to.

"Yeah," Kylee said shortly. "My weird eyes. They'd kill me back at Port Authority because of my infection. Call me a freak."

Kalico winced at the anger in the girl's voice. "What did you find back there? Any sign of the creature?"

Kylee's voice was like stone. "Tell me what happened, Kalico. All of it. Everything you remember about how my mom and dad died."

Kalico felt her way forward across the wiggling roots, step by step. "Mark was standing up high. Looking for any sign of you and Talina. It hit him from the side. Like a long black fire hose swinging down from the high branches. The tip was a black spike, like a horn. It speared clear through his chest and literally ripped him upward so hard it tore the rifle from his hands."

"Your mother wouldn't come down," Muldare added. "I was headed back up to drag her, and that black spike hit her from behind. Took maybe two, three seconds, to yank her up into the branches."

"Got a step now, Kalico," Kylee's voice was flat. "Don't trip over that bottom root. Sling your rifle and climb like a monkey. I'll tell you when you reach the top." A pause. "What did it look like? A nightmare?"

"No." Kalico felt her way up the roots. "That's the spooky thing. Private Muldare fired a burst at the branches after it took your dad. Nothing. We couldn't see a body, a shape, just the branches up there. If any of the rounds hit it, it didn't react."

"Mom wouldn't come down?"

"She just stood there, shouting for your father."

"That's the top, Kalico. Sling your leg over. Muldare? You're next. That's it. That's the root. Now climb."

Kalico felt her way over the root, eerily aware that one of those firehose-thick tentacles could shoot down from the black, could skewer her, and no one would even know. They'd just hear the falling rifle, and she'd be gone. Vanished into the blackness.

"It's something we've never seen," Kalico said as she felt her way down to the flat root mat. "Did you find any sign back there?"

"Nothing," Kylee said, voice clipped. "Neither did Flute. Just a couple of drops of blood. All spattered wide."

"I'm sorry, Kylee." Kalico stopped, staring around in the blackness, wondering where the girl could be, and even worse, where the hell was the damn quetzal? That monster could be right at her shoulder.

Kylee softly, bitterly, asked, "Why the hell were they out here to start with? What did those people up there want to do to you?"

"Going to cut our throats and eat us," Muldare growled. "And me, personally, I'm about to go explosive on the whole lot of them."

"You won't be doing it alone," Kylee said. "I think Flute and I are going to pay them a little visit. Sort of a remembrance of Mom and Dad."

"Kylee," Kalico said. "Don't start something—"

"'Bout time!" Kylee raised her voice and called. "What took you?"

Kalico turned, seeing the yellow haze of a handheld light as it shone through the roots.

Talina's voice carried: "Hey, I got soft meat with me. Didn't want him stepping into a you're screwed vine. Might have given the poor plant indigestion."

Kalico vented a sigh of relief. Felt her heart settle back where it belonged in her chest. She watched as Talina crested a batch of roots, shone her light back, and took a second gander as Derek Taglioni clambered woodenly over the roots, a long rifle swinging on his back.

"You brought *him* out into this mess?"

"Wasn't exactly my preferred plan," Talina told her, shining the light around. "Good to see you, Private."

"Ma'am," Muldare said respectfully.

"What's the plan?" Kalico asked.

"We're beating feet," Talina said. "If we don't get the hell off this floodplain, back on the basalt, we're dead."

"Yeah," Kalico agreed. "Someplace where the trees aren't as thick and tall. Where that *thing* can't hide and pick us off one by one."

"Where's Kylee and Flute?" Talina asked.

"They were . . ." Kalico glanced around, following Talina's flash as it searched the surroundings.

"Kylee?" Talina called.

Kalico felt that deadening of the heart. If she was headed up to Tyson, going to pay Batuhan and his people back for her parents, it would be a . . .

"Over here," Kylee called. "We've got a path out of here. And I think we need to go. Soonest."

"Go," Kalico ordered Muldare. "Then you, sir," she told Taglioni. "I'll bring up the rear."

"Middle of the night like this? That could get you killed," Talina told her wryly.

"Yeah? So what couldn't?"

62

Dek's feet might have turned to wood for all the feeling they had. His coordination was shot. For a time, all he prayed for was the opportunity to lay down on the soft root mat, close his eyes, and let the rhizomes entomb him in their gentle caress as he dropped off to sleep.

Have I ever been this exhausted?

And it seemed like there was no end to it. Endless forest. Endless toil. Danger on all sides.

You can do this. Gut it out.

He focused his entire universe down on the bobbing flashlight beam, its wavering shadows as they leaped and jerked on either side. His Holland & Holland might have been an ungainly bar of lead. The weight of the sling felt like it was sawing its way through his shoulder.

And he'd only what? Crossed a couple of kilometers of forest?

Panting, he kept forcing one foot ahead of the other, jaws clenched with determination. It was just walking, following in Talina's footsteps. Didn't matter that they were starting up, that the way was turning rocky.

"Watch out for the chokeya vine," Kylee called back. "I severed it just above the roots. It won't latch onto you now, but you really don't want to touch it or get any of the fluids on you."

Dek blinked, looked up into the flashlight glare to see Talina Perez, rifle extended to hold the deadly plant out of the way as it flipped and twisted in death.

Climb. One foot, then the other. And for God's sake, don't stumble when you're passing that damn stem.

"How you doing, Dek?" Talina asked as he staggered his way up the trail.

"Praying we have supper reservations at Three Spires," he murmured on the way past.

"What's Three Spires?" Talina asked.

Behind him he heard Aguila's musical laughter.

"It's a plush and tony restaurant on Transluna," Aguila explained to Perez as she ducked beneath the dying vine. "Not the kind of place anyone but a Taglioni would know."

Dek managed to gin up a bit of rage at the tone in her voice. Used it to power his flagging muscles. And, miracle of miracles, it got him to the top of the steep climb. Then, reaching the flat, he stepped to the side, bent double, and propped his hands on his knees as he sucked air into his hot and starved lungs.

"How you doing?" To Dek's surprise, the voice belonged to Aguila.

"I'm thinking that being dead takes a whole lot less effort than this does."

Kalico dropped down to a crouch beside him, calling, "We need to take a break, people. On the basalt like this, we're finally off the worst of the roots."

Dek gasped, lowered himself to the bare rock. Every muscle in his body was on fire. His joints screaming and gone to rubber.

Talina's voiced carried from where she had stopped in conversation with Kylee and Muldare. "We're calling it, people. This is about as safe as we can get. Bedrock, sparse canopy. Kylee, Flute, and I will keep watch. Dek? You, Muldare, and Kalico get some sleep if you can. I know it's rock, but it beats the living shit out of roots."

"And they know we're both about to fold," Kalico muttered. "God, I'm fucking exhausted."

"Me, too. Amazing what ten years in a starship will take out of you."

"Everything but the memory of Three Spires, I guess."

Between panting breaths, he told her, "It just came back to me. I remember now. That's the first place I ever met you. You were there, on Miko's arm. My God, dressed in that radiant blue gown.

Same color as your eyes. You could have stepped straight from the spotlight at the Paris fashion show. This absolutely gorgeous woman, and so much more than Miko ever . . . Well, it doesn't matter."

Beside him, Aguila shifted. "Surprised you remember anything from that night. Let alone what I was wearing. That was what, ten years ago? Eleven?"

He tilted his head back as he gasped for air. Could see the stars between gaps in the trees. Felt so much freer to be out of the deep forest. A weight lifted off his chest.

"More like thirteen. I remember. Right down to the words I said." He made a tsking sound. "If I could go back, I'd punch that toilet-sucking silly little shit that I used to be clear into next week. Beat him to within a millimeter of his over-righteous life."

He glanced at her, saw her eyes like pits in the darkness. "I am so sorry for what I said to you." He chuckled dryly. "Sorry for so many things I did back then."

Aguila reached out. Clapped a hand on his shoulder. "If we live through this, maybe we can talk." A pause. "Assuming this humility jag isn't just a passing phase. That or some twisted strategy affected to gain you some advantage."

"Is it that difficult to trust someone?"

"Nope." She stood. "I trust a lot of people. Many of them with my life. Just not a Taglioni."

And then she rose, staggered wearily over to where Talina Perez and Kylee were talking. The big quetzal behind them was barely visible in the faint light of the hand torch. Amazing how the thing could blend into any environment.

She really was the most beautiful woman I'd ever seen.

Closing his eyes, he could remember every detail.

Right down to the loathing she'd tried so hard to hide when he opened his clap-trapping mouth and . . .

"Hell, Dek," he told himself. "If I were her, I wouldn't forgive you either."

63

When Dan Wirth had been a kid, his snot-sucking excuse of a father had periodically locked Dan in closets—and once in a storage box where he'd had to lay for three days, hungry, thirsty, and wallowing in his own urine.

This was worse.

Dan huddled in a corner of the plastic shipping box, shivering and looking up at the distant stars. To his right, the stack of shipping containers rose like an impossible wall. Through the side of the toppled box, he could see across the ferngrass to the bush. The moon was waxing gibbous and hung low in the west. The night chime was different than the day's and fit to drive him half mad.

And there, not more than a meter from the box, he could see Windman's head. The gruesome thing lay on its side facing Dan. As pale as Windman had been in life, his head was beginning to darken, the eyes having sunk dully into the skull. The worst part was the gaping mouth. Invertebrates had been crawling into it, apparently eating the tongue because they now crawled out through the severed neck as well.

Not that Dan had ever suffered a pang of guilt, but he wished he could kick the loathsome thing out of sight. Just get it the hell away.

The miracle was that he was still alive. Trapped inside a clear plastic box, in Capella's direct light throughout the long day, without water. The suffering had been encompassing. Enough to make death seem a blessing. The entire time, he'd been terrified. Nothing, absolutely nothing he had ever seen compared with watching the empty ground rise, turn itself into a quetzal, and devour copilot Windman.

Not even Dan's nightmares—and he had plenty—could compare. The abuse he'd had to endure at his father's hands? The degradation and shame of sucking his dad's prick? Hearing the man groan in delight? The mental and physical abuse? All the shit he'd had to take? Didn't hold so much as a feeble flicker of the horror of watching a man eaten alive.

He could still hear Windman's bones breaking as Whitey crushed him.

What the fuck was that? To feel one's bones snapping and splintering? It wasn't just the pain, but the unbridled horror of being eaten alive.

I hate this fucking planet.

Worse, he couldn't leave. The fart-sucking quetzals had him neatly trapped, and the shit-sucking bastards were keeping watch.

So far, he thought he'd counted three. They'd been coming and going. Whitey was easy given his wounds. The second had been smaller, had scratched gouges in the plastic trying to get to Dan. How fucking bone-rattling was that? Hearing the grating of claws in plastic, feeling it through the box? The worst part was watching, seeing the teeth, the claws, knowing that if the plastic failed, that color-flashing horror was going to tear you out of your hiding place and rip you into pieces while it ate you.

The third beast was bigger. Not Whitey's size, but close. It had tried for an hour or so to wiggle its claws into the crack of the door and spring it open. Then it had tried the air holes at the top. Actually managed to elongate a couple, but the thick plastic had held.

Off and on through the long afternoon, one or another of the quetzals had appeared, checked his box, and gone back to whatever they'd been about since the siren had gone off.

That had been no longer than fifteen minutes after Windman was eaten—just about the time Dan was realizing how much sweat a human body could make.

He had been waiting. Longing. But no all clear had sounded.

Port Authority was still on lockdown.

Until the quetzal problem was solved, no one was coming to find him.

I'm the richest and most powerful man on the planet.

What kind of fucking solace was that? Unless something changed, he was going to die of thirst or hyperthermia in a plastic box.

Or he could simply throw the door open and be eaten alive.

He was considering that very thought.

Wondered if the quetzals were even around, when movement caught his eye. Slinking low, one of the beasts appeared at the corner of the shipping containers, seemed to flow across the ground. Its hide, in a remarkable feat, mimicked the colors of the ground it crossed.

The thing jammed its nose against the now-scarred plexiglass.

Dan thought he knew this one. Didn't have to see the mangled left front leg.

Whitey.

"I really hate this planet," Dan rasped through his dry throat.

As if it understood, Whitey chittered before turning. With a kick, the big quetzal knocked Dan's box hard enough to launch it nearly a meter.

Slammed around the inside, Dan groaned, took a breath.

When he opened his eyes, the door had held. He was still safe. But, through the plastic, Windman's decomposing head was now mere inches from Dan's face.

64

Vartan blinked. His lids grated across his eyes, feeling like he had sand in them. He was laid out on his bunk in the dormitory. A fan was blowing cool air from the ceiling vent. Light reflected from the hallway. He was naked, a blanket covering his body.

Clap-trapping hell, but he was thirsty.

He smacked his lips. Pulled the blanket back and sat up.

His head hurt, and he had to pee.

As he staggered to his feet, every muscle in his body screamed. His joints might have been soldered, or at least rusted, given the way they bent when he moved.

At the sink, he drank and drank. Hobbled to the lavatory and sighed with relief as he drained his water.

Back at his bunk, he found his wrap, tied it around his waist.

"You all right?" Marta asked as he walked wearily into the small lobby out front.

She was seated by the door, staring out through one of the windows at the yard beyond. The soft glow of overhead lights illuminated the stark ground, reflected off old pieces of machinery, and finally surrendered to the night.

"What the hell happened to me?"

"You came stumbling in a little after noon. Saw Svetlana's body and collapsed. Fodor, Ctein, and I carried you here. Sent word to the Messiah that you were wounded."

He remembered Svetlana's broken body. Had hoped it had been a bad dream.

Marta glanced at him, her hazel eyes lackluster. "What happened out there? Where's the rest of your team?"

He sank into one of the chairs, rubbed his eyes. "Dead. Eaten. Buried in roots. Mars and Hap? They just vanished." A beat. "What about Petre and Tikal's teams?"

Her stare fixed on some infinity out in the darkness beyond. "They haven't come back. Haven't radioed."

"Nothing?"

"There's been gunfire off to the west. Then the airtruck reappeared. No telling if it was Shyanne coming back or someone else. It went down in the trees. Heard some more gunfire just before dark. Got to be the Supervisor's party."

"The children?"

She inclined her head toward the rear. "Got them all asleep in the back. I'm 'on guard,' whatever that means."

"I've got to get something to eat. See the Messiah." He struggled to his feet, wondering when he'd ever felt this weak, this defeated.

"Vart?" Marta looked up, an anxious glitter behind her eyes. "It's all coming apart. Everything. The universe? Being chosen? The Prophets? It was all a lie. We're dying. And we're not coming back."

She ran the tips of her fingers along the spiral of scar tissue on her breast, following it to her nipple. "Nothing there, Vart. No soul to be suckled into a reborn life. Just . . . nothing." She raised her eyes. "And do you know what that makes us?"

"Maybe the Prophets will—"

"Irdan's dead. Callista might be, too. Couldn't tell last time I was in there."

He nodded, asked, "What did you do with the rifle?"

"Left it at the admin dome."

Vartan stepped to the door, looked back. Marta's gaze was once again fixed on some infinity that lay beyond the window.

He walked out into the night, aware of the perfumed air, of the feel of the night breeze. Donovan's moon was hanging over the distant western horizon; its weak light illuminated humped treetops, cast shadows as the forest stretched into the distance.

The growling hunger that chafed his belly, the pain in his abused muscles, the desolation in Marta's eyes, it all left him empty. A sucked-out husk.

To his absolute disgust, Svetlana's broken body still lay off to the side of the admin dome door. For a moment, in the muted glow of the yard lights, he thought she moved. Looked closer, and realized her body was swarming with invertebrates.

"For the love of God!" He bent down, got one of her wrists, and with his last reserves, started dragging her off to the . . .

He hardly had an instant to react to the tickle of little feet as several of the creatures skittered up his fingers. Like fire, they began taking bites out of his skin.

With a howl, he let go of Svetlana, manically flinging his hand back and forth to sling the little beasts off.

Damn, but that hurt!

Backing away, he stared impotently at Svetlana's crumpled corpse. The yawning hollow opened wider inside him. Seemed to swallow his heart.

Flashbacks of her laughter, that dancing joy in her eyes. He'd reveled in her clever wit, in the times they'd laid in bed, holding each other, talking about the dreams they'd shared. Svetlana had been a true believer. Really thought she was the mother of the future, that she was the vessel of eternal life. That through her, the dead were reborn.

Sucking at the bites on his hand, Vartan peered at Svetlana's shadowed corpse, watched the invertebrates as they scampered into holes chewed in her flesh.

So much for the repository of the dead, for being the living grave. The dead were now being consumed by alien bugs. To be purified into insect shit.

Did I ever really believe?

Or did I just sign on to the lie to justify staying alive?

Shyanne had never believed. She'd played the game and done it well enough to survive. He'd always known her participation—good enough to fool the rest of the Will, and the Messiah, too—was a sham.

Was the fact that he'd never turned her in due to his own apostasy? Or because of what he owed her for having once been his wife? They'd loved each other back then, before the Harrowing and Cleansing. Before participating in abomination had broken that beautiful relationship.

He turned his eyes to the heavens, star-matted and stunning as it was: a wealth of Milky Way glowing in patterns of light. Shyanne had been smart enough to get out.

Or had she? Marta said the airtruck had come back to get the Supervisor.

But it hadn't left.

"Deal with it later."

He gave Svetlana's remains a final, grieving, glance and opened the door to the admin dome.

The lights hurt his eyes.

Plodding wearily down to the cafeteria, he entered. Saw Batuhan sitting in the throne, eyes on Guan Shi's emaciated body where it lay on the rear table.

The Messiah didn't look up as Vartan crossed the room, entered the kitchen to see Irdan's body laid out on one of the stainless-steel counters. The Prophet's left arm and leg had been stripped down to the bones. Not that much meat had been on them in the first place. Callista, also dead, rested just beyond, still untouched.

Additionally, in the rear corner, the completely processed skeletons of three individuals were piled atop each other, the blood-smeared bones intertwined. Someone had seen to the First Chosen killed by the Supervisor.

As if anything made sense in this madness.

It's a prion. A misshapen protein that causes dementia. Not divine revelation.

He might have had all the sensitivity of wood as he picked up Petre's old cleaver. Used it to chop through the top of Irdan's skull. Heedless of the bone chips, he grabbed the man's hair. The sound of the keen edge biting into bone sent shivers through him.

But in the end, he yanked the skullcap loose. It parted from the brain with a sucking sound. Vartan considered the Prophet's brain. Used the cleaver edge to slice it open.

What should have been pale gray and white wasn't right. Looked . . . what? Spotted? Stippled? Bits of off-colored . . . Didn't matter. Fact was, he seen healthy brain often enough to know this was wrong.

It's a disease. Not the universe.

"What do I believe?"

Vartan grunted at the irony. Walked to the rear and used a skewer to fish boiled cabbage from one of the big pots. Back in Solar System he had never been a fan of cabbage. Cold and soggy as this was, he considered it some of the finest eating he'd ever enjoyed.

Hunger—and ten years of ration along with the occasional stewed human—could do that to a person.

Full, he passed the remains of the dead Prophets and walked out to where the Messiah sat motionless, the faint whistle of his breathing audible through the gaping hole of his nose. The man's eyes were fixed on Guan Shi, as if the comatose and limp Prophet was on the verge of uttering some stunning pronouncement.

"Messiah?"

The man remained mute.

"Have any of the other teams reported in? My team, Will, Tuac, Sima, they're confirmed dead. Mars and Hap, they just disappeared. Gone. Taken by the forest. I barely made it back."

The Messiah might have been cast of stone for all the awareness he showed.

"Outside the door the invertebrates are eating Svetlana. They'll bite you if you try to touch her. I could use something, a rake maybe. A rope with a loop. We need to drag her away from the door. I can't bring her inside with all those things eating her."

Nothing.

"Messiah?"

The man's eyes—including the eerie blue one carved into his forehead—remained fixed on emptiness.

Vartan ground his teeth. Took a deep breath. "I'll figure it out on my own."

He turned, had taken a step when the Messiah, in a disjointed voice, said, "We are being tested, Second Will. The universe is winnowing away the chaff. Those who have been taken, they have been judged and found wanting. Immortality is not granted lightly."

"Found wanting?" Vartan tried to keep the incredulous tones from his voice. "Svetlana fell to her death fighting to save the airtruck. Mars, Will, Sima, and the rest of my team? There was no testing, just luck of the draw as to which of us was taken."

The Messiah raised his bone scepter. "Beware of your words, Second Will. The universe is listening."

"Messiah, two of the Prophets are dead. The third is dying. Three of the First Chosen are dead. Petre and Tikal's teams haven't returned. It's all falling apart."

"You must have faith." The words were said with simple conviction. "The universe has brought us this far. It will not let us down now."

"Messiah, have you heard anything I've said?"

"Vartan, you must trust. Believe that. Take it to your breast and hold tight."

"Messiah, we're dying like—"

"We *are* the immortal. Now, you have your duties, Second Will. You and the rest, bring me the Supervisor. I've heard that she's out there. Once we have the Supervisor, the rest of the people on Donovan, they'll fall into line."

Vartan placed a hand to his stomach, feeling the building ache. Damn it, he'd eaten too fast.

The Messiah was staring fixedly at Guan Shi.

Vartan stepped over, got a good look. Reached out and touched her half-slitted eyeball. No reaction.

"She's dead, Messiah."

Batuhan nodded slowly, sagaciously. "Then, so be it. The universe will provide. Just have faith."

65

Talina tilted her head back to better sniff the night breeze. Where Demon lurked behind her stomach, she could feel the piece of shit's tension. Rocket's presence perched on her shoulder, chittering his unease. Bits of memory, flashes of forest, glimpses of long-ago hunts played out in her imagination.

And something else. Something old and terrifying. Something *out there* in the dark. A looming danger.

She couldn't put her finger on it.

Quetzal memory.

"What is it?" she asked, concentrating on the thought. Wishing she had a direct link to the quetzal molecules instead of the hit or miss as transferRNA went through its rigmarole in search of the right information.

How the hell did that work, anyway? Too damn many pathways through the nervous system.

Dya had tried to explain it and . . .

Dya.

Dead.

That hurt. In a lot of ways.

Talina still owed the woman: On Clemenceau's orders, she'd shot Dya's first husband down in the street. Hardly seemed like she'd come close to making amends. Now Dya was dead. Smart, competent, resourceful Dya. And the loss wasn't just Kylee's, wasn't just Su's, and rest of her family's, but all of humanity's. Dya Simonov had known more about the botany, the genetics, the intricacies of TriNA. She'd been on the verge of a breakthrough with the native plants. Had barely begun to catalog her research.

Gone. Just like that.

Not to mention Mark Talbot. Steady as the stars in the sky. Talina ached for his amused smile, the wry sense of assurance the man possessed. Not to mention his skills when it came time to hunt rogue quetzals.

Where she sat off to the side, Muldare fought a whimper and cradled her arm. The thing was red, swollen. They'd hadn't been able to pull all the gotcha spines out. How the woman bore the pain and still managed to keep it together was a wonder.

Talina shifted her rifle, stepped over to where Kylee sat; the girl had her back propped against Flute's side. She looked up, eyes hot in Talina's IR vision. She'd been crying.

"How you doing, kid?"

"Really, really mad, Tal."

Behind her, Flute opened his left eye to study Talina. To say that quetzals didn't deal with death the same as humans did was an understatement. Especially given that they tended to eat their progenitors.

Talina dropped to a crouch, rifle across her knees as she listened to the night sounds. "You and Flute found where this thing got your mom and dad. Was there any clue as to what this is? Some scent? A track? Anything?"

Kylee worked her jaw. Knotted a fist. "A couple of spots of blood, and the roots were already absorbing them. Flute and I looked up. Couldn't see anything up in the branches. No thermal signature, no shape. Flute's sense of smell is a lot better than mine; he didn't catch of a hint of anything unusual. Maybe it had moved on."

Talina winced at the resentment and guilt in the girl's voice. Kylee's words echoed in Tal's memory: *"Everyone I love dies!"*

"We're going to find this thing," Talina promised. "The way Kalico and Briah described the tentacle, or whatever it was, the creature's got to be big. Something limited to deep forest where it can anchor among the high branches. And then there's the biomechanics of being able to lift a person that high that fast."

Kylee's lips were pursed, her face contorted. Now she said, "She shouldn't have been out there in the first place. *They* drove her out there. You know it just as well as I do."

At the venom in Kylee's voice, Talina took a deep breath. "You and Flute going to go on a rampage? Slicing and dicing your way through the Unreconciled? Murder every last one of them?"

"They *eat* people."

"So do quetzals. Flash killed and ate three people in the belief that he could synthesize their molecules. Learn who they were. The Unreconciled think that by eating people, they can purify them. Give them immortality. Where's the difference?"

Kylee's hot glare would have melted sialon. "I really hate you sometimes."

"Yeah, it's a pain in the ass when someone brings up all this rational, put-it-in-perspective stuff when all you want to do is go murder forty or fifty human beings. You gonna kill the kids, too?"

"Don't be an asshole, Talina."

"Right back at you, kid. Part of being a decent human being is thinking things through before you're hip-deep in the blood you've spilled." A pause. "And living with the guilt for the rest of your life."

Kylee leaned her head forward, buried her face in her hands. "There's so many things I needed to tell Mom. Tell Mark. Stuff I couldn't get myself to say. Like, I'm sorry. Like I let her down so many times. And I was there . . . stood there . . . like a fucking rock when Leaper and Diamond killed Rebecca and Shantaya. And I didn't care. I saw it! I just wanted everything and everyone to die."

"Your mother knew that. So does Su."

Talina dropped to a knee as her leg started to cramp. Carefully she scanned the surrounding trees, sorted the sounds of the night. That was the thing about having a quetzal in camp. None of the local wildlife was likely to sneak in for a snack.

"They also knew that you were different because you'd bonded with Rocket. That he's part of you, part of us." Talina tapped the side of her head. "Me, I'm a stop-gap. You're the future. You, and probably Tip and others like you. Dya understood that. Yeah, she loved you, and it broke her heart that it had to be her beloved daughter who was chosen as the bridge to the future."

"I hurt her." Kylee sniffed, wiped her nose. "Really, really hurt her."

Talina shifted her butt. "You know why she left you out there when she could have talked Kalico into sending armed marines to bring you back? It's because she trusted you. The greatest gift you ever gave your mom was letting her and Mark come visit you out at Briggs'."

"I'm tired of hurting, Talina."

"It sucks toilet water, but if you're going to really live, you're going to hurt. At least, if you're normal. Now, take Dan Wirth. He's a psychopath. Everything is all about him. No remorse. No guilt. No grief. On days like today, psychopathy sounds pretty good."

"I still want to kill cannibals."

"I hear you." Talina glared up at the high basalt escarpment where it blocked the eastern sky. "But here's the question: They were locked in a living hell, and the only path to survival led to a different kind of hell. If you or I had been there with the choices they had, what would we have chosen?"

"I don't get it."

"It's simple really: Would you have let them cut your throat and cook you? Become food for your fellow passengers? Or would you have chosen to live and cut someone else's throat, cooked, and eaten them? Choose."

"There had to be something else they could have—"

"Do you eat, or are you eaten? Pick."

Kylee glared at her. "It's never that simple."

"It was on *Ashanti*."

The girl crossed her arms, turning sullen. "Doesn't matter. When they drove Mom and Mark out into the forest, they weren't on any damn ship. Whole different rules."

Talina chuckled, her night-shifted gaze fixed on the heights above. "Yep. And before this is done, I'm going to settle with Messiah Batuhan."

"What about the rest of them?" Kylee asked.

Talina waved away a pesky night-flying invertebrate. "Well, if what we've seen so far is any indication, Donovan's slowly whittling the numbers down. And we gave them fair warning."

"And this thing out in the forest?"

"It'll have to wait its turn, but I promise you this: Its turn is coming."

"Good," Kylee whispered fiercely, "because I want to be there when we take it down."

66

Had it not been for Talina's quetzal-enhanced hearing, she wouldn't have known how long Kylee sobbed her grief. The girl had taken Flute, removed herself from the impromptu camp, and retreated up to the foot of the slope. Only then, out of sight, had she allowed herself to let go over the deaths of her mother and father.

That had been hours ago.

Talina, dozing off and on, had kept watch. The night creatures moved in the trees; night chime—so different from the sounds of the day—had risen and fallen in harmonic cadence. Briah Muldare had moaned in her sleep. Kalico, to Talina's amusement, snored. Taglioni slept with the sprawled and loose-limbed unconcern of the totally exhausted.

But nothing was as painful as Kylee's heart-wrenching grief.

The stars had wheeled most of the way across the sky when Talina stood, willing circulation back into her legs. That internal sense told her that morning was only an hour away.

Stepping gingerly, she slipped up the trail. Glanced around the bole of an aquajade. On the unyielding stone, Flute lay curled around himself like an oversized donut. The quetzal's vigilant right eye was fully fixed on Talina.

Took a moment for her to realize that deep in the curl, Kylee lay cradled. The girl's knees were drawn up to her chest, her hair splayed across the quetzal's foreleg. She might as well have been sleeping in one of those beanbag beds.

Flute's right eye regarded Talina with an unusual intensity. Seemed like nothing was getting by the quetzal on this night.

"How's she doing?" Talina asked softly.

Flute's hide flashed a deep-bruised purple, patterned with black and infrared designs. Colors and patterns Talina had never seen.

Rocket's *Wayob*—perched on Talina's shoulder—whispered, "*This is grief. Something quetzals do not feel.*"

Seemed she learned something new every day. "So, how come Flute's feeling it?"

Flute flashed the designs for "*Kylee hurt. Deep hurt. Makes eye-water. Do not tell.*"

"Yeah, I wondered how she kept it together as long as she did."

Talina sighed, stared up at the stars. So the kid had buried her head in Flute's side and bawled herself empty?

"How are you doing, Flute?"

Again he flashed the bruised purple, then black and infrared. She swore that if only quetzals had tear ducts, Flute, too, would have shed a tear.

Didn't feel grief, huh? Flute did. Mark it up to humans changing quetzals as much as quetzals changed humans?

"Hurt with Kylee." The patterns were perfectly clear in the night.

"Yeah, buddy," Talina told the quetzal. "Me, too. Keep her safe."

The beast's hide shaded into orange, quetzal for "yes."

How much pain could a kid take in life?

Kylee's words: *Everyone I ever love dies.*

One of these days, the kid was going to explode. As it was, the only creature she could allow herself to be vulnerable with was a quetzal. How screwed was that?

Talina gave Flute a parting smile, then reshouldered her rifle. As she turned to go, a single whimper passed Kylee's lips. Even in dreams, her heart was breaking.

67

The day dawned hot and humid. Salmon pink colored the thin layer of high cirrus. Dek Taglioni roused himself, surprised that he'd slept straight through on the bare stone. But by damn and hell, he hurt. Every muscle felt like it had been torn from its mooring on his bones. His hips, knees, and shoulders were sore from the hard rock.

And he was thirsty. Hungry. His coveralls emitted the ripe odors of sweat and stink.

If any solace could be found, it was that where she lay beside him, Kalico Aguila looked worse. Her thick midnight hair was a filthy tangle, her clothes smudged and stained. Something black—looked like grease—smeared her right cheek, the side of her perfect nose, and left a streak across her forehead.

Even as he watched, she blinked awake. Looked around with almost tortured eyes. The woman's face was drawn tighter than old rope. Her left cheek was lined and wrinkled from where it had pressed into the fabric of her sleeve.

She sat up, smacking her lips, tongue sounding dry as she struggled to make enough saliva to swallow. Dek read the sudden distress as she placed a hand to her stomach.

"Here," Dek told her, reaching into his web gear for the energy bar Chaco had given him. "This will help."

She shot him an uncertain look, glanced at the bar, thick as it was with roasted grain, dried blueberries, and desiccated crest meat.

"How long since you've eaten?" Dek asked.

"Since we left PA," she said, closing her eyes. "God, I swear, I can smell that bar you're holding."

She took it with a hesitant hand, shot him a wary look, and carefully bit down.

He couldn't help but grin at the expression on her face. Worked his own mouth in an attempt to conjure saliva. Finally managed a swallow.

"Where's yours?" Kalico indicated the pocket in his web gear.

"In a bit," he told her.

Quick as she was, her eyes flashed that laser-blue intensity. "You don't have another, do you?"

"I ate yesterday," he told her. "If what I hear is correct, you were lost in a cave. Already hungry."

She handed what was left back. "Here. You're going to need it."

He declined to take it. Waved absently toward the rising bulk of the Tyson escarpment. "Once we get to the top, there'll be food. I'm fine. Ate an energy bar last night before I went to sleep."

That sharpness had faded into a thoughtful appraisal. "Liar," she said softly.

To avoid any additional complications, Dek staggered to his feet. Wobbled. Wondered if every cell in his body was being tortured. Then tried not to make a face as he took in the small camp.

Talina and Muldare, rifles across their laps, were seated on basalt boulders, talking softly. Even as Dek watched, Muldare uttered a stifled gasp, made a face as she shifted her wounded arm. The thing looked horrible. Had swollen to fill her sleeve. The hand was puffy and red. How the woman managed was a miracle.

Kylee and the quetzal were gone. Around him the aquajade and dwarf chabacho trees were turning their branches and leaves toward the morning, all focused on the top of the high basalt cliff where Capella's light would appear. The chime was involved in its just-slightly-off symphony.

As he walked carefully across the uneven stone, he could feel his calves, his thighs and glutes, not to mention his back and shoulders. How long had it been since he'd hurt like this? University? When he was playing sports?

"Dek?" Talina called. "Where you going?"

"Behind these trees," he retorted over his shoulder. "And what I'm going to do is none of your business."

Looking back, here came Talina, stopping only long enough to scoop up his rifle from where he'd left it lying on the basalt.

She handed him the gun, a look of wry amusement glowing behind her alien eyes. "First, never leave your rifle out of hand while you're in the bush. Second, never step out of sight. Third, modesty has its place. But not here. Not now."

He glanced self-consciously to where Kalico Aguila was finishing the last of the energy bar and looking all the better for it. She was chuckling as she watched him squirm.

"Got it," he muttered. "So, how do I do this?"

"How about we both step around behind the trees. I'll glance around, make sure there're no slugs, no sidewinder, no gotcha vine or skewer, and that everything's copacetic. Then, while you attend to the realities of biology, I'll stand a couple of feet away and admire the surroundings. Take in a little bit of nature."

"You've got to be kidding."

"Not even slightly."

He took a deep breath. Laughed at himself. "Yes, ma'am."

As he squatted and attended to business, he glanced uncertainly at Talina. True to her word, she stood, rifle at port arms, her attention fixed on the surrounding forest.

After he'd finished, he stepped over, told her, "Thank you. Guess I've still got a whole lot to learn."

"Different world here." She gave him a wink. "Kylee's right. You've got the makings."

As he followed Talina back to the others he asked, "The makings? Of a disaster? Of a meal for a sidewinder?"

"Of a survivor," she told him. Then leaned close. "Thanks for giving that bar to Kalico. That might just get her through the day."

"Yeah. She's looking about all in."

"What about you?"

He made a face as he shifted his rifle on his sore shoulder. "Telling it straight? I feel like I've been pulled sideways through a singularity. Everything hurts."

"We can't take the easy trail up north. It'll be guarded. Too easy for them to roll rocks down on top of us, if nothing else. Assuming Kylee and Flute can find a way, we've got a hell of climb ahead of us."

"I know."

Talina stopped in front of Kalico, looked down. "You need to use the facilities?"

"No. I'm okay. Not enough water in me to run through."

Talina reached down, pulled Kalico to her feet. "You and Dek, you're the weak links. I need you two to keep an eye on each other. Help each other. Once we're up to the top, we'll get food and water one way or another. But we have to make it. All of us. Working together."

Kalico gave the woman a crooked grin. "You know, once upon a time, I was going to put you against a wall and shoot you."

Talina grinned back. "And if you had, where would you be today?"

Kalico reached out to slap palms with Talina as the security officer started toward the slope.

"Just got to get to the top," Dek told himself. "There'll be food and water up there."

"Yeah, that's the goal. Won't be too tough, just a little climb."

Kylee appeared from between the trees, trotting on her long legs. The girl's blonde hair was tied in a ponytail that bounced with each stride.

"Found a way up," she called to Talina. "Your instincts were good. Flute's up at the top, hunkered down and guarding the trail. There's some biteya and tooth flower to keep clear of, and I saw a sidewinder."

"All right, people," Talina called. "Let's get a little exercise. Muldare? You've got the six."

Dek tried to reshoulder his Holland & Holland, only to find the bruise was just as bad on his other shoulder.

Gut it out.

Three little words that he was really coming to hate.

Nevertheless he took his place, following Talina as she led the way through the scrubby aquajade and chabacho. Compared to what he'd seen back in the deep forest, these were really scrawny specimens. And he was just as happy to be able to look up and see patches of open sky on occasion.

Then they began the climb in earnest. In the beginning it meant scrambling from one toppled boulder to the next. Reaching back, giving a hand to the person following.

Within minutes, Dek was panting, a faint sheen of perspiration slicking his cheeks, neck, and chest. Water he couldn't afford to lose. The temperature had to be in the midthirties, and the humidity left his sweat to pool.

"You were going to shoot Talina Perez?" Dek asked Kalico as Talina extended her lead on the cracked rock, climbing hot on Kylee's heels.

Kalico was already panting as she made her way around a toppled boulder and stared anxiously at the heights above. "You gotta remember, we didn't have a clue about Donovan. During those two years in transition on *Turalon* I had convinced myself the colony was in rebellion, that they'd seized the missing ships. Turned themselves into a bunch of pirates."

"I see." Dek reached down. Took Kalico's hand, and pulled her up, every muscle in his body complaining.

"No, you don't. Pirates are easy. You just shoot them. We ran into something worse: libertarians. I mean how do you deal with a bunch of lunatics who take it as an article of faith that they can govern themselves?"

"So what happened?" Dek shifted the rifle, anxious lest it might slip off his shoulder, hit the rocks, and mar the lustrous finish on the expensive wood with its beautiful inlay.

Kalico scrambled up next to him, anxiety in her eyes as she realized the magnitude of the climb she was about to attempt. "I put Talina, Shig, and Yvette on trial. When the locals figured out where it was going, Talina stopped the riot just before the Donovanians murdered us. I gave them Port Authority. Figured it was the easiest way to cut my losses."

He found toe-holds, got a grip, and forced himself to climb the next little bit. Turned, and again helped Kalico. Below them, Muldare—looking thirsty and hot herself—kept staring back the way they'd come, ensuring that nothing was following behind. She had her rifle slung, was somehow managing to climb in spite of her inflamed arm.

"So how'd you end up at Corporate Mine?"

Kalico staggered, almost lost her balance. Dek pulled her close. Kept her from falling.

"Thanks. Missed my step there." She wiped a sleeve over her forehead, smeared the smear more. "*Freelander* showed up. You've heard the story about that. What you haven't heard is that I saw myself in the temple of bones. Heard myself say, 'If you go back, you will die.'"

She chuckled, voice rasping with thirst. "Strange shit happens on that ship. Thing is: I said that, all right. More than a year in the future. Used those exact words with that pus fucker Benteen."

"Why didn't you space back on *Turalon*? From what I hear, they had a fortune on board. You'd have been a hero."

She blinked, wavered. "*Freelander* scared the shit out of me. All those lost ships. Vanished. I couldn't . . . couldn't . . ."

"Yeah, I guess I'd have done the same." He made sure she wouldn't fall, tackled the next climb, and reached back. Fought a slight dizzy spell. Had he ever been this thirsty before?

Come on, Dek. You can do this.

Somehow, he got Kalico up the next steep section.

"Why the hell am I telling you this?" she wondered under her breath. "You called me 'Miko's cerulean cunt' the last time I saw you. Asked Miko if I moaned while I was sucking his cock."

"It was outside the Boardroom, wasn't it?" He snorted derisively. "Wasn't even drunk that time. Just full of hatred."

"Of me?"

"God, no. Well . . . maybe a little. There you were, the most beautiful and capable woman in Solar System, with your perfect body pressed up against Miko's. I was so damn jealous." He blinked. Looked up at the next section. Saw the tooth flower off to the side that Talina pointed to.

"Mostly," he told her, "I was full of hatred for myself. For all of my failures, for all the frustrations that I blamed on everyone else."

He pointed. "Now, watch out for that toothy thing. We've got to climb wide."

She squinted, fixed on the tooth flower. "So, what are you now?"

"I don't have the first flipping clue. As a Taglioni, I should have hated myself the most while I was cleaning toilets on *Ashanti*. That's about as far as anyone in my family could fall. And yet, there I was, in the dark, scrubbing up other people's piss and excrement. Fixing the plumbing when the shit of menials plugged it up and stirring the septic in the hydroponics. And I was proud of myself for the first time in my life."

She was giving him that half-glazed look of disbelief. Her once-perfect lips were cracked, her smudged face fatigued and drawn. Nevertheless, she let him cup his hands for her foot, boost her up onto the next ledge. The effort took all of his energy, and he came close to dropping her.

"You ever get back to Transluna," she told him, "I wouldn't confide that to Miko. He'll rub your nose in it. Figure some way of humiliating you to the point that you'd rather be dead."

Dek licked dry lips. Tried to conjure spit . . . and failed. He could feel the building headache. Thirst, he decided, was the most agonizing of suffering. "Supervisor, there's nothing for me back in that hive of serpents and spiders."

The trembling in his muscles was evident as he levered himself up onto the narrow flat beside Kalico.

"Just going to farm? Maybe go live with Chaco Briggs?" she asked.

"Both good choices. But I think I want more. Shig says I'm more of a *rajasic* by nature. Means I'm predisposed to the hedonistic and active, the spice of life. According to Shig, while I was on *Ashanti* I managed to find harmony with the tamas in my soul. Sattva, he said, would probably elude me in this lifetime." A beat. "Sometimes I wonder if Shig delights in screwing with my head."

She laughed dryly as she tackled the next cracked section of rock. "I think the universe put Shig here because it's the only place left that he fits."

"What about you? If you could be guaranteed of getting back?"

She reached down, took his hand. Not that she had a lot left to pull with. Actually made it harder for Dek to clamber his way up.

She was panting, flipped her filth-matted hair out of her face as she told him, "Success on Donovan was supposed to be my catapult.

Was going to shoot me right into a seat on the Board. Sure, I'd already won the golden plum: I'd fought my way into the position of Supervisor in charge of Transluna. That's always been a springboard. Only one place to go after that. And once I was on the Board, it would have been a matter of time before I was in the Chairman's seat."

"You still could, you know," Dek told her softly, seeing the longing in her eyes.

As quickly it was gone. "All I want at this moment is a tall glass of water and a meal. Not to mention anything that would kill this damned headache. Starting to feel like my skull is split." She paused, blinked. "Like I want to be sick. Slightly dizzy."

"Yeah." His entire body was hot. He'd have given anything for a canteen. Cool, wonderful, water.

The skepticism was back. As if it had finally occurred to her just who she'd been talking to. "So, really, why'd you give me that energy bar this morning? What was your goal in all that?"

"You needed it."

"Uh huh." She coughed hoarsely. "How about you stick to climbing, all right?"

"Sure," he agreed, wondering how he'd managed to pick a scab off such an unhealed wound. It hit him, of course, that he'd just reminded her of how badly she'd wanted that seat on the Board. What it must have cost her to make it so high up the echelon that it was dangling within her reach.

He took a deep breath, would have killed for a gulp of water.

And then the world began to whirl. A sick feeling tickled his gut with the urge to vomit.

"Whoa," he whispered. Blinked.

And started to topple . . .

THE DESERT

I was never trained in religion. My parents didn't believe in it. And Mongolia had its own history, placed as it was between the Buddhist, Taoist, Islamic, Russian Orthodox, and animistic spheres. A sort of crossroads for faiths of every kind. And through it all, the ancient magic of the steppes was constantly blowing.

I was raised to be agnostic, to look first for the laws of physics and science before any credence was given to the spiritual. That creed led me to electronics, gave me my trade.

Had taken me to the stars.

And Ashanti.

Where the universe found me. A blank canvass upon which it could compose, and finally paint. The rough sketch was, of course, the Harrowing and Cleansing, and with the gift of the Prophets, it colored between the lines, shaded, and added the subtle tones of composition that created the masterpiece that was the Irredenta.

The tool for the redemption and renovation of the universe, for its cleansing and rebirth into purity.

I do remember, however, that messiahs are always given one last test before they are granted the final revelations. For my ancestors out on the steppes, it was usually starvation and deprivation that preceded spirit visions, soul flying, and holy trance. For the Buddhists it was meditation. Fasting for the Muslims. Jesus was tempted by the devil while exiled in the desert.

Now I face my desert, my darkest moments.

I have half of the adults left who descended to Donovan from Ashanti. *Ten of the children are dead or missing. Shyanne and Tamil betrayed us and stole the airtruck.*

The universe tempts me to recant. Taunts me with the possibility that my people really are dying on Donovan, and doing so in a way that they cannot be reincarnated.

Worst of all, it has taken my Prophets from me. An act akin to stabbing out my eyes. Leaving me in a black haze of darkness where all I can do is reach out with feeble fingers in an attempt to find my way. But flail about as I might, my groping hands find only nothingness.

For all of its appearance as a lush forest full of life, spiritually Donovan is a desert. A parched waste devoid of reassurance. A land of thirst for those desperate to slake their longing for salvation.

What better place to test me?

I am panicked, frantic, and adrift.

Three of the First Chosen are murdered by that Corporate demon, their meat preserved in refrigeration in the kitchen. They await the sacrament of feasting, the moment they will be ingested, their souls to follow the path to regeneration.

My First and Third Will, along with their teams, are missing. Presumed dead. Which, I realize, is another test. I have no proof that they are really dead. The universe might produce them, like a rabbit from a hat, the moment I declare my lack of faith.

Svetlana, my second wife, has died from a fall. Perhaps it was the universe discarding her. That she'd fulfilled her duty, bringing as many of the dead back to life as she did. The children I sired from her will grow, become new vessels in which the dead can be reborn.

Vartan worries me. I've always been suspicious of his true commitment. More so since Shyanne and Tamil got away with the airtruck. I can't help but suspect Vartan allowed that to happen through omission if not direct knowledge.

In the end, I suspect that Vartan will have to be purified and reborn. But for the moment, I need him. He's the only person I have with any security training. He knows how to use a rifle.

If, somehow, the Supervisor is alive, she will come here. She must. She's the kind who does not leave unfinished business.

There is no telling why the airtruck hasn't flown up out of the forest. This morning we've not heard gunfire. Perhaps Donovan has dealt with the

Supervisor in its own way. Or something's wrong with the airtruck. The uncertainty is maddening.

Meanwhile, I must assume Aguila is alive. And she'll be coming for the radio.

But why take away my Prophets? Blind me like this? What's the point of leaving me to grope about? What am I supposed to learn?

I look up, state emphatically: "I have faith." *I repeat:* "I do not doubt!"

In my deepest soul, I believe it. Let the belief run through my veins with each beat of my heart. I will not waver. I am the repository of souls. The chosen one.

I stare at an empty cafeteria, seeing the bare tables where the Prophets once lay.

The place is so quiet. Only the hum of the air conditioning and refrigerators can be heard in the background.

The children are being kept safe in the barracks dome. I have people on watch to the north and south.

But I am not alone. I never am. The dead are with me. Living in my tissue. Waiting patiently in my loins. I am their repository.

Through me, they shall live forever.

I hear the steps, two people. One is having trouble. I can hear the sliding, half stagger.

When Marta pushes the door open, she has Shimal Kastakourias' arm over her shoulder. The woman is having trouble walking.

I wait, watch with ever growing excitement as Marta brings Shimal close, lowers her to one of the chairs at the table.

"What happened?" I ask.

Shimal stares up at me, her dark eyes panicked. "It's been getting worse, Messiah. At first, it was simple things. Dropping stuff. Stumbling."

I glance down, see Shimal's right hand. It trembles, twitches. My amazement and delight increase.

"Then, this morning"—Shimal swallows hard—"I was having trouble. Kept slurring my words. It's better now. But I just fell over. Marta said I should come to you."

Shimal blinks, the wobble of her head barely visible.

Marta, gaze stony, says, "She thinks she's turning into a Prophet."

I close my eyes, lean my head back. A surge of relief spills through my breast, fills me with delight.

Of course.

That's the lesson.

What the universe takes, it will replace.

My soul rises on a wave of rapture.

68

The attack had been cunning, audacious, a whole new tactic. It might have worked but for Pamlico Jones. He'd been watching the corner of the shipping crates where Dan Wirth had disappeared with that *Ashanti* copilot, Windman.

While Jones wasn't about to stick his nose where it didn't belong, that didn't mean the man wasn't intensely curious, Dan being who and what he was. That Dan had been outside the fence was unusual enough. When he escorted Windman around the stacked containers and out of sight, Jones figured that Windman was about to suffer "an unfortunate accident."

So he'd seen the first of the quetzals that had poked its head around the shipping containers where Wirth and Windman had vanished.

Figuring that Dan Wirth and Paul Windman were already in transition to becoming quetzal shit, Jones had jumped on com and sounded the alert.

And just in time, Allison thought as she stared down at the "Quetzal Map" where it lay spread on the conference room table. At the sound of the siren, she'd dropped everything, run full out to the admin dome. Knowing that Talina was out at Briggs' and Shig was up doing who knew what on *Freelander,* it had just been her and Yvette coordinating the search. That had been twenty-eight long hours ago.

"Still trying to absorb this," Yvette said softly as she ran her eyes across the map.

"They've never tried to rush two gates before. Let alone at the same time."

"No." Yvette placed a finger on the shuttle-field gate. "It's bad enough that one got through the Mine Gate. Wejee almost had it closed when that first quetzal darted through."

"He's just damn lucky," Allison agreed, her eyes on the square that indicated Mine Gate's location. "If that first quetzal had stopped long enough to kill Wejee, the others could have made it through."

"Well, it didn't. It just streaked into town. Wejee managed to get the gate shut, got a couple of rounds into the second quetzal, and the third fled back to the bush."

"Three on the north, three on the east," Allison mused. "Charging the gates simultaneously." She tried to understand what that meant. Realized she was irritated with herself for leaving all of this for others over the years.

So, you alive or dead out there, Dan?

The best scenario would be if he were dead. For one thing, it would be a huge relief. She would no longer have to balance on the precarious teeter-totter of living with a violent psychopath. Sometimes the stress was unbearable. Especially over the last year as Dan had begun to realize he'd reached his zenith. If he was dead out there, The Jewel, the various properties, the claims, the house, all of it would be hers.

That being the case, Ali, how are you going to keep it?

She would have to move swiftly, mercilessly. While it had been serendipitous, Kalen Tompzen knew that she was the one who had brokered his escape from the shit-filled future Aguila had consigned him to. He'd back her, follow any order she gave him.

"Drone has a hit on the IR," came Step Allenovich's voice over com. "*Yeah, it's our quetzal. Got him in the box on one of the broken haulers."*

"Watch yourselves," Yvette called. "Don't take any chances."

"Screw chances. My call is to take him out with a drone. That haul box will contain the blast, won't even so much as mar the paint. Well, okay, old as that thing is, it won't mar the rust."

"Do it." Yvette exhaled wearily. "Tough hunt this time around."

"They cleared that area early last night," Allison said thoughtfully, staring at the map.

"Maybe it got around behind them? Maybe they just missed it? Doesn't matter. What does is that the thing was so harried it never managed to kill anyone."

"Guess that just leaves Dan and Windman."

Yvette turned pensive eyes on her. "You know the odds aren't good."

"I've been running that through my mind."

"Allison, why are you here? I mean, I appreciate the help. With Talina and Shig gone, you being here freed up Step for the hunt. But, seeing you walk through that door . . . ?"

"The last person you expected?"

"Uh . . . yeah."

Allison gave her a weary smile. "Let's say I've opened my eyes to entirely new possibilities. Some of which may change even as we discover what happened when Dan and Windman stepped out back of the shipping crates."

Yvette's cool green eyes didn't waver. "Bit brazen of you, don't you think?"

"Is it my business or my occupation that you object to? Or maybe my history?"

"Stow it," Yvette muttered. "The only saint in PA is Shig, and if he were here he'd just nod pleasantly and give us that maddening smile before he started spouting off on your karma."

A muffled bang sounded.

"Cap one quetzal," Step's voice came through com.

"Steaks and leather." Yvette accessed her personal com. "Sound the all clear, but send it out that we want everyone staying frosty, armed, and ready. They could try something else."

"*Roger that,*" Two Spot's voice came through.

Yvette then asked, "Two Spot? Anything from Tal or Aguila?"

"Negative. Not a word since yesterday."

"Well, that sucks toilet water. Now we have to figure out what's become of Talina and the Supervisor. The shit never stops coming down."

Allison yawned, stretched. "Yeah, I need a couple of armed escorts. I want to see what happened out behind that container wall."

Because this was a watershed moment. If Dan was dead, fine and thank God. If, somehow, he'd managed to survive, it had become apparent to Allison that inevitably, it would be up to her to kill him herself.

69

"Tal," Muldare called softly.

Talina turned, stared back down the steep escarpment. Muldare had her good hand on Taglioni, seemed to be pressing him into the rock to keep him from pitching off the slender ledge where the man was propped. Above him, Kalico was glancing down, looking none too steady herself. Bits of detritus were stuck in the Supervisor's already filthy hair. Something Talina had never seen.

Using cracks, Talina scaled her way back down and wide around Kalico. She got her fingers into a fissure and took a good look at Taglioni. The guy's eyes were unfocused, wavering. His muscles had that loose shiver that indicated a man on the edge.

"He's spent," Muldare said. "What the hell do we do now?"

"You're not looking any too good yourself. How's the arm?"

"Like a fucking fountain of fire. The only good news is that it keeps me from knowing how gagging thirsty, hot, and tired I am."

"Dizzy spells?"

"Not yet." Muldare gave her a suffering grin. "Marines don't quit. I'll make it."

But even marines had a point of no return.

Talina glanced up. Where was the top? Maybe another thirty or forty meters? Hard to tell from this angle.

"Kylee?" she called, hoping no one was at the summit to overhear. The girl turned, stared down, wild blonde hair framing her thin face. "You and Muldare, help Kalico."

Kylee immediately began to scramble down the rocks.

"What are you going to do?" Muldare asked, voice partly slurred by thirst. The marine winced as she hitched her swollen arm around.

"You and Kylee make sure Kalico gets to the top," Talina told her. "I've got Taglioni."

"Tal, he's about to pass out."

"Yeah. I know. So's Kalico. Too long without water and now heat stroke. So, hump your butt, Marine. Get the Supervisor up and out of here. Whatever it takes."

"Yes, ma'am," Muldare mumbled hoarsely, and taking a grip with her good hand, climbed past the sagging Taglioni.

Talina took hold of the guy, could feel his heart pounding like a triphammer. "How you doing, Dek?"

"Headache's fit to kill a horse. Everything just started spinning. Anything . . . Just want . . ." He wavered, and she pushed him back against the rock.

Talina filled her lungs. Looked up to where the others were slowly and clumsily working their way up the steep ascent. Kalico was going to fail next, and then pain-wracked Muldare. It'd be a miracle if the marine made it.

So, what to do about Taglioni?

Talina shifted her feet for the best purchase possible and swung the man onto her shoulders. Damn, his limp body jammed her rifle right into the middle of her back, bruising the spine.

"C'mon," she growled to herself as she took the weight. "All that quetzal strength better be worth something."

Demon hissed from down next to her liver.

She began to climb.

Handhold by handhold she made her way up. Felt the fingers of fatigue, her own lack of water. Quetzal visions kept spinning through her head: Bits of forest. A hot plain. Heat waves rising above the bush.

Talina imagined she had claws. Visualized how they'd look fixing themselves into the rock. Recognized the reality that she had hardly slept the night before. Had spent her time aching and grieving with Kylee over Dya and Talbot. About the "thing" out in the forest that had killed them.

And now?

Here she was, climbing with two rifles and seventy kilos of dead weight in an attempt to reach the summit where an unknown number of cannibals would love nothing better than to chop them all up and turn them into a sacred lunch.

"If that doesn't suck toilet water?" she asked between gasping breaths.

Sweat beaded, ran down into her eyes as she glanced up; Kylee tugged on Kalico's arm in an attempt to get the failing Supervisor over a vertical column of stone. Muldare had her feet braced and was pushing up on Kalico's butt with her good hand.

Kalico's butt? Really? And not a single protestation of outrage?

How was that for a measure of Aguila's failing state?

Talina grinned, hoisted herself up another half body length, and felt the burn in her muscles.

"Come on," she growled down at her stomach. "What's the point of having a piece of shit like you living inside me if you can't make me superwoman?"

"Weak!" Demon's voice taunted from her gut.

"Fuck you," Talina gritted through her teeth—and stared up at the near-vertical crack that led to the top of the next boulder. The basalt was in the signature columnar fractures; the only good news being that they'd been snapped into short segments. Sort of like climbing a stack of building blocks.

She puffed for breath, charged her muscles, and told Dek, "Hang on!"

Then she tackled the climb, shutting her mind off, simply willing herself to power up the slim fissure. Sucking air, heart hammering, she flopped herself and Taglioni across the flat surface atop one of the stones.

"That's it," she told herself. "Get your wind."

Where his head hung beside hers, Taglioni slurred, "She loathes me. Despicable walking shit that I am."

"I don't loathe you," Talina told him. "You've spent the last ten years in a ship is all. So far you've impressed the hell out of me, having made it this far."

"Kalico," he whispered muzzily. "Don't blame her. I was a real maggot."

She felt him fading, his hold growing limp. "Hey! Pay attention. Wake up. Concentrate. I need you to hang on to me. Just one more climb, okay?"

He worked his dry mouth. She felt him start, as if from impending sleep. "Yeah. Awake. God, I'm thirsty. Fucking head's about to burst."

"Okay. Here we go."

She felt him tighten his grip, and with a cry she tackled the next vertical crack. Muscles burned, fingers ached as they sought a purchase; she gutted her way to the next ledge.

And the next.

Each time, it was supposed to be the last. Somehow, sag as he did, Taglioni held on. The man's weight on her rifle was like a knife-blade bearing into her back.

And then hands reached down. Got hold of Taglioni's shirt and rifle, pulled the man off Tal's back as she fought her way up and over a final ledge. Here ferngrass grew, a hollow marking the edge of the basalt flow.

With her quetzal vision she could discern Flute where he was flattened under the lip of stone, his camouflage melding with the rocks and vegetation.

Talina slipped her rifle off, flopped onto her back, and heaved for air as she stared up at the endless vault of sky. Capella's harsh light burned down, half blinding. Baking hot. Had to be forty if it was a degree.

"Screw vacuum," she gasped. "I don't want to do that again."

"We there yet?" Kalico rasped. "They can eat me. Anything to stop this headache."

"She hates me," Taglioni's voice was mumbling, and then he seemed to drift off.

"Who hates him?" Kylee asked where she lay on her belly at the top of the hollow, eyes on the approaches.

"Kalico." Talina tried to muster enough spit to swallow. Couldn't.

"Fucker . . . called me Miko's favorite slippery cunt," Kalico said through a dry whisper. "How far to water?"

"Doesn't matter"—Muldare's voice cracked—"I'll shoot any bastard tries to get in the way."

Kalico bent, tried to throw up, but only suffered from dry heaves. "Sucking snot," she whimpered. "That hurts."

Talina's heart had slowed to the point it was no longer trying to batter its way through her ribs. She smacked her dry lips, forced herself to sit up. Her fingers were torn and bloody from the climb when she picked up her rifle and crawled up next to Kylee and Flute.

People died of heat stroke. They were running out of time.

"What have we got, kid?"

Raising her head, it was to see the flat mesa top. Maybe fifty meters to the south, the first of the domes shimmered in the hot white light. A woman, wearing only a wrap around her hips, was standing in the shade of an old ramada this side of the dome.

Eat her, Demon hissed. *Moisture in her meat.*

"Go screw yourself," Talina muttered in return.

Demon chittered happily.

"There's just that one woman on guard." Kylee made a face. "What's with the scars these people have?"

Muldare, looking haggard, hitched her way up one-handed to take a look. "Marks a path for the souls of the people they eat. Or some such shit like that." The marine awkwardly unslung her rifle, laid it across the rock and tried to sight it. Hard to do one-handed on her weak side. "I could pot her from here. The way I feel? It'd be a pleasure."

"Yeah?" Talina asked, noticing how the marine's rifle wavered like a branch in the wind. Muldare'd be lucky if she could hit the dome on fully automatic, dehydrated and exhausted as she was. "And have the whole compound hear. Bet they'd come at a run. How many of them are there?"

"Maybe fifty adults? Maybe less. No telling." Muldare sucked at her dry lips, desperate eyes on the lone sentry. "If Batuhan sent all those people . . . down into the forest . . . to search for us? May only have a handful left. Look at us. Four of us got away . . . and Talbot and his wife . . . dead. That's half."

"I can handle it." Kylee reached down and pulled her long knife from its sheath. Sunlight glinted on the wicked blade's polished steel.

"Going to kill her?"

"Well, duh?" Kylee shot her a frost-blue look of disbelief. "My parents are *dead* because of these people. Mom and Mark came here to help them, and these fuckers drove them out into the forest."

Talina got a grip on Kylee's wrist. Squeezed. "No."

For a moment their gazes locked in a battle of wills. In the end, Kylee rolled her eyes, jerked her knife hand free, and asked, "So . . . what? We sing "Coming Together Under the Bower" and make like best friends? I don't think so."

Talina glanced up at Capella. Figured the time at somewhere around eleven. The temperature, mixed with the humidity, was compounded now that they were in direct sun. Taglioni was already raving, Kalico at the stage of complete heat exhaustion. Dehydrated as they were, hyperthermia would kill them within the hour.

If that guard called out, brought twenty or thirty screaming Unreconciled soldiers charging down on top of them? What were any of their chances? Flute would unleash havoc among them. Tal'd open fire on full auto, mow them down to the last man, woman, or child.

So, what's a human life worth?

Talina slithered back down, picked up Taglioni's fancy hunting rifle with its waxed walnut, gleaming gold, and fancy inlay. She studied the thing, found the dial that controlled velocity in the pistol-grip's pommel. She set it to eleven hundred feet per second. Just subsonic.

Crawling up to her place again, she laid out prone, braced the rifle's forearm on a tuft of ferngrass.

As she got a sight picture, Muldare asked, "What are you doing?"

"Making the best of a shit-load of totally bad choices."

Talina settled the self-regulating sight on the woman's head, pressed the button on the sight that compensated for distance and trajectory, and took a breath. Letting it half out, she timed her heartbeat, and in midbeat, caressed the trigger.

The rifle barely uttered a *phfft*.

In the optic, the woman's head snapped back, her eyes gone wide. She dropped like a sack of potatoes. Kicked a couple of times and began to twitch.

"Why was that better than me knifing her?" Kylee demanded, her face in a pout.

"Because it's on my soul, not yours," Talina told her. "Muldare, you stay on guard. Flute, you make sure nothing happens to them. Kylee, you're with me."

Talina laid Taglioni's gleaming Holland & Holland to one side, took her service rifle, and not waiting to see if Kylee obeyed, sprinted for the curved side of the nearest dome.

She didn't bother to look at the woman she'd shot. Her peripheral vision was more than good enough to tell her the woman hadn't been killed outright.

With Kylee hot on her heels, Talina dared not take the time to finish the job. Instead she crept around the side of the dome, found the door, and unlatched it.

She slipped inside, closed it behind Kylee, and turned to cover the hallway with her rifle. Nothing. Just an empty corridor illuminated by a few flickering light panels.

"Where are we?" Kylee wondered under her breath.

"Science dome. Probably the last place Batuhan's maniacs would inhabit," Talina whispered. "Stay behind me."

She led the way down the hall, cleared the first two conference rooms, and then ducked into the lab. Looked to see that no one was hiding behind the counters. Even searched the hood and biocontainment room.

"Check the cabinets. We need clean jars. Jugs. Anything that will hold water." Talina ripped open the closest cabinets, finding empty shelves. In the next she found a couple bottles of alcohol, solvents, and a trio of one-gallon containers of nitric acid.

"Got it!" Kylee called, popping up from behind the counter with collapsible sample jars.

At the sink, Talina turned on the tap, cupped some and sniffed the water that trickled out. Kalico's techs had gone through the systems while under Bogarten's watchful eye. Smelled okay. She cupped it, sucking down handfuls. Waited while Kylee did the same. Now it would save the Supervisor's life.

"Come on. Come on," Talina groused as the slow flow began to fill the first jug. "Kylee. Go keep watch. Be just like our luck to have somebody stumble over that dead guard's body."

"What if they've overthrown Batuhan?"

"Then I just murdered a woman for no reason." *Yeah, right. Deal with that later.* "Now, go make sure the coast's still clear. Scoot."

Kylee vanished from the room.

What if they've overthrown Batuhan?

Talina ground her teeth. Tried not to think about it.

The jugs filled with maddening slowness.

70

The soft sound of a fan finally penetrated the pounding headache. Next was a delightful and cooling mist that settled on Kalico's skin, followed immediately by a stirring of air that ran down her chest and belly, across the tops of her thighs, and all the way to her feet.

She swallowed hard, the action doubling the pain in her skull. She hadn't hurt this much since . . . since . . .

Her muzzy thoughts couldn't quite correlate the data.

"Here," a voice told her. "You need to drink again."

Kalico blinked as a hand lifted the back of her head. A glass was placed to her lips, and she sucked down the lukewarm water. Sighed as it hit her stomach. Then her head was lowered; a folded bundle of cloth served as a pillow. Overhead was a single light panel. Had to be daytime because Capella's beams were spilling in the window to her left. She lay on a low fold-out cot.

She gasped as the gentle mist settled on her skin again. Focusing, it was to see Kylee Simonov using a spray bottle to squirt Kalico's naked body.

Naked?

"Hey?" She tried to sit up. The blast of pain in her head caused her to whimper and ease her head back to the folded cloth.

"Stay put," Kylee told her. The kid had her head cocked, tangles of blonde hair falling around her shoulders. "Tal says you're going to feel like hammered shit for a while. But we've got to get you cooled down."

"Where's my clothes? Why the hell am I naked? What's going on?"

"You're in the science dome at Tyson Station. Stripping you down to the skin is the quickest way to lower your body temperature. No ice or cold water, so I get to squirt you and Dek down, then fan you to cool you off."

"Screw vacuum. What the hell happened to me?"

"Dehydration and heat," a weak voice told her from the side. She squinted against the headache, turned her head to the right to see Taglioni, his bone-thin and pale body as naked as hers where he lay on the adjoining bunk. The man looked positively miserable.

Kylee—positioned between them—turned and used her spray bottle, shooting him down from head to toe. Then she used a flat piece of plastic attached to what looked like a length of broom handle to waft air over his body.

"My head hasn't felt like this since I tried to empty a cask of Inga's whiskey all on my own," Kalico murmured. Then: "How the hell did we get here? Last I remember was on the cliff. Feeling sick. Ready to kill for a glass of water."

"Talina carried you both to the dome while Flute and I kept watch. Muldare made it on her own. She's asleep yonder."

Kalico followed Kylee's point to see Muldare. The marine was stripped down to her underwear, supine on what looked like a lab bench, a fan blowing across her body. Some kind of grease had been slathered over her swollen arm; from the angry-red color it must have hurt like a bastard.

"Drink." Kylee offered Taglioni her glass. The man finished it off. Set his head back on a small duraplast box that served him for a pillow. Then Kylee stepped over to a sink, set the empty glass under the dribbling tap, and returned with a full one.

Kalico was aware enough to suck it all down. Felt it seep through the empty hollow that was her stomach and into her aching limbs.

She asked, "If we're at Tyson, where are the Unreconciled?"

"Down at the admin dome," Kylee told her. "Tal and Flute are keeping an eye on them. Sooner or later they're going to figure out that the woman Tal shot is missing. When they do, it's really going to get complicated."

"What woman?" Taglioni asked.

Kylee turned, spared him one of her glacial-blue gazes. "They had a guard posted between us and this dome. Tal took her out with your rifle. I wanted to. She wouldn't let me."

"Took her out with my rifle?" Dek's expression indicated his confusion. "You mean, Talina shot her?"

Kylee tapped a finger to her forehead. "Pop! And down she went."

"Wasn't there some other way?" Dek asked.

"She was a cannibal. 'Cause of her, Mom and Mark are dead. What's to cry over?"

The cold tone in the girl's voice sent a shiver down Kalico's spine.

Meanwhile, Kylee shrugged, walked over, and started spraying Dek's body again. "Sure. We could have waited her out. Heat stroke being what it is, Tal, Flute, and I could have left your dead bodies down in that hollow. After dark we could have sneaked wherever we wanted. Stocked up on eats down at the garden, drank our fill from the cisterns. Slipped into the admin dome to get to the radio and sent an SOS to PA for a quick pickup down on the south end."

The girl switched her bottle for her fan, wafting it over Dek's body as she added, "So the guard is dead, and you, Kalico, and Briah are alive. Are you wishing Tal had played it the other way around?"

Dek's face had scrunched into an uncomfortable pinch. "Don't know. Hard to think rationally with this headache."

Kalico sighed as Kylee turned, sprayed her body again. She repeated, fitting the pieces together: "So, we're all in the science dome, and they're two domes away. Eventually someone's going find the dead guard's body. See that she's shot through the head. Realize where we are. This place got a back door?"

"Don't worry about the guard's body. It . . . went away. Let's just say that in the end, Donovan got her. Meanwhile we lay low. And yeah, there's a back door. But you're not ready to run. So, my advice? Go back to sleep. Tal and Flute are out there, keeping guard. We figure we're in the last place the cannibals would look for us."

"Flute is standing guard?" Kalico asked, delighted by the cool spray on her hot flesh. She felt beads of it running down the long lines of her scars. "What's he get out of all this?"

"Mostly he's fascinated," Kylee told her. "And a little worried."

"About Batuhan? This all goes sideways, Flute can fade into the forest, and they'll never find him."

"It's the forest that worries him." Kylee's face turned grim. "First, he'd be stranded here. If we don't take him, he's got no safe way back to his lineage. Normally that would be bad enough, because he'd be a rogue. The local lineages would hunt him down. Try and kill him."

"He didn't worry about that when he came here?"

"Sure. But it was only to pick up Mom and Dad and fly out. He wouldn't have been on the ground for more than a couple of hours at the most. When the airtruck was destroyed, Flute went on alert. Figured the local lineages would pick up his scent."

"Did they?"

Kylee waved the fan—cool breeze caressing Kalico's body. "That's the thing that's really got him worried. Not only did no local quetzals come after him, he didn't pick up their scent. Nothing. Not even old sign."

"I guess that's a relief." Kalico laid the back of her hand against her forehead. Wished it would ease the damn skull-splitting ache. Wished she had aspirin. She'd have given a fortune to cut the throbbing misery.

"Anything but," Kylee told her. "Flute thinks Tyson has been quetzal-free for years. Maybe all the way back to when this base was occupied."

"Flute thinks the people killed the quetzals?" Dek asked.

"In this mess of rocks and trees?" Kylee asked incredulously. "Humans wouldn't have a chance at exterminating an entire lineage. Forest is too thick. Hell, Tal's been hunting Whitey for three years in low bush, and he's still ahead of her."

"Then what's the explanation?" Kalico asked, head hurting too much to work out the intricacies.

"Flute thinks it's the thing that got Mom and Dad. Says he's got a memory. Something ancient. From the far west. He says the memory is only an image. A sort of black swinging spear shooting down from the sky."

"Sounds about right," Kalico whispered before Kylee put the

glass to her lips. As she sucked down the water, her body seemed to give up.

She closed her eyes, laid her head back.

As she drifted into sleep, she heard Dek ask, "So, Flute thinks this thing's hunted all the quetzals? What can you do about it?"

"It took my parents," Kylee told him in a voice hinting at rage. "All I have to do is figure out how to kill it dead."

71

Vartan hurried down the hallway, burst through the doors into the cafeteria. He still felt weak, his muscles so sore that he limped. But his rising panic overwhelmed any physical discomforts.

People glanced up from where they sat at the tables. In a plush recliner brought in for her use, Shimal Kastakourias sat at the head of a long table immediately to the Messiah's right. On his left, Ctein Zhoa—the last of the First Chosen—served as a pitiful reminder of the Messiah's dying prestige.

For her part, Shimal shot Vartan a look fraught with worry. Her dark eyes were almost pleading, as if she were begging for anything but the honor of being the next Prophet. Vartan had always thought her a frail, mousy woman. Her training was as a solid-state board specialist capable of diagnosing and repairing sophisticated electronics, microscopes, computers, and the like.

Ignoring the plea in her eyes, Vartan went straight to the Messiah; the man had set his bone scepter aside to drink a cup of tea from the garden.

"Messiah, we've got trouble," Vartan said.

"Such as?"

"You remember all those crates we found while searching for the Supervisor down in the basement? One had a laser microphone for listening at long distances. I was down there to get a specimen pole to drag Svetlana's body away. Saw it. Thought it might be useful given our exposed location. Maybe give us a warning if the Supervisor's party and whoever was in that airtruck might be sneaking close."

"And?"

"And I charged it. Figured out where the best vantage point would be. Went up to the roof hatch. From up there I could see the whole compound. Figured I'd keep watch as the sun set. When I turned that mic on the science dome, it picked up conversations. There are people in the science dome."

"Perhaps some of our—"

"None of our people are called Supervisor, Dek, Muldare, or Kylee."

The Messiah's lips pursed, pulling down to elongate the hole that was his nose. "They are that close?"

"They are. From the conversation I overheard, something's wrong. The Supervisor, Dek, and Muldare are hurt, somehow disabled. Maybe wounded. But, more to the point, Talina Perez and someone called Flute are sneaking around the station, apparently keeping an eye on us. In the darkness out there, they could be anywhere."

The Messiah cocked his head slightly. "Perez and the others must have come on the airtruck. Where are Dya and Talbot?"

"Apparently dead. But I'm not positive. Might be that some creature in the forest got them. Something big. Maybe, for all I know, the same thing that got Mars and Hap. I can tell you this: They are hostile and planning some kind of action against us at first light."

The Messiah gave him a sloe-eyed glance. "How do you want to handle this?"

"They'll try for the radio. Any kind of action we might attempt against them, armed as they are, we'll have a lot of our people killed."

Ctein flinched. And well he might. He'd had to strip the flesh from the dead bodies of the First Chosen. His companions, friends, and fellows.

The Messiah set his tea down. "We have the armed drone."

"We do. And they have as many as three rifles. No telling how many more if Talina Perez was in that airtruck. And if we try to rush the science dome, she and this Flute person could decimate us with flanking fire. Especially on full auto."

One of those cold trickles of fear ran down Vartan's spine. "Messiah, if Perez has linked up with the Supervisor, she knows that we tried to kill Aguila. Given that she was in the airtruck, she's been in radio contact with the rest of Donovan's people. You know what that means, don't you? They're going to be coming for us."

The Messiah inhaled sharply, the air whistling in his gaping nose. The black eyes seemed to flicker fearfully for an instant, then sharpened into that familiar cunning glint.

He turned to Shimal, who'd sat doe-eyed and uncertain through the entire conversation. "What do you think, Prophet?"

Vartan started. *Shimal? We are going to entrust our future to her?*

"These people?" Shimal asked. "They would attack us?"

Vartan sought some cue from the Messiah, got only a blank stare in return. The unblinking blue eye painted on the Messiah's forehead appeared fixed on eternity.

With nothing else to go on, Vartan said, "If they know we tried to kill the Supervisor and her party, attack would seem their most likely course of action. Think of how we'd feel if they'd tried to kill the Prophets, or even the Messiah, here?"

"And you say Supervisor Aguila is wounded?" the Messiah mused, his gaze going distant.

"She's being cared for. That's all I know."

"The science dome? That's just two domes away." Ctein's eyes shifted toward the north. "Not more than fifty meters from here. How did they get past Minette? She's supposed to be on guard up there."

"Maybe she never got the chance to warn us. Like so many, she's just gone. Vanished." Vartan drew a worried breath. "I'm really starting to hate this place."

"What about the armed drone?" the Messiah asked. "Second Will, can we use it against them? Kill them before they can strike us?"

"Not while they're in the dome. And don't forget, that Perez woman is out there somewhere. Probably waiting for reinforcements before she makes a try at us."

"How did this go so wrong?" Ctein asked under his breath. "Messiah, what do we do?"

Vartan caught a fleeting panic behind the Messiah's eyes, saw the man battle with himself, win the fight for calm. Ctein must have seen it, too, for he paled. Swallowed hard.

"Prophet?" the Messiah asked softly. "You have been touched by the universe, as were the others before you. What do you hear it say?"

Shimal's frantic gaze darted around the room, took in the people who sat at the cafeteria tables, riveted and listening. Had to see the fear reflected in their faces. The uncertainty.

The woman's voice broke as she said, "We need to be away from here. Gone. This place is death for us. Has been ever since that Supervisor brought us here."

Vartan would have laughed out loud. Be away? How? What did the woman expect? That they could just summon a shuttle? Fly off to . . . where? *Ashanti* wouldn't take them back. The Donovanians certainly didn't want them. And after they tried to kill and eat the Supervisor, she wasn't going to be in any kind of a forgiving mood.

The change, however, in the Messiah was immediate. The man smiled, a serenity in his expression. "The universe does not make mistakes. We shall leave."

He glanced Vartan's way. "Go back to your post, Second Will. Monitor our enemies. Take your rifle. It has a night optic as I remember. You should be able to see everything. If they try to break out of the science dome, shoot as many as you can. Keep them bottled up inside."

"Messiah?"

"In the meantime, we shall make our preparations."

"What preparations?" Vartan cried. "To go where? How?"

The Messiah raised a calming hand. "The universe has brought us this far. Place your trust in it, Second Will. This is just another test. One we shall pass as we have all the others. You must have faith. The universe will not let us down."

"But, don't you—"

"Have *faith,* Second Will. Now, you have your orders. I shall call on you when we're ready."

"Messiah, you can't—"

"*Faith!* Now go to your post."

Fighting his rising sense of dismay, Vartan bowed respectfully, backed away from the throne.

As he headed for the door, he glanced around. Took in the watching Irredenta. Eighteen of them, mostly pregnant or nursing women. The rest, who were outside standing watch, numbered seven—including those guarding the children in the barracks—six if Minette was gone.

Leave? To where? They had already reached the end of the line.

"What do you believe, Vartan?" he whispered under his breath. That the universe would provide?

But his only answer was silence.

72

Miguel Galluzzi turned, hearing more of the maniacal laughter. *Freelander* seemed to be compressing the air, making it hard for him to breathe. He stared frantically up and down the poorly lit hallway, past Astrogation Control. Thought he saw a thin woman staring at him from the shadows. But for the long black hair, she might have been Tyne. Or, locked in the AC, had she let her hair grow?

"Captain?" Shig asked.

Galluzzi's heart began to pound, a foul taste on his tongue. A panic like he'd never known sent a tickle through his guts. Thoughts went dead in his head. He couldn't stand it. Had to get away. Miguel turned, ran, frantic to get away from that awful door, that eerie and haunted hallway.

Mindless, he pounded down the corridor. Powered by terror. A cry strangled in his throat.

"Captain? Miguel! Stop!" Shig's voice barely penetrated the heterodyne of fear.

Crazed, thoughtless, Galluzzi's feet hammered the deck. At the companionway, he instinctively turned: an animal in desperate flight, seeking only to hide.

Taking the stairs two at a time, he rounded the landing, charged out onto the Crew Deck, and fled pell-mell down the flickering corridor. Winded, he staggered to a stop, peering fearfully up and down the dimly lit passage. Nothing. Eerily empty, as if robbed of space itself. The effect was as if part of the very air, sialon, and light were missing. The reality he saw had the curious property of being incomplete.

Well, but for the endless lines of overwritten script.

Galluzzi tried to catch his breath, wheezed. His heart fought desperately to beat its way through his ribs.

Exhausted, Galluzzi slumped against the wall, felt his trembling legs give way. He slid down the smooth surface to curl into a ball. Across from him, barely legible in the looping script, he could scry out the words: *With each breath inhale the essence of the dead.*

Tears began to well, silvering his vision. Was that what he was doing? Inhaling the dead?

Tyne Sakihara, beautiful Tyne, with her soft dark eyes, petite nose, and charming smile. Dead. Up there. A moldering skeleton?

He'd loved her with a full and uninhibited passion. Figured that ultimately, after they'd exhausted their careers, in the end they'd be together. Married. The two of them had fit together that well. Soulmates. Of course they'd taken different berths, separated for the time being. That was mandatory. Part of the sacrifice officers made in Corporate spacing.

I saw her. He ground his teeth in grief and despair. He was as sure of that as he was of gravity.

Galluzzi scrubbed at his eyes with the heels of his palms. Tried to press the image of Tyne's face from his memory.

Her voice sounded so clear she might have been standing over him: "I saw the first of the bones, you know."

Galluzzi winced, tried to tuck himself into a smaller ball, to collapse his body until he could squeeze himself completely out of the universe.

Unbidden, the image formed in his mind: a jumbled pile of macerated human bones made a meter-tall mound on the floor. They had been dumped in a confused heap in the middle of the Crew's Mess, cleared as it was of tables and chairs. A brown-haired woman wearing a shift knelt in the center of the room. She held a string to the floor. A second woman, holding the other end of the string taut, walked in a slow arc. With a scribe she marked out a perfect circle.

"We were no longer in command," Tyne's voice explained. "The decision had been made that death and life were one. That only through death could life survive. Wherever *Freelander* had gone was eternal. Tried reversing the symmetry. Didn't work."

She paused, then added, "Jem and I made the decision to euthanize the transportees. It was our last act of kindness. No one could explain why, but we were infertile. The women didn't conceive. Couldn't make *Freelander* a generation ship. So it was just us. Living off the dead."

Galluzzi clamped his eyes tight, pressed harder with his palms, but try as he might, he couldn't stop the vision. If anything, it clarified as if he were there in the Crew's Mess.

One of the women began using a vibrasaw to cut a shallow trench in the mess floor, following the scribed circle. The other began wiring the femora together, carefully choosing each for the proper length.

"Jem and I didn't want to end like that," Tyne told him. "It was crazy. The Chief Engineer used a cutting torch on the ship's AI. So we locked ourselves in the AC. Stayed there until it was clear that *Freelander* was lost. That we were going to be in that room forever."

"How could you?"

In his mind, Tyne smiled at him. Love, like he remembered so clearly, shone in her eyes. "In the end there is no right, no wrong. We are nothing more than chemical composites of carbon-based molecules that are directed by chemo-electrical impulses designed to allow the highest probability of replicating those same chemical composites. Billions and billions of us. Anything else, like ethics, morality, notions of deity, ultimate good or evil, are nothing more than abstractions. We need those delusions to mask the reality of what life is. They provide us with a sense of purpose."

The Crew's Mess was filling with people now. Crew in uniforms showing various states of repair. He watched as they began lifting the wired-together femora, raising them like a wall and fitting them into the trench excavated into the floor.

They're building that creep-freaked dome of bones!

"Do you know that I still love you?" he asked.

"Cling to whatever you have, Miguel. In the end, it's the only thing that makes existence worth enduring."

In the Crew's Mess, the *Freelander* crew were separating all of the arm bones from the jumbled pile.

73

Where she lay in the shadow of a defunct air compressor, Talina watched through her rifle's optic. She'd dialed the magnification up, which gave her a good look at the man. Maybe early forties, black hair, dark eyes. He was perched on the top of the admin dome. Every so often, he'd raise the rifle he held and use its optic to scan the compound. Most of his time he spent listening with a long-range microphone. He kept the laser fixed on the science dome window.

From the moment Talina had seen the thing, it was apparent that the Unreconciled knew exactly who was stalking around Tyson Station, and who was in the science dome.

Which meant what when it came to relative strengths and who might move on whom?

They knew Muldare, Taglioni, and Kalico had weapons. And might even know Muldare was wounded, and that Kalico was sick. If they'd heard that Talbot was dead, they'd know his weapons had been retrieved. Kylee—young though she might be—was half quetzal and enraged over the deaths of Mark and Dya. No telling what kind of havoc the kid might unleash on both the Unreconciled and herself in the process.

Talina pasted her cheek to the rifle's stock. Sighted through the optic. Took a series of deep breaths to oxygenate her blood, exhaled, and watched the dot settle on the watcher. All it would take was a couple of pounds of pressure on the trigger, and the dome-top rifleman's head would be jelly.

Maybe it was guilt over the woman she'd shot. Maybe it was the tortured expression on the man's face. The guy looked like he was wrestling with too many demons of his own. She slipped her finger back to the rest above the trigger.

The soft chittering came from behind.

Talina used her elbows to crawl back, rise to a seat, and glance at Flute. "Find anything useful?"

The quetzal flashed a pattern of infrared that read, "Young in half bubble. Three adults watch."

"Kids are in the barracks dome," she said to herself. "Not more than an hour ago, someone hurried from the admin dome to the barracks."

She ducked down as the door to the admin dome across the way opened. A handful of people, mostly women, hurried out and headed for the barracks. They were talking softly, shooting scared looks at the night as they went.

Talina heard the words, ". . . in the morning" and "Where will . . . go?" The rest was confused babble.

Talina checked the dome-top guard. His attention was fixed on the people beating feet to the barracks.

Using the distraction, Talina sprinted to the edge of the shop dome, out of the lookout's sight.

Flute, like a dark cloud, followed silently, his hide patterning the ground in perfect camouflage. Wouldn't work if the dome-top guard had his IR turned on.

At the rear of the science dome, Talina rapped three times. Waited. Rapped twice more.

Seconds later the lock clicked open, and the door swung out.

Talina sent Flute in first, then followed, locking the door behind her. The young quetzal, almost two meters at the hips, filled the hallway, claws clicking on the duraplast.

"So," Kylee asked from up front. "What did you—"

Talina put a finger to her lips.

After Flute had deposited himself in the conference room and was out of the way, Talina leaned close, whispering in Kylee's ear, "They've got a long-range microphone fixed on the lab window. They've been listening to everything we said."

Kylee's blue eyes widened as she mouthed the words, "They know we're here?"

Talina gave her a quick nod, whispered, "How're the others?"

"Sleeping." Kylee frowned, staring off toward the lab door. With a finger she beckoned Talina toward the conference room. This was on the science dome's north side, shielded from any eavesdropping by the snooper's laser mic. Closing the door, Kylee asked, "So, what are they planning?"

"Don't know. My guess? Something with explosives. They tried that on Kalico and your folks to start with. Given that we're armed, it's the best way to try and take us down." She glanced up at the ceiling. Just ordinary duraplast. Proof against wind, rain, and hail, it wouldn't stand a chance against magtex. "If they've got a demolition expert, he could crack this roof open like an eggshell."

"Eggs have shells? Thought they were just soft membranes the sperm had to get through."

"Not many chickens down at Mundo, huh?"

"Oh, you mean birds. I've seen pictures. For some reason Mom wasn't big on terrestrial ornithology."

At the mention of her mother, Kylee's eyes tightened, her jaw firming.

Talina knew that look. "Don't even think it. For the moment, we've got other responsibilities. First there's Kalico and Dek. I need you to keep them safe. Will you do that for me?"

"Those fucking cannibals killed Mom and Mark."

"How about you and I take it up with Messiah Batuhan when we get Kalico, Dek, and Muldare out of here. Deal?"

Kylee gave her that searching look. Finally said, "Deal."

"Good. Now, let's go sit next to the window where that guy on top of the dome can hear, and spin all kinds of stories about how we're attacking the dome with rifles, grenades, and seismic charges sometime in midmorning, shall we?"

"And what are we really doing?"

"Slipping out the back way about an hour before dawn. While they hit the science dome, we're flanking them at admin. At the same time they're busy blowing this place up, Flute and I are barging into the radio room to call the PA shuttle to come pick us up."

"Flute?"

"Can you think of a better way to terrorize a bunch of soft meat?"

"Wish you wouldn't use that term when you're talking about cannibals."

"Good point."

74

More than anything, Dan hated being afraid. He'd lived his entire childhood in fear. The consuming, soul-numbing kind. His pedophile father had used Dan's fear like a sharp blade to separate him from any thought of rebellion or betrayal. Wielded it masterfully to keep Dan compliant and an accomplice in the man's perverse sexual proclivities.

When, at sixteen, Dan had killed his first victim, the act washed through him like a revelation: he had power. A realization that reinforced itself like the rebar in a concrete wall when he'd stood over Asha Tan's dead body a mere year later. That he never suffered a moment's remorse was, he realized, a blessing. One that he could never fully comprehend but deeply appreciated.

Despite the bone-chilling fear in his youth, he'd never known it like he did in that plexiglass box: numbing, crushing, soul-devouring. And all the while, Windman's severed head was mashed against the plastic. The nose had been flattened against the transparency; the lips had pulled back, mouth gaping with the bugs crawling in and out and up the nostrils. Those eyes—drying, shrinking, turning gray—kept watching Dan with a haunting gaze. The damn head mocked him, belittled his impotence. A witness to Dan Wirth's total helplessness and terror.

All of it was compounded by the suffering heat, the thirst, and hopelessness.

Just when he could take no more, when he was on the verge of unlatching the door and throwing it wide, a quetzal would appear. The thing would gnaw on the box or attack it with those razor claws. Helpless and mesmerized, Dan would watch shavings of plastic curl away under the blade-like teeth or peel in strips as the claws carved off long curlicues of material.

By the time the first rays of dawn had lightened the eastern horizon, they'd chewed a hole in the corner just above Dan's head. The smell of quetzal breath had choked him.

He'd been delirious by then, fantasizing a thousand nightmarish images. In some he was back in his father's bed, hearing the old man's cooing voice as he forced Dan from one degrading act to another. Or in Hong Kong, ducking and running as Corporate security forces hunted him, chased him past piles of dead rioters, their bodies all interlaced.

Then had come the numb surrender into oblivion . . .

Windman's head was hanging in a gray haze, talking to him. The man's voice couldn't quite penetrate the plastic. Sounded muffled and indistinct.

Fucking prick. What a candy-dicked screw up. Couldn't make himself understood, even in death.

A piercing sting in Dan's arm shattered the image, caused him to start. To pay full attention.

"He's coming around." This was a woman's voice, not Windman's. "Dan?"

He knew that voice: Allison. But how had she gotten into the box with him?

He tried to speak, heard a rasping.

"Dan? Wake up."

His head hurt. When he tried to swallow, it was with effort, and a terrible taste filled his mouth.

He got his eyes open, blinked his vision clear. Saw a ceiling. And then Ali leaned over, a reserve behind her blue eyes, tension in her lips. "Dan? Can you hear me?"

"Yeah," he croaked. The rasping? That was his voice? "What the fuck?"

Raya Turnienko leaned into his field of view. "You almost died. We have you stabilized, rehydrated, and you're on an electrolyte and sucrose drip. Your organs are rebounding. You'll be weak for a day or two, but there's no permanent damage."

"I was . . . in that fucking box. Quetzals."

Allison crossed her arms, studying him with an unnerving intensity. Disoriented as Dan was, he could see the change in her. Something dangerous and new. Predatory. Reminded him of the fucking quetzals that had been chewing on that shit-sucking box.

"You know," Allison observed, "it's a miracle that you got into that arbor box. As it was, another hour or two, and you would have shut down. We'd be digging a grave for you up at the cemetery. As it is, Fred Han Chou only needs a soil auger to dig a hole big enough for Windman's head."

Dan winced. That fart-sucking head. The fricking thing was going to fill his nightmares from here on out as it was. Maybe he'd go up and piss on the thing's final resting place.

"When can I get out of here?"

"Tomorrow . . . if there are no complications," Raya told him.

To Allison, he croaked, "What's happening at The Jewel?"

"Shin, Vik, and Kalen have it under control. Everyone's delighted that you're alive."

He heard the lie in that. Fought down a cold sliver of anger. Anger? Why? What the hell did he care?

The image of three deadly eyes in a huge triangular head filled his memory. He could feel the vibrations as teeth chewed away plastic. *The snot-sucking thing wanted to eat me.*

Now that he'd made it, his people couldn't have cared less.

I've got two big safes filled with plunder.

And what was he going to do with them?

"Did Taglioni come back?"

Allison's eyebrow quivered, as if in a question. "He's out with Talina at Tyson Station. Something's gone really wrong out there. There's been no contact."

So, the rich prick was probably quetzal shit, or maybe lunch for a bunch of cannibals.

"Figures. My fucking luck." *I could have gotten out.*

NEAR THE BROOK OF KEDRON

I think of the story of the garden near the brook of Kedron. I think about it often. That place where another messiah faced his darkest hours. Of all the messiahs, his story speaks the loudest in this particular moment of tribulation.

Am I forsaken?

Have I failed the universe?

Committed some unforgiveable sin?

It cannot be pride, for I have always doubted my worthiness. Wondered why the universe chose me, of all men, to shoulder the crushing responsibility. I have always lived in terror that I might fail.

Faith has been the unyielding pillar inside me, my shield and justification. Faith is a wonderful thing: Just believe, and it will carry you through.

It always has.

And now, in the midnight of my soul, when I am shaken with doubt, I have to ask: What more do you want of me? Haven't I given enough? Haven't my people?

We have sacrificed so much, suffered, endured, and prayed in desperation. Didn't we prove ourselves through trial and fire during our incarceration on Deck Three? Didn't Prophecy promise us that we would begin anew, grow, mature, and flourish on Capella III before venturing forth in service of the universe?

What we have found here is heartbreaking. In a matter of days, so many are irretrievably dead. In defiance of Prophecy, they are lost forever. I am bereft, crying, "Why?" as I stare up at the night sky.

What if it was all a lie?

I look at the faces of my people. They are so close to desolation and defeat. More so than even during the days of the Harrowing and Cleansing.

The human soul can only endure so much: close to eight years of suffering, with only a nebulous arrival at Capella III to buoy their hopes. Like an intangible dream. But they clung to the seemingly impossible aspiration.

And then the miracle: Release from Deck Three into the light.

Only to be ultimately betrayed.

Hope, promises, anticipation.

Everything we believed.

All a deadly deception.

Was I the greatest of deceivers?

Those are the questions that haunt me. Now I am faced with a bone-numbing decision: Do I trust in the voice of an untried Prophet? Is Shimal truly the voice of the universe? She has said we need to leave.

To go . . . where?

The only avenue left that I can see is to set forth into the forest. To venture into the wilderness as the Prophets of ancient Earth did.

But, if I can believe the warnings given by Vartan, the forest is death.

What am I to do?

What do I trust?

Where is salvation for me and my people?

The universe does not make mistakes!

I must believe. I must *believe!*

75

Vartan fought to stay awake. Overhead, clouds had obscured the night sky. Lightning flashed off to the east, flickers of it illuminating tortured and twisting clouds. The heavens had turned angry, as if to express their rage against all things.

It had been so long since Vartan had seen lightning. Almost what? Two decades? Maybe more. He fixed his staggering attention on the distant flashes. Desperate to keep his eyes open.

Had he ever been this exhausted?

His head, falling forward, banged painfully off the rifle, brought him awake. Flashes strobed in wicked white that shaped the clouds into eerie lanterns. They bathed the humps of treetops, turned the forest into an impossible landscape.

As Vartan resettled himself, listening to the night chime, he felt the shudder of steps leading up to the hatch.

Ctein called, "It's me," before appearing below.

"Storm coming," Vartan told him through a yawn.

The first distant boom of thunder rolled over the forest.

Ctein turned where he stood half out of the hatch. "We're leaving just before dawn."

"That's crazy. Following Shimal out into the forest?"

"Here's the plan," Ctein told him. "The Messiah, the women, and children will form up, march down to the southern end of the mesa. They're going to take the trail down to the trees. They'll wait there. Meanwhile, you and I will hide. Watch. When the Supervisor's people find the base abandoned, they will walk out in the open. When they do, we use the drone to swoop in close, and detonate it."

Vartan rubbed his eyes, tried to get circulation back into his arms and legs. Anything to recharge his flagged energy. Shit on a shoe, his head felt full of fuzz.

"Listen to me. Ctein, I know you were among the First Chosen. But this is wrong. Batuhan is wrong. What worked on Deck Three isn't working here. Anyone who goes down that trail is going to die."

A flash of lightning betrayed the man's incredulous look. "Do you know what you're saying? The Messiah gave you an order."

More lightning flashed in arhythmical patterns in the east. The low rumbling of thunder was louder now.

"He did. And I'll do it." The gravity, the exertions, the endless hours since he'd slept last, it all came to weigh on his weary soul.

The only two women in his life—Shyanne, whom he'd married, and Svetlana whom he'd loved—were gone. One, grieving and heartbroken, had escaped to who knew what fate, the other a rotting corpse that he himself had tumbled over the edge of the cliff. He'd watched in horror as her body smacked off rocks on the way down, each impact shooting colorful specks of invertebrates and bodily fluids until the corpse came to rest on a ledge far below.

Am I really living this shit?

He chuckled hollowly. "Go on, Ctein. Tell the Messiah that I'm taking matters in hand. He's not to worry about a thing. Just follow the Prophet's instructions." A beat. "And yes, tell him I have faith in the universe."

Just not the same as he does.

76

Carrots, garlic, and cabbage weren't Dek's idea of the finest of meals, but given that A, they had taste, B, they were incredibly nutritious, and C, that he'd been half-starved, he considered it one of the finest meals he'd ever eaten.

Talina had boiled the haul in a pan over a Bunsen burner. Then she'd stood guard as he, Kalico, and Muldare had finished off the stew and guzzled water.

The headache was now at half-strength, his muscles still wobbly, but his blood sugar was climbing. All in all, one hell of an improvement over the wreck he'd been.

Talina and Kylee had saved his life—not to mention Kalico Aguila's and Briah Muldare's in the bargain. Had to admire a woman like that.

Having left the science dome via the back door, Dek followed along behind Talina as rain fell from a midnight-black sky and lightning—in shapes reminiscent of an old man's tortured and throbbing veins—streaked, banged, and boomed. Didn't matter that he was sick-puppy weak, his stomach rebellious from having overeaten. Fact was, he was alive. Lot to be said for that.

In a contrast as stark as night and day, where he'd been in danger of dying of heat prostration, cold rain now pelted him in a staccato of big drops. Lightning knotted and pulsed in momentary misery—to vanish into afterimages of blackness. He was on the verge of shivering, and his breath fogged white in the flashes of actinic light. Didn't seem fair.

With lightning illuminating the way; he stepped over a section of pipe, careful to keep his rifle covered with the tarp Talina had provided him as a sort of rain poncho. He had the thing draped over his head, held the seams together at his throat. Must have looked like a pious Roman seeking the counsel of the gods.

Behind him, Kalico splashed along in his tracks, a similar tarp keeping her from the downpour.

"Watch your step there," he told her. "Don't trip on the pipe."

"I see it," she returned in little better than a whisper.

"How you feeling? Let me know if—"

"I'm a world of better. Thought I was going to die. Never would have made it but for that energy bar you gave me. Thanks for that. I owe you."

"My pleasure."

"Shhh!" Talina turned back, irritated.

Yeah, right. Some sort of distance microphone. As if they'd be heard over the roar of the rain where it beat on domes, in puddles, and racketed on old equipment. Not to mention the banging thunder, the crashing of the skies.

"Careful," Talina hissed, pointed. "That's the cliff right there."

Dek squinted through the fold in his tarp, caught the contrast between rock and dark pre-dawn empty space. He stepped right, veering away from the edge. Wouldn't that be the shits? Travel all this way, survive *Ashanti*, the forest, and heat stroke, just to fall to his death because of a misstep?

They were edging along the eastern side of the mesa, slipping between occasional aquajade trees that clung to the precipice. The figuring was that the Unreconciled would be planning an assault on the science dome, would be expecting them to sneak down the western side of the escarpment where the line of sheds would provide cover.

Briah Muldare—arm in a sling—brought up the rear. Holding her weapon one-handed, she kept sweeping her IR-enhanced rifle sight back and forth to ensure they weren't being followed.

Kylee and the quetzal had vanished somewhere into the storm.

Dek stumbled over an irregularity, caught himself just shy of sprawling face-first, and wished mightily for night vision.

The looming side of a shipping container brought him up short.

Talina took him by the hand, led him forward and into the dark interior. Then she collected Kalico and Briah, saying, "I want you to stay here. Out of the rain. We're opposite the admin dome. From the front of the container you've got an effective field of fire in all directions. They can't take you by surprise, and they'd be idiots to try and rush you."

"And if they do?" Briah asked.

"We shoot them down," Kalico growled.

Dek winced, realizing what a slaughter it would be given Muldare's and Kalico's fully automatic weapons. At least for as long as the ammo lasted. Not to mention if the right-handed Muldare could even control the recoil with her weak-side left hand. Then there was Kalico's pistol, his Holland & Holland, and finally his pistol.

"Dek," Talina said.

"Yes?"

"The only threat to your position here is that rifle they took from Carson. Your job is to shoot whomever wields it. Take your time, breathe, and barely touch the trigger. Yours is the most accurate weapon we have at distance."

He took a nervous breath. "Right."

Talina laid a hand on his shoulder, was staring him in the eyes—though in the darkness all he saw was two dark spots in her night-shadowed face. Her voice dropped. "You understand, don't you?"

"Understand?"

"That when they tried to blow up the Supervisor, Dya, Talbot, and Muldare, it was for keeps. Just like when they killed Carson. It's not academic. Not a game. You're going to have to kill people before they kill you."

"I understand." Just saying it sent a ripple through his soul.

"You're sure?" Muldare asked as she peered out into the night. "You're the weak link here. The rich boy who never had blood on his hands. You hesitate at the wrong moment, we all die as a result."

Kalico said, "I could take the H&H. I've become a pretty good shot with a rifle. Save you the—"

"I got it," Dek said through a hard exhale, feeling his heart begin to race. "I kill the person with Carson's rifle. Make sure they can't use it against us." He raised a hand to still any reply. "Listen, I lived for years with the knowledge of what the Unreconciled were doing down on Deck Three. Had nightmares about them sneaking up in the middle of the night. Cutting me open while I was alive. And eating my . . . Well, never mind. I got this, okay?"

Talina slapped him on the shoulder. "You're becoming my favorite Taglioni."

"And how many of us have you met?"

"Just you. Talk about having an unfair advantage, huh?"

"What's your plan, Tal?" Kalico asked.

"Link up with Kylee and Flute. They're out on the flank, keeping watch. Once the cannibals move on the science dome, we make our play for the radio." She smacked a hand to her rifle. "With this and a quetzal, I'm pretty sure that I can get in and out. Once Flute roars and flashes his collar, I may not even have to kill anyone."

"Assuming Carson's weapons are deployed against the science dome," Kalico finished. "If their shooter is in the admin hallway when you burst in, that would change the equation."

"There's that." Talina shifted, stepping out into the rain. "As long as we see each other at the same time, it all comes down to who's faster. Their shooter, or me."

"Good luck," Kalico said softly as the woman vanished into the night.

Dek slipped out of his tarp, laid it to the side.

Muldare had taken a position at the open door. With her sore arm braced, she squatted against one wall as she swept the area between them and the admin dome with her IR sight.

Dek slipped his Holland & Holland from his shoulder, checked the charge and the setting.

"And now we wait, huh?"

Muldare said, "I've just scanned that roof hatch Talina told us about. It's closed. From now 'till dawn, it's just a matter of me spotting him before he can spot us. But hopefully that shooter is preoccupied, preparing to blow the shit out of the science dome. They do that, and rush the ruins, we got them."

"How's the arm?"

"Fucking hurts. I tell you, after this, I can stand anything. Raya could pull my teeth and I wouldn't need an anesthetic."

Dek, his rifle across his lap, sank down, back to the wall beside Kalico. "We come all this way. Cross thirty light-years, survive by the skin of our teeth, and we're trying to kill each other?"

Muldare whispered, "We gave them every chance. Came here to help them. Sometimes you gotta stamp out rot where you find it." Under her breath, she added, "Come on, fuckers. Step out and give me an excuse to shoot, will you?"

Lightning strobed again, illuminating the admin dome across the way. In that instant, Dek saw someone emerge. "Got movement."

He pulled up his rifle. Used the sight's IR to watch a woman hunch against the rain and run toward the barracks dome next door.

"Wonder what that's all about?"

"That's where the children are," Muldare said. "Assuming our intelligence is right."

"Children," Dek whispered. "So, we kill all the adults? What are we going to do with the kids? Murder them, too? Hold them responsible for the accident of their birth?"

In the back, Kalico murmured, "Scarred like they are, they're branded for life. No matter where they go, what they do, they'll be known as man-eaters from here on out. Talk about outcasts, there's no coming back from that kind of stigma."

"I wouldn't want 'em around," Muldare muttered under her breath. "It'd give me the creep-freaks every time I saw them."

Lightning almost blinded him: Thunder cracked in a detonation that jarred him half out of his skin. Might have been a condemnation from the gods.

77

With careful fingers, Vartan inserted his hand-crafted detonator and pressed it into the square of magtex with gentle and even force. As he did, the storm roared; waves of rain kept pounding the dome overhead. He huddled in the radio room, squinting in the dim illumination provided by the last functioning light panel.

What was he forgetting? His fatigue-addled brain wasn't working. Be a miracle if he didn't blow himself up.

On the table sat the radio. The last link to the outside world. The place Aguila's people would ultimately try for.

He started as a violent crash of thunder shivered the dome around him. Rattled him clear to his bones. Left him panting, scared half out of his wits. Loud bangs that sent the heart skipping weren't a good combination when fooling around with explosives.

It was the Messiah's order. Vartan should have thought of booby-trapping the radio room. Should have been stone-cold obvious. That he hadn't was a sign of his exhaustion. His fear and despair.

The Messiah's latest orders were that they leave at first light. Just as soon as they could see. Ctein would lead the way, followed by the women and the children. Then the Prophet and Batuhan, with Vartan and the three remaining men in the rear. The supposition was that in that order, Shimal would be protected.

Shimal, for God's sake? She was the Prophet now? The universe's voice to humanity?

Prior to her first muscle spasms, her growing problems with co-ordination, she'd been notable only for her fertility, having borne the Messiah four children in the eight years of their captivity in *Ashanti.* What possible reason did the universe have for choosing a woman as meek and submissive as Shimal?

To look at her now that she'd been chosen was to see the fear bright in her dark eyes, the quivering of her jaws, and disquiet on her thin face. From her expression, she was more prone to throwing up than imparting the universe's wisdom.

And she orders us to leave?

Under his breath, Vartan whispered, "Damn it, Messiah, why don't you listen to sense?"

Where would they find food? According to the reports, nothing but some of the local animals was edible. Not to mention descending the south trail to the forest.

The forest?

Vartan been there. Watched his team die and vanish before his eyes. Petre's team had taken the north trail. And disappeared without a trace. This wasn't symmetry inversion, not even null singularity physics. The math was simple: leave this place and die.

Now, based on Shimal's utterance in a moment of confusion and terror, the Unreconciled were going to trust themselves to that self-same horror? They were going to believe that the universe would protect them?

Vartan blinked against the gritty feeling in his eyes. Wiped his hands on his loin wrapping, and carefully prepared a length of thin copper wire from a spool he'd found in one of the sheds. This he tied to the detonator. Stringing it out, he tied the other end to the chair leg.

Whoever pulled out the chair would topple the block of magtex. As it tilted, the battery would shift, closing the circuit. And bang!

Checking his handiwork, Vartan used a wad of wrapping paper to conceal his bomb where it sat in the corner.

Not that he was much of a demolitions man, but he figured the corner of the room would help to direct the force of the blast against whomever might pull out the chair.

He heard steps. Looked up. Marta, her expression as lined and worried as Vartan had ever seen, stood in the doorway. "You about ready? There's a graying in the east. We can see well enough to go."

"It's raining like hell out there."

"And we don't want to be here when the Supervisor's people attack. We've got maybe an hour before they charge out of the science dome and start shooting."

He sniffed, tried to rub the exhaustion from his eyes. Took two tries to stagger to his feet. "You ever wonder how we got to this point?"

"We are the chosen," she said, repeating the words as rote. "The forces of darkness are going to resist. They have no other recourse. Until we bring about the Annihilation and Purification, even the atoms will oppose us."

"Spoken like a true believer," he said as he lifted the heavy rifle from where he'd leaned it against the doorjamb. Outside in the hallway, he picked up the drone controls. Wondered if the thing could even fly in the storm. Damn it, if the drone was grounded, they'd lost their most potent defense.

Marta's hazel eyes barely flickered. "And what are you, Vartan? You're the only one of the Messiah's Will left. What else do we have but faith? Those people out there want us *dead*!"

"Not that we left them with much choice."

She indicated the drone controls. "That going to work?"

"Hope so. Outside of the booby traps, it's our only chance. I might shoot one or two, but they'll get me in the end."

In a voice like acid, she said, "So good to know that you're optimistic. Shall I go tell the Messiah we're ready?"

"I guess . . . Well, hell, why not?" Vartan winced, forced himself to plod wearily down the hallway to the double doors that opened out front.

Peering through the windows, he could barely make out the faint shapes of aquajade across the flat, the square outline of the old shipping container. From this angle, he couldn't see the low hump of the barracks where Bess Gutierrez and the other women should have been preparing the children.

The children. Eighteen of them left. The rest taken by Donovan. Some vanished, others dead in pain and suffering.

"They were supposed to be the future. Immortal."

The futility of it all, like lead in his heart, left him on the verge of weeping. He could see each and every one of those kids' faces. Thin little girls and boys, the ones who'd laughed and jumped their way down the steps as they left *Ashanti*. Who'd bounced and played in Capella's light. All that hope, about to be extinguished in Batuhan's mad dash to the forest.

So much for the Revelation of immortality.

Flashes of lightning, like a staccato, illuminated the yard outside. Thunder banged, rolled, and echoed in reply.

No one in their right mind would stumble out into a downpour like this.

Come dawn, the Supervisor's people were coming. They'd be toting rifles, and as he'd heard through the long-distance mic, they'd be coming for blood.

He remembered the look in Shyanne's eyes as she pleaded with him to leave. Not for the first time since she'd stolen the airtruck, he wondered if she hadn't been the smart one.

"Ah, Second Will!"

Vartan turned at the Messiah's enthusiastic call. The man came strolling down the hallway, his bone scepter in hand. Behind him came Ctein—the last of the First Chosen. Then Shimal, her arm interlocked with Marta's.

Time to go.

It hit home like a thrown rock: The Messiah was leaving the throne of bones behind. No one remained to carry it.

Vartan slung the rifle, retrieved a hooded poncho he'd hung by the door, and draped it over his shoulders. No way he could bring the rifle into action, covered as it was, but he'd be damned if he'd be soaked to the bone. And more to the point, he needed two hands for the drone control. He'd be last in line. Awaiting the moment the Supervisor's group charged the admin doors.

He had to time it just right. Dive the thing—kamikaze like—right into the middle of them before he hit the detonator switch. One shot. Damn it, he *had* to do this right.

Vartan led the way out into the deluge, rain battering at the hood. Barely able to see, he slopped his way to the barracks, praying that the Messiah would declare the weather too wretched for the evacuation.

78

"Tal?" Kalico's voice sounded in Talina's com bud. *"Batuhan, two men, and two women, just left the admin dome. They're headed south. Can't see Carson's rifle, but one of the men was holding something in two hands. Some kind of controls."*

Talina wiggled into the lee of one of the sheds, partially sheltered from the downpour. Peering around the corner, she watched the cannibals splash their sodden way to the barracks, where one by one they ducked inside. Draped as he was in a poncho that shadowed his face, she couldn't be sure if the last one in line was the dark-haired shooter, or carried a weapon, but he did hold something in his hands.

Accessing her com, she said, "Sort of argues against them making a try for the science dome, doesn't it? Unless they've decided to relocate the Messiah out of harm's way."

"Roger that. Makes us wonder where all the rest of them are. They had twenty-five men, right? Lost three to Talbot, and another fled to the Briggs place. We saw one being eaten by a tooth flower."

"Yeah, and you'd figure that Donovan got a few more of them along the way." She made a face. "But how many?"

"Maybe a lot, Tal. Think about it. They've only had women on guard. Is that because the men are missing or reassigned to some other task?"

"Like preparing a hot welcome for us when we arrive outside the admin dome?"

"Got me. Wish we had a drone."

"Yeah. Me, too. Listen, we're not in a hurry. I'm going to slip over to where Kylee's keeping watch. Maybe she and Flute know something."

"Roger that."

It took Talina ten minutes to ghost her way around the sheds to the south side where Kylee was supposed to be. Even then, she almost missed the girl.

"Ta Li Na. You going somewhere? Or just enjoying the rain after being half cooked for a couple of days?"

Talina craned her neck, which let cold water run down into one of the last warm and dry places on her body. Kylee lay belly-down under a piece of duraplast sheeting. Stared up as a flash of lightning illuminated her stony blue eyes.

"What do you see, kid? According to our count we're suddenly short of a bunch of cannibal men. Like all the ones we expected to make an attack on the science dome."

Kylee shifted her duraplast, water sheeting down the back. "I've got nothing." She hooked a thumb. "Flute, however, is prowling the rim. He could give a fuck about a bunch of human-eating humans. Something out in the forest's got him creep-freaked."

Talina glanced out at the dark trees beyond the escarpment. "Our mystery beast?"

"I catch a whiff," Kylee told her. "Just every once in a while when the wind's right. Nothing I've ever smelled before. Nothing that triggers quetzal memory with an image. It's more of a scary feeling. The biochemical kind that says, 'Run!'"

"Yeah, I've smelled it, too. Like rotted blood mixed with old hunger."

The rain began to let up, easing from a head-beating downpour to a gentler soaking. Looking east, the first graying of dawn cast silhouettes across the station.

"How about one menace at a time? We're not out of this mess yet. Let's deal with—"

"Tal?" Kalico's voice interrupted. *"Got action. Batuhan and a bunch of women and kids are pouring out the doors of the barracks. Looks like twenty, maybe twenty-five of them. All lining out in the rain and headed south."*

"What about the men?"

"Muldare counts three in addition to the Messiah. Where are you?"

"South of the domes, just north of the farm."

"They should be in your sight any second now. We're making a try for the radio."

"Hey! Wait! We're still missing a bunch of—"

"There's three of us, Tal. Armed. Tired. And pissed off. Besides, they're not expecting us this early."

Talina's heart skipped. "Damn it, Kalico, wait for me."

"Too late, Tal. We're going. Fast. Before they can react."

"Kalico?"

Nothing.

"What's happening?" Kylee asked.

"Kalico's making a try for the radio. I just hope she—"

"Yeah, well you might want to get under cover. Here comes trouble."

Talina spun, staring north. Seeing the first woman leading the way past the geology dome. And behind her came a parade of children.

Talina had barely ducked behind a rusted evaporator when a hollow detonation—as distinct from thunder as could be—carried on the gently raining air.

79

The downpour had let up enough that Vartan could chance the drone. As the Messiah's column plodded south through the wet and mud, he activated the flying bomb.

Using thumbs, he directed it up, the camera penetrating the early-dawn gloom with ease.

After it rose above the admin dome, he sent it scooting north to the science dome. Studying the image, he let it circle the building. Peered into the windows, finding all of the rooms dark.

Didn't mean the foe wasn't still hidden inside, but somehow, he doubted it.

Damn it. They were spread too thin. The smart play would have been to have someone up in the admin dome hatch with the long-distance mic. Someone to keep watch.

Instead he'd been called down to make bombs.

So what to do? Somewhere the Supervisor's killers were loose in the compound, armed to the teeth, and prepared to unleash a blood bath.

Got to find them.

Vartan blinked against his fatigue as he sent the drone high, turned its camera down. He had to believe they'd try for the radio.

"Come on, think, damn it. Where would they be?"

What would have prompted them to leave the safety of the science dome, head out into the teeth of the storm?

What was the old adage? That the best time to attack was before the crack of dawn?

When else would the supposedly unsuspecting Unreconciled be as vulnerable? Their sentries dozing? Groggy with sleep? Most still in their beds?

He switched the flight path, taking the drone south to focus on the approaches to the admin dome. Saw the first furtive figure burst from the shipping container, making a run for the admin doors.

"Gotcha!" Vartan's thumbs sent the drone plummeting as two other figures charged out in the wake of the first. Now it was just a matter of timing.

As the camera angle zoomed, he fixed on the first figure in line. She ran with that swinging stride of a woman. Long black hair was soaked, matted to her back. Had to be the Supervisor.

A feeling of giddy glee filled him.

He was descending too fast, applied lift, and watched the drone shiver as it struggled to slow.

The trick was to get all three as they reached the doors.

As the image continued to zoom, Vartan applied more power to the fans in an effort to achieve a hover.

Wasn't working.

Too much weight with the magtex? The batteries too old? Some complication with the rain?

As Vartan fought the controls, the straining drone must have given itself away. In the camera, the Supervisor looked up. Must not have seen the dropping drone against the storm-dark sky. Seemed to be searching.

Desperate as he was to get them all, the drone was falling too fast. He set his index finger on the switch. Was about to press when the Supervisor threw herself face-first into the mud.

The image vanished an instant before the boom of the explosion echoed through the soft patter of the rain.

Vartan stared at his finger. Tried to remember if he'd pushed the button. Couldn't. God, he was so tired. So defeated.

I just want this all to end.

THE BETRAYAL OF KALKI

At the sound of the explosion behind us, I turn to stare back through the falling rain. My warrior has prevailed. Not being versed in such things I wonder if the detonation was the drone or one of the booby traps we left in the admin dome.

Either way, the Supervisor, or someone in her party, has received the final comeuppance.

Everyone has halted, looking back across the farm field with its wealth of crops.

I stare up at the graying sky as raindrops patter on my head and face. How long has it been? Twenty? Thirty years? The last time I felt rain on my head was outside Ulaanbataar. And then it was but for a moment as I ran for cover.

Here, now, I tilt my head to the falling drops. Water runs down through my hair, trickles across my face. I can feel it trace down the scars, following the path of souls. A symbol of life and renewal.

I need to see this for what it is, not the disaster that I have been fearing it to be. I have a new Prophet, though she has yet to experience the depth of her gift. As with Irdan, Callista, and Guan Shi, she will learn and finally surrender herself to the universe.

I have the children. The immortal ones. How silly of me not to recognize that it is they who are of greatest importance. Not the adults. All of which causes me to ask if I have mistakenly interpreted the Revelation. But it seemed so simple: Adults who could reproduce would be the logical repositories for the souls and flesh of the dead.

Think, now. Be smart. Just because the universe has turned my attention to the children for the moment doesn't negate the value of the adults. Ctein and I remain. As do the women. Nine of them. And, though not among the Chosen, there are Vartan, Fodor Renz, and Marcus Santanna. The five of us men would not remain if we were not to be the vehicles through which the dead are inseminated into the women.

Though how all but Ctein and I ended up as repositories eludes me. Irdan's Prophecy back in the early days on Deck Three made it clear that the First Chosen and I were to be the breeders.

But if that been the case, wouldn't my First Chosen still be alive? Has the universe been waiting to correct my *mistake?*

"Come!" I cry. "Let us move on."

As they start forward, many of the children are shivering in the downpour, their hair plastered to their heads, arms tight about their chests. I see that some are crying. The women are burdened with the neonates and those too small to walk. Many carry two in hastily contrived slings. All but Marta; I have assigned her to assist Shimal.

The women look miserable, their hair streaming water from locks that lay tight against their skin. Gooseflesh covers their arms, their nipples tight from the cold. Each is wracked by shivers as they plod through the mud in clumsy footwear.

In the rear come Marcus and Fodor, each bearing a pack that contains food for the journey. I have no idea what the universe will provide for us when we reach the forest floor. All I know is that forests have always been rich in resources. I have faith. The universe will provide.

As we pick our way past the five big solar collectors, lightning traces a brilliant design across the roiling clouds. The instant, bone-jarring bang of thunder scares the children into sobs and tears. One little girl drops to the mud, screaming her terror as tears mix with rain on her face.

A woman pulls her up, fearful that one of the slugs will get her.

I can only suspect that the girl will learn something from this. Perhaps it is a wake-up call for her reborn soul. A way to trigger some forgotten memory that will remind her of who she was before the Cleansing.

Up ahead I can see Ctein in the lead. He has reached the head of the trail that leads down the steep and rocky slope. There, he hesitates, looking back to ensure that we are all following.

I am about to wave him ahead when I hear a shout behind me.

Turning, I see Vartan coming at a trot. Everyone stops, staring back. The women are shivering, teeth chattering as they shift the children they carry.

"Yes, First Will?" I call back—realizing only at this moment that Vartan is the only one of the Will left.

"We can't do this," Vartan declares in a most insistent voice.

"Excuse me?"

The man has a tortured look on his weary face as he trots up, feet splashing in the puddles. He stares out at me from under a poncho patterned by droplets and trickling water. The ugly military rifle is in his hands. Vartan's dark eyes are like holes in his face. "I said we can't do this."

A tight sensation in my chest is like my heart crabbing sideways and constricting. "The Prophet has told us—"

"Fuck Prophecy!"

I blink, suddenly find it hard to breathe. Has he gone insane?

Vartan looks past me. "Go on! All of you. Back to the barracks! Get those kids inside, and get them warm and fed."

"They'll do no such thing!" I roar. "You are relieved! You are condemned. I declare you an apostate!"

In a shockingly mild voice, he says, "All right." Then, ignoring me, orders, "All of you! Turn about. Head back."

"No!" I scream so loudly the hole in my nose whistles. I look to Shimal. "Prophet? What does the universe decree?"

Shimal is looking terrified, her dark eyes pleading as she shifts them from Vartan to me. "I . . . I . . ."

"Speak!"

"I . . ."

Vartan bellows, "She's not *a Prophet. None of them were. It's a disease. A protein that eats holes in a person's brain. Don't you get it?"*

I thrust my bone scepter at him, declaring, "You are an abomination!"

"Fuck you! We're not the Chosen. It's all a pus-sucking lie!" His face is tortured; tears, not rain streak down his cheeks.

"The universe does not *make mistakes!" I roar back at him, stepping up to face him. To my growing horror, he doesn't so much as wince.*

"The universe doesn't give a shit about us. It never did. That bastard Galluzzi trapped us on Deck Three. And we did what we had to in order to survive. It was a shitty deal, filled with shitty choices, and we're what's left."

"The universe—"

"Is fucked!" He steps forward, thumping the heavy rifle against my gut. "The Supervisor and the others, they told us the truth: This place is killing us. And if you go down that trail, into that forest, not a one of you will be alive by nightfall."

"You don't know—"

"I've been *there! I've seen! Petre was the best of us. His team, Tikal's team, my team, are dead because they went down there. You get it?"*

"Hand me that rifle." I reach for the weapon.

"I'll see you in hell first, Batuhan." He shoves me backward, retreating a step and bringing the rifle up. To the others, he shouts, "Now, turn around. Get the kids back to safety. Dry off and get warm."

"You . . ." I swallow, trying to muster words from a fear-clogged throat. "You . . ."

Vartan says through an emotion-tight voice, "You're delusional, don't you get it? You've convinced yourself it's real? That you're special? It's a lie, it's ugly, and it's finished."

"You defy *the universe?" I cry, reeling, seeking the right words. Panic, like a paralytic wave, rolls through me.*

"I'm right here," Vartan looks up at the storm-brooding sky and lifts a knotted fist. "You want me? I'm right here! Blast me down! I dare you!"

The women gasp, actually cowering back, fearful eyes going to the heavens.

I, too, stare up, but only see twisting and torn-looking low clouds scudding off toward the west. I pray, with all my heart, for lightning to strike, to char Vartan down to the blackened bones.

Instead a soft and misty rain settles on us like dew.

I gape, suffer a physical pain in my chest. The world seems to have gone oddly gray. A sick feeling, like I am going to throw up, turns my stomach sour.

Vartan's display of the rifle is all the authority he needs as he orders, "All of you, get those children back to the barracks. Get them warm. Then make them breakfast. That's an order."

"But I . . ."

My objection is silenced by a single thunderous shot from the rifle that hisses past my ear. I cannot move. Every muscle locked tight.

But the others do, all shuffling past me and Vartan. Fear burns bright in their eyes as they glance my way. Vartan's hot gaze they ignore.

To my surprise Ctein and Shimal remain, apparently as stunned as I am.

"When we get back," I manage to say, "You will pay for this."

Vartan shakes his head, lips pursed. "Not you. Or you, either, Ctein. You preach faith?" He gestures with the rifle. "Go on. Take the path. If I see either of you up here again, I'm putting a bullet right through you.

And when I do, there's no immortality. Just rot and Donovan's invertebrates."

He points the muzzle at my chest. I stare into the dark bore, a crawly tingle deep inside where the bullet will strike.

I turn to go, my feet oddly leaden.

As Ctein and I step over the edge, Vartan hollers, "Remember? The universe doesn't make mistakes!"

80

Talina slipped out of sight behind the concrete foundation of one of the solar collectors as the Unreconciled hurried past, some on the verge of running. As they slopped their way through the mud, they kept looking fearfully over their shoulders, as if the furies of hell were going to be in hot pursuit.

Talina leaned her head back, considered.

Well, well, call it a spur-of-the-moment Reformation.

As the last of the women, almost stumbling from fatigue, trudged past with two children in slings on her shoulders, Talina stepped out. Walking carefully, she took in the poncho-clad man as he peeled back his hood. Dark hair. Yep, the shooter.

Before him stood a woman, a frail-looking thing. Hair black with rain, her thin, scarred face, pale. The woman's hands were twitching; either her jaw was spastic, or she was shivering so hard her teeth where chattering.

She caught sight of Talina, and terror glittered in her dark eyes. She gave a slight nod to the man; he turned, bringing his weapon up.

He froze at the sight of Talina's rifle, fixed as it was on his chest. The man instantly understood. The merest pressure on the trigger would blow him away.

"Put it down slowly," she told him. "I'm not in a forgiving mood, so don't fuck with me."

He swallowed hard, eased the rifle down to the damp ground.

"Now, back away. Both of you."

They did, the woman wavering, as if struggling for balance.

"You're Talina Perez," the man said.

"The same. You?"

"Vartan Omanian. I was . . . Well, I guess that doesn't matter anymore." He smiled wearily. "Go ahead. Shoot. But I'd ask that you take care of Shimal, here. She's got the prion. Nothing's her fault. Same with the women and kids."

"The prion? So you understand it?"

"Shyanne told me it was the explanation." The empty smile was back. "You heard what I told Batuhan?"

"Yeah."

"There it is. Sum and total. The universe's ultimate sick joke at our expense. So pull the trigger. I'm tired of being played for a fucking fool."

Talina lowered the rifle to her hip. "So, you've exiled Batuhan. Once I shoot you, who's in charge?"

Vartan shrugged. Glanced sidelong at Shimal and said to the woman, "Not you. The time for ranting Prophets is over."

Turning back to Talina he said, "Doesn't matter. But don't take it out on the women and kids. Irdan, he was the first Prophet. The guy was an asshole even before his brain started to go. Formulated the revolt against Galluzzi when we first realized just how fucked we were. Was one of the ringleaders when it came to murdering people he didn't find worthy back at the beginning of the Cleansing. He laid the groundwork. Batuhan backed him up."

"Someone had to object."

"Sure. And Irdan and the First Chosen slipped up behind them and cut their throats. Someone had to provide the calories that kept us alive. I think the only skeptic left is Shyanne. Hope she made it."

"She did."

He raised his arms, let them slap his sides in defeat. "I'm tired. Whatever you're going to do, do it."

She stepped forward, snaked Carson's rifle back and safely out of Vartan's reach. Keeping Vartan covered, she picked it up, slung it. "Go on. March. And help this woman. She's looking like she's about to fall over."

As Vartan took the woman's arm and started toward the domes, he said, "Listen, I don't know what you've got planned, but I'm not up to anything long and drawn-out. I really want it over. Fast. Quick. Painless."

"While I consider that, what do you think we should do with the rest of your people? Shoot them, too?"

"Pus, no! Especially not the kids. Not their fault who they are. And someone's got to deal with Batuhan—assuming he doesn't have the guts to follow his own Prophecy. The guy's a true believer. That's his power. He really thinks the universe chose him. Chose us. So if he comes back, shoot him, and be done with it."

"Anything else you want to tell me?"

"Yeah. There's a couple of booby traps in the admin dome. One in the kitchen in the freezer, another in the radio room."

"Yeah. I know."

"How?"

"Com." She tapped an ear. "Muldare tells me the bomb in the radio room didn't go off when she pulled out the chair. Said it was a clever device, but the battery was dead. Didn't have enough of a charge to set off the magtex."

"Huh! Should have thought of that. Too fucking tired to think straight."

"Wasn't a complete failure on your part," Talina told him. "Muldare says she's in need of a change of underwear."

81

Galluzzi watched through the port-side window as the A-7 shuttle dropped through Donovan's stratosphere. The first red glow was forming on the shuttle's nose and wings.

Beside him, in the middle seat, Shig was staring out like a boy on his first spacing. A look of absolute rapture filled the man's round face; his grin, under other circumstances, would have been infectious.

Two days? It only seemed like a couple of hours.

Galluzzi had been shocked when he and Shig had finally stepped through the lock and into the PA shuttle. But then, that was *Freelander* for you. It screwed with time. Bent it, warped it, and stretched it out of shape.

What the hell had happened to him in there?

"She came to me," he told Shig, finally having come to grips with the revelations in the script-filled corridor.

He hadn't said a word after Shig found him weeping softly on the corridor floor. In an almost dissociative state, he'd allowed Shig to help him to his feet. Leaning on the short Indian, he'd let Shig lead him through the dark corridors of the Transportees' Deck. The phantasms no longer frightened him. *Freelander* had its own physics, its own continuum. Call it proof that the theoretical physicists were right when they said that time was a human creation used to explain the changing relationship between subatomic particles.

"By she I assume you mean Tyne Sakihara?" Shig gave him a mild look.

Galluzzi stared absently at the clouds flashing by the window. "I watched them build the dome of bones. I was there, Shig. It was that clear. I mean it was a real out-of-body experience. And Tyne was talking to me the entire time. Am I crazy?"

"No more so than any of the rest of us." Shig had a benign smile on his lips. "*Freelander* remains a mystery, and I suspect it always will. It exists as an enigma in our universe, part us, part other, and tainted by a physics we can't comprehend."

"So, is Tyne dead? She told me that life is only carbon-based molecules interacting with other molecules. That what we call thought is chemical and electrical impulses. So, if that was just me, imagining her . . ." He frowned, struggling for the words.

"Maybe she's alive and dead at the same time?" Shig arched a bushy eyebrow. "She is right, you know. The science is clear: We're biochemistry. The existence of the soul can neither be proved nor disproved through the scientific method."

"And ethics? Morality?"

"Anthropologists will tell you they are constructs that serve an adaptive purpose when it comes to social relations with one's fellows. That individual and group survival increases when there are rules and expected norms of behavior."

Galluzzi fingered his chin as they dropped down over the ocean. "When it came to ethics, her exact words were: 'Cling to whatever you have, Miguel. In the end, it's the only thing that makes existence worth enduring.'"

"Was she a student of epiphenomenolgy to begin with?"

"No. But who knows what all those years in *Freelander* might have done to her before Jem put that bullet . . . Well, never mind."

Shig's smile was reflective of a deeper amusement. "Then it appears that First Officer Sakihara's very appearance belies her epiphenomenal argument. But that said, I agree with her advice. No matter what one's philosophical or religious compass would indicate, believing makes existence worth enduring."

"She said that euthanizing the transportees was an act of kindness."

"Given the fate of *Freelander,* what do you think? You have a most unique insight, having been in Jem Orten's shoes."

"He turned his transportees into corpses, I turned mine into monsters."

"That assertion denies the Unreconciled any claim to free will. A power that, not being an omnipotent god, you do not have."

"No, I suppose I don't," Galluzzi admitted as the shuttle braked, slowed, and settled on the PA landing pad.

82

Dek hurt. The throbbing pain lay deep within—a sort of background to his jumbled thoughts.

What the hell?

Where was he?

He tried to shift. Hurt more.

"Hold still," a soothing voice ordered.

It took effort to pry his eyelids open. Seemed like they'd been glued. The pain localized—a burning sting just under his left eye. After a couple of blinks, the white haze solidified into a duraplast ceiling with a light panel overhead. The dark figure resolved into Kalico Aguila. She sat in a chair to one side, her clothing mud-splotched and filthy, hair a tangled and matted mess confined by a filthy string tied at the nape of her neck.

"What happened?"

"Seems you saved my life again. You don't remember?"

He blinked, started to reach up for the irritating pain under his eye, only to have Aguila grab his wrist. "You really don't want to touch that. You've got a shard of sialon stuck into your cheekbone. Another inch higher and it would have gone through your eye and into your brain."

"A piece of what?"

"You don't remember the drone? Shouting for me to drop flat? Standing there, sighting on the drone as it dropped down to kill me?"

Dek nodded, worked his dry lips. Oh, yeah. He'd heard the thing, how it made a fluttering sound with the rain in the fan blades. The way it had fallen, headed straight for Aguila, it sure wasn't after reconnaissance.

"Kalico! Down! Now! Drop flat!" His words echoed in his memory. He'd shouldered the Holland & Holland, the rifle having the same

pull and drop as the shotgun he'd used for clays and birds back home. The shot had been instinctive.

The thing exploded as the bullet tore through it.

And what felt like the fist of God had knocked him flat.

After that? Nothing.

"So, where am I?"

"Admin dome." Kalico stood. "Muldare called. The PA shuttle's on the way. They've been locked down over a quetzal scare, but Whitey's raid failed. They'll be here within the hour. We'll get you back to Raya's. Let her pry the sialon out of your cheekbone. Don't worry about the blood caked in your nostril. Seems there's some sort of sinus behind the bone and above the teeth that bled into your nose."

"Why does the rest of me hurt?"

"Muldare says the blast knocked you back a couple of meters. And you've got bits of shrapnel here and there that will need to be dug out. Beyond that, you're just bruised. Lucky it didn't burst your eardrums."

All right. Enough of this. He took a deep breath, swung his legs out, and sat up. Damn. The headache was as bad as that toilet-sucking hangover back in PA or maybe the one he'd barely gotten over from heat stroke. He figured, at this rate, he could make his fortune importing aspirin to Donovan.

Kalico offered him a hand. Pulled him to his feet.

Sure enough, Dek discovered a whole lot of hurt. His joints, arms, shoulders, but nothing like the searing in his cheek. He carefully prodded at the angular chunk of sialon. Could just see it at the edge of his vision when he lowered his eyes.

Weird.

"So, what's with the Unreconciled?"

"Don't know. Let's go find out." Kalico gave him a sober inspection. "You okay to walk? Not feeling dizzy or sick?"

"I'll let you know."

She took his arm, just to be sure, and led the way out into the hallway, down to the cafeteria. To one side, Batuhan's throne sat, empty, like a monstrous reminder.

Dek turned loose of Aguila, stepped over, this being the first time he'd seen the thing. At first it repulsed him. But as he looked closer, it was to realize the mind-boggling talent and artistry that had gone into the carving of it. It begged a magnifying glass to see the intricate detail.

"Tal?" Kalico asked her com. "Status?"

She listened to the reply, shot Dek a look. "Talina's in the barracks. She's got the women and children there. Only three men left. Batuhan and one other were last seen taking the trail down into the forest."

"Kylee and Flute?"

"Now there's a question. Talina just asked me the same."

"They'll show up." Dek finished his inspection of the throne. Realized he was more wobbly than he'd wanted to admit. He walked over and settled himself into a chair at one of the cafeteria tables.

Kalico was watching him, something unsettled in her laser-blue gaze. He asked, "What?"

"I think until you get back to Solar System, you're going to have a really nasty scar. Those perfect Taglioni features of yours are never going to be the same."

"Maybe it makes me look dashing. Like a knuckle-and-skull adventurer. The kind of tough man who takes life by the horns and—"

"Don't push your luck. The way you are right now I could knock you over with my little finger."

He liked the fact that she was grinning as she said it.

"Yeah, I suppose. Still, it makes a good story. But what about the Unreconciled? Think Talina's all right alone over there? I lived with these people just one deck down. They're not kind and loving at heart."

Kalico took a breath, picked at the mud flaking off of her clothing. "I'm not feeling particularly forgiving at the moment either. They've relentlessly tried to kill us. The loss of Talbot and Dya hasn't hit home yet. But it will. I'm angry, Dek. My inclination is to burn Tyson Station and everyone in it to ashes."

THE DARK SHADE OF BLACK

I am bereft.

My stumbling progress is mindless. I just force my legs to carry me. Climb down stones, leap from one purchase to the next as I flee toward . . . what?

Ctein is plodding ahead of me. His shoulders sag. His movements are clumsy, like a man whose soul has gone dead inside. I see defeat in his every movement.

I haven't a clue where I am, where I'm going. I just proceed. Panting. Howling in lonely silence.

This is a terrible place that I do not understand. I can't put a name to the green, blue, and turquoise leaves. Branches and stems turn in my direction. There is no sky. I clamp a hand to my ears to still the rising and falling harmony of the chime. It is like a madness that echoes inside my skull.

Beneath my feet green and brown roots squirm. The feeling of movement unnerves me, pushes me to the threshold of endurance.

At least I know enough to avoid the vines. Try not to touch anything.

I follow Ctein along the edge of the tumbled boulders. We've reached the bottom of the trail. Turned north, seeking to skirt the cliff. It's mostly flat here. The trees are small, barely twenty meters high. Water drips from the alien-shaped leaves.

The rain has tapered into a fine mist, sometimes ceasing altogether as patches open in the clouds and shafts of light shoot bars through the rainbow-patterned virga.

Ctein—soaked to the bone—is no more than four paces ahead. He stumbles over a stone. Walks with no more grace than if his feet were carved of wood. I hear the labored breathing as he fights the shivers. Nothing has prepared us for such arduous travel as we are engaged in. Struggling over boulders, leaping gaps, spanning roots.

The boulder has a black sheen, gray where the sides were sheltered from the downpour. Irregularities, cracks, a faint smattering of what looks like lichen.

Ctein puts his hand on it to brace his passage as he's done on countless other boulders.

Instantly, the stone is alive. Stabs some slender lance-shaped spike through Ctein's chest. As it does, two hose-like arms reach out to grab him. They pull him close upon the thorn-sharp spear until it shoots out of his back.

I see the expression on his face. The pain . . . the disbelief.

Ctein's mouth works the same way a fish's does when it is left on the bank after being pulled from the stream. His eyes have bugged wide, the scars on his cheeks sucking, hollow, and pale.

I freeze. Try to comprehend. Am stricken by a horror that locks my muscles. Starves my lungs of air.

And the boulder changes color. Morphs from an irregular-shaped rock to an amoeba kind of a thing that begins to conform to Ctein's thrashing body.

Standing there with all the will of a stump, I watch it begin to engulf Ctein's body. Stand there so long I barely manage to pull loose of the roots that are winding around my feet.

When panic overcomes my horror, I backpedal, run with all my might.

And now I am here, staggering through the dim half-light of the forest floor. I scramble over mats of roots, stare up at the distant canopy. I wonder if my mind and soul are broken.

DIVINE COMEDY

The emptiness is complete. From my head to my toes, I am as hollow as a bottle. Thoughtless. Terrified.

I can't trust anything.

Ctein taught me that.

The one word that repeats—like an echo through infinity—is "Why?"

Finally, shaking, weeping, I climb onto a meter-high knot of great roots. There, I stare up at the high branches. I raise my hands and cry, "I gave you everything!"

The chime seems to mock me.

"I bled for you!"

I point to the scars running across my skin. "Each cut stung like fire! I lived in agony in the days that followed."

I swallow against the tears.

I see constant movement up in the high canopy. The endless motion of the forest. But no illumination appears in the patterns above. No shaft of forgiving light. The universe ignores me.

"I gave everything to you!" I scream at the heedless heights. "Everything."

Yet the universe did nothing as Vartan betrayed me.

Should I have made him shoot me?

But if I had, what would have become of the dead? I carry *these people. They* live *in my flesh. Their souls reside in the scars that line my body. I am their living grave.*

That was the promise. The sacred bond. The reason the universe chose me. Chose us. We were the end, and the beginning.

"What happened?" I ask through the sobs that wrack me. "Why did you betray us? Was it me? Was I unworthy?"

I listen desperately, hoping to hear the universe answer. Surely there must be words, but I can decipher nothing in the maddening rising and falling of the chime.

I have to have faith.

If I do not, I have nothing.

"The universe does not make mistakes."

But I cannot conceive its purpose. My soul has gone dark. Black beyond blackness. Hopeless beyond hopelessness.

I rise wearily, start picking my way down the slowly flexing roots.

I am almost at the bottom when a voice calls, "You might not want to step down right there. A sidewinder will get you."

I freeze, look up.

She is a girl. Blonde. Early teens? Her blue eyes are hard, seem to be oddly intense. Inhuman in both size and color.

She wears some sort of leather pants and cloak. Her shirt is a kind of rough fabric I can't place a name to. She perches on a pile of knotted roots off to my left.

As I gape, she says, "Wow! I thought I knew the definition of butt ugly. Seeing you gives it a whole new twist."

"Who . . . who are you?" For a moment I reel, hoping beyond hope that this curious girl is the universe's answer to my prayers.

"Kylee Simonov." She cocks her head. "Dya was my mother. Talbot was my dad. You tried to blow them up." She gestures around. "Chased them out here."

"Why are you here?"

"Um, you might want to move that right foot. Another thirty seconds, and you're never taking another step for the rest of your life. Which won't be more than about three minutes from now."

I look down, tear my foot away from the grasping roots.

A warbling, whistling sound can be heard off to the right; she again cocks her head. Smiles grimly. "Come on. This way."

I do my best to keep up as she scampers across the roots headed in the direction of the sound. I wonder at the grace, the seemingly effortless way she moves. A wild creature at home in her element.

"So," she calls over her shoulder. "What's with that stupid eye painted on your forehead? That meant to creep-freak the congregation? Let you sleep through the sermons when they think you're watching?"

"The eye allows me to see the purpose behind the Prophets."

"Got it. Makes the poor saps think you see God when the brain-damaged goons babble."

"Do you know who I am?" I snap, beginning to anger.

"One stupid fuckhead if you ask me."

I stop short. "Don't use that tone with me! I am the last and the first, the Chosen, the Messiah who—"

"You're quetzal crap, fool. You let your buddy back there walk right up to a skewer. Stood there like a lump while it stuck him through the chest and started to eat him. Would have stepped right on that sidewinder. Would have been a root-mummy by now if I hadn't told you to move your foot."

I blink.

She looks back. "So, you following? Or are you even more stupid than I thought."

I start after her, hearing my labored breath whistling through my nose hole. "You going to kill me?" I ask. "Because of what happened to your mother and father?"

"Nope. Not that I don't want to, but there's that part of Talina inside me. You think you're the living repository for the dead? You oughtta try quetzal molecules sometime. Same effect, but you don't need the scars. And the way you were wailing back there? All the pain and sacrifice shit? I'd guess you'd think it was a bargain."

"The universe doesn't make mistakes."

"The universe doesn't give a shit. Don't you get it, butt ugly? You were trapped on a starship. Not enough food. And, yeah, I'd probably come down on the side of eating, rather than being eaten. I'm a spoiled brat when it comes to saving my skin. Been out here too long where life and death are immediate kinds of problems."

"Little girl, you—"

"Watch that vine. That's gotcha. Not that the scars it leaves behind would stand out against what you've already got, but the spines burn like liquid fire."

I weave wide of the hair-covered vine.

"You don't understand Revelation," I mutter. "To be filled with the rapture of true knowledge. To feel the presence of the universe inside your body. My failing was that in the end I wasn't worthy. Believe—as I do—in the Revelation, and the only explanation is that I wasn't devoted enough. But why the universe chose me remains—"

"Piss poor picking on the universe's part," she interrupts. "You sacrificed.

You had faith. You're the repository. You suffered. It's all about you, huh? You. You. You. You." She glances back from the top of the roots she's scaling. "And you drove my mom and dad out here to die."

As I crest the top of the roots, she's already down the other side. I am reaching the point where if I can get close enough, I am going to reach out, grab her by the neck, and watch her alien-strange eyes bug out as I strangle her.

That warbling whistle sounds. Closer now. Where she stands on the root mat below, she seems to be listening. She alters her course slightly as she starts off in the direction of the sound.

I wonder if I should follow. But looking around, I haven't a clue as to where I am. Which direction is which. Nor have I seen anything edible. Wherever the foul child is headed, there will be food there. Shelter.

Exhaustion saps my limbs. That trembling that comes from hunger and low blood sugar robs my muscles. How many hours has it been since I slept? I'm not used to the exertion. I've sat too long on my throne.

I still have faith. The universe doesn't make mistakes. The child is wrong when it comes to that.

I am out here to learn an important lesson. Whatever it is, it's not something this insolent forest urchin can teach.

We climb up over a particularly high knot of roots, many as thick around as oil drums. They are contorted around each other in a dense ball.

Kylee leaps down the other side in a remarkable display of agility. She spins around at the bottom, seems to stare at a shadowed hollow among the roots across the way, and turns back, saying, "Stop right there at the top. Catch your breath where you won't get caught by the roots."

Winded as I am, my heart thumping at the exertion, I gasp for breath. I'm delighted for a chance to rest. And here I can be assured that nothing is going to ensnare me.

"Thanks, I was running out of energy."

"Guess it doesn't take much to be a cannibal, huh? Especially when you don't have to work for it. Just set off an explosive and cut up the victims. Chuck them in the stewpot, and you're made."

"You really are a despicable child. Where are you taking me, anyway? Ah, you have that airtruck out here somewhere, don't you? Is that it? You think I can fly it for you?"

She is staring thoughtfully at me. Tilts her head back, gaze going higher as if she's seeking some answer from above. "Mom came out to Tyson to help you and your people. Dad was along to keep her and Aguila safe. You're a clap-trapping idiot. And on Donovan, stupidity's a death sentence."

I stare down at her. Glance around, lest this is some kind of trap. I'm not going to play this game any longer. Looking back over my shoulder, I realize I can take a line of sight across the clearing, and another, and another, and make my way back to the Tyson mesa.

At this, I smile. The universe has not forgotten me. It has brought me here to teach me the way home. A metaphor.

I need to let Vartan have his moment, and then I will return, wiser, better suited to do the universe's work.

The dark side of blackness begins to lift from my soul. As always, faith has carried me through.

"Go on about your business, little girl. The universe has taught me what I need to know. It has shown me the way to save the dead. What it means to be chosen. And despite what you think, the universe really doesn't make mistakes."

I catch the blur in the corner of my eye. Hear the rush of something ripping through the air. Just as I fix on the curving length, it hits me. The point spears through my chest, overwhelms even the pain of Initiation.

My vision smears sideways as my body is jerked heavenwards. I see Kylee's face dropping away. With punctured lungs I can't even scream.

I am lifted, rocketing into the branches. My vision fills with images of green, an interlacery of branches.

As I rush into them, I catch a curious odor, like rotten blood. Then the eyes appear, magically, as if forming from the leaves themselves. Huge, deep, and blue-black, like holes into eternity.

My last coherent thought as a gaping, tooth-filled mouth opens is that I am being eaten alive. And then . . . the universe . . .

Kylee flinched at the violence of the attack. Watched Batuhan's body flop under the force as the black spear on the end of the tentacle shot clear through the man's chest, right out among the three lines tattooed between the spirals on his breasts.

As the cannibal was lofted skyward, Kylee sniffed. Caught the faint taint of rotten blood. The old memory tripped, something monstrous and ancient.

Horrified, she watched as the cannibal was jerked high. Saw the three great eyes appear, as if opening out of the leaves and branches. Dark, powerful, and remorseless.

In but an instant, the retracting tentacle stuffed Batuhan into a black hole of a mouth. And as quickly it vanished, merging back into an image of branches, leaves, and vines.

For a long moment, the terrible eyes fixed on Kylee. Filled with cold promise, they seemed to drain her soul, suck her life away into some numbing eternity.

An instant later, they were gone.

From where he'd hidden, Flute vented a harmonic of fear. The sound brought Kylee back to this reality. She shivered, tensed, half expecting that diving tentacle to stab down from above.

But nothing. She might have been looking up at pristene upper story.

"So much for happy endings, huh?" she said. "Guess those only exist in fairy tales."

The soft tremolo sounded from the hollow beneath the roots.

"Yeah." Kylee kept her eyes on the spot where Batuhan disappeared into the high branches. "It's still in the same place. Remarkable how well it blends in. Doesn't hardly show up in the UV or IR either."

Flute's body seemed to emerge out of the background as the quetzal dropped its camouflage; dull patterns flashed over its body, the ruff held flat to the neck. Time to go.

"I agree. But keep low. That thing's dangerous."

As the quetzal streaked out from the hollow, it paused only long enough for Kylee to leap onto its back. Flute skirted the root knot, leaped a low tangle, and raced east.

"Hope it doesn't have such good aim when it comes to moving targets."

83

Vartan straightened, reached his hand around, and pressed on the small of his back. Overhead, Capella burned down with a fierce intensity. Vartan's skin had begun to brown, a process they'd been warned about after the first bad sunburns. The basket before him was half full of green beans. That left him with another half an hour's worth of picking.

He caught a flash in distance to the northeast, high over the trees. Stepped out from the confusion of crops and walked to the edge of the landing pad.

As it came closer, Vartan made out the airtruck. Watched it circle, hover, and slowly settle. Fans still spun up, the occupants waited, as if for some sign.

Spreading his arms wide in a gesture of open-handed surrender, Vartan braved the outwash from the fans. Almost had the hat ripped off his head.

Only then did the fans spool down, and the cab door opened.

Shyanne climbed down, landing with a sprightly jump. She was dressed in some sort of handcrafted fabric that looked more like burlap than any kind of clothing Vartan could put name to. Behind her came Tamil Kattan. The Sri Lankan glanced warily about as Shyanne gave Vartan a cocky grin and walked forward.

"Didn't figure to see you again," Vartan told her.

"Or I you." She flipped her brown hair back to expose the Initiation scars on her face. Sorrow and defeat lay behind her umber-colored eyes. "Chaco and Madison were fair. Did their best actually. But you remember that day when Perez told us that we were no long Irredenta? That's not quite true."

"How's that? We're off the ship."

Her gaze went distant. "This is the only place left for us, Vart. What we did up there on *Ashanti*? There're things that forever set a group of people apart. A history that can't be bridged. Not in the eyes of others. It's a stigma we can't outrun, can't outlive."

"That bad, huh?"

"Hey, they tried." Shyanne gave a weary shrug. "But the revulsion? It's always in their eyes. You can see it in the unguarded moments. The hesitation. The lack of trust that—no matter how they try and hide it—can't be overcome."

He bit his lip. Nodded. Turned to look where the women were standing in the fields, waiting. Unwilling to come forward after years of domination by Batuhan.

Shyanne gave him that old brown-eyed scrutiny. "Hear that you're in charge now."

"Someone has to be."

"Tamil and I, we'd like to come back. Is that a possibility? I mean . . . there's Svetlana. What happened to her and Hakil. I know that you and she were . . ."

Vartan chuckled under his breath. "She believed. We all did to one extent or another. But here's the thing: If we can't find it in ourselves to forgive one another, how do we expect the Donovanians to? It's got to start somewhere."

She gave him a weary smile. Turned to Tamil and said, "Guess you can unload our luggage."

Vartan looked up, saw Talina Perez in the doorway, her hand resting on her pistol. "Hello, Security Officer. How's Dek Taglioni?"

"Looks like he'll get away with a juicy scar. How are things?"

"Little Tina Brooks lost a lower leg to a slug. We finally got the bleeding stopped after we amputated. Looks like she'll live."

"That's tough."

Shyanne asked, "Who did the amputation?"

"I did. Scared the hell out of me."

"Then, maybe you're glad to have me back after all. I'm the closest thing you've got to a doctor. Not much else a veterinary tech can do on a planet with no dogs, cats, cattle, or horses."

Tamil was at the rear of the airtruck, had opened the hatch and was laying out what looked like leather suitcases.

Talina said, "Just so you know, we're going to be flying out west.

Whatever that thing is in the forest, the one that got Talbot and Dya, Kylee thinks she knows how to find it. Didn't want you thinking we were after you."

"After you?" Shyanne asked.

Vartan took a deep breath, that lingering unease in his gut. "Let's just say that when the Supervisor and her party took their leave of Tyson Station they weren't in a forgive-and-forget mood."

"No happy endings, huh?"

"Nope." Vartan looked up. "Officer Perez, I'm saying this now, and I'll continue to say it. As long as I am alive, any and all are welcome at Tyson. No one, under any circumstance, will be turned away. PA or Corporate. That includes you, Security Officer. You want to hunt that thing? You're welcome to use Tyson as a base."

Talina's curiously shaped face reflected hesitation. "Thanks. I'll pass the word. Meantime, I've got to be going."

"Sure you won't stay for lunch?"

Perez's alien-dark eyes narrowed. "Don't press your luck."

With that she stepped back inside, closed the cab door, and began to spool up the fans as Tamil battened the back hatch and lugged the leather cases away.

As the airtruck rose, circled, and headed back to the northwest, Shyanne cryptically asked, "Did you have to invite her for lunch?"

"It's only beans and cabbage."

He turned, leading the way toward the admin dome. Truth was, he was glad to have her back. He needed someone to remind the women that they'd been people before the Messiah's tyranny had turned them into breeding stock. Shyanne would be just the woman to do it.

84

As the shuttle settled into its berth, Derek Taglioni couldn't keep a smile from bending the corners of his lips. The feel of the ship comforted him. Hard as that was to believe.

"Hard dock. Hard seal," Ensign Naftali told him.

Ashanti's always-pleasant voice announced, "*Welcome aboard*" through the speakers.

"Good to be back," Dek called. "Missed you, old friend."

"*We missed you as well, Dek. First Officer Turner has been appraised of your arrival and will meet you in the Captain's Lounge.*"

Dek unstrapped, glanced over at Dan Wirth, seeing devious wariness in the psychopath's clever eyes. "You sure you want to do this?"

"Hey, I almost died in a plastic box while a bunch of overgrown lizards chewed on it. Lead forth, and let us begin." Wirth rose and extended a hand that Dek precede him. "Whole lot better arrival than that last departure from *Turalon*. I barely got off that bucket with my balls intact."

"Woman trouble, I take it?" Dek acknowledged Naftali's salute and led the way to the hatch.

"Is there any other kind?" Wirth asked, pausing long enough to adjust his quetzal-hide vest and its garish chains.

"Oh, yeah. Cannibals hunting you, jealous relatives, Corporate regulations." A beat. "An illegally assumed identity to cover a murder."

"Don't get funny."

Dek gave the man a flippant raise of the eyebrows. "Come on. Let's get this started."

As Dek led the way past the hatch, it was into a different *Ashanti*. The sialon had been scrubbed, the air smelling slightly astringent. Taking the lift, it was like a homecoming. The feel of the ship, so familiar after all those years. And at the same time, she was different. Smelled more earthy? Green? Alive?

But when it came to different, so was he: tanned, muscular, with a glaring pink scar under his left eye. Dr. Turnienko had repaired the bone in what she'd called his left maxilla. A scar he'd indeed have, but not a dent.

As they stepped out of the lift on the Command Deck, Wirth muttered, "I'd hate to discover that armed security personnel with a warrant for my arrest waited behind one of the doors. If that happened, you know I wouldn't hesitate to blow a hole right through you before they killed me."

Wirth danced his fingers on the grip of the holstered pistol at his belt. And true, he was fast enough that Dek wouldn't stand a chance.

Reaching the Captain's Lounge hatch, Dek turned. "Here's what you need to know: My cousin, Miko, is a smart, crafty, clever, and cunning monster. A craftier and more clever monster than I. And believe me, when it came to being a plotting pit viper, I tried. He despised me, with good reason."

"Not exactly a scintillating recommendation of character that you're giving him, or yourself, is it?"

"And you have a right to talk?" Dek arched a questioning brow. "By now your container with all the plunder is being loaded in the cargo deck with a Taglioni seal prominently displayed on it. It will only be opened by Taglioni agents in Transluna, and its contents will be reported straight to Miko."

"Yeah, yeah, and from there—with your recommendation and Miko's blessing—your people can buy my safe return. That's a shitload of plunder. In terms of Solar System, it's worth billions. You get your ten percent. But that's just a pittance compared to what's to come."

"I get more than that. I slap Miko right across his perfectly sculpted face. And I do it with wealth the likes of which he's never seen. There is no way you can understand what that means to me." Dek saw the hesitation in Wirth's eyes, and added, "Come on, Dan. In your world it's all about you. Heartless, without remorse. The high and rarified circles of power that make up Transluna are just the place for you. So, in a sense, getting you back to Solar System is my way of paying them all back."

"And to think some would call you petty."

Dek opened the door, ushered Wirth into the small room, and shook hands with Ed Turner. "Hey, old friend. Good to see you again."

"My God! Your face. I'd heard you were wounded. That's . . . horrible!"

"It's healing. Ed, this is Dan Wirth. Dan, Ed Turner is the finest First Officer to space with in the entire universe."

Turner shook hands with Wirth, offered seats, and Dek dropped into his familiar spot. "Hear you're in the captain's chair to take *Ashanti* back to Solar System."

Turner settled into Galluzzi's chair. "I don't know what Miguel's doing. I think getting here was just too much. That it broke something in his spirit. He's been living down in PA. Keeping a low profile at Shig's place."

"Hope you don't have as interesting a ride getting back."

"I'll take my chances. I'm just not a dirtie. And besides, you should see Deck Three. We ripped out the bulkheads, put in light panels, hauled up dirt. Turned the whole thing into a farm to augment the hydroponics. And we're going back as a skeleton crew. About fifteen of our people, another ten of Torgussen's when *Vixen* matches with us next week. If we get stranded somewhere, we can survive for decades."

"Naw. If you've planned for it, it won't happen. My bet? You're back off Neptune in two-and-a-half years." Dek reached into his pocket and handed Turner the data cube. "This is important. I'm entrusting it to you, and you alone. Seal it in the captain's pouch. Mark it urgent delivery to Boardmember Miko Taglioni or whoever his successor on the Board might be."

Turner's washed-out blue eyes held Dek's for a moment. Then he glanced at Wirth. Nodded. Took the data cube. "It will be done."

"And as I speak, there's a container being transferred from the shuttle to the cargo deck. It, too, bears the Taglioni seal. Make sure it is immediately delivered to my family's agents."

"Yes, sir."

"Happy spacing, Ed."

Turner frowned slightly. Studied the cube. "Dek? You sure you don't want to go with us? You almost died down there as it is."

"Positive. You'd be surprised at what I found down there."

"Like . . . what?"

"A whole new world." Dek stood.

Wirth followed, shaking Turner's hand. "Good to meet you. Before you space, drop by The Jewel. We'll set you up right. Have Angelina give your cock the milking of a lifetime. On the house, First Officer."

"Uh, yeah. Thanks."

Outside the hatch, Wirth jerked a thumb back at the lounge. "Maybe he didn't get it? Outside of Ali, Angelina's the best on the planet. And it's not like just anyone gets free tail from her."

"Well, Dan. Not everyone's a connoisseur." Dek slapped the man on the back. "Come on. Let's get out of here before Turner gets any ideas about warrants and men with guns."

85

The last shuttle left Port Authority on a cloudy morning, rising through rain squalls before bursting out into Capella's bright light and ascending from the puffy white mounds of cumulus. Within minutes it shot through the stratosphere and into the darkening threshold of vacuum.

In the copilot's seat, Miguel Galluzzi watched the familiar patterns of stars form in all of their swirling majesty, the nebulae, galaxies, and dark matter stretching across his view. Capella was a glaring orb to the left as the shuttle changed attitude.

Where was . . .? Ah, yes. There. *Freelander* hung just over Donovan's horizon. A small ball against the background of stars. Even from this distance, it didn't look right. Having seen orbiting ships his entire career, Galluzzi couldn't put his finger on the difference. As if the thing was eating light.

He wondered if, in the infinite eventuality of time, the leak would drain his universe away, siphon it slowly into whatever hellish existence *Freelander* had passed through. If it did, what would happen to the essence of his beloved Tyne Sakihara? It turned out that he had to believe that he was more than molecules and electrochemical stimuli. Indeed, he'd decided what he'd cling to.

In silent tribute, Galluzzi raised a hand and snapped off a salute just before the vessel passed out of sight.

After *Freelander* he would never again see the universe through jaded eyes. Was that redemption? Or revelation?

"Thank you, Shig," he whispered under his breath.

Memory of the little brown man with the round face and unruly hair would remain chiseled in Miguel Galluzzi's heart and soul until he took his last breath. How, in all of creation, could luck have placed him into such knowing, caring, and competent hands?

The shuttle rolled under Ensign Naftali's skilled command.

Ashanti appeared in view. Dead ahead. *Vixen*'s shuttle was just departing, returning back to the survey ship. It would have just deposited those crew members who'd opted to ride *Ashanti* home.

Their return created an interesting dilemma for The Corporation. The *Vixen* crew were owed an absolute fortune: sixty to seventy years' wages, including mission bonus, including overtime for service beyond stated period of contract, and compounded interest. And they were still in the prime of their careers.

Leave that to the Board to figure out.

Galluzzi grinned.

Naftali turned down *Ashanti*'s routine request to assume control of the shuttle prior to docking.

To Galluzzi's supreme satisfaction, the ensign settled them into the bay without so much as a quiver. The familiar vibrations told him the shuttle was locked down.

"Hard dock, hard seal," Naftali told him, turning in the command seat. "Welcome home, sir."

Galluzzi gave the ensign a wink, stood, and made his way to the hatch. There, Dan Wirth waited, his quetzal vest buttoned, the priceless rhodium and gold chains gleaming in the light. The man was smiling, boyish, which accented the dimple in his chin. A curious reservation lay behind his brown eyes.

"I'll see that you are assigned to Dek's old quarters," Galluzzi told him. "Best in the ship, as befitted a Taglioni."

"What about when we get to Neptune?"

"You are to be delivered directly to Taglioni agents. No customs."

Wirth's smile beamed in triumph. "Should be quite a ride."

Galluzzi paused as the hatch was undogged. "I do hope that you know what you're doing. You have quite the unsavory reputation as a gambler, cutthroat, and con man. But you do understand what you're getting into, don't you?"

"Biggest game of my life, Cap." Wirth gave him a wink. "And, yeah, I promise. I won't so much as lift a card with any of the crew on the way back."

The hatch swung open. Turner, Smart, and AO Tuulikki stood

waiting in dress uniform. They saluted in unison, and Turner said, "Welcome aboard, sir."

"Good to be back." Galluzzi studied Turner's watery eyes. "I'm not here to bump you out of the captain's chair, Ed. I'm happy to let you take her back to Solar System."

Turner and others were watching him warily.

"You all right, sir?" Paul Smart asked.

"Oddly, Paul, never better."

"Thought, given the way you left, that we'd be lucky to ever see you again," Tuulikki told him. "What happened down there?"

Galluzzi clasped his hands behind him, rocking up on his toes. "The Unreconciled were right about one thing: The universe continually teaches us. Sometimes you have to lose yourself to find yourself."

Turner winced. "Not sure I understand."

"No, Captain Turner," Galluzzi told him, "I don't suppose you do. And that's the crying shame of it. Now, why don't you good people show Mr. Wirth here to his cabin and take us home?"

With that he strode past them, headed for the lift that would take him to Crew Deck.

86

Sitting behind the big chabacho-wood desk, Allison leaned back in Dan's chair. With a long fingernail she tapped at her incisor teeth and studied the empty corner where Dan's safes had stood. The room looked remarkably empty without them.

She glanced at the ledger book on the desk. Business was down fifteen percent since Dan's departure.

Dan's last words echoed in her memory: *"Taglioni's got a way to fix it for me. I'm going back before I'm inclined to cut that beautiful throat of yours, or worse, wake up with your knife sticking out of my heart. You, babe, are going to run my interests here. Fifty-fifty. And don't fuck with me, or I'll send someone back to slit you open from your ribs clear down to your cunt."*

All of which gave her hope. If plunder was what it took to get Dan back to Transluna in spite of his background, she'd be a shoo-in when the day came.

At a hesitant knock, she closed the ledger, calling, "Come in."

Dek Taglioni stepped through the door and hesitated, looking around the room. "It's just not the same without those brooding safes, is it?"

"I have Lawson welding me up a new one. Sturdier legs this time."

He walked over, glanced at the whiskey in its blown-glass decanter. "You mind?"

"Help yourself." She arched a trim eyebrow. "I assume your visit has some purpose beyond a free drink?"

"Just thought I'd drop in and see how things are." He poured two glasses, bringing her one. Then he seated himself across from her.

She gave him a smile as she met his yellow-green eyes. The healing scar on his cheek didn't spoil his good looks, if anything the blemish added to the allure. Lifting the whiskey in mock salute, she said, "So, spill it. What irresistible proposition have you come to dazzle me with?"

"Straight to business, I see."

"In my world, business is all there is. So, here you are. A rich Taglioni. Handsome as all get out, and with that cute dimple in your chin. Dan's gone. Thank you very much. So, what's your pitch?"

"I did you a favor." He spread his arms, palms up to indicate the room around them. "Must be a relief to sleep at night without having to tread on eggshells. There's easier ways to make a living than playing Russian roulette with a stone-cold psychopath."

"Living with Dan has been both terrifying and educational . . . and I survived four years of it. Trust me, once I figured out what he was, I never underestimated what he was capable of." She gave him a narrow smile. "Or any man, for that matter. All of which leaves me very wary of you."

"I was wondering if you might need any of my . . ."

Another knock at the door. This one insistent. Kalen Tompzen called, "I've got him, ma'am."

"Excuse me." She stood, calling, "Kalen, bring him in."

She stepped to the back table, dropped her hand to the shelf built into the wall.

Tompzen—his face like a mask—opened the door and straight-armed Pavel Tomashev into the room.

The part-time miner, hunter, and prospector had a reddening bruise under his right eye. The man's chamois-hide shirt and pants were filthy and scuffed, as if he'd been dragged for a distance in the street.

Pavel blinked, swallowed hard, and fixed his eyes on Allison. "Hey, listen. I'm sorry. I wasn't thinking when I shot off my mouth. So, like, Ali, I won't do it again."

Pavel's exact words had been, *"If sweet Ali thinks I give a shit, she can come suck my cock."*

Allison gave him a humorless smile. "No. You won't. But your stupid fucking mouth aside, you walked out on Shin Wong owing the house almost five hundred siddars. Four hundred, ninety-seven to be exact. Is that right Kalen?"

"Yes, ma'am. And another fifteen that he stiffed Vik for drinks."

Tomashev winced. "Yeah, yeah. Five twelve altogether. Listen. I was drunk. Shit happens when I get drunk. I'll bring it around soon as I can round it up."

"Put your hand out on the table. That's it. Palm down. Perfect." She smiled, fingers curling around the handle where the pick hammer lay on the shelf. With a fluid move, she swung the geologist's hammer in an arc. Drove the sharp point through the back of his hand, through flesh, bone, and tendons, and into the wood beneath.

Pavel let out a blood-curdling scream, tried to jerk his hand away. Immediately gave that up as a bad idea. He stared at his impaled hand, wide-eyed and panting. Just as he drew breath to protest, Kalen laid the blade of his knife against the man's gulping Adam's apple.

Allison leaned close. "Pavel, you will pay us what you owe us. Immediately. Now, the talk around town is that with Dan gone, sweet little Ali's going to be an easy mark. Not nearly so scary as that psychopathic throat-cutting Dan Wirth was."

She paused, watching the fear-sweat bead on Pavel's face. "What do you think? Should I give Kalen that special nod of the head that says, 'Do it?' You know, just so people know that sweet Ali's not a fainthearted little flower that just anyone can pluck?"

The man's bugged eyes were fixed on the spiked hammer. Blood was beginning to seep out around the steel. "N—No. I got the plunder, Ali. Don't need no throat-cutting. I'm good for it."

"I figured you'd be. Not to mention that I know how it is to be a little drunk. I've done some foolish things myself when deep in the cups." She gave him a saucy wink. "So it's a good thing I'm sober, huh? If I'd been drunk—and pissed off like I am now—I'd be even more enraged when I sobered up tomorrow and had to clean up all of your stinking blood."

She worked the point of the hammer loose and pulled it free; Pavel clutched his bleeding hand to his chest.

"But, you're right about one thing: It's not the same as when Dan was in charge. He'd have thrown you out in the alley to bleed. I wouldn't do that."

"Y-Yes?"

She told Kalen, "Take Pavel over to Raya's. Have her set his bones, sew his tendons together, and what have you. We don't want him lamed up, not when that latest strike of his out in the Blood Mountains is showing color. And wait, seems to me that The Jewel has a half interest in the proceeds from that claim, right, Pavel?"

"Y—Yes, ma'am. It's in the papers. Dickered it with Dan."

"Nice to know your memory is good. Now, don't let anything else slip your mind."

She gave Kalen the nod, and he removed his knife, steered the weeping Pavel Tomashev out, and closed the door.

Allison, sighed, inspected the blood dripping from her pick hammer, and wiped it clean with a rag. Retreating to her desk, she laid the hammer on the ornate wood with a clunk and seated herself before retrieving her whiskey. "Sorry. Like I said. I only do business these days."

Taglioni had an amused twist to his perfect lips. "Good. Because, along with cadging a free drink, I'm here for business. Now that Dan's gone, would you have any objection to me running a game at your tables now and then?"

"House gets fifty percent of your take."

"Twenty-five. Not to mention that being the only Taglioni on the planet, my presence brings a certain cachet to the place."

"I think we can see our way clear for thirty-five. Same as the tables pay off. Any *other* interests?"

Here it came. How long before he wanted to bed her? Tonight? Or was he thinking to make a longer play of it? Try and convince her it was true love?

To her surprise, he said, "Nope. That will do. At least for now. Sometime, in the future, as things progress, however, I'd like to talk to you about some of the properties you hold." He stood, tossing off his whiskey. "But that is for another day."

At the door, he gave her a respectful salute with his index finger. "Good night, Allison."

And then he was gone.

"Oh, brave new world," she told herself, and drained the last of her whiskey.

87

Kalico Aguila strode down the avenue, gravel crunching under her feet. She'd just left the shuttle, coming through the gate in the forefront of her weekly rotation up from Corporate Mine. Things were going well. Thanks, in part, to the brand-new mucking machines that had been included in *Ashanti*'s cargo manifest.

Also, and most auspicious, were the cacao seeds that had been included along with the agricultural supplies. Of less value were the two heavy-duty gleaners. Giant machines built for harvesting grain fields. Neither of the monsters could manage a complete turn without exceeding the limits of a local Port Authority grain field.

But then, this was Donovan.

Toby Montoya was eyeing both of the beasts, a gleam in his eyes. He was just waiting for the next time something broke at Corporate Mine, something that required his skill to fix. When it did, he'd be rubbing his hands in anticipation of the chance to dicker the harvesters away from Kalico. No telling what he'd make out them. Dump trucks? Brush hogs? Or something even more outlandish?

When it came to imagination on Donovan, The Corporation could have learned a thing or two.

"There you are!"

Kalico turned in time to see Dek Taglioni step out of the gunsmith's shop. The scion of wealth and privilege wore a quetzal-hide cape, a claw-shrub-fiber shirt embroidered with colorful quetzals, and knee-high boots. Pouches hung from his belt, and the wooden grip of his fancy pistol was polished to a sheen.

"Derek Taglioni," she replied as he walked up, a grin bending the scar on his cheek. "Thought you were out at Briggs' place."

"Back in town. Wanted to be sure that Wirth got off without issue. Had some other business. Trip's a lot faster in an airplane. Made my life easier after Pamlico Jones finally got it unpacked."

"Making yourself right at home out there, I take it?" She shot him a sidelong glance. The scar would slowly whiten, adding to his rakish charm. His hair was longer, and he now wore it combed back.

"Been out with Kylee and Tip. Made a couple of passes over the forest out west of Tyson. Been dangling biosensors down into the trees. Took us a couple of times, but we've got it. We can find the damn thing."

"You're talking about the beast that killed Dya and Talbot?" Memory of that day still plagued her nightmares.

"Kylee pegged it. The day she and Flute lured Batuhan into its lair, she caught a faint whiff. Called it a 'rotten blood' smell. It's something we've never seen. Huge. Probably arboreal. The sensor indicates it's about fifty meters across, has some sort of adaptation that allows it to cling to branches."

"I was there. Looking right at where Dya's body vanished."

"And you know how good Donovanian life is at camouflage, right? This thing is different. And it's smart. Bems, skewers, they freeze in place. This thing moves. Like it knows when we're looking for it."

Big as it was supposed to be? Muldare's shots should have hit it somewhere.

"Buy you supper?" he asked as they came even with Inga's.

"Sure." She said it without thinking, only to be shocked when she realized how comfortable she felt with him.

He caught the look she was giving him as he held the door. "What?"

"Who the hell are you?"

Quick as he was, he caught her meaning and bit off a laugh. "Not really sure these days, but I'm working on it. Make you a deal?"

"Yeah?"

"If I ever find out, I'll let you know."

She took the lead, heels rapping as she led the way down the stairs. Passing tables, she called out greetings to people, answered their waves, surprised that Dek got his share of smiles and hellos.

She perched herself on her usual high stool, Dek climbing up beside her.

"Amber ale and a whiskey?" Inga asked, striding toward them.

"And a supper special," Dek called, "Plus whatever Kalico wants."

"Chili," Kalico called.

"You buying?" Inga asked.

Dek tossed a ten-SDR onto the bar. "Keep the change."

After Inga flipped her towel up over her shoulder and bellowed, "Special and a bowl of chili" at the top of her lungs, she lumbered back toward her taps.

"Keep the change? What are you doing for a living?"

"Hunting. A little prospecting. Spending time with Kylee, Tip, and Flute in the bush when they'll let me. It's the airplane that makes the difference. Locked away in its crate in cargo, I couldn't trade it off back when I thought we were all going to die. Don't know what I'm going to do with the exercise equipment and the entertainment center. I'd set up a theatre, but stupid me, I can't access Corp-net for content."

"What could you have been thinking?"

"That Donovan would be a cruder sort of Solar System. The kind of place where a cruder sort of man could be top dog. I'll never be that naïve again. Which is why I'm so taken with the bush."

"It's a miracle that you're still alive, you know."

"Nothing is as sobering as being human on Donovan. But I'm learning. I suppose in the end the odds will get me."

"Talbot said the same thing," she said softly. "And they did."

Dek took his beer as Inga set the drinks on the battered chabacho bar. He clinked it to the rim of Kalico's glass. "To Mark Talbot. And living every day as if it's the last."

"What the hell were you thinking, getting Dan Wirth a berth on *Ashanti*?"

"He wanted to go back. I gave him the chance."

"Why?"

"He was getting bored, Supervisor. The man is no one's fool. He'd risen as high as he can rise on Donovan. He knows better than to fiddle with PA or Corporate Mine because the minutia of everyday operations would drive him to insanity. He was the king of his heap. But what's the point of being the richest man in the universe if he's stuck on Donovan where no one cares?"

She felt that old wariness begin to stir down inside. "And what's your angle?"

"Completely mercenary. I like it here. As we just determined, given my penchant for the bush, I'm a short-timer before a bem, a skewer, a flock of mobbers, a quetzal, or some other weirdness gets me. But when I come to town, I want to spend time with Shig, you, Talina, and enjoy the place. If PA is to have any long-term prospects, Wirth had to go."

"What made you think he'd screw it up?"

"Bored? Frustrated? Eventually he'd have gone sideways at the worst possible moment. Someone would have pissed him off on the wrong day. It would wound my soul if, in a fit of pique, he'd have killed Shig." He fixed his yellow-green eyes on hers. "Or you."

"Thought you didn't like me."

"People change. I did." He gave her a noncommitted shrug. "So the best way to avoid Wirth's kind of trouble was to get him off the planet. He's a sick fart sucker, and he thinks he can play the big game in Corporate politics. Maybe he can. I give him a ten-percent chance of living out his first year."

"How do you figure that?"

"Because I just shipped two entire safes full of his plunder off to Transluna under a Taglioni seal. Of course, I get my share. Miko and the family get theirs. Makes us the richest family in Solar System. And Dan still has tens of billions of SDRs to play with. He's out of contract. Makes him a pain in the ass for the Board, but they'll deal."

"Or have him suffer some unforeseen accident." She saw the brilliance of it. "Should have thought of that myself. There's no way they can hush up that kind of wealth. The story will get out that a petty criminal, out of contract, returned from Donovan as the wealthiest man in Solar System. That's going to shake the Board to its roots. If a scum like Wirth can accomplish what he has, what could a talented, educated, capable, and well-backed individual achieve?"

He was smiling, something smug about it.

"Ah!" Kalico smacked the bar. "Well played. Miko will be wondering exactly that about you. Derek Taglioni, with all the family advantages, is loose and ungoverned on Donovan. Given the way Miko's going to twist and fret about what you're doing out here, he won't get a good night's sleep until he can send a ship and find out."

"Hey, Miko can sleep in peace. Me? I'm just a local hunter and prospector."

For a moment, perplexed, she studied him. "For a newcomer, your acumen amazes me."

Dek shrugged, sipped his beer. "Like I said. I like it here. I don't want it ruined."

"And how do I fit into your calculus?"

"You're right where you need to be. You don't know it yet, but you've found your place, and it's found you."

"I still want to be Chairman of the Board."

The corners of his lips twitched in amusement. "Who wouldn't? At least for a week or two. Unfortunately, once Donovan sank its claws into you"—he ran a finger along the scar on the back of her hand—"the woman who would have been Chairman was forever altered into something greater."

She shivered, surprised by the daring of his touch. "Greater?"

"As Chairman you'd be a master when it came to the intrigue; you'd revel in the accolades. But your heart would remain unfulfilled, your triumphs oddly vacuous. Each victory somehow hollow and bland in aftertaste."

She shifted uncomfortably, took a swig of Inga's whiskey. Savored it. "Who the hell do you think you are? Shig?"

"I'll never be that insightful, but he'd agree."

"Okay, guru, where the hell is my perfect destiny?"

"Right here. Living. Totally and unabashedly. Not only does Donovan need you, but you're complete as a human being. Vibrant. If you ever gave it up to go back to Transluna, it would rip a hole in your soul."

"You a psychotherapist now?"

He smiled as the food was set before them. "I cheat. I come from your world. It's an unfair advantage."

"I cheat, too. You're a Taglioni. Leopards don't change their spots." She took a spoonful of chili.

"The fact that you let me buy you supper is a start."

"Let alone that you saved my life . . . how many times?"

"Only a toilet-sucking boor would bring that up in a craven attempt to curry favor. I have other qualities." He pulled out another ten-SDR coin. "I'm turning into a pretty good hunter as well. Look! Earned by my skill and hard labor."

"Miko'd scoff."

"That pus bucket can fuck a skewer."

"Excuse me?"

"Sorry. Too much time around Kylee." A twinkle filled his eye. "I have to fly back out to Briggs' tomorrow. Got a job to do. Well, assuming the cannibals at Tyson don't eat us. Have supper with me when I get back? My treat?"

"Why should I make a habit of this?"

"Hey, I'm not just any soft meat. When I go hunting it's with a quetzal and two teenagers."

Kalico threw her head back and laughed in a way she hadn't in years. Dek Taglioni? Well, hell, who knew?

88

The forest had taken on an ominous feel. In the dim quarter-light of the forest floor, the air pressed on a person, hot, almost syrup-thick. Kylee swallowed hard. Experienced that prickle of anxiety running through her muscles as she climbed up onto the root tangle. Perched on high, she balanced. With her quetzal-enhanced vision, she searched the high canopy. Up there, in the tracery of branches. She could sense it: the old, dark memory.

If she closed her eyes, she could feel a cold and hollow hunger. Something ancient. A sentience so alien it tickled her soul with feathers of terror.

Didn't count that it was a matter of honor, that she owed this to Mom and Mark. Fact was, she'd rather be back at Briggs' with Tip and Flute. Safe. Not here in the dim forest, knowing that she was being hunted.

Flute had been willing, would have endured another flight, taken a chance at being killed. That he knew the risks, would have done it for her, said something about quetzals.

Maybe, because she'd said no when every fiber of her being wanted him here with her, it said something about her, too.

The chime rose and fell, ending in its uniquely atonal harmony. She was learning. Each region of Donovan where she'd traveled had its own unique chime, always a composite of the different species. The Tyson chime was as much a signature as Mundo's.

A faint rime of perspiration dampened her cheeks, her neck and chest. Warily, she shifted, following the slow twist of the root mass beneath her feet. Something called out in the heights, the sound low and warbling. Tree clinger? Hopper? Some unknown creature?

She tensed her muscles, flexed her legs as she shifted her balance in time to the root's movements. Her heart was thumping, driving adrenaline-charged blood through her veins.

"Hey!" she shouted. "Fucker! You up there! Come get me, you piece of shit!"

Kylee could imagine Talina's reaction. The woman always cringed when Kylee cursed. As if she'd forgotten just who taught her those choice words to start with. Madison would be horrified. But then, Madison was tens of kilometers away.

And this was personal.

Cupping her hands around her mouth, Kylee thundered, "Asshole!"

There, was that movement? A shift in the IR, a change of pattern? She'd have sworn the branches wavered for an instant. Not the sort of thing a quetzal would notice, but human eyes, trained by eons of terrestrial evolution caught the wavering shift of image.

"There you are!" She pointed. "Right there. Ha! I see you! Got your ass now."

Even vigilant as she was, she almost missed it. Was looking at the body. Not down below. Not where the spike appeared out of nothingness, curling toward her with ferocious speed.

Fast as she was, the thing missed her by a bare finger's width as it ripped past. She barely caught herself, dropping to one hand to keep from losing her balance on the high root. Shot a look to follow the ropy black barb as it was pulled up high again.

"Got it?" Kylee called.

"Got it!" Talina's head popped up on the other side of a clump of roots no more than thirty meters away. She braced her rifle on the top, sighted, and released a cracking volley as she emptied a magazine.

Staring up, Kylee watched the IR shift as the rounds hit home, drove deep, and exploded.

The creature sucked up its wounded part, rolling it up inside a fold of hide. How damn big was that thing? Those rounds would have torn a quetzal in two.

Kylee tensed as the black tip of the tentacle came whipping down again. Instinctively, she dropped down in front of the top root. Timed it and skipped sideways.

The impact as the sharp spear drove into the barrel-thick root toppled her from her hold. She fell, bounced off a root, and threw herself backward onto the mat below.

The whole mass went crazy as quetzal shit. She scrambled backward in a crab walk, watching the massive root, impaled as it was. The tentacle kept tugging, trying to break free. Would have, but the root, like a giant rolling drum, twisted around itself. Acting like a capstan it wound the impaled tentacle tight, trapping it.

From overhead, a deafening shriek sounded.

Even as the roots under Kylee's hands and feet erupted in movement, a thrashing began shaking the branches above. The sound of snapping, the rattle of leaves, a whipping back and forth as branches cracked overwhelmed the chime.

Careening for balance, Kylee found her feet. Arms extended, she scampered across the now-writhing mess, barely avoided being trapped as she fled over a bundle of interwoven roots.

Over the tumult, she heard Talina's voice shouting into com: "Dek? Where are you?"

Kylee raced across an open space, vaulted another bundle of roots, and barely skipped out of the way as a sidewinder whipped out from a hollow.

Heart hammering, she beat feet for the next tangle—and somehow got across before they convulsed with the intensity of God pulling the Gordian knot tight.

Panting, she located Talina, saw the woman backpedaling, struggling for balance on the squirming footing as she kept her eyes skyward.

Kylee chanced a glance. Followed the trapped tentacle up to where the great beast clung among the whipping branches. How big? Maybe fifty meters across the body. The legs weren't legs but elongated tissue that ended in prehensile tentacles that wrapped around the high branches. Even in its extreme, the creature tried to mimic its surroundings, but the patterns were off, almost random, like a riot of alternating shapes.

"Dek?" Talina screamed.

Even as she did, the sound of the airplane was faintly audible over the creature's ear-splitting screams and the thrashing forest.

Kylee bit her lip, fought for balance, then turned and ran again as the roots began to roil.

"Run!" she shouted at Talina. Saw her friend turn, bolting across the traumatized roots. Together they scrambled across a high tangle of trunk-thick roots.

"Come on, Dek!" Talina said between ragged pants. "Where the hell are you?"

"He'll . . ." Over her shoulder, Kylee caught a glimpse of the tentacle thinning under the tremendous strain. It broke. The meaty parting of tissue and tendon like a clap of thunder. With the power of severed elastic, the trapped length snapped down onto the bundled roots. Above, the remaining stump shot up into the creature's body, its path marked by spewing fluids.

Then movement. Something big. Indistinct and incredibly fast. Accompanied by crashing and tearing, branches were being whipped back only to lash angrily forward. The entire canopy seemed to erupt.

"What the hell?"

"Kylee!" Talina screamed. "Duck!"

The detonation blasted downward as the branches where the beast had been were torn asunder. In the deafening explosion's roar came a clutter of broken branches, shredded leaves, and cascading detritus.

"Fucking run!" Talina shouted. And turning, she sprinted, leaping roots, pounding her way up tangles.

Kylee was right with her, matching her step for step.

"That's for Mom and Dad, you piece of shit," Kylee averred, and then she put all of her efforts toward speed as agitation spread through the roots like a tsunami racing toward a distant shore.

A last thought was: *This whole thing might have been a mistake.*

Any second now, the roots were going to be too wild, the footing too precarious. All it would take was a single misstep . . .

89

Dek yanked back on the stick, worked the rudder, and pulled a couple of gs as he rolled back over the forest. He'd dropped the charge perfectly. Had taken the time to ensure it was right on the money.

He could see the exact spot the magtex had detonated and torn a hole in the canopy. Trees were shredded, leaves torn, the forest reacting like a stone had been dropped into a pond. The agitation spread out in a giant ring. A meteor impact into an ocean would look that way.

"Talina?" he called. "Did we get it?"

No answer.

Instead, he checked the instruments. Should have been organic material blasted all over the place. Chunks of torn tissue, given the mass they'd calculated for the creature. His readings showed some animal tissue, lots of tree organics, of course.

"But not enough creature guts and goo," he murmured as he banked around for another look.

It was the angle of the light. He saw it. Like a V just ahead of the expanding tsunami of tree agitation.

He straightened, settled the airplane's nose on the point of the vee, and dropped down. His remote sensors made the tag. Got the same readings as when he'd flown the survey that originally pinpointed the creature's location. The difference this time was a lot of heat. Something big, moving fast.

But what the hell?

How could something that big travel that fast? And yes, he was getting a trail of animal proteins. The monster was wounded. Bleeding. Leaking. Whatever.

He dropped his airspeed to just above stall speed to try and keep pace. Couldn't. Had to circle.

"Dek?"

"Tal? You all right?"

"Fucking crazy down here." She sounded out of breath. *"Remind us not to be on the ground underneath one of these things next time we bomb it."*

"Yeah, well, I've got some bad news for you."

"How's that?"

"It got away. It's wounded, headed almost due west through the treetops. And Tal? It's moving along at about thirty kph."

Silence.

Finally, Talina's voice, almost sounding defeated, replied, *"Shit! What the hell is this thing?"*

"I don't know. I've got the recordings, but Talina? My take? That thing knew the second I dropped that charge. Like it knew exactly when to cut its loses and run."

Silence.

Then, "*I just told Kylee. Is it still moving?"*

"Affirmative. Doesn't seem to be slowing in the slightest. Just headed west like it's on a mission. And moving in a hell of a hurry."

"*Roger that. Maybe* Vixen *can pick it up on the long-range sensors. How's your fuel?"*

"About sixty percent in the powerpack."

"Yeah. We've done all we can here. See you back in PA."

Dek ground his teeth, glared down at where the agitation in the trees marked the creature's path. "What the hell are you?"

And more to the point, where was it going?

And how could it have known it was being bombed from above?

EPILOGUE

Inga's tavern was running on full throttle that night. And regular as clockwork, it was Hofer who'd been too deep in his cups. While he'd give you the shirt off his back when he was sober, the guy had a tendency to let his mouth overload his ass when he was drunk.

Now it was some poor ship's tech who was catching it; out of contract on *Ashanti,* he'd stayed behind to try his luck.

"Hey!" Talina bellowed. She pulled her pistol, banged it on the chabacho-wood bar. "You stop that shit, Hofer, or I'm gonna smack your head into next week! Now, beat feet. Take your sorry chapped ass home and put it in bed! I see you out again tonight, and *maybe* Raya will be able to put the pieces back together!"

Inga's went quiet as a tomb. People staring.

Three tables away, Hofer, almost reeling on his feet, craned his head in Talina's direction. The man's eyes—glittering with drink—widened in an owlish manner. He swallowed hard. With careful fingers, he let loose of the Skull he'd jerked off the bench and was about to punch in the face.

"Yeah, yeah," he muttered. Paused to straighten the Skull's rumpled uniform shirt, and on unsteady feet, wobbled his way toward the door.

"You!" Talina barked, pointing with the pistol. "Soft meat, you're no better. Get your candy ass out of here, or you'll be carried. Got it?"

The Skull, maybe in his midthirties, gulped. Not knowing what else to do, he snapped off a salute and slurred, "Yes, ma'am."

Then he, too, started for the exit on unsteady feet. Made it only to the foot of the stairs, bent, and heaved his guts all over the stone floor. Groans and catcalls went up from around the room.

Fitzroy and one of the Hmongs grabbed him by the armpits, hustling him up the stairs.

Talina reholstered her pistol and turned back to her glass of stout. The poor sod would probably find himself atop the nearest shipping crate come morning. No one just pitched a drunk onto the ground. Not in PA. Too much chance of a slug, you know.

Talina sighed, rubbed her forehead.

She'd seen Kalico down the bar talking to Pamlico Jones. Probably something about the *Ashanti* cargo. It hadn't turned out to be the mother lode everyone had hoped for. But for some lights, the six airtrucks, a couple pieces of ludicrous farm equipment, and the cacao seeds, most of the inventory turned out to be in support of the Maritime Unit.

Boats, underwater vehicles, diving pods, and the like were all good and well for Michaela's team out in the ocean where they'd dropped their main pod. Not so good for PA and Corporate Mine.

"Hear you missed the beast that got Talbot and Dya." Kalico appeared at Talina's elbow and hitched herself up on her stool, a half-glass of whiskey already in hand.

"Dek and I went over the video. It *knew*. No doubt about it. The thing snapped its trapped tentacle off and fled the moment Dek dropped his charge. Oh, and there's this. Memo to Supervisor: Do *not* be standing below when you try to blow arboreal monsters out of the trees in deep forest."

"A little hairy?"

"That's the closest I've been to dead in a while. Kylee and I made it. Barely. That entire forest went apeshit. As fast as we were hauling ass, we'd have been dead a couple of times over if the tooth flowers, sidewinders, and gotcha vines hadn't been hanging on for dear life." Talina grunted. "How stupid can we be? And this far into the game?"

Kalico shook her head. "I keep seeing that huge black *thing*. How it stuck through their bodies. Jerked them like eiderdown into the air."

"Yeah, well it's still out there to creep-freak your dreams. *Vixen* wasn't in position to track it. Kylee's pissed."

"Knowing something's out there is half the battle."

Talina toyed with her stout glass. "Heard that *Ashanti* inverted symmetry today. Think they'll make it?"

"Don't know. But with each ship, the odds get better. Dek sent Wirth back as bait. If *Ashanti* pops back in Solar System's space, it will be the richest treasure ship in all of human history. But it's Wirth's plunder that will focus the Board. Donovan will be the center of their every thought and ambition."

Talina raised her glass. "To the lily-assed Board. Maybe they can send us chickens again. I miss eggs, and I think we're smart enough to keep the hens from eating the invertebrates this time around."

"How were the cannibals doing?"

"Passable. At least they didn't interfere with the monster hunt. I think they're starting to realize just what a rough row they have to hoe out there. That woman, Shyanne, I think we can deal with her."

Kalico fingered the scar that ran down her jaw. "It's a new calculus. We've got two new settlements. Michaela Hailwood wants me to see the Maritime Unit as soon as she gets it fully functional. Talking with her, I get the feeling that some of her people are already getting antsy. Like Corporate Mine, I'm going to have to set up a rotation for them."

"Sure." Talina smiled grimly. "Hey, with the cannibals, the Maritime Unit, and the *Ashanti* crew who stayed, we're back to a thousand people. Not to mention a real living Taglioni."

"Dek come back with you?"

"Nope. He stayed out at Briggs' claim. I guess Chaco showed him a real promising vein in the next canyon. Dek said he wanted to get some ore samples for assay."

"Oh."

Talina arched a brow. "Heard you and he went for a long walk the other night."

"I don't know what to do with him." Kalico gave her an evaluative look. "What he did with Wirth? He's thinking five moves ahead. And don't for a minute buy this humble I-wanna-be-a-Wild-One shit. He's a Taglioni. He can't help himself. That's still hidden down there inside him somewhere."

"Maybe. My take? He belongs to Donovan now. Like the Unreconciled, he's never going back."

"How so?"

"He and Flute have exchanged blood."

"He tell you that?"

"Didn't have to. I saw the wound. And I know it was voluntary. Which leaves you with a question for yourself: You ever going back?"

Kalico's gaze went blank, staring into some infinity in her mind. "Dek tells me I can't."

"And?"

"Scares me right down to my bones."

"Welcome to Donovan."

TO MY FATHER

JAMES J. MAPES

THIS BOOK

IS DEDICATED IN GRATITUDE

AND LOVE

Printed in the United States of America by Kingsport Press, Inc., Kingsport, Tenn.

HANS BRINKER

OR

The Silver Skates

A STORY OF LIFE IN HOLLAND

by

MARY MAPES DODGE

Illustrated by

CYRUS LEROY BALDRIDGE

Illustrated Junior Library

GROSSET & DUNLAP · PUBLISHERS

NEW YORK

13

Flight and Rescue: BRICHAH

CONTEMPORARY JEWISH
CIVILIZATION SERIES
In cooperation with
Institute of Contemporary Jewry,
Hebrew University of Jerusalem

MOSHE DAVIS, *Editor*

Flight and Rescue: BRICHAH

Yehuda Bauer

RANDOM HOUSE · *New York*

FIRST EDITION

9 8 7 6 5 4 3 2

Published in the United States by Random House, Inc., New York,
and simultaneously in Canada
by Random House of Canada Limited, Toronto.

Library of Congress Catalog Card Number: 74-85602

Manufactured in the United States of America
by The Haddon Craftsmen, Inc.,
Scranton, Pennsylvania

Typography and binding design
by Mary M. Ahern

To the memory of my friend

MULAH AGIN,

who fell at Gaza,

June 1967

PREFACE

Between 1944 and 1948, after their liberation from the Nazis, some 250,000 Jews fled from Eastern Europe to the countries of Central Europe—Germany, Austria and Italy. Their goal, generally speaking, was Palestine. This mass movement was usually effected by illegal or half-legal ways, and it included not only men but encumbered families with children and old people. The outcome of these wanderings was necessarily uncertain, for at the time Palestine was not open to these refugees, nor did any other country open its gates to accept them. This uncertainty and the fact that the move took place after the war, and not during any period of armed struggle, from countries that professed their desire to see the Jews stay and participate in their national recovery, make the move a highly unusual phenomenon. It was probably the largest illegal move of its kind during the past few decades, and it was known by the Hebrew name *Brichah* (literally, "flight"), which referred to two distinct things: one was the mass move itself, and the other the name of the organization that was behind most, but by no means all, of this migratory movement. The fact that both the unorganized migration and the underground organization were known by the same name caused some confusion, which of course was helpful to the men who led the organized move because it tended to increase the security gained from vagueness of information as to their existence.

The antecedents of Brichah in both senses used here lay in the tragedy that befell the Jewish people in the thirties and forties of the present century. During the early years of Nazi Germany, Jews crossed borders illegally into Belgium, Holland, France and Luxembourg. In 1938, when the Germans expelled large numbers of Polish Jews from Germany, many others tried to cross into Poland illegally because the anti-Semitic government of Poland would not let them enter the country openly, although they had been Polish citizens. German Jews driven into no man's lands on the Czech borders, Polish Jews driven by the Poles out of border territories annexed from Czechoslovakia in 1938, Slovak and Hungarian Jews expelled by their respective countries into

Hungary or Slovakia and refused entrance there—in many of these and similar cases Jews were forced to try to save themselves by illegal entry into one or the other of the countries concerned. When war broke out, Jews fled in large numbers from German zones of occupation in Poland to Soviet zones, and from Poland to Lithuania, which remained neutral and independent until annexed by the Soviet Union in 1940. While most of this migration was unorganized and individual, there were also recognizable nuclei of organized groups, usually of Zionist youth movements or, in some cases, of political parties. In 1942, another movement of Jews took place from Slovakia to the relative safety of Hungary, and in 1944, when Hungary was occupied by the Germans, the move was in the opposite direction—back into Slovakia. Similar escape routes existed in the west, where Jews threatened by Nazi deportations tried to escape into Switzerland or Spain. The element of organization became more and more evident as time went on; the Zionist youth movements were primarily responsible for this development. Often these wartime escapes were organized as part of an overall program of resistance which included armed action, hiding of people—mainly children—and various types of unarmed resistance.

These precursors of the postwar migrations merit attention in their own right. There is a qualitative difference between all of them and Brichah. They took place in different parts of Europe without relation to each other, with no overall political design motivating them. Moreover, they were—by and large—motivated by the elementary desire to escape death at the hands of the Germans. Brichah was also partly motivated by anti-Semitism; but when all is said and done, there was a world of difference between even the worst kind of postwar anti-Semitism and the war of extermination waged against the Jews by the Germans. The motivations of Brichah were based on the question of how to live, because the overwhelming will to live was there. We shall try to show the way in which the Jews in the postwar world tried to escape not from death to life, but from unsatisfactory or even dangerous conditions to what was hoped would be a better future. It is in this sense that the postwar migrations present an altogether different picture.

A word is in order about the sources used in this study of an illegal movement. The Brichah material in the Haganah archives in Tel Aviv was used extensively, and thanks are due for permission to do so to Lieutenant Colonel Gershon Rivlin and Dr. Yehuda Slutzky. This was supplemented by the private materials of Mr. Ephraim Dekel, one of the European commanders of the Brichah. Dr. Alexander Bein and Dr. Michael Hyman made possible the use of the files in Central Zionist Archives in Jerusalem. No less important was the material found in the archives of the American Jewish Joint Distribution Committee (JDC) in New York, to which access was given by the late Moses A. Leavitt. A large part of the documentation comes from the files of YIVO (Jewish Scientific Institute) in New York, where work was facilitated through the friendliness of Dr. Jacob Robinson and Mr. Eliezer Lifshitz. The vast Yad Va'Shem archives in Jerusalem also contained some Brichah materials, and the Joint Research Institute of Yad Va'Shem and the Hebrew University provided me with a scholarship and a travel grant which made possible the early stages of the research. For this I must thank Professor Israel Halperin, who suggested the Brichah as a theme worthy of research; Dr. Jacob Robinson, scientific adviser to the institute; and the late Dr. Shaul Esh. The Moreshet archives at Givat Haviva were another important source. Major sources for this book were oral testimonies, some of which were collected by the Haganah and Moreshet archives, but most of which were collected by myself and, under my supervision, by Mr. Yosef Heller and Mr. Aharon Kedar, and which are deposited with the Oral History Division of the Institute of Contemporary Jewry. Without the help especially of Mr. Kedar this book would never have been written. Thanks are also due to Rabbi Abraham J. Klausner, who put his private papers at my disposal, Rabbi Eugene J. Lipman, Rabbi Herbert Friedman, Rabbi Judah Nadich, Rabbi Philip S. Bernstein and many others who gave me diaries and important documents or copies of them that were in their possession.

Throughout the work done on this book, Professor Moshe Davis, head of the Institute of Contemporary Jewry at the Hebrew University in Jerusalem, helped in word and deed. As editor of the series in which this book appears, and in his

personal capacity as friend and colleague, he has my sincere thanks.

Finally, any book written by a member of an Israeli kibbutz is always something of a collective effort. For years the membership of my kibbutz has suffered my lectures on Brichah and shared every new discovery; their support and intelligent criticism enabled me to avoid, hopefully, at least some of the pitfalls inherent in a description of a mass movement. Their friendly and intense interest in what I was doing was a reward in itself.

Y. B.
Kibbutz Shoval, Israel

CONTENTS

Flight and Rescue: B R I C H A H

1. The Beginnings

By the autumn of 1944, after the defeat of the Polish rebellion at Warsaw, the Red Army stood on the Vistula, having liberated Lithuania, White Russia, the western Ukraine and parts of eastern Poland since the beginning of that year. In this whole area, once densely populated by Jews, only a few now remained. They were mostly Jewish partisans, or family groups of noncombatants who had hidden in the forests, or Jews who had been hiding in the villages by denying their Jewish identity, and children, mostly orphans, who had been kept alive by peasant families. The reason for hiding children might have been either simple humanity or the hope of a reward in the Hereafter if a Jewish child was converted, or material reward. Often it was a combination of all three.[1]

Among the first towns liberated in that part of the Ukraine that had been Polish prior to 1939 was Rovno. There, in early February 1944, several thousands of partisans joined the regular Red Army to conquer the town. Among them were some 300 to 400 Jews, about 250 of whom are said to have remained in the town after liberation.

The first weeks of liberation were a period of shock and despair in the face of desolation and ruins of what had once been a large Jewish community. There were instances of drunkenness and licentiousness, and the survivors asked

themselves—Why did we remain alive? What was the point of living at all, and what was the sense in any attempt at re-creating an individual and communal life in such a place?

It seems that this first period of demoralization had to come and go before any attempt could be made to face the new conditions. Ultimately, probably some weeks after liberation, a change came. One of the partisans was a man by the name of Eliezer Lidovsky.[2] He had been a member of the left-wing Zionist youth movement *Dror (Freiheit)* before the war, but had had no contact with his former friends during the partisan period. His closest associates were his brother Abraham and a former member of the Communist youth group, "Pasha" (Yitzhak) Rajchmann, who had changed his outlook during the war. The area was under Soviet rule, and any movement out of the area or the country was illegal and considered an act of treason. Any organization that was not sponsored by the party or government was either suspicious or illegal as well, and, of course, Zionism or anything related to it had been specifically outlawed in the Soviet Union since the late twenties. In these circumstances the only legal form of organization for a Jewish group with any social or political tendencies was a religious community. The group that slowly came into being through the leadership of the Lidovsky brothers and Rajchmann was not in any sense religious; but a young rabbi was brought from among the survivors of the nearby community of Dubna and under his name a religious community was established that could serve as a cover for other activities.

Eliezer Lidovsky and his friends did not take long to arrive at the conclusion that life for Jews in that area had become a practical and psychological impossibility. The Nazi occupation had left behind it a heritage of anti-Semitism; Ukrainian nationalist bands under the leadership of one Bandera were attacking Soviet officials and Jews. Because it was difficult to reestablish life on the ruins of Rovno Jewry, they concluded that they should seek to escape somehow. A meeting took place at the home of a local doctor, and seven out of the nine people present agreed with E. Lidovsky. As a result, a cooperative of fourteen members was

officially registered, ostensibly to form an artisan guild for future artisan production—another device to secure some legal basis for operations. The cooperative obtained a house which became a center for the reception and care of refugees returning from hideouts and villages, and more especially, some 300 orphans who had been hidden in the surrounding area with peasants. The synagogue became the property of the newly established religious community, and another haven and soup kitchen were established there. All this was arranged and made possible by ex-partisans, Lidovsky's friends, who were now running the town administration. The group became more numerous, and at its core were twelve people who, in secret and in a somewhat theatrical manner, swore allegiance to the idea of going to Palestine with as many other Jews as feasible.

In May, permission was obtained for 350 Jews, among them officers and men of the Red Army, to go outside the town and rearrange decently the mass graves of Rovno's 20,000 murdered Jews. A memorial meeting was held at the end of the day, and Lidovsky—according to his account—spoke of the need to leave these graves and find a new place to live in; the hint, it seems, was well taken.

In the summer, a group of five partisans was sent from Rovno to look for a suitable border-crossing between Cernauti (Czernowitz) and Rumania. This was a logical action: Rumania was the nearest foreign country geographically, and transportation to the frontier was relatively easy, if one discounted slow trains, breakdowns, overcrowding, frequent secret-police checks and, mainly, Bandera's nationalist Ukrainian bands who would occasionally stop trains and seek out Jews in order to kill them. Rumania had been an ally of Hitler Germany until 1944, when, on August 23, the young king, Michael, reading the writing on the wall, suddenly switched sides and proclaimed himself an ally of Russia and the West. Prior to that, in order to instigate sabotage activity among the Jews against the Germans and their allies and to try to rescue Allied fliers shot down over Rumania, a group of Palestinian Jewish parachutists were sent in by the British. After the change in the Rumanian attitude, they

were joined, in September and October of 1944, by two Palestinian "journalists," who were actually emissaries of bodies in Palestine dealing with Zionist political propaganda and immigration, legal and illegal. One of them, Moshe Agami, now became the head of the Palestine emissaries.

Agami was a member of Kibbutz Kfar Gileadi on the Lebanese border with Palestine where he had had a great deal of experience in smuggling in Jewish immigrants. A very energetic man with considerable organizational ability and a flair for undercover work, Agami was the nearest Palestinian representative to the liberated parts of the Ukraine. Lidovsky and his friends had heard of Palestinian emissaries, or *shlihim* (plural of *shaliah,* "emissary") in Bucharest (though Agami's name was not then known to them). They therefore decided to try to reach Rumania.

The five partisans from Rovno reached Cernauti and became workers on the only railway that connected Rumania with the Soviet Union. A group of Zionist youth movement members who had survived was organized to help them. Zionist youth movements had a long history, dating to the twenties or even further back. They differed in their political outlook, but they had in common the desire to educate their charges for a future life in Palestine and, for most of them, on a kibbutz. Apart from the right-wing Betar,* which served as a recruiting ground for Palestine's anti-British Irgun† group, and the liberal or center Noar Zioni, which tended to identify itself with the line of Dr. Weizmann, the moderate leader of the Zionist movement, all the movements were left of center. The Hashomer Hatzair and Dror

---

* Betar is the Hebrew abbreviation for Trumpeldor League, named after a Jewish national hero who fell in the defense of a Palestine settlement in 1920. Betar is also the name of an ancient Jewish town near Jerusalem, center of the Bar Kochba rebellion against the Romans in the second century C.E.

† Irgun Zvai Leumi (National Military Organization), an anti-British militant minority group, was active from 1944 to 1948, and was responsible for a large number of attacks on British targets in Palestine.

BALTIC SEA
LITHUANIA
U.
Kovno
Vilna
Lida
Minsk
Grodno
BYELORUSSIA
Baranovichi
S.
Warsaw
Luninets
POLAND
Lublin
Rovno
S.
Dubno
Przemysl
Lwow
CZECHO -
SLOVAKIA
UKRAINE
Cernauti
HUNGARY
R.
RUMANIA
International boundaries
Soviet republican boundaries
Dr. Amarant's journey
0
MILES
100
Bucharest
BLACK SEA

movements* were left-wing socialist and strongly identified with the Palestinian left-wing kibbutz movements. Gordonia† was a more moderate socialist group, also with strong kibbutz affiliations in Palestine. Even the religious youth movement, B'nai Akiva,‡ was left-oriented and sent its youngsters to the religious kibbutzim in Palestine. All these youth movements had become very powerful in the last prewar years in Eastern Europe and had played a central part in Jewish resistance during the Nazi period. It was therefore only natural that the Rovno partisans should seek out survivors from among these groups to help them in their quest for a way out of the Soviet Union. In Cernauti it was mainly the membership of Noar Zioni and Hashomer Hatzair groups that provided such help, and with their enthusiastic assistance small-scale migrations began trickling into Rumania.

During the summer, Eliezer Lidovsky attempted to collect money from Moscow Jews for his relief work in Rovno. He met with members of the Jewish Antifascist Committee, which had been set up by the Soviet government to gather support from world Jewry for the Soviet war effort against the Nazis. Members of the committee, such as the great actor Shlomo Michoels and the writer Itzik Feffer, saw him, but they seemed to Lidovsky to have been well aware of their precarious position in the latently anti-Semitic milieu of the Stalin dictatorship (both of them were later killed in Stalin's anti-Jewish purge), and they could not help. However, the Moscow synagogue had at its disposal large sums

---

* Hashomer Hatzair (Young Guardian), the oldest of the youth movements, founded in 1913; a pro-Soviet but non-Communist group favoring a peaceful arrangement with the Arabs in Palestine. Together with Dror (Freedom, or, in Yiddish, *Freiheit*), it represented the majority of Palestine's kibbutz movement. Between them, the two organizations accounted for a large proportion of resistance movements against the Nazis.

† Named after A. D. Gordon, Tolstoyan philosopher and one of the founding fathers of the kibbutz movement.

‡ B'nai Akiva means children of Akiva. Named after Rabbi Akiva ben Joseph (c. 40 C.E.–135), an illustrious rabbinic sage.

of money which had been given to it by Jews so that relief could be granted in deserving cases; unfortunately the treasurer in charge refused Lidovsky's plea, probably because of fear of the authorities, and donated the money to the Red Army instead. Lidovsky returned to Rovno with empty hands, but he was determined to carry on, despite the tremendous obstacles.

In the meantime, on July 13, Vilna (Vilnius), the capital of Lithuania since 1940, was liberated. In the Rudniki forests, some distance from Vilna, a partisan detachment of former ghetto rebels had fought as part of the Lithuanian partisan forces. Originally, there had been a Jewish brigade under the command of Abba Kovner, the last commander of the Vilna ghetto rebellion. Kovner was twenty-three years old at the time of liberation. Scion of a family of Talmudic scholars, he had had a Yiddish and Hebrew education, in addition to his knowledge of Lithuanian culture and language. He was a member of the executive committee of Hashomer Hatzair in Poland and Lithuania, and by the time war broke out had already made a name for himself as a poet in both Hebrew and Yiddish. A small, wiry man with a gaunt face and a long, sharp nose, long and curly black hair and deep-brown eyes, he was the prototype of a Jewish intellectual. The first call to Jewish rebellion had issued from Kovner's fiery pen, in December 1941; it was his call, transmitted to Warsaw, which brought about the first stirrings leading ultimately to the great Warsaw ghetto rebellion and to others that followed. A wonderful orator and a man of culture and taste, his imagination tended sometimes to lead him into tremendous schemes that turned out to be unrealistic. In the forest, his proud assertion of Jewish identity among the partisans soon led to a clash with Soviet authority which, as time went on, tightened its control over the guerrillas. The Soviets were as opposed to the existence of nationally oriented Jewish fighting units as—peculiarly enough—the British were, at the same time, in Palestine. They apparently wanted to belittle as much as possible the contribution of the Jews in the so-called Lithuanian units (the Lithuanian people were, on the whole, collaborating with the Germans, and the partisans consisted mainly of Russian soldiers who

had escaped from POW camps, Soviet parachutists and Jews, with only a very few Lithuanians). Kovner's detachment was split into several *otriads* (companies), and he remained the commander of one of them, called The Avenger. Despite Soviet policy, national cohesion was maintained in the various *otriads* that had made up the original Jewish fighting group.

Within a still smaller underground circle, Abba Kovner, and two girls—Vitka Kempner and Ruzhka Korczak—saw themselves as the secretariat of Hashomer Hatzair. Vitka had been the first person in Lithuania to blow up a German army train, near Vilna in 1942, and she was to become Kovner's wife after the war. Ruzhka, too, had been one of the subordinate commanders in the ghetto and a member of the directing committee. Now, on the eve of Vilna's liberation, apparently on July 3, the three met in the forest "as if [they] were an elected leadership of a large body and a heavy public responsibility rested upon [them]."[3] Kovner suggested an approach to the Red Army to raise a Jewish parachutist detachment to fight behind enemy lines on German territory. The two girls objected—such a unit would take the dozen or so men of the Hashomer Hatzair movement who had survived and lead them on to a suicide mission, leaving the girls, who were a majority among the survivors, behind and alone. They demanded that after liberation they should start to make their way to Palestine. Kovner agreed that Palestine was the goal, but he wished to postpone this until the end of the war. The "meeting" decided differently: ". . . one of our first moves would be to collect those who had survived, and against my vote we resolved to devote every effort to pave a way to Palestine as soon as possible. Secretly we transmitted the message by word of mouth that our people should, on the liberation of Vilna, see themselves as coming under our command."[4]

The decision applied not only to Hashomer Hatzair and its periphery but was soon extended also to other survivors of Zionist youth groups, including those from the Kovno ghetto who were stationed in a nearby forest and to whom Ruzhka brought the word.

There was something quite extraordinary in this decision

taken by three youngsters in a forest on the eve of their own liberation; it was presumptuous, self-confident and, on the whole, rather naïve, as though it were such a simple matter to take the Jews out of Soviet Lithuania—in 1944—to Palestine. It was not till much later that the importance of that determination and, indeed, audacity, became evident.

There was a difference between Rovno and Vilna, the two places where Brichah began. In Rovno, Eliezer Lidovsky had emerged as the leading personality after liberation, and without previous contacts or planning, had begun to organize a group whose aim it was to leave Russia for Palestine. In Vilna, the case was different. There had been youth movements, there had been a ghetto rebellion, a partisan fighting unit—the decision had come about, prior to liberation, as a logical outcome of years of youth movement work and was taken by a tightly knit youth group who had their own contacts among similar groups of survivors. However, after liberation, Vilna and Rovno went through much the same development. The Soviet authorities had prepared the administration for the liberated areas while the survivors were still in the forest. This was especially true of Lithuania, where in the last stages of the partisan war highly placed Lithuanian Communists appeared and chose people for responsible positions. For young Jews, even for those of known Zionist convictions, positions of power and authority beckoned. This was due to the fact that there simply were not enough Lithuanians sufficiently loyal to the U.S.S.R., and certainly a very small proportion of the local intelligentsia were pro-Soviet. Some Jews did accept these offers and stayed on afterward, but most of the youngsters accepted only temporary positions, tying themselves to the regime as little as possible. At first, of course, Jews were friendly to the regime and participated wholeheartedly in the irregular, and very forceful, activities of the Soviets to punish at least some of those who had lent wholehearted support to the Germans.[5]

It was during that first period of a honeymoon between the regime and the Jewish remnant that Kovner met a number of important Soviet personalities. He met, apart from writers such as Ilya Ehrenburg, an emissary from Malen-

kov's office, the party secretariat, and it became clear to him that after a short while concessions would begin to be made to local nationalism and the prospects for Jewish ex-partisans would probably dim considerably. Kovner also tried, despite the decision in the forest, to interest the Soviets in his parachutist scheme. But the answer, quite possibly given in all sincerity, was that Jews had suffered enough and that the remnants should not be further decimated, especially as action behind German lines in East Prussia would be more or less equivalent to suicide. Generally speaking, the attitude of the Soviet military—headed by Marshal Cherniakhovsky, himself probably Jewish—was friendly. This may at least partly explain the real friendship that developed between Kovner and Professor Rabielsky, a famous psychiatrist, who was serving with Cherniakhovsky's headquarters. Rabielsky was an old and faithful Bolshevik, but also a very warm-hearted Jew. To him Kovner revealed his plans for an exodus from Lithuania, collecting other Jews on the way. Rabielsky was shocked—Kovner should not endanger himself and his friends by a foolhardy adventure which could only lead to prison and suffering. It was unnecessary in any case—soon "we shall all travel officially via Odessa" because official Russian policy toward Zionism would change.[6] Kovner listened, but was not deterred.

Members of the widening Zionist circle were being released from the army and proceeded to occupy important positions in the administration. A Jewish orphanage was founded, with Rabielsky's help. So was a Jewish museum, where Kovner himself and the Yiddish poet Suzkover were trying to collect scattered remnants of the important materials that had been part of the Jewish Scientific Institute (YIVO) at Vilna. New materials were collected there, too, dating from the holocaust, and the hope was to get them out of Russia together with the people. In the meantime, the original group expanded considerably, and a coordinating committee (*koordinazia*) was established. This was in fact a re-creation of the old ghetto rebellion command without, of course, the Communists and the Bund, the large non-Zionist Jewish working-class group in Eastern Europe, who after the war tended to side with the Jewish Communists on

the issue of opposing the exodus of Jews to Palestine. The *koordinazia* was composed of members of the Noar Zioni liberal Zionists and the right-wing Betar, apart from Kovner's own Hashomer Hatzair group. From the towns of Kovno and Siauliai (Shavli) survivors came to Vilna; emissaries were sent to other towns in the area, such as Grodno and Bialystok, in preparation for a move.

News began to arrive of Jews from the Russian interior—people who had been deported by the Soviets before the German invasion to labor camps because of their Zionist or middle-class affiliations, soldiers in the Red Army who had heard of the existence of a Jewish community at Vilna and, mainly, Jews in Soviet Central Asia. Hundreds of thousands of Jewish refugees, both Polish and Soviet Jews, congregated in that area during the war, chiefly in and around Tashkent. Some, like the Hashomer Hatzair group, had been directed there by a deliberate decision of their leadership when the Germans invaded the Soviet Union. Others simply wanted to be somewhere where it was warm and food problems were less acute than elsewhere, and where there were known to be other Jews. Kovner thought that attempts should be made to get in touch with all these centers. This was dramatized by the arrival of a postcard written on the bark of a tree from a distant labor camp in Mari, in northern Russia—someone had heard of Vilna and wanted to know whether there were any chances of getting there.

Before he started sending people to places such as Central Asia, Kovner had to decide what to do about about the many Jewish soldiers in the Red Army who had originally been Lithuanian or Polish Jews and who were only too eager to join Kovner's scheme. Kovner definitely discouraged any attempts to leave the army before the war was over. His position was that there would be time for joining the exodus when the war was over and the Germans defeated. For the time being, his plans embraced only those men who had been released from the Red Army and, of course, older people and women—the others, he felt, should fight.

Another obstacle to be overcome before his plans could materialize was the depression and despair of the survivors, or at least many of them. As in Rovno, there were some in

Vilna who sought relief for their emotions in dissipation and drunkenness or in a quick return to a cynical quasi-normalcy of black marketeering and smuggling. The death that surrounded them as they surveyed their old homes and the streets that had once teemed with Jews—their own friends, relatives and acquaintances—was a reality to which they could not readily adjust. As one of them said: "Who will release us from the pain in our hearts, from the lonesomeness and destruction that call out at us from every street corner and every clod of earth? Around us victory trumpets are blown every day. There is a tremendous desire to live again, and we—we try to run away from ourselves. Can one demand that we eat flesh off the altar of death? When we heard of the liberation of Kovno, we rushed there like mad. Each one went to his home with a pounding heart. We went to our house in Milados 7. Heaps of rubble and burnt bricks —that is all that remained. . . . An émail-covered plaque, with the number 7 inscribed on it in shining white, remained, as though to protest the destruction of the house and its occupants."[7]

It was this reality of graveyards and bitter memories, more than anything else, that made the survivors decide to leave. "In the evening we met in a small flat temporarily occupied by one of our people. The few remnants of the Lithuanian movement met there, partisans who returned from the forest and those that had survived miraculously. They heard me tell them the reason for my coming, the decision to concentrate the remnants in Vilna, the steps taken for immediate flight from here. With excitement they heard the instructions to leave this town of theirs to which they had returned so recently and prepare themselves for yet another journey, a journey that may perhaps bring them to a promised shore. No one demurred, no hesitation was evident. It seemed that they all had just been waiting for a word, a communication, a clear-cut order to leave. A peculiar atmosphere of common fate and deep mutual affection seemed to surround us in this alien house, in the midst of a large and alien city, surrounded by loneliness."[8] This was Kovno, and the story repeated itself in all the other places where Kovner was sending his emissaries.

It was not merely the aftermath of the disappearance of communities, families and friends that made the people go. "In the village of Eisiskes in the Vilna area five of the few Jews who had survived were found murdered. Their bodies were brought to Vilna for burial. In some of the pockets of their clothes the following inscription, in Polish, was found: 'This will be the fate of all surviving Jews' (*Taki los spotka wszystkich pozostalych Zydow*); and the authorities are contemplating a concentration of all the Jews in Vilna because they are incapable of protecting them in the small towns and villages from bands of Polish and Lithuanian nationalists."[9] Anti-Semitism seemed to increase after liberation. The seed that the Nazis had sown had fallen on fertile ground, and the Nazis had shown to many nationalists how simple the matter of getting rid of the Jews could be. Anti-Semitism was quite clearly one of the reasons that made people take the risks of a flight from the Soviet Union.

Even among those who had joined the Soviet administration in the first days after liberation there soon were some who decided that this had been a mistake. For one thing, there was mistrust of the Soviets dating from the period in the forest, when the treatment of Jews had often been unfriendly, and on occasion even murderous. It now became increasingly clear that as the hold of the regime strengthened over the country suppression of all Jewish expression would increase. But Kovner was careful not to let people who had found jobs with the administration withdraw from their positions. Some of them were useful as couriers because of their relative freedom of movement; others, and especially those in the secret police apparatus, were vital in their ability to obtain documents and signatures.[10]

After the first rounds of visits to places around Vilna had been completed, and after the organizational setup had been established, messengers were sent to spy out the way to Rumania. Again, even though there was no knowledge in Vilna of the Rovno group and its activities, they had heard rumors about Bucharest and the Palestinians there. Some individuals were sent to the Rumanian border via Minsk and Kiev, but the main attempt was made via Lida, Baranovichi, Rovno, Lwow and Cernauti. The two messengers were

Ruzhka Korczak and Dr. Shmuel Amarant, a gaunt and scholarly man, an experienced teacher who had become a partisan and had fought along with the others until liberation. It seems that the two left Vilna on November 6 and reached Lida on the following day, Revolution Day. In Rovno they discovered the Lidovsky brothers and their friends, and though the reports from Cernauti were not very encouraging, they decided to carry on nevertheless, accompanied by Abraham Lidovsky, who would try to cross into Rumania with Ruzhka. Amarant was to return—this had been decided back in Vilna—and report on the details of the route. In every larger center they set up reception points with some Jewish survivors for those who would follow. Then, via Stanislawow and Kolomeja they reached Cernauti (Czernowitz) toward the end of November.[11]

There was the physical difficulty of moving through war-devastated areas infested by Bandera's Ukrainians with forged documents showing them to be correspondents of the Moscow Yiddish paper *Emes*. But quite apart from this, there was the fact that in these former centers of Jewish life which Amarant and Ruzhka had known so well there were hardly any Jews that had survived. In Luninets "we only met one Jewish woman, she was the only member of the community left alive. She was the widow of the local doctor, but she had gone insane, and we could not get a full story out of her, only a mess of incoherent detail."[12] In Cernauti they stayed with a local rabbi, Meir Kahan, a fervent Zionist who introduced them to the group of youngsters who were actually engaged in the work of transferring people across the border. The contact that was established there with the Noar Zioni and Hashomer Hatzair people enabled Ruzhka and Abraham Lidovsky to attempt the border-crossing. Despite some mishaps, the Ukrainian guides brought them into Rumanian territory, and they reached Bucharest on the last day of November or the first of December.

In Bucharest the Palestinians were preparing a transport of close to a thousand legal immigrants for Palestine who were about to leave on the S.S. *Taurus*. Ruzhka did not stay in Bucharest for more than a couple of days. One of the *shlihim* (Palestine emissaries) suggested that she go to Pal-

estine, and on the following day arranged for her to meet Moshe Agami, the chief *shaliah,* at the railway station, where he would be loading the immigrants onto the train. In the hectic atmosphere of emigrants in the throes of leaving their former homes, Agami told her that she would perform a vital function by going to Palestine without waiting for her Vilna friends and telling the leadership there all she knew about the ghetto, partisans, resistance and the new move toward the shores. Her Vilna friends, he said, would be able to get on without her, whereas in Palestine nobody really knew what had happened in eastern Poland and Lithuania and what the situation was there now. Ruzhka boarded the ship on the certificate of a woman who changed her mind at the last moment, and Abraham Lidovsky got on it in a similar way. They reached Haifa on December 12, 1944.

In the meantime, Amarant had returned to Vilna at the end of November, convinced that he had been instrumental in opening the route to Rumania. The decision was taken to start sending out groups to Cernauti, and again it was Amarant, this time accompanied by his wife, who went first. They were in Rovno on December 11, and by the middle of the month they reached Cernauti.[13] They were followed by the first organized groups leaving Vilna after them. Unknowingly, they were walking into a trap.

Amarant had come to know a Cernauti doctor to whom Rabbi Kahan had confided his plans. The man was, as it turned out, an agent of the Soviet political police, the NKVD. Appointed to be the physician of the group of youngsters who were organizing the convoys that crossed the borders, he was able to keep the NKVD informed. In addition, the Soviet guards had caught a convoy that had crossed the border with the help of some anti-Soviet Ukrainians—it was never made clear whether this group belonged to the Cernauti organization or whether it was a group of people who had organized themselves privately. However that may be, some of the Jews caught there led the investigators to one of the flats where some of the youngsters who were generally responsible for these crossings lived. These were arrested, but most of them managed to run away while they were being led through the streets. Now the doctor

agent helped out, and the NKVD uncovered another flat with more Zionist youths. Amarant, who arrived in the middle of all this, made the fatal mistake of trying to take the bull by the horns and going to the doctor to ask him point-blank whether he was a traitor. He then tried to leave the town but was arrested on the outskirts. Fortunately he managed to send a cable to the assembly point at Lwow—and as a result, further groups coming down from Vilna stopped in their tracks and awaited further instructions.

In the end, eleven men and women faced trial at Cernauti, among them Rabbi Kahan and Dr. Amarant. It is not our purpose here to tell the story of the trial—suffice it to say that when it was held in May 1945 the accused were charged with belonging to Hashomer Hatzair (which most of them did not) and *koordinazia* (only Amarant had any knowledge of who was known by that name as the steering committee in Vilna) and with trying to take Jews out of the Soviet Union—which was true enough. However, all this came under the heading of counterrevolutionary activity. Amarant seems to have defended his Zionist viewpoint and admitted only to having wanted to leave the Soviet Union because of the unsettled political situation. Surprisingly enough, he was acquitted, but not released, and was subsequently sentenced to ten years in a second trial on the same charge, in the spring of 1946. Through various maneuvers, financial and otherwise, the accused were released some two years after their arrest, in September 1946.[14]

The Cernauti arrests necessitated an immediate change in directions. Thanks to Amarant's last cable the groups moving toward Cernauti were redirected back into Poland and began to converge on Lublin. Lublin had been liberated on July 23, 1944, and had become the seat of the PKWN—the Polish Committee of National Liberation, the future left-wing government of Poland. One of the committee's members was Dr. Emil Sommerstein, an old-time Zionist politician of the center or right-of-center General Zionist party from the Polish district of Galicia; he had been arrested by the Soviets in 1939, had spent some two years in prison and had then been taken straight from the camp to become responsible for the reconstruction desk in the incipient left-wing regime. He was in fact the representative of

the Jews on the committee, and rumors had it that he had established contact with the West, and even with Jerusalem. Actually, there was some truth in this: on August 24, 1944, a cable signed by Sommerstein had reached Jerusalem,[15] and after that, irregular contact was maintained between him and the Jewish Agency Rescue Committee. Aid was sent to him from Jerusalem and from the JDC (American Jewish Joint Distribution Committee, the major Jewish relief and rehabilitation agency in the United States) in the form of packages, letters and money.

In the autumn, the Rovno group sent "Pasha" Rajchman and Eliezer Lidovsky to Lublin to get in touch with Sommerstein. The meeting was most disappointing: a frightened, trembling old Jew begged Lidovsky not to involve him in anything that might send him back to the prison he had left such a short while ago.[16] Later attempts to draw Sommerstein into some kind of contact with Brichah were no more successful. In early 1945 another meeting took place with Brichah representatives and one of them relates: "An impressive-looking Jew with a patriarch's beard was sitting there, and he said in Polish (we spoke Yiddish and he answered in Polish): 'Children, what on earth do you want of me? How do I know that I will return to this room if I leave it? . . . Let us not talk, he said, the walls might hear. Contacts? What contacts are you talking about? I shall be happy if you give me some contacts.' Simply—a broken man. He was scared, he was trembling."[17]

The Rovno and Vilna groups came to Lublin, generally speaking, in December 1944. Kovner left Vilna suddenly, having been warned of his impending arrest as a result of a betrayal to the NKVD. His name was prominently mentioned at the Cernauti trial, and he was lucky to get away before the authorities caught up with him. In Poland he was, or thought himself, safer. Vitka Kempner, his deputy and future wife, left a month after him, in early January—by air! At about the same time, the first group of returnees from Central Asia arrived in Lublin.

One of Kovner's emissaries was a young girl by the name of Cesia Rosenberg. It was her task to try to find members of youth movements who had gone to Central Asia early in the war and bring them, if possible, to Vilna. She had no

addresses, only the names of two men, Mordechai Rosman and Shlomo Kless. Rosman she knew, from her youth movement days in Vilna, but Kless was unknown to her. Traveling on false papers as a reporter of the Moscow Yiddish paper *Einigkeit* looking for, of all things, Yiddish type reportedly evacuated to Tashkent, and dressed in Red Army uniform, she tried to reach Moscow. The recollection of another journey was fresh in her memory. During the war, Kovner had tried to smuggle out news of what was happening to the Vilna Jews to Moscow. Cesia, a fair-haired, blue-eyed girl, along with a friend, had tried to get to the Russian lines and tell their story to the Soviet high command. Posing as Germans, they got about halfway to the front when they were stopped and interrogated by the Nazis. Miraculously, Cesia had escaped and returned to Vilna—and now here she was, retracing her steps after the war. She traveled with military transport, protected part of the way by ordinary Soviet soldiers who sensed that there was something wrong with her papers, and finally reached Moscow. At the Kazan railway station she asked, on the strength of her documents, for a ticket to Tashkent. The official became suspicious and asked her to return later. The second time, she was told to leave her documents behind and return later; now it was clear to her that if she came again she would be running the risk of arrest. She was in Moscow, in a railway station crowded with thousands of soldiers in the last winter of the war, without documents and with no friends to turn to. She did have money, but that might turn out to be a very mixed blessing if she was caught. Her poor knowledge of Russian did not exactly increase her confidence.

It is now necessary to introduce another group, those whom Cesia had set out to find. In Central Asia there were indeed, among many tens of thousands of Jewish refugees, some three hundred to four hundred young *halutzim,**

---

* *Halutzim* is the Hebrew word for "pioneers"; this was the general name given to members of those Zionist youth movements whose aim was to settle on a kibbutz in Palestine. In Palestine, the term was used for settlers in the various kinds of cooperative or communal settlements (kibbutz or *moshav,* the small-holders cooperative).

mostly from Hashomer Hatzair, with a sprinkling of Dror members. These had set up an efficient and rather ingeniously organized illegal body. They had originally come to Tashkent because it was near the Iranian and Afghan borders, and therefore "next door," in their imagination at least, to Palestine. But soon enough they found out that it was impossible to leave the Soviet Union by that route, and they therefore tried to join a Polish army which had been organized in Russia in 1941 and 1942 and which had moved out into the Middle East from there in order to assist the British Army. For a variety of reasons, mainly technical hitches and just plain bad luck, only very few managed to get out with the Poles. The "Movement Afar," as they called themselves, now organized itself on the principles of mutual help, productive occupations (so as to avoid living off the black market) and the intention of leaving as soon as possible. Ultimately some central members were arrested, and when one of these was freed the danger arose that the police would ferret out the members of the group behind the façade of false names and addresses. In the autumn of 1944 the situation became unbearable, and it was decided that the time had come to move back to Poland. Lublin now seemed to be the easiest way to Palestine. A postcard received from Palestine also contained a clear instruction to move to Lublin. In addition, in Moscow the Yiddish paper *Einigkeit* published an article by Ilya Ehrenburg about his meeting with Jewish partisans at Vilna, and also a snapshot taken on the occasion. It was therefore clear now that Jews—partisans—had survived at Vilna, though the fact that Abba Kovner was their commander was not yet known.[18]

Preparations were now speeded up. With the help of bribes, places were obtained for members of the group in units joining the left-wing Polish Army (the Poles would not take Jews into these forces in 1944 for fear of equating communism with Jews in the minds of the liberated Polish population). The first three men reached Lublin probably at the beginning of December. The second group of five men, including Shlomo Kless and Mordechai Rosman, appears to have reached Moscow toward the end of December. They were part of a transport of twenty-three "Poles"

(during the journey it became clear that they were all Jews traveling on non-Jewish papers) who now settled down at the Kazan railway station to wait for their train—a process that might take a number of days. Their escort, two Soviet officers, were in the meantime engaged in a profitable piece of trade. Thousands of soldiers were milling about at the huge station, and many of them were spending their nights in the heated waiting rooms, while, outside, Moscow froze under its white winter cover. The fact that three out of the five Zionists in the group were sought by the NKVD all over the country did not make their position any easier. At the station one of them saw a pretty young girl soldier walking in the crowd. Their first interest was entirely masculine, but soon the girl became "suspect" in their eyes as one of them. Following her they overheard her conversation with the official who refused her the ticket. Her bad Russian gave her away, but any attempt to establish contact with her was met with decided reticence. At last they tried Yiddish, whereupon she volunteered the information that she came from Vilna and that she knew Abba Kovner; then she admitted that he had sent her. The girl could, of course, be a trap—she might have become involved with the NKVD. But then she said she was looking for Kless and Rosman. She would not believe that she was actually speaking to Kless and rather childishly asked him for his papers to prove it. The two men who had spoken to her now brought her to Rosman. There was immediate mutual recognition, and then all the barriers were down. She now boarded the train back to Poland as the "relative" of one of the soldiers. On the train she told them the story of the ghetto and the slaughter, of the rebellion and the partisans, and gave them Abba Kovner's little booklet *Flammen in Asch* (Flames in the Ash)—they cried like children, for hours. Then they told their story, and now a plan materialized: Abba Kovner would want them to go to Lublin, and they would see how to carry on once they got there.

There is something very extraordinary about this chance meeting in Moscow. Two streams met there—the Zionist youth movement driven into a far-away diaspora and the fighting remnant of Lithuanian and Polish Jewry; they were

both motivated by the desire to emigrate and build new foundations for a personal and national existence. Only the actual meeting was accidental; the urge to find each other, the common yearning for a common goal and, finally, the amazing readiness to risk prison and Siberia rather than leave comrades behind, this feeling of responsibility for others—all of this was not accidental at all. It was one of the results and, indeed, a logical consequence of years of education, suffering and fighting.

In early January of 1945 there were already organized beginnings of Jewish life in Lublin—if indeed it could be called life. A public soup kitchen and asylum—the Peretz-Heim—was opened by a central Jewish committee set up by the new regime. Jews were reaching Lublin from all over the liberated eastern part of Poland—from hiding places, partisan units and the few liberated slave-labor camps in the area, and now also from Vilna, Rovno and Central Asia. Prewar patterns of public life now tended to repeat themselves, ghostlike, in a nightmarish sort of way. A Jewish population of 3.3 millions in 1939 had had a variety of political institutions, political parties and so on. Now, in January 1945, there were all of 7,000 Jews in liberated eastern Poland. These were usually sole survivors of families, very often also of whole towns and communities—disillusioned and bitter. Against the somber background of the miserable soup doled out at Peretz-Heim, an attempt was made to "elect" committees and appoint "representatives" of parties that reflected the fullness of prewar conditions. But the conditions were there no more, the parties and their programs were ashes strewn all over the Polish earth. The representatives represented things that were dead, never to rise again, and the whole routine of activity seemed to many to be mere shadow-play on the gray edge of nothingness.

The Jewish Central Committee was the result of Communist initiative. This is not to say that the PPR (Polish Workers' Party—the Polish CP) had any real influence among the Jewish survivors. The individuals representing them and the Bund—in close-knit alliance—were very largely imposed by the regime. Yet the committee did some useful work from the outset, providing some sort of social service with what-

ever limited funds the new government could spare. Also, the committee and Sommerstein, its chairman, were deemed important by the government for their share in the respectable front that the new regime wanted to present vis-à-vis the Western powers, whose recognition was now eagerly sought. This applied also to religious life, and Rabbi Kahanne of Lwow was appointed chief military chaplain and, unofficially, civilian coordinator of religious matters for Jews.

The Central Committee went through stages of organization and ultimately a parity between Zionists and non-Zionists was achieved, with Sommerstein as chairman. This was no small success, considering the supremacy of the PPR (Communists); nevertheless it did not really represent the Jews, because only a small proportion among them supported the Communist and Bundist half of the committee, as Brichah was so amply to prove. The PPR slogan was that Jews should participate in the socialist reconstruction of a progressive and peace-loving Poland. This would probably have attracted large numbers of Jews in prewar Poland. But this good-will had been liquidated, along with the Jewish population itself, and not without the support of many Poles, including large sections of the Polish right-wing underground. Only the Polish left, known as the People's Guard, had supported the Jewish ghetto fighters during the war to the best of its very limited capability. The new postwar regime tried to carry on this tradition of struggle against anti-Semitism, but they were very weak themselves, precariously balanced, as they were, on top of Soviet bayonets amid an anti-Soviet and anti-Semitic population.

On January 17, 1945, the liberation of Warsaw began. In Lublin arrived the last remnants of the leadership of the Warsaw ghetto rebellion—Yitzhak Zuckerman, the tall and moustachioed deputy commander of the uprising, and Ziviah Lubetkin, a heroine in her own right, and Zuckerman's wife. These two now joined the others, Kovner, Lidovsky, Rosman and Kless, in what now became a symposium that went on for several days and nights. Apart from sharing experiences and facts, discussions were held of an ideological nature. There was absolute unanimity on the crucial question of emigration to Palestine. The Zionist solution

seemed to be borne out by the experience of the holocaust, in which the best-known ghetto rebellions were initiated by persons largely motivated by Zionist ideology. Why, asked Zuckerman, had mass murder of Jews been possible? "Because we are a cursed people, a people who sleep when they should work, work when they should fight, who have so little feeling for something that every little non-Jewish child has got deep in his blood: the bond with a little piece of earth he calls his own." Who had fought in the Warsaw ghetto? Of the twenty-two fighting groups, said Zuckerman, there was one of the Noar Zioni; and of the twenty-one others with leftist inclinations eight had been non-Zionist; all the rest were left-wing Zionist youth movement people. "In other words: has our movement stood the test of history? It has. Has the right education been given? It has. Our movement has stood the test of peace and the test of fighting at times of war. What are the conclusions? . . . 90% of the workers and the youth fell in the struggle with the dream of a Jewish Palestine before their eyes—the Palestine of the Ein Harod* and Mishmar Ha'emek."[19]

Beyond these points, there were differences of opinion in Lublin. Should they or should they not participate in the setting up of committees and all the other paraphernalia of organized community life? Kovner and many of his partisan friends saw in the bustling activities of busy budding little bureaucrats a kind of desecration of the memory of the dead, a cheapening of the experiences they had been through. Indeed, there seems to have been a time in Lublin when Kovner and others were seriously considering self-destruction. But this thought was overcome, and they became deeply committed to two ideas—revenge and flight. Life seemed justified only if some attempt was made to take revenge on the German people in such a way as to leave a lasting impression on its history and show that Jewish blood would not be spilled in vain. There was no point in simply killing a few, or even a few hundred, known Nazis. In the darkness of the despair of men and women who had seen their people—

* Ein Harod, Mishmar Ha'emek—two kibbutzim (collective settlements) in the Jezreel Valley of northern Israel.

practically all their people—brutally massacred, the only meaning of revenge, and therefore of life, could be the mass destruction of Germans in the same way that the Germans had murdered Jews. The Germans had given rise to Nazism. Millions of Germans must have known, millions therefore should suffer. This could only be done by using poison. Schemes were talked about, plans were laid for putting this into action, but this could not be done in Lublin. One had to go to Germany to do it, and the war was still not over.

Then there was the second idea that had already begun to be put into practice—the idea of taking people out of the East and bringing them to the shores, toward Palestine. The two—revenge and flight—were connected. You could not talk of revenge openly, not even to Jews. The small group of forest guerrilla leaders who sought revenge had to hide their activities behind another façade, that of flight (Brichah). Not that they did not believe in Brichah—they most fervently did. But they would use Brichah to get closer to Germany, and would only go to Palestine if and when they survived the consequences of their avenging missions.

Brichah was common ground to everyone in Lublin; revenge was not. This was quite unconnected with party or ideological affiliations. Ranged on Kovner's side were partisans from his own Hashomer Hatzair movement, the right-wing Betar and the liberal Noar Zioni, and young partisans who had no affiliations at all and could not care less about them. Against Kovner were the "Asiatics," as they came to be called—members of Hashomer Hatzair and Dror who were now coming back from Central Asia after the meeting in Moscow with Cesia Rosenberg. (This latter group merits closer analysis because of its later importance in Brichah.)[20]

When the first groups reached Lublin, a very risky attempt was made to arrange for the departure of the rest of the group from Central Asia. The first man to reach Lublin from Tashkent, Raphael Feldman, returned there with written instructions to his Hashomer Hatzair group to try to reach Poland by all means. He was followed by others, and it was largely due to these missions that some three to four hundren "Asiatics" arrived in Lublin between January and April and joined the Brichah there.

They were much more of a closely knit group than even the partisans; their loyalty to each other and to their movement had withstood the test of illegality in the Soviet Union. They returned to Poland with the very clear idea that all they wanted was to get out and go to Palestine, and settle on a kibbutz once they got there.

In Palestine, their movement of Hashomer Hatzair was opposed at that stage to the idea of a Jewish state in a partitioned Palestine and advocated a kind of federal arrangement with the Arabs. Their movement also could be described as pro-Soviet. The "Asiatics" combined a deep loyalty to their movement with a very decided dissent from these two political precepts—they were disillusioned with the Soviet Union and they had no objection at all to a Jewish state. When they met with Kovner in Lublin, they saw in him a hero, one of their own, a man whom they were eager to see as their leader. He agreed with them in their political attitudes, but then, somehow, a wall seemed to rise between them. Kovner was becoming secretive, he was beginning to talk cryptically about tasks other than simply leaving Poland and going to Palestine, and while they continued to admire his tremendously impressive personality, they neither could nor particularly wanted to understand his schemes of revenge. His motives were hidden from them, in Lublin and later. His desire to shake the Jewish world to its foundations, to change its outlook on life so that the lesson of those years should be learned and never forgotten, the preoccupation of this humanist writer and poet and guerrilla leader with death and revenge—this was beyond them, and they moved away from him, respectfully and with no rancor, forming their own distinct coterie. They emphasized the youth movement, education, Hebrew—the old stand-bys of the Zionist youth movement. Kovner did not oppose this; in fact, he even made some half-hearted gestures to aid in the reestablishment of youth groups. But this was not for him; this had been before the deluge, and nothing could bring that world back from the dead.

There was, then, this one agreement in Lublin: whatever the motives, there had to be an exodus, a flight, a Brichah. And so, probably in the last week of January 1945, a new

koordinazia was founded to replace the old Vilna one, a committee to direct the movement out of Poland. Kovner was the undisputed head, but he did not wish to run the Brichah himself. The "Asiatics" were more than eager to take over that work. Kovner still remained there, in the background, and nobody doubted his authority; but the actual running of the exodus was left to one of the "Asiatics" group—Mordechai Rosman (who met Cesia Rosenberg in Moscow), small, hefty, energetic Rosman, with his quick, darting gray eyes. Everyone agreed to the nomination, and with it the Lublin symposium came to an end.

The route to Rumania had to be spied out. This did not wait for the termination of the discussions, and during the third week in January Kovner sent three young partisans south into the Carpathian mountains and over the border. Chief among them was a young man by the name of Velvele Rabinowitz from Vilna; he led his comrades through Krosno in Poland to Humene in Slovakia, then to Chust in Subcarpathia and to Sighet and Satu Mare in Rumania. In Bucharest they found Moshe Agami, the main *shaliah*; then Velvele returned to Lublin and reported that the way was clear.[21] The first group apparently left immediately for Rumania and laid down the final route and the methods of getting there—posing as returnees from camps in Poland and places in the west, going "home" to Rumania or, more usually, to Greece or Bulgaria (Rumania was too near, and they did not know any Rumanian). This camouflage, which became known as "the Greek bluff," was apparently believed by the Soviet authorities.

At first, groups that started out on their way to Rumania came to Lublin; but soon, probably in February, the center of Brichah was transferred to Cracow, because Lublin was the center of the government and it was best to be as secretive as possible—which was easier in Cracow. From Cracow, Rosman established transit centers in Poland itself at Rzeszow and Tarnow in eastern Galicia, and the groups were sent there after being briefed at headquarters. The briefing included a general explanation of the dangers that would be encountered, a stern warning not to take any money or documents or to speak Russian, Polish or Yiddish.

The only language that the refugees were allowed to speak was Hebrew, which for the purpose became the local variety of Greek. The groups would then pass on to Krosno or Sanok; Krosno was the more usual "point" near the Polish border, and there "Ben" (Moshe Meiri), a diminutive, black-haired and very cheerful "Asiatic" was waiting for them with a small staff to give them a place to sleep and a bite to eat. From there, the people would cross the Carpathian mountains, by train, truck or, partly, on foot. This was arranged either with Russian soldiers who were suitably impressed with large, red forged seals of the Red Cross, or won over simply by some minor bribes combined with genuine sympathy.[22] The documents were forged at Cracow by some experts, also "Asiatics," who had had considerable experience in the art of forgery during their efforts to get out of the Soviet Union. The documents, in a number of languages, showed the refugees to be Greek Jews liberated from German camps and destined for Athens, Salonika or Larissa.

Crossing the mountains was the most difficult part of the trip. Bandera's bands were still roaming the forests, and no Jew could expect to be spared by them. In Slovakia, on the other hand, there was relative safety. There, the little town of Humene provided a shelter in the form of a hospital which had been founded by some Czech Jewish doctors. Soon a man was sent there from Budapest, a member of the left-wing Dror youth group by the name of Zvi Prisant. He saw to it that people received a minimum of food and some rest, and were then sent on their way to Tokay in Hungary. Then came Oradea Mare, a Rumanian border town, and then the train to Bucharest.

Back in Cracow, Rosman was responsible to the *koordinazia* committee, representing the various movements and groups. Its task was to determine how many people should leave at any given time and according to what "key" of percentages people should be taken into the groups from the various movements. This was important, both because there were more individuals who wanted to leave than there were groups to accommodate them, and mainly because the fierce particularism of the various factions had to be amicably

adjusted. Everyday arrangements and operational control were vested in the commander, but slowly a small staff developed that shared the work with him—a treasurer, and two or three aides. The financing was ingenious—the refugees would deposit their money with the Brichah, because it would have been foolhardy to carry it on their persons while illegally crossing borders. They were given little slips of paper with Hebrew scribbling on them, and these were then honored in Bucharest by the Palestinian emissaries there. These sums in turn were obtained, at first, from the Jewish Agency in Jerusalem, which had a rescue committee that collected money from the Palestinian Jews; later on, additional sums were obtained from the JDC (American Jewish Joint Distribution Committee) to pay for the "transients'" food and clothing. Occasionally, couriers such as Velvele would bring hard currency in cash from Bucharest to Cracow. What was amazing was the implicit trust of these people —who had so little trust in anyone in those post-war years— in an organization run by youngsters who gave them slips of paper in exchange for whatever property they had.

On March 1, 1945, the central partisan group, with Kovner, Vitka Kempner, Eliezer Lidovsky and Zivia Lubetkin, passed through Sanok, disguised as Bulgarian partisans trying to return home.

As a result of betrayal by a local informer they were arrested by the NKVD. A long interrogation at the local police station followed, lasting about thirty-six hours. They were accused of smuggling, and of desertion from the Red Army. Their situation was becoming hourly more critical because by that time Kovner and Lidovsky were also being sought by the NKVD in connection with their activities in Vilna and Rovno, and because they had been prominently mentioned in the Cernauti trial and their true identities might be revealed. The Bulgarian disguise was wearing rather thin, and the only thing that seemed to be in their favor was the fact that they obviously knew the partisan lore intimately. At one point a gray-haired colonel entered the room, listened to the interrogation for some time, then bent over and whispered something in the ear of the interrogating officer. Soon afterward, the partisans were given orders to turn around

and follow an escort. The escort led them down long flights of stairs, and then they came to some sort of cellar. There a clerk was sitting at a little table, writing. Each one was asked to approach the table, was asked some questions, and then led off into the darkness at the other side of the room. The man who later told the story was the last one in the group. He went up to the table and the clerk asked him, "Where did you want to go?" Why does he want to know, thinks the partisan, they are going to send me to "the white bears" (Siberia) in any case. "To Petach Tikvah,"* he answers. "Where is Petach Tikvah?" asks the clerk. "Far, far away," he answers. The clerk shrugs his shoulders and writes out a railway ticket: Sanok–Petach Tikvah. The line of partisans leave the room, are led out to a courtyard, and from there to the street. At the gate of the station, the old colonel appears and says in good Yiddish, "Go and bless you, children."

Group after group, usually of ten or fifteen or twenty people, passed into Rumania; by the end of April 2,000 to 3,000 Jews had arrived there, mostly partisans and "Asiatics," but partly also concentration camp victims from western Poland, or people who had hidden in Poland—Jews who heard that other Jews were organizing a movement to leave the country, and they joined, or followed. The number of organized partisans and "Asiatics" was, according to a reasonably reliable estimate, about 1,200; these, on arrival in Rumania, remained in "kibbutzim," groups living more or less communally, inspired by the Palestine kibbutz idea.[23]

In Poland and Lithuania, in the meantime, the situation had changed. In Vilna, after the departure of the partisans and their followers, a small center remained that continued to assist the exodus of Vilna Jews into Poland. It is very difficult to estimate the number of those who left Vilna at the end of 1944 and the beginning of 1945, but the most probable figure is around 300 to 400, of whom about 100 were partisans from the Vilna and Narocz forests.

In Rumania, the period between liberation (August 1944) and the arrival of the first groups of the Polish Brichah had

---

* Petach Tikvah—a town near Tel Aviv.

brought with it new developments. At the end of August a North Transylvanian Refugees Committee was set up with the knowledge and consent of the Red Cross in Bucharest. In early November eleven representatives of the committee started a tour of northern Transylvania to discover what was left of the Jewish population that had been destroyed by the Germans earlier in the year in the mass extermination of Hungarian Jewry. They found only 6,000 survivors of a large and ancient population, and those remnants were in part prisoners of war in Russian camps because they had been recruited into forced labor battalions by the Hungarians and taken prisoner along with the regular Hungarian Army. Weeks passed in efforts to alleviate the conditions in the area and to rescue the "Hungarians" from their POW camps. These efforts were only partly successful and some of these unfortunates were taken into the interior of Russia, together with some Jews from Bukovina and Bessarabia, where they were used as forced laborers.[24]

In Bucharest this committee was connected not only with the Red Cross, but also with Agami and the Palestine emissaries. It was Agami, apparently, who had the idea of sending an official train to Poland and other places in order to repatriate Rumanian Jewish refugees; such a train would also be able to bring non-Rumanian Jews to Rumania legally. With the help of the Red Cross and the AJDC representative a committee of Transylvanians was set up, headed by Dr. Marton and Dr. Carl. This committee, called DEFAB, obtained official permission to get a train consisting of a locomotive and twelve wagons; it looked after equipment, food, medical personnel and equipment, whereas the government (actually to an ever-increasing degree the Communist Party) provided the technical personnel. The commander of the train, nominated in fact by Agami—Yakov Shmetterer—was officially a sympathizer of the CP, and through his excellent relations with a local official who was very friendly to the idea of bringing Jewish refugees, especially Rumanians, to his area, Shmetterer was able to supplement the various official documents with a letter of recommendation from the CP. On March 24, 1945, the train moved into Hungary, complete with nurses, doctors, and supervisors from the Communist Party.

It should be remembered that at that time Eastern Europe (and later on, all of Europe) was inundated with refugees—"displaced persons"—who were trying to reach their homes. It is impossible even to estimate the number of refugees in the liberated areas of Hungary, Poland and Czechoslovakia in March 1945; suffice it to say that later, in June–July, the total number of DPs was estimated at about ten million in all of Europe. The idea, as such, of governmental help in the form of repatriation by train was to become very much accepted after VE Day. But in March this was apparently the first and only venture of its kind. This fact probably explained at least some of the difficulties. The train was stopped at the Hungarian town of Debrecen, and its passengers were accused of being smugglers. Similar trouble occurred at smaller stations along the route. But soon the train reached Humene, where the emissary of Brichah, Zvi Prisant, was able to hand over about 200 refugees to Shmetterer. A part of the train, with special locomotives, made their way across the mountainous border into Poland; the tracks had not yet been repaired properly after the fighting, and the area was infested with Bandera's Ukrainian bands. Nevertheless, they reached Nowy Sacz, and picked up some more refugees. From there they returned to Humene, and at the beginning of April they were back at Oradea Mare, their starting point.

A second journey was immediately begun, starting probably on April 7 or 8; this time the train, with an increased number of freight cars (fourteen) and equipped with documents enabling them to move throughout the whole Eastern European area, reached Poland without delay. Around the middle of the month they arrived at Cracow.

Mr. Shmetterer did not keep a diary, and there is little detailed documentation regarding the dates of his voyages or the number of refugees brought by him to various countries from Poland. However, it is clear that at the beginning of May he reached Auschwitz camp, where he met a very sympathetic woman doctor in charge of the hospital. He was able to take with him some of the survivors, mainly Rumanians and Hungarians, but was arrested at Cracow by an overzealous Russian commander. After much argument he was allowed to leave, on May 7, but with a Russian lieu-

tenant as escort, whose task it was to bring the train to Russia for further investigation. Shmetterer himself tells the story with a somewhat tragicomic effect: by the time they reached Rumania, the Russian was both drunk and utterly convinced that these were real refugees who were really being brought to Hungary and Rumania. The train never went to Russia, of course, and strings were pulled to save the Russian officer from the wrath of his superiors. He was placed in a secure position in Rumania and, apparently, prospered there as part of the army of occupation.[25]

Shmetterer's third, or fourth, journey brought him into direct contact with the Brichah command in Cracow. By this time, Mordechai Rosman had left Poland, and Moshe Meiri ("Ben") was appointed his successor. Agami provided Shmetterer with Ben's address, and one day about the middle of May Shmetterer appeared there. Ben had not been advised of the affair, and was convinced that he had been found out by the police at last. In the end he went to see the train, and was overwhelmed by the audacity and the possibilities of the venture. The train now became what it had been intended to be—principally a vehicle for Brichah, especially Brichah of orphans and groups of young people. The complexion of Brichah was changing in any case—the partisans and rebels were being replaced by concentration camp victims, orphans and people who had hidden with Aryan documents. During April and May Shmetterer's train transferred people mainly of the latter sort—together, of course, with whatever few Rumanian refugees could be found. By the end of this operation, September 1945, he had repatriated or transferred some 5,000 Jews from Poland to Rumania and Hungary.

The Shmetterer train was used, among other things, for transporting children, mainly orphans, and sick people or invalids. Four hundred and thirty-three children were transported in the fall of 1945 to the American sector of Germany rather than to Rumania (on the Rumanian Red Cross train!), and a group of youths with amputated limbs came to Rumania from Czestochowa in Poland. These train journeys directed the attention of Brichah people to the general problem of children and youths in postwar Poland. It was

soon clear that these young people were utterly broken in spirit and that some kind of moral regeneration was needed. This was of course to be the task of youth movements and children's homes. But in many cases it was quite clear that the promise of Brichah to take the youngsters out and, hopefully, to Palestine, acted as a tonic.

> At Czestochowa we found a group, mainly of girls, with but a few boys. They were there in that camp and they did not want to budge. I must say that I received a shock there that I have not overcome to this day. They did not want to leave the place. They did not believe that the Germans would not return. The war was not over yet. 'Where should we go? Here we have a place to live and some food to eat.' [One of us] tried to persuade them. The thing that in the end broke the ice was that he lied to them and told them we were emissaries from Palestine. My language is too poor to describe what happened after that. We sat and cried, all of us. That was the discussion—crying, that was all. The moment they heard we were from Palestine, we could not disillusion them, we could not tell them that we were only talking about Palestine. They overwhelmed us, kissed us, these children—they thought they were already on the way to Palestine.[26]

Meanwhile, the situation of the 2,000 to 3,000 people who had come across into Rumania was growing from bad to worse. There had been some legal immigration into Palestine throughout 1944, but the ship on which Ruzhka Korczak had gone, the *Taurus,* was the last legal ship to leave. There was no machinery in existence to promote illegal immigration at that stage from a country in which the Soviets were now reaching for ultimate control. It became more and more difficult to stay on, and there was definite threat of demoralization among the refugees. They were living on provisions paid for with money from the Jewish Agency in Jerusalem and JDC. There was plenty of time for ideological discussions.

Kovner was still in charge in Rumania, and though Rosman was the Brichah commander in Poland, Kovner's influence was great in Poland too. He was an original thinker, unfettered by preconceived political notions, despite his

membership in a definite movement and his loyalty to it. In Lublin he had already put forward the notion of political unity of the East European survivors. Now in Rumania Kovner put these ideas into a coherent form. The basic idea underlying his concept of unity was the common fate of the Jewish people under the Nazis. "In the Ghettoes the murderers made no difference between Jews and Jews. This is the reason that we found amongst ourselves a common language in Ghetto and forest. This mutual understanding we want to bring to all Jewish communities."[27] If the Nazis had seen the Jews as one, so should the Jews who survived. This unity had a central purpose: to teach the Jewish world the lesson of the holocaust. This concept of the "lesson of the holocaust" was essentially irrational. Kovner was a poet and a dreamer; and his followers, captivated by Kovner's impressive oratory and his self-effacing honesty, usually understood only half of what he was saying—the terminology of the intellectual leader remained obscure to these fighters and partisans. But he had been their leader in the forests, and they were confident that he knew what he was talking about, even if they did not; moreover, he was talking about unity, and the holocaust, and they were profoundly moved. There really seemed to be no need to evince understanding of the many foreign words that their leader and some of his close associates used.

The lesson of the holocaust, which Kovner wanted to teach the Jewish world, consisted of a number of points. First and foremost was the thought that the holocaust would recur in a different form at some not-too-distant future. "We have the feeling that somewhere, not so very far away, a new mass murder is being prepared; it will come at the next political upheaval, and it makes no difference what nation will start it. . . . We feel with all our senses the breath of the knife. . . . Masses of millions of many nations have seen how it is done: how easily, how simply, how quietly."[28] Liberalism and equality of rights were dead; socialism had proved no obstacle to mass murder. Any political upheaval would repeat what had happened recently. Modern means of mass destruction had made possible what in previous centuries had been a murderous desire only: the mass destruction of that unwanted minority—the Jews.

If this was the major precept, one might perhaps expect that the logical conclusion would be nihilism, or even a kind of Jewish fascism. In a typically, traditionally Jewish way, however, that kind of solution was interpreted away—there was a way out, and that way could only be achieved by the exercise of individual and national virtues. If another holocaust was in the offing, then the logical conclusion was that the Jewish world must prepare for it. The trouble with the Jewish people prior to the holocaust had been that nobody had prepared them to resist it. "The lesson of the holocaust lies not only in the warning which it contains but also in the remembrance of the horror of finding ourselves unprepared to meet the danger. We were broken human beings even before the knife touched the neck of our people. What was so hard was not the sufferings of death, but this going towards it unprepared. . . . it cost us so much blood." In time, Kovner said, the secret of mass destruction would be revealed, but no one would ever know the true quality of life lived in the expectation of death. "The most terrible thing in the holocaust was not the murder, but the life on the very edge of death, the feeling of being humbled, the fall, the feeling of turning into dust even before the actual destruction."[29] The expectation of this kind of experience should be transmitted to the Jewish people and they should thus prepare themselves for the next time. Their reaction would then be to fight, not as before, just at the last moment; they must prepare themselves for major resistance now. The old parties and movements were incapable of teaching that lesson. It would take a unified movement of survivors to teach that. "The teacher of our time is a teacher of blood, and we are his pupils. We have learnt that in order to fight one does not have have to shout for years about fighting."[30] This would be the mission of the East European Jewish survivors all over the Jewish Diaspora. At the same time, a refuge had to be created and quickly fortified in the national homeland of the Jews in Palestine. To do that, Brichah had to play a vital part, it would have to become a mass popular movement, forceful, with a clear aim and an appropriate organizational framework. The remnants of the Jewish people would then concentrate in Palestine and rebuild their national existence there.

Kovner saw a major obstacle in the apathy of the Jewish populations who had not suffered in the holocaust. He related a story about the time he had been in a small Rumanian town where he and his friends sought out the local synagogue to meet Jews. They had been shocked to find trade in foreign currencies and all kinds of business being transacted in front of the Ark (the holiest part in the Jewish synagogue). "We then understood that only a mass movement with a tremendous, if simplified, emotional appeal could possibly move people like that. Any kind of movement needs a certain proportion of purity. There was no purity in these people." And, he added, "millions were part of the destruction, only hundreds saw it coming, only dozens understood its meaning and now, after having left the ruins of Lithuania and Poland and having reached this living community in Roumania, we saw: nobody bothered to remember it. . . . We felt the pain in our faces from the cold, cellar-like wind blowing at us from that Jewry, who live as though nothing had happened, as though before the Flood, as though there never had been a Flood. As though nothing had happened, the shopkeeper opens his little shop, as though nothing had happened children are brought into the world, people express a crusty and crumpled sort of sorrow—and turn to their empty little happinesses."[31]

The words seemed to resemble those of the prophets of old, but the deeds had to take account of the realities of 1945; and so an organization was formed, on April 26, called the "Organization of the East European Remnants." Officially, this was a unified Zionist movement where members of different political groups would cooperate to achieve such standard Zionist aims as a Jewish state, immigration to Palestine, Hebrew culture and the like. In Palestine, members of the group would perhaps prefer to live in groups rather than disperse among the Jewish population. It was understood, however, that the official program was a minor aspect of the movement. The "Remnants" were out to *change* the Jewish world; concrete politics was definitely secondary. Kovner, unlike some of his more extreme collaborators, harbored no illusions as to the possibilities of unifying the Jewish world by his "Remnants"—"We do not

dream the childish dream of coming and uniting parties by the magic of our word; we do not have a proper political program to offer."[32] The "Remnants" were a moral movement, rather than a political one.

The idea of unity as a logical answer to the problems raised by the mass destruction was evident all over Jewish Europe after the war. Organizations similar in some ways to the "Remnants" developed in a number of countries. In Poland, a center group composed largely of the liberal Noar Zioni, the religious movement of B'nai Akiva, and some left-of-center movements was formed and gave itself the name of *Ichud* (Unity). The left-wing groups of Hashomer Hatzair and Dror, together with other smaller movements joined in the *Liga* (League for a Labor Palestine). Similar moves for temporary or permanent unification took place in Germany and France. However, none of them tried to probe as deeply as the "Remnants" into the experiences they had been through, and in a very real sense the "Remnants" provided the only statements we have for a state of mind that prevailed throughout Jewish Europe at the time.

The "Remnants" split when they met the Palestinian emissaries (*shlihim*) and confronted the solid reality of Palestinian Jewry. Jewish life in Palestine, and elsewhere, and the ideologies and parties which resulted were the products of a living community facing real issues. The experience of European Jewry, harrowing and awesome as it was, could not be made to fit the Palestinian community and did not offer any solutions for its problems. No wonder then, that the confrontation with the Palestinian *shlihim* in Rumania broke the back of the "Remnants." Later Kovner was to speak bitterly of the victory of vested political interests, of the fact that there had been *shlihim* in Rumania who tried "to turn us into a tool in the hands of this or that faction."[33] What happened was that the Palestinians simply did not understand the motives behind Kovner's efforts. Coming from a faction-ridden Jewish community in Palestine, they suspected some hidden party-political motive somewhere in the ideology of the "Remnants." The fact was that Kovner and most of his closest associates were members of movements which in Palestine were in opposition to the ruling

moderate Labor Party, Mapai. It was therefore assumed that Kovner's real intention must be to bring the "Remnants" into the group opposing Mapai. This was clearly suggested by Agami, the chief *shaliah* in Bucharest.[34] In his reports to Palestine he stated that the "Remnants" were bound to disintegrate because the various movements had begun to organize their separate groups and in Poland the "Liga" had been set up which united the Labor youth groups in opposition to all the others, and that therefore there was no longer any room for the "Remnants." This was, in a way, true. The different groups, under the influence of at least some of the Palestinians, began to organize separately just in case the "Remnants" did break up. Moreover, many of the rank-and-file members simply did not understand Kovner's involved arguments and lofty motives. The movement was doomed before it had properly started, but its influence remained. It had had, as one of its major tenets, the aim of furthering Brichah on a unified, non-sectional basis. This persisted long after the "Remnants" disbanded. The disappearance of the movement had another consequence as well: Kovner had tried to found a political movement, and this had now failed—he was therefore free to pursue his twin dream of revenge and Brichah. To do so, he had to leave Rumania, because there could be neither emigration nor revenge from that country.

In Italy, so Kovner and his friends heard, there was a Jewish brigade, recruited from Palestine, which was part of the British Eighth Army. The war ended on May 8. The brigade had arms, an organization, potential power. It was imperative to get in touch with them. There were two routes that might lead to Italy: Yugoslavia and Hungary. Another aim would be to explore the route to Greece because Greece was so near to Palestine; but missions that were sent south to the Greek border revealed that the British had a very strong hold there and that a mass move was impossible. There remained Italy.

On April 24, Kovner sent to Yugoslavia a group of young partisans under Mulia Ben Hayim, one of Kovner's chief lieutenants. Mulia arrived in Belgrade and immediately sent on one of his men. This was a colorful personality, a fair-

haired Vilna partisan by the name of Pinhas Zeitag, more commonly known as "Pinieh the Yellow." Pinieh reached Split on May 13, and from there got in touch with the brigade, which was encamped at the time at Tarvisio in northern Italy.

In the meantime, Mulia Ben Hayim succeeded in communicating with the head of the Jewish community of Belgrade who offered help and contacts with the Government Repatriation Office. Armed with forged Rumanian Red Cross documents and passing as citizens of Western countries on their way home, Brichah now used the Yugoslav route as one of two main avenues toward Italy. People went from Arad and Timisoara in Rumania via Belgrade and Zagreb to Trieste; they were helped by the Yugoslav authorities, who very quickly saw through the thin disguise but placed no obstacles in the way of the partisans and their followers. At the same time Mordechai Rosman, who had left Cracow on V-E Day for Rumania, was sent to Budapest. There he found a full-fledged organization, dating from the underground days of Nazi-occupied Hungary, composed of members of Zionist youth movements (again, typically, members of Hashomer Hatzair, Gordonia and Dror, and similar movements). These had been instrumental in effecting the flight of many Jews to Slovakia and Rumania during the last year of the war, apart from rescue operations in Budapest itself. Nominally, the Palestinian parachutist Yoel Palgi was at their head, but he was about to leave Hungary and the actual work was done in any case by local people. Rosman now undertook to facilitate the transfer of a large proportion of the Rumanian group through Budapest to Graz and Italy, and thus revived the local organization which now became part and parcel of Brichah.

The Brigade in Italy, and other Jewish Palestinian units of the British Army there, had by now become aware of the existence of the partisan group in Rumania. A small delegation was sent to Bucharest to suggest that the group try to reach Italy. The delegation of four arrived in Bucharest just as the preparatory work in Belgrade and Budapest had been concluded, and the leadership—Kovner, Eliezer Lidovsky and Haim Lazar—were about to leave for Budapest.

They arrived there about the middle of June, stayed for a few weeks, and arrived in Italy via Austria (the town of Graz) about July 15.

The first circle closed. Palestine, in the persons of its emissaries and soldiers, had not found the way to the remnants of fighting Jewry in Eastern Europe. Zionist propaganda emanating from Palestine had not, as Britain was to suggest later on, moved the Jews to leave Poland and Lithuania and start a movement toward the shores and Palestine. Motivated by their experiences, based on their Zionist education (in many cases) in prewar years, the East European Jewish partisans and youth movement members, and the "Asiatics" and other survivors of the catastrophe had found their way to the Palestinians in Rumania and Italy. With them they brought the concept of Brichah, and a primitive but very effective organizational framework for putting this concept into practice. Undoubtedly, Palestine formed the basis of their hopes and their ultimate goal. Without it their Zionist outlook made no sense. But it was important for them, in later times, to point out the fact that they had come themselves, that they had found among themselves the forces and the leadership to leave their former countries and embark on the flight toward other and, hopefully, safer shores.

2. The Survivors

During the last months of the existence of the Third Reich, large numbers of non-Germans—slave laborers, voluntary laborers, prisoners of war, foreign volunteers for the Nazi crusade, concentration camp inmates—were being brought into the ever-decreasing *Lebensraum* of Germany, Austria and the Bohemian-Moravian "protectorate." Among these were Jewish inmates of concentration camps. (There were very few Jews hiding their Jewish identities among the slave laborers or the voluntary laborers, and of course none among the various kinds of pro-Nazis.) Their number is conservatively estimated at about 75,000,[1] but there may have been a few thousand more; they were found in several camps, including the more important ones at Ravensbruck, Terezin (liberated by the Russians), Bergen-Belsen (liberated by the British), Dachau, Allach, Kauffering, Buchenwald, Mauthausen and Ebensee (liberated by the Americans). In the south especially, the Nazis had made last-minute attempts to transfer these unfortunates to their Tyrolean redoubts in order to use them as slave laborers to build fortifications. These marches of prisoners were interrupted by the advancing Allied armies, so that many of the camp inmates were actually liberated in scattered localities while being moved, on foot, on railway freight cars, or in tempo-

rary encampments. Those remaining in the actual camps were liberated in the five weeks between the beginning of April and the end of the war on May 9, 1945. Buchenwald was freed on April 11, Bergen-Belsen on the 15th, Dachau on the 29th and Mauthausen on May 3.

The free Jewish world had very little knowledge of what was going on behind the enemy lines. Rumors and reports tended to be contradictory and confusing. In Holland and Poland, for instance, very few Jews were left alive, whereas in France about half of the Jews managed to escape death at Nazi hands. There was justified apprehension that as the Germans approached their inevitable defeat they would revenge themselves at the expense of the still-surviving Jews. The knowledge that Hitler wanted all camps destroyed together with their inhabitants caused frantic efforts to prevent such a disaster. The World Jewish Congress negotiated with Himmler through his physician, Kersten, and with the aid of the Swedish government. The representatives in Switzerland and elsewhere of the War Refugee Board, set up by President Roosevelt, tried to act through the International Red Cross, and were also backed by the American Jewish Joint Distribution Committee and other bodies. Undoubtedly these efforts saved the lives of many thousands. And yet it seems that the discovery of tens of thousands of surviving Jews when the camps were finally liberated caught the Jewish world by surprise. One might have expected that some preparation had been made against such a possibility, but the Jewish world, shaken and disorganized, not only had not done so but did not react with necessary speed. We shall see that it took months before effective Jewish aid came to the Jewish inmates of the camps.

The Allied armies, at least, had a certain disciplined reaction in such cases, and the knowledge that they would find millions of displaced persons in Germany and Austria prepared them in some ways, inadequate as they proved to be, to deal with these problems. Yet, despite the detailed information available all over the free world about conditions in the concentration camps, the actual uncovering of the horrors caused both shock and surprise and revealed a psychological unpreparedness—people had been inclined to dis-

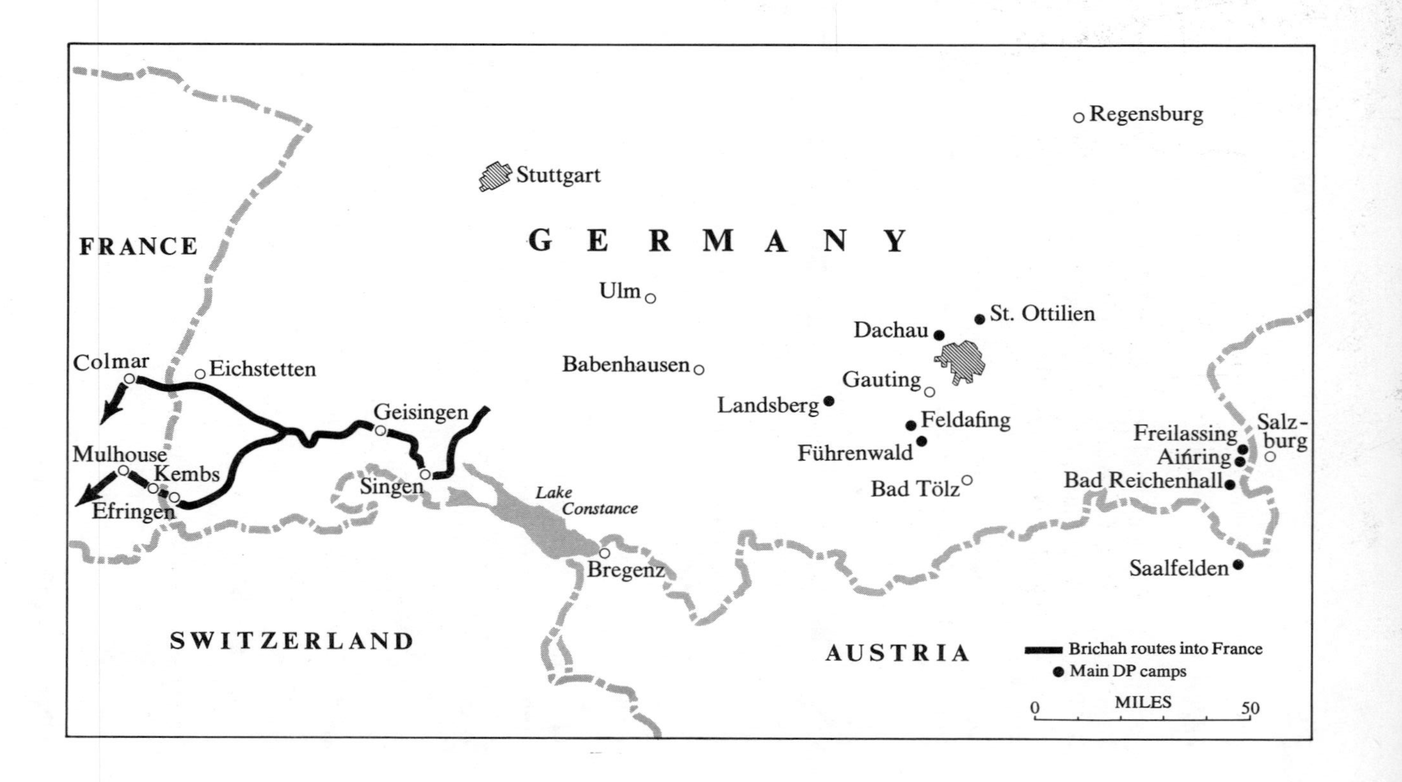

Main Jewish DP Camps in Bavaria, 1945

count the worst stories as atrocity propaganda and were aghast to see that the stories had in fact been understatements.

The first problem that had to be faced was that of health. In Bergen-Belsen, for instance, 13,000 people, mostly Jews, died *after* liberation. This was caused by the systematic starvation and its inevitable results during the very last weeks of Nazi rule. A similar situation obtained in Mauthausen, Dachau and most of the other camps. In some instances the inmates were even deprived of water during the last days before liberation. The Allies were therefore faced with epidemics, mainly typhoid, in almost every camp. Many people lost their lives after liberation because they stuffed themselves with food they could not digest. It must also be remembered that most of the medical staff with the Allied armies were not prepared for the kind of problems encountered in the liberated camps. They had been equipped to meet the requirements of soldiers wounded or suffering disease in the course of a modern war. The results of maltreatment, hunger, thirst and—with the exception of Belsen—forced labor were something most doctors would not normally have encountered in the course of their work. The commanders of the Allied armies threw their best personnel in large numbers into these camps, and the medical units did the very best they could to save as many lives as possible. Thus, Brigadier General Glynn Hughes, Montgomery's chief medical officer, called in regular medical teams of front-line units (while fighting was still going on) and had volunteer medical students flown in from Britain to help at Bergen-Belsen. More than anyone else, he was responsible for saving thousands of lives in the extraordinary conditions of the camp after liberation. American medics did a tremendous job in the camps they liberated, and at Dachau the 116th and 127th Evacuation Hospital Units and the 10th Field Hospital Unit worked for weeks to save the lives of large numbers of people, most of whom again were Jews. The same is true of Major Kuzmin and his unit at Terezin and other Soviet medical units.

The policy of the Western armies under General Dwight D. Eisenhower toward displaced persons was in effect: to return

them to their countries of origin with the least possible loss of time. According to one source, there were at that time in Germany and Austria some 10,422,000 displaced persons of various origins—not counting German refugees; and another 656,000 were dispersed in the rest of Europe and the Middle East.[2] This vast mass of suffering humanity threatened the world with enormous problems of food and housing if they were allowed to winter where they were. The repatriation policy was therefore logical and, indeed, inevitable.

The existence of these displaced millions was a well-known fact long before the Normandy invasion in June 1944. The Western Allies had encountered the problem for the first time in North Africa in late 1942; in 1943, when the United Nations Relief and Rehabilitation Administration (UNRRA) was set up, this served as a kind of study and pilot project. Accordingly, UNRRA was given the double task of providing help to the stricken countries liberated from the enemy through their respective governments and of aiding the Allied armies in their treatment of DP problems by providing administrative, medical and welfare teams to work with the DPs. Under separate agreements with SHAEF (Supreme Headquarters Allied Expeditionary Forces) it was stipulated, however, that these teams would have to be "called forward" by the armies and be subject to military regulations. Food, clothing and accommodation were in any case reserved for army jurisdiction, so that the UNRRA teams could not be more than half-civilian adjuncts to the military. The Soviet army never requested any UNRRA group for refugee work and simply repatriated the DPs as soon as they were pronounced medically fit for transport. As long as they were in Soviet transit camps, the DPs enjoyed better rations and treatment than even Red Army soldiers, but they were got rid of as quickly as possible.

In the West, after some early attempts, a special Displaced Persons Executive (DPX) was set up at SHAEF, which clarified procedures for the benefit of unit commanders in an administrative memorandum dated April 16, 1945.[3] DPs were defined as Allied subjects outside their homelands, and now this category also included stateless people (of

whom there was a large proportion among Jews). People outside their usual place of domicile but within the borders of their country were called refugees. This category was later to include Germans evicted from East European countries as well. The memorandum introduced another category, that of "persecutees," or persons persecuted because of race, religion or political opinions, whatever their citizenship. This category was now recognized as equal in rights to the DPs, which in practice meant that German Jews would not be considered enemies but would be accorded treatment equal to that of DPs. Also, the principle was stated that apart from Soviet citizens and war criminals no person was to be returned home against his will.

On April 13, two days after uncovering the horrors of Buchenwald (the first concentration camp to be liberated by the Western armies), a SHAEF order called for special efforts to find other such camps and rush medical aid and food to them. On April 22 the army emphasized "the importance of proper care for persons uncovered who were confined on political or religious grounds." Three weeks after Buchenwald, Dachau was free, and on May 9 the war was over. On May 8 a DPX cable to army units stated that "the care of displaced persons was a principal Allied objective," and requested that the treatment of these people be improved. Immediately afterward, repatriation commenced.

A tremendous dispersal began; millions of people went home, by any and every means available—by plane or train, motor transport or animal-drawn carts, on horseback and on foot. The roads and rails of Europe, damaged as they were, were clogged with these vast masses of humanity streaming in every direction. The Jews, a minority among these multitudes, were found in dozens of camps. The policy of repatriation affected them just as it affected all the others. This policy, at least on the part of SHAEF, was based on what seem to have been three mistaken presuppositions: one, that all these people had left their homes against their will; second, that they were therefore eager to return home; third, that their governments and their fellow citizens in their countries of origin would welcome them back. For a certain proportion of DPs these were fictions kept up for adminis-

trative convenience long after their fallacies had been exposed. The DP category included very different kinds of people; there were persons who had collaborated with the Germans, served in their armies or gladly volunteered to work in their industries—these included large numbers of Ukrainian and Baltic S.S. members, Poles, Hungarians and others, who were now understandably unwilling to face punishment in their own countries. They all tried to utilize the clause in the DP regulations permitting them to refuse repatriation. Many of these individuals, who later found refuge in various Western countries, had been responsible to no small degree for the murder of Jews while serving their German masters. They were now classed as DPs together with deported slave laborers, POWs, and Nazi victims generally. These others formed, of course, the vast majority of those who came under the DP category. Most of the bona fide DPs were most eager to return home, and only a small proportion of them refused to return, whether for ideological reasons or because of the prospects of higher standards of life elsewhere. Representatives of the new governments with an increasingly marked left-wing hue were of course sparing no effort to get their citizens to return to their countries. Knowledge of the provision regarding the option not to be repatriated was often withheld from DPs generally, including Jews. The Western armies evinced no great desire to be saddled with nonrepatriable DPs, and they often aided the foreign missions. When these efforts of persuasion failed, they resorted to bribery by promising prospective repatriants special rations or to threats. This was done by local commanders in contravention of clear orders from higher quarters not to force people into repatriation against their will.[4] The provision about Soviet citizens having to return was unclear, because various interpretations as to who was a Soviet citizen depended on the borders recognized as those of the Soviet Union. During the summer of 1945 citizens of Baltic countries, those of eastern Poland and soon even Ukrainians were, by stages, exempted from forceful repatriation.

Because of the tendency in actual practice to contradict orders from above, Jews were often forced to return "home"

against their will. We do not lack descriptions of the welcome they received in Poland and Lithuania. One report relates the story of a group of Jews who were pressed into repatriation. At the frontier they were met by a government official who informed them that they had all been sentenced to death for collaboration with the enemy, but as the war had been won the head of the government had graciously commuted their sentence to three years of hard labor or a commensurate service in certain army departments so that reparation could be made for their crimes. Then men were separated from their families, loaded into trucks and sent away. A few escaped by jumping into the river near the frontier and returned to the camp to warn their brethren against a similar fate. Another example deals with a Polish Jewish couple, who had been partisans. Upon returning to their township, they found that only six out of sixteen hundred Jewish families had survived. An evening of welcome was organized by the Jewish families. On that evening the Jews were all murdered by their neighbors, except for the couple and a child of ten. When these three arrived at a DP camp in Austria, they were placed among their "fellow nationals," the Poles.[5]

A Lithuanian Jew by the name of Froimtschik from a DP camp at Salzburg summed it all up at a meeting of DPs: "I have already come back from my 'Fatherland.' There are hundreds, even thousands who, like myself, have felt for themselves what we can expect in our former homes."[6]

The impression is easily created that there was a general reluctance of Jews to be repatriated, no matter what country they came from. Nothing could be further from the truth. Generally speaking, this reluctance was limited to Jews from Poland and Lithuania, while Jews from Western Europe, Czechoslovakia, and even Hungary and Rumania were in most cases eager to return home. However, these Jews formed a minority of Jewish camp survivors, and the majority, composed largely of Polish and Baltic Jews, took a different attitude.

Practically, all the regulations notwithstanding, the attitude toward Jews in camps depended on the officer in command. Faced with reams of regulations and circulars, many

officers had given up trying to keep up with the plethora of military laws and rules devised for them. This certainly applied to those who were unfortunate enough to be made responsible for DP camps. Food rations, for instance, officially stood at two thousand calories per DP daily, and this was to be derived from the German economy by confiscation. In fact this depended on the initiative of the commander, availability of food and the Germans' ingenuity in evading orders. As far as the Jews were concerned, their problem seemed at first wholly insignificant. Out of some ten million DPs, there were about 80,000 Jews in the area when repatriation began. It is interesting, however, to note certain different tendencies among the various levels of command. In the top ranks sympathy with Jews seems to have been deepest, with certain notable exceptions. The rank and file, too, were likely to be very friendly at first. Difficulties were usually experienced in the middle ranks, the captains and majors, where hostile and occasionally even anti-Semitic attitudes were sometimes though by no means generally shown.[7]

A SHAEF cable of June 6 complains that field commanders ignored the instructions about help to the concentration camps and the equalization of status between DPs and persecutees. Every person carrying a release card from a concentration camp was entitled to admittance in DP camps set up by the army.[8] Children were to be removed from Germany immediately; this directive resulted in arrangements to send the first 535 Jewish children from Buchenwald and Hillersleben (Belsen survivors) to France and other children to Switzerland. U.S. soldiers were taken to the camps on guided tours to see for themselves that Nazi horrors had not been invented by Allied propaganda.

Jews were not recognized as a separate nationality. This apparently had been discussed before the Normandy invasion and the decision had been reached that separate camps would be organized only for citizens of Allied countries. Later, separate Baltic and Ukrainian camps were to be set up. But as the question whether Jews were a nationality was considered to be a controversial point, Jews were to be classed with their "fellow citizens" and placed in the appro-

priate camps.[9] They were not included in a corrected list of nationalities sent out on June 7. On June 20, however, the category of "non-repatriables" (those who in accordance with previous regulations exercised their right to refuse repatriation) was officially introduced. Special centers were to be set up for them, and there would be about 500,000 such people, mainly Poles, Balts and Jews. On June 29 another order added that "teams such as the Joint Distribution Committee for Jewish centers" and other special UNRRA teams would go to these new camps.[10]

This indicates that in contradiction to existing regulations Jewish centers or concentrations had in fact come into existence. Other army material makes it clear that regulations regarding the non-repatriation option were disregarded, especially in the area of General Patton's Third Army, where "direct" methods of solving problems tended to be favored. Also, it becomes obvious that no official Jewish bodies, such as the JDC, had arrived in the camps during these first months. This does not include the Palestinian Jewish soldiers, of whom more will be said later. At any rate, it is clear that no official representatives of Jewish organizations came to say a word of encouragement to the Jewish survivors. May passed, June arrived, July went by—and the refugees asked (and, by the way, are still asking): Why did no one come to bring us a greeting, a sign of sympathy? Where were the Joint (JDC), the World Jewish Congress, the Zionist organization and all the rest? These are searching questions, and it is not easy to answer them.[11]

It has already been mentioned that the Jewish world was in every way unprepared to meet the survivors' problems. There was also the impossibility of legally entering former enemy territory without Army agreement; and, any significant help in food and medicines had to be legal or it would be totally inefficient. The JDC, on its part, turned to UNRRA and the Army for permits for their teams to enter the camps. We have record of a number of such requests and their rejection.[12] The Army tended to see in any civilian intrusion an unwelcome complication in a situation that was already difficult enough; it therefore did not at all favor the idea of having large numbers of UNRRA people inter-

fere in a semiautonomous manner with the job of looking after the DPs. UNRRA on its side did not want to exacerbate its strained relations with the Army any further by introducing "private" agencies that would enjoy independent powers in their association with the Army. The JDC was by no means the only "private" organization that had applied—there were also organizations that were Catholic, Polish Catholic, Protestant and Quaker. It would seem, however, that the fact that Jews were not considered to be a separate national group had something to do with the reluctance to let in specifically Jewish teams even after the June 29 cable. Such officially Jewish participation was apparently thought to create a problem which could perhaps be avoided altogether by repatriation. In June a small JDC team did actually enter Buchenwald and work there for a short time. It was this team that arranged the transport of children to France that was previously mentioned. In this particular instance the legalistic procedure to which some of the JDC staff were still wedded almost caused a tragedy when the French government tried to appropriate these children and hand them over to Catholic institutions. This was prevented both by the children and their own leaders and by some of the JDC staff.[13] It should, however, be immediately added that this was an isolated incident; with very few exceptions, JDC in the postwar era, under the European leadership of Dr. Joseph J. Schwartz, quietly abandoned its extreme legalism and supported the activities of Jews and their organizations in Europe, despite the opposition of some governments. In its attempts to enter the camps, however, JDC was in a difficult position: as a leading American philanthropic institution with an almost semiofficial status, it could not possibly act in opposition to the U.S. Army, nor would that have made any sense from a practical point of view because without Army help no supplies could be brought in. On the other hand, JDC people often lacked the necessary ingenuity and gamesmanship to utilize fully the loopholes given in the chaotic situation of the summer of 1945. Thus the first permanent JDC mission arrived in Belsen in early July, and the first team for the U.S. sector—roughly the whole of present-day southeastern part of West

Germany—arrived in Munich on August 4.[14] Other organizations came even later. Palestinian emissaries arrived illegally in Vienna in October, and the official Jewish Agency mission got to Germany only in November. UNRRA itself became a significant factor in Germany only in July–August, for reasons which we have already seen. Of the leaders, only Eliahu Dobkin of the Agency came to Germany for a few days in July. In the north, a small Jewish relief unit came from Britain to work in Belsen, under the formidable leadership of Lady Henriques, a social welfare worker and an extreme assimilationist, whose relations with the DPs tended to be strained. It is a fact that at least for three months the survivors, especially in the U.S. zone, were without any real contact with the Jewish world, with the sole exception of the Jewish Brigade from Palestine, and even they arrived in Germany only six weeks after liberation.

The concentrations of Jews hinted at in the June 29 cable had been established before that and without any organized help from the outside.

The two problems facing the rescued immediately on liberation were physical convalescence and the tracing of relatives. In a large collection of letters from Buchenwald written on May 6,[15] a tremendous urge to reestablish family contacts is apparent. People are looking forward to seeing their homes again—home is a house, a room, relatives, friends—and this is a primary need of great force. Many letters seem to indicate an amazing lack of awareness of the mass extermination; it was as though it was understood that whatever may have happened to others, the writer and his own relatives and friends were safe and sound. It is difficult to say whether this really mirrored a lack of knowledge or, more plausibly perhaps, an irrational reaction to facts that were too terrible to contemplate rationally, as though the death of a nation had been but a nightmare from which the writer had happily awakened. Generally speaking, Jews who were liberated in the camps or elsewhere wanted to know first of all what had happened to their dear ones. We know that there were many —how many we do not know—who went to Poland on repatriation trains not in order to stay there but merely to look

for relatives, and who then returned to Germany. These journeys seem to have been limited to Poland, Lithuania and Latvia, and we lack proof of any significant movement to other countries with the object of returning to Germany afterwards.

It is by no means easy to give a statistical picture of Jewish displaced persons. There was continual flux—Jews were repatriated, others returned to camps in ways already described. Polish and other Jews arrived in Germany legally from places such as Terezin and other camps liberated by the Soviets. Buchenwald passed into Russian hands as the zone boundaries were fixed; Dachau, Allach, Kauffering were emptied of their former inmates. Some Jews did not dare identify themselves as such in former forced-labor groups or in DP camps that had Polish and other anti-Semitic elements. Despite their protests others were counted as nationals of their respective countries of origin. The accepted figure for the U.S. zone in Germany and Austria in June–July is 14,000 to 15,000, though this may be just slightly too low. In Berlin there were in June probably 8,000 Jews belonging to the reconstituted Jewish community. In Belsen, 13,000 to 15,000 remained after the first exodus of the repatriates. There were perhaps a couple of thousands in the Soviet zone, a small number in the French and British zones in Austria, and some 7,000 in Vienna. In all probability the total for Germany and Austria did not exceed 50,000.[16]

The first Jews from the outside to meet the Jewish survivors were the Jewish soldiers in the liberating armies. Such encounters are reflected in private letters or reminiscences and often also in the diaries and notes written by the DPs. One of those on the scene was Harry A. Freidenberg, of Los Angeles, who was the administrative officer of the Military Government Section at U.S. Army Area Command, Vienna. Attending synagogue services in the city he became instrumental in establishing a mail and package service for the Jews,[17] as did many of the soldiers, officers and, mainly, rabbis serving as chaplains in the American Army. While the soldiers and officers did what they could to help, it was the

chaplains who, without any organizational setup for the purpose, succeeded in giving real aid. Rabbis Schenk, Schacter and, later, Robert S. Marcus worked effectively in Buchenwald. Rabbis Hazelkorn, Lipman and, indeed, about twenty-five rabbis all over the U.S. zone were the first people to whom the survivors could turn. The fact that the Jewish chaplains wore insignia representing the Tablets of the Law had a certain significance to people who had to be convinced that these symbols were no longer symbols to be used against them. Though the Jewish chaplain in the British Army occupied a less prominent place than did his counterpart in the U.S. forces, Rabbi Levy in Belsen was effective, if not as an actual helper, at least as a first contact with the outside world. There were similar contacts with Jewish soldiers and officers of the Soviet Army.[18]

The chaplain in the U.S. zone was also the first effective link in communications between the DP and the free world. The rabbis made it a practice to send and receive mail on behalf of the refugees at a time when all postal connection was forbidden—a situation that was not to change until October 1945. The packages project was introduced by most chaplains and some enterprising soldiers and officers (in the U.S. sector of Berlin, for instance), each in his own area. Friends and relatives of the initiator, and then of Jewish soldiers in his area, would be asked to send packages in the chaplain's name and postal number, and the chaplain would then distribute the packages among the DPs. This process began very early, in June–July.

Most of these donors unfortunately remained anonymous, and the practice of moving units as Army needs dictated made most of the contacts of the very first days, important as they were, temporary. Thus Dachau was liberated by the 42nd Division under General Collins; but the division moved on to the Salzburg area, where Rabbi Bohnen, who was attached to the unit, did the kind of work described above. Occasionally, these contacts were more permanent. At Tutzing, a large contingent of Jews, mainly women, was liberated by the Americans, and one of the liberators, a Jew, Lieutenant Irving Smith, was appointed commander of a DP camp at Feldafing that was to become the first Jewish camp in the zone. He had the support of Chaplain Max

Braude of the Seventh Army.[19] Most Jews, however, were liberated in the Third Army area in southern Bavaria or in the areas of Salzburg and Linz which were under the control of the 42nd and 26th Divisions respectively. It was under these conditions that Abraham J. Klausner, a young Reform rabbi, arrived in Dachau, probably in the third week of May.

Klausner had been with the Army in Germany when the war ended. He then volunteered to go to the Far East, because he thought he might be of some use there with the Jewish soldiers. Unexpectedly, and against his wishes, he was called to serve in the 116th Evacuation Hospital Unit where, he was told, there were hundreds of Jews who needed a rabbi. Not knowing where the unit was stationed, he found it difficult to believe that any U.S. military hospital could have such a high percentage of Jews. Reluctantly he went to Germany to look for his unit in the Third Army area, and after a three-day pleasure trip he arrived in Munich to find his unit. There a sergeant was trying to locate it on a large wall map. His finger, relates Klausner, wandered over the map until it stopped and pointed to—Dachau.

Klausner's story of his first days at Dachau is very similar to other accounts of chaplains in camps. His first task was to bury those whom even the devoted work of the medical team could not save. They were placed in mass graves; often names of those who died were unknown, and there was no way of identifying them. Most of the dead were Jews, but not all of them, and so a Protestant chaplain worked with Klausner on the sad assignment. Finally a Jew volunteered to take over the job of burials—by that time deaths had become much fewer and individual burials could be arranged, and the rabbi only signed the register.

The feeling of frustration must have been enormous. The young rabbi had not been equipped for this kind of work, in spirit or in substance. He had been given *mezzuzot** by the people back home to distribute to the survivors—he was ashamed even to show these, and he had nothing else to give.

The questions asked of him were not of the kind he had

---

* Plural of *mezzuza:* encased parchment scroll inscribed with two Biblical passages (Deut. 6:4–9, 11:13–21), placed on the doorposts in traditional Jewish homes.

expected; they were not about the help that had not come, the nations and governments who had talked and their words had been empty, or the Lord who had looked on while His chosen people were being slaughtered. Instead, he was asked about friends and relatives in the United States. Among his questioners was a man, so sick he could not raise himself, who asked Klausner about a brother of his who had gone to America in the good old days to become a rabbi. By a remarkable coincidence, the brother was not only known to Klausner but was actually serving as a chaplain in the neighborhood. The brothers met, and seeing the way the Dachau brother was revived by that meeting, Klausner decided to make the rounds of the camps in the zone and, with help from some of the DPs, make a list of all the inmates so as to institute a kind of tracing service.

Meanwhile Klausner's personal position changed. The hospital unit to which he was attached was transferred to a health resort for recuperation—its members had come up all the way from the battle of Anzio and richly deserved a rest. Klausner was expected to go with them. In his own words:

> And so we came to this place, it was a beautiful place, I remember. We came off a highway onto a little loading area which rose above a lake, a beautiful lake, and the trucks stopped, and everybody jumped out and started to run for the resort place in order to get better rooms, I imagine. I was a little embarrassed, I didn't feel like running. . . . I wasn't interested in resting. But I got off the truck, jumped off, and I stood there alone, and one truck turned back, and another truck, and—I don't remember how many there were, some eight trucks . . . As the last truck began to circle to move towards the highway, without really thinking—because the thought hadn't gone through my mind, it was something that just urged me—I grabbed the tail-board of the truck and I climbed aboard. And that was it. That was my last moment of being officially attached to the U.S. Army. As the trucks came back to Dachau to pick up the second unit, I jumped off the truck before it moved into Dachau; and I waited outside, and just hung around till everybody left. And when everybody had left, I walked back into Dachau. I walked over to

> the 127th Unit and I told the chaplain there that I was being reassigned to the 127th, the papers would be coming through. Did he mind if I found a corner to sleep. He didn't mind . . . .[20]

This was the beginning of a process in which Klausner was to twist and turn in the tangle of American military bureaucracy—his was a unique case of a roving chaplain with a very tenuous link to various units, an unofficial liaison between the Army and Jewish DPs, helped on by friends who prevented his being brought to book for his irregularities or from being taken out and sent away.

Meanwhile also, a large number of sick Jews were being concentrated at St. Ottilien, a Benedictine monastery used by the Nazis as a military hospital. The Nazis had taken out a group of Jews from Dachau and were bringing them to the Tyrolean mountains when the advancing Americans liberated them at a village called Schwabenhausen. A young Kovno doctor, Zalman Gruenberg, organized them there and an American captain by the name of Raymond arranged for them to go to St. Ottilien.[21] At that time St. Ottilien was being used as a hospital for German and Hungarian soldiers, and tension developed between them and the Jews. In the meantime Klausner had won the confidence not only of the commander of Dachau, Colonel Paul A. Roy, but also of the medical officer at the camp. Colonel Roy was ordered to clear the camp of its Jewish inhabitants, and Klausner took some of the sick people to St. Ottilien, thereby considerably increasing the hospital's Jewish population. By various manipulations he was also instrumental in having the hospital cleared of its German and Hungarian occupants, and it soon became a DP hospital for Jews. At St. Ottilien, the first organized activity of Jewish DPs took place; it took the form of a concert. The Kovno ghetto orchestra members, most of whom had survived, were brought to the hospital by friendly Americans, and the singer Henia Dumashkin added her voice to the first performance of the *She'erit Hapletah* (Saved Remnant), the name by which the survivors were to become generally known.[22]

Klausner soon realized that he had "to organize the picture." He wrote memoranda and letters to friends and per-

sonalities in the United States; in this he was but one of many chaplains, soldiers and officers who sought to alarm the Jewish world into action in support of their brethren in Europe. Klausner's special contribution was to activate an organization that would represent the liberated Jews and be effective, ultimately, both as an expression of the people's will and as an instrument of administration and negotiation. It should be added here that Klausner was not a Zionist; but his Jewish and humanitarian approach and the things he saw in the camps filled him with anger at a world that had allowed such things to happen, and he thought that if these few Jews wanted a separate organization and a separate life and a new country they would call their own the world was duty-bound to give it to them.

The first stumbling block on the road to achieving these tasks was lack of recognition of Jews as a separate entity. But here the problems that the military faced came to Klausner's rescue. The officer responsible for DP questions in Munich was only too glad to accept Klausner's offer to organize the Jews and take them off the hands of the military as far as discipline, movements, and so on were concerned. Following the officer's advice, Klausner obtained the use of part of the ruins of the Deutsches Museum in Munich from a French team attached to UNRRA. A few days after this, on June 24, an open-air meeting took place at the Flak-Kaserne, a DP center in Munich, to welcome the first mission of the Jewish Brigade to Germany. This was organized by a Zionist group, and Gruenberg and Klausner were there as well.

The stories about the origin of the Zionist group in Bavaria have a rather mythical quality. But it is a fact that a letter dated June 9[23] was sent off to the Zionist Executive in Jerusalem announcing the birth of a Zionist group in Bavaria. This consisted of a Lithuanian group, including Yitzhak Rattner and Yossef Lavi (Lebovitz), whose members had been together in one of the camps and had helped each other survive. Members of resistance groups from Kovno and Shavli, they had maintained their organization in the Nazi camps and had even published a clandestine, handwritten newsletter there. Apparently a foundation meeting

had taken place at the beginning of June, and a United Zionist organization had been founded. The ideas put forward by this group were very similar to those of the "Remnants" in Bucharest. Here, too, the lesson seemed to be that the Jews had to present a united front to a hostile world. There was no contact of any kind between the two bodies, and yet there was a great similarity in attitudes between them; this indeed was characteristic of the atmosphere then prevailing among the survivors generally. It should also be noted that the Zionist movement that developed in Bavaria was completely independent—as indeed that of the Brichah movement in Poland had been a few months before that—and neither Klausner nor the Brigade people had been in touch with the Zionist group until after it had become active.

This does not mean that the Zionists had it all their own way. There was a Bundist delegate at the first meeting of camp representatives, and a Bundist group was to operate at Landsberg for a long time afterward. But in general it was only natural that Polish Bundists or Communists should return to Poland in accordance with their ideology, leaving the field in the camps to Zionists or to people who were quite willing that they should be represented by Zionists.

At this point another factor must be considered: at Feldafing, not far from Munich, the first Jewish DP camp had actually come into being, with Lieutenant Irving Smith as its commander. This, too, had its origin in Dachau. We have already noted that Colonel Roy had to clear Dachau camp, and Klausner in fact undertook to move its inmates to other places. In return he was given a certain measure of command over what he considered to be the necessary supplies which would have to be given to the DPs. His first care was for the sick, and apart from transferring some of these to St. Ottilien, he also managed to obtain, again by a variety of means, the hospital at Gauting, near Munich, to house the many tubercular patients at Dachau. He transferred the other people mainly to Feldafing and Landsberg. Smith at Feldafing was very much in accord with the idea of a Jewish camp, and so was Chaplain Braude. The process of making Feldafing a Jewish camp involved moving out the Hungarians who were there and bringing in the Dachau Jews. This

was accomplished, more or less, by July, and the camp became definitely Jewish, even though it still had a minority of non-Jews.[24]

Smith ran Feldafing in a rather high-handed fashion, but there was no doubt that he meant well for his charges. Later, accusations were leveled at him that he had handed the camp over to strong men who had used their positions of authority as overseers in the Nazi concentration camps to the detriment of other camp inmates. A dubious position was also held by a German woman, Ethel Otto, who served as Smith's aide. Yet Smith ran a relatively well-organized camp under difficult conditions.

This, then, was the situation in Bavaria in mid-June: Jews were beginning to concentrate in certain of the Bavarian camps—Feldafing, Landsberg (where a Jewish section of the camp was growing in numbers), Buchberg, Wels in Austria, St. Ottilien and Dachau. A Zionist group had been established by Rattner and his friends; at St. Ottilien Dr. Gruenberg had a Jewish hospital, and Klausner was engaged in plans to organize the refugees, to publish a list of survivors and to transfer the survivors of Dachau to Jewish centers. Then the Brigade arrived.

Of Palestine's 500,000 Jews, 25,700 had volunteered to join the British Army and had been accepted (others had volunteered, but for political reasons the British were reluctant to accept Jews into their army). After much struggling and through sheer obstinacy most of these Jews were finally organized in Jewish units, most of them with Hebrew as the official language in the unit. These units, with a few exceptions, were not allowed to fight at the front, not because they were expected to fight poorly, but probably because the British feared they would fight well and thus be able to present a moral claim after the war for political concessions. However, as the details of the destruction wrought by the Nazis came in, Churchill increasingly insisted on giving some kind of political or military compensation to the Jews. After several false starts the British finally announced, in September 1944, that a Jewish Brigade would be set up. They took the three existing Palestinian battalions to form the core of the

new unit, added other Jewish soldiers and a number of non-commissioned officers, officers and technical personnel, as well as some special units taken from non-Jewish British Army units, and the Brigade was established under the command of Brigadier Benjamin, a regular Jewish officer of the British Army. There were as many as 7,000 Jews in the unit, but this was not the only Jewish group in Italy in the winter of 1944–45. Jewish transport units and engineers were also in Italy, as were some members of ATS (auxiliary service for women). From an internal Jewish point of view the significance lay in the fact that most of the Jewish officers and N.C.O.'s had been suggested to the British by the Agency from among Haganah members. Besides, each larger unit had a Haganah commander, who was not at all necessarily identical with the highest-ranking Jewish officer. The overall command of the Haganah in Italy in 1946, for instance, was in the hands of a sergeant (Eliyahu Ben-Hur). In addition, one must always remember the tremendous Jewish passion for political factions, and any committees that were formed had to take into account the various political movements.

In October 1944, the newly formed Brigade was in training near Fiuggi in southern Italy. By that time, 7,000 refugees had been uncovered, among them some 1,400 at Ferramonti.[25] The Palestinian Jewish soldiers made it their business to look after these survivors, help them in every way, try to educate the youth among them and establish the young people, wherever the Zionist idea was predominant, on training farms—all this, of course, in cooperation with the Italian Jews (or those among them who were able and willing to help) and the JDC. This activity, like all others, necessitated a committee, and this committee had to be carefully balanced to give representation to the various parties. The Brigade had such a committee, but the other units now joined as well, and on October 29, 1944, at a meeting in Fiuggi the Center for the Diaspora (*Merkaz Lagolah*) was founded in the presence of two representatives of the JDC (Arthur Greenleigh and Max Pearlman).[26] The task of this committee was to bring aid and comfort to refugees and conduct Zionist education activities among them. Unoffi-

cially the idea of organizing illegal immigration was ever-present, and naturally the Merkaz thought of itself as a representative of the Haganah and all its branches as well.

The Brigade, though organized very late in the war, yet managed to do some fighting in the last stages of the struggle in Italy. It went into action on March 4 on the Senio River and fought there almost until the general collapse of the German Army. Naturally, the Merkaz was inactive during that time. Immediately following the end of the war, the Brigade was stationed at Tarvisio, on the Austrian-Italian-Yugoslav border. Three weeks passed from that May 8 on which the war ended, and the Brigade, stationed on the very frontier of Austria, had no knowledge of what was happening in the regions north of it. Then, on May 29, four adventurous soldiers came back to camp, having traveled through parts of Yugoslavia and Austria, and reported that they had seen some camps and a number of survivors. On June 1, the emissaries of the Rumanian "remnants" arrived on the border. A day before, 98 Jewish refugees had been found at Villach, just over the Austrian border from Tarvisio. They were brought to the Brigade, and the greetings they and the "Remnants" brought from thousands of people made the Merkaz and other soldiers realize that they had additional tasks before them. And yet, this realization dawned upon them slowly. As late as June 4 a general meeting was held at Tarvisio, at which soldiers' delegates demanded that they return home to Palestine when their normal turn came under British regulations. Some soldiers said that the Brigade might have a task to fulfill with the survivors, but their words were not heeded.[27]

This peculiar state of affairs changed as the month of June advanced. It was decided to send a delegation to the Rumanian "Remnants" group, and four soldiers left Tarvisio on June 13. They arrived in Bucharest just as Kovner and his people were about to leave Rumania for Italy. In the meantime a legendary figure arrived from Palestine, a man for whom the British had been looking for about two years—a Haganah member called Yehuda Arazi. Arazi was quite different from the usual Haganah man. He was definitely not a left-winger, as were most Haganah officers; he

was something of an aristocrat in taste and manners, and was to feel more at home in the country houses of Italian nobles who became his friends than with his collaborators who had been soldiers and refugees. He had been in charge of acquiring arms for the Haganah during the war and had run into trouble. The British knew him well—he had been a police officer in the British forces in Palestine—and he had to hide for a long time in a Palestinian kibbutz. Finally he had had enough of this kind of passivity and volunteered to go to Italy to organize illegal immigration there.

Illegal immigration was not run by the Haganah directly. It was organized by an institution known as *Mossad Le'Aliyah Beth* (Institute for "B" [illegal] immigration) which had been founded in 1938 by the *Histadruth* (Jewish Federation of Labor in Palestine). Soon, during the first years of the war, Mossad had been broadened beyond the Labor groups and had become a national institution controlled by the political department of the Jewish Agency and run by a committee representing the various political parties. The commander of Mossad—from its inception in 1938 and right through to 1948—was Shaul Avigur, who had been one of the two Haganah commanders in the early thirties and was one of the central figures in Jewish Palestine. The link with Haganah was functional: Mossad members were Haganah members as a matter of course and were almost always recruited from the Haganah with the latter's consent. To the ordinary Palestinian Jew the organizational niceties meant very little, and as the whole setup was of course clandestine, it seemed as though in fact the Haganah was responsible for "B" immigration as well.

Arazi arrived in Italy disguised as a Jewish sergeant. When he got to Tarvisio he sought out Hoter-Yishai, a former Haganah lawyer who now was a major in the second battalion of the Brigade. Hoter-Yishai, who knew Arazi very well, says he did not recognize his friend, so perfectly had he changed his external appearance. When at last they got down to business, Arazi explained to him his mission: he wanted to organize illegal emigration to Palestine. Of course he knew that there were very few survivors, and even those who survived were so demoralized that few would probably

want to go to Palestine clandestinely; yet he hoped that Hoter-Yishai would find, say, 5,000 Jews in Europe who would be willing to undertake the dangerous journey.[28]

The complete lack of comprehension of the true situation among the Jewish survivors in Europe surely cannot be illustrated better than by citing this story about the "5,000 people" who might possibly want to go to Palestine illegally. In fact, between 1945 and the establishment of the State of Israel on May 14, 1948, 69,000 Jews[29] made the journey by boat (apart from "illegals" who came on false passports, overland or by air), and the number would have been considerably greater had there been enough ships and money. But none of this, of course, was even dreamt of in June 1945.

Arazi's mission, the "Remnants' " delegation, the 98 Jews in Villach—all these prompted Hoter-Yishai to try to organize a search mission into Austria and Germany. This of course had to be carefully camouflaged, as there were not only grave suspicions on the British side (perfectly justified ones, one might add) but the mission would have to enter American-occupied territory—and what would a British soldier with the "Palestine" tag be doing in the U.S. zone of Germany? The solution was to find relatives of those Brigade soldiers, and there were many of them, who had been born in Germany and Austria. A list of such people was on hand, and the brigadier gave his permission (it is a bit doubtful whether he actually believed what he was told, and it is more probable that he guessed the real reasons for the mission and did not want to interfere). And so, on June 20, a group of five men with Hoter-Yishai at the head left Italy, went through Austria, visiting camps on the way, and arrived in Munich probably on the 22nd.[30] The rumors and some eye-witness reports of the camps that had filtered through to the Brigade were one thing; the sight of thousands of Jews, many of them still in the striped uniforms of the camps, poorly fed, suffering the overt and brutal anti-Semitism of Polish or Baltic centers, and living under constant threat of repatriation to their "homes"—this was a different thing altogether. It was a shattering experience. The soldiers were received everywhere in an almost worshipful spirit and they themselves were later unable to describe their meetings with the survivors in dispassionate terms.

The Jews had been so long under Nazi influence and rule that they had begun involuntarily to accept notions about their inferiority. The Jew had been the lowest creature on earth in the Nazi world, and abandoned to humiliation and destruction. Now, five weeks after the end of the war, his humiliation still with him, his condition wretched, living in camps with Polish, Lettish, Lithuanian or Ukrainian murderers, he was suddenly visited by soldiers bearing the insignia of the Star of David (the official badge of the Brigade), the same badge that he had been made to wear as the badge of shame. True, most of them had seen Jews before, soldiers of the liberating armies, and especially American chaplains, rabbis who had as their insignia the Tablets of the Law. But these had been individual Jews in large armies; here came Jews who were fighting as Jews, not as Americans or British or Russians. The impact beggared description.

The tour of the camps had some practical results as well—everywhere Hoter-Yishai tried to improve living conditions for the Jews, brought to the attention of commanders the option of non-repatriation open to the DPs, and tried to achieve segregation, and thereby protection, for the Jews. There is even ground for assuming that it was Hoter-Yishai's intervention at the Frankfurt headquarters of SHAEF that was instrumental in producing a repeat order, dated June 29, to lower-command echelons restating in clear language the right of DPs to refuse repatriation. In all these activities Hoter-Yishai was followed by other Jewish units' teams, which came to Germany in July and August.

In Munich, Hoter-Yishai met Klausner. The two men found they had much in common, and a plan of cooperation was speedily evolved. It should perhaps be emphasized that the approach of these two men to the problem of the DPs was not identical. Hoter-Yishai was, after all, an emissary of Zionist bodies, even though he had had no actual contact with them, apart from the talk with the man from Mossad. But he knew that he was acting in the Zionist spirit. He wanted to help the refugees, and he also knew that his deeply felt humanitarian aim was inextricably bound up with a political approach and a national philosophy. Klausner's point of departure was different—he wanted to help the "people," as he always called them, and as they were

bent on going to Palestine, they should be helped to go there. Unencumbered with knowledge of the intricacies of internal Zionist politics, Klausner tended to support a radical, even extreme Zionism, which he felt was more in line with his own moral fervor. The problem for him was a world problem, the means of solving it had to be political; for the soldiers there were no two sides to the problem. To them the political means were humanitarian because the survivors would continue to be victimized if they were not used. The Zionist way of looking at things fitted perfectly the situation of 1945—the world was literally closed to Jews, and only the hard road to Palestine might be opened. Empirically, even non-Zionists could easily accept such a solution. All this was of course never explicit, and people did not have time for intelligent formulae and philosophical analyses. Klausner and Hoter-Yishai were men of action, and discussions centered on money and gasoline rather than on Zionist theory.

In actual fact, of course, the help given by the Brigade was necessarily very small. The Brigade claims to have provided Klausner or the camps with some materials procured in Italy by highly irregular procedures. Also, food and blankets were collected from the soldiers who gave up their rations for the DPs—their behavior was quite extraordinary. But all they did was pathetically little. And it is true that their main influence was exerted by their very presence and by the Palestine-centered attitude this encouraged.

At the meeting of June 24 held at the Flak-Kaserne, Klausner arranged for DP representatives interested in a survivors' organization to meet at Feldafing on July 1. At this point, however, a hitch occurred. The officer in charge of DP matters in the Third Army area asked Klausner to appear before him. "He understood," Klausner says, "that I wanted to organize. . . . But, he said, unfortunately we cannot permit you to proceed. . . . I was told, then, that I could not set up this organization. And as I walked to the door—I thanked him, he explained that this was the ruling of the Army—as I walked to the door, and my back was towards him, he said to me: 'but do a good job.' So I smiled, thanked him again, and walked out . . . And we were in business."[31]

Then, on Sunday, July 1, 1945, some three dozen people came to Feldafing from various camps in Germany and Austria, and a meeting took place on a kind of porch in one of the buildings. Those present were Max Braude (the senior chaplain of the Seventh Army), a representative of the Brigade and, of course, Smith, the Feldafing commander. The usual long speeches were made, and Smith especially insisted that if the Jews kept their camps clean they would be treated well and, like the Feldafing people, would be getting Red Cross packages. At this, Gruenberg and Klausner became angry, got up and dissolved the meeting. The delegates assembled later in a kitchen in the camp without Smith, and after reports from the camps had been heard a central committee of the liberated Jews in the U.S. zone was elected. The Zionist attitude of all but one of the speakers is interesting to note. Klausner stated that there were at that point about 825,000 DPs in the U.S. zone, among them 15,000 Jews; that there was a legal possibility of refusing repatriation, provided Soviet citizenship could not be proved. The committee elected represented not only the camps but also the main groups by country of origin (*Landsmannschaften*). In fact, however, the Lithuanian contingent predominated; this is important in view of the central role played by Lithuanian Jews with their very strong Zionist background in survivors' organizations generally in postwar Europe. The Austrian camps at first joined the committee but were later to separate to form a very unstable committee of their own at Salzburg.[32]

The new committee moved to Munich and began its organization. The Deutsches Museum was made ready on July 11. Departments were then formed, such as those for health, tracing, food, clothing, culture and education, transport and religion. Later on, various other functions were added, and Yosef Lavi, among others, was appointed as liaison with the Brichah. The various departments could do very little at first, because Klausner was for some time the only one who could get things going by virtue of his chaplain's uniform and rank.

Sometime in the middle of July a blow fell: the Flak-Kaserne Jews received an order to move north for repatriation to their "homeland." Klausner was asked to intervene.

For what happened then we have to rely mainly on Klausner's testimony: He says he advised the officer in charge not to use force and to tell his superiors of the determined opposition encountered. This led to a summons to Klausner to appear before the commanding officer who, as it turned out, had his orders from Patton's HQ to clear Munich of DPs. The colonel is reported to have told Klausner that he had no Jews at all—only such people as Lithuanians and Poles and proved this by pointing to an official list of all nationalities recognized by the U.S. Army. Klausner then asked him who was causing all the trouble at Flak-Kaserne if there were no Jews, whereupon the colonel dismissed the rabbi. As a result, when the trucks came to take away the DPs, they found only a few dozen out of the original 1,200. This incident is of some importance, as it not only asserted Jewish truculence and independence with regard to official regulations but also contributed in a practical way to the Central Committee's work, because the people from Flak now dispersed in Munich and became the obvious choice as workers at the Central Committee's offices.[33]

Meanwhile, the Dachau situation had been solved with the help of Colonel Roy. In the course of these activities, Klausner, helped by some of the people who now were working with him, got hold of Nazi or discarded American materials and supplies, and used them to give the first clothes, shoes and minimal amenities to the Jews. This was done by methods that were, to put it mildly, highly unorthodox—but it is quite obvious that in the situation then prevailing this was the only way such items could be obtained for a group that had been the most underprivileged of the underprivileged and therefore was thought to need a correspondingly better treatment now. The lists of survivors collected by Klausner were published on June 26, in a volume called simply *She'erit Ha-pletah* (The Spared Remnant).

In the meantime, Brigade soldiers had prepared a general Jewish conference to meet in St. Ottilien on July 25. A first official Jewish representative, Eliahu Dobkin of the immigration department of the Jewish Agency, was present. Participants were brought in Brigade vehicles from all over

Germany to what was to be the only all-German conference of Jewish DPs. Among those who came was a small delegation from Bergen-Belsen, in the British sector, to which we must now turn our attention.

After the dead had been buried and some of the living repatriated, Belsen was the camp with the largest Jewish population in Germany—some 13,000 to 15,000 people. With the Jews in the camp were Polish DPs, and the main struggle of the Jewish committee of the camp for quite some time was to obtain recognition by the British of the right of the Jews to a separate existence. The British attitude, at first no different from that prevailing in the U.S. zone, hardened progressively under the influence of the growing strain of Anglo-Jewish relations over the Palestine issue. Basically, the British attitude combined a very humane, nondiscriminatory approach with a violent opposition to Jewish nationalism. A memorandum of the Chief of Staff office of the British Zone Command (no date, probably October–November 1945) states succinctly:

> It is undesirable to accept the Nazi theory that the Jews are a separate race. Jews, in common with all other religious sects, should be treated according to their nationality rather than as a race or a religious sect. Thus for repatriation purposes they will be the responsibility of National Liaison officers, and should any Jews be proved stateless or be unwilling to return to their country of origin they will be provided for by the Intergovernmental Committee on Refugees. Jews should be accommodated in camps appropriate to their nationality rather than to their race or religion. Any form of racial or religious segregation will only give rise to anti-Jewish feeling and may well have far-reaching repercussions.[34]

There is no reason to doubt the sincerity of the British approach. It was made up of a real distaste for what was considered to be a result of Nazi propaganda, blended with the feeling that a whole historical attitude to Jews which found its expression in the Balfour policy of regarding the Jews as a people, or nation, had been a vast political error. The bureaucratic mind then translated this into a set of rules and regulations which tended to prevent Jews in the British

zone from somehow arranging their lives as they wished. Here, however, the British found a very formidable opponent in the shape of a very small but very efficient and forceful Jew from Bendzin, a man of about thirty-five years of age, with piercing gray eyes and a strong physique: Yosef (Yossel) Rosensaft. Rosensaft is one of those controversial characters conditioned by the holocaust that one finds in postwar European Jewish history. He was an idealist in the sense that he was absolutely determined that "his" Jews should get a fair deal, that they should not be bullied by anti-Semitic Poles at Belsen or by pro-Jewish but anti-Zionist British anywhere. (Later, he was to be determined to save them from the inequities of Israeli bureaucracy.) A former member of a left-wing Zionist group, he was determined that Jewish children should have Jewish schools to go to, that health should be looked after by Jewish doctors, and he was to do everything he could to alleviate their lot when they finally reached whatever destination they chose—whether it was America or Israel. His courage, steeled in the political "bunker" of Auschwitz, knew no bounds—he was fully the equal of the all-powerful British officials in wit and intellect, though he had little formal education and could speak no language correctly except for his native Yiddish. He ruled the camp with an iron hand; he was accused of being a dictator, but he was elected and reelected again and again because in a very real sense, with all his ruthlessness toward strangers and love for his own kind, he was truly one of the people and they had confidence in him. Of course he had enemies among Jews; he was ambitious and did not like opposition. But in Belsen he did a tremendous job; he forced the British, after months of wrangling, to recognize his camp as a Jewish camp, prevented anyone from knowing the real number of the camp's inhabitants and thus got more rations than Belsen was actually entitled to—a very popular stratagem in the DP camps, but Yossel Rosensaft was a past master in this. When an attempt was made at St. Ottilien to create a representative Jewish body from all the camps, Yossel opposed it. He would not be run by a committee sitting in Munich. And so he created a committee of his own, representative of the whole British zone, which in fact meant the big Belsen camp and some

small German Jewish communities, which were now run from Belsen by Rosensaft and his associates with a benevolent but strong hand. This at first seemed to be a serious matter, because Belsen in July 1945 had about the same number of DPs as all the camps in the U.S. zone put together. But the picture changed very quickly. By the end of the year, close to 100,000 Jews were to crowd the U.S. zones, and by 1947 Belsen and the British zone were a small section of the Jewish DP population. And yet, Belsen is a story of great importance which still waits to be told.[35]

The St. Ottilien conference was intended as a public demonstration, and as such it did its job: in the early morning of of the 26th, the participants went to the infamous Hitler beer cellar in Munich and there, among Jewish Law scrolls pilfered by the Nazis from synagogues all over Europe, a proclamation was read in the presence of foreign press correspondents dealing with the demand of the liberated Jews to be allowed to emigrate to Palestine. This was very impressive and received a good press—but apart from the demonstration, St. Ottilien had other tasks to fulfill. The business begun at Feldafing was now completed, and the officers of the Central Committee ("ZK"—the capital letters of its Yiddish title) were confirmed in their jobs. Dr. Gruenberg was president and was to remain in this position till his emigration to Palestine in late 1946. A serious discussion on DP problems started, with 94 delegates present who represented some 40,000 Jews from all over Germany and Austria. The speeches showed how much conditions varied even in the same zone. Austrian representatives complained of very bad treatment at American hands, of food rations rated officially at 1,200 calories but actually worth less than that starvation ration; stories were told of lack of clothing, of degradation and anti-Semitism. Conditions in German U.S. zone camps seemed to vary a great deal. Landsberg and Feldafing reported crowded conditions, bad food, harsh restrictions on movement at the hands of American armed guards. Frankfurt and Langenzell, on the other hand, reported friendliness and compassion and favored treatment. Klausner summed it all up by saying that the American Army had in fact no policy toward the Jewish DPs. Dobkin's speech was

particularly interesting: he was very cautious and told his listeners that Palestinian certificates were nowhere in sight, and he emphasized the possibility of an all-out struggle to gain entrance into Palestine. Characteristically, there was no political discussion—to Jewish survivors in 1945 there was absolutely no question about political aims.[36] Jews had to have their national state, and whether the Jew who said this would actually go there or not made no difference whatsoever. This widely held conviction lent support to the Zionist coloring of the ZK and the German camps—and this, as we shall see, was a precondition for the success of Brichah.

3. *Refuge in Germany*

Contemporary Jewish history seems to abound in tragic paradoxes. Not the least of these is the fact that the DP camps in Germany and Austria—and especially those in the U.S. sectors—situated in the lands where the major destroyers of European Jewry originated, became the haven for hundreds of thousands of Jews, a vast transit camp into which the Brichah was to lead the survivors of East European Jewry.

On the face of it, there would seem to be little reason for the U.S. government or Army to allow the entrance of additional people into their zones of occupation at a time when their major effort was directed toward getting rid of those that were there already. The position of the Army was indeed difficult enough. They had some 825,000 DPs still on their hands by the time August had passed and the majority of the DPs had mercifully been repatriated. Those remaining DPs were Poles, Balts, Ukrainians and Jews. At the same time, the Americans were facing the beginning of an influx of German refugees deported from Poland, Czechoslovakia and other countries. In addition, German towns were damaged or ruined, and German economy generally was a shambles. In the autumn of 1945, an additional influx, this time of Jews, began to worry the authorities. The Ger-

man refugees they had to accept because they were being deported in accordance with the Potsdam Conference resolutions to which the United States had agreed. Our question must be: why did they allow the Jews to add to their burdens?

At the beginning of June, news from Germany reaching Jewish organizations and leaders in the United States were disquieting indeed. Jews were apparently being badly treated, were not recognized as a special group with special problems, and their future was entirely uncertain. The aid of the Secretary of the Treasury, Henry W. Morgenthau, Jr., was enlisted, and it was he who persuaded President Truman through Joseph C. Grew, Assistant Secretary of State, that an investigation be made into the situation of the camps generally and their Jewish inmates in particular.[1] The situation must be seen against the American background as well. Truman had become President in April and his grasp of matters was still uncertain. This was to be expected particularly in regard to problems of a secondary nature such as the DP camps in Germany. His innate humanitarianism, his pro-Jewish proclivities and a very acute political instinct which made him pay attention to the grievances, real or imagined, of an influential minority group were factors that influenced his acceptance of demands presented by Jewish interests. On June 22, Truman wrote to Earl G. Harrison, dean of the Law School at the University of Pennsylvania and U.S. representative on the Intergovernmental Committee on Refugees, who was about to be sent to investigate conditions in Europe on behalf of the State Department; the letter approved of the mission and added that Harrison should pay special attention to the situation of the Jewish DPs in the camps. At the instance of Harrison, the State Department, on July 2, asked Dr. Joseph J. Schwartz, European director of the JDC, to assist him in the mission. Assistance was also asked of Patrick M. Malin, deputy director of the Intergovernmental Committee (IGCR), and Herbert Katzki, later with the JDC, who was active in the work of the War Refugee Board (WRB). Schwartz went to visit north Germany and other areas, whereas Harrison concentrated on the U.S. zones in Bavaria and Austria. An itinerary was arranged for

Harrison by the Third Army, and if Harrison had followed it he would probably have seen very little of the actual conditions in the camps. However, Colonel Richmond of G-6, an acquaintance of Klausner, told the rabbi about the proposed itinerary. Klausner went to the hotel where Harrison had gone on his arrival in Munich, and the results were a night-long discussion and a change of itinerary. Klausner now accompanied Harrison on his tour, and his influence is clearly discernible in the language of Harrison's report. Harrison returned to the United States before Schwartz did and handed in a preliminary report to the President before August 3. Schwartz submitted his report to Harrison on the 19th, and the final report was submitted on the 24th. It made a devastating impression. Harrison charged the Army thus: "As matters now stand, we appear to be treating the Jews as the Nazis treated them, except that we do not exterminate them. They are in concentration camps in large numbers under our military guard, instead of SS troops. One is led to wonder whether the German people, seeing this, are not supposing that we are following or at least condoning Nazi policy." This was very exaggerated and hardly fair to the U.S. Army, but at the same time Harrison did bring out some of the real grievances, as for instance the fact that the Jews were treated as nationals of countries whose peoples, or at least a percentage of them, had cooperated in their slaughter. "There is," Harrison said, "a distinctly unrealistic approach to the problem. Refusal to recognize the Jews as such has the effect, in this situation, of closing one's eyes to their former and more barbaric persecution, which has already made them a separate group with greater needs . . . Many Jewish displaced persons and other possibly nonrepatriables are living under guard behind barbed-wire fences in camps of several descriptions (built by Germans for slave laborers and Jews), including some of the most notorious of the concentration camps, amid crowded, frequently unsanitary and generally grim conditions, in complete idleness, with no opportunity, except surreptitiously to communicate with the outside world, waiting, hoping for some word of encouragement and action in their behalf." Harrison said that food was miserable, clothing deficient,

and that no attempt was being made to grapple with the problem of the Jewish refugees' ultimate fate. To Harrison, who saw the Labour government in power in Britain, the solution seemed simple. Had not the Labour Party declared in 1944, and again in 1945, that it aimed at unlimited Jewish immigration into Palestine so that that country could be established as a Jewish state? Had they not declared that the Arabs should be encouraged to move out as the Jews moved in—something which no Zionist leader had ever demanded? What simpler way of solving the problem than sending most of the Jewish DPs to Palestine, where they were declaring they wanted to go! "Now that such large numbers are no longer involved and if there is any genuine sympathy for what these survivors endured, some reasonable extension or modification of the British White Paper of 1939 ought to be possible without too serious repercussions." The United States should "express its interest in and support of" a proposal to settle a large number of Jews in Palestine, and in this connection the number 100,000 was mentioned, based upon a Jewish Agency memorandum submitted to the British government. Harrison also recommended that the United States "should, under existing immigration laws, permit reasonable numbers of such persons to come here, again particularly those who have family ties in this country." With an almost audible sigh of relief, Harrison added, "As indicated earlier, the number who desire emigration to the United States is not large."[2]

The demand for 100,000 immigration certificates for Palestine was to turn into a political shibboleth of great importance. It had apparently originated in an interview of Churchill with Weizmann on November 4, 1944, when talk was centered on a plan for 1.5 million immigrants to be allowed into Palestine within fifteen years. This was made more explicit in a Jewish Agency memorandum of June 18, 1945. Now, through some medium—possibly Schwartz or the Jewish Agency directly—the figure was introduced into international politics by the Harrison report. Truman, in turn, picked up the demand and pledged his support for the 100,000. There were, as we have seen, about 50,000 Jews in Germany and Austria at that time, and it is

quite clear that the granting of 100,000 certificates by the British would have solved the problem for the existing DPs and also for the American army and government. Even some Jews from Poland and other places might have benefited. The U.S. administration would have scored well with the politically important Jewish element, would have rid itself of a serious political embarrassment in Germany and satisfied the Zionists without actually doing anything to support the political aim of Zionism—the establishment of a Jewish State. The immigration of the 100,000 would still have left a majority of Arabs in Palestine (approximately 900,000, compared with 600,000 plus 100,000 Jews), and would thus have solved a real and burning humanitarian problem without prejudging the Palestine issue or embarrassing the British position. It seems that Britain committed a grave political mistake in her refusal to accept the 100,000. She might have avoided an unpleasant wrangle with the United States and a number of European states; she would have taken the edge off the Zionist demands; and she would still have been left with much the same situation in Palestine to deal with. In August, with 50,000 Jews in the Western zones, the 100,000 might well have been the solution to the whole problem. After the British refusal, however, the Brichah put into Germany many tens of thousands of Jews, and by that time the problem had grown so much that the original concept was completely vitiated. It should perhaps be added, in parentheses, that the Jewish Agency was well aware of all these implications. It soon came to regard its proposal of the 100,000 as rather less than wise and was very much afraid that the British might accept it. Even in 1946 such an acceptance would probably have taken the edge off the pressure exercised by the Jewish DP camps on the United States and Britain; the Agency had to support its own demand—vocally—but it was British obstinacy that saved it from the results of its own proposals.

Harrison's report caused a great stir; on August 3, Secretary of War Stimson sent a cable to Eisenhower informing him of the gist of the accusations against the Army. For the rest of the month, inquiries and pressures continued to mount at Eisenhower's HQ in Frankfurt and culminated in

a Presidential rebuke bearing the dateline of August 31. Truman wrote, "While Mr. Harrison makes due allowance for . . . the huge task of mass repatriation [which occupied the Army since liberation], he reports conditions which now exist and which require prompt remedy. These conditions, I know, are not in conformity with policies promulgated by SHAEF, now Combined Displaced Persons Executive. But they are what actually exists in the field. In other words, the policies are not being carried out by some of your subordinate officers." Truman then complained of the fact that adequate German housing was not requisitioned for the Jews and that many of them were still being kept on the sites of the former concentration camps. He suggested frequent inspection tours to remedy intolerable situations. Finally, Truman pledged to make an effort "to have the doors of Palestine opened to such of these displaced persons as wish to go there."[3]

The Army had been badly burned and its reactions were immediate. On August 5, and again on the 22nd, new orders were issued recognizing the right of Jews to be housed in separate camps and reiterating previously issued regulations to ensure a satisfactory treatment of the DPs. The policy of transferring Jews out of former camps was now speeded up, and the use of armed U.S. guards at the gates gradually discontinued. In most camps, Jewish unarmed guards took their place. To be quite truthful, Eisenhower's replies to Truman (August 10 and October 6) contained some just criticisms of Harrison's report. Most Jews had been moved out of the concentration camps into DP camps; the food, while bad, was not inedible as Harrison had implied; and generally the treatment was not parallel to that of the S.S. by a very long way. Also, the Army acted very quickly in response to Presidential pressure. In any case, the Army was no welfare establishment, and young officers and other ranks could not be expected to cope with human problems that baffled experienced social and medical workers and political leaders. Yet Harrison's report jolted Army commanders dealing with DP matters at all levels, and the quick improvement, though creating no paradise and indeed leaving the situation just bearable, proved that the conditions prevailing

before the report had not been inevitable. Tens of thousands of Jews could be thankful for the moral indignation of a Protestant humanitarian which had bettered to an appreciable degree their physical conditions and their political prospects.

For some time the Army had a very bad press in the United States on DP problems. This caused a chain reaction in Germany, where officers were removed and disciplined for disregarding regulations concerned with DP problems. The tendency developed, therefore, to handle DP matters with kid gloves, especially after Eisenhower's visit to Feldafing camp on September 17. Army publicity saw to it that swarms of reporters informed the American public of the general's impressions and comments. There is no doubting the sincerity of the upper reaches of the Army's hierarchy in their efforts to improve the lot of the DPs within the given limits. This perhaps was at least partly fed also by a vague feeling of guilt at not having been able to prevent the horrors that had led to the creation of the DP problem. The feeling was, it seems, that these people had a right to be looked after rather better than they had been; a corollary of this was the attitude shown by many American combat soldiers toward the influx of Jews when that came to pass in the autumn. The fear of a repetition of the Harrison episode, which triggered the attacks by the press, and the complex reactions to the Jewish problem generally were the main reasons for the removal of obstacles in the way of the Brichah.

As a matter of fact, this situation was brought to a head very early in Brichah movements toward the U.S. zone. On August 21 a move started by Brichah people to get some 650 Jews in four trainloads across zone boundaries near Pilsen in Czechoslovakia. The New York *Post* reported on October 2 that "the top authorities of the XXII Corps requested permission to ship these Jews to Germany where special camps for Jews were being erected. But General Patton's headquarters ordered them shipped back to Poland." The eviction apparently occurred on August 24, enforced by the 8th Armored Division. "Pitiful scenes" ensued, the official explanation being that the move had been unan-

nounced and there was no room in Germany for these Jews. In the course of passive resistance offered by the Jews, blows were dealt and heads bloodied. The Jews were finally shipped back beyond the Russian boundary line, whence, of course, they penetrated back again into Germany on foot and in small groups.[4] This was the last time that U.S. authorities in Germany tried to use force against Jews to prevent them from entering the zone. The outcry in the American press quickly put a stop to such efforts; it was simply not worth the adverse publicity and possible Congressional or even Presidential intervention to send back a few hundreds or thousands of Jewish refugees fleeing, for whatever reason, from the East. The argument was now turned upside down, as it were: the Army was taking care of a defeated and bombed country into which refugees—Germans—were now being sent. They had some hundreds of thousands of foreign DPs on their hands; a few thousand more Jews were inconvenient and might cause more trouble but were preferable to another Harrison report and newspaper scandal. The refugees, as their spokesmen pointed out time and time again, could be stopped only by application of brute force. But no American general in 1945 would order his troops to fire on Jewish persecutees fleeing from the East. This was also a question of morale, and after the strongly emphasized anti-Nazi propaganda one simply could not shoot at Jews.

We have as yet no documentary evidence of an actual order to let Jews into the U.S. zone in the fall of 1945. But we do have it on fairly good authority that such an order was transmitted orally, and that would explain the behavior of the American forces after August. This also tallies with events in Austria in the autumn, to which we must now turn.[5]

The U.S. Army in Austria was under the command of General Mark Clark, and its position vis-à-vis Eisenhower and the U.S. forces European Theater (USFET), the successor of SHAEF in the American sectors, was one of virtual independence. The treatment of Jews differed significantly between the areas of the two occupying divisions, the 26th and the 42nd ("Rainbow Division"). The Salzburg area of the 42nd Division could, by October, boast of certain amenities, a package project instituted by Chaplain Rabbi Eli

Bohnen and by the benevolent interest of the very friendly commander, General Harry J. Collins, even to the extent of aid in executing cultural programs. A modest project of employment for the idle DPs had also been set in motion. The area comprised a camp in Salzburg (Camp Riedenburg), to which others were soon to be added, and several smaller concentrations. The Linz area, controlled by the 26th Division, was by comparison in a very bad way. There was no Jewish chaplain, and his place was temporarily taken by a corporal, Katzmann, who did his best but lacked status. He was helped by a Lieutenant Hillman, who really had no right to interfere at all in Jewish affairs. There were a number of camps: in the area of Wels there were Lichtenegg 1 and 2, which were bad enough, but two other camps at Hart and Haag near Leonding were worse and had been "recommended for closing after recent inspection because of overcrowding and poor sanitary conditions."[6] They housed about 640 Jews, who saw the area in which they were living slowly converted into one large sea of autumn mud. Nearby was a camp called Asten, housing Germans, Rumanians and Hungarians, all of them either Nazis or Nazi collaborators, who had been voluntary workers at German military installations at the camp for three years with full wages. James P. Rice, the young representative of the JDC in the area, reported: "The facilities at Asten are the finest I have seen in any camp which I have visited in France, Italy and Austria." Nearby, in Linz itself, there was an apartment house project called Bindermichl which was actually intended for families and which had been offered to the Jews on condition that they be treated as Austrians—that is, that they receive 1,200 calories (which was contrary to Eisenhower's instructions). In any case, there were very few families among the Jews, as they were mostly ex-concentration-camp inmates.

The man who was ultimately responsible—under the commanding officer of the 26th Division, General Rinehart—for DP problems was the chief of staff, a Colonel Epes, whose attitude does not seem to have been very sympathetic toward the Jews. According to Rice, Epes was doubtful about the responsibility of the United States, and the United

Nations generally, toward the Jewish ex-concentration-camp inmates because these were not United Nations nationals but mostly stateless people who did not want to go home (and thus relieve the U.S. Army generally and Colonel Epes particularly of their burdensome presence); on the other hand he was quite clear that the Germans and other enemy nationals or collaborators at Asten were U.S. charges and had to be treated well. If the Jews did not want to go to their former homes, they would either be treated as Austrians or else had to accept whatever was given to them. On October 3, the Hart and Haag inmates were to have been moved to an abandoned German camp called "Camp No. 55" without any previous warning or consultation, but the UNRRA zone welfare officer had managed to persuade Colonel Epes to postpone this till October 6. Rice arrived on the scene on the 3rd, and a round of conferences began with Epes and others. On the 5th, Rice and the UNRRA team responsible for the Hart and Haag camps visited Camp 55 and found it shocking—muddy, "still surrounded with barbed wire and dotted with pill-boxes . . . leaky roofs and broken windows." The UNRRA physician thought that no more than half of the Hart and Haag people could possibly be put into the new place, and said so in an adverse report to Epes. Rice agreed, and the Jewish committee simply refused to move from their old camp, bad as it was. It must be borne in mind that this kind of opposition even to very unjust Army measures was by no means usual in postwar Europe. The military therefore retorted "that the residents would definitely have to go to No. 55 and that their men were to be armed with live ammunition to enforce this order." Rice tried in vain to avert the danger by a further interview with Epes. Epes insisted that Rice should convince the Jews to move peacefully. Rice was in a very delicate situation: he was understood to be a kind of semiofficial representative of the Jews, trying to "interpret" their wishes to the military, but at the same time he was under U.S. Army discipline as a social worker attached to UNRRA. Furthermore, his American citizenship made him fully aware of his duty of loyalty to his country's armed forces. Rice therefore agreed to talk to the people but declared

that he was not convinced he would succeed. It appears that he made a very sincere effort to "interpret" the Army to the Jews. The Jews, however, were indignant and bitter and he made no headway. On October 6 in the morning, Rice appeared at the camp to be present while the inmates were moved; on arrival he found that the inhabitants of the camps had gone to demonstrate in front of divisional headquarters in Linz—it is quite clear that they did not trust Rice enough to confide their plans in him and he was therefore surprised by this unforeseen development. The demonstration was orderly and dignified, and a committee was invited for discussions with a major of the DP section who showed tact and understanding. He promised to let them into the apartments and to provide some minimal furniture, provided they accepted the 1,200-calorie starvation rations—which they did. In return, the order to move to Camp No. 55 was canceled.

During all that time Rice had tried unsuccessfully to reach the officer in charge of all DP matters in the U.S. zone in Austria. Now, in the afternoon, he sent off a cable to the Paris AJDC headquarters with a summary of what had happened. The cable reported in terse language that on October 5 "JDC has suggested military postpone movement to avoid any incidents"; that the military had disregarded this and that a demonstration had led to a cancellation of the original order. The cable ended on an ominous note: "Believe situation in whole Upper Austria requires close attention at this time."

There is no doubt that had this cable reached the eyes of any American newspaperman, he would certainly have given the situation in Upper Austria his "close attention." This may not have been Rice's intention, but that would certainly have been the outcome. For the Army, a public scandal—*after* the Harrison report and *after* Truman's letter to Eisenhower—was the last thing it wanted. It is therefore hardly surprising that events occurred with great swiftness, after the cable went off. At 3 A.M. on October 6 General Clark himself telephoned Rice and asked him to have the cable "withheld as he felt that the contents of the cable might create an incorrect impression if it reached the press."

The truth was, of course, that the cable might have created a correct impression, and therefore Clark's chief of staff, General Brann, was whisked to Linz, where he called a meeting at which the general commanding the 26th Division and his chief of staff were publicly reprimanded in Clark's name for having "failed to carry out the program he had ordered on behalf of the DP's, especially the Jewish refugees."

This was not all. Next day, October 7, another meeting took place, this time in Vienna, at which Clark himself stated that "he intended that President Truman's orders shall be carried out in the American zone of Austria not only because they were orders, but because he himself was in sympathy with the principle that the Jews had been most persecuted by the Nazis and would therefore be entitled to first consideration." According to Eisenhower's and Truman's directives, the Jews should be getting both German apartments *and* DP rations (2,000 calories), and that was what was now ordered to take place at the Bindermichl project. The 42nd divisional commander, General Collins, had brought his Jewish chaplain, Eli Bohnen, with him, and he was now able to point out the achievements of his unit in this sphere. At the end of the meeting Rice had an interview with Clark, who declared that the solution of the DP camp problem was now top priority. He invited Rice to ask for the help of the highest Army authorities if necessary. A committee composed of General Hume (G-5), James P. Rice and Rabbi Bohnen then chose suitable sites for the Jewish camp inmates which included some very luxurious places in the resort area of Bad Gastein.

We can see in this incident the same forces at work as in Germany. There was fear of adverse publicity for the Army, and there was also genuine sympathy with the plight of the Jews. At the same time, the dignified but resolute behavior of the Jews themselves was also a factor. The Brichah had nothing whatever to do with this incident, but it was this that changed very radically the climate of opinion and made most American officers very wary of a clash with Jews. One can hardly exaggerate the influence of the incident on Army policy toward Jews in Austria at a moment when Brichah was just beginning to operate in the American zone.

It was at that time, too, that physical conditions eased for all of the DPs in the American zones. On September 30, the Harrison report was published in the American press, and the Army reacted to this event by issuing orders (on September 18 and 19, and October 15), valid for Germany and Austria, which fixed the DP ration at 2,300 calories, provided the persecutees with 2,500 calories and put the burden of housing on the Germans by requiring Army officers to requisition German dwellings for the use of DPs. This improvement in physical conditions, relative as it was, contributed to the beginnings of large-scale Brichah movements into Germany and Austria. These movements into Austria increased considerably in October, exactly at the time that the Linz episode took place.

The increase in Jewish infiltration caused a reaction among American military authorities. They began to fear that hundreds of thousands of Jews would flood the U.S. zones. A report from Prague says that Jewish influence was brought to bear on the Americans via Czech officials to induce the U.S. zone authorities to accept Jews.[7] In November a crisis was reached in Vienna. General Foster Tate, Clark's chief of staff, contacted James P. Rice and Dr. Sachs, the JDC representative in Vienna, and told them that it might be necessary to jail all Jews who crossed the border illegally, not only because this was a serious offense but because the Army could not expand the already overcrowded new facilities for Jews. Fortunately at this very time Dr. Schwartz (head of the JDC European office), together with Dr. Sachs, had arrived in Austria and, at the request of Mr. Rice, immediately proceeded to Vienna for conferences. He was able to point out to General Tate and General Clark the reasons why Jews were leaving Poland based on his own recent visit to that country. He suggested that Jews who escaped the Nazi terror would not be intimidated by border guards. Schwartz seems to have talked very bluntly, but the Americans were not convinced. On the 25th, the zonal border between the Russians and the Americans near Linz, on the Enns River, was the scene of a passive struggle by three trainloads of 150 Jews each to enter the American zone. The Americans refused to admit them; whereupon the Russians returned the Jews to Vienna. This caused a

sharp reaction by the Brichah commander in Austria, Arthur Ben Nathan, who caused demonstrations and disorders to take place in a DP camp at Linz. Colonel Stevens of the U.S. DP section in Vienna, who up till then had been rather friendly, now asked Ben Nathan to come to him; this showed that he knew who the responsible person was. But Stevens could make no headway. The Brichah knew that no American colonel would want his name associated with the shooting of Jews, and Brichah itself could not have stopped the movement of Jews even if it had wanted to, which it emphatically did not.

Stevens had to retreat, and the way was opened for another conference with the JDC representatives. "The new unofficial policy of the Army on transients was laid down by General Tate. The Army would provide transient shelters in Vienna, Linz and Salzburg, with minimum but adequate food and shelter. . . . In return, the Army expected the transients would not filter into the newly established settlements [that is, those that had been established after the Linz affair in October. Further, the Army expected] that the movement would be fairly regular, so that shelters would not become overcrowded, and create possibilities of difficulties and bad publicity for the Army. This plan was accepted by Dr. Schwartz after unofficial discussions with leaders of the Brichah in Vienna."[8]

In Germany, too, a similar development took place at the same time. In November General Truscott, commanding the Third Army, asked for instructions regarding the Jewish infiltrees and was told to establish special centers for them "but to reject non-Jewish infiltrees," presumably as these would come not as a result of any national or racial persecution but because of political disagreements with the left-wing governments of Eastern Europe. However, he was also to reject "all persons, whether Jews or non-Jews who had already been repatriated" and were now coming back to Germany. Further detailed instructions were requested of Washington, but there was for a long time no further pronouncement on the problem by the government.[9]

It is obvious that this situation caused some second thoughts in Washington; there does not seem to have been

a clear-cut policy on Jewish infiltration into the U.S. zones, although it must have been obvious that such infiltration might well upset the whole equilibrium of U.S. policy toward the Jews. The State Department, represented by Major General Hilldring, Assistant Secretary of State, was in consultation with Jewish leaders, who had but the slightest knowledge of the mood and organization of the Jewish survivors in Eastern Europe. An apparently decisive meeting took place on December 20, between Hilldring and the JDC leaders Dr. Schwartz and Moses A. Leavitt. They were told that the matter was now being taken up by President Truman and Dean Acheson. Two hundred fifty thousand refugees were now expected to arrive, according to an estimate made by Judge Simon H. Rifkind, and the State Department was most apprehensive. Schwartz stated that he felt that the maximum number of refugees would not exceed 50,000. This number, Hilldring indicated, the Army was willing to absorb. In fact, though there never was a formal announcement, unofficial sources intimated to the Jewish organizations that if the monthly influx did not exceed 5,000 the Army would make no difficulties at the border.

The whole question of infiltration was vitally influenced by yet another event that took place in October—the visit to Frankfurt of David Ben Gurion, then chairman of the Jewish Agency Executive in Palestine.

Harrison's report in August was a first American intimation that the two problems of Jewish DPs and the future of Palestine were in fact interrelated and, indeed, formed one indivisible complex. As to Palestine, the summer of 1945 was an important watershed in its troubled history. Since 1939 the official policy of Great Britain in Palestine was embodied in the so-called MacDonald White Paper of May 17, 1939. This document envisaged the creation of an independent Palestinian state after a transition period of ten years, during which 75,000 more Jewish immigrants would be allowed to enter Palestine if they did not strain the economic absorptive capacity of the country. On attaining independence, therefore, Palestine would be a state with an Arab majority of about a million inhabitants and a minority

of Jews (about 600,000), to which special minority rights would be guaranteed. According to the Land Transfer Regulations published on February 27, 1940, which were conceived as a supplement to the White Paper, Jews were allowed to buy land only in 5 percent of western Palestine, the other 95 percent of the area being either forbidden altogether or so severely restricted as to be practically out of bounds to Jews. Further Jewish immigration after the 75,000 had come in was, of course, dependent upon Arab consent, but by a typical maneuver the British provided for Palestinian independence on the condition that law and order be maintained. In other words, if the Jews objected violently, the Arabs might not get their independence and the country would be retained by the British. The White Paper effectively curtailed Jewish immigration to Palestine during the war, that is, at a time when every immigrant was another life saved from Nazi hell. This fact was interpreted in Jewish Palestine as a form of passive British complicity in Nazi crimes, and it created a feeling of intense bitterness toward Britain. The Jewish Agency tried to reestablish cooperation with Britain during the war, both by recruiting volunteers to serve—in Jewish units—in the British Army and also by carrying on an intensive political campaign of persuasion. Despite the friendliness of Churchill and the pro-Zionism of the Labour Party, the wartime coalition government did not change the political status determined by the White Paper. Anti-Zionists in the Conservative Party, in the government offices and among British civilian and military personnel in the Middle East neutralized the pro-Zionism of the Prime Minister. In 1943 and 1944, a British Cabinet committee discussed postwar policies in Palestine and arrived at the conclusion that partition was the only solution. This committee represented all three major British parties, Conservative, Labour and Liberal, and its report was the result of prolonged discussions. Anthony Eden's Foreign Office objected to partition because it was considered a pro-Zionist solution, but the committee persevered, and when the report reached the Cabinet the consensus was positive toward the proposed solution. It was decided, however, that no action should be taken before the end of the war. Then, on Novem-

ber 6, 1944, Churchill's close friend, Lord Moyne, a member of the Cabinet and a serious contender for leadership of the Conservative Party who was the British Middle Eastern representative, was murdered in Cairo by two members of the extremist Stern Group ("Fighters for the Freedom of Israel").

Moyne's murder has since been glorified as a heroic deed by devoted partisans fighting against oppression, but the hard fact is that this murder destroyed whatever chance there still may have been to achieve some kind of partition of Palestine with British help or at least through British neutrality. The Stern Group, barely 300 members strong, the only Jewish group anywhere that had actually tried to come to a political and military agreement with Nazi Germany in late 1940 and early 1941 out of its extreme hatred for Britain, had a quite disproportionate influence on the development of the Palestine imbroglio. Churchill denied that the murder would influence his attitude, but there can be no doubt at all that despite the denial the murder removed him from the scene as a vocal supporter of Zionism. When, therefore, the Labour Party came to power in July 1945, the Palestine question was very much back where it had been before the wartime coalition had come into office.

The Labour Party had a very extreme pro-Zionist platform, written by Hugh Dalton, foreign expert and prospective foreign minister. This platform had been approved by the Party in 1944 at its annual convention and provided for the establishment of Palestine west of the Jordan as a Jewish state, from which the Arabs would be encouraged to move out as the Jews moved in. Specifically, the White Paper was to be abolished immediately and Jewish immigration allowed to stream freely into the country so as to turn the Jews into a majority. The Zionist representation in London was not very happy about the platform, which went far beyond anything the most extreme Zionists had ever said (in public). However, that was the responsibility of the Labour Party, and there were good reasons to hope that at least some part of this grandiose program would be put into practice.

Labour won the general election of 1945 with a tremen-

dous majority; but Clement Attlee, the new Prime Minister, was well aware of the internal and external difficulties facing the new government. He came to power in the midst of the Potsdam Conference with Truman and Stalin with full knowledge of the discords and tensions between the Soviets and their Western allies. He had to have a strong man at his side as foreign minister, someone who could present unpopular policies to a reluctant party. Attlee himself was a very quiet, intellectual type and not the kind of man who would normally fill the post of leader; he was a compromise candidate. The man he chose to be foreign minister was Ernest Bevin, self-made man, trade unionist and economist, slated to be chancellor of the exchequer. Dalton, the foreign affairs expert, was given Bevin's economic job in the Labour government.

Bevin's nomination critically affected the Palestine problem, although one should take care not to exaggerate the influence of individuals and personalities on issues as complex as this. Bevin's record on Zionism was positive, and he certainly was no enemy to start with; at the same time he had no real knowledge of the Middle East generally and the Palestine problem in particular. His Foreign Office experts explained to him that a pro-Zionist line on Palestine might involve Britain in a struggle with the rising Arab nationalists and that a Zionist state could be created only at great cost and with Britain's willingness to send large numbers of troops to protect the Jews against the Arabs. Uncertain as to what the policy was to be, Bevin caused a new committee to be nominated; composed of several Cabinet ministers, it started its work at the beginning of August 1945 and reported back to the Cabinet in the middle of September. Throughout all that time—July, August and September—the future of Palestine was in abeyance. It was during that time, too, that Harrison made his report and that a Zionist World Conference met in London, under the chairmanship of Chaim Weizmann, the veteran Zionist leader, to appraise and approve of the line taken by the Zionist movement. The Zionists demanded a Jewish state in the whole of western Palestine and the immediate abolition of the White Paper and the Land Transfer Regulations. However, as the weeks

went by, disquieting rumors about the Labour government's position in Palestine began to circulate. In Palestine, the Zionist underground, Haganah, patched up its quarrels with the dissident armed groups of the NMO (Irgun) and the FFI (Sternists) so as to present a united front to the British in case the Labour Party defaulted on its extravagant promises. The architect of this new Resistance Movement, as it called itself, in Palestine was Ben Gurion, while Weizmann's support was half-hearted and limited. On September 16, Attlee replied to Truman's request to allow 100,000 Jewish survivors of the holocaust to enter Palestine as a humanitarian act: the reply was a refusal and at the same time a plea to the U.S. government to share with Britain the burden of finding a settlement to the Palestine problem. On the 18th, Reuter's reported that the British Cabinet committee had made its decision: Palestine was to become, ultimately, a country with an Arab majority having treaty relations with the British so as to preserve the military bases which the Empire was then building there. Jewish immigration was to be set at a maximum 1,500 monthly, or 18,000 yearly, thus making the Jews a permanent minority of about one-third of the population. The White Paper policy was, in essence, to be continued; and all the promises so eloquently promulgated on public platforms by Britain's Socialists were discarded. On September 21, this policy was discussed and approved by the full Cabinet, with Dalton and Bevan of the party's left wing opposing. The die was cast. Britain had in effect declared war on the Zionist movement, and the Palestinian Jews now reacted: the Resistance Movement began a series of armed actions, starting with the liberation of illegal immigrants at Athlit concentration camp near Haifa on October 10; other actions were to follow in the winter and spring of 1945–46.

Officially, these armed actions were the work of "terrorists," over whom the Jewish Agency exercised no control whatever. As for the Haganah activities, Dr. Moshe Sneh was commander and a member of the Jewish Agency Executive, and the overall control was exercised by Ben Gurion as chairman. The money for the Resistance Movement came from the Agency budget, raised partly from abroad.

Ben Gurion was in London when the decision was taken to activate the Resistance Movement. He then moved to Paris and then to Germany—to the U.S. zone. Accompanied by Rabbi Judah Nadich of the Mossad and Ruth Kluger, he arrived in Frankfurt on October 19. There in the meantime an official adviser to the commanding general on Jewish affairs had been appointed at the suggestion of the major American Jewish organizations. The adviser was Judge Simon H. Rifkind, who was now to take the place of the temporary adviser, Rabbi Nadich. The Jewish position at SHAEF was therefore fairly strong, and Ben Gurion had the advantage of being advised by the two official representatives of American Jewry with access to General Smith and General Eisenhower. On the 19th, Ben Gurion saw the two generals and immediately suggested to them that as there were large numbers of Polish Jews infiltrating into the zone, the Army should officially allow them to enter. He also made a fantastic proposal that a certain region in Germany be cleared of Germans and that Jews be allowed to take their place, thus providing a refuge for East European Jews fleeing from their countries of origin. The generals apparently asked him to formulate his suggestions in the form of a memorandum, which he submitted on the 25th, on the eve of his departure from Germany. It was phrased so as to win approval by Americans in positions of authority: it asked for a measure of self-government for the Jewish camps; it asked for what amounted in fact to a permission to provide paramilitary training in the camps under the guise of physical exercise; it emphasized the cultural needs of the refugees and it repeated the proposal of creating a kind of Jewish enclave in southern Germany. These were the specific proposals, but the whole tone of the memorandum was calculated to create the impression that the Jews were unanimous in their demand for settlement in Palestine and that they had to be treated as a nationality.

Ben Gurion was, it appears, perfectly justified in taking the attitude that he did. The response he met when visiting a number of camps—chiefly Zeilsheim, Landsberg and Feldafing—was tremendous. We happen to have a firsthand account by an impartial observer, Major Irving Heymont,

at that time commander of the camp at Landsberg. Heymont is a Jew and was at that time a regular Army officer. While apparently he never denied his Jewishness, he did not emphasize it either, and only a few of his comrades knew that he was a Jew. With his assimilationist background, he had never been interested in Jewish politics, and when Ben Gurion came to Landsberg, Heymont was a calm and shrewd observer. In a letter written to his wife on that day he writes: "The camp was visited by Mr. Ben-Gurion—the head of the Zionist organization in Palestine [*sic*]. To the people of the camp he is God. It seems that he represents all of their hopes of getting to Palestine. He had just come from England where he had been negotiating with the British Government to allow more Jews to enter Palestine. Mr. Ben-Gurion's visit came as a complete surprise. I did not get word of his visit through Army channels until about an hour after he had arrived. The first I knew of his coming was when we noticed the people streaming out to line the street leading from Munich. They were carrying flowers and hastily improvised banners and signs. The camp itself blossomed out with decorations of all sorts. Never had we seen such energy displayed in the camp. I don't think that a visit by President Truman could cause as much excitement."

Heymont led Ben Gurion through the camp and "gave him a straight story without glossing over anything." He was impressed by the Zionist leader's quick grasp of the essentials of the situation. He had, Heymont wrote, "a keen insight and a practical approach to problems." Before leaving he commented that the psychological problems that would have to be faced in Palestine when these people got there would be tremendous: "A voyage on a boat does not transform people." But Ben Gurion said a month later, on November 21, at a Jewish Agency Executive meeting in Jerusalem that he had never been so encouraged as he was in Germany—these refugees really wanted to go to Palestine, and they were now concentrated in a military zone where the commanders showed the greatest sympathy for their fate and future. He quoted General Walter Bedell Smith as saying that the American Army would not stop

infiltrees from coming in. Ben Gurion immediately seized on this essential point. Rifkind, he said, had told him that his proposal of creating a kind of Jewish state in Germany would not have the slightest chance of acceptance, but that did not matter because, as he said, he had "told our people who deal with these matters to bring the refugees in quickly. That will be the major factor for the Americans to demand their removal to Palestine. . . . It is possible to bring there all the European Jews, from everywhere, without any difficulty. . . . If we manage to concentrate a quarter of a million Jews in the U.S. zone, it would increase the American pressure [on the British] not because of the economic problem—that does not play any role with them—but because they see no future for these people anywhere but in Palestine."[10]

This, then, was the major practical result of Ben Gurion's German visit: through Ephraim Frank, a Palestinian *shaliah* and a representative of the Brichah in Germany who had just arrived there, a binding decision was handed down by the chairman of the Jewish Agency Executive and the accepted leader of the movement. What had been going on since the summer, namely, the movement of refugees toward Germany, was now transformed into a policy with a rather clearly defined aim. The fact of Ben Gurion's approval and the clarity of his political vision undoubtedly influenced the Brichah. We find evidence of this in the protocols of the Brichah commanders' meetings at the beginning of November in Vienna and Prague, where these directives were discussed and enthusiastically approved.

This was the situation in Germany and Austria, as it had developed by the end of 1945.

Ben Gurion's influence was extremely important, but a parallel decision, to direct at least some of the refugees into Germany was taken rather early, probably in July, by the Brigade Committee, which formed the major constituting body of the Merkaz Lagolah, the Jewish soldiers' committee for aid to DPs. From a Jewish point of view, the decision was logical. The Brigade was faced with an influx of refugees from Rumania and Poland on the one hand and from the DP camps on the other. There was simply not

enough room for all these people in Italy. A reservoir had to be created in a place which would clearly be a transit area and would be regarded as such by the refugees. At the same time they would be relatively well treated. The U.S. zones fulfilled all of these conditions. However, with all due respect to the Brigade, it must be said that Brichah at that moment was hardly the kind of organization that would obey orders from a center, especially a center in Italy. The Polish Brichah had very little contact with the Brigade and yet it, too, started turning toward Germany in August.

From June onward and through August, there was a movement of Jews from Germany to Italy. It was organized only very slightly—Jews simply wanted to leave Germany and go to a coast whence immigration to Palestine might be easier. We know of a number of individuals and groups who used contacts in the American Army and managed to reach Austria. The situation being still very chaotic, these people usually managed to reach those areas where the Brigade soldiers could pick them up and bring them to Italy. In Italy they were received by soldiers who worked under the Merkaz Lagolah which established a transit camp at Pontebba, near Tarvisio, the Brigade's main camp. This had originally been a POW camp, which the Brigade had taken over, and there, at considerable personal sacrifice to the Jewish soldiers, the transients were given food, blankets and, to some extent, clothes. From there they were infiltrated into UNRRA and British Army DP camps, first at Modena and other places in the north, and then to a number of seaside resorts in the south, around Bari.

These movements were a curious blend of the unorganized and the organized. Our best estimate is that from about the middle of June and up to the middle of August 15,000 Jews entered Italy. The Merkaz Lagolah organized part of this movement through the Palestinian transport units and the Brigade under a number of pretexts. Of course, any empty trucks returning to Italy from legitimate Army business in Austria were loaded with refugees, but such opportunities were also artificially created in various ways. Also, refugees were occasionally given uniforms and even soldiers' paybooks and smuggled across the Austrian borders. Very soon

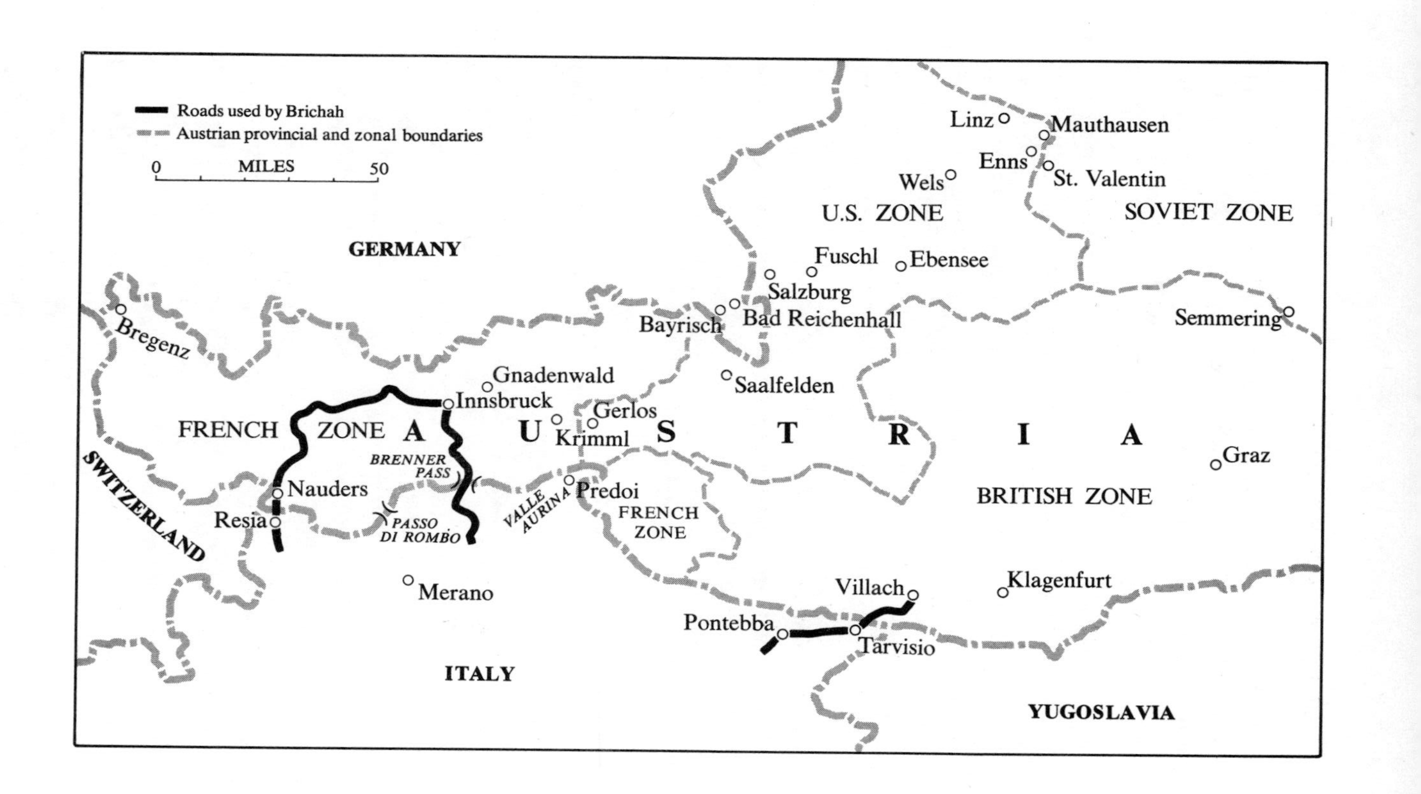

The Roads into Italy

the Merkaz Lagolah delegated one of its members, Yehiel Duvdevani, to supervise all these activities. This included not only transport, but also the Pontebba home and the transit south. Duvdevani in turn asked Mordechai Surkiss to take over the actual border-crossing part of the job. Soon Surkiss became the person in charge of Brichah activities of the Palestinian soldiers. The work was done very efficiently, and at great personal risk and sacrifice; the principle was that all this had to be done outside of and after proper fulfillment of the normal military duties of the officers and soldiers involved so that no shadow would be cast on the Jewish military unit. The farthest point reached by Brigade trucks was Salzburg; but usually refugees were picked up in southern Austria, near Graz or Klagenfurt, and then brought across the border. Apart from this movement, large numbers of refugees came on their own to the border or even across it, and a trickle of about 200 a month made the trip from Rumania via Yugoslavia.

Where did these people come from? From Brigade reports we learn that about 6,000 to 7,000 came from the camps in Germany and Austria; the rest were Rumanian Jews, partisans of the "Remnants" group in Rumania, and Polish or Hungarian Jews who came via Budapest after May.[11]

These activities of the Palestinians could not, of course, remain undetected. They aroused controversy not only with non-Jews but with Jews as well. One of the American Jewish chaplains, Marvin M. Reznikoff, accused his own community and invited anyone to "ask any GI returning from Italy how much the Palestinian soldiers have done and how little American money and aid have come to the rescue." The chief representative of the JDC in Italy during those summer months, Reuben Reznik, was indeed a controversial figure, and the Palestinians, who generally got on very well with the American organization, strongly objected to him. In October, Judah Magnes, the president of the Hebrew University, intervened with JDC leadership in New York and Reznik was transferred. His replacement was Charles Passman, an American Jew who had settled in Palestine, and there were no more complaints. But there seem to have been many complaints the other way around: a number of Amer-

ican and British Jews of extreme assimilationist tendencies began to oppose the Palestinians and took exception to the illegal "traffic" that was bringing thousands of refugees to a land from which they obviously hoped to get to Palestine, illegally if necessary. "There is a group of Zionists," one of them complained, "who are consciously and actively trying to stir up a tremendous wave of world-wide antagonism towards the Jew in the hope that this antisemitism will force greater immigration into Palestine than ever before—not merely from European countries, but [and this, of course, was the main cause for great worry!] also from America." And a British Jewish chaplain, a certain S. Pimontel, complained that the "Palestine elements" were "responsible for inciting lawlessness and disorder among the refugees," that they "took a leading hand in organising the unlawful entrance into Austria and the creation of an impossible position for Jewish refugees in Italy thereby hoping to force the hand of the military government in securing entrance into Palestine."[12]

These complaints mirrored, of course, the opinions of many non-Jewish Army officers; the important point in them was the widely held belief that the refugees were being goaded by clever and dangerous propaganda originating with the Palestinians. The Palestinians themselves thought differently. Hoter-Yishai says that "the presence of the Brigade was necessary as an encouragement and as proof of the connection between the Jews and the Brigade, and through it with Palestine; but they were certainly not in need of Palestinian help to get themselves organised. They did that themselves in a most effective way." In effect, the Brigade scarcely did more than somehow regulate the flow of the DPs into Italy. True, for political reasons it was interested in this flow, but it did not originate it. On July 22, the Brigade received the order to leave Tarvisio and move to Belgium to join the British Army there. But the flow of refugees did not cease: it was not dependent solely on the presence of the Palestinian soldiers.

This does not mean that the Brigade was particularly happy about the refugees, especially those from the German camps who now came into Italy. Hoter-Yishai says that he

thought that "5,000 Jews such as these in Palestine, with the then existing Jewish population there, can turn the country into one big lunatic asylum." One of the main tasks of the soldiers was therefore to institute for the refugees a program of reeducation, training and readjustment with the help of their considerable prestige among them. On the whole these programs were quite successful. In time some 3,000 refugee youngsters became agricultural trainees on farms set up by the soldiers and paid for largely by the JDC. Of course, the educational program was very definitely Zionist—which was in line with the wishes of the DPs themselves. However, this also created a difficulty: Arazi and his men did not manage to organize large-scale illegal immigration into Palestine at first, and between August 1945 and the end of the year only 1,036 people left Italy for Palestine on Mossad boats. As the autumn months progressed, the soldiers in charge were afraid that their whole program would be endangered by the lack of substantial emigration from Italy, with dire effects on the DPs' moral stamina and Zionist enthusiasm. "Let it be clear to you," wrote Duvdevani to the Mossad command in Palestine on September 9, "that if there is no change in the situation and no immigration into Palestine, many will return [to their countries of origin], and the whole thing will fail from a practical and political viewpoint." But then Duvdevani generally had a very pessimistic view of the quality of human material in the DP camps; fortunately he was proved wrong. It took another half year before illegal immigration to Palestine from Italy became really significant, but none of the DPs returned to their countries of origin and no demoralization set in in the camps in Italy.[13]

The big problem in the summer months was not the unorganized influx from Germany but the partisan-led groups that started coming to Italy over two principal routes: Yugoslavia and Hungary. The main group went through Budapest. There the wartime organization (known as *Tiyul,* "excursion") for smuggling Hungarian Jews to Slovakia and Rumania was revived. The leaders of the youth movements in the Hungarian capital who had organized that move—men like Moshe Pil (Alpan), Raffi Ben-Shalom, Zvi Gold-

farb and Peretz Revesz—were still in Budapest, and they were now joined by representatives of the organized Brichah from Poland. In June, Mordechai Rosman, the commander of the Polish Brichah, came to Budapest from Rumania, and took over the direction of Polish groups via Szentgotthard into Austria and Graz, all of which were at that time under Russian occupation. Hungarian youth movements and Polish partisans worked well together. An efficient transit system was organized to cross the border from Hungary to Austria, guarded by Red Army soldiers. This was done with the help of friendly contacts with frontier guards, largish amounts of good vodka and assorted items like leather jackets, wrist watches (to which Russian soldiers were always very partial) and hams. Thousands of Brichah people ("Brichniks") converged in July and August on Graz, where they found a first home in the great Hotel Weitzer under the leadership of the redoubtable Pinieh the Yellow (Pinhas Zeitag). The idea of going to Graz was a very obvious one. It was known that the town would be handed over to the British, and the intention was to fill Graz with Jews who, on the day of the transfer, would suddenly find themselves in the British zone of occupation. This would save them a difficult border-crossing from the Russian zone to the British zone, and hopefully would ease the further move to Italy, which was under British-American influence. The transfer did indeed take place on August 8, but the British would not allow these refugees to cross the Italian border. By September the Graz people had become DPs distributed in a number of camps in the neighborhood of the town. With the help of some anti-Zionist Jewish officers the British and American armies appear to have gained some insight into the workings of Brichah, and the partisans near and in Graz were affected. Internal troubles now began to arise. Pinieh the Yellow was a colorful personality: a swashbuckling young partisan with yellow hair—resourceful and very brave, but also unscrupulous and insolent. His considerable organizational talent was amply shown in the establishment of the Graz center, but he was now being accused by many people that he had used his position for personal gain, taking watches and money from refugees supposedly to bribe the frontier guards but actually to put them in his own pocket.

The Graz affair shows up some of the moral and political problems of the Brichah. It seems that here, at the beginning of the mass move, certain attitudes were developed that vitally influenced later developments. A rule from which the Brichah very rarely deviated was that the people were not required to pay for their migration through Europe. Generally speaking, Brichah officers came out of the Brichah as poor as they entered it, and the few exceptions, if discovered, were dealt with very strictly. Expenses were paid, and a certain amount of clothing supplied, but that was about all. No wages were paid. These were very strict measuring rods for an underground organization that conducted its operations to an appreciable extent on the basis of bribery. We have seen that Graz was no exception, and the *Dai chas* ("Give your watch") of the Russian soldiers had to be satisfied from some source. Pinieh argued that he had used the articles he took from the refugees to good purpose. However, Surkiss ordered an investigation which was conducted by Pinieh's "peer" and an "Asiatic," Israel Eichenwald. Very little could be proved either way, but the suspicion was sufficient. The principle that Brichah was a national organization whose members must never be under the merest shadow of suspicion asserted itself. Pinieh was removed, and Eichenwald, an equally resourceful but considerably more level-headed man, was appointed commander by Abba Kovner in Italy with Surkiss's agreement.[14]

By September, then, there were some 12,000 Jews in the Graz area. Only a few of these had come there from Rumania. After May the Polish Brichah no longer sent their people to Rumania but straight to Budapest, via Humene or Zilina-Bratislava in western Slovakia. Among these newer arrivals from Poland the ex-partisan element no longer predominated. The people who now came were families, often formed of individual surviving members of former family groupings destroyed in the holocaust, children and members of youth movements. The youth groups were also organized in the typical "kibbutz" form of the first Brichah groups. They now formed the organizational, cultural and moral backbone, and this was especially true of Graz. Eichenwald preferred to rely on them rather than on the emotionally more unstable partisan element. The situation

in Graz soon became unpleasant. The Italian frontier, so close at hand, was a seemingly insurmountable obstacle. The Alps with their few well-guarded passes offered little prospect of illegal frontier-crossings to which the Brichah had by then become accustomed. Food rations were small; the British-zone camps bore no comparison with even the worst of the camps in the American zone; and winter was in the offing. In charge of the camps was an anti-Zionist Jewish major, who made life difficult for the refugees and their leaders. As winter approached Eichenwald tried to get the JDC to send supplies to the area, but despite frantic appeals to Paris he met with little success; Reuben Reznik, the JDC representative, could or would help very little. The Polish Red Cross tried to capitalize on the situation and persuade the refugees to support the London Poles' anti-Communist crusade in return for certain quantities of food. The fact that their underground friends in Poland constituted the anti-Semitic murder gangs did not seem to deter them; but of course they met with refusal. However, some help came from the Merkaz Lagolah, and an important source of aid was the British Red Cross, which cared for children and women who kept arriving in Graz and gave them certain foods and items that the soldiers and Eichenwald could not obtain.

The constant flow of refugees into Graz was another problem, because Eichenwald had in fact no control over it. The British were getting rather desperate, too, and one day in September, previous attempts at cajoling or threatening Eichenwald into somehow stopping the flow having failed, they suggested to him that some of his people be transferred to the American zone! The Americans were rich, they would look after these Jews; Eichenwald asked for permits, but he did not get them. He was told that those who got these Jews into the British zone would have to see to it that they got into the American one, and all the British would do would be to facilitate the move on the British side. The plan was adopted, but not very many Jews went to the Salzburg area occupied by the Americans. This was, after all, not what they wanted—they wanted to go to Italy, and Italy was closed.

In the meantime, the British were forced to open more

camps; Hotel Weitzer in Graz was cleared of the refugees, and camps were established at Judenburg, Leibnitz, Villach, Trofaiach and Graz. In these camps, committees were elected and educational work organized. Schools were opened and sheets were stenciled to provide text material in a tremendous effort to prevent demoralization. There were cases where Eichenwald used his partisans to beat up black market operators.

In the end, however, Italy remained the only possible answer. In the month of October a first great attempt was made in what had now become good Brichah tradition: a train was bought (by bribery) from the Austrians, and 1,200 refugees were put on it. They traveled from Villach to Tarvisio in Italy. There the Italian police received orders from the British to return the refugees. The police had no choice —they had to do their duty, but they had to carry every individual refugee bodily back into the train before they could return it. The result was decisive—the Italian guards were quite willing, after this experience, to be bribed into admitting the refugees. With the connivance of some friendly British officers, trucks were obtained and transports organized to bring the people across the border. This process, which started in late October, went on in the cold months of November, December and January. Occasionally, footpaths running parallel to the road were used. By the end of January, only some 2,000 refugees remained in the British zone of Austria. The rest had gone to Italy, and a certain number to the U.S. zone. In March, Eichenwald left and a Palestinian emissary took over from him.

By the end of 1945 there were probably 20,000 refugees in Italy. English pressure notwithstanding, the number had grown since the big influx in the summer and despite the fact that some had left for Palestine. The soldiers were now considerably less in evidence in Italy than they had been previously, and they tended to concentrate more and more on illegal migration to Palestine. By the end of the year, the initiative of finding new ways into Italy was passing slowly from the Graz area to the American zone, where Salzburg had grown into a central point of the Brichah. (This will be discussed later in the Austrian context.)

At the end of the war two lone emissaries from Palestine reached Italy: Levi Argov (Kopelevitch) and Moshe Ben David. They had been sent by the opposition group of Hashomer Hatzair to contact their movement in Europe and, despite opposition from Haganah headquarters in Palestine, had managed to smuggle themselves into Italy. There the inner political tensions of Zionism mattered very little. The two men, dressed in British uniforms, got themselves transferred to the north of Italy as interpreters at a German base which was then, just after the German surrender, being taken over by the Allies. The idea was that they should try to carry on from there to Czechoslovakia, their final destination. However, in the north of Italy, they happened to meet a Dutch Jew, a Red Cross worker by the name of Van Harten. Van Harten had already been to liberated Hungary and expected the two young men to go there first. He led them into a cellar where a number of boxes were stored and from one of them he took thick wads of notes and stuffed 10,000 British pound notes into the rucksacks of the speechless youngsters. They never questioned the source of the money, and they do not seem to have doubted the genuineness of the banknotes, which had obviously been taken from the Germans—and that was enough. They left northern Italy and went to Salzburg; there they changed into refugees' clothing and made their way on a repatriation convoy via Czechoslovakia to Budapest. They made immediate contact with the Brichah organization and paid a debt which Van Harten had asked them to settle for him. The money they brought served as the first batch of funds to be acquired by Brichah, first in Budapest and then in Slovakia; the notes were gradually converted into local currency as the need arose. Ben David stayed in Bratislava and worked there mainly for his youth movement. Argov, on the other hand, became a full-time Brichah worker, and he now (in June–July) set about the task of coordinating Brichah activities in Hungary, Austria and Czechoslovakia; in fact, he became the self-appointed, but recognized, coordinator of these movements. Together with a number of local people, some of whom had preceded him, he established good relations with Czech and Slovak officials. One of these, a Czech Zion-

ist, unsuspectingly took some of the Van Harten money for a visit to England as a member of an official Czech delegation. Soon he found himself the subject of an unpleasant investigation. The money, it seemed, was counterfeit.

On hearing the news, Argov quickly got rid of the money. After a time, the truth emerged: Van Harten had laid hands on part of a German stock of counterfeit English money. The forgery had been done under duress by Jewish inmates in the Sachsenhausen concentration camp, where these unfortunates were forced by the Germans to turn their skill into a weapon for Germany. Most of these Jews were murdered by the Nazis before the end of the war, but some survived to tell the tale. Van Harten had somehow got hold of the money but had neglected to tell Argov that it was counterfeit.

When relating the story of the organizational setup of the Brichah in the so-called transit countries—Hungary, Czechoslovakia and Austria—one must remember that in the chaotic conditions of the summer of 1945 all organization was tentative and fluid, and an illegal group like the Brichah worked more on the basis of mutual understanding and coordinated moves than as an institution with the usual hierarchy. The influx of people coming from Poland was not publicized at all, except perhaps by scribbled notes on pieces of paper (*zettelach* in Yiddish) a couple of days prior to arrival. The task was clear: the survivors of Polish Jewry were on the move, and most of them wanted to go someplace near a shore whence emigration to Palestine might become feasible. But Italy had filled up; infiltration into Germany became inevitable. The basis for the transition from the move into Italy to the move into Germany can be seen by examining another migratory movement—that centered on the American zone of occupation in Czechoslovakia in the summer of 1945.

The first and major worry as far as repatriation in the Czech lands was concerned was the fate of the 29,300 inmates of the Terezin (Theresienstadt) concentration camp and ghetto who had been liberated by the Soviet Army on May 10. In the chaos of the first few days some 3,700 people left the camp individually; then Major Kuzmin took over and a

proper hospital was established in Terezin. A typhoid epidemic had broken out and only the quick and devoted action by a Soviet team (under Dr. Hernstein and Dr. Kaliuzhny) prevented disaster; even so, 500 people lost their lives. Then repatriation started, and trains left Terezin for Hungary, Rumania, Germany and other places. There were, however, special problems concerning two groups: older people from Germany who had nowhere to go in their home towns and were helpless because of their physical and mental condition; and Polish Jews, mostly young people, who did not want to go "home."

In Prague in the meantime a Brichah office had come into existence at the old Jewish community center of Jozefovska Street No. 7. Originally composed of Jewish youths who had returned from Terezin, the office staff was reinforced by a number of young men, among whom was a Slovak Jewish partisan, Bubu Landau, who had been sent there by Argov at the beginning of June and who soon gained prominence. Landau maintained good relations with the repatriation office of the Ministry of Social Welfare, where Jews and non-Jews alike were usually helpful toward Zionist aspirations. Refugees trying to go west and south were treated the same way as bona fide repatriants and given food and lodgings by the ministry. About the beginning of July, Hoter-Yishai appeared in Prague.

The western part of Bohemia was occupied by American forces during the last days of fighting, and there they stayed for some five months. The main town in their zone was Pilsen (Plzen). This political and geographical fact was too obvious to be missed by Palestinians in Europe at that time. Consequently, Hoter-Yishai and his friends began looking for someone who would take over the task of facilitating movement of Jews toward the shores through that area. In Paris, meanwhile, a Jewish Agency office had been established where the person in charge was Ruth Kluger, a veteran member of Mossad. She again was looking for people she could send to Germany to be unofficial representatives of the Agency and, if suited for the work, for Mossad as well. Her choice was Sylvia Neulander, the Red Cross worker who had taken the Hillersleben children to

Buchenwald and then to France. Ruth Kluger asked her to work for Zionist interests in Germany and suggested that she meet the Brigade people at Munich. This was probably during Hoter-Yishai's first trip there, that is, toward the end of June. Miss Neulander met Rabbi Lifshitz and Hoter-Yishai, and was asked to get somehow to the Pilsen area and set up a transit point there. She went back to Paris and got herself assigned to the XVIII Corps at Pilsen as a Soldiers' Club organizer on behalf of the Red Cross. There, while selling (and soon giving) coffee and doughnuts to American soldiers, she began orienting refugees for moves toward DP camps in Germany or toward Italy en route to Palestine. There were two clearly discernible parts of this work. One was to speak to Jews being repatriated from the British zone of Germany—where the British did not want them—to Poland. These people were usually unsure of themselves, and Miss Neulander considered it her duty to enlighten them on whatever she knew of conditions in Poland. As a result, some continued on the repatriation trains, but many remained at Pilsen and went back to DP camps in the U.S. zone. The other part of her work was more difficult and in the long run more important. She began organizing the transfer of Jewish refugees across the border between the zones.

At first these transports came only partly organized or not organized at all. But it was soon obvious to Miss Neulander that she alone could not possibly cope with the problem, and she therefore looked around for help. This she found in a young Reform rabbi, Eugene J. Lipman, who was attached to the XVIII Corps. With the help of Jewish GIs transportation, food and other necessities were obtained, and Jewish refugees were brought into Karlov, the DP camp at Pilsen, and from there to Salzburg in Austria, where they were taken over by the Brigade people and brought to Italy. The first transport appears to have gone on July 4. The people who were transferred made a depressing impression at first. They were "miserable specimens, because all the initiative and drive is gone." These were largely Jews who had been liberated in the forced labor camps in the Sudeten area, and their physical and mental condition was still very bad. However, this began to improve after a short while.

From about July 10 transports began to go regularly every second day. Lipman then went to Prague and got in touch with the Brichah people. It was actually his and Miss Neulander's work that gave a sense of perspective to the rather confused Brichah youngsters in Prague.

By the middle of July, only a few thousand of the former Terezin inmates were left there. It was about that time that a Jewish lieutenant of the U.S. Army by the name of Kopelowitz got an assignment to transfer the older German Jews from Terezin to a special DP camp in Bavaria. In the process he went to Bohemia and after presenting his documents to Major Kuzmin he took out his 700 old people and transferred them to a camp at Deggendorf. Bubu Landau made use of the fact of this legal transfer. He obtained Kopelowitz's agreement to intervene on behalf of the Polish Jews and others who did not want to be repatriated and cover their exit from Terezin by his official documents. He then approached Kuzmin and talked to him openly; he explained to him the past and possible future of these Polish Jews and told him about Palestine and the desire of these people to go there. From the Polish delegation in Prague he got a paper signed by a Polish Jew who worked there that the Poles would not insist on the repatriation of the people at Terezin. In the end Kuzmin agreed, and a most unusual document was drawn up, bearing the date of July 28. Covering himself by the attached American and Polish documents, the major insisted in his letter that the Jews concerned be transferred to the American zone, whence the Joint Distribution Committee (that is, Landau, who appeared there supposedly as a representative of the JDC, to which he was unknown) would "repatriate them *only to Palestine*" (in the Russian original: *repatriirovat ikh TOLKO V PALESTINU*). The signatures of Kuzmin, Landau and another man were appended. The transport was taken out accordingly and brought to Pilsen.

In the meantime, however, the Salzburg program was stopped by the American military. On July 26 two transports were turned back and Lipman received "a bawling out from the DP officers there." It was therefore agreed that the Terezin transports should go to German DP camps, where indeed they went.[15]

Lipman and Neulander both left the scene on the last day of July and went to a Zionist conference in London. When that ended, they did not return to their old post at Pilsen. Their place was taken by Brichah members, who opened a transit point at Karlovy Vary (Karlsbad) to take care of people en route for the border at Pilsen. By that time the Brigade was in Italy no longer, and the Italian border was closed. There was therefore no alternative in any case—the people had to be sent to Germany. In August occurred the great clash with the Americans which has been mentioned before. It was not the only one, but it was the one that reached American newspapers and the situation became easier after it. However, Pilsen was no longer a good "point," and in August another border was, to use a Brichah expression, "opened." This was the town of As, in the westernmost tip of Bohemian territory. There another young woman came to the fore, a nineteen-year-old refugee whose name was Miriam Fried. She hailed from Poznan in western Poland, and her story up to that point was the usual one of ghetto, hunger, murder of relatives, concentration camp and ultimate liberation. She had gone back "home" only to find there was nothing to go back to. Now she volunteered for Brichah work and was sent to As. For a time Rosman, who came over from Budapest, was responsible for the Karlovy Vary–As route, but he left for Munich in the early autumn, and Moshe Laufer, another Polish Jewish refugee, became the local commander. Miriam Fried at As quickly made a reputation for herself for utter fearlessness and great diplomatic skill. She made friends with the frontier guards and also with Czech officers, ranging right up to some generals. She also had contacts with the Americans, who left their Bohemian enclave in October and were now on the other side of the frontier from As. At first under Laufer, then alone, she was in charge of As for about two years.

It is very difficult to estimate the number of people who went through the Pilsen zone boundary and through As before the American withdrawal. No records were kept at that time, and as most of the crossings were completely illegal and the chaos in Germany still great, no really reliable estimate can be formed by comparing the reported number

of Jews in various DP camps in the U.S. zone at different times. Our own guess would be that during the Lipman-Neulander episode (July 4–July 31) some 2,000 people at the most went to Salzburg or Germany. For the months of August, September and October roughly the same number can be taken as a reasonable and conservative estimate.

❧

4. Poland

After the end of the war, Polish Jewry* underwent many changes. Jews were liberated from camps, emerged from hiding places and crossed the border from Germany (to a very limited extent). From the Soviet Union came the Polish Army bringing with it thousands of Jewish soldiers and many civilians who, under one pretext or another, managed to cross the Polish-Russian border. By August 1945 there were in Poland some 80,000 Jews, of whom 13,000 were serving in the Polish Army.[1]

The new regime's hold over the country was very weak. It was supported by the few Communists and by a left-wing section of the prewar Socialist Party (PPS). It was perfectly obvious that the majority of the population, and especially the peasants, were very much opposed to the government. The right-wing A.K. (Armja Krajowa) and the fascist NSZ (Narodowe Sily Zbrojowe) resumed their armed activities, this time with the object of driving the Soviets and their Polish allies out of the country. An era commenced of what

---

* In an earlier chapter we left the story of the Polish Brichah at the point where Rosman departed, at the beginning of May, and "Ben" (Moshe Meiri of the "Asiatics") was appointed as the secretary, or rather the "coordinator" (*merakez*), of Brichah.

in fact was civil war. Soon only the larger towns were in the government's hands, whereas the countryside generally and the Carpathian mountain range in particular were controlled by the insurgents. The old A.K. had dissolved, and the successor organizations assumed various names, such as WIN. Despite the existence among them of some moderate social democratic or liberal elements, these organizations were predominantly right-wing, and they tended to continue the old, violent and bloody prewar Polish anti-Semitism, fortified and barbarized by the example set by the Nazi conquerors.

The Jews were now an easy target indeed. Having dwindled to an insignificant percentage of the population, they were completely dependent on the protection afforded by the government. And the government, lacking the support of any significant segment of Polish society, had to turn—very reluctantly—to the Jews to fill many administrative posts. No figures exist on the percentage of Jews in government employ, but it is safe to assume that they were fairly large; in any case there were proportionately many more Jews in the administration than non-Jews.[2] In the higher ranks the powerful ministers of the interior and of economic planning, Jakub Berman and Hilary Minc, were of Jewish origin. Being Communists, they were of course far removed from any sympathy with specifically Jewish aspirations—they considered themselves soldiers of the revolution. Jakub Berman is supposed to have said in an argument with Rabbi Kahane after the Kielce pogrom (discussed below): "If you think I am a Jew, you are mistaken. My father and my mother were Jews, and it so happens that I am working for my ideal in Warsaw. Tomorrow I may be in Peking and the day after in New York, and in another week's time I may be sitting in Prague, for the glory of an idea that one day will pervade the whole world."[3] Non-Jewish Communists were generally more accessible and friendly to Jews speaking in the name of Jews than these two ministers. But the fact of their Jewish origin served as a butt for attacks of the WIN and fascist NSZ on the regime. Jews and Communists were equated in right-wing propaganda in the well-worn Nazi manner. The Jew-hatred of many Poles, and especially among the peasantry, was now whipped up for anti-government attacks. This of course tended to make the Jews even

more dependent on the government, and their situation became difficult in the extreme.

The first serious anti-Jewish outbreaks occurred in Cracow. On August 11, riots occurred and a Jewish school was burned down. This followed the distribution of leaflets by the underground forces chiding Cracow for not activating its anti-Jewish committee. The WIN leaflets declared that the riots had been instigated by Jews and the "perpetrators were the Jews themselves and the NKVD [Russian secret police]." Several Jews were killed, and similar though lesser outbreaks were recorded in Radom and Czestochowa. Contemporary reports relate how members of the right-wing groups went through villages where individual Jews or small groups tried to maintain a foothold and encouraged actions against the Jews in the name of the London government-in-exile of the anti-Communist Poles. An official government summary (unpublished) said that between November 1944 and October 1945, 351 Jews had been murdered in Poland, 79 in the Kielce district, 64 in the Lublin district, 57 in the Warsaw area, 51 in the Lodz district and 3 in newly acquired Silesia. At Opatow the local Jewish committee building was attacked; riots occurred at Nowy Sad (August 20), again at Cracow (August 20), at Sosnowice (October 25) and at Lublin (November 19). The fascist NSZ declared in a leaflet on March 25, 1945 that it was a sign of patriotism to kill Jews. These official accounts and documents complete the picture we get from the reports of the welcome accorded to those Jews who returned to Poland from the DP camps.[4]

A majority of the 80,000 Polish Jews found themselves living in a trap. Their old homes and occupations were gone —indeed they had not amounted to much before the war— the country was in the throes of a political and economic and, possibly, even military revolution or a civil war. They were living in a huge graveyard of relatives and friends and now here they were, hated, hunted and murdered wherever the government's authority could be flouted. The concept of the Brichah and Kovner's somber visions of another holocaust seemed utterly vindicated by events. There was no need for the Brichah to make propaganda urging Jews to leave Poland. Jews by the thousands joined the Zionist organizations whose representatives made up the Brichah com-

mittee in order to be sent out of the country. In the summer and autumn of 1945 the Brichah could scarcely do more than maintain some vague control of organization and direction over a movement that threatened to overwhelm it.

The desire to leave was so strong, the urge and need so great, that people had no patience to wait for the slowly growing Brichah apparatus. Moreover, not every Jew who wanted to get out was a Zionist or wished to join one of the organizations. And so another much smaller exodus began—unorganized, private, where operators took money from the fugitives, brought them to the borders and either smuggled them out or left them there to fend for themselves.[5] This kind of "private" Brichah is variously estimated to have led 10,000 to 30,000 Jews into Germany in the second half of 1945,[6] mainly via Stettin (Szczecin) in the north but also by other routes. We have practically no record of this movement; the operators were anonymous and they could not be traced. They were living in a postwar atmosphere in Germany where fortunes were made and lost by trade in cigarettes or foodstuffs conducted between the Western zones of occupation and countries such as Poland. Operators who transported Jewish refugees over the frontiers saw them as no more than a sideline to their "normal" business. A whole underworld existed at the time, composed largely of Germans and East Europeans, and they were trying, among many other things, to take advantage of the desire of Jews to leave Poland. It is true to say that despite the efforts of these smugglers their importance was no more than marginal in the overall picture of Jewish migration, but the Brichah documents contain accounts of bitter struggles against them. Some of them tried to use Brichah facilities to move from country to country. Of course, when they were caught by Brichah people, they were refused any further help. But who could control some of the smaller fry? They simply went via another Brichah point, or to a different country.[7]

The vast majority of Jews not only went by Brichah routes; their property was so small and their panic so great that they showed no inclination at all to engage in anything but flight.

The Brichah headquarters moved out of Cracow after the

Main Brichah Routes Out of Poland

pogrom there to Lodz, where the largest Jewish community was now concentrated. Close contact was maintained with the Zionist representatives on the official Central Committee of Polish Jews. In the early autumn, too, the first orphan homes were founded by the Zionists; a fantastic battle now began in order to save for Jewry some of the thousands of Jewish orphans who were being raised as Christians in religious institutions or by private families to whom they had been entrusted by their parents before their destruction. By various means, legal or not quite legal, hundreds of these orphans were assembled. The Central Committee's children's homes, supported by the government, also provided education for Jewish orphans, but this was Communist- and Poland-oriented, and therefore rejected by the Zionists. The Brichah considered it to be their most sacred task to take these children out of Poland. Most of the orphan homes were therefore placed in Upper Silesia, near the Czech border and in the area acquired by Poland after the war, where the Communists on the Central Committee dreamed of setting up an autonomous Jewish region.

"Ben," the Brichah secretary in Poland after May, was the man under whom the decisive shift in the direction of the Brichah occurred. From May to about August, people were sent via Slovakia to Austria or via Bohemia to the U.S. zone, but generally the numbers were not large. The largest group, that at Graz, was composed partly of the residue of the original partisan group in Rumania and the later arrivals from Hungary who had come via Slovakia as well. Now a number of refugees who came via Bratislava and Vienna filtered through at the Semmering, where the Russian and British zones of occupation met, and passed through to Graz to swell the numbers there. The move generally did not pick up till August, and then the change came. It cannot be proved that any instructions were passed to Poland from the Brigade, but it appears that the Polish Brichah did not need any such instructions—it was obvious that the Italian border was closed and the only place where people could be sent to was the U.S. zone of Germany. In August, then, Brichah was beginning to move people to Germany.

According to figures prepared by the Polish Brichah for

the Twenty-second Zionist Congress in December 1946, some 111,537 Jews left Poland with the organized Brichah movement between the beginning of July 1945 and the end of September 1946. The statistics do not always tally with similar figures we find in diaries and summaries written during that period, but they are close enough to show us the approximate size of the movement. In July 1945, 4,600 people left, in August the figure reached a record 9,875 (over 10 percent of Polish Jewry). It then dropped to 6,475 in September, but rose again to 9,760 in October. Then it tapered off as the cold weather came, and as we shall soon see, various political impediments materialized; in November 520 left, and in December 2,050.[8]

Up till September, the whole movement was run without the presence of a single person from the Palestine center. However, in early October, the first *shaliah* arrived—Isser Ben Zvi. A kibbutz member (at that time) of the dominant Mapai group, he was sent to Poland to take over command of the Brichah. He had arrived in Europe on an illegal immigration boat after the successful landing of the immigrants on the Palestinian shore; he came together with a group of *shlihim* who were to deal with various underground activities, ranging from political missions to educational work with children. Shortly after the arrival of Ben Zvi, other emissaries representing different shades of opinion of the faction-ridden Zionist movement came to Poland. The most important of these was "Alexander" of the left-wing Kibbutz Meuchad movement to which the youth movement of Dror was affiliated in Poland (and which we have already met in the persons of Yitzhak Zuckerman and Zivia Lubetkin who had distinguished themselves in the Warsaw ghetto rebellion). Alexander was a colorful personality; he had been arrested by the Russians in Vilna in 1940 trying to organize border-crossings for Jewish refugees there. He was released in 1941 and went to Central Asia. There he boarded a ship with Polish civilians attached to the Polish Anders Army and arrived in Iran. After joining Jewish Agency representatives at Teheran, his information was utilized to advance a project of sending food parcels to Polish Jewish refugees in Soviet Central Asia; he then moved illegally to

Palestine, where he joined a kibbutz. Now, barely two years later, he came to Poland as a "Palestinian" emissary. In other countries the influx of Palestinian *shlihim* was by no means an unmixed blessing. Often these emissaries engaged in party politics and created or increased tensions where few existed before. Poland suffered relatively little from this kind of trouble. True, Ben Zvi was a member of Mapai, and in Poland at that time Mapai was a minority group; Ben Zvi therefore made some moves to strengthen youth movements connected with his particular group and tried to split the Dror movement which tended to be leftist. This, however, was soon discovered, the relevant correspondence became common knowledge and Ben Zvi took greater care afterward.

Generally speaking, internal relations in the Brichah were not disturbed by the Palestinians. A tendency to establish a separate organization of the right-wing Ichud group was finally averted in August at the Zionist Conference in London, where the liberal leader Yitzhak Gruenbaum influenced his people in Poland to abstain from any splitting of the Polish Brichah. The Revisionists, whose parent body was still outside of the Zionist movement at that time, had a representative on the Brichah committee, although, being considered a right-wing organization, they were not allowed to operate legally in Poland. But the core of the Brichah was the labor wing, and its youth movements. These, while operating their own youth groups in the country, cooperated with Brichah. There were two bodies whose functions tended to overlap: a political committee, composed of the representatives of parties and movements; and a Brichah "center," a command which was normally composed of three or four persons. With the coming of the Palestinians, there were two developments. First, the rather hazy allegiance of Brichah to Mossad became clearly defined, because the *shlihim* were very definitely sent by Mossad. This linking of the Brichah with the organization that dealt with illegal immigration was logical and inevitable. Second, the Brichah apparatus began to function more efficiently with the introduction of a painstaking bookkeeping department, which took careful account of monies spent and people transferred.

The actual control of Brichah was not much changed by the coming of the *shlihim*. That control still remained vested in the local people; Ben left in September, and another "Asiatic," Tuviah Cohen, took over. He was now "coordinator," and Ben Zvi "director." Theoretically Ben Zvi was the commander, but in fact the better knowledge of local conditions by the local people made him turn mainly to overall political problems and money matters. There was no antagonism, and indeed the *shlihim* were regarded with something of a mixture of respect and awe—after all, they had really lived in Palestine. This situation changed as the local old-timers slowly moved on and out of Poland themselves. Progressively the *shlihim* took over, and by the late spring of 1946 it was definitely the *shlihim* who were running the Brichah. Under Ben Zvi and Alexander, the Brichah command numbered eleven members: the commander, the coordinator, three accountants and cashiers, two more *shlihim* and four others, representing various groups and parties. While nominal control remained in the hands of Ben Zvi, Alexander took over more and more and soon became the dominant figure on the scene. His background—he was a "local" Polish Jew, an "Asiatic" and a Palestinian *shaliah*—made him acceptable to all.

The system of operation was uniform all over the country. Central points, called "stores," would be designated in larger towns. People would be assembled there in groups, and spend some time there—a day or two, or up to a week—and then move on to a place near the border. There another shelter would await the group, and from it they would be led to the border itself, where a local point would be established in a village or hamlet. Smugglers from among the local population would only be used initially to show the Brichah teams the route. Once a route was studied, it was preferred to dispense with professional smugglers. The task of the Brichah man or woman who actually led the group across the border was to establish contact with Brichah people from the other side and hand over the group to them. These would then bring the people in trucks or on foot to assembly centers or straight to a railway station.

For the individual who wanted to join a Brichah group

there would be a choice of two possible procedures. Either he would join a Zionist group which would put him on the waiting list for Brichah or he would manage to contact a Brichah member and join one of the groups that had no distinct affiliation. In both cases a period of waiting would be required till the person's turn came. The groups, especially the Zionist ones, were known as *kibbutzim*. Some of these were tightly knit social units where friendships had developed over a period of preparation at some farm of one of the youth movements in Poland or even during the war period previous to that. Many of these groups did actually intend to settle on a Palestinian kibbutz, but most of them were simply influenced by the popularity of the kibbutz, without really comprehending its principles, and were organized in a kind of loose group structure. Each person in such a group would be given a number and a list of things to take and, more important, things he was not to take for his journey. Polish or Russian documents, photographs and letters, money and valuables, military decorations—all these were supposed to be left behind. But these regulations were often disregarded. The problem of money and valuables was very serious—Jews had sold their last possessions before leaving Poland and had perhaps bought a new suit or converted their money into gold pieces or rings. This, of course, was dangerous, because frontier guards and smugglers were on a lookout for these items. The Brichah therefore occasionally transferred the possessions of refugees legally. Speed and safety of actual transfer of these items that had little bulk were ensured by some simple arrangements: a few genuine passports and visas, and good connections with frontier guards. Often, however, the people would not listen, and occasionally things were lost on the way. One principle was strictly adhered to: people were not required to pay for their passage with the Brichah.

On a lower level, the coordinator had a list of groups on hand who were ready to go as well as reports from the points at the borders as to the capacity of transfer and dates. These two would be matched and local Brichah commanders would get their instructions on little pieces of paper with Hebrew scribbling. A very primitive but very effective code was used.

The central office had a radio transmitter but this was often out of action, and in any case it was never used for transmitting instructions in Poland itself. The principle was that each member of the Brichah would know as little as possible about the way Brichah worked. At the most a point, or "store," would be uncovered and therefore lost. These, however, changed very often anyway as points had to be closed because border-crossings had been discovered. It is also a fact that although the Poles and later the British wanted to find out details about the Brichah, they never managed to do so, and excepting one single instance did not succeed in smuggling agents into the organization. There was no betrayal, and not only was very little known about the organization but even its very existence was often doubted.*

Brichah was organized in four sectors: the north, including the town of Szczecin (Stettin); some minor points to the south of it, such as Zary (Sorau) and Zgorzelec (Goerlitz), which were also considered as transition points to the west;

---

* This impenetrability of the Brichah was not uniquely characteristic of that organization only. There was a definite tradition of Jewish solidarity dating back to the Middle Ages, when the hostility of the surrounding world created psychological barriers of great importance between the Jew and his neighbors. This found expression in the contempt the Jews felt for a spy for the gentile world; an informer, a *moisser* (the Yiddish rendering of a Hebrew word) was the lowest creature. To be branded as a *moisser* could be a terrible calamity for the individual in the closely knit Jewish community. Even during the Second World War the number of Nazi agents among Jews was minimal and they were usually known. It is interesting to note that in France, for instance, where the general resistance movement suffered considerably from the infiltration of enemy agents, the Jewish maquis (Armée Juive) were free of them. The same is true for Belgium, Germany and Poland, where Jewish resistance groups were very seldom confronted with internal problems of *agents provocateurs*. It is even more interesting to note that the same phenomenon existed in Palestine as far as the Jewish underground organizations there were concerned. One of the prerequisites of successful operation for Brichah as an illegal organization was quite clearly the absence of danger from spies and agents.

the area of Walbrzych and Kudowa and their environs in the south, on the border between Silesia and Bohemia; and the mountainous Carpathian region, especially the area south and west of Krosno and Nowy Sacz where the first border-crossings of the Brichah had been organized into Slovakia and which were never quite abandoned. December and the early months of 1946 were marked by the necessity of finding a "green border," that is, one that could be passed, usually on foot, illegally in the fullest sense of the term. During those winter months it seemed to the Polish Brichah that the mass migration would cease, that soon the point would come when Jews would no longer wish to risk the dangerous path of illegal exit from Poland. Two factors intervened to prevent this possibility: first, the continued political unrest in Poland, and second, the mass repatriation from Soviet Russia. The right-wing terror groups created a kind of coordinating committee called the PKOP. In January 1946 a congress was held of the PSL, the peasant party grouped around Stanislaw Mikolajczyk, the anti-Communist member of the government. This showed that the mass peasant party probably had the support of a large proportion of the country's population and served as a rallying point for the right-wing underground. On February 25, 1946, negotiations for a political truce between Mikolajczyk and the Communist-led left were broken off, and agitation started for a plebiscite to be held on June 30 which was widely regarded as a political trial of strength. In this situation the terror against the Jews was continually increasing, and the pressure for leaving the country, which had been weakened by bad weather and perhaps also by slightly improved political conditions during the winter, again increased considerably in the spring. Second, contrary to expectations, the repatriation from the Soviet Union of Polish nationals, including many Jews, was begun. This had been the subject of negotiations between the Polish and Soviet governments in June and July 1945, and as early as June 20 Ber Mark, the well-known leftist Jewish intellectual and later head of the Warsaw Jewish Historical Institute, had cabled to his friends from Moscow that the agreement was about to be signed and that there would be no discrimination against the estimated 500,000

Polish Jews who were then thought to be residing in the Soviet Union.[9] The actual beginning of the repatriation was delayed for quite a while, perhaps partly because of the disorganization prevailing in Poland, and people therefore were somewhat skeptical about it. In February, however, the first groups arrived. The figure of 500,000 Jews in Soviet Russia turned out to have been vastly exaggerated. In fact, there were in 1945/46 about 200,000 Polish Jews in the Soviet Union, most of them concentrated in Central Asia. Of these, between February and September 1946 an estimated 175,000 returned to Poland. Nobody knew in advance the extent to which the Soviets would allow these Jews to leave, and nobody could know how many of these people themselves would prefer to stay where they were rather than start their wanderings all over again. Certainly nobody could foretell what these Jews would want to do once they reached Poland, if they did come. The Central Committee in Warsaw made frantic efforts preparing places of settlement in Silesia for the newcomers, plans were made for their absorption in crafts and industries; thought was given to education and cultural problems. The idea of Jewish settlement in Poland on new territory where they could build a national life of their own was in itself an attractive one to many Jews. The fact that such a settlement would not be as exposed to anti-Semitic outrages as would be a dispersal of Jews in Polish towns and villages was also important. And it must be said that the Jewish Communists and the Bundists who cooperated with them made every effort to make this venture succeed. For this they obtained important help from the JDC and the government. And yet, despite some initial success, the settlement idea never really got off the ground. There were several reasons why the repatriants preferred the hard road to Palestine via Germany to the lures of Silesia.

First, they had come out of the Soviet Union with very bitter memories. They had indeed seen the worst sides of the Soviet regime—many had been in forced labor camps as anti-Communist suspects or "bourgeois elements"; all of them had undergone severe privations during the starvation years of the war when many refugees had died of epidemics and starvation; and in Central Asia their status as refugees

engaging in black market operations to keep themselves alive had aroused anti-Semitism on the part of the local population. Then came the shock of Poland—the old story of graveyards, near and dear ones lost, the hopelessness of starting again in such an environment, the virulent hatred of so many Poles—all these factors militated against their staying. True, they let themselves be shipped to new centers or they stayed in Lodz and tried to make a living in their former occupations or learn new trades. But many of them immediately joined groups that would ultimately lead them to Brichah and out of Poland. At the railway stations in Warsaw or Lodz, propagandists of the Central Committee and those of the Zionists competed quite openly for the newcomers. Communist newspapers in Yiddish tried to influence them, as did Zionist publications; but generally speaking, the Communist side did not really have a chance. The problem was not that these people wanted to stay but that they shunned the dangers inherent in the illegal operations of the Brichah, especially in the spring of 1946. They had had enough of dangers and sufferings. Unlike those Polish Jews who had been under direct Nazi rule, they were not single remnants of large families but members of families, who now came out of Russia with children, and sometimes grandchildren, and they did not relish the idea of illegal border-crossings. The number of those who left Poland in the spring went up, but it went up slowly—from a low of 452 in January the figure rose to 954 in February and 820 in March, 1,098 in April, 3,502 in May and 8,000 in June.[10] While, therefore, there was a basic readiness to leave the country, this readiness was not unconditional, and the majority of repatriants were content to sit on their suitcases waiting for a legal way to leave Poland.

During that winter and spring of 1945 and 1946, Poland's borders became stabilized. As far as the Brichah was concerned, this was marked by the establishment of more efficient frontier guards and the replacement of Red Army soldiers by Polish officials who were apt to be rather more sophisticated than the simple souls who accepted a bottle of vodka and any impressive-looking document with a *bolshaya petchat* (large seal) in lieu of a proper document of travel.

The Polish frontier guards were of course under the control of Soviet officers, chosen from among Polish-speaking Soviet nationals or reliable Polish Communists, some of whom were Jews. Occasionally an arrangement could be made with such an area commander, but generally the political police, the UB, was becoming more vigilant over the exits from the country, and illegal or half-legal crossings became practically impossible. The special attention that the regime now paid to the borders was not directed against the Jews but paradoxically against the Jews' enemies, the right-wing bands who, for obvious reasons, tried to maintain open doors for themselves at the frontiers. But the results were the same—the postwar chaos as far as frontiers were concerned was now a thing of the past, and given the confused Jewish policy of the Polish government, border-crossing became increasingly dangerous.

Brichah turned to the so-called green borders. During the period now under review, "points" were opened and closed depending on local conditions. Dozens of Brichah members scoured the borders of Poland for possible exits. Wherever a weak link in the chain of guards indicated a possibility, attempts were made to find appropriate crossings. These were then held open until they were "burnt"—betrayed by the local populace, found out by the guards, discovered through carelessness of the refugees.

All these activities demanded money. Until the summer of 1945 the major source of financing was the funds supplied by the Jewish Agency Rescue Committee. This committee had been established in Palestine in 1942, originally for the purpose of supporting the families of Palestinian Jewish soldiers in the British Army. When, in late 1942, the facts of the mass murder of European Jewry became known, the fund received its final name, Mobilization and Rescue Fund, and large amounts of money were transferred during the war to Istanbul and Switzerland from the small and relatively poor Jewish community in Palestine to help in rescue operations. When the war ended, these monies were expended on what was considered a natural sequel to wartime rescue, namely, the mass move out of Eastern Europe in the general direction of Palestine. In 1945, and until the JDC

took over the major burden of direct and indirect financing of the refugees, the Rescue Fund provided an estimated 300,000 pounds (or over one million dollars)[11] for the various activities in Europe, which of course included not only Brichah but relief as well.

After October 1945, JDC funds were made available to refugees on the move, at first irregularly and intermittently, by providing the transients with food and clothing. Later on, this was done in an organized fashion, through a treasurer of the Jewish Agency, Pinchas Ginzburg, who disbursed the funds from his office in Geneva to various refugee committees in the different countries. From October 1945 to June 1946 a total of $136,571 was received by Poland for aiding refugees.[12]

Brichah officials received no salaries, only food and a minimum of clothing and some pocket money, and were therefore very "cheap." This very strict attitude was occasionally carried to extremes. A case was recorded of a Brichah worker on the Czech border being fired by a *shaliah* because he had taken Polish cigarettes to the Czech side, exchanged them there for money and bought himself a sorely needed coat. The principle was that no Brichah worker had the right to utilize his position at the border for any private purpose whatsoever.

Food for the "points" and "stores" was often obtained from the JDC under various guises, such as support of Zionist youth training groups, children and especially orphan homes, and various other institutions. This, of course, was not included in the Brichah budgets. About two-thirds of the JDC budget for Poland ($37 million out of $50 million in 1946) went to institutions operated by the official Communist-dominated Central Committee. The other third was given to the Zionist and religious groups, and quite large sums of this found their way, indirectly, to the refugees who turned to the Brichah. The fact that most Brichah points were located in Zionist agricultural training centers also helped: the actual food for Brichah workers and for the transients in these centers was provided by the JDC, without the JDC's knowledge.

It should be pointed out that the JDC had to be slowly

convinced of the need for Jews to become refugees again. Dr. Joseph J. Schwartz's suspicions stemmed not only from the great American institution's fear of refugee movements but also from early assessments that the majority of repatriants from the Soviet Union were likely to stay in Poland. In early 1946 the American Bundist leader Jacob Patt visited Poland; misled by the propaganda of his Bundist friends there, he had visions of a brilliant future for the repatriants in the Silesian districts. Influenced by his report, JDC Secretary Moses A. Leavitt wrote to Schwartz on March 15 that according to his information "these repatriants will probably take root in Poland and remain there, whereas single survivors without family will in all likelihood want to move to Palestine and other destinations."[13]

The New York leadership of the JDC was informed of the general trend of the exodus, but was not aware of the details or the organizational setup. The way it looked from New York was that these Jews were transients who would be leaving Poland in any case, with or without JDC assistance. JDC, as a humanitarian organization, had to help them on their difficult journeys with food, clothing and medical supplies. Obviously, without the help of the great philanthropic Jewish organization and the moral support of American Jewry it brought with it, things would have been considerably more difficult for them. Schwartz's personality was undoubtedly a vital factor in mobilizing JDC's help. He influenced his New York colleagues and convinced them to go along with him in supporting the migratory movement. Schwartz himself was quite certain that, even without the JDC, Brichah would operate and succeed. But JDC could alleviate the hard lot of the wandering masses of people, and this was what it set out to do under his leadership.

The Communists and their Bundist allies did all they could to prevent the mass exodus from Poland—they employed threats and promises, and they also invested a great deal of praiseworthy productive effort in trying to create a meaningful life in Silesia for the returning Jews from Soviet Asia. In May 1946 a delegation representing the Communist and Zionist wings of the Central Committee left for the United States mainly in order to arouse American Jewry to

greater support of Polish Jews. The JDC, in its turn, could not but support *all* Polish Jews. Besides, had it not supported the Communists it is hardly likely that it could have lent its support to the Zionist wing or the religious groups.

One of the more fascinating episodes in the history of the Polish Brichah was the story of the northern route, leading from Stettin (Szczecin) to Berlin.[14] Stettin is a port on the Baltic Sea, situated at the mouth of the Oder. It became the border town between the new Polish territories and eastern Germany, and for Brichah this meant a border between Poles and Russians. The route, as well as Berlin at the end of it, was known in Brichah code as *hazir* ("swine," perhaps derived from the nearby town of Swinemünde). In Stettin there were a handful of Jews, mostly survivors of concentration camps in the neighborhood, who, after their release, found a niche for themselves in the ruined town. The route was actually started by private operators very early after the end of the war. Brichah started there in a half-hearted way; a building was taken over where refugees could be housed, and some people were sent there early in August 1945. This, however, proved to be one case where Brichah failed. The smugglers caused the Brichah considerable trouble. For a relatively short period of time Brichah groups were even forced to use these operators as intermediaries to get trucks for the 120 kilometers to Berlin. The attitude of the Russians was another grim problem. Despite occasional attempts to explain to them the difference between smuggling and the flight of war victims from Poland, they proved to be utterly insensitive to refugee problems. However, few Soviet officers cared about the migration, and ordinary soldiers were certainly not concerned with any struggle against it if they themselves could make profit out of it. The journey to Berlin was itself by no means without dangers. Often when the Russians caught a truck they would simply steal the passengers' belongings and then let the victims go. Sometimes, in the middle of such a journey being made by forty persons on a tarpaulin-covered vehicle, the smuggler guide would stop the truck and refuse to go on until he was given additional money. Nevertheless, this way, with all its dangers, was taken by 7,000 Jews until November 1945. During

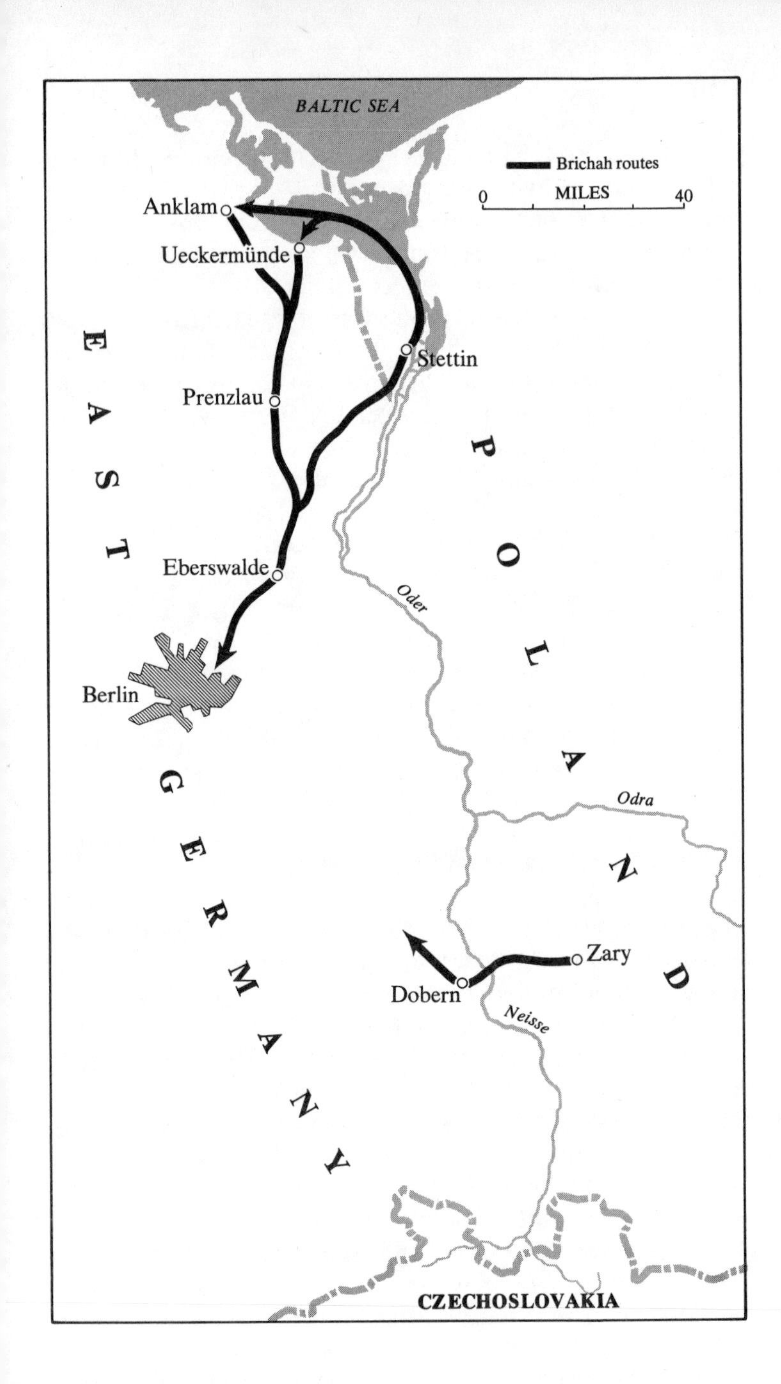

The Stettin Brichah Route

that month, new Brichah people were sent to Stettin, and a bitter struggle with the speculators started which lasted until well into the spring of 1946. By that time, Brichah organized its own truck transports, and established its own contacts with Polish and Soviet soldiers.

In contrast to Stettin, Berlin was organized from the very beginning on quite a different basis. The Polish Brichah sent a man there in early August 1945, and by the winter an efficient group of eight persons were working there. There were three transit camps, housed in buildings of the old Jewish community: one in Iranienstrasse in the French sector and two in the Russian sector. They were in terrible condition, but they were the best that could be had, and they were therefore used. In the U.S. zone of the city an UNRRA repatriation camp for all nationalities opened in October under an American named Charles J. Taylor. Until then, most of the Jews who arrived in Berlin stayed in the houses in the Russian zone or elsewhere in the city. The Brichah was trying to find a way out of Berlin and into the American zone, but this was not easy. At the same time, some help was obtained from the Berlin Jewish community, which numbered about 7,000 persons who thought of themselves as Jews. It was a very odd community, and the whole tragedy of the Nazi period seemed to be reflected in the statistics of these Jews: 1,628 had come back from concentration camps; 1,321 had found hiding places in the city with honest and humane German families; 2,126 (some of these had been sterilized by the Nazis) had married non-Jews but had no children and were therefore exempt from deportation; and 1,995 were married to non-Jews and had children. The rest were non-German Jews who had arrived in Berlin after the war.[15] Most of these people were also members of an organization that called itself *Opfer des Faschismus*,* which was entitled to certain help and material benefits. This organization was to play a significant role in the Brichah. The

* "Victims of Fascism," a Communist-led organization of ex-concentration camp inmates and other sufferers from the Nazi regime whose members were entitled to certain privileges in food, housing and transport.

community was in charge of the transient centers and was trying to look after the transients with the help of the *Opfer des Faschismus* and other groups. Among these was a private aid organization set up by a Jewish American sergeant, David J. Eisenberg, who started a scheme of sending five-pound parcels from the United States to the Jews in Berlin. In the first months after liberation Eisenberg's project alone got some 5,000 packages into starving Berlin.

On October 15, Philip S. Skorneck, the first representative of the JDC, arrived in the city. He appears to have gone to work with tremendous zeal; he attached Eisenberg to his staff and thus brought the package project under the control of a recognized relief agency. He got in touch with the several occupation authorities in the divided city and tried to get their cooperation in alleviating the condition of the refugees in the crowded transients' camps. He also contacted the Brichah people, and it appears that it was agreed that efforts be made to get large numbers of Jews out of Berlin and into west Germany. Skorneck himself reports that he intervened with the French, who closed the unsatisfactory camp in their zone and opened a much better place at Wittenau in their sector. He then "was able to arrange with Mr. Taylor, director of the UNRRA transit camp, to ship 50 Jews a day and subsequently 100 Jews a day. Actually, through personal arrangements with other UNRRA staff members, we were able to ship between 140 and 200 a day."[16] Taylor had been shipping some 15 to 30 Jews a day to the west even prior to that, but Skorneck's intervention was now decisive. By the end of December, 5,000 Jews had been transferred out of the city ostensibly as German citizens returning to the Western zones of occupation. Once in the British zone, they usually went to Bergen-Belsen, received food from the Brigade soldier stationed there for that purpose—with the full knowledge of the Jewish camp committee—and then infiltrated into the American zone by train or truck. Officially this movement came to an end when the British authorities declared on December 5 that they would not let through any more Jews and closed the transfer point at Hesslingen to them. Whereupon the U.S. authorities in Frankfurt instructed their people in Berlin that no more Jews were to

be allowed to come through Berlin into the U.S. zone in Germany.

Brichah sources make it clear that the continued flow of Jews into Berlin bore no relation to the strict attitude of the British and the Americans. In other words, there was no decision, such as we have seen in relation to southern Germany and Austria, to break down the resistance of the occupying powers to the admission of refugees. But the results were the same. Brichah carried more Jews into Berlin, about 250 to 300 a day during the last weeks of December. In fact, most Jews who left Poland during December and January came via Berlin. Soon there were 5,000 Jews in the city, and more were coming in daily. The *Kommandatura* (Berlin City Council of the occupying powers) finally met and decided to grant them a ration of 1,600 calories a day. Then a discussion started as to what should be done about them. The Russians declared that the problem was not of their making and they had no interest in it. The British did not recognize the existence of a problem of a specifically Jewish character at all: "It was simply a matter of Polish nationals who were leaving their homeland and should be forced to return there." The French stated that they were sympathetic but were poor in materiel and could not help. The U.S. attitude was: "We don't have a Polish-Jewish problem because none of them are living in the U.S. sector of Berlin and we don't want to have a Jewish problem, so we will not permit them to live in the U.S. sector!"[17]

On January 4, 1946, the Russians finally forced a solution. They suddenly announced to the 2,500 Jews in the two transit homes in their zone that they would be taken to a Russian DP camp at Prenzlau (near the new Polish border) on January 7. No Jews who had escaped from Poland or who had arrived from Soviet Asia could have any doubt that the Russians intended to ship the Jews considerably farther east than Prenzlau. However, it was quite contrary to Russian practice to announce such a move two and a half days prior to its execution; the aim quite obviously was to get the Jews to leave their sector. In this they succeeded. A wealthy German Jew gave the JDC a place called the Swedish pavilion in the suburb of Wannsee (where the

famous Nazi conference on the murder of European Jewry took place in January 1942). On January 7 no Jews were left in the Russian sector; most of them had moved into the French sector or to the Swedish pavilion, and 250 left illegally as German Jews for the British zone. What followed is best told in Mr. Skorneck's own words: "I notified the US Military Government authorities that a Committee of Jews had come to tell me that they had established themselves in the US Sector and wanted help from the US authorities. These authorities, who had for weeks been trying to prove that the Joint was responsible for the movement of Jews from Poland to Berlin, became immediately convinced that the Joint [JDC] was responsible for the movement of Jews from the Russian Sector to the US Sector of Berlin. For two days they refused to do anything except to order us to curtail our activities. We were ordered not to operate in any sector but the US Sector. I was personally ordered to work completely through military channels and not to see anyone outside those channels without prior permission from Colonel Howley, the Military Governor, or General Baker, the Commanding General of the US Sector of Berlin. The Military Government for the US Zone at the same time ordered us to discontinue our mail service, the petrol allowances for our vehicles were discontinued because of a technicality, and we were subjected to an investigation from a large group of CIC agents, our telephones were monitored, our mail was opened and read, but the authorities were unable to prove that the Joint had anything to do with the movement of Jews. Hundreds of Jews who were questioned said that the Joint had advised them that it could do nothing to help them, since the Kommandatura had ordered that they were not to move from one sector to another."[18]

Finally, it was the problem involving some 200 women who were either in the later stages of pregnancy or had young children and who had established themselves at the Swedish pavilion that broke the American resistance. The husbands of these women were refugees from the two homes in the Russian sector, but the Americans demanded that the women return to the Russian zone, Prenzlau notwithstanding. "The women became panic stricken and rushed to the

Joint office for advice. They were told to refuse to go and when they did so, the next morning the UNRRA team director refused to move them by force. . . . After three days, the US authorities opened the camp in the US Sector which it calls an 'Infiltree Camp.' " The resistance of the U.S. authorities to Jewish infiltration of their Berlin sector was effectively broken. From January 1946 the U.S. section of Berlin, like its counterpart in southern Germany, became a safe haven for Jewish refugees. Ultimately, because of the threat of a public scandal and the humanitarian interest in the Jewish question in the United States, as well as the sympathy with the Jews in their struggle against Britain and the knowledge of actions of the Nazi era, it was very difficult for the American military to persist for very long, in the face of determined opposition, in a policy of refusing the Jews access to the U.S.-controlled areas in Germany. At the new camp, which was called Schlachtensee, a temporary organization of Jews was created, along the lines of the camp committees in Bavaria. However, the kind of people who came to Berlin differed greatly from those who reached Bavaria via the other routes. There were fewer young people and Zionist youth movement groups, and more people with families; also, there were more people coming to Berlin who had had no affiliation with any organized group in Poland. Moreover, Berlin attracted some smugglers who tried to penetrate Wittenau in the French zone and Schlachtensee as well. A prolonged struggle ensued which ended in the early spring when the chief of the largest smugglers' group was kidnapped by the Brichah and taken to Wittenau, where he was beaten up. After this, the smugglers and their like avoided the official camps.

In contrast to this unsavory group there were Jews of the finest type, notably a Hebrew teacher by the name of Krochmalnik, who did a tremendous job in influencing his fellow DPs to fight the temptations of black marketeering, smuggling and other forms of crime. His school for children of all ages and the cultural activities he supervised helped the Brichah to overcome the difficulties inherent in the abnormal and illegal situations that tended to demoralize the refugees.

The nature of the black market in Berlin affected the Brichah to a considerable degree. Corruption among the military of the occupying powers was general and open. The main means of exchange was the cigarette. A carton of American cigarettes was worth 1,500 marks (officially the dollar was worth 10 marks, unofficially 300 marks); people did not want money, which was worthless, and preferred cigarettes. Thus, Russian soldiers smuggling Jews into the city would accept a pack of cigarettes per Jew. There was an average of 40 Jews per truck, and this of course meant a corresponding number of packs of cigarettes.

In the second half of January an important organizational change occurred: the Brigade sent a man to Berlin to take over the "point" from the Polish Brichah, and the Polish Brichah in its turn sent a girl (Rega Globman) to run a new "point" together with a Brigade man at Hannover in the British zone. This was done mainly in order to ease the financial burden of the Polish Brichah but also because Brigade people had an easier time with English-speaking military personnel than did the Polish Jews. After some changes, Yitzhak Ram ("Peretz") became the commander of Berlin's Brichah. During the months of December 1945 to March 1946, 8,000 Jews were smuggled into Berlin from Stettin, largely by truck. Exit from Berlin was more difficult. In the course of the December–January crisis, described above, Taylor had ceased transporting Jews in UNRRA vehicles, and Brichah had recourse to an illegal route. Refugees were transported to Weferlingen, near the Russian-British zonal frontier, and then on foot over the actual border into Helmstedt. There they boarded trains to Hannover and Celle for the Bergen-Belsen camp, or—from January on—via the Hannover Brichah "point" to the U.S. zone. This route was taken by some 4,000 people to the end of March, when it was uncovered by the Russians and had to be discontinued. The Russians intended their move to stop Germans and others, but it hit the Brichah incidentally as well.

The Brichah devised a new ruse to ease the situation. At the official transit point of Heiligenstadt near the British zonal border they established two representatives with forged

documents of the *Opfer des Faschismus* committee. This committee was now recognized as a semiofficial repatriation agency, mainly of course for Germans. Jews therefore went to Heiligenstadt as Germans returning to the West, were given appropriate documents by the "representatives" of the committee, and with the connivance of some local officials 5,000 Jews were thus transferred to Hannover between the beginning of April and June 30. On the latter date an order forbade further repatriation of Germans from zone to zone, and this avenue was henceforth closed. UNRRA was called upon again. At first, Taylor agreed to transfer small numbers of Jews to the British zone, but in April a new arrangement was arrived at with a Jewish UNRRA director, Harold Fishbein, who had become responsible for the Schlachtensee camp. At first Fishbein adhered strictly to regulations, so strictly, in fact, that Skorneck had to complain to the commanding general about his reluctance to stretch his orders even to the slightest degree. But this changed later on, and UNRRA transport was provided for Jews to leave for the British zone. It is unlikely that the American authorities were unaware of this semilegal move, and it looks as though they tacitly supported an operation that would free them of the pressure of Jewish DPs in their area of Berlin. Up to the end of June, some 8,000 Jews were sent by this safe route.

In the meantime, the stream of refugees from Stettin continued unabated and, indeed, in ever-increasing numbers. The distance was only 120 kilometers from the Polish border to Berlin, but the strengthening of Russian control over the area made the journey more hazardous. In April and May Russian interference with the Brichah became very serious. It seems that at the time the smugglers and speculators were also increasing their operations. The Russians thought of the Brichah as just another group of smugglers, and if they caught a group on the way their usual policy was to release the refugees but to arrest the leader, if they could identify him. Nevertheless, in the middle of April, 60 refugees were caught and held in a Russian prison for two months before they were released. On May 5 they managed to catch another group, whose leader was a member of the central Brichah committee in Poland of the right-wing Ichud group.

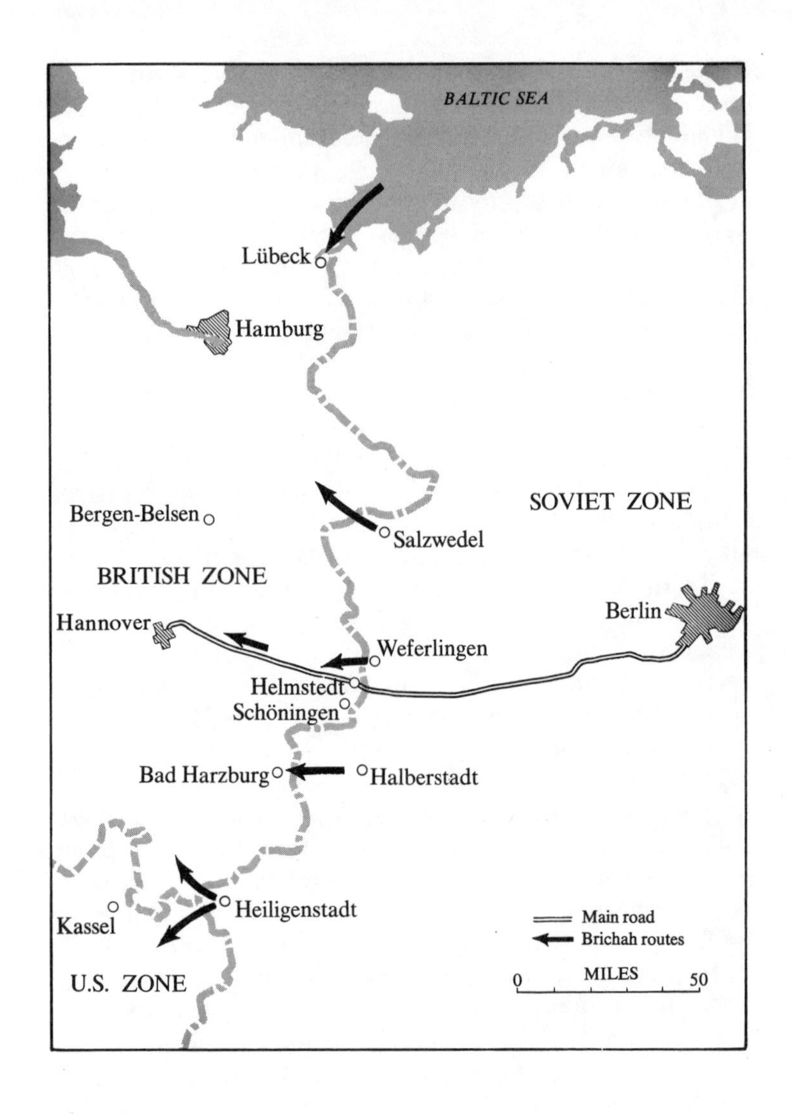

Brichah Routes into the British Zone, Germany

He had been involved in an attempt to take Jews out of the Lwow area which had been annexed by the Soviet Union. His identity was revealed, and he spent some twelve years in Soviet prisons as a result.

In order to make the transit easier, various stratagems were resorted to. Post office trucks were used to transport especially important groups, mainly children (1,500 children were brought into Berlin in the spring of 1946). The route was varied. People were brought by boat or rail to Ueckermuende, thence by truck to Eberswalde, and then by train to Berlin. However, as this proved to be inadequate, two points were established south of Stettin—one at Zary (Sorau) and one at Zasieki. Both were tried as transfer points in March and April. In the end the old route by truck from Stettin was found to be the best one, and it functioned till June 10. In the course of time Brichah began to use trucks owned by the organization rather than relying on Soviet vehicles. But at the beginning of June a few of these were caught, and the lack of funds forced Brichah to cease operations in Stettin. From June 10 and until the third week of July no more refugees were brought into Berlin.

How did the Brichah manage to operate in Berlin? Who helped the emissaries from the Brigade and the Polish Jewish youngsters who did the actual work? First of all, there were the chaplains: Rabbi Herbert Friedman and Rabbi Meyer Abramowitz. Friedman was stationed in Berlin from early spring until July 1946, when he became the aide to Rabbi Philip S. Bernstein, the official Jewish adviser to General Joseph McNarney, the commanding general of U.S. forces in Germany. Friedman soon got in touch with the Brigade people whose center was in the French zone, and he put his house at the disposal of the Brichah. Trucks, along with gasoline, tires and spare parts, were stored there, and the chaplain was also instrumental in obtaining some of these. His help went further: payment for transport was made in cigarettes, and the Brichah obtained these partly through gifts from Jewish soldiers of the occupying armies and partly by mail from the United States—in all these activities Friedman's help was well-nigh decisive. Although nothing he did was actually illegal, he ran considerable risks in

being in touch in this way with an underground organization and obtaining funds (that is, cigarettes) for its operations. This kind of help was continued by his successor, Rabbi Abramowitz (a Palestine-born Jew), and the Brichah reports were full of praise for the two chaplains.[19] Another crucial factor was the JDC. We have seen that under Skorneck the JDC actually saved the Brichah from a real danger of defeat. When Skorneck had to leave at the end of February, his place was taken by a JDC team headed by Eli Rock. While most of the actual money expended by the JDC went to the Berlin Jewish community, it seems that much of the working time of the JDC team was taken up with helping transients brought in by Brichah. The 1,600 calories officially supplied at Schlachtensee were supplemented by additional rations, and blankets, sheets and other items were provided. More important even than these was the day-to-day contact with the authorities established by the JDC and utilized by the refugees whenever difficulties arose. JDC was the representative of all these fleeing Jews, and it took up cudgels in their behalf whenever necessary. The policy of JDC was certainly one of strict legality and obedience to military rule, but in practice, while its loyalty to the American authorities was never in the slightest doubt, it saw itself as the only group that could present and "interpret" the grievances and problems of Jewish persecutees to the authorities. Typically, while a fair amount of criticism of the JDC was heard occasionally throughout the camps of the U.S. zone, little or none was ever voiced in Berlin; the group of JDC workers there were looked upon by their fellow Jews as worthy representatives of the American Jewish community. Stettin was really a case by itself, as far as the Brichah was concerned; all the points south of it presented a different picture.

South of Stettin, along the Oder-Neisse border with East Germany, only two attempts were made by Brichah to take the heavy load off the dangerous Stettin route. In early 1946 a couple of energetic young men of the organization, Meir Yocht and Yosef Schechter, were sent to the town of Zary (Sorau) on the main railway line leading from Breslau

(Wroclaw) to Berlin and established a "kibbutz" there; this was an agricultural training farm manned by members of the Dror pioneer youth movement "simply to get the Germans [at that time there were still German civilians there as well as administrators] accustomed to the idea that there are Jews in the place."[20] Using the local knowledge of a Jewish doctor who lived there, they established a relationship with Polish officials, especially police and security personnel. Just after Passover (April–May) of 1946, Jews were brought to the "kibbutz," then by train to the town of Tuplice on the actual border, and thence by Polish Army trucks (for which sums of money would be paid) or by boat over the Neisse River to the East German town of Döbern. From there the refugees were brought to Berlin. However, this route was too expensive because the Poles and Russians had to be bribed. Finally one of the transports was caught by some zealous Polish officials when it happened to cross the river on a night when the Poles were having a celebration on the water with plenty of lights. The mass arrest caused a scandal. This happened probably in late May or early June, and it was the end of the Zary episode. Not more than about 400 people crossed the border at that particular point.

The "point" at Zgorzelec (Görlitz), which served as a crossing point into eastern Germany in the direction of Dresden and the Western zones, had an even more ephemeral existence. Organized Brichah used this point rarely, mainly because of the difficulties in crossing eastern Germany into the Western zones. Besides, it seems that such small "points" were not really very useful for the Brichah, because ever since the fall of 1945 the main centers of Brichah activity lay on the southwestern and southern borders of Poland, especially in the Silesian-Bohemian borderland.

Organized Brichah movements in Silesia started from the general direction of Katowice not later than August 1945. Prior to that, there had been unorganized crossings, but apart from the fact that they occurred we know very little about them. At first, groups of between twenty and forty persons, disguised as Greeks, went via Dziedzice or Zebrzydowice, two small railroad junctions on the tracks leading to Zilina in Slovakia; another main point on the same rail-

road was Bohumin. From these places, once the border was crossed, the groups went on to Bratislava.[21] The railroad was an easy and speedy way, provided you had the right documents. These again were expertly forged in Katowice and took the form of Red Cross lists with an accompanying letter certifying that the particular group of Greek nationals concerned was passing through Czechoslovakia on the way home. The same ruse was used also in Silesia, where in the fall of 1945 a road was opened via Walbrzych (Waldenburg) to Broumov and Nachod on the Czech side of the border, and thence to Prague and As. This route was considerably more difficult because the border was crossed on foot. The Greek camouflage was correspondingly flimsier, and it is very doubtful whether the rather sophisticated Czechs actually swallowed the stories they were told. But they did not seem to care very much, and their attitude is one to which we shall have to return again later on. In late November a Brichah man in Prague estimated that up to that time a total of 20,000 people had passed through Prague. Of these some 7,000 had gone via As, and the rest had been sent by train either through Pilsen or via Bratislava to Austria. He further estimated that 17,000 had gone with the organized Brichah, and 3,000 with smugglers.[22]

On the Bohumin-Zilina route the Greek story was apparently taken seriously for quite a while, and in Bratislava the Brichah man was officially designated as a Greek interpreter. The language used as a local variety of Greek was of course Hebrew; this gave the Jews a chance to revel in the full use of the famed Jewish sense of humor, which had survived even the holocaust. "Greek" names such as Roshashanitis, Misheberach or Nebbachos* flourished, and Jews who had no knowledge of Hebrew recited prayers to each other in lieu of conversation when in the company of strangers. And it is a fact that when in November real Greeks crossed the border from Poland they were refused entry be-

---

* Rosh Hashanah is the Jewish New Year; *Misheberach,* in this sense, is a popular allusion to the opening words of the synagogue prayer for the welfare of an individual; *Nebboch* (Yiddish) means an unfortunate, a man to be pitied.

cause their documents, being unlike the forged ones, were suspect and the language they spoke sounded different from the one to which the border guards were accustomed.[23]

In Bratislava, the Jews were housed in a hotel in the center of the town given to them by the Slovak Ministry of Social Welfare; the venerable structure was known as Hotel Jelen, and apart from the refugees, its population consisted of a very large number of small but omnipresent and unpleasant creatures, which fact led the human occupants to call the place Hotel La Wanz (*wanz* being the Yiddish word for louse). Because postal connections in Europe were still very uncertain, the refugees left their names and presumed future whereabouts on the walls of the hotel. Thus the walls of the building became a veritable tracing bureau, primitive but effective. Passing groups of infiltrees would first of all go to read the names and addresses on the walls in the hope of finding relatives or friends who might have passed on the same route before them. Then they would add their own particulars so as to provide information for others. On one of these walls a Brichah man once discovered a rhyme with the typical bittersweet Jewish humor:

Die Welt is rund, ohn a Eck
Moishe sich mich, ich bin a Greck

The globe is cornerless and sleek,
Just try and find me, Moish, I'm a Greek[24]

The "Greeks" were sent along all the way from Poland with the small slips of paper called *parols* (passes), where a very simple code (numbers and Hebrew letters) would tell Brichah people on the border and in Bratislava the number of persons in the group, the destination and the desired method of transportation. The *parol* was always in the hands of the group leader, chosen from among the refugees, and it would send the people on the journey from Katowice or Lodz to Vienna or Munich, and no further passport was needed.

In November the Greek method collapsed, though not completely, for we find evidence of Greek documents being

used well into 1946. The difficulties during the winter months mounted, until they seemed absolutely insurmountable. The diary of one of the central Brichah figures, Tuvia Cohen, gives us a fair picture of the pessimistic mood. "The situation is growing more serious every day," because "the number of Jews wanting to leave is getting larger" and the possibilities of border-crossing do not increase to the same extent.[25] "Points" were opened, only to be closed again as frontier guards caught small groups trying out the new routes. Then, in January, Walbrzych was reopened, and simultaneously another route, that of Kladzko via Bad Kudowa to Nachod, was tried and found suitable. Two men did outstanding service at these two "points": Avraham Sadeh, an intellectual, and Menahem Shmulewitz, a daredevil and typical underground worker.

It took some time before these two Silesian "points" became really important. The first problem was to arrive at an understanding with the Czech side. Here, two Nachod Jews entered the picture, Messrs. Pick and Beck. They were quite simply local Jewish people, who volunteered to explain to the local officials the problem of Jews fleeing from the other side. In this they were eminently successful, and the good-natured Czechs declared themselves willing to cooperate. We shall have occasion to see that they took good care to get backing in Prague for what they did at the frontier, but Pick and Beck were instrumental in getting their good will and readiness to enter into the whole situation. The use of a wooden shack and, later, a small hotel was obtained to serve as a temporary resting place for the refugees on their way to the railway station in the town. A whole camp was to be erected later for the same purpose. The *parols* during those winter months stated quite plainly that the refugees were destined for "Pick and Beck," the code name for the little Czech town of Nachod with its friendly, compassionate officials who helped the people onto trains that took them to Bratislava and beyond. Only a portion of the infiltrees would be allowed to go to Prague and As: from about January-February the Nachod crowd, by and large, was headed for Bratislava.[26]

During this time, the original border points of the Bri-

chah—Krosno, Krynica, Nowy Sacz, Nowy Targ, on the eastern border of the Polish Carpathian mountains—were not abandoned. However, these difficult mountain passes were suitable during those winter months only for the young and the adventurous. Then in March a crisis developed. The Polish security police, which up to that time had not paid much attention to the illegal movement of Jews out of the country, discovered that the headquarters of the Brichah was situated in Katowice. Escaping arrest in the nick of time, the *shlihim* and the coordinator, Tuvia Cohen, moved to Bitum on March 12. Hardly had they begun to reorganize when on the 23rd, a group of people trying out a new route through the large Moravian town of Moravska Ostrava were arrested by the police. Among them were two members of the Brichah center, one of them the Palestinian *shaliah* Yohanan Cohen who had gone there in order to meet with the Czech Brichah and coordinate movements. Viewed from the Polish angle this was a heavy blow. Some of the Brichah people laid the blame at the door of a suspected informer in its ranks, the only such case in its history. Apparently the man was warned by the Brichah and then thoroughly beaten up and told to disappear, which, it seems, he did.[27] Brichah was on the move again, this time to Lodz, and then it split: the *shlihim* remained in Lodz, which became the overall center, but Cohen stayed in Katowice, his old haunt, and gave the direct orders for movement from there—acting, it seems, on the old soldier's maxim that no shell-crater is ever hit twice.

The group arrested at Moravska Ostrava was interrogated in such a way that it became clear they had been denounced as—of all things—Nazis escaping from a Polish prison camp to Germany. Even after the mistake had been made clear and their identities as Jews revealed, the Czechs were reluctant to let them go. This time, it seems, there were suspicions that these were Soviet citizens escaping from the U.S.S.R., and in any case they had crossed the border illegally. They were finally released after weeks in Czech prisons.

During this time, in March, April and May, with the spring weather melting the snow in the Tatra mountains,

the desire of the Jews to leave Poland became stronger. We have evidence that suggests that smugglers, both Jews and Poles, capitalized on this wish to leave and organized border-crossings in the region of Piwniczna and Krynica, where the mountains were not too high and the railroad to Bratislava could be reached if one got to the Slovak townships of Bardejov or Plavec. I. F. Stone, in his book *Underground to Palestine,* claims to have met some people who came by that route, and Cohen mentions these unorganized groups in his diary.[28] The Brichah organization, too, turned to this part of the border. Krosno was tried again and abandoned, and then the "wild" route of Piwniczna was utilized, with a "point" established at Nowy Sacz. The Brichah was still exploring the best route in that area when on the night of May 3 disaster struck: a picked group of twenty-six members of the Gordonia youth movement were stopped south of Nowy Sacz by Polish fascists, taken off their truck and thirteen of them brutally murdered. The rest managed to get away, though some were wounded.[29] The story quickly became known all over Jewish Poland, but the results were quite different from what might have been expected: the Tatra route was abandoned, but during the days immediately following the tragedy a sudden influx of Jews came into Kudowa on the Silesian border. In an unorganized way and helped partly by local smugglers, some 800 people crossed the border into Bohemia between May 10 and May 16. It was an uncontrollable panic flight, indicative of things to come. The Brichah had to organize that border very quickly if it did not want to lose whatever control it had over the exodus. The problem of course was the illegality of the crossing, and the impossibility of doing anything really big in such conditions. At that point, on May 6, Ben Zvi, the Brichah commander, suggested at a Brichah center meeting in Lodz that the organization prepare a demonstrative, open mass crossing of the Silesian border sometime in the near future. This would be a march of 10,000 to 15,000 people, and no government could possibly stop it unless firearms were used—and then of course the whole problem would become part of the political struggle around the Jewish question. "The proposal," wrote Tuvia Cohen, "is

a very serious one, but difficult to put into operation; but we shall have to return to it, otherwise we will not be able to escape from our present predicament."[30]

The Brichah saw the absolute necessity of using the Kudowa border but feared an outright clash with the Poles —unless the mass protest envisaged by Ben Zvi was staged. The groundwork for such a solution was actually laid in March, when Cohen and a girl who was in charge of Kladzko got in touch with a couple of Soviet officers serving in the Polish frontier gendarmerie. Cohen's contact was a colonel; and after a long discussion in which all the cards were laid on the table, the colonel, shaken by what he heard from the Brichah man, intervened to free some Brichah people who had been arrested in the middle of March near Kudowa. He was, as it happened, responsible for the whole stretch of the border which was the main area of operations of the Brichah—from Cieszyn to Kladzko. In March he opened the transit point for the Brichah at the Polish town of Glucholazy, not far from Cieszyn, but for a number of reasons the Brichah operated this point for a short time only. Along with another officer he gave further help in May. An army truck would be used to transport the Jews as close to the border as possible, and then the way was free for the actual crossing. It is uncertain whether the officers informed their superiors of the action taken by them, and on the face of it there would seem to be no special reason why they should have told anyone. And yet this is a moot point—it is rather unlikely that a policy of inaction which allowed many hundreds of people to cross the borders should have remained a secret. One must remember that these officers were at the same time incorruptible, good Communists and loyal servants of their government. It is more reasonable to suppose that the question of how to treat the vexatious Jewish escape problem had been asked in Warsaw or even Moscow and answered. We do not know the exact nature of the answer, but we do know about the actual policy of the frontier guards: provided the Jews did not meet any guards on their way, and the helpful officers usually saw to it that they did not, the authorities let the Jews go. We do not hear of any large-scale move on the part of the security organs to hamper the Brichah after March.[31]

The Silesian Border

This attitude on the part of the frontier guards did not, of course, mean that everything was smooth sailing on the Silesian border. One must not forget that the Jewish Communists and their Bundist allies saw the ground cut from under them with the intensification of Jewish escapes from Poland. These two parties claimed to represent the Jewish "masses." If these masses disappeared, whom would they represent? No voting was possible among Jews in Poland at the time, but if the Jews voted with their feet and simply left the country, then the whole ideology of Poland as the homeland for the Polish Jews, their culture and their Yiddish language, and all the rest of the ideological baggage of Jewish Communism and Bundism in Poland simply collapsed. Apart from oral propaganda and pressure exerted on the Soviet repatriants as they came to Lodz and Silesia, the Communists used two other means of trying to influence their fellow Jews. One was the Jewish press. Thus, *Unsere Stimme,* the organ of the Bund in Poland, said on June 4, 1946 in a typical article "We accuse the Zionists of spreading and sowing despair and weakness among the Jewish masses purposely; of causing panic and a psychosis of fear, and this at a time when Jewish culture is flourishing in Poland." The Communist Yiddish paper *Dos Naje Lebn* instituted a veritable campaign against the Zionists in February and March, but this, too, was of no avail. However, there was a third way of curbing the Zionist influence: by building a new life for the returning Jews in the Silesian district where they were sent. Now, it happened that this area included Walbrzych and Kladzko; in other words, the paradise for Polish Jews was being created exactly in those areas where the greatest possibilities existed for escaping from it. A very good example was the town of Walbrzych itself, where a man by the name of Cybulie, a very active and energetic chairman of the local Jewish committee nominated by the government, tried everything in his power to stop the border-crossings. First he tried propaganda; when this had no effect, he then said he would organize a soup kitchen for the transients (presumably with JDC funds) so as to control the movement and choke it from within. "Then they said that we [the Brichah] were in league with some soldiers

and were robbing the refugees."[32] There were scuffles, and sometimes arrests resulted from this enmity. In the end, however, these inter-Jewish squabbles had little effect on the exodus. The basic truth was that the Jews wanted to go, and no set of self-appointed officials could stop them. Thus, in late May and June, the Kladzko-Kudowa and the Walbrzych areas became the major transit points of Brichah crossings into Bohemia. It was at this point that, on July 4, 1946, the pogrom of Kielce burst upon Polish Jewry.

5. The Transit Countries

Except for the Stettin route, the road from Poland to Germany (or Italy) led through the so-called transit countries, Czechoslovakia and Austria. Not only Polish Jews but also Slovak, Hungarian and Rumanian Jews were leaving their country of origin. The country farthest from Germany in this respect was Rumania, and the Jews leaving that country for the West passed through Hungary and Yugoslavia. The story of the escape is both complicated and unique, and resplendent with exotic-sounding names.

Mass movements of Jews into Rumania were not limited to Abba Kovner's partisans—indeed, purely quantitatively the Polish Jews were a minority. In May 1945 the Soviets opened the Cernauti border to allow a repatriation of people from Bessarabia, now part of the Soviet Moldavian Republic, who opted for Rumanian citizenship. During the late spring and early summer, an estimated 17,000 Jews availed themselves of this opportunity and swelled the number of penniless refugees in Rumania. In the course of the year, 4,400 former residents of Subcarpathian Russia—the easternmost tip of the former Czechoslovakia which was now

also part of the Soviet Ukraine, fled to Rumania. They were joined by 2,400 people from Hungarian Transylvania and another 2,400 from Hungary proper, all of whom had moved without any kind of organization.[1]

The motives were various. Besides the economic problem, there was the fear of anti-Semitism (especially in the notoriously anti-Semitic sections of northern Transylvania), and there were factors reminiscent of Poland because the Nazis and their Hungarian allies had thoroughly exterminated Hungarian and Transylvanian Jewry, and the survivors—like their Polish brethren—could hardly be expected to return "home." The Hungarian pogroms came later and were much less publicized than those in Poland, but the atmosphere was tense. In Slovakia the situation was no better. On September 24, 1945, an anti-Jewish pogrom occurred at the town of Topolciany, and the local paper *Vestnik* ascribed the occurrence, during which forty-nine people were wounded and Jewish property (whatever there was of it) destroyed, to the "fact" that Jews had poisoned Christian children. This was, of course, a simple and straightforward revival of medieval superstitions, and it was directed especially against a Jewish physician, Dr. Karel Berger. Ultimately the government intervened, the individuals responsible were punished, and the people apologized to the doctor. But the damage was done; as a result of the incident, attacks on Jews spread to other places, such as Chinorany, Krasno-nad-Nitrou and Nedenovce. The Czech press tried to avoid mention of these incidents, and similar occurrences were treated in the same way in other East European countries. But the news spread among the Jews like wildfire; and while their living conditions even before the war had caused them to seek refuge in overseas countries whenever and wherever possible, the desire to leave now became even stronger. This desire did not affect all areas of a given country to the same degree. It would be generally true to say that older people and people who were living in the bigger cities were less likely to leave than others. But the Brichah estimated that between the summer of 1945 and July 1946 some 15,000 Jews left Rumania and the same number left Hungary. Another source puts the Hungarian exodus

through Vienna from July 1945 through May 1946 at about 6,500. There were other routes as well, and the total number fleeing Hungary up to July 1946 would then be about 10,000. The statistics are vague in the extreme, but it seems that from these two countries 20,000 to 30,000 people left illegally during the period mentioned.[2]

During the passage of Kovner's partisans, Brichah "points" were established both at Budapest and at Belgrade. The Yugoslav transit seems to have been dormant after the departure of Ben Haim (see Chapter 1) for Italy in the summer of 1945. In October and November the Yugoslav route was reopened. This was apparently done from both the Rumanian and Yugoslav sides. Agami, the *shaliah* in Bucharest, relates that his colleagues received the cooperation of some high security officials in this. Why this should have been so one can only guess: the Jews were trying to leave Rumania anyway, and perhaps the incipient Communist regime saw in them an element which would be difficult to absorb in the new society they were trying to build. Jews were middle-class people and small artisans; on top of that, their presence created tensions and enmities. There was absolutely no suggestion of any expulsion; the official attitude was that if they wanted to leave there was no point in preventing them from doing so. And incidentally, Jewish refugees from areas outside Rumania would presumably be the first to go, thereby solving a local refugee problem. Illegal emigration of Jews from Rumania with Palestine as a goal was nothing new to Rumanians; it had gone on throughout the war, and in a way this new phase was really a continuation of a certain tradition. There is, of course, no doubt that such decisions could not be taken by the Rumanian authorities without Soviet knowledge and consent. But more about that later.

Through the Rumanian Deputy Minister of the Interior an agreement was reached with the Yugoslavs to open their country to this kind of transit.[3] At the same time, a Palestinian *shaliah,* Leibl Abramovsky, arrived in Belgrade. Leibl was helped by the respected and popular head of the Belgrade Jewish community, Dr. Alkalay, who was a Zionist. Through him a local relationship was established

with the security organs, and again Red Cross documents (forged, of course) were used. Officially, this was a transit of Western Jewish repatriants to their homelands. Leibl established Brichah points at Jimbolia on the Rumanian side of the border and at Kikinda on the Yugoslav side. He also tried to reopen the Hungarian gate into Yugoslavia—a few transports had got through Szeged in Hungary to Subotica and Novi Sad in May—and he went to Budapest for the purpose. From there he returned to Belgrade with a transport of a hundred people and went on to Greece to try to open a new way to the Mediterranean. He succeeded, and the railway through Skoplje and Bitulj (Bitola) to Salonika was envisaged by the Brichah as a great opportunity for a direct way to Palestine. Three transports were sent on that route in November-December 1945. The details are obscure, but it appears that the British soon realized who these people were, and effectively sealed the rail entry. Greece had to be abandoned as a Brichah center, and Leibl returned to Belgrade.

In the meantime, in November, a central figure of Mossad, Ehud Avriel, had come to Yugoslavia. Avriel was an old hand at illegal immigration. From Vienna he had been instrumental in sending transports in 1938 and 1939 to Palestine, and he now acted as a roving ambassador to Shaul Avigur, commander of Mossad. In Yugoslavia the boundaries between Brichah and illegal immigration under Mossad were blurred, and Leibl Abramovsky was responsible for both phases of the program. Avriel's task was to try to ease the way through direct negotiations with central personalities on the Yugoslav scene. Talks were held by both Avriel and Abramovsky with Mose Pijade, the Jewish-born Communist theoretician and close friend of President Tito. Oddly enough, these talks were prompted by an untoward incident, which could have destroyed all the work that had been done in Yugoslavia till then: two Yugoslavs, non-Jews, who were opponents of the regime and who had been accused of collaboration with the Nazis, were inadvertently smuggled out into Italy because the Brichah people thought them to be Jews. The Yugoslav authorities were understandably upset about this and one of the chief purposes of

the talks with Pijade was to clear up the matter of this incident. Pijade was friendly but cautious. He understood that the Jews, an essentially middle-class people, could best become "productivized" in the communist sense if they went to a country of their own. By that time, too, the armed struggle between the Jews and the British in Palestine was filling the front pages of Europe's newspapers, and the Yugoslavs saw this in terms of a liberation struggle against British imperialism. Pijade paved the way for an understanding with other Yugoslav officials, and then the Croat Republican authorities (in the federal structure of the Yugoslav state) were informed of the sympathy with which the government regarded the unofficial moves of Jews. This was very important because the route of the Brichah went from Belgrade or Subotica to Zagreb, capital of Croatia, where a Brichah point was established. From there people were sent via Ljubljana to the Trieste area in Italy. Between November and February, small-scale moves took place regularly from Rumania and Hungary to Italy via Yugoslav territory.

In February 1946, another *shaliah* arrived from Palestine to take over the central direction of the Brichah and Mossad work in Belgrade, while Abramovsky remained responsible for Croatia. The new *shaliah* was Yakov Ben Yehuda. At first, things went on very much as before, but in April the British finally put an end to the Trieste transfers. The Italian route was now blocked, but the idea occurred to the Mossad that the friendly attitude of the Yugoslavs might be usefully exploited for illegal immigration.

New negotiations took place, and again Avriel was called in to conduct them. They did not take very long, and soon permission was granted to establish a closed transit camp near Zagreb for Jews who were being "repatriated" to Palestine. In May the Mossad ship *Haganah* took 2,600 illegal immigrants from the tiny fishing village of Baka on the Dalmatian coast and transported them to Palestine. Here again, the basis for Yugoslav sympathy was the intensifying struggle in Palestine against the British. However, another point should be mentioned which influenced the Yugoslavs at least marginally: during the war, Croatia had been the scene of slaughter of a majority of Yugoslav Jewry mainly by the

Croatian fascists, the Ustasha. Tito, himself a Croat, was the leader of the great partisan uprising in the country, and many Jews among the survivors fought in the ranks of the partisans. There seems to have been a certain feeling of compassion, combined with guilt feelings, which had some influence on the Yugoslav attitude. Serbia, on the other hand, had been well known during the war as a country where Jews could always count on the friendly help of the local population. There never was any question of anti-Semitism in Serbia, and the Yugoslav state after the war continued this tradition. While these may not have been decisive factors in the official attitude displayed toward Brichah, the climate of opinion undoubtedly helped.[4]

At the beginning, Hungary and Austria were one Brichah area. There were no clear-cut hierarchical structures of command during the first months of Brichah; the local Hungarian group, Mordechai Rosman of the Polish Brichah, and Levi Argov from Palestine all cooperated and divided the work among themselves. Soon, however, functions became slightly more clearly defined. Rosman moved on into Bohemia, the local people became absorbed in their youth movement work, and Argov was left to set up the Brichah apparatus in the transit countries. We have already seen how this operated in Czechoslovakia.

As far as Austria was concerned, the problem was rather more complicated because of the division of the country into four zones of occupation. Vienna, the capital—like Berlin—was also divided into zones. The British zone in southern Austria became independent of Argov under Eichenwald and the Italian group of Jewish soldiers. But there was a need for a "point" at Vienna, preferably in a western section of the city, whence transports could leave for the American sector at Salsburg or Linz and then go on to either Germany or Italy. The exact dates are not quite clear, but it seems that in early June Argov sent a young Polish partisan, Yitzhak Wenglishevsky, to establish a "point" in Vienna. There, in the meantime, the Jewish Community (*Israelitische Kultusgemeinde* or IKG) had fallen into the hands of a small group of Jewish Communists by

default. The community itself consisted of about 2,000 professed Jews, some 300 of whom had been allowed to remain in the city by the Nazis till its conquest by the Russians, and some 7,000 half-Jews, baptized Jews and non-Jewish widows of Jews killed by the Nazis.[5] This sorry remnant of a community of 175,000 in 1938 was utterly disorganized and could in no way help the thousands of Jewish transients who now began to pour into the city. At first these concentration camp victims, mainly Hungarian Jews, moved from west to east, back to their former homes. In these moves they were helped by a small committee of Hungarian Jews headed by a Viktor Schwartz. Another and less important beginning was made by a Rumanian group. Wenglishevsky does not seem to have adjusted himself to the big city with its many and complicated problems, and the job he was doing did not satisfy Argov. The Vienna "point" had to be strengthened, and there was a man in Budapest who was thought to be the right choice for such a job: Bronislaw Teichholz, a Polish Jewish refugee from Lwow (Lemberg). Teichholz's story up to that point was similar to the accounts of other refugees, though of course like all the personal stories of the holocaust it was extraordinary in itself. He had been a minor official of the Nazi-nominated Jewish Council at Lwow for a short time, but he left the city and joined a band of fugitives, Jews and non-Jews, near the Polish-Hungarian border who called themselves partisans but were apparently little more than an armed band roving the Carpathian forests. Early in 1943 some of them, including Teichholz, crossed the border into Hungary because the Germans were getting uncomfortably close. Teichholz was arrested and brutally interrogated at Munkacz (Mukacevo). However, he had the good fortune to be transported to Budapest, and there he managed to escape from a hospital. He got in touch with Polish Jewish refugees in the city who were being helped by the local Zionist Emergency Committee. Teichholz became the central figure in the Polish Jewish underground organization, whose main task was to provide food, clothing and documents to the illegal refugees. When the Germans came in 1944, Teichholz became part of the Zionist underground that tried to save as many Buda-

pest Jews as possible by forging documents. With the Russians shelling the city, he escaped to the Slovak border, armed with forged "Aryan" papers, and after serving the Russians as an interpreter he finally became a worker for the Hungarian Red Cross. As such he was sent to Rumania about May 1945 but returned from there when it became clear that the Rumanian Red Cross was already active in helping Jews. He was on the point of being sent to Vienna by the Red Cross when Argov approached him and told him to go to Vienna as a Brichah man.

Teichholz was different from the other Brichah people. First, he was older; he could not be regarded as a youth movement member. Nor did he rank as a partisan, despite his forest episode. It was hard to make him out, and some Brichah people regarded him with something less than confidence. In a way, he was like Jossel Rosensaft of Bergen-Belsen, even to the point of physical resemblance. Without asking many questions about finances or organization he went on to Vienna, where he found Schwartz and his committee and began to help them in taking care of transients now beginning to move from east to west. He set up a headquarters in the center of the city near the municipal buildings at the Frankgasse. It did not take him very long to become a kind of coordinator between Schwartz's committee and the others. Then one day a transport of people arrived who were too numerous to be accommodated in the same way as their predecessors had been. They were huddled in one of Vienna's railway stations, starving and with no shelter to go to. In desperation, Teichholz went to a very sympathetic young American officer, and after some wrangling he was shown the former Jewish hospital donated by the Rothschild family many years ago. In the half-destroyed building there were some German prisoners, but Teichholz moved in anyway and obtained some food from the Americans. He was in business.

An organization had to be set up to take care of the transients, but it was quite clear to Teichholz that without official help no organization could possibly be effective. On the other hand, to create just another one of the multifarious Jewish societies would not do, either. Teichholz had been a

Red Cross man of sorts. He now got together a group of representatives of existing societies: the Communists from the Jewish community organization (*Israelitische Kultusgemeinde*); Viktor Schwartz; representatives, either self-appointed or otherwise, of existing or nonexistent Rumanian and Polish groups. He then approached the Vienna municipality. Playing very shrewdly on the fact that these people were mostly deeply anti-Semitic and therefore obsessed with a guilt complex (altogether justified, one might add), he got Karl Steinhardt, deputy burgomaster, and another man to join his group. On August 21 he founded the International Committee for Transient Ex-Concentration Camp Inmates and Refugees. The officers elected were nonentities; Teichholz was secretary. On August 29, the committee, known by its German initials as IK, received official recognition by the Austrian government, after some negotiations with its reputedly anti-Semitic Minister of the Interior, the Socialist Helmer. During those first weeks the DP section of the American Army was still hesitant about Teichholz and his IK, and the Rothschild hospital had not yet been definitely handed over to them. But the Americans gave blankets and some food, and in the end they became convinced that the IK was doing a reasonably good job. Rather than being saddled with Jewish transients themselves they decided to hand the hospital over to the IK, on September 18, and promised to continue giving food (1,500 calories daily per person) and medicines and occasional other help. Teichholz had the hospital cleaned up, arranged for the housing of a maximum number of people, had the heating, pipes, cooking facilities, windows and other items seen to, and obtained the services of qualified medical personnel. A master of group politics and an excellent administrator, he had lists made of all the people who passed through the hospital. It seems that these lists are reliable, and according to them 573 people were accommodated in July, 1,551 in August and 2,120 in September. The advent of winter brought the slackening of the Brichah flow, and 1,293 came and left in October, 1,410 in November and 1,714 in December—a total of 8,661 since the beginning of Teichholz's activities.[6]

In the IK, Teichholz was the undisputed master. A headstrong man, he made enemies as well, but his efficient administration made it impossible for them to dislodge him. Like Rosensaft in Belsen, Teichholz was utterly devoted to his job and to the welfare of "his" refugees. He became quite a power in Vienna, and even the JDC failed to touch him. A JDC report of September referred to "the so-called International Committee" which two JDC people "believe is completely unreliable."[7] However, the JDC had no choice in the matter; Teichholz now had the advantage of having established a working relationship with the head (Captain Healey) of the Viennese DP section at U.S. Army headquarters, was enjoying the support of the Austrians, was de facto custodian of the transients, and last but not least had managed to obtain the collaboration of the Communist heads of the Jewish *Kultusgemeinde*. The leaders of the *Kultusgemeinde* had removed from his post the unofficial representative (Dr. Tuchmann) of the JDC by accusing him of collaboration with the Nazis, and they tried—unsuccessfully—to get hold of the JDC warehouses, where some of the 75 tons of supplies shipped by the JDC into Austria by the end of August had landed. When, in October, the JDC offices were opened in Vienna, Teichholz was the unchallenged ruler of the Rothschild hospital.[8]

Until the end of October, Teichholz was, so far as the Brichah organization was concerned, the deputy of the ineffectual commander Wenglishevsky in charge of transients' relief. The whole operation was run from Budapest and Bratislava by Argov, who realized that this was an untenable situation. Teichholz was, after all, not an ordinary Brichah worker; he was older, more experienced and, from the Brichah point of view, less reliable, despite the fact that in all situations he had always proved to be loyal. When, therefore, the Mossad sent more Palestinian *shlihim* to Central Europe, two of them, Ephraim Frank and Asher Ben Nathan ("Arthur"), were sent to Vienna. After a short while, Frank was sent to Germany, and Arthur remained the commander in Vienna. Arthur had great personal advantages. He had been born and bred in Vienna and even

had an Austrian passport. He was at the same time a Palestinian citizen and was in Vienna legally as representative of Hebrew daily papers. His English was excellent, and his personal appearance imposing—he looked considerably more like an Austrian nobleman than a Jewish underground operator. From the first moment of his arrival, on November 1, there was never the slightest doubt as to who was the commander of the Brichah, and Teichholz now became what he was intended to be: a deputy in charge of a special operation. As such he was now responsible for the personal safety of the Brichah workers, mostly Polish Jewish youngsters, working with Arthur from their headquarters at Fankgasse 2, camouflaged as a transients' center affiliated with the Rothschild hospital. Teichholz got the money, the clothes and the food, reported on movements and helped prepare plans for the move from Vienna into other parts of Austria, because it was quite clear from the start that the Brichah transports could not remain in the city and had to be moved either to the U.S. zones or Italy.

Wenglishevsky had been responsible for Vienna only, but Brichah "points" had been established outside of Vienna in other parts of Austria. While Graz under Eichenwald was connected both with Budapest and the Italian-based Jewish soldiers, no such clearly defined relationship existed with Salzburg (in the American zone) and Innsbruck (in the French zone). In late July 1945, the local Jewish committee of the American zone was aiding those people who were coming through in an unorganized fashion from Germany to Italy or, from late August on, from Vienna to either Italy or Germany. Polish ex-members of youth movements established a transit point at Salzburg, with the help of Chaplain Bohnen (who did not want to know anything about their illegal activities but helped out with lodgings and food). Soldiers were sent by Mordechai Surkiss from Italy and the British sector of Austria, where one of the transport units of Jewish soldiers was stationed. These "points" were not very well organized, however, and a certain proportion at least of the work was done by two young men who had no contact with the Brichah. Here, in fact, was one of those relatively infrequent cases where bitter inter-Zionist feuds affected

Brichah operations. The opposition movement of the Zionist Right, the Revisionists, and their youth organization (Betar) were part and parcel of the Polish and Lithuanian Brichah, and their comrades among the Jewish soldiers also operated within the framework of the Merkaz Lagolah; however, in Austria and Germany no unified Jewish underground had as yet been set up, and two Betar youngsters, operating from Salzburg and Innsbruck, were the de facto border smugglers of the Brichah on the route to Italy. There were complaints against them, both personal and "political" (that is, they were prone to concentrate, to the detriment of other groups, on getting their own Betar comrades across). Just at that time, in late October, a young Betar man, Abba Gefen (Weinstein), arrived from Lithuania; he had quite a record as a partisan and had come across from Vilna in the general Brichah movement. As he was considered reliable, he was offered the post of commander of the Salzburg area by the local people. Before accepting he made the trip to the Milan office of Arazi and saw Surkiss and other soldiers as well. Assured of the support of Surkiss, he then returned to Salzburg and started operations. At this point, the majority groups in the Zionist setup, as represented on the Merkaz Lagolah, wanted to make sure that the Betar would relinquish its controlling role on the crucial Austro-Italian border. In order to put a new arrangement into effect, Surkiss sent Muliah Ben Haim, the former Brichah commander from Yugoslavia, into Austria to come to a formal agreement with Gefen. Ben Haim arrived on November 9, and at the new Jewish camp of Bad Gastein an agreement was signed. This gave the Betar people a 50 percent control over border-crossings from Austria to Italy. Had this arrangement remained in force, the Austrian Brichah would have become a faction-ridden coalition, with Betar given a stranglehold over the most crucial transit points. This, however, was not to be.

Ben Haim reported to Arthur in Vienna, because Arthur claimed the right to have ultimate control over what was happening all over Austria. The very next day and the following day (November 10–11), all the principals—Gefen, Ben Haim, Arthur, and some of the soldiers—met again,

this time at Linz. After a long discussion, the Bad Gastein agreement was shelved, and a simple new agreement was signed which was to be important not only for Austria but for all other areas. It provided for a recognition of command exercised by Palestinian *shlihim* everywhere. On the borders and in the vital DP camps Palestinian *shlihim* consequently took over, except for Salzburg, where Gefen was to be left in charge until his resignation in November 1947—proof that he was *persona grata* with the *shlihim*. The local commanders were nominated by agreement between the Merkaz Lagolah and Arthur, who, moreover, introduced innovations in the system of control. Arthur was a scion of a new tradition in the Palestinian underground, and he declared that all the camp committees had to be subservient to commanders nominated by the Brichah. This was effected very quickly and very efficiently, and while there were to be occasional camp committee elections, these were to be always subject to Brichah control. Arthur, through his people in the Austrian camps, controlled the situation. It was this policy which enabled him to bring his struggle with the American military to a successful conclusion. It must be borne in mind that this was by no means accepted Brichah procedure: in Germany, Italy and Czechoslovakia, local communities or DP camps were self-governing, and Brichah never dreamed of turning them into instruments for its purposes. In Austria, Arthur argued, conditions were different. The camp population was in constant flux; this was the major transit stage in Europe; and Brichah had to exercise direct control. Moreover, Arthur told Surkiss and his men very bluntly that he was the commander of Austrian operations and would brook no interference from anyone. His immediate superior was Argov, who would head the unified command being evolved for the transit countries. Merkaz Lagolah was given the sole task of selecting its *shlihim* for Austria and effecting transports into Italy.[9]

As fall approached and passed, and winter came on, the situation crystallized in the American zone of Austria. Following the intervention of General Mark Clark, the camps in the American sector could be rated as fair to very good. In

the latter category were the two camps at Bad Gastein and the Bindermichl apartment houses at Linz; there were other camps too, but the general conditions in the U.S. zone of Austria were not bad at all, that is, by DP standards. The statistics varied; a report of Brichah in early 1946 spoke of less than 5,000 people in the U.S. zone, with some 2,000 in the British zone and a few hundred in the French zone. There also were some 7,000 native Jews or half-Jews, mainly in Vienna.[10] It is therefore clear that Austria was in every sense a transit country; people usually did not stay there any length of time, because they were moved on, either to Germany or to Italy.

During the latter half of 1945 Brichah movements into Vienna came from two directions: either via Bratislava and a wooden footbridge over the Danube between the villages of Devinska Nova Ves in Slovakia and Marchegg in Austria, or by road or rail from Budapest, usually via Sopron. The Bratislava route was the main road for Polish Jews, and a Brichah report put the number of those who passed through the city in 1945 at 13,043.[11] The bridge at Marchegg, originally opened under Argov in the early summer of 1945, was actually the major transit point of Brichah in all Europe, and the Brichah was vitally interested in keeping it open. Transport from the bridge to Vienna was no problem; it was only a half-hour's bus or tram ride to the city.

The transit from Hungary was more difficult. At first, trains from Budapest via Sopron to Wiener Neustadt were used, with Brichah people in Russian uniforms accompanying the refugees. It seems that some of the Hungarian authorities knew what was going on, but after all, Brichah was taking Jews *out* of Hungary, and there was little objection to that. However, Brichah people became careless and arrogant, and on one occasion they fired on some Hungarian soldiers who were trying to stop them; immediately following this, it was discovered that one of the Brichah workers had taken—probably for a consideration—two Hungarians over the border who had been Nazi collaborators. As in Yugoslavia and Poland, such incidents were serious and generally the Brichah did all it could to avoid them. The Brichah worker was fired, but that did not help: the rail

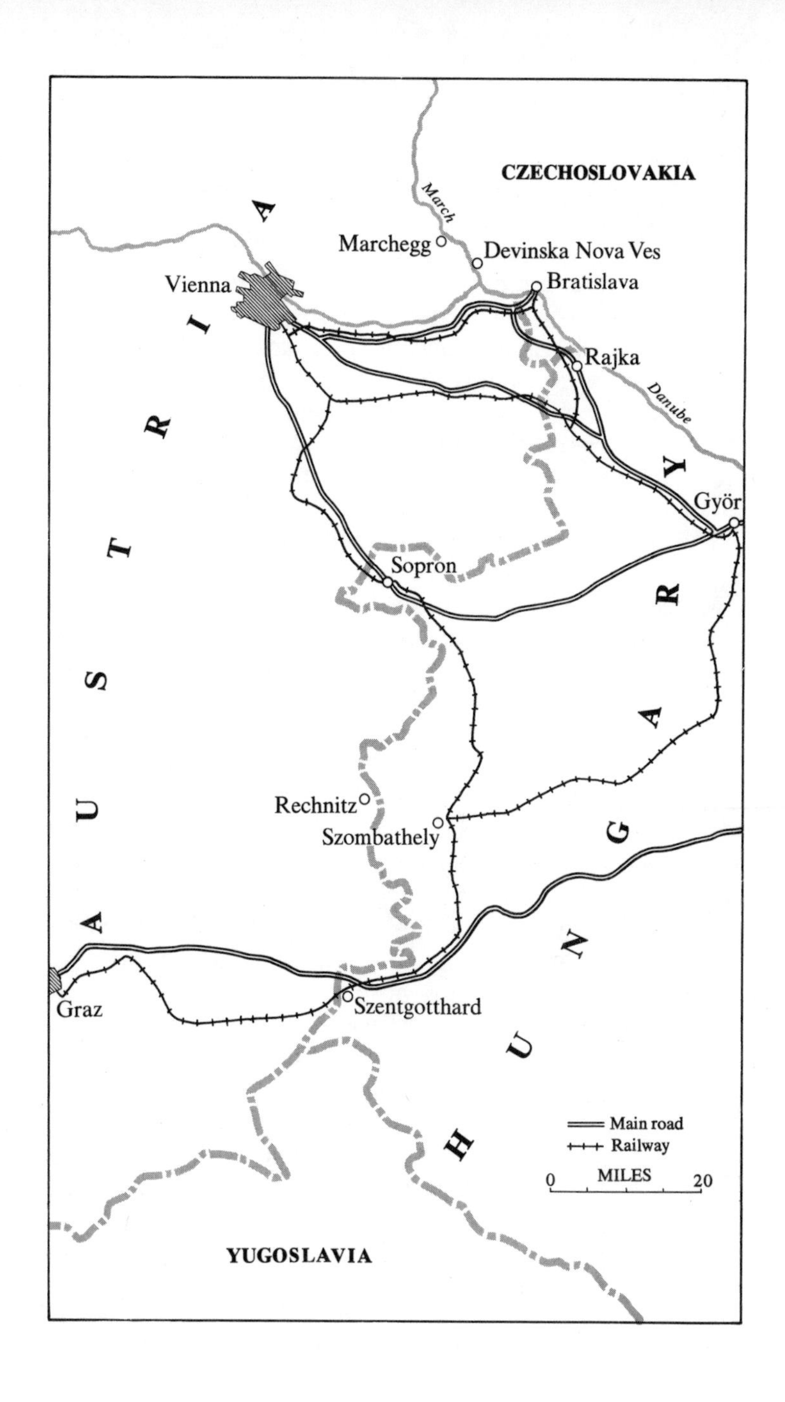

Bratislava–Vienna–Graz

route was closed. This happened in March 1946, and with the coming of spring Brichah had to find alternative routes. For about two months until the end of April, it used a small Austrian border station called Rechnitz, which was off the beaten track and to which people came by car or bus or even on foot from the rail junction of Szombathely. Hungarian and Rumanian Jews were brought there in groups of eighty and led across a little bridge on the border according to an arrangement with the local Russian soldiers. Ultimately, however, a Russian soldier was arrested, and with him some Brichah people. One of them, Kalman Weiss, was put into a forced labor battalion involved in road construction, and he faced the prospects of a very long journey eastward. Fortunately the prisoners were allowed to enter a small beer-house on the road where Weiss managed to get very friendly with a servant girl working at the bar; she helped him to get to a telephone, and he contacted Arthur, who had been trying to locate him. In Western spy-story fashion, two cars were brought to the place; one whisked Weiss off, and then he changed into the other. He was spirited away beyond the reach of the Russians. However, the Rechnitz point was "burnt." Subsequently a less romantic but more secure "point" was found at Rajka, on the Gyor-Bratislava-Vienna railroad, where a continuous flow of small groups, fifteen to twenty strong, could cross into Austria.[12]

The problem of the Russian zone did not end with the refugees' arrival in Vienna. It must be remembered that Vienna was an international island in the Russian zone, and in order to reach the American zone in the west one had to cross the Russian part of Austria which stretched to the Enns River. Once the refugees got into Vienna the problem was how to get them out of there to one of the western zones of occupation. To all of this the attitude of the Russians was crucial.

Early transports from Vienna went with the general stream of repatriation under one guise or another—as Italians, or Spaniards, or Germans. But soon this kind of unorganized flow could no longer continue. The first really large concentration of Brichah in Austria was, as we have seen, at Graz. The problem was how to get to that town. The

Russian-British zonal border was at Semmering, normally a resort for the wealthy on the border between two Austrian provinces. The railway from Vienna came down to the town of Semmering, and then there was a three-kilometer stretch of no man's land, after which rail service could be obtained down to Graz on the British side. The Soviet officer responsible for the border point was a Jew by the name of Moshkowitz, a convinced Communist and Russian patriot. However, Argov managed to talk to him, and it appeared that he was prepared to allow the crossing of Jews into the British zone for ideological reasons. He argued that if there were nationalistic Jews who were disillusioned with all that Europe had to offer them, then—considering the suffering they had been through—they had the right to do what they wanted, although he personally disagreed with their choice. On the other side of the border, Argov found a Palestinian interpreter for the British, a man called Kaplan, whose task it was to be in constant touch with the Russians. Having found two necessary aides, Moshkowitz and Kaplan, Argov started operations. The Jews would arrive at Semmering, walk the three kilometers to the British train and then arrive at Graz. This went on without serious interruptions till October, when Kaplan unwittingly exposed the system. He wanted to make his charges more comfortable—why should they walk the distance to the British train? So without authorization he told the Austrian train engineer to move the train right up to the border at Semmering. The interesting point is that as long as all these operations were done by underlings, nobody bothered very much about them. It was the British officer in charge who noticed that his trains were moving up to the border without his approval. He began investigating and found out what was going on. The result, of course, was the closing of the border.

Argov rushed in from Budapest to try to straighten out the mess, and met his Soviet friend Moshkowitz. According to Argov, this is what Moshkowitz told him: "The failure here represents exactly the difference between the Russian and the British armies. We knew we would win, so we found bread, shoes, boots, trains, but mainly what we did was walk over corpses and so we defeated Hitler. The British also

knew how to win, but they could not do it without a 'cup of tea' at four o'clock; they would lose the war if they did not have it. Here, Jews want to go to Palestine—let them make the effort, let them go another three kilometers! But no, they had to have their 'cup of tea,' they had to have a train call for them. The Russians," said Moshkowitz, "do not like 'cups of tea,' and they said: stop!" It seems that Argov took the lecture to heart—and indeed there was a lot of truth in it. Little conveniences had to be foregone if Jews were to be moved en masse. But the Semmering "point" remained closed from October 1945 on.[13]

In the meantime another border—on the Enns River—was opened. At first, Jews crossed the bridge between the Russian and American sectors there, but it was found to be safer to cross by boat. It was during that time, in November, that the Americans tried vainly to ban Brichah from their sector. We have seen how Colonel Stevens in Vienna had to yield and how the U.S. authorities allowed Jews in afterward. The route was nevertheless difficult, because while the Americans did not want to clash with the Jews they were not eager at all to let them in, either. The procedure was usually that the Jews would come by train to St. Valentin in the Russian sector, then they would either cross the Enns by boat or would walk a fairly long distance to the little town of Urfahr and then cross over to Linz. The Russian attitude, too, was quite unpredictable. Michael Yitzhaki, one of the local Brichah workers who had established a very good working relationship with Russian officers, was originally a Polish Jew from an area that had been annexed by the Soviet Union; the Russians were very strict about Soviet citizens not leaving their country and the young man escaped arrest by mere accident. This was at St. Valentin, probably in early 1946, and after Yitzhaki's escape the "point" had to be completely reorganized. Again, in March 1946, the Americans tried to stop the Brichah, but they had to reopen the route when a trainload of fifty refugees threatened to cause trouble.[14]

Once in the American sector the refugees entered transients' camps. These must be distinguished from the permanent camps for the "original" Jewish DPs set up after

the Linz incident in October 1945, because the Americans insisted that while they had an obligation to the ex-concentration camp inmates whom they had liberated, there was no such obligation to the persecutees fleeing from the East. In order to separate the groups, the Army had two sets of camps: the camps at Bad Gastein and Bindermichl and a large camp at Salzburg ("New Palestine"); and the transients' camps, mainly at Mulln near Salzburg, where accommodations and food were on a lower level than in the permanent camps. At the same time, while transients were "discouraged" from staying, the Americans had in fact no control over the population in the camps; it was the Brichah who decided when and how to take out "permanent" DPs and put "transients" in their stead. But the numbers remained more or less stable, as the Brichah had no desire to annoy the American authorities unnecessarily by breaking a gentleman's agreement whereby the Austrian camps would not be allowed to grow. This agreement meant that the Brichah had to get the people out of Austria into Germany or Italy, and it was more or less adhered to till the summer of 1946.

The movement from Austria was effected with the connivance of the American authorities in Austria and sometimes at least against the wishes of the American Third Army in Germany. This peculiar situation enabled the Brichah to play off the Americans in Austria against the Americans in Germany, and it had no scruples in doing so. The actual transfers were partly legal, and for quite some time buses or trains took groups of refugees openly over the border into Germany; however, this was supplemented by illegal border-crossing, which was simple enough on the winding mountainous border in the Salzburg area. There, right across on the German side, were two large transit camps, one at Saalfelden and the other at Ainring. In both, Palestinian soldiers were established by the Brichah and they received the groups sent from Salzburg by Gefen and his team. Even if a group was caught—which sometimes happened—no harm was done. They would return to Salzburg and cross the next night. According to Gefen, between November 1945 and May 1946, over 10,000 people passed his "point."

One thousand remained in the area (in contravention of the gentleman's agreement with the Army); about 7,000 left for Germany; and 2,332 crossed into Italy.[15]

The illegal crossings from Salzburg to Ainring were made with the guidance of four young Polish and Lithuanian Jewish refugees, who learned the topography of the area very thoroughly and who, like most of the border guides of the Brichah, had great reserves of courage and qualities of leadership. The name of at least one of them should be mentioned, that of Yonah (Yonah'le) Eisenberg, who became a legendary figure among the DPs. It seems that he became so well known that when the Americans caught him with a group, they would return him without investigation straight to Mulln, because they knew who he was. One night, apparently early in March 1946, he was caught with his group by an American sergeant and an Austrian policeman. The sergeant had to work hard to persuade the Brichah man in charge of the Mulln camp to take back the refugees, and it was apparent that he would be careful in the future not to get involved in preventing illegal crossings by Jews. But the Austrian was a problem: in 1946 the Austrian police were beginning to become more effective, and lack of cooperation on their part might have been unpleasant. Gefen therefore undertook to talk to the policeman; it turned out that he had been a soldier on the German side, and though—like many others—he did not admit to any hostility toward Jews during the war, he did not—unlike many others—deny that he had had knowledge of the mass murder. Playing on his guilt feelings, Gefen convinced the man that he should cooperate in helping his former enemies (as he had been taught to see them) by enabling them to reach the haven of the German camps. He was humorously christened "Moishele," and played an important part in keeping the illegal crossings into Germany going smoothly.[16]

There was coordination between the Salzburg Brichah and the command in Vienna. However, one of the interesting points in the history of this mass migration is the fact that in reality no one, not even Arthur in Vienna or Argov in Bratislava, had any real control over the flow of people. At one point, in January it appears, the Czech-Austrian

border was suddenly closed by the Russians—Argov believes this was in response to British pressure, but we have no documentary evidence of it—yet the flow into Austria did not therefore cease. When at any point Brichah appeared, even temporarily, helpless Jews arranged to cross on their own, in small groups and in various ways. The flow into Salzburg never stopped. When in March the Americans attempted to stop the influx by refusing to grant permits to enter their zone from Vienna, it was Gefen's office that forged American documents of transit, complete with the seal of the USFA (United States Forces Austria) HQ, so expertly that it took the Americans quite some time to realize what was happening. At the same time it must be strongly emphasized that were it not for the basic unwillingness of the U.S. Army to engage in any kind of serious quarrel with the Jews all these little subterfuges would hardly have worked. The Army was simply unwilling to take the political risk involved in difficulties with the Jews, and that was the decisive factor.[17]

The crossing into Italy was both more difficult and more important for the Brichah. Germany might be a temporary haven, but it was Italy that was the main assembly point for illegal transports to Palestine, and it was there that the Brichah wanted to transfer those who were considered capable of making the difficult sea trip on the rickety boats of the Mossad. When Gefen began operations in Salzburg in early November, the border was "controlled" by the two members of the Betar organization, which has been mentioned before. The official route via the Brenner Pass was, of course, closed to Jews, as it was controlled by the British. In the assignment of occupation zones to the Allied armies, the whole southern border of Austria had been divided between the British and the French, except for a small stretch of a few miles south of Krimml. This was due to the fact that the zones followed the demarcation lines between the Austrian provinces; Carinthia was British, Tyrol French, and Salzburg American. The Salzburg province included the thin wedge of territory near Krimml, but at first it looked as though this was impassable—there were no roads on the

Austrian side and hardly a road on the Italian side (in the Aurina valley). With the Brenner closed, at least officially, the only solution was to resort to various subterfuges. These consisted—after the departure of the Brigade and other Palestinian units—of attaching freight cars loaded with Jewish refugees to trains carrying Italians who were being repatriated to their country. These groups were given forged Italian documents by two young Betar men, and with the help of suitable bribes, people were smuggled across as Italians at the official border-crossing, the Brenner. In Italy they would go to Milan, and thence to the UNRRA camps for Jews, mostly in the south.

These two young men who provided the refugees with forged documents were rather unsavory characters. The "official" Brichah had not sent them there; they were self-appointed, and even the Betar had no control over them. They smuggled Brichah groups across without charge, but they accepted money from speculators and swindlers who used the easy way to Italy for their illicit trades. This was of course anathema to Brichah, and it had been precisely to avoid this that the accord at Linz with the Betar had been signed by Arthur, the Brigade people and Abba Gefen. For a short time, Gefen and one of the soldiers who worked with him tried to "reform" the two men at Innsbruck; from November 17 on, a few transports were smuggled across in the "usual" way. A small Jewish camp at Innsbruck was used as an assembly point, and when an overflow threatened people with starvation (the French gave very minimal rations for forty people only, and when there were more at the little house of Rennweg No. 40, Innsbruck, there was trouble), some of the refugees were moved to a farmhouse above Innsbruck in a little place called Gnadenwald, where close to a hundred Jewish youngsters were living in what was a mixture of a DP camp and an agricultural training point.

The arrangements with the two men at Innsbruck were not working out. Border guards at the Brenner were becoming suspicious of the Jewish transports because of the smugglers, some of whom were finally caught. When one day a man was caught with $30,000 on him, the French and the

Italians decided that this was too much and forbade transit for Jews. The presence of a few underworld characters reflected on the legitimacy of the passage of the genuine refugees and caused difficulties. All these people were Jews, and the border guards could not be expected to make the necessary distinction. It was only after transit into Italy was stopped that Gefen fired his erstwhile comrades. Unfortunately, they took with them the forged seals and the secrets of their contacts with guards and officers, and thus the Brenner was finally closed.

In the meantime, people continued to be sent to Innsbruck, and the outlook was not bright. In this situation the private action of an individual showed the way. One of the refugees organized a small group of young men and set out to cross the border at Nauders, on the Swiss-Italian-Austrian frontier. Gefen and his Brigade friends at Mulln and Innsbruck decided to explore this new possibility. With the help of some friendly Americans of the 42nd Division, permission was obtained for thirty-five people to go to a "TB sanitarium" at Merano. However, this was an American permission, and a French permit was needed too. Gefen rather naïvely tried to get such a permit through a local JDC representative. The French asked the British, and they of course refused. The process of attempting to get legal papers might have vitiated the whole idea, but luckily it seems that the Nauders French guard knew nothing of technicalities when Gefen approached him with the American paper only. Gefen explained to the Frenchman that he was an UNRRA worker bringing TB-infected Jewish ex-concentration camp inmates to Merano, and the French let the group pass. On the Italian side there were no difficulties because there was an American pass, and so the people got into Italy. On his way back, Gefen became rather friendly with the Frenchman on the border and made a point of telling him the truth about the transport. The French officer showed sympathy and understanding, and it seemed that a new major infiltration point had been opened. However, a second transport of forty-five people was stopped by the Italians, who now demanded an Italian seal on the document. With the help of the French officer they allowed just

that one group into Italy, but it was clear that another method would have to be found. This time everything was prepared thoroughly. The Salzburg Brichah boasted of two first-class specialists in document-forging, and a suitable paper was prepared, with American, French and even Italian seals.

The first Nauders group had passed on January 9, 1946. It was now the 30th of the month, and heavy snow almost put an end to all transportation on the border. Nevertheless, 105 refugees, including 40 children, were sent across. This time the journey almost ended in tragedy. During a short stop in the town of Landeck, some soldiers overheard the children chattering in Polish in the closed, tarpaulin-covered trucks. They were sure Polish infiltrators were heading for Italy and they were determined to stop them. They telephoned the frontier guards, and when the trucks appeared, shots were fired to stop them. The drivers, scared to death, accelerated instead of stopping, whereupon the soldiers fired in earnest. One of the adults was wounded, and it was a miracle that the children escaped unscathed. The French were angry, but they let the convoy pass. On the other side, however, the trucks could not continue and the refugees had to be brought in horse-drawn vehicles to the nearest railway station at Sluderno. From January 30 until March, no more attempts were made to cross into Italy.

When transports started rolling again toward Italy, the route taken was Nauders, and the necessary papers were "home-made" documents, purporting this time to originate with a British mission at Salzburg. The date was March 6, and a total of 221 people were brought across within a few days. Then a problem appeared. The German Brichah command, headed by Ephraim Frank, a Palestinian who had come to Europe together with Arthur Ben Nathan, wanted to have 1,000 *chalutzim* (young pioneers), members of Zionist youth movements, leave Germany and cross into Italy to join one of the illegal immigration ships. After some discussion, it was decided that these should come via Bregenz in the Vorarlberg district of Austria, where the French commander happened to be Jewish. At Innsbruck and Bregenz feverish negotiations started. We do not know why,

but on April 1 the French announced that they would let through as many Jews as would want to go over into Italy but that after three days they would close the border. Between the 2nd and the 5th, some 700 people were rushed through to Merano, and then Germany had to be advised to stop sending people, as the French had closed the border. Fortunately, however, Frank failed to get in touch with a group of some 400 who were already on the way, and these managed to cross into Italy despite the expired time limit. By the 6th, then, 1,100 refugees had arrived in Italy. The Brichah now became more audacious. On the 14th, two big convoys with a total of 590 refugees crossed the Nauders border with forged documents. This time they went on trucks that had been painted with British Army signs, and the Brichah people were all in British Army uniforms and had army documentation on them. The convoy had been organized mainly by the soldiers—Ben Haim, Zvi Pines and others—and Gefen was in charge of the actual crossing. Everything went off smoothly and only the Merano "hospital" point was terribly overcrowded. A further group of 360 crossed in the same way from the French zone in Germany via Bregenz to Landeck and Nauders; they, too, swelled the numbers at Merano, but that was a relatively simple matter involving only some inconvenience and temporary hardship. On April 14 another group was sent to Innsbruck, the idea being to utilize the Nauders arrangement and transfer them to Italy. But this time they were stopped by a British sergeant at Resia, on the Italian side, and returned to Austria. Ironically, Yonah'le Eisenberg, who had been sent there to save the situation, was caught by the Americans dressed in British Army uniform and with papers under four different names. This was too much even for the Americans, and Yonah'le was tried by a military court. Through the intervention of an American captain who was working with Gefen, the young daredevil was released, but not without some anxious moments for the Brichah point at Salzburg. This actually was the end of a phase, of the first attempts to cross into Italy. With the end of May, small-scale infiltration by Brichah came to an end.[18] According to Brichah figures, 1,500 people passed through Salz-

burg during the second half of May; in June, 5,000 did so, and in July 11,000. Obviously, the scale of operations was changing.[19] The first stage of Brichah operations in Austria had ended, and while the Brichah could be satisfied with the overall picture of the move of East European Jews into Austria and Germany, the relatively small number of those whom it managed to smuggle into Italy posed a problem which would have to be dealt with later.

Did these refugees really want to go to Palestine? Or was it rather merely a desire to leave their countries of origin? What was the role of Zionist propaganda in their attitude?

The question of the importance of Zionist ideology must be seen against the background of the Jewish refugee's mentality generally. In Austria there were, as we have seen, two kinds of Jews: the "settled" ones at Bad Gastein, Bindermichl and "New Palestine" (Salzburg); and the transients at Mulln and other places. In the course of time the "settled" Jews became involved in a process of demoralization caused by their aimless and senseless existence in DP camps, where their food and lodgings were good, and their occupation nil. They were not allowed to leave, to emigrate or become involved in any kind of productive life. Coming from concentration camps or hideouts, deprived of their families and backgrounds by the Nazi scourge, they became a quarrelsome, faction-ridden group with an acute sense of insecurity and uncontrolled aggressions. Quite a number of them began to engage in illicit trade and black marketeering, which were more or less the only remunerative pursuits open to them. The morally stronger and healthier types concentrated on the only alternative, which was Zionist ideology and education, as a means of preparation for a future meaningful existence. Small wonder, then, that the Zionist organizations and factions became the mainstays of a shaky communal discipline. The youth movements managed to concentrate among their membership the best elements in the camps, even though this was done with much petty politicking and backbiting. The movements promoted a national-spiritual ideal, inculcated a sense of moral rectitude and pride of achievement and, of course, provided most of those utterly selfless young men and women who actually

did the Brichah work, and did it with initiative and drive—it was they who were much more important for the Brichah work than the leaders and commanders. Consequently, it was they also and the Zionist-oriented groups generally that ran the camps, provided election platforms for camp committees and created a state of affairs where a non-Zionist or anti-Zionist Jewish group simply could not exist. Not that there was any hint of undemocratic procedure involved in preventing such groups to be set up—it was merely unthinkable, in the atmosphere of the camps, that a non-Zionist group could make any headway. There were, at the beginning, some small Bundist groups in a few places. But these people, insofar as their opinions were sincerely held, went back to Poland in the early stages, and many more simply reacted to the overwhelming evidence of the Polish pogroms and turned away from their erstwhile convictions.[20]

At first the idea of a unified Zionist group was generally accepted, as a parallel to the "Remnants" in Bucharest or the Zionists in Germany. But in practice the unity of such an overall organization was obstructed by the inevitable assertion of factional loyalties. True, there was in existence a Central Committee for Austria in Salzburg, but it was generally held to be inefficient and it never attained the prominence achieved by the Munich committee. In effect, the individual camps were held together only by the Brichah, and within the camps the different political groups vied with each other for supremacy. In a very real sense, this was all to the good, because the several groups aroused the most intense loyalty and sense of comradeship among the people, and thus served as a kind of substitute for family and town ties that had been destroyed. Each youth movement, especially, was a warm nest of friendship and purity in a hostile world, and the close relationships enabled these groups to radiate an influence which was on the whole of a very healthy nature.

All this did not mean that everybody really wanted to go to Palestine. An inquiry at Bindermichl, probably in late 1945, showed that of 1,375 who declared their intentions 1,291 wanted to go to Palestine as their first choice, and 65 wished to go to the United States, the rest preferring a num-

ber of other countries. Asked to identify a second choice, only 111 responded, of whom 65 indicated Palestine to be their second choice, and 32 opted for the United States. An Army investigation conducted early in 1946 showed similar results: of 5,057 DPs whose answers were obtained, 4,948 wished to go to Palestine, and 109 to other places.[21] It must, however, be stated that Army questionnaires were treated as political challenges, especially when they came prior to the appearance in Austria of the Anglo-American Commission; there is clear evidence that the Brichah, like all the other Zionist organizations, did everything to convince the Jews that they should opt for Palestine, if only for appearances' sake. Yet, whoever knows the complicated democratic structure of Jewish society will realize that it would have been next to impossible to make Jews act the way the Jewish Agency wanted them to if there had not been a very deep feeling among the vast majority that in fact their response to the questionnaire was genuinely their own. The argument therefore cuts both ways: there undoubtedly was pressure from Brichah and Zionist parties on the one hand, but this would merely have created a terrific opposition in the camps had the people generally not agreed with Zionist policies. At the same time, there was no 99 percent victory, and that itself seems to point to the relative reliability of the figures. On the whole it can be stated quite safely that while the pro-Palestine sentiment in those early days, before the opportunities of emigration to the United States appeared, was perhaps not as great as some of the figures would indicate, it was powerful enough to be representative of the large majority of the camp inmates.

The third of the transit countries, and in many ways the most important one from the Brichah point of view, was Czechoslovakia. The internal situation as seen generally and from a Jewish angle, was unique and advantageous for the kind of activity Brichah engaged in. The country was ruled by an uneasy coalition between Communists, Socialists and Liberals, but there were important differences of approach even within the political bodies. In Slovakia, the separatist movement dominated by the right was still fairly strong,

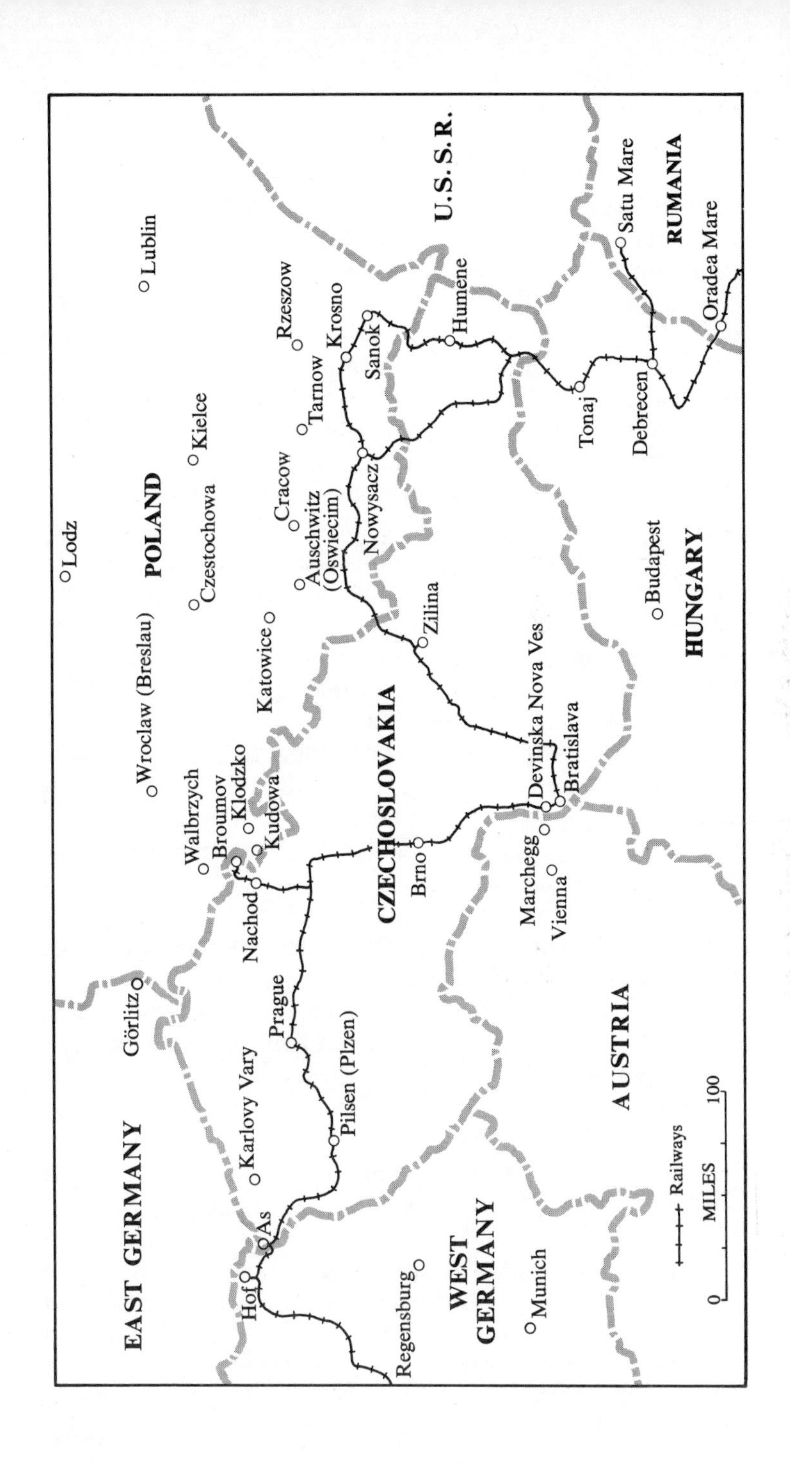

Czechoslovakia as a Transit Country

and tended to carry on the anti-Semitic tradition of the "independent" Slovak state that the Catholic priest Jozef Tiso had set up under a Nazi protectorate in 1939. The result, paradoxically, was that antifascism and progressive thinking generally came to be identified, among other things, with a pro-Jewish attitude. Also, the part played by Jewish partisans in the fighting in the Slovak mountains in 1944–45 was very considerable: it is reliably estimated that 2,000 out of 15,000 partisans were Jews—at a time when the total Jewish population in Slovakia was 20,000 and in the process of being further decimated by the Nazis.[22] Partisans were enjoying special rights in post-liberation Slovakia, and because many of the Jewish partisans were connected with Zionist movements their influence was quite considerable. In the "historic lands" of Bohemia and Moravia, with their higher standard of living and greater sophistication, a distinction was made between those Czechs who had been in the country during the war and those who had fled to the safety of London or Moscow. Our witnesses stressed the sympathy shown to Jews by those who had been to the camps, and attributed some of the support by the Czechs to this factor. A major supporter of the Brichah in Czechoslovakia was Jan Masaryk, Foreign Minister and main representative of the liberal wing. Masaryk had a long history of friendship, political and personal, with Zionism generally and with Dr. Weizmann in particular. He was not the kind of person to renege on his friends, especially as help to the Jews was part and parcel of his policy of reestablishing the image created by his father, Thomas G. Masaryk, of a humanistic, liberal Czech republic. Yet at the same time, Masaryk had no illusions about the limited extent of Jewish political influence in the West, a fact that serves to emphasize the element of humanitarianism in his Jewish policy.[23]

The Jewish situation in the country was chaotic. The easternmost, Carpathian section of the country had seceded and joined the Soviet Union; whereupon most of the surviving Jews, estimated at 13,000, fled the country into Hungary and Czechoslovakia. Some 6,000 were estimated to have moved to the "historic lands," and this was to create some problems later on when the Czech government declared

these people to be Soviet citizens and therefore liable to repatriation to Soviet Russia.[24] The Slovak communities, whatever was left of them, took some time to reorganize, and in Prague the remnants of the ancient Jewish community were trying to find their way in new and bewildering circumstances. The Prague Jewish Council set up by the Nazis had to be dissolved, its property had to be taken over; the government tended to see as Germans those Jews who had declared themselves to be of German nationality in 1930, before Hitler came to power, and therefore as people liable to expulsion. Efforts had to be made to protect those Jews who had opted for Jewish nationality because the new government declared that it did not want national minorities —the new state was to be a country of Czechs and Slovaks only. This situation, and the pogroms in Slovakia already referred to, caused a slow exodus: some people left for the West, some went with the Brichah, and some stayed till the establishment of Israel and left only after that event. There was no anti-Semitism in Bohemia, and certainly none in government circles. Quite naturally, therefore, Prague became the center of Brichah activities.

We have had occasion to see that the Greek camouflage was wearing rather thin in the fall of 1945, and quite simply no Jews could have passed to Bratislava or Prague had it not been for the aid and sympathy extended by the Czechs. At first, this was a matter for some highly placed Zionist officials employed in the Ministry for Social Welfare, headed by Jan Soltez, a friendly and helpful Communist. His successor, Zdenek Nejedly, also a Communist, was to maintain the same attitude. One of our witnesses claims that the government sent an official to the border at Nachod apparently sometime in November 1945 to investigate the Greeks that were coming over from Poland with their Red Cross documents. It is said that this official reported that it could not be proved definitely that these people were not Greeks.[25] Whether this Schweikish interlude actually occurred may be in doubt, but the spirit was certainly there. Toward the end of November, it appears, the government had to have some assurance that the mass move of Jews would ultimately be paid for by someone. (On the move itself, there

was never any question but that it would not be stopped.) However, for important discussions with top officials of the government local Brichah commanders could hardly be used. Luckily, there was at that time in Prague a JDC representative named Harry Viteles, who had had many years' experience as bank manager in Palestine and was an expert on cooperative institutions; he knew the kibbutz people representing the Brichah better perhaps than any other American representative. The Brichah brought the problems involved to his attention just at the point when Masaryk was in London. The Czechs, reported Viteles, were prepared to let the Jews in, provided they were sure no refugees would stay in their territory; they were supplying the transients with food and were providing transportation through their country to points of exit, but they wanted assurance that they would be reimbursed for these expenses. The Czech UNRRA was asking London UNRRA headquarters whether UNRRA should lay out the money, and Viteles suggested that Masaryk should clarify the situation while he was in London. This, however, does not seem to have been done, for we find Viteles reporting on December 14 that in a talk with him Masaryk was in effect repeating his demand for "unlimited maintenance guarantee and guarantee of departure."[26] Negotiations proceeded throughout December not only with the Czech UNRRA but also with the Intergovernmental Committee for Refugees, which was prepared to consider the Jewish persecutees entering Czechoslovakia as refugees from persecution within the committee's mandate and to care for them accordingly. Finally the Prague UNRRA people, with Dr. Elfan Rees as the moving spirit, decided to accept responsibility. On January 17, Viteles cabled: "UNRRA Prague informed Czech authorities UNRRA now required [to] care for persons unsuccessfully repatriated." UNRRA asked the government to establish two assembly centers for 2,000 transients: one (Nachod) on the northeastern border, another (As) on the Bavarian border. This was apparently made dependent on the agreement of the American Army to permit the entry of the Jewish refugees into the U.S. zone. Our sources do not tell us whether official American agreement was received

or whether Czech UNRRA acted with the express agreement of UNRRA headquarters; the likelihood is that they did not. Argov relates the story of an interview with Masaryk in which the Foreign Minister agreed to a procedure whereby UNRRA would somehow, sometime, repay the costs incurred in feeding and transporting the refugees. During all of that time Nachod remained open, and so did other transit points near Moravska Ostrava. At Prague a transit camp was established at Hloubetin, at the expense of the government, which served mainly as a temporary station for those destined for As and the Bavarian border. This rather vague and indeterminate arrangement prevailed from January to July 1946. It must have cost the Czechs a very considerable sum of money for trains and food, and they earned the sympathy and gratitude of the Jews.[27]

The internal organization of the Brichah in Czechoslovakia was also affected by the presence of the JDC. Landau and Yitzhak Sela (a Palestinian) were joined in October by two Palestinians, Elhanan Gafni and Aharon Ofri, and these, together with a Polish boy by the name of Nat Friedman, who was in charge of relations with the Czechs, constituted the Brichah office. Officially most of them were JDC employees. The JDC office was run by a number of sympathetic and understanding Americans, the most important of whom was Israel G. Jacobson, who arrived in the spring of 1946. Bratislava was run by a few Poles (Yosef Marcus, Menachem Shmulewitz), and the whole area was under the general aegis of Argov.

The Brichah had started as an organization set up by East European survivors of the holocaust with a minimum of machinery. Slowly, as 1945 passed, the soldiers and the Palestinian *shlihim* of Mossad made their influence felt, and toward the end of the year all the countries of Central and Eastern Europe had their Palestinian Brichah commanders. The time had clearly come to set up a much more efficient centralized organization. However, efforts to do so ran into snags that can only be explained by the complications of the Zionist political structure.

The Jewish Agency in 1945 was a coalition of four main political forces. Mapai, the moderate Labor Party, predom-

inated, and its leader, Ben-Gurion, was the chairman of the Agency's Executive; the major posts in the Agency were held by other Mapai members: Moshe Sharett was head of the Political Department, Eliezer Kaplan head of the Economic Department, and Eliahu Dobkin head of the Immigration Department. The Progressive wing of the General Zionist Party was the second major force; Weizmann, its head, was the president of the Zionist World Organization and of the Jewish Agency (the two were identical by that time). Yitzhak Gruenbaum, veteran leader of Polish Jewry, stood at the head of the Polish Department, which had merged with the Jewish Agency Rescue Committee. He was supposed to be in charge of rescue activities both during and immediately following the war, and one of his lieutenants, Haim Barlas, was the official head of the Jewish Agency mission at Istanbul, which during the war had been the main point of contact between Palestine Jewry and the European Jews. Dr. Moshe Sneh, at that time still considered to be a General Zionist,[28] was head of the Security Department and the head of the Haganah National Command. The center or right of center of General Zionism was very strong in America, where Rabbi Abba Hillel Silver was the predominant figure. The Mizrahi Religious Party was represented by the forceful personality of Rabbi Maimon, and usually found itself in full support of Mapai's political line (though there were disagreements on religious issues). The Mossad was under Shaul Avigur, a Mapai stalwart, and Avigur was quite determined that Mossad should be responsible for all underground activities in Europe. Gruenbaum, as head of the Rescue Committee dominated by the General Zionists, was supplying most of the money to Brichah until late in 1945. These funds had been collected mainly in Palestine, though one third came from the United States, and a certain amount came from South Africa as well. They were intended for rescue work during the war, but a considerable amount was left over and further collections were made after the end of the fighting. Gruenbaum's conception was that the JDC was a non-Zionist organization, and that the way it administered relief might have a vital influence on the future political orientation of the

European survivors. He thought therefore that the Rescue Committee should enter the relief field and not let the JDC monopolize it. Brichah was now seen as the major avenue of rescue, because the situation in Eastern Europe was regarded as a continuation of the holocaust under postwar conditions. The Committee had paid for the *shlihim,* it was supplying the funds, and it had a long-term policy; all of which made Gruenbaum determined not to let Mapai conduct the Brichah through the Mossad to its own future credit.[29]

The situation was further complicated by several minor issues and one major one. The chief problem was that the Polish situation simply did not admit of a hierarchical arrangement whereby final decisions on Poland would be made hundreds of miles away. The Polish situation was *sui generis,* and neither Ben Zvi nor Alexander, not to mention the "Asiatics" and Partisans, would hear of a centralized command. The transit countries, on the other hand, demanded such centralization. Here the minor issues appeared. Together with quite a number of the founding fathers of Brichah, such as Kovner, the "Asiatics," Eichenwald, Rosman, "Ben," and Ben Haim, Argov was a member of the left-wing opposition party of Hashomer Hatzair, and, moreover, had reached Europe against the express wish of the Haganah Command. The other issue was that the Palestinian soldiers also wanted to have a say and claimed some authority by virtue of their excellent organization and discipline, and the strength of their own Merkaz Lagolah committee, which had designated Surkiss as head of the Brichah. Rescue Committee funds had in fact been disbursed first by Agami in Bucharest and then by Surkiss. But Surkiss was Mapai and therefore not acceptable to Gruenbaum.

In the summer of 1945 Gruenbaum came to Paris, where he found a Mossad office run by Ruth Kluger. After Ben Gurion's visit to Germany, Gruenbaum decided to act, and called a European meeting of Brichah commanders. This took place between the 21st and the 25th of December 1945 in Paris, with about forty participants. Most of the more important area commanders were there, and Haim Barlas. Gruenbaum accused the East European command-

ers of discrimination against some of the right-wing and orthodox groups, but it seems that the very energetic answers and some proofs convinced him that there was little foundation for these accusations. There was general agreement that there should be a central committee of the Brichah in Europe, especially for the transit countries, and Argov was indicated as the obvious choice. But it appeared that Gruenbaum wanted to run the Brichah more or less by himself, and he suggested a committee consisting of himself, Barlas and Ruth Kluger (as Mossad representative), with its seat in Paris. Pino Ginzburg and others objected. The *shlihim* had been sent by the Mossad—the Rescue Committee had merely financed the operation—and they were going to obey only those who had sent them. The East Europeans were bewildered and did not really understand the politics involved. Ben Gurion intervened and as Chairman of the Executive vetoed the arrangement.[30]

What happened after the abortive effort in Paris is not quite clear, but it seems that the attempts made even before Paris, in November, to establish a Brichah secretariat in Central Europe continued. In January, Avriel, Avigur's deputy, arrived in Prague with Ben Zvi from Poland, and it was decided to proceed immediately with the setting up of a secretariat that would be responsible in the main for the transit countries. Argov, being a member of a minority group in Palestine, was not to have sole responsibility, and Sela, and later Ofri and Gafni, also were made members of the secretariat that was established at Bratislava. But they in turn elected Argov to be their secretary, and so Argov at last became formally what he had long been in fact: the central figure in the European Brichah. A stocky, powerful man with broad shoulders, slow and deliberate in manner and speech, a good judge of people and a man of considerable administrative capabilities, Argov was certainly a good choice for the difficult post. In Europe, far from the central bodies of the Zionist parties in Palestine, the party coloring mattered very little. These men and women had by now become a group with an esprit de corps of its own, and the task they saw before them was to change the essence of Brichah in the future. In their estimation

they had helped thousands to move "without any direction having been given by [them]." They said, "We organized the moves to go with the stream. . . . From now on we should direct it towards places whence immigration [to Palestine] should be possible. This means to direct and select that human material that should go to the shores from which immigration takes place."[31] This meant in fact, of course, that while the select few would go to Italy, Yugoslavia or Greece, the rest would continue to go to Germany. But from now on Brichah would carefully choose those who were to board illegal immigration ships. At the same time, stringent economy and accurate bookkeeping were to be introduced.

In late December, Dr. Joseph J. Schwartz of the JDC agreed to supply the local Jewish bodies dealing with refugees with some funds. The JDC, as such, did not wish to deal with the problem of helping the refugees reach camps or the borders. As a humanitarian organization, it held to its purpose of providing funds for the feeding and clothing of the refugees. The sums were very small, compared with the total expenditure of the JDC. In December, Schwartz promised the Brichah $75,000 for the three months of January–March 1946 to cover expenses for transients in Central Europe (exclusive of Poland). The money was paid to the Jewish Agency in Geneva, and from there it found its way to Bratislava or Prague, and finally to refugee camps. The administration of Brichah was paid for by funds supplied by the Agency itself. A strict accounting procedure was instituted; it reflected, among other things, the way in which the dollars obtained in Switzerland were converted into local currency to make them last as long as possible.[32] The same financial principles as those followed in Poland were observed. No Jew was required to pay for Brichah transportation, and the Brichah workers themselves received no wages at all beyond the cost of their food and clothing and some pocket money. The number of workers grew, but the cases of what the strict Brichah rules considered to be personal corruption were very, very few—and these were efficiently dealt with.

The JDC did more than pay directly for an increasing

part of the refugees' needs. It subsidized the work of the Teichholz group in the Rothschild hospital in Vienna, by supplying food in Bratislava and at the bridge at Marchegg on the way to Austria, and supplemented Czech rations at Nachod, Broumov and Hloubetin, thus helping to finance refugee transports. Other aid was supplied by the Czechs, by the American Army who gave the major part of the food to Teichholz and his camp and to the transit camps in their zones, and by the UNRRA in Italy and in other places where it had some contact with "transients."

6. *Politics and the Displaced Persons*

In late autumn of 1945 some important changes occurred in the administration of the DP camps in Germany. UNRRA (the United Nations Relief and Rehabilitation Agency) had signed an agreement with the Army on November 11, 1944, in which it undertook to administer those camps handed over to it and look after the problems of health, welfare, registration and repatriation. This agreement was gradually being put into practice in the fall of 1945, but of course the Army still retained general supervision and responsibility for food and housing. The Army's administration was also changing. From October 1, 1945, the Interallied Combined Displaced Persons Executive ceased to exist, and control over DP affairs in Germany was no longer unified. In the American zones the DP branch of G-5 (Military Government) took over.

It was in October that Brichah into Germany began to be really effective; by coincidence it seems also to have been in October that the Army began to consider what should happen to the hard core of the so-called non-repatriables, who could not or would not return to their original domi-

ciles. These were estimated at 224,000 out of the 474,000 still in Germany.[1] The two concepts clashed: one could not accept the increasing flow of refugees (up to 400 daily in December) into the zone and at the same time embark on a program of rehabilitation and vocational training for the non-repatriables predicated on the assumption that the DP population was now permanent and had to be treated as such. As we have seen, the Army was waiting for some kind of directive, and this seems to have come in December[2]—the Jews were to be admitted. But this did not necessarily mean that the newcomers would get the same treatment as the "old" DPs. For one thing, DPs were considered to be people who had been displaced by reason of war, whereas the newcomers had come from liberated postwar Poland or Hungary and therefore were obviously not entitled to DP treatment. Military handbooks used the term "persecutees," too, but these were defined as people "who had been subject to discrimination and ill-treatment because of race, religion, political beliefs or activities in favor of the United Nations."[3] This implied that only people persecuted at Nazi hands were to be covered by the definition, whereas Jews fleeing from Eastern Europe, though they may have been victims of Nazism, were fleeing not because of the Nazis but because of conditions they found upon liberation. There therefore seems to have been a tendency at first to create such conditions as would make prospective migrants think twice before undertaking the journey to Germany. Military Government Law 161, published in December, decreed that special centers be created for the persecutees fleeing from the East with somewhat lower daily rations and where the new arrivals would await whatever was in store for them. Yet in February 1946 "new instructions directed that all Jews who had infiltrated into the US zone were to be provided for in Jewish centers with the same standards of food, shelter and care" as were provided for the DPs. In other words, there was to be no difference between the groups, who were now considered as one.[4]

Behind this seemingly dry administrative problem there lay a human drama that vitally influenced the Brichah's history. During October and November new arrivals simply

infiltrated into the existing camps and created grave problems of overcrowding. The commander of Landsberg, Major Heymont, wrote in his diary that he would contact his commanding officer "and cry on his shoulder for the umpteenth time. Again he will undoubtedly call corps headquarters. They, in turn, will probably again call UNRRA who now has the responsibility. In the meantime the camp has the problem of caring for the newcomers and bulges some more at the seams."[5] The Army was reluctant at first to establish the centers for new infiltrees, and the instructions of February 1945 mentioned above were the result of a crisis that came to a head at Landsberg in early December.

One of the most respected members of the UNRRA team at Landsberg was a New York psychiatrist named Dr. Leo Srole. Appalled by what he saw of the conditions at Landsberg, Dr. Srole tendered his resignation to UNRRA and the Army in early December. This aroused a wave of protest in the camp, whose occupants had admiration and affection for the doctor. They declared they felt "that at long last they had with them an American who understood their problems,"[6] and the Central Committee at Munich demanded an investigation into Srole's charges.

Srole made a number of points in his letter of resignation regarding the Landsberg conditions. He declared that there was danger of epidemics because of the unsanitary conditions prevailing at the camp; he protested the overcrowding and the custom of two or more people sleeping in one bed; he protested the use of "dark cellars, cold corridors and wooden shacks condemned as unfit for the use of German POWs [for the housing of refugees]"; and he objected to the unbalanced diet and inadequate clothing.[7] The charge was serious, and it threatened the Army in the zone with another version of the Harrison report. The Army therefore reacted vigorously.

On December 6 Lieutenant General Walter Bedell Smith, Eisenhower's chief of staff in Germany, arrived for a surprise inspection tour of Landsberg. Mindful of the political purpose of his visit, which was to prevent another scandal, he brought with him not only high Army officers (including the Surgeon General, General Albert Kenner, and General Lucian Truscott, commanding officer of the Third Army)

but also Judge Rifkind, his Jewish adviser, and an army of reporters and photographers. In a visit lasting several hours he discovered that there was no more danger of an epidemic at Landsberg than anywhere else in Europe, that unsanitary conditions were the fault of the demoralized inmates, chiefly of the new arrivals, that the food was palatable, though not sufficiently varied, and that the UNRRA staff was a group of people with considerable good will but with utter lack of experience and efficiency in handling large numbers of people and their problems.[8] Smith and the other visitors were appalled at the unwillingness of the refugees to help themselves and organize their lives in a reasonably decent manner; they obviously could not grasp the significance of the problems and attitudes of these individuals resulting from their experiences in Poland, Russia or Germany. Major Irving Heymont, by that time ex-commander of Landsberg, who was also present, says that Srole could have made much more carefully investigated charges which would have been entirely truthful and that it was unfortunate that he had chosen to exaggerate, thus leaving himself open to exposure by the military. However, Heymont added, "perhaps Dr. Srole is much smarter than we appreciate. He has not caused any real harm—in fact he may be responsible for accelerating the establishment of additional camps to care for the newcomers."[9]

The main point of the Smith visit to Landsberg was the policy he stated to reporters at the end of his tour of the camp. In handling the Jewish DPs, he said, the Army had been moving from the rescue phase (feeding, housing, clothing, nursing back to health) to the rehabilitation phase (schooling, vocational training, recreation) when the new influx came. "The Army felt that the rehabilitation program could only be continued if the newcomers were denied admittance to the camps." If they were permitted to come, the resources were only sufficient for another rescue phase. Did anyone suggest, he added, that the newcomers be kept out of the zone by force?[10] Truscott declared during the Landsberg visit that he was surprised his men had not yet set up new camps for the newcomers, and after the visit the Third Army moved swiftly to correct the situation.

The situation was complicated by Judge Rifkind's inter-

vention. Asked by the Army as to the number of Jewish refugees that might be expected to arrive in the American zone, he made an unofficial survey among the various agencies and personalities and came up with a figure of 250,000 to 300,000.[11] This was taken very seriously by the Army, and the Army newspaper *Stars and Stripes* even carried a story in its issue of December 8 that 100,000 Jews might be expected to come during the winter and that the ultimate figure might be as high as 350,000. The figure of 250,000 was also mentioned by Hilldring of the State Department, who was obviously repeating the figures received from Rifkind.[12] However, the attitude of the Army was clear by that time—there were, said the *Stars and Stripes,* three possibilities: to close the border, to leave it only "relatively" open, or to offer "the US zone as a haven and staging area where Jews could prepare for settlement by a thorough rehabilitation program. Of these three courses, the last is regarded as most compatible with American official aims."[13]

At the same time that these developments took place there was a shift in the sympathy that the higher officers had had for the Jews. Army sources made it increasingly clear that the Jewish exodus was somehow organized. The Berlin crisis described above occurred in December. And the UNRRA leadership was by no means very friendly toward the Jews. This did not apply to the head of UNRRA, Lieutenant General Sir Frederick E. Morgan, who had been Eisenhower's chief of logistics during the invasion preparations. He did, of course, share the attitude of the British Army toward Jews and seems to have been an ardent supporter of the hard line of the British government in Palestine, but people who worked with him testified that he was a warm human being, eager to help those whom fate had turned into displaced persons.

On January 2, 1946, Morgan called a press conference in Frankfurt. The aim of the conference was to appeal to world public opinion to urge governments to somehow solve the problem of homelessness of the estimated 400,000 remaining DPs in Germany. Morgan dealt with the human aspects of the situation and stated that if the DPs stayed in Germany for a long time they would become a tremendous

problem; he strained his point somewhat in arguing that this might well be the seed of a third world war. He then proposed that some international organization be given the job of settling the question. This was the formal part of Morgan's interview.

After reading his statement and responding to some needling by the reporters, the general, an apparently inexperienced politician, aired his views on the problem of the Jewish refugees. Exactly what he said or how he qualified what he did say will probably never be known, because the reporters picked out only the more sensational bits. It is clear, however, that he did insist that his personal impression of the Berlin situation was that these Jews were well dressed, well fed and had "pockets bulging with money."[14] UNRRA representatives had been unable, he said, to find a single concrete example of a pogrom inside Poland. According to one of the reporters, he added that "the Jews seem to have organized a plan enabling them to become a world force—a weak force numerically, but one which will have a generating power for getting what they want."[15] There was evidence of an organization behind Jewish migration, and the idea was to have a Jewish exodus out of Europe. He added that the governments in Britain, the United States, Australia and other places should try to absorb these people.

These statements created a tremendous storm on both sides of the Atlantic. The London *Star* headed its leader with the word STUPID.[16] The *News Chronicle,* one of England's most liberal papers, said on January 3 that the general had either said too little or too much. The Manchester *Guardian* (January 4) termed Morgan's remarks "childish nonsense" at best, "and at worst too close an echo of Hitler's ravings." American reactions generally were very bitter. Eddie Cantor, the performer, said in a paid advertisement in the *New York Times* of January 4, "I thought that Hitler was dead." Max Lerner in *PM* of January 3 demanded that the Labour government in Britain make it clear that they do not "share the views of Hitler and General Morgan on how to 'solve' the problem" of Europe's Jews.

It was therefore hardly surprising that the regional European office of UNRRA in London "felt obliged to call for

his [Morgan's] resignation."[17] The Zionist leadership, the offices of the World Jewish Congress and representatives of other Jewish organizations were also obviously after General Morgan's head.

Morgan fought back. He denied that he was anti-Semitic, he charged that he had been misquoted (though he never restated what he had actually said), and he refused to resign.[18] Appealing over the head of the London office of UNRRA to Governor Herbert H. Lehman, head of the UNRRA organization, he demanded a hearing of his side of the case.

Behind the scenes a struggle began, of which we have but the barest outline. In order to understand it and its implications for the Brichah, we must see first of all what was actually behind Morgan's statement. There is no doubt that Morgan was a very conscientious and sympathetic man who was trying to do his best for the various groups of DPs. L. S. B. Shapiro of the *New York Times* summed up the affair in his very carefully phrased article of January 7. He made it clear that Morgan's remarks had been made in a question-and-answer period after the actual news conference, that they had been made casually and had been accompanied by qualifications which had been omitted in the reports, and that therefore all the quotes and misquotes had been presented entirely out of context. Shapiro accused Morgan merely of failing "to appreciate the repercussions that have developed by his unguarded remarks made before a gathering of correspondents."[19] Here Morgan was depicted as a kind of innocent in Newspaperland. Shapiro was not the only one to come to his defense; the head of the JDC operations in Germany. Jacob L. Trobe, also intervened. On January 4 he met with Morgan, apparently at the latter's invitation.[20] In his report to the JDC, Trobe said that he had told Morgan some harsh things about the unfortunate interview, but he added that the general's resignation "will have an unhealthy byproduct as it may be [wrongly] interpreted [that] certain groups [are] out to get him." He also said that Morgan was "honest, nonmalicious [and] nonantisemitic."[21] The report was sent not only to the JDC but also directly to the American head office of UNRRA and

was divulged to the press.[22] Trobe's position was interpreted as being a defense of Morgan, despite his condemnation of the actual remarks made at the disastrous interview. The JDC office, following the old JDC line of keeping out of politics, disavowed Trobe but did nothing to discipline him. In fact, Trobe's intervention was welcomed by Lehman, UNRRA's head, who had been a co-founder and a central figure in JDC councils for three decades.

Moreover, it appears that unofficially hints were dropped by American military people to Rifkind and others that the Army would take a very dim view of a successful Jewish campaign to dislodge Morgan. It is not unlikely that the desire to maintain good relations with the Army moved both Rifkind and Trobe to intervene with Lehman and provide a Jewish counter to the attacks on the hapless general.[23] In the end, Morgan refused to resign and went to America, where he conducted negotiations with Lehman on January 26 and 27. On the 28th a letter appeared in the *New York Times* over Morgan's signature which said that the general had only the best of intentions and would fulfill his duties impartially. There was no retraction of what he had said nor even an explanation of what he actually did say, and the matter was officially closed.

It seems clear that Morgan's statement was influenced by the opinions held by his staff and by American officers with whom he worked. At least one of our sources[24] indicates that a number of anti-Communist Poles supporting the exiled London government and who were no great friends of Jews were working at UNRRA, and moreover General Mickelsen, the head of the DP administration at American headquarters, was reported to be unfriendly to Jewish DPs.[25] Immediately following the general's interview, however, new attempts were made to get at the truth and a spate of reports on Jewish DPs were prepared. Among these the most significant was a report by the head of UNRRA's research division, Jay B. Krane, to General Morgan, dated January 18.[26] Krane arrived at the conclusion that "there is widespread anti-Semitism in Poland" and that the question whether the refugees who happened to be questioned were themselves victims of any such manifestations was immaterial; the fear

was there and that was the main problem. At the same time he corroborated Morgan's impression that the refugee movement was "not spontaneous but that it [was] part of a deliberate plan to bring the questions of the future of the Jews and of Zionism to a head." UNRRA officials in Bavaria, two of whom were Jews, reported similar findings.[27] Because of these reports the American military began to assume that the refugee movement was indeed politically directed, though they were aware of its background of persecution which justified it. In consequence, pro-Jewish sentiment began to cool somewhat, especially in the lower ranks of command. It is true that probably only a Jew—Lehman—could have saved Morgan in early 1946 because of a desire not to make too strong a Jewish issue out of the affair. But this apparently had no influence on the officers' mentality, and anti-Jewish sentiments increased. Morgan's statements had "left its impression on the mind of the military authorities and UNRRA personnel."[28]

This changed or changing attitude was manifested in a growing number of incidents that marred the relations between the DPs and the American authorities in the spring of 1946. On the American side it could be argued that much of the ill feeling could be laid at the door of the Jews themselves, whose activities on the black market increased as their situation remained static. A short list of some of the incidents will suffice to illustrate the disharmony. On March 28, there was a scuffle with the military at Oberammingen after a fight between Jews and Germans; on the same day American MPs beat up some Jews at Wolfrathshausen after a misunderstanding; in Landsberg, at the end of April, there was fighting and twenty Jews were arrested in the aftermath of a Jewish mass protest against the disappearance and suspected abduction by Germans of two young Jews near the camp (it was found afterward that the two young men had simply left the place without telling anyone); on March 25 a group of Jews were transferred from Fürth to Bamberg under rather grim conditions which showed a certain callousness on the part of the military; and on the 29th a young Jew was killed in Stuttgart in a scuffle that involved German police and American MPs. Similar incidents occurred in

May at Cham, Munich and other places.[29] Dr. Gruenberg of St. Ottilien was moved to declare at a Central Committee meeting on June 9 in Munich that "the attitude of the Military Government towards the Jews has unfortunately worsened considerably."[30] It is interesting, however, to note that these strains and stresses had no measurable influence on the infiltration of Jews in the U.S. zones. It is quite possible that had the situation in Poland and elsewhere become stabilized, the continuation of the Jewish flow into Germany would have been affected by the changing attitude of the American military. But the situation in Eastern Europe did not change for the better, and in these circumstances the riots and blows exchanged in Germany had no significant effect.

In the meantime, important political developments affecting the situation of Jewish DPs and the Brichah had taken place on the international scene. After three months of confidential negotiations about the Palestine problem and the refugees, Attlee wrote to Truman on October 5 that the British government had devoted much attention and thought to the two problems and had found that they were not necessarily connected.[31] On the 19th the British suggested the creation of an Anglo-American inquiry commission rather than the type of royal commission which had investigated Palestine in 1937. Britain was in the throes of a severe economic crisis and could not fulfill its obligations to its American ally without the latter's economic and political aid. Its commitments were overstretched, and its adjustment to second-class power status was a very painful one. The Labour government clearly desired American support for its policies, and in order to overcome Truman's reluctance to commit the United States to any actions in the Mediterranean area it proposed a joint appraisal of the refugee problem. Specifically the British proposal was to study the Jewish situation in Europe, find out how many Jews could be resettled in their countries of origin and then examine the immigration possibilities, in Palestine and elsewhere. As far as Palestine was concerned, the commission was to determine the conditions and limits of any Jewish immigration there.

The British proposal gave Palestine a very modest place in the labors of the proposed commission. It was clear that the British hoped that the American commission members would come around to the British point of view when they examined conditions in the Holy Land. In this they were strengthened by papers submitted by researchers of the semi-official Royal Institute of International Affairs (Chatham House); one of these even went so far as to suggest that many Jews would now leave Palestine for their countries of origin in Europe.[32] However, Truman did not agree with this formulation, and he tended to defend the connection between the DP problem and Palestine, to which he therefore wanted to give a central position in the inquiry. He also insisted on as much speed as possible in reaching practical political conclusions. During Attlee's visit to the United States in early November 1945 these points were thrashed out and an agreement was reached.

On November 13 Foreign Minister Bevin announced in the House of Commons the setting up of an Anglo-American Committee of Inquiry. This was also the first official government pronouncement on Palestine and the Jewish refugees since the Labour Party came into power. Bevin made a great effort to separate the refugee problem from the Palestine issue. The Jewish problem, as far as he was concerned, had started with Hitler and would end with Hitler's downfall. The immediate solution had to be that the Jews return to their homelands. "We cannot accept the view," he said, "that the Jews should be driven out of Europe and should not live again in these countries without discrimination and give their ability and their talents towards building the prosperity of Europe."[33] Apart from thus prejudging the issue that the committee was supposed to study, Bevin also made clear that Palestine could not possibly absorb all those Jews who wanted to go there. However, the 1,500 permits that the British government had offered the Jewish Agency on August 25 would still be issued, and Bevin hoped the Arabs would agree to that measure of Jewish immigration. The task of the committee would be to report within a hundred and twenty days and suggest a temporary solution to both the refugee and the Palestine problems so that time would be gained to find permanent solutions later on.

The official declarations were disappointing enough for the Jews; they meant a further delay, more suffering in the camps and a dangerous postponement of the problem's resolution for the Jews of Palestine. It also seemed that Truman had fallen into a British trap or perhaps wanted to get out of his commitments to the Jews by having a committee which would probably arrive at a conclusion acceptable to Britain. Beyond the political aspect, however, a great deal of emotion was stirred up by some remarks made by Bevin in the course of a short and informal press conference after his announcement. He said among other things that the Jews should not jump to the head of the queue and thus gave expression to his utter ignorance of the whole problem. His remarks were interpreted bitterly in Jewish circles as an affront or even as an anti-Semitic outburst.

It was in this atmosphere that the committee began its sessions. It was composed of six English and six American members, most of whom had had no contact whatsoever with the problems concerning the Jews or Palestine. The official work of the committee began on January 5, 1946 in Washington, and sessions with witnesses were held there and in London until February 4. After London, the committee split up into a number of sections and visited the DP camps in the various zones of Germany, except the Soviet zone; some groups also visited Austria, Poland and Czechoslovakia. The impression they gained was more or less the same: the Jews wanted to go to Palestine, and they very emphatically did not want to be returned to their homelands. What was obvious to every American officer in Germany had to be laboriously rediscovered. In the process, one must add, the Jewish Agency representatives helped along with persuasion, propaganda and pressure in the various camps. Not that the pressure was necessary for many of the Jews; but the tremendous majorities in which the Jews protested that their aim was Palestine were the result of a great deal of intensive political work. Most of those who did not themselves want to go to Palestine were persuaded quite easily that for the sake of the majority they should also join in the general opinion to present a united Jewish front to the committee members. One JDC worker put it that parents with Zionist-oriented children said, "I don't particularly want

to go to Palestine but I think it is good for the children."[34] In one camp, it is reported, an anti-Zionist social worker was spirited away for a weekend with her boyfriend when the commission members were about to arrive, and similar incidents are said to have occurred in other places. During the whole of their journeying in Europe, commission members were under constant Jewish pressure of persuasion and discussions. So much so, in fact, that one of the commission's members is reported to have declared that if the Jewish attempt to influence him had lasted much longer he would have definitely turned against the Jews.

On the whole, however, the effect of the DP camps on the committee members was shattering—the human tragedies they saw and the general determination for Palestine were so vivid that it was quite clear that no amount of propaganda could have created the scene merely for their benefit. Especially important was the visit of some members to Poland at the beginning of February. There, after much haggling, the Jewish Communists agreed at last to accede to the Zionist demands because had they not done so they would have made their position untenable among their fellow Jews in the country. An impressive demonstration of some 20,000 Jews in Lodz crowned the visit. It was quite clear that there was a poisoned anti-Semitic atmosphere in Poland and that the Polish government was trying to stand by the Jews but was quite unable to do so successfully. A question often asked during the visit was, How were these Jews leaving Poland? Ultimately, however, the question was immaterial because, as the committee members found out, the exodus itself was apparently unavoidable. All Jewish organizations in Poland, and not only the Zionists, were infected with the Palestine bug, as one committee member put it.

Figures gained by questionnaires of various agencies were quoted to prove the point that most Jews wanted to go to Palestine. An UNRRA questionnaire elicited the information that of 19,311 Jews asked, 96.8 percent stated a preference for Palestine, and only 393 wanted to go to the United States.[35] Mickelsen, head of the American DP section, confirmed from Army sources that most of the Jews would go

to Palestine if they were given the choice. His figures were that 60 percent would choose Palestine, 20 percent other overseas countries, and 14 percent were estimated to be undecided; only 1 percent might go back to their countries of origin.[36]

On February 17, members of the committee met again in Vienna. The Americans demanded that the committee issue an interim report then and there that would probably have included a demand for increased emigration to Palestine. This was prevented by the English members, though they also had seen the situation in the camps, and the committee moved on to Palestine to continue its study there.

The final report of the committee was presented on April 22 to the two governments. Its main recommendation was that Britain should immediately admit 100,000 immigrants into Palestine; other recommendations spoke of ultimately creating in Palestine a binational regime based on a mutual understanding between Jews and Arabs, and of allowing Jews in the meantime to immigrate into the country under certain conditions, even after the 100,000 had been admitted. The report as it stood came as a great shock to the Labour government. Instead of the American members following the lead of the British ones, it seemed obvious that the opposite had taken place. The British government had no intention of allowing 100,000 Jews into Palestine and thereby endangering its position in the Middle East vis-à-vis the Arab countries. A series of maneuvers followed whose general aim was to achieve British aims with as little loss of face for Truman as possible. A group of experts headed by Henry F. Grady was sent by Truman to discuss the committee's report, but their English counterparts persuaded them to accept a plan that would practically have meant leaving Palestine under British rule and given the Jews a very small area into which to bring further immigrants. This plan had been submitted to the committee during its deliberations and rejected by it, but now called the Morrison Plan, it was intended to become official Anglo-American policy. Despite heavy British pressure, however, Truman did not accept the plan, mainly because of the determined opposition of Jews and of the American members of the now de-

funct committee. The final American rejection of the British plan came on August 8, 1946, and this brought the Palestine problem and the question of the future of the Jewish DPs back to where it had been in late 1945.

Politically, therefore, the refugees in Europe went through alternating phases of hope and disappointment. There was disappointment over the very fact that a committee was needed to investigate what to Europe's Jews seemed so obvious, but there was great hope in that at least some of the committee's recommendations would be put into practice. And there was the final disappointment when British political maneuvers brought to naught all hopes of an early legal emigration to Palestine. The danger began to be evident that if nothing happened in the sphere of emigration to Palestine, the desperate refugees might turn away from the Zionist dream and seek their fortunes in other countries.

The problem of finding solutions other than Palestine for the DPs had been brought up often. There was, however, a marked reluctance by prospective countries to accept these Jewish war-victims as immigrants, because they were very largely a demoralized element who, moreover, did not have the necessary training for jobs available in the various countries. Estonians, Letts, Poles and Ukrainians were accepted by Canada, Britain or South America as agricultural laborers, miners or factory hands. But who would want Jewish tailors and cobblers, especially when they had not practiced their skills for years? In this situation it was Truman who tried to do at least some justice to outraged humanitarianism by allowing some Jewish immigration into the United States. There was, of course, the American immigration law, which restricted the number of immigrants by a complicated quota system. Few Jews would have been qualified to enter the United States under such a system. Moreover, Congress was not very eager in those years to accept new immigrants. Truman therefore tried to let in as many DPs as possible without actually changing the existing law. He issued an Executive Order on December 22, 1945, the intention of which was to grant priority on existing quotas to the DPs. The German and Austrian quotas and the Polish quota amounted to a total of about 39,000. It was intended that a large num-

ber of DPs should come into the United States under this combined quota, but it seems that the effort was largely sabotaged at the lower administrative levels in the government. Not more than about 45,000 DPs entered the United States between the end of 1945 and the Displaced Persons Act of July 1, 1948. Of these, an authoritative source claims, 12,649 were Jews (between May 1946, when the first ship with Jewish immigrants sailed with 439 Jews from Bremen and until October 1948, when the effects of the bill passed on July 1 were felt).[37] During 1946, only 9,500 Jewish refugees left Germany by legal or illegal means.[38]

The initial report of the Anglo-American committee was received with great joy by the inmates of the camps because of its stress on the speedy emigration to Palestine of 100,000 Jews. The disappointment that came after the British refused to implement the report was, of course, shattering. The Jewish Agency had to be wary of two possible outcomes of these developments: one was that the refugees, disappointed in their hopes of reaching Palestine, might start to move heaven and earth to get into other countries; the other was that in the absence of a constructive solution a demoralization might set in that would throw the refugees back to the mental state they were in at liberation—or worse—and exacerbate anti-Semitism among Americans, Germans and others. These dangers were quite real and were explicitly pointed out in discussions held within the Agency.[39] As far as the disposition of the refugees to go to countries other than Palestine was concerned, this was very well known. The Zionist ideology argued that in the modern world there simply would be no country that would accept large-scale Jewish immigration for a variety of reasons, mainly economic and social. The American attitude, and of course that of Britain and the Latin American countries, proved this to be correct. However, before all these problems could be weighed properly, the Kielce pogrom broke out and a set of new and vast problems arose which catapulted Brichah into a position of tremendous importance.

7. The Great Exodus

Kielce is an old Polish town of medium size; here in olden times the bishop's seat and the Jewish quarter coexisted quite peacefully. In the period between the world wars, however, relations deteriorated there as everywhere else in Poland, and then came the great slaughter and the Jews of Kielce were no more. After the war, survivors trickled back —from the forests, from Russia, from the camps—and with them came others who had not lived there before. Altogether, Kielce was little more than a transit point for Jews, and in the spring of 1946 there were no more than about 200 Jews in the town of 50,000.

On the morning of July 4, 1946, a nine-year-old boy named Henryk Blaszczyk, the son of a shoemaker, appeared at the local militia (police) station. The story he told was hair-raising: he said that he had been held captive by Jews for two days, that he could identify the place of his detention as Planta Str. No. 7 (the Jewish Committee's house), that he had been held there in a cellar and that he had seen other Christian children murdered there by the Jews, presumably for ritual purposes. The amazing thing was that the commander of the militia accepted the testimony of the boy without any doubt (was it not well known that Jews murdered Christian children for ritual purposes?). The commander ordered his militiamen to go to the committee's

house and surround it from all sides. The boy, of course, went along too. As a crowd began to assemble the boy expounded his story, with no sign of disapproval by the militia, to an incensed audience. The crowd became a mob, a priest appeared on the scene and did nothing to calm the audience, and soon the attitude of the mob toward the occupants of the house became threatening.

In the house at the time there were staff members of the committee and a "kibbutz" group of youngsters who were preparing to leave Poland at the next opportunity. They do not seem to have had weapons, but members of the Jewish committee in the rooms upstairs had some small arms which they were licensed to carry.

At about 11:15 A.M. the crowd, including the militiamen, attacked the building. The defenseless "kibbutz" members were dragged outside and a number of them were brutally murdered, including a man by the name of Weinreb who had been a lieutenant in the Russian Army and had fought all the way from Stalingrad to Berlin. The mob then pillaged the "kibbutz" quarters, and finding very little of any value there, turned to the rooms upstairs. There, the committee staff were assembled in the office. Some Army officers who had joined the mob walked in and took the arms away from the Jews, promising them at the same time that they would protect them from the mob. When they left the house, the mob surged into the upper story and dragged out those they could lay hands on. Outside, in the courtyard, the Jews were done to death with bricks, knives and sticks. Other Jews managed to escape into a room where they barricaded themselves. A number of Jewish officials ran into the telephone room where the chairman of the committee, Dr. Kahana, was trying to reach the office of the regional commander (*woiewod*). The commander's deputy, a man by the name of Urbanowicz, promised them help. By that time fifteen people had already been killed and a larger number wounded. When the commotion increased, Dr. Kahana tried to reach the bishop's palace. He was told that the bishop was out of town (this was later disputed). While he was on the phone the mob broke into the room and killed him. Others managed to get into the barricaded room.

It seems that in the meantime some Army detachments had arrived. There was divided opinion among the officers. Whereas an officer called Mucha was trying to calm the mob and reassure the Jews, other Army officers insisted on bringing them out into the courtyard. The Jews had no choice but to obey, as the soldiers were armed. Outside, the mob had grown into a huge mass of thousands of people. Workers from two nearby factories, including one of the managers, a well-known socialist, came and joined the crowd. Again, the Jews who were brought out were attacked; some were killed and others wounded. A remnant escaped and ran back into the building, defending themselves with bare hands as best they could. There they barricaded themselves; at this point, at last, a detachment of soldiers came, dispersed the mob and rescued the Jews who were still alive. In the meantime other Jews had been attacked and some killed in other parts of Kielce and at the little railway station of Piekuszow nearby. When evening came and relative calm was restored, 41 Jews and 4 Poles were dead, and many dozens injured. More blood would certainly have been shed if the Polish government had not reacted so swiftly.[1]

The Kielce story is told very dramatically by Yitzhak Zuckerman, the chief representative of the Zionist groups on the Jewish Central Committee of Poland. We met Zuckerman, the erstwhile deputy commander of the Warsaw ghetto rebellion, when he, together with Abba Kovner, set up the Brichah in Lublin. Now, in July 1946, he was the man most respected and valued by the Polish government who could speak in the name of the Zionist movement. In Palestine the British had cracked down on the Haganah, the underground Jewish military organization there, which was trying to get more Jews into the country at the time. On June 29 the British arrested numerous Jews and searched for arms caches; in the process, they caused much damage in Jewish settlements. More important, they obviously meant their action to be understood as an expression of their implacable hostility to any Jewish immigration leading to the establishment of an independent Jewish political community. Zuckerman convinced even the Communist members of the Polish Central Committee to go with him to Poland's Prime Minis-

ter, Osobka-Morawski, to ask for Poland's help in the struggle against the British. This, it so happened, occurred on July 4. According to Zuckerman: "The discussion was very friendly, when the ringing of a telephone bell suddenly interrupted us. . . . We were sitting in a very elongated room. He went to one of the telephones, heard some report, and suddenly grew pale. He said something into the receiver, went over to us and said: 'Gentlemen, there is a pogrom at Kielce!' "[2]

Zuckerman went to Kielce immediately with medical help. It was found that on that July 4 individual Jews had been attacked in the neighborhood of the town as well, so that the possibility of a premeditated attempt at eliminating the Jewish population presented itself immediately. A special train was sent from Cracow to take the wounded away to Lodz; it was surrounded with special security measures because it was clear that the underground opposition was out to kill the Jews and might attack the train. Accompanied by Polish Army detachments commanded by a Polish-speaking Russian officer, the train reached Lodz and the wounded were hospitalized there. In the meantime, planeloads of high officials arrived from Warsaw to participate in the burial services and to start a purge of local officials. A quick investigation resulted in summary sentences for a number of participants in the pogrom, nine of whom were sentenced to death and executed on July 14.

It is, of course, true that, as we have already seen, small-scale pogroms had been occurring in Poland ever since the end of the war. Individual Jews had been attacked, beaten and murdered, especially on trains or in smaller townships or villages. But here in Kielce, in broad daylight, a ritual murder story had caused a massacre which few had believed was still possible in postwar Poland. It seemed clear that the political opposition to the Communist regime had used the anti-Semitism of the population to harass the government by inflaming the Jewish problem. Underground publications attested to the violent anti-Semitism of the opposition;[3] however, the attitude of the main opposition force, the Catholic Church, was not clear. The Church had great sympathy for the underground organizations, and it was traditionally

anti-Semitic. At the same time, there always had been some persons in the Catholic hierarchy, and more especially many simple priests, who acted in a humane fashion toward the Jews, both during and after the war. It was clear that a pronouncement by the Cardinal-Primate of Poland, August Hlond, might be more effective in containing pogroms than all the security measures of the weak leftist government.

Rabbi Kahane of Warsaw had tried to speak to Hlond before Kielce, but Hlond had not agreed to receive him. The rabbi thereupon wrote him asking for a pastoral letter against pogroms to be sent out; but the Primate refused to do so. A similar request by Joseph Tennenbaum, representing Polish Jews in the United States, was also refused. One should perhaps mention in this connection that Hlond had been in exile in France during the war and had apparently participated in some rescue activities in behalf of individual Jews at that time. Now, however, on July 11, he held a press conference on the Kielce pogrom, and his attitude was rather different. First, said Hlond, the Catholic Church was against all murder, in Poland or elsewhere, whether acts were committed against Jews or Poles or others. Second, the Kielce events showed, according to Hlond, that there was no racism behind the pogrom. The reasons were tragic, and the prelate expressed his sorrow and pain at the unhappy events. Third, the Church authorities in Kielce had behaved with great wisdom and circumspection, had helped the authorities in the preservation of peace and had read a message from the bishop on the Sunday following the outrage demanding peace and order. As a result, it was claimed, no disturbances had occurred after July 4. (Yet, Prime Minister Osobka-Morawski said, according to the *New York Times* of July 9, that Prince Adam Cardinal Sapieha of Cracow had refused a French request to sign an appeal against pogroms.)

The fourth point in Hlond's statement was in many ways the most interesting. Poles had saved Jews from the Nazis at the risk of their own lives. But anti-Semitism was, Hlond said, "to a great extent due to Jews who today occupy leading positions in Poland's government and endeavor to introduce a governmental structure that a majority of the people

do not desire." This was a dangerous game, he said, and might cost the Jews a great deal; and while it was true that some Jews were suffering as a result of the present unrest in Poland, Poles were suffering incomparably more. Apart from some expressions of pious hopes for a more peaceful future, the Primate gave no indication of his condemnation of the pogrom as directed specifically against Jews.[4] It seemed to be the Primate's view that Jews were either Communists or supporters of Communism and that the fault of the pogroms rested with them.

The reaction of Polish Jewry was an immediate and overwhelming desire to leave Poland as quickly as possible. In actual fact this degenerated into a panic. The weakness of the government, its incapacity to protect the lives of peaceful citizens of Jewish extraction, had been openly demonstrated. The attitude of the clergy as exemplified by Hlond showed that the Church, if it was not directly connected with those sponsoring the pogroms, would certainly do nothing to prevent them and that its attitude would continue to be based on the traditional, prewar form of extreme anti-Semitism. Caught between Communism and its right-wing opposition, the vast majority of Jews felt that Poland had become too inhospitable to tarry there longer than was absolutely necessary. What turned this realization into panic was the acute feeling of vulnerability, of being abandoned by all powers capable of protecting them. And this feeling was strengthened by what was reported to be the reaction of Polish officialdom. There was deep dismay—indeed disbelief—that a medieval pogrom could happen in an ordinary Polish town in what had been assumed to be a civilized country.[5]

It should perhaps be stressed that the mass movement out of Poland had been picking up through the late spring, even before the Kielce pogrom. The figure of 8,000 refugees for June quoted above[6] seems to be an approximation only, but compared with the 3,502 for May it indicates the rising tide of mass flight. Nevertheless, the change that came with Kielce was unmistakable: it seems that in July at least 19,000 people left with the organized Brichah; in August

35,346 and in September 12,379 left Poland.[7] However, these figures are incomplete. The Stettin transients did not always pass Berlin where they could be counted, and thousands went via Lübeck directly into western Germany. Then there were additional thousands who fell into the hands of private speculators or professional smugglers, or were organized by separatist groups. The Stettin group could be estimated at about 10,000, and about the same number again, or perhaps slightly less, crossed with smugglers. Then there were Hungarian Jews, and a smaller number of Rumanian and Slovakian Jews who joined the mass exodus. The JDC reported from Czechoslovakia[8] that over 14,000 Hungarian Jews passed the Bratislava point in the three months of the massive flight. This figure contradicts the Vienna statistics that mention 4,576 Hungarian and 800 Rumanian Jews for that period[9]—but it must be noted that not all Jews passed through the Vienna Rothschild hospital where the count was taken. It would seem that in all an estimate of between 90,000 and 95,000 Jewish refugees from Eastern Europe to the so-called DP countries of Germany, Austria and Italy during July, August and September 1946 would be conservative and reasonable.

The change in the whole character of the movement out of Poland caught the Brichah unprepared. Literally overnight its organization had to adapt itself to dealing with illegal crossings of numbers twice to three times as large as those to which it had been accustomed. Apart from the smaller "points," Brichah operated mainly on two "fronts": Stettin-Berlin and the Silesian border into Czechoslovakia. For many reasons the latter route was preferred—it was nearer the new centers of Jewish settlement in Poland (many of the repatriants from Russia were being settled just there, in Lower Silesia); the crossing was into friendly Czechoslovakia rather than into Berlin via the Russian zone of Germany, and the route to the U.S. zone in Germany or Austria was much easier via the south. Kladzko and Walbrzych, near the Czech border, now became the two major "points." In Kladzko, Luba Geller and Max Krochmal received the groups sent to them from places like Katowice or Lodz; they would provide them with lodging and

some food, and then transfer them to either of three small places on the border—Grodek, Miedzylesie or Kudowa. A spa beautifully situated in the hills and forests of the border mountain ranges, Kudowa was the main point of departure. There Yisrael Ridelnik had his headquarters. The routes were well known to the youngsters who worked with Krochmal and Ridelnik; they were themselves the "boys from the forest" and did not need any professional smugglers to guide them across the "green," unguarded parts of the border. The main problem was the border guards; many of these were by no means loyal to the government and were quite capable of participating in anti-Semitic ventures of various kinds. These had to be bribed. Ridelnik later described the situation thus: "If he [the guard] received a large bribe—he worked with us; if he felt like it and imagined he was still living in the Nazi era and he can both receive money from the Jews and then also shoot at them, well, sometimes he did that too."[10] The crossings were dangerous, and many were wounded. But the pressure was such that the work continued despite everything. A similar situation obtained in Walbrzych, from which, as in the case of Kladzko, people went to the small border town of Frydlant, whence the border crossing was effected.

There were many stories of heroism and tragedy. One sad case was that of the friendly mayor of Kudowa, a non-Jew, who had lived in the place during the Nazi occupation. At that time a concentration camp of Jewish girls existed at Kudowa, and he, who was then an ordinary worker, would go by and supply the girls with bread and other food as much as he could. When liberation came, he took care of the girls until they slowly dispersed. As time went on, he fell in love with one of the girls in the group. When Brichah started to operate at Kudowa, the girl became torn between her feelings of gratitude to the Pole and her dislike of Poland. The Brichah commander decided to make use of his friendship with the Polish mayor to ease his way to the border. Of course by this time the mayor was someone of influence. So when the girl came to the Brichah and asked their help to get away, the Brichah commander tried to persuade her to stay. In the meantime the relation-

ship between the two men had become one of real friendship and the Brichah official began to feel he could not misuse a friend and moreover that he would do him a great injustice if he granted the girl's request. What had started as a cynical use of a human situation became an involved emotional problem. The girl became more and more insistent, and the Pole of course knew that she could not get away without the help of the Brichah. In the end the girl had her way—it was, after all, her right to insist on having control over her own life. The Brichah commander removed her by stealth, and later had to face the Pole, who accused him of bad faith. But the mayor continued to support the Brichah, and the commander tried to make up for what he had done, knowing that he could not have done otherwise.[11]

That month of July was the worst on the Silesian frontier. Of course, the police and the border guards knew exactly what was happening, but their attitude was full of contradictions. Because they had no clear-cut instructions on how to deal with these Jews, they used the situation to their own very concrete advantage. This meant dangerous nightly crossings and heavy work for the Brichah youngsters. As an illustration of such a night crossing, the story of Avraham Sadeh of Walbrzych is apposite.

> We left by rail, in the morning, with about 100 youths, complete with their flags—just a pleasant outing. Then we visited, as it were, a children's home near the frontier. After having spent the whole day there, we made preparations as though we were to spend the night at the home; but when the night came, we went out towards the border. It was a great thing to see these youngsters ascend the hills there; and when we finally climbed on top, we went down on the other side where there were a few houses of Poles and then a wood; inside that wood there was a line of felled trees and that was the border. We only had a few hundred yards to cover, but when we approached the houses we saw a commotion there. which was unusual for that quiet place. Then we saw that the soldiers were there, having some kind of festivity together with the local inhabitants; by the sound of their singing we knew they were drunk. We told the kids to lie down in the

> field and two of us approached the place to see what was going on. We saw that a large number of people was there but that they were about to leave on their horse carts. We could not bypass the hamlet, so we decided to wait till the guests left and the inhabitants went to sleep. This of course took time, and the kids were trembling with cold; there was a heavy dew, and the soldiers did not seem to be in a hurry. Somebody suggested that we return; but we decided against it —the soldiers might meet us or see us, and the way up to the hamlet had been difficult enough. At last the soldiers sat in their carts and started shooting in the air. They were laughing and screaming and we were trembling with cold—the kids must have been scared. We told them to retreat slowly through the field to a ditch further away from the soldiers; they did that in perfect discipline, and then we waited for three full hours. The soldiers just sat in their carts, drank and fired in the air towards the fields and the ditch where we lay. I was no longer afraid of falling into their hands but I was trembling at the thought of one of these stray bullets hitting one of the youngsters who had not had a single quiet day for the last six years, who had been wandering all over Eastern Europe and now, when they were on the point of finally leaving Poland . . . The dirt track for the carts passed right near where we we lying. They went off at last, still shooting; the kids lay down flat at the bottom of the ditch. They themselves removed everything of light color from themselves, and the soldiers passed by without seeing anything. Two of us went into the hamlet and saw that everyone was asleep. Quickly we made the frontier and delivered the youngsters on the other side. When we got there, the sun was up already.[12]

During July, then, the Jews began streaming into Czechoslovakia in ever-increasing numbers, not only via Kladzko or Walbrzych to Nachod in Bohemia, but also in small groups via Moravska Ostrava in Moravia, and Zilina and Poprad in Slovakia. All this presented the Czech government with a very serious problem. Even since January the Czechs had been supplying most of the food, the shelter and special trains to ship the refugees through their country. This had been done on the understanding, verbally confirmed

by Elfan Rees, the repatriation officer of UNRRA attached to the Czech ministries of Social Welfare, Labor, Foreign Affairs and Interior, "that a special allocation would be forthcoming from UNRRA, Washington" to cover these expenses.[13] With the help of some Jewish officials of the Repatriation Office of the Ministry of Social Welfare and also of Jan Masaryk, the Minister for Foreign Affairs, and other pro-Jewish Czech officials, this arrangement had worked until early July. The prime negotiator on the Jewish side was Gaynor I. Jacobson, the American head of the JDC in Prague, on whose staff most of the Brichah commanders either worked or were registered. Jacobson knew of the Brichah operations but only in a general way. He knew he had the Brichah men on his staff but did not know what their functions were and who else was involved. His task was to see to it that refugees who actually crossed the border into Czechoslovakia were properly cared for and shipped on to Bratislava and Vienna. He had no special liking for the role of a "front" for the Brichah, but he thought it his duty to help the refugees as far as possible. Being gifted with a persuasive tongue, great diplomatic tact and a quick mind and having deep compassion for the refugees, he became quite naturally the official negotiator in behalf of the refugees. Utilizing his contacts with U.S. Ambassador Laurence A. Steinhardt, Jan Masaryk and a number of Communist officials, he became an effective mediator between the various interests. Jacobson says[14] that Rees's verbal agreement came on June 1, apparently in response to some worried inquiries on the part of minor officials who had been spending money on the refugees without any proper authorization. On that day, too, Jacobson and Rees visited Nachod, the main gate of entry. Apart from being feted there by the mayor, and having to consume certain quantities of alcohol in the process, Jacobson agreed for the JDC to supplement government rations to the refugees, provide some medical help and participate in improving the housing facilities in Nachod.

On July 7 the deputy director-general of UNRRA in Europe, Mary Gibbons, came to Prague. In the course of her discussions she was asked whether the Czechs would

indeed be reimbursed for their expenses in what was officially known as "unsuccessful repatriation" (that is, the Jews had been repatriated to Poland but had refused to remain there—they had become refugees again and were crossing the Czech border). Miss Gibbons declared that this must have been a misunderstanding; UNRRA certainly was not committed to any such expenses, and the Czechs should pay for them out of their normal UNRRA allocations or, in other words, they should pay for them themselves. "The immediate result of this statement by Miss Gibbons," noted Jacobson, "was great anxiety among the lower echelons of Governmental employees who had been carrying out the program of aid to Polish transients without authorization from their chiefs, the heads of the various ministries."[15] Jacobson thereupon went to Masaryk and Vlado Clementis, his Communist deputy. Masaryk promised that everything would be done to keep the border open and that he would personally pay tribute to the various officials who had been assisting in this important work. To quote Jacobson again: "At the government meeting on July 16 he informed the Cabinet that Czechoslovakia must remain a haven of refuge for these Jews fleeing from terror. If Czechoslovakia was to close its borders he, Minister Masaryk, would resign."[16] Clementis also supported Masaryk, after being assured that the refugees would not stay in the country longer than the time it took to transport them out of it. Even before the government meeting, Jacobson decided to press his head office, via Dr. Joseph J. Schwartz, to get another commitment by UNRRA that would annul the impression created by Miss Gibbons. The problem in Prague was complicated by the fact that the head of UNRRA in Czechoslovakia was a Russian, whose name was Alexeiev. He was not eager to assume any responsibility of his own and declared that he must await the ruling of UNRRA authorities.

In New York and Washington, JDC got to work to see what UNRRA could do to unscramble the Czech situation. On July 15, JDC cabled to Schwartz that the new head of UNRRA, Fiorello La Guardia, had left the United States but that the head office of UNRRA had reassured the JDC that the Czechs were expected to assist postwar refugees and

that they had the right to request additional supplies for that purpose. The Czechs had made no such requests to date, but they were expected to do so.[17] Alexeiev now expressed his willingness, despite the continuing lack of a formal letter from UNRRA headquarters, to ask the Czechs not to discontinue the work of aiding the refugees. Jacobson then met with Professor Zdenek Nejedly, the Minister for Social Welfare, a Communist who had suffered under the Nazi occupation (he later became the head of the Czechoslovak Academy of Sciences). Nejedly was very friendly, and he tried—unsuccessfully—to get telephoned approval of the other ministries to a continuation of the Nachod arrangements. The real objections seemed to come from Dr. Vaclav Toman, Deputy Minister of the Interior, the Communist official responsible for internal security. Jacobson went to his house and heard Toman's fears that anti-Communist and anti-Polish Ukrainians were coming across the Tatra mountains disguised as Jewish refugees; it seemed also that members of the Polish right-wing opposition were infiltrating in the same way. Toman even suggested that Jacobson discuss the matter with the Polish ambassador in Prague, but Jacobson refused. Toman also considered the possibility of moving the refugees from Nachod to As on the Czech-German border so that they would reach the DP camps in the U.S. zone directly rather than via the tortuous route through Vienna. Schwartz tried to discuss this with U.S. military officials in Germany, but General McNarney, the U.S. commander there, refused his consent—while he would not prevent the entry of Jewish refugees into his zone, he would also do nothing to invite them to come, and an arrangement for the transit of refugees at As would be interpreted as an invitation by the U.S. zone authorities.[18]

In further conferences with the Czech officials Jacobson was told that a bill for 21 million Czech crowns would be submitted to UNRRA and was reassured at the same time that the Czech program would not be interrupted without consulting the JDC. On July 26[19] a Cabinet meeting took place where the matter was discussed and finally decided. It was very clearly stated that the transients would not be allowed to stay on Czech soil for longer than an absolute

minimum of time; Masaryk was told to find out the attitude of the Polish government and to be in touch with UNRRA on the question of payments. The British and American governments were to be requested to find as quickly as possible permanent places of settlement for these refugees. The operative clause of the decision, however, stated quite clearly that Nejedly's ministry should take care of the transients and provide transportation through Czech territory. The fact that the large Communist contingent in the government, including Klement Gottwald, supported this decision is, of course, very important. One can but guess at the motives for this attitude. Obviously, any Jewish infiltration into Palestine would cause trouble there for the British, and this was welcomed by pro-Communist or pro-Soviet politicians. At the same time, however, other motives seem to have been present as well. Many Czech politicians, including such people as Nejedly, Antonin Zapotocky, the future Communist President of Czechoslovakia, and others, had gone through the Nazi hell, which was still fresh in their minds in 1946. Generally speaking, the feeling in Czechoslovakia toward Jewish refugees was friendly for that reason, and this was probably a factor. At any rate, Communist and non-Communist ministers and officials cooperated to make this extraordinary arrangement possible, knowing full well the opposition of Britain to this mass move of Jews.

In the end, UNRRA paid only $250,000 for the expenses borne by the Czechs. This sum was apparently paid at the end of September 1946, while the actual expenses came to 52,406,750 crowns up to that date (or about $1,048,000).[20] As far as is known, the Czechs were never reimbursed for the rest of the sums expended.

Unknown to Jacobson—and probably to the Brichah commanders in Czechoslovakia—a parallel series of negotiations were taking place in Poland. These began immediately after Kielce. Zuckerman relates[21] how he chanced to talk to a high U.B. (Polish Security) official on the plane back to Warsaw after the funeral of the Kielce victims. The burden of the conversation was, he says, that the Poles were unable, though willing, to protect the Jews in Poland, but

were not allowing them to leave the country legally. It was true that the Polish government was issuing passports freely to anyone who could show he had an entry visa to a foreign country. However, after all, this was the major trouble—the Jews had no way of getting official permits to go anywhere. The U.B. official appears to have reported the casual conversation to his superiors, and these then invited Zuckerman for a series of talks. It seems that the security organs saw the Jews as a liability in their struggle against the anti-Communist opposition and were prepared to let them go, provided they could get some kind of official backing for the move. They suggested to Zuckerman that he turn to the Deputy Minister of Foreign Affairs, Zygmunt Modzilewski, an old Polish Communist who was on friendly terms with him. However, Zuckerman pointed out that the Polish Foreign Ministry was desperately trying to remain on good terms with Britain because the Polish gold reserves were in England and the Poles were trying to get them back. With Britain violently opposed to Jewish mass moves designed to infiltrate into Palestine, there was no chance that the Foreign Ministry would accede to a request by Zuckerman to facilitate exit of Jews out of Poland. The U.B. thereupon suggested that the Defense Minister, Marian Spychalski, might be more friendly. Spychalski had been an important commander of the left-wing resistance movement during the German occupation. His relations with Zuckerman were also friendly and Zuckerman agreed to go to see him.[22] Accompanying him was Dr. Adolf Berman, head of the leftist Poale Zion Party (a Zionist-Socialist organization in Poland), who happened to be the brother of Jakub Berman, the Communist strong man in the government. The problem that arose in the discussions was the question of responsibility. Zuckerman was a member of the Jewish Central Committee in his own right, as the former commander of the surviving ghetto fighters; in fact, as the leader of the *chalutz* he represented the Zionist-Socialist youth movements, but he could not involve them in an activity which might expose them to all kinds of persecution later on. Before the meeting with Spychalski he did not even have time to consult the Brichah people, and

so he assumed personal responsibility for the arrangements. Spychalski agreed immediately on his own to open the border without involving the Foreign Ministry. A Russian general of Polish extraction, General Czerwinski, who barely spoke Polish and was the commander of the border police, was called in and a meeting was set up for a later date to determine the details of a semi-legal arrangement. The interesting aspect of this discussion with Spychalski was, according to Zuckerman, Spychalski's request to determine the border-crossing on the Czech border, and not at Stettin. The reason he gave was that there were Soviet officials at Stettin and this might get the Poles into trouble.

Following the meeting with Spychalski, a deputy of Zuckerman (Stepan Grayek, also a survivor of the Warsaw ghetto rebellion) met with the Russo-Polish general, and they determined the area where the crossing should be made. In the meantime Zuckerman had called a meeting of the Brichah commanders at his home in Warsaw, and there the details were discussed. It was decided that the person who should arrange the details with the Poles should be the Palestinian *shaliah* Alexander. Alexander appeared before the Poles as a member of the Jewish United Workers' Party, not as a representative of the Brichah. This was the name under which the Poale Zion Party was known in Poland, and the choice of name was felicitous because of its similarity to the United Workers' Party, which was the official name of the Polish Communist Party. The result was that many simple Polish officials thought that Alexander was a member of the official hierarchy, and he of course did nothing to dispel that illusion.

His first task was to see to the practical arrangements for opening the border, and this had to be done with the U.B. (security police) and the border guards. He first went to Czerwinski. Czerwinski arranged for two majors to be detailed to accompany him to the frontier to choose the actual spot for the crossings. The task was to find a crossing that would be convenient geographically and at the same time be remote enough to prevent the British from finding out about it. The two officers, a U.B. man and Alexander then went to the border in Alexander's car. At Breslau (Wroclaw)

they were assured that the regional commander would agree to any arrangements they might make; then they came down to Lower Silesia. At each point successively removed from central authority the identity of Alexander in the eyes of the local officials became more obscure.[23] In Warsaw he had to appear as the Jewish partner in the arrangement; but at Kladzko, where the officer in charge was the same Russo-Polish officer who had unofficially helped the Brichah before,[24] or in Kudowa, Alexander—with his fair hair, blond moustache and excellent Polish—could well have been some kind of security official himself. He appeared to be the most active and prestigious person in the group and did most of the talking; so naturally the superiority of his position was enhanced as the survey proceeded. In the end the crossing at Kudowa was approved, though the Brichah worked at Frydlant as well. It was further determined that the Jews should arrive at the border itself early in the morning, about 6 A.M., and the security people would see to it that nobody else appeared in the vicinity at that time. A simple procedure was devised for customs checking and identification. All the refugees had to have a slip of paper marked with Alexander's facsimile stamp. Both sides agreed that good care should be taken not to allow non-Jewish Poles, opponents of the regime, to cross and that no gold or foreign money should be taken out of the country.

Alexander was at that time the deputy of Ben Zvi as the Brichah's commander in Poland, but in fact it was he who organized the movement. Ben Zvi dealt largely with money matters and was therefore mainly in Warsaw or Lodz; he visited the border only on occasion after the original accommodation had been arrived at. His local deputies now took over; but before they did, Alexander crossed the border into Nachod and saw for himself the extent to which Nachod was capable of handling a large inflow. This must have been during the last few days of July, because the Czech Brichah people there assured him that they were quite capable of handling the influx and did not expect any trouble from the Czech government.[25]

According to Jacobson,[26] the opening of the Polish border occurred on July 30. The outflow of Jews in August and

September was henceforth conducted on a semilegal basis by the Poles.

The Polish agreement, in contradistinction to the Czech one, was a very peculiar affair indeed. It appears that the Czech government was not aware, as late as July 26, of the readiness of the Poles to let the Jews out.[27] The two governments were therefore acting simultaneously but quite independently of each other. Indeed, given the Czech dislike of Poland, their commiseration with the victims of Polish terrorism could not have been very much to the Poles' liking. But the most interesting part is the secrecy with which the Poles wished to surround the whole affair—secrecy not only as far as the British were concerned but even their own Foreign Office. In other words, the security organs and the Foreign Office, both directed by Communists, were working at cross purposes. Again, as in the Czech case, the motives must be a matter of conjecture. But the involvement of a Russian officer such as Czerwinski could not have been achieved without the knowledge and approval of the Russians. The U.B. in 1946 also could hardly have acted without at least the tacit approval of their Russian mentors. All this seems to point to a definite Russian policy: they would not encourage the Jews to move out, but neither would they do anything drastic to prevent the exodus. Behind this there was the consideration that the Eastern states were only beginning to build their new regimes and could not as yet be considered as socialist countries. It was therefore possible to admit that certain national problems had not been solved there, and the possibility of emigration, especially if it was connected with a national movement with anti-imperialist overtones in the Middle East, could be admitted as well. This of course did not apply to the Jews of the Soviet Union itself. There it was axiomatic to declare that the country was socialist, and therefore no national problems existed and that there was no reason why Jews or anyone else should leave because the Jewish problem had been solved. It was this mixture of ideological and political motivation that seems to have been behind the Soviet policy toward the Brichah. At the same time, the admission by any Communist regime that it was too weak to protect its citizens or

that a minority under its rule had no choice but to leave the country was also an impossibility. The solution was a compromise: the agreement with Zuckerman was a purely verbal one; absolutely nothing was written down and indeed great care was taken by all the officials involved that no tangible evidence should exist of their involvement in the whole affair.

The practical problem facing the Brichah was how to organize the exodus in the most efficient way. In order to enable it do so, Zuckerman came before the Central Committee of the Jews in Poland, with its Communist and Bundist majority, and demanded that the official Jewish committees, largely run by the two anti-Zionist groups, be advised to give help to those leaving the country. This open and brazen avowal of the desire to leave brought a tremendous verbal onslaught against the Zionists. The Jewish Communists did not know that their government had agreed to the exodus, but after a first very stormy meeting they inquired and were told of the new situation. Disciplined Communists that they were, they took a very quiet and passive line at the second meeting of the Central Committee, and only the Bundists were left to voice their disagreement. In the end the committee decided, with a heavy heart, to provide some measure of assistance to those who were leaving. More important, it obtained the full assistance of the JDC in Poland from which it received two trucks and large amounts of extra clothing and food.[28]

The security problem was another aspect which the Brichah took seriously. Zuckerman was very much opposed to the practice of Brichah men's bribing local Polish soldiers in order to facilitate the transit. Now he had achieved an agreement that made this particular way of getting people out of the country unnecessary—or so he thought. But it appears that the Brichah people could not always count on the official support of the U.B.; they had to deal with local officials, and these were likely to put obstacles in the way of the fleeing Jews. Warsaw was far away, and the official was right there. What could one do? The necessity for bribing venal officials existed even after the agreement with the government. But on the problem of non-Jewish Poles' trying to

smuggle themselves out along with Jews there was no disagreement. The Brichah was very eager to avoid any breach of the agreement on this point, and when they did discover the occasional Pole they handed him over to the police. Even before Kielce, this had been a problem, and on one occasion the Brichah had killed a German S.S. man who had posed as a Jew and tried to cross the frontier out of Poland.[29] Now the vigilance sharpened considerably and the Poles acknowledged the efficiency of the Brichah in this matter. On the other hand, it was impossible to eliminate completely the work of the private operators, and we find echoes of their operations even on the well-organized Silesian border; the pressure to leave Poland was simply too great and the facilities of the Brichah did not satisfy everyone.

Practically speaking, Walbrzych and Kladzko could accommodate some 3,500 or 4,000 people at a time, when all the possibilities were utilized. From these "stores," or assembly places, trucks came to fetch the Jews for the trip to Kudowa or Frydlant. At Kudowa the Jews sometimes spent the night and rose very early in the morning in order to cross the border at the appointed time. An issue of clothes was usually handed out before the crossing, and people were required to hand over documents, cigarettes and the like to the Brichah representatives. Such items often constituted the last possessions of the refugees, as they had to sell all their belongings before leaving the country and invest the money in some small but valuable articles. It was forbidden to take out money, whether Polish or foreign, and the Brichah people insisted that the Polish regulations on this point should be strictly observed. Most refugees complied; some few did not, and these were occasionally caught by the Polish guards (the Czechs were not interested in money; but they were very strict with regard to cigarettes). The whole process was based on a certain amount of mutual trust because there was very little time for customs examinations. By about 10 to 10:30 A.M. the last Jews had to be passed on to the other side. It was very difficult—in fact, impossible—to have proper customs control of thousands of people at a little post manned by a couple of customs officers. There was, however, little need for customs examinations in any case.

The amount of property the Jews had hardly warranted a control at all.

From Kudowa the Jews moved on to Nachod, again by truck, and were then accommodated there for a few hours until the trains took them further on.[30]

A second border point operated out of Wałbrzych and Frydlant (Friedland) into Broumov on the Czech side of the border. There trains brought the refugees to a distance of about one mile from the border. Luggage, children, women and old people were brought to the border post by cart, and the rest went on foot. The arrangement was that the people would arrive in the evening, pass the Polish inspection and then stay at the border post overnight. Next morning they would pass on to the Czech side for customs and then be brought by tractor to Broumov, which was about six miles away. The number that passed through Wałbrzych was smaller than that via Kudowa, but the arrangements were essentially the same. At Frydlant, too, only two soldiers and one officer supervised the transit, and the customs checking was perfunctory.[31]

A serious problem arose with the attempted flight of many soldiers and officers from the Polish, or even the Russian, army or police forces. On principle, the Brichah refused to deal with these cases because of the agreement with the Polish authorities. Of course, Brichah had no way of knowing the identities of those who registered with it beyond certain superficial indications. It therefore happened that individuals went with groups crossing the border whom Brichah would have refused to take had their true identities been known.

There were of course troubles. Not all Polish officers at the border were sympathetic. The reason for such attitudes was not far to seek: there was no doubt at all during those summer months that it was the illegal Brichah organization that was actually in control of the border, and quite naturally some of the officers in charge did not like it at all. At Frydlant, Brichah men would prepare a small fuel tank each morning for the Czech tractor that brought the refugees to Broumov. One morning, the fuel tank was found to have been emptied at night—it was found later that this had been

done by the Polish officer in charge. No fuel was to be had on the Czech side, and the refugees, many of whom simply could not walk the six miles to Broumov, were sitting with their bundles on Czech territory and were getting nervous. The Brichah man then suggested that the Czech police officer go to Polish Frydlant on his motorcycle to get fuel. This was against regulations, because a Czech officer had no business in Poland without a permit. The Czech then asked the Brichah man to come with him in case of trouble—an indication of the status of the Brichah at that time.

At Frydlant the two men on the motorcycle happened, by pure accident, to run into a group of high Polish officers who were checking the arrangements at the border. The Brichah man's explanations were unsatisfactory, and the border was immediately closed. It took a great deal of talking and apologizing to open it again. More serious was the mood among the refugee group. A Brichah man had informed them that they would have to go back to Frydlant. An argument ensued, blows were exchanged and a nervous Brichah man took out his gun and fired in the air. Just at that critical moment the Brichah commander at Frydlant arrived and managed to calm both the refugees and the Brichah man. The fuel was obtained, and the refugees moved on.[32]

At Nachod, the technique was quite simple; every transport had to go through a reception center when it arrived from the Kudowa border about 10 A.M., and in the afternoon a train would be ready to take about 1,000 people to Bratislava. The sick were cared for and sometimes remained behind for treatment. Everyone was given food, information was handed out and personal problems that arose in this mass of humanity were attended to. The people who worked at the actual center were largely JDC people, mostly Americans who had been sent over to do social welfare work. They adapted, it seems, exceedingly well to the hectic conditions of Nachod and Broumov. At Nachod, an inadequate barracks was supplemented by another barracks paid for by the JDC, and there those refugees who could not be accommodated in the daily trains of 1,000 to Bratislava were lodged overnight. This happened quite often in August;

the total registered for Nachod and Broumov during that month, according to the JDC statistics, came to 30,568.[33] On one hectic day in August 3,800 people came,[34] and on one occasion the Broumov camp had to accommodate 2,600 people for ten days. The relationship between the JDC and the Brichah workers was cordial,[35] and in fact JDC vehicles were often used by Brichah workers to get the people from the border into the camps. During the month of August, too, a special orthodox group, the Lubavicher Hassidim, came along, and the workers were all impressed by the good humor and discipline they showed. The Lubavicher are a sect of the ultra-orthodox followers of the rabbis of the Shneerson family, whose original home was Lubavich in the Soviet Union. Some 3,000 people belonging to the group managed to leave Russia in 1946, led by one of their rabbis. In line with their philosophy of religion and life they shunned no work and adapted themselves to any situation. They passed the Czech border in groups of 150 to 300 people, and created a great impression on the Brichah workers, most of whom were nonbelievers. The stories told about them by the workers[36] relate mainly to their behavior when faced with shortage of food (they would not touch their food until every one of the 800 refugees then in Nachod had received his share) and to the fortitude with which they bore the tragedy of the only death at Broumov when a Czech policeman accidentally fired into a crowd of people and killed the wife of a Lubavicher hassid.

One of the problems in Nachod was the tendency of many of the refugees to rebel against the restriction forbidding them to leave the organized groups throughout their stay in the country. Some would wander off on their own in Nachod or even try to "escape" into Prague, mostly in connection with personal arrangements. And while it is true that the number of people who tried to do this was relatively small, they presented a problem out of all proportion to their numbers. Brichah workers in Nachod had to chase after them in the streets of the little town or try to prevent them from boarding trains going to Prague. In the capital itself, their arrival complicated contacts with the Czech Repatriation Office, though the officials there, led by a Zionist,

Dr. Gordon, were friendly enough. The procedure as far as the central Prague Brichah office was concerned consisted of receiving the number of arrivals at Nachod by telephone and then making out lists of names—any names—that would fit the number reported. A copy of these lists would then be sent to the Repatriation Office; another copy would be used to document the number of people on the train out of Nachod and a third would be shown the Czech border officials on the way out of the country. A somewhat humorous sidelight to this was the fact that the lists were typed by a non-Jewish secretary who of course knew very well—as did all the officials concerned—that the lists and the real people had absolutely nothing in common.[37]

In Prague, in the meantime, the Brichah workers—Landau, Friedman and others—together with Jacobson, were working on the problem of those refugees who somehow managed to stay behind in the city. It must not be forgotten that small numbers of people were sent all the time via Prague to As on the Czech-German border, and others had some temporary or less temporary business in Prague. Moreover, there would be the transports sent by separatist groups who either did not cooperate with the Brichah or only pretended to do so. Chief among these was the orthodox Agudat Yisrael, which at that time still had reservations about the Zionist way of looking at things, and which often directed their charges to look for an overseas haven other than Palestine. The Brichah, while definitely Palestine-oriented, never asked questions as to the aim of any Jew escaping from Eastern Europe. Everyone had to be helped, and when Agudat Yisrael transports arrived in Prague, as they often did, with inadequate documents and loud demands to be helped, whether by the JDC or by the Brichah, they were a burden to the Brichah and Jacobson, but one they simply could not escape. As far as the Brichah was concerned, there was in its attitude to these people a definite element of calculated policy. If these orthodox people from Poland aroused too much attention and became a problem for the Czech police, they might make the situation dangerous for the Brichah as such. They had to be removed from Czechoslovakia as quickly as possible. This

of course was not done by the Brichah, which had no means of obtaining legal documents—the JDC had to step in and try to obtain visas, and it seems that only a small proportion of the Prague refugees utilized the Brichah procedures. The work of helping these people was done under JDC auspices; all the money came from the JDC, and Jacobson was the official interpreter of Jewish situations to all authorities concerned. After much difficulty, Jacobson succeeded in obtaining two camps near Prague, at Hloubetin and Dablice, for his Orthodox charges. But it was still necessary to maintain a ramshackle hostel in the heart of the city to put up a number of rabbis at some considerable expense in small hotels.

The problem of the Orthodox refugees in Prague was dramatized by the arrival in Prague on August 28 of 488 Polish orphans and 101 members of an educational staff under the leadership of the Palestinian Chief Rabbi Yitzhak Halevi Herzog.[38] Herzog had gone to Europe in May 1946, mainly to remove Jewish orphans from convents, monasteries and private Catholic homes in France and Belgium who had been converted, or were in danger of being converted, by priests and nuns who had no qualms about saving the children's souls for Catholicism after saving their bodies from destruction at the hands of the Nazis. In France, Herzog had an interview with Minister Georges Bidault on July 26,[39] and seems to have understood that the French government had promised him visas for 500 souls from Poland: 250 children and 250 Talmudic scholars. He did receive $25,000 from the JDC and some vague promises from English Orthodox bodies for a plan to bring these children and youths out of Poland. A conference in Prague yielded an agreement by the Czechs (Herzog says he saw Gottwald himself on this problem) to grant a stay of six weeks to the group. The children for the transport were chosen by Jewish religious leaders in Poland, and Herzog himself brought them out of Katowice into Czechoslovakia with the full permission of the Poles.

Upon arrival, the children were thrown on the JDC for supplies. "Although Rabbi Herzog had informed us," writes Jacobson, "that everything had been arranged with the

Czech authorities and with UNRRA to provide all that was necessary for the children, this did not prove to be the case."[40] The children arrived in Prague in a pitiful state; members of the Brichah team were assigned to supervise the distribution of food, shoes and other necessities. The visas that the rabbi had thought had been promised him were not forthcoming, and on September 24 the Czechs declared that the children had to move on; they had obtained transit visas on the strength of an alleged French promise, which now had to be implemented. The religious Vaad Hatzalah (Rescue Committee), run by rabbis in France and Belgium and an offshoot of an American organization, promised to look after the children in France and said that visas would be available for the children to go to Belgium. On September 30 it became clear that there were no Belgian visas (the JDC had undertaken to look after the 250 destined for Belgium). In the end the French granted the necessary visas and the children arrived at Strasbourg. Nothing had been prepared against their coming, and some 350 were sent to a hostel at Aix-les-Bains, while an abandoned chateau near Strasbourg was found for most of the others.[41]

In addition to the Orthodox element, there were Jewish refugees in Prague who were mainly from Hungary and Rumania and who had somehow managed on their own to leave their countries of origin. These presented another difficult problem, as many of them had no funds at all and had to be accommodated at the camps; others did have visas to France but no transportation money, though they had hoped that the Vaad Hatzalah representatives would care for them. These had to be shipped out of the country as quickly as possible. Prague, therefore, was a great headache for both the Brichah and the JDC, but it involved only a very small minority passing through Czechoslovakia in the summer of 1946. The great exodus going through never touched Prague at all; it went directly to Bratislava, was accommodated there at the famous Hotel Jelen and then brought by train to the wooden bridge across the Danube at Devinska Nova Ves. Thirty-six hours after crossing the Czech border at Nachod or Broumov, the refugees would find themselves crossing

the Slovak border into the hamlet of Marchegg in Austria. There they would board a train or, later, a bus or a tram to reach Vienna and the Rothschild hospital.

The understanding with the Poles concerning Jews leaving Polish territory presumed that there would be no attempts to cross the border illegally once the Polish-Czech border was open. Moreover, General Spychalski in his talk with Zuckerman had emphasized the point that it would not be desirable for Poland to have Jews move via Stettin, as they would have to cross Russian-controlled territory and this might cause complications.

The Brichah never had any intentions of relying on the Polish government in order to move Jews out from Poland. Its whole existence up to the Kielce affair was proof of its conviction that until an open and general exodus was freely allowed it would see to it that whenever Jews wanted to leave they could do so. There was therefore no thought of disbanding the small "points" that existed along the Carpathian mountain range on the border between Poland and Slovakia, and there was certainly no let-up in the Brichah work in the Stettin area. In fact, as we have seen, a new Brichah team had moved in at the end of May, and the new commanders had immediately entered the fray against the smugglers in order to open the way by truck through about 120 miles of road to Berlin.

The team was probably the largest of any Brichah group on the Polish frontier. There were fourteen members—eleven men and three women. The commander between May and July 1946 was Yakov Erner ("Tulek"), a small, thickset man of great personal integrity, much beloved by his comrades for his kindliness and friendliness. He was a hard worker and quite efficient, but it seems that by July a different kind of commander was needed. After a short period of about four weeks when a Palestinian soldier served as commander, Mordechai Mittelman took over. A big, athletic man with broad shoulders and a perpetual scowl on his face, he had been active in student Zionist circles in Poland in his youth and had spent years in Soviet prisons for Zionist activities. He was well versed in the art of con-

spiracy, and his ability to make decisions quickly and effectively was essential for operating in a difficult place such as Stettin. Mittelman was a difficult person, but the situation in which he worked was not simple either; the man obviously fitted the task. Erner had welded the workers together into an efficient team, and Mittelman continued in the same tradition. The customary political backbiting between adherents of different Zionist factions had no place in Stettin; members of all the groups cooperated to guide out of Poland as many Jews as possible.

At the end of June an organization by the name of PUR began operating in Poland. PUR was the governmental repatriation commission, charged with the job of expelling the Germans out of the territories annexed by Poland after the Potsdam agreement. An important branch of PUR was located in Stettin, and large transports of Germans began leaving the town through the Russian zone into Lübeck in the British zone. Most of these went by rail, but a few also went by boat. It was immediately apparent to the Brichah that here was a great opportunity to send Jews out of the country with as few complications as possible. Stettin began to be resettled by Poles, and the government directed a large number of Jewish repatriants from the Soviet Union into the town. By early July some 20,000 Jews had been brought into Stettin, and the JDC in Poland, under William Bein, an American citizen, had to throw in large amounts of supplies in order to keep alive the thousands of people who had been put into a half-destroyed and empty town with no industry or commerce to speak of. However, the very existence of a relatively large Jewish community, complete with its Communist-dominated local Jewish committee, Jewish club and social services, provided a useful background for Mordechai Mittelman, Yakov Erner and other Brichah members. A number of abandoned houses were designated as temporary homes for groups in transit, and a final assembly point was selected—this was a house whose front had been destroyed by a bomb but whose rear part had remained whole. The fact that the third and fourth stories of the building were occupied could not readily be seen from the street. Here the prospective emigrants were held incommunicado for a night

before their departure. To an ever-increasing degree the departure procedure now involved PUR. First, a forged letter was fabricated[42] which purported to come from the mayor of one of the suburbs of Warsaw; it declared that a number of German citizens of Jewish descent wished to be repatriated to Germany. Then a couple of Brichah men went to the regional and local representatives of PUR in Stettin and explained to them, in the name of the Jewish committee (which, of course, was unaware of what was going on), that a large number of German Jewish citizens, or stateless persons who had resided in Germany before the war and had left all their property there, were desirous of returning to Germany where they hoped to retrieve property and positions which had been usurped by the Nazis. Therefore, they said, these persons should not only be allowed to utilize the PUR facilities but also to receive priority in transportation. In addition, the Brichah succeeded in having three members of its staff infiltrate the local PUR authority; one of these who belonged to the Brichah command in Stettin became deputy manager of the PUR. The way this was done was by getting in touch with two young Polish officers working with PUR who turned out to be Jews; Alexander himself came to Stettin to talk to them and they became part of the Brichah structure in the town. Another important contact was a high U.B. officer, a Pole, who shielded the refugees from harm, whether at the hands of Russians or Poles or Germans.[43]

At first the numbers sent via PUR were small, not more than 100 to 200 people on trains that carried 1,500 Germans to western Germany. The Jews were kept separately inside the PUR camp until the train came, and then they usually managed to obtain a separate carriage or compartments. An attempt was made to have at least one German-speaking Jew in the transport who would then become the representative of the whole group. The others would be assigned new names, personal life histories and names of towns in Germany where they purportedly came from. They even had instructions on what to say in case of a slip-up, such as did happen occasionally, especially after they arrived in Lübeck. They were to say that they had received the

forged documents in Lodz and to describe exactly the man who gave them the papers. There would, of course, be no resemblance whatsoever between the description and the Brichah workers in Lodz.[44]

These arrangements withstood the acid test of a grave incident in August, when a central PUR commission came to Stettin on the very day that a Polish PUR worker recognized one of the "German" Jews as his neighbor from a Polish town. The whole group of 500 was detained, and ten leaders and the confiscated documents were flown to Warsaw for a thorough checking. A participant relates how "the *starosta* [mayor—the man who supposedly issued the documents in Warsaw] carefully examined the document, twirled his long moustache and finally answered with great confidence: 'the stamp is mine, the signature is mine, the paper comes from my stationery, only the serial number does not fit.' To which the security officer answered, 'Mr. Starosta, should we keep 500 Jews under arrest because of a clerical error in your office?' 'Of course not,' said the Starosta."[45] As time went on, the Brichah people became bolder. Soon the numbers grew, and at one time 1,200 Jews were sent on a train that was supposed to carry 1,500 Germans out of Poland.

These proceedings did not pass unnoticed in the British sector of Germany where the Jews arrived from Stettin. In order to check upon the eligibility of the repatriants, the British obtained the right to send a captain and a sergeant to Stettin. This of course stymied the operation considerably, and though our sources are mainly reminiscences which must be approached very critically, at least one of the stories with a ring of authenticity would indicate that the British did not succeed completely in blocking the PUR for the Brichah. One Sunday, says the commander of the Stettin Brichah at the time,[46] the Brichah decided to send 1,200 people, the largest group ever to be sent through PUR. On Saturday evening a party was thrown by the Jewish Committee at a large café in town. Polish artists from the State Theater and, of course, the English members of the PUR team were invited. Dancing and entertainment lasted far into the night; the Brichah commander left the party quietly

and went to his prepared group of infiltrees. At 6 A.M. they were all at PUR to be checked and processed, and the train came shortly afterward. The Polish commander waited for his British colleague until 7 A.M., when he received a telephone call from the stationmaster who said he could hold the train no longer. The commander agreed to send the train off (the phone call had come from a Brichah man who spoke in the name of the absent railwayman). At noon the British captain appeared, apologizing profusely, and received a report saying that the transport had gone off and that everything was in perfect order. All concerned were pleased with the outcome.

The PUR transports were mostly sent by rail straight into the British zone. There the Jewish refugees would go to Hannover or to Bergen-Belsen, where Brichah points would send them on by train into the American zone of Germany. This method of transfer was stopped in the autumn of 1946, when the British discontinued accepting PUR trains. The Brichah then tried to send Jews via PUR into the Russian zone and from there by train into the French zone, but this proved impossible and by October 1946 the whole PUR operation ceased, as far as the Brichah was concerned.

In the meantime, the old truck route was renewed and additional sea routes were operated out of Stettin; all these passed Berlin and therefore were affected by what was happening in that city. The major problem of transportation concerned the trucks; these had formerly been Russian or Polish Army vehicles whose drivers had been bribed to take refugees on their empty runs into Berlin (on the way back they would bring equipment and goods that the Russian forces were dismantling and taking out of defeated Germany). This had been proved unsatisfactory because cases had multiplied where the drivers handed over the refugees to the Russian police, and kept the bribe. Brichah therefore bought their own trucks in Poland and used Brichah drivers for them, under a variety of pretexts. This was very expensive, however, and there was of course always the risk that trucks that were caught would be confiscated by the Soviets. In Berlin, trucks were much cheaper, and so Brichah began using Berlin vehicles, for which the Berlin Brichah paid

out of funds that were at least partly collected locally (Stettin was accused of not repaying the full amount to the Berlin group—a point which was hotly contested between the Polish-controlled Stettiners and the Berlin team which was under Palestinian command). Truck transport under these conditions began to operate again on July 20, after a long pause caused by arrests and interference on the part of the Russians. The Russians seemed to ignore the operation, although they must have been fully aware of what was going on. Soon the Schlachtensee DP camp in the U.S. sector of the city was overcrowded; it contained 5,000 people instead of the 3,000 for whom it had been intended. The Americans were again faced with the choice of either stopping the infiltration by force or opening another camp. Again, as in so many instances prior and subsequent to this situation, they chose to open a new camp—at Tempelhof. This was done on August 15, and within two weeks 4,000 more Jews came into the American sector, filling Tempelhof to capacity and beyond. In late August and early September, despite UNRRA efforts to move some of the Jews, the situation was very difficult in both camps. Nevertheless, Yitzhak Ram ("Peretz"), the Brichah commander, continued pouring in refugees from Stettin until September 15, when an incident occurred which to all intents and purposes ended the Stettin-Berlin movement.

On that date three trucks with refugees were stopped by the Russians and all the people were arrested. After a great deal of argument the drivers, the trucks and the refugees were set free. The Brichah guides, who by that time were well known to the Russian police, were kept behind in jail. Again, this mishap was due to some Jewish smugglers who had been caught the same day shipping goods through to Berlin. The Russians at first identified the Brichah guides as smugglers, but in the course of the interrogation the true character of the Brichah work was revealed, and the three guides were sent on a very long journey eastward[47] from which they did not return for many years. The Russians tried to catch the whole of the Brichah command by freeing Jewish prisoners on condition that they find out who the Brichah commanders were. Two Jews they tried to use as

informers came to the Brichah post in Berlin and reported what the Russians wanted, whereupon they were immediately transferred to the U.S. zone and into safety. Interventions on the part of influential Jewish personalities were of no avail either—the Russians apparently became even more suspicious and the Brichah work became only a trickle, dragging on desultorily through October, until in early November the Polish command decided that the operation was too costly and almost all work ceased.[48]

On a small scale, Brichah attempted a number of other subterfuges to get Jews out of Poland. One of these was the transport by boat. At the end of July a boatload of children was sent to the small port of Ueckermünde, and from there the train took them to Berlin. One more boat was sent in this way, and then increased Russian control over the port made the route impossible. Two more boats were sent to another port, Anklam, also in eastern Germany, from which one group went via the Oder Canal to Berlin and the other by train. This seemed to be a more promising route, but the Polish Brichah command declared the operation to be too costly for the reduced means of the Brichah. Also, at the end of August, another incident had occurred which was typical of the hazards of the Stettin operations. Yitzhak Ram and Yosef Nissenbaum, both from the Berlin Brichah, decided to try another boat route and entered into negotiations with some Russian sailors on one of the river boats. After reaching an agreement with them, they took the boat ride to Berlin together with ten refugees, mainly teachers, from Stettin. Before they reached German territory, the Russian sailors said they needed fuel and asked the passengers to wait for them on shore because they could not ask for fuel with Jewish refugees on board. Nissenbaum and two other Brichah men stayed on board. As they were moving away from the shore, three armed Russians who had hidden themselves in the engine room came up and forced the three men at gunpoint into the Oder. When the three hit the water, the Russians opened fire on them and Nissenbaum was killed.

Meanwhile, in Berlin, the local DP committee was doing yeoman service in handling the newcomers, especially the

1,200 or so children who had come partly by boat and partly by truck in August and September. The transfer to the British zone via Heiligenstadt had stopped in June, and Fishbein, the head of the UNRRA camp, was promising to get the Jews out but was meeting tremendous obstacles in the form of British reluctance to have these Jews come via their zone. Most of the additional burden fell on the shoulders of Eli Rock and his co-workers of the JDC, and Rabbi Mike Abramowitz, the American chaplain. In the end, UNRRA received American permission to transfer large numbers of Jews straight into the U.S. zone rather than into the British area. The move started in late August, and by November UNRRA had shipped 8,000 people in trucks, as well as two special transports: one taking 2,000 children (some were orphans and some were accompanied by parents); and the other a special group of 300 sick persons. A few hundred youngsters from the youth movements went illegally via Schoeningen on the border of the British zone. In all, considerably more than 10,000 people left Berlin between August and November. Nevertheless, the influx was greater still: during the same period of time the Brichah estimated the numbers of those reaching the city from Stettin at 16,000, so that at the end of November there were still 7,000 Jews in the Berlin camps at Wittenau in the French zone, and at Schlachtensee and Tempelhof. An additional number of DPs had dispersed in the city itself.[49]

We have already seen that the people who came to Berlin were of a different kind from the ones who crossed the Czech border further south with Polish connivance. A proportion of them were brought in by smugglers, and many others were not organized in any way but were simply individuals who were trying to get out of Poland. A prominent worker for UNRRA observed even at the Czech-Polish border that not many of the refugees "gave any special preference for Palestine as their final destination." They wanted to go to the U.S. zone mainly because they hoped from there to be able to reach some overseas country, preferably the United States or Britain. A preference for Palestine existed only because other avenues of exit from Europe seemed to be closed. "An offer of a British or American visa would

very quickly and painlessly have cancelled those preferences."[50] Brichah people complained of the large number of unsavory characters among the people they were bringing in, and it was mainly these who refused to move on and stayed behind in the city to live on the black market. But it must be remembered that the reluctance to move out of Berlin which became more and more marked as the summer progressed was also due to the negative reports the refugees were receiving by mail from friends and relatives in the overcrowded camps of the American sector in Germany.

8. *Diplomatic Interludes*

In 1946 Rabbi Philip S. Bernstein was the spiritual head of a large congregation in Rochester, New York. During the war he had been responsible for the program of sending Jewish chaplains to the U.S. Armed Forces and had acquired experience in dealing with things military. He was a stocky man, slow-spoken, calm and dignified, and he was impressively erudite. When Judge Simon H. Rifkind retired from his post as adviser on Jewish affairs to the U.S. Theater Commander in Europe in April 1946, the five major American Jewish organizations, which had asked Judge Rifkind to take on the job, now offered the vacant post to Rabbi Bernstein. The rabbi took four months' leave of absence from his congregation (he stayed over a year, as it turned out) and departed for Germany in May. The first problem that confronted him was the changing attitude of the American Army in Germany to the Jewish refugees. As we have seen before, while the higher commanders were friendly and in many ways still affected by what had happened during the war, this could not be said of the officers on the lower levels and of the men, most of whom by the spring of 1946 were

people who had seen nothing of the war. There was, as Rabbi Bernstein put it, "a great deal of resentment and irritation with regard to the displaced persons. They were felt to be trouble makers, they were regarded as radicals, they were irritating the Germans, they were making the task of the U.S. armed forces much more difficult and the word 'Zionist' was anathema to them, they did not quite understand what it meant. They associated it with communism." One of the first actions that the new adviser took was to give a lecture to top army brass at the home of General Clarence Huebner, who became the chief of staff to the theater commander General McNarney.[1] Similar attempts to persuade the American military were made by other Jewish personalities on different levels; however successful these lectures and essays in persuasion were, it is hardly likely that they changed the ideas and prejudices of those at whom they were directed. But the problem of relations between the military and the Jews was quickly overshadowed by another question which became more and more pressing as the summer approached: the problem of infiltration into the U.S. zone from the East.

The attitude of the Army to infiltration was outwardly tolerant but by no means friendly. Housing was very limited in Germany because of the destruction by bombing. The Army did not like the idea of Jewish DPs coming in from the East and taking up the housing. "In fact, if anything they wanted the Germans to have more housing rather than less."[2] The generally mistrustful attitude created the danger that the increasing influx would be made extremely unwelcome. The new troublemakers coming from the East were even worse than those that were already in Germany. They were a motley crowd, constantly squabbling among themselves, bitter and disillusioned after years of suffering, disease and starvation in Soviet Russia, disorganized and rather wild—hardly an appealing sight to the military eye. Compared with the docile, disciplined Germans they looked even worse.

This situation was worsened by the attitude of UNRRA in Germany, still under the command of Sir Frederick Morgan. It seems that General Morgan, after the scandal in

January, was understandably not too friendly toward the Jewish infiltrees. In addition, it seems fairly obvious that he was politically out of sympathy with the Zionist ideals that inspired the politically conscious among the migrants, and he knew that Germany was considered by a majority of them as a stepping stone to Palestine—which, of course, ran counter to Britain's policy.[3] There was an unofficial oral understanding that if the rate of infiltration did not exceed 5,000 monthly, the Army would make no difficulties. Rabbi Bernstein, who apparently thought that this arrangement was a top secret of the U.S. Army, reaffirmed the understanding in great confidence to Haim Yahil, the head of the official Jewish Agency mission in Germany, who had arrived there in November 1945.[4] In June the Brichah increased its flow into Germany, and even without the Kielce pogrom it was clear that a larger number of people would be coming. May and June were the months after the publication of the Anglo-American Commission of Inquiry's report which came out in favor of an immigration of 100,000 into Palestine. Not even the greatest pessimists thought that Britain would renege completely on her promise to implement a unanimous report. As a result, both the Jewish Agency people in Germany and the Jews in Poland thought that at least a significant emigration from Germany to Palestine would be likely. This combination of pressure from Poland and opportunity for emigration made it vital that the Americans should keep their zone open for the infiltrees, who undoubtedly would come in larger numbers than the 5,000 monthly. There was apparently a fear on Yahil's part that the Americans might make the emigration of the 100,000 conditional on the stoppage of illegal infiltration. In order to forestall such a policy, he thought that maximum pressure should be brought to bear on the Americans to allow larger numbers to enter their zone. Here again, as in so many instances throughout this story, the political and humanitarian considerations coincided: Yahil knew very well that if he did not succeed the Jews would come anyway, because nobody, including the Zionists themselves, could stop them, and the only result of closing the borders would be increased suffering and bitterness. The

solution to the problem of the Jewish DPs was necessarily political, and he was determined to do everything in his power to facilitate Jewish emigration to Palestine which, in the absence of any other solution, was the only way out. The danger of the U.S. Army's changing its policy of the open door to Germany was real; as Yahil said, the Jews would have "to increase [their] pressure in order to renew the Eisenhower policy."[5] He explained to his colleagues that everything had to be done to avoid a clash with the Americans, but not at the price of stopping the movement across Europe. About the middle of June Rabbi Bernstein visited Berlin, and there he was shown groups of children who had come across from Poland. Shaken by that experience, Bernstein asked Yahil to come to Frankfurt and estimate the size of the migration problem. Yahil did so and concluded that probably some 200,000 Jews would leave their countries if conditions ripened; 40,000 were to be expected in the U.S. zone within the next three months—almost three times the 5,000-a-month figure which had been accepted until then by the military. Bernstein undertook to present the problem to the Army, and on June 26 he came back and said that General McNarney had agreed to the figure mentioned.[6]

All this of course happened before the Kielce pogrom on July 4 made all these arrangements obsolete. It appears that a meeting of Brichah leaders, including representatives from Eastern Europe, took place in Germany immediately following Kielce and that they decided on a plan to take 80,000 to 100,000 people out of Poland.[7] Yahil thereupon went to Frankfurt again to see Rabbi Bernstein and tell him that the figures would have to be revised upward. The Rabbi was now in a very awkward situation. He was an American citizen and held a courtesy rank in the Army. It was his duty to interpret the Army's policies to the DPs and their representatives and to advise the Army on Jewish matters. But he was certainly not a representative of Jewish interests or organizations in Europe in the U.S. Armed Forces, and as an American citizen his first duty was loyalty to Army policies. He had warned General McNarney that if he felt that his conscience did not allow him to carry on in his post he would so inform the authorities and resign. However, though

walking a tightrope, Bernstein was an experienced man of the world who knew something of the psychology of men and was therefore no mean diplomat. During two hectic weeks in July he prepared his next moves in the face of mounting Army difficulties. The Army, one report said, on July 18, "is not able to cope with [the influx] on the basis of sheer food and shelter. I believe that in the next week or ten days, there will be some action taken and I am hopeful that Washington will be able to prevail upon military authorities in Berlin to keep the frontier open, as they sincerely seem to want to do."[8]

A few days after Kielce, Rabbi Bernstein was contacted by Henry Montor, a well-known American Jewish leader. Montor urged Bernstein to go to Poland immediately in order to see the situation for himself. Whether or not it was intended as such—as it probably was—this was a very good move as far as Bernstein's relations with the Army were concerned, because he would then have the full moral authority to ask the Army to revise his own previous figures if he returned from Poland with a clear personal conviction regarding the exodus from that country. Taking Rabbi Herbert Friedman with him and with the blessing of General McNarney, a visit to Poland was arranged. This took place between the 23rd and 30th of July.[9] He visited Lodz and Warsaw, and was impressed by the wave of anti-Semitism and the accompanying "incitement"[10] by the Catholic Church. He talked with various Jewish political leaders and visited the districts of Silesia, where the Jewish committees controlled by the Communists hoped to settle the Jews; he claims that he visited the "points at which Jews begin their emigration which brings them ultimately to the U.S. zone in Germany."[11] The number of Jews in Poland he estimated at 160,000, and he thought that some 100,000 would move out of Poland within a year and that some 60,000 of these would migrate between August and October. This latter estimate proved to be slightly exaggerated because Brichah figures indicate that some 44,000 people left Poland in those three months. Considerably less than 100,000 did in fact leave that country in the year starting August 1946, but on the other hand Bernstein did not take into account the flight

of Jews from other East European countries. Bernstein recommended that the U.S. Army be prepared to accept the Jewish refugees he expected to arrive in the West, and that facilities for absorbing them should be expanded also in the U.S. zone of Austria, in the French and British zones, and beyond that in Italy and France. Agencies such as the JDC and the Jewish Agency were expected to provide such aid as they could. In his general observations included in the report Rabbi Bernstein urged that no panic psychology "to save the Jews of Poland" should be encouraged, and in this he clearly took a line differing from that of the Zionists. A deliberate program to get all the Jews to leave Poland would be "unwise, impractical and dangerous," and among the reasons for this view he included two that are of special interest. One was that he found that not all the Jews wished to leave Poland. Specifically, Rabbi Treistman, one of the religious leaders in the country, told him that the Jews of Silesia were likely to stay (in fact, it seems that the ratio of those leaving Silesia was no different from that in other districts). Another reason was that "a public acceptance of emigration . . . might establish the precedent by which anti-Semites in other countries might initiate pogroms in order to bring about the emigration of all Jews"[12]—a fear that was typical of the leadership of American Jewry generally and which had been voiced by people close to the American Jewish Committee and the JDC during prewar years as well. The view expressed what was perhaps an unconscious feeling of insecurity even in enlightened countries where there was no imminent danger of anti-Jewish feeling.

The proposals of Rabbi Bernstein underwent a certain amount of discussion in military circles. At the same time, pressure by Jewish groups was put on the State Department, where General John H. Hilldring was the Assistant Secretary of State in charge of DP affairs and was thoroughly sympathetic to Jewish DPs. On July 31 he wrote a letter to the JDC which reflected the thinking of the State Department. He expressed the hope that the number of persecutees entering the U.S. zone would be kept at a minimum, but he added that the policy of the government was definitely to keep the door open to those who came. The letter was written, of

course, before Bernstein's report came in; but it is understandable that in the light of State Department policy the report's recommendations were accepted, though not without misgivings.[13] In those early August days a delegation of Jewish leaders went to Washington and was presented by Dean Acheson with a whole list of the tremendous difficulties the Jewish persecutees from Poland were causing the Army. There, as in Hilldring's letter, an appeal was made to the American Jewish leaders to do something to stop the infiltration.[14] The assumption of the Americans that the JDC or other American Jewish bodies could do anything to stop the movement was, of course, quite mistaken. It was true that the JDC was, by now, the main source of funds for the feeding and movement of fleeing Jews, but it had absolutely nothing to do with Brichah operations, nor could it influence its decisions. This fact was clearly stated in the JDC's answer to Hilldring's letter,[15] which said, among other things, that "the JDC has never participated in any organizing of this movement. However, it is our policy to assist wherever possible, to the fullest extent of our resources [those Jews who are in distress]." Dr. Schwartz, the JDC's European chairman, was quoted as saying "that nothing short of shooting could prevent this movement." The disclaimer of the JDC does not seem to have been believed by the U.S. Army, but we know that it was perfectly true.

Jewish pressure was by no means the only one that had to be taken into account in Germany. Britain, too, became active in that crucial summer of 1946. An attempt was made in the British press to present the refugees as hoodlums influenced by the Jewish "terrorists" who were fighting Britain in Palestine. They were depicted as being young and tough, and it was charged that "their racial arrogance and their ambitions are similar to those of the Nazi youth and for the same reasons."[16] Articles such as this were part of a general atmosphere in Britain, where most of the population supported Foreign Minister Bevin's anti-Zionist policies. In early August, British diplomacy became very active. Russian diplomats in Rumania were approached in an effort to stop illegal emigration from that country. Similar approaches were made to Czechoslovakia, Italy and, of course, Poland.[17]

The chief effort of the British was directed, however, toward their American allies, and in this on August 6 the British seemed to have attained a real success: despite his desire to avoid a head-on clash with the Jews and to follow State Department policy, General McNarney yielded to British pressure to the extent of making a public declaration to the effect that "all organized movement of Jewish refugees will be turned back from the American zones of Germany and Austria in the future." In order to make his point quite clear, he added that the "United States had never adopted a policy of the American zone being a station on the way to Palestine or any other place." The Russians, he noted, had promised to give their cooperation in preventing such movement.[18] Unorganized movement of genuine refugees would continue to be allowed as before. The British followed up on McNarney's declaration three days later; Air Marshal Sholto Douglas declared the British zone closed to all movement of Jewish refugees from the East.[19] British and even some American press organs justified these moves and took a stand that was clearly anti-Zionist. Don Cook in the New York *Herald Tribune* of August 8 explained that the Jewish DPs cost the American taxpayer $80 million yearly; the London *Times* declared on the 9th that it did not seem that the organizers of the Jewish movement were motivated by humanitarian motives and that therefore the British and American policies were entirely proper. And the *Daily Mail* enlarged on the fact that no German war criminals had been found among the Jewish refugees "yet."[20] It seems that McNarney thought his new policy would combine two elements that would make it successful: he would not stop "genuine" Jewish refugees from entering his zone—though he left it very unclear as to who would determine the "genuineness" of Jewish refugees—and yet he would put an end to the unceasing pressure of the large-scale and presumably organized movement from the East. At the same time he would please the British, though he did not go so far as Sholto Douglas who, not satisfied with the sealing of his zone, deprived the 5,000 or so Jewish refugees already in the British zone of DP rations and threatened any new entrants with a similar withdrawal of DP privileges.

McNarney's declaration caused a storm among Jewish bodies. The American Jewish Committee, the most conservative of the American Jewish organizations, declared there was no organized movement from the East and protested McNarney's stand. The American Zionists and Rabbi Bernstein more realistically put pressure both on the military in Germany and, mainly, on the government in Washington to change the Army's policy to fit Hilldring's and other officials' previous statements. Rabbi Stephen S. Wise, the Zionist leader, went to Frankfurt, Rabbi Bernstein to Washington, and the representatives of other Jewish bodies made their views known, publicly and privately. It was Washington that made McNarney retreat, mainly because it was perfectly clear that the result might be serious clashes between the refugees and American troops trying to seal the borders. As we have seen, the Brichah itself, at that point, had no control whatever over the masses that were seeking to leave Poland, and all it could do was to direct the flow. It could not have stopped it had it wanted to—which of course it did not.[21]

The result of all this pressure was a recantation which took the form of a reinterpretation by McNarney of what he had said on the 6th. This took place on August 21,[22] when the American press was treated to a tortured explanation, which was that in actual fact what the general had meant was that the groups coming should not be larger than 100—the definition of an organized movement being 100 or more at a time—and that he would not agree to groups coming from the British or French zones where they could not be considered as persecuted, but he would accept (and had never meant not to accept) those who came from Poland, where, as everyone knew, there was indeed an unbearable situation for the Jews. The British were left looking rather foolish, and Brichah operations, which had not been stopped by the first declaration, now adopted what some commanders termed the "100 rule," that is, that groups going across, mainly from Vienna to the U.S. zone in Austria, very often numbered precisely 99 souls in order to qualify as bona fide refugees.

The situation in Austria became especially precarious as

a result of the mass influx. The U.S. Army there was less capable physically of handling the refugees than in Germany, and by early August General Mark Clark reported to McNarney that the limit of accommodation in the Austrian camps had been reached at 27,000 Jewish refugees and further transports would have to be sent elsewhere.[23] McNarney agreed and undertook to accept 5,000 Jewish refugees who would presumably arrive soon. This arrangement, which at first took the form of a temporary step, became a fixed policy on August 12, when the Army in Germany began taking over from Austria all surplus Jewish DPs. The maximum capacity in Austria was fixed at 30,000, and any number beyond that was sent on at Salzburg into Bavaria. In this way, until late in September, 33,860 Jewish refugees officially entered Germany. Smaller numbers, amounting to about 7,000 people, were sent from Austria by the Brichah illegally or by means of various subterfuges.[24]

The overcrowding of the Austrian camps, where physical conditions were now much worse than in the German camps, caused real hardship for the refugees. General Clark therefore had a great deal of backing by various organizations, including the JDC, when he tried to make Washington intervene diplomatically in Poland and Czechoslovakia in order to stop the flow temporarily, or at least to try to regulate it. This was actually done, and on August 19 and 20 the U.S. Embassy in Poland, headed by Ambassador Lane, who happened to be very much out of sympathy with the left-wing government in Poland, intervened—first with the deputy foreign minister and then with the Prime Minister, Osobka-Morawski. The Americans asked for a regulation of the flow, which they assumed must be well known to the government. At the same time they informed the JDC representatives in Poland that they were intervening in Czechoslovakia in the same spirit and told them that the JDC in New York had agreed to try as far as possible to regulate the exodus. On the 23rd, the Poles sent a liaison officer on Jewish questions, a Colonel Wrzosz, to help arrange a solution with the Americans. However, Wrzosz had not very much to say beyond some platitudes about the traditional friendship between Poles and Jews and the hope that more Jews would

stay in the future because the government was seeing to it that the security situation would improve. In any case, he was responsible only for internal problems, and arrangements concerning exit from the country had to be dealt with by the Foreign Office.[25] But apparently the Foreign Office was more receptive to American pressure, which now came on top of the British variety; and the same was true of the Czechs. After the tremendous flow into Austria during the first six days of August, which reached the figure of about 10,000, members of the American embassy approached Jacobson in Prague and asked him to do his best to regulate the exodus. On or about the 14th of the month, the Americans even closed temporarily the borders of their zones to further entrance of refugees,[26] and similar temporary closings of the frontiers occurred a number of times during August (10 and 13)[27] on the Polish-Czech borders and again during the last week of September.[28] The two governments, the Polish and the Czech, were rather hesitant in this complicated situation. The Czechs wanted to present a humanitarian image to the world and many of them had real sympathy with the Jewish refugees. They had no wish to comply with British or even American requests if they could help it. On the other hand, they could not disregard American wishes if they did not want to be faced with the danger of seeing the Jewish persecutees stay in Czechoslovakia for lack of permission to proceed to Germany. The Poles, too, thought they should be sympathetic to the Jews. The Polish consul-general in New York even went so far as to say that "the crossing of the border by Jews who do not want to wait for the legal procedure would in no case be hindered."[29] Both countries' governments were walking the tightrope between conflicting interests and conflicting emotions, but the net result from the Jewish point of view was that, temporary closings of borders notwithstanding, Jews were streaming through with little difficulty during the crucial months.

Rabbi Bernstein's relations with the Army made it mandatory for him to try to accommodate the Army's interests wherever possible. It was quite clear that the Army wanted the Jews or as many of them as possible to move on beyond Germany. While movement of large numbers was dependent

on the solution of the large issues, Bernstein was expected to attempt to settle at least some of the refugees in places other than Germany and to do his best to prevent too large a flow of Jews to converge on the overcrowded U.S. zones in Germany and Austria. This policy of, to put it frankly, getting rid of the Jews, led the Army to support not only the attempts made to remove the refugees by legal means but to connive at illegal exit as well, as long as this was not done too blatantly.

Rabbi Bernstein put forward two schemes to ease the pressure on the American zone: one envisaged the acceptance of 10,000 refugees by the Czechs, whereas the other sought to place 25,000 in Italy. Bernstein, accompanied by Jacobson, went to Prague in late August, and on September 3 they saw the Communist leader Klement Gottwald. The proposal was that the Czechs accept 10,000 people in camps in the Sudeten area, which was then being cleared of its German inhabitants. Bernstein thought that the JDC should take the responsibility of feeding these people, but the JDC refused to guarantee such action—the argument being that this was a tremendous expense and that this kind of mass feeding operation could not be undertaken by a private agency such as the JDC which depended on voluntary contributions. Gottwald demanded not only some kind of guarantee that food would be supplied but insisted mainly on the assumption of responsibility by a U.S. government agency which would make sure that if these Jews were unable to find another place to go to after a certain period of time they would be accepted into the American zone. Bernstein went back to Germany, and a telephone call from Frankfurt empowered Jacobson to tell the Czechs that General McNarney agreed "to accept these Jewish DPs in the US zone of Germany as of July 1st, 1947, if so requested." The JDC, after some exchange of correspondence, agreed to provide supplementary food. Then there was a prolonged period of silence on the part of the Czech government until November 11, when Gottwald wrote his agreement to the project, specifying, however, that he would like to be officially requested by the American government to undertake the program. Ambassador Steinhardt, upon receipt of advice

from Washington, filed such a letter with the Czech Foreign Office on December 2, but by that time the Brichah from Poland had died down, and the program was never implemented.[30]

Rabbi Bernstein's success in Italy was no greater. Negotiations started in the latter half of August, and there the U.S. representatives intervened from the outset. The original proposal was the acceptance of 25,000 Jewish refugees into the country. The Italian government rejected the proposal out of hand at the end of the month.[31] The reason given was scarcity of food in the country and the unavailability of UNRRA funds with which to buy food abroad. Actually, the Italians said, there were already 25,000 Jewish refugees in the country, and they had done their share. These figures, in point of fact, were vastly exaggerated. A JDC count of heads in early September yielded the information that there were some 10,365 people in the camps and the agricultural training centers, and an estimate of Jewish DPs living in the cities in early December set their number as 5,618.[32] These figures were considerably smaller than the official estimates because higher registration in the camps meant more food—when people left or died or settled temporarily in towns they continued to be carried on the registers and rations were taken in their names. The Italian government was well aware of the facts, but in order to prevent further mass immigration into Italy it chose to disregard them. Illegal immigration into the country from Austria was also a trickle, compared with the mass movements taking place in Central Europe. From January to the end of August 1946, 6,032 Jews were estimated by the Brichah to have crossed the Italian border, and between September and the end of the year another 7,250 were to come. These came largely by the Nauders route from the French sector, and others came on occasion through other border points under a variety of pretexts.[33] Bernstein did not give up hope; he proposed that a smaller number, 10,000, be taken by the Italians. The food problem he tried to solve by asking the JDC to assume the feeding burden. When he got no positive response from the JDC to this proposal, he complained sharply (September 8) of the shortsightedness of the New York committee

and argued that the relationship with the Army in Germany would be made much easier if he succeeded in placing some Jews outside of that country. Also, he added, these people had to be supported in Germany or Austria, and providing for them in Italy would not be such a tremendous additional burden. Moses A. Leavitt, the JDC's secretary in New York, thereupon asked Dr. Schwartz to send him a cable which would counter Bernstein's arguments and could be shown to the Rabbi. Schwartz obliged on September 30, and poured large quantities of cold water on the rabbi's plans. The 10,000 would cost some $210,000 a month, which he, Schwartz, did not have, and in any case the mass movement from Poland was abating and many refugees had even returned to Poland. Under those conditions there was no point in pursuing Bernstein's plans any further—and indeed they were quietly dropped.[34]

In his attempts to alleviate the situation for Jews, both for those on the move and for those who had to or intended to stay in Poland, Rabbi Bernstein asked for an audience with Pope Pius XII. The audience took place on September 11, at the papal resort of Castel Gandolfo. The Pope described the murder of the Jews during the war as "dreadful" and said, "It was a great pity." Rabbi Bernstein's purpose was to bring up the subject of Kielce and ask the Pope to issue, either personally or through the Polish hierarchy, a condemnation of pogroms. The pogrom, too, was "dreadful," the Pope said, and the Church condemned all violence. He then told the rabbi that the Church was in difficulty itself in Poland and that it, too, did not have freedom from fear. Decrying the hostile attitude of the Soviet government and the new regimes in Eastern Europe, he declared that the freedom-loving nations would have to guard against the new brand of nationalism in Russia. It was difficult to communicate with Polish Catholics because of the Iron Curtain, but he assured Bernstein that he would instruct the Polish Church to take positive action against anti-Semitism. In addition, he promised to intercede with the Italian government regarding the acceptance of the 10,000 refugees into the country. It is impossible to say whether the Pope did actually intervene, and if so, to what extent, both in Poland

and Italy. It is clear at any rate that if he did so his intervention was secret and yielded no results at all.[35]

After his failure to achieve his goals with the various governments and the Pope, Rabbi Bernstein returned to the United States and was granted an appointment to see President Truman on October 11. This interview was rather significant because it brought out the thinking of both participants in a fairly clear way. Bernstein praised the top commanders of the Army in Europe for the good job they were doing under difficult circumstances and the cooperation which they unfailingly offered. There was some discussion of the material welfare of the DPs in the U.S. zone, and then the talk turned to Palestine (of which more later). Rabbi Bernstein proceeded to complain about British action to block not only immigration into Palestine but even the resettlement of Jews in Europe; he was obviously referring to their opposition to the Italian scheme, and he went on to say, "I am sorry to report that no government in Europe with whom I have dealt on temporary settlement projects is prepared to accept these Jews on a permanent basis." Truman's reply was that he could not understand it; after all, the Jews were good citizens in the United States and would be assets to any country. The rabbi then remarked that the world was sick and the attitude toward the Jews was a symptom of the sickness; Truman agreed. Cynics may read politics into these words, but there does not seem to be any ground for doubting the sincerity of the President in this short encounter.[36] The conclusion may have been banal, but it was perfectly true.

Those first August days of 1946 were crucial, in more ways than one, to the development of the Palestine problem, leading up as they did to the creation of the State of Israel. On June 29, the British had attacked the Haganah and driven its leader, Dr. Moshe Sneh, into exile in Paris. Ben-Gurion, who happened to be in Paris at the time of the British crackdown, called an expanded Jewish Agency executive to meet with him there on August 1. Weizmann, who was ill and in London, maintained daily contact with the deliberations in France. By that time Paris had become the center of opera-

tions for the Mossad and Brichah: Shaul Avigur was there, and as head of the Mossad he exercised a growing authority over Brichah operations, with Mordechai Surkiss in the role of a roving commander-inspector. The executive meeting was not attended by Dr. Abba Hillel Silver, then head of the American Zionist Emergency Council, the chief spokesman of American Zionist activists. The deliberations in Paris were stormy and gloomy. Afterward Dr. Nahum Goldmann was to speak of a "tragic decision taken in what was regarded as a desperate situation" and, for once, Silver agreed and talked of the "terrible situation in which we found ourselves at the moment, in which all the cards seemed to be stacked against us."[37] The lines of communication with the British government had been definitely severed by the British action of June 29, and even the moderate Goldmann stated that "Jews had come to feel that the continuation of British rule in Palestine was intolerable."[38] The attitude of the Soviets to the whole Palestine problem was at the time quite unclear; there simply were no contacts of any significance and the Agency was in the dark as to the intentions of the Soviet government. What caused the greatest concern was the attitude of the United States. Truman had shown great interest in the DPs in Europe. This, as we have pointed out, was a mixture of a very genuine humanitarian attitude with the ardent desire, shared especially by the Army, to get rid of the Jewish DPs. One of the American members of the Anglo-American committee related in a public speech how General Tate, Clark's chief of staff in Austria, had pleaded with the committee in February, "Gentlemen, for God's sake, help us! We are at the end of our rope. . . . The American Army authorities pleaded with us . . . to clean out those camps."[39] But neither the State Department nor the White House would go beyond the DP problem in their search for solutions. Symptomatic of this attitude was a discussion Truman had with nine Congressmen from New York who called on him on July 30. He was reported to have been sympathetic to the plight of the homeless Jews, but when they brought up the general subject of Palestine he was "inattentive" and suggested at one point that the reason for their call was political.[40] By early August this had gone even

further—he had, after much British prodding, become involved in two attempts to help the British in solving the Palestine problem: the investigations by the Anglo-American committee and the Brook-Grady negotiations. On both occasions he had been let down, mainly by the British, but he also intensely disliked the pressures that were put on him by the Jews. There seems to have been a tendency in the administration to take a back seat and lose interest in the whole problem. This certainly was the burden of the reports that came to the Agency out of Washington.[41] The Jews, therefore, felt completely alone and abandoned by all their "friends."

The mass exodus from Poland was a very important factor contributing to the Agency's assessment of the situation. As Dr. Stephen S. Wise stated on August 4 in Paris, during the most crucial of the discussions of the Executive, he had been a lifelong opponent of the partition of Palestine in all its forms. However, he confessed "to a harrowing sense of guilt," because he felt that if the Zionist movement had supported the idea of partition strenuously enough before the war a state might have been created there which could have saved many who became victims of Hitler's Germany. "Perhaps now," he said, "if we have a little State of our own, enabling us to issue passports, etc., we may save half of the survivors in Europe."[42] The greatest influence on many of those present appears to have been that of Rabbi Maimon, the venerable leader of Mizrahi, the religious group in Palestine's Jewry, who asked whether those present had the right, by sticking to a solution which was at best a possibility for a remote future, to abandon to their fate those tens of thousands who were now fleeing from the East and see them lost to the Jewish people. His own answer was that he had come reluctantly to the conclusion that mainly for the sake of the suffering Jews of Europe the Agency had to agree to the partition of Palestine.[43] On the morning of August 5 the Agency in Paris voted, Ben-Gurion and Sneh abstaining and one other member voting against, to adopt a set of proposals submitted by Dr. Nahum Goldmann. The important clause in the declaration was that "the Executive is prepared to discuss a proposal for the

establishment of a viable Jewish State in an adequate area of Palestine."[44]

Armed with this new proposal, which replaced the old Agency stand that all of Palestine west of the Jordan should be made a Jewish state by allowing mass immigration into it, Goldmann flew to Washington to try to convince the American government to take a positive stand toward these new suggestions. In a series of discussions held there on the 6th and 7th, Goldmann seems to have gone beyond his brief. He was supposed to indicate to the Americans that the Jews would discuss partition if it was offered by others; instead, he directly suggested partition as the Agency proposal. Silver, no great friend of Nahum Goldmann in any case, was very angry. His argument was that if the Jews suggested anything at all, it would immediately be taken as a maximum demand and would then have to go through the inevitable process of being whittled down. On the other hand, other Jewish representatives argued that Goldmann did well to break the ice—Secretaries Patterson and Acheson showed themselves favorable to partition, and the danger of American lack of interest in the whole problem was thus avoided. Judge Joseph Proskauer, head of the American Jewish Committee, who participated in Goldmann's conversations in Washington, agrees with this interpretation, though, of course, it is hard to say what exactly was meant when the Americans talked of their general acceptance of the partition idea.[45] Rumor had it that the United States had put out feelers to see what the British reaction to the proposal was, and a telegram from Truman to Ambassador Averell Harriman was said to have expressed American agreement with the idea of partition.[46] What happened between the middle of August and early October is not quite clear, in the absence of official documentation. However, as far as the Jews were concerned, the time was used to try to press the British into making some concessions and to get American approval expressed publicly. After long negotiations, Truman did publish a statement, on October 4, which had great importance in the evolution of the intertwined DP and Palestine problems. The statement was obviously very carefully phrased and bore all the marks of State

Department editing. It said that, as far as partition went, "a solution along these lines would command the support of public opinion in the United States. I cannot believe that the gap between the [Jewish Agency and the British] proposals which have been put forward is too great to be bridged by men of reason and good-will. To such a solution our Government could give its support." In addition, Truman demanded immediate "substantial immigration" into Palestine.

The statement meant one thing, and was generally interpreted to mean quite another. In the statement itself, the U.S. government indicated quite clearly that it would support a solution which was worked out as a compromise between the Agency proposal of partition and the British-sponsored Morrison-Grady Plan (which meant, as was pointed out earlier, the stifling of Zionist endeavor in Palestine); exactly as Silver and his friends had foretold and feared, the partition plan had become a political maximum, and the practical solution would be an even further Jewish retreat. However, this was not the way the declaration was popularly interpreted. Public opinion in both America and Britain interpreted American policy to be generally favorable to partition, which was now considered to be the pro-Jewish solution; by the same token American policy was thought of as basically opposed to that of Britain. This, at any rate, was clearly what the British themselves thought. Bevin was furious at American intervention, and declared that the British government "could not continue with this stigma of failure. They [the British] were the subject of every New York election and the butt of every international relation. They had been asked to take in 100,000 people, but promised no support except financial. . . . If the President had not put forward the request for 100,000 certificates, they might already have had a settlement. He [Bevin] thought that request was most unfortunate. The Arabs would not accept partition. Was he to force it on the Arabs with British bayonets? He was not prepared to do that. He would try to get agreement, otherwise they would hand back the Mandate to UNO."[47] Bevin felt he was being pressed by American-backed demands for partition and

large-scale immigration, both of which ran counter to British policy in the Middle East. Defeated and isolated, unable to reach an agreement with both Jews and Arabs, he could only think of handing the mandate back to the U.N., with the hope, apparently, of getting a mandate back that would be "better" from his point of view. The specter of an American-Soviet alliance against Britain on the Palestine and refugee issue had not yet arisen.

This picture of British isolation was compounded by the obvious failure of British diplomacy in the summer of 1946 to persuade the Continental countries to put an end to Jewish mass migration. Britain even failed to stop illegal immigration into Palestine, despite her policy, after August 12, of deporting illegal immigrants to Cyprus, where large detention camps were set up for the purpose. Brichah was feeding these activities, and the British failed to stop all such moves. It was clear that the sympathy of Europeans generally was most definitely with the Jews and against the British.

It can therefore be said that it was not only the Jews who found themselves at an impasse in August 1946. The Americans, too, were facing a problem and the British were equally embarrassed. The Americans were prepared to adopt the partition proposal as basis for a compromise and thus thought they had a policy; the British thought themselves under American pressure and were quickly led into a position where they had no policy at all. In Europe, in the meantime, the Jewish masses took heart as the struggle for immigration continued unabated in the little ships; Jewish leadership saw ways out of the impasse, and a Zionist Congress was called to meet in Basel and engage in that favorite Jewish pastime of party debate and political hairsplitting. For that congress, which met in December, the Brichah prepared another meeting, a first European assembly of Brichah commanders, where a new organizational setup was established. But between August and December, a number of things happened, and to these we must now turn.

9. *Displaced Persons*

It is extremely difficult to estimate the total number of refugees who came during the great panic exodus and their distribution in Germany and Austria; but one reliable estimate[1] puts the number of those who eventually reached Germany at 70,000 and those who stayed in Austria at 20,000—all in the U.S. zones and Berlin. In addition, some 4,000 settled in the British zones, mainly in Germany, and others in Italy and France. Of those who entered the U.S. zone in Germany, most came through Austria because, as we have seen, the Nachod–Bratislava–Vienna route led to Germany via the U.S. zone in Austria, where the two regions of Linz and Salzburg shared between them the burden of accommodating the transients. In the Linz area, there had been only two camps (at Bindermichl and Enns), which had been set up after the scandal of October 1945 and which provided a fairly decent standard of living for their inmates. Now, under pressure from the waves of transients streaming in from Vienna, four camps were set up to provide merely temporary shelter and where standards were kept very low to discourage anyone from staying too long. Another five transient camps were set up in the Salzburg area, where conditions were similar to those at Linz. At Salzburg, too, the permanent camps set up previously, notably the one at

Bad Gastein, the health resort, provided conditions which stood in glaring contrast to those prevailing in the transient centers.

From May 1946 to January 1947, a total of 62,950 transient Jews (of which 53,000 came between July and October) were registered by the Salzburg Brichah. Some 11,700 of these stayed in the Salzburg area at the end of the period. (An additional 16,000 to 17,000 stayed behind at Linz; these were not included in the Salzburg figures.) Of the rest, 45,000 left legally or illegally for Germany, 5,500 went to Italy, and 750 went to Belgium and France on semilegal documents (that is, legal documents obtained under false pretenses).[2] Brichah in the U.S. zone was forced to devote its attention to getting the people out of the zone as speedily as possible because of the desperate shortage of supplies in the camps. The JDC representative at Salzburg, a young and energetic American named Leon D. Fisher, said that the Army and the JDC had been taken completely by surprise by the size and complexity of the problem. The "supplies were ridiculously inadequate, and at first failed hopelessly and completely to meet the demands of a starving, disturbed transient population."[3] This improved only gradually later in autumn. Throughout the zone the Austrians at first gave maximum rations of about 1,200 calories per person (about half of the necessary minimum) and the Army supplemented this by 500 more calories, until in the autumn the feeding was improved by the Army's addition of 1,550 calories and by the JDC's supplement of 800 calories from its own supplies. As for the general situation, "it is impossible adequately to describe the general conditions of chaos and confusion that existed here at the time, and the countless frantic attempts to meet this critical situation. . . . Attempts to control and limit the surge of population into the already extremely overcrowded area were mostly futile. The Jews fleeing the pogroms in Poland did so with a determination that allowed for no such retardation at the borders of Austria by the military authorities."[4]

Brichah in the U.S. zone was generally under the command of ex-members of the Palestinian units, mostly the Brigade. Most of the time in the spring and summer of

1946 Linz was under the command of Ephraim Rosen, an ex-Brigade soldier. In Salzburg, which was in many ways a more important Brichah point, other soldiers were in charge until May, when Abba Gefen took over the contacts with the American military and the JDC. The Brigade soldier Uri Fried became responsible for other branches of the work, until in September another soldier, Zemach Harari, took overall command. Harari was a heavyset, slow-moving and very intelligent man, and a master of human relations. He and Gefen got on very well together, despite the fact that they belonged to different political factions and had different backgrounds: Gefen had been a Lithuanian Jewish guerrilla fighter, whereas Harari was a member of a fairly prosperous kibbutz in the Jordan valley in Palestine. In any case, it would be a grave mistake to see Brichah relationships in terms of hierarchical order; as in many underground organizations, command in the Brichah was a vague thing, and informal status was considerably more important than a formal title. Ben Nathan was still the commander in Austria, and he would come to Salzburg to participate in crucial discussions or intervene with the Americans. But there was confidence enough in the Salzburg people to let them arrange everything according to their own lights. The tasks were, after all, quite clear: to get as many people as possible into Germany and Italy so that they would not stay behind in the terrible conditions of the Austrian transit camps.

The importance of Salzburg lay in its geographical position: toward it led the main Brichah route in Europe from Vienna, and from it the two routes to Germany in the north and west and Italy in the south. Had the American Army intended to interfere with Brichah activities, this would have been an ideal spot to do so. Fortunately for the Brichah, there was an American officer in Salzburg who was very sympathetic to it: Captain Stanley K. Novinsky, a Polish-Catholic American, and deputy to the officer in charge of the DP camps in the Salzburg area. It seems that at first Novinsky was none too friendly to the mass movement of the Jews, but the Brigade soldiers who were in charge of the Brichah's external relations in early 1946 convinced

him of the inevitability of the migration. Working in close contact with them and, after May, with Gefen, Novinsky became an ardent and convinced supporter of the Brichah; he had a very high regard for the self-sacrifice and idealism of the men and women who were engaged in the clandestine operation, and he did his best to help them. It was of course in the interest of the U.S. Army in Austria to send the Jews to Germany, and Novinsky willingly obtained the necessary papers and even obtained the signatures. But if this had become known to top officers in Germany they would have remonstrated vehemently with the Austrian command, which was, needless to say, quite unaware of any papers' being provided for movement of Jews to Germany at this stage, in May 1946. So in order to avoid any unpleasantness for Novinsky, his papers were used only to get past the checkpoint on the Austrian side, and for the German side another document was used that was issued by one of the Salzburg transit camps and bore Gefen's signature. This was stopped by the Americans on the German side on May 28, when they declared that only papers countersigned by the 42nd Division—commanded by pro-Jewish General Collins, and Novinsky's outfit—would be considered valid. With the help of Novinsky, this was obtained as well, and transports went on to Germany until June 18.

On the same day, Yonah'le Eisenberg, the daring young ex-partisan from Lithuania and the most experienced of the Brichah boys at Salzburg, was sent with a transport of 130 people, and then with another group of 106 to cross into Germany. The second transport was caught by the American guards at Freilassing on the German side of the border, and it was obvious that they would not be let off this time. Yonah'le saw the American troops ready to arrest his group at the railway station and gave his people instructions to disperse. This they did, and only some eighteen were actually arrested, but Yonah'le himself was among them. They were placed in custody at the nearest command post at Bad Reichenhall; when Gefen heard about this, he immediately went into Germany himself in order to get Yonah'le out of prison. However, when he got to the American commander, a Lieutenant Evans, he was arrested too. Yonah'le was put

under pressure—he got only one meal a day in prison, and was placed in a cell with German criminals—and it seemed that worse would follow. At this point Gefen got word out to Novinsky about the trouble they were in, and Novinsky informed the JDC representative, Leon D. Fisher. It was Fisher who, basing himself on Novinsky's authority, got the two Brichah men out of prison. However, transports stopped temporarily, and Brichah sent people over illegally, which was not too difficult to do in the mountainous area of the Salzburg border.[5]

The Brichah took an attitude of reciprocity in its relationship with Novinsky and Major Schutz, his superior. In June, Brichah consented to prevent anti-British demonstrations in the zone in return for a promise of future cooperation. The promise was made good toward the end of June, when first one and then another legal transport were arranged to go from Austria to Germany. In both cases the Brichah introduced more people into the group than they had permission for. This went on through the month of July, with the situation in Austria becoming grimmer by the day, as the effects of the July 4 pogrom at Kielce began to be felt. Ben Nathan tried to help out from Vienna by obtaining some "Bolivian" visas which would enable Jews to get to Belgium or France, but all he managed to do was to send 250 people to Belgium—a mere drop in the bucket.

The basic change in the position of the Salzburg Brichah came with the official agreement between the U.S. commands in Germany and in Austria to transfer thousands of Jewish refugees from Austria into Germany. After August 12, when that arrangement went into effect, Gefen and his friends became more or less official representatives of the Jews. Their position was especially strong because they were in actual control of the DP camps in the area; in this they were unlike the Brichah in Germany, which claimed no direct control over the camps there. The difference lay in the fact that the Austrian camps were temporary and much worse than those in Germany, and demoralization was likely to spread in them—such, at least, was the rationalization used by the Salzburg Brichah, and the camps were simply Brichah camps. This in turn gave the organization a

leverage of influence vis-à-vis the American military; relations now were very good in any case, and toward the middle of August Gefen began talks with Novinsky and his superiors to allow the creation of a new legal body to represent the refugees and provide an official Jewish partner for the Army in its transfer operations of Jews throughout the zone in Austria. This body, the Committee for Assistance to Jewish Refugees (CAJR), was officially organized on August 27, and was given a house in Salzburg, means of transportation, telephone and official documentation so as to help the Army in its complicated tasks concerning the Jewish refugees.[6] The Army was in fact greatly interested in avoiding too much direct contact with the DPs and left all the administrative detail and the handling of human relations to the Jews themselves. Novinsky himself, we are told by Gefen and Ben Nathan,[7] even went as far as to accept the rather peculiar conception Brichah had of law and order and obedience to the law. Brichah generally—and not only Brichah in Austria—saw it as the supreme moral right of Jews, after what had happened to them in the war, to move toward Palestine or, at any rate, out of the lands of their oppression. Military regulations by foreign armies were not binding upon them, and for once, after a long history of obedience to others, the Jews would obey only their own institutions, which were at that time clandestine. The moral right of the non-Jew to tell the Jews what to do and where to go or stay had lapsed, and it was in this light that all problems of legality were approached. Foreign as this concept may have been to Jews from Western democratic countries, it was accepted unquestioningly by those hundreds of thousands who were connected with Brichah or with other manifestations of an independent Jewish nationalism. Novinsky and other friends may not have fully comprehended this in its theoretical formulation, but they evinced humane understanding for the position in practice. Such an attitude, it must be added, was found almost only among American officers—the French, British or Russians showed no sympathy whatsoever for this point of view.

One incident which Gefen relates is characteristic both of this basic philosophy and the special problems posed by

a close relationship with the Americans.[8] The Americans were of course intent on closing Jewish camps, so as to prevent Jews from staying in their zone. In September, they suddenly closed one of their Salzburg camps without informing the Brichah in advance. Coincidentally, at that point the American counterintelligence (CIC) came to Gefen complaining of the lack of cooperation from the Jews. It developed that the CIC was beginning to interrogate the Jews about Communism, Communist leanings and information about Communist countries. Gefen himself was very far removed from even the slightest sympathy with Communism, and most of the people who had, after all, been repatriated from Russia after spending the war years there, shared this point of view. However, there was a marked reluctance in giving information to Americans, even to the point of refusing them material help (rooms in the camps to conduct interrogations, for instance). In replying to the CIC, Gefen said that it was quid pro quo for the unfriendly act of closing down camps against the wishes of the Brichah; but he admitted that in any case he would not be prepared to influence the Jews to give evidence to the American intelligence people—he was not prepared to be a pawn in a big power game and supply information about third parties. If the Jews wanted to give evidence, that was their business; if they did not wish to do so, that was their business again—he would not influence them either way.

In September the legal transfer into Germany ceased, or almost ceased, and Brichah had to depend again on subterfuges, forged documents, and illegal crossings. But at the end of September, Brichah from the East was declining sharply, and large-scale movements were no longer the order of the day.

People came to Germany via three main channels: through Austria via Salzburg to Bavaria; via the Prague–As–Hof–Munich route; and from the British zone in the north down into the American zone. The last route brought together the people who came from Berlin with those who came on the repatriation ships or trains as "Germans" straight from Stettin. In Bergen-Belsen in the British zone the quiet,

scholarly Kurt Levin was officially responsible for the welfare activities of the Jewish Agency team in the DP camps. Less officially, he served as liaison for the Brichah. Rega Globman, a Brichah girl at Hannover, cooperated with Brigade soldiers in setting up a well-functioning Brichah apparatus. She was a small, intelligent young woman and a perfect choice for the difficult assignment. Simple repatriation documents were used in getting people southward into the U.S. zone by train, and when the trains were stopped by the Americans in the summer, by truck. However, the situation was complicated to a considerable degree by the fact that a group of speculators got two large transports totaling some 1,600 Polish Jews out of Poland and by train via Wroclaw (Breslau) into the British zone at Uelzen. The Brichah personnel were very angry indeed. Not only did the smugglers promise their victims that they would be royally received in the Western zones but they also robbed them of some $50 to $100 per head and, moreover, made the British aware of the border-crossings. Fortunately, the transport was put into a camp at Dettmold, near the American-British zonal frontier, and the Brichah people managed to smuggle out the newly arrived people in small batches into Frankfurt, the next "point" in the U.S. zone. The speculators, of course, disappeared without a trace.

Jewish refugees who arrived in the British zone faced some difficult choices if they could not be transported southward immediately. As "infiltrees" they were not recognized by the British as coming within the DP category at all and were therefore dispersed in small communities among Germans and received the German starvation ration—if they could pay for it, which normally they could not. Many Jews did manage to obtain DP papers of one kind or another; many were hidden in the large Bergen-Belsen camp where they received help; and the destitute were aided by the JDC. The fact was that the British military authorities were most unfriendly to the Jews, and David Wodlinger, a Canadian and the JDC representative in the zone, declared that while the British were not actually anti-Semitic "it has been found that the German welfare authorities are generally more understanding and helpful in connection with problems of German Jews than are the British authorities."[9]

It has been emphasized that conditions in the British zones and the U.S. zone in Austria were poor, but this is not to imply that those in the U.S. zone of Germany were ideal. The American Army had not, after all, been set up to fulfill the functions of a welfare agency—and yet in a way this was exactly what was expected of it as far as the DPs were concerned. It was responsible for "basic amenities"—food, lodging and transportation. At the same time, American policy toward Germany was changing as the international atmosphere chilled to cold war temperature. "I want to concentrate on the job in hand, and that is to reconstitute the German economy as rapidly as possible," General McNarney is reported to have said to an American visitor in June.[10] The signs multiplied that this was indeed the American policy in Germany, until on September 6 Secretary of State Byrnes made his famous speech at Stuttgart which in a sense served as an official American declaration of the cold war—which, unofficially, had been going on, of course, for quite some time.

Under these new conditions the DP problem put the Army in a very difficult position: if it favored the DPs, and that could essentially be done only at German expense, the new policy of favoring Germany might be harmed. At the end of 1945 the situation had looked a great deal easier; there had been 313,000 DPs in Germany at that time, of whom only some 50,000 were Jews, the rest being mainly Poles and Balts. The Army had even thought of closing all the camps in the spring, except for those of the persecutees, that is, Jews, but then winter had come and with the further deterioration of the German economy many DPs who had until then lived outside the camps now came to them in search of food and fuel. Then the Jewish influx came, and by the end of 1946, despite some repatriation of non-Jews, the Army found itself with over 400,000 DPs on its hands in the U.S. zone and Berlin alone.[11] Torn between the conflicting policies of assuaging the Germans and providing for the DPs, the Army had to do a tightrope-walking act, and armies are notoriously bad at that kind of exercise. At first the Army opposed the opening of new camp facilities on the theory that new camps would encourage infiltrees to move into the zone in even larger numbers, implying that

overcrowded camps might have a salutary effect in keeping infiltrees away. When this did not work, the Army and UNRRA opened temporary camps in July at Landshut, Cham and eight other places, mainly in the Munich area. These camps were appallingly ill equipped. Tents were put up in open fields, sanitation was primitive, medical assistance poor, and on top of an almost intolerable situation came a wet German summer and the camps became seas of mud. Cham and Landshut were located between Munich and the Czech border, and Jews from the camps in the Munich area came to them to take their friends and relatives to the relative comfort of their permanent DP locations. Thus, Jacob Isaac Herszkowicz of Feldafing camp received a probably not very welcome plea, dated September 12, from his cousins Lea and Zelda and their families in Cham. They asked him to rescue them from their predicament: "Until three weeks ago we lived in Lodz and it is now three weeks that we wander around. Whatever the place we stay in one day we are sure to be at another place the next day; they drag us from one place to another. We had hoped we would forget camp life for a bit but we have had opportunity to be reminded again. Where we were brought today we have to live in a field in which they put up tents and we live like Gypsies. We cannot leave here. We are supposed to stay for two weeks and then be sent on—where, no one knows."[12]

In early July the Army gave up its attempt to postpone the establishment of permanent camps.[13] In June only three were put up, but in July thirteen were established; in August and September seven were set up each month, and then in October and November another eight. In all, thirty-eight camps were set up by the Army during the mass influx, largely in Army barracks, old POW camps or similar facilities. As these camps were established the temporary ones were slowly abandoned, including Cham and Landshut (in September). However, even in November, an American visitor, sent by UNRRA director La Guardia, had the doubtful pleasure of visiting a so-called transit camp at Funk-Kaserne in Munich which he had seen in July and been told it would be closed. There he found a "large ga-

rage, which in the summertime had housed some 1,800 Displaced Persons with washing and latrine facilities sufficient only for a family of ten or twelve." Now the additional ordeal of cold weather was added. On a top floor, there were 800 beds placed almost side by side. A makeshift wood-burning stove billowed forth smoke all over "this wretched hell-hole." In the midst of all this walked a woman director trying to ease people's burdens, comforting and aiding, herself as haggard and worn-out as the refugees themselves.[14]

Of course not all the camps were like the one at Funk-Kaserne. But many were, even the "permanent" camps. An incident concerning one of them found its way into the press. This happened at a God-forsaken POW camp called Babenhausen, where people were brought on the last day of September from a transit camp by train. When they saw their new "home" from their warm train—barbed-wire fence, stables, tin shacks, tents and all—they declared they would not budge. Chaplains, Army people, Rabbi Bernstein and even the commander of the Third Army, Lieutenant General Geoffrey S. Keyes, were brought in to persuade the DPs to enter the camp. That night, after much coaxing, nine hundred of the thousand who were on the train agreed to go into the camp, after being promised that the fence would be removed and the facilities improved. A few days later a second train was brought and again the same argument ensued. Finally most of the people entered the camp, and a remnant of 225 who refused were shipped to another place ("Did we flee for our lives for this?" they asked).[15] Pocking, the largest camp in the zone, housed 8,500, and Rabbi Friedman, aide to Rabbi Bernstein, reported on November 15 that there was no fuel there and the barracks were substandard.

The Army was not necessarily being callous; they were simply trying to do two conflicting jobs at the same time. The new policy of friendship with the Germans precluded a return to the Eisenhower line of evicting Germans from decent housing projects to make room for their Jewish victims, and so literally nothing remained but to house the Jews in makeshift garages, stables and barracks or huts. In

the British zone the basic sympathy of at least the top levels of Army command that was evident in the American zone was lacking; elementary rapport between officialdom and the camp inmates was absent. Solomon M. Gelber, the JDC representative at Bergen-Belsen, told the story of how the local UNRRA director, a Mr. Wheatman, suddenly confronted the Jews with the demand that they evacuate the brick barracks in which they were living and move into Nissen huts (tin huts which were actually quite reasonable accommodations, but which of course were much less comfortable than the solid brick buildings into which the Jews had been moved from the Belsen camp). Gelber remonstrated, but "Mr. Wheatman was cold and unfriendly to my suggestion that the ultimatum was unjust and that it should be re-examined. He said that there were many people in England who would love to live in Nissen huts and that he himself had done so during the war. He could, therefore, see no reason why the Jews objected. I pointed out to him that I myself have lived in Nissen huts throughout the war and I would have no objection if he had ordered me to a Nissen hut, but I felt it was unfair to relegate Jewish DPs to such conditions after so many years in concentration camps. He advised me that the concentration camp reason had been used too often, and I explained to him that it had to be used often only because there still remain those who are unmindful of its existence." When Wheatman threatened to use force, Gelber answered by using the most effective Jewish weapon of those postwar years: he said he would advise the press, who would then undoubtedly flock to the scene and report that Wheatman had created the difficulty. Wheatman retreated, and different quarters were found for the British unit that was to have taken over the Jews' barracks.[16] The point in citing this exchange of unpleasantries is to illustrate the British official's lack of comprehension of the concentration camp psychology, which was ridden with inferiority complexes and resulting aggressiveness, of people who regarded any removal to new surroundings that were not an improvement over their present dwellings as a new threat to their still-shaky sense of security and self-respect.

Some of the higher officials exhibited the same lack of sympathy. General Sir Frederick Morgan, UNRRA chief for Germany, for instance, who had made that unhappy statement on Jewish refugees early in the year, had not changed his opinions since then. There were also reports circulating that he wanted to hand over all UNRRA's tasks to the occupation armies because he was expecting a clash with the Russians soon. Then, in August, he overstepped the limits of prudence by leaking a story to the papers accusing his own organization, UNRRA, of serving as an umbrella for Russian agents. There were, of course, Russians and East Europeans on UNRRA's staff, because it was an international organization, and no doubt many of these people were used as sources of information for their countries' various agencies. But La Guardia, who had had very little sympathy for the British general to start with, and who was not held back by scruples as his Jewish predecessor, Governor Lehman, had been, took the opportunity and fired Morgan summarily.[17] This was very welcome news to Jews all over the DP camps.

In this atmosphere of gathering clouds, morale in the DP camps was sinking rapidly. Physical conditions, bad as they were, were not the only, perhaps not even the main, cause of this decline. The hopes that had accompanied the panic flight from Poland seemed to have been dashed. Palestine was closed: from August 12 on, the British deported every Mossad ship they caught (only two managed to enter Palestine unobserved in 1946) to Cyprus, where they set up detention camps for the refugees. Morale was sagging, and a JDC observer said that what was "happening is that people are getting more and more discouraged daily . . . the feeling of frustration is reaching the stage where it is demoralizing."[18] People had food and basic clothing, but little else. To acquire other things that were called amenities but were in fact in many ways essentials of civilized existence, such as toilet articles, bed sheets and pillows, some extra clothing and books, one had recourse either to the distribution of such items by the JDC or to the black market. The market was actually gray rather than black; literally everyone engaged in it—Germans, Americans, DPs. One simply

could not exist without it. The people who supplied this gray market with quantities of goods, both the large and small operators, were unscrupulous in their manipulations and were largely responsible for the demoralization of the refugees. The big operations were in the hands of Germans, but in the Jewish camps themselves there was a whole substructure of minor operators.

The fight against demoralization was primarily a Jewish task. It was of course made possible by JDC funds that supported morale-building activities, but the actual use of the monies and the implementation of the programs was in the hands of the DPs themselves. This was where the Central Committee of Liberated Jews in Munich, founded a year earlier by Rabbi Klausner, became primarily effective. The U.S. zone, which was the committee's bailiwick, had become the main area of concentration of Jewish DPs in Germany. Some 70,860 people arrived between June and the end of October 1946, and at the end of the year, the zone had about 140,000 Jews, of whom 70 percent were estimated to be living in camps. There were 57 such camps, apart from 15 special children's centers, 39 agricultural training farms and 27 hospitals and sanatoriums. The training farms were populated by about 3,000 members of Zionist youth movements who were training for agricultural pioneering in Palestine. The tremendous health and social welfare problems of this transient community were indicated by the relatively large number of children's centers and health institutions. Despite these problems, the existence of the children's centers in particular reflected an encouraging trend in the Jewish refugees' demographic structure. There had been literally no children under six when the Jews were liberated in 1945. By the end of 1946, such children accounted for 8.5 percent of the Jewish population, and another 12 percent were between the ages of six and seventeen.[19] This was due to the fact that whereas in 1945 Jews in Germany and Poland were survivors of the Nazi regime and remnants of families whose children had been exterminated by the Germans with great thoroughness, the 1946 arrivals came from Russia where they had spent the war years. When they returned, they

came in families with children. Quite apart from this factor, however, was the tremendous urge of young people among the liberated Jews—and practically only young people had survived—to rebuild their lives and found new families and thus regain in part at least what they had so tragically lost. The result was an epidemic of marriages and births, a tremendous urge in women to bear children, and as many of them as possible. By the end of 1946, there were 26,506 children in the U.S. zone, of whom 5,703 were labeled as "unaccompanied," that is, either orphaned or sent ahead from Poland by parents who would follow later on.[20] Close to 1,000 babies were being born each month in that winter.

All these factors placed entirely new tasks before the Central Committee. The last elections to the committee had taken place late in 1945, and by the summer of 1946 the committee could no longer be held representative of the Jewish population; yet no elections could be held while the chaotic influx was in process. Dr. Zalman Gruenberg, the committee's chairman, had gone to Palestine in July, when it seemed that the 100,000 entry permits to Palestine asked for by Truman would be granted and preparations to receive them in their new country were deemed essential. But Gruenberg stayed in Palestine to be near his son who was dying of leukemia in a hospital there; and the leadership of the committee was taken over by men like Dr. Samuel Gringausz, a formidable and popular lawyer from Landsberg, and Dr. Avraham (Abrasha) Blumovicz, a physician and the only genuine resistance fighter among the committee's membership. Also among the committee's members was Aryeh Nesher (Retter), aged twenty-one, who was secretary and who took over relations with the U.S. Army. Nesher had set up a model community at Regensburg, where black market operations did not take root. In July, too, Klausner was forced to leave Munich after a bitter personal quarrel with the JDC representative there, and the committee had to stand on its own feet. At first, no great love was lost between it and the JDC, but the two organizations supplemented each other, the JDC providing the funds and supplies and the committee the purpose and the self-government which alone could make the Jews form a self-

respecting community. In the face of disillusionment and threatening demoralization, the committee in Munich had local elections held in each camp to provide for self-government. Nominees of the committees then manned schools, cultural institutions and internal courts; they also engaged in religious activities and provided internal policing with JDC funds and expert advice. The Central Committee itself undertook some activities which had a more than transitory value. A series of books were published under its auspices—again with JDC funds—in such fields as poetry and religion, which brought out some of the most constructive elements of DP life. Jacob Kaplan, another of the Lithuanian core of the Committee's supporters, published his *Fun Letzten Churben* (Of the Late Catastrophe), a journal that for the first time attempted to deal calmly and scientifically with the destruction of European Jewry. The political party structure, despite or perhaps precisely because of its factionalism, was another morale-building force. The Unity Zionist Party, founded immediately after liberation, which had to all intents and purposes monopolized the political scene, identified with the moderate socialist Mapai Party of Palestine (led by Ben-Gurion). In 1946 a host of other political groups appeared, all of them Zionist and all of them identifying with one or the other of the Palestinian Jewish political factions. In a way, the existence of all these groups guaranteed a means of self-expression and a vehicle for camp democracy, and also a safety valve for a largely unemployed and emotionally disturbed population.

The U.S. Army, prodded energetically by Rabbi Bernstein, was on the whole officially sympathetic to the Central Committee and on September 7 recognized it[21] as the representative of the liberated Jews in the zone. The new definition of the committee's functions by that act of recognition put some limitations on its claims of authority, but it now had independent access to the Army through Colonel George R. Scithers, a special liaison officer assigned to it. From the Brichah point of view this was a vital achievement: the committee was now a useful go-between between Brichah and the Army in all practical things that mattered—organization, transportation and movement of refugees.

There seems to be little doubt that without the committee the Brichah would have been unable to use the zone as the chief reservoir for Jews fleeing from Eastern Europe. The relationships between the two groups, channeled partly through Yahil's Palestinian welfare workers, was excellent. Officially the committee was of course independent of Yahil's team. In fact, because of the committee's Zionist persuasion, Yahil's word carried a great deal of weight in the committee's councils. Moreover, the Palestinian group was officially part of UNRRA and was suitably equipped with transportation and uniforms; these were very useful for Brichah work, especially while Ephraim Frank was commander of Brichah in Germany because Frank was in Germany illegally. This did not impair his authority, which was exercised with the full support of Yahil on the one hand and the committee on the other. The committee's liaison man with Brichah was Yosef Lavi, another Lithuanian Zionist, who arranged the preparatory work for Brichah movements, such as choosing candidates for Italy and France through the various political groups. Frank was in charge of the main Brichah "points" at Frankfurt, Hof (on the German side of the As border with Czechoslovakia), Freilassing and Bad Reichenhall on the border with the U.S. zone in Austria, and the "points" on the route to France. Having set up the basic organization, Frank left Germany and his place was taken by Willy Ritter in June 1946. Ritter, like Frank, was also a Palestinian kibbutz member. He was a scholarly, bespectacled man who was later to become a physics professor at the Haifa Technical Institute. Ritter's advantage was that he had come in officially as a member of the Palestinian welfare team and had an official standing as an emigration officer of UNRRA, which of course in a sense he was. He was thus better able to use the services of the Palestinians, who were people of high caliber who had been specially chosen for their aptitude for welfare and social work; their work for Brichah was certainly incidental to their main task, but for Brichah it was essential to have their guidance and expert advice when problems arose in the emotionally charged atmosphere of the DP camps.

Rabbi Bernstein's unsuccessful attempts to ease the Army's

burden by placing some of the refugees in countries other than Germany (except for one scheme, which also failed, to transfer 2,500 children from Germany to Norway) dealt with refugees who had not yet come to Germany but were likely to go there.[22] Legal opportunities for leaving Germany were not very bright in 1946, and Brichah had an important share in whatever exodus there was. The Americans did not place any serious obstacles in the way of the Brichah; and there were quite a few Americans who, unofficially, helped. There were 6,200 DPs who left Germany by Brichah routes in 1946; 3,400 of these went to Italy by way of Austria, and 2,800 to France. In addition, there was legal immigration into Palestine from the camps, which started about May 1946 and accounted for some 2,500 people by July 1947. These immigrants, among whom children's transports had priority, were processed by the Palestinian welfare team of the Jewish Agency under Yahil. In addition, 5,210 others went from Germany to all the other countries legally with the help of the JDC and the Jewish immigration society HIAS. Another 6,042 left Germany in similar fashion between January and July 1947, and an estimated 3,500 left by legal means on their own in 1946 and early 1947. For 1946 alone, all these figures would show that approximately 14,500 people left Germany by one means or another, or about 8 percent of the Jewish population of the U.S. zone; some 35 to 40 percent of these went by Brichah routes.[23]

As far as France was concerned, the Frankfurt "point" and several small "points" in the French zone marked the exit into that country. At Frankfurt, there was a succession of Brigade soldiers who were responsible for the operations. However, from late 1945 to the middle of 1947, a Hebrew-speaking ex-Lithuanian DP, Zev Birger, was there and did a great deal of the actual work. Until about the middle of 1946 Frankfurt simply passed on refugees coming down from the British zone into the Munich area where most of the camps were situated. When the big movement began, Frankfurt began to get more detailed instructions from Ritter as to what to do with the arrivals, how to distribute them and where. Planning and execution of policy thereby became much more effective. The actual "point" was located

in a school, and from there Birger and his comrades maintained their operations with the help of both the Americans and Germans. Not much cash was needed, and blankets, food and gasoline were obtained from UNRRA, the JDC or Frankfurt municipality. Birger himself wore an UNRRA uniform and served officially as an emigration officer, an end result of an unusual history. He had been liberated from a concentration camp and was stopped in late 1945 by Americans as he was trying to cross their zonal borders in western Czechoslovakia. His knowledge of languages proved useful and he became an official translator in the 88th U.S. Infantry Division. He became friendly with a number of officers who enabled him to don a uniform, receive arms and even undergo some training. By that time the unit, originally stationed in Bohemia, was transferred to the west and was demobilizing its men and sending them home. Birger was offered an opportunity to emigrate to America by a simple though irregular procedure. However, he declined, and used his military standing to join UNRRA. An individualist and a strong character, he worked in close friendship with the men of the Brigade. His relations with the Germans enabled him to pull off some rather unusual tricks. At one time he was asked by Munich to get 500 gallons of gasoline—a most difficult assignment. He took with him another Brichah man, Dov Nishri, who was dressed in good civilian clothes, and entered the office of the German supply department of Frankfurt municipality. There he put on a show of great deference to his well-dressed friend, and proceeded to ask the German official for 500 gallons of gasoline, which in 1946 was an astronomical amount to ask from a German city. When the German demurred, Birger "translated" his remarks into Hebrew and Nishri started shouting at Birger—also in Hebrew. There was hardly a need now to translate into German—obviously the civilian was some very important personage in the Allies' setup. The German was suitably impressed and the gasoline was obtained without further difficulty.[24]

The smuggling of people out of Germany into France was a very complicated business. Luckily the Brichah people had the help of certain American personnel, who provided them

with trucks and gasoline. The man behind the operation was a slight, daredevil kibbutz member from Palestine by the name of Simcha Even-Dar, who established a series of "points" in the French zones, starting from Lake Constance. The country road from Singen and Geisingen brought the refugees to the Efringen border point; there they were received by another Palestinian from the religious kibbutz of Tirath-Zvi and brought to Colmar.[25] This was already well within French territory; and with the connivance of French government officials who disagreed with British policy in Palestine, the people were brought into Lyons and from there to Marseilles.

This route began to be used in May 1946. Refugees were brought in only when a ship was actually about to sail, and therefore much careful Mossad planning went into these transports from Germany into France. The forged South American visas which gave the French the official excuse to admit the Jews into France were not issued until the illegal ship was ready to receive the load, so that the whole operation was purely Mossad, and the Brichah as such did not operate in France at all: from the moment the people arrived at the French border, operational responsibility passed into Mossad hands.

It must be added that the organized Brichah transports were only part of the crossings into France. Other DPs managed to get legal papers of various kinds and got into a France whose government was hospitable to them. This unorganized movement was by no means Palestine-centered; on the contrary, most of the people who thus came in intended to use Paris as a starting point for emigration to the Americas or to stay in France and settle there, as indeed many of them did.

The general policy of Brichah in 1946 was dominated by two main purposes: to send the mass of the refugees into the U.S. zone in Germany so as to create there a large reservoir of Jewish population that by its very existence would exercise a growing pressure on Palestine's closed doors; and secondly, to send a continual trickle of would-be immigrants to France and Italy whence most of the Mossad ships sailed for their illegal runs to Palestine. Generally speaking, a total

of 69,878 people were transported by sixty-five Mossad ships out of Europe and North Africa between the summer of 1945 and May 1948, when Israel came into existence. In 1946, twenty-two ships brought 21,711 people, and of these, eleven ships brought 7,451 persons from Italy, and four others sailed out of France with 3,777 on board. Brichah had to bring the people into these countries, or fill the camps with other candidates to take the place of those that left. In Italy this was much simpler than in France, because the DP camps in Italy were maintained by UNRRA—later by IRO—and the JDC, whereas there were no DP camps in France. Italy was therefore a main goal of Brichah activities; in 1946, despite all the difficulties, 13,282 people were smuggled in, of whom 7,250 came after July.[26]

Transit to Italy was beset with problems. The Italian government became increasingly independent of Allied control, and had to deal with unemployment and economic chaos. They were very much opposed to the idea of Jewish refugees coming into the country. However, there were kind and humanitarian Italians who did not take official policy too seriously. Many Italian officials knew exactly what Brichah was and helped it, in defiance of explicit orders and without receiving any kind of compensation. The problem for Brichah therefore was to find the right type of border and, more important, the right kind of Italian official or policeman.

Above Solbad Hall near Innsbruck, on a forest-covered hillside, lies the tiny village of Gnadenwald. It consists of a few homesteads, a couple of inns and an eighteenth-century church. In 1945 a local hotel called Wiesenhof was taken over by a Jewish agricultural training group. The group soon left for Italy, but others came and it became a central point for Brichah operations in the French zone. Soon a second hotel (Gnadenwalder Hof), just a few hundred yards away, was added, and the two houses became Brichah centers of great importance. Their position was ideal: they were centrally located, but the main road to Innsbruck was three miles away. The three miles are steep and uninviting and narrow; moreover, above Gnadenwald rise hundreds of feet of forested mountains. It was hard to take Gnadenwald by

surprise because Brichah lookouts could always warn people of trucks or cars puffing up the steep incline; also, it was easy to slip into the woods. The peasants were friendly because the Jews bought up the local produce; the old village headman, owner of another inn, was an anti-Nazi of sorts, and the priest was most understanding as well. The JDC gave blankets and cash, the French and the Austrians gave basic rations; Gnadenwald was an ideal spot in every way.

In July, after months of searching for a way to get into Italy, a square-shouldered, compact little Turkish Jew by the name of Sami Levy came to Gnadenwald.[27] He knew neither Yiddish nor German, but he spoke excellent French and passable Italian; and he was a no-nonsense man (years later he was to become Ben Gurion's bodyguard). Sami was not sent to Gnadenwald by the Mossad or by Surkiss of the Brigade, but by yet another illegal body, *the* illegal body, in fact—the European command of Haganah. This command had been set up some months previously: its aims were to train young Jews for paramilitary activity in Palestine and at the same time provide for the possible need for self-defense against anti-Semitic attacks in Europe. Also, in 1946 the possibility of actions against the British in Europe could not be discounted, and Haganah was preparing for that eventuality. The slackening of movement into Italy was a setback for Haganah as well as for Brichah, because most of Haganah's training centers were located in Italy. Sami was therefore sent to find new ways through the mountains, and a jurisdictional dispute soon started as to which organization should be responsible for Gnadenwald. Sami remained loyal to his Haganah commander, but it soon became clear that it was Brichah, that is, Ben Nathan from Vienna and the Salzburg people, who controlled the situation.

Sami brought with him seven Brigade soldiers, all of whom became Brichah workers.[28] With their help he began in a manner characteristic of him, to clear out a nest of black marketeers who had preempted the Wiesenhof hotel. They were supported by some Polish DPs from a nearby camp and told Sami that if he did not leave them alone they would use their guns on him. Sami told them that he and his friends had guns, too, and proceeded to burn their

stock of cigarettes. The intimidated smugglers disappeared, never to be heard of again. He then brought in a group ("kibbutz") of idealistic young people from Poland, members of one of the youth movements, and with their help created a different atmosphere from the one he had found when he got to Gnadenwald.

Sami began by trying to use the Brenner Pass, despite the fact that this was the main road leading from Austria to Italy and was of course very closely guarded by the Americans, British and Italians. He tried to smuggle people across by bypassing the actual frontier post; besides the physical difficulties, which were formidable in themselves and involved some tricky climbing over wet and treacherous paths—it was summer—the problem of finding paths that would accommodate larger numbers proved insurmountable. There was no point in bringing over groups of ten or fifteen hardy young men or women. He then tried to organize a transport of three trucks, loaded eighty people on them and had an Italian collective visa forged to get them through. This was good enough for the French, the Americans and the British, but the Italian border guard at the Brenner insisted on getting in touch with the Ministry of the Interior in Rome to verify the visa. Fortunately, he could not reach the ministry, and Sami was able to beat a dignified retreat, declaring he could not let his eighty people wait on trucks while telephone calls were being put through to Rome and adding that he would be back later. He never came back, of course.

With the Brenner no longer possible, Sami tried other routes; there were two other roads leading across the frontier in the general area of Innsbruck, at Passo di Rombo and at Nauders. Footpaths could be used around either of these, but after a few tryouts he settled for the old route at Nauders which had been used by Gefen and his friends up till May. By the end of July, however, there were no more British guards there, and it was easier to cope with the French, Austrian and Italian patrols than with the British. Sami got hold of trucks—some were Brigade vehicles which he obtained from the Haganah, and some were American trucks from Munich. These he equipped with new license plates, and using some imagination, painted the JDC in-

signias on them *and* the inscription "Headquarters, US Forces, French Zone, Austria." Having thus occupied the French zone in Austria in the name of the American Army, he then quite logically proceeded to don the uniform of an American captain, and was ready for action; there were no American MPs in the French zone near Innsbruck and he was quite safe.

His major problems were fuel, spare parts and repairs for his trucks, and these he solved by having a repair shop installed in Gnadenwald. His Brigade pals became the drivers, and he started shipping refugees across the border. His destination on the other side was the little holiday resort of Merano, where there was a TB hospital set up by the JDC. The Italian police knew of its existence and it seemed quite logical to them that large numbers of Jews should be sent from Germany and Austria to be cured of the terrible illness on Italian soil. And if one hospital was conceded, surely there could be more, to accommodate the growing demand as shown by the large numbers of Jews who apparently were in need of recuperation. That was the basis on which Sami operated, until one fine day one of his trucks was caught by the French, the vehicle confiscated and the people arrested. It did not take him too long to talk his way through to the French police and free his driver and the truck—the refugees the French had freed very gladly. He appeared there as the American captain whose driver had inadvertently driven across into Italy with the wrong papers; but the important part of the adventure was that Sami got to know the French security officer responsible for the whole border region, and with this man he struck up an intimate friendship. Before long the Frenchman was told the truth about the whole operation, and he became an ardent supporter of Sami and the Brichah; in fact, he became almost a member of the organization, just as Novinsky had further north. He even gave Sami an Austrian policeman to accompany the trucks to the border. Thus Sami operated his Gnadenwald project for the rest of the year. He obtained food from the French and from the JDC, and by going into the American zone in his captain's uniform he demanded and received gasoline for the "French zone"—in time he be-

came known to American Army personnel who never suspected the genuineness of his American disguise. Contrary to Brichah operations everywhere else, Sami's achievements grew rather than diminished as winter came on, and in 1947 Gnadenwald was to become a focal point for what remained of the Brichah in Central Europe in that year.

10. *The Slow Decline*

The panic created in Poland by Kielce slowly subsided. In the great struggle for the control of Poland the leftist government was gaining the upper hand, and life and property were becoming safer in the war-torn country. The incentives for Jews to leave Poland illegally, with not much more than the clothes on their backs, were disappearing. On the other hand, as the autumn of 1946 progressed, news coming back from the DP camps of Germany and, chiefly, Austria became less and less encouraging. Descriptions of overcrowding, shoddy barracks and tent cities, inadequate food and lack of prospects to leave for Palestine or America were filtering back to Lodz and Warsaw. Why leave reasonably decent homes in Poland for camps in Germany under such conditions? Many Jews in Poland were still thinking of emigration, but there was no longer such a desperate hurry. They would go ultimately, but they wanted to go legally, in an organized and orderly fashion. The mad rush across borders was no longer necessary; some people even came back from Germany—probably not more than a few thousand at the most, but still they came back and fortified the resolution of many people to adopt an attitude of wait and see.[1] In the newly Polish areas of Silesia, taken over from the Germans, the increasingly Communist-dominated Central Committee of Polish Jews, with the help of the JDC,

began to be more successful than before in building up a closely populated Jewish settlement, which seemed to promise some kind of security and permanence. The Jews still had their suitcases packed, but they were no longer standing by them; they were sitting on them, and they might possibly start unpacking if conditions improved.

Brichah from Poland declined in numbers. In November, only 2,545 left the country; in December 1946, 1,897 left; in January 1947, 1,029; and in February, 1,700.[2] Stettin had practically closed, though a few people carried on there in order to keep the connection open. In Silesia only one "point," the one at Kladzko, was maintained. Only determined Zionists were leaving now. The Poles were becoming rather uneasy about the semilegal arrangement that had been initiated during the Kielce period. In December there were occasions when they closed the border. On January 19, 1947, elections were held that ended in a crushing defeat of the anti-government forces. From now on, the regime could exercise fuller control both over the country internally and also over its borders, and it did not hesitate to do so. The Ministry for Foreign Affairs was especially eager to close the illegal and semilegal exit routes. It was under constant pressure from the British, and it was clear that the problem of the Polish gold reserves, held by the British, was a factor as well. The Deputy Minister of Foreign Affairs, Olszewski, claimed that his ministry had had no information as to what had actually been happening, and the confusion was made greater by the fact that Adolf Berman, one of the two Jewish leaders who had originally arranged the exit, was the Zionist brother of the Communist and anti-Zionist Jakub Berman, who was thought to have given his consent to the arrangement because of the kinship—but nothing could have been further from the truth. When Olszewski "found out" that the arrangement was an unofficial one with the security police, he told the commander of the border police to come to see him. The general, sensing something wrong, sent his two aides with Alexander to face the music. Quite innocently, Alexander walked into the trap and had to listen to a long diatribe against Brichah in general and himself in particular. The border was to be closed.

The time was the middle of February. There still were hundreds, if not more, of Zionist youths who were trying to get out. Nine hundred Jews were allowed to slip quickly through the border, and on February 22, 1947, the border was finally closed.[3] The last vestiges of the great panic exodus had gone.

The atmosphere in Poland in early 1947 was not conducive to large-scale illegal activity. It became increasingly difficult to evade the watchful eyes of the regime. At the time of the January 1947 elections, the Polish Brichah received word of the impending visit of three important visitors: Yisrael Galili, chief of the National Command of the Haganah in Palestine, Yigal Alon, commander of the Palmach, the main force of the Haganah, and Ephraim Dekel, the new European commander of the Brichah, of whom more later. The three men did not go to the trouble of obtaining official entry permits—it is hardly likely they would have gotten them—and they entered Poland by Brichah routes. They wanted to see for themselves how Brichah operated, they wanted to see something of the survivors of Polish Jewry and, last but not least, they wanted to visit Auschwitz. Alexander had to maneuver them in and out of Polish towns, trembling all the while that by some accident Galili and Alon, the top commanders of the Jewish underground in Palestine, might be captured. The fact that neither of them spoke Polish did not make his task any easier. On the night before the elections they had to go by train to the frontier to leave the country, but just in front of the railway station in a Polish town they were stopped by gendarmes who suspected them to be anti-government saboteurs on some destructive mission. Had they been caught, the results might well have been disastrous; it was only through Alexander's presence of mind that the situation was saved. He drew a gun (for which he had a license) and thereby diverted attention away from the two mute Palestinians. He then was able to produce proper documents issued in the name of the Jewish United Workers' Party (the name, as we have seen, tended to dispel suspicion) and the other members of the little group were no longer involved. The gendarmes apologized and the incident was settled; but it clearly showed that

the former chaos had definitely given way to order and that the old methods of Brichah operations had not much further chance of success.[4]

All this did not mean that the Brichah simply ceased operations. There was, as the figures show, a trickle of border-crossings into Czechoslovakia from the Kladzko region in Silesia. Throughout 1947, the Brichah statistics showed that 9,315 were taken across.[5] Some went on to As, but the majority traveled the well-worn route that led them to Bratislava and Vienna. Most of these refugees were young people, members of Zionist youth movements who did not flinch at the prospects of dangerous crossings and long jail sentences. But the older people, including members of Zionist parties who still had hopes of maintaining their legality in the new Poland, began to fear the consequences of a clash with the government over illegal exit, and as the year went on, opposition to Alexander and the Brichah increased. Alexander reported at the time that while "*chalutzic* (pioneering) elements demand the immediate reopening of the border, the Zionist parties are definitely opposed to our actions because they are afraid they will be closed down if there is Brichah movement, and they have been warned by the Government in this sense."[6] The climate of Jewish opinion had definitely changed, and Brichah had to try other ways and means.

In Warsaw there was an official emigration office of the Jewish Agency whose task was to administer the distribution of the few legal certificates of entry to Palestine that the Agency could send to it. In that office, Alexander opened his own branch, and tried to get legal visas to West European or South American countries that would enable people to get out of Poland as legal emigrants, reach Western Europe and then proceed to Palestine from there. By May he had 2,000 such visas, and then he received another bunch from the friendly representative of a Central American government, who knew of course that these immigrants would never arrive in his country in any case. However, in order to leave, people had to have Polish passports, and the Poles were by no means eager to provide these, though there never was a blanket refusal. The lady who was responsible for the issue of passports at the Polish Foreign Office would

receive the forms, promise action, and then proceed at a snail's pace, each application lying for many months before the documents were issued. Many of those for whom passports were asked would be members of Zionist youth movements, and these would get impatient and cross the borders illegally. Then, when the passports finally arrived they would no longer be in the country and that fact would have to be hushed up. In all, according to the visa office report, only 1,075 people left Poland in 1947, out of some 4,000 for whom foreign visas could be had.[7]

Another attempt was made through direct negotiations with the Polish officials. This was again the province of Zuckerman and his colleagues, but these negotiations brought no results. Toward the autumn of 1947 illegal crossings were again tried, but the number remained small. Brichah in Poland had become a mere trickle, carrying on well into 1948, when another 2,300 managed to cross the borders. As a mass movement of the Jewish people, as a historical phenomenon, it was dead.[8]

Brichah hierarchy and organization had never been very clearly defined. Country commanders (often called *merakzim,* or coordinators) had owed a vague allegiance to either the Bratislava secretariat with Levi Argov at its head or to Mordechai Surkiss of the Brigade, or to both. Ultimately, they all acknowledged they were connected to Mossad, the illegal immigration authority which had appointed most of them. Most of the founders of the movement, the survivors of the holocaust—such as Kovner, Ben, Lidovsky—had gone on to Palestine or else had taken on new tasks of a political kind. Their places had largely been taken by Palestinians. Ever since early 1946, occasional conferences of Brichah commanders took place (usually in Bratislava), where movements were coordinated, coding of messages and money transfers were arranged and methods of transit determined. There was remarkably little discussion of general policy, because it seemed that the general task was quite clear: to get the Jews out of Eastern Europe and either concentrate them in the DP countries or bring them to the shores of the Mediterranean. In 1946 a first attempt was also made to nominate a Brichah commander for all of Europe, and

the man chosen was Pinhas Rashish, a local labor leader and politician from Petah-Tikvah, near Tel Aviv. This proved to be a dismal failure, and Rashish did not last more than a few weeks; the commanders did not accept his authority, his grasp of the situation was inadequate, and generally an esprit de corps had developed with which he did not know how to cope. By April 1946 Rashish was on his way back to Palestine, and Brichah continued to exist without a formal command hierarchy throughout its most heroic period.

Paradoxically, the organization of Brichah came after it had fulfilled its major task, that is, after the autumn of 1946. With the increasing bitterness of the anti-British struggle, Mossad assumed practical control of all illegal activities in Europe. Shaul Avigur, the Mossad commander, was a small, rotund man with tremendous will power; one of the old-time pioneers of the upper Jordan valley, he had been one of the two effective members of the Haganah command until 1938, when he became head of the Mossad. Quiet, secretive and very efficient, he maintained personal and, usually, very friendly relations with most of the Mossad emissaries. His headquarters were in Paris, and his responsibilities embraced Mossad, Brichah, the acquisition of arms for the Haganah, and Haganah in Europe itself. It was he who decided to use the forthcoming 22nd Congress of the Zionist Movement in Basel in December 1946 to effect a reorganization of the illegal Jewish organizations.

The 22nd Congress was probably the most crucial Zionist meeting in the pre-Israel era. Outwardly, the problem was whether the Zionist movement would agree to give up its claim to the whole of Palestine and proclaim its readiness to accept the partition of that country; also, whether or not it would accept an invitation by the British to participate in yet another round of three-cornered conversations with them and the Arabs. In fact, however, the issues went deeper: at issue was the question of how best to resist British pressure, and therefore who should lead the movement—the "activists" who advocated a strong anti-British line and were led by Ben-Gurion and Rabbi Abba Hillel Silver of the United States, or the gradualist, essentially pro-British

forces led by Weizmann and Goldmann. A majority of the groups represented admitted privately that if partition was feasible they would accept it. The question of the conferences with the British and Arabs was also essentially a smokescreen, as was shown later when those who had opposed them, and had gained a majority at the Congress for their stand, promptly went to London, with Ben Gurion at the head, to conduct the talks which they had opposed. As happens so often, the real issues were hidden by political maneuvering because they could not be discussed openly. The moderates lost, Weizmann resigned from the presidency of the Zionist movement, and the Ben Gurion group took over. After the Congress, in January, the last talks with the British failed in London, and in February the Labour government handed the whole problem to the U.N., hoping for an international mandate to pursue their essentially pro-Arab and anti-Zionist policies.

Avigur was a staunch supporter of Ben Gurion, and most of the Brichah commanders, whatever their political affiliations, supported a fairly energetic line of Jewish "activism." They all met at Basel, where they were introduced to a new man who was to be the commander of Brichah in Europe. His name was Ephraim Dekel, outwardly the most unlikely figure for such a job: a balding, jovial, folksy, round little man with merry brown eyes—hardly the prototype of an underground commander. Moreover, he had what for a Brichah commander was the most unlikely occupation—he had for years been the commander of the Tel Aviv fire brigade. However, the Jewish fire brigade in Palestine had been one of the more effective fronts for Haganah, and Dekel had organized the intelligence service of the Tel Aviv Haganah and then become the effective head of the Haganah intelligence on a country-wide basis. It was he who in a daring raid on the British command post at Sarafand stole British documents on their proposed action against the Haganah in the spring of 1946, copied the papers and returned them without being noticed at all by the British. But by the summer of that year the British were on his trail and he had to leave the country. Reporting to Avigur in Paris, he received the assignment to head Brichah. Up to the time of the Basel

Congress he toured the countries where Brichah operated, gathering his impressions and making copious notes. After Basel, he reorganized the movement on a hierarchic basis. Argov terminated his work as Dekel took over, and a new reign began. Dekel introduced sound bookkeeping, evolved efficient methods of communication and proper covers for illegal activity. His Palestine experience stood him well, and the genuine high regard which he had for his predecessors made him popular among the old-timers. Ben-Zvi had left Poland, and Alexander was now in charge in name as well as in fact. The other countries now had well-established Palestinian commanders with whom Dekel soon found common language. At the discussions in Basel special stress was laid on transit to Italy and France to supply passengers for Mossad ships. Also at Basel, an exhibition was organized by Argov for the benefit of reliable Congress delegates to show the character and extent of Brichah activities. The self-confidence of Brichah was clearly shown in the exhibit, which was seen by hundreds of people yet not a word of it reached unauthorized ears.

Dekel maintained his position at the head of Brichah throughout 1947; opinions regarding his efficiency must have been divided because two attempts were made throughout the year to curtail his authority. Argov was brought back from Palestine to take over the leadership, but in a struggle behind the scenes Dekel managed to maintain his position and Argov was removed from the stage. Another man, a daredevil ex-Brigade man by the name of Yisrael Carmi, was brought in to take over part of Dekel's job. But when on April 25, 1947, he was caught with 300 DPs in seven trucks trying to cross the German border into Austria because he attempted to crash through a side-road guarded by Austrians without first arranging the transfer locally, it was decided that he was not quite the right man for the job. Yahil in Germany had to work hard to get the drivers, the trucks and Carmi released. To make matters worse, Carmi used the forged signature of an important Norwegian UNRRA functionary on his homemade documents; it so happened that the man was a good friend of Yahil's and very pro-Jewish. At his next encounter with Yahil, the Nor-

wegian talked for a long time about many other matters, but when he was about to leave he turned to Yahil and remarked—according to Yahil—"By the way, should you accidentally meet some people who deal with transportation documents, you might tell them that the name 'Smith' is also a very good name." The incident effectively settled the personnel problem of Brichah command and Dekel remained in charge.

The relationship of Brichah to Mossad also underwent a change. In 1946, Brichah was equal in importance for actual illegal immigration to Palestine which was what Mossad was also supporting, whereas in 1947, under Dekel, it became an adjunct to the more important Mossad work. In Paris Mossad was run by two men, Avigur and Avriel, with others (usually members of different political groups) occasionally sitting in on decision making. Control was now tight and increasingly efficient, and very definitely in the hands of Mossad. Mossad asserted itself even vis-à-vis Dr. Moshe Sneh, the former head of the Haganah National Command, who had to flee from Palestine on June 29, 1946, and was still nominally in charge of underground affairs, especially in Europe. He was not a member of the ruling Mapai party but belonged to the centrist General Zionists, and he never quite managed to become a member of the inner circle.

Until the autumn of 1946, Poland had been the major source of Brichah; but even then up to 20 percent of the refugees were of other than Polish origin, about equally divided between Hungary, Rumania and other countries (Czechoslovakia, Yugoslavia). With the decline of the Polish Brichah those other elements became increasingly important. It must be remembered that the regimes in Hungary and Rumania were no more popular than that in Poland, and there were obvious parallels between the position of the Jews in all three countries. In Hungary, Palestine *shlihim* had been in charge of Brichah ever since the original wartime leaders of the local Zionist youth groups left in late 1945. In 1946 Yonah Rosen and after him Yehuda Talmi were operating out of the office of a youth group called Esrah which served as a "front" organization for Brichah activities. On the

whole, in early 1946, there were no great difficulties, but the Hungarians assumed that anti-government elements would not use Brichah routes to leave the country. In March, however, a trainload of 500 refugees was stopped on its way to Austria, and some Hungarian fascists were found posing as Jews—they had gone to such lengths as having themselves circumcised and having facial changes made through surgery. As a result of the incident, the Brichah activists, including Rosen, were arrested. Talmi, who was outside of Hungary at the time, returned at the direct behest of Ben-Gurion and went to the police to explain that no bad faith was involved in the mishap. The Communists, however, demanded what in effect was ransom money, and in the end a large amount ($20,000) was paid as a "contribution" to the Communist Party. After this, relations improved again and an agreement was reached which opened certain border points for crossing into Yugoslavia and Austria. The people who wanted to leave were largely poor Jews (many from the provinces rather than Budapest), children and Zionist youth groups. The organization was haphazard, and not more than educated guesses are available as to numbers. It seems that up to the end of 1946, between 15,000 and 18,000 Hungarian Jews left the country, mostly via Austria, but some also through Subotica to Yugoslavia.[9] Toward the end of 1946 the flow of Hungarian Jews out of their country ceased, in a way reflecting a similar trend in Poland. The reason in Hungary was largely economic. Inflation, which had completely ruined the Hungarian economy (and had been artificially advanced by the Communists as a means of expropriation of the wealthier classes), was stopped by a monetary reform. An immediate improvement in the economic life followed, and with it an important cause for leaving disappeared. Hungary embarked on a course of stronger control by the new regime which gradually stifled the relative liberalism in Jewish matters. The fact that many of the leading lights of Hungarian communism were Jews was a negative factor because these Jews felt they had to prove that they had no sympathy whatever for any Jewish interests. A man like Zoltan Vas, the effective ruler of Budapest, put increasing restrictions on Brichah although he did

not hesitate to use its services to rescue his own relatives.[10] But quite apart from the growing hostility on the part of Jewish Communists, Brichah in Hungary, as in Poland, was hamstrung by the apparent hopelessness of emigration prospects generally and the fact that DP camps were not more alluring than even a miserable existence in Hungary.

In early 1947, therefore, the task of enabling East European Jews to leave their countries appeared fairly hopeless. The UN was about to discuss the Palestine question in April, and until then there was no way of getting to Palestine except by illegal immigration, and there were already enough candidates for that in the DP camps. Unless driven out by new crises, East European Jews would no longer move in large numbers. In fact, only one Brichah route remained: the Bratislava-Vienna route, and it was on that route that an interesting incident occurred in early 1947 which highlighted both the possibilities and the limitations of Brichah.

There was a narrow wooden bridge on the Danube, between the Slovak village of Devinska Nova Ves and the Austrian township of Marchegg, which had been used by over 100,000 Jewish refugees throughout 1946. On the Slovak side there was a wooden barracks where people could wait until passage was cleared. The winter of 1946–47 was especially severe, and although the Brichah flow had dwindled considerably, the trickle that came had to be transferred from point to point as before. In January 1947 disaster struck: ice floes on the rivers brought down the flimsy structure of the bridge. It was impossible to use the main bridge for semi-legal traffic, and soon over 300 refugees accumulated in the barrack on the Slovak side, cold, hungry and desperate. After a week or so of frantic efforts to find a solution, Brichah workers found another village, Zahorska Ves, further north on the border, where only the Morava, a Danube tributary, had to be crossed by boat. A number of transports were dispatched on that route and they got through safely.

In the meantime, the problem of the collapsed bridge brought Dekel to the scene. Both the Austrians and the Slovaks wanted the bridge restored, but neither would agree to pay the cost or come to any agreement at all regard-

ing the matter. Dekel offered to rebuild the bridge, or rather to advance the money. Surprisingly, the offer was accepted by both sides and in March 1947 the bridge over the Danube between Czechoslovakia and Austria was rebuilt—by a Jewish underground organization smuggling Jewish refugees from one of the countries into the other. The bridge has been known ever since as Ephraim's bridge.[11]

The largest Jewish population in postwar Europe was that of Rumania, estimated at about 400,000 people. Their economic situation was extremely bad, because even in prewar Rumania anti-Semitism had driven numerous Jewish traders and artisans into abject poverty; the war years had impoverished the Jews even further and many had been wiped out by the Germans. Jews from the Rumanian province of Bukovina had been driven into the Rumanian-occupied Ukraine (Transnistria), and only a third of these returned after the war. There were many thousands of destitute people, returnees from camps, widows and invalids, and then the new leftist regime began expropriating the small Jewish enterprises, thus driving more Jews into the ranks of the poor. The situation was worsened by a series of disastrous droughts in the immediate postwar period which helped to feed the traditional anti-Semitism of the Rumanian peasant. Some 40 to 45 percent of Rumanian Jews were receiving aid from the JDC in early 1947, and about one third were estimated to be completely destitute.[12] It was inevitable that there would be rising pressure from the demoralized Jewish multitude for escape anywhere at almost any price. Yet the authorities, although tolerating Zionist emissaries in their country and expressing occasional sympathy for Jewish national aims in Palestine, made difficulties for the Mossad man, Moshe Agami, who was trying to organize illegal boats to leave for Palestine. The last such ship, the *Max Nordau,* had sailed in May 1946, and since then the Jews felt bottled up in a hopeless situation. Though there were no actual outbreaks of anti-Semitism, fear of pogroms was uppermost in many minds. The JDC secretary, Moses A. Leavitt, told of interviewing a young Rumanian refugee in Hungary and asking her why she had left Rumania. The answer was that she had left because of

the pogroms. When Leavitt pointed out to her that there had been no pogroms, the answer, reputedly, was that she had meant the future, not the past, pogroms.[13]

In this situation, in early 1947, an exodus started from Rumania. Measured by Polish standards it was very small indeed. According to Brichah figures, some 800 arrived in Vienna in April, 900 in May, 1,697 in June, 4,238 in July, and 4,186 in August. Then the figures began to decline, showing 1,670 for September, 2,571 for October and 2,046 for November. After that, the movement became a mere trickle. The Rumanian refugee movement accounted for a total close to 19,000 in 1947, and it was the last large influx into the DP countries that the Brichah had to deal with. However, it presented the Brichah with complications that accounted in part for its final demise.

The fact of the matter was that the Brichah had very little to do with the Rumanian exodus. Actually, as the Brichah man responsible in Rumania reported, "we tried to stop this movement, but failed. We thought there should be direct immigration (to Palestine) but the people go to Vienna. They get there barefoot and torn, but if they get some bread and other food there they consider themselves saved. We are now holding the Jews back and in actual fact are sinning against them."[14] What happened was that groups of Jews from the Rumanian provinces, with the help of local Jewish dignitaries in border towns, either bribed border officials to let them out or evaded the guards. From the border, they entered Hungary and made their own way to Budapest. At Budapest they usually arrived penniless, or almost so, because the journey to that point deprived the small groups of whatever means they had. By March or April 1947, the Budapest JDC had become very much aware of the problem, and as they did not want the attention of the authorities focused on the Rumanians, they rented a large house on the outskirts of the city to house them. In theory, 60 people could be housed there, but reports had it that in fact as many as 600 occasionally crowded the shelter. A minimum of food was provided, and the Hungarian Brichah provided some forms of transport to the Austrian border. Crossing that particular border was not simple because Hungarian

and Austrian guards would rob the refugees of any valuables they still possessed, and even occasionally of the clothes on their backs. And yet only in Austria did the real problems begin.

The first question for Brichah was that of its own attitude to the flow from Rumania. This in turn was influenced by the drastic step taken by General Clay on April 16, when he announced that as of April 21 new refugees filtering into the American zones of occupation would not be admitted to DP centers, nor would they receive food from U.S. sources. There was a pointed reference in the announcement that the United States was not closing the borders to refugees, but it was clear that in effect such official closing was superfluous once a policy of nonadmittance to DP status was rigidly followed. Clay's action came as a result of administrative and financial difficulties, because Congress refused to allocate additional large sums for the care of refugees.[15] The new order also meant that new refugees arriving in Vienna would not get the automatic clearance to enter the U.S. zone in Austria and would therefore be bottled up in the capital, with nobody responsible for their welfare except, presumably, the JDC. It must be stressed, however, that the April 21 regulation was not designed specifically to meet the Rumanian emergency because, as the figures show, the large-scale influx did not start until after April 21. Brichah commanders were deeply divided on the Rumanian issue. The general idea of the Jewish underground was that Rumanian Jews should be taken out by sea and that there was no point in having them come to Germany to swell the camp population there. The Rumanian government's policy, too, was not unequivocal, and as the spring turned into summer it appeared that they would not give their consent to the renewal of seaborne emigration unless the illicit exit stopped. The Rumanian Brichah workers demanded that help be given to the transients on purely humanitarian grounds. Arthur Ben Nathan from Vienna, on the other hand, declared that "we can decide not to help them. These Jews don't want to go to Palestine, they are fleeing from Roumania." Brichah, he thought, should make up its mind whether or not to help, and if the decision was to help, it

should take over the whole operation, from Rumania to Austria, and thus do away with the disorders and sufferings that attended the unorganized movement.[16] The important point in these statements, repeated in discussions by many Brichah people, was the assumption that the Rumanian Jews were a demoralized group and would make bad settlers in Palestine even if they went there. Most of them did not in fact want to go to Palestine, although they quite spontaneously indicated their identification with Palestine when visited in Vienna by members of the United Nations Special Committee for Palestine (nominated by the UN in April to suggest a solution to the Palestine and Jewish refugee problems). Finally, at the Brichah meeting at Fuschl in Austria in May 1947, Sneh declared that Brichah would have to support the Rumanian movement. "Our primary aim is to serve immigration to Palestine, [but] our secondary aim is to save Jewish people and we must help them to move from place to place."[17] Avigur and Dekel concurred, and so from about May on, Brichah took over the guidance of refugee groups from the Rumanian border to Vienna.

A number of paradoxical situations developed as a result of the hesitations of Brichah. Leavitt, who visited Hungary for the JDC in May, was told by the refugees that they had had no help from Brichah; as a result, he—the representative of a law-abiding American agency who had no wish to be involved in Jewish underground activities—promised to intervene with Brichah headquarters to get them to control the situation.[18] In Austria, on the other hand, Brichah representatives had a very hard time convincing the Americans that they had nothing to do with this particular influx. The Americans on their part saw the movement as part of a conspiracy against themselves, in line with previous Brichah tactics and designed to break the April 21 ruling. The effects of the cold war were also apparent. The Russians were none too happy about the movement of refugees because they suspected American encouragement to Rumanian citizens fleeing their country. The Americans on the other hand tried to utilize the influx as a source of valuable information on Communism. Some American officers again seem to have thought of the movement as strictly a

Communist infiltration ruse and there was considerable opposition to it on those grounds. As the new commander of the Austrian Brichah, Amos Rabel, said, "the possibility of utilizing this stream of humanity for political purposes was, of course, more important in their eyes, than to look after the welfare of these refugees, whose living conditions were appalling."[19] Brichah refused to cooperate with any such cold-war activities.

The purely physical problem was tremendous, despite the relatively small number of the refugees. Because of the barring of refugees from the American zone in Austria, the Jewish camps in Vienna had to absorb them, at least temporarily. In April the U.S. DP section abdicated its responsibility, and for the whole of June even the Rothschild hospital was closed because the Americans would not hand it back to the Teichholz committee; these moves were part of an attempt to pressure the initiators of the infiltration, whoever they were, to stop it. The camps under Teichholz could hold no more than about 1,500 people under normal conditions, but by the end of June there were 2,696 people in them. By the end of July the number snowballed to 6,643, and at the end of August there were 6,897 persons crowded in such a way that each had about eight square feet of "space."[20] UNRRA ended its existence on June 30, and its successor organization, IRO (International Refugee Organization), had not yet taken over. Without American, UNRRA or IRO aid, the Austrian government had no intention of helping, and was in fact prevented with difficulty from closing the border. The burden of feeding the destitute refugees fell solely upon Harold Trobe's team of JDC workers in Vienna. Trobe, a veteran JDC worker, rushed food and some clothes to Vienna to stave off starvation. The distribution of supplies and the medical supervision were carried out by the Teichholz group itself, which, as we have seen, was a front for the Brichah. There was a real danger of epidemics, but these were avoided by the medical personnel, especially after the Rothschild hospital was returned in late June to Teichholz by the Americans.

In the meantime a great deal of discussion took place in Washington, and between the JDC, UNRRA-IRO and the

U.S. Army. Essentially, the State Department, represented by General Hilldring, favored a transfer all at once of all the Rumanian refugees to the U.S. zone in Austria; the War Department on the other hand hedged by asking for a clear recommendation by General Keyes, the new commander in Austria, on the question. But when Keyes did ask for such a transfer of the refugees, the War Department rejected it, despite or perhaps because of the Russian agreement to let the people through the Russian zone.[21]

The people had to be moved from Vienna; and for lack of any legal solution, Brichah undertook to smuggle them out. A first large transport of 200 people was sent across the Russo-American zonal border near Steyr in June, and another 500 followed. The second transport was caught by the Americans, but another attempt to send them through succeeded. The Russians were quite indifferent and they neither aided nor prevented the infiltration. However, when they thought they knew the identity of the organizer, or Brichah representative, they would not hesitate to arrest him—usually, they knew, these people came from Poland and might be former members of the Polish or Russian armies. But the Brichah man on the border was an old hand, an ex-partisan by the name of Niatek Friedman, and though he escaped being caught only by the skin of his teeth more than once, he did escape every time. Throughout July and August the illegal transfer went on, with American resistance to it gradually weakening. What finally won the Brichah a grudging American acquiescence was the fact that the Rumanians were absorbed in the existing camps without the need for additional food supplies, and also that most of them did not stay but moved on to Germany and Italy. By the end of the year Yahil in Germany estimated that 8,000 each had finally settled in the camps in Germany and Austria, and 4,000 had gone on to Italy. The general attitude of the camp populations to the new influx was commendable—they were receiving more rations than their numbers warranted, the percentage of additional calories being anything up to 30 percent, and these extra rations they now gave to the new arrivals. Only in some instances were Rumanians identified as such by the Americans and sent to special Ger-

man refugee centers, including infamous Dachau, where they were put in a camp together with German expellees from Eastern Europe. Such instances of a strict adherence to the April 21 order were rare, however, and even those who were caught were ultimately brought over to Jewish camps and absorbed among the "old" DPs, given forged identity cards and given the rations and clothing that the other DPs received. This was largely done by the Central Committee in Munich who regarded this to be their obvious duty.

In the meantime, too, the food situation in Vienna itself had been solved; the Americans had decided to exercise pressure on the Austrian government to provide the basic rations to the new infiltrees, and it was understood that this would be taken out of the stocks that IRO would provide for Austria. The JDC undertook to supplement the extremely low rations of 1,550 calories provided by the Austrians with an additional 600 calories, and thereby the load on the voluntary agency was somewhat reduced.

The Rumanian episode was the last large-scale migration from Eastern Europe into the DP countries of Germany, Austria and Italy. But if the usefulness of Brichah as an instrument for bringing Jews into that area was coming to an end, it was still a major force for Zionist policies in Central and Southern Europe. Two areas of activity remained; Brichah continued to bring Jews from Germany and Austria to the illegal immigration ships that sailed from Italian and French ports. Therefore the Italian and French borders occupied a large part of the attention of Dekel and his colleagues during 1947.

The first step in any move to get Jews from Germany to Italy was, of course, the crossing from Germany into Austria. As we know, this was a two-way flow, especially since Rumanian infiltrees in 1947 had to be smuggled out of Austria and into Germany. On the other hand, people who went in the opposite direction were persons chosen to go on illegal immigration ships in Italy. At first, these were mostly young people, but as time went on, the German Brichah changed its policy largely because it had to take into account the morale in the camps. On the one hand it had to leave some

of the young enthusiasts in the camps, but on the other, some hope had to be given to families with children, and even older people as well. On the whole, however, whatever the age, the groups that started out for Italy were people who were prepared to undergo a great deal of hardship to reach their goal.

Instrumental in enabling the refugees to cross into Austria were some of the American personnel in the area, especially Captain Novinsky and the chaplain Rabbi Eugene Cohen. With their help, semi-official ruses were found to explain why people had to move in opposite directions on the border. A particularly good way of dealing with the problem was found when it was discovered that an Austrian DP camp at Saalfelden on the Austro-German border could best be reached from Salzburg by a road that led into a corner of Germany separating the two places. On April 11, 1947, Rabbi Cohen took a convoy of DPs across from Salzburg to Saalfelden with official permission. On the way, however, the convoy stopped at Bad Reichenhall, another DP camp in German territory, and there the people who were to go into Germany left the trucks and their places were taken by others who had to leave Germany and go to Austria. The convoy then went on to Saalfelden, arriving there with the same number of persons—but only different ones—that had left Salzburg. It took the American authorities quite some time before they discovered what was afoot, but when they did they looked the other way, at least for some time. Their attitude generally wavered between extremes of friendliness and hostility, except, of course, for Novinsky and some of his friends. In January 1947, for instance, they threatened Gefen and his colleagues from the Salzburg Brichah that they would close down the border altogether if further illicit crossings occurred. But Gefen was not particularly impressed. Since October 1946 he and his outfit had even been using British uniforms, with tacit U.S. approval, and any scandal that occurred would inevitably have involved American personnel as well. Also, if Brichah was forced underground, it could no longer provide the Americans with the welcome service of officially looking after the DPs, whereby they could ensure some semblance of order in the camps and

on the routes. Besides, the Americans knew very well that short of the use of force Brichah could not be stopped.[22] As far as the DP camps were concerned, Brichah felt that in any case its position there was much too exposed, and so it agreed to hand over the actual administration of the camps to local elected committees, in accordance with the wishes of the inmates. On January 17, 1947, elections were held all over the U.S. zone, and a new Central Committee was chosen, with Brichah as the unofficial power behind the throne.

Because the relations with the Army were uncertain, new and independent ways had to be found across the mountainous border. One of these crossings was again proof of Brichah ingenuity. At two small places lying on each side of the border, Bayrisch-Gmain and Gross-Gmain, two children's homes were established. Some of the educators were accomplices, and "in the course of chasing a ball" the border that was the brook was crossed. Crossings at that point occurred often in broad daylight, camouflaged by perfectly genuine children's activities.[23]

From Saalfelden, the problem was how to get to Innsbruck or rather Gnadenwald, Sami Levy's stronghold. There again it was the question of overcoming the opposition of the French occupation authorities who were glad not to have a Jewish problem on their hands and who had no intention of allowing one to develop. The difficulties with the French were largely resolved by forged documentation, occasional crossings of zonal borders on foot and, to a considerable degree, arrangements worked out with local Austrian rail officials that allowed for small groups to enter the French zone under various guises. All these stratagems were met with increasing severity by the French authorities, until in April all movement into the French zone ceased. The Brichah had arrived at an impasse, and if it was not broken no movement into Italy could take place.

In the light of these developments a decision was taken to force the hand of the French with a daring feat. Ben Nathan, Levy from Gnadenwald and Gefen from Salzburg, as well as other local Brichah representatives, sent eighteen Brichah men to Saalfelden. There, under the general com-

mand of Yisrael Ridelnik, who had been the Brichah man on the Silesian border during the time of the Kielce exodus, 500 refugees were chosen who consented to be the path-breakers. Of these, three men were picked to examine the paths leading down from the mountaintops on the zonal border near the little township of Gerlos; this was done and the breakthrough was planned to take place early in the morning. On May 7, 1947, 518 men and women left Saalfelden by trucks, divided into ten groups of 50 refugees with their Brichah leaders, and moved into the Gerlos mountains on the American side. There they dismounted and marched through the night until, early in the morning, they reached the French side. On their way they accidentally ran into two Austrian policemen, overpowered them and took away their rifles, but let them go. This almost proved to be a fatal mistake, because the Austrians managed to establish radio contact with the French, who now sent more Austrians to stop the Jews as near to the zonal border as possible. An early morning fog helped, however, and the Jews managed to get to the main Gerlos road, a few miles inside the French zonal territory. After a short scuffle with some Austrian police they were encircled by French troops who had been given the alarm by a French officer. The people were then brought to Gerlos, where they established themselves in an open field. In the afternoon they had a ceremony in honor of VE Day (May 8), with French and Jewish flags displayed. At first the French did not allow any water or food to be brought to the compound. When the restriction was lifted, the Jews declared a hunger strike based on demands to be transported to the Italian frontier. Negotiations were started, at which the Jews declared they had come from the British zone and in any case they would not go to the Ameircan sector. During the day Sami Levy, who was dressed in his American uniform, appeared with Chaplain Cohen, supposedly to calm the people but in fact to tell them in Hebrew that they were to stay where they were. As night approached the morale remained high. Forced to stay in the open, the people lit fires and sat around them singing, and somehow the night passed. In the morning the French made a determined effort to get the people to move into trucks that

would take them back into the American zone, despite the fact that the Americans refused to take them—Gefen had been very active in convincing the American authorities to refuse the French request. Four leaders of the group, including the immediate commander, Abraham Giora, were lured away by the French by the promise of negotiations, but instead were put into jail. Then tanks were brought in and they advanced on the crowd to force them into the waiting trucks. But a number of girls threw themselves down in front of the tanks and dared them to advance. The French commander, shaken, gave the order to desist and the tanks withdrew. Thus passed May 9, by which time, of course, the story had spread and was swiftly becoming a sensational press item. On that day, food was accepted only by the few children and some people who had fallen sick. All the rest continued a hunger strike that was threatening to become very troublesome for the French. In the background, negotiations were started between the French commanding general, Voizard, and the JDC representative, Jean Bernstein (who was rather annoyed at not having been informed by the Brichah beforehand of what was about to happen, but who very valiantly did whatever was needed of him). The French suggested a transfer to Gnadenwald, and Bernstein consented. There was no difficulty with the refugees, because Gnadenwald was in the French zone and they had made their point that they would not be stopped from passing through the zone on their way to Italy. Accordingly, on May 10, the people were transferred to Gnadenwald without further incident.

This was not, however, the end of the story. The French were determined not to be defeated by a few hundred unarmed Jews; and on Friday the 15th they told Bernstein that the next morning, a Saturday, the Jews would be moved to the U.S. zone in accordance with an agreement reached between the French and American armies. Bernstein informed Sami Levy, and Sami immediately organized passive resistance. The approaches to Gnadenwald were strewn with nails, causing a large number of punctured tires as the trucks brought 170 soldiers and gendarmes to the camp. The refugees were housed in a large, rambling building; among them

was a man who had fought at Stalingrad, an expert in building barricades, who was told by Levy to prepare a barricade, and he proceeded to do so. All the people were concentrated in the upper stories of the building and all the lower floors were jammed with furniture, stones and other material. It took the French guards hours to break through, and the continuous threat of the refugees to set fire to the building was taken quite seriously by the attackers. Ultimately, of course, after a whole day's operation, the 500 unarmed Jews were finally forced out of the building one by one and lifted bodily into the trucks and to Saalfelden.

The affair ended in complete victory for the Brichah: the French had learned their lesson and they had no wish to repeat the Gerlos performance. In two separate negotiations, one conducted by Sami Levy in Innsbruck and one by Ben Nathan in Vienna, the French agreed to let groups of 40 people a day pass through their zones. This was soon stretched to 60 and then 100, and in fact the French zone became an area of transit. Thus Gerlos was one of the great Brichah victories in the battle of the borders.[24]

Once in the French zone of Austria, the Jews had to get into Italy. According to Brichah statistics,[25] the total number of Jewish refugees who crossed the Austrian border into Italy in 1947 was 16,913. The routes taken were via Nauders and neighboring areas of the French zones, and the methods of transit were no different from what they had been in the previous year. The aim was again to get to Merano, where the Brichah center, camouflaged as a TB hospital, would accept the transients and send them on their journey to Milan and points south.

Italy, from the Brichah point of view, was the final goal for its operations. Once there, refugees were taken over by the Mossad delegates, still led, as they had been since 1945, by the redoubtable Yehuda Arazi. The Central Committee of Jewish refugees in Italy, a democratically elected body, looked after day-to-day internal affairs of the refugees' camps, and UNRRA and the JDC provided the basic necessities of life for their inmates. But actual control lay in the hands of the Mossad, which determined the most important question in the refugees' life: When would the next illegal

boat sail for Palestine? For DPs in Austria or Germany, Italy was almost the Promised Land itself, a most important stepping-stone on their road away from the miserable existence of the overcrowded camps. Therefore there were many people who were willing to go to some lengths in order to cross the Alpine borders into Italy.

The commander of the Italian Brichah was a Palestinian, Isashar Haimowitz. His main tasks were the provision of funds, men and transport to the border points, liaison with Mossad and contact with the Italian authorities wherever necessary. The commander of the Merano "point" was a young ex-Brigade soldier, Danny Laor, who, like Sami Levy, had been sent to the Brichah from European Haganah command, and he was very well acquainted with the Italian scene generally. Like Sami he sported an American uniform, conducted local negotiations with Italian police officers and generally became a fairly well-known figure on the northern border of Italy. His Brichah "point" at Hotel Terminus in Merano, with its spacious courtyard, supported around thirty permanent Brichah workers and their fifteen trucks, inherited from the Brigade or "organized" later. If gas could not be obtained on forged military documents from military gas stations, it had to be bought on the black market. No wages were paid to the workers (including Danny of course), in line with Brichah custom elsewhere—only expenses were covered. A shortwave radio provided communications with trucks on their way and other stations.

Danny's main headache was the multiplicity of Italian police. There were the *carabinieri,* essentially a gendarme rather than a police force. Then there was the *publica sicurezza,* or security police, also active on the borders, and lastly the *dogana,* or customs police. All of these stationed their forces not only on the actual borders but also in areas adjacent to the borders, and occasionally refugees were seized as far back from the frontier as Milan itself. The trouble was that there was bitter competition among the three forces, and when one of them managed to catch a group illegally crossing the borders, the others were taunted for not having been efficient enough to do the same. This system of competition made difficulties for the refugees,

who had to dodge three sets of guards, each eager to prove that it was more efficient than the others. On the more hopeful side of the picture, however, were Danny's relations with some of the regional commanding officers which were very good; he had helped to track down Nazi and Italian war criminals, and had gained their friendship and trust.

In the late autumn of 1946, the Nauders route had already been threatened by ever-increasing difficulties. Brichah was looking for an alternative route, and at first it tried the little-used Passo di Saas, some 60 kilometers east of Nauders; this, however, was not good enough, and other outlets were sought. At this point it occurred to a young Palestinian that because of historically drawn frontiers, there was actually a five-mile stretch of territory where the U.S. zone in Austria abutted directly on Italian territory. South of the resort township of Krimml and sandwiched between the French and British zones, a narrow valley, the Krimmler Tal, led past three wonderful waterfalls to a tourist hut, the Tauernhaus. From there two alternative paths led up to a height of over 2,600 meters where the Italian border was crossed. On the other side lay the tiny hamlet of Kasern (Casere), in the Valle Aurina, populated by German Tyrolese chafing under Italian rule. From Krimml there was no road, only a footpath. On the Italian side, a very narrow road led to the village of Prettau, and from then on the road up the valley to Kasern was little better than a dirt track. The distance between Krimml and Kasern was about 25 difficult, cold and wet kilometers.[26] A group of hardy pioneers, about thirty strong, actually tried out the new route before winter set in at the end of 1946 and made the crossing impossible.

It was quite easy to reach the border from the Austrian side: trucks could bring the refugees from Saalfelden to Krimml, all within the U.S. zone, and then the footpath would lead them on to the Tauernhaus, where an accommodating Austrian would put them up for appropriate payment. The problem was the Italian side, because the Aurina valley at that point was full of the various kinds of Italian police whose main task was to watch over the restive Tyrolese Germans.

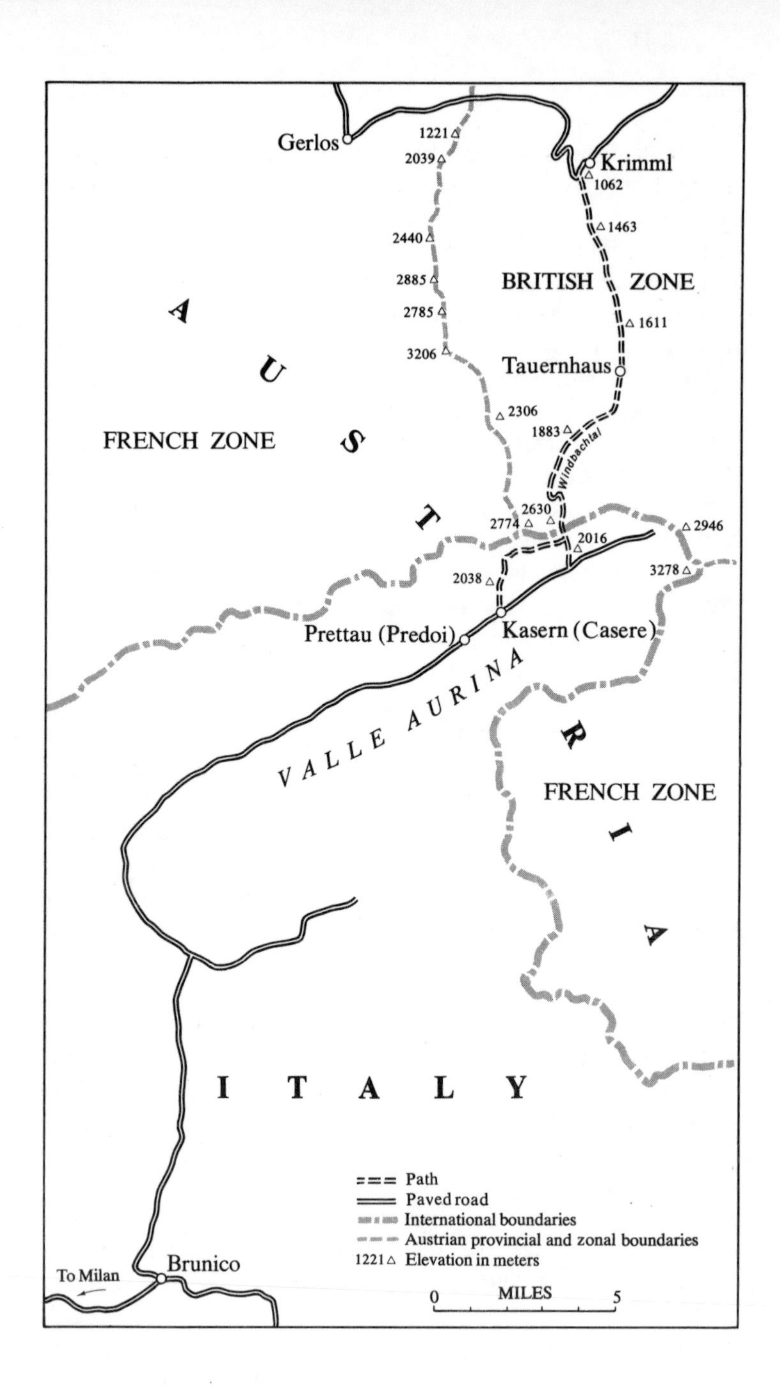

The Krimml–Kasern Route

What followed looked like a story from a bad thriller. Danny Laor, the "American" officer, started to visit the valley and its few taverns in early 1947, making friends with local policemen in the process. Slowly, he let it be known that he was looking for a quiet place in the mountains where American officers could recuperate. Various places were offered to him by local residents and police officers identified with the small hotels in the area, but Danny maintained that all these were not secluded and quiet enough. Finally, a newly won officer friend brought him up to Kasern, and showed him the hotel of Donna Maria, an efficient Tyrolese hotelkeeper. One of the three stories of the hotel was occupied by the *publica sicurezza,* but the top story was free. Next to the hotel was a peasant's house, very suitable for Danny's purposes. He now set his officer friend to work and requisitioned the peasant's house in the name of the American Army. The peasant received a handsome fixed rent for the house and moved out. In addition, the top story of Casa di Casere, the hotel, was rented, and a number of well-chosen blond "Americans" from the Merano group came in to prepare the place for the recuperating American officers. Soon the food for the police was prepared and paid for by the new staff as well, and a couple of accordionists even provided much-needed entertainment. The stage was set, and the trial run could begin.

One spring evening the first group of 150 refugees crossed the Alps and arrived at Kasern. The idea was that they should be caught by the police and interned at the hotel. But the police never expected anyone but occasional smugglers to cross the mountains, and the refugees had to go up to the hotel and more or less demand to be arrested before the police caught on. Overjoyed by the capture of such a large group, the officer in charge then faced the problem of what to do with them. There was no room at the hotel, so he asked the "Americans" whether they would agree to accommodate the people temporarily at the other house. The "Americans" obliged. No trucks could reach Kasern and the question was what to do next. The regional officer was called—and here Danny's contacts were effective and the idea was suggested to ask the "American" officer to

suggest something. Danny obliged: he would transport the refugees back to the border, but of course not over the Alpine footpaths; he would bring them to the official Brenner crossing in trucks. The people were then marched and partly transported by small jeeps to Prettau, and from there Brichah trucks, appropriately painted, took them to "the Brenner," that is, to Milan and the DP camps of Italy.

The ruse had worked beyond all expectations and the road was open. People were now brought regularly, sometimes several times a week, to Krimml, and then they trudged for many hours in the valley to the Tauernhaus. There they stayed the night, and next morning they began the difficult ascent to the border, crossing down into Kasern in the afternoon or at sunset. At first this was thought to be no route for the weak and the old or very young. But slowly, as experience increased efficiency even weaker people, and once even a whole transport of families with children, were successfully brought over the high mountain pass into Italy without mishap. On the Italian side, the comedy continued to be played with a great deal of fruitful imagination. The local sergeant was promised advancement, and when by pure accident he was transferred to a better post at the end of about half a year, he was sure that the "American" officer had engineered it. Early in the spring, Danny commandeered the whole of Prettau village to widen and improve the road so that the trucks might come right up to Kasern to pick up the people. This was done, and in return for their help, the local police received a jeep from the Brichah, with which to accompany the trucks with the refugees part of the way to "the Brenner." The area officer was of course never in doubt about the true identity of the "Americans." Sometime after the transfers began, the local people also began to realize who the "Americans" were; but they were never quite sure, and in any case, if the affair blew up the blame would fall on the security police who had let themselves be fooled for months by impostors. So they continued to cooperate with Danny, pretending they believed in the story about a helpful and humane American who happened to be willing to help out a local refugee problem. Brichah sources insist that the regional officers were convinced of the moral

right of the Jewish refugees to cross borders in their quest for a way to Palestine; bribery, so widely used in Poland or Hungary, was never resorted to. Occasional favors were performed, presents exchanged, but even in these cases everything was above board.

An additional factor in the success of the Aurina valley crossing was the enmity of the local Germans to the Italians. Not all the transports were "caught" by the police. Some bypassed Kasern and made straight for Prettau with the help of the German peasants, who disliked the way in which the ordinary policemen treated the refugees. By that time the movement of trucks in and out of the village was a daily occurrence and several transports did not even have to go through the pretense of being captured by the Italians.

During the year 1947, some 5,000 people, or about one-third of the total number of refugees crossing into Italy, came via Kasern. In the autumn, as the first snowfalls made the footpaths dangerous and the road into Kasern impassable, the operation was terminated. The American captain (he had upgraded himself to major in the meantime, complete with battle ribbons which he put on upside down, as he later found out when a friendly and genuine American officer pointed out the error to him) withdrew from the valley, the house was derequisitioned and Donna Maria deprived of her well-paying guests.

Until late in 1947, Brichah managed to maintain its untarnished neutrality in relation to the various Zionist factions. Despite the fact that in Palestine the Haganah and the more radical, right-wing-oriented IZL (Irgun), were at loggerheads over the best way to oppose the British policy, Brichah had cooperated with the Revisionists, generally identified as the main political defender of the IZL, and Betar, its youth movement and main recruiting ground for IZL. Thus, in Austria, Abba Gefen in Salzburg was actually a Betar representative in the Brichah, and other functionaries locally were also members of Betar. Occasional complaints of one or the other of the movements about supposed discrimination in the number of people transferred over frontiers were never taken too seriously.

However, in 1947, IZL began operating in Europe under a Palestinian delegate, Yakov Fershtay, whose headquarters were in Italy. There is doubt about whether Fershtay thought that Betar was getting an unfair deal from the Brichah or whether he wanted to emphasize IZL's independence and rivalry with the Haganah-controlled Brichah organization; whatever the reason he apparently sent word to Austria that independent Betar crossings should be organized. From some of the evidence it seems that a local decision was made to capture Gnadenwald for the IZL as the main transit point into Italy. Sami Levy, himself quite nonpolitical, had made a number of enemies among the Betar group because he was adamant on punishing smugglers who had been trying to lead small groups of Jews over the mountains on "his" routes in return for large money payments. Some of the smugglers had contact with Betar people who apparently thought that these would lead them toward an independent frontier-crossing organization. On September 21, 1947, Sami caught a group of what appeared to him to be smugglers, and interned seven of them in Gnadenwald. It seems they were beaten up and then four of them were released. The others were to be released soon thereafter. It is not quite clear whether any of these people were Betar members, but at any rate Betar immediately "adopted" the smugglers and organized a group of embittered young men, largely Rumanians who had just arrived from Vienna and who were looking for a way in which to express their resentment at the world in general. This group surprised the peaceful Gnadenwald camp on September 27 and announced that they were taking over the place. Sami was not present that day, but other Palestinians who happened to be there tried to resist the takeover. The Betar group was armed, and in the scuffle a shot was fired which killed a young Palestinian, Eitan Avidov, who had just arrived from Palestine. A few others were wounded, some money was taken and then the raiders, obviously frightened by what had happened, got away. The French, who had to be alerted, arrested a large number of people. A few youths were tried and given prison sentences.[27]

The repercussions of this incident on the Brichah were

serious. Unrest and local incidents spread in Austria, Germany and Italy. In Italy, the Brichah commander and a foreign visitor were taken by surprise at the Jewish Agency headquarters in Milan and beaten up. There were fistfights in a number of camps, and a tremendous bitterness began to develop. It would not be correct to say that the Gnadenwald murder spelled the demise of Brichah; but its internal structure was thereby weakened, and it had to rely on methods it had never employed before: the bringing in of armed guards to certain frontier points, and an intelligence system directed toward its own members. After September 1947 Brichah in Austria and Italy declined for other reasons, but as far as its internal structure was concerned, the Gnadenwald incident had struck a blow from which Brichah never recovered.

The second main route to the shores of the Mediterranean, apart from the road to Italy, led from Germany to France. A slow and unorganized trickle of infiltration had brought 10,000 Jews into France from late 1946 to the end of 1947. But these, by and large, were not candidates for Mossad ships. What was needed was organized transports of candidates from DP camps for such ships, and a great opportunity came when an old Chesapeake Bay steamer, the *President Garfield,* was bought by Mossad in America and brought over to Europe. The British immediately identified it as a potential Jewish ship, and in order to dispel their suspicion, the *President Garfield* made a few commercial runs between France and North Africa. In the meantime, the possibilities of sending the ship to the Balkans were investigated, but the Americans were pressing Mossad to take Jews out of the German camps, and in the end that pressure proved too strong. Yahil had the idea of a run from Bremen, which was an American enclave in northern Germany. The Army seemed to agree with the idea, but at the last moment someone informed Washington about it, and of course the War Department immediately squashed the notion of a Jewish illegal ship leaving from an American-controlled harbor.[28] In the end, the ship was to sail from the French harbor of Sete, and the problem was how to get the people to it without arousing too much attention.

Mossad had created in France a so-called Jewish Refugees' Welfare Society, supposedly registered in the United States, with a roster of imaginary names for its officers and a very handsome letterhead. Through this organization, it had obtained the agreement of some South American and African consulates to give visas to Jews some of which at least were bona fide. In June 1947, 1,700 such visas were given to Mossad, which handed them over to the German Brichah. With a tremendons logistic effort, vigorously aided by the Palestinian volunteers under Yahil and the Central Committee, 5,000 people were chosen in the German DP camps, brought to a staging area near the French border without American knowledge and then shipped into France. The 1,700 people with visas were transported by train, quite openly, to Marseilles, and well over 3,000 went in three motorcades illegally. It so happened that just at that time there was a strike of transport workers in the south of France, but when the Mossad emissaries explained the situation the French workers let the refugees through. Of the 5,000 people, 600 were kept behind for later ships, 200 children were distributed in children's homes in France, and the other 4,200 boarded the *President Garfield,* now renamed *Exodus '47*.[29]

The transshipment of the *Exodus* passengers to France was the last big effort of Brichah in Germany. Toward the end of 1947, the Palestine problem seemed nearer solution. The UN Special Committee on Palestine had reported in favor of the partition of Palestine into Jewish and Arab states, and on November 29, 1947, the UN Assembly accepted that solution by a larger than two-thirds majority. The Israeli war of independence started, and with it a train of events that made Brichah superfluous. It came only just in time. More than two years of camp life had caused a severe deterioration of the DPs' morale. The urge to go to Palestine had weakened, and many wanted to go to the United States instead. Abraham S. Hyman, aide to the Jewish Adviser in Germany, commented cynically but truthfully at the end of 1947 that "the emergence of the Jewish State has, in my opinion, not substantially affected the *Drang nach Amerika*. I would say that now, given equal opportu-

nity to go to Palestine and to the States, 50% would join the unfortunate Galuth Jews in America."[30] Jewish Agency personnel concurred with these estimates, and had it not been for the actual establishment of Israel on May 14, 1948, the situation might have become extremely critical. As it was, salvation for the DPs, reprieve from the continuing embarrassment of the presence of Jewish DPs to the U.S. Army and an avoidance of anti-Semitic outbreaks, especially in Austria, were all achieved by the creation of Israel. As soon as the chance for a free immigration to that country became a real possibility, most Jews chose it; and there was no longer any need for clandestine border-crossings through half of Europe. Soon Israeli consulates began distributing visas, and Brichah slowly shrank to nothingness.

Not quite, though. From Hungary and Poland, and later from Czechoslovakia, a trickle of Jews continued to come through 1948 and 1949. According to the Viennese Brichah, 2,511 Jews came into Austria illegally in 1948, 8,548 in 1949, and 1,576 in 1950. The last European commander of Brichah, Meir Sapir, had to deal with this slight movement in 1948–49. His main task, however, was to wind up Brichah affairs, and send its 2,000 workers to Israel. Most of them went there, but some ended up in the Diaspora which they had vowed to leave, some in the affluent countries of the West, a very few even in Europe. But the vast majority of that devoted army of young people came to Israel—they who had braved danger from man and nature to bring their fellow Jews from lands of absolute insecurity to those of relative and temporary safety so that they might there congregate until the way to Palestine became open. Brichah never really died officially—it just withered away, a mass movement that ceased to exist when it was no longer needed simply because it had achieved its end.

Afterword

How many people came with Brichah, organized and unorganized? It is very difficult to give a precise answer. The fact that the Jews in the DP camps were unwilling ever to be accurately counted combines with the fact that Brichah was an illegal organization and its statistics were therefore incomplete and were sometimes not more than vague estimates. In August 1945 some 50,000 Jews, DPs and local residents, were in Germany and Austria. At the end of 1947 the JDC counted 169,960 Jews in the German DP camps and communities of all zones, and Brichah's more accurate count in Austria was 23,216. Brichah estimated the number in Italy, exclusive of Italian Jews, to be about 15,000 (IRO estimated it at 25,000!). JDC estimates of DPs who had infiltrated into France and Belgium and were then living there was a conservative 15,000. Until the end of 1948 a total of 12,849 Jews came to the United States under Truman's special DP directive, and 36,664 emigrated illegally to Palestine from French and Italian shores. Between 1945 and 1948, 7,169 Jews came to Canada, 15,131 to Latin America and 6,453 to Australia, most of them presumably DPs—this however was assisted immigration only. All this would give a total of about 300,000 Jews who were either in the so-called DP countries of Austria, Germany and Italy

or had been there between 1945 and 1948.[1] This estimate might err on the conservative side, but if it is only approximately correct, then the number of people who came from Eastern Europe with Brichah would be at least 250,000.[2]

Brichah turned the DP countries into temporary havens for Jewish men and women and children who could not find any permanent home. The fact that no country was willing to receive these homeless Jews ultimately led to the opening of Palestine and its metamorphosis into Israel. The Anglo-American Committee of Inquiry had suggested that most of the DPs should go to Palestine as far back as the spring of 1946. The United Nations Special Commission on Palestine had said much the same thing in the summer of 1947 and had linked this to a majority proposal that wished to see a Jewish state established in Palestine which would be capable of absorbing the DPs. The United States, especially after it had adopted its new policy of friendship toward West Germany, had a stake in seeing the Jewish DPs taken out of that country, but this could not be done without immigration into Palestine. The pressure of the United States on Britain to allow the DPs to go to Palestine, combined with the pressure of illegal immigration (largely again by DPs) and armed action by the Jewish underground in Palestine, in turn led Britain to hand over the Palestine problem to the United Nations in February 1947. Russian interest in seeing the British removed from Palestine and American desire to settle the refugee question, coupled with the pressure of Jewish and non-Jewish public opinion in the United States, led to the decision of the U.N. Assembly to partition Palestine and establish a Jewish state there. It was this decision, taken on November 29, 1947, that enabled the Palestinian Jews, together with thousands of DP immigrants, to battle for Israel's independence and win it. At the beginning and at the center of this chain of events stands the mass movement of the Jewish survivors of the holocaust as one of the most significant, if indeed not *the* most significant, of the factors leading up to Israel's establishment.

The important point, and one which we tried to stress, was that Brichah's leaders were fully aware of the general trend of the historical events in which they were taking part.

At the same time, while they directed the flow of people, they did not instigate the exodus. In a very real sense, they were themselves the product of the mass movement—not its prime movers. The movement was conditioned by anti-Semitism and economic deprivation, by the mass murders that preceded it and their political and psychological consequences. The originators and leaders of Brichah, and behind them the leaders of the Zionist movement, were duty-bound to help their brethren, fleeing panic-stricken from Eastern Europe. What they did was to channel this flow intelligently into a reservoir that would turn the very misery of the people into a powerful weapon that would lead them to a new and better life, and thus achieve a basic humanitarian aim by political and national means. In the end it was the people, the Jewish survivors themselves, who had to show indomitable will to live in order to surmount all the tremendous obstacles they were facing. The will to live, fortunately, was there.

Glossary

Agudat Yisrael Ultra-orthodox, originally anti-Zionist, but later non-Zionist, political organization, founded in 1912. Very influential in Poland prior to the Second World War, It veered toward Zionism after the war and organized itself as a political party in Israel.

American Jewish Joint Distribution Committee Abbreviated to AJDC, or JDC; philanthropic agency founded in 1914 to aid Jews in need all over the world.

Betar Zionist youth movement emphasizing military education. Affiliated (until the 1940s) with the Revisionist Party and acknowledging the authority of Ze'ev Jabotinsky, Jewish nationalist, orator and man of letters.

Bnai Akiva Zionist religious youth movement with a moderately left-wing hue, allied to the Palestinian religious kibbutz movement.

Bund *Algemener Yiddisher Arbeter-Bund,* anti-Zionist Socialist Jewish Workers' Party in Poland prior to the Second World War.

Dror Zionist youth movement affiliated to the left-wing Kibbutz Meuchad federation of kibbutzim in Palestine (and today in Israel); also known by its Yiddish name, *Freiheit* (Freedom).

FFI Fighters for the Freedom of Israel (Hebrew acronym: LHY), also known as the Stern Group; extreme radical anti-British underground in Palestine which was founded in 1940 by Abraham Stern (killed in 1942).

Gordonia Zionist movement of a moderate non-Marxist socialist tendency, affiliated with Mapai and the Hever Hakvutzot federation of kibbutzim in the Palestine of the 1940s.

Haganah *Irgun Haganah Ha'ivrit Be'Eretz Israel* (Hebrew Defense Organization in Palestine), underground military organization of the overwhelming majority of the Jewish population in Palestine, controlled by the Jewish Agency for Palestine.

Halutzim Pioneers, name for those who chose to serve the Zionist cause primarily through agricultural settlement of a collectivist nature.

Hashomer Hatzair Young Guardsman, oldest Zionist youth movement; left-wing socialist and Marxist; affiliated with the Kibbutz Artzi federation of kibbutzim in Palestine.

HIAS Hebrew Sheltering and Immigrant Aid Society, founded in 1902 in New York; dedicated to helping Jewish immigrants all over the world and especially those bound for the United States.

Histadruth *Hahistadrut Haklalit shel Ha'ovdim ha'ivrim be'eretz Israel*, founded in 1920; a federation of agricultural and industrial enterprises owned by trade unions and workers.

IGCR (Intergovernmental Committee for Refugees), founded through American initiative in the wake of the Evian Conference on refugees held in 1938. In the aftermath of World War II its purpose was to implement the agreement reached in the 1943 Bermuda Conference between the United States and United Kingdom on the care and resettlement of stateless refugees.

IRO (International Refugee Organization), successor organization to UNRRA. Founded in 1947 by interested nations, it participated in the upkeep of DP camps and the emigration of Jews to Israel and other countries.

Israelitische Kultusgemeinde Wien (IKG), Jewish community in Vienna.

IZL *Irgun Tzvai Leumi* (National Military Organization), also known simply as Irgun. Founded in 1931, it became in the 1940s a radical anti-British underground military organization in Palestine and abroad. Originally allied to the Revisionist Party (see below), it cut off this relationship in 1941.

JDC *See* American Jewish Joint Distribution Committee.

Jewish Agency for Palestine Founded in 1929 as a partnership between Zionists and non-Zionist Jews for the upbuilding of Palestine. By the 1940s it had in fact become synonymous with the Zionist movement and served as its political executive body and prime mover in fund-raising.

Lubavicher Hasidim (Habad), a very important Hasidic sect, whose original home was the small township of Lubavich in the Ukraine. Founded early in the nineteenth century, it is a proselytizing movement not averse to Zionism; its center has been New York since the late twenties, when the Rabbi of Lubavich came to the United States.

Mapai Founded in 1930; chief political party in the Zionist movement and in Palestine with a moderate socialist tendency. Led since 1944 by David Ben Gurion.

Merkaz Lagolah (lit., Center for the Diaspora), the central committee established in 1944 by the Palestinian-Jewish soldiers in the British Army for the purpose of helping refugees and victims of the holocaust.

Mossad *Mossad Le'Aliyah Beth* (Institute for "B" [illegal] Immigration). Founded in late 1938, it was entrusted by Haganah, and later by the Jewish Agency, with the task of organizing illegal immigration of Jews into Palestine.

Noar Zioni Zionist youth movement of a nonsocialist liberal tendency.

Poale Zion Party (Workers of Zion Party), moderate labor party of the Zionist movement outside Israel; run in fact by Mapai, the Palestinian (later Israeli) party. Not to be confused with the radical left-wing Poale Zion, which was especially active in Poland.

PPR Polish United Workers' Party, official name of the Polish Communist Party.

PPS Polish Socialist Party, split into two wings after World War II, with the left under Josef Cyrankiewicz joining the PPR.

PUR Polish Repatriation Committee, whose main task was to evict the German minorities from Poland after the Second World War.

Revisionist Party Founded 1925 by Ze'ev Jabotinsky; radical right-wing party demanding the foundation of a Jewish state on both sides of the Jordan.

shlihim (Plural of *shaliah*), emissaries of Zionist bodies, legal and illegal, from Palestine.

UNRRA (United Nations Relief and Rehabilitation Administration), founded in 1943 by the United Nations to administer relief to war-stricken areas and populations.

Vaad Hatzalah, or **Vaad Hahatzalah** Organization of Orthodox rabbis in the United States to aid and rescue Orthodox groups in Europe and Asia during and after the holocaust.

ZK *Zentralkomitaet,* the Central Committee of Liberated Jews in Bavaria. Founded in July 1945, its main headquarters was at Munich. Not to be confused with the Central Committee of Polish Jews, founded in Lublin in 1944, which was the central representative of Polish Jewry after liberation.

Notes

Sources for the material in this section have been abbreviated as follows:

ATH	Haganah Archives at Tel Aviv
ATH-AB	Brichah Archive at ATH
AZ	Central Zionist Archives
H	Oral Documentation Center of the Hebrew University's Institute of Contemporary Jewry
JDC, Gen. & Emerg.	American Jewish Joint Distribution Committee files: General and Emergency
JTA	Jewish Telegraphic Agency
M	Moreshet Archives at Givat Haviva
PM	The author's private files
YIVO	Jewish Scientific Institute (Yiddishes Wissenshaftliches Institut), New York

Chapter 1

1 See *Yalkut Moreshet,* Vol. 1, No. 2 (April 1964): "Hatzlav" (The Cross) by Nesia Orlowicz-Reznik, pp. 96–105, and "Sipura

shel Halina" (Halina's Story), pp. 137–142, by the same author—two examples from a fairly large literature dealing with children during the catastrophe that befell European Jewry.

2 The Rovno story is based on three separate interviews with Eliezer Lidovsky, two of which are at the Oral Documentation Center of the Hebrew University's Institute of Contemporary Jewry and one at the Haganah Archives at Tel Aviv. Also see interview with Yitzhak Avidov (H).

3 A summary of the story of the Vilna partisans will be found in *Lehavot Baefer* (Flames in the Ash) by Ruzhka Korczak (Merhavia, 1965), especially pp. 205 ff. Her book is based on a wealth of documentary material and uses 36 testimonies of witnesses. The quotation in our text comes from Kovner's testimony, No. 2 (H), p. 1, confirmed by Ruzhka Korczak (H).

4 Abba Kovner, *ibid.,* p. 2.

5 See Abba Gefen, *Porzei Hamachsomim* (Tel Aviv, 1961), pp. 47–48; also testimonies of Eliezer Lidovsky (H) and Dov Levin (H).

6 See Nesia Orlowicz-Reznik: *Ima, hamutar kvar livkot?* (Mother, May I Weep Now?) (Israel, no date, 1965?), p. 11, and her testimony (M). See also Kovner's testimony, No. 2 (H), p. 9, and No. 1 (H), pp. 2–3.

7 Dov Levin in *Sefer Hapartizanim* (The Partisans' Book) (Israel, 1962), p. 257.

8 Ruzhka Korczak, *Lehavot Baefer,* p. 304.

9 *Ibid.,* p. 305.

10 See, for instance, testimony of Avraham Yashpan (H).

11 The story of the journey to Czernowitz is based on some documents in the possession of Dr. Amarant, now in Haifa, Israel, and testimonies of Dr. and Mrs. Amarant, Ruzhka Korczak and Avraham Yashpan (H).

12 Amarant testimony (H), p. 2.

13 *Ibid.,* pp. 5–6.

14 *Ibid.,* and confidential information given to the author.

15 Correspondence between the Jewish Agency Rescue Committee and Dr. Sommerstein (AZ, File S26/1248).

16 Lidovsky testimony No. 1 (H), pp. 33–34.

17 Yisrael Gal testimony (H), pp. 17–19.

18 This summary is based on a group of seven confidential testimonies (H): S. K., S. M., G. M., Y. G., M. R., Y. E., Y. Ei. An account of the episode was published in *Sefer Hashomer Hatzair*

(Merhavia, 1961), Vol. 2, pp. 226–250. The Ehrenburg interview was published in the *Einigkeit* of July 27, 1944.

19 Yitzhak Zuckerman to Kibbutz Meuchad, June 20, 1945, PM (material in possession of the author which will be handed over to Moreshet Archives).

20 Tel-Amal Symposium (collective interview) (H), pp. 11–12, 19, 25, 27, and Mordechai Rosman (H), pp. 19–21, 27. The description of the arguments and disagreements in Lublin has been taken largely from interviews with Zuckerman, Kovner, Kless, Gal (H) and Moshe Meiri (M).

21 Moshe Agami in Brichah meeting, December 12, 1946, at Basel (ATH); also interview with Agami, No. 1 (H), pp. 12, 16, 45. The incident is mentioned in interviews (H) with Rosman and Eichenwald, and Agami reported on his meeting with the three partisans in his letter to Palestine of January 21, 1945 (ATH).

22 Description of the route in the early days will be found in an interview (M) with Meiri and interviews (H) with Dov Levin, Yisrael Eichenwald, Shlomo Kless and Mordechai Munkacz.

23 The estimates of numbers are based on a report by Agami, May 30, 1945 (ATH) and an unsigned report in the "Krasner material," dated August 19, 1945 (ATH). The reports do not agree and the numbers quoted are somewhere between the two, arrived at by checking partial figures and fragments.

24 Report by Baruch Kaminker, January 15, 1945 (ATH–AB, Rumanian File). See also interview with Yakov Shmetterer (H).

25 Report (in German) by Yakov Shmetterer, undated (1948?), attached to his testimony (H), with supporting statements by Agami and an unsigned and undated (summer 1945?) "Report on a Visit to Poland" (in German) in ATH form the main basis for the story.

26 Yisrael Gal (H), pp. 11–12.

27 Hayim Lazar (leader of the Betar movement in Vilna and one of Kovner's associates in Lublin and Rumania), protocol of the meeting of the partisans with the Jewish Brigade, July 18, 1945 (M).

28 For the first quotation, see note above; for the second, see Kovner's speech, "Die Shlichess fun die Letzte" (The Mission of the Last Survivors), July 17, 1945 (M).

29 *Ibid.*

30 Velvele Rabinowitz at a Lublin *koordinazia* meeting, April 26, 1945, in Biletzky file (M).

31 "Die Shlichess fun die Letzte," see Note 28.

32 *Ibid.*

33 See above, Note 27, Kovner's speech.

34 Agami letter, May 30, 1945 (ATH).

Chapter 2

1 Malcolm J. Proudfoot, *European Refugees* (New York: Macmillan, 1957), p. 306. Proudfoot was not only a sociologist but a member of the staff at Allied Headquarters dealing with DP problems. He acknowledges, however, that his is no more than an intelligent guess. The Nazis themselves put the figure at 600,000 (!), according to the Musy report (M), but this is clearly impossible; Musy claims that the figure was given to him by Schellenberg, chief of S.S. intelligence and an important deputy of Himmler, and by Himmler himself, probably in February or March 1945. During the few weeks between that date and liberation, many thousands of Jews died on the marches and from hunger and disease.

2 Proudfoot, *op. cit.*, p. 189.

3 This memorandum (M) was originally published on December 28, 1944, and amended in April 1945. Excerpts were published in a stenciled brochure for students, *Machanot Ha'akurim Begermania, 1945–48* (Institute of Contemporary Jewry, Hebrew University, 1962–63), pp. 1–6. A summary of the other SHAEF cables quoted below will be found in SHAEF Memorandum on stateless and non-repatriables, August 5, 1945, DPG–117 (M), *ibid.*, pp. 7–12.

4 See President Truman's letter to General Eisenhower, August 31, 1945, published in the *New York Times* of September 30, 1945. Also Leo W. Schwarz, *The Redeemers* (New York: Farrar, Straus, 1953), pp. 24–26; and interviews with Aharon Hoter-Yishai, Rabbi Abraham J. Klausner (H).

5 According to the "Report of the Inquiry for Soldiers' Relatives," by A. Hoter-Yishai and Rabbi Jacob Lifshitz, July 1, 1945 (M), published in *Machanot,* pp. 27–41.

6 Protocol of the St. Ottilien meeting, July 25, 1945, DPG–21 (M).

7 See, for instance, Sylvia Neuberger's account of problems encountered with some of the American officers in transporting children, June 9, 1945 (AZ–S26/1296); also interview with Rabbi Bohnen (H), and Schwartz, *ibid.*, who clearly regards Patten as the exception among the top-ranking generals. More material will be

found in the ZK Protocols, especially DPG–67, 94, 95 (YIVO Archives, Schwartz material).

8 The issuance of such release cards had not been authorized by any Army authority, but they were actually given to survivors, especially at Mauthausen in Austria. These cards were easy to forge, and such forgeries were later used for clandestine or unauthorized movement of Jews who had never been to concentration camps (interviews with Levi Argov, Moshe Ben David, Ben Asher (H)).

9 Proudfoot, *op. cit.,* p. 110. This was especially the considered opinion of the British: "The fact that Jews can, as a race, be identified by certain characteristics, and that political developments, and in particular the National Socialist racial doctrine, have given them peculiar problems of importance in international politics are not sufficient reasons for treating 'Jews' as a separate national category" (Sir George Rendel, on behalf of the British authorities, to UNRRA, August 11, 1944, quoted by R. Hilberg in *The Destruction of East European Jewry* (Chicago: Quadrangle Books, 1961, p. 732). This may have been contrary to the policies of Balfour or Churchill, but it was in line with the thought on these matters as expressed in the policy of the 1939 White Paper on Palestine (Great Britain Command Paper, 6019).

10 Quotations from SHAEF Memorandum of August 5, 1945 (see Note 3).

11 See interview with Joseph Rosensaft (H); the Agudas Yisrael representative in Europe, Yakov Griffel, wrote on August 29, 1945 (AZ–S26/1296) that in view of the failure of the Jewish bodies to enter Germany in time "every serious and decent person must in the future refuse to be regarded as a 'saviour' of these people in these circumstances." The same point of view is presented in interviews with Rabbi Klausner, Y. Lavi and others (H).

12 These requests were made in May (DPG–145); in June the JDC was told to apply directly to the individual American armies. The Third and Seventh Armies, in whose occupation territories most of the liberated Jews were concentrated, refused these requests (the refusal is dated July 4).

13 The JDC team reached Buchenwald on June 13. Three JDC teams were subsequently permitted to enter the First and Twelfth Army areas, but there were very few Jews there. The Buchenwald transport of children was joined by another group that had been brought down from Hillersleben, where a train carrying some

thousands of evacuees from Belsen had been liberated by the Americans. The whole group numbered 535 children, of whom 400 were taken over by OSE, the Jewish health and child-care organization, founded in Eastern Europe and now the central Jewish body of its kind in France; 100 children were to become wards of the French government, and the 94 Hillersleben children were chosen for that transport. Catholic welfare organizations tried to take them over and there were apparently grounds to believe that they would become good Catholic French. In the end, after a protracted struggle in which the older children played a prominent part, their desire to live in Jewish surroundings and go to Palestine prevailed. The whole story is related in detail by S. Neuberger (see Note 7) and Ruth Kluger, cable of June 11, 1945 (Mossad, ATH).

14 Even after their arrival, it took months for the JDC to bring in supplies in appreciable quantities, because of the reluctance of Army authorities, who were concerned about transport difficulties and considerations of equity (the question arose why the Jews should be getting more supplies than other DPs). The comment of Yossel Rosensaft (see below) on the inability of the JDC to provide large-scale relief is reported to have been: "Listen, if you can't give us food and you can't give us things, give us some Yiddish typewriters so we can criticize the Joint to the Jews of the world" (Interview with Jacob L. Trobe [H]).

15 DPG–1.

16 Martin Hauser, special Report about the situation of Jewish Refugees, June 20, 1945 (ATH); Berlin reports of Philip Skorneck, JDC, representative, February 21, 1946 (JDC); reports by Hoter-Yishai and Klausner, June 24, 1945 and July 1, 1945 (in *Machanot* —see Note 3). More material will be found in DPG–614.

17 Letter by Freidenberg to Rabbi Max Nussbaum, Hollywood, May 25, 1947, and JDC File Austria, 1946–47.

18 Ephraim Dekel, Bin'tiv Ha'Brichah (Tel Aviv, 1958), pp. 71–73, 461–466.

19 Interview with Rabbi Klausner (H); Schwartz, *op. cit.*, pp. 17–23, 38–39, and information from Mr. Max Braude to this author (February 15, 1967).

20 Interview with Rabbi Klausner, first tape (H).

21 Report of Dr. Z. Gruenberg to the Jewish World Congress, May 31, 1945 (DPG–21).

22 Schwartz, *op. cit.*, p. 8.

23 DPG–167.

24 Klausner, second tape.

25 M. Sharett at the Jewish Agency Executive meeting, 4/22/45; Moshe Mosinsohn report, Brichah Archive (ATH, Italy File, December 1944).

26 Interviews with Y. Duvdevani and M. Hadash (H) and material kindly provided by M. Hadash (diary notes)—Yad Vashem Archive, 2/1–1, 20 I.

27 See previous note.

28 A. Hoter-Yishai interview, p. 2; Arazi mentioned the number 5,000 and says "and I remember that when he mentioned that number, I asked him if he really believed that we could find in all of Europe 5,000 such people." Sharett stated at the Jewish Agency Executive meeting mentioned in Note 25, above, that "if there were a practical possibility for illegal immigration from Italy, we would have no candidates for it there."

29 I am indebted to Dr. Yehuda Slutsky of the Haganah Archives, Tel Aviv, for providing me with a list of illegal ships and the numbers on each ship.

30 See Notes 26 and 28, and *Sefer Hahitnadvuth,* edited by Z. Shefer and Y. Lamdan, Jerusalem, 1949, pp. 737–744, 766–784, and testimony by Yeshayahu Weinberg (H).

31 Klausner, second tape (H).

32 Feldafing Protocol (DPG–94); ZK Protocol, August 8, 1945 (DPG–9); also Klausner, second tape. A previous effort to found a similar organization had been made by a man by the name of Friedheim, a Polish Jewish solicitor; this had taken place at the beginning of June, but had failed. Friedham was now given a prominent role in the first Central Committee, and he was later the head of the local committee in Munich.

33 Schwartz, *op. cit.,* pp. 27–28, 325, mentions this and a similar occurrence at Buchberg. The details are filled in by Klausner and Y. Lavi (H).

34 The memorandum was addressed to the Undersecretary of State for War and signed by Maj. Gen. R. H. Dewing.

35 Interviews with Y. Rosensaft, Jacob L. Trobe, Rabbi I. Levy, Rabbi Zvi Azaryah (H) and report by Harry Viteles, April 1946 (JDC, Reports, 1946).

36 Schwartz, *op. cit.,* pp. 30–31, 326; DPG–21 and 61, also 112 for the protocol and descriptions of the gathering.

Chapter 3

1 Harry S. Truman, *Years of Decisions* (1955), p. 235.

2 The Harrison report appeared in the Department of State Bulletin 13, September 30, 1945, and in a number of daily newspapers (*New York Times*) of the same date. The quotations are taken from that source. Additional information was obtained in interviews with Dr. Schwartz, Rabbi Klausner (H) and Mr. Katzki (PM).

3 For the Weizmann–Churchill interview of November 4, 1944, see Weizmann Archives, File 1944. The Jewish Agency memorandum referred to was published in *The Jewish Case before the Anglo-American Committee of Inquiry on Palestine* (Jerusalem, 1947), pp. 313 ff. The Stimson cable was made available to the author through the kindness of Rabbi Judah Nadich. Truman's comments were published in the *New York Times* of September 30.

4 New York *Post,* October 2, 1945. Klausner promised in a letter dated September 9 to make the incident public; it is not impossible that he may have been one of the prime movers in the publicity surrounding the incident. JTA carried an item on the incident on the same date as Klausner's letter. A letter from the War Department in answer to the inquiry of a private citizen (DPG–141, January 8, 1946) quotes the number of 650 as having been returned. The reason stated in the letter for not admitting the refugees was lack of accommodations in Germany. See also interview with Zev Landa (Bubu Landau) (H).

5 "General Collins told us that an order had come down *orally* from a higher headquarters which he would not name, that our division was to facilitate the passage of Jews across Austria so that they might proceed on their way" (Rabbi Eli A. Bohnen, in a letter to the author, April 14, 1965).

6 The Linz story is based on a number of reports in JDC, 8–19 (Austria, 1945), mainly Rice's report of October 14, 1945; the quotations in the text to the next footnote mark are taken from that report, except for the quote of the Oct. 6 cable which is taken from the same file. See also oral interviews with Rabbi Eli Bohnen and James P. Rice (H) which shed additional light on the incident.

7 J. Griffel (representative of the Agudat Yisrael) reported his trip to Prague (October 1945) that in order to prevent the closing

of the Czech-Bavarian border a number of steps had been taken, among others an intervention by a Jewish member of the American legation, Hugh Weisgal, with Major Schoenborn of the Czechoslovak Repatriation office. Schoenborn apparently tried to influence General Wood of the Third Army to agree to the entry of Jews to Bavaria (AZ–S26/1189).

8 Interview with A. Ben Nathan (H); report of A. Ben Nathan to the Brichah command, June 29, 1946 (ATH–AB); the quotations are from a report by James P. Rice, *Brichat* (sic) *or Alyiah Bet* (JDC, Gen. & Emerg. Austria, 1946/47), no date (May 1946?); interviews with Dr. J. J. Schwartz and J. P. Rice (H).

9 The quotations are taken from a confidential report to UNRRA by Jay D. Krane on Jewish Infiltrees, January 18, 1946 (in a report by Dr. J. J. Schwartz to the JDC, March 31, 1946, in JDC, Gen. & Emerg., 1946). See also the report of Leavitt and Schwartz on the conversation with Hilldring (JDC, Gen. & Emerg., 1945).

10 The material on Ben Gurion's visit is taken from the following sources: L. Schwarz, *op. cit.,* pp. 50–54; Ben Gurion's memorandum (H), obtained from Judge Simon H. Rifkind with Ben Gurion's consent; further interviews (H) with Judge Rifkind, Mr. Eno, R. Kluger (Eliav) and Rabbi Nadich; Major Heymont's diary, October 22 (the diary has been placed at my disposal through the kindness of Mr. S. Gringausz of New York City). Protocols of the Brichah, November 8–9, 1945 (ATH).

11 *Sefer Hahitnadvut,* especially articles by Bankover, Surkiss and Pines; also Duvdevani correspondence (ATH).

12 Rabbi Reznikoff's letter, October 27, 1945 (JDC, Italy File, 1946); the second quotation is taken from a letter from Major Berham Goldsmith to Mrs. Udo Reinach ("who gave $50,000 to UJA this year," as the JDC file puts it rather pointedly), who then sent it to Mrs. David Levy for transmittal to the JDC (*ibid.*); Pimontel's letter was sent to Rev. M. Berman, M. B. E., no date (PM).

13 Hoter-Yishai interview (H), p. 10; Duvdevani correspondence, September 5, 1945, (ATH).

14 Interviews with Israel Eichenwald, Mordechai Surkiss (H). Letter of Eichenwald to JDC, August 30, 1945 (AZ, S/26/1080). Two letters of Rosman to Eichenwald, August 27, 28, 1945 (ATH–AB, Austria File). The figure of 12,000 is an approximation only and many other conflicting figures are quoted (see for instance Duvdevani-Mossad correspondence [ATH], especially September

and October). The JDC reported 11,000 for Graz on October 31, 1945 (JDC, Reports 1945). When Duvdevani came to Graz to announce that Pinieh had been removed, he is said to have used the expression· "The king is dead—long live the king!" to which the Jews replied, "Aweg a ganev, gekummen a ganev" (one thief gone, another thief has come)—Eichenwald, p. 14. The footpath used by the Brichah on the Austrian border was at Passo di Pramollo.

15 The forged money story is based on the accounts of Argov, Ben David, Landa(u) and Van Harten (H); I am indebted to N. Orlowitz for additional confidential information. On Terezin, see M. Lagus-J. Polak, *Mesto za Mrizemi* (Prague, 1964), pp. 280 ff. The Terezin agreement of July 28, 1945 has been printed by E. Dekel, *op. cit.*, p. 72. The Pilsen events are based on Mrs. E. Elitzur's interviews with S. Neulander (H) and Rabbi Lipman (PM). I am indebted to Rabbi Lipman for his permission to use his private letters which enabled me to specify dates.

Chapter 4

1 An anonymous and undated report (PM) from Cracow (probably late May or early June 1945) puts the number of Polish Jews at 40,000, with 15,000 on the way from Germany. An authoritative summary by the Jewish Central Committee, August 15, 1945 (PM), gave the results of a census undertaken on June 15 which put the number of Jews at 73,955. Of these, 18,633 registered in the Lodz district (practically all of these lived in the town of Lodz); about 13,000 were serving in the Army (over 15 percent of the total Jewish population). The figures are borne out by a Merkaz Lagolah report (ATH) of August 7 in which the number of Jews outside the army is estimated at 60,000. To these figures must be added people who did not register as Jews, because they were unwilling to do so for security reasons or for convenience sake. Between June and August, too, some people arrived from the Soviet Union and some from Germany. The figure of 80,000 therefore seems a reasonable approximation.

2 See for instance Y. Heller's interview with Rabbi David Kahane (H), where a list of Jewish officials, mainly in the Defense Forces, is discussed.

3 *Ibid.*, p. 21.

4 On the pogroms in Cracow and elsewhere see Y. Griffel's report (AZ–S26/1296, August 29, 1945); also a report (PM), by a member of the Rumanian Committee (no date) entitled *Reiseeindrücke und Betrachtungen über die Lage in Polen,* p. 1; Ben's letter to Mossad in Palestine, August 13, 1945 (ATH). Anti-Semitic pamphlets and detailed descriptions and dates of pogroms, as well as an internal government circular *Objawy Antysemityzmu w Polsce i Walka z Nimi* (fall 1945), were presented to the Hebrew University's Oral History Department by Rabbi D. Kahane.

5 See Notes on an Interview with Rabbi Gorodetzky (H) where a typical incident of this kind is described.

6 See below, Note 8.

7 *Detailed Report on the Transit* by Yitzhak (Sela), Levi (Argov) and Elhanan (Gafni), March 23, 1946, p. 16 (ATH). On the smugglers generally, see especially a report by Yoav (ATH–AB, Germany File); also testimonies of Y. Erner and B. Teichholz (H).

8 The figures are taken from the report of the Brichah to the 22nd Zionist Congress at Basel, December 1946 (ATH). Lower figures were used by Alexander and Y. Cohen in their respective reports (ATH–AB).

9 E. Dekel, *op. cit.,* p. 23. According to Dekel, an agreement between the Soviets and the Poles regarding repatriation was signed on July 6, 1945.

10 See above, Note 8. The description about the reception of repatriants leans heavily on the testimonies (H) of Alexander, T. Cohen and S. Weiner (M).

11 This is no more than an estimate. The summary of financial expenditure of the Rescue Committee (S26/1268) does not list Brichah, for obvious reasons, as the recipient of sums sent abroad. Its total expenditures from 1942 to October 1946 came to £1,750,734. Of its receipts £518,348 came from the U.S.; therefore about 30 percent of all its expenditures must be credited to that country. Between October 1945 and October 1946, £111,008 were spent on "help to the Diaspora," £99,378 for "aid to refugees abroad" and £82,348 to the Merkaz Lagolah. Some additional sums were spent earlier on for Brichah, from about March or April 1945. Thus we know that in March 1945 £60,000 were sent to Rumania mainly for Brichah activities (S 26/1238b, May 9, 1945). On February 2, 1946 Dobkin of the Immigration Department of the agency made the statement to the Rescue Com-

mittee that up to that point £250,000 had been spent on Brichah (*ibid.*); if we add to that the period from early 1946 to October of that year, we arrive at the £300,000 mentioned in the text. This includes the JDC funds; of course the JDC did not know that its funds had enabled the committee to support Brichah.

12 Y. Cohen's report, April 3, 1947 (ATH–AB).

13 Quotations from L. Argov (H), p. 11, and M. A. Leavitt's letter (JDC, Poland File), 1946.

14 The Stettin story is based on the following main sources: Report by Yoav, early 1947, on Berlin (ATH–AB, Germany File); interviews (H) with Yisrael Harkovsky, Mordechai Mittelman, Yakov Schechter, Yitzhak Ram and Yakov Erner, and interview with Rabbi Herbert Friedman (M); and Philip S. Skorneck, report on Berlin, February 21, 1946 (JDC, Germany 1946). While there is some documentation on the Berlin side of the story, the whole of the Stettin episode had to be culled from oral testimonies.

15 The figures appear in the Skorneck report mentioned in Note 14.

16 Skorneck, p. 7.

17 *Ibid.*, p. 9.

18 *Ibid.*, p. 11.

19 See above, Note 14. Also the personal papers of Rabbi Friedman, who very kindly allowed the author to make use of them.

20 Y. Schechter (H), p. 6, and M. Yocht (H).

21 E. Dekel, *op. cit.*, p. 25, and testimonies of M. Sharon (ATH), Argov (H), Sela (H).

22 Y. Steiner (Sela) report (ATH–AB, Czechoslovakia File); a report by the JDC on May 1, 1946 (Czechoslovakia, 1946) states that between July and November 18,000 people had passed through the country.

23 The Greek story is told by Dekel (*op. cit.*, pp. 37 ff., 67 ff). Also testimonies by Menahem Sharon and Avraham Sadeh (ATH). There is hardly a witness who did not have his own tale about the Greek episode—these tales seem to have multiplied and assumed a rather mythical character.

24 Testimony of Yosef Marcus (ATH), who also wrote down the ditty.

25 Cohen Diary, February 1946.

26 For Pick and Beck see Landau's testimony (H), first tape, p. 15; JDC Czechoslovakia File, Reports 1946/47; and report by

I. G. Jacobson for May/June 1946, p. 19. See also testimony of Ann Borden (PM).

27 For the Moravska Ostrava incident, see testimonies by T. Cohen (M), Y. Cohen and Alexander (H).

28 I. F. Stone, *Underground to Palestine* (New York, 1947), pp. 90–91. Cohen Diary, April 13, May 18.

29 This incident, reported on May 10 in the Hebrew daily *Davar,* was the biggest of its kind up to that time, but it should be emphasized that it was but one manifestation of the upsurge of anti-Semitic feeling in Poland in the spring of 1946. The Polish *Rzeczpospolita* reported on February 27, 1946 that the NSZ had killed a Jew by the name of Grungras at Nowy Targ, near Nowy Sacz; Dr. Yishai, the official representative of the Jewish Agency in Poland, reported on May 30 that "not a week passes without a number of Jews being killed on buses, on roads, or even on the streets in towns and houses. The murders are committed by A.K. men whose influence is on the increase. The Government is fighting them vigorously, but their strength is nevertheless growing, and the first victims are the Jews" (PM). An article in the Yiddish *The Day* of New York (February 10, 46) reported 363 Jews killed in Poland in 1945, and in early 1946 this was on the increase.

30 Cohen Diary, May 6.

31 Testimonies of Tuvia Cohen and Shania Gringross. Yisrael Ridelnik, another commander at Kudowa in late spring, maintain that the help received from local Polish officers was almost always gained through bribes. But Ridelnik operated on a purely local level, and there is no necessary contradiction to the story in the text—Ridelnik would not have had any contact with area commanders of the border guards (H).

32 Testimony of A. Sadeh (ATH).

Chapter 5

1 The figures are taken from the Brichah Files (ATH): "Report from Russia," May 16, 1946; report on Rumania, April 23, 1946; and Dr. C. Jancu's letter to Y. Holzmann in Palestine, April 20, 1946. According to a report prepared by Mossad for submission to the Anglo-American Commission of Inquiry, February 19, 1946 (ATH, Mossad Files, Rumania), about 115,000 Rumanian Jews were prepared to leave for Palestine, 36,959 heads of families and

21,927 single individuals having registered with the Bucharest Palestine Office of the Jewish Agency (which in effect was run by the Mossad). There is no way of checking the accuracy of these figures, but the desire to leave Rumania, while weaker than in Poland, was undoubtedly fairly widespread.

2 Report: *The Essence of Brichah, 1948* (ATH–AB, Krassner File) provides general contemporary background material. The details of the Slovak pogrom were taken from confidential material at the disposal of the author, and the Slovak *Vestnik*. The Vienna figures are based on a Teichholz report in File KAuV/119 in the Vienna Jewish Community archives at the General Jewish Historical Archives (Hebrew University, Jerusalem). The same figures, with some explanations are found in the Ben Nathan report, no date, 1947? (ATH–AB, Austria Files). They were then repeated by others. The other figures estimating the flux of refugees from Hungary and Rumania are contained in Agami's report at Basel, December 12, 1946 (ATH–AB).

3 M. Agami (H), first tape, p. 27. This is also mentioned by Ben Haim (M).

4 There are practically no documents on the Yugoslav operation. The information was therefore obtained through interviews with S. Ben Haim, L. Abramovsky, Y. Ben Yehuda, E. Avriel, L. Argov and Dr. Alkalay (H).

5 James P. Rice report, September 20, 1945, JDC, 8–19, pp. 5–6. Also R. Reznik, *ibid.,* September 15, 1945 report.

6 The foregoing is based on the following sources: a memorandum by B. Teichholz to Dr. Joseph J. Schwartz dated November 8, 1945, on the setting up of the IK; KAuV/25 (see Note 2, above), which contains letters and memoranda from the period August 1945 to January 1946 confirming the details of the Teichholz memo. Additional information will also be found in KAuV/120 and in another report by Teichholz, November 3, 1947 (ATH–AB, Austria Files). This has been supplemented by oral interviews (H) with L. Argov, B. Teichholz, A. Ben Nathan. The figures for refugees will be found in KAuV/119 and 120 (see above, Note 2). Teichholz claimed that the total number of people who passed through Vienna was 13,901. The additional 250 persons were supposed to have come through Vienna before July, i.e., before Teichholz came there and before an organization existed to receive them. This seems to be pure conjecture. However, the Bratislava figures (ATH–AB, Czecho-

slovakia File), which have no date but were probably prepared for the Basel meeting, show the following numbers as having passed through that town: July 1945, 1,320, August, 2,126, September, 3,085, October, 2,829, November, 1,930, December, 1,753, or a total of 13,043. The majority of these must have gone through Vienna, but some of them may not have visited the Rothschild hospital—there was a transit place for refugees at the Social-Democratic center at the Goldschlaegergasse. The others would have gone via the Semmering to Graz in the early months, or directly to Linz. A comparison between the two sets of figures reveals that the Bratislava set is larger in every instance except for the month of December. Generally speaking, statistics at both places were fairly reliable, so that the conclusion would be that up to December there were other routes besides Vienna and the Rothschild hospital. In early 1946, between January and the end of May, 10,003 people were registered at the Rothschild hospital, bringing the total to 18,664. Of these, 12,855 declared they came from Poland (about 65 percent), the rest mainly from Hungary and Rumania.

7 Rice report, see Note 5.

8 *Ibid.;* also report by Bienenfeld, no date (summer 1945?), JDC 9–18.

9 The early Austrian story is based on oral interviews (H) with L. Argov, B. Teichholz, A. Ben Nathan. The Salzburg section is amply documented in Report by Abba Gefen, 1947 (ATH–AB, Austrian File), and A. Gefen, *Porzei Hamachsomim* (Tel Aviv, 1961), pp. 13–17, 22–25, 32–39, 55–68.

10 Letter to Artzi, January 12, 1946 (ATH–AB, Austrian File). Compare with report of Melvin S. Goldstein, February 22, 1946 (JDC, Austria, Gen. & Emerg., 1946).

11 See above, Note 6.

12 Ben Nathan Report (see Note 2) and testimony (H). The numbers of those coming through from Hungary are not ascertainable from our sources.

13 This story is based on Argov's testimony, which has been proved to be very accurate wherever it could be checked against other sources. Credence is therefore given to it in this case as well.

14 See above, Note 12, and testimony of Michael Yitzhaki (H).

15 Gefen report; see Note 9 for figures. See also Ben Nathan (H).

16 A. Gefen, *Porzei Hamachsomim,* pp. 74–81.

17 *Ibid.,* pp. 63–74, 82–85, 91–99, 106–110.

18 *Ibid.;* also E. Frank (H).

19 *Ibid.*, p. 169.

20 On the subject of demoralization in the camps, oral interviews with A. Klausner (H), A. Hymań (PM), S. Gringausz (PM) were consulted. A vast amount of documentation exists concerning the individual DP camps in Austria and Germany at the YIVO archives in New York. Only samples of this were read for the purpose of the present work, but they tended to confirm the opinions and judgments summarized in the text.

21 YIVO, Austria DP camps, 5–1 (no date). Similar polls were conducted on a partial basis at the same time in various places. Major John W. Denny of the 42nd Division reported to the Anglo-American Commission of Inquiry on February 1, 1946, that he had investigated 1,941 persons in three camps and found that 95 percent wished to go to Palestine. A similar report was submitted by Major Otis P. Gray for Upper Austria. Of a total of 3,360 persons, 3,104 opted for Palestine. The American officer stated quite categorically that "all foreign Jews in the area do not wish to return to their former homes," and the fact that during the past two months 4,550 Jews had passed through the area "to a very uncertain future" seemed to indicate that no pressure would have been sufficient to produce that effect and that there must have been very compelling reasons that had nothing to do with Zionist propaganda (Rice Report, February 12, 1946, JDC, Austria, 1946).

22 E. Kneza, in Y. Suhl, *They Fought Back* (New York, 1967), p. 181.

23 See for instance Y. Sela (H), L. Argov (H), N. Friedman (H) and I. G. Jacobson (PM).

24 Dr. Breslauer Report, October 9, 1945 (M).

25 Z. Landau (H), p. 16. Landau claims that the official was sent by Masaryk. It should be noted parenthetically that, while Bohemia and Moravia were safe as far as Jewish lives were concerned, almost a mass hysteria did exist among Jews in Slovakia. Thus, JTA brought a report on January 25, 1946, that a pogrom at Snina in Slovakia had caused the deaths of sixteen persons. I have not found any other mention of the incident or indeed evidence that a place by the name of Snina exists. The very fact that such a report should have been published by a usually reliable press agency shows something of the atmosphere then prevailing.

26 Incoming cables, Paris, December 10, 14, 1945 (JDC, Czech Refugees, 1945/46).

27 The quotation is from a Viteles cable, January 17, 1946

(ibid.). Other information will be found in Report of May 1, 1946, testimonies by Argov, Landau and Sela (JDC, Czechoslovakia, 1946).

28 Sneh was a very close collaborator of Mapai in 1946, and his membership in the nonsocialist General Zionist Party seems to have been nominal. He was to move further left in 1947/48, when he joined the Mapam Party, and in 1952/53 he left Mapam and after a short interlude joined the Israeli Communist Party. In 1946 these tendencies were not evident, however.

29 AZ S26/1238b, protocols of meetings, May 9, 1945, October 1, 1945; S26/1238, date undecipherable, probably September 1944, and the following protocol of October 3, 1944. At these meetings it was Ben-Gurion who declared quite clearly that the Jewish Agency and its Rescue Committee should under no circumstances take over the relief work which was the job of the JDC. The task of all the branches of the Jewish Agency was to bring Jews to Palestine, and nothing else.

30 The December decisions and reports on the meeting in Paris are in AZ–S26/1238. See also S26/1230, 1082 and 1231. Two letters (ATH) of Pino Ginzburg dated November 6, 1945, and January 2, 1946, are also important. A summary, received on March 23, 1946 in Palestine, was presented at a meeting of the Brichah at Bratislava (ATH, Mossad Files). Argov's testimony is again very important in this connection.

31 Letter signed by Argov, Sela and Gafni, received on March 23, 1946 (ATH–AB). See also Bulletin received on the same date; also Sela's letter, November 29, 1945 (*ibid.*).

32 Based on testimonies (H) of Argov, Sela, Gafni and Ofri, and the Bratislava protocol referred to in Note 30, above.

Chapter 6

1 Col. Harold E. Potter, Chief Historian, "Displaced Persons," in *Occupation Forces in Europe Series, 1945–1946*.

2 See above, page 89.

3 *Administrative Memorandum,* No. 39, SHAEF, revised, April 16, 1945, paragraphs 5, 32.

4 See Note 1, above.

5 Irving Heymont, *After the Deluge* (Diary), p. 186.

6 Letter of Central Committee (Munich) to Judge Rifkind, December 5, 1945 (YIVO, D–1 and PM).

7 General Smith's *Memorandum for Lt. Gen. Frederick E. Morgan,* no date, December 7, 1945? (PM).

8 *Ibid.*

9 Heymont, *op. cit.,* p. 242.

10 *Ibid.,* p. 237.

11 Interview with Judge Simon H. Rifkind (H); Viteles Report (JDC, Gen. & Emerg. Germany, 1946), p. 20; Gruenbaum to Sharett, January 6, 1946 (AZ–S26/1296).

12 Interview of Dr. Schwartz and Mr. Leavitt with Gen. Hilldring, December 20, 1945 (JDC, Gen. & Emerg., Germany).

13 Robert Marshall in *Stars and Stripes,* December 8, 1945.

14 London *Evening Standard,* January 2, 1946.

15 *Ibid.*

16 *Star,* January 3, 1946.

17 *News Chronicle,* January 5, 1946.

18 Manchester *Guardian,* January 5, 1946.

19 *New York Times,* January 7, 1946.

20 Interview with Jacob L. Trobe (H), pp. 2–4; Trobe cable, January 4, 1946 (YIVO, DPG–65).

21 *Ibid.*

22 *News Chronicle,* January 5, 1946.

23 Interview with Trobe (H), p. 4; and confidential information put at the author's disposal.

24 Résumé of (PM) interview with Ilya Dijour.

25 Interview with Trobe (H), p. 4; Philip Skorneck's letter to Benjamin B. Goldman, November 22, 1946 (YIVO, DPG–65).

26 JDC, Gen. & Emergency, Germany, 1946.

27 Samuel Zissman, UNRRA Regional Director, 20th Corps, and Helena Matouskova, Supervisor of Jewish Camps, UNRRA, Third Army.

28 Report by Harry Viteles (JDC), May 11, 1946.

29 Schwartz, *op. cit.,* pp. 104–110; Legal aid report (O. A. Mintzer), YIVO, DPG–22, May 30, 1946; *JTA Bulletin,* June 10, 1946.

30 Protocol of Council meeting of the Central Committee, June 9, 1946 (YIVO, DPG–105).

31 Francis Williams, *A Prime Minister Remembers* (London, 1961), p. 191.

32 I. F. Stone in *PM* of January 6, 1946. See also RIIA: *The Importance of the Middle East and the Interests of the Commonwealth in the Middle East, Preparatory Papers for an Unofficial Commonwealth Relations Conference* (Chatham House, 1945).

33 House of Commons, *Hansard,* November 13, 1945.

34 Interview with Mrs. Ann Borden (PM).

35 Azriel Karlebach, *Duach Va'adath Hahakirah* (Tel Aviv, 1946), p. 275.

36 Memo of DP Office of the U.S. Army, U.S. zone of Germany, to the Anglo-American Committee, February 1946 (YIVO, DPG–54).

37 Mark Wischnitzer, *Visas to Freedom* (New York, 1956), p. 213. However, the same author mentions in another book (*To Dwell in Safety,* p. 349) that the number of Jews who received visas between March 31, 1946, and October 1, 1947, was 14,958. It is not clear whether this refers to DPs only or to Jews generally.

38 Dov Levin's interview with Dr. Haim Yahil (H), p. 55.

39 Yahil—lecture on Brichah, 1947, in Yahil material (ATH–AB).

Chapter 7

1 The details about the Kielce pogrom are based on Rabbi David Kahane's article in *Hatzofe,* July 6, 1956; a testimony of an anonymous witness who fled from Kielce to Germany (Stamsried Jewish Committee's Historical Commission, PM); oral testimonies of Alexander and Yitzhak Zuckerman (H), and the *New York Times,* July 5–July 16, 1946.

2 Zuckerman (H), II, p. 2.

3 Photostats obtained from Rabbi Kahane (H). A good example is a leaflet entitled *Poles!* which claims that 60,000 Jews arrived in Lodz (actually the Jewish population there, even at the height of the repatriation from Russia, never surpassed the 30,000 mark), that they had been given factories and houses and that they now were the police in the town. These were the same Jews that had shot at the Poles at the East (the Ukrainian parts annexed by Poland) in 1920/21. The great opponents of the Poles were the PPR (Communists), whereas in the east the Ukrainians were continuing to murder Poles. But there was hope from Turkey and the West, because the Soviet Union had been decisively weakened by the war. These allies would remove the "treacherous cliques at whose head stands the Jew Bierut" (*zradziecka klika na czele z zydem Bierutem*) —Bierut, the president of Poland, was of course not a Jew. But that did not matter, it was convenient to combine the hatred of Jews and

Communists to achieve propagandist ends. The pamphlets ended with acclaiming the exile government in London.

4 *New York Times,* July 12, 1946; a full record of the interview will be found in Rabbi Kahane's materials (H).

5 Interview with Alexander (H), 11, p. 12. The *New York Times* said on July 5 that "Polish spokesmen frankly and ashamedly declare that it is not safe to live in small Polish towns."

6 See Chapter 4, Note 10. The figures for May and July are detailed, whereas the June figures are everywhere given in round numbers. The discrepancies between various sources are great. Yochanan Cohen (ATH–AB), April 3, 1947, has the figure of 18,000 for June which seems to be a typographical error (Tuvia Cohen's diary [MandPM] for July 1 has the figure of 8,500). The error seems to have been transferred to others. Our other sources for the statistical picture are Ephraim Dekel in *Mahut haBrichah* (ATH–AB), and a 1947 report by Alexander on the Brichah from Poland, *ibid.*

7 The figure for July was taken from Yochanan Cohen, *ibid.;* Dekel (see Note 6) has 17,505, but this does not seem to include Stettin. The August figure is Dekel's, and this time he specifically mentions Stettin. The September figure is taken from the same source. The main source for Stettin is a report by "Yoav" (pseud.), written in early 1947 (ATH–AB, Germany File). He mentions 16,000 as the number of Jews who passed through Berlin from Stettin between July and November 1946. This excludes those who went from Stettin directly to Lübeck. If "Yoav's" figure is accepted, the figures arrived at in the text would have to be revised upward. A compilation by the JDC, Report by Gaynor I. Jacobson, 1946 (YIVO, DPG–57), p. 20, puts the number of transients through the Czech lands only (i.e., without those who entered Slovakia directly via the Tatra mountains) at 66,000. Add 16,000 for Stettin, 10,000 for Stettin-Lübeck and the Hungarians, etc. (see below), and the total will be around 100,000.

8 Jacobson Report (see Note 7), p. 22: he counts 13,528 Hungarians for July and August, and another 630 for September.

9 Arthur Ben Nathan, *Report on Austria 1947* (ATH, AB–Austria).

10 Yisrael Ridelnik, interview (H), I, p. 22.

11 *Ibid.,* p. 31.

12 Avraham Sadeh, interview (ATH), p. 10.

13 Jacobson Report, p. 13.

14 JDC, Gen. & Emerg., 1946–47, Czechoslovakia File, Reports and Report by G. I. Jacobson for May and June 1946, p. 35.

15 G. I. Jacobson, July 26, 1946, memorandum (*ibid.*).

16 G. I. Jacobson, *Saving Europe's Jews,* no date (ATH–AB, Czechoslovakia File).

17 JDC, Gen. & Emerg. Czechoslovakia 1946, cable no. 316.

18 YIVO, DPG–57, Jacobson Report, p. 15.

19 *Ibid.* See also E. Dekel, *op. cit.,* pp. 81–82, where a Hebrew translation of an official paper issued by the Czechoslovak Prime Minister's office regarding the session of July 25 (*sic*) is printed. However, Dekel gives no indication of his sources and it was therefore impossible to check the accuracy of the translation.

20 Dekel, *op. cit.,* pp. 84–85. Again, while the authenticity of the documents is hardly in question, no sources are indicated and the original could not be consulted.

21 Zuckerman (H) II, p. 6.

22 *Ibid.,* p. 8.

23 Alexander interview (H), II, p. 13.

24 See Chapter 4.

25 Alexander, II, pp. 16–18.

26 YIVO, DPG–57, Jacobson Report, p. 15. See also Zuckerman interview (H), II, p. 10.

27 This seems to be the conclusion one can draw from the document published in Dekel, p. 82, if the translation is accurate. In that document the Foreign Minister of Czechoslovakia is asked to find out what the policy of Poland is toward the flight of these "unsuccessful repatriants." If the Czechs had known about the imminent opening of the borders, there would presumably have been little occasion for such a decision by the Czech cabinet.

28 Zuckerman (H), II, pp. 10–15.

29 *Ibid.,* I, p. 37. Ridelnik (H), I, p. 13, says that with the opening of the frontier nothing really changed as far as the Polish border guards were concerned. "Possibly the danger of them killing somebody diminished after Kielce. But the illegality continued despite the fact that the form of the exit out of Poland had changed. . . . There was a kind of 'legal robbery'—they used to take away from the Jew his last possessions and say: 'listen, this I am going to take.' The taking was completely arbitrary, and therefore the bribing had to be continued . . . I think that for us, the local people—as the

Palestinian shlihim used to call us—these things were clearer and better understood. We had not received the Western, Anglo-Saxon kind of education. We had emerged from the little townships of Poland, we had come from the Siberian steppes and we knew exactly with whom we had to deal there on the borders."

30 The above account is based on the accounts (H) of Alexander, Krochmal, Kravchik and Ridelnik, and also of Sadeh (ATH). The person actually responsible at Kudowa was a girl by the name of Shania Sheinberg (H—see interview).

31 Sadeh, pp. 11 ff.

32 *Ibid.*, p. 14.

33 Jacobson Report, p. 17 (YIVO, DPG–57).

34 *Ibid.*, p. 15, and interview with Mrs. Ann Borden (PM).

35 Interviews with Ann Borden and Leah Assa (H).

36 Nati Friedman, interview, p. 7 (H), Aharon Ofri, interview, p. 29 (H).

37 Ofri, p. 22.

38 Jacobson Report, p. 18 (YIVO, DPG–57); S. Z. Shragai, *Massa Hatzalah* (May 1947, Jerusalem)—an account of Rabbi Herzog's trip to Europe in 1946; JDC, Gen. & Emerg.; Czechoslovakia 1946, incoming cables, Prague 8.10.46, Paris 26.12.46.

39 The story as told in Shragai, *op. cit.*, of Bidault hanging his head and in tears as the venerable rabbi lectured him on the inequities of the Christian world is not altogether convincing, but it is of course quite likely that an interview of some kind did actually take place.

40 Jacobson, *op. cit.*, p. 18.

41 *Ibid.*

42 Dekel, *op. cit.*, p. 42, where a facsimile of a forgery is reproduced.

43 Alexander (H), I, pp. 41 ff.; M. Mittelman, *The Brichah in Stettin,* July 1963 (mimeographed), p. 4, and Yakov Erner, interview (H).

44 Mittelman, *op. cit.*, p. 4.

45 *Ibid.*, p. 5.

46 *Ibid.*

47 See "Yoav" report (ATH–AB Germany File); Erner, p. 17, adds that the Jews who traveled in the trucks betrayed their Brichah guides and told the Russians that these were the people who had

brought them across the frontier. One of the boys who were caught there, Yossef Ozikowski, spent some eleven years in Siberia before returning to Poland, and arrived in Israel in the late fifties (*ibid.*).

49 "Yoav," p. 17. Alexander, in his 1947 report (ATH–AB) has completely different figures for the Szczecin-Berlin route: July, 5,158; August, 5,032; September, 335; October, 625; total, 11,150. It is of course possible that the difference may be explained by the people who were brought in by smugglers.

48 "Yoav," pp. 6–9.

50 Elfan Rees, *Abusing the Jews—A Plea for Refugees, 1946* (mimeographed), Chap. 3 ("Abusing the Jews—The Refugee Racket"). See also interview with Ann Borden and "Yoav" report (ATH–AB, Germany File).

Chapter 8

1 Interview with Rabbi Bernstein (H), p. 2.

2 *Ibid.*, p. 3.

3 Chaim Yahil: *Brichah,* no date (1947?), p. 1 (ATH–AB, Germany File).

4 Yahil, *loc. cit.*, p. 2.

5 *Ibid.*

6 *Ibid.*, p. 4; *New York Times,* June 27, 1946, where McNarney was quoted as "offering temporary haven and assistance to these persecutees." This did not mean, however, that things went smoothly: on May 5, Secretaries Patterson (War) and Acheson (State) told Dr. Wise and Dr. Goldmann, representatives of the World and American Jewish Congresses as well as of the Jewish Agency, "that because of the talk of admitting into Palestine 100,000 Jews, they anticipate an increased infiltration of Jewish refugees into the American zone of occupation which, if it should develop into great proportions would exceed the ability of the American Army to handle the matter and would probably necessitate a revision of American policy" (AZ–Z–5/1172).

7 Yahil, *ibid.*

8 Letter by Moses A. Leavitt to Isaac Levy, July 18, 1946 (JDC, Gen. & Emerg., 1946).

9 For the preceding as well as the following, see interview with Rabbi Bernstein (H), pp. 4–5; also *Report on Poland, Memorandum to General Joseph T. McNarney,* August 2, 1946. The report

reached the Secretaries of State and War and General Mark Clark (the *New York Times* of June 24 had carried an item according to which "high U.S. officers" had told 12 U.S. editors and newspaper executives that the United States in Germany faced the possibility of "3 million Jews" coming at the rate of 10,000 a month; this was termed "one of the gravest problems facing U.S. occupation authorities." Whether motivated by conscious or unconscious anti-Semitism or by simple alarmism, one of the by-products of Rabbi Bernstein's report was that it scotched this kind of irresponsible talk.

10 Interview with Rabbi Bernstein (H), p. 4. In the "report," Bernstein stated (p. 5) that "Cardinal Hlond in effect condoned the Kielce pogroms."

11 *Ibid.*, p. 2. See also interview with William Bein (H). What Rabbi Bernstein saw were "stores" at Kladzko and Rychbach. The commander of the Brichah in Poland, Isser Ben Zvi, reported that "danger is threatening that the Americans will try to close the borders. Dr. Bernstein was here with us and left with a firm decision to fight for our cause." Ben Zvi met the rabbi, but was of course not introduced as commander of the Brichah (ATH—Mossad, Poland, Ben Zvi report, August 7, 1946).

12 Bernstein "Report," p. 7.

13 John H. Hilldring to JDC, Gen. & Emerg., 1946, July 31, 1946.

14 Notes on interview with Moses A. Leavitt (H).

15 Edward M. Warburg to John H. Hilldring, August 23, 1946 (JDC, Gen. & Emerg., 1946).

16 London *Daily Mail,* July 9, 1946.

17 London *Times,* August 9, 1946, *Daily Mail,* August 10, 1946, *Daily Telegraph,* August 9, 1946.

18 *New York Times,* August 10, 1946, JTA, August 12, 1946.

19 Don Cook in the New York *Herald Tribune,* August 9, 1946; also *New York Times,* August 10, 1946.

20 *Daily Mail,* August 16, 1946.

21 Interview with Dr. Joseph J. Schwartz (H), August 14, 1962—"The retreat was due to pressure from Washington. Definitely. There was a time when we went to Hilldring and the President and Morgenthau and everybody that was around. They understood that it shouldn't be done and then they told the Army not to do it."

22 *New York Times,* August 22, 1946. The Manchester *Guardian* quoted McNarney as saying that "although it is not our function to

arrange for organized mass transfer of non-Germans to the U.S. zone I will continue to grant shelter and care to persecuted persons filtering to the U.S. zone."

24 Report of Abba Gefen, 1947 (ATH–AB, Austria File). Leo W. Schwarz to UNRRA, November 11, 1946 (JDC, Gen. & Emerg. Germany).

25 Report by W. Bein re note of the American Embassy to the Polish Foreign Ministry, August 19, 1946; report on a conference with Mr. Keith of the American Embassy, August 20, 1946; W. Bein's letter to Dr. J. J. Schwartz, August 23, 1946; conference between Ambassador Lane, Colonel Wrzosz and W. Bein, August 23, 1946 (JDC, Gen. & Emerg. Poland, 1946).

26 Dorothy Greene's report to JDC, N.Y., August 14, 1946 (JDC, Czechoslovakia, 1946). Miss Greene reported that the borders to the U.S. zones were temporarily closed.

27 JTA, August 14, 1946—according to Prague radio the Czech border had been closed at British request.

28 In a cable from Paris (JDC, Czech Refugees, File 45/46) Schwartz blamed the border difficulties on "Island pressure" and the "desire [of] Pat's boys for brief respite" ["Pat's boys" were the War Department] and "Island" referred to Britain.

29 Mr. Jan Galewicz, quoted in the Jewish *Morning Journal* of September 15, 1946.

30 Jacobson Report, July 1, 1947 (YIVO–DPG–58); and undated report by Jacobson (ATH–AB, Czechoslovakia File); and interview with G. I. Jacobson, 1962 (H).

31 New York *Herald Tribune*, August 28, 1946; and letter of September 3 by Jacob L. Trobe (JDC, Italy File, September–December 1946).

32 *Ibid.*, Trobe to David N. Key, U.S. chargé d'affaires in Rome; and *ibid.*, December 1946 report.

33 Report on Italy (by Surkiss?) in ATH–AB, Italy File.

34 JDC, Italy File, September–December 1946: P. S. Bernstein to M. A. Leavitt, September 8; Leavitt to Schwartz, September 20; and Schwartz to Leavitt, September 30.

35 Rabbi Bernstein's memorandum to Joseph T. McNarney, September 14, 1946, on an audience with Pope Pius XII. On the 10,000, see also JDC, Italy File, for report by Blanche Bernstein (a JDC worker, unrelated to the rabbi) to New York, August 19, who remarked that the project was under discussion with the Italians

and the U.S. authorities, but the British objected ("Islanders know and will scream").

36 Rabbi Bernstein's memorandum to Joseph T. McNarney, October 18, 1946, on an interview with President Truman. I am grateful to Rabbi Bernstein for his kind permission to use the documents quoted in this and the preceding footnote.

37 AZEC meeting, August 7, 1946 (AZ—Z-5/1172).

38 *Ibid.*

39 Speech by Bartley Crum at Madison Square Garden, June 12, 1946 (AZ—Z-5/1171).

40 *New York Times,* July 31, 1946.

41 Memorandum by Eliahu Elath, October 4, 1946 (Weizmann Archives).

42 Protocol of Jewish Agency Executive, August 4, 1946, Archive of the Jewish Agency, Jerusalem.

43 *Ibid.,* and quoted in a report by Dr. Stephen S. Wise, August 24 (AZ—Z-5/1171).

44 AZ—Z-4/15,170.

45 Proskauer: *A Segment of My Times* (New York, 1950), pp. 242 ff.

46 See above, Note 41.

47 Protocol of meeting in London at the Foreign Office, October 1, 1946 (Weizmann Archives).

Chapter 9

1 See below, Note 19. See also Yahil (ATH–AB), p. 5.

2 Gefen report (ATH) and report by Harold Nordlicht from Linz, September 9, 1946 (JDC). The figures agree more or less with the 85,316 registered with the Rothschild hospital in Vienna as having passed through Austria in 1946. If it can be assumed that the number of people passing through Salzburg in 1946 came to about 70,000, then the addition of the Linz number brings the total up to about the Rothschild hospital figure.

3 Report by Leon D. Fisher, December 10, 1946 (JDC).

4 *Ibid.* This, by the way, was an internal report to a Jewish organization, and one can safely discount the possibility that it was intended in any way for propaganda.

5 Gefen, *op. cit.*, pp. 111–126; Dekel, *op. cit.*, pp. 157–166, 472–474.

6 Gefen, *op. cit.*, pp. 122–160.

7 Gefen, *loc. cit.*, and Ben Nathan report (ATH).

8 *Ibid.*, p. 144.

9 October 29, 1946 (YIVO, DPG–57). The Hannover story is based largely on testimony by Rega Globman (ATH) based on her diary. See also interview with E. Frank (H). She says her "point" effected the transit of 34,000 Jewish refugees into the American zone; however, her figures are inconsistent, and therefore of doubtful validity. Her story that British authorities were less than friendly toward the Jews is borne out by many others (see further discussion in this chapter), including Ira A. Hirschmann—see his book *The Embers Still Burn* (New York, 1949), pp. 120 ff.

10 Hirschmann, *op. cit.*, p. 69. He says that Lucius D. Clay, at that time McNarney's aide, also declared to him that "my orders are to reconstitute the German economy without delay" (p. 109).

11 U.S. Army memorandum on the DP Question, August 26, 1946 (YIVO, DPG–145).

12 For the Herszkowicz letter, see PM; J. C. Hyman of the JDC wrote to Ira Hirschmann on July 18, 1946 (JDC, Gen. & Emerg., Germany, 1946) that thousands were coming in, and there was "a tremendous bottleneck, because the Army has not made adequate preparations to receive these people, knowing full well that they were bound to come in. The Army had to be jacked up."

13 Hirschmann, *op. cit.*, p. 130.

14 *Ibid.*, pp. 166–167.

15 Report (October 4, 1946) on Babenhausen, Rabbi Friedman to Rabbi Bernstein (Friedman papers); *ibid.*, a note (October 1, 1946) by Friedman entitled "The Silence at Babenhausen." I am grateful to Rabbi Friedman for permission to use these sources.

16 Gelber report, June 28, 1946 (PM, JDC).

17 Hirschmann, *op. cit.*, pp. 143–144.

18 Joseph Levine report, July 10, 1946 (YIVO, DPG–23).

19 ATH–AB, "Han'didah Hagdolah"; the figures quoted are the lowest ones available. Other agencies, such as UNRRA, went up as much as 175,000 for the U.S. zone, and even Yahil said there were 153,000 (in a speech at Basel, November 12, 1946, ATH). JDC had higher figures as well; these discrepancies arose primarily because of the high proportion of "angels" (Yiddish: *Malochim*), that is, people who had left or died but continued to be carried on the camp lists in order to obtain their rations—a ruse that was re-

peated in all refugee centers. It is interesting to note that only 80 percent of the Jews came from Poland, or, in other words, about 28,000 came from Hungary, Rumania and other countries. The figures quoted for the camps were taken from *Der Joint in Daitshland* (YIVO–DPG–163).

20 Susan Pettiss, December 5, 1946 (YIVO–DPG–421).

21 Schwartz, *op. cit.*, pp. 148–156. The Committee applied for recognition as early as March 14, 1946 (YIVO–D–1–24, letter of Treger and Retter to UNRRA).

22 Bernstein report, September 13, 1946 (JDC).

23 *Hayetziah veha'aliyah le'Eretz Yisrael,* no date, probably 1947 (ATH–AB, Germany File).

24 Interview Zev Birger (H) and confirmation by Dov Nishri.

25 Interviews (H) with Birger, Ritter and Even-Dar (ATH), and Notes on Interview with Hy Wachtel (H).

26 See Chapter 8, Note 33.

27 Ben Nathan Report (ATH).

28 This and the following are based on the ATH reports of Ben Nathan and Abba Gefen, and on an interview with Sami Levy (H). Additional material: interview with Joseph J. Silber (H), and A. Gefen's book.

Chapter 10

1 Joseph J. Schwartz in Country Directors Meeting of the JDC, Paris, September 26–27, 1946 (JDC General Files). Malka Shapiro, one of the Palestinian welfare workers in Germany, says, "There was never a concrete answer to the question 'when will we go to Palestine?' " (ATH). The morale was kept up by rather devious methods: "Individuals were transferred to a transit camp where they waited weeks and months until a date was set at which they were moved—to another camp, just to create the illusion of movement." Appeals came from Poland to return there. Thus, the Wroclaw (Breslau) Jewish Community (i.e., the Communist group there) told the people in the camps that clearly they had had "no intentions to emigrate and [they] would not have had to go from one degrading camp to another had [they] not been carried away by the panic which was created by certain reactionary elements in order to make political capital out of [their] sufferings." The authors of the appeal, by contrast, thought of themselves as "proud citizens of

Polish democracy" and called on the camp inmates to rejoin them (Vienna *Juedische Nachrichten,* April 23, 1947).

2 Alexander's report (ATH–AB); Alexander at the Brichah meeting February 28–March 1, 1947 (ATH–AB, Protocols).

3 *Ibid.,* protocol of meeting at Fuschl, May 10, 1947. Interviews: Zuckerman (H), II, p. 25, Alexander (H), III, pp. 2–6.

4 Alexander, *ibid.*

5 The statistics are based on Dekel's figures (ATH–AB).

6 Alexander at Fuschl, May 10, 1947.

7 *Ibid.,* and Alexander (H), III, pp. 21 ff.; also interview with David Schiff (H).

8 Figures for 1948–49 are from JDC, Czech file reports (in 1948, in July 98 crossed to Nachod, 90 in August, 399 in September, 625 in October, 603 in November and 512 in December). See also Zuckerman (H), II, pp. 31 ff.

9 Interviews with Dr. Shimshon Natan and Yehuda Talmi (H); and Yehuda Talmi ("Aryeh") at the Brichah conference at Basel, December 13, 1946 (ATH–AB, Protocols).

10 Interview with Talmi (H), pp. 10–12, and interview with J. J. Schwartz, August 8, 1962 (H), I, p. 21.

11 Interview with Yosef Markus (ATH); Markus, *Hatzalah* (report) Bratislava, February 1948 (ATH); Shlomo Friedman report (ATH–AB); Dekel, *op. cit.,* pp. 94–96.

12 Dr. Moshe Sneh at Brichah Conference, November 1947, Bratislava (ATH–AB, Protocols).

13 M. A. Leavitt, note on interview, 1962 (H).

14 Yizhak Ben Efraim ("Menu") at the Fuschl Conference, May 10, 1947 (ATH–AB, Protocols).

15 *Stars and Stripes,* April 17, 1947.

16 Ben Nathan at Fuschl.

17 *Ibid.*

18 see above, Note 13.

19 Rabel, Report on Austria, April 1947–March 1948 (ATH–AB, Austrian File).

20 General Historical Archive, Jerusalem, KAuV/120 and RA/119 (Vienna).

21 Exchanges of cables in JDC, Austria, 1947.

22 Gefen, *op. cit.,* pp. 171–188. The trading of threats occurred at a meeting between Gefen and Schutz, the U.S. officer in charge of the DP section at a meeting in January.

23 *Ibid.*, pp. 204 ff. Interview with Michael Shur-Ami (H), p. 26.

24 The Gerlos story is based on the following sources: memo by Jean Bernstein to Harold Trobe, May 19, 1947 (YIVO, DPG–170); Gefen, *op. cit.*, pp. 221 ff.; Ben Nathan, Report on Austria (ATH–AB); *ibid.*, Abraham Giora, Report on the Gerlos incident; interviews: Michael Shur-Ami (H), Yakov Shuster (ATH), Ben Nathan (H), I, p. 25, Yisrael Ridelnik (H), II, pp. 24–26, and Sami Levy (H), pp. 16–20.

25 ATH–AB, Italy File.

26 The main source for the Kasern story is a series of three interviews with Dan Laor (H). Supporting material will be found in reports by A. Ben Nathan on Austria (ATH–AB); by Amos Rabel in March 1948 (*ibid.*), and by Isaschar Haimowitz at Fuschl, May 10, 1947 (ATH–AB, Protocols). See also interview with Yisrael Ridelnik (H), II, pp. 20–23; Israel Feinbuch report, Dekel material (ATH–AB); *Daily Telegraph,* October 14, 1947; and the author's investigation on the spot, August 24, 1962, coupled with an interview with the brother of the Prettau hotel-owner. Donna Maria, or Frau Marie, unfortunately refused to be interviewed.

27 Material on the Gnadenwald incident is concentrated in the Innsbruck Murder Case file (ATH–AB and PM), where a number of leaflets are collected. See also testimonies by Sami Levy (H), Yakov Farshtay (H) and Ridelnik (H), II, pp. 27–28.

28 Interview with Haim Yahil (H), VII, pp. 5–6.

29 The Brichah part of the Exodus story will be found in Yahil, *loc. cit.*, interview with Ephraim Frank (H), pp. 30–33, a speech by H. Yahil (ATH), no date (1948?), on the Exodus affair, and a telegram, July 7, 1947, of Mossad (ATH—Mossad material) reporting the successful completion of the refugees' transfer to Marseilles.

30 Abraham S. Hyman to Rabbi Philip S. Bernstein, December 19, 1947 (Herbert Friedman papers).

Afterword

1 The figures are based on a number of sources, the main ones being JDC statistical abstracts; Ilya Dijour's mimeographed article *Jewish Migration in the Post-War World,* put out by the United Hias Service (no date, 1961?); and material in the ATH–AB, mainly figures quoted by Amos Rabel and Ephraim Dekel. Another computation would be to total the known figures of the organized

Brichah movement. According to Teichholz, 122,000 Jews went through Vienna between 1945 and August 1948 (Amos Rabel puts it at 123,000 until October 1947); Stettin counted 42,000, and another 15,000 by the Polish repatriation. An approximate 20,000, at least, went through As. The Brigade in 1945 brought 15,000 from the DP camps to places north of the Italian border, and 12,000 spent the winter of 1945–46 at Graz. The Yugoslavian Brichah reported a total of 4,500 as having passed through that country until the middle of 1947. All this would give us a total of at least 230,000 who came by organized transports. With the addition of those who came by unorganized transports, a figure of at least 250,000 emerges.

2 That is, 300,000 minus the 50,000 who were there in August 1945.

3 JDC, Saly Mayer Archive, Files 16 and 58.

Oral Documentation

The history of an underground organization presents special difficulties. Much of the factual material was never committed to paper, and some of the written documentation was created to mislead the reader. It was therefore both necessary and very useful to supplement the written record with a large number of oral interviews. This in itself is a difficult and treacherous path for a historian to take, because the memory of the interviewee may be faulty or there may even be intent to mislead or to glorify one's own actions. It was therefore necessary to check and countercheck these personal memoirs by comparing them with other interviews. The writer was fortunate in having at his disposal the facilities of the Oral History Division of the Institute of Contemporary Jewry, of which he is the Scientific Director, and the whole-hearted cooperation of Dr. Geoffrey Wigoder, the Administrative Director of the Division, and of Mr. Aharon Kedar, Secretary. A total of 114 persons (listed below) were interviewed by the author or under his supervision; most of the interviews were tape-recorded. In addition, three more interviews were recorded by the author for Moreshet Archives. When not marked otherwise, the interviews are kept at the Oral History Division. (See p. 326 for key to abbreviations of other sources.)

"Alexander" (pseud.)
Aryeh Abramovsky
Moshe Agami
Ruth Aliav (Kluger)
Yehuda Alkalay
Shmuel Amarant
Aharon Assa
Leah Assa
Yitzhar Avidov
Ehud Avriel
Zvi Azaryah
Moshe Ben David
Asher (Arthur) Ben Nathan
Sarah Benyamini
Yakov Ben Yehuda
Philip S. Bernstein
Zev Birger
Eli A. Bohnen
Ann Borden (Liepah)
Max Braude
Tuvia Cohen
Ilya Dijour (PM)
Yehiel Duvdevani
Yakov Erner
Yisrael Eichenwald
Fishel Farber
Rivka Farber
Yakov Fershtay
Ted Feder
Ephraim Frank
Naphtali Friedman
Herbert Friedman
Miriam Fuchs
Yisrael Gal
Michael Gelber
Luba Geller
Zev Geller
Shania Gringross
Meir Gordon
Zev Hadari
Mordechai Hadash
Jacques van Harten
Lady Henriques
Aharon Hoter-Yishai
Gaynor I. Jacobson
David Kahane
Leibl Kariski (M)
Herbert Katzki (PM)
Vitka Kempner
Abraham J. Klausner
Shlomo Kless
Pinhas Koppelberg
Abba Kovner
Ruzhka Korczak
Moshe Kravchik
Max Krochmal
Zev Landa (Landau)
Daniel Laor
Moses A. Leavitt (PM)
Yosef Lavi
Sami Levy
Jehuda Levy
Dov Levin
Louis E. Levinthal
Aryeh Lichtig
Eliezer Lidovsky
Eugene J. Lipman
Shlomo Mann
Moshe Meiri (M)
Evelyn Mitzman (PM)
Mordechai Mittelman
Mordechai Munkacz
Robert Murphy (PM)
Judah Nadich
Shimshon Nathan
Stanley K. Novinsky
Aharon Ofri
Nesia Orlowicz-Resnik
Charles Passman

Shmuel Potek
Yitzhak Ram
Simon H. Rifkind
James P. Rice
Yisrael Ridelnik
Zev Ritter
Mordechai Rosman
Avigdor Rubinstein
Joseph Rosensaft
Yitzhak Sela
Yosef Schechter
Zvi Shiloah
Yakov Shmetterer
Joseph J. Schwartz
Leo W. Schwarz
Uri Schweitzer
Bronislaw Teichholz
Yehuda Talmi
Jacob Trobe
Tel-Amal Symposium—with five participants
Hy Wachtel
Yeshayahu Weinberg
Yeshayahu Weiner (M)
David Winshelbaum
Haim Yahil
Avraham Yashpan
Zvi Yehieli
Eliahu Yonas
David Zimand
Yitzhak Zuckerman

Selected Bibliography

Anglo-American Committee of Inquiry on Palestine. Report, April 20, 1946.

Attlee, Clement. *As It Happened*. London, 1954.

Bach, Julian. *America's Germany: An Account of the Occupation*. New York, 1946.

Begin, Menachem. *The Revolt*. London, 1951.

Crum, Bartley C. *Behind the Silken Curtain*. New York, 1947.

Crossman, Richard. *Palestine Mission*. New York, 1947.

Dekel, Ephraim. *Bin'tiv Habrichah*. Tel Aviv, 1958.

———. *Sridei Herev*. Tel Aviv, 1963.

Dijour, Ilya. *Jewish Migration in the Post-War World*. New York: United HIAS, no date. Mimeographed.

Frank, Gerold. *The Deed*. New York, 1963.

Gefen, Abba. *Porzei Hamachsomim*. Tel Aviv, 1961.

Dalton, Hugh. *High Tide and After*. London, 1962.

Hilberg, Raoul. *The Destruction of European Jewry*. Chicago, 1961.

Hirschmann, Ira A. *The Embers Still Burn*. New York, 1949.

The Jewish Case Before the Anglo-American Committee of Inquiry. Jerusalem, Jewish Agency, 1947.

Horowitz, David. *State in the Making*. New York, 1953.

The Importance of the Middle East. RIIA (Chatham House), 1945.

Interests of the Commonwealth in the Middle East. RIIA (Chatham House), 1945.
Karlebach, Azriel. *Duah Va'adat Ha'hakirah.* Tel Aviv, 1946.
Katz, Shmuel. *Yom Ha'esh.* Israel, 1966.
Korczak, Ruzhka. *Lehavot Ba'efer.* Merhavia, 1965.
Kimche, Jon and David. *Both Sides of the Hill.* London, 1960.
Lagus, Karel and Polak, Josef. *Mesto Za Mrizemi.* Prague, 1964.
Mahanot Ha'akurim Be'Germania, 1945–1948. Jerusalem, Institute of Contemporary Jewry, Hebrew University, 1962. Mimeographed.
Mardor, Meir. *Shlihut Alumah.* Tel Aviv, 1957.
Nadich, Judah. *Eisenhower and the Jews.* New York, 1953.
Orlowicz-Resnik, Nesia. *Ima, Hamutar Kvar Livkot?* Israel, no date (1965?).
Pinson, Koppel S. "Jewish Life in Liberated Germany," *Jewish Social Studies,* Vol. IX, No. 2, 1947.
Potter, Harold E. *Displaced Persons.* Occupation Forces in Europe, Series 1945/6.
Proskauer, Joseph. *A Segment of My Times.* New York, 1950.
Proudfoot, Malcolm J. *European Refugees.* New York, 1957.
Rees, Elfan. *Abusing the Jews: A Plea for Refugees.* London, 1946. Mimeographed.
Schechtman, Joseph B. *The U.S. and the Jewish State Movement.* New York, 1966.
Schwarz, Leo W. *The Redeemers.* New York, 1953.
———. *The Root and the Bough.* New York, 1949.
Sefer Hahitnadvut. Jerusalem, 1949. Shefer and Lamdan.
Sefer Hapartizanim. Israel, 1962.
Sefer Hashomer Hatzair. Merhavia, 1961.
Shragai, S. Zalman. *Massa Hahatzalah.* Jerusalem. 1947.
Sington, Derrick. *Belsen Uncovered.* London, 1946.
Stone, I. F. *Underground to Palestine.* New York, 1947.
Suhl, Yuri. *They Fought Back.* New York, 1967.
Truman, Harry S. *Memoirs.* London, 1956.
Vernant, Jacques. *The Refugee in the Post-War World.* London, 1953.
Warren, Helen. *The Buried Are Screaming.* New York, 1948.
Williams, Francis. *A Prime Minister Remembers.* London, 1961.
———. *Ernest Bevin, Portrait of a Great Englishman.* London, 1952.

Wischnitzer, Mark. *To Dwell in Safety*. New York, 1948.
———. *Visas to Freedom*. New York, 1956.
Yalkut Moreshet, I–VI (published in Israel, 1963–1967).
Zaar, Isaac. *Rescue and Liberation; America's Part in the Birth of Israel*. New York, 1954.
Zemar (Harari). *Israel, 1953*. Memorial brochure.

Index

About the Author

YEHUDA BAUER was born in 1926 in Prague, Czechoslovakia. He went to Palestine in 1939, studied at Hugim Secondary School in Haifa, served in Palmach (Haganah forces), and in 1945 entered Hebrew University, where he studied history, philosophy and English. He continued his studies (1946–1968) at the University of Wales at Cardiff. He returned to fight in the Israeli war of independence (1948–1949) and then went back to Cardiff to take an M.A. in 1950. Dr. Bauer remained in England until the end of 1951 in connection with Zionist Youth work. In 1952, he joined Kibbutz Shoval in Negev, and in 1955–1960 he wrote his doctoral thesis, *The Palmach Against the Background of Zionist Policies, 1939–45.* He received his doctorate in 1961. He taught various kibbutz seminars from 1954 to 1964. He joined the Institute of Contemporary Jewry at the Hebrew University in 1962. He is presently lecturer, research fellow and co-director of the Oral Documentation Department, Research Department of the History of Zionism and the Yishuv.

PREFACE

This little work aims to combine the instructive features of a book of travels with the interest of a domestic tale. Throughout its pages the descriptions of Dutch localities, customs, and general characteristics have been given with scrupulous care. Many of its incidents are drawn from life, and the story of Raff Brinker is founded strictly upon fact.

While acknowledging my obligations to many well-known writers on Dutch history, literature, and art, I turn with especial gratitude to those kind Holland friends, who, with generous zeal, have taken many a backward glance at their country for my sake, seeing it as it looked twenty years ago, when the Brinker home stood unnoticed in sunlight and shadow.

Should this simple narrative serve to give my young readers a just idea of Holland and its resources, or present true pictures of its inhabitants and their everyday life, or free them from certain current prejudices concerning that noble and enterprising people, the leading desire in writing it will have been satisfied.

Should it cause even one heart to feel a deeper trust in God's goodness and love, or aid any in weaving a life, wherein, through knots and entanglements, the golden thread shall never be tarnished or broken, the prayer with which it was begun and ended will have been answered.

M. M. D.

A LETTER FROM HOLLAND

AMSTERDAM, July 30, 1873

Dear Boys and Girls at Home:

If you all could be here with me today, what fine times we might have walking through this beautiful Dutch city! How we should stare at the crooked houses, standing with their gable ends to the street; at the little slanting mirrors fastened outside of the windows; at the wooden shoes and dogcarts near by; the windmills in the distance; at the great warehouses; at the canals, doing the double duty of streets and rivers, and at the singular mingling of trees and masts to be seen in every direction. Ah, it would be pleasant, indeed! But here I sit in a great hotel looking out upon all these things, knowing quite well that not even the spirit of the Dutch, which seems able to accomplish anything, can bring you at this moment across the ocean. There is one comfort, however, in going through these wonderful Holland towns without you—it would be dreadful to have any of the party tumble into the canals; and then these lumbering Dutch wagons, with their heavy wheels, so very far apart: what should I do if a few dozen of you were to fall under *them?* and, perhaps, one of the wildest of my boys might harm a stork, and then all Holland would be against us! No. It is better as it is. You will be coming, one by one, as the years go on, to see the whole thing for yourselves.

Holland is as wonderful today as it was when, more than twenty years ago, Hans and Gretel skated on the frozen Y. In fact, more wonderful, for every day increases the marvel of its not being washed away by the sea. Its cities have grown, and some of its peculiarities have been brushed away by contact with other nations; but it is Holland still, and always will be—full of oddity, courage and industry—the pluckiest little country on earth. I shall not tell you in this letter of its customs, its cities, its palaces, churches, picture galleries, and museums—for these are described in the story—except to say that they are here still, just the same, in this good year 1873, for I have seen them nearly all within a week.

Today an American boy and I seeing some children enter an old house in the business part of Amsterdam, followed them in—and what do you think we found? An old woman, here in the middle of summer, selling hot water and fire! She makes her living by it. All day long she sits tending her great fires of peat and keeping the shining copper tanks above them filled with water. The children who come and go, carry away in a curious stone pail their kettle of boiling water and their blocks of burning peat. For these they give her a Dutch cent, which is worth less than half of one of ours. In this way persons who cannot afford to keep a fire burning in hot weather may yet have their cup of tea or coffee and their bit of boiled fish and potato.

After leaving the old fire-woman, who nodded a pleasant good-bye to us, and willingly put our stivers in her great outside pocket, we drove through the streets enjoying the singular sights of a public washing day. Yes, in certain quarters of the city, away from the canals, the streets were lively with washerwomen hard at work. Hundreds of them in clumsy wooden shoes, with their tucked-up skirts, bare arms and close-fitting caps, were bending over tall wooden tubs that reached as high as their waists —gossiping and rubbing, rubbing and gossiping—with perfect unconcern, in the public thoroughfare, and all washing with cold water instead of using hot, as we do. What a grand thing it would be for our old fire-woman if boiling water were suddenly to become the fashion on these public washing days!

And now good-bye. Oh! I must tell you one more thing. We found today in an Amsterdam bookstore this story of Hans Brinker told in Dutch. It is a queer-looking volume, beautifully printed, and with colored pictures, but filled with such astonishing words that it really made me feel sorry for the little Hollanders who are to read them.

Good-bye, again, in the touching words of our Dutch translator with whom I'm sure you'll heartily agree: *Toch ben ik er mijn landgenooten dank baar voor, die mijn arbeid steeds zoo welwillend outvangen en wier genegenheid ik voortdurend hoop te verdienen.*

Yours affectionately,

THE AUTHOR.

CONTENTS

HANS BRINKER

OR

The Silver Skates

I
HANS AND GRETEL

On a bright December morning long ago, two thinly clad children were kneeling upon the bank of a frozen canal in Holland.

The sun had not yet appeared, but the gray sky was parted near the horizon, and its edges shone crimson with the coming day. Most of the good Hollanders were enjoying a placid morning nap; even Mynheer van Stoppelnoze, that worthy old Dutchman, was still slumbering "in beautiful repose."

Now and then some peasant woman, poising a well-filled basket upon her head, came skimming over the glassy surface of the canal; or a lusty boy, skating to his day's work in the town, cast a good-natured grimace toward the shivering pair as he flew along.

Meanwhile, with many a vigorous puff and pull, the

brother and sister, for such they were, seemed to be fastening something upon their feet—not skates, certainly, but clumsy pieces of wood narrowed and smoothed at their lower edge, and pierced with holes, through which were threaded strings of rawhide.

These queer-looking affairs had been made by the boy Hans. His mother was a poor peasant woman, too poor even to think of such a thing as buying skates for her little ones. Rough as these were, they had afforded the children many a happy hour upon the ice; and now as with cold, red fingers our young Hollanders tugged at the strings—their solemn faces bending closely over their knees—no vision of impossible iron runners came to dull the satisfaction glowing within.

In a moment the boy arose, and with a pompous swing of the arms, and a careless "Come on, Gretel," glided easily across the canal.

"Ah, Hans," called his sister plaintively, "this foot is not well yet. The strings hurt me on last market day; and now I cannot bear them tied in the same place."

"Tie them higher up, then," answered Hans, as without looking at her he performed a wonderful cat's-cradle step on the ice.

"How can I? The string is too short."

Giving vent to a good-natured Dutch whistle, the English of which was that girls were troublesome creatures, he steered toward her.

"You are foolish to wear such shoes, Gretel, when you have a stout leather pair. Your klompen [1] would be better than these."

"Why, Hans! Do you forget? The father threw my beautiful new shoes in the fire. Before I knew what he had done they were all curled up in the midst of the burning peat. I can skate with these, but not with my wooden ones. Be careful now——"

Hans had taken a string from his pocket. Humming a

[1] Wooden shoes.

tune as he knelt beside her, he proceeded to fasten Gretel's skate with all the force of his strong young arm.

"Oh! oh!" she cried, in real pain.

With an impatient jerk Hans unwound the string. He would have cast it upon the ground in true big-brother style had he not just then spied a tear trickling down his sister's cheek.

"I'll fix it—never fear," he said, with sudden tenderness, "but we must be quick; the mother will need us soon."

Then he glanced inquiringly about him, first at the ground, next at some bare willow branches above his head, and finally at the sky now gorgeous with streaks of blue, crimson and gold.

Finding nothing in any of these localities to meet his need, his eye suddenly brightened as, with the air of a fellow who knew what he was about, he took off his cap and removing the tattered lining, adjusted it in a smooth pad over the top of Gretel's worn-out shoe.

"Now," he cried triumphantly, at the same time arranging the strings as briskly as his benumbed fingers would allow, "can you bear some pulling?"

Gretel drew up her lips as if to say "Hurt away," but made no further response.

In another moment they were laughing together, as hand in hand they flew along the canal, never thinking whether the ice would bear or not, for in Holland, ice is generally an all-winter affair. It settles itself upon the water in a determined kind of way, and so far from growing thin and uncertain every time the sun is a little severe upon it, it gathers its forces day by day and flashes defiance to every beam.

Presently, squeak! squeak! sounded something beneath Hans' feet. Next his strokes grew shorter, ending ofttimes with a jerk, and finally, he lay sprawling upon the ice, kicking against the air with many a fantastic flourish.

"Ha! ha!" laughed Gretel, "that was a fine tumble!" But a tender heart was beating under her coarse blue jacket and, even as she laughed, she came, with a graceful sweep, close to her prostrate brother.

"Are you hurt, Hans? Oh, you are laughing! Catch me now"—and she darted away shivering no longer, but with cheeks all aglow and eyes sparkling with fun.

Hans sprang to his feet and started in brisk pursuit, but it was no easy thing to catch Gretel. Before she had traveled very far, her skates, too, began to squeak.

Believing that discretion was the better part of valor, she turned suddenly and skated into her pursuer's arms.

"Ha! ha! I've caught you!" cried Hans.

"Ha! ha! I caught *you,"* she retorted, struggling to free herself.

Just then a clear, quick voice was heard calling "Hans! Gretel!"

"It's the mother," said Hans, looking solemn in an instant.

By this time the canal was gilded with sunlight. The pure morning air was very delightful, and skaters were gradually increasing in numbers. It was hard to obey the summons. But Gretel and Hans were good children; without a thought of yielding to the temptation to linger, they pulled off their skates, leaving half the knots still tied. Hans, with his great square shoulders, and bushy yellow hair, towered high above his blue-eyed little sister as they trudged homeward. He was fifteen years old and Gretel was only twelve. He was a solid, hearty-looking boy, with honest eyes and a brow that seemed to bear a sign "goodness within" just as the little Dutch zomerhuis [1] wears a motto over its portal. Gretel was lithe and quick; her eyes had a dancing light in them, and while you looked at her cheek the color paled and deepened just as it does upon a bed of pink and white blossoms when the wind is blowing.

As soon as the children turned from the canal they could see their parents' cottage. Their mother's tall form, ar-

[1] Summerhouse.

rayed in jacket and petticoat and close-fitting cap, stood, like a picture, in the crooked frame of the doorway. Had the cottage been a mile away, it would still have seemed near. In that flat country every object stands out plainly in the distance; the chickens show as distinctly as the windmills. Indeed, were it not for the dykes and the high banks of the canals, one could stand almost anywhere in middle Holland without seeing a mound or a ridge between the eye and the "jumping-off place."

None had better cause to know the nature of these same dykes than Dame Brinker and the panting youngsters now running at her call. But before stating *why*, let me ask you to take a rocking-chair trip with me to that far country where you may see, perhaps for the first time, some curious things that Hans and Gretel saw every day.

II
HOLLAND

HOLLAND is one of the queerest countries under the sun. It should be called Odd-land or Contrary-land, for in nearly everything it is different from other parts of the world. In the first place, a large portion of the country is lower than the level of the sea. Great dykes or bulwarks have been erected, at a heavy cost of money and labor, to keep the ocean where it belongs. On certain parts of the coast it sometimes leans with all its weight against the land, and it is as much as the poor country can do to stand the pressure. Sometimes the dykes give way, or spring a leak, and the most disastrous results ensue. They are high and wide, and the tops of some of them are covered with buildings and trees. They have even fine public roads upon them, from which horses may look down upon wayside cottages. Often the keels of floating ships are higher than the roofs of the dwellings. The stork clattering to her young on the house peak may feel that her nest is lifted far out of danger, but the croaking frog in neighboring bulrushes is nearer the stars than she. Water bugs dart backward and forward above the heads of the chimney swallows; and willow trees seem drooping with shame, because they cannot reach as high as the reeds near by.

Ditches, canals, ponds, rivers and lakes are everywhere to be seen. High, but not dry, they shine in the sunlight, catching nearly all the bustle and the business, quite scorning the tame fields stretching damply beside them. One is tempted to ask, "Which is Holland—the shores or the water?" The very verdure that should be confined to the land has made a mistake and settled upon the fishponds. In fact the entire country is a kind of saturated sponge or, as the English poet, Butler, called it——

> "A land that rides at anchor, and is moor'd,
> In which they do not live, but go aboard."

Persons are born, live and die, and even have their gardens on canalboats. Farmhouses, with roofs like great slouched hats pulled over their eyes, stand on wooden legs with a tucked-up sort of air, as if to say "We intend to keep dry if we can." Even the horses wear a wide stool on each hoof to lift them out of the mire. In short, the landscape everywhere suggests a paradise for ducks. It is a glorious country in summer for barefooted girls and boys. Such wading! Such mimic ship sailing! Such rowing, fishing and swimming! Only think of a chain of puddles where one can launch chip boats all day long, and never make a return trip! But enough. A full recital would set all young America rushing in a body toward the Zuider Zee.

Dutch cities seem at first sight to be a bewildering jungle of houses, bridges, churches and ships, sprouting into masts, steeples and trees. In some cities vessels are hitched like horses to their owners' doorposts and receive their freight from the upper windows. Mothers scream to

Lodewyk and Kassy not to swing on the garden gate for fear they may be drowned! Water roads are more frequent there than common roads and railways; water fences in the form of lazy green ditches enclose pleasure ground, polder and garden.

Sometimes fine green hedges are seen; but wooden fences such as we have in America are rarely met with in Holland. As for stone fences, a Dutchman would lift his hands with astonishment at the very idea. There is no stone there, excepting those great masses of rock that have been brought from other lands to strengthen and protect the coast. All the small stones or pebbles, if there ever were any, seem to be imprisoned in pavements or quite melted away. Boys with strong, quick arms may grow from pinafores to full beards without ever finding one to start the water rings or set the rabbits flying. The water roads are nothing less than canals intersecting the country in every direction. These are of all sizes, from the great North Holland Ship Canal, which is the wonder of the world, to those which a boy can leap. Water omnibuses, called *trekschuiten,*[1] constantly ply up and down these roads for the conveyance of passengers; and water drays, called *pakschuyten,*[1] are used for carrying fuel and merchandise. Instead of green country lanes, green canals stretch from field to barn and from barn to garden; and the farms or *polders,* as they are termed, are merely great lakes pumped dry. Some of the busiest streets are water, while many of the country roads are paved with brick. The city boats with their rounded sterns, gilded prows and gaily painted sides are unlike any others under the sun;

[1] Canalboats. Some of the first named are over thirty feet long. They look like green houses lodged on barges, and are drawn by horses walking along the bank of the canal. The trekschuiten are divided into two compartments, first and second class, and when not too crowded the passengers make themselves quite at home in them; the men smoke, the women knit or sew, while children play upon the small outer deck. Many of the canalboats have white, yellow, or chocolate-colored sails. This last color is caused by a preparation of tan which is put on to preserve them.

and a Dutch wagon with its funny little crooked pole is a perfect mystery of mysteries.

"One thing is clear," cries Master Brightside, "the inhabitants need never be thirsty." But no, Odd-land is true to itself still. Notwithstanding the sea pushing to get in, and the lakes struggling to get out, and the overflowing canals, rivers and ditches, in many districts there is no water fit to swallow; our poor Hollanders must go dry, or drink wine and beer, or send far into the inland to Utrecht, and other favored localities, for that precious fluid older than Adam yet young as the morning dew. Sometimes, indeed, the inhabitants can swallow a shower when they are provided with any means of catching it; but generally they are like the albatross-haunted sailors in Coleridge's famous poem of "The Ancient Mariner"—they see

"Water, water, everywhere,
Nor any drop to drink!"

Great flapping windmills all over the country make it look as if flocks of huge sea birds were just settling upon it. Everywhere one sees the funniest trees, bobbed into fantastical shapes, with their trunks painted a dazzling white, yellow or red. Horses are often yoked three abreast. Men, women and children go clattering about in wooden shoes with loose heels; peasant girls who cannot get beaux for love, hire them for money to escort them to the Kermis; [1] and husbands and wives lovingly harness themselves side by side on the bank of the canal and drag their pakschuyts to market.

Another peculiar feature of Holland is the dune or sand hill. These are numerous along certain portions of the coast. Before they were sown with coarse reed grass and other plants, to hold them down, they used to send great storms of sand over the inland. So, to add to the oddities, farmers sometimes dig down under the surface to

[1] Fair.

find their soil, and on windy days *dry* showers (of sand) often fall upon fields that have grown wet under a week of sunshine.

In short, almost the only familiar thing we Yankees can meet with in Holland is a harvest song which is quite popular there, though no linguist could translate it. Even then we must shut our eyes and listen only to the tune which I leave you to guess.

"Yanker didee dudel down
Didee dudel lawnter;
Yankee viver, voover, vown,
Botermelk und Tawnter!"

On the other hand, many of the oddities of Holland serve only to prove the thrift and perseverance of the people. There is not a richer or more carefully tilled garden spot in the whole world than this leaky, springy little country. There is not a braver, more heroic race than its quiet, passive-looking inhabitants. Few nations have equaled it in important discoveries and inventions; none has excelled it in commerce, navigation, learning and science—or set as noble examples in the promotion of education and public charities; and none in proportion to its extent has expended more money and labor upon public works.

Holland has its shining annals of noble and illustrious men and women; its grand, historic records of patience, resistance and victory; its religious freedom, its enlightened enterprise, its art, its music and its literature. It has truly been called "the battlefield of Europe"; as truly may we consider it the asylum of the world, for the oppressed of every nation have there found shelter and encouragement. If we Americans, who after all are homeopathic preparations of Holland stock, can laugh at the Dutch, and call them human beavers, and hint that their country may float off any day at high tide, we can also feel proud, and say they have proved themselves heroes, and that their country will *not* float off while there is a Dutchman left to grapple it.

There are said to be at least ninety-nine hundred large windmills in Holland, with sails ranging from eighty to one hundred and twenty feet long. They are employed in sawing timber, beating hemp, grinding, and many other kinds of work; but their principal use is for pumping water from the lowlands into the canals, and for guarding against the inland freshets that so often deluge the country. Their yearly cost is said to be nearly ten millions of dollars. The large ones are of great power. The huge, circular tower, rising sometimes from the midst of factory buildings, is surmounted with a smaller one tapering into a caplike roof. This upper tower is encircled at its base with a balcony, high above which juts the axis turned by its four prodigious, ladder-backed sails.

Many of the windmills are primitive affairs, seeming sadly in need of Yankee "improvements"; but some of the new ones are admirable. They are so constructed that, by some ingenious contrivance, they present their fans, or wings, to the wind in precisely the right direction to work with the requisite power. In other words, the miller may take a nap and feel quite sure that his mill will study the wind, and make the most of it, until he wakens. Should there be but a slight current of air, every sail will spread itself to catch the faintest breath; but if a heavy "blow" should come, they will shrink at its touch, like great mimosa leaves, and only give it half a chance to move them.

One of the old prisons of Amsterdam, called the Rasphouse, because the thieves and vagrants who were confined there were employed in rasping logwood, had a cell for the punishment of lazy prisoners. In one corner of this cell was a pump and, in another, an opening through which a steady stream of water was admitted. The prisoner could take his choice, either to stand still and be drowned, or to work for dear life at the pump and keep the flood down until his jailer chose to relieve him. Now it seems to me that, throughout Holland, Nature has introduced this little diversion on a grand scale. The Dutch have always been forced to pump for their very existence and probably must continue to do so to the end of time.

Every year millions of dollars are spent in repairing dykes and regulating water levels. If these important duties were neglected the country would be uninhabitable. Already dreadful consequences, as I have said, have followed the bursting of these dykes. Hundreds of villages and towns have from time to time been buried beneath the rush of waters, and nearly a million persons have been destroyed. One of the most fearful inundations ever known occurred in the autumn of the year 1570. Twenty-eight terrible floods had before that time overwhelmed portions of Holland, but this was the most terrible of all. The unhappy country had long been suffering under Spanish tyranny; now, it seemed, the crowning point was given to its troubles. When we read Motley's history of the Rise of the Dutch Republic we learn to revere the brave people who have endured, suffered and dared so much.

Mr. Motley in his thrilling account of the great inundation tells us how a long-continued and violent gale had been sweeping the Atlantic waters into the North Sea, piling them against the coasts of the Dutch provinces; how the dykes, tasked beyond their strength, burst in all directions; how even the Hand-bos, a bulwark formed of oaken piles, braced with iron, moored with heavy anchors and secured by gravel and granite, was snapped to pieces like packthread; how fishing boats and bulky vessels floating up into the country became entangled among the trees, or beat in the roofs and walls of dwellings, and how at last all Friesland was converted into an angry sea. "Multitudes of men, women, children, of horses, oxen, sheep, and every domestic animal, were struggling in the waves in every direction. Every boat and every article which could serve as a boat was eagerly seized upon. Every house was inundated, even the graveyards gave up their dead. The

Hans rode the towing—horses on the canals

living infant in his cradle, and the long-buried corpse in his coffin, floated side by side. The ancient flood seemed about to be renewed. Everywhere, upon the tops of trees, upon the steeples of churches, human beings were clustered, praying to God for mercy, and to their fellowmen for assistance. As the storm at last was subsiding, boats began to ply in every direction, saving those who were struggling in the water, picking fugitives from roofs and

treetops, and collecting the bodies of those already drowned." No less than one hundred thousand human beings had perished in a few hours. Thousands upon thousands of dumb creatures lay dead upon the waters; and the damage done to property of every description was beyond calculation.

Robles, the Spanish Governor, was foremost in noble efforts to save life and lessen the horrors of the catastrophe. He had formerly been hated by the Dutch because of his Spanish or Portuguese blood, but by his goodness and activity in their hour of disaster, he won all hearts to gratitude. He soon introduced an improved method of constructing the dykes, and passed a law that they should in future be kept up by the owners of the soil. There were fewer heavy floods from this time, though within less than three hundred years six fearful inundations swept over the land.

In the spring there is always great danger of inland freshets, especially in times of thaw, because the rivers, choked with blocks of ice, overflow before they can discharge their rapidly rising waters into the ocean. Added to this the sea chafing and pressing against the dykes, it is no wonder that Holland is often in a state of alarm. The greatest care is taken to prevent accidents. Engineers and workmen are stationed all along in threatened places and a close watch is kept up night and day. When a general signal of danger is given, the inhabitants all rush to the rescue, eager to combine against their common foe. As, everywhere else, straw is supposed to be of all things the most helpless in the water, of course in Holland it must be rendered the mainstay against a rushing tide. Huge straw mats are pressed against the embankments, fortified with clay and heavy stone, and once adjusted, the ocean dashes against them in vain.

Raff Brinker, the father of Gretel and Hans, had for years been employed upon the dykes. It was at the time of a threatened inundation, when in the midst of a terrible storm, in darkness and sleet, the men were laboring at a weak spot near the Veermyk sluice, that he fell from the scaffolding, and was taken home insensible. From that hour he never worked again; though he lived on, mind and memory were gone.

Gretel could not remember him otherwise than as the strange, silent man, whose eyes followed her vacantly whichever way she turned; but Hans had recollections of a hearty, cheerful-voiced father who was never tired of bearing him upon his shoulder, and whose careless song still seemed echoing near when he lay awake at night and listened.

III
THE SILVER SKATES

DAME BRINKER earned a scanty support for her family by raising vegetables, spinning and knitting. Once she had worked on board the barges plying up and down the canal, and had occasionally been harnessed with other women to the towing rope of a pakschuyt plying between Broek and Amsterdam. But when Hans had grown strong and large, he had insisted upon doing all such drudgery in her place. Besides, her husband had become so very helpless of late that he required her constant care. Although not having as much intelligence as a little child, he was yet strong of arm and very hearty, and Dame Brinker had sometimes great trouble in controlling him.

"Ah! children, he was so good and steady," she would say, "and as wise as a lawyer. Even the burgomaster would stop to ask him a question, and now alack! he don't know his wife and little ones. You remember the father, Hans, when he was himself—a great brave man—don't you?"

"Yes, indeed, mother, he knew everything, and could

do anything under the sun—and how he would sing! Why, you used to laugh and say it was enough to set the windmills dancing."

"So I did. Bless me! how the boy remembers! Gretel, child, take that knitting needle from your father, quick; he'll get it in his eyes maybe; and put the shoe on him. His poor feet are like ice half the time, but I can't keep 'em covered, all I can do——" and then half wailing, half humming, Dame Brinker would sit down, and fill the low cottage with the whir of her spinning wheel.

Nearly all the outdoor work, as well as the household labor, was performed by Hans and Gretel. At certain seasons of the year the children went out day after day to gather peat, which they would stow away in square, brick-like pieces, for fuel. At other times, when homework permitted, Hans rode the towing-horses on the canals, earning a few stivers[1] a day; and Gretel tended geese for the neighboring farmers.

Hans was clever at carving in wood, and both he and Gretel were good gardeners. Gretel could sing and sew and run on great, high, homemade stilts better than any girl for miles around. She could learn a ballad in five minutes, and find, in its season, any weed or flower you could name; but she dreaded books, and often the very sight of the figuring-board in the old schoolhouse would set her eyes swimming. Hans, on the contrary, was slow and steady. The harder the task, whether in study or daily labor, the better he liked it. Boys who sneered at him out of school, on account of his patched clothes and scant leather breeches, were forced to yield him the post of honor in nearly every class. It was not long before he was the only youngster in the school who had not stood at least *once* in the corner of horrors, where hung a dreaded whip, and over it this motto:

"Leer, leer! jou luigaart, of dit endje touw zal je leeren!"[2]

[1] A stiver is worth about two cents of our money.

[2] Learn! learn! you idler, or this rope's end shall teach you.

It was only in winter that Gretel and Hans could be spared to attend school; and for the past month they had been kept at home because their mother needed their services. Raff Brinker required constant attention, and there was black bread to be made, and the house to be kept clean, and stockings and other things to be knitted and sold in the market place.

While they were busily assisting their mother on this cold December morning, a merry troop of girls and boys came skimming down the canal. There were fine skaters among them, and as the bright medley of costumes flitted by, it looked from a distance as though the ice had suddenly thawed, and some gay tulip bed were floating along on the current.

There was the rich burgomaster's daughter Hilda van Gleck, with her costly furs and loose-fitting velvet sack; and, near by, a pretty peasant girl, Annie Bouman, jauntily attired in a coarse scarlet jacket and a blue skirt just short enough to display the gray homespun hose to advantage. Then there was the proud Rychie Korbes, whose father, Mynheer van Korbes, was one of the leading men of Amsterdam; and, flocking closely around her, Carl Schummel, Peter and Ludwig [1] van Holp, Jacob Poot, and a very small boy rejoicing in the tremendous name of Voostenwalbert Schimmelpenninck. There were nearly twenty other boys and girls in the party, and one and all seemed full of excitement and frolic.

Up and down the canal, within the space of a half mile they skated, exerting their racing powers to the utmost. Often the swiftest among them was seen to dodge from under the very nose of some pompous lawgiver or doctor, who with folded arms was skating leisurely toward the town; or a chain of girls would suddenly break at the approach of a fat old burgomaster who, with gold-headed cane poised in air, was puffing his way to Amsterdam. Equipped in skates wonderful to behold, with their su-

[1] Ludwig, Gretel, and Carl were named after German friends. The Dutch form would be Lodewyk, Grietje, and Karel.

perb strappings, and dazzling runners curving over the instep and topped with gilt balls, he would open his fat eyes a little if one of the maidens chanced to drop him a curtsy, but would not dare to bow in return for fear of losing his balance.

Not only pleasure seekers and stately men of note were upon the canal. There were workpeople, with weary eyes, hastening to their shops and factories; market women with loads upon their heads; peddlers bending with their packs; bargemen with shaggy hair and bleared faces, jostling roughly on their way; kind-eyed clergymen speeding perhaps to the bedsides of the dying; and, after a while, groups of children, with satchels slung over their shoulders, whizzing past, toward the distant school. One and all wore skates excepting, indeed, a muffled-up farmer whose queer cart bumped along on the margin of the canal.

Before long our merry boys and girls were almost lost in the confusion of bright colors, the ceaseless motion, and the gleaming of skates flashing back the sunlight. We might have known no more of them had not the whole party suddenly come to a standstill and, grouping themselves out of the way of the passers-by, all talked at once to a pretty little maiden, whom they had drawn from the tide of people flowing toward the town.

"Oh, Katrinka!" they cried, in a breath, "have you heard of it? The race—we want you to join!"

"What race?" asked Katrinka, laughing. "Don't all talk at once, please, I can't understand."

Everyone panted and looked at Rychie Korbes, who was their acknowledged spokeswoman.

"Why," said Rychie, "we are to have a grand skating match on the twentieth, on Mevrouw[1] van Gleck's birthday. It's all Hilda's work. They are going to give a splendid prize to the best skater."

"Yes," chimed in half a dozen voices, "a beautiful pair of silver skates—perfectly magnificent—with such hand-

[1] Mrs. or Madame (pronounced Meffrow).

some black straps and shining silver bells and buckles!"

"*Who* said they had bells?" put in the small voice of the boy with the big name.

"*I* say so, Master Voost," replied Rychie.

"So they have"—"No, I'm sure they haven't"—"*Oh,* how can you say so?"—"It's an arrow"—"And Mynheer van Korbes told *my* mother they had bells"—came from sundry of the excited group; but Mynheer Voostenwalbert Schimmelpenninck essayed to settle the matter with a decisive—

"Well, you don't any of you know a single thing about it; they haven't a sign of a bell on them, they——"

"Oh! oh!" and the chorus of conflicting opinion broke forth again.

"The girls' pair are to have bells," interposed Hilda quietly, "but there is to be another pair for the boys with an arrow engraved upon the sides."

"*There!* I told you so!" cried nearly all the youngsters in a breath.

Katrinka looked at them with bewildered eyes.

"Who is to try?" she asked.

"All of us," answered Rychie. "It will be such fun! And you must, too, Katrinka. But it's schooltime now, we will talk it all over at noon. Oh! you will join of course."

Katrinka, without replying, made a graceful pirouette, and laughing out a coquettish, "Don't you hear the last bell? Catch me!"—darted off toward the schoolhouse, standing half a mile away, on the canal.

All started, pell-mell, at this challenge, but they tried in vain to catch the bright-eyed, laughing creature who, with golden hair streaming in the sunlight, cast back many a sparkling glance of triumph as she floated onward.

Beautiful Katrinka! Flushed with youth and health, all life and mirth and motion, what wonder thine image, ever floating in advance, sped through one boy's dreams that night! What wonder that it seemed his darkest hour when, years afterward, thy presence passed from him forever.

IV

HANS AND GRETEL FIND A FRIEND

At noon our young friends poured forth from the schoolhouse intent upon having an hour's practicing upon the canal.

They had skated but a few moments when Carl Schummel said mockingly to Hilda:

"There's a pretty pair just coming upon the ice! The little ragpickers! Their skates must have been a present from the king direct."

"They are patient creatures," said Hilda gently. "It must have been hard to learn to skate upon such queer affairs. They are very poor peasants, you see. The boy has probably made the skates himself."

Carl was somewhat abashed.

"Patient they may be, but as for skating, they start off

pretty well only to finish with a jerk. They could move well to your new *staccato* piece, I think."

Hilda laughed pleasantly and left him. After joining a small detachment of the racers, and sailing past every one of them, she halted beside Gretel who, with eager eyes, had been watching the sport.

"What is your name, little girl?"

"Gretel, my lady," answered the child, somewhat awed by Hilda's rank, though they were nearly of the same age, "and my brother is called Hans."

"Hans is a stout fellow," said Hilda cheerily, "and seems to have a warm stove somewhere within him, but *you* look cold. You should wear more clothing, little one."

Gretel, who had nothing else to wear, tried to laugh as she answered:

"I am not so very little. I am past twelve years old."

"Oh, I beg your pardon. You see I am nearly fourteen, and so large for my age that other girls seem small to me, but that is nothing. Perhaps you will shoot up far above me yet; not unless you dress more warmly, though—shivering girls never grow."

Hans flushed as he saw tears rising in Gretel's eyes.

"My sister has not complained of the cold; but this is bitter weather they all say"— and he looked sadly upon Gretel.

"It is nothing," said Gretel. "I am often warm—too warm when I am skating. You are good, jufvrouw,[1] to think of it."

"No, no," answered Hilda, quite angry at herself. "I am careless, cruel; but I meant no harm. I wanted to ask you—I mean—if——" and here Hilda, coming to the point of her errand, faltered before the poorly clad but noble-looking children she wished to serve.

"What is it, young lady?" exclaimed Hans eagerly. "If there is any service I can do, any——"

[1] Miss or young lady (pronounced yuffrow). In studied or polite address it would be jongvrowe (pronounced youngfrow).

"Oh! no, no," laughed Hilda, shaking off her embarrassment, "I only wished to speak to you about the grand race. Why do you not join it? You both can skate well, and the ranks are free. Anyone may enter for the prize."

Gretel looked wistfully at Hans, who tugging at his cap answered respectfully:

"Ah, jufvrouw, even if we could enter, we could skate only a few strokes with the rest. Our skates are hard wood, you see" (holding up the sole of his foot), "but they soon become damp, and then they stick and trip us."

Gretel's eyes twinkled with fun as she thought of Hans' mishap in the morning, but she blushed as she faltered out timidly, "Oh, no, we can't join; but may we be there, my lady, on the great day to look on?"

"Certainly," answered Hilda, looking kindly into the two earnest faces, and wishing from her heart that she had not spent so much of her monthly allowance for lace and finery. She had but eight kwartjes [1] left, and they would buy but one pair of skates, at the furthest.

Looking down with a sigh at the two pairs of feet so very different in size, she asked:

"Which of you is the better skater?"

"Gretel," replied Hans promptly.

"Hans," answered Gretel, in the same breath.

Hilda smiled.

"I cannot buy you each a pair of skates, or even one good pair; but here are eight kwartjes. Decide between you which stands the best chance of winning the race, and buy the skates accordingly. I wish I had enough to buy better ones—good-bye!" and, with a nod and a smile, Hilda, after handing the money to the electrified Hans, glided swiftly away to rejoin her companions.

"Jufvrouw! jufvrouw van Gleck!" called Hans in a loud tone, stumbling after her as well as he could, for one of his skate strings was untied.

[1] A kwartje is a small silver coin worth one-quarter of a guilder, or ten cents in American currency.

Hilda turned, and with one hand raised to shield her eyes from the sun, seemed to him to be floating through the air, nearer and nearer.

"We cannot take this money," panted Hans, "though we know your goodness in giving it."

"Why not indeed?" asked Hilda, flushing.

"Because," replied Hans, bowing like a clown, but looking with the eye of a prince at the queenly girl, "we have not earned it."

Hilda was quick-witted. She had noticed a pretty wooden chain upon Gretel's neck.

"Carve me a chain, Hans, like the one your sister wears."

"That I will, lady, with all my heart. We have whitewood in the house, fine as ivory. You shall have one tomorrow," and Hans hastily tried to return the money.

"No, no," said Hilda decidedly. "That sum will be but a poor price for the chain," and off she darted, outstripping the fleetest among the skaters.

Hans sent a long, bewildered gaze after her; it was useless, he felt, to make any further resistance.

"It is right," he muttered, half to himself, half to his faithful shadow, Gretel. "I must work hard every minute, and sit up half the night if the mother will let me burn a candle; but the chain shall be finished. We may keep the money, Gretel."

"What a good little lady!" cried Gretel, clapping her hands with delight. "Oh! Hans, was it for nothing the stork settled on our roof last summer? Do you remember how the mother said it would bring us luck and how she cried when Janzoon Kolp shot him? And she said it would bring him trouble. But the luck has come to us at last! Now, Hans, if the mother sends us to town tomorrow you can buy the skates in the market place."

Hans shook his head. "The young lady would have given us the money to buy skates, but if I *earn* it, Gretel, it shall be spent for wool. You must have a warm jacket."

"Oh!" cried Gretel, in real dismay, "not buy the skates! Why, I am not often cold! Mother says the blood runs up and down in poor children's veins humming 'I must keep 'em warm! I must keep 'em warm.'

"Oh, Hans," she continued with something like a sob, "don't say you won't buy the skates, it makes me feel just like crying—besides, I want to be cold—I mean I'm real, awful warm—so now!"

Hans looked up hurriedly. He had a true Dutch horror of tears, or emotion of any kind, and, most of all, he dreaded to see his sister's blue eyes overflowing.

"Now mind," cried Gretel, seeing her advantage, "I'll feel awful if you give up the skates. *I* don't want them. I'm not such a stingy as that; but I want *you* to have them, and then when I get bigger they'll do for me—oh-h—count the pieces, Hans. Did ever you see so many!"

Hans turned the money thoughtfully in his palm. Never in all his life had he longed so intensely for a pair of skates, for he had known of the race and had, boylike, fairly ached for a chance to test his powers with the other children. He felt confident that with a good pair of steel runners, he could readily distance most of the boys on the canal. Then, too, Gretel's argument was so plausible. On the other hand, he knew that she, with her strong but lithe little frame, needed but a week's practice on good runners, to make her a better skater than Rychie Korbes or even Katrinka Flack. As soon as this last thought flashed upon him, his resolve was made. If Gretel would not have the jacket, she should have the skates.

"No, Gretel," he answered at last, "I can wait. Some day I may have money enough saved to buy a fine pair. You shall have these."

Gretel's eyes sparkled; but in another instant she insisted, rather faintly:

"The young lady gave the money to *you*, Hans. I'd be real bad to take it."

Hans shook his head resolutely as he trudged on, causing his sister to half skip and half walk in her effort to keep beside him; by this time they had taken off their wooden "rockers," and were hastening home to tell their mother the good news.

"Oh! *I* know!" cried Gretel, in a sprightly tone. "You can do this. You can get a pair a little too small for you, and too big for me, and we can take turns and use them. Won't that be fine?" and Gretel clapped her hands again.

Poor Hans! This was a strong temptation, but he pushed it away from him, bravehearted fellow that he was.

"Nonsense, Gretel. You could never get on with a big pair. You stumbled about with these, like a blind chicken,

before I curved off the ends. No, you must have a pair to fit exactly, and you must practice every chance you can get, until the twentieth comes. My little Gretel shall win the silver skates."

Gretel could not help laughing with delight at the very idea.

"Hans! Gretel!" called out a familiar voice.

"Coming, mother!" and they hastened toward the cottage, Hans still shaking the pieces of silver in his hand.

On the following day, there was not a prouder nor a happier boy in all Holland than Hans Brinker, as he watched his sister, with many a dexterous sweep, flying in and out among the skaters who at sundown thronged the canal. A warm jacket had been given her by the kind-hearted Hilda, and the burst-out shoes had been cobbled into decency by Dame Brinker. As the little creature darted backward and forward, flushed with enjoyment, and quite unconscious of the many wondering glances bent upon her, she felt that the shining runners beneath her feet had suddenly turned earth into fairyland, while "Hans, dear, good Hans!" echoed itself over and over again in her grateful heart.

"By den donder!" exclaimed Peter van Holp to Carl Schummel, "but that little one in the red jacket and patched petticoat skates well. Gunst! she has toes on her heels, and eyes in the back of her head. See her! It will be a joke if she gets in the race and beats Katrinka Flack, after all."

"Hush! not so loud!" returned Carl, sneeringly. "That little lady in rags is the special pet of Hilda van Gleck. Those shining skates are her gift, if I make no mistake."

"So! so!" exclaimed Peter, with a radiant smile, for Hilda was his best friend. "She has been at her good work there, too!" And Mynheer van Holp, after cutting a double 8 on the ice, to say nothing of a huge P, then a jump, and an H, glided onward until he found himself beside Hilda.

Hand in hand, they skated together, laughingly at first, then staidly talking in a low tone.

Strange to say, Peter van Holp soon arrived at a sudden conviction that his little sister needed a wooden chain just like Hilda's.

Two days afterward, on Saint Nicholas' Eve, Hans, having burned three candle ends, and cut his thumb into the bargain, stood in the market place at Amsterdam, buying another pair of skates.

V

SHADOWS IN THE HOME

Good Dame Brinker! As soon as the scanty dinner had been cleared away that noon, she had arrayed herself in her holiday attire in honor of Saint Nicholas. "It will brighten the children," she thought to herself, and she was not mistaken. This festival dress had been worn very seldom during the past ten years; before that time it had done good service, and had flourished at many a dance and Kermis, when she was known, far and wide, as the pretty Meitje Klenck. The children had sometimes been granted rare glimpses of it as it lay in state in the old oaken chest. Faded and threadbare as it was, it was gorgeous in their eyes, with its white linen tucker, now gathered to her plump throat, and vanishing beneath the trim bodice of blue homespun, and its reddish brown skirt bordered with black. The knitted woolen mitts, and the dainty cap showing her hair, which generally was hidden, made her seem almost like a princess to Gretel, while Master Hans grew staid and well-behaved as he gazed.

Soon the little maid, while braiding her own golden tresses, fairly danced around her mother in an ecstasy of admiration.

"Oh, mother, mother, mother, how pretty you are! Look, Hans! isn't it just like a picture?"

"Just like a picture," assented Hans cheerfully, *"just* like a picture—only I don't like those stocking things on the hands."

"Not like the mitts, brother Hans! why, they're very important—see—they cover up all the red. Oh, mother, how white your arm is where the mitt leaves off, whiter than mine, oh, ever so much whiter. I declare, mother, the bodice is tight for you. You're growing! You're surely growing!"

Dame Brinker laughed.

"This was made long ago, lovey, when I wasn't much thicker about the waist than a churn dasher. And how do you like the cap?" turning her head from side to side.

"Oh, *ever* so much, mother. It's b-e-a-u-tiful! See, the father is looking!"

Was the father looking? Alas, only with a dull stare. His vrouw turned toward him with a start, something like a blush rising to her cheeks, a questioning sparkle in her eye. The bright look died away in an instant.

"No, no," she sighed, "he sees nothing. Come, Hans" (and the smile crept faintly back again), "don't stand gaping at me all day, and the new skates waiting for you at Amsterdam."

"Ah, mother," he answered, "you need many things. Why should I buy skates?"

"Nonsense, child. The money was given to you on purpose, or the work was—it's all the same thing. Go while the sun is high."

"Yes, and hurry back, Hans!" laughed Gretel. "We'll race on the canal tonight, if the mother lets us."

At the very threshold he turned to say, "Your spinning wheel wants a new treadle, mother."

"You can make it, Hans."

"So I can. That will take no money. But you need feathers, and wool and meal, and——"

"There, there! That will do. Your silver cannot buy everything. Ah! Hans, if our stolen money would but come back on this bright Saint Nicholas' Eve, how glad we would be! Only last night I prayed to the good Saint——"

"Mother!" interrupted Hans in dismay.

"Why not, Hans! Shame on you to reproach me for that! I'm as true a Protestant, in sooth, as any fine lady that walks into church, but it's no wrong to turn sometimes to the good Saint Nicholas. Tut! It's a likely story if one can't do that, without one's children flaring up at it—and he the boys' and girls' own saint. Hoot! mayhap the colt is a steadier horse than the mare?"

Hans knew his mother too well to offer a word in opposition, when her voice quickened and sharpened as it did now (it was often sharp and quick when she spoke of the missing money), so he said gently:

"And what did you ask of good Saint Nicholas, mother?"

"Why, to never give the thieves a wink of sleep till they brought it back, to be sure, if he's power to do such things, or else to brighten our wits that we might find it ourselves. Not a sight have I had of it since the day before the dear father was hurt—as you well know, Hans."

"That I do, mother," he answered sadly, "though you have almost pulled down the cottage in searching."

"Aye; but it was of no use," moaned the dame. "'*Hiders* make best finders.'"

Hans started. "Do you think the father could tell aught?" he asked mysteriously.

"Aye, indeed," said Dame Brinker, nodding her head, "I think so, but that is no sign. I never hold the same belief in the matter two days. Mayhap the father paid it off for the great silver watch we have been guarding since that day. But, no—I'll never believe it."

"The watch was not worth a quarter of the money, mother."

"No, indeed; and your father was a shrewd man up to the last moment. He was too steady and thrifty for silly doings."

"Where *did* the watch come from, I wonder," muttered Hans, half to himself.

Dame Brinker shook her head, and looked sadly toward her husband, who sat staring blankly at the floor. Gretel stood near him, knitting.

"That we shall never know, Hans. I have shown it to the father many a time, but he does not know it from a potato. When he came in that dreadful night to supper he handed the watch to me and told me to take good care of it until he asked for it again. Just as he opened his lips to say more, Broom Klatterboost came flying in with word that the dyke was in danger. Ah! the waters were terrible that holy Pinxter week! My man, alack, caught up his tools and ran out. That was the last I ever saw of him in his right mind. He was brought in again by midnight, nearly dead, with his poor head all bruised and cut. The fever passed off in time but never the dullness—*that* grew worse every day. We shall never know."

Hans had heard all this before. More than once he had seen his mother, in hours of sore need, take the watch from its hiding place, half resolved to sell it, but she had always conquered the temptation.

"No, Hans," she would say, "we must be nearer starving than this before we turn faithless to the father!"

A memory of some such scene crossed her son's mind now; for, after giving a heavy sigh, and filliping a crumb of wax at Gretel across the table, he said:

"Aye, mother, you have done bravely to keep it—many a one would have tossed it off for gold long ago."

"And more shame for them!" exclaimed the dame indignantly. "*I* would not do it. Besides, the gentry are so hard on us poor folks that if they saw such a thing in our hands, even if we told all, they might suspect the father of——"

Hans flushed angrily.

"They would not *dare* to say such a thing, mother! If they did—I'd——"

He clenched his fist, and seemed to think that the rest of his sentence was too terrible to utter in her presence.

Dame Brinker smiled proudly through her tears at this interruption.

"Ah, Hans, thou'rt a true, brave lad. We will never part company with the watch. In his dying hour the dear father might wake and ask for it."

"Might *wake,* mother!" echoed Hans, "wake—and know us?"

"Aye, child," almost whispered his mother, "such things have been."

By this time Hans had nearly forgotten his proposed errand to Amsterdam. His mother had seldom spoken so familiarly with him. He felt himself now to be not only her son, but her friend, her adviser.

"You are right, mother. We must never give up the watch. For the father's sake, we will guard it always. The money, though, may come to light when we least expect it."

"Never!" cried Dame Brinker, taking the last stitch from her needle with a jerk, and laying the unfinished knitting heavily upon her lap. "There is no chance! One thousand guilders—and all gone in a day! One thousand guilders. Oh! what ever *did* become of them? If they went in an evil way, the thief would have confessed by this on his dying bed—he would not dare to die with such guilt on his soul!"

"He may not be dead yet," said Hans soothingly. "Any day we may hear of him."

"Ah, child," she said in a changed tone, "what thief

would ever have come *here?* It was always neat and clean, thank God! but not fine; for the father and I saved and saved that we might have something laid by. 'Little and often soon fills the pouch.' We found it so, in truth; besides, the father had a goodly sum, already, for service done to the Heernocht lands, at the time of the great inundation. Every week we had a guilder left over, sometimes more; for the father worked extra hours, and could get high pay for his labor. Every Saturday night we put something by, except the time when you had the fever, Hans, and when Gretel came. At last the pouch grew so full that I mended an old stocking and commenced again. Now that I look back, it seems that the money was up to the heel in a few sunny weeks. There was great pay in those days if a man was quick at engineer work. The stocking went on filling with copper and silver—aye, and gold. You may well open your eyes, Gretel. I used to laugh and tell the father it was not for poverty I wore my old gown. And the stocking went on filling, so full that sometimes when I woke at night, I'd get up, soft and quiet, and go feel it in the moonlight. Then, on my knees, I would thank our Lord that my little ones could in time get good learning, and that the father might rest from labor in his old age. Sometimes, at supper, the father and I would talk about a new chimney and a good winter-room for the cow; but my man forsooth had finer plans even than that. 'A big sail,' says he, 'catches the wind—we can do what we will soon,' and then we would sing together as I washed my dishes. Ah, 'a smooth sea makes an easy rudder.' Not a thing vexed me from morning till night. Every week the father would take out the stocking, and drop in the money and laugh and kiss me as we tied it up together. Up with you, Hans! there you sit gaping, and the day a-wasting!" added Dame Brinker tartly, blushing to find that she had been speaking too freely to her boy. "It's high time you were on your way."

Hans had seated himself and was looking earnestly into

her face. He arose, and, in almost a whisper, asked: "Have you ever *tried,* mother?"

She understood him.

"Yes, child, often. But the father only laughs, or he stares at me so strange I am glad to ask no more. When you and Gretel had the fever last winter, and our bread was nearly gone, and I could earn nothing, for fear you would die while my face was turned, oh! I tried then! I smoothed his hair, and whispered to him soft as a kitten, about the money—where it was—who had it? Alack! he would pick at my sleeve, and whisper gibberish till my blood ran cold. At last, while Gretel lay whiter than snow, and you were raving on the bed, I screamed to him—it seemed as if he *must* hear me—'Raff, where is our money? Do you know aught of the money, Raff?—the money in the pouch and the stocking, in the big chest?' But I might as well have talked to a stone—I might as——"

The mother's voice sounded so strangely, and her eye was so bright, that Hans, with a new anxiety, laid his hand upon her shoulder.

"Come, mother," he said, "let us try to forget this money. I am big and strong—Gretel, too, is very quick and willing. Soon all will be prosperous with us again. Why, mother, Gretel and I would rather see thee bright and happy than to have all the silver in the world—wouldn't we, Gretel?"

"The mother knows it," said Gretel, sobbing.

VI
SUNBEAMS

DAME BRINKER was startled at her children's emotion; glad, too, for it proved how loving and true they were.

Beautiful ladies, in princely homes, often smile suddenly and sweetly, gladdening the very air around them; but I doubt if their smile be more welcome in God's sight than that which sprang forth to cheer the roughly clad boy and girl in the humble cottage. Dame Brinker felt that she had been selfish. Blushing and brightening, she hastily wiped her eyes, and looked upon them as only a mother can.

"Hoity! Toity! pretty talk we're having, and Saint Nicholas' Eve almost here! What wonder the yarn pricks my fingers! Come, Gretel, take this cent,[1] and while Hans is trading for the skates you can buy a waffle in the market place."

[1] The Dutch cent is worth less than half of an American cent.

"Let me stay home with you, mother," said Gretel, looking up with eyes that sparkled through their tears. "Hans will buy me the cake."

"As you will, child, and Hans—wait a moment. Three turns of the needle will finish this toe, and then you may have as good a pair of hose as ever were knitted (owning the yarn is a grain too sharp) to sell to the hosier on the Heireen Gracht.[1] That will give us three quarter-guilders if you make good trade; and as it's right hungry weather, you may buy four waffles. We'll keep the Feast of Saint Nicholas after all."

Gretel clapped her hands. "That will be fine! Annie Bouman told me what grand times they will have in the big houses tonight. But we will be merry too. Hans will have beautiful new skates—and then there'll be the waffles! Oh-h! Don't break them, brother Hans. Wrap them well, and button them under your jacket very carefully."

"Certainly," replied Hans, quite gruff with pleasure and importance.

"Oh! mother!" cried Gretel in high glee, "soon you will be busied with the father, and now you are only knitting. Do tell us all about Saint Nicholas!"

Dame Brinker laughed to see Hans hang up his hat and prepare to listen. "Nonsense, children," she said, "I have told it to you often."

"Tell us again! oh, *do* tell us again!" cried Gretel, throwing herself upon the wonderful wooden bench that her brother had made on the mother's last birthday. Hans, not wishing to appear childish, and yet quite willing to hear the story, stood carelessly swinging his skates against the fireplace.

"Well, children, you shall hear it, but we must never waste the daylight again in this way. Pick up your ball, Gretel, and let your sock grow as I talk. Opening your ears needn't shut your fingers. Saint Nicholas, you must

[1] A street in Amsterdam.

know, is a wonderful saint. He keeps his eye open for the good of sailors, but he cares most of all for boys and girls. Well, once upon a time, when he was living on the earth, a merchant of Asia sent his three sons to a great city, called Athens, to get learning."

"Is Athens in Holland, mother?" asked Gretel.

"I don't know, child. Probably it is."

"Oh, no, mother," said Hans respectfully. "I had that in my geography lessons long ago. Athens is in Greece."

"Well," resumed the mother, "what matter? Greece may belong to the king, for aught we know. Anyhow, this rich merchant sent his sons to Athens. While they were on their way, they stopped one night at a shabby inn, meaning to take up their journey in the morning. Well, they had very fine clothes—velvet and silk, it may be, such as rich folks' children, all over the world, think nothing of wearing—and their belts, likewise, were full of money. What did the wicked landlord do, but contrive a plan to kill the children, and take their money and all their beautiful clothes himself. So that night, when all the world was asleep, he got up and killed the three young gentlemen."

Gretel clasped her hands and shuddered, but Hans tried to look as if killing and murder were everyday matters to him.

"That was not the worst of it," continued Dame Brinker, knitting slowly, and trying to keep count of her stitches as she talked, "that was not near the worst of it. The dreadful landlord went and cut up the young gentlemen's bodies into little pieces, and threw them into a great tub of brine, intending to sell them for pickled pork!"

"Oh," cried Gretel, horror-stricken, though she had often heard the story before. Hans still continued unmoved, and seemed to think that pickling was the best that could be done under the circumstances.

"Yes, he pickled them, and one might think that would have been the last of the young gentlemen. But no. That night Saint Nicholas had a wonderful vision, and in it he saw the landlord cutting up the merchant's children. There was no need of his hurrying, you know, for he was a saint; but in the morning he went to the inn and charged the landlord with the murder. Then the wicked landlord

confessed it from beginning to end, and fell down on his knees, begging forgiveness. He felt so sorry for what he had done that he asked the saint to bring the young masters to life."

"And did the saint do it?" asked Gretel, delighted, well knowing what the answer would be.

"Of course he did. The pickled pieces flew together in an instant, and out jumped the young gentlemen from the brine tub. They cast themselves at the feet of Saint Nicholas and he gave them his blessing, and—oh! mercy on us, Hans, it will be dark before you get back if you don't start this minute!"

By this time Dame Brinker was almost out of breath and quite out of commas. She could not remember when she had seen the children idle away an hour of daylight in this manner, and the thought of such luxury quite appalled her. By way of compensation she now flew about the room in extreme haste. Tossing a block of peat upon the fire, blowing invisible dust from the table, and handing the finished hose to Hans, all in an instant——

"Come, Hans," she said, as her boy lingered by the door, "what keeps thee?"

Hans kissed his mother's plump cheek, rosy and fresh yet, in spite of all her troubles.

"My mother is the best in the world, and I would be right glad to have a pair of skates, but"—and, as he buttoned his jacket, he looked, in a troubled way, toward a strange figure crouching by the hearthstone—"if my money would bring a meester [1] from Amsterdam to see the father, something might yet be done."

"A meester would not come, Hans, for twice that money, and it would do no good if he did. Ah! how many guilders I once spent for that; but the dear, good father would not waken. It is God's will. Go, Hans, and buy the skates."

Hans started with a heavy heart, but since the heart was young, and in a boy's bosom, it set him whistling in less than five minutes. His mother had said "thee" to him, and that was quite enough to make even a dark day sunny. Hollanders do not address each other, in affectionate intercourse, as the French and Germans do. But Dame Brinker had embroidered for a Heidelberg family in her girlhood, and she had carried its "thee" and "thou" into her rude home, to be used in moments of extreme love and tenderness.

Therefore, "What keeps thee, Hans?" sang an echo song beneath the boy's whistling, and made him feel that his errand was blest.

[1] Doctor (dokter in Dutch) called meester by the lower class.

VII
HANS HAS HIS WAY

Broek, with its quiet, spotless streets, its frozen rivulets, its yellow brick pavements, and bright wooden houses, was near by. It was a village where neatness and show were in full blossom; but the inhabitants seemed to be either asleep or dead.

Not a footprint marred the sanded paths, where pebbles and sea shells lay in fanciful designs. Every window shutter was closed as tightly as though air and sunshine were poison; and the massive front doors were never opened except on the occasion of a wedding, christening, or a funeral.

Serene clouds of tobacco smoke were floating through hidden apartments, and children, who otherwise might have awakened the place, were studying in out-of-the-way corners, or skating upon the neighboring canal. A few peacocks and wolves stood in the gardens, but they had never enjoyed the luxury of flesh and blood. They were cut out in growing box, and seemed guarding the grounds with a sort of green ferocity. Certain lively automata, ducks, women and sportsmen, were stowed away in summerhouses, waiting for the springtime, when they could be wound up, and rival their owners in animation; and the shining, tiled roofs, mosaic courtyards and polished house trimmings flashed up a silent homage to the sky, where never a speck of dust could dwell.

Hans glanced toward the village, as he shook his silver kwartjes, and wondered whether it were really true, as he had often heard, that some of the people of Broek were so rich that they used kitchen utensils of solid gold.

He had seen Mevrouw van Stoop's sweet cheeses in market, and he knew that the lofty dame earned many a bright, silver guilder in selling them. But did she set the cream to rise in golden pans? Did she use a golden skimmer? When her cows were in winter quarters, were their tails really tied up with ribbons?

These thoughts ran through his mind as he turned his face toward Amsterdam, not five miles away on the other side of the frozen Y.[1] The ice upon the canal was perfect; but his wooden runners, so soon to be cast aside, squeaked a dismal farewell, as he scraped and skimmed along.

When crossing the Y, whom should he see skating toward him but the great Dr. Boekman, the most famous physician and surgeon in Holland. Hans had never met him before, but he had seen his engraved likeness in many of the shopwindows of Amsterdam. It was a face that one could never forget. Thin and lank, though a born Dutchman, with stern, blue eyes, and queer, compressed lips, that seemed to say "no smiling permitted," he certainly was not a very jolly or sociable looking personage, nor one that a well-trained boy would care to accost unbidden.

But Hans *was* bidden, and that, too, by a voice he seldom disregarded—his own conscience.

[1] Pronounced eye, an arm of the Zuider Zee.

"Here comes the greatest doctor in the world," whispered the voice. "God has sent him; you have no right to buy skates when you might, with the same money, purchase such aid for your father!"

The wooden runners gave an exultant squeak. Hundreds of beautiful skates were gleaming and vanishing in the air above him. He felt the money tingle in his fingers. The old doctor looked fearfully grim and forbidding. Han's heart was in his throat, but he found voice enough to cry out, just as he was passing:

"Mynheer Boekman!"

The great man halted, and sticking out his thin underlip, looked scowlingly about him.

Hans was in for it now.

"Mynheer," he panted, drawing close to the fierce-looking doctor, "I knew you could be no other than the famous Boekman. I have to ask a great favor——"

"Humph!" muttered the doctor, preparing to skate past the intruder. "Get out of the way—I've no money—never give to beggars."

"I am no beggar, mynheer," retorted Hans proudly, at the same time producing his mite of silver with a grand air. "I wish to consult with you about my father. He is a living man, but sits like one dead. He cannot think. His words mean nothing—but he is not sick. He fell on the dykes."

"Hey? what?" cried the doctor, beginning to listen.

Hans told the whole story in an incoherent way, dashing off a tear once or twice as he talked, and finally ending with an earnest——

"Oh, do see him, mynheer. His body is well—it is only his mind—I know this money is not enough; but take it, mynheer, I will earn more—I know I will. Oh! I will toil for you all my life, if you will but cure my father!"

What was the matter with the old doctor? A brightness like sunlight beamed from his face. His eyes were kind and moist; the hand that had lately clutched his cane, as if preparing to strike, was laid gently upon Hans' shoulder.

"Put up your money, boy, I do not want it—we will see your father. It is a hopeless case, I fear. How long did you say?"

"Ten years, mynheer," sobbed Hans, radiant with sudden hope.

"Ah! a bad case; but I shall see him. Let me think. To-day I start for Leyden, to return in a week, then you may expect me. Where is it?"

"A mile south of Broek, mynheer, near the canal. It is only a poor, broken-down hut. Any of the children thereabout can point it out to your honor," added Hans, with a heavy sigh. "They are all half afraid of the place; they call it the idiot's cottage."

"That will do," said the doctor, hurrying on, with a bright backward nod at Hans, "I shall be there. A hopeless case," he muttered to himself, "but the boy pleases me. His eye is like my poor Laurens. Confound it, shall I never forget that young scoundrel!" And, scowling more darkly than ever, the doctor pursued his silent way.

Again Hans was skating toward Amsterdam on the squeaking wooden runners; again his fingers tingled against the money in his pocket; again the boyish whistle rose unconsciously to his lips.

"Shall I hurry home," he was thinking, "to tell the good news, or shall I get the waffles and the new skates first? Whew! I think I'll go on!"

And so Hans bought the skates.

VIII INTRODUCING JACOB POOT AND HIS COUSIN

Hans and Gretel had a fine frolic early on that Saint Nicholas' Eve. There was a bright moon; and their mother, though she believed herself to be without any hope of her husband's improvement, had been made so happy at the prospect of the meester's visit, that she had yielded to the children's entreaties for an hour's skating before bedtime.

Hans was delighted with his new skates, and in his eagerness to show Gretel how perfectly they "worked" did many things upon the ice that caused the little maid to clasp her hands in solemn admiration. They were not alone, though they seemed quite unheeded by the various groups assembled upon the canal.

The two Van Holps, and Carl Schummel were there, testing their fleetness to the utmost. Out of four trials Peter van Holp had beaten three times. Consequently Carl, never very amiable, was in anything but a good humor. He had relieved himself by taunting young Schimmelpenninck who, being smaller than the others, kept meekly near them, without feeling exactly like one of the party; but now a new thought seized Carl, or rather he seized the new thought and made an onset upon his friends.

"I say, boys, let's put a stop to those young ragpickers from the idiot's cottage joining the race. Hilda must be crazy to think of it. Katrinka Flack and Rychie Korbes are furious at the very idea of racing with the girl; and for my part, I don't blame them. As for the boy, if we've a spark of manhood in us we will scorn the very idea of——"

"Certainly we will!" interposed Peter van Holp, purposely mistaking Carl's meaning, "who doubts it? No fellow with a spark of manhood in him would refuse to let in two good skaters just because they were poor!"

Carl wheeled about savagely:

"Not so fast, master! and I'd thank you not to put words in other people's mouths. You'd best not try it again."

"Ha! ha!" laughed little Voostenwalbert Schimmelpenninck, delighted at the prospect of a fight, and sure that, if it should come to blows, his favorite Peter could beat a dozen excitable fellows like Carl.

Something in Peter's eye made Carl glad to turn to a weaker offender. He wheeled furiously upon Voost.

"What are you shrieking about, you little weasel! You skinny herring you, you little monkey with a long name for a tail!"

Half a dozen bystanders and byskaters set up an applauding shout at this brave witticism; and Carl, feeling that he had fairly vanquished his foes, was restored to partial good humor. He, however, prudently resolved to defer plotting against Hans and Gretel until some time when Peter should not be present.

Just then, his friend, Jacob Poot, was seen approaching. They could not distinguish his features at first; but as he was the stoutest boy in the neighborhood there could be no mistaking his form.

Out jumped the gentlemen!

"Halloo! here comes Fatty!" exclaimed Carl, "and there's someone with him, a slender fellow, a stranger."

"Ha! ha! that's like good bacon," cried Ludwig. "A streak of lean and a streak of fat."

"That's Jacob's English cousin," put in Master Voost, delighted at being able to give the information, "that's his English cousin, and, oh! he's got such a funny little name—Ben Dobbs. He's going to stay with him until after the grand race."

All this time the boys had been spinning, turning, "rolling" and doing other feats upon their skates, in a quiet way, as they talked; but now they stood still, bracing themselves against the frosty air as Jacob Poot and his friend drew near.

"This is my cousin, boys," said Jacob, rather out of breath—"Benjamin Dobbs. He's a John Bull and he's going to be in the race."

All crowded, boy-fashion, about the newcomers. Benjamin soon made up his mind that the Hollanders, notwithstanding their queer gibberish, were a fine set of fellows.

If the truth must be told, Jacob had announced his cousin as "Penchamin Dopps," and called him a "Shon Pull," but as I translate every word of the conversation of our young friends, it is no more than fair to mend their little attempts at English. Master Dobbs felt at first decidedly awkward among his cousin's friends. Though most of them had studied English and French, they were shy about attempting to speak either, and he made very funny blunders when he tried to converse in Dutch. He had learned that *vrouw* means wife; and *ja,* yes; and *spoorweg,* railway; *kanaals,* canals; *stoomboot,* steamboat; *ophaalbruggen,* drawbridges; *buiten plasten,* countryseats; *mynheer,* mister; *tweegevegt,* duel or "two fights"; *koper,* copper; *zadel,* saddle; but he could not make a sentence out of these, nor use the long list of phrases he had learned in his "Dutch dialogues." The topics of the latter were fine, but were never alluded to by the boys. Like the poor fellow who had learned in Ollendorf to ask in faultless German "Have you seen my grandmother's red cow?" and when he reached Germany discovered that he had no occasion to inquire after that interesting animal, Ben found that his book-Dutch did not avail him as much as he had hoped. He acquired a hearty contempt for Jan van Gorp, a Hollander who wrote a book in Latin to prove that Adam and Eve spoke Dutch; and he smiled a knowing smile when his uncle Poot assured him that Dutch "had great likeness mit Zinglish but it vash much petter languish, much petter."

However, the fun of skating glides over all barriers of speech. Through this, Ben soon felt that he knew the boys well; and when Jacob (with a sprinkling of French and English for Ben's benefit) told of a grand project they had planned, his cousin could now and then put in a "ja," or a nod, in quite a familiar way.

The project *was* a grand one, and there was to be a fine opportunity for carrying it out; for, besides the allotted holiday of the Festival of Saint Nicholas, four extra days were to be allowed for a general cleaning of the schoolhouse.

Jacob and Ben had obtained permission to go on a long skating journey—no less a one than from Broek to The Hague, the capital of Holland, a distance of nearly fifty miles! [1]

"And now, boys," added Jacob, when he had told the plan, "who will go with us?"

"I will! I will!" cried the boys eagerly.

"And so will I!" ventured little Voostenwalbert.

"Ha! ha!" laughed Jacob, holding his fat sides, and shaking his puffy cheeks, "*you* go? Such a little fellow as you? Why, youngster, you haven't left off your pads yet!"

Now in Holland very young children wear a thin, padded cushion around their heads, surmounted with a frame-

[1] Throughout this narrative distances are given according to our standard, the English statute mile of 5,280 feet. The Dutch mile is more than four times as long as ours.

work of whalebone and ribbon, to protect them in case of a fall; and it is the dividing line between babyhood and childhood when they leave it off. Voost had arrived at this dignity several years before; consequently Jacob's insult was rather too great for endurance.

"Look out what you say!" he squeaked. "Lucky for you when you can leave off *your* pads—you're padded all over!"

"Ha! ha!" roared all the boys except Master Dobbs, who could not understand. "Ha! ha!"—and the good-natured Jacob laughed more than any.

"It ish my fat—yaw—he say I bees pad mit fat!" he explained to Ben.

So a vote was passed unanimously in favor of allowing the now popular Voost to join the party, if his parents would consent.

"Good night!" sang out the happy youngster, skating homeward with all his might.

"Good night!"

"We can stop at Haarlem, Jacob, and show your cousin the big organ," said Peter van Holp eagerly, "and at Leyden, too, where there's no end to the sights; and spend a day and night at The Hague, for my married sister, who lives there, will be delighted to see us; and the next morning we can start for home."

"All right!" responded Jacob, who was not much of a talker.

Ludwig had been regarding his brother with enthusiastic admiration.

"Hurrah for you, Pete! It takes you to make plans! Mother'll be as full of it as we are when we tell her we can take her love direct to sister Van Gend. My! but it's cold," he added, "cold enough to take a fellow's head off his shoulders. We'd better go home."

"What if it is cold, old Tender-skin?" cried Carl, who was busily practicing a step which he called the "double edge." "Great skating we should have by this time, if it was as warm as it was last December. Don't you know if it wasn't an extra cold winter, and an early one into the bargain, we couldn't go?"

"I know it's an extra cold night anyhow," said Ludwig. "Whew! I'm going home!"

Peter van Holp took out a bulgy gold watch, and holding it toward the moonlight as well as his benumbed fingers would permit, called out:

"Halloo! it's nearly eight o'clock! Saint Nicholas is about by this time, and I, for one, want to see the little ones stare. Good night!"

"Good night!" cried one and all, and off they started, shouting, singing, and laughing as they flew along.

Where were Gretel and Hans?

Ah! how suddenly joy sometimes comes to an end!

They had skated about an hour, keeping aloof from the others, quite contented with each other, and Gretel had exclaimed, "Ah, Hans, how beautiful! how fine! to think that we both have skates! I tell you the stork brought us good luck!"—when they heard something!

It was a scream—a very faint scream! No one else upon the canal observed it, but Hans knew its meaning too well. Gretel saw him turn white in the moonlight as he hastily tore off his skates.

"The father!" he cried. "He has frightened our mother!" and Gretel ran after him toward the house as rapidly as she could.

IX

THE FESTIVAL OF SAINT NICHOLAS

WE all know how, before the Christmas tree began to flourish in the home life of our country, a certain "right jolly old elf," with "eight tiny reindeer," used to drive his sleigh-load of toys up to our housetops, and then bound down the chimney to fill the stockings so hopefully hung by the fireplace. His friends called him Santa Claus, and those who were most intimate ventured to say "Old Nick." It was said that he originally came from Holland. Doubtless he did; but, if so, he certainly, like many other foreigners, changed his ways very much after landing upon our shores. In Holland, Saint Nicholas is a veritable saint, and often appears in full costume, with his embroidered robes glittering with gems and gold, his miter, his crosier and his jeweled gloves. *Here* Santa Claus comes rollicking along, on the twenty-fifth of December, our holy Christmas morn. But in Holland, Saint Nicholas visits earth on the fifth, a time especially appropriated to him. Early on the morning of the sixth, he distributes his candies, toys and treasures, then vanishes for a year.

Christmas Day is devoted by the Hollanders to church rites and pleasant family visiting. It is on Saint Nicholas' Eve that their young people become half wild with joy and expectation. To some of them it is a sorry time, for the saint is very candid, and if any of them have been bad during the past year, he is quite sure to tell them so. Sometimes he carries a birch rod under his arm and advises the parents to give them scoldings in place of confections, and floggings instead of toys.

It was well that the boys hastened to their abodes on that bright winter evening, for in less than an hour afterward, the saint made his appearance in half the homes of Holland. He visited the king's palace and in the selfsame moment appeared in Annie Bouman's comfortable home. Probably one of our silver half dollars would have purchased all that his saintship left at the peasant Bouman's; but a half dollar's worth will sometimes do for the poor what hundreds of dollars may fail to do for the rich; it makes them happy and grateful, fills them with new peace and love.

Hilda van Gleck's little brothers and sisters were in a high state of excitement that night. They had been admitted into the grand parlor; they were dressed in their best, and had been given two cakes apiece at supper. Hilda was as joyous as any. Why not? Saint Nicholas would never cross a girl of fourteen from his list, just because she was tall and looked almost like a woman. On the contrary, he would probably exert himself to do honor to such an august-looking damsel. Who could tell? So she sported and laughed and danced as gaily as the youngest, and was the soul of all their merry games. Father, mother and grandmother looked on approvingly; so did grandfather, before he spread his large red handkerchief over his face, leaving only the top of his skullcap visible. This kerchief was his ensign of sleep.

Earlier in the evening all had joined in the fun. In the general hilarity, there had seemed to be a difference only in bulk between grandfather and the baby. Indeed a shade of solemn expectation, now and then flitting across the faces of the younger members, had made them seem rather more thoughtful than their elders.

Now the spirit of fun reigned supreme. The very flames danced and capered in the polished grate. A pair of prim candles that had been staring at the astral lamp began to wink at other candles far away in the mirrors. There was a long bellrope suspended from the ceiling in the corner, made of glass beads netted over a cord nearly as thick as your wrist. It generally hung in the shadow and made no sign; but tonight it twinkled from end to end. Its handle of crimson glass sent reckless dashes of red at the papered wall, turning its dainty blue stripes into purple. Passers-by halted to catch the merry laughter floating, through curtain and sash, into the street, then skipped on their way with a startled consciousness that the village was wide awake. At last matters grew so uproarious that the grandsire's red kerchief came down from his face with a jerk. What decent old gentleman could sleep in such a racket! Mynheer van Gleck regarded his children with astonishment. The baby even showed symptoms of hysterics. It was high time to attend to business. Madame suggested that if they wished to see the good Saint Nicholas they should sing the same loving invitation that had brought him the year before.

The baby stared and thrust his fist into his mouth as mynheer put him down upon the floor. Soon he sat erect, and looked with a sweet scowl at the company. With his lace and embroideries, and his crown of blue ribbon and whalebone (for he was not quite past the tumbling age), he looked like the king of the babies.

The other children, each holding a pretty willow basket,

formed at once in a ring, and moved slowly around the little fellow, lifting their eyes, meanwhile, for the saint to whom they were about to address themselves was yet in mysterious quarters.

Madame commenced playing softly upon the piano; soon the voices rose—gentle, youthful voices—rendered all the sweeter for their tremor:

"Welcome, friend! Saint Nicholas, welcome!
Bring no rod for us, tonight!
While our voices bid thee, welcome,
Every heart with joy is light!

Tell us every fault and failing,
We will bear thy keenest railing,
So we sing—so we sing—
Thou shalt tell us everything!

Welcome, friend! Saint Nicholas, welcome!
Welcome to this merry band!
Happy children greet thee, welcome!
Thou art glad'ning all the land!

Fill each empty hand and basket,
'Tis thy little ones who ask it,
So we sing—so we sing—
Thou wilt bring us everything!"

During the chorus, sundry glances, half in eagerness, half in dread, had been cast toward the polished folding doors. Now a loud knocking was heard. The circle was broken in an instant. Some of the little ones, with a strange mixture of fear and delight, pressed against their mother's knee. Grandfather bent forward, with his chin resting upon his hand; grandmother lifted her spectacles; Mynheer van Gleck, seated by the fireplace, slowly drew his meerschaum from his mouth, while Hilda and the other children settled themselves beside him in an expectant group.

The knocking was heard again.

"Come in," said Madame softly.

The door slowly opened, and Saint Nicholas, in full array, stood before them. You could have heard a pin drop! Soon he spoke. What a mysterious majesty in his voice! what kindliness in his tones!

"Karel van Gleck, I am pleased to greet thee, and thy honored vrouw Kathrine, and thy son and his good vrouw Annie!

"Children, I greet ye all! Hendrick, Hilda, Broom, Katy, Huygens, and Lucretia! And thy cousins, Wolfert, Diedrich, Mayken, Voost, and Katrina! Good children ye have been, in the main, since I last accosted ye. Diedrich was rude at the Haarlem fair last fall, but he has tried to atone for it since. Mayken has failed of late in her lessons, and too many sweets and trifles have gone to her lips, and too few stivers to her charity box. Diedrich, I trust, will be a polite, manly boy for the future, and Mayken will endeavor to shine as a student. Let her remember, too, that economy and thrift are needed in the foundation of a worthy and generous life. Little Katy has been cruel to the cat more than once. Saint Nicholas can hear the cat cry when its tail is pulled. I will forgive her if she will remember from this hour that the smallest dumb creatures have feeling and must not be abused."

As Katy burst into a frightened cry, the saint graciously remained silent until she was soothed.

"Master Broom," he resumed, "I warn thee that boys who are in the habit of putting snuff upon the foot stove of the schoolmistress may one day be discovered and receive a flogging——"

[Master Broom colored and stared in great astonishment.]

"But thou art such an excellent scholar, I shall make thee no further reproof.

"Thou, Hendrick, didst distinguish thyself in the archery match last spring, and hit the Doel,[1] though the bird was swung before it to unsteady thine eye. I give thee credit for excelling in manly sport and exercise—though I must not unduly countenance thy boat racing since it leaves thee too little time for thy proper studies.

"Lucretia and Hilda shall have a blessed sleep tonight. The consciousness of kindness to the poor, devotion in their souls, and cheerful, hearty obedience to household rule will render them happy.

"With one and all I avow myself well content. Goodness, industry, benevolence and thrift have prevailed in your midst. Therefore, my blessing upon you—and may the New Year find all treading the paths of obedience, wisdom and love. Tomorrow you shall find more substantial proofs that I have been in your midst. Farewell!"

With these words came a great shower of sugarplums, upon a linen sheet spread out in front of the doors. A general scramble followed. The children fairly tumbled over each other in their eagerness to fill their baskets. Madame cautiously held the baby down in their midst, till the chubby little fists were filled. Then the bravest of the youngsters sprang up and burst open the closed doors—in vain they peered into the mysterious apartment—Saint Nicholas was nowhere to be seen.

Soon there was a general rush to another room, where stood a table, covered with the finest and whitest of linen damask. Each child, in a flutter of excitement, laid a shoe upon it. The door was then carefully locked, and its key hidden in the mother's bedroom. Next followed good night kisses, a grand family procession to the upper floor, merry farewells at bedroom doors—and silence, at last, reigned in the Van Gleck mansion.

Early the next morning, the door was solemnly unlocked and opened in the presence of the assembled household,

[1] Bull's-eye.

when lo! a sight appeared proving Saint Nicholas to be a saint of his word!

Every shoe was filled to overflowing, and beside each stood many a colored pile. The table was heavy with its load of presents—candies, toys, trinkets, books and other articles. Everyone had gifts, from grandfather down to the baby.

Little Katy clapped her hands with glee, and vowed, inwardly, that the cat should never know another moment's grief.

Hendrick capered about the room, flourishing a superb bow and arrows over his head. Hilda laughed with delight as she opened a crimson box and drew forth its glittering contents. The rest chuckled and said "Oh!" and "Ah!" over their treasures, very much as we did here in America on last Christmas Day.

With her glittering necklace in her hands, and a pile of books in her arms, Hilda stole toward her parents and held up her beaming face for a kiss. There was such an earnest, tender look in her bright eyes that her mother breathed a blessing as she leaned over her.

"I am delighted with this book, thank you, father," she said, touching the top one with her chin. "I shall read it all day long."

"Aye, sweetheart," said mynheer, "you cannot do better. There is no one like Father Cats. If my daughter learns his 'Moral Emblems' by heart, the mother and I may keep silent. The work you have there is the Emblems—his best work. You will find it enriched with rare engravings from Van de Venne."

[Considering that the back of the book was turned away, Mynheer certainly showed a surprising familiarity with an unopened volume, presented by Saint Nicholas. It was strange, too, that the saint should have found certain things made by the elder children, and had actually placed them upon the table, labeled with parents' and grandparents' names. But all were too much absorbed in happiness to notice slight inconsistencies. Hilda saw, on her father's face, the rapt expression he always wore when he spoke of Jakob Cats, so she put her armful of books upon the table and resigned herself to listen.]

"Old Father Cats, my child, was a great poet, not a writer of plays like the Englishman, Shakespeare, who lived in his time. I have read them in the German and very good they are—very, very good—but not like Father Cats. Cats sees no daggers in the air; he has no white women falling in love with dusky Moors; no young fools sighing to be a lady's glove; no crazy princes mistaking respectable old gentlemen for rats. No, no. He writes only sense. It is great wisdom in little bundles, a bundle for every day of your life. You can guide a state with Cats' poems, and you can put a little baby to sleep with his pretty songs. He was one of the greatest men of Holland. When I take you to The Hague I will show you the Kloosterkerk where he lies buried. *There* was a man for you to study, my sons! He was good through and through. What did he say?

" 'O, Lord, let me obtain this from Thee
To live with patience, and to die with pleasure!' [1]

"Did patience mean folding his hands? No, he was a lawyer, statesman, ambassador, farmer, philosopher, historian, and poet. He was keeper of the Great Seal of Holland! He was a—Bah! there is too much noise here, I cannot talk"—and mynheer, looking with astonishment into the bowl of his meerschaum—for it had "gone out"—nodded to his vrouw and left the apartment in great haste.

The fact is, his discourse had been accompanied throughout with a subdued chorus of barking dogs, squeaking cats and bleating lambs, to say nothing of a noisy ivory cricket that the baby was whirling with infinite delight. At the last, little Huygens, taking advantage of the increasing loudness of mynheer's tones, had ventured a blast on

[1] O Heere! laat my dat van uwen hand verwerven,
Te leven met gedult, en met vermaak te sterven.

his new trumpet, and Wolfert had hastily attempted an accompaniment on the drum. This had brought matters to a crisis, and well for the little creatures that it had. The saint had left no ticket for them to attend a lecture on Jakob Cats. It was not an appointed part of the ceremonies. Therefore when the youngsters saw that the mother looked neither frightened nor offended, they gathered new courage. The grand chorus rose triumphant, and frolic and joy reigned supreme.

Good Saint Nicholas! For the sake of the young Hollanders, I, for one, am willing to acknowledge him and defend his reality against all unbelievers.

Carl Schummel was quite busy during that day, assuring little children, confidentially, that not Saint Nicholas, but their own fathers and mothers had produced the oracle and loaded the tables. But *we* know better than that.

And yet if this were a saint, why did he not visit the Brinker cottage that night? Why was that one home, so dark and sorrowful, passed by?

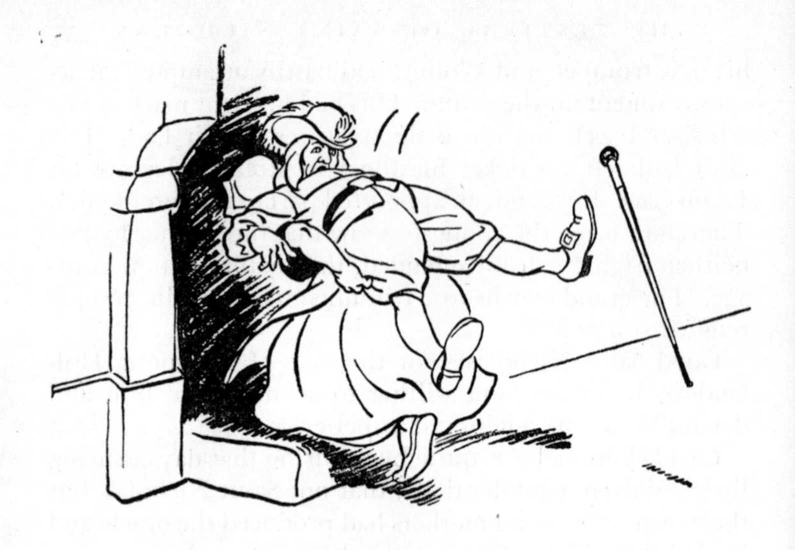

X

WHAT THE BOYS SAW AND DID IN AMSTERDAM

"ARE we all here?" cried Peter, in high glee, as the party assembled upon the canal early the next morning, equipped for their skating journey. "Let me see. As Jacob has made me captain, I must call the roll. Carl Schummel—— You here?"

"Ya!"

"Jacob Poot!"

"Ya!"

"Benjamin Dobbs!"

"Ya-a!"

"Lambert van Mounen!"

"Ya!"

"[That's lucky! Couldn't get on without *you,* as you're the only one who can speak English.] Ludwig van Holp!"

"Ya!"

"Voostenwalbert Schimmelpenninck!"

No answer.

"Ah! the little rogue has been kept at home. Now, boys, it's just eight o'clock—glorious weather, and the Y is as firm as a rock—we'll be at Amsterdam in thirty minutes. One, two, three—START!"

True enough, in less than half an hour they had crossed a dyke of solid masonry, and were in the very heart of the great metropolis of the Netherlands—a walled city of ninety-five islands and nearly two hundred bridges. Although Ben had been there twice since his arrival in Holland, he saw much to excite wonder; but his Dutch comrades, having lived near by all their lives, considered it the most matter-of-course place in the world. Everything interested Ben: the tall houses with their forked chimneys and gable ends facing the street; the merchants' warerooms, perched high up under the roofs of their dwellings, with long, armlike cranes hoisting and lowering goods past the household windows; the grand public buildings erected upon wooden piles driven deep into the marshy ground; the narrow streets; the canals everywhere crossing the city; the bridges; the locks; the various costumes, and, strangest of all, shops and dwellings crouching close to the fronts of the churches, sending their long, disproportionate chimneys far upward along the sacred walls.

If he looked up, he saw tall, leaning houses, seeming to pierce the sky with their shining roofs; if he looked down, there was the queer street, without crossing or curb—nothing to separate the cobblestone pavement from the footpath of brick—and if he rested his eyes halfway, he saw complicated little mirrors (*spionnen*) fastened upon the outside of nearly every window, so arranged that the inmates of the houses could observe all that was going on in the street, or inspect whoever might be knocking at the door, without being seen themselves.

Sometimes a dogcart, heaped with wooden ware, passed him; then a donkey bearing a pair of panniers filled with crockery or glass; then a sled driven over the bare cobblestones (the runners kept greased with a dripping oil rag so that it might run easily); and then, perhaps, a showy, but clumsy family carriage, drawn by the brownest of Flanders horses, swinging the whitest of snowy tails.

The city was in full festival array. Every shop was gorgeous in honor of Saint Nicholas. Captain Peter was forced, more than once, to order his men away from the tempting show windows, where everything that is, has been, or can be thought of in the way of toys was displayed. Holland is famous for this branch of manufacture. Every possible thing is copied in miniature for the benefit of the little ones; the intricate mechanical toys that a Dutch youngster tumbles about in stolid unconcern would create a stir in our Patent Office. Ben laughed outright at some of the mimic fishing boats. They were so heavy and stumpy, so like the queer craft that he had seen about Rotterdam. The tiny trekschuiten, however, only a foot or two long, and fitted out, complete, made his heart ache—he so longed to buy one at once for his little brother in England. He had no money to spare; for, with true Dutch prudence, the party had agreed to take with them merely the sum required for each boy's expenses, and to consign the purse to Peter for safekeeping. Consequently Master Ben concluded to devote all his energies to sight-seeing, and to think as seldom as possible of little Robby.

He made a hasty call at the Marine school and envied the sailor students their full-rigged brig and their sleeping berths swung over their trunks or lockers; he peeped into the Jews' Quarter of the city, where the rich diamond cutters and squalid old-clothesmen dwell, and wisely resolved to keep away from it; he also enjoyed hasty glimpses of the four principal avenues of Amsterdam—the Prinsen Gracht,

Keizers Gracht, Heeren Gracht and Singel. These are semicircular in form, and the first three average more than two miles in length. A canal runs through the center of each, with a well-paved road on either side, lined with stately buildings. Rows of naked elms, bordering the canal, cast a network of shadows over its frozen surface; and everything was so clean and bright that Ben told Lambert it seemed to him like petrified neatness.

Fortunately the weather was cold enough to put a stop to the usual street-flooding, and window-washing, or our young excursionists might have been drenched more than once. Sweeping, mopping and scrubbing form a passion with Dutch housewives, and to soil their spotless mansions is considered scarcely less than a crime. Everywhere a hearty contempt is felt for those who neglect to rub the soles of their shoes to a polish before crossing the doorsill; and, in certain places, visitors are expected to remove their heavy shoes before entering.

Sir William Temple, in his memoirs of "What passed in Christendom from 1672 to 1679," tells a story of a pompous magistrate going to visit a lady of Amsterdam. A stout Holland lass opened the door, and told him in a breath that the lady was at home and that his shoes were not very clean. Without another word, she took the astonished man up by both arms, threw him across her back, carried him through two rooms, set him down at the bottom of the stairs, seized a pair of slippers that stood there and put them upon his feet. Then, and not until then, she spoke, telling him that her mistress was on the floor above, and that he might go up.

While Ben was skating, with his friends, upon the crowded canals of the city, he found it difficult to believe that the sleepy Dutchmen he saw around him, smoking their pipes so leisurely, and looking as though their hats might be knocked off their heads without their making any resistance, were capable of those outbreaks that had taken place in Holland—that they were really fellow countrymen of the brave, devoted heroes of whom he had read in Dutch history.

As his party skimmed lightly along he told Van Mounen of a burial riot which in 1696 had occurred in that very city, where the women and children turned out, as well as the men, and formed mock funeral processions through the town, to show the burgomasters that certain new regulations, with regard to burying the dead, would not be acceded to—how at last they grew so unmanageable and threatened so much damage to the city that the burgomasters were glad to recall the offensive law.

"There's the corner," said Jacob, pointing to some large buildings, "where, about fifteen years ago, the great cornhouses sank down in the mud. They were strong affairs, and set up on good piles, but they had over seventy thousand hundredweight of corn in them; and that was too much."

It was a long story for Jacob to tell and he stopped to rest.

"How do you know there were seventy thousand hundredweight in them?" asked Carl sharply. "You were in your swaddling clothes then."

"My father knows all about it," was Jacob's suggestive reply. Rousing himself with an effort, he continued, "Ben likes pictures. Show him some."

"All right," said the captain.

"If we had time, Benjamin," said Lambert van Mounen in English, "I should like to take you to the City Hall, or *Stadhuis*. There are building-piles for you! It is built on nearly fourteen thousand of them, driven seventy feet into the ground. But what I wish you to see there is the big picture of Van Speyk blowing up his ship—great picture."

"Van *who?*" asked Ben.

"Van Speyk. Don't you remember? He was in the height of an engagement with the Belgians, and when he found that they had the better of him and would capture his ship, he blew it up, and himself too, rather than yield to the enemy."

"Wasn't that Van Tromp?"

"Oh, no. Van Tromp was another brave fellow. They've a monument to him down at Delftshaven—the place where the Pilgrims took ship for America."

"Well, what about Van Tromp? He was a great Dutch admiral, wasn't he?"

"Yes, he was in more than thirty sea fights. He beat the Spanish fleet and an English one, and then fastened a broom to his masthead to show that he had swept the English from the sea. Takes the Dutch to beat, my boy!"

"Hold up!" cried Ben. "Broom or no broom, the English conquered him at last. I remember all about it now. He was killed somewhere on the Dutch coast in an engagement in which the British fleet was victorious. Too bad," he added maliciously, "wasn't it?"

"Ahem! where are we?" exclaimed Lambert, changing the subject. "Halloo! the others are way ahead of us—all but Jacob. Whew! how fat he is! He'll break down before we're halfway."

Ben, of course, enjoyed skating beside Lambert, who though a stanch Hollander, had been educated near London, and could speak English as fluently as Dutch; but he was not sorry when Captain van Holp called out:

"Skates off! There's the Museum!"

It was open, and there was no charge on that day for admission. In they went, shuffling, as boys will when they have a chance, just to hear the sound of their shoes on the polished floor.

This Museum is in fact a picture gallery where some of the finest works of the Dutch masters are to be seen, besides nearly two hundred portfolios of rare engravings.

Ben noticed, at once, that some of the pictures were hung on panels fastened to the wall with hinges. These could be swung forward like a window shutter, thus enabling the subject to be seen in the best light. The plan served them well in viewing a small group by Gerard Douw, called the "Evening School," enabling them to observe its exquisite finish and the wonderful way in which the picture seemed to be lit through its own windows. Peter pointed out the beauties of another picture by Douw, called "The Hermit," and he also told them some interesting anecdotes of the artist, who was born at Leyden in 1613.

"Three days painting a broom handle!" echoed Carl in astonishment, while the captain was giving some instances of Douw's extreme slowness of execution.

"Yes, sir, three days. And it is said that he spent five in finishing one hand in a lady's portrait. You see how very bright and minute everything is in this picture. His unfinished works were kept carefully covered, and his painting materials were put away in airtight boxes as soon as he had finished using them for the day. According to all accounts, the studio itself must have been as close as a bandbox. The artist always entered it on tiptoe, besides sitting still, before he commenced work, until the slight dust caused by his entrance had settled. I have read somewhere that his paintings are improved by being viewed through a magnifying glass. He strained his eyes so badly with this extra finishing that he was forced to wear spectacles before he was thirty. At forty he could scarcely see to paint, and he couldn't find a pair of glasses anywhere that would help his sight. At last, a poor old German woman asked him to try hers. They suited him exactly, and enabled him to go on painting as well as ever."

"Humph!" exclaimed Ludwig indignantly, "that was high! What did *she* do without them, I wonder?"

"Oh," said Peter, laughing, "likely she had another pair. At any rate she insisted upon his taking them. He was so grateful that he painted a picture of the spectacles for her, case and all, and she sold it to a burgomaster for a yearly allowance that made her comfortable for the rest of her days."

"Boys!" called Lambert, in a loud whisper, "come look at this Bear Hunt."

It was a fine painting by Paul Potter, a Dutch artist of

the seventeenth century, who produced excellent works before he was sixteen years old. The boys admired it because the subject pleased them. They passed carelessly by the masterpieces of Rembrandt and Van der Helst, and went into raptures over an ugly picture by Van der Venne, representing a sea fight between the Dutch and English. They also stood spellbound before a painting of two little urchins, one of whom was taking soup and the other eating an egg. The principal merit in this work was that the young egg eater had kindly slobbered his face with the yolk for their entertainment.

An excellent representation of the "Feast of Saint Nicholas" next had the honor of attracting them.

"Look, Van Mounen," said Ben to Lambert, "could anything be better than this youngster's face? He looks as if he *knows* he deserves a whipping but hopes Saint Nicholas may not have found him out. That's the kind of painting *I* like; something that tells a story."

"Come, boys!" cried the captain. "Ten o'clock, time we were off!"

They hastened to the canal.

"Skates on! Are you ready? One, two—halloo! where's Poot?"

Sure enough where *was* Poot?

A square opening had just been cut in the ice not ten yards off. Peter observed it, and without a word skated rapidly toward it. All the others followed, of course.

Peter looked in. They all looked in; then stared anxiously at each other.

"Poot!" screamed Peter, peering into the hole again. All was still. The black water gave no sign; it was already glazing on top.

Van Mounen turned mysteriously to Ben.

"Didn't he have a fit once?"

"My goodness! yes!" answered Ben, in a great fright.

"Then, depend upon it, he's been taken with one in the Museum!"

The boys caught his meaning. Every skate was off in a twinkling. Peter had the presence of mind to scoop up a capful of water from the hole, and off they scampered to the rescue.

Alas! They did indeed find poor Jacob in a fit—but it was a fit of sleepiness. There he lay in a recess of the gallery, snoring like a trooper! The chorus of laughter that followed this discovery brought an angry official to the spot.

"What now! None of this racket! Here, you beer barrel, wake up!" and Master Jacob received a very unceremonious shaking.

As soon as Peter saw that Jacob's condition was not serious, he hastened to the street to empty his unfortunate cap. While he was stuffing in his handkerchief to prevent the already frozen crown from touching his head, the rest of the boys came down, dragging the bewildered and indignant Jacob in their midst.

The order to start was again given. Master Poot was wide awake at last. The ice was a little rough and broken just there, but every boy was in high spirits.

"Shall we go on by the canal or the river?" asked Peter.

"Oh, the river, by all means," said Carl. "It will be such fun; they say it is perfect skating all the way, but it's much farther."

Jacob Poot instantly became interested.

"*I* vote for the canal!" he cried.

"Well, the canal it shall be," responded the captain, "if all are agreed."

"Agreed!" they echoed, in rather a disappointed tone—and Captain Peter led the way.

"All right, come on. We can reach Haarlem in an hour!"

XI

BIG MANIAS AND LITTLE ODDITIES

WHILE skating along at full speed, they heard the cars from Amsterdam coming close behind them.

"Halloo!" cried Ludwig, glancing toward the rail track, "who can't beat a locomotive? Let's give it a race!"

The whistle screamed at the very idea—so did the boys—and at it they went.

For an instant the boys were ahead, hurrahing with all their might—only for an instant, but even *that* was something.

This excitement over, they began to travel more leisurely and indulge in conversation and frolic. Sometimes they stopped to exchange a word with the guards who were stationed at certain distances along the canal. These men, in winter, attend to keeping the surface free from obstruction and garbage. After a snowstorm they are expected to sweep the feathery covering away before it hardens into a marble pretty to look at but very unwelcome to skaters. Now and then the boys so far forgot their dignity as to clamber among the icebound canalboats crowded together in a widened harbor off the canal, but the watchful guards would soon spy them out ond order them down with a growl.

Nothing could be straighter than the canal upon which our party were skating, and nothing straighter than the long rows of willow trees that stood, bare and wispy, along the bank. On the opposite side, lifted high above the surrounding country, lay the carriage road on top of the great dyke built to keep the Haarlem Lake within bounds; stretching out far in the distance, until it became lost in a point, was the glassy canal with its many skaters, its brown-winged iceboats, its push-chairs and its queer little sleds, light as cork, flying over the ice by means of iron-pronged sticks in the hands of the riders. Ben was in ecstasy with the scene.

Ludwig van Holp had been thinking how strange it was that the English boy should know so much of Holland. According to Lambert's account, he knew more about it than the Dutch did. This did not quite please our young Hollander. Suddenly he thought of something that he believed would make the "Shon Pull" open his eyes; he drew near Lambert with a triumphant:

"Tell him about the tulips!"

Ben caught the word *"tulpen."*

"Oh! yes," said he eagerly, in English, "the Tulip Mania—are you speaking of that? I have often heard it mentioned, but know very little about it. It reached its height in Amsterdam, didn't it?"

Ludwig moaned; the words were hard to understand, but there was no mistaking the enlightened expression on Ben's face. Lambert, happily, was quite unconscious of his young countryman's distress as he replied:

"Yes, here and in Haarlem, principally; but the excitement ran high all over Holland, and in England too for that matter."

"Hardly in England,[1] I think," said Ben, "but I am not sure, as I was not there at the time."

"Ha! ha! that's true, unless you are over two hundred years old. Well, I tell you, sir, there was never anything like it before nor since. Why, persons were so crazy after tulip bulbs in those days that they paid their weight in gold for them."

"What, the weight of a man?" cried Ben, showing such astonishment in his eyes that Ludwig fairly capered.

"No, no, the weight of a *bulb*. The first tulip was sent here from Constantinople about the year 1560. It was so much admired that the rich people of Amsterdam sent to Turkey for more. From that time they grew to be the rage, and it lasted for years. Single roots brought from one to four thousand florins; and one bulb, the Semper Augustus, brought fifty-five hundred."

"That's more than four hundred guineas of our money," interposed Ben.

"Yes, and I know I'm right, for I read it in a translation from Beckman, only day before yesterday. Well, sir, it was great. Everyone speculated in tulips, even the bargemen

[1] Although the Tulip Mania did not prevail in England as in Holland, the flower soon became an object of speculation and brought very large prices. In 1636, tulips were publicly sold on the Exchange of London. Even as late as 1800, a common price was fifteen guineas for one bulb. Ben did not know that in his own day a single tulip plant, called the "Fanny Kemble," had been sold in London for more than seventy guineas.

Mr. Mackay in his "Memoirs of Popular Delusions" tells a funny story of an English botanist who happened to see a tulip bulb lying in the conservatory of a wealthy Dutchman. Ignorant of its value, he took out his penknife and, cutting the bulb in two, became very much interested in his investigations. Suddenly the owner appeared, and pouncing furiously upon him, asked him if he knew what he was doing. "Peeling a most extraordinary onion," replied the philosopher. "Hundert tousant tuyvel!" shouted the Dutchman, "it's an Admiral Van der Eyk!" "Thank you," replied the traveler, immediately writing the name in his notebook. "Pray are these very common in your country?" "Death and the tuyvel!" screamed the Dutchman, "come before the Syndic and you shall see!" In spite of his struggles the poor investigator, followed by an indignant mob, was taken through the streets to a magistrate. Soon he learned to his dismay that he had destroyed a bulb worth 4,000 florins ($1,600). He was lodged in prison until securities could be procured for the payment of the sum.

and rag women, and chimney sweeps. The richest merchants were not ashamed to share the excitement. People bought bulbs and sold them again at a tremendous profit without ever seeing them. It grew into a kind of gambling. Some became rich by it in a few days, and some lost everything they had. Land, houses, cattle and even clothing went for tulips when people had no ready money. Ladies sold their jewels and finery to enable them to join in the fun. Nothing else was thought of. At last the States-General interfered. People began to see what geese they were making of themselves, and down went the price of tulips. Old tulip debts couldn't be collected. Creditors went to law, and the law turned its back upon them; debts made in gambling were not binding, it said. Then there was a time! Thousands of rich speculators reduced to beggary in an hour. As old Beckman says, 'the bubble burst!"

"Yes, and a big bubble it was," said Ben, who had listened with great interest. "By the way, did you know that the name tulip came from a Turkish word signifying turban?"

"I had forgotten that," answered Lambert, "but it's a capital idea. Just fancy a party of Turks in full headgear, squatted upon a lawn—perfect tulip bed! Ha! ha! capital idea!"

["There," groaned Ludwig to himself, "he's been telling Lambert something wonderful about tulips—I knew it!"]

"The fact is," continued Lambert, "you can conjure up quite a human picture out of a tulip bed in bloom, especially when it is nodding and bobbing in the wind. Did you ever notice it?"

"Not I. It strikes me, Van Mounen, that you Hollanders are prodigiously fond of the flower to this day."

"Certainly. You can't have a garden without them; prettiest flower that grows, *I* think. My uncle has a magnificent bed of the finest varieties at his summerhouse on the other side of Amsterdam."

"I thought your uncle lived in the city?"

"So he does; but his summerhouse, or pavilion, is a few miles off. He has another one built out over the river. We passed near it when we entered the city. Everybody in Amsterdam has a pavilion somewhere, if he can."

"Do they ever live there?" asked Ben.

"Bless you, no! They are small affairs, suitable only to spend a few hours in on summer afternoons. There are some beautiful ones on the southern end of the Haarlem Lake—now that they've commenced to drain it into polders, it will spoil *that* fun. By the way, we've passed some red-roofed ones since we left home. You noticed them, I suppose, with their little bridges, and ponds and gardens, and their mottoes over the doorway."

"They make but little show, now," continued Lambert, "but in warm weather they are delightful. After the willows sprout, uncle goes to his summerhouse every afternoon. He dozes and smokes; aunt knits, with her feet perched upon a foot stove, never mind how hot the day; my cousin Rika and the other girls fish in the lake from the windows, or chat with their friends rowing by; and the youngsters tumble about, or hang upon the little bridges over the ditch. Then they have coffee and cakes; besides a great bunch of water lilies on the table—it's very fine, I can tell you; only (between ourselves), though I was born here, I shall never fancy the odor of stagnant water that hangs about most of the summerhouses. Nearly every one you see is built over a ditch. Probably I feel it more, from having lived so long in England."

"Perhaps I shall notice it, too," said Ben, "if a thaw comes. This early winter has covered up the fragrant waters for my benefit—much obliged to it. Holland without glorious skating wouldn't be the same thing to me at all."

"How very different you are from the Poots!" exclaimed Lambert, who had been listening in a sort of brown study, "and yet you are cousins—I cannot understand it."

"We *are* cousins, or rather we have always considered ourselves such, but the relationship is not very close. Our grandmothers were half sisters. *My* side of the family is entirely English, while his is entirely Dutch. Old Great-grandfather Poot married twice, you see, and I am a descendant of his English wife. I like Jacob, though, better than half of my English cousins put together. He is the truest-hearted, best-natured boy I ever knew. Strange as you may think it, my father became accidentally acquainted with Jacob's father while on a business visit to Rotterdam. They soon talked over their relationship—in French, by the way—and they have corresponded in that language ever since. Queer things come about in this world. My sister Jenny would open her eyes at some of Aunt Poot's ways. Aunt is a thorough lady, but so different from mother—and the house, too, and furniture, and way of living, everything is different."

"Of course," assented Lambert complacently—as if to say, "You could scarcely expect such general perfection anywhere else than in Holland"—"but you will have all the more to tell Jenny when you go back."

"Yes, indeed. I can say one thing—if cleanliness is, as they claim, next to godliness, Broek is safe. It is the cleanest place I ever saw in my life. Why, my Aunt Poot, rich as she is, scrubs half the time, and her house looks as if it were varnished all over. I wrote to mother yesterday that I could see my double always with me, feet to feet, in the polished floor of the dining room."

"Your *double!* that word puzzles me; what do you mean?"

"Oh, my reflection, my apparition. Ben Dobbs number two."

"Ah, I see," exclaimed Van Mounen. "Have you ever been in your Aunt Poot's grand parlor?"

Ben laughed. "Only once, and that was on the day of my arrival. Jacob says I shall have no chance of entering it again until the time of his sister Kenau's wedding, the week after Christmas. Father has consented that I shall remain to witness the great event. Every Saturday Aunt

Poot, and her fat Kate, go into that parlor and sweep, and polish, and scrub; then it is darkened and closed until Saturday comes again; not a soul enters it in the meantime; but the *schoonmaken,* as she calls it, must be done, just the same."

"That is nothing. Every parlor in Broek meets with the same treatment," said Lambert. "What do you think of these moving figures in her neighbor's garden?"

"Oh, they're well enough; the swans must seem really alive gliding about the pond in summer; but that nodding mandarin in the corner, under the chestnut trees, is ridiculous, only fit for children to laugh at. And then the stiff garden patches, and the trees all trimmed and painted. Excuse me, Van Mounen, but I shall never learn to admire Dutch taste."

"It will take time," answered Lambert condescendingly, "but you are sure to agree with it at last. I saw much to admire in England, and I hope I shall be sent back with you to study at Oxford; but take everything together, I like Holland best."

"Of course you do," said Ben, in a tone of hearty approval, "you wouldn't be a good Hollander if you didn't. Nothing like loving one's country. It is strange, though, to have such a warm feeling for such a cold place. If we were not exercising all the time we should freeze outright."

Lambert laughed.

"That's your English blood, Benjamin. *I'm* not cold. And look at the skaters here on the canal—they're red as roses, and happy as lords. Halloo! good Captain van Holp," called out Lambert in Dutch, "what say you to stopping at yonder farmhouse and warming our toes?"

"Who is cold?" asked Peter, turning around.

"Benjamin Dobbs."

"Benjamin Dobbs shall be warmed," and the party was brought to a halt.

XII
ON THE WAY TO HAARLEM

On approaching the door of the farmhouse the boys suddenly found themselves in the midst of a lively domestic scene. A burly Dutchman came rushing out, closely followed by his dear vrouw, and she was beating him smartly with a long-handled warming pan. The expression on her face gave our boys so little promise of a kind reception that they prudently resolved to carry their toes elsewhere to be warmed.

The next cottage proved to be more inviting. Its low roof of bright red tiles extended over the cow stable, that, clean as could be, nestled close to the main building. A neat, peaceful-looking old woman sat at one window, knitting. At the other could be discerned part of the profile of a fat figure that, pipe in mouth, sat behind the shining little panes and snowy curtain. In answer to Peter's subdued knock, a fair-haired, rosy-cheeked lass in holiday attire opened the upper half of the green door (which was divided across the middle) and inquired their errand.

"May we enter and warm ourselves, jufvrouw?" asked the captain respectfully.

"Yes, and welcome," was the reply, as the lower half of the door swung softly toward its mate. Every boy before entering rubbed long and faithfully upon the rough mat, and each made his best bow to the old lady and gentleman at the windows. Ben was half inclined to think that these personages were automata like the moving figures in the garden at Broek; for they both nodded their heads slowly, in precisely the same way, and both went on with their employment as steadily and stiffly as though they worked by machinery. The old man puffed, puffed, and his vrouw clicked her knitting needles, as if regulated by internal cogwheels. Even the real smoke issuing from the motionless pipe gave no convincing proof that they were human.

But the rosy-cheeked maiden. Ah! how she bustled about. How she gave the boys polished high-backed chairs to sit upon, how she made the fire blaze up as if it were inspired, how she made Jacob Poot almost weep for joy by bringing forth a great square of gingerbread and a stone jug of sour wine! How she laughed and nodded as the boys ate like wild animals on good behavior, and how blank she looked when Ben politely but firmly refused to take any black bread and sauerkraut! How she pulled off Jacob's mitten, which was torn at the thumb, and mended it before his eyes, biting off the thread with her white teeth, and saying, "Now it will be warmer," as she bit; and finally, how she shook hands with every boy in turn and (throwing a deprecating glance at the female automaton) insisted upon filling their pockets with gingerbread!

All this time the knitting needles clicked on, and the pipe never missed a puff.

When the boys were fairly on their way again, they came in sight of Zwanenburg Castle with its massive stone front, and its gateway towers, each surmounted with a sculptured swan.

"Halfweg,[1] boys," said Peter, "off with your skates."

"You see," explained Lambert to his companion, "the Y and the Haarlem Lake meeting here make it rather trouble-some. The river is five feet higher than the land—so we must have everything strong in the way of dykes and sluice

gates, or there would be wet work at once. The sluice ar-rangements here are supposed to be something extra—we will walk over them and you shall see enough to make you open your eyes. The spring water of the lake, they say, has the most wonderful bleaching powers of any in the world; all the great Haarlem bleacheries use it. I can't say much upon that subject—but I can tell you *one* thing from per-sonal experience."

"What is that?"

"Why, the lake is full of the biggest eels you ever saw—

[1] Halfway.

He sprang upon her

I've caught them here, often—perfectly prodigious! I tell you they're sometimes a match for a fellow; they'd almost wriggle your arm from the socket if you were not on your guard. But you're not interested in eels, I perceive. The castle's a big affair, isn't it?"

"Yes. What do those swans mean? Anything?" asked Ben, looking up at the stone gate towers.

"The swan is held almost in reverence by us Hollanders. These give the building its name, Zwanenburg—swan castle. That is all I know. This is a very important spot; for it is here that the wise ones hold council with regard to dyke matters. The castle was once the residence of the celebrated Christiaan Brünings."

"What about *him?*" asked Ben.

"Peter could answer you better than I," said Lambert, "if you could only understand each other, or were not such cowards about leaving your mother tongues. But I have often heard my grandfather speak of Brünings. He is never tired of telling us of the great engineer—how good he was, and how learned, and how when he died the whole country seemed to mourn as for a friend. He belonged to a great many learned societies, and was at the head of the State Department entrusted with the care of the dykes, and other defenses against the sea. There's no counting the improvements he made in dykes and sluices and water mills, and all that kind of thing. We Hollanders, you know, consider our great engineers as the highest of public benefactors. Brünings died years ago; they've a monument to his memory in the cathedral of Haarlem. I have seen his portrait, and I tell you, Ben, he was right noble-looking. No wonder the castle looks so stiff and proud. It is something to have given shelter to such a man!"

"Yes, indeed," said Ben. "I wonder, Van Mounen, whether you or I will ever give any old building a right to feel proud. Heigho! there's a great deal to be done yet in this world and some of us, who are boys now, will have to do it. Look to your shoe latchet, Van, it's unfastened."

XIII
A CATASTROPHE

It was nearly one o'clock when Captain van Holp and his command entered the grand old city of Haarlem. They had skated nearly seventeen miles since morning, and were still as fresh as young eagles. From the youngest (Ludwig van Holp, who was just fourteen) to the eldest, no less a personage than the captain himself, a veteran of seventeen, there was but one opinion—that this was the greatest frolic of their lives. To be sure, Jacob Poot had become rather short of breath, during the last mile or two, and perhaps he felt ready for another nap; but there was enough jollity in him yet for a dozen. Even Carl Schummel, who had become very intimate with Ludwig during the excursion, forgot to be ill-natured. As for Peter, he was the happiest of the happy, and had sung and whistled so joyously while skating that the staidest passers-by had smiled as they listened.

"Come, boys! it's nearly tiffin[1] hour," he said, as they neared a coffeehouse on the main street. "We must have something more solid than the pretty maiden's gingerbread"—and the captain plunged his hands into his pockets as if to say, "There's money enough here to feed an army!"

"Halloo!" cried Lambert, "what ails the man?"

Peter, pale and staring, was clapping his hands upon his breast and sides—he looked like one suddenly becoming deranged.

"He's sick!" cried Ben.

"No, he's lost something," said Carl.

Peter could only gasp, "The pocketbook, with all our money in it—it's gone!"

For an instant all were too much startled to speak.

Carl at last came out with a gruff——

"No sense in letting one fellow have all the money. I said so from the first. Look in your other pocket."

"I did—it isn't there."

"Open your underjacket——"

Peter obeyed mechanically. He even took off his hat and looked into it—then thrust his hand desperately into every pocket.

"It's gone, boys," he said at last, in a hopeless tone. "No tiffin for us, nor dinner either. What is to be done? We can't get on without money. If we were in Amsterdam I could get as much as we want, but there is not a man in Haarlem from whom I can borrow a stiver. Don't one of you know anyone here who would lend us a few guilders?"

Each boy looked into five blank faces. Then something like a smile passed around the circle, but it got sadly knotted up when it reached Carl.

"That wouldn't do," he said crossly. "I know some people here, rich ones, too, but father would flog me soundly, if I borrowed a cent from anyone. He has 'An honest man need not borrow," written over the gateway of his summerhouse."

[1] Lunch.

"Humph!" responded Peter, not particularly admiring the sentiment just at that moment.

The boys grew desperately hungry at once.

"It wash my fault," said Jacob, in a penitent tone, to Ben. "I say first, petter all de boys put zair pursh into Van Holp's monish."

"Nonsense, Jacob; you did it all for the best."

Ben said this in such a sprightly tone that the two Van Holps and Carl felt sure he had proposed a plan that would relieve the party at once.

"What? what? Tell us, Van Mounen," they cried.

"He says it is not Jacob's fault that the money is lost—that he did it for the best, when he proposed that Van Holp should put all of our money into his purse."

"Is that all?" said Ludwig dismally. "He need not have made such a fuss in just saying *that.* How much money have we lost?"

"Don't you remember?" said Peter. "We each put in exactly ten guilders. The purse had sixty guilders in it. I am the stupidest fellow in the world; little Schimmelpen-ninck would have made you a better captain. I could pom-mel myself for bringing such a disappointment upon you."

"Do it then," growled Carl. "Pooh," he added, "we all know it was an accident, but that doesn't help matters. We must have money, Van Holp—even if you have to sell your wonderful watch."

"Sell my mother's birthday present! Never! I will sell my coat, my hat, anything but my watch."

"Come, come," said Jacob pleasantly, "we are making too much of this affair. We can go home and start again in a day or two."

"*You* may be able to get another ten-guilder piece," said Carl, "but the rest of us will not find it so easy. If we go home, we stay home, you may depend."

Our captain, whose good nature had not yet forsaken him for a moment, grew indignant.

"Do you think I will let you suffer for my carelessness,"

he exclaimed. "I have three times sixty guilders in my strongbox at home!"

"Oh, I beg your pardon," said Carl hastily, adding in a surlier tone, "Well, I see no better way than to go back hungry."

"I see a better plan than that," said the captain.

"What is it?" cried all the boys.

"Why, to make the best of a bad business and go back pleasantly, and like men," said Peter, looking so gallant and handsome as he turned his frank face and clear blue eyes upon them that they caught his spirit.

"Ho! for the captain," they shouted.

"Now, boys, we may as well make up our minds there's no place like Broek, after all—and that we mean to be there in two hours—is that agreed to?"

"Agreed!" cried all, as they ran to the canal.

"On with your skates! Are you ready? Here, Jacob, let me help you."

"Now. One, two, three, start!"

And the boyish faces that left Haarlem at that signal were nearly as bright as those that had entered it with Captain Peter half an hour before.

XIV

HANS

DONDER and Blixin!" cried Carl angrily, before the party had skated twenty yards from the city gates, "if here isn't that wooden-skate ragamuffin in the patched leather breeches. That fellow is everywhere, confound him! We'll be lucky," he added, in as sneering a tone as he dared to assume, "if our captain doesn't order us to halt and shake hands with him."

"Your captain is a terrible fellow," said Peter pleasantly, "but this is a false alarm, Carl—I cannot spy your bugbear anywhere among the skaters. Ah! there he is! Why, what is the matter with the lad?"

Poor Hans! His face was pale, his lips compressed. He skated like one under the effects of a fearful dream. Just as he was passing, Peter hailed him:

"Good day, Hans Brinker!"

Hans' countenance brightened at once. "Ah! mynheer, is that you? It is well we meet!"

"Just like his impertinence," hissed Carl Schummel, darting scornfully past his companions, who seemed inclined to linger with their captain.

"I am glad to see you, Hans," responded Peter cheerily, "but you look troubled. Can I serve you?"

"I have a trouble, mynheer," answered Hans, casting down his eyes. Then lifting them again with almost a happy expression, he added, "But it is Hans who can help Mynheer van Holp *this* time."

"How?" asked Peter, making, in his blunt Dutch way, no attempt to conceal his surprise.

"By giving you *this,* mynheer"—and Hans held forth the missing purse.

"Hurrah!" shouted the boys, taking their cold hands from their pockets to wave them joyfully in the air. But Peter said "Thank you, Hans Brinker," in a tone that made Hans feel as if the king had knelt to him.

The shout of the delighted boys reached the muffled ears of the fine young gentleman who, under a full pressure of pent-up wrath, was skating toward Amsterdam. A Yankee boy would have wheeled about at once and hastened to satisfy his curiosity. But Carl only halted, and with his back toward his party wondered what on earth had happened. There he stood, immovable, until, feeling sure that nothing but the prospect of something to eat could have made them hurrah so heartily, he turned and skated slowly toward his excited comrades.

Meantime Peter had drawn Hans aside from the rest.

"How did you know it was my purse?" he asked.

"You paid me three guilders yesterday, mynheer, for making the whitewood chain, telling me that I must buy skates."

"Yes, I remember."

"I saw your purse then; it was of yellow leather."

"And where did you find it today?"

"I left my home this morning, mynheer, in great trouble, and as I skated, I took no heed until I stumbled against some lumber, and while I was rubbing my knee I saw your purse nearly hidden under a log."

"That place! Ah, I remember, now; just as we were passing it I pulled my tippet from my pocket, and probably flirted out the purse at the same time. It would have been gone but for you, Hans. Here"—pouring out the contents—"you must give us the pleasure of dividing the money with you."

"No, mynheer," answered Hans. He spoke quietly, without pretense or any grace of manner, but Peter, somehow, felt rebuked, and put the silver back without a word.

"I like that boy, rich or poor," he thought to himself, then added aloud, "May I ask about this trouble of yours, Hans?"

"Ah, mynheer, it is a sad case—but I have waited here too long. I am going to Leyden to see the great Dr. Boekman."

"Dr. Boekman!" exclaimed Peter in astonishment.

"Yes, mynheer, and I have not a moment to lose. Good day!"

"Stay, I am going that way. Come, my lads! Shall we return to Haarlem?"

"Yes," cried the boys eagerly—and off they started.

"Now," said Peter, drawing near Hans, both skimming the ice so easily and lightly as they skated on together that they seemed scarcely conscious of moving, "we are going to stop at Leyden, and if you are going there only with a message to Dr. Boekman, cannot I do the errand for you? The boys may be too tired to skate so far today, but I will promise to see him early tomorrow if he is to be found in the city."

"Ah, mynheer, that would be serving me indeed; it is not the distance I dread, but leaving my mother so long."

"Is she ill?"

"No, mynheer. It is the father. You may have heard it;

how he has been without wit for many a year—ever since the great Schlossen Mill was built; but his body has been well and strong. Last night the mother knelt upon the hearth to blow the peat (it is his only delight to sit and watch the live embers; and she will blow them into a blaze every hour of the day to please him). Before she could stir, he sprang upon her like a giant and held her close to the fire, all the time laughing and shaking his head. I was on the canal; but I heard the mother scream and ran to her. The father had never loosened his hold, and her gown was smoking. I tried to deaden the fire, but with one hand he pushed me off. There was no water in the cottage or I could have done better; and all that time he laughed—such a terrible laugh, mynheer; hardly a sound, but all in his face. I tried to pull her away, but that only made it worse. Then—it was dreadful, but could I see the mother burn? I beat him—beat him with a stool. He tossed me away. The gown was on fire! I *would* put it out. I can't remember well after that; I found myself upon the floor and the mother was praying. It seemed to me that she was in a blaze, and all the while I could hear that laugh. My sister Gretel screamed out that he was holding the mother close to the very coals. *I* could not tell! Gretel flew to the closet and filled a porringer with the food he liked, and put it upon the floor. Then, mynheer, he left the mother and crawled to it like a little child. She was not burnt, only a part of her clothing. Ah, how kind she was to him all night, watching and tending him. He slept in a high fever, with his hand pressed to his head. The mother says he has done that so much of late, as though he felt pain there. Ah, mynheer, I did not mean to tell you. If the father was himself, he would not harm even a kitten."

For a moment the two boys moved on in silence.

"It is terrible," said Peter at last. "How is he today?"

"Very sick, mynheer."

"Why go for Dr. Boekman, Hans? There are others in Amsterdam who could help him, perhaps. Boekman is a famous man, sought only by the wealthiest and they often wait upon him in vain."

"He *promised,* mynheer, he promised me yesterday to come to the father in a week. But now that the change has come, we cannot wait—we think the poor father is dying. Oh! mynheer, you can plead with him to come quick. He will not wait a whole week and our father dying, the good meester is so kind."

"So kind!" echoed Peter, in astonishment. "Why, he is known as the crossest man in Holland!"

"He looks so because he has no fat, and his head is busy, but his heart is kind, I know. Tell the meester what I have told you, mynheer, and he will come."

"I hope so, Hans, with all my heart. You are in haste to turn homeward, I see. Promise me that should you need a friend, you will go to my mother, at Broek. Tell her I bade you see her; and, Hans Brinker, not as a reward, but as a gift, take a few of these guilders."

Hans shook his head resolutely.

"No, no, mynheer. I cannot take it. If I could find work in Broek or at the South Mill I would be glad, but it is the same story everywhere—'Wait till spring.'"

"It is well you speak of it," said Peter eagerly, "for my father needs help at once. Your pretty chain pleased him much. He said, 'That boy has a clean cut; he would be good at carving.' There is to be a carved portal to our new summerhouse, and father will pay well for the job."

"God is good!" cried Hans in sudden delight. "Oh! mynheer, that would be too much joy. I have never tried big work—but I can do it—I know I can."

"Well, tell my father you are the Hans Brinker of whom I spoke. He will be glad to serve you."

Hans stared in honest surprise.

"Thank you, mynheer."

"Now, captain," shouted Carl, anxious to appear as good-humored as possible, by way of atonement, "here we are in the midst of Haarlem, and no word from you yet.

We await your orders, and we're as hungry as wolves."

Peter made a cheerful answer, and turned hurriedly to Hans.

"Come, get something to eat, and I will detain you no longer."

What a quick, wistful look Hans threw upon him! Peter wondered that he had not noticed before that the poor boy was hungry.

"Ah, mynheer, even now the mother may need me, the father may be worse—I must not wait. May God care for you"—and, nodding hastily, Hans turned his face homeward and was gone.

"Come, boys," sighed Peter, "now for our tiffin!"

XV

HOMES

It must not be supposed that our young Dutchmen had already forgotten the great skating race which was to take place on the twentieth. On the contrary, they had thought and spoken of it very often during the day. Even Ben, though he had felt more like a traveler than the rest, had never once, through all the sight-seeing, lost a certain vision of silver skates which, for a week past, had haunted him night and day.

Like a true "John Bull," as Jacob had called him, he never doubted that his English fleetness, English strength, English everything, could at any time enable him, on the ice, to put all Holland to shame, and the rest of the world, too, for that matter. Ben certainly was a superb skater. He had enjoyed not half the opportunities for practicing that had fallen to his new comrades; but he had improved his share to the utmost; and was, besides, so strong of frame, so supple of limb, in short, such a tight, trim, quick, graceful fellow in every way, that he had taken to skating as naturally as a chamois to leaping, or an eagle to soaring.

Only to the heavy heart of poor Hans had the vision of the silver skates failed to appear during that starry winter night and the brighter sunlit day.

Even Gretel had seen them flitting before her as she sat beside her mother through those hours of weary watching —not as prizes to be won, but as treasures passing hopelessly beyond her reach.

Rychie, Hilda and Katrinka—why, they had scarcely known any other thought than "The race! the race! It will come off on the twentieth!"

These three girls were friends. Though of nearly the same age, talent and station, they were as different as girls could be.

Hilda van Gleck you already know, a warmhearted, noble girl of fourteen. Rychie Korbes was beautiful to look upon, far more sparkling and pretty than Hilda, but not half so bright and sunny within. Clouds of pride, of discontent and envy had already gathered in her heart, and were growing bigger and darker every day. Of course these often relieved themselves very much after the manner of other clouds. But who saw the storms and the weeping? Only her maid, or her father, mother and little brother—those who loved her better than all. Like other clouds, too, hers often took queer shapes, and what was really but mist and vapory fancy assumed the appearance of monster wrongs and mountains of difficulty. To her mind, the poor peasant girl Gretel was not a human being, a God-created creature like herself—she was only something that meant poverty, rags and dirt. Such as Gretel had no right to feel, to hope; above all, they should never cross the paths of their betters—that is, not in a disagreeable way. They could toil and labor for them at a respectful distance, even admire them, if they would do it humbly, but nothing more. If they rebel, put them down; if they suffer, don't trouble me about it, was Rychie's secret motto. And yet how witty she was, how tastefully she dressed, how charmingly she sang; how much feeling she displayed (for pet kittens and rabbits), and how completely she could bewitch sensible, honest-minded lads like Lambert van Mounen and Ludwig van Holp!

Carl was too much like her, within, to be an earnest admirer, and perhaps he suspected the clouds. He, being deep and surly, and always uncomfortably in earnest, of course preferred the lively Katrinka, whose nature was made of a hundred tinkling bells. She was a coquette in her infancy, a coquette in her childhood, and now a coquette in her school days. Without a thought of harm, she coquetted with her studies, her duties, even her little troubles. They shouldn't know when they bothered her, not they. She coquetted with her mother, her pet lamb, her baby brother, even with her own golden curls—tossing them back as if she despised them. Everyone liked her, but who could love her? She was never in earnest. A pleasant face, a pleasant heart, a pleasant manner—these only satisfy for an hour. Poor, happy Katrinka! such as she tinkle, tinkle so merrily through their early days; but Life is so apt to coquette with them in turn, to put all their sweet bells out of tune, or to silence them one by one!

How different were the homes of these three girls from the tumbling old cottage where Gretel dwelt. Rychie lived in a beautiful house near Amsterdam, where the carved sideboards were laden with services of silver and gold, and where silken tapestries hung in folds from ceiling to floor.

Hilda's father owned the largest mansion in Broek. Its glittering roof of polished tiles, and its boarded front, painted in half a dozen various colors, were the admiration of the neighborhood.

Katrinka's home, not a mile distant, was the finest of Dutch countryseats. The garden was so stiffly laid out in little paths and patches that the birds might have mistaken it for a great Chinese puzzle with all the pieces spread out ready for use. But in summer it was beautiful; the flowers made the best of their stiff quarters, and, when the gardener was not watching, glowed and bent and twined about each other in the prettiest way imaginable. Such a tulip bed! Why, the Queen of the Fairies would never care for a grander city in which to hold her court! But Katrinka preferred the bed of pink and white hyacinths. She loved their freshness and fragrance, and the lighthearted way in which their bell-shaped blossoms swung in the breeze.

Carl was both right and wrong when he said that Katrinka and Rychie were furious at the very idea of the peasant Gretel joining in the race. He had heard Rychie declare it was "disgraceful, shameful, too bad!" which in Dutch, as in English, is generally the strongest expression an indignant girl can use; and he had seen Katrinka nod her pretty head, and heard her sweetly echo "shameful, too bad!" as nearly like Rychie as tinkling bells can be like the voice of real anger. That had satisfied him. He never suspected that had Hilda, not Rychie, first talked with Katrinka upon the subject, the bells would have jingled as willing an echo. She would have said, "Certainly, let her join us," and would have skipped off thinking no more about it. But *now* Katrinka with sweet emphasis pronounced it a shame that a goose-girl, a forlorn little creature like Gretel, should be allowed to spoil the race.

Rychie, being rich and powerful (in a schoolgirl way), had other followers, besides Katrinka, who were induced to share her opinions because they were either too careless or too cowardly to think for themselves.

Poor little Gretel! Her home was sad and dark enough now. Raff Brinker lay moaning upon his rough bed, and his vrouw, forgetting and forgiving everything, bathed his forehead, his lips, weeping and praying that he might not die. Hans, as we know, had started in desperation for Leyden to search for Dr. Boekman, and induce him, if possible, to come to their father at once. Gretel, filled with a strange dread, had done the work as well as she could, wiped the rough brick floor, brought peat to build up the slow fire, and melted ice for her mother's use. This accomplished, she seated herself upon a low stool near the bed, and begged her mother to try and sleep awhile.

"You are so tired," she whispered, "not once have you closed your eyes since that dreadful hour last night. See, I have straightened the willow bed in the corner, and spread everything soft upon it I could find, so that the mother might lie in comfort. Here is your jacket. Take off that pretty dress, I'll fold it away very carefully, and put it in the big chest before you go to sleep."

Dame Brinker shook her head without turning her eyes from her husband's face.

"I can watch, mother," urged Gretel, "and I'll wake you every time the father stirs. You are so pale, and your eyes are so red—oh, mother, *do!*"

The child pleaded in vain. Dame Brinker would not leave her post.

Gretel looked at her in troubled silence, wondering whether it were very wicked to care more for one parent than for the other—and sure, yes, quite sure, that she dreaded her father, while she clung to her mother with a love that was almost idolatry.

"Hans loves the father so well," she thought, "why cannot I? Yet I could not help crying when I saw his hand bleed that day, last month, when he snatched the knife—and now, when he moans, how I ache, ache all over. Perhaps I love him, after all, and God will see I am not such a bad, wicked girl as I thought. Yes, I love the poor father—almost as Hans does—not quite, for Hans is stronger and does not fear him. Oh, will that moaning go on forever and ever! Poor mother, how patient she is; *she* never pouts, as I do, about the money that went so strangely. If he only could, just for one instant, open his eyes and look at us, as Hans does, and tell us where mother's guilders went, I would not care for the rest. Yes, I would care; I don't want the poor father to die, to be all blue and cold like Annie Bouman's little sister—I *know* I don't. Dear God, I don't want father to die."

Her thoughts merged into a prayer. When it ended, the poor child scarcely knew. Soon she found herself watching a little pulse of light at the side of the fire, beating faintly but steadily, showing that somewhere in the dark pile there

was warmth and light that would overspread it at last. A large earthen cup filled with burning peat stood near the bedside; Gretel had placed it there to "stop the father's shivering," she said. She watched it as it sent a glow around the mother's form, tipping her faded skirt with light, and shedding a sort of newness over the threadbare bodice. It was a relief to Gretel to see the lines in that weary face soften as the firelight flickered gently across it.

Next she counted the windowpanes, broken and patched as they were; and finally, after tracing every crack and seam in the walls, fixed her gaze upon a carved shelf made by Hans. The shelf hung as high as Gretel could reach. It held a large leather-covered Bible, with brass clasps, a wedding present to Dame Brinker from the family at Heidelberg.

"Ah, how handy Hans is! If he were here he could turn the father some way so the moans would stop. Dear! dear! if this sickness lasts, we shall never skate any more. I must send my new skates back to the beautiful lady. Hans and I will not see the race," and Gretel's eyes, that had been dry before, grew full of tears.

"Never cry, child," said her mother soothingly. "This sickness may not be as bad as we think. The father has lain this way before."

Gretel sobbed now.

"Oh, mother, it is not that alone—you do not know all—I am very, very bad and wicked!"

"*You,* Gretel! you so patient and good!" and a bright, puzzled look beamed for an instant upon the child. "Hush, lovey, you'll wake him."

Gretel hid her face in her mother's lap, and tried not to cry.

Her little hand, so thin and brown, lay in the coarse palm of her mother's, creased with many a hard day's work. Rychie would have shuddered to touch either, yet they pressed warmly upon each other. Soon Gretel looked up with that dull, homely look which, they say, poor children in shanties are apt to have, and said in a trembling voice:

"The father tried to burn you—he did—I saw him, and he was *laughing!*"

"Hush, child!"

The mother's words came so suddenly and sharply that Raff Brinker, dead as he was to all that was passing round him, twitched slightly upon the bed.

Gretel said no more, but plucked drearily at the jagged edge of a hole in her mother's holiday gown. It had been burned there. Well for Dame Brinker that the gown was woolen.

XVI

HAARLEM—THE BOYS HEAR VOICES

REFRESHED and rested, our boys came forth from the coffeehouse just as the big clock in the square, after the manner of certain Holland timekeepers, was striking two with its half-hour bell for half past two.

The captain was absorbed in thought, at first, for Hans Brinker's sad story still echoed in his ears. Not until Ludwig rebuked him with a laughing "Wake up, grandfather!" did he reassume his position as gallant boy leader of his band.

"Ahem! this way, young gentlemen!"

They were walking through the streets of the city, not on a curbed *sidewalk,* for such a thing is rarely to be found in Holland, but on the brick pavement that lay on the borders of the cobblestone carriage way without breaking its level expanse.

Haarlem, like Amsterdam, was gayer than usual, in honor of Saint Nicholas.

A strange figure was approaching them. It was a small man dressed in black, with a short cloak; he wore a wig and a cocked hat from which a long crape streamer was flying.

"Who comes here?" cried Ben. "What a queer-looking object."

"That's the aanspreeker," said Lambert. "Someone is dead."

"Is that the way men dress in mourning in this country?"

"Oh, no! The aanspreeker attends funerals, and it is his business, when anyone dies, to notify all the friends and relatives."

"What a strange custom."

"Well," said Lambert, "we needn't feel very badly about this particular death, for I see another man has lately been born to the world to fill up the vacant place."

Ben stared. "How do you know that?"

"Don't you see that pretty red pincushion hanging on yonder door?" asked Lambert in return.

"Yes."

"Well, that's a boy."

"A boy! What do you mean?"

"I mean that here in Haarlem whenever a boy is born the parents have a red pincushion put out at the door. If our young friend had been a girl instead of a boy the cushion would have been white. In some places they have much more fanciful affairs, all trimmed with lace, and even among the very poorest houses you will see a bit of ribbon or even a string tied on the door latch——"

"Look!" almost screamed Ben, "there *is* a white cushion, at the door of that double-jointed house with the funny roof."

"I don't see any house with a funny roof."

"Oh, of course not," said Ben. "I forget you're a native;

but all the roofs are queer to me, for that matter. I mean the house next to that green building."

"True enough, there's a girl! I tell you what, captain," called out Lambert, slipping easily into Dutch, "we must get out of this street as soon as possible. It's full of babies! They'll set up a squall in a moment."

The captain laughed. "I shall take you to hear better music than that," he said. "We are just in time to hear the organ of St. Bavon. The church is open today."

"What, the great Haarlem organ?" asked Ben. "That will be a treat indeed. I have often read of it, with its tremendous pipes, and its vox humana[1] that sounds like a giant singing."

"The same," answered Lambert van Mounen.

Peter was right. The church was open, though not for religious services. Someone was playing upon the organ. As the boys entered, a swell of sound rushed forth to meet them. It seemed to bear them, one by one, into the shadows of the building.

Louder and louder it grew until it became like the din and roar of some mighty tempest, or like the ocean surging upon the shore. In the midst of the tumult a tinkling bell was heard; another answered, then another, and the storm paused as if to listen. The bells grew bolder; they rang out loud and clear. Other deep-toned bells joined in; they were tolling in solemn concert—ding, dong! ding, dong! The storm broke forth again with redoubled fury—gathering its distant thunder. The boys looked at each other, but did not speak. It was growing serious. What was that? *Who* screamed? *What* screamed—that terrible, musical scream? Was it man or demon? Or was it some monster shut up behind that carved brass frame—behind those great silver columns—some despairing monster begging, screaming for freedom? It was the Vox Humana!

At last an answer came—soft, tender, loving, like a mother's song. The storm grew silent; hidden birds sprang

[1] An organ stop which produces an effect resembling the human voice.

forth filling the air with glad, ecstatic music, rising higher and higher until the last faint note was lost in the distance.

The Vox Humana was stilled; but in the glorious hymn of thanksgiving that now arose one could almost hear the throbbing of a human heart. What did it mean? That man's imploring cry should in time be met with a deep content? That gratitude would give us freedom? To Peter and Ben it seemed that the angels were singing. Their eyes grew dim, and their souls dizzy with a strange joy. At last, as if borne upward by invisible hands, they were floating away on the music, all fatigue forgotten, and with no wish but to hear forever those beautiful sounds, when suddenly Van Holp's sleeve was pulled impatiently and a gruff voice beside him asked:

"How long are you going to stay here, captain, blinking at the ceiling like a sick rabbit? It's high time we started."

"Hush!" whispered Peter, only half aroused.

"Come, man! Let's go," said Carl, giving the sleeve a second pull.

Peter turned reluctantly; he would not detain the boys against their will. All but Ben were casting rather reproachful glances upon him.

"Well, boys," he whispered, "we will go. Softly now."

"That's the greatest thing I've seen or heard since I've been in Holland!" cried Ben enthusiastically, as soon as they reached the open air. "It's glorious!"

Ludwig and Carl laughed slyly at the English boy's *wartaal,* or gibberish; Jacob yawned; Peter gave Ben a look that made him instantly feel that he and Peter were not so very different after all, though one hailed from Holland and the other from England; and Lambert, the interpreter, responded with a brisk—

"You may well say so. I believe there are one or two organs nowadays that are said to be as fine; but for years and years this organ of St. Bavon was the grandest in the world."

"Do you know how large it is?" asked Ben. "I noticed that the church itself was prodigiously high and that the organ filled the end of the great aisle almost from floor to roof."

"That's true," said Lambert, "and how superb the pipes looked—just like grand columns of silver. They're only for show, you know; the *real* pipes are behind them, some big enough for a man to crawl through, and some smaller than a baby's whistle. Well, sir, for size, the church is higher than Westminster Abbey, to begin with, and, as you say, the organ makes a tremendous show even then. Father told me last night that it is one hundred and eight feet high, fifty feet broad, and has over five thousand pipes; it has sixty-four *stops,* if you know what they are, *I* don't—and three keyboards."

"Good for you!" said Ben. "You have a fine memory. *My* head is a perfect colander for figures; they slip through as fast as they're poured in. But other facts and historical events stay behind—that's some consolation."

"There we differ," returned Van Mounen. "I'm great on names and figures, but history, take it altogether, seems to me to be the most hopeless kind of jumble."

Meantime Carl and Ludwig were having a discussion concerning some square wooden monuments they had observed in the interior of the church. Ludwig declared that each bore the name of the person buried beneath, and Carl insisted that they had no names, but only the heraldic arms of the deceased painted on a black ground, with the date of the death in gilt letters.

"I ought to know," said Carl, "for I walked across to the east side, to look for the cannon ball which mother told me was embedded there. It was fired into the church, in the year fifteen hundred and something, by those rascally Spaniards, while the services were going on. There it was in the wall, sure enough, and while I was walking back I noticed the monuments. I tell you they haven't a sign of a name upon them."

"Ask Peter," said Ludwig, only half convinced.

"Carl is right," replied Peter, who, though conversing with Jacob, had overheard their dispute. "Well, Jacob, as I was saying, Handel the great composer chanced to visit Haarlem and of course he at once hunted up this famous organ. He gained admittance, and was playing upon it with all his might, when the regular organist chanced to enter the building. The man stood awestruck; he was a good player himself, but he had never heard such music before. 'Who is there?' he cried. 'If it is not an angel or the devil, it must be Handel!' When he discovered that it *was* the great musician, he was still more mystified! 'But how is this?' said he. 'You have done impossible things—no ten fingers on earth can play the passages you have given; human hands couldn't control all the keys and stops!' 'I know it,' said Handel coolly, 'and for that reason, I was forced to strike some notes with the end of my nose.' Donder! just think how the old organist must have stared!"

"Hey! What?" exclaimed Jacob, startled when Peter's animated voice suddenly became silent.

"Haven't you heard me, you rascal?" was the indignant rejoinder.

"Oh, yes—no—the fact is—I heard you at first. I'm awake now, but I do believe I've been walking beside you half asleep," stammered Jacob, with such a doleful, bewildered look on his face, that Peter could not help laughing.

XVII
THE MAN WITH FOUR HEADS

After leaving the church, the boys stopped near by, in the open market place, to look at the bronze statue of Laurens Janszoon Coster, who is believed by the Dutch to have been the inventor of printing. This is disputed by those who award the same honor to Johannes Gutenberg of Mayence; while many maintain that Faustus, a servant of Coster, stole his master's wooden types on a Christmas Eve, when the latter was at church, and fled with his booty, and his secret, to Mayence. Coster was a native of Haarlem, and the Hollanders are naturally anxious to secure the credit of the invention for their illustrious townsman. Certain it is that the first book he printed is kept by the city in a silver case wrapped in silk, and is shown with great caution as a most precious relic. It is said he first conceived the idea of printing from cutting his name upon the bark of a tree, and afterward pressing a piece of paper upon the characters.

Of course Lambert and his English friend fully discussed this subject. They also had a rather warm argument concerning another invention. Lambert declared that the honor of giving both the telescope and microscope to the world lay between Metius and Jansen, both Hollanders; while Ben as stoutly insisted that Roger Bacon, an English monk of the thirteenth century, "wrote out the whole thing, sir, perfect descriptions of microscopes and telescopes, too, long before either of those other fellows were born."

On one subject, however, they both agreed: that the art of curing and pickling herrings was discovered by William Beukles of Holland, and that the country did perfectly right in honoring him as a national benefactor, for its wealth and importance had been in a great measure due to its herring trade.

"It is astonishing," said Ben, "in what prodigious quantities those fish are found. I don't know how it is here, but on the coast of England, off Yarmouth, the herring shoals have been known to be six and seven feet deep with fish."

"That *is* prodigious, indeed," said Lambert, "but you know your word 'herring' is derived from the German *heer,* an army, on account of a way the fish have of coming in large numbers."

Soon afterward, while passing a cobbler's shop, Ben exclaimed:

"Halloo! Lambert, here is the name of one of your greatest men over a cobbler's stall! Boerhaave—if it were only Hermann Boerhaave instead of Hendrick, it would be complete."

Lambert knit his brows reflectively, as he replied:

"Boerhaave—Boerhaave—the name is perfectly familiar; I remember, too, he was born in 1668, but the rest is all gone, as usual. There have been so many famous Hollanders, you see, it is impossible for a fellow to know them all. What was he? Did he have two heads? Or was he one of your great, natural swimmers like Marco Polo?"

"He had *four* heads," answered Ben, laughing, "for he was a great physician, naturalist, botanist and chemist. I am full of him just now, for I read his life a few weeks ago."

"Pour out a little, then," said Lambert, "only walk faster, or we shall lose sight of the other boys."

"Well," resumed Ben, quickening his pace and looking with great interest at everything going on in the crowded street. "This Dr. Boerhaave was a great anspewker."

"A great *what?*" roared Lambert.

"Oh, I beg pardon. I was thinking of that man over there, with the cocked hat. He's an anspewker, isn't he?"

"Yes. He's an aanspreeker, if that is what you mean to say. But what about your friend with the four heads?"

"Well, as I was going to say, the doctor was left a penniless orphan at sixteen without education or friends."

"Jolly beginning!" interposed Lambert.

"Now don't interrupt. He was a poor friendless orphan at sixteen, but he was so persevering and industrious, so determined to gain knowledge, that he made his way, and in time became one of the most learned men of Europe. All the—— What is that?"

"Where? What do you mean?"

"Why, that paper on the door opposite. Don't you see? Two or three persons are reading it; I have noticed several of these papers since I've been here."

"Oh, that's only a health bulletin. Somebody in the house is ill, and to prevent a steady knocking at the door, the family write an account of the patient's condition on a placard, and hang it outside the door, for the benefit of inquiring friends—a very sensible custom, I'm sure. Nothing strange about it that I can see. Go on, please. You said 'All the'—and there you left me hanging."

"I was going to say," resumed Ben, "that all the—all the —how comically persons do dress here, to be sure! Just look at those men and women with their sugar-loaf hats—

and see this woman ahead of us with a straw bonnet like a scoop shovel tapering to a point in the back. Did ever you see anything so funny? And those tremendous wooden shoes, too—I declare she's a beauty!"

"Oh, they are only back-country folk," said Lambert, rather impatiently. "You might as well let old Boerhaave drop, or else shut your eyes."

"Ha! ha! Well, I was *going* to say—all the big men of his day sought out this great professor. Even Peter the Great when he came over to Holland from Russia to learn shipbuilding, attended his lectures regularly. By that time Boerhaave was professor of Medicine and Chemistry and Botany in the University of Leyden. He had grown to be very wealthy as a practicing physician; but he used to say that the poor were his best patients because God would be their paymaster. All Europe learned to love and honor him. In short, he became so famous that a certain mandarin of China addressed a letter to 'The illustrious Boerhaave, physician in Europe,' and the letter found its way to him without any difficulty."

"My goodness! That is what I call being a public character. The boys have stopped. How now, Captain van Holp, what next?"

"We propose to move on," said Van Holp. "There is nothing to see at this season in the Bosch. The Bosch is a noble wood, Benjamin, a grand park where they have most magnificent trees, protected by law. Do you understand?"

"Ya!" nodded Ben, as the captain proceeded——

"Unless you all desire to visit the Museum of Natural History, we may go on the grand canal again. If we had more time it would be pleasant to take Benjamin up the Blue Stairs."

"What are the Blue Stairs, Lambert?" asked Ben.

"They are the highest point of the Dunes. You have a grand view of the ocean from there, besides a fine chance to see how wonderful these Dunes are. One can hardly believe that the wind could ever heap up sand in so remarkable a way. But we have to go through Bloemendal to get there—not a very pretty village, and some distance from here. What do you say?"

"Oh, I am ready for anything. For my part, I would rather steer direct for Leyden, but we'll do as the captain says—hey, Jacob?"

"Ya, dat ish goot," said Jacob, who felt decidedly more like taking another nap than ascending the Blue Stairs.

The captain was in favor of going to Leyden.

"It's four long miles from here. (Full sixteen of your English miles, Benjamin.) We have no time to lose if you wish to reach there before midnight. Decide quickly, boys —Blue Stairs or Leyden?"

"Leyden," they answered, and were out of Haarlem in a twinkling, admiring the lofty, towerlike windmills and pretty countryseats as they left the city behind them.

"If you really wish to see Haarlem," said Lambert to Ben, after they had skated awhile in silence, "you should visit it in summer. It is the greatest place in the world for beautiful flowers. The walks around the city are superb; and the 'Wood' with its miles of noble elms, all in full feather, is something to remember. You need not smile, old fellow, at my saying 'full feather'—I was thinking of waving plumes, and got my words mixed up a little. But a Dutch elm beats everything; it is the noblest tree on earth, Ben—if you except the English oak."

"Aye," said Ben solemnly, "*if* you except the English oak"—and for some moments he could scarcely see the canal because Robby and Jenny kept bobbing in the air before his eyes.

XVIII
FRIENDS IN NEED

MEANTIME, the other boys were listening to Peter's account of an incident which had long ago occurred [1] in a part of the city where stood an ancient castle, whose lord had tyrannized over the burghers of the town to such an extent that they surrounded his castle and laid siege to it. Just at the last extremity, when the haughty lord felt that he could hold out no longer, and was preparing to sell his life as dearly as possible, his lady appeared on the ramparts and offered to surrender everything, provided she was permitted to bring out, and retain, as much of her most precious household goods as she could carry upon her back. The promise was given, and forth came the lady from the gateway bearing her husband upon her shoulders. The burghers' pledge preserved him from the fury of the troops, but left them free to wreak their vengeance upon the castle.

[1] Sir Thomas Carr's Tour through Holland.

"Do you *believe* that story, Captain Peter?" asked Carl, in an incredulous tone.

"Of course, I do; it is historical. Why should I doubt it?"

"Simply because no woman could do it—and, if she could, she wouldn't. That is *my* opinion."

"And *I* believe there are many who *would*. That is, to save anyone they really cared for," said Ludwig.

Jacob, who in spite of his fat and sleepiness, was of rather a sentimental turn, had listened with deep interest.

"That is right, little fellow," he said, nodding his head approvingly. "I believe every word of it. I shall never marry a woman who would not be glad to do as much for *me*."

"Heaven help her!" cried Carl, turning to gaze at the speaker. "Why, Poot, three *men* couldn't do it!"

"Perhaps not," said Jacob quietly, feeling that he had asked rather too much of the future Mrs. Poot. "But she must be *willing*, that is all."

"Aye," responded Peter's cheery voice, "willing heart makes nimble foot—and who knows, but it may make strong arms also."

"Pete," asked Ludwig, changing the subject, "did you tell me last night that the painter Wouwerman was born in Haarlem?"

"Yes, and Jacob Ruysdael and Berghem too. I like Berghem because he was always good-natured—they say he always sang while he painted, and though he died nearly two hundred years ago, there are traditions still afloat concerning his pleasant laugh. He was a great painter, and he had a wife as cross as Xantippe."

"They balanced each other finely," said Ludwig, "he was kind and she was cross. But, Peter, before I forget it, wasn't that picture of St. Hubert and the Horse painted by Wouwerman? You remember father showed us an engraving from it last night."

"Yes, indeed; there is a story connected with that picture."

"Tell us!" cried two or three, drawing closer to Peter as they skated on.

"Wouwerman," began the captain oratorically, "was born in 1620, just four years before Berghem. He was a master of his art, and especially excelled in painting horses. Strange as it may seem, people were so long finding out his merits that, even after he had arrived at the height of his excellence, he was obliged to sell his pictures for very paltry prices. The poor artist became completely discouraged, and, worse than all, was over head and ears in debt. One day he was talking over his troubles with his father-confessor, who was one of the few who recognized his genius. The priest determined to assist him, and accordingly lent him six hundred guilders, advising him at the same time to demand a better price for his pictures. Wouwerman did so, and in the meantime paid his debts. Matters brightened with him at once. Everybody appreciated the great artist who painted such costly pictures. He grew rich. The six hundred guilders were returned, and in gratitude Wouwerman sent also a work which he had painted, representing his benefactor as St. Hubert kneeling before his horse—the very picture, Ludwig, of which we were speaking last night."

"So! so!" exclaimed Ludwig, with deep interest. "I must take another look at the engraving as soon as we get home."

At that same hour, while Ben was skating with his companions beside the Holland dyke, Robby and Jenny stood in their pretty English schoolhouse, ready to join in the duties of their reading class.

"Commence! Master Robert Dobbs," said the teacher, "page 242. Now, sir, mind every stop."

And Robby, in a quick childish voice, roared forth at schoolroom pitch:

"LESSON 62. THE HERO OF HAARLEM

"Many years ago, there lived in Haarlem, one of the principal cities of Holland, a sunny-haired boy, of gentle

Haarlem shall not be drowned

disposition. His father was a *sluicer,* that is, a man whose business it was to open and close the sluices, or large oaken gates, that are placed at regular distances across the entrances of the canals to regulate the amount of water that shall flow into them.

"The sluicer raises the gates more or less according to the quantity of water required, and closes them carefully at night, in order to avoid all possible danger of an oversupply running into the canal, or the water would soon overflow it and inundate the surrounding country. As a great portion of Holland is lower than the level of the sea, the waters are kept from flooding the land only by means of strong dykes, or barriers, and by means of these sluices, which are often strained to the utmost by the pressure of the rising tides. Even the little children in Holland know that constant watchfulness is required to keep the rivers and ocean from overwhelming the country, and that a moment's neglect of the sluicer's duty may bring ruin and death to all."

["Very good," said the teacher. "Now, Susan."]

"One lovely autumn afternoon, when the boy was about eight years old, he obtained his parents' consent to carry some cakes to a blind man who lived out in the country, on the other side of the dyke. The little fellow started on his errand with a light heart, and having spent an hour with his grateful old friend, he bade him farewell and started on his homeward walk.

"Trudging stoutly along by the canal, he noticed how the autumn rains had swollen the waters. Even while humming his careless, childish song, he thought of his father's brave old gates and felt glad of their strength, for thought he, 'if *they* gave way, where would father and mother be? These pretty fields would be all covered with the angry waters—father always calls them the *angry* waters; I suppose he thinks they are mad at him for keeping them out so long.' And with these thoughts just flitting across his brain, the little fellow stooped to pick the pretty blue flowers that grew along his way. Sometimes he stopped to throw some feathery seed ball in the air, and watch it as it floated away; sometimes he listened to the stealthy rustling of a rabbit, speeding through the grass, but oftener he smiled as he recalled the happy light he had seen arise on the weary, listening face of his blind old friend."

["Now, Henry," said the teacher, nodding to the next little reader.]

"Suddenly the boy looked around him in dismay. He had not noticed that the sun was setting: now he saw that his long shadow on the grass had vanished. It was growing dark, he was still some distance from home, and in a lonely ravine, where even the blue flowers had turned to gray. He quickened his footsteps; and with a beating heart recalled many a nursery tale of children belated in dreary forests. Just as he was bracing himself for a run, he was startled by the sound of trickling water. Whence did it come? He looked up and saw a small hole in the dyke through which a tiny stream was flowing. Any child in Holland will shudder at the thought of *a leak in the dyke!* The boy understood the danger at a glance. That little hole, if the water were allowed to trickle through, would soon be a large one, and a terrible inundation would be the result.

"Quick as a flash, he saw his duty. Throwing away his flowers, the boy clambered up the heights, until he reached the hole. His chubby little finger was thrust in, almost before he knew it. The flowing was stopped! 'Ah!' he thought, with a chuckle of boyish delight, 'the angry waters must stay back now! Haarlem shall not be drowned while *I* am here!'

"This was all very well at first, but the night was falling rapidly. Chill vapors filled the air. Our little hero began to tremble with cold and dread. He shouted loudly; he screamed 'Come here! come here!' but no one came. The cold grew more intense, a numbness, commencing in the tired little finger, crept over his hand and arm, and soon his whole body was filled with pain. He shouted again, 'Will no one come? Mother! mother!' Alas, his mother, good, practical soul, had already locked the doors, and had fully resolved to scold him on the morrow for spending the night with blind Jansen without her permission. He tried to whistle. Perhaps some straggling boy might heed the signal; but his teeth chattered so, it was impossible. Then he called on God for help; and the answer came, through a holy resolution—'I will stay here till morning.' "

["Now, Jenny Dobbs," said the teacher. Jenny's eyes were glistening, but she took a long breath and commenced:]

"The midnight moon looked down upon that small solitary form, sitting upon a stone, halfway up the dyke. His head was bent but he was not asleep, for every now and then one restless hand rubbed feebly the outstretched arm that seemed fastened to the dyke—and often the pale, tearful face turned quickly at some real or fancied sounds.

"How can we know the sufferings of that long and fearful watch—what falterings of purpose, what childish terrors came over the boy as he thought of the warm little bed at home, of his parents, his brothers and sisters, then looked into the cold, dreary night!

"If he drew away that tiny finger, the angry waters, grown angrier still, would rush forth, and never stop until they had swept over the town. No, he would hold it there till daylight—if he lived! He was not very sure of living. What did this strange buzzing mean? and then the knives that seemed pricking and piercing him from head to foot? He was not certain now that he could draw his finger away, even if he wished to.

"At daybreak a clergyman, returning from the bedside of a sick parishioner, thought he heard groans as he walked along on the top of the dyke. Bending, he saw, far down on the side, a child apparently writhing with pain.

" 'In the name of wonder, boy,' he exclaimed, 'what are you doing there?'

" 'I am keeping the water from running out," was the simple answer of the little hero. 'Tell them to come quick.'

"It is needless to add that they did come quickly and that——"

["Jenny Dobbs," said the teacher, rather impatiently, "if you cannot control your feelings so as to read distinctly, we will wait until you recover yourself."

"Yes, sir!" said Jenny, quite startled.]

It was strange; but at that very moment, Ben, far over the sea, was saying to Lambert:

"The noble little fellow! I have frequently met with an account of the incident, but I never knew, till now, that it was really true."

"True! Of course it is," said Lambert, kindling. "I have given you the story just as mother told it to me, years ago. Why, there is not a child in Holland who does not know it. And, Ben, you may not think so, but that little boy represents the spirit of the whole country. Not a leak can show itself anywhere either in its politics, honor, or public safety, that a million fingers are not ready to stop it, at any cost."

"Whew!" cried Master Ben, "big talking that!"

"It's *true* talk anyway," rejoined Lambert, so very quietly that Ben wisely resolved to make no further comment.

XIX
ON THE CANAL

THE skating season had commenced unusually early; our boys were by no means alone upon the ice. The afternoon was so fine that men, women, and children, bent upon enjoying the holiday, had flocked to the grand canal from far and near. Saint Nicholas had evidently remembered the favorite pastime; shining new skates were everywhere to be seen. Whole families were skimming their way to Haarlem or Leyden or the neighboring villages. The ice seemed fairly alive. Ben noticed the erect, easy carriage of the women, and their picturesque variety of costume. There were the latest fashions, fresh from Paris, floating past dingy, moth-eaten garments that had seen service through two generations; coal-scuttle bonnets perched over freckled faces bright with holiday smiles; stiff muslin caps, with wings at the sides, flapping beside cheeks rosy with health and contentment; furs, too, encircling the whitest of throats; and scanty garments fluttering below faces ruddy with exercise. In short, every quaint and comical mixture of dry goods and flesh that Holland could furnish seemed sent to enliven the scene.

There were belles from Leyden, and fishwives from the border villages; cheese women from Gouda, and prim matrons from beautiful countryseats on the Haarlemmer Meer. Gray-headed skaters were constantly to be seen; wrinkled old women, with baskets upon their heads; and plump little toddlers on skates clutching at their mother's gowns. Some women carried their babies upon their backs, firmly secured with a bright shawl. The effect was pretty and graceful as they darted by, or sailed slowly past, now nodding to an acquaintance, now chirruping, and throwing soft baby talk to the muffled little ones they carried.

Boys and girls were chasing each other, and hiding behind the one-horse sleds that, loaded high with peat or timber, pursued their cautious way along the track marked out as "safe." Beautiful, queenly women were there, enjoyment sparkling in their quiet eyes. Sometimes a long file of young men, each grasping the coat of the one before him, flew by with electric speed; and sometimes the ice squeaked under the chair of some gorgeous old dowager, or rich burgomaster's lady, who, very red in the nose, and sharp in the eyes, looked like a scare-thaw invented by old Father Winter for the protection of his skating grounds. The chair would be heavy with foot stoves and cushions, to say nothing of the old lady. Mounted upon shining runners it slid along, pushed by the sleepiest of servants, who, looking neither to the right nor the left, bent himself to his task while she cast direful glances upon the screaming little rowdies who invariably acted as bodyguard.

As for the men, they were pictures of placid enjoyment. Some were attired in ordinary citizen's dress; but many looked odd enough with their short woolen coats, wide breeches, and big silver buckles. These seemed to Ben like little boys who had, by a miracle, sprung suddenly into manhood, and were forced to wear garments that their astonished mothers had altered in a hurry. He noticed, too, that nearly all the men had pipes, as they passed him whizzing and smoking like so many locomotives. There was every variety of pipes from those of common clay to the most expensive meerschaums mounted in silver and gold. Some were carved into extraordinary and fantastic shapes, representing birds, flowers, heads, bugs, and dozens of other things; some resembled the "Dutchman's pipe" that grows in our American woods; some were red, and many were of a pure snowy white; but the most respectable were those which were ripening into a shaded brown. The deeper and richer the brown, of course the more honored the pipe, for it was a proof that the owner, if honestly shading it, was deliberately devoting his manhood to the effort. What pipe would not be proud to be the object of such a sacrifice!

For a while, Ben skated on in silence. There was so much to engage his attention that he almost forgot his companions. Part of the time he had been watching the ice-boats as they flew over the great Haarlemmer Meer (or Lake), the frozen surface of which was now plainly visible from the canal. These boats had very large sails, much larger, in proportion, than those of ordinary vessels, and were set upon a triangular frame furnished with an iron "runner" at each corner—the widest part of the triangle crossing the bow, and its point stretching beyond the stern. They had rudders for guiding, and brakes for arresting their progress; and were of all sizes and kinds, from small, rough affairs managed by a boy, to large and beautiful ones filled with gay pleasure parties, and manned by competent sailors, who, smoking their stumpy pipes, reefed and tacked and steered with great solemnity and precision.

Some of the boats were painted and gilded in gaudy style and flaunted gay pennons from their mastheads; others white as snow, with every spotless sail rounded by the wind, looked like swans borne onward by a resistless current. It seemed to Ben as, following his fancy, he watched one of these in the distance, that he could almost hear its helpless, terrified cry, but he soon found that the sound arose from a nearer and less romantic cause—from an iceboat not fifty yards from him, using its brakes to avoid a collision with a peat sled.

It was a rare thing for these boats to be upon the canal and their appearance generally caused no little excitement among skaters, especially among the timid; but today every iceboat in the country seemed afloat or rather aslide, and the canal had its full share.

Ben, though delighted at the sight, was often startled at the swift approach of the resistless, high-winged things threatening to dart in any and every possible direction. It required all his energies to keep out of the way of the passers-by, and to prevent those screaming little urchins from upsetting him with their sleds. Once he halted to watch some boys who were making a hole in the ice preparatory to using their fishing spears. Just as he concluded to start again, he found himself suddenly bumped into an old lady's lap. Her push-chair had come upon him from the rear. The old lady screamed, the servant who was propelling her gave a warning hiss. In another instant Ben found himself apologizing to empty air; the indignant old lady was far ahead.

This was a slight mishap compared with one that now threatened him. A huge iceboat, under full sail, came tearing down the canal, almost paralyzing Ben with the thought of instant destruction. It was close upon him! He saw its gilded prow, heard the schipper shout, felt the great boom fairly whiz over his head, was blind, deaf and dumb all in an instant, then opened his eyes, to find himself spinning some yards behind its great, skatelike rudder. It had passed within an inch of his shoulder, but he was safe! safe so see England again, safe to kiss the dear faces that for an instant had flashed before him one by one—father, mother, Robby and Jenny—that great boom had dashed their images into his very soul. He knew now how much he loved them. Perhaps this knowledge made him face complacently the scowls of those on the canal who seemed to feel that a boy in danger was necessarily a *bad* boy needing instant reprimand.

Lambert chided him roundly.

"I thought it was over with you, you careless fellow! Why don't you look where you are going? Not content with sitting on all the old ladies' laps, you must make a Juggernaut of every iceboat that comes along. We shall have to hand you over to the aanspreekers yet, if you don't look out!"

"Please don't," said Ben, with mock humility; then, seeing how pale Lambert's lips were, added in a low tone:

"I do believe I *thought* more in that one moment, Van Mounen, than in all the rest of my past life."

There was no reply, and, for a while, the two boys skated on in silence.

Soon a faint sound of distant bells reached their ears.

"Hark!" said Ben. "What is that?"

"The carillons," replied Lambert. "They are trying the bells in the chapel of yonder village. Ah! Ben, you should hear the chimes of the 'New Church' at Delft; they are superb—nearly five hundred sweet-toned bells, and one of the best carillonneurs of Holland to play upon them. Hard work, though; they say the fellow often has to go to bed from positive exhaustion, after his performances. You see, the bells are attached to a kind of keyboard, something like they have on pianofortes; there is also a set of pedals for the feet. When a brisk tune is going on, the player looks like a kicking frog fastened to his seat with a skewer."

"For shame," said Ben indignantly.

Peter had, for the present, exhausted his stock of Haarlem anecdotes, and now, having nothing to do but to skate, he and his three companions were hastening to "catch up" with Lambert and Ben.

"That English lad is fleet enough," said Peter. "If he were a born Hollander he could do no better. Generally these John Bulls make but a sorry figure on skates. Halloo!

Here you are, Van Mounen; why, we hardly hoped for the honor of meeting you again. Whom were you flying from in such haste?"

"Snails," retorted Lambert. "What kept you?"

"We have been talking; and, besides, we halted once to give Poot a chance to rest."

"He begins to look rather worn out," said Lambert in a low voice.

Just then a beautiful iceboat with reefed sail, and flying streamers, swept leisurely by. Its deck was filled with children muffled up to their chins. Looking at them from the ice you could see only smiling little faces imbedded in bright-colored, woolen wrappings.

They were singing a chorus in honor of Saint Nicholas. The music, starting in the discord of a hundred childish voices, floated, as it rose, into exquisite harmony:

"Friend of sailors, and of children!
  Double claim have we,
As in youthful joy we're sailing,
  O'er a frozen sea!
        Nicholas! Saint Nicholas!
          Let us sing to thee!

While through wintry air we're rushing,
  As our voices blend,
Are you near us? Do you hear us,
  Nicholas, our friend?
        Nicholas! Saint Nicholas!
          Love can never end!

Sunny sparkles, bright before us,
  Chase away the cold!
Hearts where sunny thoughts are welcome,
  Never can grow old.
        Nicholas! Saint Nicholas!
          Never can grow old!

Pretty gift and loving lesson,
  Festival and glee,
Bid us thank thee as we're sailing
  O'er the frozen sea.
        Nicholas! Saint Nicholas!
          So we sing to thee!"

XX
JACOB POOT CHANGES THE PLAN

THE last note died away in the distance. Our boys, who in their vain efforts to keep up with the boat had felt that they were skating backward, turned to look at one another.

"How beautiful that was!" exclaimed Van Mounen.

"Just like a dream!" said Ludwig.

Jacob drew close to Ben, giving his usual approving nod, as he spoke: "Dat ish goot. Dat ish te pest vay. *I* shay petter to take to Leyden mit a poat!"

"Take a boat!" exclaimed Ben, in dismay. "Why, man, our plan was to *skate*, not to be carried like little children."

"Tuyfels!" retorted Jacob, "dat ish no little—no papies—to go for poat!"

The boys laughed, but exchanged uneasy glances. It

would be great fun to jump on an iceboat, if they had a chance; but to abandon so shamefully their grand undertaking—who could think of such a thing?

An animated discussion arose at once.

Captain Peter brought his party to a halt.

"Boys," said he, "it strikes me that we should consult Jacob's wishes in this matter. He started the excursion, you know."

"Pooh!" sneered Carl, throwing a contemptuous glance at Jacob. "Who's tired? We can rest all night at Leyden."

Ludwig and Lambert looked anxious and disappointed. It was no slight thing to lose the credit of having skated all the way from Broek to The Hague, and back again; but both agreed that Jacob should decide the question.

Good-natured, tired Jacob! He read the popular sentiment at a glance.

"Oh! no," he said, in Dutch. "I was joking. We will skate, of course."

The boys gave a delighted shout, and started on again with renewed vigor.

All but Jacob. He tried his best not to seem fatigued, and, by not saying a word, saved his breath and energy for the great business of skating. But in vain. Before long, the stout body grew heavier and heavier—the tottering limbs weaker and weaker. Worse than all, the blood, anxious to get far as possible from the ice, mounted to the puffy, good-natured cheeks, and made the roots of his thin, yellow hair glow into a fiery red.

This kind of work is apt to summon Vertigo, of whom good Hans Andersen writes—the same who hurls daring young hunters from the mountains, or spins them from the sharpest heights of the glaciers, or catches them as they tread the steppingstones of the mountain torrent.

Vertigo came, unseen, to Jacob. After tormenting him awhile, with one touch sending a chill from head to foot, with the next scorching every vein with fever, she made the canal rock and tremble beneath him, the white sails bow and spin as they passed, then cast him heavily upon the ice.

"Halloo!" cried Van Mounen. "There goes Poot!"

Ben sprang hastily forward.

"Jacob! Jacob, are you hurt?"

Peter and Carl were lifting him. The face was white enough now. It seemed like a dead face—even the good-natured look was gone.

A crowd collected. Peter unbuttoned the poor boy's jacket, loosened his red tippet, and blew between the parted lips.

"Stand off, good people!" he cried. "Give him air!"

"Lay him down," called out a woman from the crowd.

"Stand him upon his feet," shouted another.

"Give him wine," growled a stout fellow who was driving a loaded sled.

"Yes! yes, give him wine!" echoed everybody.

Ludwig and Lambert shouted in concert:

"Wine! wine! Who has wine?"

A sleepy-eyed Dutchman began to fumble mysteriously under the heaviest of blue jackets, saying as he did so:

"Not so much noise, young masters, not so much noise! The boy was a fool to faint off like a girl."

"Wine, quick!" cried Peter, who, with Ben's help, was rubbing Jacob from head to foot.

Ludwig stretched forth his hand imploringly toward the Dutchman, who with an air of great importance was still fumbling beneath the jacket.

"*Do* hurry! He will die! Has anyone else any wine?"

"He *is* dead!" said an awful voice from among the bystanders. This startled the Dutchman.

"Have a care!" he said, reluctantly drawing forth a small blue flask. "This is schnapps. A little is enough."

A little *was* enough. The paleness gave way to a faint flush. Jacob opened his eyes, and, half bewildered, half ashamed, feebly tried to free himself from those who were supporting him.

There was no alternative, now, for our party but to have their exhausted comrade carried, in some way, to Leyden. As for expecting him to skate any more that day, the thing was impossible. In truth, by this time each boy began to entertain secret yearnings toward iceboats, and to avow a Spartan resolve not to desert Jacob. Fortunately a gentle, steady breeze was setting southward. If some accommodating schipper [1] would but come along, matters would not be quite so bad after all.

Peter hailed the first sail that appeared; the men in the stern would not even look at him. Three drays on runners came along, but they were already loaded to the utmost. Then an iceboat, a beautiful, tempting little one, whizzed past like an arrow. The boys had just time to stare eagerly at it when it was gone. In despair, they resolved to prop up Jacob with their strong arms, as well as they could, and take him to the nearest village.

At that moment a very shabby iceboat came in sight. With but little hope of success, Peter hailed it, at the same time taking off his hat and flourishing it in the air.

The sail was lowered, then came the scraping sound of the brake, and a pleasant voice called out from the deck:

"What now?"

"Will you take us on?" cried Peter, hurrying with his companions as fast as he could, for the boat was "bringing to" some distance ahead. "Will you take us on?"

"We'll pay for the ride!" shouted Carl.

The man on board scarcely noticed him except to mutter something about its not being a trekschuit. Still looking toward Peter he asked:

"How many?"

"Six."

"Well, it's Nicholas' Day—up with you! Young gentleman sick?" He nodded toward Jacob.

"Yes—broken down—skated all the way from Broek," answered Peter. "Do you go to Leyden?"

[1] Skipper. Master of a small trading vessel—a pleasure boat or iceboat.

"That's as the wind says. It's blowing that way now. Scramble up!"

Poor Jacob! if that willing Mrs. Poot had only appeared just then, her services would have been invaluable. It was as much as the boys could do to hoist him into the boat. All were in at last. The schipper, puffing away at his pipe, let out the sail, lifted the brake, and sat in the stern with folded arms.

"Whew! How fast we go!" cried Ben. "This is something like! Feel better, Jacob?"

"Much petter, I tanks you."

"Oh, you'll be as good as new in ten minutes. This makes a fellow feel like a bird."

Jacob nodded, and blinked his eyes.

"Don't go to sleep, Jacob; it's too cold. You might never wake up, you know. Persons often freeze to death in that way."

"I no sleep," said Jacob confidently, and in two minutes he was snoring.

Carl and Ludwig laughed.

"We must wake him!" cried Ben. "It is dangerous, I tell you. Jacob! Ja-a-c——"

Captain Peter interfered, for three of the boys were helping Ben for the fun of the thing.

"Nonsense! don't shake him! Let him alone, boys. One never snores like that when one's freezing. Cover him up with something. Here, this cloak will do. Hey, schipper?" and he looked toward the stern for permission to use it.

The man nodded.

"There," said Peter, tenderly adjusting the garment, "let him sleep. He will be frisky as a lamb when he wakes. How far are we from Leyden, schipper?"

"Not more'n a couple of pipes," replied a voice, rising from smoke like the genii in fairy tales (puff! puff!). "Likely not more'n one an' a half (puff! puff!) if this wind holds" (puff! puff! puff!).

"What is the man saying, Lambert?" asked Ben, who

was holding his mittened hands against his cheeks to ward off the cutting air.

"He says we're about two pipes from Leyden. Half the boors here on the canal measure distances by the time it takes them to finish a pipe."

"How ridiculous."

"See here, Benjamin Dobbs," retorted Lambert, growing unaccountably indignant at Ben's quiet smile. "See here, you've a way of calling every other thing you see on *this* side of the German ocean 'ridiculous.' It may suit *you*, this word, but it doesn't suit *me*. When you want anything ridiculous just remember your English custom of making the Lord Mayor of London, at his installation, count the nails in a horseshoe to prove *his learning*."

"Who told you we have any such custom as that?" cried Ben, looking grave in an instant.

"Why, I *know* it, no use of anyone telling me. It's in all the books—and it's true. It strikes me," continued Lambert, laughing in spite of himself, "that you have been kept in happy ignorance of a good many ridiculous things on *your* side of the map."

"Humph!" exclaimed Ben, trying not to smile. "I'll inquire into that Lord Mayor business when I get home. There must be some mistake. B-r-r-roooo! How fast we're going. This is glorious!"

It was a grand sail, or ride, I scarce know which to call it; perhaps "fly" would be the best word; for the boys felt very much as Sindbad did when, tied to the roc's leg, he darted through the clouds; or as Bellerophon felt when he shot through the air on the back of his winged horse Pegasus.

Sailing, riding, or flying, whichever it was, everything was rushing past, backward—and, before they had time to draw a long breath, Leyden itself, with its high-peaked roofs, flew halfway to meet them.

When the city came in sight it was high time to waken the sleeper. That feat accomplished, Peter's prophecy came to pass. Master Jacob was quite restored and in excellent spirits.

The schipper made a feeble remonstrance when Peter, with hearty thanks, endeavored to slip some silver pieces into his tough, brown palm.

"Ye see, young master," said he, drawing away his hand, "the regular line o' trade's *one* thing, and a favor's another."

"I know it," said Peter, "but those boys and girls of yours will want sweets when you get home. Buy them some in the name of Saint Nicholas."

The man grinned. "Aye, true enough, I've young 'uns in plenty, a clean boatload of them. You are a sharp young master at guessing."

This time, the knotty hand hitched forward again, quite carelessly, it seemed, but its palm was upward. Peter hastily dropped in the money and moved away.

The sail soon came tumbling down. Scrape, scrape went the brake, scattering an ice shower round the boat.

"Good-bye, schipper!" shouted the boys, seizing their skates and leaping from the deck one by one. "Many thanks to you!"

"Good-bye! good-b—— Here! stop! I want my coat."

Ben was carefully assisting his cousin over the side of the boat.

"What is the man shouting about? Oh, I know, you have his wrapper round your shoulders!"

"Dat ish true," answered Jacob, half jumping, half tumbling down upon the framework, "dat ish vot make him sho heavy."

"Made *you* so heavy, you mean, Poot?"

"Ya, made you sho heavy—dat ish true," said Jacob innocently, as he worked himself free from the big wrapper. "Dere, now you hands it mit him straits way and tells him I voz much tanks for dat."

"Ho! for an inn!" cried Peter, as they stepped into the city. "Be brisk, my fine fellows!"

XXI

MYNHEER KLEEF AND HIS BILL OF FARE

The boys soon found an unpretending establishment near the Breedstraat (Broad Street) with a funnily painted lion over the door. This was the Roode Leeuw, or Red Lion, kept by one Huygens Kleef, a stout Dutchman with short legs and a very long pipe.

By this time they were in a ravenous condition. The tiffin, taken at Haarlem, had served only to give them an appetite, and this had been heightened by their exercise, and swift sail upon the canal.

"Come, mine host! give us what you can!" cried Peter rather pompously.

"I can give you anything—everything," answered Mynheer Kleef, performing a difficult bow.

"Well, give us sausage and pudding."

"Ah, mynheer, the sausage is all gone. There is no pudding."

"Salmagundi, then, and plenty of it."

"That is out also, young master."

"Eggs, and be quick."

"Winter eggs are *very* poor eating," answered the inn-keeper, puckering his lips and lifting his eyebrows.

"No eggs? Well—caviare."

The Dutchman raised his fat hands: "Caviare! That is made of gold! Who has caviare to sell?"

Peter had sometimes eaten it at home; he knew that it was made of the roe of the sturgeon, and certain other large fish, but he had no idea of its cost.

"Well, mine host, what have you?"

"What have I? Everything. I have rye bread, sauerkraut, potato salad and the fattest herring in Leyden."

"What do you say, boys?" asked the captain. "Will that do?"

"Yes," cried the famished youths, "if he'll only be quick."

Mynheer moved off like one walking in his sleep, but soon opened his eyes wide at the miraculous manner in which his herring were made to disappear. Next came, or rather went, potato salad, rye bread and coffee—then Utrecht water flavored with orange, and, finally, slices of dry gingerbread. This last delicacy was not on the regular bill of fare; but Mynheer Kleef, driven to extremes, sol-emnly produced it from his own private stores, and gave only a placid blink when his voracious young travelers started up, declaring they had eaten enough.

"I should think so!" he exclaimed internally, but his smooth face gave no sign. Softly rubbing his hands, he asked: "Will your worships have beds?"

"Will your worships have beds?" mocked Carl. "What do you mean? Do we look sleepy?"

"Not at all, master; but I would cause them to be warmed and aired. None sleep under damp sheets at the Red Lion."

"Ah, I understand. Shall we come back here to sleep, captain?"

Peter was accustomed to finer lodgings; but this was a frolic.

"Why not?" he replied. "We can fare excellently here."

"Your worship speaks only the truth," said mynheer with great deference.

"How fine to be called 'your worship,' " laughed Ludwig aside to Lambert, while Peter replied:

"Well, mine host, you may get the rooms ready by nine."

"I have one beautiful chamber, with three beds, that will hold all of your worships," said Mynheer coaxingly.

"That will do."

"Whew!" whistled Carl when they reached the street.

Ludwig started. "What now?"

"Nothing, only Mynheer Kleef of the Red Lion little thinks how we shall make things spin in that same room to-night. We'll set the bolsters flying!"

"Order!" cried the captain. "Now, boys, I must seek this great Dr. Boekman before I sleep. If he is in Leyden it will be no great task to find him, for he always puts up at the Golden Eagle when he comes here. I wonder that you did not all go to bed at once. Still, as you are awake, what say you to walking with Ben up by the Museum or the Stadhuis?"

"Agreed," said Ludwig and Lambert; but Jacob preferred to go with Peter. In vain Ben tried to persuade him to remain at the inn and rest. He declared that he never felt "petter," and wished of all things to take a look at the city, for it was his first "stop mit Leyden."

"Oh, it will not harm him," said Lambert. "How long the day has been—and what glorious sport we have had. It hardly seems possible that we left Broek only this morning."

Jacob yawned. "I have enjoyed it well," he said, "but it seems to me at least a week since we started."

Carl laughed, and muttered something about "twenty naps."

"Here we are at the corner; remember, we all meet at the Red Lion at eight," said the captain, as he and Jacob walked away.

XXII

THE RED LION BECOMES DANGEROUS

THE boys were glad to find a blazing fire awaiting them upon their return to the Red Lion. Carl and his party were there first. Soon afterward Peter and Jacob came in. They had inquired in vain concerning Dr. Boekman. All they could ascertain was that he had been seen in Haarlem that morning.

"As for his being in Leyden," the landlord of the Golden Eagle had said to Peter, "the thing is impossible. He always lodges here when in town. By this time there would be a crowd at my door waiting to consult him. Bah! people make such fools of themselves!"

"He is called a great surgeon," said Peter.

"Yes, the greatest in Holland. But what of that? What of being the greatest pill choker and knife slasher in the world? The man is a bear. Only last month on this very spot, he called me *a pig*, before three customers!"

"No!" exclaimed Peter, trying to look surprised and indignant.

"Yes, master—*a pig*," repeated the landlord, puffing at his pipe with an injured air. "Bah! if he did not pay fine prices and bring customers to my house I would sooner see him in the Vleit Canal than give him lodgment."

Perhaps mine host felt that he was speaking too openly to a stranger, or it may be he saw a smile lurking in Peter's face, for he added sharply:

"Come, now, what more do you wish? Supper? Beds?"

"No, mynheer, I am but searching for Dr. Boekman."

"Go find him. He is not in Leyden."

Peter was not to be put off so easily. After receiving a few more rough words, he succeeded in obtaining permission to leave a note for the famous surgeon, or rather, he *bought* from his amiable landlord the privilege of writing it there, and a promise that it should be promptly delivered when Dr. Boekman arrived. This accomplished, Peter and Jacob returned to the Red Lion.

This inn had once been a fine house, the home of a rich burgher; but, having grown old and shabby, it had passed through many hands, until finally it had fallen into the possession of Mynheer Kleef. He was fond of saying as he looked up at its dingy, broken walls, "Mend it, and paint it, and there's not a prettier house in Leyden." It stood six stories high from the street. The first three were of equal breadth but of various heights, the last three were in the great, high roof, and grew smaller and smaller like a set of double steps until the top one was lost in a point. The roof was built of short, shining tiles, and the windows, with their little panes, seemed to be scattered irregularly over the face of the building, without the slightest attention to outward effect. But the public room on the ground floor was the landlord's joy and pride. He never said, "Mend it, and paint it," there, for everything was in the highest condition of Dutch neatness and order. If you will but open your mind's eye you may look into the apartment.

Imagine a large, bare room, with a floor that seemed to be made of squares cut out of glazed earthen pie dishes, first a yellow piece, then a red, until the whole looked like a vast checkerboard. Fancy a dozen high-backed wooden chairs standing around; then a great hollow chimney place all aglow with its blazing fire, reflected a hundred times in the polished steel firedogs; a tiled hearth, tiled sides, tiled top, with a Dutch sentence upon it; and over all, high above one's head, a narrow mantelshelf, filled with shining brass candlesticks, pipe lighters and tinderboxes. Then see, in one end of the room, three pine tables; in the other, a closet and a deal dresser. The latter is filled with mugs, dishes, pipes, tankards, earthen and glass bottles, and is guarded at one end by a brass-hooped keg standing upon long legs. Everything dim with tobacco smoke, but otherwise clean as soap and sand can make it. Next picture two sleepy, shabby-looking men, in wooden shoes, seated near the glowing fireplace, hugging their knees and smoking short, stumpy pipes; Mynheer Kleef walking softly and heavily about, clad in leather knee breeches, felt shoes and a green jacket wider than it is long; then throw a heap of skates in the corner, and put six tired, well-dressed boys, in various attitudes, upon the wooden chairs, and you will see the coffeeroom of the Red Lion just as it appeared at nine o'clock on the evening of December 6, 184—. For supper, gingerbread again; slices of Dutch sausage, rye bread sprinkled with anise seed, pickles, a bottle of Utrecht water, and a pot of very mysterious coffee. The boys were ravenous enough to take all they could get, and pronounce it excellent. Ben made wry faces, but Jacob declared he had never eaten a better meal. After they had laughed and talked awhile, and counted their money by way of settling a discussion that arose concerning their expenses, the captain marched his company off to bed, led on by a greasy pioneer boy who carried skates and a candlestick instead of an axe.

One of the ill-favored men by the fire had shuffled toward

the dresser, and was ordering a mug of beer, just as Ludwig, who brought up the rear, was stepping from the apartment.

"I don't like that fellow's eye," he whispered to Carl. "He looks like a pirate, or something of that kind."

"Looks like a granny!" answered Carl in sleepy disdain.

Ludwig laughed uneasily.

"Granny or no granny," he whispered, "I tell you he looks just like one of those men in the 'voetspoelen.' "

"Pooh!" sneered Carl, "I knew it. That picture was too much for you. Look sharp now, and see if yon fellow with the candle doesn't look like the other villain."

"No, indeed, his face is as honest as a Gouda cheese. But, I say, Carl, that really was a horrid picture."

"Humph! What did you stare at it so long for?"

"I couldn't help it."

By this time the boys had reached the "beautiful room with three beds in it." A dumpy little maiden with long earrings met them at the doorway, dropped them a curtsy, and passed out. She carried a long-handled thing that resembled a frying pan with a cover.

"I am glad to see that," said Van Mounen to Ben.

"What?"

"Why, the warming pan. It's full of hot ashes; she's been heating our beds."

"Oh! a warming pan, eh! Much obliged to her, I'm sure," said Ben, too sleepy to make any further comment.

Meantime, Ludwig still talked of the picture that had made such a strong impression upon him. He had seen it in a shopwindow during their walk. It was a poorly painted thing, representing two men tied back to back, standing on shipboard, surrounded by a group of seamen who were preparing to cast them together into the sea. This mode of putting prisoners to death was called *voetspoelen,* or feet washing, and was practiced by the Dutch upon the pirates of Dunkirk in 1605; and, again, by the Spaniards upon the Dutch, in the horrible massacre that followed the siege of Haarlem. Bad as the painting was, the expression upon the pirates' faces was well given. Sullen and despairing as they seemed, they wore such a cruel, malignant aspect that Ludwig had felt a secret satisfaction in contemplating their helpless condition. He might have forgotten the scene by this time but for that ill-looking man by the fire. Now, while he capered about, boylike, and threw himself with an antic into his bed, he inwardly hoped that the voetspoelen would not haunt his dreams.

It was a cold, cheerless room; a fire had been newly kindled in the burnished stove, and seemed to shiver even while it was trying to burn. The windows, with their funny little panes, were bare and shiny, and the cold, waxed floor looked like a sheet of yellow ice. Three rush-bottomed chairs stood stiffly against the wall, alternating with three narrow wooden bedsteads that made the room look like the deserted ward of a hospital. At any other time the boys would have found it quite impossible to sleep in pairs, especially in such narrow quarters; but tonight they lost all fear of being crowded, and longed only to lay their weary bodies upon the feather beds that lay lightly upon each cot. Had the boys been in Germany instead of Holland they might have been covered, also, by a bed of down or feathers. This peculiar form of luxury was at that time adopted only by wealthy or eccentric Hollanders.

Ludwig, as we have seen, had not quite lost his friskiness; but the other boys, after one or two feeble attempts at pillow firing, composed themselves for the night with the greatest dignity. Nothing like fatigue for making boys behave themselves.

"Good night, boys!" said Peter's voice from under the covers.

"Good night," called back everybody but Jacob, who already lay snoring beside the captain.

"I say," shouted Carl, after a moment, "don't sneeze, anybody. Ludwig's in a fright!"

"No such thing," retorted Ludwig in a smothered voice. Then there was a little whispered dispute, which was ended by Carl saying: "For *my* part, I don't know what fear is. But you really are a timid fellow, Ludwig."

Ludwig grunted sleepily, but made no further reply.

It was the middle of the night. The fire had shivered itself to death, and, in place of its gleams, little squares of moonlight lay upon the floor, slowly, slowly shifting their way across the room. Something else was moving also, but they did not see it. Sleeping boys keep but a poor lookout. During the early hours of the night, Jacob Poot had been gradually but surely winding himself with all the bed covers. He now lay like a monster chrysalis beside the half-frozen Peter, who, accordingly, was skating with all his might over the coldest, bleakest of dreamland icebergs.

Something else, I say, besides the moonlight, was moving across the bare, polished floor—moving not quite so slowly, but quite as stealthily.

Wake up, Ludwig! The voetspoelen pirate is growing real!

No. Ludwig does not waken, but he moans in his sleep.

Does not Carl hear it—Carl the brave, the fearless?

No. Carl is dreaming of the race.

And Jacob? Van Mounen? Ben? No. They, too, are dreaming of the race; and Katrinka is singing through their dreams—laughing, flitting past them; now and then a wave from the great organ surges through their midst.

Still the thing moves, slowly, slowly.

Peter! Captain Peter, there is danger!

Peter heard no call; but, in his dream, he slid a few thousand feet from one iceberg to another, and the shock awoke him.

Whew! How cold he was! He gave a hopeless, desperate tug at the chrysalis. In vain; sheet, blanket and spread were firmly wound about Jacob's inanimate form. Peter looked drowsily toward the window.

"Clear moonlight," he thought. "We shall have pleasant weather tomorrow. Halloo! what's that?"

He saw the moving thing, or rather something black crouching upon the floor, for it had halted as Peter stirred.

He watched in silence.

Soon it moved again, nearer and nearer. It was a man crawling upon hands and feet!

The captain's first impulse was to call out; but he took an instant to consider matters.

The creeper had a shining knife in one hand. This was ugly; but Peter was naturally self-possessed. When the head turned, Peter's eyes were closed as if in sleep; but at other times nothing could be keener, sharper than the captain's gaze.

Closer, closer crept the robber. His back was very near Peter now. The knife was laid softly upon the floor; one careful arm reached forth stealthily to drag the clothes from the chair by the captain's bed—the robbery was commenced.

Now was Peter's time! Holding his breath, he sprang up and leaped with all his strength upon the robber's back, stunning the rascal with the force of the blow. To seize the knife was but a second's work. The robber began to struggle, but Peter sat like a giant astride the prostrate form.

"If you stir," said the brave boy in as terrible a voice as he could command, "stir but one inch, I will plunge this knife into your neck. Boys! Boys! wake up!" he shouted, still pressing down the black head, and holding the knife at pricking distance, "give us a hand! I've got him! I've got him!"

The chrysalis rolled over, but made no other sign.

"Up, boys!" cried Peter, never budging. "Ludwig! Lambert! Thunder! Are you all dead?"

Dead! not they. Van Mounen and Ben were on their feet in an instant. "Hey? What now?" they shouted.

"I've got a robber here," said Peter coolly. "(Lie still, you scoundrel, or I'll slice your head off!) Now, boys, cut out your bed cord—plenty of time—he's a dead man if he stirs."

Peter felt that he weighed a thousand pounds. So he did, with that knife in his hand.

The man growled and swore, but dared not move.

Ludwig was up, by this time. He had a great jack-knife, the pride of his heart, in his breeches pocket. It could do good service now. They bared the bedstead in a moment. It was laced backward and forward with a rope.

"I'll cut it," cried Ludwig, sawing away at the knot. "Hold him tight, Peter!"

"Never fear!" answered the captain, giving the robber a warning prick.

The boys were soon pulling at the rope like good fellows. It was out at last—a long, stout piece.

"Now, boys," commanded the captain, "lift up his rascally arms! Cross his hands over his back! That's right—excuse me for being in the way—tie them tight!"

"Yes, and his feet too, the villain!" cried the boys in great excitement, tying knot after knot with Herculean jerks.

The prisoner changed his tone. "Oh—oh!" he moaned, "spare a poor sick man. I was but walking in my sleep."

"Ugh!" grunted Lambert, still tugging away at the rope. "Asleep, were you? Well, we'll wake you up."

The man muttered fierce oaths between his teeth—then cried in a piteous voice, "Unbind me, good young masters! I have five little children at home. By Saint Bavon I swear to give you each a ten-guilder piece if you will but free me!"

"Ha! ha!" laughed Peter.

"Ha! ha!" laughed the other boys.

Then came threats—threats that made Ludwig fairly shudder, though he continued to bind and tie with redoubled energy.

"Hold up! mynheer housebreaker," said Van Mounen in a warning voice. "That knife is very near your throat. If you make the captain nervous, there is no telling what may happen."

The robber took the hint, and fell into a sullen silence.

Just at this moment the chrysalis upon the bed stirred and sat erect.

"What's the matter?" he asked, without opening his eyes.

"Matter!" echoed Ludwig, half trembling, half laughing. "Get up, Jacob. Here's work for you. Come sit on this fellow's back while we get into our clothes; we're half perished."

"What fellow? Donder!"

"Hurrah for Poot!" cried all the boys, as Jacob, sliding quickly to the floor, bedclothes and all, took in the state of affairs at a glance, and sat heavily beside Peter on the robber's back.

Oh, didn't the fellow groan then!

"No use in holding him down any longer, boys," said Peter, rising, but bending as he did so to draw a pistol from his man's belt. "You see, I've been keeping guard over this pretty little weapon for the last ten minutes. It's cocked and the least wriggle might have set it off. No danger now. I must dress myself. You and I, Lambert, will go for the police. I'd no idea it was so cold."

"Where is Carl?" asked one of the boys.

They looked at one another. Carl certainly was not among them.

"Oh!" cried Ludwig, frightened at last, "where is he? Perhaps he's had a fight with the robber, and got killed."

"Not a bit of it," said Peter quietly, as he buttoned his stout jacket. "Look under the beds."

They did so. Carl was not there.

Just then they heard a commotion on the stairway. Ben hastened to open the door. The landlord almost tumbled in; he was armed with a big blunderbuss. Two or three lodgers followed; then the daughter, with an upraised frying pan in one hand and a candle in the other; and, behind her, looking pale and frightened, the gallant Carl!

"There's your man, mine host," said Peter, nodding toward the prisoner.

Mine host raised his blunderbuss, the girl screamed, and Jacob, more nimble than usual, rolled quickly from the robber's back.

"Don't fire," cried Peter, "he is tied, hand and foot. Let's roll him over, and see what he looks like."

Carl stepped briskly forward, with a blustering "Yes. *We'll* turn him over, in a way he won't like. Lucky we've caught him!"

"Ha! ha!" laughed Ludwig. "Where were you, Master Carl?"

"Where was I?" retorted Carl angrily. "Why, I went to give the alarm, to be sure!"

All the boys exchanged glances; but they were too happy and elated to say anything ill-natured. Carl certainly was bold enough now. He took the lead while three others aided him in turning the helpless man.

While the robber lay, face up, scowling and muttering, Ludwig took the candlestick from the girl's hand.

"I must have a good look at the beauty," he said, drawing closer, but the words were no sooner spoken than he turned pale and started so violently that he almost dropped the candle.

"The voetspoelen!" he cried. "Why, boys, it's the man who sat by the fire!"

"Of course it is," answered Peter. "We counted our money before him like simpletons. But what have we to do with voetspoelen, brother Ludwig? A month in jail is punishment enough."

The landlord's daughter had left the room. She now ran in, holding up a pair of huge wooden shoes. "See, father," she cried, "here are his great ugly boats. It's the man that we put in the next room after the young masters went to bed. Ah! it was wrong to send the poor young gentlemen up here so far out of sight and sound."

"The scoundrel!" hissed the landlord. "He has disgraced my house. I go for the police at once!"

In less than fifteen minutes two drowsy-looking officers were in the room. After telling Mynheer Kleef that he must appear early in the morning with the boys and make his complaint before a magistrate, they marched off with their prisoner.

One would think the captain and his band could have slept no more that night; but the mooring has not yet been found that can prevent youth and an easy conscience from drifting down the river of dreams. The boys were too much fatigued to let so slight a thing as capturing a robber bind them to wakefulness. They were soon in bed again, floating away to strange scenes made of familiar things. Ludwig and Carl had spread their bedding upon the floor. One had already forgotten the voetspoelen, the race—everything; but Carl was wide awake. He heard the carillons ringing out their solemn nightly music, and the watchman's noisy clapper putting in discord at the quarter hours; he saw the moonshine glide away from the window, and the red morning light come pouring in, and all the while he kept thinking: "Pooh! what a goose I have made of myself!"

Carl Schummel, alone, with none to look or to listen, was not quite so grand a fellow as Carl Schummel strutting about in his boots.

Jacob sat beside Peter

XXIII
BEFORE THE COURT

You may believe the landlord's daughter bestirred herself to prepare a good meal for the boys next morning. Mynheer had a Chinese gong that could make more noise than a dozen breakfast bells. Its hideous reveille, clanging through the house, generally startled the drowsiest lodgers into activity, but the maiden would not allow it to be sounded this morning:

"Let the brave young gentlemen sleep," she said, to the greasy kitchen boy. "They shall be warmly fed when they awaken."

It was ten o'clock when Captain Peter and his band came straggling down one by one.

"A pretty hour," said mine host gruffly. "It is high time we were before the court. Fine business this for a respectable inn. You will testify truly, young masters, that you found most excellent fare and lodgment at the Red Lion?"

"Of course we will," answered Carl saucily, "and pleasant company, too, though they visit at rather unseasonable hours."

A stare and a "humph!" was all the answer mynheer made to this, but the daughter was more communicative. Shaking her earrings at Carl she said sharply:

"Not so very pleasant either, master traveler, if one could judge by the way *you* ran away from it!"

"Impertinent creature!" hissed Carl under his breath, as he began busily to examine his skate straps. Meantime the kitchen boy, listening outside at the crack of the door, doubled himself with silent laughter.

After breakfast the boys went to the Police Court, accompanied by Huygens Kleef and his daughter. Mynheer's testimony was principally to the effect that such a thing as a robber at the Red Lion had been unheard of until last night; and as for the Red Lion, it was a most respectable inn, as respectable as any house in Leyden. Each boy, in turn, told all he knew of the affair, and identified the prisoner in the box as the same man who entered their room in the dead of night. Ludwig was surprised to find that the robber was a man of ordinary size—especially after he had described him, under oath, to the court as a tremendous fellow, with great square shoulders, and legs of prodigious weight. Jacob swore that he was awakened by the robber kicking and thrashing upon the floor; and, immediately afterward, Peter and the rest (feeling sorry that they had not explained the matter to their sleepy comrade) testified that the man had not moved a muscle from the moment the point of the dagger touched his throat, until, bound from head to foot, he was rolled over for inspection. The landlord's daughter made one boy blush, and all the court smile, by declaring that, "if it hadn't been for that handsome young gentleman there" (pointing to Peter) they "might have all been murdered in their beds; for the dreadful man had a great, shining knife most as long as Your

Honor's arm," and *she* believed "the handsome young gentleman had struggled hard enough to get it away from him, but he was too modest, bless him! to say so."

Finally, after a little questioning and cross-questioning from the public prosecutor, the witnesses were dismissed, and the robber was handed over to the consideration of the Criminal Court.

"The scoundrel!" said Carl savagely, when the boys reached the street. "He ought to be sent to jail at once. If I had been in your place, Peter, I certainly should have killed him outright!"

"He was fortunate, then, in falling into gentler hands," was Peter's quiet reply. "It appears he has been arrested before under a charge of housebreaking. He did not succeed in robbing this time, but he broke the door fastenings, and that I believe makes a burglary in the eye of the law. He was armed with a knife, too, and that makes it worse for him, poor fellow!"

"Poor fellow!" mimicked Carl. "One would think he was your brother!"

"So he is my brother, and yours, too, Carl Schummel, for that matter," answered Peter, looking into Carl's eye. "We cannot say what me might have become under other circumstances. *We* have been bolstered up from evil, since the hour we were born. A happy home and good parents might have made that man a fine fellow instead of what he is. God grant that the law may cure and not crush him!"

"Amen to that!" said Lambert heartily, while Ludwig van Holp looked at his brother in such a bright, proud way that Jacob Poot, who was an only son, wished from his heart that the little form buried in the old church at home had lived to grow up beside him.

"Humph!" said Carl, "it's very well to be saintly and forgiving, and all that sort of thing, but I'm naturally hard. All these fine ideas seem to rattle off me like hailstones—and it's nobody's business, either, if they do."

Peter recognized a touch of good feeling in this clumsy concession; holding out his hand, he said in a frank, hearty tone:

"Come, lad, shake hands, and let us be good friends even if we don't exactly agree on all questions."

"We do agree better than you think," sulked Carl, as he returned Peter's grasp.

"All right," responded Peter briskly. "Now Van Mounen, we await Benjamin's wishes. Where would he like to go?"

"To the Egyptian Museum," answered Lambert, after holding a brief consultation with Ben.

"That is on the Breedestraat. To the Museum let it be. Come, boys!"

XXIV
THE BELEAGUERED CITIES

"This open square before us," said Lambert, as he and Ben walked on together, "is pretty in summer, with its shady trees. They call it the Ruine. Years ago it was covered with houses, and the Rapenburg Canal, here, ran through the street. Well, one day a barge loaded with forty thousand pounds of gunpowder, bound for Delft, was lying alongside, and the bargemen took a notion to cook their dinner on the deck; and before anyone knew it, sir, the whole thing blew up, killing lots of persons and scattering about three hundred houses to the winds."

"What!" exclaimed Ben. "Did the explosion destroy three hundred houses!"

"Yes, sir, my father was in Leyden at the time. He says it was terrible. The explosion occurred just at noon, and was like a volcano. All this part of the town was on fire in an instant, buildings tumbling down, and men, women and children groaning under the ruins. The king himself came to the city and acted nobly, father says, staying out in the streets all night, encouraging the survivors in their efforts to arrest the fire, and rescue as many as possible from under the heaps of stone and rubbish. Through his means a collection for the benefit of the sufferers was raised throughout the kingdom, besides a hundred thousand guilders paid out of the treasury. Father was only nineteen years old then; it was in 1807, I believe, but he remembers it perfectly. A friend of his, Professor Luzac, was among the killed. They have a tablet erected to his memory, in Saint Peter's Church, further on—the queerest thing you ever saw—with an image of the professor carved upon it representing him just as he looked when he was found after the explosion."

"What a strange idea! Isn't Boerhaave's monument in Saint Peter's also?"

"I cannot remember. Perhaps Peter knows."

The captain delighted Ben by saying that the monument was there and that he thought they might be able to see it during the day.

"Lambert," continued Peter, "ask Ben if he saw Van der Werf's portrait at the Town Hall last night?"

"No," said Lambert, "I can answer for him. It was too late to go in. I say, boys, it is really wonderful how much Ben knows. Why, he has told me a volume of Dutch history already. I'll wager he has the siege of Leyden at his tongue's end."

"His tongue must burn then," interposed Ludwig, "for if Bilderdyk's account is true it was a pretty hot affair."

Ben was looking at them with an inquiring smile.

"We are speaking of the siege of Leyden," explained Lambert.

"Oh, yes," said Ben eagerly, "I had forgotten all about it. This was the very place. Let's give old Van der Werf three cheers. Hur——"

Van Mounen uttered a hasty "Hush!" and explained that, patriotic as the Dutch were, the police would soon have something to say if a party of boys cheered in the street at midday.

"What! not cheer Van der Werf?" cried Ben indignantly. "One of the greatest chaps in history? Only think! Didn't he hold out against those murderous Spaniards for months and months! There was the town, surrounded on all sides by the enemy; great black forts sending fire and death into the very heart of the city—but no surrender! Every man a hero—women, and children, too, brave and fierce as lions—provisions giving out, the very grass from between the paving stones gone—till people were glad to eat horses and cats and dogs and rats. Then came the plague—hundreds dying in the streets—but no surrender! Then when they could bear no more—when the people, brave as they were, crowded about Van der Werf in the public square begging him to give up, what did the noble old burgomaster say? 'I have sworn to defend this city, and with God's help, *I mean to do it!* If my body can satisfy your hunger, take it, and divide it among you—but expect no surrender so long as I am alive.' Hurrah! hur——"

Ben was getting uproarious; Lambert playfully clapped his hands over his friend's mouth. The result was one of those quick india-rubber scuffles fearful to behold, but delightful to human nature in its polliwog state.

"Vat wash te matter, Pen?" asked Jacob, hurrying forward.

"Oh! nothing at all," panted Ben, "except that Van Mounen was afraid of starting an English riot in this orderly town. He stopped my cheering for old Van—"

"Ya! ya—it ish no goot to sheer—to make te noise for dat. You vill shee old Van der Does' likeness mit te Stadhuis."

"See old Van der Does? I thought it was Van der Werf's picture they had there."

"Ya," responded Jacob, "Van der Werf—vell, vot of it! Both ish just ash goot——"

"Yes, Van der Does was a noble old Dutchman, but he was not Van der Werf. I know he defended the city like a brick, and——"

"Now vot for you shay dat, Penchamin? He no defend te citty mit breek, he fight like goot soltyer mit his guns. You like make te fun mit effrysinks Tutch."

"No! no! no! I said he defended the city *like* a brick. That is very high praise, I would have you understand. We English call even the Duke of Wellington a brick."

Jacob looked puzzled; but his indignation was already on the ebb.

"Vell, it ish no matter. I no tink, before, soltyer mean breek, but it ish no matter."

Ben laughed good-naturedly, and seeing that his cousin was tired of talking in English, he turned to his friend of the two languages.

"Van Mounen, they say the very carrier pigeons that brought news of relief to the besieged city are somewhere here in Leyden. I really should like to see them. Just think of it! At the very height of the trouble if the wind didn't turn, and blow in the waters, and drown hundreds of the Spaniards, and enable the Dutch boats to sail in right over the land with men and provisions to the very gates of the city. The pigeons, you know, did great service, in bearing letters to and fro. I have read somewhere that they were reverently cared for from that day, and, when they died, they were stuffed, and placed for safekeeping in the Town Hall. We must be sure to have a look at them."

Van Mounen laughed. "On that principle, Ben, I suppose when you go to Rome you'll expect to see the identical goose who saved the Capitol. But it will be easy enough to see the pigeons. They are in the same building with Van der Werf's portrait. Which was the greatest defense, Ben, the siege of Leyden or the siege of Haarlem?"

"Well," replied Ben thoughtfully, "Van der Werf is one of my heroes; we all have our historical pets, you know, but I really think the siege of Haarlem brought out a braver, more heroic resistance even, than the Leyden one; besides they set the Leyden sufferers an example of courage and fortitude, for their turn came first."

"I don't know much about the Haarlem siege," said Lambert, "except that it was in 1573. Who beat?"

"The Spaniards," said Ben. "The Dutch had stood out for months. Not a man would yield, nor a woman either for that matter. They shouldered arms and fought gallantly beside their husbands and fathers. Three hundred of them did duty under Kanau Hesselaer, a great woman,

and brave as Joan of Arc. All this time the city was surrounded by the Spaniards under Frederic of Toledo, son of that beauty, the Duke of Alva. Cut off from all possible help from without, there seemed to be no hope for the inhabitants, but they shouted defiance over the city walls. They even threw bread into the enemy's camps to show that they were not afraid of starvation. Up to the last they held out bravely, waiting for the help that never could come—growing bolder and bolder until their provisions were exhausted. Then it was terrible. In time hundreds of famished creatures fell dead in the streets, and the living had scarcely strength to bury them. At last, they made the desperate resolution that, rather than perish by lingering torture, the strongest would form in a square, placing the weakest in the center, and rush in a body to their death, with the faint chance of being able to fight their way through the enemy. The Spaniards received a hint of this, and believing there was nothing the Dutch would not dare to do, they concluded to offer terms."

"High time, I should think."

"Yes, with falsehood and treachery they soon obtained an entrance into the city, promising protection and forgiveness to all except those whom the citizens themselves would acknowledge as deserving of death."

"You don't say so!" said Lambert, quite interested. "That ended the business, I suppose."

"Not a bit of it," returned Ben, "for the Duke of Alva had already given his son orders to show mercy to none."

"Ah! there was where the great Haarlem massacre came in. I remember now. You can't wonder that the Hollanders dislike Spain when you read of the way they were butchered by Alva and his hosts, though I admit that our side sometimes retaliated terribly. But as I have told you before, I have a very indistinct idea of historical matters. Everything is utter confusion—from the Flood to the battle of Waterloo. One thing is plain, however, the Duke of Alva was about the worst specimen of a man that ever lived."

"That gives only a faint idea of him," said Ben, "but I hate to think of such a wretch. What if he *had* brains, and military skill, and all that sort of thing! Give me such men as Van der Werf, and— What now?"

"Why," said Van Mounen, who was looking up and down the street, in a bewildered way. "We've walked right past the Museum, and I don't see the boys. Let us go back."

XXV
LEYDEN

THE boys met at the Museum, and were soon engaged in examining its extensive collection of curiosities, receiving a new insight into Egyptian life, ancient and modern. Ben and Lambert had often visited the British Museum, but that did not prevent them from being surprised at the richness of the Leyden collection. There were household utensils, wearing apparel, weapons, musical instruments, sarcophagi, and mummies of men, women, and cats, ibexes and other creatures. They saw a massive gold armlet that had been worn by an Egyptian king at a time when some of these same mummies, perhaps, were nimbly treading the streets of Thebes; and jewels and trinkets such as Pharaoh's daughter wore, and the children of Israel borrowed when they departed out of Egypt.

There were other interesting relics, from Rome and Greece, and some curious Roman pottery which had been discovered in digging near The Hague—relics of the days when the countrymen of Julius Caesar had settled there. Where have they not settled? I for one would hardly be astonished if relics of the ancient Romans should some day be found deep under the grass growing round the Bunker Hill monument.

When the boys left this Museum, they went to another and saw a wonderful collection of fossil animals, skeletons, birds, minerals, precious stones and other natural specimens, but as they were not learned men, they could only walk about and stare, enjoy the little knowledge of natural history they possessed, and wish with all their hearts they had acquired more. Even the skeleton of the mouse puzzled Jacob. What wonder? He was not used to seeing the cat-fearing little creatures running about in their bones—and how could he ever have imagined their necks to be so queer?

Besides the Museum of Natural History, there was Saint Peter's Church to be visited, containing Professor Luzac's memorial, and Boerhaave's monument of white and black marble, with its urn and carved symbols of the four ages of life, and its medallion of Boerhaave, adorned with his favorite motto "Simplex sigillum veri." They also obtained admittance to a tea garden, which in summer was a favorite resort of the citizens, and passing naked oaks and fruit trees, ascended a high mound which stood in the center. This was the site of a round tower now in ruins, said by some to have been built by Hengist the Anglo-Saxon king, and by others to have been the castle of one of the ancient counts of Holland.

As the boys walked about on the top of its stone wall, they could get but a poor view of the surrounding city. The tower stood higher when, more than two centuries ago, the inhabitants of beleaguered Leyden shouted to the watcher on its top their wild, despairing cries, "Is there any help? Are the waters rising? What do you see?"

And for months he could only answer, "No help. I see around us nothing but the enemy."

Ben pushed these thoughts away; and, resolutely looking down into the bare tea garden, filled it in imagination with gay summer groups. He tried to forget old battle clouds, and picture only curling wreaths of tobacco smoke, rising from among men, women and children enjoying their tea and coffee in the open air. But a tragedy came in spite of him.

Poot was bending over the edge of the high wall. It would be just like him to grow dizzy and tumble off. Ben turned impatiently away. If the fellow with his weak head knew no better than to be venturesome, why, let him tumble. Horror! what meant that heavy, crashing sound?

Ben could not stir. He could only gasp:

"Jacob!"

"Jacob!" cried another startled voice and another. Ready to faint, Ben managed to turn his head. He saw a crowd of boys on the edge of the wall opposite—but Jacob was not there!

"Good heavens!" he cried, springing forward, "where is my cousin?"

The crowd parted. It was only four boys, after all. There sat Jacob in their midst, holding his sides and laughing heartily.

"Did I frighten you all?" he said in his native Dutch. "Well, I will tell you how it was. There was a big stone lying on the wall and I put my—my foot out just to push it a little, you see—and the first thing I knew, down went the stone all the way to the bottom, and left me sitting here on top with both my feet in the air. If I had not thrown myself back at that moment, I certainly should have rolled over after the stone. Well, it is no matter. Help me up, boys."

"You are hurt, Jacob!" said Ben, seeing a shade of seriousness pass over his cousin's face as they lifted him to his feet.

Jacob tried to laugh again. "Oh, no—I feels little hurt ven I stant up, but it ish no matter."

The monument to Van der Werf in the Hooglandsche Kerk was not accessible that day; but the boys spent a few pleasant moments in the Stadhuis, or Town Hall, a long irregular structure somewhat in the Gothic style, uncouth in architecture, but picturesque from age. Its little steeple, tuneful with bells, seemed to have been borrowed from some other building and hastily clapped on as a finishing touch.

Ascending the grand staircase the boys soon found themselves in rather a gloomy apartment, containing the masterpiece of Lucas van Leyden, or Hugens, a Dutch artist, born three hundred and seventy years ago, who painted well when he was ten years of age, and became distinguished in art when only fifteen. This picture, called the Last Judgment, considering the remote age in which it was painted, is truly a remarkable production. The boys, however, were less interested in tracing out the merits of the work than they were in the fact of its being a triptych—that is, painted on three divisions, the two outer ones swung on hinges so as to close, when required, over the main portion.

The historical pictures by Harel de Moor and other famous Dutch artists interested them for a while, and Ben had to be almost pulled away from the dingy old portrait of Van der Werf.

The Town Hall, as well as the Egyptian Museum, is on the Breedestraat, the longest and finest street in Leyden. It has no canal running through it, and the houses, painted in every variety of color, have a picturesque effect as they stand with their gable ends to the street; some are very tall, with half of their height in their steplike roofs; others crouch before the public edifices and churches. Being clean, spacious, well-shaded and adorned with many elegant mansions, it compares favorably with the finer portions of Amsterdam. It is kept scrupulously neat; many of the gutters are covered with boards that open like trap doors; and it is supplied with pumps surmounted with shining brass ornaments kept scoured and bright at the public cost. The city is intersected by numerous water roads formed by the river Rhine, there grown sluggish, fatigued by its long travel; but more than one hundred and fifty stone bridges reunite the dissevered streets. The same world-renowned river, degraded from the beautiful, free-flowing Rhine, serves as a moat around the rampart that surrounds Leyden, and is crossed by drawbridges at the imposing gateways that give access to the city. Fine broad promenades, shaded by noble trees, border the canals and add to the retired appearance of the houses behind, heightening the effect of scholastic seclusion that seems to pervade the place.

Ben, as he scanned the buildings on the Rapenburg Canal, was somewhat disappointed in the appearance of the great University of Leyden. But when he recalled its history—how, attended with all the pomp of a grand civic display, it had been founded by the Prince of Orange as a tribute to the citizens for the bravery displayed during the siege; when he remembered the great men in religion, learning and science who had once studied there, and thought of the hundreds of students now sharing the benefits of its classes and its valuable scientific museums—he was quite willing to forego architectural beauty, though he could not help feeling that no amount of it could have been misplaced on such an institution.

Peter and Jacob regarded the building with even a deeper, more practical interest, for they were to enter it as students, in the course of a few months.

"Poor Don Quixote would have run a hopeless tilt in this part of the world," said Ben, after Lambert had been pointing out some of the oddities and beauties of the suburbs—"it is all windmills. You remember his terrific contest with one, I suppose."

"No," said Lambert bluntly.

"Well, I don't either, that is, not definitely. But there was something of that kind in his adventures, and if there wasn't, there should have been. Look at them, how frantically they whirl their great arms—just the thing to excite the crazy knight to mortal combat. It bewilders one to look at them; help me to count all those we can see, Van Mounen. I want a big item for my notebook"—and after a careful reckoning, superintended by all the party, Master Ben wrote in pencil, "Saw, Dec.,—184— ninety-eight windmills within full view of Leyden."

He would have been glad to visit the old brick mill in which the painter Rembrandt was born; but he abandoned the project upon learning that it would take them out of their way. Few boys as hungry as Ben was by this time would hesitate long between Rembrandt's home a mile off and tiffin close by. Ben chose the latter.

After tiffin, they rested awhile, and then—took another, which, for form's sake, they called dinner. After dinner the boys sat warming themselves, at the inn; all but Peter, who occupied the time in another fruitless search for Dr. Boekman.

This over, the party once more prepared for skating. They were thirteen miles from The Hague and not as fresh as when they had left Broek early on the previous day; but they were in good spirits and the ice was excellent.

XXVI
THE PALACE AND THE WOOD

As the boys skated onward, they saw a number of fine countryseats, all decorated and surrounded according to the Dutchest of Dutch taste, but impressive to look upon, with their great, formal houses, elaborate gardens, square hedges, and wide ditches—some crossed by a bridge, having a gate in the middle to be carefully locked at night. These ditches, everywhere traversing the landscape, had long ago lost their summer film, and now shone under the sunlight like trailing ribbons of glass.

The boys traveled bravely, all the while performing the surprising feat of producing gingerbread from their pockets and causing it to vanish instantly.

Twelve miles were passed. A few more long strokes would take them to The Hague, when Van Mounen proposed that they should vary their course by walking into the city through The Bosch.

"Agreed!" cried one and all—and their skates were off in a twinkling.

The Bosch is a grand park or wood, nearly two miles long, containing the celebrated House in the Wood—*Huis in't Bosch*—sometimes used as a royal residence.

This building, though plain outside for a palace, is elegantly furnished within, and finely frescoed—that is, the walls and ceilings are covered with groups and designs painted directly upon them while the plaster was fresh. Some of the rooms are tapestried with Chinese silk, beautifully embroidered. One contains a number of family portraits, among them a group of royal children who in time were orphaned by a certain axe which figures very frequently in European history. These children were painted many times by the Dutch artist Van Dyck, who was court painter to their father, Charles the First of England. Beautiful children they were. What a deal of trouble the English nation would have been spared had they been as perfect in heart and soul as they were in form!

The park surrounding the palace is charming, especially in summer, for flowers and birds make it bright as fairyland. Long rows of magnificent oaks rear their proud heads, conscious that no profaning hand will ever bring them low. In fact the Wood has for ages been held as an almost sacred spot. Children are never allowed to meddle with its smallest twig; the axe of the woodman has never resounded there. Even war and riot have passed it reverently, pausing for a moment in their devastating way. Philip of Spain, while he ordered Dutchmen to be mowed down by hundreds, issued a mandate that not a bough of the beautiful Wood should be touched. And once when in a time of great necessity the State was about to sacrifice it to assist in filling a nearly exhausted treasury, the people rushed to the rescue, and nobly contributed the required amount rather than that the Bosch should fall.

What wonder, then, that the oaks have a grand, fearless air? Birds from all Holland have told them how, elsewhere, trees are cropped and bobbed into shape—but *they* are untouched. Year after year, they expand in unclipped luxuriance and beauty; their wide-spreading foliage, alive with song, casts a cool shade over lawn and pathway, or bows to its image in the sunny ponds.

Meanwhile, as if to reward the citizens for allowing her to have her way for once, Nature departs from the invariable level, wearing gracefully the ornaments that have been reverently bestowed upon her. So the lawn slopes in a velvety green; the paths wind in and out; flower beds glow and send forth perfume; and ponds and sky look at each other in mutual admiration.

Even on that winter day the Bosch was beautiful. Its trees were bare, but beneath them still lay the ponds, every ripple smoothed into glass. The blue sky was bright overhead, and as it looked down through the thicket of boughs, it saw another blue sky, not nearly so bright, looking up from the dim thicket under the ice.

Never had the sunset appeared more beautiful to Peter than when he saw it exchanging farewell glances with the windows and shining roofs of the city before him. Never had The Hague itself seemed more inviting. He was no longer Peter van Holp, going to visit a great city, nor a fine young gentleman bent on sight-seeing; he was a knight, an adventurer, travel-soiled and weary, a Hop-o'-my-Thumb grown large, a Fortunatus approaching the enchanted castle where luxury and ease awaited him—for his own sister's house was not half a mile away.

"At last, boys," he cried, in high glee, "we may hope for a royal resting place—good beds, warm rooms and something fit to eat. I never realized before what a luxury such things are. Our lodgings at the Red Lion have made us appreciate our own homes."

XXVII
THE MERCHANT PRINCE AND THE SISTER-PRINCESS

WELL might Peter feel that his sister's house was like an enchanted castle. Large and elegant as it was, a spell of quiet hung over it. The very lion crouching at its gate seemed to have been turned into stone through magic. Within, it was guarded by genii, in the shape of red-faced servants, who sprang silently forth at the summons of bell or knocker. There was a cat, also, who appeared as knowing as any Puss-in-Boots; and a brass gnome in the hall whose business it was to stand with outstretched arms ready to receive sticks and umbrellas. Safe within the walls bloomed a Garden of Delight, where the flowers firmly believed it was summer, and a sparkling fountain was laughing merrily to itself because Jack Frost could not find it. There was a Sleeping Beauty, too, just at the time of the boys' arrival; but when Peter, like a true prince, flew lightly up the stairs, and kissed her eyelids, the enchantment was broken. The princess became his own good sister, and the fairy castle just one of the finest, most comfortable houses of The Hague.

As may well be believed, the boys received the heartiest of welcomes. After they had conversed awhile with their lively hostess, one of the genii summoned them to a grand repast in a red-curtained room, where floor and ceiling shone like polished ivory, and the mirrors suddenly blossomed into rosy-cheeked boys as far as the eye could reach.

They had caviare now, and salmagundi, and sausage and cheese, besides salad and fruit and biscuit and cake. How the boys could partake of such a medley was a mystery to Ben; for the salad was sour, and the cake was sweet; the fruit was dainty, and the salmagundi heavy with onions and fish. But, while he was wondering, he made a hearty meal, and was soon absorbed in deciding which he really preferred, the coffee or the anisette cordial. It was delightful, too—this taking one's food from dishes of frosted silver and liqueur glasses from which Titania herself might have sipped. The young gentleman afterward wrote to his mother that, pretty and choice as things were at home, he had never known what cut glass, china and silver services were until he visited The Hague.

Of course Peter's sister soon heard of all the boys' adventures. How they had skated over forty miles and seen rare sights on the way; how they had lost their purse and found it again. How one of the party had fallen and given them an excuse for a grand sail in an iceboat; how, above all, they had caught a robber, and so for a second time saved their slippery purse.

"And now, Peter," said the lady, when the story was finished, "you must write at once to tell the good people of Broek that your adventures have reached their height, that you and your fellow travelers have all been taken prisoners."

The boys looked startled.

"Indeed, I shall do no such thing," laughed Peter. "We must leave tomorrow at noon."

But the sister had already decided differently, and a Holland lady is not to be easily turned from her purpose. In short, she held forth such strong temptations, and was so bright and cheerful, and said so many coaxing and unanswerable things, in both English and Dutch, that the boys were all delighted when it was settled that they should remain at The Hague for at least two days.

Next the grand skating race was talked over; Mevrouw van Gend gladly promised to be present on the occasion. "I shall witness your triumph, Peter," she said, "for you are the fastest skater I ever knew."

Peter blushed and gave a slight cough, as Carl answered for him.

"Ah, mevrouw, he is swift, but all the Broek boys are fine skaters—even the ragpickers"—and he thought bitterly of poor Hans.

The lady laughed. "That will make the race all the more exciting," she said. "But I shall wish each of you to be the winner."

At this moment her husband Mynheer van Gend came in, and the enchantment falling upon the boys was complete.

The invisible fairies of the household at once clustered about them whispering that Jasper van Gend had a heart as young and fresh as their own, and if he loved anything in this world more than industry, it was sunshine and frolic. They hinted also something about his having a heart full of love and a head full of wisdom, and finally gave the boys to understand that when mynheer said a thing he meant it.

Therefore his frank "Well, now, this is pleasant," as he shook hands with them all, made the boys feel quite at home and as happy as squirrels.

There were fine paintings in the drawing room and exquisite statuary, and portfolios filled with rare Dutch engravings; besides many beautiful and curious things from China and Japan. The boys felt that it would require a month to examine all the treasures of the apartment.

Ben noticed with pleasure English books lying upon the table. He saw also over the carved, upright piano, life-sized portraits of William of Orange and his English queen, a sight that, for a time, brought England and Holland side by side in his heart. William and Mary have left a halo round the English throne to this day, he the truest patriot that ever served an adopted country, she the noblest wife that ever sat upon a British throne, up to the time of Victoria and Albert the Good. As Ben looked at the pictures, he remembered accounts he had read of King William's visit to The Hague in the winter of 1691. He who sang the Battle of Ivry had not yet told the glowing story of that day, but Ben knew enough of it to fancy that he could almost hear the shouts of the delighted populace as he looked from the portraits to the street, which at this moment was aglow with a bonfire, kindled in a neighboring square.

That royal visit was one never to be forgotten. For two years William of Orange had been monarch of a foreign land, his head working faithfully for England, but his whole heart yearning for Holland. Now, when he sought its shores once more, the entire nation bade him welcome. Multitudes flocked to The Hague to meet him—"many thousands came sliding or skating along the frozen canals from Amsterdam, Rotterdam, Leyden, Haarlem, Delft." [1] All day long the festivities of the capital were kept up, the streets were gorgeous with banners, evergreen arches, trophies, and mottoes of welcome and emblems of industry. William saw the deeds of his ancestors and scenes of his own past life depicted on banners and tapestries along the streets. At night, superb fireworks were displayed upon the ice. Its glassy surface was like a mirror. Sparkling fountains of light sprang up from below to meet the glittering cascades leaping upon it. Then a feathery fire of crimson

[1] Macaulay's *History of England.*

and green shook millions of rubies and emeralds into the ruddy depths of the ice—and all this time the people were shouting, "God bless William of Orange. Long live the King!" They were half mad with joy and enthusiasm. William their own prince, their stadtholder, had become the ruler of three kingdoms; he had been victorious in council and in war, and now, in his hour of greatest triumph, had come as a simple guest to visit them. The king heard their shouts with a beating heart. It is a great thing to be beloved by one's country. His English courtiers complimented him upon his reception. "Yes," said he, "but the shouting is nothing to what it would have been if Mary had been with me!"

While Ben was looking at the portraits, Mynheer van Gend was giving the boys an account of a recent visit to Antwerp. As it was the birthplace of Quentin Matsys, the blacksmith who for love of an artist's daughter studied until he became a great painter, the boys asked their host if he had seen any of Matsys' works.

"Yes, indeed," he replied, "and excellent they are. His famous triptych in a chapel of the Antwerp cathedral, with the Descent from the Cross on the center panel, is especially fine; but I confess I was more interested in his well."

"What well, mynheer?" asked Ludwig.

"One in the heart of the city, near this same cathedral, whose lofty steeple is of such delicate workmanship that the French emperor said it reminded him of Mechlin lace. The well is covered with a Gothic canopy surmounted by the figure of a knight in full armor. It is all of metal, and proves that Matsys was an artist at the forge as well as at the easel; indeed, his great fame is mainly derived from his miraculous skill as an artificer in iron."

Next, mynheer showed the boys some exquisite Berlin castings, which he had purchased in Antwerp. They were *iron jewelry,* and very delicate—beautiful medallions designed from rare paintings, bordered with fine tracery and openwork—worthy, he said, of being worn by the fairest

The giant was thrown into the Scheld

lady of the land. Consequently the necklace was handed with a bow and a smile to the blushing Mevrouw van Gend.

Something in the lady's aspect, as she bent her bright young face over the gift, caused mynheer to add earnestly:

"I can read your thoughts, sweetheart."

She looked up in playful defiance.

"Ah! now I am sure of them. You were thinking of those noblehearted women, but for whom Prussia might have fallen. I know it by that proud light in your eye."

"The proud light in my eye plays me false, then," she answered. "I had no such grand matter in my mind. To confess the simple truth, I was only thinking how lovely this necklace would be with my blue brocade."

"So! so!" exclaimed the rather crestfallen spouse.

"But I *can* think of the other, Jasper, and it will add a deeper value to your gift. You remember the incident, do you not, Peter? How when the French were invading Prussia and for lack of means the country was unable to defend itself against the enemy, the women turned the scale by pouring their plate and jewels into the public treasury——"

"Aha!" thought mynheer, as he met his vrouw's kindling glance. "The proud light is there, now, in earnest."

Peter remarked maliciously that the women had still proved true to their vanity on that occasion, for jewelry they would have. If gold or silver were wanted by the kingdom, they would relinquish it and use iron, but they could not do without their ornaments.

"What of that?" said the vrouw, kindling again. "It is no sin to love beautiful things, if you adapt your material to circumstances. All *I* have to say is, the women saved their country and, indirectly, introduced a very important branch of manufacture. Is not that so, Jasper?"

"Of course it is, sweetheart," said mynheer, "but Peter needs no word of mine to convince him that all the world over women have never been found wanting in their country's hour of trial, though (bowing to mevrouw) his own countrywomen stand foremost in the records of female patriotism and devotion."

Then, turning to Ben, the host talked with him in English of the fine old Belgian city. Among other things, he told the origin of its name. Ben had been taught that Antwerp was derived from *ae'nt werf* (on the wharf), but Mynheer van Gend gave him a far more interesting derivation.

It appears that about three thousand years ago, a great giant, named Antigonus, lived on the river Scheld, on the site of the present city of Antwerp. This giant claimed half the merchandise of all navigators who passed his castle. Of course some were inclined to oppose this simple regulation. In such cases, Antigonus, by way of teaching them to practice better manners next time, cut off and threw into the river the right hands of the merchants. Thus handwerpen (or hand-throwing), changed to Antwerp, came to be the name of the place. The escutcheon or arms of the city has two hands upon it; what better proof than this could one have of the truth of the story, especially when one wishes to believe it!

The giant was finally conquered and thrown into the Scheld by a hero called Brabo, who, in turn, gave a name to the district known as Brabant. Since then the Dutch merchants have traveled the river in peace; but I, for one, thank old Antigonus for giving the city so romantic an origin.

When Mynheer van Gend had related in two languages this story of Antwerp, he was tempted to tell other legends—some in English, some in Dutch; and so the moments, borne upon the swift shoulders of gnomes and giants, glided rapidly away toward bedtime.

It was hard to break up so pleasant a party, but the Van Gend household moved with the regularity of clockwork. There was no lingering at the threshold when the cordial "Good night!" was spoken. Even while our boys were mounting the stairs, the invisible household fairies again clustered around them, whispering that system and regularity had been chief builders of the master's prosperity.

Beautiful chambers with three beds in them were not to be found in this mansion. Some of the rooms contained two, but each visitor slept alone. Before morning, the motto of the party evidently was, "Every boy his own chrysalis," and Peter, at least, was not sorry to have it so.

Tired as he was, Ben, after noting a curious bellrope in the corner, began to examine his bedclothes. Each article filled him with astonishment—the exquisitely fine pillow spread trimmed with costly lace and embroidered with a gorgeous crest and initial, the *dekbed* cover (a great silk bag, large as the bed, stuffed with swan's-down) and the pink satin quilts, embroidered with garlands of flowers. He could scarcely sleep for thinking what a queer little bed it was, so comfortable and pretty, too, with all its queerness. In the morning he examined the top coverlet with care, for he wished to send home a description of it in his next letter. It was a Japanese spread, marvelous in texture as well as in its variety of brilliant coloring, and worth, as Ben afterward learned, not less than three hundred dollars.

The floor was of polished wooden mosaic, nearly covered with a rich carpet bordered with thick black fringe. Another room displayed a margin of satinwood around the carpet. Hung with tapestry, its walls of crimson silk were topped with a gilded cornice which shot down gleams of light far into the polished floor.

Over the doorway of the room in which Jacob and Ben slept was a bronze stork who, with outstretched neck, held a lamp to light the guests into the apartment. Between the two narrow beds, of carved whitewood and ebony, stood the household treasure of the Van Gends, a massive oaken chair upon which the Prince of Orange had once sat during a council meeting. Opposite stood a quaintly carved clothespress, waxed and polished to the utmost, and filled with precious stores of linen; beside it a table holding a large Bible, whose great golden clasps looked poor compared with its solid, ribbed binding made to outlast six generations.

There was a ship model on the mantelshelf, and over it hung an old portrait of Peter the Great, who, you know, once gave the dockyard cats of Holland a fine chance to look at a king, which is one of the special prerogatives of cats. Peter, though Czar of Russia, was not too proud to work as a common shipwright in the dockyards of Saardam and Amsterdam, that he might be able to introduce among his countrymen Dutch improvements in shipbuilding. It was this willingness to be thorough in even the smallest beginnings that earned for him the title of Peter the Great.

Peter the little (comparatively speaking) was up first, the next morning; knowing the punctual habits of his brother-in-law, he took good care that none of the boys should oversleep themselves. A hard task he found it to wake Jacob Poot; but after pulling that young gentleman out of bed, and, with Ben's help, dragging him about the room for a while, he succeeded in arousing him.

While Jacob was dressing, and moaning within him, because the felt slippers, provided him as a guest, were too tight for his swollen feet, Peter wrote to inform their friends at Broek of the safe arrival of his party at The Hague. He also begged his mother to send word to Hans Brinker that Dr. Boekman had not yet reached Leyden, but that a letter containing Hans' message had been left at the hotel where the doctor always lodged during his visits to the city. "Tell him, also," wrote Peter, "that I shall call there again, as I pass through Leyden. The poor boy seemed to feel sure that 'the meester' would hasten to save his father, but we, who know the gruff old gentleman better, may be confident he will do no such thing. It would be a kindness to send a visiting physician from Amsterdam to the cottage at once, if Jufvrouw[1] Brinker will consent to receive any but the

[1] In Holland, women of the lower grades of society do not take the title of Mrs. (or Mevrouw) when they marry, as with us. They assume their husband's name, but are still called Miss (Jufvrouw, pronounced yuffrow).

great king of the meesters, as Dr. Boekman certainly is.

"You know, mother," added Peter, "that I have always considered Sister van Gend's house as rather quiet and lonely; but I assure you, it is not so now. Sister says our presence has warmed it for the whole winter. Brother van Gend is very kind to us all. He says we make him wish that he had a houseful of boys of his own. He has promised to let us ride on his noble black horses. They are gentle as kittens, he says, if one have but a firm touch at the rein. Ben, according to Jacob's account, is a glorious rider, and your son Peter is not a very bad hand at the business; so we two are to go out together this morning mounted like knights of old. After we return, Brother van Gend says he will lend Jacob his English pony and obtain three extra horses; and all of the party are to trot about the city, in a grand cavalcade, led on by him. He will ride the black horse which father sent him from Friesland. My sister's pretty roan with the long white tail is lame and she will ride none other; else she would accompany us. I could scarcely close my eyes last night after sister told me of the plan. Only the thought of poor Hans Brinker and his sick father checked me—but for that I could have sung for joy. Ludwig has given us a name already—the Broek Cavalry. We flatter ourselves that we shall make an imposing appearance, especially in single file. . . ."

The Broek Cavalry were not disappointed. Mynheer van Gend readily procured good horses; and all the boys could ride, though none were as perfect horsemen (or horseboys) as Peter and Ben. They saw The Hague to their hearts' content; and The Hague saw them—expressing its approbation, loudly, through the mouths of small boys and cart dogs; silently, through bright eyes that, not looking very deeply into things, shone as they looked at the handsome Carl, and twinkled with fun as a certain portly youth with shaking cheeks rode past "bumpetty, bumpetty, bump!"

On their return, the boys pronounced the great porcelain stove in the family sitting room a decidedly useful piece of furniture, for they could gather round it and get warm without burning their noses or bringing on chilblains. It was so very large that, though hot nowhere, it seemed to send out warmth by the houseful. Its pure white sides and polished brass rings made it a pretty object to look upon, notwithstanding the fact that our ungrateful Ben, while growing thoroughly warm and comfortable beside it, concocted a satirical sentence for his next letter, to the effect that a stove in Holland must of course resemble a great tower of snow or it wouldn't be in keeping with the oddity of the country.

To describe all the boys saw and did on that day and the next, would render this little book a formidable volume indeed. They visited the brass cannon foundry, saw the liquid fire poured into molds and watched the smiths who, half naked, stood in the shadow, like demons playing with flame. They admired the grand public buildings and massive private houses, the elegant streets, and noble Bosch—pride of all beauty-loving Hollanders. The palace with its brilliant mosaic floors, its frescoed ceilings and gorgeous ornaments, filled Ben with delight; he was surprised that some of the churches were so very plain—elaborate sometimes in external architecture, but bare and bleak within with their blank, whitewashed walls.

If there were no printed record, the churches of Holland would almost tell her story. I will not enter into the subject here, except to say that Ben—who had read of her struggles and wrongs, and of the terrible retribution she from time to time dealt forth—could scarcely tread a Holland town without mentally leaping horror-stricken over the bloody steppingstones of its history. He could not forget Philip of Spain nor the Duke of Alva even while rejoicing in the prosperity that followed the Liberation. He looked in the meekest of Dutch eyes for something of the fire that once lit the haggard faces of those desperate, lawless men, who wearing with pride the title of "Beggars," which their oppressors had mockingly cast upon them, became the terror of land and sea. In Haarlem, he had wondered that the air did not still resound with the cries of Alva's three thousand victims. In Leyden, his heart had swelled in sympathy as he thought of the long procession of scarred and famished creatures who after the siege, with Adrian van der Werf at their head, tottered to the great church to sing a glorious anthem because Leyden was free! He remembered that this was even before they had tasted the bread brought by the Dutch ships. They would praise God first, then eat. Thousands of trembling voices were raised in glad thanksgiving. For a moment, it swelled higher and higher—then suddenly changed to sobbing—not one of all the multitude could sing another note. But who shall say that the anthem, even to its very end, was not heard in heaven!

Here, in The Hague, other thoughts came to Ben—of how Holland in later years unwillingly put her head under the French yoke, and how, galled and lashed past endurance, she had resolutely jerked it out again. He liked her for that. What nation of any spirit, thought he, could be expected to stand such work, paying all her wealth into a foreign treasury and yielding up the flower of her youth under foreign conscription. It was not so very long ago, either, since English guns had been heard booming close by in the German Ocean; well—all the fighting was over at last. Holland was a snug little monarchy now in her own right, and Ben, for one, was glad of it. Arrived at this charitable conclusion, he was prepared to enjoy to the utmost all the wonders of her capital; he quite delighted Mynheer van Gend with his hearty and intelligent interest—so, in fact, did all the boys, for a merrier, more observant party never went sight-seeing.

XXVIII
THROUGH THE HAGUE

THE picture gallery, in the Maurits Huis,[1] one of the finest in the world, seemed only to have flashed by the boys during a two hours' visit, so much was there to admire and examine. As for the royal cabinet of curiosities, in the same building, they felt that they had but glanced at it though they were there nearly half a day. It seemed to them that Japan had poured all her treasures within its walls. For a long period, Holland, always foremost in commerce, was the only nation allowed to have any intercourse with Japan. One can well forego a journey to that country if he can but visit the Museum at The Hague.

Room after room is filled with collections from the Hermit Empire—costumes peculiar to various ranks and pursuits, articles of ornament, household utensils, weapons, armor and surgical instruments. There is also an ingenious

[1] A building erected by Prince Maurice of Nassau.

Japanese model of the Island of Desina, the Dutch factory in Japan. It appears almost as the island itself would if seen through a reversed opera glass, and makes one feel like a Gulliver coming unexpectedly upon a Japanese Lilliput. There you see hundreds of people in native costumes, standing, kneeling, stooping, reaching—all at work, or pretending to be—and their dwellings, even their very furniture, spread out before you, plain as day. In another room a huge tortoise-shell baby house, fitted up in Dutch style and inhabited by dignified Dutch dolls, stands ready to tell you at a glance how people live in Holland.

Gretel, Hilda, Katrinka, even the proud Rychie Korbes, would have been delighted with this; but Peter and his gallant band passed it by without a glance. The war implements had the honor of detaining them for an hour; such clubs, such murderous krits, or daggers, such firearms, and, above all, such wonderful Japanese swords, quite capable of performing the accredited Japanese feat of cutting a man in two at a single stroke!

There were Chinese and other Oriental curiosities in the collection. Native historical relics, too, upon which our young Dutchmen gazed very soberly, though they were secretly proud to show them to Ben.

There was a model of the cabin at Saardam in which Peter the Great lived during his short career as a shipbuilder. Also, wallets and bowls—once carried by the "Beggar" Confederates who, uniting under the Prince of Orange, had freed Holland from the tyranny of Spain; the sword of Admiral van Speyk who about ten years before had perished in voluntarily blowing up his own ship; and Van Tromp's armor with the marks of bullets upon it. Jacob looked around, hoping to see the broom which the plucky admiral fastened to his masthead—but it was not there. The waistcoat which William Third[1] of England

[1] William, Prince of Orange, who became King of England, was a great-grandson of William the Silent, Prince of Orange, who was murdered by Geraerts (or Gerard) July 10, 1584.

wore during the last days of his life, possessed great interest for Ben; and one and all gazed with a mixture of reverence and horror-worship at the identical clothing worn by William the Silent when he was murdered at Delft by Balthazar Geraerts. A tawny leather doublet and plain surcoat of gray cloth, a soft felt hat, and a high neck ruff from which hung one of the "Beggars'" medals—these were not in themselves very princely objects, though the doublet had a tragic interest from its dark stains, and bullet holes. Ben could readily believe, as he looked upon the garments, that the Silent Prince, true to his greatness of character, had been exceedingly simple in his attire. His aristocratic prejudices were, however, decidedly shocked when Lambert told him of the way in which William's bride first entered The Hague.

"The beautiful Louisa de Coligny, whose father and former husband both had fallen at the Massacre of St. Bartholomew, was coming to be fourth wife to the Prince, and of course," said Lambert, "we Hollanders were too gallant to allow the lady to enter the town on foot. No, sir, we sent (or rather my ancestors did) a clean, open post-wagon to meet her, with a plank across it for her to sit upon!"

"Very gallant indeed!" exclaimed Ben, with almost a sneer in his polite laugh—"and she the daughter of an admiral of France."

"Was she? Upon my word I had nearly forgotten that. But, you see, Holland had very plain ways in the good old time; in fact, we are a very simple, frugal people to this day. The Van Gend establishment is a decided exception, you know."

"A very agreeable exception, I think," said Ben.

"Certainly, certainly. But, between you and me, Mynheer van Gend, though he has wrought his own fortunes, can afford to be magnificent, and yet be frugal."

"Exactly so," said Ben profoundly, at the same time stroking his upper lip and chin, which latterly he believed had been showing delightful and unmistakable signs of coming dignities.

While tramping on foot through the city, Ben often longed for a good English sidewalk. Here, as in the other towns, there was no curb, no raised pavement for foot travelers—but the streets were clean and even, and all vehicles were kept scrupulously within a certain tract. Strange to say, there were nearly as many sleds as wagons to be seen, though there was not a particle of snow. The sleds went scraping over the bricks or cobblestones; some provided with an apparatus in front for sprinkling water, to diminish the friction, and some rendered less musical by means of a dripping oil rag, which the driver occasionally applied to the runners.

Ben was surprised at the noiseless way in which Dutch laborers do their work. Even around the warehouses and docks there was no bustle, no shouting from one to another. A certain twitch of the pipe, or turn of the head or, at most, a raising of the hand, seemed to be all the signal necessary. Entire loads of cheeses or herrings are pitched from cart or canalboat into the warehouses without a word; but the passer-by must take his chance of being pelted, for a Dutchman seldom looks before or behind him while engaged at work.

Poor Jacob Poot, who seemed destined to bear all the mishaps of the journey, was knocked nearly breathless by a great cheese, which a fat Dutchman was throwing to a fellow laborer; but he recovered himself, and passed on without evincing the least indignation.

Ben professed great sympathy on the occasion, but Jacob insisted that it was "notting."

"Then why did you screw your face so when it hit you?"

"What for screw mine face?" repeated Jacob soberly. "Vy, it vash de—de——"

"The what?" insisted Ben maliciously.

"Vy, de—de—vat you call dis, vat you taste mit de nose?"

Ben laughed.

"Oh, you mean the smell."

"Yesh. Dat ish it," said Jacob eagerly. "It wash de shmell. I draw mine face for dat!"

"Ha! ha!" roared Ben, "that's a good one. A Dutch boy smell a cheese. You can never make me believe *that!*"

"Vell, it ish no matter," replied Jacob, trudging on beside Ben in perfect good humor. "Vait till you hit mit cheese—dat ish all."

Soon he added pathetically, "Penchamin, I no likes be call Tutch—dat ish no goot. I bees a Hollander."

Just as Ben was apologizing, Lambert hailed him.

"Hold up! Ben. Here is the fish market. There is not much to be seen at this season. But we can take a look at the storks if you wish."

Ben knew that storks were held in peculiar reverence in Holland, and that the bird figured upon the arms of the capital. He had noticed cart wheels placed upon the roofs of Dutch cottages to entice storks to settle upon them; he had seen their huge nests, too, on many a thatched gable roof from Broek to The Hague. But it was winter now. The nests were empty. No greedy birdlings opened their mouths—or rather their heads—at the approach of a great white-winged thing, with outstretched neck and legs, bearing a dangling something for their breakfast. The longbills were far away, picking up food on African shores; and before they would return in the spring, Ben's visit to the land of dykes would be over.

Therefore he pressed eagerly forward, as Van Mounen led the way through the fish market, anxious to see if storks in Holland were anything like the melancholy specimens he had seen in the Zoological Gardens of London.

It was the same old story. A tamed bird is a sad bird, say what you will. These storks lived in a sort of kennel, chained by the feet like felons, though supposed to be honored by being kept at the public expense. In summer they were allowed to walk about the market, where the fish stalls were like so many free dining saloons to them.

Untasted delicacies in the form of raw fish and butcher's offals lay about their kennels now, but the city guests preferred to stand upon one leg, curving back their long neck and leaning their head sidewise, in a blinking reverie. How gladly they would have changed their petted state for the busy life of some hard-working stork mother, or father, bringing up a troublesome family on the roof of a rickety old building, where flapping windmills frightened them half to death every time they ventured forth on a frolic.

Ben soon made up his mind, and rightly, too, that The Hague with its fine streets and public parks, shaded with elms, was a magnificent city. The prevailing costume was like that of London or Paris, and his British ears were many a time cheered by the music of British words. The shops were different in many respects from those on Oxford Street and the Strand, but they often were illumined by a printed announcement that English was "spoken within." Others proclaimed themselves to have London stout for sale—and one actually promised to regale its customers with English roast beef.

Over every possible shop door was the never-failing placard, "Tabak te Koop" (tobacco to be sold). Instead of colored glass globes in the windows, or high jars of leeches, the drugstores had a gaping Turk's head at the entrance—or, if the establishment were particularly fine, a wooden mandarin entire, indulging in a full yawn.

Some of these queer faces amused Ben exceedingly; they seemed to have just swallowed a dose of physic; but Van Mounen declared he could not see anything funny about them. A druggist showed his sense by putting a *Gaper* before his door, so that his place could be known at once as an "apotheek" and that was all there was about it.

Another thing attracted Ben—the milkmen's carts. These were small affairs, filled with shiny brass kettles or stone jars, and drawn by dogs. The milkman walked meekly beside his cart, keeping his dog in order, and delivering the milk to customers. Certain fish dealers had dogcarts, also, and when a herring dog chanced to meet a milk dog, he invariably put on airs and growled as he passed him. Sometimes a milk dog would recognize an acquaintance before another milk cart across the street, and then how the kettles would rattle, especially if they were empty! Each dog would give a bound and, never caring for his master's whistle, insist upon meeting the other halfway. Sometimes they contented themselves with an inquisitive sniff, but generally the smaller dog made an affectionate snap at the larger one's ear, or a friendly tussle was engaged in by way of exercise. Then woe! to the milk kettles, and woe! to the dogs!

The whipping over, each dog, expressing his feelings as best he could, would trot leisurely back to his work.

If some of these animals were eccentric in their ways, others were remarkably well behaved. In fact, there was a school for dogs in the city, established expressly for training them; Ben probably saw some of its graduates. Many a time he noticed a span of barkers trotting along the street with all the dignity of horses, obeying the slightest hint of the man walking briskly beside them. Sometimes, when their load was delivered, the dealer would jump in the cart, and have a fine drive to his home beyond the gates of the city; and sometimes, I regret to say, a patient vrouw would trudge beside the cart, with fish basket upon her head, and a child in her arms—while her lord enjoyed his drive, carrying no heavier burden than a stumpy clay pipe, the smoke of which mounted lovingly into her face.

XXIX
A DAY OF REST

THE sight-seeing came to an end at last, and so did our boys' visit to The Hague. They had spent three happy days and nights with the Van Gends, and, strange to say, had not once, in all that time, put on skates. The third day had indeed been one of rest. The noise and bustle of the city was hushed; sweet Sunday bells sent blessed, tranquil thoughts into their hearts. Ben felt, as he listened to their familiar music, that the Christian world is one, after all, however divided by sects and differences it may be. As the clock speaks everyone's native language in whatever land it may strike the hour, so the church bells are never foreign if our hearts but listen.

Led on by those clear voices, our party, with Mevrouw van Gend and her husband, trod the quiet but crowded streets, until they came to a fine old church in the southern part of the city.

The interior was large and, notwithstanding its great stained windows, seemed dimly lighted, though the walls were white, and dashes of red and purple sunshine lay brightly upon pillow and pew.

Ben saw a few old women moving softly through the aisles, each bearing a high pile of foot stoves which she distributed among the congregation by skillfully slipping out the under one, until none were left. It puzzled him that mynheer should settle himself with the boys in a comfortable side pew, after seating his vrouw in the body of the church, which was filled with chairs exclusively appropriated to the women. But Ben was learning only a common custom of the country.

The pews of the nobility and the dignitaries of the city were circular in form, each surrounding a column. Elaborately carved, they formed a massive base to their great pillars standing out in bold relief against the blank, white walls beyond. These columns, lofty and well-proportioned, were nicked and defaced from violence done to them long ago; yet it seemed quite fitting that, before they were lost in the deep arches overhead, their softened outlines should leaf out as they did into richness and beauty.

Soon, Ben lowered his gaze to the marble floor. It was a pavement of gravestones. Nearly all the large slabs, of which it was composed, marked the resting places of the dead. An armorial design engraved upon each stone, with inscription and date, told whose form was sleeping beneath, and sometimes three of a family were lying one above the other in the same sepulcher.

He could not but think of the solemn funeral procession winding by torchlight through those lofty aisles, and bearing its silent burden toward a dark opening whence a slab had been lifted, in readiness for its coming. It was something to feel that his sister Mabel, who died in her flower, was lying in a sunny churchyard, where a brook rippled and sparkled in the daylight and waving trees whispered together all night long; where flowers might nestle close to the headstone and moon and stars shed their peace upon it, and morning birds sing sweetly overhead.

Then he looked up from the pavement and rested his eyes upon the carved, oaken pulpit, exquisitely beautiful in design and workmanship. He could not see the minister—though, not long before, he had watched him slowly ascending its winding stair—a mild-faced man wearing a ruff about his neck, and a cloak reaching to the knee.

Meantime the great church had been silently filling. Its pews were somber with men and its center radiant with women in their fresh Sunday attire. Suddenly a soft rustling spread through the building. All eyes were turned toward the minister now appearing above the pulpit.

Although the sermon was spoken slowly, Ben could understand little of what was said; but when the hymn came, he joined in with all his heart. A thousand voices lifted in love and praise offered a grander language that he could readily comprehend.

Once he was startled, during a pause in the service, by seeing a little bag suddenly shaken before him. It had a tinkling bell at its side, and was attached to a long stick carried by one of the deacons. Not relying solely upon the mute appeal of the poor boxes fastened to the columns near the entrance, this more direct method was resorted to, of awakening the sympathies of the charitable.

Fortunately Ben had provided himself with a few stivers, or the musical bag must have tinkled before him in vain.

More than once, a dark look rose on our English boy's face that morning. He longed to stand up and harangue the people concerning a peculiarity that filled him with pain. Some of the men wore their hats during the service, or took them off whenever the humor prompted, and many put theirs on in the church as soon as they arose to leave. No wonder Ben's sense of propriety was wounded; and yet a higher sense would have been exercised had he tried to feel willing that Hollanders should follow the customs of their country. But his English heart said over and over again, "It is outrageous! It is sinful!"

There is an angel called Charity who often would save our hearts a great deal of trouble if we would but let her in.

XXX
HOMEWARD BOUND

On Monday morning, bright and early, our boys bade farewell to their kind entertainers and started on their homeward journey.

Peter lingered awhile at the lion-guarded door, for he and his sister had many parting words to say.

As Ben saw them bidding each other good-bye, he could not help feeling that kisses as well as clocks were wonderfully alike everywhere. The English kiss that his sister Jenny gave when he left home had said the same thing to him that the Vrouw van Gend's Dutch kiss said to Peter. Ludwig had taken his share of the farewell in the most matter-of-fact manner possible, and though he loved his sister well, had winced a little at her making such a child of him as to put an extra kiss "for mother" upon his forehead.

He was already upon the canal with Carl and Jacob. Were they thinking about sisters or kisses? Not a bit of it. They were so happy to be on skates once more, so impatient to dart at once into the very heart of Broek, that they spun and wheeled about like crazy fellows, relieving themselves, meantime, by muttering something about "Peter and donder" not worth translating.

Even Lambert and Ben who had been waiting at the street corner began to grow impatient.

The captain joined them at last; they were soon on the canal with the rest.

"Hurry up, Peter," growled Ludwig. "We're freezing by inches—there! I knew you'd be the last after all to get on your skates!"

"Did you?" said his brother, looking up with an air of deep interest—"clever boy!"

Ludwig laughed, but tried to look cross, as he said, "I'm in earnest. We must get home sometime this year."

"Now, boys," cried Peter, springing up, as he fastened the last buckle. "There's a clear way before us! We will imagine it's the grand race. Ready! One—two—three—START!"

I assure you very little was said for the first half hour. They were six Mercuries skimming the ice. In plain English they went like lightning—no, that is imaginary too. The fact is, one cannot decide what to say when half a dozen boys are whizzing past at such a rate. I can only tell you that each did his best, flying, with bent body, and eager eyes, in and out among the placid skaters on the canal, until the very guard shouted to them to "Hold up!" This only served to send them onward with a two-boy power that startled all beholders.

But the laws of inertia are stronger even than canal guards.

After awhile Jacob slackened his speed—then Ludwig—then Lambert—then Carl.

They soon halted to take a long breath, and finally found themselves standing in a group gazing after Peter and Ben who were still racing in the distance as if their lives were at stake.

"It is very evident," said Lambert, as he and his three companions started on again, "that neither of them will give up until he can't help it."

"What foolishness!" growled Carl, "to tire themselves at the beginning of the journey. But they're racing in earnest—that's certain. Halloo! Peter's flagging!"

"Not so!" cried Ludwig. "Catch him being beaten!"

"Ha! ha!" sneered Carl. "I tell you, boy, Benjamin is ahead."

Now if Ludwig disliked anything in this world, it was to be called a boy—probably because he was nothing else. He grew indignant at once.

"Humph, what are *you*, I wonder. There, sir! *now* look and see if Peter isn't ahead!"

"*I* think he *is,*" interposed Lambert, "but I can't quite tell at this distance."

"*I* think he isn't!" retorted Carl.

Jacob was growing anxious—he always abhorred an argument—so he said in a coaxing tone, "Don't quarrel—don't quarrel!"

"Don't quarrel!" mocked Carl, looking back at Jacob as he skated. "Who's quarreling? Poot, you're a goose."

"I can't help that," was Jacob's meek reply. "See! they are nearing the turn of the canal."

"*Now* we can see!" cried Ludwig in great excitement. "Peter will make it first, I know."

"He can't—for Ben is ahead!" insisted Carl. "Gunst! That iceboat will run over him. No! he is clear! They're a couple of geese anyhow. Hurrah! they're at the turn. Who's ahead?"

"Peter!" cried Ludwig joyfully.

"Good for the captain!" shouted Lambert and Jacob.

And Carl condescended to mutter:

"It *is* Peter after all. I thought, all the time, that head fellow was Ben."

This turn in the canal had evidently been their goal, for the two racers came to a sudden halt after passing it.

Carl said something about being "glad that they had sense enough to stop and rest"—and the four boys skated on in silence to overtake their companions.

All the while, Carl was secretly wishing that he had kept on with Peter and Ben, as he felt sure he could easily have come out winner. He was a very rapid, though by no means a graceful skater.

Ben was looking at Peter with mingled vexation, admiration and surprise, as the boys drew near.

They heard him saying in English:

"You're a perfect bird on the ice, Peter van Holp. The first fellow that ever beat me in a fair race, I can tell you!"

Peter, who understood the language better than he could speak it, returned a laughing bow at Ben's compliment, but made no further reply. Possibly he was scant of breath at the time.

"Now, Penchamin, vat you do mit yourself? Get so hot as a firebrick—dat ish no goot," was Jacob's plaintive comment.

"Nonsense!" answered Ben. "This frosty air will cool me soon enough. I am not tired."

"You are beaten, though, my boy," said Lambert in English, "and fairly, too. How will it be, I wonder, on the day of the grand race?"

Ben flushed, and gave a proud, defiant laugh, as if to say:

"This was mere pastime. I'm *determined* to beat then, come what will!"

XXXI

BOYS AND GIRLS

By the time the boys reached the village of Voorhout which stands near the grand canal, about halfway between The Hague and Haarlem, they were forced to hold a council. The wind, though moderate at first, had grown stronger and stronger, until at last they could hardly skate against it. The weather vanes throughout the country had evidently entered into a conspiracy.

"No use trying to face such a blow as this," said Ludwig. "It cuts its way down a man's throat like a knife."

"Keep your mouth shut, then," grunted the affable Carl, who was strong-chested as a young ox. "I'm for keeping on."

"In this case," interposed Peter, "you must consult the weakest of the party rather than the strongest."

The captain's principle was all right, but its application

was not flattering to Master Ludwig. Shrugging his shoulders, he retorted:

"Who's weak? Not I, for one—but the wind's stronger than any of us. I hope you'll condescend to admit that!"

"Ha! ha!" laughed Van Mounen, who could barely keep his feet. "So it is."

Just then the weather vanes telegraphed to each other by a peculiar twitch—and, in an instant, the gust came. It nearly threw the strong-chested Carl; it almost strangled Jacob; and quite upset Ludwig.

"This settles the question," shouted Peter. "Off with your skates! We'll go into Voorhout."

At Voorhout they found a little inn with a big yard. The yard was well bricked, and, better than all, was provided with a complete set of skittles, so our boys soon turned the detention into a frolic. The wind was troublesome even in that sheltered quarter, but they were on good standing-ground, and did not mind it.

First a hearty dinner—then the game. With pins as long as their arms, and balls as big as their heads, plenty of strength left for rolling, and a clean sweep of sixty yards for the strokes—no wonder they were happy.

That night Captain Peter and his men slept soundly. No prowling robber came to disturb them; and, as they were distributed in separate rooms, they did not even have a bolster battle in the morning.

Such a breakfast as they ate! The landlord looked frightened. When he had asked them where they "belonged," he made up his mind that the Broek people starved their children. It was a shame, "such fine young gentlemen, too!"

Fortunately the wind had tired itself out, and fallen asleep in the great sea cradle beyond the Dunes. There were signs of snow; otherwise, the weather was fine.

It was mere child's play for the well-rested boys to skate to Leyden. Here they halted awhile, for Peter had an errand at the Golden Eagle. He left the city with a lightened heart; Dr. Boekman had been at the hotel, read the note containing Hans' message, and departed for Broek.

"I cannot say it was your letter sent him off so soon," explained the landlord. "Some rich lady in Broek was taken bad very sudden, and he was sent for in haste."

Peter turned pale.

"What was the name?" he asked.

"Indeed, it went in one ear and out of the other—for all I hindered it. Plague to people who can't see a traveler in comfortable lodgings, but they must whisk him off, before one can breathe."

"A lady in Broek, did you say?"

"Yes," very gruffly. "Any other business, young master?"

"No, mine host—except that I and my comrades here would like a bite of something and a drink of hot coffee."

"Ah," said the landlord sweetly, "a bite you shall have, and coffee too, the finest in Leyden. Walk up to the stove, my masters—now I think again—that was a widow lady—from Rotterdam, I think they said, visiting at one Van Stoepel's if I mistake not."

"Ah!" said Peter, greatly relieved. "They live in the white house by the Schlossen Mill. Now, mynheer, the coffee, please!"

"What a goose I was," thought he, as the party left the Golden Eagle, "to feel so sure it was my mother. But she may be somebody's mother, poor woman, for all that. Who can she be, I wonder?"

There were not many upon the canal that day, between Leyden and Haarlem. However, as the boys neared Amsterdam, they found themselves once more in the midst of a moving throng. The big ysbreeker [1] had been at work for the first time that season, but there was any amount of skating ground left yet.

[1] Icebreaker—A heavy machine armed with iron spikes for breaking the ice as it is dragged along. Some of the small ones are worked by men—but the large ones are drawn by horses—sixty or seventy of which are sometimes attached to one ysbreeker.

"Three cheers for home!" cried Van Mounen, as they came in sight of the great Western Dock (Westelijk Dok). "Hurrah! Hurrah!" shouted one and all. "Hurrah! Hurrah!"

This trick of cheering was an importation among our party. Lambert van Mounen had brought it from England. As they always gave it in English, it was considered quite an exploit and, when circumstances permitted, always enthusiastically performed, to the sore dismay of their quiet-loving countrymen.

Therefore, their arrival at Amsterdam created a great sensation, especially among the small boys on the wharfs.

The Y was crossed. They were on the Broek canal.

Lambert's home was reached first.

"Good-bye, boys!" he cried, as he left them. "We've had the greatest frolic ever known in Holland."

"So we have. Good-bye, Van Mounen!" answered the boys.

"Good-bye!"

Peter hailed him. "I say, Van Mounen, the classes begin tomorrow!"

"I know it. Our holiday is over. Good-bye, again."

"Good-bye!"

Broek came in sight. Such meetings! Katrinka was on the canal! Carl was delighted. Hilda was there! Peter felt rested in an instant. Rychie was there! Ludwig and Jacob nearly knocked each other over in their eagerness to shake hands with her.

Dutch girls are modest and generally quiet; but they have very glad eyes. For a few moments, it was hard to decide whether Hilda, Rychie or Katrinka felt the most happy.

Annie Bouman was also on the canal, looking even prettier than the other maidens, in her graceful peasant's costume. But she did not mingle with Rychie's party; neither did she look unusually happy.

The one she liked most to see was not among the new-comers. Indeed, he was not upon the canal at all. She had not been near Broek since the Eve of Saint Nicholas, for she was staying with her sick grandmother in Amsterdam, and had been granted a brief resting spell, as the grandmother called it, because she had been such a faithful little nurse night and day.

Annie had devoted her resting spell to skating with all her might toward Broek, and back again, in the hope of meeting her mother or some of her family on the canal, or, it might be, Gretel Brinker. Not one of them had she seen, and she must hurry back, without ever catching a glimpse of her mother's cottage; for the poor helpless grandmother, she knew, was by this time moaning for someone to turn her upon her cot.

Where can Gretel be? thought Annie, as she flew over the ice; she can almost always steal a few moments from her work at this time of day. Poor Gretel! What a dreadful thing it must be to have a dull father! I should be woefully afraid of him, I know—so strong, and yet so strange!

Annie had not heard of his illness. Dame Brinker and her affairs received but little notice from the people of the place.

If Gretel had not been known as a goose-girl she might have had more friends among the peasantry of the neighborhood. As it was, Annie Bouman was the only one who did not feel ashamed to avow herself by word and deed the companion of Gretel and Hans.

When the neighbors' children laughed at her for keeping such poor company, she would simply flush when Hans was ridiculed, or laugh in a careless, disdainful way; but to hear little Gretel abused always awakened her wrath.

"Goose-girl, indeed!" she would say. "I can tell you any of you are fitter for the work than she. My father often said last summer that it troubled him to see such a bright-eyed, patient little maiden tending geese. Humph! She would not harm them, as you would, Janzoon Kolp;

and she would not tread upon them, as you might, Kate Wouters."

This would be pretty sure to start a laugh at the clumsy, ill-natured Kate's expense; and Annie would walk loftily away from the group of young gossips. Perhaps some memory of Gretel's assailants crossed her mind as she skated rapidly toward Amsterdam, for her eyes sparkled ominously and she more than once gave her pretty head a defiant toss. When that mood passed, such a bright, rosy, affectionate look illumined her face that more than one weary workingman turned to gaze after her, and to wish that he had a glad, contented lass like that for a daughter.

There were five joyous households in Broek that night.

The boys were back safe and sound; and they found all well at home. Even the sick lady at neighbor Van Stoepel's was out of danger.

But the next morning! Ah, how stupidly school bells will ding-dong, ding-dong, when one is tired.

Ludwig was sure he had never listened to anything so odious. Even Peter felt pathetic on the occasion. Carl said it was a shame for a fellow to have to turn out when his bones were splitting. And Jacob soberly bade Ben "Goot-pye!" and walked off with his satchel as if it weighed a hundred pounds.

XXXII
THE CRISIS

WHILE the boys are nursing their fatigue, we will take a peep into the Brinker cottage.

Can it be that Gretel and her mother have not stirred since we saw them last? That the sick man upon the bed has not even turned over? It was four days ago and there is the sad group just as it was before. No, not precisely the same, for Raff Brinker is paler; his fever is gone, though he knows nothing of what is passing. Then they were alone in the bare, clean room. Now there is another group in an opposite corner.

Dr. Boekman is there, talking in a low tone with a stout young man who listens intently. The stout young man is his student and assistant. Hans is there also. He stands near the window respectfully waiting until he shall be accosted.

"You see, Vollenhoven," said Dr. Boekman, "it is a clear case of—" and here he went off into a queer jumble of Latin and Dutch that I cannot conveniently translate.

After awhile, as Vollenhoven looked at him rather blankly, the learned man condescended to speak to him in simpler phrase.

"It is probably like Rip Donderdunck's case," he explained, in a low, mumbling tone. "He fell from the top of Voppelploot's windmill. After the accident the man was stupid, and finally became idiotic. In time he lay helpless like yon fellow on the bed, moaned, too, like him, and kept constantly lifting his hand to his head. My learned friend Von Choppem performed an operation upon this Donderdunck, and discovered under the skull a small dark sac, which pressed upon the brain. This had been the cause of the trouble. My friend Von Choppem removed it—a splendid operation! You see, according to Celsus—" and here the doctor again went off into Latin.

"Did the man live?" asked the assistant respectfully.

Dr. Boekman scowled. "That is of no consequence. I believe he died, but why not fix your mind on the grand features of the case? Consider a moment how—" and he plunged into Latin mysteries more deeply than ever.

"But, mynheer," gently persisted the student, who knew that the doctor would not rise to the surface for hours unless pulled at once from his favorite depths. "Mynheer, you have other engagements today, three legs in Amsterdam, you remember, and an eye in Broek, and that tumor up the canal."

"The tumor can wait," said the doctor reflectively. "That is another beautiful case—a beautiful case! The woman has not lifted her head from her shoulder for two months—magnificent tumor, sir!" The doctor by this time was speaking aloud. He had quite forgotten where he was.

Vollenhoven made another attempt.

"This poor fellow on the bed, mynheer. Do you think you can save him?"

"Ah, indeed, certainly," stammered the doctor, suddenly perceiving that he had been talking rather off the point—"certainly, that is—I hope so."

"If anyone in Holland can, mynheer," murmured the assistant with honest bluntness, "it is yourself."

The doctor looked displeased—growled out a tender request for the student to talk less, and beckoned Hans to draw near.

This strange man had a great horror of speaking to women, especially on surgical matters. "One can never tell," he said, "what moment the creatures will scream or faint." Therefore he explained Raff Brinker's case to Hans and told him what he believed should be done to save the patient.

Hans listened attentively, growing red and pale by turns, and throwing quick, anxious glances toward the bed.

"It may *kill* the father—did you say, mynheer?" he exclaimed at last, in a trembling whisper.

"It may, my boy. But I have a strong belief that it will cure and not kill. Ah! if boys were not such dunces, I could lay the whole matter before you, but it would be of no use."

Hans looked blank at this compliment.

"It would be of no use," repeated Dr. Boekman indignantly. "A great operation is proposed; but one might as well do it with a hatchet. The only question asked is, 'Will it kill?' "

"The question is *everything* to us, mynheer," said Hans, with tearful dignity.

Dr. Boekman looked at him in sudden dismay.

"Ah! exactly so. You are right, boy, I am a fool. Good boy. One does not wish one's father killed—of course not. I am a fool."

"Will he die, mynheer, if this sickness goes on?"

"Humph! this is no new illness. The same thing growing worse every instant—pressure on the brain—will take him off soon like *that,*" said the doctor, snapping his fingers.

"And the operation *may* save him," pursued Hans. "How soon, mynheer, can we know?"

Dr. Boekman grew impatient.

"In a day, perhaps, an hour. Talk with your mother, boy, and let her decide. My time is short."

Hans approached his mother; at first, when she looked up at him, he could not utter a syllable; then turning his eyes away he said in a firm voice:

"I must speak with the mother alone."

Quick little Gretel, who could not quite understand what was passing, threw rather an indignant look at Hans, and walked away.

"Come back, Gretel, and sit down," said Hans sorrowfully. She obeyed.

Dame Brinker and her boy stood by the window while the doctor and his assistant, bending over the bedside, conversed together in a low tone. There was no danger of disturbing the patient. He appeared like one blind and deaf. Only his faint, piteous moans showed him to be a living man. Hans was talking earnestly, and in a low voice, for he did not wish his sister to hear.

With dry, parted lips, Dame Brinker leaned toward him searching his face, as if suspecting a meaning beyond his words. Once she gave a quick, frightened sob that made Gretel start, but, after that, listened calmly.

When Hans ceased to speak, his mother turned, gave one agonized look at her husband, lying there so pale and unconscious, and threw herself on her knees beside the bed.

Poor little Gretel! what did all this mean? She looked with questioning eyes at Hans; he was standing, but his head was bent as if in prayer—at the doctor; he was gently feeling her father's head, and looked like one examining some curious stone—at the assistant; the man coughed and turned away—at her mother. Ah! little Gretel, that was the best you could do—to kneel beside her and twine your warm, young arms about her neck—to weep and implore God to listen.

When the mother arose, Dr. Boekman, with a show of trouble in his eyes, asked gruffly, "Well, jufvrouw, shall it be done?"

"Will it pain him, mynheer?" she asked in a trembling voice.

"I cannot say. Probably not. Shall it be done?"

"It may *cure* him, you said, and—mynheer, did you tell my boy that—perhaps—perhaps"—she could not finish.

"Yes, jufvrouw, I said the patient might sink under the operation; but we will hope it may prove otherwise." He looked at his watch. The assistant moved impatiently to the window. "Come, jufvrouw, time presses. Yes, or no?"

Hans wound his arm about his mother. It was not his usual way. He even leaned his head against her shoulder.

"The meester awaits an answer," he whispered.

Dame Brinker had long been the head of her house in every sense. Many a time she had been very stern with Hans, ruling him with a strong hand, and rejoicing in her motherly discipline—*now* she felt so weak, so helpless. It was something to feel that firm embrace. There was strength even in the touch of that yellow hair.

She turned to her boy imploringly.

"Oh, Hans! What shall I say?"

"Say what God tells thee, mother," answered Hans, bowing his head.

One quick, questioning prayer to Heaven rose from the mother's heart. The answer came.

She turned toward Dr. Boekman.

"It is right, mynheer. I consent."

"Humph!" grunted the doctor, as if to say, "You've been long enough about it." Then he conferred a moment with his assistant, who listened with great outward deference but was inwardly rejoicing at the grand joke he would have to tell his fellow students. He had actually seen a tear in "old Boekman's" eye.

Meanwhile Gretel looked on in trembling silence; but when she saw the doctor open a leathern case, and take out one sharp, gleaming instrument after another, she sprang forward.

Gretel was known as the "goose-girl"

"Oh, mother! The poor father meant no wrong. Are they going to *murder* him?"

"I do not know, child," screamed Dame Brinker, looking fiercely at Gretel. "I do not know."

"This will not do, jufvrouw," said Dr. Boekman sternly, and at the same time he cast a quick, penetrating look at Hans. "You and the girl must leave the room. The boy may stay."

Dame Brinker drew herself up in an instant. Her eyes flashed. Her whole countenance was changed. She looked like one who had never wept, never felt a moment's weakness. Her voice was low but decided. "I stay with my husband, mynheer."

Dr. Boekman looked astonished. His orders were seldom disregarded in this style. For an instant his eye met hers.

"You may remain, jufvrouw," he said in an altered voice.

Gretel had already disappeared.

In one corner of the cottage was a small closet where her rough, boxlike bed was fastened against the wall: none would think of the trembling little creature crouching there in the dark.

Dr. Boekman took off his heavy coat; he filled an earthen basin with water and placed it near the bed. Then turning to Hans he asked, "Can I depend upon you, boy?"

"You can, mynheer."

"I believe you. Stand at the head, here—your mother may sit at your right—so," and he set a chair near the cot.

"Remember, jufvrouw, there must be no cries, no fainting."

Dame Brinker answered him with a look.

He was satisfied. "Now, Vollenhoven."

Oh! that case with the terrible instruments. The assistant lifted them. Gretel, who had been peering, with brimming eyes, through the crack of the closet door, could remain silent no longer.

She rushed frantically across the apartment, seized her hood, and ran from the cottage.

XXXIII

GRETEL AND HILDA

It was recess hour. At the first stroke of the schoolhouse bell, the canal seemed to give a tremendous shout, and grow suddenly alive with boys and girls. The sly thing, shining so quietly under the noonday sun, was a kaleidoscope at heart, and only needed a shake from that great clapper to start it into dazzling changes.

Dozens of gaily clad children were skating in and out among each other, and all their pent-up merriment of the morning was relieving itself in song and shout and laughter. There was nothing to check the flow of frolic. Not a thought of schoolbooks came out with them into the sunshine. Latin, arithmetic, grammar, all were locked up for an hour in the dingy schoolroom. The teacher might be a noun if he wished, and a proper one at that, but *they* meant to enjoy themselves. As long as the skating was as perfect as this, it made no difference whether Holland were on the North Pole or the Equator; and, as for philosophy, how could they bother themselves about inertia and gravitation and such things, when it was as much as they could do to keep from getting knocked over in the commotion.

In the height of the fun, one of the children called out: "What is that?"

"What? Where?" cried a dozen voices.

"Why—don't you see? That dark thing over there by the idiot's cottage."

"I don't see anything," said one.

"I do," shouted another. "It's a dog!"

"Where's any dog?" put in a squeaky voice that we have heard before. "It's no such thing—it's a heap of rags."

"Pooh! Voost," retorted another gruffly, "that's about as near the fact as you ever get. It's the goose-girl, Gretel, looking for rats."

"Well, what of it?" squeaked Voost. "Isn't *she* a bundle of rags, I'd like to know?"

"Ha! ha! Pretty good for you, Voost! You'll get a medal for wit yet, if you keep on."

"You'd get something else, if her brother Hans were here. I'll warrant you would!" said a muffled-up little fellow, with a cold in his head.

As Hans was *not* there, Voost could afford to scout the insinuation. "Who cares for *him*, little sneezer? I'd fight a dozen like him any day, and you in the bargain."

"You would, would you? I'd like to catch you at it," and, by way of proving his words, the sneezer skated off at the top of his speed.

Just then a general chase after three of the biggest boys of the school was proposed—and friend and foe, frolicsome as ever, were soon united in a common cause.

Only one of all that happy throng remembered the dark little form by the idiot's cottage. Poor, frightened Gretel! She was not thinking of them, though their merry laughter floated lightly toward her, making her feel like one in a dream.

How loud the moans were behind the darkened window! What if those strange men were really killing her father!

The thought made her spring to her feet with a cry of horror!

"Ah! no," she sobbed, sinking upon the frozen mound of earth where she had been sitting, "mother is there, and Hans. They will care for him. But how pale they were. And even Hans was crying!

"Why did the cross old meester keep *him,* and send me away," she thought. "I could have clung to the mother and kissed her. That always makes her stroke my hair and speak gentle, even after she has scolded me. How quiet it is now! Oh, if the father should die, and Hans, and the mother, what *would* I do?" and Gretel, shivering with cold, buried her face in her arms, and cried as if her heart would break.

The poor child had been tasked beyond her strength during the past four days. Through all, she had been her mother's willing little handmaiden, soothing, helping and cheering the half-widowed woman by day, and watching and praying beside her all the long night. She knew that something terrible and mysterious was taking place at this moment, something that had been too terrible and mysterious for even kind, good Hans to tell.

Then new thoughts came. Why had not Hans told her? It was a shame. It was *her* father as well as his. She was no baby. She had once taken a sharp knife from the father's hand. She had even drawn him away from the mother on that awful night when Hans, big as he was, could not help her. Why, then, must she be treated like one who could do nothing? Oh, how very still it was—how bitter, bitter cold! If Annie Bouman had only stayed home instead of going to Amsterdam, it wouldn't be so lonely. How cold her feet were growing—was it the moaning that made her feel as if she were floating in the air!

This would not do—the mother might need her help at any moment!

Rousing herself with an effort, Gretel sat upright, rubbing her eyes and wondering—wondering that the sky was so bright and blue—wondering at the stillness in the cottage—more than all, at the laughter rising and falling in the distance.

Soon she sank down again, the strange medley of thought growing more and more confused in her bewildered brain.

What a strange lip the meester had! How the stork's nest upon the roof seemed to rustle and whisper down to her! How bright those knives were in the leathern case—brighter perhaps than the silver skates. If she had but worn her new jacket she would not shiver so. The new jacket was pretty—the only pretty thing she had ever worn. God had taken care of her father so long, He would do it still, if those two men would but go away. Ah, now the meesters were on the roof, they were clambering to the top—no—it was her mother and Hans—or the storks—it was so dark who could tell? and the mound rocking, swinging in that strange way. How sweetly the birds were singing. They must be winter birds, for the air was thick with icicles—not one bird—but twenty. Oh! hear them, mother—wake me, mother, for the race—I am so tired with crying, and crying——

A firm hand was laid upon her shoulder.

"Get up, little girl!" cried a kind voice. "This will not do, for you to lie here and freeze."

Gretel slowly raised her head. She was so sleepy that it seemed nothing strange to her that Hilda van Gleck should be leaning over her, looking with kind, beautiful eyes into her face. She had often dreamed it before.

But she had never dreamed that Hilda was shaking her roughly, almost dragging her by main force; never dreamed that she heard her saying, "Gretel! Gretel Brinker! you *must* wake!"

This was real. Gretel looked up. Still the lovely delicate young lady was shaking, rubbing, fairly pounding her. It must be a dream. No, there was the cottage—and the stork's nest, and the meester's coach by the canal. She could see them now quite plainly. Her hands were tingling, her feet throbbing. Hilda was forcing her to walk.

At last Gretel began to feel like herself again.

"I have been asleep," she faltered, rubbing her eyes with both hands and looking very much ashamed.

"Yes, indeed, entirely too much asleep," laughed Hilda, whose lips were very pale, "but you are well enough now. Lean upon me, Gretel; there, keep moving, you will soon be warm enough to go by the fire. Now let me take you into the cottage."

"Oh, no! no! no! jufvrouw, not in there! The meester is there. He sent me away!"

Hilda was puzzled, but she wisely forbore to ask at present for an explanation. "Very well, Gretel, try to walk faster. I saw you upon the mound; but I thought you were playing. That is right, keep moving."

All this time the kindhearted girl had been forcing Gretel to walk up and down, supporting her with one arm, and, with the other, striving as well as she could to take off her own warm sacque.

Suddenly Gretel suspected her intention.

"Oh, jufvrouw! jufvrouw!" she cried imploringly. "*Please* never think of such a thing as *that*. Oh! please keep it on. I am burning all over, jufvrouw! I really am burning. Not burning exactly, but pins and needles pricking all over me. Oh, jufvrouw, don't!"

The poor child's dismay was so genuine that Hilda hastened to reassure her.

"Very well, Gretel, move your arms then—so. Why, your cheeks are as pink as roses, already. I think the meester would let you in now, he certainly would. Is your father so very ill?"

"Ah, jufvrouw," cried Gretel, weeping afresh, "he is dying, I think. There are two meesters in with him at this moment, and the mother has scarce spoken today. Can you hear him moan, jufvrouw?" she added, with sudden terror. "The air buzzes so I cannot hear. He may be dead! Oh, I do wish I could hear him!"

Hilda listened. The cottage was very near, but not a sound could be heard. Something told her that Gretel was right. She ran to the window.

"You cannot see there, my lady," sobbed Gretel eagerly. "The mother has oiled paper hanging inside. But at the other one, in the south end of the cottage, you can look in where the paper is torn."

Hilda in her anxiety ran round, past the corner where the low roof was fringed with its loosened thatch.

A sudden thought checked her.

"It is not right for me to peep into another's house in this way," she said to herself; then softly calling to Gretel, she added, in a whisper, "You may look—perhaps he is only sleeping."

Gretel tried to walk briskly toward the spot, but her limbs were trembling. Hilda hastened to her support.

"You are sick, yourself, I fear," she said kindly.

"No, not sick, jufvrouw, but my heart cries all the time now, even when my eyes are as dry as yours. Why! jufvrouw, your eyes are not dry! Are you crying for *us!* Oh, jufvrouw, if God sees you! Oh! I know father will get better now," and the little creature, even while reaching to look through the tiny window, kissed Hilda's hand again and again.

The sash was sadly patched and broken, a torn piece of paper hung halfway down across it. Gretel's face was pressed to the window.

"Can you see anything?" whispered Hilda at last.

"Yes—the father lies very still, his head is bandaged and all their eyes are fastened upon him. Oh, jufvrouw!" almost screamed Gretel, as she started back, and by a quick, dexterous movement shook off her heavy wooden shoes, "I *must* go in to my mother! Will you come with me?"

"Not now, the bell is ringing. I shall come again soon."

Gretel scarcely heard the words. She remembered for many a day afterward the bright, pitying smile on Hilda's face, as she turned away.

XXXIV
THE AWAKENING

An angel could not have entered the cottage more noiselessly. Gretel, not daring to look at anyone, slid softly to her mother's side.

The room was very still. She could hear the old doctor breathe. She could almost hear the sparks as they fell into the ashes on the hearth. The mother's hand was very cold but a burning spot glowed on her cheek; and her eyes were like a deer's—so bright, so sad, so eager.

At last there was a movement upon the bed, very slight, but enough to cause them all to start. Dr. Boekman leaned eagerly forward. Another movement. The large hand, so white and soft for a poor man's hand, twitched—then raised itself steadily toward the forehead.

It felt the bandage, not in a restless, crazy way, but with a questioning movement that caused even Dr. Boekman to hold his breath. Then the eyes opened slowly.

"Steady! steady!" said a voice that sounded very strange to Gretel. "Shift that mat higher, boys! Now throw on the clay. The waters are rising fast—no time to——"

Dame Brinker sprang forward like a young panther.

She seized his hands, and leaning over him, cried, "Raff! Raff, boy, speak to me!"

"Is it you, Meitje?" he asked faintly. "I have been asleep, hurt, I think. Where is little Hans?"

"Here I am, father!" shouted Hans, half mad with joy. But the doctor held him back.

"He knows us!" screamed Dame Brinker. "Great God! he knows us! Gretel! Gretel! Come, see your father!"

In vain Dr. Boekman commanded "Silence!" and tried to force them from the bedside. He could not keep them off.

Hans and his mother laughed and cried together, as they hung over the newly awakened man. Gretel made no sound, but gazed at them all with glad, startled eyes. Her father was speaking in a faint voice.

"Is the baby asleep, Meitje?"

"The baby!" echoed Dame Brinker. "Oh, Gretel, that is *you!* And he calls Hans, 'little Hans.' Ten years asleep! Oh, mynheer, you have saved us all. He has known nothing for ten years! Children, why don't you thank the meester?"

The good woman was beside herself with joy. Dr. Boekman said nothing; but as his eye met hers, he pointed upward. She understood. So did Hans and Gretel.

With one accord they knelt by the cot, side by side. Dame Brinker felt for her husband's hand even while she was praying. Dr. Boekman's head was bowed; the assistant stood by the hearth with his back toward them.

"Why do you pray?" murmured the father, looking feebly from the bed, as they rose. "Is it God's day?"

It was not Sunday; but his vrouw bowed her head—she could not speak.

"Then we should have a chapter," said Raff Brinker, speaking slowly and with difficulty. "I do not know how it is. I am very, very weak. Mayhap the minister will read to us."

Gretel lifted the big Dutch Bible from its carved shelf.

Dr. Boekman, rather dismayed at being called a minister, coughed and handed the volume to his assistant.

"Read," he muttered. "These people must be kept quiet or the man will die yet."

When the chapter was finished, Dame Brinker motioned mysteriously to the rest by way of telling them that her husband was asleep.

"Now, jufvrouw," said the doctor in a subdued tone, as he drew on his thick woolen mittens, "there must be perfect quiet. You understand. This is truly a most remarkable case. I shall come again tomorrow. Give the patient no food today," and, bowing hastily, he left the cottage, followed by his assistant.

His grand coach was not far away; the driver had kept the horses moving slowly up and down by the canal nearly all the time the doctor had been in the cottage.

Hans went out also.

"May God bless you, mynheer!" he said, blushing and trembling. "I can never repay you, but if——"

"Yes, you can," interrupted the doctor crossly. "You can use your wits when the patient wakes again. This clacking and sniveling is enough to kill a well man, let alone one lying on the edge of his grave. If you want your father to get well, keep 'em quiet."

So saying, Dr. Boekman, without another word, stalked off to meet his coach, leaving Hans standing there with eyes and mouth wide open.

Hilda was reprimanded severely that day for returning late to school after recess, and for imperfect recitations. She had remained near the cottage until she heard Dame Brinker laugh, until she had heard Hans say, "Here I am, father!" and then she had gone back to her lessons. What wonder that she missed them! How could she get a long string of Latin verbs by heart, when her heart did not care a fig for them, but would keep saying to itself, "Oh, I am so glad! I am so glad!"

XXXV
BONES AND TONGUES

BONES are strange things. One would suppose that they knew nothing at all about school affairs, but they do. Even Jacob Poot's bones, buried as they were in flesh, were sharp in the matter of study hours.

Early on the morning of his return they ached through and through, giving Jacob a twinge at every stroke of the school bell, as if to say "Stop that clapper! There's trouble in it." After school, on the contrary, they were quiet and comfortable; in fact, seemed to be taking a nap among their cushions.

The other boys' bones behaved in a similar manner—but that is not so remarkable. Being nearer the daylight than Jacob's, they might be expected to be more learned in the ways of the world. Master Ludwig's, especially, were like beauty, only skin deep; they were the most knowing bones you ever heard of. Just put before him, ever so quietly, a grammar book with a long lesson marked in it, and immediately the sly bone over his eyes would set up such an aching! Request him to go to the garret for your foot stove, instantly the bones would remind him that he was "too tired." Ask him to go to the confectioner's, a mile away, and *presto!* not a bone would remember that it ever had been used before.

Bearing all this in mind you will not wonder when I tell you that our five boys were among the happiest of the happy throng pouring forth from the schoolhouse that day.

Peter was in excellent spirits. He had heard through Hilda of Dame Brinker's laugh and of Hans' joyous words, and he needed no further proof that Raff Brinker was a cured man. In fact the news had gone forth in every direction, for miles around. Persons who had never before cared for the Brinkers, or even mentioned them, except with a contemptuous sneer or a shrug of pretended pity, now became singularly familiar with every point of their history. There was no end to the number of ridiculous stories that were flying about.

Hilda, in the excitement of the moment, had stopped to exchange a word with the doctor's coachman, as he stood by the horses, pommeling his chest and clapping his hands. Her kind heart was overflowing. She could not help pausing to tell the cold, tired-looking man that she thought the doctor would be out soon; she even hinted to him that she suspected—only suspected—that a wonderful cure had been performed—an idiot brought to his senses. Nay, she was *sure* of it—for she had heard his widow laugh—no, not his widow, of course, but his wife—for the man was as much alive as anybody, and, for all she knew, sitting up and talking like a lawyer.

All this was very indiscreet. Hilda in an impenitent sort of way felt it to be so.

But it is always so delightful to impart pleasant or surprising news!

She went tripping along by the canal, quite resolved to

repeat the sin, *ad infinitum,* and tell nearly every girl and boy in the school.

Meantime, Janzoon Kolp came skating by. Of course, in two seconds, he was striking slippery attitudes, and shouting saucy things to the coachman, who stared at him in indolent disdain.

This, to Janzoon, was equivalent to an invitation to draw nearer. The coachman was now upon his box gathering up the reins and grumbling at his horses.

Janzoon accosted him.

"I say. What's going on at the idiot's cottage? Is your boss in there?"

Coachman nodded mysteriously.

"Whew!" whistled Janzoon, drawing closer. "Old Brinker dead?"

The driver grew big with importance, and silent in proportion.

"See here, old pincushion, I'd run home yonder and get you a chunk of gingerbread if I thought you could open your mouth."

Old pincushion was human—long hours of waiting had made him ravenously hungry. At Janzoon's hint, his countenance showed signs of a collapse.

"That's right, old fellow," pursued his tempter, "hurry up—what news—old Brinker dead?"

"No—CURED! got his wits," said the coachman, shooting forth his words, one at a time, like so many bullets.

Like bullets (figuratively speaking) they hit Janzoon Kolp. He jumped as if he had been shot.

"Goede Gunst! you don't say so!"

The man pressed his lips together, and looked significantly toward Master Kolp's shabby residence.

Just then Janzoon saw a group of boys in the distance. Hailing them in a rowdy style, common to boys of his stamp all over the world, whether in Africa, Japan, Amsterdam or Paris, he scampered toward them, forgetting coachman, gingerbread, everything but the wonderful news.

Therefore by sundown it was well known throughout the neighboring country that Dr. Boekman, chancing to stop at the cottage, had given the idiot Brinker a tremendous dose of medicine, as brown as gingerbread. It had taken six men to hold him while it was poured down. The idiot had immediately sprung to his feet, in full possession of all his faculties, knocked over the doctor, or thrashed him (there was admitted to be a slight uncertainty as to which of these penalties was inflicted), then sat down and addressed him for all the world like a lawyer. After that he had turned and spoken beautifully to his wife and children. Dame Brinker had laughed herself into violent hysterics. Hans had said, "Here I am, father, your own dear son!" and Gretel had said, "Here I am, father, your own dear Gretel!" and the doctor had afterward been seen leaning back in his carriage looking just as white as a corpse.

XXXVI
A NEW ALARM

When Dr. Boekman called the next day at the Brinker cottage, he could not help noticing the cheerful, comfortable aspect of the place. An atmosphere of happiness breathed upon him as he opened the door. Dame Brinker sat complacently knitting beside the bed, her husband was enjoying a tranquil slumber, and Gretel was noiselessly kneading rye bread on the table in the corner.

The doctor did not remain long. He asked a few simple questions, appeared satisfied with the answers, and after feeling his patient's pulse, said, "Ah, very weak yet, jufvrouw; very weak, indeed. He must have nourishment. You may begin to feed the patient, ahem! not too much, but what you do give him let it be strong and of the best."

"Black bread we have, mynheer, and porridge," replied Dame Brinker cheerily; "they have always agreed with him well."

"Tut! tut!" said the doctor, frowning, "nothing of the kind. He must have the juice of fresh meat, white bread, dried and toasted, good Malaga wine, and—ahem! The man looks cold—give him more covering, something light and warm. Where is the boy?"

"Hans, mynheer, has gone into Broek to look for work. He will be back soon. Will the meester please be seated?"

Whether the hard polished stool offered by Dame Brinker did not look particularly tempting, or whether the dame herself frightened him, partly because she was a woman, and partly because an anxious, distressed look had suddenly appeared in her face, I cannot say. Certain it is that our eccentric doctor looked hurriedly about him, muttered something about "extraordinary case," bowed, and disappeared, before Dame Brinker had time to say another word.

Strange that the visit of their good benefactor should have left a cloud, yet so it was. Gretel frowned, an anxious childish frown, and kneaded the bread dough violently, without looking up. Dame Brinker hurried to her husband's bedside, leaned over him, and fell into silent but passionate weeping.

In a moment Hans entered.

"Why, mother," he whispered in alarm, "what ails thee? Is the father worse?"

She turned her quivering face toward him, making no attempt to conceal her distress.

"Yes. He is starving—perishing. The meester said it."

Hans turned pale.

"What does this mean, mother? We must feed him at once. Here, Gretel, give me the porridge."

"Nay!" cried his mother distractedly, yet without raising her voice, "it may kill him. Our poor fare is too heavy for him. Oh, Hans, he will die—the father will *die* if we use him this way. He must have meat, and sweet wine, and a dek-bed. Oh, what shall I do, what shall I do?" she sobbed, wringing her hands. "There is not a stiver in the house."

Gretel pouted; it was the only way she could express sympathy just then. Her tears fell one by one into the dough.

"Did the meester say he *must* have these things, mother?" asked Hans.

"Yes, he did."

"Well, mother, don't cry, *he shall have them;* I shall bring meat and wine before night. Take the cover from my bed. I can sleep in the straw."

"Yes, Hans; but it is heavy, scant as it is. The meester said he must have something light and warm. He will perish. Our peat is giving out, Hans. The father has wasted it sorely, throwing it on when I was not looking, dear man."

"Never mind, mother," whispered Hans cheerfully. "We can cut down the willow tree and burn it, if need be; but I'll bring home something tonight. There *must* be work in Amsterdam, though there's none in Broek. Never fear, mother; the worst trouble of all is past. We can brave anything now that the father is himself again."

"Aye!" sobbed Dame Brinker hastily drying her eyes, "that is true indeed."

"Of course it is. Look at him, mother, how softly he sleeps. Do you think God would let him starve, just after giving him back to us. Why, mother, I'm as *sure* of getting all the father needs as if my pocket was bursting with gold. There, now, don't fret." And hurriedly kissing her, Hans caught up his skates and slipped from the cottage.

Poor Hans! Disappointed in his morning's errand, half sickened with this new trouble, he wore a brave look, and tried to whistle as he tramped resolutely off with the firm intention of mending matters.

Want had never before pressed as sorely upon the Brinker family. Their stock of peat was nearly exhausted, and all the flour in the cottage was in Gretel's dough. They had scarcely cared to eat during the past few days—scarcely realized their condition. Dame Brinker had felt so sure that she and the children could earn money before the worst came that she had given herself up to the joy of her husband's recovery. She had not even told Hans that the few pieces of silver in the old mitten were quite gone.

Hans reproached himself, now, that he had not hailed the doctor when he saw him enter his coach and drive rapidly away in the direction of Amsterdam.

"Perhaps there is some mistake," he thought. "The meester surely would have known that meat and sweet wine were not at our command; and yet the father looks very weak—he certainly does. I *must* get work. If Mynheer van Holp were back from Rotterdam I could get plenty to do. But Master Peter told me to let him know if he could do aught to serve us. I shall go to him at once. Oh, if it were but summer!"

All this time Hans was hastening toward the canal. Soon his skates were on, and he was skimming rapidly toward the residence of Mynheer van Holp.

"The father must have meat and wine at once," he muttered, "but how can I earn the money in time to buy them today? There is no other way but to go, as I *promised,* to Master Peter. What would a gift of meat and wine be to him? When the father is once fed, I can rush down to Amsterdam and earn the morrow's supply."

Then came other thoughts—thoughts that made his heart thump heavily and his cheeks burn with a new shame. "It is *begging,* to say the least. Not one of the Brinkers has ever been a beggar. Shall I be the first? Shall my poor father just coming back into life learn that his family have asked for charity—he, always so wise and thrifty? No," cried Hans aloud, "better a thousand times to part with the watch.

"I can at least borrow money on it in Amsterdam!" he thought, turning around. "That will be no disgrace. I can find work at once, and get it back again. Nay, perhaps I can even *speak to the father about it!"*

This last thought almost made the lad dance for joy.

Why not, indeed, speak to the father? He was a rational being now. "He may wake," thought Hans, "quite bright and rested—may tell us the watch is of no consequence, to sell it of course! Huzza!" and Hans almost flew over the ice.

A few moments more and the skates were again swinging from his arm. He was running toward the cottage.

His mother met him at the door.

"Oh, Hans!" she cried, her face radiant with joy, "the young lady has been here with her maid. She brought everything—meat, jelly, wine and bread—a whole basketful! Then the meester sent a man from town with more wine, and a fine bed and blankets for the father. Oh! he will get well now. God bless them!"

"God bless them!" echoed Hans, and for the first time that day his eyes filled with tears.

XXXVII
THE FATHER'S RETURN

That evening Raff Brinker felt so much better that he insisted upon sitting up awhile on the rough, high-backed chair by the fire. For a few moments there was quite a commotion in the little cottage. Hans was all-important on the occasion, for his father was a heavy man, and needed something firm to lean upon. The dame, though none of your fragile ladies, was in such a state of alarm and excitement at the bold step they were taking in lifting him without the meester's orders that she came near pulling her husband over, even while she believed herself to be his main prop and support.

"Steady, vrouw, steady," panted Raff. "Have I grown old and feeble, or is it the fever makes me thus helpless?"

"Hear the man!" laughed Dame Brinker, "talking like any other Christian. Why, you're only weak from the fever, Raff. Here's the chair, all fixed snug and warm; now. sit thee down—hi-di-didy—there we are!"

With these words, Dame Brinker let her half of the burden settle slowly into the chair. Hans prudently did the same.

Meanwhile Gretel flew about generally, bringing every possible thing to her mother to tuck behind the father's back and spread over his knees. Then she twitched the carved bench under his feet, and Hans kicked the fire to make it brighter.

The father was "sitting up" at last. What wonder that he looked about him like one bewildered. "Little Hans" had just been almost carrying him. "The baby" was over four feet long, and was demurely brushing up the hearth with a bundle of willow wisps. Meitje, the vrouw, winsome and fair as ever, had gained at least fifty pounds in what seemed to him a few hours. She also had some new lines in her face that puzzled him. The only familiar things in the room were the pine table that he had made before he was married, the Bible upon the shelf, and the cupboard in the corner.

Ah! Raff Brinker, it was only natural that your eyes should fill with hot tears even while looking at the joyful faces of your loved ones. Ten years dropped from a man's life are no small loss; ten years of manhood, of household happiness and care; ten years of honest labor, of conscious enjoyment of sunshine and outdoor beauty, ten years of grateful life—one day looking forward to all this; the next, waking to find them passed and a blank. What wonder the scalding tears dropped one by one upon your cheek!

Tender little Gretel! The prayer of her life was answered through those tears. She *loved* her father from that moment. Hans and his mother glanced silently at each other when they saw her spring toward him and throw her arms about his neck.

"Father, *dear* father," she whispered, pressing her cheek close to his, "don't cry. We are all here."

"God bless thee," sobbed Raff, kissing her again and again. "I had forgotten that!"

Soon he looked up again, and spoke in a cheerful voice. "I should know her, vrouw," he said, holding the sweet young face between his hands, and gazing at it as though he were watching it grow. "I should know her. The same blue eyes, and the lips, and, ah! me, the little song she could sing almost before she could stand. But that was long ago," he added, with a sigh, still looking at her dreamily, "long ago; it's all gone now."

"Not so, indeed," cried Dame Brinker eagerly. "Do you think I would let her forget it? Gretel, child, sing the old song thou hast known so long!"

Raff Brinker's hands fell wearily and his eyes closed, but it was something to see the smile playing about his mouth, as Gretel's voice floated about him like an incense.

It was a simple air; she had never known the words.

With loving instinct she softened every note, until Raff almost fancied that his two-year-old baby was once more beside him.

As soon as the song was finished, Hans mounted a wooden stool and began to rummage in the cupboard.

"Have a care, Hans," said Dame Brinker, who through all her poverty was ever a tidy housewife. "Have a care, the wine is there at your right, and the white bread beyond it."

"Never fear, mother," answered Hans, reaching far back on an upper shelf, "I shall do no mischief."

Jumping down, he walked toward his father, and placed an oblong block of pine wood in his hands. One of its ends was rounded off, and some deep cuts had been made on the top.

"Do you know what it is, father?" asked Hans.

Raff Brinker's face brightened. "Indeed, I do, boy! It is the boat I was making you yest—alack, not yesterday, but years ago."

"I have kept it ever since, father; it can be finished when your hand grows strong again."

"Yes, but not for you, my lad. I must wait for the grandchildren. Why, you are nearly a man. Have you helped your mother, boy, through all these years?"

"Aye, and bravely," put in Dame Brinker.

"Let me see," muttered the father, looking in a puzzled way at them all, "how long is it since the night when the waters were coming in? 'Tis the last I remember."

"We have told thee true, Raff. It was ten years last Pinxter week."

"Ten years—and I fell then, you say. Has the fever been on me ever since?"

Dame Brinker scarcely knew how to reply. Should she tell him all? Tell him that he had been an idiot, almost a lunatic? The doctor had charged her on no account to worry or excite his patient.

Hans and Gretel looked astonished when the answer came.

"Like enough, Raff," she said, nodding her head, and raising her eyebrows, "when a heavy man like thee falls on his head, it's hard to say what will come—but thou'rt well *now,* Raff. Thank the good Lord!"

The newly awakened man bowed his head.

"Aye, well enough, mine vrouw," he said, after a moment's silence, "but my brain turns somehow like a spinning wheel. It will not be right till I get on the dykes again. When shall I be at work, think you?"

"Hear the man!" cried Dame Brinker, delighted, yet frightened, too, for that matter. "We must get him on the bed, Hans. Work, indeed!"

They tried to raise him from the chair, but he was not ready yet.

"Be off with ye!" he said, with something like his old smile (Gretel had never seen it before). "Does a man want to be lifted about like a log? I tell you before three suns I shall be on the dykes again. Ah! there'll be some stout fellows to greet me. Jan Kamphuisen and young Hoogsvliet. They have been good friends to thee, Hans, I'll warrant."

Hans looked at his mother. Young Hoogsvliet had been dead five years. Jan Kamphuisen was in the jail at Amsterdam.

"Aye, they'd have done their share no doubt," said Dame Brinker, parrying the inquiry, "had we asked them. But what with working and studying, Hans has been busy enough without seeking comrades."

"Working and studying," echoed Raff, in a musing tone. "Can the youngsters read and cipher, Meitje?"

"You should hear them!" she answered proudly. "They can run through a book while I mop the floor. Hans there is as happy over a page of big words as a rabbit in a cabbage patch; as for ciphering——"

"Here, lad, help a bit," interrupted Raff Brinker. "I must get me on the bed again."

XXXVIII
THE THOUSAND GUILDERS

NONE seeing the humble supper eaten in the Brinker cottage that night would have dreamed of the dainty fare hidden away near by. Hans and Gretel looked rather wistfully toward the cupboard as they drank their cupful of water and ate their scanty share of black bread; but even in thought they did not rob their father.

"He relished his supper well," said Dame Brinker, nodding sidewise toward the bed, "and fell asleep the next moment. Ah, the dear man will be feeble for many a day. He wanted sore to sit up again, but while I made show of humoring him, and getting ready, he dropped off. Remember that, my girl, when you have a man of your own (and many a day may it be before that comes to pass), remember you can never rule by differing; 'humble wife is husband's boss—' Tut! tut! never swallow such a mouthful as that again, child; why, I could make a meal off two such pieces. What's in thee, Hans? One would think there were cobwebs on the wall."

"Oh, no, mother, I was only thinking——"

"Thinking, about what? Ah, no use asking," she added in a changed tone. "I was thinking of the same a while ago. Well, well, it's no blame if we *did* look to hear something by this time about the thousand guilders; but, not a word—no—it's plain enough he knows naught about them."

Hans looked up anxiously, dreading lest his mother should grow agitated, as usual, when speaking of the lost money; but she was silently nibbling her bread and looking with a doleful stare toward the window.

"Thousand guilders," echoed a faint voice from the bed. "Ah, I am sure they have been of good use to you, vrouw, through the long years while your man was idle."

The poor woman started up. These words quite destroyed the hope that of late had been glowing within her.

"Are you awake, Raff?" she faltered.

"Yes, Meitje, and I feel much better. Our money was well saved, vrouw, I was saying. Did it last through all these ten years?"

"I—I—have not got it, Raff, I——" She was going to tell him the whole truth, when Hans lifted his finger warningly and whispered:

"Remember what the meester told us; the father must not be worried."

"Speak to him, child," she answered, trembling.

Hans hurried to the bedside.

"I am glad you are feeling better," he said, leaning over his father. "Another day will see you quite strong again."

"Aye, like enough. How long did the money last, Hans? I could not hear your mother. What did she say?"

"I said, Raff," stammered Dame Brinker in great distress, "that it was all gone."

"Well, well, wife, do not fret at that; one thousand

guilders is not so very much for ten years, and with children to bring up; but it has helped to make you all comfortable. Have you had much sickness to bear?"

"N-no," sobbed Dame Brinker, lifting her apron to her eyes.

"Tut—tut, woman, why do you cry?" said Raff kindly. "We will soon fill another pouch, when I am on my feet again. Lucky I told you all about it before I fell."

"Told me what, man?"

"Why, that I buried the money. In my dream just now, it seemed I had never said aught about it."

Dame Brinker started forward. Hans caught her arm.

"Hist! mother," he whispered, hastily leading her away, "we must be very careful." Then, while she stood with clasped hands waiting in breathless anxiety, he once more approached the cot. Trembling with eagerness he said:

"That was a troublesome dream. Do you remember *when* you buried the money, father?"

"Yes, my boy. It was before daylight on the same day I was hurt. Jan Kamphuisen said something, the sundown before, that made me distrust his honesty. He was the only one living besides mother who knew we had saved a thousand guilders, so I rose up that night and buried the money—blockhead that I was ever to suspect an old friend!"

"I'll be bound, father," pursued Hans in a laughing voice, motioning to his mother and Gretel to remain quiet, "that you've forgotten where you buried it."

"Ha! ha! not I, indeed. But good night, my son, I can sleep again."

Hans would have walked away, but his mother's gestures were not to be disobeyed, so he said gently:

"Good night, father. Where did you say you buried the money? I was only a little one then."

"Close by the willow sapling behind the cottage," said Raff Brinker drowsily.

"Ah, yes. North side of the tree, wasn't it, father?"

"No, the south side. Ah, you know the spot well enough, you rogue. Like enough you were there when your mother lifted it. Now, son, easy; shift this pillow—so. Good night."

"Good night, father!" said Hans, ready to dance for joy.

The moon rose very late that night, shining in, full and clear, at the little window; but its beams did not disturb Raff Brinker. He slept soundly, and so did Gretel. As for Hans and his mother, they had something else to do.

After making a few hurried preparations, they stole forth with bright expectant faces, bearing a broken spade and a rusty implement that had done many a day's service when Raff was a hale worker on the dykes.

It was so light out of doors they could see the willow tree distinctly. The frozen ground was hard as stone, but Hans and his mother were resolute. Their only dread was that they might disturb the sleepers in the cottage.

"This ysbreker is just the thing, mother," said Hans striking many a vigorous blow, "but the ground has set so firm it'll be a fair match for it."

"Never fear, Hans," she answered, watching him eagerly. "Here, let me try awhile."

They soon succeeded in making an impression; one opening, and the rest was not so difficult.

Still they worked on, taking turns and whispering cheerily to one another. Now and then Dame Brinker stepped noiselessly over the threshold and listened, to be certain that her husband slept.

"What grand news it will be for him," she said, laughing, "when he is strong enough to bear it. How I should like to put the pouch and the stocking, just as we find them, all full of money, near him this blessed night, for the dear man to see when he wakens."

"We must get them, first, mother," panted Hans, still tugging away at his work.

"There's no doubt of that. They can't slip away from us

now," she answered, shivering with cold and excitement, as she crouched beside the opening. "Like enough we'll find them stowed in the old earthen pot I lost long ago."

By this time Hans, too, began to tremble, but not with cold. He had penetrated a foot deep for quite a space on the south side of the tree. At any moment they might come upon the treasure.

Meantime the stars winked and blinked at each other as if to say, "Queer country, this Holland! How much we do see, to be sure!"

"Strange that the dear father should have put it down so woeful deep," said Dame Brinker, in rather a provoked tone. "Ah, the ground was soft enough then, I warrant. How wise of him to mistrust Jan Kamphuisen, and Jan in full credit at the time. Little I thought that handsome fellow with his gay ways would ever go to jail! Now, Hans, let me take a turn. It's lighter work, d'ye see, the deeper we go? I'd be loath to kill the tree, Hans; will we harm it, think you?"

"I cannot say," he answered gravely.

Hour after hour, mother and son worked on. The hole grew larger and deeper. Clouds began to gather in the sky, throwing elfish shadows as they passed. Not until moon and stars faded away and streaks of daylight began to appear did Meitje Brinker and Hans look hopelessly into each other's face.

They had searched thoroughly, desperately, all round the tree; south, north, east, west. *The hidden money was not there!*

XXXIX
GLIMPSES

ANNIE BOUMAN had a healthy distaste for Janzoon Kolp. Janzoon Kolp, in his own rough way, adored Annie. Annie declared she could not "to save her life" say one civil word to that odious boy. Janzoon believed her to be the sweetest, sauciest creature in the world. Annie laughed among her playmates at the comical flapping of Janzoon's tattered and dingy jacket; he sighed in solitude over the floating grace of her jaunty blue petticoat. She thanked her stars that her brothers were not like the Kolps; and he growled at his sister because she was not like the Boumans. They seemed to exchange natures whenever they met. His presence made her harsh and unfeeling; and the very sight of *her* made him gentle as a lamb. Of course they were thrown together very often. It is thus that in some mysterious way we are convinced of error and cured of prejudice. In this case, however, the scheme failed. Annie detested Janzoon more and more at each encounter; and Janzoon liked her better and better every day.

"He killed a stork, the wicked old wretch!" she would say to herself.

"She knows I am strong and fearless," thought Janzoon.

"How red and freckled and ugly he is!" was Annie's secret comment when she looked at him.

"How she stares, and stares!" thought Janzoon. "Well, I am a fine, weather-beaten fellow, anyway."

"Janzoon Kolp, you impudent boy, go right away from me!" Annie often said. "I don't want any of your company."

"Ha! ha!" laughed Janzoon to himself, "girls never say what they mean. I'll skate with her every chance I can get."

And so it came to pass that the pretty maid would not look up that morning when, skating homeward from Amsterdam, she became convinced that a great burly boy was coming down the canal toward her.

"Humph! if I look at him," thought Annie, "I'll——"

"Good morrow, Annie Bouman," said a pleasant voice.

[How a smile brightens a girl's face!]

"Good morrow, Master Hans, I am right glad to meet you."

[How a smile brightens a boy's face!]

"Good morrow again, Annie. There has been a great change at our house since you left."

"How so?" she exclaimed, opening her eyes very wide.

Hans, who had been in a great hurry, and rather moody, grew talkative and quite at leisure in Annie's sunshine.

Turning about, and skating slowly with her toward Broek, he told the good news of his father. Annie was so true a friend that he told her even of their present distress, of how money was needed, and how everything depended upon his obtaining work, and he could find nothing to do in the neighborhood.

All this was not said as a complaint, but just because she was looking at him, and really wished to know. He could not speak of last night's bitter disappointment, for that secret was not wholly his own.

"Good-bye, Annie!" he said at last. "The morning is going fast, and I must hasten to Amsterdam and sell these skates. Mother must have money at once. Before nightfall I shall certainly find a job somewhere."

"Sell your new skates, Hans!" cried Annie. "You, the best skater around Broek! Why, the race is coming off in five days!"

"I know it," he answered resolutely. "Good-bye! I shall skate home again on the old wooden ones."

Such a bright glance! So different from Janzoon's ugly grin—and Hans was off like an arrow.

"Hans, come back!" she called.

Her voice changed the arrow into a top. Spinning around, he darted, in one long, leaning sweep, toward her.

"Then you really are going to sell your new skates if you can find a customer?"

"Of course I am," he replied, looking up with a surprised smile.

"Well, Hans, if you *are* going to sell your skates," said Annie, somewhat confused, "I mean if you——well, I know somebody who would like to buy them, that's all."

"Not Janzoon Kolp?" asked Hans, flushing.

"Oh, no," she pouted, "he is not one of my friends."

"But you *know* him," persisted Hans.

Annie laughed. "Yes, I know him, and it's all the worse for him that I do. Now please, Hans, don't ever talk any more to me about Janzoon. I hate him!"

"Hate him! *You* hate anyone, Annie?"

She shook her head saucily. "Yes; and I'll hate you too, if you persist in calling him one of my friends. You boys may like him because he caught the greased goose at the Kermis last summer, and climbed the pole with his great, ugly body tied up in a sack, but I don't care for such things. I've disliked him ever since I saw him try to push his little sister out of the merry-go-round at Amsterdam; and it's no secret up *our* way who killed the stork on your mother's roof. But we mustn't talk about such a bad, wicked fellow. Really,

The money was not there

Hans, I know somebody who would be glad to buy your skates. You won't get half a price for them in Amsterdam. *Please* give them to me. I'll take you the money this very afternoon."

If Annie was charming even when she said "hate," there was no withstanding her when she said "please"; at least Hans found it to be so.

"Annie," he said, taking off the skates, and rubbing them carefully with a snarl of twine before handing them to her, "I am sorry to be so particular; but if your friend should not want them, will you bring them back to me today? I must buy peat and meal for the mother early tomorrow morning."

"My friend *will* want them," laughed Annie, nodding gaily, and skating off at the top of her speed.

As Hans drew forth the wooden "runners" from his capacious pockets and fastened them on as best he could, he did not hear Annie murmur, "I wish I had not been so rude; poor, brave Hans. What a noble boy he is!" And as Annie skated homeward filled with pleasant thoughts, she did not hear Hans say, "I grumbled like a bear. But bless her! some girls are like angels!"

Perhaps it was all for the best. One cannot be expected to know everything that is going on in the world.

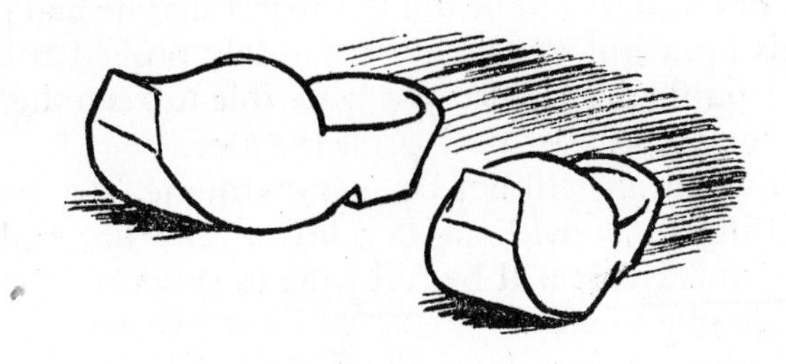

XL
LOOKING FOR WORK

LUXURIES unfit us for returning to hardships easily endured before. The wooden runners squeaked more than ever. It was as much as Hans could do to get on with the clumsy old things; still he did not regret that he had parted with his beautiful skates, but resolutely pushed back the boyish trouble that he had not been able to keep them just a little longer, at least until after the race.

"Mother surely will not be angry with me," he thought, "for selling them without her leave. She has had care enough already. It will be full time to speak of it when I take home the money."

Hans went up and down the streets of Amsterdam that day, looking for work. He succeeded in earning a few stivers by assisting a man who was driving a train of loaded mules into the city, but he could not secure steady employment anywhere. He would have been glad to obtain a situation as porter or errand boy, but though he passed on his way many a loitering, shuffling urchin, laden with bundles, there was no place for him. Some shopkeepers had just supplied themselves; others needed a trimmer, more lightly built fellow (they meant better dressed, but did not choose to say so); others told him to call again in a month or two, when the canals would probably be broken up; and many shook their heads at him without saying a word.

At the factories he met with no better luck. It seemed to him that in those great buildings, turning out respectively such tremendous quantities of woolen, cotton and linen stuffs, such world-renowned dyes and paints, such precious diamonds cut from the rough, such supplies of meal, of bricks, of glass and china—that in at least one of these, a strong-armed boy, able and eager to work, could find somethink to do. But no—nearly the same answer met him everywhere. "No need of more hands just now. If he had called before Nicholas' Day they might have given him a job, as they were hurried then; but at present they had more boys than they needed." Hans wished they could see, just for a moment, his mother and Gretel. He did not know how the anxiety of both looked out from his eyes, and how more than once, the gruffest denials were uttered with an uncomfortable consciousness that the lad ought not to be turned away. Certain fathers, when they went home that night, spoke more kindly than usual to their own youngsters, from memory of a frank, young face saddened at their words; and before morning one man actually resolved that if the Broek boy came in again he would instruct his head man Blankert to set him at something.

But Hans knew nothing of all this. Toward sundown he started on his return to Broek, uncertain whether the strange, choking sensation in his throat arose from discouragement or resolution. There was certainly one more chance. Mynheer van Holp might have returned by this time. Master Peter, it was reported, had gone to Haarlem the night before to attend to something connected with the great skating race. Still Hans would go and try.

Fortunately, Peter had returned early that morning. He was at home when Hans reached there, and was just about starting for the Brinker cottage.

"Ah, Hans!" he cried as the weary boy approached the door. "You are the very one I wished to see. Come in and warm yourself."

After tugging at his well-worn hat, which always *would* stick to his head when he was embarrassed, Hans knelt down, not by way of making a new style of Oriental salute, nor to worship the goddess of cleanliness who presided there, but because his heavy shoes would have filled the soul of a Broek housewife with horror. When their owner stepped softly into the house, they were left outside to act as sentinels until his return.

Hans left the Van Holp mansion with a lightened heart. Peter had brought word from Haarlem that young Brinker was to commence working upon the summerhouse doors immediately. There was a comfortable workshop on the place and it was to be at his service until the carving was done.

Peter did not tell Hans that he had skated all the way to Haarlem for the purpose of arranging this plan with Mynheer van Holp. It was enough for him to see the glad, eager look rise on young Brinker's face.

"I *think* I can do it," said Hans, "though I have never learned the trade."

"I am *sure* you can," responded Peter heartily. "You will find every tool you require in the workshop. It is nearly hidden yonder by that wall of twigs. In summer when the hedge is green, one cannot see the shop from here at all. How is your father today?"

"Better, mynheer—he improves every hour."

"It is the most astonishing thing I ever heard of. That gruff old doctor is a great fellow after all."

"Ah! mynheer," said Hans warmly, "he is more than great. He is good. But for the meester's kind heart and great skill my poor father would yet be in the dark. I think, mynheer," he added, with kindling eyes, "surgery is the very noblest science in the world!"

Peter shrugged his shoulders. "Very noble it may be, but not quite to my taste. This Dr. Boekman certainly has skill. As for his heart—defend me from such hearts as his!"

"Why do you say so, mynheer?" asked Hans.

Just then a lady slowly entered from an adjoining apartment. It was Mevrouw van Holp arrayed in the grandest of caps, and the longest of satin aprons ruffled with lace. She nodded placidly as Hans stepped back from the fire bowing as well as he knew how.

Peter at once drew a high-backed oaken chair toward the fire, and the lady seated herself.

There was a block of cork on each side of the chimney place. One of these blocks he placed carefully under his mother's feet.

Hans turned to go.

"Wait a moment, if you please, young man," said the lady. "I accidentally overheard you and my son speaking, I think, of my friend Dr. Boekman. You are right, young man. Dr. Boekman has a very kind heart. You perceive, Peter, we may be quite mistaken in judging of a person solely by his manners, though a courteous deportment is by no means to be despised."

"I intended no disrespect, mother," said Peter, "but surely one has no right to go growling and snarling through the world, as they say he does."

"They say. Ah, Peter, 'they' means everybody or nobody. Surgeon Boekman has had a great sorrow. Many years ago he lost his only child, under very painful circumstances, a fine lad, except that he was a thought too hasty and high-spirited. Before then Gerard Boekman was one of the most agreeable gentlemen I ever knew."

So saying, Mevrouw van Holp, looking kindly upon the

two boys, arose and left the room with the same dignity with which she had entered.

Peter, only half convinced, muttered something about "the sin of allowing sorrow to turn all one's honey into gall," as he conducted his visitor to the narrow side door. Before they parted, he advised Hans to keep himself in good skating order, "for," he added, "now that your father is all right, you will be in fine spirits for the race. That will be the prettiest skating show ever seen in this part of the world. Everybody is talking of it; you are to try for the prize, remember."

"I shall not be in the race, mynheer," said Hans, looking down.

"Not be in the race! Why not, indeed?" and immediately Peter's thoughts swept on a full tide of suspicion toward Carl Schummel.

"Because I cannot, mynheer," answered Hans, as he bent to slip his feet into his big shoes.

Something in the boy's manner warned Peter that it would be no kindness to press the matter further. He bade Hans "good-bye," and stood thoughtfully watching him as he walked away.

In a minute Peter called out:

"Hans Brinker!"

"Yes, mynheer."

"I'll take back all I said about Dr. Boekman."

"Yes, mynheer."

Both were laughing. But Peter's smile changed to a look of puzzled surprise when he saw Hans kneel down by the canal and put on the wooden skates.

"Very queer," muttered Peter, shaking his head as he turned to go into the house. "Why in the world doesn't the boy wear his new ones?"

XLI

THE FAIRY GODMOTHER

THE sun had gone down quite out of sight when our hero—with a happy heart but with something like a sneer on his countenance, as he jerked off the wooden "runners" —trudged hopefully toward the tiny hutlike building, known of old as the idiot's cottage.

Duller eyes than his would have discerned two slight figures moving near the doorway.

That gray, well-patched jacket and the dull blue skirt covered with an apron of still duller blue, that faded, close-fitting cap, and those quick little feet in their great boat-like shoes, they were Gretel's of course. He would have known them anywhere.

That bright coquettish red jacket, with its pretty skirt, bordered with black, that graceful cap bobbing over the gold earrings, that dainty apron, and those snug leather shoes that seemed to have grown with the feet—why if the Pope of Rome had sent them to him by express, Hans could have sworn they were Annie's.

The two girls were slowly pacing up and down in front of the cottage. Their arms were entwined, of course, and their heads were nodding and shaking as emphatically as if all the affairs of the kingdom were under discussion.

With a joyous shout, Hans hastened toward them.

"Huzza, girls, I've found work!"

This brought his mother to the cottage door.

She, too, had pleasant tidings. The father was still improving. He had been sitting up nearly all day, and was now sleeping, as Dame Brinker declared, "just as quiet as a lamb."

"It is my turn now, Hans," said Annie, drawing him aside after he had told his mother the good word from Mynheer van Holp. "Your skates are sold and here's the money."

"Seven guilders!" cried Hans, counting the pieces in astonishment. "Why, that is three times as much as I paid for them."

"I cannot help that," said Annie. "If the buyer knew no better, it is not our fault."

Hans looked up quickly.

"Oh, Annie!"

"Oh, Hans!" she mimicked, pursing her lips, and trying to look desperately wicked and unprincipled.

"Now, Annie, I know you would never mean that! You must return some of this money."

"But I'll not do any such thing," insisted Annie. "They're sold, and that's an end of it." Then seeing that he looked really pained she added in a lower tone:

"Will you believe me, Hans, when I say that there has been no mistake—that the person who bought your skates *insisted* upon paying seven guilders for them?"

"I will," he answered; and the light from his clear blue eyes seemed to settle and sparkle under Annie's lashes.

Dame Brinker was delighted at the sight of so much silver, but when she learned that Hans had parted with his treasures to obtain it, she sighed, as she exclaimed:

"Bless thee, child! That will be a sore loss for thee!"

"Here, mother," said the boy, plunging his hands far into his pockets, "here is more—we shall be rich if we keep on!"

"Aye, indeed," she answered, eagerly reaching forth her hand. Then, lowering her voice, added, "We *would* be rich but for that Jan Kamphuisen. He was at the willow tree years ago, Hans—depend upon it!"

"Indeed, it seems likely," sighed Hans. "Well, mother, we must give up the money bravely. It is certainly gone; the father has told us all he knows. Let us think no more about it."

"That's easy saying, Hans. I shall try, but it's hard, and my poor man wanting so many comforts. Bless me! How girls fly about. They were here but this instant. Where did they run to?"

"They slipped behind the cottage," said Hans, "like enough to hide from us. Hist! I'll catch them for you! They both can move quicker and softer than yonder rabbit, but I'll give them a good start first."

"Why, there *is* a rabbit, sure enough. Hold, Hans, the poor thing must have been in sore need to venture from its burrow this bitter weather. I'll get a few crumbs for it within."

So saying, the good woman bustled into the cottage. She soon came out again, but Hans had forgotten to wait, and the rabbit after taking a cool survey of the premises had scampered off to unknown quarters. Turning the corner of the cottage, Dame Brinker came upon the children. Hans and Gretel were standing before Annie, who was seated carelessly upon a stump.

"That is as good as a picture!" cried Dame Brinker halting in admiration of the group. "Many a painting have I seen at the grand house at Heidelberg not a whit prettier. My two are rough chubs, Annie, but *you* look like a fairy."

"Do I?" laughed Annie, sparkling with animation. "Well then, Gretel and Hans, imagine I'm your godmother just paying you a visit. Now I'll grant you each a wish. What will you have, Master Hans?"

A shade of earnestness passed over Annie's face as she looked up at him; perhaps it was because she wished from the depths of her heart that for once she could have a fairy's power.

Something whispered to Hans that, for the moment, she was more than mortal.

"I wish," said he solemnly, "I could find something I was searching for last night."

Gretel laughed merrily. Dame Brinker moaned, "Shame on you, Hans!" and passed wearily into the cottage.

The fairy godmother sprang up and stamped her foot three times.

"Thou shalt have thy wish," said she, "let them say what they will." Then with playful solemnity, she put her hand in her apron pocket and drew forth a large glass bead. "Bury this," said she, giving it to Hans, "where I have stamped, and ere moonrise thy wish shall be granted."

Gretel laughed more merrily than ever.

The godmother pretended great displeasure.

"Naughty child," said she, scowling terribly. "In punishment for laughing at a fairy, *thy* wish shall not be granted."

"Ha!" cried Gretel in high glee, "better wait till you're asked, godmother. I haven't made any wish!"

Annie acted her part well. Never smiling, through all their merry laughter, she stalked away, the embodiment of offended dignity.

"Good night, fairy!" they cried again and again.

"Good night, mortals!" she called out at last as she sprang over a frozen ditch, and ran quickly homeward.

"Oh, isn't she—just like flowers—so sweet and lovely!" cried Gretel, looking after her in great admiration. "And to think how many days she stays in that dark room with her grandmother! Why, brother Hans! What is the matter? What are you going to do?"

"Wait and see!" answered Hans as he plunged into the cottage and came out again, all in an instant, bearing the spade and ysbreker in his hands. "I'm going to bury my magic bead!"

Raff Brinker still slept soundly; his wife took a small block of peat from her nearly exhausted store, and put it upon the embers. Then opening the door, she called gently:

"Come in, children."

"Mother! mother! See here!" shouted Hans.

"Holy St. Bavon!" exclaimed the dame, springing over the door-step. "What ails the boy!"

"Come quick, mother," he cried, in great excitement, working with all his might, and driving in the ysbreker at each word. "Don't you see? *This* is the spot—right here on the south side of the stump. Why didn't we think of it last night? *The stump* is the old willow tree—the one you cut down last spring because it shaded the potatoes. That little tree wasn't here when father—Huzza!"

Dame Brinker could not speak. She dropped on her knees beside Hans just in time to see him drag forth—*the old stone pot!*

He thrust in his hand and took out—a piece of brick—then another—then another—then, the stocking and the pouch, black and moldy, but filled with the long-lost treasure!

Such a time! Such laughing! Such crying! Such counting, after they went into the cottage! It was a wonder that Raff did not waken. His dreams were pleasant, however, for he smiled in his sleep.

Dame Brinker and her children had a fine supper, I can assure you. No need of saving the delicacies now.

"We'll get father some nice fresh things tomorrow," said the dame, as she brought forth cold meat, wine, bread and jelly, and placed them on the clean pine table. "Sit by, children, sit by."

That night Annie fell asleep wondering whether it was a knife Hans had lost, and thinking how funny it would be if he should find it, after all.

Hans had scarcely closed his eyes, before he found himself trudging through a thicket; pots of gold were lying all around, and watches, and skates, and glittering beads were swinging from every branch.

Strange to say, each tree, as he approached it, changed into a stump, and on the stump sat the prettiest fairy imaginable, clad in a scarlet jacket, and blue petticoat.

XLII
THE MYSTERIOUS WATCH

SOMETHING else than the missing guilders was brought to light on the day of the fairy godmother's visit. This was the story of the watch that for ten long years had been so jealously guarded by Raff's faithful vrouw. Through many an hour of sore temptation she had dreaded almost to look upon it, lest she might be tempted to disobey her husband's request. It had been hard to see her children hungry and to know that the watch, if sold, would enable the roses to bloom in their cheeks again. "But nay," she would exclaim, "Meitje Brinker is not one to forget her man's last bidding, come what may."

"Take good care of this, mine vrouw," he had said, as he handed it to her—that was all. No explanation followed, for the words were scarcely spoken, when one of his fellow workmen rushed into the cottage, crying, "Come, man! the waters are rising! You're wanted on the dykes."

Raff had started at once, and that, as Dame Brinker has already told you, was the last she saw of him in his right mind.

On the day when Hans was in Amsterdam looking for work, and Gretel, after performing her household labors, was wandering about in search of chips, twigs—anything that could be burned, Dame Brinker with suppressed excitement had laid the watch in her husband's hand.

"It wasn't in reason," as she afterward said to Hans, "to wait any longer, when a word from the father would settle all; no woman living but would want to know how he came by that watch." Raff Brinker turned the bright, polished thing over and over in his hand—then he examined the bit of smoothly ironed black ribbon fastened to it; he seemed hardly to recognize it. At last he said, "Ah, I remember this! Why, you've been rubbing it, vrouw, till it shines like a new guilder."

"Aye," said Dame Brinker, nodding her head complacently.

Raff looked at it again. "Poor boy!" he murmured, then fell into a brown study.

This was too much for the dame. "Poor boy!" she echoed, somewhat tartly. "What do you think I'm standing here for, Raff Brinker, and my spinning awaiting, if not to hear more than that?"

"I told ye all, long since," said Raff positively, as he looked up in surprise.

"Indeed, and you never did!" retorted the vrouw.

"Well, if not, since it's no affair of ours, we'll say no more about it," said Raff, shaking his head sadly. "Like enough while I've been dead on the earth, all this time, the poor boy's died and been in heaven. He looked near enough to it, poor lad!"

"Raff Brinker! If you're going to treat me this way, and I nursing you and bearing with you since I was twenty-two years old, it's a shame; aye, and a disgrace," cried the vrouw, growing quite red, and scant of breath.

Raff's voice was feeble yet. "Treat you *what* way, Meitje?"

"What way," said Dame Brinker, mimicking his voice and manner, "what way? Why, just as every woman in the world is treated after she's stood by a man through the worst, like a——"

"Meitje!"

Raff was leaning forward, with outstretched arms. His eyes were full of tears.

In an instant Dame Brinker was at his feet, clasping his hands in hers.

"Oh, what have I done! Made my good man cry, and he not back with me four days! Look up, Raff! Nay, Raff, my own boy, I'm sorry I hurt thee. It's hard not to be told about the watch after waiting ten years to know; but I'll ask thee no more, Raff. Here, we'll put the thing away that's made the first trouble between us, after God just giving thee back to me."

"I was a fool to cry, Meitje," he said, kissing her, "and it's no more than right ye should know the truth. But it seemed like it might be telling the secrets of the dead to talk about the matter."

"Is the man—the lad—thou wert talking of dead, think thee?" asked the vrouw, hiding the watch in her hand, but seating herself expectantly on the end of his long foot bench.

"It's hard telling," he answered.

"Was he so sick, Raff?"

"No, not sick, I may say; but troubled, vrouw, very troubled."

"Had he done any wrong, think ye?" she asked, lowering her voice.

Raff nodded.

"Murder?" whispered the wife, not daring to look up.

"He said it was like to that, indeed."

"Oh! Raff, you frighten me. Tell me more, you speak so strange, and you tremble. I must know all."

"If I tremble, mine vrouw, it must be from the fever. There is no guilt on my soul, thank God!"

"Take a sip of this wine, Raff. There, now you are better. It was like to a crime, you were saying."

"Aye, Meitje, like to murder; *that* he told me himself. But I'll never believe it. A likely lad, fresh and honest-looking as our own youngster, but with something not so bold and straight about him."

"Aye, I know," said the dame gently, fearing to interrupt the story.

"He came upon me quite sudden," continued Raff. "I had never seen his face before, the palest, frightenedest face that ever was. He caught me by the arm. 'You look like an honest man,' says he."

"Aye, he was right in that," interrupted the dame, emphatically.

Raff looked somewhat bewildered.

"Where was I, mine vrouw?"

"The lad took hold of your arm, Raff," she said, gazing at him anxiously.

"Aye, so. The words come awkward to me, and everything is half like a dream, ye see."

"S-stut! What wonder, poor man," sighed the dame, stroking his hand. "If ye had not head enough for a dozen, the wit would never had come to ye again. Well, the lad caught ye by the arm, and said ye looked honest (well he might!). What then? Was it noontime?"

"Nay; before daylight—long before early chimes."

"It was the same day you were hurt," said the dame. "I know it seemed you went to your work in the middle of the night. You left off, where he caught your arm, Raff."

"Yes," resumed her husband, "and I can see his face this minute—so white and wild looking. 'Take me down the river a way,' says he. I was working then, you'll remember, far down on the line, across from Amsterdam. I told him I was no boatman. 'It's an affair of life and death,' says he. 'Take me on a few miles—yonder skiff is not locked, but it may be a poor man's boat and I'd be loath to rob him!' (The words might differ some, vrouw, for it's all like a dream.) Well, I took him down; it might be six or eight miles, and then he said he could run the rest of the way on shore. I was in haste to get the boat back. Before he jumped out, he says, sobbing-like, 'I can trust you. I've done a thing—God knows I never intended it—but the man is dead. I must fly from Holland.' "

"What was it, did he say, Raff? Had he been shooting at a comrade, like they do down at the University of Göttingen?"

"I can't recall that. Mayhap he told me; but it's all like a dream. I said it wasn't for me, a good Hollander, to cheat the laws of my country by helping him off that way; but he kept saying, 'God knows I am innocent!' and looked at me in the starlight as fair, now, and clear-eyed as our little Hans might—and I just pulled away faster."

"It must have been Jan Kamphuisen's boat," remarked Dame Brinker dryly. "None other would have left his oars out that careless."

"Aye, it was Jan's boat, sure enough. The man will be coming in to see me Sunday, likely, if he's heard; and young Hoogsvliet too. Where was I?"

[It was lucky the dame restrained herself. To have spoken at all of Jan after the last night's cruel disappointment would have been to have let out more sorrow and suspicion than Raff could bear.]

"Where were you? Why, not very far, forsooth—the lad hadn't yet given ye the watch—alack, I misgive whether he came by it honestly!"

"Why, vrouw," exclaimed Raff in an injured tone, "he was dressed soft and fine as the prince himself. The watch was his own, clear enough."

"How came he to give it up?" asked the dame, looking uneasily at the fire, for it needed another block of peat.

"I told ye just now," he answered with a puzzled air.

"Tell me again," said Dame Brinker, wisely warding off another digression.

"Well, just before jumping from the boat, he says, handing me the watch, 'I'm flying from my country as I never thought I could. I'll trust you because you look honest. Will you take this to my father—not today but in a week, and tell him his unhappy boy sent it; and tell him if ever the time comes that he wants me to come back to him, I'll brave everything and come. Tell him to send a letter to—to'—there, the rest is all gone from me. I *can't* remember where the letter was to go. Poor lad! poor lad," resumed Raff, sorrowfully taking the watch from his vrouw's lap, as he spoke—"and it's never been sent to his father to this day."

"I'll take it, Raff, never fear—the moment Gretel gets back. She will be in soon. What was the father's name, did you say? Where were you to find him?"

"Alack!" answered Raff, speaking very slowly, "it's all slipped me. I can see the lad's face, and his great eyes, just as plain—and I remember his opening the watch, and snatching something from it and kissing it—but no more. All the rest whirls past me; there's a kind of sound like rushing waters comes over me when I try to think."

"Aye. That's plain to see, Raff; but I've had the same feeling after a fever. You're tired now—I must get ye straight on the bed again. Where *is* the child, I wonder?"

Dame Brinker opened the door, and called, "Gretel! Gretel!"

"Stand aside, vrouw," said Raff, feebly, as he leaned forward, and endeavored to look out upon the bare landscape. "I've half a mind to stand beyond the door just once."

"Nay, nay," she laughed, "I'll tell the meester how ye tease, and fidget and bother, to be let out in the air; and, if he says it, I'll bundle ye warm tomorrow, and give ye a turn on your feet. But I'm freezing you with this door open. I declare if there isn't Gretel with her apron full, skating on the canal, like wild. Why, man," she continued almost in a scream, as she slammed the door, "thou'rt walking to the bed without my touching thee! Thou'lt fall!"

The dame's "thee" proved her mingled fear and delight, even more than the rush which she made toward her husband. Soon he was comfortably settled under the new cover, declaring, as his vrouw tucked him in snug and warm, that it was the last daylight that should see him abed.

"Aye! I can hope it myself," laughed Dame Brinker, "now you have been frisking about at that rate." As Raff closed his eyes, the dame hastened to revive her fire, or rather to dull it, for Dutch peat is like a Dutchman, slow to kindle, but very good at a blaze when once started. Then putting her neglected spinning wheel away, she drew forth her knitting from some invisible pocket and seated herself by the bedside.

"If you could remember that man's name, Raff," she began cautiously, "I might take the watch to him, while you're sleeping; Gretel can't but be in soon."

Raff tried to think; but in vain.

"Could it be Boomphoffen," suggested the dame. "I've heard how they've had two sons turn out bad—Gerard and Lambert?"

"It might be," said Raff. "Look if there's letters on the watch; that'll guide us some."

"Bless thee, man," cried the happy dame, eagerly lifting the watch, "why, thou'rt sharper than ever! Sure enough. Here's letters! L. J. B. That's Lambert Boomphoffen, you may depend. What the J is for I can't say; but they used to be grand kind o' people, high-feathered as fancy fowl. Just the kind to give their children all double names, which isn't Scripture anyway."

"I don't know about that, vrouw. Seems to me there's long mixed names in the Holy Book, hard enough to make out. But you've got the right guess at a jump. It was your way always," said Raff, closing his eyes. "Take the watch to Boompkinks and try."

"Not Boompkinks, I know no such name; it's Boomphoffen."

"Aye, take it there."

"Take it there, man! Why, the whole brood of 'em's been gone to America these four years. But go to sleep, Raff; you look pale and out of strength. It'll all come to you, what's best to do, in the morning.

"So, Mistress Gretel! Here you are at last!"

Before Raff awoke that evening, the fairy godmother, as we know, had been at the cottage, the guilders were once more safely locked in the big chest, and Dame Brinker and the children were faring sumptuously on meat and white bread and wine.

So the mother, in the joy of her heart, told them the story of the watch as far as she deemed it prudent to divulge it. It was no more than fair, she thought, that the poor things should know, after keeping the secret so safe, ever since they had been old enough to know anything.

XLIII
A DISCOVERY

THE next sun brought a busy day to the Brinkers. In the first place, the news of the thousand guilders had of course to be told to the father. Such tidings as that surely could not harm him. Then while Gretel was diligently obeying her mother's injunction to "clean the place fresh as a new brewing," Hans and the dame sallied forth to revel in the purchasing of peat and provisions.

Hans was careless and contented; the dame was filled with delightful anxieties caused by the unreasonable demands of ten thousand guilders' worth of new wants that had sprung up like mushrooms in a single night. The happy woman talked so largely to Hans on their way to Amsterdam, and brought back such little bundles after all, that he scratched his bewildered head as he leaned against the chimney piece, wondering whether, "bigger the pouch, tighter the string" was in Jakob Cats, and therefore true, or whether he had dreamed it when he lay in a fever.

"What thinking on, Big-eyes?" chirruped his mother, half reading his thoughts as she bustled about, preparing the dinner. "What thinking on? Why, Raff, would ye believe it, the child thought to carry half Amsterdam back on his head. Bless us! he would have bought as much coffee as would have filled this fire pot. 'No—no—my lad,' says I, 'no time for leaks when the ship is rich laden'—and then how he stared—aye—just as he stares this minute. Hoot, lad! fly around a mite. Ye'll grow to the chimney place with your staring and wondering. Now, Raff, here's your chair at the head of the table, where it should be, for there's a man to the house now—I'd say it to the king's face. Aye, that's the way—lean on Hans; there's a strong staff for you! Growing like a weed too, and it seems only yesterday since he was toddling. Sit by, my man, sit by."

"Can you call to mind, vrouw," said Raff, settling himself cautiously in the big chair, "the wonderful music box that cheered your working in the big house at Heidelberg?"

"Aye, that I can," answered the dame, "three turns of a brass key, and the witchy thing would send the music fairly running up and down one's back—I remember it well. But, Raff" (growing solemn in an instant), "you would never throw our guilders away for a thing like that?"

"No, no, not I, vrouw; for the good Lord has already given me a music box without pay."

All three cast quick, frightened glances at one another and at Raff. Were his wits on the wing again?

"Aye, and a music box that fifty pouchful would not buy from me," insisted Raff. "And it's set going by the turn of a mop handle, and it slips and glides around the room, everywhere in a flash, carrying the music about till you'd swear the birds were back again."

"Holy St. Bavon!" screeched the dame, "what's in the man?"

"Comfort and joy, vrouw, that's what's in him! Ask

Gretel, ask my little music box Gretel if your man has lacked comfort and joy this day."

"Not he, mother," laughed Gretel. "He's been *my* music box, too. We sang together half the time you were gone."

"Aye, so," said the dame, greatly relieved. "Now, Hans, you'll never get through with a piece like that; but never mind, chick, thou'st had a long fasting. Here, Gretel, take another slice of the sausage; it'll put blood in your cheeks."

"Oh! Oh! mother," laughed Gretel, eagerly holding forth her platter, "blood doesn't grow in girls' cheeks—you mean roses—isn't it roses, Hans?"

While Hans was hastily swallowing a mammoth mouthful in order to give a suitable reply to this poetic appeal, Dame Brinker settled the matter with a quick:

"Well, roses or blood it's all one to me, so the red finds its way on your sunny face. It's enough for mother to get pale and weary-looking, without——"

"Hoot, vrouw," spoke up Raff hastily, "thou'rt fresher and rosier this minute than both our chicks put together."

This remark though not bearing very strong testimony to the clearness of Raff's newly awakened intellect, nevertheless afforded the dame intense satisfaction; the meal accordingly passed off in the most delightful manner.

After dinner, the affair of the watch was talked over and the mysterious initials duly discussed.

Hans had just pushed back his stool, intending to start at once for Mynheer van Holp's, and his mother had risen to put the watch away in its old hiding place, when they heard the sound of wheels upon the frozen ground.

Someone knocked at the door, opening it at the same time.

"Come in," stammered Dame Brinker, hastily trying to hide the watch in her bosom. "Oh, is it you, mynheer! Good day! The father is nearly well, as you see. It's a poor place to greet you in, mynheer, and the dinner not cleared away."

Dr. Boekman scarcely noticed the dame's apology. He was evidently in haste.

"Ahem!" he exclaimed, "not needed here, I perceive. The patient is mending fast."

"Well he may, mynheer," cried the dame, "for only last night we found a thousand guilders that's been lost to us these ten years."

Dr. Boekman opened his eyes.

"Yes, mynheer," said Raff. "I bid the vrouw tell you, though it's to be held a secret among us, for I see you can keep your lips closed as well as any man."

The doctor scowled. He never liked personal remarks.

"Now, mynheer," continued Raff, "you can take your rightful pay. God knows you have earned it, if bringing such a poor tool back to the world, and his family, can be called a service. Tell the vrouw what's to pay, mynheer; she will hand out the sum right willingly."

"Tut! tut!" said the doctor kindly. "Say nothing about money. I can find plenty of such pay any time, but gratitude comes seldom. That boy's 'Thank you,' " he added, nodding sidewise toward Hans, "was pay enough for me."

"Like enough ye have a boy of your own," said Dame Brinker, quite delighted to see the great man becoming so sociable.

Dr. Boekman's good nature vanished at once. He gave a growl (at least, it seemed so to Gretel) but made no actual reply.

"Do not think the vrouw meddlesome, mynheer," said Raff. "She has been sore touched of late about a lad whose folks have gone away, none know where; and I had a message for them from the young gentleman."

"The name was Boomphoffen," said the dame eagerly. "Do you know aught of the family, mynheer?"

The doctor's reply was brief and gruff.

"Yes. A troublesome set. They went long since to America."

"It might be, Raff," persisted Dame Brinker timidly,

"that the meester knows somebody in that country, though I'm told they are mostly savages over there. If he could get the watch to the Boomphoffens with the poor lad's message, it would be a most blessed thing."

"Tut, vrouw, why pester the good meester, and dying men and women wanting him everywhere? How do ye know ye have the true name?"

"I'm sure of it," she replied. "They had a son Lambert, and there's an L for Lambert and a B for Boomphoffen on the back; though to be sure there's an odd J too, but the meester can look for himself."

So saying, she drew forth the watch.

"L. J. B.!" cried Dr. Boekman, springing toward her.

Why attempt to describe the scene that followed! I need only say that the lad's message was delivered to his father at last—delivered while the great surgeon was sobbing like a little child.

"Laurens! My Laurens!" he cried, gazing with yearning eyes at the watch as he held it tenderly in his palm. "Ah, if I had but known sooner! Laurens a homeless wanderer—Great Heaven! he may be suffering, dying at this moment! Think, man, where is he? Where did my boy say the letter must be sent?"

Raff shook his head sadly.

"Think!" implored the doctor. Surely the memory so lately awakened through his aid could not refuse to serve him in a moment like this.

"It is all gone, mynheer," sighed Raff.

Hans, forgetting distinctions of rank and station, forgetting everything but that his good friend was in trouble, threw his arms round the doctor's neck.

"I can find your son, mynheer. If alive, he is *somewhere.* The earth is not so very large. I will devote every day of my life to the search. Mother can spare me, now. You are rich, mynheer; send me where you will."

Gretel began to cry. It was right for Hans to go; but how could they ever live without him?

Dr. Boekman made no reply, neither did he push Hans away. His eyes were fixed anxiously upon Raff Brinker. Suddenly he lifted the watch, and with trembling eagerness attempted to open it. Its stiffened spring yielded at last; the case flew open, disclosing a watch paper in the back bearing a group of blue forget-me-nots. Raff, seeing a shade of intense disappointment pass over the doctor's face, hastened to say:

"There was something else in it, mynheer, but the young gentleman tore it out before he handed it to me. I saw him kiss it as he put it away."

"It was his mother's picture," moaned the doctor. "She died when he was ten years old. Thank God! the boy had not forgotten. Both dead? It is impossible!" he cried, starting up. "My boy is alive. You shall hear his story. Laurens acted as my assistant. By mistake he portioned out the wrong medicine for one of my patients—a deadly poison—but it was never administered, for I discovered the error in time. The man died that day. I was detained with other bad cases until the next evening. When I reached home, my boy was gone. Poor Laurens!" sobbed the doctor, breaking down completely, "never to hear from me through all these years. His message disregarded. Oh, what must he have suffered!"

Dame Brinker ventured to speak. Anything was better than to see the meester cry.

"It is a mercy to know the young gentleman was innocent. Ah! how he fretted! Telling you, Raff, that his crime was like unto murder. It was sending the wrong physic he meant. Crime indeed! Why, our own Gretel might have done that! Like enough the poor young gentleman heard that the man was dead—that's why he ran, mynheer. He said, you know, Raff, that he never could come back to Holland again, unless"—she hesitated—"ah, your honor, ten years is a dreary time to be waiting to hear from——"

"Hist, vrouw!" said Raff sharply.

"Waiting to hear," groaned the doctor, "and I, like a fool, sitting stubbornly at home, thinking he had abandoned me. I never dreamed, Brinker, that the boy had discovered the mistake. I believed it was youthful folly—ingratitude—love of adventure, that sent him away. My poor, poor Laurens!"

"But you know all, now, mynheer," whispered Hans. "You know he was innocent of wrong, that he loved you and his dead mother. We will find him. You shall see him again, dear meester."

"God bless you!" said Dr. Boekman, seizing the boy's hand. "It may be as you say. I shall try—I shall try—and, Brinker, if ever the faintest gleam of recollection concerning him should come to you, you will send me word at once?"

"Indeed we will!" cried all but Hans, whose silent promise would have satisfied the doctor even had the others not spoken.

"Your boy's eyes," he said, turning to Dame Brinker, "are strangely like my son's. The first time I met him it seemed that Laurens himself was looking at me."

"Aye, mynheer," replied the mother proudly. "I have marked that you were much drawn to the child."

For a few moments the meester seemed lost in thought; then, arousing himself, he spoke in a new voice:

"Forgive me, Raff Brinker, for this tumult. Do not feel distressed on my account. I leave your house today a happier man than I have been for many a long year. Shall I take the watch?"

"Certainly you must, mynheer. It was your son's wish."

"Even so," responded the doctor, regarding his treasure with a queer frown, for his face could not throw off its bad habits in an hour—"even so. And, now, I must be gone. No medicine is needed by my patient; only peace and cheerfulness, and both are here in plenty. Heaven bless you, my good friends! I shall ever be grateful to you."

"May Heaven bless you, too, mynheer, and may you soon find the dear young gentleman," said Dame Brinker earnestly, after hurriedly wiping her eyes upon the corner of her apron.

Raff uttered a hearty "Amen!" and Gretel threw such a wistful, eager glance at the doctor that he patted her head as he turned to leave the cottage.

Hans went out also.

"When I can serve you, mynheer, I am ready."

"Very well, boy," replied Dr. Boekman with peculiar mildness. "Tell them, within, to say nothing of what has just passed. Meantime, Hans, when you are with your father, watch his mood. You have tact. At any moment he may suddenly be able to tell us more."

"Trust me for that, mynheer."

"Good day, my boy!" cried the doctor, as he sprang into his stately coach.

"Aha!" thought Hans, as it rolled away, "the meester has more life in him than I thought."

XLIV
THE RACE

THE twentieth of December came at last, bringing with it the perfection of winter weather. All over the level landscape lay the warm sunlight. It tried its power on lake, canal and river; but the ice flashed defiance and showed no sign of melting. The very weathercocks stood still to enjoy the sight. This gave the windmills a holiday. Nearly all the past week they had been whirling briskly; now, being rather out of breath, they rocked lazily in the clear, still air. Catch a windmill working when the weathercocks have nothing to do!

There was an end to grinding, crushing and sawing for that day. It was a good thing for the millers near Broek. Long before noon they concluded to take in their sails, and go to the race. Everybody would be there—already the north side of the frozen Y was bordered with eager spectators; the news of the great skating match had traveled far and wide. Men, women and children in holiday attire were flocking toward the spot. Some wore furs, and wintry cloaks or shawls; but many, consulting their feelings rather than the almanac, were dressed as for an October day.

The site selected for the race was a faultless plain of ice near Amsterdam, on that great arm of the Zuider Zee which Dutchmen, of course, must call the Eye. The townspeople turned out in large numbers. Strangers in the city deemed it a fine chance to see what was to be seen. Many a peasant from the northward had wisely chosen the twentieth as the day for the next city trading. It seemed that everybody, young and old, who had wheels, skates or feet at command, had hastened to the scene.

There were the gentry in their coaches, dressed like Parisians, fresh from the Boulevards; Amsterdam children in charity uniforms; girls from the Roman Catholic Orphan House, in sable gowns and white headbands; boys from the Burgher Asylum, with their black tights and short-skirted harlequin coats.[1] There were old-fashioned gentlemen in cocked hats and velvet knee breeches; old-fashioned ladies, too, in stiff, quilted skirts and bodices of dazzling brocade. These were accompanied by servants bearing foot stoves and cloaks. There were the peasant folk arrayed in every possible Dutch costume—shy young rustics in brazen buckles; simple village maidens concealing their flaxen hair under fillets of gold; women whose long, narrow aprons were stiff with embroidery; women with short, corkscrew curls hanging over their foreheads; women with shaved heads and close-fitting caps, and women in striped skirts and windmill bonnets. Men in leather, in homespun, in velvet and broadcloth; burghers in model European attire, and burghers in short jackets, wide trousers and steeple-crowned hats.

There were beautiful Friesland girls in wooden shoes

[1] This is not said in derision. Both the girls and boys of this institution wear garments quartered in red and black, alternately. By making the dress thus conspicuous, the children are, in a measure, deterred from wrongdoing while going about the city. The Burgher Orphan Asylum affords a comfortable home to several hundred boys and girls. Holland is famous for its charitable institutions.

and coarse petticoats, with solid gold crescents encircling their heads, finished at each temple with a golden rosette, and hung with lace a century old. Some wore necklaces, pendants and earrings of the purest gold. Many were content with gilt or even with brass, but it is not an uncommon thing for a Friesland woman to have all the family treasure in her headgear. More than one rustic lass displayed the value of two thousand guilders upon her head that day.

Scattered throughout the crowd were peasants from the Island of Marken, with sabots, black stockings, and the widest of breeches; also women from Marken with short blue petticoats, and black jackets, gaily figured in front. They wore red sleeves, white aprons, and a cap like a bishop's miter over their golden hair.

The children often were as quaint and odd-looking as their elders. In short, one-third of the crowd seemed to have stepped bodily from a collection of Dutch paintings.

Everywhere could be seen tall women, and stumpy men, lively faced girls, and youths whose expression never changed from sunrise to sunset.

There seemed to be at least one specimen from every known town in Holland. There were Utrecht water bearers, Gouda cheesemakers, Delft pottery men, Schiedam distillers, Amsterdam diamond cutters, Rotterdam merchants, dried-up herring packers, and two sleepy-eyed shepherds from Texel. Every man of them had his pipe and tobacco pouch. Some carried what might be called the smoker's complete outfit—a pipe, tobacco, a pricker with which to clean the tube, a silver net for protecting the bowl, and a box of the strongest of brimstone matches.

A true Dutchman, you must remember, is rarely without his pipe on any possible occasion. He may for a moment neglect to breathe, but when the pipe is forgotten, he must be dying indeed. There were no such sad cases here. Wreaths of smoke were rising from every possible quarter. The more fantastic the smoke wreath, the more placid and solemn the smoker.

Look at those boys and girls on stilts! That is a good idea. They can see over the heads of the tallest. It is strange to see those little bodies high in the air, carried about on mysterious legs. They have such a resolute look on their round faces, what wonder that nervous old gentlemen, with tender feet, wince and tremble while the long-legged little monsters stride past them.

You will read in certain books that the Dutch are a quiet people—so they are generally. But listen! Did ever you hear such a din? All made up of human voices—no, the horses are helping somewhat, and the fiddles are squeaking pitifully (how it must pain fiddles to be tuned!), but the mass of the sound comes from the great vox humana that belongs to a crowd.

That queer little dwarf going about with a heavy basket, winding in and out among the people, helps not a little. You can hear his shrill cry above all the other sounds, "Pypen en tabac! Pypen en tabac!"

Another, his big brother though evidently some years younger, is selling doughnuts and bonbons. He is calling on all pretty children far and near to come quickly or the cakes will be gone.

You know quite a number among the spectators. High up in yonder pavilion, erected upon the border of the ice, are some persons whom you have seen very lately. In the center is Madame van Gleck. It is her birthday, you remember; she has the post of honor. There is Mynheer van Gleck, whose meerschaum has not really grown fast to his lips—it only appears so. There are grandfather and grandmother whom you met at the Saint Nicholas fete. All the children are with them. It is so mild they have brought even the baby. The poor little creature is swaddled very much after the manner of an Egyptian mummy, but it can crow with delight, and when the band is playing, open and shut its animated mittens in perfect time to the music.

Grandfather, with his pipe and spectacles and fur cap, makes quite a picture as he holds baby upon his knee.

Hans is ahead!

Perched high upon their canopied platforms, the party can see all that is going on. No wonder the ladies look complacently at the glassy ice; with a stove for a footstool one might sit cozily beside the North Pole.

There is a gentleman with them who somewhat resembles Saint Nicholas as he appeared to the young Van Glecks on the fifth of December. But the saint had a flowing white beard; and this face is as smooth as a pippin. His

saintship was larger around the body, too, and (between ourselves) he had a pair of thimbles in his mouth, which this gentleman certainly has not. It cannot be Saint Nicholas after all.

Near by, in the next pavilion, sit the Van Holps with their son and daughter (the Van Gends) from The Hague. Peter's sister is not one to forget her promises. She has brought bouquets of exquisite hothouse flowers for the winners.

These pavilions, and there are others besides, have all been erected since daylight. That semicircular one, containing Mynheer Korbes' family, is very pretty, and proves that the Hollanders are quite skilled at tentmaking, but I like the Van Glecks' best—the center one—striped red and white, and hung with evergreens.

The one with the blue flags contains the musicians. Those pagodalike affairs, decked with sea shells and streamers of every possible hue, are the judges' stands, and those columns and flagstaffs upon the ice mark the limit of the race course. The two white columns twined with green, connected at the top by that long, floating strip of drapery, form the starting point. Those flagstaffs, half a mile off, stand at each end of the boundary line, cut sufficiently deep to be distinct to the skaters, though not enough so to trip them when they turn to come back to the starting point.

The air is so clear it seems scarcely possible that the columns and flagstaffs are so far apart. Of course the judges' stands are but little nearer together.

Half a mile on the ice, when the atmosphere is like this, is but a short distance after all, especially when fenced with a living chain of spectators.

The music has commenced. How melody seems to enjoy itself in the open air! The fiddles have forgotten their agony, and everything is harmonious. Until you look at the blue tent it seems that the music springs from the sunshine, it is so boundless, so joyous. Only when you see the staid-faced musicians do you realize the truth.

Where are the racers? All assembled together near the white columns. It is a beautiful sight. Forty boys and girls in picturesque attire darting with electric swiftness in and out among each other, or sailing in pairs and triplets, beckoning, chatting, whispering in the fullness of youthful glee. A few careful ones are soberly tightening their straps; others halting on one leg, with flushed, eager faces suddenly cross the suspected skate over their knee, give it an examining shake, and dart off again. One and all are possessed with the spirit of motion. They cannot stand still. Their skates are a part of them and every runner seems bewitched.

Holland is the place for skaters, after all. Where else can nearly every boy and girl perform feats on the ice that would attract a crowd if seen in Central Park? Look at Ben! I did not see him before. He is really astonishing the natives; no easy thing to do in the Netherlands. Save your strength, Ben, you will need it soon. Now other boys are trying! Ben is surpassed already. Such jumping, such poising, such spinning, such india-rubber exploits generally! That boy with a red cap is the lion now; his back is a watch spring, his body is cork—no, it is iron, or it would snap at that! He is a bird, a top, a rabbit, a corkscrew, a sprite, a flesh-ball, all in an instant. When you think he's erect he is down; and when you think he is down he is up. He drops his glove on the ice and turns a somersault as he picks it up. Without stopping, he snatches the cap from Jacob Poot's astonished head and claps it back again "hind side before." Lookers-on hurrah and laugh. Foolish boy! It is arctic weather under your feet, but more than temperate overhead. Big drops already are rolling down your forehead. Superb skater as you are, you may lose the race.

A French traveler, standing with a notebook in his hand, sees our English friend, Ben, buy a doughnut of the dwarf's brother, and eat it. Thereupon he writes in his notebook that the Dutch take enormous mouthfuls, and universally are fond of potatoes boiled in molasses.

There are some familiar faces near the white columns. Lambert, Ludwig, Peter and Carl are all there, cool and in good skating order. Hans is not far off. Evidently he is going to join in the race, for his skates are on—the very pair that he sold for seven guilders! He had soon suspected that his fairy godmother was the mysterious "friend" who bought them. This settled, he had boldly charged her with the deed, and she, knowing well that all her little savings had been spent in the purchase, had not had the face to deny it. Through the fairy godmother, too, he had been rendered amply able to buy them back again. Therefore Hans is to be in the race. Carl is more indignant than ever about it, but as three other peasant boys have entered, Hans is not alone.

Twenty boys and twenty girls. The latter by this time are standing in front, braced for the start, for they are to have the first "run." Hilda, Rychie and Katrinka are among them—two or three bend hastily to give a last pull at their skate straps. It is pretty to see them stamp, to be sure that all is firm. Hilda is speaking pleasantly to a graceful little creature in a red jacket and a new brown petticoat. Why, it is Gretel! What a difference those pretty shoes make, and the skirt, and the new cap. Annie Bouman is there too. Even Janzoon Kolp's sister has been admitted —but Janzoon himself has been voted out by the directors, because he killed the stork, and only last summer was caught in the act of robbing a bird's nest, a legal offense in Holland.

This Janzoon Kolp, you see, was— There, I cannot tell the story just now. The race is about to commence.

Twenty girls are formed in a line. The rollicking music has ceased.

A man, whom we shall call the crier, stands between the columns and the first judges' stand. He reads the rules in a loud voice:

"THE GIRLS AND BOYS ARE TO RACE IN TURN, UNTIL ONE GIRL AND ONE BOY HAVE BEATEN TWICE. THEY ARE TO START IN A LINE FROM THE UNITED COLUMNS—SKATE TO THE FLAG-STAFF LINE, TURN, AND THEN COME BACK TO THE STARTING POINT; THUS MAKING A MILE AT EACH RUN."

A flag is waved from the judges' stand. Madame van Gleck rises in her pavilion. She leans forward with a white handkerchief in her hand. When she drops it, a bugler is to give the signal for them to start.

The handkerchief is fluttering to the ground. Hark!

They are off!

No. Back again. Their line was not true in passing the judges' stand.

The signal is repeated.

Off again. No mistake this time. Whew! how fast they go!

The multitude is quiet for an instant, absorbed in eager, breathless watching.

Cheers spring up along the line of spectators. Huzza! Five girls are ahead. Who comes flying back from the boundary mark? We cannot tell. Something red, that is all. There is a blue spot flitting near it, and a dash of yellow nearer still. Spectators at this end of the line strain their eyes and wish they had taken their post nearer the flagstaff.

The wave of cheers is coming back again. Now we can see! Katrinka is ahead!

She passes the Van Holp pavilion. The next is Madame van Gleck's. That leaning figure gazing from it is a magnet. Hilda shoots past Katrinka, waving her hand to her mother as she passes. Two others are close now, whizzing on like arrows. What is that flash of red and gray? Hurrah, it is Gretel! She, too, waves her hand, but toward no gay pavilion. The crowd is cheering, but she hears only her father's voice, "Well done, little Gretel!" Soon Katrinka, with a quick merry laugh, shoots past Hilda. The girl in yellow is gaining now. She passes them all, all except Gretel. The judges lean forward without seeming to lift their eyes from their watches. Cheer after cheer fills the air; the very columns seem rocking. Gretel has passed them. She has won.

"GRETEL BRINKER, ONE MILE!" shouts the crier.

The judges nod. They write something upon a tablet which each holds in his hand.

While the girls are resting—some crowding eagerly around our frightened little Gretel, some standing aside in high disdain—the boys form in a line.

Mynheer van Gleck drops the handkerchief this time. The buglers give a vigorous blast!

The boys have started.

Halfway already! Did ever you see the like!

Three hundred legs flashing by in an instant. But there are only twenty boys. No matter, there were hundreds of legs I am sure! Where are they now? There is such a noise one gets bewildered. What are the people laughing at? Oh, at that fat boy in the rear. See him go! See him! He'll be down in an instant, no, he won't. I wonder if he knows he is all alone; the other boys are nearly at the boundary line. Yes, he knows it. He stops! He wipes his hot face. He takes off his cap and looks about him. Better to give up with a good grace. He has made a hundred friends by that hearty, astonished laugh. Good Jacob Poot!

The fine fellow is already among the spectators gazing as eagerly as the rest.

A cloud of feathery ice flies from the heels of the skaters as they "bring to" and turn at the flagstaffs.

Something black is coming now, one of the boys—it is all we know. He has touched the vox humana stop of the crowd; it fairly roars. Now they come nearer—we can see the red cap. There's Ben—there's Peter—there's Hans!

Hans is ahead! Young Madame van Gend almost crushes the flowers in her hand; she had been quite sure that Peter would be first. Carl Schummel is next, then Ben, and the youth with the red cap. The others are pressing close. A tall figure darts from among them. He passes the red cap, he passes Ben, then Carl. Now it is an even race between him and Hans. Madame van Gend catches her breath.

It is Peter! He is ahead! Hans shoots past him. Hilda's eyes fill with tears. Peter *must* beat. Annie's eyes flash proudly. Gretel gazes with clasped hands—four strokes more will take her brother to the columns.

He is there! Yes, but so was young Schummel just a second before. At the last instant, Carl, gathering his powers, had whizzed between them and passed the goal.

"CARL SCHUMMEL, ONE MILE!" shouts the crier.

Soon Madame van Gleck rises again. The falling handkerchief starts the bugle; and the bugle, using its voice as a bowstring, shoots off twenty girls like so many arrows.

It is a beautiful sight, but one has not long to look; before we can fairly distinguish them they are far in the distance. This time they are close upon one another; it is hard to say as they come speeding back from the flagstaff which will reach the columns first. There are new faces among the foremost—eager, glowing faces, unnoticed before. Katrinka is there, and Hilda, but Gretel and Rychie are in the rear. Gretel is wavering, but when Rychie passes her, she starts forward afresh. Now they are nearly beside Katrinka. Hilda is still in advance; she is almost "home." She has not faltered since that bugle note sent her flying; like an arrow still she is speeding toward the goal. Cheer after cheer rises in the air. Peter is silent but his eyes shine like stars. "Huzza! Huzza!"

The crier's voice is heard again.

"HILDA VAN GLECK, ONE MILE!"

A loud murmur of approval runs through the crowd, catching the music in its course, till all seems one sound, with a glad rhythmic throbbing in its depths. When the flag waves all is still.

Once more the bugle blows a terrific blast. It sends off the boys like chaff before the wind—dark chaff, I admit, and in big pieces.

It is whisked around at the flagstaff, driven faster yet by the cheers and shouts along the line. We begin to see what is coming. There are three boys in advance this time, and all abreast. Hans, Peter and Lambert. Carl soon breaks the ranks, rushing through with a whiff! Fly, Hans; fly, Peter; don't let Carl beat again. Carl the bitter, Carl the insolent. Van Mounen is flagging, but you are strong as ever. Hans and Peter, Peter and Hans; which is foremost? We love them both. We scarcely care which is the fleeter.

Hilda, Annie and Gretel, seated upon the long crimson bench, can remain quiet no longer. They spring to their feet—so different, and yet one in eagerness. Hilda instantly reseats herself; none shall know how interested she is, none shall know how anxious, how filled with one hope. Shut your eyes then, Hilda—hide your face rippling with joy. Peter has beaten.

"PETER VAN HOLP, ONE MILE!" calls the crier.

The same buzz of excitement as before, while the judges take notes, the same throbbing of music through the din—but something is different. A little crowd presses close about some object, near the column. Carl has fallen. He is not hurt, though somewhat stunned. If he were less sullen he would find more sympathy in these warm young hearts. As it is they forget him as soon as he is fairly on his feet again.

The girls are to skate their third mile.

How resolute the little maidens look as they stand in a line! Some are solemn with a sense of responsibility, some wear a smile half bashful, half provoked, but one air of determination pervades them all.

This third mile may decide the race. Still if neither Gretel nor Hilda wins, there is yet a chance among the rest for the silver skates.

Each girl feels sure that this time she will accomplish the distance in one-half the time. How they stamp to try their runners! How nervously they examine each strap! How erect they stand at last, every eye upon Madame van Gleck!

The bugle thrills through them again. With quivering eagerness they spring forward, bending, but in perfect balance. Each flashing stroke seems longer than the last.

Now they are skimming off in the distance.

Again the eager straining of eyes, again the shouts and cheering, again the thrill of excitement as, after a few moments, four or five, in advance of the rest, come speeding back, nearer, nearer to the white columns.

Who is first? Not Rychie, Katrinka, Annie, nor Hilda, nor the girl in yellow—but Gretel—Gretel, the fleetest sprite of a girl that ever skated. She was but playing in the earlier race, *now* she is in earnest, or rather something within her has determined to win. That lithe little form makes no effort; but it cannot stop—not until the goal is passed!

In vain the crier lifts his voice—he cannot be heard. He has no news to tell—it is already ringing through the crowd. *Gretel has won the silver skates!*

Like a bird she has flown over the ice, like a bird she looks about her in a timid, startled way. She longs to dart to the sheltered nook where her father and mother stand. But Hans is beside her—the girls are crowding round. Hilda's kind, joyous voice breathes in her ear. From that hour, none will despise her. Goose-girl or not, Gretel stands acknowledged Queen of the Skaters!

With natural pride Hans turns to see if Peter van Holp is witnessing his sister's triumph. Peter is not looking toward them at all. He is kneeling, bending his troubled face low, and working hastily at his skate strap. Hans is beside him at once. "Are you in trouble, mynheer?"

"Ah, Hans! that you? Yes, my fun is over. I tried to tighten my strap—to make a new hole—and this botheration of a knife has cut it nearly in two."

"Mynheer," said Hans, at the same time pulling off a skate, "you must use my strap!"

"Not I, indeed, Hans Brinker," cried Peter, looking up, "though I thank you warmly. Go to your post, my friend, the bugle will sound in a minute."

"Mynheer," pleaded Hans in a husky voice, "you have called me your friend. Take this strap—quick! There is not an instant to lose. I shall not skate this time—indeed I am out of practice. Mynheer, you *must* take it"—and Hans, blind and deaf to any remonstrance, slipped his strap into Peter's skate and implored him to put it on.

"Come, Peter!" cried Lambert, from the line, "we are waiting for you."

"For madame's sake," pleaded Hans, "be quick. She is motioning to you to join the racers. There, the skate is almost on; quick, mynheer, fasten it. I could not possibly win. The race lies between Schummel and yourself."

"You are a noble fellow, Hans!" cried Peter, yielding at last. He sprang to his post just as the white handkerchief fell to the ground. The bugle sends forth its blast, loud, clear and ringing. Off go the boys!

"Mine Gott," cries a tough old fellow from Delft. "They beat everything, these Amsterdam youngsters. See them!"

See them, indeed! They are winged Mercuries every one of them. What mad errand are they on? Ah, I know; they are hunting Peter van Holp. He is some fleet-footed runaway from Olympus. Mercury and his troop of winged cousins are in full chase. They will catch him! Now Carl is the runaway—the pursuit grows furious—Ben is foremost!

The chase turns in a cloud of mist. It is coming this way. Who is hunted now? Mercury himself. It is Peter, Peter van Holp; fly, Peter—Hans is watching you. He is sending all his fleetness, all his strength into your feet. Your mother and sister are pale with eagerness. Hilda is trembling and dares not look up. Fly, Peter! The crowd has not gone deranged, it is only cheering. The pursuers are close upon you! Touch the white column! It beckons—it is reeling before you—it——

"Huzza! Huzza! Peter has won the silver skates!"

"PETER VAN HOLP!" shouted the crier. But who heard him? "Peter van Holp!" shouted a hundred voices, for he was the favorite boy of the place. "Huzza! Huzza!"

Now the music was resolved to be heard. It struck up a lively air, then a tremendous march. The spectators, thinking something new was about to happen, deigned to listen and to look.

The racers formed in single file. Peter, being the tallest, stood first. Gretel, the smallest of all, took her place at the end. Hans, who had borrowed a strap from the cake boy, was near the head.

Three gaily twined arches were placed at intervals upon the river facing the Van Gleck pavilion.

Skating slowly, and in perfect time to the music, the boys and girls moved forward, led on by Peter.

It was beautiful to see the bright procession glide along like a living creature. It curved and doubled, and drew its graceful length in and out among the arches—whichever way Peter, the head, went, the body was sure to follow. Sometimes it steered direct for the center arch, then, as if seized with a new impulse, turned away and curled itself about the first one; then unwound slowly and bending low, with quick, snakelike curvings, crossed the river, passing at length through the fartherest arch.

When the music was slow, the procession seemed to crawl like a thing afraid; it grew livelier, and the creature darted forward with a spring, gliding rapidly among the arches, in and out, curling, twisting, turning, never losing form until, at the shrill call of the bugle rising above the music, it suddenly resolved itself into boys and girls standing in double semicircle before Madame van Gleck's pavilion.

Peter and Gretel stand in the center in advance of the others. Madame van Gleck rises majestically. Gretel trembles, but feels that she must look at the beautiful lady. She cannot hear what is said, there is such a buzzing all around her. She is thinking that she ought to try and make a curtsy, such as her mother makes to the meester, when suddenly something so dazzling is placed in her hand that she gives a cry of joy.

Then she ventures to look about her. Peter, too, has something in his hands. "Oh! oh! how splendid!" she cries, and "Oh! how splendid!" is echoed as far as the people can see. Meantime the silver skates flash in the sunshine, throwing dashes of light upon those two happy faces.

Mevrouw van Gend sends a little messenger with her bouquets. One for Hilda, one for Carl, and the others for Peter and Gretel.

At sight of the flowers the Queen of the Skaters becomes uncontrollable. With a bright stare of gratitude, she gathers skates and bouquet in her apron, hugs them to her bosom, and darts off to search for her father and mother in the scattering crowd.

XLV
JOY IN THE COTTAGE

PERHAPS you were surprised to learn that Raff and his vrouw were at the skating race; you would have been more so had you been with them on the evening of that merry twentieth of December. To see the Brinker cottage standing sulkily alone on the frozen marsh, with its bulgy, rheumatic-looking walls, and its slouched hat of a roof pulled far over its eyes, one would never suspect that a lively scene was passing within. Without, nothing was left of the day but a low line of blaze at the horizon. A few venturesome clouds had already taken fire, and others, with their edges burning, were lost in the gathering smoke.

A stray gleam of sunshine slipping down from the willow stump crept stealthily under the cottage. It seemed to feel that the inmates would give it welcome if it could only get near them. The room under which it hid was as clean as clean could be. The very cracks in the rafters were polished. Delicious odors filled the air. A huge peat fire upon the hearth sent flashes of harmless lightning at the somber walls. It played in turn upon the great leathern Bible, upon Gretel's closet-bed, the household things on their pegs, and the beautiful silver skates and the flowers upon the table. Dame Brinker's honest face shone and twinkled in the changing light. Gretel and Hans, with arms entwined, were leaning against the fireplace, laughing merrily, and Raff Brinker was dancing!

I do not mean that he was pirouetting or cutting a pigeon wing, either of which would have been entirely too undignified for the father of a family; I simply affirm that while they were chatting pleasantly together Raff suddenly sprang from his seat, snapped his fingers and performed two or three flourishes very much like the climax of a Highland fling. Next he caught his vrouw in his arms and fairly lifted her from the ground in his delight.

"Huzza!" he cried, "I have it! I have it! It's Thomas Higgs. That's the name! It came upon me like a flash. Write it down, lad, write it down!"

Someone knocked at the door.

"It's the meester," cried the delighted dame. "Goede Gunst! how things come to pass!" Mother and children came in merry collision as they rushed to open the door.

It was not the doctor, after all, but three boys, Peter van Holp, Lambert and Ben.

"Good evening, young gentlemen," said Dame Brinker, so happy and proud that she would scarcely have been surprised at a visit from the king himself.

"Good evening, jufvrouw," said the trio, making magnificent bows.

"Dear me!" thought Dame Brinker as she bobbed up and down like a churn dasher, "it's lucky I learned to curtsy at Heidelberg!" Raff was content to return the boys' salutations with a respectful nod.

"Pray be seated, young masters," said the dame, as Gretel bashfully thrust a stool toward them. "There's a lack of chairs as you see, but this one by the fire is at your service, and if you don't mind the hardness, the oak chest is as good a seat as the best. That's right, Hans, pull it out."

By the time the boys were seated to the dame's satisfaction, Peter, acting as spokesman, had explained that they were going to attend a lecture at Amsterdam, and had stopped on the way to return Hans' strap.

"Oh, mynheer," cried Hans earnestly, "it is too much trouble. I am very sorry."

"No trouble at all, Hans. I could have waited for you to come to your work tomorrow, had I not wished to call. And, Hans, talking of your work, my father is much pleased with it; a carver by trade could not have done it better. He would like to have the south arbor ornamented also, but I told him you were going to school again."

"Aye!" put in Raff Brinker emphatically, "Hans must go to school at once—and Gretel as well—that is true."

"I am glad to hear you say so," responded Peter, turning toward the father, "and very glad to know that you are again a well man."

"Yes, young master, a well man, and able to work as steady as ever—thank God!"

[Here Hans hastily wrote something on the edge of a time-worn almanac that hung by the chimney place.]

"Aye, that's right, lad, set it down. Figgs! Wiggs! Alack! Alack!" added Raff in great dismay, "it's gone again!"

"All right, father," said Hans, "the name's down now in black and white. Here, look at it, father; mayhap the rest will come to you. If we had the place as well, it would be complete"; then turning to Peter, he said in a low tone, "I have an important errand in town, mynheer, and if——"

"Whist!" exclaimed the dame, lifting her hands, "not to Amsterdam tonight, and you've owned your legs were aching under you. Nay, nay—it'll be soon enough to go at early daylight."

"Daylignt indeed!" echoed Raff. "That would never do. Nay, Meitje, he must go this hour."

The vrouw looked for an instant as if Raff's recovery was becoming rather a doubtful benefit; her word was no longer sole law in the house. Fortunately, the proverb, "Humble wife is husband's boss," had taken deep root in her mind; even as the dame pondered, it bloomed.

"Very well, Raff," she said smilingly, "it is thy boy as well as mine. I've a troublesome house, young masters."

Just then Peter drew a long strap from his pocket.

Handing it to Hans he said in an undertone, "I need not thank you for lending me this, Hans Brinker. Such boys as you do not ask for thanks—but I must say you did me a great kindness, and I am proud to acknowledge it. I did not know," he added laughingly, "until fairly in the race, how anxious I was to win."

Hans was glad to join in Peter's laugh—it covered his embarrassment and gave his face a chance to cool off a little. Honest, generous boys like Hans have such a stupid way of blushing when you least expect it.

"It was nothing, mynheer," said the dame, hastening to her son's relief. "The lad's whole soul was in having you win the race, I know it was!"

This helped matters beautifully.

"Ah, mynheer," Hans hurried to say, "from the first start I felt stiff and strange on my feet; I was well out of it so long as I had no chance of winning."

Peter looked rather distressed.

"We may hold different opinions there. That part of the business troubles me. It is too late to mend it now, but it would be really a kindness to me if——"

The rest of Peter's speech was uttered so confidentially that I cannot record it. Enough to say, Hans soon started back in dismay, and Peter, looking very much ashamed, stammered out something to the effect that he would keep them, since he won the race, but it was "all wrong."

Here Van Mounen coughed, as if to remind Peter that lecture hour was approaching fast. At that same moment Ben laid something upon the table.

"Ah," exclaimed Peter, "I forgot my other errand. Your sister ran off so quickly today that Madame van Gleck had no opportunity to give her the case for her skates."

"S-s-t!" said Dame Brinker, shaking her head reproachfully at Gretel, "she was a very rude girl, I'm sure."

[Secretly, she was thinking that very few women had such a fine little daughter.]

"No, indeed," laughed Peter, "she did exactly the right thing—ran home with her richly won treasures—who would not? Don't let us detain you, Hans," he continued, turning around as he spoke; but Hans, who was watching the father, seemed to have forgotten their presence.

Meantime, Raff, lost in thought, was repeating under his breath, "Thomas Higgs—Thomas Higgs, aye, that's the name. Alack! if I could but tell the place as well."

The skate case was elegantly made of crimson morocco, ornamented with silver. If a fairy had breathed upon its tiny key, or Jack Frost himself designed its delicate tracery, they could not have been more daintily beautiful. FOR THE FLEETEST was written upon the cover in sparkling letters. It was lined with velvet, and in one corner was stamped the name and address of the maker.

Gretel thanked Peter in her own simple way; then, being quite delighted and confused, and not knowing what else to do, lifted the case, carefully examining it in every part. "It's made by Mynheer Birmingham," she said after a while, still blushing and holding it before her eyes.

"Birmingham!" replied Lambert van Mounen, "that's the name of a place in England. Let me see it.

"Ha! ha!" he laughed, holding the open case toward the firelight, "no wonder you thought so; but it's a slight mistake. The case was made at Birmingham, but the maker's name is in smaller letters. Humph! they're so small, I can't read them."

"Let me try," said Peter, leaning over his shoulder. "Why, man, it's perfectly distinct. It's T—H—it's T——"

"Well," exclaimed Lambert triumphantly, "if you can read it so easily, let's hear it, T—H, what?"

"T. H—T. H. Oh! why, Thomas Higgs, to be sure," replied Peter, pleased to be able to decipher it at last. Then, feeling they had been behaving rather unceremoniously, he turned toward Hans.

Peter turned pale! What was the matter with the people? Raff and Hans had started up, and were staring at him, in glad amazement. Gretel looked wild. Dame Brinker, with an unlighted candle in her hand, was rushing about the room, crying, "Hans! Hans! Where's your hat? Oh, the meester! Oh, the meester!"

"Birmingham! Higgs!" exclaimed Hans. "Did you say Higgs? We've found him! I must be off."

"You see, young masters," panted the dame, at the same time snatching Hans' hat from the bed, "you see—we know him—he's our—no, he isn't—I mean—oh, Hans, you must go to Amsterdam this minute!"

"Good night, mynheers," panted Hans, radiant with sudden joy, "good night—you will excuse me, I must go. Birmingham—Higgs—Higgs—Birmingham," and seizing his hat from his mother, and his skates from Gretel, he rushed from the cottage.

What could the boys think, but that the entire Brinker family had suddenly gone crazy!

They bade an embarrassed "good evening," and turned to go. But Raff stopped them.

"This Thomas Higgs, young masters, is a—a person."

"Ah!" exclaimed Peter, quite sure that Raff was the most crazy of all.

"Yes—a person—a—ahem!—a friend. We thought him dead. I hope it is the same man. In England, did you say?"

"Yes, Birmingham," answered Peter. "It must be Birmingham in England."

"I know the man," said Ben, addressing Lambert. "His factory is not four miles from our place—a queer fellow—still as an oyster—doesn't seem at all like an Englishman. I've often seen him—a solemn-looking chap, with magnificent eyes. He made a beautiful writing case once for me to give Jenny on her birthday. Makes pocketbooks, telescope cases, and all kinds of leatherwork."

As this was said in English, Van Mounen of course translated it for the benefit of all concerned, noticing meanwhile that neither Raff nor his vrouw looked very miserable, though Raff was trembling, and the dame's eyes were swimming with tears.

You may believe the doctor heard every word of the story, when later in the evening he came driving back with Hans. "The three young gentlemen had been gone sometime," Dame Brinker said, "but like enough, by hurrying, it would be easy to find them coming out from the lecture, wherever that was."

"True," said Raff, nodding his head, "the vrouw always hits upon the right thing. It would be well to see the young English gentleman, mynheer, before he forgets all about Thomas Higgs. It's a slippery name, d'ye see? One can't hold it safe a minute. It come upon me sudden and strong as a pile driver, and my boy writ it down. Aye, mynheer, I'd haste to talk with the English lad; he's seen your son many a time—only to think on't!"

Dame Brinker took up the thread of the discourse.

"You'll pick out the lad quick enough, mynheer, because he's in company with Master Peter van Holp; and his hair curls all up over his forehead like foreign folk's, and, if you hear him speak, he talks kind of big and fast, only it's English; but that wouldn't be any hindrance to your honor."

The doctor had already lifted his hat to go. With a beaming face, he muttered something about its being just like the young scamp to give himself a rascally English name; called Hans "my son," thereby making that young gentleman happy as a lord, and left the cottage with very little ceremony, considering what a great meester he was.

The grumbling coachman comforted himself by speaking his mind, as he drove back to Amsterdam. Since the doctor was safely stowed away in the coach, and could not hear a word, it was a fine time to say terrible things of folks who hadn't no manner of feeling for nobody, who were always wanting the horses a dozen times of a night.

XLVI
MYSTERIOUS DISAPPEARANCE OF THOMAS HIGGS

HIGGS' factory was a mine of delight for the gossips of Birmingham. It was a small building, but quite large enough to hold a mystery. Who the proprietor was, or where he came from, none could tell. He looked like a gentleman, that was certain, though everybody knew he had risen from an apprenticeship, and he could handle his pen like a writing master.

Years ago he had suddenly appeared in the place a lad of eighteen—learned his trade faithfully, and risen in the confidence of his employer—been taken in as a partner soon after his time was up—and, finally, when old Willett died, had assumed the business on his own hands. This was all that was known of his affairs.

It was a common remark among some of the good people that he never had a word to say to a Christian soul; while others declared that though he spoke beautifully, when he chose to, there was something wrong in his accent. A tidy man, too, they called him, all but for having that scandalous green pond alongside of his factory, which wasn't deep enough for an eel, and was "just a fever nest, as sure as you live."

His nationality was a great puzzle. The English name spoke plain enough for *one* side of his house, but of what manner of nation was his mother? If she'd been an American, he'd certainly have had high cheekbones and reddish skin; if a German, he would have known the language, and Squire Smith declared he didn't; if French (and his having that frog pond made it seem likely), it would come out in his speech. No—there was nothing he could be but Dutch. And strangest of all, though the man always pricked up his ears when you talked of Holland, he didn't seem to know the first thing about the country when you put him to the point.

Anyhow, as no letters ever came to him from his mother's family in Holland, and as nobody living had ever seen old Higgs, the family couldn't be anything much. Probably Thomas Higgs himself was no better than he should be, for all he pretended to carry himself so straight; and for their parts, the gossips declared, they were not going to trouble their heads about him. Consequently Thomas Higgs and his affairs were never-failing subjects of discussion.

Picture, then, the consternation among all the good people, when it was announced by "somebody who was there and ought to know," that the postboy had that very morning handed Higgs a foreign-looking letter, and the man had "turned as white as the wall; rushed to his factory, talked a bit with one of the head workmen, and without bidding a creature good-bye, was off bag and baggage before you could wink, ma'am." Mistress Scrubbs, his landlady, was in deep affliction. The dear soul became quite out of breath while speaking of him. "To leave lodgin's in that suddent way, without never so much as a day's warnin' which was what every woman who didn't wish to be trodden underfoot, which thank Hevving wasn't *her* way, had a perfect right to expect; yes, and a week's warnin' now you mention it, and without even so much as sayin', 'Many thanks to you, Mistress Scrubbs, for all past kindnesses,' which was most numerous, though she said it who shouldn't say it; leastwise she wasn't never no kind of a person to be lookin' for thanks every minnit. It was really scanderlous, though to be sure Mister 'iggs paid up everythin' to the last farthin' and it fairly brought tears to her eyes to see his dear empty boots lyin' there in the corner of his room, which alone showed trouble of mind for he always stood 'em up straight as solgers, though bein' half-soled twice they hadn't of course been worth takin' away."

Whereupon her dearest friend, Miss Scrumpkins, ran home to tell all about it. And, as everybody knew the Scrumpkinses, a shining gossamer of news was soon woven from one end of the street to the other.

An investigating committee met, that evening, at Mrs. Snigham's—sitting, in secret session, over her best china. Though invited only to a quiet "tea," the amount of judicial business they transacted on the occasion was prodigious. The biscuits were actually cold before the committee had a chance to eat anything. There was so much to talk over, and it was so important that it should be firmly established that each member had always been "certain sure that something extraordinary would be happening to that man yet," that it was nearly eight o'clock before Mrs. Snigham gave anybody a second cup.

XLVII
BROAD SUNSHINE

One snowy day in January, Laurens Boekman went with his father to pay his respects to the Brinker family.

Raff was resting after the labors of the day; Gretel, having filled and lighted his pipe, was brushing every speck of ash from the hearth; the dame was spinning; and Hans, perched upon a stool by the window, was diligently studying his lessons. It was a peaceful, happy household whose main excitement during the past week had been the looking forward to this possible visit from Thomas Higgs.

As soon as the grand presentation was over, Dame Brinker insisted upon giving her guests some hot tea; it was enough to freeze anyone, she said, to be out in such crazy, blustering weather. While they were talking with her husband she whispered to Gretel that the young gentleman's eyes and her boy's were certainly as much alike as four beans, to say nothing of a way they both had of looking as if they were stupid and yet knew as much as a body's grandfather.

Gretel was disappointed. She had looked forward to a tragic scene, such as Annie Bouman had often described to her, from storybooks; and here was the gentleman who came so near being a murderer, who for ten years had been wandering over the face of the earth, who had believed himself deserted and scorned by his father—the very young gentleman who had fled from his country in such magnificent trouble, sitting by the fire just as pleasant and natural as could be!

To be sure, his voice had trembled when he talked with her parents, and he had met his father's look with a bright kind of smile that would have suited a dragon killer bringing the waters of perpetual youth to his king; but after all he wasn't at all like the conquered hero in Annie's book. He did not say, lifting his hand toward heaven, "I hereby swear to be forever faithful to my home, my God and my country!" which would have been only right and proper under the circumstances.

All things considered, Gretel was disappointed. Raff, however, was perfectly satisfied. The message was delivered; Dr. Boekman had his son safe and sound; and the poor lad had done nothing sinful after all, except in thinking his father would have abandoned him for an accident. To be sure, the graceful stripling had become rather a heavy man. Raff had unconsciously hoped to clasp that same boyish hand again; but all things were changed to Raff, for that matter. So he pushed back every feeling but joy, as he saw father and son sitting side by side at his hearthstone. Meantime, Hans was wholly occupied in the thought of Thomas Higgs' happiness in being able to be the meester's assistant again; and Dame Brinker was sighing softly to herself, wishing that the lad's mother were alive to see him—such a fine young gentleman as he was; and wondering how Dr. Boekman could bear to see the silver watch getting so dull. He had worn it ever since Raff handed it over, that was evident. What had he done with the gold one he used to wear?

The light was shining full upon Dr. Boekman's face. How contented he looked; how much younger and brighter than formerly. The hard lines were quite melting away. He was laughing, as he said to the father:

"Am I not a happy man, Raff Brinker? My son will sell out his factory this month, and open a warehouse in Amsterdam. I shall have all my spectacle cases for nothing."

Hans started from his reverie. "A warehouse, mynheer! And will Thomas Higgs—I mean—is your son not to be your assistant again?"

A shade passed over the meester's face, but he brightened with an effort, as he replied:

"Oh, no, Laurens has had quite enough of that. He wishes to be a merchant."

Hans appeared so surprised and disappointed that his friend asked good-naturedly:

"Why so silent, boy? Is it any disgrace to be a merchant?"

"N—not a disgrace, mynheer," stammered Hans—"but——"

"But what?"

"Why, the other calling is so much better," answered Hans, "so much nobler. I think, mynheer," he added, kindling with enthusiasm, "that to be a surgeon, to cure the sick and crippled, to save human life, to be able to do what you have done for my father, is the grandest thing on earth."

The doctor was regarding him sternly. Hans felt rebuked. His cheeks were flushed; hot tears were gathering under his lashes.

"It is an ugly business, boy, this surgery," said the doctor, still frowning at Hans. "It requires great patience, self-denial and perseverance."

"I am sure it does," cried Hans, kindling again. "It calls for wisdom too, and a reverence for God's work. Ah, mynheer, it may have its trials and drawbacks—but you do not mean what you say—it is great and noble, not ugly! Pardon me, mynheer. It is not for me to speak so boldly."

Dr. Boekman was evidently displeased. He turned his back on the boy, and conferred aside with Laurens. Meanwhile the dame scowled a terrible warning at Hans. These great people, she knew well enough, never like to hear poor folk speak up so pertly.

The meester turned around.

"How old are you, Hans Brinker?"

"Fifteen, mynheer," was the startled reply.

"Would you like to become a physician?"

"Yes, mynheer," answered Hans, quivering with excitement.

"Would you be willing, with your parents' consent, to devote yourself to study, to go to the University—and, in time, be a student in my office?"

"YES, mynheer."

"You would not grow restless, think you, and change your mind just as I had set my heart upon preparing you to be my successor?"

Hans' eyes flashed. "No, mynheer, I would not change."

"You may believe him, there," cried the dame, who could remain quiet no longer. "Hans is like a rock, when once he decides; and as for study, mynheer, the child has almost grown fast to his books of late. He can jumble off Latin already, like any priest!"

The doctor smiled. "Well, Hans, I see nothing to prevent us from carrying out this plan, if your father agrees."

"Ahem," said Raff, too proud of his boy to be very meek, "the fact is, mynheer, I prefer an active, out-of-door life myself. But if the lad's inclined to study for a meester, and he'd have the benefit of your good word to push him on in the world, it's all one to me. The money's all that's wanting, but it mightn't be long, with two strong pair of arms to earn it, before we——"

"Tut! tut!" interrupted the doctor, "if I take your right-hand man away, I must pay the cost, and glad enough will

I be to do it. It will be like having *two* sons—eh, Laurens? One a merchant and the other a surgeon—I shall be the happiest man in Holland! Come to me in the morning, Hans, and we will arrange matters at once."

Hans bowed assent. He dared not trust himself to speak.

"And, Brinker," continued the doctor, "my son Laurens will need a trusty, ready man like you when he opens his warehouse in Amsterdam; someone to oversee matters, and see that the lazy clowns round about the place do their duty. Someone to—— Why don't you tell him yourself, you rascal!"

This last was addressed to the son, and did not sound half as fierce as it looks in print. The rascal and Raff soon understood each other perfectly.

"I'm loath to leave the dykes," said the latter, after they had talked together awhile, "but you have made me such a good offer, mynheer, I'd be robbing my family if I let it go past me."

Take a long look at Hans as he sits there staring gratefully at the meester, for you shall not see him again for many years.

And Gretel—ah, what a vista of puzzling work suddenly opens before her! Yes, for dear Hans' sake she will study now. If he really is to be a meester, his sister must not shame his greatness.

How faithfully those glancing eyes shall yet seek for the jewels that lie hidden in rocky schoolbooks! And how they shall yet brighten and droop at the coming of one whom she knows of now only as the boy who wore a red cap on that wonderful day when she found the silver skates in her apron!

But the doctor and Laurens are going. Dame Brinker is making her best curtsy. Raff stands beside her, looking every inch a man as he grasps the meester's hand. Through the open cottage door we can look out upon the level Dutch landscape all alive with the falling snow.

CONCLUSION

OUR story is nearly told. Time passes in Holland just as surely and steadily as here; in that respect no country is odd.

To the Brinker family it has brought great changes. Hans has spent the years faithfully and profitably, conquering obstacles as they arose, and pursuing one object with all the energy of his nature. If often the way has been rugged, his resolution has never failed. Sometimes he echoes, with his good old friend, the words said long ago in that little cottage near Broek: "Surgery is an ugly business"; but always in his heart of hearts lingers the echo of those truer words, "It is great and noble! It awakes a reverence for God's work!"

Were you in Amsterdam today, you might see the famous Dr. Brinker riding in his grand coach to visit his patients; or, it might be, you would see him skating with his own boys and girls upon the frozen canal. For Annie Bouman, the beautiful, frankhearted peasant girl, you would inquire in vain; but Annie Brinker, the vrouw of the great physician, is very like her—only, as Hans says, she is even lovelier, wiser, more like a fairy godmother than ever.

Peter van Holp, also, is a married man. I could have told you before that he and Hilda would join hands and glide through life together, just as years ago, they skimmed side by side over the frozen, sunlit river.

At one time, I came near hinting that Katrinka and Carl would join hands. It is fortunate now that the report was not started, for Katrinka changed her mind, and is single to this day. The lady is not quite so merry as formerly, and, I grieve to say, some of the tinkling bells are out of tune. But she is the life of her social circle, still. I wish she would be in earnest, just for a little while, but no; it is not her nature. Her cares and sorrows do nothing more than disturb the tinkling; they never waken any deeper music.

Rychie's soul has been stirred to its depths during these long years. Her history would tell how seed carelessly sown is sometimes reaped in anguish, and how a golden harvest may follow a painful planting. If I mistake not, you may be able to read the written record before long; that is, if you are familiar with the Dutch language. In the witty but earnest author whose words are welcomed at this day in thousands of Holland homes, few could recognize the haughty, flippant Rychie who scoffed at little Gretel.

Lambert van Mounen and Ludwig van Holp are good Christian men, and, what is more easily to be seen at a glance, thriving citizens. Both are dwellers in Amsterdam, but one clings to the old city of that name, and the other is a pilgrim to the new. Van Mounen's present home is not far from Central Park, and he says if the New Yorkers do their duty the park will, in time, equal his beautiful Bosch, near The Hague. He often thinks of the Katrinka of his boyhood, but he is glad now that Katrinka, the woman, sent him away; though it seemed at the time his darkest hour. Ben's sister Jenny has made him very happy, happier than he could have been with anyone else in the wide world.

Carl Schummel has had a hard life. His father met with reverses in business; and as Carl had not many warm friends, and, above all, was not sustained by noble principles, he has been tossed about by Fortune's battledore until his gayest feathers are nearly all knocked off. He is a bookkeeper, in the thriving Amsterdam house of Boekman and Schimmelpenninck. Voostenwalbert, the junior partner, treats him kindly; and he, in turn, is very respectful to the "monkey with a long name for a tail."

Of all our group of Holland friends, Jacob Poot is the only one who has passed away. Good-natured, truehearted and unselfish to the last, he is mourned now as heartily as he was loved and laughed at while on earth. He grew to be very thin before he died; thinner than Benjamin Dobbs, who is now portliest among the portly.

Raff Brinker and his vrouw have been living comfortably in Amsterdam for many years—a faithful, happy pair; as simple and straightforward in their good fortune as they were patient and trustful in darker days. They have a zommerhuis near the old cottage and thither they often repair with their children and grandchildren on the pleasant summer afternoons when the pond lilies rear their queenly heads above the water.

The story of Hans Brinker would be but half told, if we did not leave him with Gretel standing near. Dear, quick, patient little Gretel! What is she now? Ask old Dr. Boekman, he will declare she is the finest singer, the loveliest woman in Amsterdam; ask Hans and Annie, they will assure you she is the dearest sister ever known; ask her husband, he will tell you she is the brightest, sweetest little wife in Holland; ask Dame Brinker and Raff, their eyes will glisten with joyous tears; ask the poor, the air will be filled with blessings.

But, lest you forget a tiny form trembling and sobbing on the mound before the Brinker cottage, ask the Van Glecks; they will never weary telling of the darling little girl who won the silver skates.

[illegible]

Carl Schurz had had a hard life. His brother went with [illegible]

[illegible]

Of all the [illegible] of Highland Brigade, [illegible]

[illegible] particular among the poets.

[illegible]

[illegible]

Baldridge